GONE TO GRAVEYARDS

an epic novel of the Korean War

BREWSTER
MILTON
ROBERTSON

Also by Brewster Milton Robertson

Rainy Days and Sundays
The Grail Mystique
A Posturing of Fools

Published in the United States by Mangus Hollow Books
POB 1689
Auburn, Alabama 36831
mangushollow@islc.net

This is a work of the author's imagination. Names, characters, places and incidents either are the products of the author's imagination or are used fictitiously. Those who believe they see themselves or someone else in this book are mistaken.

Author's Notes

The reader is reminded the action in this novel takes place almost 60 years ago and the descriptions of the highways and towns and cities relate to a far-less sophisticated time.

The author will pay the sum of $500.00 to the first reader who can provide a copy of the photograph of 2nd Lts. Paul Golden Price and Brewster Milton Robertson at the Seattle-Tacoma airport standing with Marilyn Monroe in the doorway of the airplane which transported the leading actors—Robert Mitchum, Rory Calhoun, and Marilyn Monroe—of the major Oscar Preminger motion picture, *River of No Return*, from Hollywood, California, to locations near Edmonton, Canada, in Banff and Jasper National Parks sometime in late June or early July 1953.

Cover art and interior book design by Brewster Milton Robertson. Technical consultantion on cover mechanical by Kenton Argabright Robertson. Digital rendition of cover mechanical by Jon Crenshaw. Author photo by Tippy Lunsford Photography.

First Edition 2011
Printed in the United States of America

1 3 5 7 9 10 8 6 4 2

Library of Congress Cataloging-in-Publication Data
Robertson, Brewster Milton
Gone to graveyards: an epic novel of the Korean War / by Brewster Milton Robertson
p. cm.
ISBN 978-0-615-44535-9
1.   Fiction – War and military 2. Fiction – Historical 3. Fiction

LCCN 2011922302

Dedication

For my wife Charlotte, my true love, my inspiration and counsel and Chumbley, our endearing, cavalierly-alpha English Bulldog.

———

For my spiritual brother and lifelong friends Al and Nancy Stump.

———

For Rick Robotham, my erudite longtime good friend.

———

For 2nd Lt. Paul Golden Price, my intrepid comrade in arms, who posed with Marilyn Monroe and me in the doorway of a DC-3 at the SeaTac Airport in the early summer of 1953.

WHERE HAVE ALL THE SOLDIERS GONE?
LONG TIME PASSING
WHERE HAVE ALL THE SOLDIERS GONE?
LONG TIME AGO
WHERE HAVE ALL THE SOLDIERS GONE?
GONE TO GRAVEYARDS EVERY ONE
WHEN WILL THEY EVER LEARN?
WHEN WILL THEY EVER LEARN?

Pete Seeger and Joe Hickerson, (inspired by lines from an old Ukranian folksong quoted in *And Quiet Flows the Don*, the novel by Mikhail Sholokhov.)

"POWER TENDS TO CORRUPT AND ABSOLUTE POWER CORRUPTS ABSOLUTELY."
Lord Acton, (Letter to M. Creighton, April/5/1887).

"TO EVERY MAN UPON THIS EARTH
DEATH COMETH SOON OR LATE."
Lays Of Ancient Rome by Thomas Babington Macaulay

"I was always embarrassed by the words sacred, glorious, and sacrifice and the expression in vain. We had heard them, sometimes standing in the rain almost out of earshot, so that only the shouted words came through, and had read them, on proclamations that were slapped up by billposters over other proclamations, now for a long time, and I had seen nothing sacred, and the things that were glorious had no glory and the sacrifices were like the stockyards in Chicago if nothing was done with the meat except to bury it. There were many words that you could not stand to hear and finally only the names of places had dignity. Certain numbers were the same way and certain dates and these with the names of the places were all you could say and have them mean anything. Abstract words such as glory, honor, courage, or hallow were obscene beside the names of rivers, the numbers of regiments and the dates."

A Farewell to Arms by Ernest Hemingway.

GONE
TO
GRAVEYARDS

an epic novel of the Korean War

MANGUS
HOLLOW
BOOKS

AUBURN, ALABAMA

FOREWORD

As a newly-commissioned Lieutenant in the U.S. Army Medical Service Corp, I first met Brewster Milton Robertson at the Army Medical Field Service School in San Antonio, Texas in January 1953. Following MFSS, we served together at Camp Pickett, Virginia, and in July 1953, flew together to Japan and on to Korea. In Korea, I was assigned to a Mobile Army Surgical Hospital (MASH), an hour north of Seoul, and Robertson was assigned to the 121st Evacuation Hospital, just south of Seoul across the Han River from Kimpo AFB, where we served from July to November 1953, when we both were released from active duty and sent back home.

It is a travesty of history that the Korean War has come to be known as the "Forgotten War." Incredibly today, over a half-century after the Korean truce was signed, daily headlines portend the ominous threat of North Korea's nuclear ambition while UN troops still anxiously patrol the Demilitarized Zone at the 38th Parallel.

Most of the meager legacy of written history about the so-called "Forgotten War" would have current and future generations believe the Korean War began on June 25, 1950, when the North Koreans crossed the 38th Parallel into Seoul, and ended slightly over one year later on July 10, 1951, the date both sides sat down at negotiating tables at Panmunjom, a village a few miles north of Seoul.

This is the farthest thing from the truth.

During the ensuing two years of bickering between the negotiators before the truce was finally signed on July 27, 1953, the bitter and bloody fighting continued to rage—literally within a day's march of the truce tents themselves—on meaningless land features nicknamed Old Baldy, Pork Chop Hill, Whitehorse Mountain, Bloody Ridge, Iron Triangle, Heartbreak Ridge, et. al., with a mind-boggling total loss of life and limb to over 400,000 American and UN soldiers and an estimated 1,200,000 of the North Korean and Chinese, as well.

Revealing long-kept-secret atrocities eclipsing the Vietnam massacres at My Lai and My Khe, Brewster Milton Robertson's novel, **Gone to Graveyards**, examines under the burning glass, the soul-scarring psychological and physical toll the carnage this reprehensible conflict exacted upon a world still quaking under the shadow of mushroom clouds—delivering after a half-century clouded in obscurity, the all-encompassing history of the Korean War.

Paul Golden Price
1184 North Ludlow Road
Urbana, OH 43078
November 15, 2010

BOOK ONE

PROLOGUE

HIS BALD, FRECKLED PATE betraying a fondness for warmer climes, the lean, white-bearded man stood on the top step of the Lincoln Memorial, squinting against the morning sunshine down the length of the Mall. After a long moment, he pulled a dog-eared envelope from the inner pocket of his topcoat and reread the engraved invitation.

THE PRESIDENT OF THE UNITED STATES REQUESTS THE PRESENCE OF YOUR COMPANY FOR DINNER AT THE WHITE HOUSE 7PM, FRIDAY, OCTOBER 22, 2010. SOCIAL HOUR AT 6PM *RSVP 202/456-1414*

"Please wear your military ribbons..." was penciled underneath.

Slowly refolding the card, he replaced it in his pocket and carefully made his way down the steps. With a brief glance toward the Vietnam Wall to his left, he skirted the corner of the Reflecting Pool and walked a short distance through the newly-turning trees and took a seat on a park bench beside a sculptural group of soldiers on combat patrol with weapons at the ready. In the near-distance, fallen leaves from the trees covered the paths around the Tidal Basin in a mosaic carpet of red and brown and gold, producing a somber backdrop to the metallic figures frozen into a stark monument to a "Forgotten War."

Pulling the collar of his coat high against the chill breeze blowing from the Tidal Basin, he unfolded the newspaper and, in one of those curious circumstances of coincidence, was confronted with a bitter reminder of America's half-century-long penance for her unresolved blunders in Korea.

The Washington Post
Friday, October 22, 2010
US ADMIRAL WARNS AGAINST ANOTHER NKOREA NUKE TEST
By HYUNG-JIN KIM
The Associated Press
Friday, October 22, 2010, 5:49 AM

SEOUL, South Korea -- If North Korea carries out a third nuclear test, it would seriously undermine international and regional security, the U.S. Pacific commander warned Friday.

Adm. Robert Willard's comments were prompted by a South Korean newspaper report that said a U.S. spy satellite detected activity at the North's main nuclear test site and that a detonation could occur in three months. South Korean officials played down the report, saying the activity didn't seem unusual.

Responding to questions about the report, Willard told reporters that North Korea's nuclear capabilities pose a grave threat to the region and that another atomic bomb test - which would be the country's third - would be a "very serious matter."

    Tensions between the Koreas -- which are still technically at war because the 1950-53 Korean War ended with a truce, not a peace treaty -- have been high in recent months following the sinking of a South Korean warship that killed 46 sailors. Seoul blamed the sinking on North Korea, which denied involvement.

Refolding the newspaper and staring blankly at the metallic figures, Collier Boyd Ramsay's mind drifted back nearly sixty years to June 27, 1950. Just home from college, he had been twenty-one years old and had been looking forward to his approaching wedding day.

CHAPTER ONE

THE ROANOKE TIMES
Roanoke, Virginia, Tuesday, June 27, 1950
NORTH KOREAN FORCES PUSH INTO SEOUL
By Russell Brines

TOYKO, TUESDAY, JUNE 27 (AP) – Tank-led Korean Communist troops today entered Seoul and the United States-sponsored government prepared to flee to the south.

As the South Korean capital tottered, a United States fighter shot down a Russian-made plane over Seoul's Kimpo Airport.

————————

"WHAT THE BLOODY HELL!" In Roanoke, Virginia, on the morning of June 27, 1950, Collier Boyd Ramsay picked up *The Roanoke Times* anxious to read Slammin' Sam Snead's latest Golf Tips and was ill-prepared to read the headline about the North Korean invasion of South Korea. Too young to be drafted into the Army during WWII, young Ramsey had since avoided the draft by virtue of a college exemption. Only a few weeks home from two years of studying commercial art at Richmond Professional Institute and counting down the days of the remaining five weeks until his wedding day, Collier had just started to work with his aunt Jackie Ramsay Anderson's husband, Ralph, who was a full-generation older and held a minor supervisory position in the Freight office of the N&W railroad. Collier was helping his uncle, who also brought home extra money moonlighting as a show-card artist with the Kroger Company, a well-known Ohio supermarket chain. Even before Collier finished reading the front-page article in *The Roanoke Times*, he began to worry how this disturbing news might affect his smug plans for the future.

Not that it mattered all that much to young Collier Ramsay or, for that matter, to most Americans, but—partly due to incompetence at the White House and Pentagon and partly due to the International Date Line which created a thirteen-hour time difference in the Orient—the news reports of the outbreak of war in Korea in the American papers were already more than one day old. Meanwhile, at the same time halfway around the world in Japan, some 75,000 draftees, newly assigned to General Douglas MacArthur's American Eighth Army, may have been a few hours more up-to-date and somewhat better informed, but, justifiably, they were a great deal more upset to get the news.

Shamefully, even though it was never generally revealed to the American public during MacArthur's lifetime—and certainly never known to young Collier Ramsay—these badly disheveled ranks of MacArthur's once-proud Far Eastern forces and the drastically-reduced state of the ill-trained and poorly-equipped standing American military forces around the world were due almost entirely to the petty prejudices of the small-town Midwesterner American President, Harry S. Truman.

Like a number of college-aged Americans who had been too young to vote in the 1948 election, Collier Ramsay had never been overly impressed with Truman, who at times he found to be downright embarrassing. Even so, Collier would have been more than a little surprised to have learned that the sitting president was, of all things, secretly anti-military.

Collier and a majority of the voting public would most likely have felt a trifle deceived to have learned that, contrary to HST's much-publicized political portfolio predicated upon his exemplary service as a National Guard Artillery officer during World War I, as an eager high-school student in Independence, Missouri, Truman had been rejected by both West Point and Annapolis. Scarred by this teenage trauma, the basically insecure Truman henceforth nurtured a secret smoldering resentment for the entire American military establishment, with particular loathing for the Army and a venomous hatred for the elitist corps of officers trained at West Point.

Reelected to his second term as a United States senator in 1940, near the beginning of WWII, Truman founded and chaired a committee to investigate waste and mismanagement in military procurement. He later boasted that this probe—which became widely known as the Truman Committee—saved the country $15-billion and countless lives on the battlefield.

Elected as Franklin Delano Roosevelt's Vice President in 1944, and subsequently taking the Oval Office after FDR's untimely death on April 12, 1945, barely four months later, in mid-August, Truman reluctantly approved the dropping of A-Bombs on Hiroshima and Nagasaki, quickly bringing about Japan's surrender and the end of war with Japan.

Unfortunately for the country's unsuspecting military, pandering to a war-weary citizenry clamoring to get their sons and daughters back home offered Truman the perfect platform from which the newly-ascended Commander-in-Chief could methodically set into motion his quest to exact vengeance upon America's armed services. Before the country had scarcely settled into a peacetime lifestyle, Truman lost little time in exercising his new powers to take action on his clandestine contempt for the military. All in the sacred name of "national fiscal responsibility," at the end of his first three years in office, Truman had ruthlessly slashed military budgets and reduced America's standing forces—Army, Navy, Air Force and Coast Guard—from 12 million at the end of WWII to a total standing force of only 1.5 million by December 1948.

Still a carefree teenager, Collier Ramsay had been preparing to enter his senior year in high school when, on August 10, 1945, barely one day after the nuclear bombing of Nagasaki and a mere four days prior to the Japanese surrender, Russia—pushing to establish a visible communist presence in the Far East—officially entered the war against Japan and immediately occupied both Korea and Manchuria. This swift subversive action raised alarms with Truman and the Joint Chiefs of Staff (JCS) in Washington that Stalin was looking to control the entire Korean peninsula. This prompted the Pentagon to arbitrarily propose the land mass be divided in half with the north-south dividing line randomly placed at the 38th Parallel. With troops already occupying the northern provinces of Korea—but not at all ready for an overt confrontation with Washington—Moscow promptly accepted the proposal without objection.

To protect the nation's hard-won interest, the JCS—not really prepared for an occupation of Korea, but wary that the Soviets might try to overrun the entire peninsula—immediately ordered the Army's XXIV Corps stationed on Okinawa to proceed directly to Korea for occupation of the territory below the 38th Parallel.

Like a vast number of Americans in 1945 who had very likely never heard of Korea, all this international geopolitical maneuvering was of little interest to young

Collier Ramsay. However, on both sides of the 38th Parallel, the Koreans—who had already suffered some forty years of Japanese occupation—were immediately outraged by these ill-thought-out, offensively cavalier arrangements. After two full years of haggling over a solution to the stalemate in the original U.S. proposal of unification of Korea, with open elections and withdrawal of occupation troops, in September of 1947, the Soviets offered to enter into a mutual withdrawal of forces. After more internal debate, Washington agreed to a plan for free elections on both sides of the 38th Parallel, thereby leaving Korea still divided, but freeing the people to home rule.

With Dr. Syngman Rhee in the South and Kim Il Sung in the North duly elected in free elections on their respective sides of the 38th Parallel, in September 1948, both American and Russian troops began withdrawing from Korea. On July 1, 1949, a token force designated the Korean Military Advisory Group (KMAG) of about 500 officers and enlisted men under the command of Brigadier General W. Lynn Roberts was left behind to oversee the establishment of the Republic of Korea (ROK) Army. Despite repeated warnings from Syngman Rhee and KMAG intelligence that Kim was building a formidable Russian-armed-and-trained military presence, Washington paid little attention, supplying the KMAG-supported ROK with castoff, out-dated, and poorly-maintained military equipment and arms.

Already moving toward his seventieth birthday in the spring of 1949, General Douglas MacArthur, the egocentric and battle-weary commander of Far Eastern Forces, was forced to stand by helplessly as Truman decimated the military, watching his Far Eastern Eighth Army being reduced to an unwieldy—rather inept and poorly-prepared—conglomerate of four ill-matched divisions.

Not only had the White House's secret vendetta against the military downsized these four peacetime divisions from a regular combat strength of 18,800 to only 12,500 soldiers, but a great majority of these GIs were 1948-1949 draftees and not especially well-trained. As if matters weren't already bad enough in June of 1950, the usually competent MacArthur had never gotten around to implementing his optimistic plans to transform his dwindling troops into a cohesive fighting force. Meanwhile, in South Korea, General Roberts' KMAG troops had been reduced to about 250 men.

During the intervening years since WWII, Collier Ramsay's attention had been focused on girls, sports, his struggles with academia and how to avoid being drafted into the post-war military, and his on-again-off-again romance with Emma Lowell—not to mention the occasional thought about what he really wanted to do with the rest of his life. Thus, on the 26th of June, 1950, when the North Koreans launched a surprise invasion of American-supported South Korea, Collier Ramsay was oblivious that MacArthur's ragtag Eighth Army was in something of a shambles. Like most of his friends, Collier was unmindful that the indigenous South Korean ROK forces had grown to almost 100,000 soldiers, and uncaring that this ill-supported, under-trained ROK force was wasting most of its dwindling ammo and gasoline pursuing renegades and robbers all over the South Korean boondocks and rice paddies.

Away for a weekend in Independence, Missouri, Harry S. Truman—typically thin-skinned and straighforward—took the news of the Communist invasion rather personally, assuming immediately that it was ordered from Moscow. He returned to Washington, vociferously vowing to those within earshot: "We are going to fight..." and "We can't let the U.N. down..." and "By God, I'm going to let them have it."

The North Korean aggression caused such a panic in Washington, by the time Truman arrived back at the White House, the Pentagon had already authorized MacArthur to send two shiploads of ammo to South Korea without first receiving presidential approval. At a hastily-called meeting of fourteen of the top advisors at the temporary presidential residence in Blair House, Truman and his advisors decided that the U.S. would not let Stalin's affront to American prestige go unchallenged. In short order, it was summarily agreed that MacArthur would:

1. Continue sending supplies to prevent the loss of Seoul.
2. Send a "survey party" to Korea to assess their needs.
3. Provide naval and air support to prevent the loss of Seoul and ensure   the safety of U.S. dependents and non-combatants.
4. The Navy's Seventh Fleet would sail from the Philippines to Japan to beef up MacArthur's naval support.

When he received this four-point Blair House communiqué the following day, MacArthur immediately dispatched aging, ailing General John Church with a survey party of twelve officers and two enlisted men to Kimpo Airfield near Seoul. Warned in flight that Kimpo might already be in enemy hands, the pilot wisely diverted to Suwon airfield some twenty miles to the south.

Under false assurances that the ROK Army was a superior, well-trained fighting force, Church was utterly staggered to find that the South Korean military was in complete disarray and South Korean President Syngman Rhee had taken refuge on Jeju, a resort island off the southern coast. Church immediately took charge, trying to restore some semblance of order to total chaos.

Alarmed by Church's distressing news of North Korean Communist superiority and the impending fall of Seoul, on June 29, MacArthur personally flew to Suwon. Upon landing, he asked to be driven to the south bank of the Han River where, under personal attack by enemy mortar fire, he observed Seoul in flames.

Returning to Tokyo determined to recommend that Washington should commit troops and air power to Korea without further delay, MacArthur arose early on the morning of June 30 and drafted a chilling report describing his reconnaissance of the Korean combat zone and stating that the ROK Army was incapable of mounting a defense against the North Korean Communist Army. If the ROK forces were not reinforced immediately, the shortage would threaten the total defeat of the South Korean Republic. He followed this dire appraisal with the terse recommendation that he be allowed to immediately move one Regimental Combat Team (RCT) into the Han River area and/or the Seoul-Suwon corridor to stem the advance while he rushed two full, combat-ready divisions to South Korea.

In Washington during that same time period, Army Chief of Staff, General "Lightning" Joe Collins and his fellow Joint Chiefs in Washington had reached basically the same conclusion, committing American air and naval power to operate against enemy targets beyond the 38th Parallel and also authorizing MacArthur to dispatch "essential" communication and service units and "such

Army combat and service forces as required" to ensure the retention of the "general area Pusan-China" with all judicious haste.

Fatefully, the operational caveat that these units should be limited to a "defensive role" was not included in the original cable.

While Collier Boyd Ramsay and one-hundred-fifty-five million fellow Americans slept blissfully unaware of the portending effect upon their future, Chief of Staff Collins was summoned in the middle of the night to the Pentagon to read MacArthur's brash communiqué which, in essence, proposed that the nation go to war. Well aware that MacArthur's troops were anything but combat-ready— and all foregoing JCS decisions not to engage in war with Asians on Asian soil notwithstanding—incredibly, Collins raised no objections. Future historians would later judge Collins' indecision to be one of the most mind-boggling snafus in the annals of American military history.

Sadly, this was only a hint of the long-running nightmare yet to come.

THE ROANOKE TIMES
Roanoke, Virginia, Wednesday, June 28, 1950
DRAFT EXTENSION GIVEN SPEEDY HOUSE APPROVAL
WASHINGTON, WEDNESDAY, JUNE 28 (AP) – War in Korea broke a Senate-House deadlock over a draft extension today and propelled a broadened one-year extension through the House...

THE TIMES REGISTER
Salem, Virginia, Friday, June 30, 1950
REDS OPEN KOREAN WAR

"Judas H. Priest! What next?" Collier Boyd Ramsay blurted in exasperation as he stared with dismay at the local headlines about Congress's extension of the military draft and the war in Korea. Standing in his Aunt Jackie's kitchen, a golden latticework of early-morning sunshine splashing across the wallpaper, he frowned as an icy lump of anxiety slowly formed in his belly.

"Where's Korea, anyway?" Jacqueline Ramsay Anderson asked. A scant half-dozen years older than Collier, his Aunt Jackie was Collier's father's youngest sister.

"I remember seeing an article in an old *National Geographic*. It's somewhere near Japan and the Chinese mainland, I think," Collier grunted, scowling as he anxiously perused the news.

"Do you think this war could change your standing in the draft?" Collier's aunt remarked, as if she could read his mind.

"I'm not really sure. I'm only back from Richmond two weeks. I still have a regular college student deferment," he muttered fretfully. "I guess, in a pinch, I could always register at Roanoke College to hold on to my exemption."

"Getting married might actually help your draft status," his aunt offered hopefully.

"By George, I think you may be right," Collier brightened. "I surely believe it might."

CHAPTER TWO

THE ROANOKE TIMES
Roanoke, Virginia, Friday, July 21, 1950

GENERAL DEAN AMONG MISSING AS
NORTH KOREANS OVERRUN TAEJON

By FRANK TREMAINE

TOKYO, Friday, July 21 (UP) - American Forces have abandoned Taejon and established a new defense line four miles southeast which already is under heavy Communist attack, Gen. Douglas MacArthur announced today...

Among those who have not been accounted for since the withdrawal was Maj. Gen. William F. Dean, commanding general of 24th Division troops on the Taejon front...

FIRST TEL AVIV, NOW SOME PLACE CALLED TAEJON? Why couldn't the stuffed shirts in Washington let the Jews and Orientals settle their own problems? In Salem, Virginia, on the morning of July 21, 1950, Collier Ramsay's fiancé, Emma Lowell, her head awhirl with details still undone before her wedding day, regarded news of the fighting in Korea as just some brushfire on the other side of the world. Emma had no inkling that over the ensuing weeks and months, this national apathy would quickly change.

What Emma Lowell—and the rest of America—was never privy to, was that three weeks before, on June 30, President Harry S. Truman was already up at 5:00 A.M. when General Collins received MacArthur's urgent request to commit ground troops to Korea.

By 9:30 that morning, Truman had reconvened the JCS, and, scarcely before MacArthur's Tokyo HQ received the official Washington "go-ahead" sending essentially only a token expedition of American ground forces to Korea, to the astonishment of all present—but true to his impulsive, self-important persona of a former WWI artillery Captain—the sitting American president announced MacArthur should be authorized to commit "any and all ground forces under his command necessary to get the job done."

Implausibly, the Joint Chiefs of Staff offered no objection.

When the meeting adjourned, Truman lost little time informing the press and broadcast media that the Air Force had been authorized to attack targets in North Korea with a naval blockade for the entire Korean coast. The 24th Division under the command of General William F. Dean—who had served a year in the post-WWII occupation of Korea—was selected to be the first American fighting force to enter the conflict.

On July 1, Task Force Smith—an advance Regimental Combat Team (RCT) of 406 of General Dean's poorly-trained and under-equipped soldiers under the command of Colonel Brad Smith—was flown into the port of Pusan on the southern tip of the Korean peninsula. The pervasive stink of roadside rice paddies fertilized with human feces filling their nostrils, on July 3, these ruefully inept troops were transported by rail and truck to the frontlines near Taejon. Supported by only one lone, forlorn battery of 134 men and six 105-mm howitzers from Miller Perry's Field Artillery Battalion, Task Force Smith was ordered to push forward to take a position on the Seoul-Pusan highway just north of Osan. Verging near the edge of panic as they encountered large groups of ROK deserters fleeing south, Smith's untested soldiers celebrated July 4 slogging through bone-chilling rain and mud.

The morning of July 5—only a month before her wedding date—Emma Lowell remained oblivious to the fact that Task Force Smith had scarcely begun to dig in near Osan, before it was attacked by a column of North Korean People's Army infantry led by Russian-built T-34 tanks. With only ten antiquated 2.36-inch bazookas and Perry's artillery, Task Force Smith was pathetically overmatched. After a morning of futile resistance using outmoded weapons and faulty ammo against the T-34s, Brad Smith gave the order to withdraw. In broad daylight, with untested troops under blistering fire, discipline collapsed, and attempts at an orderly withdrawal proved to be a disaster. Distinguished by inspiring instances of personal heroics by Brad Smith and other individuals in their initial American Army encounter with the NKPA, Task Force Smith was completely wiped out in a matter of a few hours. Word of the humiliating defeat and the ensuing cowardice quickly spread like an insidious pestilence exerting a profound effect on the already-dismal morale at the front.

Meanwhile, suffering from abominable weather and lack of suitable transport, the remaining 21st and 34th regiments of Dean's 24th Division finally began arriving by fits and starts. By the end of the first week, Bill Dean, clearly failing to demonstrate a grasp of intelligent battlefield strategy, suffered the unforgivable mortification of having wasted over 3000 (dead, wounded, captured, or missing) of the 5000 soldiers under his command while squandering truckloads of irreplaceable equipment.

By July 13, the North Koreans had suffered only minor losses in pushing their advance fifty miles further south to the new American defensive positions near the Kum River. During the first week of combat, MacArthur reported the dire conditions in Korea to the JCS with an urgent request for reinforcements of a field army of four full divisions with ancillary supporting services. Given the sad state of the standing military, MacArthur's request had a sobering effect on the JCS, and Truman immediately dispatched Army General Joe Collins and Air Force General Hoyt Vandenberg to fly to Tokyo and Korea to survey the situation.

Arriving in Tokyo the morning of July 13, the generals listened to MacArthur's plea for two field armies—as well as a pitch for enough troops and material to defeat the NKPA and unify Korea.

Leaving MacArthur with a sobering reminder of the sorry state of America's existing worldwide military forces, Collins and Vandenberg flew with Eighth Army commander, Johnnie Walker, to an airfield near the Eighth Army field HQ at Taegu, Korea, about halfway between Taejon and Pusan, to confer with commanding General Dean. Neither Dean nor Walker was optimistic, but Walker believed they could retreat to a more defensible line and defend and hold a perimeter around Pusan long enough for reinforcements to arrive. After only an hour on the ground in Korea, Collins and Vandenberg headed back to Tokyo where they briefly conferred again with MacArthur before returning to Washington.

On July 14—about the same time Collins and Vandenberg were reporting to the White House they did not believe MacArthur needed two divisions—on the Korean front, the NKPA was launching an assault on the Kum River line.

Somewhat rested and resupplied, over the next four days, the well-organized North Koreans came screaming across the river shredding all three regiments of Dean's 24th Division—sending them into full and totally disorganized retreat.

Meanwhile back in Virginia, bride-to-be Emma Lowell—like most of the rest of the English-speaking world reading *New York Herald Tribune* news correspondent Marguerite Higgins' dispatches from the front—was becoming vaguely aware that a new term, "bug out," was creeping into the language.

On the morning of July 18, General Dean hastily regrouped his woefully demoralized stragglers at Taejon. Dean was determined to try to hold the position until he could be reinforced by the 1st Cavalry Division which Eighth Army Commander, Johnnie Walker, had reported was landing three-quarters of the way across the peninsula at Pohang on the Sea of Japan. The holding of Taejon against the superior NKPA, like the rest of Dean's and Walker's tactical and strategic plans, turned out to be only a desperate pipedream. The NKPA launched its attack on Taejon the morning of July 19, and by the following day, July 20, they had completely encircled and overrun Bill Dean's badly-decimated troops, scattering them like rabbits into the surrounding rice paddies and hills.

When the smoke cleared, General William F. Dean was nowhere to be found.

Dreading her appointment for a pre-marital physical and fitting for a diaphragm, Emma Lowell wheeled into the parking lot of the College Avenue Medical Arts building in Salem and breathed a sigh as she set the gearshift lever of her brand-new Ford sedan into Park and gave the steering wheel a loving pat. Emma was proud of that little car. She had purchased it with her newfound independence of being a *bona fide* employee of the local Veterans Administration Hospital—her first real job as a professional Registered Nurse. When she thought about it, it was still hard to believe that the VA Hospital had actually recruited her because of her performance on the state nursing exams. A graduate of the nursing school at Lewis-Gale Hospital, Emma had achieved the second-highest score on her state boards in Richmond the previous September.

So now why was a little thing like a pelvic exam and the fitting of a diaphragm bothering her, an honest-to-god professional nurse?

As she gathered up her purse, she glanced nervously back at the front-page headline of *The Roanoke Times*, "GENERAL DEAN AMONG MISSING AS NORTH KOREANS OVERRUN TAEJON", on the seat beside her. The anxiety of having all five of her brothers and one of her four sisters overseas in the combat zone during World War II was still fresh in her mind. Now, as if she didn't already have enough to worry about, the recent turn of events in Korea was beginning to look serious. Her fiancé, Collier Ramsay, had told her to relax, pointing out that married men were exempt from peacetime draft—getting married sealed the deal. But, she had reminded him, they had drafted married men with children in World War II.

It was impossible to get Collier to take life seriously.

They'd been going steady since their junior year at Andrew Lewis, but, despite the fact that she loved him, Collier was exasperating and she had never really expected him to amount to much. In high school, he'd played all sports and had wanted someday to be a coach. Then, when he did the drawings for their high school annual, he thought he might want to become an artist. Either ambition seemed okay until he went off to Bluefield Junior College to play basketball and Lida, his snobby mother, made him take Pre-Med.

He had performed quite well academically at Bluefield. But when he graduated with his junior college diploma, he had finally decided he wanted to pursue his ambition to become an artist. When he told his parents he wanted to transfer to Richmond Professional Institute of the College of William and Mary, Emma was not surprised when his father, who had always encouraged him to be his own man, had intervened on his behalf with the ambitious, status-conscious Lida. So, after graduating from Bluefield, he had transferred to RPI, switching his major from pre-Med to Advertising Art. If that weren't irresponsible enough, at RPI, he had roomed briefly with the former captain of a fancy, prep-school golf team and taken up golf. Now that he was home and working with his uncle for a national supermarket chain, all he talked about was playing golf and going to New York and becoming the second-coming of Norman Rockwell.

Emma, already in nursing school, had had her heart set on him becoming a doctor and had little empathy for his following what she considered such a frivolous dream. It made her downright furious that he had practically had a hissy when she told him she wanted to take up golf, too. He had some nerve—he really wasn't all that good at golf. And, when you got right down to it, he wasn't so hot as a commercial artist for that matter.

Collier acted so superior and was such a dreamer. But he was a fantastic lover—so fantastic, sometimes her need for him and the sheer recklessness of their clandestine lovemaking made her very nervous, afraid their outrageous behavior would be discovered.

In that regard, just last evening, her oldest brother, L.E. Jr., and his wife, Shasta, had dropped by for an overnight stopover en route to their mountain retreat near Asheville. As usual, Emma had stepped aside and given them the use of her bedroom.

Emma was quite accustomed to giving up things. The youngest of ten children—the only one still living at home—she had spent most of the twenty-two years of her young life wearing her older sisters' hand-me-downs and taking a back seat to all nine of her older siblings. But now, by darn—she shook her head in an involuntary gesture of resolve—with her secure, well-paying nursing job at the VA and her wedding less than two weeks away, all that was about to change.

It was only eleven more days now. Her tummy did a little flip just thinking about it.

She and Collier had found a cozy, furnished apartment in south Roanoke on the side of Mill Mountain just across the river from Victory Stadium and had already begun moving their linens and kitchen articles. Not counting the dorm in nursing school, the only place she had ever lived was at home with five brothers and four sisters. Just the prospect of having a place of her own brought a little smile to her face. And she really hadn't done a lot of smiling lately.

Over the past month as her wedding date grew closer, she had been plagued with awakening in the early hours of the morning, her mind anxiously worrying if she were doing the right thing. Recalling this morning's conversation with Shasta, her smug sister-in-law, over a hurried breakfast of cold cereal, hardly eased Emma's unsettled state of mind.

"So, you're actually going to marry that self-styled juvenile Don Juan? Have you heard the tales about his substitute seventh grade teacher? I really thought you were smarter than this, Emma. It's not too late, you know?" Shasta had regarded her coolly over the rim of her coffee cup. "You're not PG are you? You can trust me, Emma. I won't tell."

"Pregnant!" she had exploded. "What kind of girl do you think I am?"

"C'mon Emma, who do you think you're kidding? You've been letting Collier Ramsay into your panties since your junior year in high school. You forget I lived right here in this house the whole time you were dating until after L.E., Jr. came home from the war. That boy couldn't keep his hands off of you—much less keep that thing in his pants. You think I didn't know you did it on this very kitchen table with us playing cards in the living room. If your daddy had known, he would have skinned you both alive."

"How dare you, Shasta! I'm still a virgin. We've never gone all the way," she had protested weakly, feeling the rush of color creep up her neck.

Struggling not to cast a guilty glance down at the red-linoleum top of the old kitchen table in question, Emma had wondered what Shasta—or Collier for that matter—would say if they found out about Trey Moseley. The son of Simpkins Moseley, Sr., a senior staff physician at the VA Hospital, Simpkins Moseley III, Trey, a good-looking, but very conceited—despite being rather short, and wearing expensive elevator shoes—medical student serving an externship at Lewis-Gale, had lured her into the intern's quarters and seduced her late one night, year before last while she was still in training and only the two of them had been working on the medical floor. At the time, Collier was away in Richmond and they had been in the middle of one of their silly periodic lovers' quarrels. After the Napoleonic bantam rooster had finished thrusting his reedy pencil-penis into her and she was still lying on the bed with her uniform pushed up above her waist, confused by discovering she actually enjoyed the experience, she quickly dismissed any thoughts of the career-destroying consequences of lodging a complaint against the well-connected fledgling physician. Then, since Moseley's assault had occurred when she and Collier were not getting along very well, she had continued to submit herself to the arrogant medical student almost nightly for the remaining six weeks of his externship—long past the time she had patched up her quarrel with Collier.

Thankfully, she had not heard from the high-handed little weasel since, but the guilty memory did nothing to help Emma's stomach ache.

"Look, Shasta, I'm warning you. Don't you dare spread those trashy rumors. Collier and I have never...I swear..."

"Okay, okay. No big deal. Just calm down...from the looks of you, you're already a nervous wreck. Anyway, I wish you both all the best. With this thing in Korea, you're going to need it."

It was mostly true what Shasta had said about her sexual permissiveness with Collier. Almost from the very beginning of their courtship, Emma had let him do almost anything he wanted except enter her vagina. God, she shivered with pleasure, remembering the first time he had touched her down there. But it was also true that she had steadfastly drawn the line; as much as she had wanted him to, she had never let Collier actually put his penis inside her.

Still, even if she had succeeded in keeping his penis outside her vaginal passageway, she shuddered remembering how often he would lose control and ejaculate all over her belly and her thighs. She had carried wads of Kleenex in her purse, and they had sweated the arrival of her period practically every month for six long years while they finished high school and she finished training and he finished college.

What troubled her now were her hateful sister-in-law's trashy innuendos about Collier's sexual history. Collier had told her about the rich lawyer's daughter having a crush on him in seventh grade. But what was this about a substitute seventh-grade teacher?

Had he really told her everything?

If he were keeping secrets from her, maybe it served him right that she had let Trey Moseley put his skinny penis all the way into her. It would probably kill smug Mister Collier Ramsey if he ever found out about that.

Rousing from her troubling reveries, Emma checked her watch again and opened the car door. She needed to get moving. It was already five until nine and her appointment with Esther Brown was for nine sharp. As she closed the car door, a final worried glance at a newspaper headline, "**LOCAL MARINES GET ORDERS FOR ACTIVE DUTY,**" did absolutely nothing to ease her stomach ache. And, the stress of wedding plans had certainly not helped her chronic constipation, making her nagging problem with painful hemorrhoids worse.

CHAPTER THREE

THE ROANOKE TIMES
Roanoke, Virginia, Friday, July 28, 1950
AMERICANS DRIVEN BACK 25 MILES

NORTH KOREANS PUSH TOWARD PORT OF PUSAN
By FRANK TREMAINE

TOKYO, Friday, July 28 (UP) – A lightning thrust by Communist forces along the southeast coast of Korea today drove American troops back 25 miles to within 50 miles of the port of Pusan...

100,000 DRAFTEES SOUGHT BY ARMY
Wanted in September and October;
Enlistments Frozen for a Year

THE ROANOKE TIMES
Roanoke, Virginia, Friday, August 4, 1950
RED JAB AGAINST NEW U.S. POSITIONS HALTED

TOKYO, Friday, August 4 (AP) – A heavy Red attack was repulsed early today by the U.S. 25th Division, hurriedly shifted from the north to the crucial southern front 35 miles west of the vital port of Pusan.

Fast-moving North Korean forces elsewhere began shelling new riverfront positions along a shortened, 125-mile front in the shrinking beachhead of southern Korea.

FRETTING OVER HAVING TO TRAVEL into the heart of a polio epidemic raging all over southwestern Virginia, on the eve of his honeymoon, Collier Ramsay scarcely took notice of the disquieting news that Commanding General William F. Dean was still missing after the Eighth Army debacle around Taejon. For that matter, he was only superficially aware that during their first few weeks in Korea, the American Army was suffering a horrendous bloodbath at the hands of the North Korean Communist invaders.

Besides losing 3000 of the 24th Division's original 5000 troops in their humiliating 'bugout' from their initial positions near Osan—with an additional loss of 1150 of the 4000 troops deployed in the attempt to hold Taejon—by the time American commanders had fallen back fifteen miles to positions at the Division Command Post at Yongdong on July 22 and assessed their losses, they could only account for 8,660 of the total of 15,965 personnel committed.

Although General William Kean's 25th Division was landing in Pusan from July 10 to July 12 and could have provided important reinforcements for General Dean's beleaguered and overmatched 24th Division, uppermost in the minds of MacArthur and the JCS was to stop the NKPA advance and establish a perimeter around the lower peninsula protecting innocent American civilians hoping to evacuate through the port of Pusan. With that objective in mind, most of Kean's 25th were sent directly north to defend the Eighth Army CP at Taegu, diverting a small detachment to secure the port of Pohang where the 1ˢᵗ Cavalry Division was scheduled to land on July 18.

High hopes were riding on the 1ˢᵗ Cav under the command of Hobart R. Gay, an aging, ailing, one-eyed, two-star General who had been George Patton's chief-of-staff and also had the questionable distinction of having been riding in the car with Patton when he was fatally injured near Manheim, Germany in December 1945. Upon Gay's landing, General Johnnie Walker ordered the general to attack directly up the Taegu-Taejon road, south of Kean's 25ᵗʰ Division.

Luckily for both Kean's 25ᵗʰ Division and Gay's 1ˢᵗ Cav, the NKPA had paused to regroup after the capture of Taejon, affording General Church the opportunity to provide the shattered elements of Bill Dean's 24ᵗʰ Division with a chance to withdraw to Taegu for a well-deserved rest.

Their reprieve was short-lived.

On the morning of July 23, the regrouped NKPA tank-led infantry pushed south and eastward again along both highways toward Taegu. Dressed like peasants and infiltrating like guerilla bands by commingling with multitudes of fleeing civilians and deserting ROK soldiers, large numbers of NKPA troops were able to attack from all sides—sometimes even from the rear.

For the green, untested Americans and their badly discombobulated leaders, these guerilla tactics were a nightmare, resulting in panic-driven, indiscriminate massacres of innocent civilians.

After heavy fighting all day, the Communists overran and surrounded the leading elements of the newly-deployed 1ˢᵗ Cav. Finally, on the night of July 24-25, after suffering heavy losses of both troops and equipment, some of the survivors managed to fight their way clear. By dawn July 25, however, the North Koreans had overwhelmed three of the four American battalions. Despite their devastating losses, by the end of the day on July 26, the 1ˢᵗ Cav had regrouped and taken more defensible positions.

During this same period, back in Virginia, Collier Ramsay was totally preoccupied with setting up a silkscreen shop over the Kroger store in the old farmer's market area of downtown Roanoke and helping Emma move their new bed linens and everyday china into the furnished apartment in the old residential section across the Roanoke River from Victory Stadium in south Roanoke and remained oblivious that on the other side of the world, the armored-led Red infantry had launched a massive attack on Bill Kean's 25ᵗʰ Division, just dug in on the high ground along the Kumchon-Hamchang road. Although repeatedly overrun, the two-battalion 27ᵗʰ Infantry Wolfhounds under Mike Michaelis were able to fight a skillfully-conducted holding action, significantly slowing the Red offensive.

Celebration was cut short, however, as by July 26, the entire 25ᵗʰ Division front was under punishing attack. Fortuitously, at this point, the North Koreans split off two crack divisions in an attempt to encircle the Eighth Army by swinging south to the coast and capturing Pusan.

With the goal of capturing Pusan by mid-August to celebrate the fifth anniversary of the liberation of Korea from Japan, on August 4, the NKPA had spread its forces along the defensive Pusan Perimeter and were preparing for an all-out attack. Although the remaining NKPA forces continued to pound the retreating 25ᵗʰ and 1ˢᵗ Cav Divisions, forcing them back another twenty-five miles, the NKPA's fatal tactical blunder provided General Walker the opportunity to make a strategic redeployment of his troops, spreading them across a wider front.

This shaky, historic "Pusan Perimeter" eventually proved to be the decisive turning point of the war.

Thursday evening, the third of August, after Emma and her parents, and the last of the other guests from Lida's wedding rehearsal dinner finally pulled out of the driveway, Collier walked out on the darkened front porch and smoked a cigarette before he followed his parents upstairs and went to bed. But, although exhausted both physically and emotionally, sleep would not find him. All day long, disquieting recriminations and misgivings about going through with his marriage to Emma had prowled his consciousness like a pack of wild dogs circling a slaughter house.

It was not too late to back out of this. If he got in the car right now and just bugged out for parts unknown, he could be in Washington or New York or even halfway to Florida before anyone would miss him.

He could just picture the pandemonium at the church and all the self-righteous "I-told-you-so" smirks on the faces of those who were always warning Emma that he wasn't good enough for her—snidely telling her he'd never amount to anything.

But no! He buried his head in a pillow; no way could he back out now. Anyway, if things didn't work out, divorces were pretty easy to get nowadays.

And not good enough! What the hell? From the very beginning, he'd been the first male who had treated Emma with any decency. Somewhere down the line, he'd make those bastards eat their words. Someday he was going to make a real name for himself as a famous illustrator. It would serve the self-righteous bastards right.

Besides, it really wasn't that he didn't care for Emma. Even though from the very beginning, he had recognized that they were worlds apart intellectually and spiritually, he did love her...well...as much as he was capable of loving anyone, he supposed.

What bothered him most was her all-consuming self-righteous goodness and purity. How could he possibly live up to that? And, deep down, she was a "man hater."

Although Emma was practically a saint and had a good head on her shoulders, anyone with half a brain could see she was pathologically repressed. It all came down to the fact that she hated her father, L.E. Lowell, Sr. As a result—although she was quick to deny it—Emma essentially mistrusted all males. Collier understood that subconsciously this deeply-ingrained suspicion also included him. Still, despite her psychological repression, that was not to say that Emma was some species of airhead. After all, she had graduated fourth in their high-school class of one hundred and forty-four.

He had graduated forty-fourth. Yet, he was uncomfortably aware he was light years smarter and far more sophisticated than Emma. By the time he was eight he had out-spelled everyone in the entire Fort Lewis Elementary School and skipped the third grade. When he was ten—going on eleven—sixth graders in all the county schools, including Roanoke, Salem and Vinton, had taken Achievement tests, and his mother, who was President of the PTA, blabbed to everyone that he had scored the highest I.Q. in the entire county. It was not only embarrassing, but caused Collier all sorts of trouble. From that time forward, his well-intended teachers kept throwing those test results up to him in their frustrated efforts to inspire him to make better grades.

Besides, being smart didn't necessarily make a person good, and it most certainly hadn't made him virtuous.

It came as no surprise to Collier that when they began dating, Emma had been a virgin.

So to keep her good opinion, he had lied to her about his own virginity.

Although he had been only sixteen, his own sexual history weighed down on him like the stone ceiling of a medieval torture chamber. It would have shocked his bride-to-be to know that while he never dated girls in high school before his first date with her, he had been sexually initiated at age five by the adventuresome seven-year-old daughter of his family's next-door neighbor. This delightfully-titillating relationship continued off and on until he was in the third grade when his eager tutor's family moved back up north. From fourth to sixth grade, he'd been lucky enough to enjoy a few sparsely-scattered, earthy barn-loft sexual encounters with a succession of mostly older farm girls in their rural community five miles west of Salem.

In the seventh grade, there had been Miss Alma Sandhurst.

The year following Collier's infamous I.Q. testing, Miss Sandhurst—a pleasantly shaped young substitute teacher from Farmville State Teachers College whose otherwise pretty face was marred by a smattering of tiny acne scars—had caught him reading smutty books his seventh-grade classmates, Doris Sink and Nancy Parrish, had pilfered from someone, most likely their parents. The girls were at least two years older and very sexy to Collier's soon-to-be twelve-year-old mind. After class, Miss Sandhurst had taken the girls aside, given them a stern talking-to and had told them to take the books back where they belonged.

Instead of a similar perfunctory scolding, Miss Sandhurst had kept him after school sitting in front of her desk, his heart filled with dread while she busied herself with paperwork.

"Did you read those naughty books, Collier?" trying to look quite stern, she had asked after perhaps an hour when she finally put her papers aside.

"Yes'm...some of 'em," he had replied, his head down.

"What made you want to read them?" Miss Sandhurst persisted.

"Uhmm...ah...what do you mean, Ma'am?"

"Did you already know about the things in those books...the naughty things men and women do with each other?"

"Well...sort of...but I...ah..." he had stammered, not knowing what to say.

"Have Nancy and Doris suggested you get together with them outside of school?" Miss Sandhurst got up from her desk and walked over and closed the door. He watched fascinated as she slowly turned the key, then walked back and stood in front of him, her sensual hips squarely in front of his nose.

"Well, Collier, have they?"

"No, Ma'am...uhmm...they...uh..." he tried to lie, his hopes gone a-glimmering.

"Look at me, Collier. Have you ever done any of those naughty things with girls?" Now, gazing down at him with her mouth slightly open, she seemed to be having trouble breathing.

"No, Ma'am..." staring up over her ripe bosom, he had found it difficult to speak.

"Collier, have you ever seen a *real* woman naked?" Her voice hoarsened as she started fiddling with the buttons of her tight white blouse. Gazing intently down at him, she slowly unbuttoned her blouse halfway, shrugging the straps of her slip and brassiere off her shoulders, fully exposing her cantaloupe-sized breasts.

"No, Ma'am...ah..." he had croaked.

"Oh, Collier, baby, just look at you," she whispered hoarsely, staring at the bulge in the crotch of his corduroys.

Looking down, he had hung his head, embarrassed that his penis had suddenly grown rock hard, pushing his pants out in front.

"I'm sorry, Ma'am...I...I can't help it," he had half-sobbed with shame.

"Unbutton your pants, Collier," she had commanded, gently.

"Ma'am?..."

"Unbutton your pants, I want to show you about those naughty books," she repeated and reaching up under the skirt of her dress, she pulled her white panties down, stepping completely free of them.

Fumbling clumsily, he had scarcely unloosed himself before she had straddled him and he had felt his organ slipping inside her tight, wet passage. Before he could even catch his breath, a great burst of skyrockets went off inside his head as he felt himself gushing inside her.

"Oh, I'm sorry, Ma'am! I...I couldn't help it..." he cried, but she quickly shushed him by putting her mouth on his, ramming her tongue inside as she rode him hard.

"Promise you'll never tell, Collier," she had cautioned sometime later, kissing her finger and pressing it to his lips as she let him out of her car at the school bus stop near his home.

At school the following morning, Miss Sandhurst had scarcely glanced at him as she left Doris and Nancy in their seats in the back of the room and quietly moved Collier to a seat near the front away from the window.

For the remainder of Miss Sandhurst's two-month-long practicum, Collier continued to hope she would keep him after-school again, but his hopes were in vain. Then, just as suddenly as she had come into his life, one morning she was gone.

Collier had never heard from her again.

After the episode with Miss Sandhurst in the seventh grade, there had been a brief, mostly platonic and one-sided, relationship with a wealthy lawyer's daughter—which consisted mostly of her nanny picking him up in their expensive Chrysler station wagon at his parent's home and delivering him to her daddy's impressive estate on the river near Fort Lewis School. Under the watchful eye of the faithful nanny, there had been absolutely no hanky-panky. After they entered eighth grade at Andrew Lewis High School, the lawyer's daughter ran with a more sophisticated crowd whom she knew from belonging to the country club. Up until his junior year when he started dating Emma, Collier had dedicated most of his time and effort to athletics.

While he gave it no particular importance, Collier would have to admit he had always been invested with a robust sexual curiosity—a state of consciousness which he found as ordinary as breathing. Although he was not predatory and most certainly not obsessive—if you didn't count daily masturbation—he was undeniably opportunistic. Consequently, from the beginning, his solicitous attentions to affection-starved Emma were subconsciously subverted to finding the quickest way inside the tight crotch band of her freshly-laundered, white, cotton, Fruit-of-the-Loom panties—a goal which had turned out to be far easier accomplished than he had ever imagined. On their second date, their first real date actually, he had been astounded when goody-two-shoes Emma had let him put his hand on—and then inside—her nicely-filled, hand-me-down Maidenform bra.

Less than a month passed before she was regularly petting him to orgasm.

Amazingly, this quickly led to Emma allowing him to place his penis inside her labia while her hand firmly directed his throbbing organ directly to her clitoris. This exercise resulted in a countless succession of orgasmic accidents with endless ensuing recriminations and anxieties always followed by virtuous vows of future celibacy. Quite predictably, no matter how sincere, these solemn resolutions were always short-lived.

But regardless how they had sweated over her tardy periods each month and how loudly Emma continued to protest, "We can't go on taking these crazy chances!" the actual quitting was akin to trying to divert a moth from a flame. And, she had done little to help the situation—after all, wasn't she almost a half-year older and a devout Episcopalian?

About the only success they'd had in controlling their wanton coupling was that no matter how hard he tried, Emma refused to allow him to ram his perpetually turgid penis inside her tight vagina. Even on those rare occasions when he had persuaded her to just let him try, she would quickly pull back complaining, "Stop, Honey! It hurts."

Although he found her protests downright maddening, no matter how he wheedled and complained that it was going to happen soon enough, Emma had steadfastly refused to give in.

Collier was careful never to betray any hint of his physical intimacy with Emma to anyone—not even his brother Jim ever had a clue. For that matter, he was sure none of his buddies would have believed him even if he had told them. Or if they would have believed him, they would have shunned him like a pariah for defiling her purity and innocence. In the small-town south, a woman's reputation was everything.

Unwaveringly, for the remainder of their Junior and Senior years at high school, Collier had remained true to Emma. When she entered nursing training after graduation from high school, the restrictive life Emma had to live in the dorm of the nursing school at Lewis-Gale Hospital had caused Collier a lot of sexual frustration. But it was going away to Bluefield College the first week of September that ultimately precipitated the breakdown of his fidelity to her. Even though he boarded the N&W passenger train in Salem headed for college with firm resolve to be true to his sweetheart, the separation of a two-hour train ride with the attending anonymity and opportunity proved to be too much temptation for his raging, male hormonal overload.

On his first day at college, he had hardly deposited Uncle Bob's borrowed travel-weary, saddle-leather suitcase on his dormitory bed before he and Bob Ullman, one of his prospective basketball teammates from New York, caught a bus downtown to reconnoiter the soda fountain at Goodykoontz' drugstore, reputed to be an after-school hangout for the high-school crowd. In less than an hour by the electric clock over the oversized, marble soda fountain, Collier had fallen hopelessly in lust with Betty Jean Kitts, a curvaceous flaming redhead and rising senior at Beaver High. Like Collier's father in Roanoke, Betty Jean's daddy worked for the N&W railroad in Keystone, a small West Virginia coal camp about twenty miles outside of Bluefield. To avail herself of the best public education available amidst a wasteland of sub-standard schools in the surrounding coal fields, BeeJay rode on her daddy's railroad pass, commuting daily by train to attend the prestigious senior high school in Bluefield.

On most weekends, the good-looking redhead stayed over with her almost equally attractive schoolmate, Gladys Coffman, to enjoy the ball games and other social life with their classmates. Gladys lived with her brother and his wife in their modest cottage in a middleclass residential section out near the college. Gladys' brother was an accountant with a local firm, but he frequently took his wife home to Charleston for weekends, leaving Gladys and BeeJay to their own devices. Suitably impressed that Collier and Bob were honest-to-goodness college men, BeeJay wasted no time in introducing Gladys to Bob Ullman and the girls invited their newfound college boyfriends to meet them that evening at the opening game of the high-school football season. After the game, the girls invited the boys to join them at Gladys' house, informing them with a wink that Gladys' brother and sister-in-law were spending the weekend in Charleston.

"Just to keep our nosy neighbors happy," once inside her brother's house, Gladys turned on a small lamp in the living room and tugged Bob into the darkness of an unlit adjoining room.

"Follow me," BeeJay whispered to Collier, pulling him by the hand into what turned out to be the kitchen. Before his eyes had a chance to adjust to the darkness, she was tonguing him hotly, full in the mouth, grinding her pelvis against his lower abdomen. After a long moment of this wildly erotic exercise, she stepped back and unfastened Collier's hands from behind her back.

Speechless, Collier watched as she pulled her sweater over her head and tossed it aside. Without hesitation she quickly unsnapped her bra and released her breasts which, by the streetlight filtering through the blinds over the kitchen sink, Collier could see were incredibly well-formed with large, pale-pink aureola, the nipples erect and jutting ceilingward. Tossing her bra in the general direction of her sweater, she guided Collier's hands to her blue-veined, alabaster breasts and rubbed her hips hard against his granite-hard erection.

"Do you like me?" Her words were lost inside his mouth as she resumed tonguing him hotly.

"Uhmm..." he murmured against her busy tongue. The feel of her smooth, swollen breasts drove him half-crazy, but when he tried to lean down to suck her nipples, she pulled him urgently to the floor.

"Hurry, get undressed." Resting on her knees, she began taking off her skirt and panties. In a heartbeat, she was bending over him buck-naked, pulling off his jeans and jockey briefs.

"Go slow...I've never gone all the way...I still have my cherry..." she whispered as she rolled onto her back, raised her arms and spread her legs wide, inviting him.

"Are you sure you want this?..." Collier stammered. She had him firmly by the penis guiding him into her wetness.

"You talk too much..." she muttered.

"Wait...I'm gonna come..." He felt as if he would explode as his penis slowly made headway into the tight hot space between her legs.

"No...don't..." Beejay pushed against his chest until he had withdrawn his organ. Then she began pumping his penis with her hand as he spewed a geyser of semen all over her white belly. After the flow of juices finally subsided, she got up and left the kitchen. When she came back, she had a damp, warm washcloth and a clean hand towel and cleaned him. When she finished, she placed the towel and washrag on the floor beside them and pulled him over on top of her again.

Not surprisingly, Collier found his erection undiminished as she began slowly guiding him inside her once again.

Fortunately the college had no curfews or any requirement for permission to stay away from the dorm overnight. The four of them ran around naked the remainder of the night and most of Saturday. Gladys' brother had left the girls plenty of food in the house and they cooked when they were hungry. The rest of that night and all day and night Saturday they remained naked having frequent sex, but there was no swapping partners. They slept in short naps, took the occasional shower with the girls and ate from time to time. That's the way it went for the entire weekend.

Collier thought he had died and gone to heaven.

For the entire month of September and halfway into October, their weekends became regular orgies until Gladys's brother and sister-in-law walked in unexpectedly early one Sunday morning and found all four of them gloriously naked in the same bed.

That of course had been the end of that. Collier and Bob left, shaking in their loafers and thanking their lucky stars Gladys' brother had not reported them to the college administration.

Before Christmas vacation, Collier had another brief, but steamy dalliance with sweetly-carnal Dorrie Donovan, a day-student at the college whose daddy ran a used-car lot. Their sweaty coupling in the backseat of Dorrie's secondhand low-mileage Oldsmobile sedan had been exciting until she started pestering him to accompany her to Sunday services at the First Baptist church where his mother's second cousins were prominent members. Quickly confessing that he was reuniting with his hometown sweetheart, Collier assured Dorrie he hoped they would always be good friends and walked away with a sigh of relief.

Following close upon his split with Dorrie, there had been the early autumn night at a house party of high-school students when he had given in to the urging of classmate, Bob Hemmings, and let himself be talked into accompanying three carloads of teenagers, tipsy on the contents of an old-fashioned, galvanized-zinc washtub full of Purple Jesus—a popular concoction of gin and Welch's grape juice—as they embarked on an depraved excursion to a secluded fire trail halfway up East River Mountain.

Once there, he watched in open-mouthed amazement as the bench-like backseat cushions of two of the cars were dragged out on the slag-cindered parking ground and the only girls, Annie and Ginnie—the depressingly homely daughters of a prominent Bluefield physician and a local merchant—quickly stripped naked and lay down on the bench seats, docilely waiting with their legs spread wide apart.

Declining the opportunity to go first with either—or both girls—of his choosing, Collier would never forget standing by in disgust as Hemmings—the other "honored guest"—stepped to the head of the line and accepted "firsts" with Annie, the doctor's daughter. Then, amid cheers and giggles, one-by-one, the two girls took on the entire entourage of fourteen males punctuating the chill night air with loud, vulgar exhortations of encouragement.

To his everlasting credit—and Hemmings' insulting comments notwithstanding—Collier had refused to participate in the degrading gang-bang.

Thinking back now, he smiled remembering that one of the girls had presented Hemmings with a dose of clap.

That revolting episode had put Collier on the straight-and-narrow for awhile, at least.

But this conscientious renewed vow of monogamous fidelity to Emma was not to last forever.

The ensuing summer between graduating Bluefield and matriculating at RPI, youthful *naiveté*, the kindest word for *utter stupidity* he could think of, had cost him golden opportunities with two slightly-older water nymphs—Natalie Bowman, an absolutely breathtaking, Jean-Harlow blonde, and Mary Kay O'Brien, an auburn-haired, green-eyed jungle cat—at the Red Cross National Aquatic School held at Minnehaha Springs, West Virginia, where he had been afforded a scholarship to obtain his Water Safety Instructor's certification. Sometimes he still woke in the middle of the night with his loins—and his heart—throbbing at the recollection of those two openly-inviting young women who had done everything but knock him over the head and drag him into the bushes. Remembering, he blushed with mortification for his awkwardness.

As unsophisticated as he had been back then, he had let them both get clean away.

"You really blew your chance with me, you jerk. I'm in the book on Quackenbos Street in D.C. Call me if you're ever up my way," Bowman had whispered in his ear when he danced with her in the recreation room that last night at Minnehaha Springs.

Mary Kay had written him as soon as he got back home and invited him to come to the Fall Dances at Iowa State in Ames. It would have been easy enough. He could have used his father's railroad pass to get there, but, then, there was a matter of finding the money, and he didn't have a tux. Besides, he had been certain Emma would find him out.

Last night in the kitchen, he had been amazed at how many long-forgotten names had come floating up from the past. There had been so many minor peccadilloes, he had actually lost count. It made him tremble to think that in less than an hour, one of his casual dalliances would actually be standing at the altar as one of Emma's bridesmaids.

It didn't matter that he was more intelligent and sophisticated than Emma. In her childlike innocence, compared to him she was a veritable saint. But, brought up under the influence of the mindless Baptist faith, Collier also understood that good Episcopal Emma's repression was magnified by an all-consuming Protestant guilt twice the size of New York City.

Collier would have violently protested any suggestion that men usually look to replace their mother when choosing a mate. By comparison, his mother, Lida, was a self-centered hypochondriac who spent the first fourteen years of Collier's life lying around in bed "sick" most of the time. Love did strange things to people. Collier had never really understood why his father lavished the neurotic shrew with almost servile adoration. Unbelievably selfish, his mother would sometimes call Fort Lewis Elementary School when he was only a fourth grader and have him sent home with the first graders on the noon bus to do the family washing and other household chores. From time to time, at odd moments, Collier stopped and shook his head just thinking it over. Yet, when he did mull it over, he had to admit his mother did have some redeeming qualities. He would be the first to thank her for teaching him Emily Post's book of etiquette, cover-to-cover, before he entered first grade—that little treasure of education had invested him with confidence in all manner of pretentious social situations.

When he was fourteen, Collier's mom had actually gotten a job at the county courthouse to help pay for his college. Even so, she was still pretty much a vain, self-absorbed woman.

It was almost incomprehensible to Collier that Emma's father—a man who held the lofty position of regional plant manager of the telephone company—could be so completely reprehensible. In sharp contrast, Collier's own father, Harry Collier Ramsay, was the best all-around father a boy could ask for. As far as Collier was concerned, his father ought to be on the cover of *Time* magazine as "all-time husband and father of the fucking millennium."

The youngest of ten children in a highly screwed-up family system headed by the most selfish, coldest, alcoholic SOB anyone could possibly imagine, Emma had every reason to hate her daddy. For years, L.E. Lowell, Sr. spent virtually every weekday evening at the Elks Club in Roanoke squandering a large portion of his executive salary on booze and cards. In the entire six years they had dated, Collier had never seen the boozy old reprobate come home before midnight on a workday.

During that same period, Emma's mother had never had a new dress. It should have come as no surprise to Collier that Mother Emma's youngest daughter—with grim poetic symmetry, her own namesake—had never owned a new dress until their senior year in high school when Collier bought her one for Christmas with money he made working hard labor during the summer.

Faintly athletic-looking with pear-sized breasts, Emma had thin lips and a straight nose. One thing for certain, Emma Lowell certainly would not be considered ugly by any stretch of the imagination. Although she was not movie-star-pretty and not exactly what you'd call stylish by current *Harper's Bazaar* standards, now that she could afford to shop at B. Forman, Sons and Irving Saks, Emma was actually rather attractive if you liked the outdoorsy type.

Despite her distrust of men, he really did care deeply for Emma. From the beginning, he had literally smothered his sadly-neglected, emotionally-deprived sweetheart with attention.

In his heart-of-hearts, Collier Boyd Ramsay knew himself to be a simple and very decent guy. His innocent philandering to the contrary, Collier had a deep, abiding respect for Emma Lowell. She was a good girl with an impeccable reputation. In absolute awe of her strong work ethic, her overall seriousness and Puritan goodness, Collier held Emma's reputation sacrosanct. As proof of his respect, during the entire two years he had spent at RPI, he had not once been unfaithful to her on a campus fairly crawling with sophisticated, wantonly-uninhibited, and heart-stoppingly beautiful women.

In Collier's simplistic, chauvinistic way of rationalizing things, the two sides of his persona were completely separate. Perhaps his history was not exactly unblemished, but his harmless indiscretions were quite understandable and most certainly were forgivable. Although plagued by transient pangs of conscience for his unpremeditated—if not unwilling—transgressions against Emma, Collier would have been wounded to think that anyone thought him shallow.

This morning, his gut churning from butterflies the size of B-29s, Collier had risen even before his father was up and slipped into a pair of cutoff jeans and a ragged tee shirt and had waded through the hip-high, dew-laden grass and weeds in the pasture between his parent's house and Grandma Boyd's old home place, toward the wire fence separating the field from the main tracks of the N&W railroad. His parents' house stood on a four-acre tract stretching from the River Road to the railroad—a gift to his folks from Grandma Boyd. Building their house was made possible by a separate gift of $1250 from his Grandma Ramsey, taken from the $10,000 death benefit the N&W paid her when Granddaddy Ramsey was killed in a horrific train wreck at Glade Spring. He had heard his daddy say that a steel rod pierced Granddaddy Ramsey's mangled body, also scalded by the burst boiler of the steam locomotive. At his wake and funeral, the casket had been kept securely closed.

Pausing astraddle the top barbwire strand to look back on the field which had been the first training ground for his skills at punting a football farther and higher than anyone at the local high school, he scaled the sturdy wire barrier and crossed the double railroad tracks gleaming like silver ribbons in the morning sun light. Stopping in the middle of the tracks to gaze westward, he reflected briefly on the fateful December Sunday the Japanese had bombed Pearl Harbor.

With his father and his kid brother, Jim, early that bone-chilling December morning, they had trudged these same tracks across the long, narrow trestle over the Roanoke River, carrying two whippy, ancient crosscut saws the two miles to his great-grandmother's place where they had labored the long, cold, damp afternoon sawing discarded railroad ties into stove-length blocks. Split into two-foot-long pieces using sharpened axes and a battered, homemade wooden maul and cold steel wedges, this rich, creosote-impregnated wood provided the fuel for the proud old matriarch's simple existence. Burning coal oil in her lamps and using wood to fire her ancient, cast-iron cook stove and the potbellied stove which heated her primitive, rudimentary farmhouse, his fiercely independent great-grandmother had never allowed electricity in her home. She also used the firewood to heat the water in the black iron pots she used for boiling clothes under the grape arbor out back. Stubbornly self-sufficient to her last breath, only when she finally took too sick to be left alone, would Octavia Augusta Argabright let the family move her to Grandma Boyd's front bedroom to die.

"The Japs bombed Pearl Harbor," an anxious chorus had greeted them with the news late that afternoon when they returned home to find his mother and his Aunt Blanche huddled in front of the secondhand—almost good as new—Silvertone radio.

Blinking hard to chase the haunting memories of that day and the ensuing years living under the shadow of war, this morning Collier had jumped the shallow ditch on the far side of the tracks and scrambled up the weedy, opposite bank, scaling a second barbwire fence and deftly slipping unscathed between the strands of the sagging, inner barbwire cattle barrier on the other side.

Some things, like riding a bicycle, are never forgotten. He smiled, recalling his crusty Grandpa Boyd's trite—but nonetheless wise—old adage. For the college-educated offspring of country folk, climbing expertly through barbwire fences was undoubtedly a trick genetically double-helixed deep into Collier's protoplasm.

Safely through the menacing wire, glancing up, he had surveyed the terrain around him. Stretching before him, the spiked stubs of the newly-harvested cornstalks stood like toy soldiers rising in neat ranks up the slope. Letting his gaze wander upward, he could see where, three-quarters of the way to the summit, the recently-cultivated field gave way to a tangled thicket of wild-blackberry brambles.

When he was still a boy, his father had picked seemingly endless buckets of those big, juicy blackberries which the womenfolk made into jams and dark-blue jellies. Fondly savoring the memory, he wagered to himself that his dad still picked those berries every season.

A dozen yards beyond the impenetrable blackberry vines, the beginning of the tree line of virgin woods crowned the crest of the hill. It was a lovely morning. Except for a line of towering thunderheads on the rim of the distant horizon, the sky was virtually cloudless. Far above the tree line, a lone hawk was a mere speck, circling lazily against the high, near-colorless, sky. Moving a few steps closer, he could hear the soughing of a gentle breeze stirring in the treetops. Far off, a half-imagined timpani of thunder echoed whispers of his long-lost innocence.

This morning those woods had beckoned him. Spellbound, as he began slowly climbing, in a twinkling, he was transported back in time.

The summer he was twelve, with his younger brother, Jim, and a neighbor's son, Carl—who was several years older and came daily with a phlegmatic, totally indifferent, dappled-gray plow horse named Nell—together they had made a crop of corn on this very same abominable piece of Virginia hillside. That summer's inglorious labor had been an altogether uninspiring fate for a rather suppressed, romantic male of twelve.

Day after day, each morning at seven, Collier, his brother and Carl and the old mare showed up to face the seemingly-endless prospect of unbearably hot, undistinguished days. Beginning at the top of this rock-encrusted, reddish-clay hillside, they had plowed and hoed their way, cornstalk by cornstalk, down the hardscrabble slope. For most of the summer, the three of them and the horse labored and sweated like galley slaves, struggling vainly to keep the indomitable scourge of morning glory vines and farmer's wiregrass from their mindless lusting to ententacle the cornstalks in a death embrace. Rats on a treadmill, top to bottom, the cycle took them perhaps two weeks. Each time they reached the bottom row, there was no celebration. They had simply turned and marched back to the top to begin chopping at the weeds again.

To Collier's melodramatic, pubescent mind, that summer's toil called up the tortures of Dante's *Inferno* that Miss Sandhurst had shown them during seventh-grade art appreciation. The labor itself was totally unredeeming, for the land was completely unsuitable for growing anything worthwhile—even the morning glories and wiregrass seemed sustained only by pure meanness.

For Collier and his brother, theirs was an exercise in futility; once the crop was harvested, even the weeds appeared to lose interest and languish. In the end, the corn was destined to be fed to the livestock—a rather pointless objective in his pragmatic adolescent view as it would be he and his brother who eventually would wind up spending the dreary winter carting the sorry corncobs and fodder to the hogs and chickens and cows.

Finally, one hot day—just as unceremoniously as it had begun—without fanfare, the ordeal ended. Collier and his brother had simply shouldered their hoe and stood staring blankly as Carl perfunctorily unhitched old Nell from the plow. The three of them wiped the sweat from their eyes with their shirts and all trudged silently away from the field.

In due time, the grownups came and harvested the scraggly crop and hauled it off.

That summer, Collier had put away forever most of what was his childhood, making a solemn vow he would never put his hands in dirt again.

A scant week later, he had begun riding the school bus five miles into town to enter Andrew Lewis High School, the big, consolidated county school in Salem, where he would demonstrate his budding skills in kicking and throwing balls of every shape and size.

And discover girls.

Continuing to make his way awkwardly upward across the rocky hillside, this morning—when at last he had reached the topmost of the cornrows—at the edge of the maze of blackberries, there was scattered a disarray of lunch bags, candy wrappers and soft-drink bottles. Two rusting cans with pork'n beans labels and two smaller ones which had contained Vienna sausages had been tossed aside. This tacky litter gave mute evidence that crops *still* did not make themselves. Idly kicking at the refuse, he had continued along the border of the blackberry thicket to where he could see just the trace of a narrow, beaten-down track leading through the tangle to the deeper shadows at the edge of the woods.

Feeling a little foolish—a college man about to be married and dreaming of finding his destiny in New York—he had picked his way gingerly through the bramble-strewn pathway toward the tree line. When he had finally threaded his way through the thorny gauntlet and reached the leafy overhang, he turned and looked back down the hill. Standing there, slightly bemused—or becharmed—he breathed the freshening scent of honeysuckle mixed with cooler breaths of the approaching summer storm. Feeling strangely astraddle a chasm in time, the panorama of his youth had stretched below him like a display in some cosmic department-store window.

Growing up in this valley had been magical. By the time he was twelve, he had heard Texas Gladden sing at least twenty verses of Barbara Allen one night at a school entertainment. He had started school with her son, Irvin, in Miss Billie Northcross's first grade at the Fort Lewis School. His Aunt Blanche had told him Texas Gladden was famous and a bunch of important people had come down from the Library of Congress to make recordings of her singing. He could still see her—a rather large, country woman whose neck was already beginning to show the signs of goiter—standing up there on the stage singing *a cappella*, her voice as musical as a bell. He thought back on the wonderful nights when his mother had gone to PTA meetings or some other woman's thing at the church or at the home of some woman-friend, and his father would let him and his brother stay up listening to the rip-roaring saga of Bonnie and Clyde or John Dillinger or Pretty Boy Floyd on the *Gangbusters* show. A couple of years back, he had actually seen the bullet-riddled car in which Bonnie and Clyde had been killed on display on the sidewalk in front of the Harold Depkin's Ford dealership in Salem. Not too long afterwards, he had seen Hermann Goering's massive, custom-built, 1943 Mercedes-Benz touring car on display there, too.

And there was the time his parents took the family into Roanoke to see Robert Wadlow, the world's tallest man. A barker on the stage said the giant was nearly nine-feet-tall, and Collier believed him. When he was eleven and in seventh grade, he had read in the paper that Wadlow had died. The paper said he was only twenty-two years old and eight-feet-eleven inches tall. That was the same year his daddy had taken Jimmy and him into Roanoke one Sunday night to see Bullet Bill Dudley, the University of Virginia All-American tailback. He had actually shaken Dudley's massive hand. The very next year, Dudley was named Outstanding College Player of the Year for the entire country.

His twelfth summer had been a confusing year. Big for his age and blessed with an awkward athletic grace, for reasons he had never quite understood, his parents had always pushed him ahead in school. In previous summers, he had left the swimming hole early and put in a lot of serious practice at throwing and kicking balls. But, during that momentous, enchanted summer, things had subtly changed. He had begun to sprout dark, wiry hairs in funny places, and his voice had started playing tricks on him. He had advanced from the Bobbsey Twins, Tom Swift and Nancy Drew, and now in the evenings, he was reading less of Robin Hood and Tarzan—smuggling copies of *God's Little Acre* and *For Whom the Bells Toll* out of his Aunt Blanche's hand-me-down county library housed in the Roanoke County Woman's Club on the hill across the road from the badly rundown Lakeside amusement park.

His Aunt Blanche had been the founding librarian of that first library of the county back in 1932. Through her selfless efforts, Blanche had since gone on to become the functional director of the countywide system consisting of at least a half-dozen branch libraries and several bookmobile routes shedding the light of literacy into the rural areas.

And, in the evenings, Collier was spending a lot of time hanging around Girlie Stump, an older farm girl directly across the river. Girlie thought he was thirteen and he had been content to let her go on believing it. One night, crossing the river in a weather-beaten rowboat, she'd told him he was beautiful and had pressed her lips against his mouth, hungrily tasting him.

After that, he had never been quite the same.

But at twelve, he still often daydreamed of being a pearl diver on a South Sea island or a movie star or a dashing fighter pilot, and he would sometimes slip off alone to play out his dreamy fantasies in these woods at the top of this wretched cornfield. Here, shadowed by the fear of discovery, he had built a primitive lean-to and self-consciously donned a homemade loin cloth torn from one of his mother's discarded sheets. Cutting the thick grapevines at their roots, he had gone swinging through the trees, playing his solitary game of Tarzan.

That was the summer he had walked out of Fort Lewis Baptist Church the Sunday evening just before making a commitment to the Boy Scouts. Although he continued his nightly, childish ritual of asking "God" to bless his parents and his brother and the rest of his family and to help him succeed in whatever earthly enterprise he might currently be involved—with a fervent sign-off request for forgiveness of an ever-mounting list of damning sins, most particularly that of habitual masturbation, and for help in becoming a better person, although secretly he hoped he would not become *too* good—that infamous Sunday essentially had ended his commitment to organized religion forever.

This morning, from that hilltop, taking in the sweeping vista out across the sunlit country landscape, the memories had been strangely seductive. With a parting look at the railroad tracks and his parents' house sitting far below, he had stepped through the leafy curtain. Inside the tree line, it had been as if a door had closed behind him, shutting away the lively chorus of birdcalls and insect sounds. Those who have been in the woods can never forget the timeless, fairy-like setting of leaf-strewn, mossy floors, huge vines and lacy ferns. Emitting a peculiar green luminescence filtering down through the leaves, the forest encompassed a magical universe all its own as the setting suddenly called to Collier's mind the time he and Emma had been at a cabin party just on the far side of those very mountains across the valley. That drizzly afternoon, deep in the dripping woods out of sight from the cabin, they had found a giant boulder, perhaps ten-feet high and flat on top. Covered by a plastic raincoat and stark naked in the warm pewter mist, they had shut out the world.

He had been sixteen. There would never be another time like that for him.

"*God help us both, Emma; that moment was so incredibly special...*" he breathed the words half-aloud to the curious mockingbird perched in the tree above him.

"Collier, please hurry, Darling! It would be unforgivable to be late for one's own wedding," his mother's insistent voice reverberated up the wide stairwell for at least the tenth time in the past five minutes.

Sweat fast wilting his starched tux shirt and trickling down his spine, Collier reached to turn off the radio just as the local DJ interrupted Nat King Cole crooning *Mona Lisa*:

"THE ROANOKE MARINE RESERVE UNIT HAS BEEN PUT ON STANDBY ALERT AS PRESIDENT TRUMAN ANNOUNCED TODAY THAT GENERAL WALKER WITH REINFORCEMENTS FROM THE FIRST CAVALRY DIVISION AND RESERVE ROK TROOPS ON THE WESTERN FRONT, HAVE OUTMANEUVERED THE NORTH KOREAN INVADERS AND ESTABLISHED A STRONG PERIMETER POSITION AROUND THE SOUTHERNMOST PORT OF PUSAN. PRESIDENT TRUMAN STATED THAT U.N. FORCES HAVE THE SITUATION WELL IN HAND..."

Momentarily troubled by the announcement, he was sobered to hear that a bunch of his buddies in the local Marine Reserves had just been called to standby alert. Just who did Washington think they were fooling anyway? He'd seen the maps in the local paper and knew Pusan was a last-ditch stand.

"Collier..." his mother called again. She was clearly losing patience now.

"Keep your girdle on, old girl...I'm on my way," he answered with a deep sigh as he turned off the radio and the little electric fan and headed for the stairs.

Still brooding about the upsetting news from Korea as they drove up to the rear door of the parish house of St. Paul's Episcopal Church, it brought Collier some small comfort to know that married men would be far down the list for the military draft.

The good news was that in less than an hour, he would be a happily married man.

Before midnight, he would be stretched buck-naked on the pristine white sheets of the exotic, all-white bridal suite of The Governor Tyler Inn in Radford. From that moment forever after, he would be faithful to Emma and devote every spare waking instant trying to perfect his abilities as an illustrator. Never mind he was going have to get her some golf clubs and drag her out to the course sometimes. Every night the rest of his interminable future, he would be able to sleep naked in bed with his penis inside the delectable, unattainable—not to mention well-employed and owner of a brand-new Ford—Emma Lowell.

Now, was that a dream come true, or what?

CHAPTER FOUR

The Roanoke World-News
Roanoke, Virginia, Friday Afternoon, September 15, 1950
AMERICANS HALF WAY TO SEOUL AFTER
AMPHIBIOUS LANDING BEHIND REDS
Marines, Infantry Under MacArthur Storm Into Inchon

TOKYO, Friday, September 15 (AP) - American Marines and infantry stormed ashore at the big North Korean port of Inchon Friday, 165 miles behind the lines of the North Korean Communists in a bold nutcracker operation intended to crush the life out of the Red invaders.

The Americans knifed quickly eastward toward Seoul, the Red held capital 22 miles inland.

Invasion Strategy
MacArthur Plans to Crush Reds Between Two Armies
By Russell Brines

WITH GENERAL DOUGLAS MACARTHUR ON THE INCHON FRONT, Korea, Sept. 15 (AP) - General MacArthur returned to combat today to direct a bold military gamble which he says may break the back of the North Korean Army...

SOMEWHAT PREOCCUPIED by the vagaries of being newly married and by the unanticipated, rapidly-expanding responsibilities of his first real job as an artist, after he and Emma returned home from their honeymoon, Collier Ramsay gave only rather superficial notice to the newspaper headlines about MacArthur's brilliant military coup in Korea.

Making the grave tactical error of splitting its ten-division force into two spearheads with a main two-division thrust to the southwest, in an early-August flanking maneuver designed to capture Masan and Pusan, the North Korean People's Army apparently received no intelligence reports that the American Army's 2nd Infantry Division, the Army 5th RCT, and a Marine Regimental Combat Team with independent tank battalions were all landing at Pusan. This powerful fighting force encompassed a total of five regiments (fifteen battalions) of infantry, six battalions of artillery and an anti-aircraft battalion, more than a few tank battalions, some combat engineers and assorted other support groups—in total, around 30,000 troops.

Even before these fresh reinforcements were in place, Johnnie Walker made a hasty redeployment of the 25th Division, led by combat-savvy Mike Michaelis's Wolfhounds, to reinforce John Church's badly-depleted 24th, already heavily-besieged in the defense of Masan. Arriving in the area on August 1 to find the south road to Pusan now open, Michaelis wasted little time in taking charge. In a bloody two-day battle, the Americans secured both the north and south roads, thus blocking the North Koreans from enjoying a cakewalk into Pusan.

By mid-August—no little thanks to the bravery and vigilance of the Wolfhounds—it had become apparent to the JCS that by reducing pressure in the northwest sector against the defense of Taegu, the NKPA had played into the unwitting, uncommonly lucky, Eighth Army Commanding General, Johnnie Walker's, hands.

But, even with 30,000 well-equipped reinforcements, fighting to hold the Pusan Perimeter was far from over. With renewed fervor from August to mid-September, the NKPA launched a series of all-out attacks on allied positions along the Perimeter, driving the American forces back and capturing the cities of Pohang and Jinju. During this period, the overrun of the CP at Taegu seemed so severely threatened that the Eighth Army moved HQ to Pusan, and the situation seemed so precarious that many prominent South Korean refugees—including President Syngham Rhee—fled Pusan for the neighboring Japanese Tsushima Islands. Even with massive troop reinforcements and armor exacting an incredible toll of casualties on the attacking NKPA, it was not until mid-September that it became evident that American and ROK troops would be able to hold the line.

When the smoke finally cleared, the price, however, had been costly.

Spearheaded by an advanced party of Marines, when MacArthur finally landed forces at Inchon on September 15, cutting off the almost 100,000 North Korean troops from their main supply lines, America had already suffered 20,000 combat casualties, 4280 of whom were corpses rotting beside Korean hills and rice paddies.

Rubbing the sleep from his eyes, Collier felt the tension in his gut ease as he read the comforting news of MacArthur's bold attack behind North Korean lines. Still exhausted from staying up well past midnight cutting silkscreen stencils for last-minute changes to the Kroger "Weekend-Specials" window banners, he had gotten up groggily at 6 AM to take Emma to work so he could use the car during the day. He had told her that since his father was bringing them a generous bounty of green beans and squash and tomatoes from his garden into work, he would stop by the General Offices of the N&W to pick up the produce then run by the apartment to put them in their fridge to keep them fresh.

But that was only an excuse.

He really wanted the car so he could go hit golf balls at the driving range before picking her up around 3:00 to take her with him to the Salem Municipal golf course.

He hated the petty dishonesty of sneaking around on Emma, but she could be such a tight-ass bitch. She practically had a hissy-fit when he brought up the idea of spending fifty bucks on an annual family membership at the rinky-dink, nine-hole, sand-green Salem Muni. No manner of argument about how much they would save from the daily green fee of fifty cents for nine holes—or seventy-five cents for all day—could make her change her mind. She would simply pitch another of her fits if she knew he was going to squander his lunch money on two buckets of range balls to apply the latest tips from Slammin' Sam Snead's newspaper column in an unending and thus-far futile attempt to correct his horrendous banana ball.

What he really hated most of all was that he had to start taking Emma to the golf course in the first place. When he first came home from Richmond and bought himself a cheap set of Wilson Sam Snead Autograph clubs wholesale from Nelson Hardware, she protested. Then he made the mistake of taking her over to The Greenbrier to watch Sam Snead, Porky Oliver and the flamboyant fashion-plate, Jimmy Demeret, compete in the Greenbrier Open. After she got a look at all of the fashionable, well-dressed people in that lush, well-manicured setting, she began nagging him to let her play, too.

Emma just couldn't understand that golf was a serious undertaking which men did together—not some silly social event like her monthly bridge club where girls just sat around and gossiped or giggled about cooking, clothes and breastfeeding. In the end, he had given in and gotten her a cheap J.C. Higgins starter set of a three-wood, three-, five- and nine-iron, and a putter from Sears Roebuck and he sometimes took her along late weekday afternoons after work.

The exercise turned out to be a world-class disaster. As athletic as she had been in high school playing softball, tumbling on the gymnastics team and swimming and diving, Emma was just plain hopeless at golf.

Still, it had paid off in another way. Since he took her along weekday afternoons, he held his ground and insisted that he be allowed to play with his buddies on Saturday mornings and Sundays while she was at church. Even so, he had to compromise by going to church with her one Sunday each month.

The issue was actually bigger than the golf.

What really chapped his rosy-red pucker was that she never let him forget she was the dominant breadwinner. At the VA, Emma was pulling down nearly three-hundred a month. Despite the fact he had enabled Kroger to increase the availability of their window banners from the eight stores in the Roanoke Valley to include all fifty-five stores in the region—and he was now going into the office once a week to do the spiffy new layouts for their double full-page weekly newspaper spreads—the tightwad bastards still refused to increase his hourly rate one nickel above the measly seventy-five-cents-an-hour minimum wage. Treating professionally-trained commercial artists like common laborers was downright humiliating. He was fairly itching to tell Kroger to get screwed, but he didn't have any other legitimate job prospects.

God knows, he had looked hard enough.

By the time he went by the silkscreen shop over the Kroger store on the Market Square to make certain the weekly window banners had been picked up, the sun was almost directly overhead when he made an abortive attempt at a spur-of-the-moment call on the "Art Director" at Stone Printing, a large lithographic press. Housed in a forbidding grey-granite fortress located on Jefferson Street, Stone Printing was located several blocks north of the wide multi-track crossing of the N&W mainline. Directly across Jefferson Street from the impeccably-kept grounds of the elegant Hotel Roanoke, the ugly granite edifice was just beyond the first of the two architecturally-mismatched brick buildings incorporating his father's workplace in the General Offices of the N&W. Owned and operated by the N&W as a prestigious tourist destination, the Hotel Roanoke was Roanoke's answer to the C&O's famous Greenbrier.

As sizeable and well-known as Stone Printing was—with huge accounts in New York and other major cities—this morning when he called at the tiny front-reception window, Collier
had been flabbergasted to learn that the lithographic press actually had no art director. Even worse, when he was ushered back to the cubbyhole office of their production manager, he was quickly informed that they didn't have a single commercial artist on their staff.

"Most of our art work comes to us camera-ready from big city agencies. What little commercial art we buy locally is mostly hand-lettered logotypes and headlines. For these, we Despite the fact he had enabled Kroger to increase the availability of their window banners from the eight stores in the Roanoke Valley to include all fifty-five stores in the region—and he was now going into the office once a week to do the spiffy new layouts for their double full-page weekly newspaper spreads—the tightwads at Kroger still refused to increase his hourly rate one nickel above the measly seventy-five-cents-an-hour minimum wage. Treating professionally-trained commercial artists like common laborers was downright humiliating. He was fairly itching to tell Kroger to get screwed, but he didn't have any other legitimate job prospects.

God knows, he had looked hard enough.

By the time he went by the silkscreen shop over the Kroger store on the Market Square to make certain the weekly window banners had been picked up, the sun was almost directly overhead when he made an abortive attempt at a spur-of-the-moment call on the art director at Stone Printing, a large lithographic press.

As sizeable and well-known as Stone Printing was—with huge accounts in New York and other major cities—this morning when he called at the tiny front-reception window, Collier depend almost exclusively upon Bill Paxton—he lives right up the road in Salem," the production manager told him. From the examples of contracted freelance art work the production manager showed him, Collier knew their requirements were way out of his league.

Collier quickly thanked him for his time and left feeling discouraged and depressed.

Now, hurrying down the sidewalk toward town, weaving in and out of the office workers heading into the heart of the shopping district on lunchtime errands, he moved past the newer, buff-colored brick N&W office tower next door to Stone Printing, silently thanking his lucky stars that at least he had not shown his pitiful folio of sample illustrations to the Production Manager. He was ashamed to admit that he was far too shaky and would starve to death if he had to make his living hand lettering. In Mr. Engel's and Mr. Hull's lettering classes at RPI, he had barely gotten by. Compared to the highly professional work the Production Manager had shown him at Stone Printing, his pathetic efforts were something akin to third runner-up in a kindergarten contest.

Rising eight or nine stories above the hillside, the lighter-colored-brick N&W office tower was several stories taller than the older, red-brick companion building bordering the railroad tracks, the site of his father's big office bullpen. The older, red-brick building stood on the corner, at the intersection of Jefferson and Railroad Avenue, overlooking the ten-track-wide crossing of the N&W's main line. Just to the east of the Jefferson Street crossing, a hundred yards on up the hill across Railroad Avenue from the Hotel Roanoke, were the boarding platforms of the sooty, smoke-redolent old passenger station. Up ahead, the crossing gate arms were lowered as a long coal train rattled slowly eastbound while impatient office workers on restricted lunch breaks scurried up and down the steep stairs of the overhead pedestrian crosswalk bridging the railroad tracks.

This formidable collection of buildings on the hill overlooking the impressive downtown skyline of an ill-assorted assemblage of vintage and modern offices, hotels, restaurants, department stores, shops and movie houses made an eloquent statement that Roanoke was indeed a thriving "railroad town"—the center of commerce and shopping for the entire, predominantly-agrarian countryside of southwest Virginia.

Hurrying down the long, sloping sidewalk, Collier had hopes of dashing in to pick up the promised bounty from his father's garden before his dad went on lunch break. His father's desk was located about halfway up a long center aisle separating two rows of desks. With luck, he would just make it before the noon whistle blew at the East End Shops and could avoid prolonging the unavoidable father-son chit-chat. It wasn't that he didn't love his old man. The awful reality was—with his embarrassingly ill-fitting, blousy dress shirts carelessly stuffed in his wrinkled suit pants and the sleeves rolled up above the elbows—Harry "Cocky" Ramsay always looked like a hayseed.

No matter that Collier's father was well-respected by his co-workers and almost everybody else in Roanoke County, and, for that matter, big-shot politicians and bleacher- and box-seat baseball fans in damned near the whole Commonwealth of Virginia, the nickname "Cocky" related to a minor astigmatism which gave him a slightly cockeyed look and was not related to anything about his father's dress or demeanor. No matter that Collier worshipped the ground his father walked on, to him, Cocky's appearance was downright humiliating.

A deacon in their historic little Fort Lewis Baptist church, the driving force of Fort Lewis School's annual Lion's Club Follies and a fanatic Byrd Democrat and zealot party organizer, around their home in the county west of Salem, Cocky Ramsay was something of an icon. He and his longtime ball-playing buddy, Smokey Joe Woods, had almost single-handedly brought the minor league baseball team to Roanoke. Cocky was a veritable legend among the local sandlot baseball leagues and, in his constant need to bring home some extra bucks, he was well-known as an umpire in the city leagues.

None of these virtues relieved Collier of his snobbish hang-up.

All of his father's well-deserved recognition notwithstanding, the shameful truth was that Collier was ashamed of his old man's unpardonable sartorial negligence and folksy, plainspoken behavior. Paradoxically, the thing that made Collier so uncomfortable was that he understood his father's lack of pretension was firmly grounded in the man's unapologetic honesty about himself. His father was comfortable in his own skin, and Collier envied the peace of mind he understood must go with that.

With a biographic history worthy of a Horatio Alger, Jr. novel, Harry Milton Ramsay had been born March 8, 1899, the oldest of ten children, to Ocie Ellen and Charlie M. Ramsay—the family legend had it that the M was merely an initial, representing no real name—a fireman (and sometimes engineer) on the powerful steam-driven locomotives of the Radford Division of the N&W Railroad. Because Charlie periodically suffered cruelly-debilitating exacerbations of rheumatoid arthritis, little Harry had been forced to drop out of school in the third grade, going to work as a "call boy" for the railroad. It was hard to imagine, but at eight years of age, young Harry was providing almost sole support for his parents and five, eventually to become nine, siblings by pedaling a second- or third-hand bike around Roanoke in the bleak hours of the morning waking train crews scheduled to make their run.

By the time he was fourteen, Harry Ramsay was working a full-time job in the railroad's East End Shops and had already become a legend for his baseball talent on the local sandlots. When he was seventeen, Harry escaped service in World War I because—continuing to be the principal breadwinner for his parents and nine siblings—he had taken wartime employment packing gunpowder into artillery shell casings in a munitions plant in distant Hopewell, Virginia.

Back home and twenty-one in the post WWI-era before there were rules about age restrictions and academic eligibility, a group of affluent local alumni took up a collection and sent Harry, a third-grade dropout, on "athletic scholarship" to exclusive Fork Union Military Academy to beef up their war-depleted athletic programs.

At FUMA, all athletic scholarships were not equal. Although Cocky quickly became a legend around the elitist Virginia prep league, he was required to wash dishes in the kitchen and shovel coal into the boilers of the school's heating system to pay for his room and board. This shameful exploitation lasted only a year before Cocky's father's arthritis flared up, and Cocky was called home to resume the role of family breadwinner.

With only these insubstantial prep-school credentials to qualify him, soon Collier's dad was offered a clerical job in the railroad's general offices due to his prodigious skills on the diamond. Surprisingly, with a previously-undiscovered gift for numbers, Cocky quickly became a self-taught whiz on the newfangled Burroughs portable adding machines.

In the spring of 1927, because of his well-earned importance at his clerical work, the N&W granted Cocky a temporary leave of absence to play the baseball season with Danville in the Piedmont League. When he returned to his regular job in the fall, he met and fell hopelessly in love with the primly-cultured Lida Gertrude Boyd, the daughter of self-described "land-owning Virginia aristocrats"—a local euphemism for "poor but proud"—who lived out in the country along Roanoke River, about five miles west of Salem. With the solemn promise to the equally-smitten, but infinitely more practical, Lida, that he would not waste his time trying to make a career playing baseball, they were married two days before Christmas. Just over a year later, on the twenty-fifth of January, 1929, Collier Boyd Ramsay was born.

Fortuitously, following the ensuing stock market crash on Black Friday in November 1929, the coal-carrying N&W and C&O railroads remained reasonably strong, and, although shamefully underpaid, Cocky Ramsay remained quite secure at his modern electric calculator throughout the subsequent depression years of the early thirties.

Although now married with two sons, and securely employed at the N&W, Cocky's lifelong love of sports never wavered. During the summer of 1938, Cocky purchased six season tickets to Duke University's home football games and sold five of them to kindred sports-loving office members, offering a package deal which included roundtrip transportation in the family sedan to Durham—a roundtrip of about 300 miles—plus lunch and dinner of huge Dagwood sandwiches and fried chicken Lida helped Cocky prepare at home. Not only did the self-styled entrepreneur make a few bucks profit on the deal, he was able to see Duke go through a spectacular season that has gone down in the annals of big-time college football history. That well-remembered 1938 season the Duke team—dubbed the "Iron Dukes" by sportswriters—galloped through a nine-game regular schedule undefeated, untied and unscored-upon before losing in the final minute, 7 to 3, to Southern California in Pasadena, California, at the celebrated Rose Bowl.

Duke was invited back to play the Rose Bowl in 1942, but due to the Japs hitting Pearl Harbor on December 7, scarcely three weeks prior to the game, with realistic fear that Japanese submarines might shell—or their carrier-launched planes might bomb—the event in a demoralizing attack, the Rose Bowl committee decided to move the event to Duke Stadium in Durham rather than give the Japs a moral victory by canceling the event altogether. Again, seizing upon this remarkable serendipity, Cocky got on the telephone with the Duke Athletic office, purchased a dozen tickets, recruited one of his office-mates to drive a second car and sold out his offer for an once-in-a-lifetime moment in history.

All during the thirties, Adolph Hitler had been orchestrating the prelude to another war in Europe, stirring to life the Nazi party with his poisonous ranting for "Aryan purity" giving rise to dark clouds of anti-Semitism. Testing his Nazi muscle in the Spanish Revolution, eventually led to the Blitzkrieg invasion of Poland, the Netherlands and—with an unholy alliance with Benito Mussolini of Italy—the surprisingly effortless fall of France. Now, drunk with aspirations for ruling all of Europe, the ranting megalomaniac's lust for power quickly escalated into an all-out air assault on Great Britain—soon followed by Japan's entry into the conflict with the sneak attack on Pearl Harbor.

Several years back, during one of Collier's visits home from college, his father had confided to him that the day following Pearl Harbor, he had tried to enlist as a physical education instructor in all four branches of the military, but at age forty-two with a wife and two young sons, all four services had turned him down, deeming him too old for service.

His entire life, from third grade on, Cocky had gone to heroic lengths to keep both his army of hungry sisters and brothers and his own family above the poverty line. To his everlasting credit, the first eleven years of Collier's existence, every Saturday and Sunday morning, their selfless father rose before dawn to work overtime at the office, supplementing his meager $100 monthly salary. To Collier's everlasting embarrassment, at Christmastime, Cocky sold greeting cards and wrapping paper to other office workers, members of the church and any neighbors he could collar—and, of course, in baseball season there was always the five dollars a game Cocky took in, umpiring for the city leagues. To manage eking out a comfortable existence during the Depression years, Cocky bought canned goods from the Damaged Freight Warehouse, and in season, Cocky also sold produce to his co-workers from a garden he grew on Grandma Boyd's property. The first summer in their solid new, brick, Williamsburg Colonial house on the large plot of land Grandma Ramsay had given them, Cocky Ramsay planted their sprawling, half-acre front yard in tomatoes. Every evening that summer, Collier and his brother had picked—and carefully packed—baskets of fancy tomatoes his father sold at the office, peddling the excess baskets at the bustling city farmer's market just a block off Jefferson Street, downtown. To insure Collier and Jim had the advantages of their more affluent playmates, Cocky brought used, although new-looking, bats and balls and gloves home from the office baseball team. And he was a genius at making homemade kites with marvelous sticks he brought home from the N&W office carpenter shop.

Shortly after they had moved into their new house, as 4-H Club projects when Collier was in the seventh grade, Collier had kept chickens and Jimmy had raised hogs. When Collier and his brother moved on to high school, their "city-boy-gone-wild-over-farming" dad had eagerly taken over both of these projects. At one time, Cocky had as many as 100 laying hens and 73 hogs of varying ages on the back end of their four-acre property.

Over recent years, however, his Dad and Mom had undertaken the project of converting their backyard into a formal garden with azaleas and boxwoods. Consequently, his father's livestock inventory—along with the accompanying aroma of hog and chicken shit—had gradually subsided, but Cocky steadfastly continued to raise a garden and sell tomatoes and green beans to the office force.

After Collier transferred to commercial art curriculum at RPI, it had become increasingly harder for him to be face-to-face with his dad as he was plagued with a hollow feeling inside his gut that he had let his daddy down and he would never justify the sacrifices Cocky had made for him. For self-centered Collier, his love-hate relationship with his father was an emotional Gordian Knot. Although he despised himself for harboring such feelings, Collier understood he was too much the product of his mother's haughty disdain for what she considered demeaning physical labor.

The other cancer gnawing at Collier's soul was that no matter how hard he had strived for their approval, his jockstrap father and his father's longtime baseball sidekick, Cricket LaPrade, had always favored his younger brother, Jimmy. Even old Grandpa Boyd preferred Jimmy—always hugging and teasing him with "My name's Jimmy, take all you gimme."

When Collier was fifteen and at war with the new high-school coach, he had organized a pick-up team of his buddies—including Jimmy, then only thirteen. Even though their father knew practically nothing about basketball, they had asked him to sponsor them in an "under sixteen" Saturday league at the YMCA. Collier still burned with resentment recalling the day he had scored a record-high thirty-three points in a single game. On the way home, instead of acknowledging his achievement, his father had angrily berated him for his selfishness at not giving his brother the chance to score more points. Thinking back on it now gave Collier satisfaction to know that his record thirty-three points still stood.

His cheeks still burned with phantom pain recalling when he was sixteen and, suffering some mostly-imagined transgression, his mother had cancelled his plans to take the bus into town to see Emma, ordering him upstairs to his room. When his father had come home from work, Collier had heard his vindictive mother down in the kitchen recounting his greatly-exaggerated sins to his father. He had listened seething with resentment to his father's footsteps marching resignedly up the stairs to confront his son with his most recent crimes against his mother.

"What's this your mother's telling me about your latest insolence?" His father asked without preamble as soon as he set foot inside the room.

"Ask her; you married the selfish bitch," Collier scarcely remembered getting the words out of his mouth when his father struck him a single backhand blow with his blacksmith-like right forearm, knocking him head over heels across both twin beds to land upside down against the wall on the far side of the wide room. It had been the last time he had complained to his father about his self-centered mother's sometimes totally irrational, hateful behavior.

Despite his continued failure to attract his father's favor, although he was almost two years older and two years ahead of Jimmy in school, Collier had done his best to include his younger brother in his sphere of friends and activities. A talented athlete, Jimmy, had come into his own when Collier was a senior, and, as a tenth grader, he began earning playing time in all the major high-school sports. For that reason, it had never occurred to Collier that Jim regarded him with big-brother hero-worship and would feel abandoned when Collier headed off to Bluefield. Totally unsuspecting of the effect his absence might have on his brother, Collier had come home for Thanksgiving that first year at college to find his brother hanging out with a gang of unwashed, high-school jocks who spent too many evenings at the Apartment Camps, a disreputable local beer joint and hot-pillow motel whose dissolute management thought nothing of selling beer to underage high-school kids. His well-intended efforts to talk some sense into his sullen, abandoned brother had fallen on deaf ears, serving only to widen the chasm between them. Further attempts at reconciliation had resulted in Collier finally losing his temper and knocking Jim over a six-foot-high hedge. The next morning before he left to go back to school, he informed their clueless father, "Your fair-haired boy is out of control. You'd better pay more attention to what's going on."

Cocky promptly grounded the wayward Jim and began laying down the law. By the time basketball season got underway, Jim was well on his way to cleaning up his act.

Although the incident of knocking Jim over the hedge strained their relationship for a time, after awhile, things gradually got back to normal. In his sophomore year, Jim came along when Harry and Lida brought Emma to Princeton, West Virginia, on Thanksgiving night to see Collier start for Bluefield in an exhibition game against the University of West Virginia with the All-American, Leland Bird. Driving back to Roanoke after the game, they all had a good laugh at Collier's expense, kidding him about how a Mountaineer freshman named Fred Schaus—an overage WWII veteran who had already played a lot of service ball—had made him look pretty bad. Collier later took comfort from the fact that Schaus made All-American the following year, in 1949, before leaving UWV to make his mark with the fledgling National Basketball Associations' Fort Wayne Pistons.

His relationship with his brother apparently healed, Collier took great pride over the following year-and-a-half as Jim went on to make All-District in basketball before he graduated.

Unfortunately, however, what had begun as a promising sophomore year for Collier at Bluefield began turning sour right after the varsity basketball team returned early from Christmas break for a few days extra practice. Horace Fanning, the totally-incompetent coach, who—like a predominance of faculty at the fanatical Baptist school—had been hired largely because he was a self-nominated lay preacher and also enrolled in ministerial courses. Like his nefarious predecessor, Bill Judy, Fanning lived with his wife and son in the men's dorm acting as proctor. Hopelessly insensitive, the artless Fanning had developed an annoying habit of dropping into basketball players' rooms in the evenings, unannounced, snooping for evidence of misbehavior and submitting the aggravated occupants to tiresome monologues on accepting Christ as one's true personal savior.

Growing more than a little tired of Fanning's boorish snooping, in a moment of divine—or perhaps Satanic—inspiration, Collier bought an ubiquitous calendar artist's portrait of Jesus, in a cheap 8 x 10 imitation-gold picture frame, at the local Kresge's Five and Dime. Arriving back at the dorm, he autographed the insipid portrait "*To my good pal, Collier,*" and signed it: "*J. C.*" in a flowing script. With the picture prominently displayed on his dresser top, between a studio portrait of Emma and a snapshot of his family, Collier sat back and waited for Fanning's next snooping foray.

Rumblings of this outrageous sacrilege had spread among his dorm mates, and word went out the next time Fanning started his prowl. By the time the unwitting coach reached Collier's room, a crowd of at least eight or nine of his buddies had gathered, eager to see the oafish, sycophantic coach's reaction.

Overjoyed to find such a throng gathered in one room and completely mistaking the expectant energy for an atmosphere of welcoming camaraderie,

Fanning stepped into the room and immediately set about his usual practice of making himself an all-around pain in the ass. Perhaps ten or fifteen minutes passed before his gaze finally fell upon the doctored portrait on Collier's dresser and his face lit up with the rapt expression of a Baptist missionary about to baptize an unwashed heathen. Making a beeline directly across the room, when he got close enough to see the inscription, his mouth flew open, and he stood there almost apoplectic, unable to utter a sound. Finally, after a very pregnant moment, Fanning turned and left without a word, the muffled sound of suppressed guffaws following him all the way down three flights of stairs.

The rest of the week, Collier and his teammates walked on eggshells around the deserted, snow-covered campus going to the intense two-a-day practices waiting for the other shoe to drop, but no further mention was ever made. The only tangible repercussion was that Fanning's uninvited dormitory sorties were ended—for the rest of that year at least.

Collier should have known, however, for Baptists, it is written that no transgression goes unpunished. With school back in session after New Year's break, Fanning enlisted Collier and several other teammates to officiate games in the campus intramural league. One evening early in January, acting as impromptu coach of his woefully-inept son's team, Fanning began making a complete ass of himself, loudly complaining and criticizing Collier for almost every call against the boy and his teammates.

Toward the end of the first half, Collier had had enough. The next time Fanning came running onto the floor, protesting Collier's call of flagrant foul against his clumsy son, Collier reflexively launched a serious haymaker at the coach. Fortunately, Collier's other teammate officiating the game caught his arm, deflecting Collier's fist, preventing him from actually striking Fanning. Luckily, the president of the college was in the stands and witnessed Fanning's abominable behavior. Later, upon sober reflection, Collier considered it a minor miracle that he had only been kicked off the basketball team—not sent home from school in disgrace. What really hurt him the most was being forced stand alone in the crowd at the train station listening to the speeches and the band playing, the night in March when his teammates left to play in the national junior college tournament in Springfield, Missouri.

After graduating high school, Jim—no longer "Jimmy" with every inch of his spindly, six-three frame a pure symphony of motion on the court—because of a misplaced sense of sacrifice inspired by their father's struggle to finance Collier's last two years at RPI, turned down a full scholarship at William & Mary and stayed at home to play for Buddy Hackman, the converted football coach at the academically-oriented Roanoke College. However altruistic, this misguided decision turned out to be an utter disaster. Hackman tried to fit him into an antiquated offense that was passé before iron hoops had replaced peach baskets. Somewhat embittered—and not without justification—Jim quit the team early in his sophomore season and reverted to hanging out at the frat house and the local poolroom.

Collier finally regained some optimism about his brother's future, three weeks before, when Jim had been best man at his wedding. At the reception, to everyone's surprise, Jim had broken the news that he and his frat brother, Milan C. Hitt, Jr., had decided to give law school a try. Like the proverbial leaf in a windstorm, following the wedding, his star-crossed brother headed off to law school at T.C. Williams in Richmond on the back of Hitt's old Harley. Thinking about Jim now, as he walked through the wide doors of his father's office building, Collier held his breath. With less than a month gone by, the margins of his most recent note from his brother were tinged with discontent. Now, as he crossed the lobby, Collier shuddered to think how it would effect their dad if he knew Jim had written that he was already disenchanted with reading the law. This damned ruckus in Korea also heightened Collier's concerns. As a married man, he felt secure, but he was worried about his brother. Collier had never been much of a religious man, but every night he breathed a fervent prayer that his kid brother would stay in law school.

Rejecting the creaky elevator just inside the lobby, Collier—trying hard not to inhale the strong vapor of the industrial-strength, pine-scented cleaning fluid—took the wide steps two at a time to the third floor. Crossing the broad landing, he entered the cavernous bullpen of the Transportation Department. Inside, he stopped short, puzzled to find most of the employees gathered around a radio in the break area, back near the Supervisor's office.

"Hi, Dad. I came to get my goodies. What's up?" Collier asked as Cocky saw him and stepped out to greet him.

"MacArthur just landed at Inchon near Seoul. Old "Dugout Doug's" doing an end run on the North Koreans, taking some heat off the breakout from the Pusan perimeter. We were listening, trying to find out if the Roanoke Marine Reserves are among the landing force. Some of my baseball boys are in that outfit," his father said with a worried look.

"That whole thing is a damned screw-up," Collier said, then added, "Well, at least now we won't have to worry about Jim getting caught up in all that mess."

"I certainly hope you're right. Hold on, I'll get your vegetables," his father agreed, turning to get Collier the promised vegetables from his garden.

CHAPTER FIVE

The Roanoke World-News
Friday Afternoon, November 24, 1950
**MacArthur: "Tell the Boys...They'll
Eat Christmas Dinner at Home"**
By Relman Morin

TOKYO, November 24 (AP) – General Douglas MacArthur boldly flew the length of the Yalu River boundary between North Korea and Red Manchuria today in an unarmed plane.

At the Ninth Corps area in Korea he said to Maj. Gen. John B. Coulter: "Tell the boys when they reach the Yalu, they are going home. I want to make good on my statement they are going to eat Christmas dinner at home."

FOLLOWING MACARTHUR'S AUDACIOUS LANDING at Inchon on September 15, the badly-depleted, badly-demoralized North Korean Peoples Army—in one of the finest, most noteworthy actions of the war—were helplessly caught in a giant nutcracker operation between Johnnie Walker's Eighth Army in the south and MacArthur's northern envelopment. Finally, on September 26, the Eighth Army caught up to them just south of Suwon, and, although some token resistance ensued, a vast majority of the enemy fled into the eastern mountains. Even so, more than 100,000 prisoners were taken. By September 30, the NKPA ceased to exist south of Seoul and the Han River.

On September 27, without waiting for the introduction of a resolution before the UN, Truman officially had the JCS cable MacArthur the authorization to invade North Korea with the specified objective of "destruction of the North Korean Armed Forces." On September 30—the same day the British introduced a resolution to the UN authorizing crossing the 38th Parallel—after receiving approval from Washington, MacArthur broadcast to the NKPA from Tokyo a strongly-worded ultimatum of surrender.

By October 1, after liberating Kimpo airfield and clearing the capital city of Seoul of the enemy, MacArthur's forces had already pushed a short distance north of the 38th Parallel. In the absence of a response to a surrender ultimatum to the NKPA—and, without bringing the issue before the UN General Assembly, but with strong admonitions that he keep his mouth shut to the press—the JCS cabled MacArthur: "We want you to feel unhampered tactically and strategically to proceed north of the 38th Parallel."

In China, Premier Chou En-lai made a public declaration to the Chinese people that they would absolutely not tolerate foreign aggression in Korea nor would they "supinely tolerate seeing their neighbors being savagely invaded by imperialists." Privately, Chou told the Indian ambassador to Peking that if UN forces other than ROKs crossed the 38th Parallel, China would send troops to North Korea.

When this message was relayed through secure diplomatic channels, after serious consideration and despite CIA reports of Chinese troops north of the Yalu River, the powers in Washington paid little attention, giving little credence to what they considered an idle threat.

However, with MacArthur's forces receiving only token opposition from the rapidly-disintegrating NKPA, but with some nagging concerns about MacArthur's battle plan which encompassed spectacular troop landings to the west at Chinnampo near the North Korean capital of Pyongyang and eastward at Wonsan and Iwon on the Sea of Japan—and the far-fetched yet worrisome possibility of Chinese intervention from across the Yalu River—Truman, convinced by his staff that it would be good politically, summoned MacArthur to Wake Island for a mid-October meeting. After a brief private sit-down with Truman which reiterated convictions from both parties there was little to fear from Chinese intervention, there was a formal meeting of a more general nature considering the post-war rehabilitation of the Korean people. On October 15, Truman and MacArthur shook hands with an air of celebration and boarded aircraft for long flights home.

During his Wake Island meeting with Truman and the JCS and the return flight home, MacArthur had absolutely no inkling that some 300,000 Chinese soldiers—supported by modern tanks and state-of-the-art Russian MIG aircraft— were making quiet preparations to cross the Yalu into North Korea.

Upon landing in Tokyo, MacArthur quickly discovered that his unnecessarily political and unnecessarily complicated strategy to finish taking North Korea was not going at all according to plan. On the eastern front, while the Navy waited for wooden-hulled minesweepers to arrive from Japan to clear the heavily-mined Wonsan harbor, the hapless Marines were forced to sail in circles for seven full days battling an outbreak of dysentery.

In the western sector, when Hap Gay's 1ˢᵗ Cav—embroiled in the useless politics of which unit would take Pyongyang—finally crossed the Taedong river on October 20, they found the ROKs had already slipped across and beaten them all to the punch. By October 23, the NKPA was now apparently virtually non-existent, and John Church's 24ᵗʰ Division had moved north through the rugged mountainous landscape beyond Sukchon to the Chongchon River at Sinanju.

Then on October 25 and again on the 29th, American forces were unexpectedly attacked by strong NKPA infantry supported by new T-34 tanks and self-propelled guns.

On October 29, after turning the Reds back with close support from the Air Force, the report from frontline commanders that two Chinese soldiers were among the eighty-nine prisoners taken was not treated seriously by Charles Willoughby, MacArthur's G-2 (Chief of Intelligence) nor any of the other rear-area intelligence officers. Even after flying in by chopper and personally interviewing the Chinese POWs, Willoughby dismissed them as being of no importance.

However, warily pushing on toward the Yalu on October 31, the same regiment encountered and punched through another road block manned by another powerful NKPA force estimated at about 5000 men.

On the following morning of November 1 about eighteen miles south of the Yalu, Brad Smith's RCT—given the honor of leading a triumphant American march to the Manchurian border—met with comparable strong resistance from a similarly well-equipped, well-organized, tank-led force of some 500 NKPA.

Almost simultaneously on the extreme right flank, a pair of ROK regiments blundered headlong into two divisions of the Chinese Communist Forces (CCF), each at full strength of around 30,000 men. Despite having broken into full retreat, the ROKs managed to take prisoners who verified to General Almond the

ROK estimates of their number. Refusing to believe Peking would enter the war at this late date, Willoughby continued to minimize this credibly-verified intelligence of incursion by the CCF.

The fatal irony was that while MacArthur's Tokyo G-2 scoffed at the ROK reports of such large numbers of fully-armed CCF south of the Yalu, the actual number was then approaching 300,000. Even worse and even more incredible, despite many daily reconnaissance flights, these forces would go virtually undetected for the next several weeks as the badly-battered Eighth Army and X Corps were being resupplied as they regrouped in new positions along the Sinanju-Kunu-Yongwan-Hamhung line.

To add to the chaos, under the virtually impossible caveat that there be no violation of the Manchurian border, MacArthur—without consulting the JCS—ordered the Far East Air Force (FEAF) to launch a firestorm of mass destruction on every possible remaining target inside the shrunken North Korean perimeter, including the Korean (southern) side of the dozen bridges across the Yalu River.

Just a few hours before this mission was to begin, FEAF commander, General George E. Stratemeyer—aware that MacArthur's orders were in direct violation of the JCS directive to stay "well clear" of the Manchurian border—got word of the impending operation to the Air Force Chief of Staff in Washington.

Washington was flabbergasted.

Not only had MacArthur flagrantly exceeded his authority, but he was also jeopardizing White House plans to protest Chinese intervention before the Security Council of the UN General Assembly. Hastily, the JCS cabled MacArthur to postpone all bombing of targets within five miles of the Manchurian border.

Resenting JCS intervention with his masterminding the war, MacArthur fired off a blistering cable to Washington:

Men and materiel in large force are pouring across all bridges over Yalu from Manchuria. This movement not only jeopardizes but threatens the ultimate destruction of the forces under my command...The only way to stop this reinforcement...is the destruction of these bridges...Every hour that this is postponed will be paid for dearly in American and other United Nations blood...Under the gravest protest that I can make, I am suspending this strike and carrying out your instructions...

In a parting shot, he scornfully confronted the JCS:

I cannot overemphasize the disastrous effect, both physical and psychological, that will result from the restrictions which you are imposing. I trust that the matter will be immediately brought to the attention of the President as I believe your instructions may well result in a calamity of major proportions for which I cannot accept responsibility without his personal and direct understanding of the situation.

The Oval Office and JCS were stunned, but even so—caught on the eve of an off-year election which threatened loss of Democratic control in the Senate—Truman succumbed to political pressure, and gave MacArthur authority to bomb the three Sinuiju bridges crossing the Yalu. (Not to be confused with the advanced Eighth Army position at Sinanju some miles south in the northwestern sector).

Ironically, the impotent air strikes on the Yalu Bridges were a humiliating failure. Not only did the Air Force and Navy bombers fail miserably to make effective hits on these structures, but by November 19, the Yalu had frozen solid enough to allow vehicular traffic. Contributing to this fiasco, air strikes on the neighboring towns and villages were killing innocent women and children while failing completely to kill or detect the CCF effectively camouflaged among the tortuous ridges and valleys of the rugged 7,000-foot mountains.

With American forces regrouping and totally unaware of the nightmare awaiting them on the eve of the planned Eighth Army Offensive, November 23 came and passed with the Americans enjoying a traditional Thanksgiving Day dinner of shrimp cocktail, roast turkey and dressing with gravy, cranberry sauce, assorted pumpkin and mincemeat pies, and fruitcakes and candies. Some units were also afforded a shot of whiskey. The next day MacArthur flew into Sinanju to be on hand for the push-off of the attack, touring the front in the numbing cold.

Within earshot of war correspondents, MacArthur told IX Corp Commander, General John Coulter: *"Tell the boys when they reach the Yalu, they are going home. I want to make good on my statement they are going to eat Christmas dinner at home."*

From the beginning, Emma knew snobby Collier hated living in the rundown Hamilton Terrace neighborhood populated largely with blue-collar workers and elderly retirees who had spent their entire lives there. When one of the doctors at the VA told her about a one-bedroom unit coming available at the ultra-modern Franklin Heights Apartments, Emma was not surprised that her choosy hubby fairly jumped at the chance to move from the dingy, depressing, roach-infested, furnished apartment on Hamilton Terrace.

As luck would have it, they had not been required to sign a long-term lease at Hamilton Terrace. However, since their first apartment had been furnished, there arose the problem of having to acquire furniture. The cosmic winds continued to favor them, and the planets all came into alignment just at the right moment as Emma unexpectedly received a nice increase in salary, more than covering the sizeable increase in rent, with a little left over to apply to furniture.

Best of all—although Lida purely hated anything but antiques—to celebrate their move up in class, Collier's stuck-up mother chipped in with a substantial down payment on a one-of-a-kind modern sofa and matching chair in a colorful rust- and olive-green-hued Aztec (or perhaps Mayan) print displayed in the window of the Grand Piano Company—a set Collier had been fairly drooling over. Too fancy for the local unwashed masses, after sitting in the store window for three months at least, the avant-garde set had recently been marked down to half-price.

Then—exacting a solemn promise that they not breathe a word to Harry—Lida had slipped them the extra money to pay the cost of a full-sized bed with Simmons Beautyrest box springs and mattress. Secretly ecstatic at selling the white-elephant sofa and chair—which was showing signs of fading from being so long in the window—the salesman at Grand Piano threw in a rather unstylish limed-oak headboard and bed frame and matching chest of drawers to sweeten the deal.

With the money saved as the result of this largesse, they picked up a cheap chrome and Formica dinette set at a bargain store near the city market.

Then—just when Emma thought everything was perfect—to her great annoyance, Collier decided at the very last minute he wanted to paint the living room chocolate brown before they moved in. At first, she pitched a fit over the idea, but she finally gave in with his promise to repaint it immediately if it turned out to be as hideous as she imagined. Taking no chances that she would change her mind, the very next morning Collier and two of his buddies had completed the entire paint job while she was at work, managing to keep it hush-hush until the living room furniture was delivered the next day. When she saw the finished result, Emma had to admit she should never question Collier's aesthetic judgment. The way the dark chocolate walls set off the *avant-garde* designer furniture made the room look as if it were right off the cover of *House Beautiful.*

The remaining odds and ends of furniture delivered by the respective dealers, the rest of the move went like clockwork, and they settled in, spending the first night in their new bed in their new apartment the Monday before Thanksgiving. To celebrate, when Emma got home from the VA that evening, Collier broiled rib-eyes in the oven—served with baked potatoes and sour cream and a mess of late-arriving pole beans from his father's garden. Emma privately conceded that whatever deficiencies Collier had as a breadwinner, he made up for in the kitchen, as she had never even learned to properly scramble an egg.

Cozily ensconced in their new address a full two days before Thanksgiving, they were all set.

Or so Emma thought.

Late Thanksgiving morning, they had stopped by her parents for the traditional gathering of almost the entire Lowell family before going on to Collier's parents for the time-honored sit-down dinner. The only one of Emma's siblings missing was Jaynie, who was almost five years older than Emma. Because of some real or imagined transgression which remained a dark mystery, Jaynie had left for California right after her high school graduation and had only come home once for a visit, leaving tight-lipped the following morning, swearing never to return.

Except for her mother, Collier despised Emma's family, and she honestly couldn't blame him. While they had been courting in high school, her insensitive brothers and sisters had made them both miserable with their off-color remarks and otherwise generally rude behavior. For this reason, if her father or any of her siblings were present, Emma always tried to make visits to her parents as brief as possible without being insultingly obvious.

"Looks like MacArthur has the Commies on the run in Korea—guess that will keep you safe at home from yet another war," L.E., Jr. had snidely remarked to Collier when he and Emma first arrived.

An R.O.T.C. graduate of Virginia Polytechnic Institute in nearby Blacksburg, L.E., Jr. was still a colonel in the tidewater-area Army reserve and never lost a chance to remind Collier that he had commanded a battalion of Engineers at Normandy on D-Day which went on to help liberate Berlin. He had brought back over a thousand photos of combat scenes, with particular emphasis on gruesome images of rotting, dead corpses from both sides to prove it.

"Yeah, well..." Collier nodded noncommittally refusing to be baited into defending his courage and patriotism. With a sly smile, he continued, "Have you seen the new movie *Battleground*, L.E? I thought it was the best Hollywood version of combat I've ever seen. I'm curious to have your firsthand opinion of how it really was at the Bulge."

Collier hadn't been hoodwinked by L.E., Jr.'s war stories. He knew that L.E., Jr.'s outfit had not landed until at least a full week after the Normandy beachhead was cleared of mines. L.E., Jr. had spent the entire push to Germany, including the siege of Bastogne, safely out of artillery range of the retreating Germans.

"Hmmpf!" L.E., Jr., cleared his throat as color crept up his neck, "Those damn Hollywood faggots don't know the first thing about real war."

"Well...I don't know. Some Sergeant who was with General Anthony McAuliffe when he answered the German surrender ultimatum with, "Nuts!" was quoted as saying it was the real thing."

"Just Hollywood bullshit!" L.E., Jr.'s face was blood red now.

"If you say so, L.E.," Collier condescended.

"C'mon, Shasta, get Daddy moving. We're going to miss the kickoff," obviously uncomfortable now, L.E., Jr. turned and called impatiently over his shoulder,

Being a faithful contributor to the VPI Alumni Association garnered L.E., Jr. good tickets to the annual pomp and ceremony of the VPI-VMI Turkey Day clash at Roanoke's Victory Stadium. Not one of the Lowells knew the first thing about football or any other sport. The VPI Gobblers football program had fallen on hard times over the past three years, posting a string of embarrassing losses and only one win. For the Lowells, going to the game was just another excuse to drink too much and make all-around jackasses of themselves.

"I know you like to support your Gobblers, L.E., but they're no match for the Keydets this year. I'll give you six points and take VMI." Collier knew he was getting L.E., Jr.'s goat and he didn't want to lose the advantage. "You could save yourself a lot of trouble and stay here. You can get just as drunk here and avoid that damn traffic snarl coming home. At your age, you don't need to aggravate your blood pressure."

"Age? Blood pressure? What the hell do you know about my age and blood pressure?"

"Well...I didn't mean to upset you..." Collier said, solicitously.

It was all Emma could do not to laugh out loud. Collier enjoyed ruffling L.E., Jr.'s feathers. It was sweet payback for the many miserable hours she had suffered with her family.

CHAPTER SIX

THE ROANOKE TIMES
Roanoke, Virginia, Friday, December 1, 1950
U.S. WILL USE ATOM BOMB IF NECESSARY
New Defense Line Set Up 30 Miles From Pyongyang
CHINESE REDS SNAP TRAP IN NORTHEAST
By LIEF ERICKSON

SEOUL, Friday, December 1 (AP) - The bulk of the 110,000 U.S. Eighth Army today set up a new defense line in northwest Korea 30 miles north of Pyongyang against pursuing Chinese Communists...

FRIDAY, NOVEMBER 24 (the day following Thanksgiving), the ink was scarcely dry on the newspaper and magazine headlines heralding his "Home by Christmas" promise, when MacArthur—at X Corp CP to observe the kickoff of the Eighth Army's final push to the Manchurian border—again grabbed headlines by arrogantly and irresponsibly flying through North Korean airspace to the Yalu River before returning to his HQ in Tokyo.

He reported seeing only a merciless wasteland with no sign of Chinese Communist Forces.

On November 24 and 25—the first thirty-six hours of what was being looked upon as a stroll through the northern mountains to the Yalu—elements of the Eighth Army met fairly light and generally sporadic enemy resistance, reporting gains ranging from about two to eight miles. Somewhat weary from negotiating the extremely rugged terrain with weapons and equipment—many of them still supplied with only summer-weight fatigues in numbing temperatures dropping into the mid-teens—after dusk, exhausted soldiers who couldn't find Korean huts for shelter huddled together around makeshift fires desperate for any way to stay warm. With only half-hearted patrols, the Americans had pretty much buttoned down for the night when the proverbial excrement hit the fan.

Around 2000 hours (8:00 P.M.), with massive force and guns blazing, the CCF came swarming out of the foothills, screaming and blowing bugles, banging pans, shaking rattles and shooting off flares, exacting horrific losses and taking few prisoners. After two days of struggling to retreat across a wide front against overwhelming odds with a great cost of life and weapons, it became obvious to the stunned, disorganized and disoriented frontline commanders that the CCF were threatening complete encirclement. Despite overwhelming evidence back at HQ that the CCF were present in superior numbers, the supercilious Eighth Army G-2 still dismissed CCF participation as being limited to a small number of isolated "volunteers" and "stragglers" and ordered X Corps to proceed with the launch of the ill-fated Chosin Reservoir offensive on the morning of November 27.

Inside the Chosin, waiting until the right tactical moment and again attacking from all directions still blowing bugles and exploding flares, CCF hordes scrambled down from the high ground like ants, catching the vastly outnumbered Marines totally unprepared. Despite putting up a courageous fight and killing great numbers of Chinese, the seemingly inexhaustible CCF multitudes kept coming.

Finally surrounded, the gallant Americans were reduced to utter shambles.

Early the morning of November 28, Washington received a communiqué from MacArthur confirming that the CCF had committed at least 200,000 troops to North Korea with the clear intent of pushing UN forces back in an "undeclared war." MacArthur cabled that the desperate situation immediately demanded a switch in strategy from offensive to defensive mode.

From that moment, White House confidence in MacArthur was in immediate decline.

Ironically, that same day before the setting sun cast the long shadow of the Washington Monument across the iced-over reflecting pool, Joe Stalin's diabolical machinations to bring about Chinese intervention in Korea—threatening the advent of WWIII—had set America on an all-out course of military rearmament which continued until the end of the so-called Cold War and resulting in Russia's ultimate decline.

Meanwhile in North Korea, legions of CCF had completely overrun the American-led troops and sent them fleeing south in desperate disarray, leaving thousands of ROK and X Corps troops trapped inside the "Frozen Chosin" Resevoir.

THE ROANOKE TIMES
Roanoke, Virginia, Sunday, December 3, 1950
UN FORCES FACE TRAPS IN NORTH

To Emma, sitting at the kitchen table just before leaving for work the Wednesday before Christmas, absently bundling newspapers she had saved for the local Boy Scouts paper drive, the grim headlines served as a sobering reminder of the dire gravity of the Korean situation. She was suddenly jolted to attention as centered just below the fold was a photo of one of Collier's rival footballers from Jefferson Senior High School.

PAUL MARTIN DIES IN KOREA
Cpl. Paul Edward Martin, USMCR – popular Roanoke athlete and leader of youth – was killed in action in Korean area Nov. 28.
An official confirmation of his death was received yesterday from Marine Headquarters in Washington...

More alert now and wondering if Collier had heard about Paul Martin's death, Emma continued to peruse headlines as she stacked the papers neatly for bundling.

THE ROANOKE TIMES
Roanoke, Virginia, Monday, December 4, 1950
UN RETREATS FROM PYONGYANG

THE ROANOKE TIMES
Roanoke, Virginia, Tuesday, December 5, 1950
PYONYANG FALLS IN FACE OF RED HORDE

THE ROANOKE TIMES
Roanoke, Virginia, Sunday, December 10, 1950
ALLIED FORCES CANNOT HALT CHINESE REDS

THE ROANOKE TIMES
Roanoke, Virginia, Saturday, December 16, 1950
TRUMAN SAYS NATION IN GRAVE DANGER

THE ROANOKE TIMES
Roanoke, Virginia, Sunday, December 17, 1950
TRUMAN PROCLAIMS NATIONAL EMERGENCY

"National emergency!" Emma sniffed half-aloud in the empty kitchen at the three-day-old headline, "So what else is new?"

Wrapping the stack of papers with twine, Emma stuffed them into a large, paper grocery bag and set the bag outside in the entrance hall. Before coming back inside, she picked up their newly-delivered morning paper, carelessly unfolding it. Glancing down, instinctively she clutched her bosom, totally unprepared for the fresh-faced image of the young Marine corporal staring back from the top of the front page.

THE ROANOKE TIMES
Roanoke, Virginia, Wednesday, December 20, 1950
Jimmy Akers, Jeff Athlete Dies in Action

Cpl. James F. (Jimmy) Akers, 20-year-old son of Mr. and Mrs. Peter L. Akers of 1801 Warrington Rd. SW was killed in action in Korea on December 2 according to word received yesterday...

Reading the bulletin about one of Collier's father's star baseballers, Emma gave a little sob and caught her breath.

This damn war was getting entirely too close for comfort.

Between last-minute Christmas shopping, the war going badly in Korea, and Collier's dubious job security, Emma was verging on total exhaustion.

Collier's dubious job security troubled Emma deeply. Although Harvey Wirtz, Kroger's local advertising manager, was using him more and more at the office to give their newspaper ad layouts a decidedly more professional look, the insincere Wirtz had done nothing to raise Collier above minimum wage, steadfastly refusing to put him on the regular payroll.

Last week, when she showed Collier a Classified Ad for an Art Department Assistant from the local Houck Agency, he stalled around, pointing out that they were probably looking for some kid right out of high school to empty trash cans, tend the paste pots and sharpen the pencils.

"Besides," he had added, "the mess in Korea makes me a poor risk for permanent employment."

On the positive side, he had been putting in extra hours at home the nights she worked three-to-eleven to make his dream of becoming a figure illustrator come true. With his mother's help again, he had recently purchased a fancy drawing desk from the Sherwin-Williams store, which supplied the silk screen materials for the Kroger operation, and set it up by the picture window in the far corner of their living room. Just this weekend, against her protests, he had her strip down to panties and bra and sketched her lying across their bed, composing a cover illustration for a paperback novel to add to his sample portfolio. The impromptu modeling session had soon led to sexual foreplay, and they had spent all afternoon both Saturday and tonight, Christmas Eve, making love—amazingly, the sexual marathon had not left her as sore as she feared it might.

Tonight, as sort of a Christmas surprise, he showed her the half-finished illustration. When she saw how provocative the painting was, she had squealed, "Collier, I will not have you showing that dirty picture to anyone."

"Don't be such a prude," He'd laughed and showed her the sexy cover illustrations for a couple of Mickey Spillane and Richard Prather paperback mysteries. Finally, she had relented after he promised to alter the woman's facial features so that they did not so closely resemble her own. Privately pleased that he had rendered her likeness to appear much more glamorous than she ever actually could be, later, in bed with the lights out, paying no mind that she was still tender from the weekend's lovemaking, she had wantonly seduced him.

Afterwards, dozing in post-coital bliss, she suddenly realized she was lying alone in bed. Her senses slowly adjusting to the darkness, she gradually became aware of the sound of the radio turned down low. Instinctively, she got out of bed and shrugged into her robe. Groping her way through the darkened living room, she found Collier sitting with his back to the kitchen door, dunking cold cornbread into a glass of buttermilk, his head bent close to the telephone.

"Hey, Honey, who's on the phone?" she asked, rubbing her eyes against the sudden light.

"Wrong number..." he muttered, replacing the receiver on the hook and reaching across the table to turn up the big Zenith Transoceanic she had given him for Christmas.

"You h-hungry?" he stammered, obviously surprised to see her.

"Uhm-m...is there any pie?" She opened the fridge. "Who would be calling at this hour?"

"Oh, just some damn drunk." Collier shrugged and pointed to the radio. "Listen to the news. Washington says the Chinese have about a blue-million troops massed at the Yalu—Truman's talking about calling up more reserves and upping the draft."

"Oh, Collier," Emma sighed, locating the pie hidden behind a bowl of last weekend's tuna salad. "Now, you'll never be able to find a real job."

CHAPTER SEVEN

Merry Christmas
THE ROANOKE TIMES
Roanoke, Virginia, Monday, December 25, 1950
CHINESE ATTACK ANEW BELOW 38TH

TOKYO, Monday, December 25 (UP) - Fresh Chinese Communist troops clashed with American forces south of the 38th Parallel on Christmas Eve and the Eighth Army braced for a massive onslaught expected at any hour along a 60-mile front...

––––––––––

LISTENING TO HIS FAMILY and the preacher talking around Lida's Christmas dinner table, Collier reflected upon how the news from Korea had drastically changed from MacArthur's braggadocio prediction: "Home by Christmas" to disheartening reports of chaos and utter disaster.

Virtually overnight, the American political and military brass had been completely blindsided by teeming hordes of Chinese Communist foot soldiers and tanks. Utterly overwhelmed and outnumbered by multitudes of ill-equipped, quilted-vested, suicidally -fanatic Chinese forces pouring across the Yalu River tooting whistles, blowing trumpets, shrilling flutes and shaking rattles like an onslaught of bloodthirsty, slant-eyed Halloween-treat-or-treaters in the middle of the bitter, northernmost North Korea winter night of November 27, U.S. forces on the Korean west coast had retreated in chaotic disarray. Before U.S. forces were finally able to rally and gather courage well over a 100 blood-soaked miles south, battered American troops had suffered losses totaling several thousand casualties.

On December 6, Marguerite Higgins—recently fired by the *New York Tribune* for refusing to leave the combat zone and now reporting for *Time*—with *Life* photographer, David Douglas Duncan, had flown into Hagaru near the Chosin Reservoir and began filing reports and photos from remote places with names like Koto and Hamhung, recording the humiliating, yet heroic, evacuation of X Corps through the east-coast port of Hungnam. In a historic naval exercise of unparalleled proportion, incredibly, before it was over, the Navy had removed 105, 000 troops; 17,500 vehicles; 350,000 tons of cargo and over 90,000 Korean civilians.

Almost immediately following the Chinese Communist ambush, headlines blazed: **TRUMAN THREATENS USE OF ATOMIC-BOMB**! Instantly, the press raised an outcry of concern for WWIII and a nuclear holocaust.

Hardly before Truman's shaken brain trust could temper the President's careless bombast with diplomacy, there rapidly ensued news of the death of General Johnnie Walker followed by reports that local Marines, Paul Martin and Jimmy Akers—youths that Collier had played ball against, and his father had coached in sandlot baseball—had been killed during the nightmare retreat from the Chosin Reservoir.

Then, to make things even more depressing, at the last minute, Jim had called to say that he was taking the train up to New York to spend Christmas with his girlfriend, Hitch, at her home on Long Island.

Collier understood that this was Jim's payback for Lida's insensitive treatment of Hitch.

Jim had met Betty Hitchcock while he was at Roanoke College, and much to Lida's disapproval of Hitch's Catholicism, they had been going hot and heavy over the two years since.

Incredible as it was, Jim had hardly begun dating Hitch when Lida had invited—summoned, actually—the unwitting girl to a confrontation and proceeded to try to break up the relationship on the basis of religious differences. Arrogantly, Lida had patronized that while she had no personal quarrel with Hitch, she couldn't allow her grandchildren to be enslaved by the Catholic Church—insinuating by tone and manner that marrying into Catholicism was the equivalent of submitting to a frontal lobotomy.

Of course, this fiasco had been tantamount to a death wish for the haughty Lida.

Jim—who, in Collier's opinion, hadn't really been all that seriously committed to Hitch prior to that point—retaliated for his mother's cavalier meddling by escalating his attentions to Hitch.

By the same token, Collier, even though he wasn't all that impressed with Hitch, had mellowed his feelings toward her following this outrageous display of arrogance on Lida's part.

Collier was sorry Jim was missing out on the family gathering because Uncle Bob, his mother's baby brother, their absolute favorite, was making a rare and reasonably sober appearance within the family circle.

John Robert Boyd, retired Army Master Sergeant and black-sheep family pet, first ran away from home in 1920 and joined the Coast Guard when he was only fourteen, only to be quickly found out and sent back home within ninety days of his enlistment.

Before another six weeks had elapsed, the oversized, rebellious young rogue ran away again. This time he went to Norfolk and joined the Army. By the time his actual age caught up to him, he was already a nineteen-year-old Staff Sergeant with the horse cavalry in South Dakota; consequently, the Army chose to look the other way.

Probably because of his lifelong battle with the bottle, a family trait on the Boyd side, John Robert had a long, illustrious history of being busted back in rank, mostly for brawling. After finally reclaiming the rank of Master Sergeant for good in 1936, he unexpectedly came marching up the driveway one sunny August day in 1940, announcing his honorable retirement at age forty, having served the required twenty years.

According to his official birth record, he was actually only thirty-four.

After spending the rest of that glorious Indian summer and a goodly part of the ensuing fall and winter sleeping off one roaring drunk after another and being brought home countless times by kindly local deputies, he began paying serious court to the unassuming Ruby Prillaman. To the open-mouthed amazement of everyone who knew him, the following summer, he suddenly eloped with Ruby, announcing that he had taken a position as an Aide in the Recreation Department of the Salem Veterans Administration Hospital.

Whether it was the new job or his marriage to Ruby or both, Bob had demonstrated a remarkable turnaround in his lifestyle when—a scant six months later—the Japanese hit Pearl Harbor on that fateful December Sunday.

By noon the following day, Army HQs in Washington had sent John Robert a telegram offering a commission as Captain and requesting that he report to Fort Meade, Maryland ASAP.

"I'd rot in hell before I'd be a friggin' officer," Bob, who proudly boasted of his "Scotch-Irish fighting blood," snorted after one quick look at the telegram and promptly got in his black secondhand Plymouth, drove into Roanoke and negotiated his reenlistment as a Master Sergeant in the Army Air Corps. After a short stay at Lackland Airfield in San Antonio, Texas, he was sent to California and on to Hawaii before he finally wound up in charge of the Officer's Mess at the airbase on Tinian Island in the South Pacific on August 5, 1945, the day the B-29, *Enola Gay*, took off for Hiroshima.

In 1946, prodigal Master Sergeant Bob Boyd returned home the family hero and retired again, immediately resuming his former job at the VA. Every August since, he had declined an invitation to the annual reunion of that historic bombing mission.

A voracious reader drunk or sober, Uncle Bob had a particular fascination for history. Subscribing to *Time*, *U.S. News & World Report* and *Life* magazines and reading the daily New York and Washington papers cover to cover, John Robert Boyd was a veritable fountain of knowledge regarding politics and current events. While it annoyed Collier that his uncle was an unrelenting bigot and a chauvinist, it also struck a resonant chord in Collier's soul that Bob Boyd was, at the core, every inch a rebel.

Throughout the course of the Christmas dinner, Collier had observed with hidden amusement his uncle's growing restlessness, obviously in dire need of a drink.

"Collie, me boyo, let's go outside and have a smoke before these women-folk put us to work." Bob pushed back his chair as soon as Lida had taken the last bite of her dessert.

Once outside in the chilly sunshine, Bob went straight around to the bed of the beat-up pickup truck he used for transporting his prize-winning Beagles to the field trials and reached under a tarp behind the driver's compartment, magically producing a half-filled pint of Crab Orchard bourbon, the rawest, cheapest booze on the Virginia ABC Store list.

"Join me in a little Christmas cheer, Boyo?" he offered, uncapping the bottle and wiping the bottle's neck with the open palm of his hand. At Collier's smiling refusal, he turned up the clear glass container and took about half of the contents in one long draught, moaning with great pleasure as he recapped the pint.

"No hard feelings, Boyo, but you really are a blot on the Boyd family's good name." He grinned good-naturedly as he replaced the liquor beneath the tarp.

Moving back around the truck, Bob refused Collier's offer of a Lucky and lit his own Pall Mall. Deeply inhaling a drag from the long cigarette, he looked around at the Blue Ridge Mountains towering on every side then shifted his gaze to the line of giant sycamores and buckeye trees lining the Roanoke River banks just across the country road.

"I guess you must be getting kind of nervous, considering all the news." Bob glanced back at Collier enigmatically.

"You mean our retreat from the Yalu?" Collier asked with a start, wondering if he had been missing something.

"Well...that's at the bottom of it, I guess, but I'm referring to the terrible loss of military manpower in the last thirty days. Now, General Johnnie Walker is dead. You know we're really hurting. Before all this started last June, that dumb, tight-ass, Kansas shoe clerk, Harry Truman, had deliberately let our standing Army dwindle to barely over a half-million half-wits and niggers. Just two weeks ago, MacArthur asked the Joint Chiefs to call up the four National Guard divisions, but the JCS has already nixed that. The friggin' Russians are making threatening noises about Japan. I say nuke the bloody Chinese Commies before they push our troops off the Korean peninsula. We're facing the real possibility of a freaking global war, anyway, Boyo. Washington will be expanding the draft call any day now." Bob shrugged, flipping his half-finished cigarette into one of Lida and Harry's prize azalea beds. "Face it, Boyo, married or not, you're only twenty-one. You'd best get your freaking affairs in order."

His chest suddenly gripped by a tight fist of fear, Collier couldn't think of a single thing to say.

That night in bed he signed off his night prayer with a fervent request that "god" would intervene between him and induction into the military.

Although he didn't have a lot of faith in divine intervention and still wasn't ready to believe Congress would draft married men, on Tuesday morning, January 2, Collier took his Uncle Bob's advice to heart and made a furtive appointment with a young orthopedic surgeon.

When he had hurt his back playing football his junior year in high school, the crusty old orthopedist, Doc Hoover, told his parents a bunch of mumbo-jumbo about him having some sort of birth defect called *spina bifida occulta*. Translated from the Latin or Greek, whatever, the term meant he was born with an incomplete fusion—a small separation—between the fifth and six lumbar vertebra. Even that, the old doc said, was abnormal—most people only had five vertebrae in the lumbar region. To further complicate this anomaly, the old specialist explained in his case this separation had resulted in a minor canting or curvature in the alignment of the spine.

"Ordinarily, this shouldn't cause a major problem with your son's daily activity, but if he got hit or twisted just the wrong way playing football, it could paralyze or cripple him for life—worst-case scenario it could conceivably kill him," Doctor Hoover had warned his parents. Of course, this medical B.S. had scared Lida into making him give up playing the rough stuff. She would have made him quit basketball, too—but there, Collier had drawn the line.

Although he had eventually ignored Doc Hoover's dire predictions and, except for an occasional backache or lingering stiffness after a basketball workout or long hours pulling a squeegee across the silk screen at the shop, he had managed to live a fairly normal life. Still, he knew the military was sensitive about back problems and he held out hope this abnormality might give him a medical deferment.

"I see the slight anomaly in your lumbar, but it doesn't amount to anything I think you can count on to give you a draft deferment," the young specialist said, holding up the X-ray film to the light and pointing with a fountain pen.

"You don't think it might cause a problem when I go through the physical stress of Basic Training?" Collier asked, disappointed.

"Well, I didn't say that. I think it could cause a lot of distress, but it's an anomaly seen in about twenty percent of the population. Sooner or later, you'll have a few sleepless nights from over exercising, but it's not likely to put you out of commission."

Collier left the doctor's office depressed and disappointed. What kind of system would take a man with a disability that would likely cause him a lot of pain?

CHAPTER EIGHT

THE ROANOKE TIMES
Roanoke, Virginia, Thursday, January 25, 1951
REDS FORCES IN CENTRAL KOREAN
MOUNTAINS PULL BACK ALONG BROAD LINE
By RUTHERFORD M. POATS

TOKYO, Thursday, January 25 (UP) – The main Communist forces in the mountains of central Korea have made a general withdrawal along a broad front, leaving a no man's land up to 20 miles wide, front dispatches reported today...

Allied patrols ranged far north of their main defense line Wednesday. They found no sizeable enemy force anywhere. Neither did air scouts. United Press Correspondent William Chapman reported early today that it had become plain the enemy had pulled back for unknown reasons.

MUCH HAD HAPPENED both at home and in Korea during the month between Christmas 1950 and Collier's twenty-second birthday, January 25, 1951.

Following General Johnnie Walker's death in a jeep crash two days before Christmas, the Joint Chiefs of Staff in Washington wasted little time in naming his replacement. Because EST is twelve hours behind Seoul time, it was still the morning of December 23 when the much-decorated, WWII paratrooper and field commander, General Matthew B. Ridgeway—who at age fifty had parachuted with his troops behind Normandy on D-Day—was named to replace Walker as Commander of the badly-beleaguered Eighth Army. At age fifty-five, well-past an acceptable age for field commanders, Ridgeway immediately took off from Washington, DC. Refueling in Tacoma, Washington, and Adak in the Aleutian Islands—where he got a fresh haircut—Ridgeway arrived in Tokyo Christmas Day and immediately conferred with MacArthur.

On the morning of December 27, he boarded a WWII relic B-17 Flying Fortress christened *Hi Penny!*—which honored his thirty-two-year-old wife—and headed for Korea. Prior to landing at his primary destination of Kimpo airfield on the Han River near Seoul, Ridgeway instructed the pilot to make a gutsy, battle-savvy reconnaissance. Flying low over the rugged, mountainous combat zone, Ridgeway was disheartened to see the scattered remnants of the vaunted Eighth Army in full flight from legions of Chinese foot soldiers trudging like quilt-jacketed ants inexorably across the craggy, snow-covered North Korean ranges.

Both I Corps on the west flank and X Corps to the east were in desperate confusion.

As the world anxiously waited over the next several weeks, little good was reported in the U.S. press. Relentlessly exacting a devastating toll, the Chinese forces continued to drive the badly-bloodied, thoroughly-demoralized and vastly outnumbered American and ROK forces from just below the Chinese border to well over several hundred miles back through Seoul and on south of the Han River. It was not until the third week in January that the newly-appointed Eighth Army commander finally managed to staunch the tide, establishing a tenuous defensive perimeter at Defense Line D, roughly along the 37th Parallel.

Back in Roanoke, although they rarely spoke of it—as if not speaking of it would make it go away—the news of increasing numbers of draft call-ups coupled with new activations of the military reserves kept Collier and Emma both on edge.

Kroger was also demanding more and more of Collier's time at the office for adding some much-needed punch to their double-page layouts. While he was drawing favorable attention from the Cincinnati home office, and the local management continually promised they were exploring ways to put him on the regular payroll, nothing had yet been forthcoming and he remained an unhappy, part-time employee drawing only minimum wage.

In the meantime, similar to his visit to Stone Printing, surreptitiously he had been making new forays to several potential markets in surrounding towns, exploring all possible employment opportunities around the area.

The results continued to be uniformly depressing.

One heartening bit of intelligence, however, had come as a surprise while dropping by Piedmont Label, a busy package and label printer in nearby Bedford. Chatting with Joe Davison at Piedmont Label, Collier discovered that although they were of separate generations, there were actually two quite successful commercial illustrators who had graced the Roanoke-Salem market.

First, he had been dumbfounded to discover that the eminent, old-time magazine illustrator, Walter Biggs, a wonderfully-gifted, impressionistic fine-artist, had been born in nearby Elliston, and, as a young man, had attended VPI before going to New York City to attend the Chase School of Art—now the New York School of Art. At Chase, Biggs had actually roomed and studied with the celebrated fine artist, George Bellows.

Long since moved from Salem and now in his mid-sixties retired in New York, Biggs had been a close contemporary of the well-known illustrator-artists, W.T. Benda, Guy Pene Dubois and Rockwell Kent. From the early '20s through the '40s, Biggs' distinctive illustrations for stories and advertisements had decorated *Cosmopolitan, Ladies Home Journal* and *Woman's Home Companion*—still the leading magazines of the day.

When he found out that the other Roanoke-area illustrator, William Paxton, Sr. still lived and worked in Salem and had done the award-winning Old Dominion Candy Company logo designs and ad illustrations, this information got Collier's undivided attention.

Even more incredible, he immediately put two and two together and realized that Paxton, Sr. was most certainly the father of his high-school Jayvee-football teammate, Billy Paxton, Jr., who had played in the backfield and made a fairly-decent wingback. Recently graduated from Roanoke College, Billy was now Salem Town Clerk at the courthouse.

Desperate to find encouragement to regain some shred of self-respect, Collier called the senior Paxton the following morning and introduced himself. Heart in his throat, he asked if he might come by for advice.

"Oh, yeah, I remember you were quarterback when Billy played JayVee. I'm always glad to meet a friend of Billy's. I could spare a couple of minutes, I guess," Paxton begrudged with perceptible resignation. "Bring some samples of your work, but I ought to warn you, I doubt I have much to offer in the way of help."

That night just before he fell asleep, Collier confided to Emma about his upcoming appointment to see Billy Paxton's dad.

"That's nice, Honey. By the way, I saw an ad in today's paper for a paint-and-art-supplies salesman at Sherwin-Williams. The pay sounded a lot better than minimum wage," she had mumbled sleepily. There was no "happy birthday" wish or further mention of Paxton or the sales job in the car the following morning en route to Emma's work.

At the appointed time, Paxton—an older, more finished version of the easygoing, rather swarthy and somewhat undersized Billy—answered the door dressed in blue jeans and a wash-faded, paint-smeared plaid shirt. Pointedly protesting that he was running behind deadline on a current illustration, he escorted Collier back through his old Victorian frame house to an ultra-modern, skylighted studio in a remodeled carriage house at the rear of his heavily-wooded property on upper Broad Street, just down from the entrance to the ivy-covered Baptist Orphanage high on the nearby hill.

Walking along the wide gallery leading into Paxton's studio, Collier gawked openmouthed at the parade of framed originals by Jon Whitcomb, James Bingham, Paul Bacon and Harvey Kidder, and a few other well-recognized illustrators of the day.

"These guys are my heroes. Wow! Nobody does the surface of water better than James Bingham," Collier exclaimed, pausing momentarily in front of a striking illustration of the deck of a warship awash in a storm-tossed sea.

"I worked with all these guys during the war in a big government studio in Manhattan. We created propaganda materials and recruiting posters and made training films for the war effort. It was a great learning experience," Paxton said, offhandedly.

Inside the studio itself, a number of Paxton's award-winning paintings for Old Dominion Candies were prominently displayed. Also, several of his impressive illustrations for well-recognized national ad campaigns were framed along the walls.

Resting on the drawing table itself was a half-finished painting of Mabry's Mill, a familiar landmark on the Blue Ridge Parkway near Roanoke.

Paxton's professionalism fairly took Collier's breath. At RPI, most of his instructors had been successful freelancers to a minor degree, but this man was clearly in a league of his own.

"As you can see, I'm way behind deadline on these paintings for the N&W calendar," the artist complained, nodding at the current work-in-progress on his drawing table.

"Okay now, let's have a quick peek at *your* masterpieces," Paxton got right down to business.

Reluctantly, Collier opened up his plain black portfolio and showed Paxton the new sample for a paperback mystery novel, another rather slick, color illustration of a John Whitcomb-like Cosmo cover girl, a black-and-white tempera of a gathering of men around a big city editor's desk and a pretty good spot illustration of a pair of skiers for a travel brochure.

Except for the new paperback cover, these samples represented his work at art school.

"Hm-m...not too bad, really. You draw pretty well—so-so, anyway. Your perspective needs work and sometimes your forms aren't quite three-dimensional. When you get back to school, work harder on modeling the rounded forms," Paxton remarked after scarcely more than a perfunctory glance.

"Thanks, I appreciate your time and good advice." The blush of his embarrassment and resentment slowly creeping up his neck, Collier rose and awkwardly collected his work.

"You know, I remember you were quite a good passer and punter in high school, but you weren't much of a runner," Paxton remarked conversationally as Collier replaced his samples in his cheap portfolio. "Coach should have told you to give the ball to Billy more. He may have been a trifle undersized, but he could really run the football."

"If Billy had been able to hold on to the football a little better, he would've gotten a better shot," Collier said without expression. Burning with humiliation and mumbling insincere expressions of appreciation, Collier assured Paxton that he could find his way back to the street. When he turned to leave, he stumbled headlong into a pixyish girl in a too-tight sweater.

"Whoops! Sorry, I...my god, Essay Whitman, what are you doing here?" Collier stammered, totally unprepared to find Sallyanne Whitman, the youngest daughter of a prominent Roanoke surgeon, standing there.

"Essay" had been one of several young girls who had taken diving lessons from him two summers back when he was life guard at LaValle's Swimming Club. Knowing he was usually without a ride into Salem, the diminutive, quite libidinous, Essay had suddenly begun showing up to give him a lift into town after the pool closed at nine.

At the time, Collier had been entertaining serious doubts about his relationship with Emma. In no time, the flirty, not-so-innocent taxi service had escalated into a steamy entanglement that ended with a storm of recriminations when he left for RPI in the fall.

"Don't be sorry, Collie. Long time, no see." The petite teen beamed up at him.

"Yeah, it has been awhile. Ah...I'm expected in Roanoke—gotta run..." Still reeling from Paxton's dismissal of his work, he brushed past Sallyanne and rushed into the deepening gloom. Blindly picking his way through the shadowy darkness around the side of the house, he refastened the white-picket gate and half-ran across Broad Street to his car parked under a streetlight.

Collier couldn't remember ever feeling so utterly hopeless in his entire life. Struggling mightily to blink back a sudden rush of tears, he started the engine and sat numbly wondering what he would tell Emma about the interview.

"Collie, will you roll this stupid window down?" Not sure how long he had been sitting there, just as he was about to let the car start rolling, he realized Sallyanne was standing there tapping on the window.

"Sorry Essay—what's up?" he asked, slowly cranking down the window.

"I think I deserve a little better. Is that the best you can do?" she glowered.

"Of course you do. Sorry, Baby, it just hasn't been a good day. What've you been up to? You okay?" he fumbled for words, not really wanting to be having this conversation.

"Oh...managing a few laughs now and then—despite my parents and teachers." She laughed.

"Sounds like you haven't changed much." Collier couldn't help but chuckle.

"Not likely. I heard you got married. I didn't get an invitation."

"Must have gotten lost in the mail. You know the Post Office in this town," he teased.

"Yeah...you're just afraid that tight-ass bitch you married might find out she wasn't the best you ever had."

His gut tightened. He wasn't at all sure he liked the way this conversation was heading.

"C'mon now, Essay—that's ancient history," he smoothed. "What's done is done."

"Easy for you to say," she protested.

Shrugging, he asked, "How come you were in Paxton's studio just now?"

"His daughter, Betty, is a good friend. I dropped in but missed her. I wanted her father to tell her I was sorry I didn't catch her home."

"Oh!" he grunted. "Well, I gotta get moving. It was really good seeing you again, Essay. I got to admit you just keep getting prettier every time we meet."

"You're just saying that to be nice, but thanks just the same. Say, now that I think about it, how about giving me a lift down to Main. I have to catch the bus."

"Sure. Come around and hop in." He didn't trust the little minx, but how could he refuse to give her a lift?

Once inside, she quickly scooted closer on the front seat, not quite snuggling, but way too close for comfort.

"How's school? What grade now?" he asked, nervously letting the car roll forward.

"Tenth. My parents shipped me off to Virginia Episcopal in Alexandria two years ago when you took off for RPI." The implication seemed to suggest the fault of her exile was his.

"I thought VES was just for boys," he blurted lamely.

"I wish! The girl's campus is a goddamn nunnery."

"Sorry, Essay—that's too bad," he commiserated, not knowing what else to say.

In the closeness of the car, her fresh-scrubbed female scent called up a montage of images of her ripe, young form, stirring a familiar tension in his groin.

"Why did you just run off without so much as a word of goodbye?" she asked.

"You were against the freaking law, and I was engaged. I didn't need an Einstein to tell me I didn't want to end up in jail." Collier pulled to the curb in front of Webber's Pharmacy at the corner of Broad and Main, and got out to use the phone booth to call Emma to tell her he hadn't forgotten their plans to go to dinner for his birthday.

No answer...probably in the shower.

"Where do you want me drop you?" he asked, sliding back under the wheel.

"I heard you tell Mr. Paxton you were going to Roanoke? Why don't I just ride with you? It would save having to take a bus."

"Look, Essay. I'd be glad to help you out, but it's my birthday. I'm running late and Emma's taking me out to dinner. I go out Lee Highway through Grandin Court to Franklin Road. That's really off the beaten path."

"Oh, no, that's perfect. My grandparents live off Brandon just after it crosses Grandin. That's really not out of your way at all," she chirped happily.

"Well, okay, then. I'll be glad to drop you off."

Crossing the Roanoke River Bridge, just beyond at the beginning of South Salem, he pulled into a dimly-lit filling station with a pay phone and dialed home again. After seven or eight rings, he hung up, retrieved his dime and dialed Emma's work number at the VA.

"Hello?..." Emma picked up on the first ring.

"Hey, Honey. What're you doing still at work?"

"Oh, Collier, Baby, I tried to call. Two RNs called in with flu. They're really in a bind here and offered to pay me double-overtime if I'd stay and pull a double," she explained.

"Alright, Honey, don't worry. I was late getting away from my session with Paxton anyway. I'm just glad you're okay."

"I hope you don't mind picking me up at eleven?"

"I'll be there...see you then." He said good-bye and hung up the phone.

Well, so much for my birthday, he mused angrily as he got back in the car and slammed the door.

"What was that for? Is everything alright?" Sallyanne asked.

"Emma had to pull an extra shift. My birthday plans are down the drain," he fumed, easing back out into the sporadic traffic.

"Oh, Collie, I'm really sorry." She reached across and patted him on the thigh.

Her touch surged into him like an electric shock.

"No big deal," he replied, instantly aware that his penis was swelling.

"Do you ever think about us, Collie?" she asked, now her voice took a softer sound.

"Hmm-m..." he murmured noncommittally.

"Are you afraid to admit it, or does that mean you don't think about me at all?"

"Well, yes, goddamn it, Essay, I do. I try not to, but sometimes I just do," he growled, knowing very well it was a big mistake to admit it.

"Well, at least I'm glad of that," she gave a little sigh. "I lie awake a lot remembering how good you felt inside me. Sometimes I touch myself down there, just thinking about us. Do you think I'm awful?"

The muscles in his belly tightened.

"Do I shock you speechless?" she asked impishly when he didn't answer. Her fingers tightened on his thigh.

"Well...uh...no, I don't think you're awful."

"I really miss you, Collie." Before he could protest, she had moved her hand and was lightly tracing the outline of his swollen member with her fingers.

"Goddamn it, Essay, don't try to start anything. It would just make things worse for both of us," he said hoarsely, making a halfhearted effort to move her hand away.

"Can't be any worse for me," she laughed a little hollow laugh, pushing away his hand and unzipping his trousers.

"My god, Essay, quit. You'll make me wreck the car," he protested weakly as she fumbled inside his pants.

"Up ahead, pull in The Riverjack," she said, still probing inside his jockey shorts.

"Okay...just quit for a minute will you, Essay, please," pleading now, he slowed in front of the rundown beer joint and drifted to a stop at the far edge of the ill-lighted parking lot.

Before he could kill the engine and cut the lights, she had completely freed his rebellious penis.

"Wait...whoa, Essay. We've got to stop..." he protested weakly.

Ignoring him, she pivoted her legs around, and, with a practiced movement of her free right hand, she deftly wriggled up her skirt, exposing her creamy thighs and a reddish glint of silky, pubic patch.

"C'mon, scoot around a little and give me room," she urged impatiently.

Now, he was beyond any thought of stopping her.

Reaching down and releasing the mechanism, he pushed back the seat to make more room. He had hardly begun to twist himself before she had risen to her knees and swung her right leg across straddling him. With her right hand, she was already deftly guiding him home.

He closed his eyes and leaned back, losing himself in the hot sweetness of her center.

"R-R-R-RRR-R-R-rrr...."

A diminishing cacophony of sound and flashing colored lights assaulted his awareness as he felt himself inching slowly into her tight cleft.

"Oh, spit!" The sudden raucous whine of a siren and the blinding sweep of the police spotlight caused Essay to crack her elbow sharply on the steering wheel as she hurriedly untangled herself, trying desperately to put herself back together.

Behind them, uniformed police were discharging from two cars with spinning red lights, rushing through the headlight glare, toward the entrance of The Riverjack.

Peering anxiously in the rearview mirror, trying to figure out what was taking place, Collier's heart almost jumped outside his chest.

"What the devil's going on back there?" Essay finally asked when it became apparent that the cops were totally oblivious to their presence.

"Looks like they're here to break up a fight or maybe a raid for illegal booze." Collier quickly zipped himself, twisting to catch a better view through the rear window.

"Damn stupid cops! Just when you were about to come," Essay giggled.

"Come? I almost had a heart attack," Collier grumbled, not at all amused.

When he was sure the cops were all inside, he started the engine and slipped back out on the highway.

"Well, at least I know you still like me," she began after they had moved by the glut of traffic waiting to get in the Lee-Hi Drive-In theater. "I'm going to be in town for the weekend. If Emma has to work, we could figure out a way to finish what we started back there..."

"Forget that, Essay. We just lucked out. Or don't you understand?"

"But, Collie, it could be your birthday present..." she teased. "How old are you, anyway?"

"Twenty-two today," he confided.

"I'm catching up with you. I'll be sixteen next month," she giggled again.

"Damn, Essay, did you ever hear of statutory rape? If those cops back there had caught us, I'd really have my ass in a sling..."

"Oh, c'mon, Collie, when did you get to be such a prude?" she pleaded.

"About five minutes ago. Forget fun and games, Essay. What's done is done." Reaching across, he gently touched her cheek.

"C'mon, Collie, no one would ever know..."

"No, Essay. Warn me when we get close to where I turn off Brandon," he said as they passed the little sign marking the Roanoke Corporate Limit.

When he had dropped her off on Brandon, he circled back by Garland's labyrinthine drug emporium across from the Grandin Theater and bought two spray cans of air freshener and a cake of deodorant soap.

First, he had to try to get Sallyanne's musky scent out of Emma's car. Then he had to take a very long shower.

CHAPTER NINE

The Roanoke World-News
Roanoke, Virginia, Friday Afternoon, April 13, 1951
MACARTHUR PLANS TO START
HOMECOMING FLIGHT MONDAY
By Russell Brines

TOKYO, Friday, April 13 (AP) –General MacArthur will fly to the United States Monday in a fighting mood to challenge the President who fired him over war policy.

THE ROANOKE TIMES
Roanoke, Virginia, Friday, April 20, 1951
MACARTHUR: "OLD SOLDIERS NEVER DIE"
FIGHTING CONTINUES TO RAGE IN KOREA

WASHINGTON, Friday, April 20 (AP) - Ending his tearful farewell speech with the line from an old British ballad,: *"Old soldiers never die, they only fade away,"* General of the Army, General Douglas MacArthur vigorously defended his Far East policy to Congress in joint session yesterday, while in Korea, troops were engaged in mop-up operations around Seoul and the fierce firefight raged on in the vicinity of Chorwan in North Korea...

DURING THE FINAL DAYS of January while Collier was trying to shake off the humiliation of having had his wife overlook his twenty-second birthday–not to mention breathing a great sigh of relief that he had been unwittingly saved from committing statutory rape with Sallyanne–halfway around the globe in Korea, the aging, but quite able, General Matthew Ridgeway was quickly getting down to the task at hand, replacing most of the war-weary Eighth Army commanders with Generals having proven WWII combat credentials.

Now reasonably rested, resupplied, reinforced and regrouped far to the south, along the 37th Parallel at Defense Line D stretching from P'yongt'aek on the west coast to Samch'ok on the east coast, on January 25, General Ridgeway launched Operation Thunderbolt, a cautious counter-offensive, probing guardedly north against suspiciously-light Chinese resistance.

By nightfall that first day, elements of the rejuvenated 7th and 8th Cav moving warily along the Suwon-Wonju road, had reached Inchon and dug in for the night, forming a tight perimeter. Heartened by this easy progress, Ridgeway audaciously moved up his reserves the following day, determined to attack in full force.

Very much to Ridgeway's vexation that MacArthur was alerting the Chinese to his plans for a full-scale offensive–and quite aware he was being upstaged by the ever-pompous old rooster–the morning of January 28, MacArthur flew into Suwon Airfield for a photo shoot, crowing to Ridgeway within well-calculated earshot of a British war correspondent, "This is exactly where I came in seven months ago...The stake we fight for now, however, is more than Korea–it is a free Asia."

Ridgeway's concern over MacArthur's reckless, irresponsible ego-posturing was well founded. After receiving almost no resistance on January 28, early on the frigid morning of January 29, Operation Thunderbolt ran headlong into strong Chinese resistance along both I and IX Corps sectors.

Taking heavy casualties in bloody fighting over the next two days, the battle finally culminated February 1, with the Eighth Army's hard-won annihilation of a complete Chinese Division at a place called the Twin Tunnels near the banks of the Han River south of Seoul.

Despite a major Chinese counterattack in the Wonju-Chipyong-ni area, in mid-February, the UN forces—with determined initiative, dogged combat and with great cost of life—finally accomplished the Second Liberation of Seoul, advancing to Phase Line Kansas just north of the 38th Parallel by mid-April.

Because of ongoing disagreement with White House strategy in the Far East, on April 11, President Truman relieved MacArthur of all commands, calling him back to Washington.

Although he didn't much subscribe to the idea of omens or various other signs portending the future, driving to pick up Emma at work late on the evening of Friday 13, Collier had seen his first-ever shooting star. While the spectacular event produced an eerie expectant feeling that his luck was about to change, he quickly dismissed the idea as nonsense. But ensuing events soon proved him wrong.

Early in February, a slightly older couple, Gerry and Bill Deeds, moved into 4-B across the hall. Quickly endearing themselves to Collier and Emma almost from the beginning, the Deeds—who were far more sophisticated, much better traveled, and infinitely more interesting than their local circle of friends—became the center of Collier and Emma's social life. By early April, most of their weekend evenings were spent in the company of their urbane new neighbors.

Working more and more at home now at his new drawing desk, Collier had convinced Kroger Company to let him enhance their weekend double-page newspaper spreads with custom hand-lettered headlines. Moreover, from time-to-time, he would render black-and-white wash drawings of major featured grocery items from off-brand suppliers when the Cincinnati office failed to supply appropriate art for paste-up. With this freedom to create, Collier gained newfound confidence and was fast becoming the postmodern Michelangelo of bacon packages and bean cans.

The circumstance of Gerry having a key to their apartment had been Emma's idea.

One evening over late dessert in the Deeds' kitchen, Emma had confided that she had a bad habit of going off to work and leaving the coffee pot on. Gerry confessed to the same absentmindedness, and it was quickly agreed that exchanging keys, so each couple could serve as watchdogs for the other would be a great idea.

To Collier's annoyance—and extreme discomfort—with Bill traveling overnight extensively throughout the week, Gerry quickly developed the distracting habit of walking in unannounced with a fresh cup of coffee on mornings Emma was at work.

"Hi, Collie! Look what I brought. Your favorite! Homemade apple pie fresh out of the oven." One morning late in April, Gerry just popped right in without bothering to knock, bearing a covered dish and interrupting his concentration on a hand-lettered caption for a newspaper ad promoting Kroger's upcoming May Day weekend specials.

"Gee, Gerry, thanks. But I'm on a tight deadline..." He purely hated to be called Collie.

"Oh, don't be such a grind," she ignored his protest with a dismissive wave of hand.

"No fooling, Gerry...I have to get this to the paper this morning..." he protested.

"All work and no play, so the saying goes. Come on, Sweetie, quit being such a grouch." To his annoyance, she set the plate on the coffee table, came over, and mussed his hair.

Reluctantly, he put down his pencil and looked up. To his complete surprise, she stepped forward and took his face in her hands and gave him a steamy, deeply-probing kiss.

"Don't forget tonight," she reminded, turning to leave.

Momentarily, he found himself totally speechless. For the life of him, he couldn't remember anything they had planned for tonight.

"What about tonight?..."

"MacArthur...his farewell speech to Congress, remember?"

"Oh yeah, but that's today, I have to work..." He vaguely recalled the four of them talking about Truman firing MacArthur when they were playing Yahtzee last evening. There had also been some conversation about Bill and Gerry's new Magnavox AM/FM Radio with its fancy record changer, but he had no recollection of making plans to listen to MacArthur's speech. Emma was headed to a seminar in Richmond and Bill left town before the crack of dawn this morning.

"WDBJ is rebroadcasting the speech tonight at eight. I'll feed you spaghetti."

"Better not count on me. I have to finish screening the weekly window banners, then finish the newspaper layouts. It's going to be a long day," Collier hedged. Her toe-curling kiss made him very uncomfortable to think of being alone with Gerry in her apartment.

"Oh, come on, Collie, surely you'll be home before eight." Giving him a reproving look, she disappeared through the door.

Although he worked at a harried pace into the early evening screening the window banners, the memory of Gerry's soul kiss left Collier with a nagging heaviness in his loins. He had fantasized having sex with his voluptuous neighbor since the moment he first laid eyes on her. He seriously doubted that bumbling old Bill was taking care of his homework. But he worked all day with the firm resolve that he was not going to jump into bed with his sexy neighbor.

When he finally made it home, it had already grown quite dark, and he could hear his phone ringing as walked up the walk. Running the last few steps, he slipped inside and turned on the lights, making a desperate grab for the phone.

"Hello?..."

"Collier...where on earth have you been? I've been trying to get you for over an hour," Emma was clearly exasperated.

"Sorry, Baby, I just this minute came through the door. I had to screen the banners this morning and nothing went right. Then I went into the office to do the newspaper layouts," he explained defensively. "I can hardly wait until tomorrow. I miss you terribly."

"Well, that's one reason I've been so anxious to reach you. I have to stay over an extra day, maybe two," she said, not very apologetically.

"Oh, crap! Why's that?" he exploded.

"Don't use that language, Collier. I heard enough of that from my brothers. Look, I don't like being out of town, but it's my job, Collier," she replied coolly, adding with a more haughty inflection. "After all, one of us has to make enough money to afford our ritzy lifestyle."

"Uh..." Collier let his protest die in his throat. He really did enjoy living in these classy apartments—he had no complaint about their lifestyle.

"And, speaking of your employment, did you call about the newspaper ad for an art supply salesman?" she quickly changed the subject.

"I called, but it was already filled," he lied resentfully. No way was he going to become a common peddler.

"Already filled? Carolyn says the ad is still running in today's *Times*," she replied mistrustfully. Carolyn Eck was a nurse at the VA.

"That's not uncommon. They can't just cancel a classified ad on one-day's notice," he fired back defensively, strongly resentful she would call her friends to check up on him.

"Well, keep an eye on the paper. Something more substantial has to come up sooner or later."

"I look every day," he replied sullenly.

"Have you called Security Envelope?" she reminded.

She was constantly trying to get him to go see the staff artist at Security Envelope Company—a small local printing company specializing in corporate letterhead stationary and their patented double-compartmented envelopes used for church offerings. The company was owned by members of Emma's boss, Dr. Simpkins Moseley's, family.

"I called twice, but their artist was tied up with clients," he lied. "I'll call again tomorrow."

"Well, anyway, I'm glad I finally got you. I really am late for a meeting. I'll call tomorrow morning, okay?" She was obviously anxious to get off the phone.

"Okay. Have a good night..." he began, but she had already broken the connection.

Before he could lower the phone back onto the cradle, it started ringing again.

"Emma?..."

"It's me, Collier," Gerry started in immediately. "Where have you been? I'm cooking us spaghetti, remember?"

"Oh, Gerry, I'm sorry. To tell the truth, I've had a killing day and had forgotten."

"All the better. You need a chance to relax and enjoy a good home-cooked meal."

"It's late, Gerry. I just got home and I'm really bushed. I need a shower. I hope you haven't gone to a lot of trouble..."

"Well, I *have* gone to a lot of trouble, and you've got to eat. Listen, Buster, you're not going to weasel out on me. Run take a shower and get comfortable. Twenty minutes, okay?" Her tight little laugh told him she obviously was in no mood to take "no" for an answer.

"Well, alright...twenty minutes. I just hope I don't fall asleep with my face in the pasta," too tired to argue he sighed and hung up. And, now that he thought about it, except for some peanut-butter crackers and a coke, he hadn't had a bite since morning.

"Don't just stand there, come in." Wearing a silky, loose-fitting Oriental gown, low-cut across the inviting canyon between her enormous breasts and sensually slit to mid-thigh on both sides, Gerry ushered him into her apartment.

"My god, that smells good! I could eat an elephant," he enthused—his senses assailed by the mouth-watering smell of simmering spaghetti sauce mingled with the tantalizing aroma of freshly-baked bread.

Bumping the door firmly shut with her curvaceous buttocks, Gerry stepped forward and gave him a sisterly peck on the cheek, lightly brushing the length of her voluptuous body against him. Then, before he could protest, she leaned into him and turned her face up and kissed him full upon the mouth, her tongue leaving little doubt of her agenda for the evening. Still burning with resentment for Emma's cavalier behavior and resigning himself to fate, Collier let himself be caught up in the kiss. Casually letting his hand slide down the small of her back, his subtle exploration confirmed she was wearing nothing at all underneath the filmy garment. And, wearing no bra to support them, her incredible breasts imposed against him unnervingly—the large stiff nipples bored into his chest, surprising him with their rigidity. Confronted with such blatant sexuality, Collier's penis protested against the confinement of the tight cotton underwear.

"C'mon on in here. Let's eat while the bread is fresh out of the oven," Gerry commanded when she finally released him, taking him by the hand into the kitchen. "We're eating in the dining alcove. Grab a plate and help yourself to the pasta and spaghetti sauce. There's plenty, so don't be shy. I'll bring the bread."

Filling his plate with a mountain of the thinnest pasta he'd ever seen and the rich-looking, red meat sauce, Collier went into the small dining area, placed his plate on the glass-topped, wrought-iron table and stood by waiting so he could hold a chair for his seductive hostess.

"Such a gentleman," she murmured sweetly. Nodding toward the grass-covered bottle of Chianti sitting on the table, she chirped conspiratorially, "I know that Emma never lets you take a drink, but I thought what she doesn't know won't hurt her. A good, rich Chianti goes nicely with spaghetti."

"You're right about that. I used to have a small glass at a little Italian restaurant near the campus in Richmond. What the hell? I confess I had the occasional beer with the gang while I was away at school," he smiled sheepishly.

"Good for you! I'd hate to drink alone." She poured both glasses half full. "Now eat!"

Digging into the food and washing it down with large swallows of the Chianti, Collier hardly came up for air. In a matter of minutes, he had devoured the entire plate, sopping up the remaining sauce with large pieces of the delicious, fresh-baked bread.

"There's plenty more...go help yourself," she smiled sweetly, only about a third of the way through eating her more ladylike helping.

"Thanks. I think I'll take you up on that. Can I bring you anything?" Pausing beside her, he took another surreptitious opportunity to appreciate her tits beneath the sexy dress.

"No thanks, I'm fine." She smiled up at him knowingly and nodded. Glancing over the rim of her wine glass, she caught him looking at her breasts and responded with an openly flirtatious look.

For just a fleeting instant, he felt like an errant schoolboy, but he refused to look away.

"Did you hear any of MacArthur's speech today while you were driving around in the car?" she resumed their conversation when he began to eat again.

"Nuh-uh..." he shook his head negatively. "I caught a snippet of commentary on the evening news, driving home. I was too tired to pay much attention...something about 'Old soldiers never die...' I got the impression that 'Dugout Doug' really stuck it to Truman and the JCS. Did you hear any of the live broadcast?"

"No. The rebroadcast will be coming on in an hour. That's plenty of time to clean up the kitchen first."

"Sure thing, let's do it. But I'm beat. Would you be upset if I just helped you clean up and went on home?" he asked.

"No, no. You don't have to help me. Take a rest. Why not stretch out on my bed and take a nap? I'll wake you when MacArthur comes on?"

"Oh...no. If I go lie down, I may not make it back up again."

"Nonsense...you have an hour. Come on now, I won't *bite*. Don't you like my company?"

"Of course I do...I...uh..." He watched those well-formed thighs peeking out of the slit skirt...and the firm cantaloupe breasts. Pure carnality.

"Come on, Collie, times a'wasting." She moved her feet apart suggestively and began picking up the plates and utensils.

"Well...okay, but I really don't want to lie down. I'll help clean up the kitchen. It'll help wake me up." Reflecting on this morning's kiss, he was reminded of the fate of the Black Widow Spider's mate. He just wanted to get the hell out of there before it was too late.

"Well, alright, if you insist..." She flashed an enigmatic smile.

Collier grabbed the remaining items from the table and followed, watching her well-rounded derriere as she bent to put the dishes in the sink. He moved in behind her and put the remaining items on the counter, entertaining a transient fantasy of raising the long slit skirt and fondling those delectable cheeks as he wantonly entered her, bent helplessly over the sink.

Lost in the lustful fantasy, he was still standing close behind when she turned to face him, and he took a tentative half-step back to give her room.

"We can just leave them for now. Let's go get comfortable. I'll do them later," she said.

"No...come on, let's do them now. I'll wash. You dry. Won't take a minute," he insisted and reached for an apron hanging on the back of a chair.

"Alright...do you do this at home? Bill has never been much to help in the kitchen. He says keeping house is women's work." She took the apron and looped the strap around his neck. Reaching around him to tie it behind his back, she pushed up against him. His caged penis was quite painful now.

"I had a lot of practice when I was just a kid. My mom was sick a lot," he mumbled, not wanting to move away.

"I hope you don't mind my saying this, but I notice Emma is not much of a hand in the kitchen."

"No...she was the youngest of ten kids. She helped with housework, but her mom did all the cooking. You're right. I surely didn't marry her for her cooking. The atrocities that girl can commit in the kitchen." He shrugged and laughed.

"Well, I'm sure she makes it up to you in other ways." She raised her eyebrows knowingly then turned back and began running hot water into the double sink. "They say that opposites attract. I knew, the first time we met, you two were as different as oil and water.

"Well...I...ah..." He blushed and looked away.

"Take the clean dishes out of the rinse water and put them in the drain rack. I always let them air dry." She pulled a plate out of the suds and slipped it into the rinse water. The drain rack was on the counter next to the sink.

He set to work rinsing dishes, mulling over what she'd said.

"What difference does it make that we're not alike, if we love each other?" he asked, after a moment.

"Nothing really. I didn't mean to strike a nerve just now...about your relationship with Emma, I mean," she paused and gave him an apologetic look. "Emma is smart enough in a conventional way, but she is practical—very down-to-earth. She obviously thinks you're wasting your time trying to be an artist. On the other hand, you're artistic and romantic—quite intellectual and talented. A dreamer. You're a sensualist too. My guess is that Emma is rather unresponsive...ah, uhm...unadventuresome in the...uhm...romance department."

Collier's first reaction was to defend Emma, but thinking it over, Gerry had pretty much nailed her dead on. He kept silent, concentrating on rinsing the dishes. They were almost finished with everything. Gerry had already started on the pots and pans.

"Sometimes I talk too much," after a long moment, she continued. "I hope I didn't hurt your feelings."

"No, no, not at all. I'm just not comfortable discussing my personal life...and what do you mean by sensualist?"

"Well, in the broadest sense, you experience life to the hilt—you take time to smell the roses. The sky, the sun, the way food smells and tastes, music, art...*sex*—everything gives you pleasure." Her emphasis on the word "sex" was obviously deliberate.

"Uhm-m? Well, I do enjoy living...what I can afford of it," he admitted sheepishly. "You don't think Emma enjoys those things? What makes you say that?"

"Emma doesn't particularly enjoy sex. She told me that herself." Gerry had finished the last of the utensils and was hanging up the apron now. "We've been in this damn kitchen long enough. Just leave these pots. I'll rinse and dry them later."

"Hold on. This won't take me half-a-minute. I don't like to leave a mess," Collier said, quickly rinsing the two cooking pots and placing them in the drain. "There now...all done."

"Thanks...you're the perfect dinner guest. Let's go get comfortable before MacArthur's speech comes on," she took him by the hand and led him back into the living room.

He followed, dying to know what Emma told her about their sex life.

"Sit here with me," she flopped on the oversized sofa, reclining against a pile of throw pillows at the far end. "Sit down and relax...you make me nervous," she scolded good-naturedly and indicated the opposite end of the sofa.

"Well...but I don't want to stay late. I've got another killing day tomorrow." He scooted into the narrow wedge at the other end of the sofa with her toes almost touching his thigh.

"Will you relax? Am I boring you? Is that it?"

"Oh, no...I'm just tired that's all." He adjusted a pillow, trying to make himself more comfortable. When he looked in her direction now, he was staring directly down the narrow vee formed by her extended legs, directly into her crotch. The pressure of his imprisoned anatomy struggling against the briefs was becoming almost unbearable now. He was going to have to leave if the discomfort increased much more.

"Now, isn't that better?" She smiled a Mona Lisa smile.

"Uhm-m..." he agreed, then blurted, "what else did Emma tell you about our...uhm... personal life?"

"Nothing really. Except that she doesn't enjoy sex, and that you are something of a sex maniac. But relax. Your secrets are safe with me." She winked broadly.

"A sex maniac? Oh, come on, Emma never said that...did she?" he asked, not at all sure she wasn't putting him on.

"Well, yes, in so many words. Are you? A satyr, I mean?" She smiled that unreadable smile again.

"Certainly not...but I admit I do enjoy sex, like any normal male. I'm sure Bill is pretty much the same."

"Are you kidding? Bill is more like Emma. Once a year would be okay by him," her lighthearted tone took on a hard edge.

"Now who's kidding who?" He looked at her incredulously.

"I wish. I'm more like you...I'm sensual too. I purely enjoy sex. Bill thinks I'm a nymphomaniac and Emma thinks you're a satyr. Maybe we should trade spouses, what do you think?"

"Huh?..." Teasing or not, the suggestion left him speechless.

"Maybe I don't appeal to you?" She sat up and leaned toward him, her billowing breasts exposed now all the way down to the top of the pale-pink aureoles.

"Well...ah...sure, I like you fine. Any man who doesn't find you attractive needs to see an ophthalmologist." He completely surprised himself with his audacity.

Spellbound, he watched as she twisted around on the sofa and pulled herself to her knees. Leaning toward him, she slowly lowered her face close and kissed him deeply, her tongue probing aggressively.

His eyes still wide open as he began to return the kiss, he felt her hands fumbling to unloose the fastener on his trousers; then she unzipped his fly and groped to free his turgid penis. When she finally managed to slip his briefs down and took a firm grip on her prize, he was so aroused he was afraid he would have an orgasm right in her hand.

"My! What a lovely specimen you have there," she exclaimed as she broke the kiss and lowered her head, slowly taking the length of him into her mouth. The ecstasy was almost more than he could bear and brought him again to the edge of release.

"Wait! I can't stand much of that..." he lifted her head from his lap.

"Look at you...I've got to have that thing inside me," she breathed in his ear as she mounted him, spreading herself, welcoming him inside her moist vagina.

She had ridden him hard for probably less than a minute when she started to moan. A moment later, he felt her shuddering to a violently-convulsive orgasm. When her orgasm subsided, she collapsed with her head on his shoulder breathing hard into his ear. After just the briefest of moments, he started pumping into her again.

"Please...no. I can't take anymore," she pleaded, but he ignored her and continued rhythmically pumping into her. Soon she quit fighting and started to respond again, coming for the second time in almost no time at all with an orgasm even more powerful than the first. "Wait," she gasped and sat up, pulling the gown over her head. Now, stripped completely naked mounted above him, the enormous breasts bounced to a wild rhythm in all their unfettered glory as she continued to move against him.

"Me, oh my, I never knew I could do it twice...much less three..." she panted, nibbling his ear. "Stop now. I mean it. I can't stand anymore," she pleaded as he continued gently thrusting his penis in and out. "Stop, I really mean it...stop..." she moaned, totally without conviction as she found herself responding yet again.

"I can't hang on. I'm going to come...do you have a diaphragm in?" he asked desperately as he felt an unbearable tension building.

"Forget that, it's not a problem. Give it to me, Collie. Let me have it all," she gasped as he exploded inside her.

To his utter disbelief, he felt her vaginal passage contracting once again.

In all his young life, Collier could not remember having such a profoundly shattering orgasm. After several minutes had elapsed, he was completely amazed to find his penis still throbbing, painfully erect, already responding anew to the tightness of Gerry's vagina.

Slowly, he resumed a rhythmic thrusting inside her.

Immediately, she began responding again. This time they both built to orgasm in a matter of a few short minutes, and Gerry finally collapsed on his chest, completely exhausted.

"Do you think I really could be a nymphomaniac?" she finally wheezed in his ear.

"Maybe...it's perfectly alright with me," he chuckled, savoring the moment, laying there exhausted, feeling the sticky perspiration between them. The last thing he heard before he fell fast asleep, was her softly snoring in his ear.

"Goddammit, Gerry, open this door! I can't find my key."

Collier came full awake at the sound of loud pounding on the door.

"Uhm-m...what?" Groggily, Gerry slowly roused and sat up, still buck naked astride him.

"Oh, shit, it's Bill," Collier gasped. "I gotta get out of here."

"Quick, out through the kitchen and over the back-porch rail." Rolling off of him, she retrieved her dress, trying desperately to untangle it.

Pulling up his slacks, Collier grabbed his shirt and shoes and was already heading for the kitchen. Out the kitchen door in record time, he quickly checked the area about ten feet below the fully-enclosed tiny back porch, peering into the darkness for anything that would make his landing hazardous. In the reflected neon light from businesses on Franklin Road, he saw nothing but an empty expanse of unmowed grass. Without looking back, he launched himself recklessly into the night, preparing to do a gymnast's roll as soon as his feet touched the ground. Landing without mishap, he lost no time in making his way down the rather long back side of the apartments, walking around to the parking area on the circular drive to the sidewalk leading back around to their unit.

Approaching their building, Collier could clearly see Bill and Gerry in animated conversation through the open drapes in their living room. Taking great pains to be quiet, he slipped into the foyer, made it back inside his own apartment and closed the door behind him before he dared breathe again.

Using the streetlight coming through the front window, he negotiated his way carefully back and fell into bed exhausted, his eyes staring into the darkness, his heart beating like a triphammer. As his breathing and heart rate returned to normal, visions of Gerry's naked body and vivid recollections of the powerful sexual encounter came flooding back over him and he came painfully erect again.

Just what the hell had he gotten himself into now?

CHAPTER TEN

THE ROANOKE TIMES
Roanoke, Virginia, Friday, April 20, 1951
MACARTHUR DEFENDS FAR EAST POLICY
By Relman Morin

WASHINGTON, Friday, April 20 (AP) - Gen. Douglas MacArthur, restrained but jut-jawed with defiance, defended his entire "Far Eastern strategy in a dramatic speech before Congress today, asserting that he had believed his views were fully shared by "our own joint chiefs of staff."

It was a fighting speech all the way.

IN RICHMOND, hurrying to meet her dinner companions, Emma Lowell Ramsay was hardly aware of the controversy over General Douglas MacArthur's recall, certainly in no way interested in his farewell speech before a joint meeting of Congress.

"Sorry to keep you, but I had to call home to tell Collier I'll be staying over," Emma apologized as she stepped off the elevator and found her VA medical director, Dr. Simpkins Moseley, Sr., his wife, Barbara, with their slightly-gnomish physician son, Simpkins III, and his wife, Laura, waiting in the lobby of the John Marshall hotel.

"No problem. Trey just got here, but come along now. My car is outside and the dinner begins in thirty minutes," the elder Moseley urged them along. Trey was a time-honored southern nickname for a son in a family bearing the same name as his grandfather and father. Now a full-fledged MD, in his obviously expensive tuxedo Trey Moseley looked like a diminutive double for Peter Lawford, the devilishly handsome British movie heartthrob.

Emma felt a flush creeping up her neck, recalling vividly her senior year in training at Lewis-Gale when the younger Moseley had forced himself on her while he was serving an externship at Lewis-Gale during Collier's first year at RPI. Inexplicably, instead of reporting him, she had quickly submitted and spent the rest of that outrageously sinful summer as his virtual sex slave.

"I must say you look simply stunning, my dear," Laura Moseley fairly gushed over the gown Emma had purchased on sale at Montaldo's earlier in the day with money she had furtively squirreled away before she married Collier.

"I'll second that," Trey chimed in, taking Emma's arm. "You look positively stunning, Emma."

Shivering at memories of Trey with his slender, pencil-penis and his soft, boyish body between her legs, Emma blushed at his compliment.

Throughout dinner and in the car returning to the John Marshall, Emma was deeply disappointed that Trey gave no subtle indication that he remembered their clandestine history. Back at the hotel, she allowed Trey to accompany her as she detoured by the front desk to ask about telephone messages before he saw her safely onto the elevators.

"Goodnight. It was good seeing you again," he said and politely shook her hand when they reached the bank of elevators. When she stepped onto the elevator and turned around, he was already halfway back across the lobby.

Inside her room, she quickly undressed and washed her face. Leaving the bathroom door ajar with only a tiny sliver of light showing, she pulled her abbreviated nightie over her head, climbed into bed and lay hugging her pillow, silently fighting back tears of disappointment as she finally drifted off to sleep.

The luminous hands on the bedside clock showed 1:29A.M. when Emma was roused by a light, insistent tapping on her door.

"Yes...who is it?" she called sleepily.

"It's me—Trey! Let me in." Quickly coming wide awake, she slipped out of bed. Shrugging into her robe, she moved to the door and peeked through the tiny, magnifying peephole. One glance confirmed the visitor was Trey.

"What on earth are you doing here?" she whispered after she took the chain off the door and let him in.

He merely shrugged as he shut the door firmly behind him and bolted it. Lifting her, he carried her across the darkened room and deposited her on the bed. Still without a word, he ripped off her robe and dropped his pants. Spreading her legs, he lifted her knees, bending her legs all the way back until her thighs were resting on her breasts, leaving her wide open and completely vulnerable as he lowered himself, guiding his slender, rock-hard penis into her already slippery-wet vagina.

"Oh, my god!" she gasped as much with surprise as pleasure as she felt his member already gushing volumes inside her.

Finally, after he had collapsed with exhaustion on her breasts, he allowed her to straighten her legs and she encircled his buttocks, refusing to release him and pulling him deeper into her. In almost no time at all, she felt him slowly begin to regain his erection, and soon, he resumed thrusting into her again. This time he brought her to the very edge of rapture, and she thought she might come, but, as always, she couldn't quite reach an orgasm before he came the second time and collapsed with a great groan.

"I told my wife I was called to the hospital," he said, rolling off the bed and pulling up his trousers. "Just like old times in Roanoke, eh?"

"I'm staying over again tonight," she said.

Without an answer, he had slipped back out the door and was gone.

Lying there in the dark, her body tingling with excitement, she began to massage her throbbing clitoris with her finger. After a long, dreamy interlude she attained some sorry semblance of relief and had almost drifted off to sleep when she realized Trey had flooded her full of semen and she was without her diaphragm.

Finally, shrugging away the niggling worry that she had left her diaphragm at home, she drifted off to sleep.

In the morning, there were only the tattered shreds of her robe and gown to confirm the reality of what had happened.

At breakfast, she idly wondered if she could purchase a diaphragm without a prescription—just in case the cavalier young physician might show up again tonight.

CHAPTER ELEVEN

THE ROANOKE TIMES
Roanoke, Virginia, Saturday, June 2, 1951
SENATE PASSES EXTENDED DRAFT
BILL SETS UP MECHANICS FOR UMT PROGRAM
Draft Age Reduced To Take 18-Year-Olds

WASHINGTON, Friday, June 1 (AP) – The Senate today stamped its final approval on a bill to extend the military draft until mid-1955 and set up the mechanics for a permanent universal military training program, reducing the draft age from 19 to 18.

FRESH CHINESE TROOPS MOVED TO WARFRONT
By Don Huth

TOKYO, Saturday, June 2 (AP) – Fresh Chinese troops were moved up Friday in defense positions guarding their rugged supply base area in North Korea. The allied advance above Parallel 38 inched ahead in deep mud.

AT 2200 HOURS MILITARY TIME on April 22, Emma—back home from Richmond, but still aroused by a kaleidoscopic montage of erotic memories from her reunion with Dr. Trey Moseley—and, Collier, ravished to near-exhaustion by the nymphomaniacal Gerry Deeds, had gone to bed with their faces turned away from each other, completely oblivious that halfway around the globe, the Chinese Communists were about to kick off a massive spring offensive with a devastating four-hour artillery bombardment in preparation for an early evening attack by three of the Red armies on U.S. I and IX Corps troops in the Seoul sector.

About the same time, on April 22 in the I Corps area, the Reds were also making a well-coordinated strategic crossing of the Imjin River.

By mid-day April 23, the Red army had pushed retreating ROK units south of Phase Line Kansas, roughly just north of the 38th Parallel. Then, on April 27, the CCF outflanked UN forces at Uijongbu, driving Commanding General Van Fleet's troops back to within four miles of Seoul, but their attack was finally blunted as they attempted to outflank Seoul to the east.

These first thrusts of the CCF spring offensive finally lost momentum after taking horrendous losses and was halted at a new line extending across from just north of Seoul to Sabangue and continuing on northeastward across the 38th Parallel to Taepo-ri on the east coast. This new line was designated No-Name-Line by General Van Fleet. Holding the ground at No-Name-Line, Van Fleet reshuffled his units for more strategic deployment of seasoned American divisions and readied his forces for a counter-offensive to move the Eighth Army back to Phase Line Kansas. However, intelligence reports that the CCF was making preparations for a counterattack caused him to decide to wait and see what the Chinese were up to.

Van Fleet's decision to hold off an attack proved to be judicious. Two weeks later, on the night of May 15—continuing well into the early morning of May 16—the CCF struck the U.S. X Corp in the central sector of the Naep'yong-ni and No-dong area with an estimated force of 24 divisions. With the ROK troops overrun by hordes of Chinese and North Koreans, once again Van Fleet redeployed his forces, moving in reserves and pounding the enemy with such a devastating rain of artillery that the enemy was forced to stop their attack.

The following day in the western sector, the CCF moved down the Pukhan River toward the Han River with a force estimated at 250,000 troops. Giving the CCF no chance to recuperate and continue the offensive, on May 18, Van Fleet opened a cautious counteroffensive, and stepwise, the enemy began pulling back. After several days of bloody combat, this maneuver was also blunted, and by May 20, the enemy had bogged down to a complete standstill. By May 31, the UN Forces had retaken their strategic positions at Phase Line Kansas just north of the 38th Parallel.

On June 1, Van Fleet began reinforcing Phase Line Kansas so as to make it virtually impenetrable, and the I and IX Corps continued with Operation Piledriver toward Phase Line Wyoming, a bulge north of Phase Line Kansas running from the Imjin River south of Ch'orwon and Kumhwa—the base of the infamous Iron Triangle—and continuing southeast. In less than two weeks, on June 11, American tank-led infantry units had reached P'yongyang, the northern apex of the Triangle, but elected to pull back when they found that the controlling high ground overlooking the city was occupied by CCF.

After this bloody, costly combat, the White House and the JCS made the decision that American forces were not to pursue aggressive tactics beyond the general area of Phase Lines Kansas and Wyoming. With South Korea once-again cleared of the invading enemy, U.S. forces were to hold their hard-won positions and maintain constant contact and vigilance to harass the enemy, but no effort would be made to move back into North Korean territory.

Over the next two years of the conflict—unmindful of the empty sacrifice of brave American and UN lives—this irresponsible, unworthy and staggeringly-costly human chess game would prove to be unforgivably cavalier.

Anticipating the disastrous outcome of this stalemate—and serving mainly to add to the stain of reckless human sacrifice—Truman asked Congress for sweeping changes in the military draft which lowered the eligible age to 18, extended the draft for five years, opening the door for universal military training.

On Saturday morning, June 2, Collier was in his Aunt Blanche's office in the Salem Library across from Tarpley's magazine store on Main Street, idly scanning a notice in the May 26 issue of the *Saturday Review* that John Steinbeck was writing a new novel for Viking Press, when he noticed the headline in the morning *Roanoke Times* about the Senate extending the military draft until 1955 and lowering the draft age from nineteen to eighteen-and-a-half.

The newspaper article said the new Senate bill stated no men under 19 would be drafted until all men under twenty-six still available to the draft pool were called up. There was no specific mention in the article of calling up married men, but that question had been a matter of considerable discussion in the press lately and seemed just a matter of time.

Reading the article gave Collier an uneasy feeling. After some consideration, he picked up the phone and called Bruce Bohon, Jr. and Doyle Pogue, his close married friends who were in the same boat in this situation. Both men had already read the news, and after brief discussion, agreed to get together at Doyle Pogue's place early that evening to give the matter further consideration.

Collier could not remember a time he hadn't known Bo—Bruce Bohon, Jr. They both had been in Wesley Givens' boys' Sunday School class at Fort Lewis Baptist Church at least two years before they entered Miss Billie Northcross' first grade at Fort Lewis Elementary.

When Collier had been skipped ahead from second to fourth grade, they no longer shared the same recesses and lunch period, and, while they continued to be Sunday school classmates and still rode the same school bus, they more or less drifted away from the closeness of being playground buddies during the scheduled classroom breaks.

During high school, they continued to see each other on the school bus and at church, and during Collier's senior year, they both played intramural baseball where Collier, a varsity basketball player, had been a rather lackluster first baseman while Bo—in a dramatic role reversal—made a damned fine catcher.

Sometime after Collier graduated high school, Bo left school to take a job at the Yale-Towne Lock Company in Salem where he quickly became skilled at electroplating.

Over the next two years with Collier away at college most of the time, except for an occasional meeting in the poolroom or on the street in town, or sometimes at church—which Collier attended as little as possible—they rarely bumped into one another.

Oddly enough, it was baseball that brought them back together.

While he had never particularly enjoyed playing baseball and found it rather boring as a spectator sport, three years before during his summer hiatus between graduating Bluefield College and transferring to art school at RPI, one Saturday afternoon, he had gone with his father up across the old iron bridge to the local baseball diamond beside the Virginian Railroad tracks in Wabun to watch his brother, Jim, play with the Salem Foundry team of the Virginia Athletic League against the local team, a ragtag group who didn't dress out very well, but played a pretty good brand of country baseball. Owning a wealth of tractors with scraper blades and miscellaneous other farm equipment, over the years, the locals had all pitched in and—complete with an admirable, heavy-wire backstop and serviceable bleachers down both first and third—carved a decent baseball diamond out of the once rock-strewn, hardscrabble, red clay field.

Quite rightly, Collier's father was proud of Jim's considerable baseball skills. On the other hand, to his father's everlasting disappointment, baseball had never really appealed to Collier in the same way he felt about basketball—or, for that matter, football, before he hurt his back.

Jim came by the game naturally. Playing as catcher and maintaining a sensational batting average above 400 that season, Jim was easily leading the VAL in both batting and RBIs. While their father loved all sports, baseball had always been his passion. Mainly pitching—but also playing regularly at first base because of his bat—Cocky had played a season in the Class D Piedmont League with Danville before he met and married their mom.

"Brother, am I glad to see you. We've got to have a right fielder. Roger Foutz, our regular guy, is running late, and we're going to have to forfeit if we can't find someone to start the game," Jim zeroed in on him when he saw Collier and their dad come strolling up.

"Oh, no, Brud...don't look at me. I can't. I mean, just look at this outfit...and my shoes are leather-soled—slick as glass," Collier protested, pointing to his street clothes and penny loafers.

"C'mon, you don't need spikes. These guys are mostly right-handed hitters. All you have to do is just stand out there and watch the girls in the bleachers. Our guy will be here before the inning is half over."

"Go on, Collier, do it. You don't want to see the Foundry have to forfeit," his father urged in a tone which insinuated letting his brother down would be tantamount to committing treason to his country.

"Well...look...I'll play first base. That's the only position I know..." Collier protested.

"That won't work. Our first baseman's solid. We need someone to take right field. Come on, man, it'll only be for the first inning, maybe less. C'mon, let's find you a fielder's glove."

Despite his protests and before he hardly knew what was happening, he was standing in the closely-mowed, native blue grass and lespedeza out behind first base, trying to adjust his fingers in the unfamiliar fielder's glove and praying that the first batter stepping up to the plate would not hit the ball his way.

Thankfully, the first hitter grounded out to short, the second batter fanned on three straight pitches and the count quickly went to two strikes and a ball on the third man at the plate.

Collier let out a big sigh of relief and reached down and plucked a straw, sticking it between his teeth. Absently, he pounded at the ill-formed pocket in the ratty fielder's glove, feeling much more at ease.

Then, before he fully brought his wandering attention back to the action on the diamond, the sharp crack of the bat meeting ball tightened his sphincter, returning his awareness to the game. Searching frantically to find the ball against the high, faded, blue summer sky, his heart sank as he finally spotted a fast-sinking line drive headed straight at him. Trying desperately to get his slick-soled shoes to gain traction in the pasture grass, he started moving toward the sinking liner, wanting to make sure he got in front of the ball, limiting the batter to a single.

Before he had taken more than a half-dozen slippery strides in his penny loafers, he suddenly realized he was faced with the quandary of having an outside shot at catching the ball. Despite all the internal arguments to play it safe going on inside his head, Collier kept striding hard with all the effort his slippery loafers would allow.

Miraculously, at the last instant, he dove for the ball and made a spectacular sliding catch.

No one was more surprised by his good luck than he was, but trotting in to the hearty congratulations of the admiring fans and the backslapping of his teammates, he looked ruefully down at his grass-stained shirt and new golf slacks, thanking his lucky stars that his meteoric career as right fielder was over.

Unfortunately, this was not to be the case.

Roger Foutz was still nowhere to be found.

"Don't sweat it, ol' Rog'll be here any minute now. He hits sixth in the regular batting rotation," brother Jimmy reassured him as Collier took the bench, praying "old Rog" would quickly show and save him from having to take the field again.

Sitting on the bench sweating blood, he relaxed when the first two batters grounded out, but he started getting very nervous as Jim doubled to deep left-center, the next man walked and the fifth batter was called safe at first on a failed sacrifice bunt leaving the bases loaded with two out.

Still no Roger.

"Let's get a batter up here," the plate umpire was in no mood to put up with foolishness.

"You're up, Ramsay," Speck Byrd, the player-manager called from the first-base coaching box.

Reluctantly, Collier stood and deliberately took his time testing the heft of three 32-inch bats hoping against hope Roger would come ambling up to save the day.

"C'mon, let's have a batter," the plate umpire was obviously getting angry now.

Avoiding the umpire's steely glare, Collier selected a bat and took his place in the batter's box.

"Nice catch out there. You robbed me of a nice clean single." Collier looked down at Bo Bohon in catcher's equipment crouching behind the plate.

"Bo...was it you that hit that liner? I made a lucky catch." Collier grinned sheepishly at his old Sunday School classmate.

"Save the old home week...it's hot out here," the ump grouched as Collier turned his attention toward the mound.

"Strike," the ump called before Collier barely had the chance to set himself.

"Ball one." Somewhat better settled now, Collier watched the next pitch come in high and way outside.

"Good eye, Collie boy," Jim encouraged loudly as he took a dangerously-long lead down the third-base line toward home plate.

"Way to look, Ramsay," Speck Byrd called from the first-base coaching box as Collier attempted to set himself, trying to control the uneasiness in his belly.

Never taking his eyes off the pitcher's hand throughout his windup, he tried to recall the things his father had attempted to teach him growing up as he took a couple of shaky practice swings.

"Ball two," the umpire called to Collier's great relief—the pitch had already gotten by him before he could decide to take a cut.

"Ball three," the ump called as the pitch came in so high and tight that Collier felt a whisper of air on his ear lobe as he ducked away at the last instant.

"Keep a good eye, babe...walk's as good as a hit," Jim kept up a busy line of chatter, taking a big lead again.

"Strike," the ump called on a smoking fastball that Collier had hoped was low out of the strike zone.

"C'mon ump, that ball was almost in the dirt," Speck Byrd continued to ride the ump.

"Be ready, brother," Jim urged as the count went to three and two.

Afterwards, Collier could never be sure whether or not the next pitch would have been in the strike zone. The ball came in a little high, but was definitely too good to let go by.

Gritting his teeth, he narrowed his eyes and swung from his heels.

Twack!

Collier would never forget the electric tingle in his hands and forearms when the wood made solid contact with the leather and the thrill of seeing the ball still rising as he moved down the first base line, then watching as it sailed completely over the surprised center fielder's head.

On the way home after the game, his excited brother and father assured him it was the longest ball they had ever seen hit in the local park. Much to Collier's secret pleasure, at family gatherings, they still talked about it now and then.

Best of all, Roger Foutz finally arrived and relieved Collier from the agony of having to go back into right field. Between innings, Collier walked over to the homemade concession stand to buy a Coke and Bo walked up to say hello.

"That was some hit," Bo said as he shook Collier's hand. "Great catch, too. I don't remember you liking baseball that much."

"I don't, really. I never played anything but first base in my life. I got pushed into filling in and just got lucky. My Granddaddy Boyd says that even a blind hog will find an acorn sometime." Collier shrugged and laughed.

"Say, we could use a first baseman. The guy who is playing there now is a converted outfielder. Why don't you play with us? We don't practice much and mostly we just play Sunday afternoons," Bo brightened as the idea took shape in his head.

"Look, Bo, thanks a lot, but I'm not really a baseball player...not at first base or any other position. Jim is the baseball player in our family," he replied.

"Who do you think you're kidding? I saw that catch and hit." Bo slapped him on the shoulder. "We're going to have a practice session next Saturday around three, right here. Come on and give it a try. We need you, man." Bo looked at him anxiously.

Collier tried to stand his ground, but no matter how adamantly he protested that he didn't want to play baseball, in the end, Bo was not to be denied.

"Collier, this is Bo. We really need a first baseman Sunday...this is an emergency," The following Thursday, Collier got a call. Before Bo would let him off the phone, he had reluctantly agreed to work out with the team on Saturday.

Saturday morning, Collier located his well-worn first baseman's mitt in a box of junk in his closet. It was still in reasonably good shape from playing the occasional game of catch with his dad and Jim at family get-togethers. Surprisingly, he enjoyed the workout. He was actually something of a "natural" with that old, but well-oiled, first baseman's mitt. With Emma finishing her final year in training and getting little time off on weekends, following the workout, Collier agreed to fill in for the team on Sunday.

That first Sunday, he had played an error-free game at first base, making several spectacular catches and getting two solid singles up the middle.

High on the sweet wine of success, Collier was hooked.

To Collier's pleasant surprise, Emma hadn't put up much of a fuss about the baseball. Even after she completed her training, on the Sundays she didn't have to work, while Collier played baseball with Bo, she took the opportunity to visit her mother. At some point that summer, she had given in and agreed to come to a game and afterwards have a hamburger with Bo and his young girlfriend, Virginia "Jenny" Francisco—a strikingly pretty bobbysoxer fresh out of Andrew Lewis High School.

From the beginning, Emma found Bo and Jenny to be good company and the routine of having a post-game burger soon developed into a comfortable ritual. Over time the friendship deepened, and last year, Bo and Jenny had decided to set a wedding date just a few weeks before Collier and Emma planned to get married.

Coincidentally, with wedding plans taking precedent, the previous summer, both Bo and Collier gave up playing summer baseball—something of a rite of passage, Collier supposed.

After their respective marriages, with Collier and Emma taking an apartment in Roanoke and Bruce and Jenny remaining in Salem, the two couples didn't see each other very often until they crossed paths at Collier's church a few weeks back at Easter. After services, they had lunch together and reminisced over old times. Inevitably, the topic quickly turned to the Korean War and the looming shadow of the military draft. With that in common, they began to see each other more frequently again. Sometime soon afterward, having burgers following an evening at the movies, the two couples ran into Marla and Doyle Pogue, another couple from high-school days who shared similar concerns over the impending threat of forced military service.

Overlooking megalomaniacal Doyle's often tiresome obsession with making money, the Pogues were very pleasant company. With his brother, Tim, Doyle ran a small, country grocery store at Hanging Rock, which had been in the family since long before the Great Depression of the early Thirties. Pogue's Grocery had been the local beer stop for years—a gathering place for hunters, fisherman and assorted colorful local ne'er-do-wells with a lot of idle time on their hands. Doyle was really the driving force behind the revitalized business and was well on his way to becoming—if not already there—a bona fide millionaire as a result of his having the foresight to buy up virtually every acre of seemingly worthless mountain acreage within miles and converting some of it to the use of magazines he leased to the state and federal highway departments for storage of blasting powder.

Overnight, Doyle's acquisitions of remote property became a virtual goldmine.

Marla was slender as a rail but had the classic good-looks and carriage of a fashion model. For all that, she was as down to earth and friendly as anyone you would ever care to know—sometimes perhaps a bit too friendly for Collier's overactive prurient imagination.

"I hear we're having dessert with the Bohons and the Pogues tonight? Both Jenny and Marla called about the newspaper articles on Congress's new laws for the military draft," Emma called him at work just before noon.

"I was going to call you during lunch. Things are looking rather iffy," Collier admitted.

That evening, looking forward to homemade apple pie and ice cream with the Pogue's, Collier wasted little time in stating his intentions to the group. "I've decided if married men actually do become eligible for the draft, I'm going to enlist, with the specific intention of going to OCS for two very good reasons. In the first place, going to OCS will delay my having to go to Korea six months at a minimum. In the second place, rank has its privilege as far as money and living conditions are concerned."

"Yeah, and they're the first to go into combat—just doubles your chances to get killed," Doyle wasted no time in voicing his opinion.

"Don't you have to have a college degree or something?" Bo offered pessimistically.

"Not at all. I don't have a degree. I called the recruiting office and checked." Collier replied.

"But don't you have to take some kind of test or something to qualify?" Bo asked suspiciously.

"Well, sure...but nothing ventured, nothing gained," Collier replied.

"Count me out. I'm no good at tests," Bo shrugged, resignedly.

"Me neither," Doyle grumbled.

"Come on, you guys. What have you got to lose?" Collier snorted. "Besides, if you wait to get drafted, you take a big chance on getting put in the damned Marines. You think Army basic training's bad? It's nothing compared to the Marines. And, if you join up, you can always choose the Navy...or even the Coast Guard, maybe."

"No Navy or Coast Guard for me. I got seasick fishing down at Nags Head," Doyle said.

"Well, it's going to be the Army for me. I'm definitely enlisting for OCS if the draft's breathing down my neck," Collier said emphatically.

"How long do you have to stay in?" Marla was the first of the wives to join in.

"The regular enlistment is only two years—same as the draft," Collier hedged.

"How long would you have to stay in if you enlist especially for OCS?" Emma was curious now.

"Well, I think you enlist for the regular two, but you have to commit to three years if you make it through OCS. After all, it costs a lot to train an officer, and the Army has to protect its investment," Collier parroted the same line the recruiting sergeant had told him over the phone this morning.

"That means if you become an officer, you have to serve at least four years," Doyle spoke right up. "No way am I going to sign away four years of my life when I can get by with two."

"Me neither," Bo echoed. "Besides, I'd never pass the test."

"Forget OCS...forget the bleeping tests, Bo. Are you just going to stand by and take a chance on getting stuck in the bloody Gyrenes?" Collier interjected with exasperation.

"Well, no. I don't want that." Bo admitted. "If it comes to that, I'll join the Army. If what you say is true, I've got nothing to lose."

"That's absolutely right," Collier said. "How about it, Doyle? How about you?"

"Makes sense to me." Doyle said.

"The recruiting sergeant said I could take the test without having to sign up. I'm thinking about taking it right away—no sense waiting until the last minute," Collier replied.

"Let me know if you're going to take that test. I just might go take it at that," Doyle chimed back in.

"Well, I don't trust them. You better make sure what you're signing..." Emma protested. "Besides, there's not a word in this article about drafting married men. What's the rush?"

"Oh, this war in Korea isn't even close to being settled. They'll be drafting married men sooner than you think," Collier said.

"I'm afraid Collier's right," Marla sighed regretfully. "Now, would anybody like some apple pie and ice cream?"

Marla flashed a glimpse of her pink-panty-clad crotch as she rose, headed to the kitchen.

"How can you take that Army officer test Monday?" Emma asked in the car on the way home. "You have an interview for the job with Security Envelope."

"Oh, yeah, I forgot. I wonder what Security Envelope will think about my draft status?" Collier replied absently.

"Oh, darn...I hadn't considered that," Emma sputtered, slumping dejectedly in her seat.

They rode in silence until they were almost home. Still thinking about Marla's little peepshow, Collier wondered idly how Emma would respond if he tried to make love to her. They hadn't had intercourse since before her trip with Doctor Moseley to the medical convention in Richmond six weeks ago.

"I've got a terrible tummy ache—I'm way overdue to start my period," Emma said as if she could read his mind.

CHAPTER TWELVE

TOKYO, Monday, June 4 (AP) - Allied troops advancing under intense Communist mortar and rifle fire took two key heights within twelve miles of Chorwan within the southwestern sector of Red Korea's Iron Triangle.

STILL REELING FROM THE NEWS that the Senate had opened the door for future Universal Military Training by passing a bill lowering the draft age to eighteen, Collier Ramsay woke up Monday morning, June 4th, totally unsuspecting that while a massive, new Allied offensive, Operation Piledriver, was being launched in the Iron Triangle sector just above the 38th Parallel, back home the Executive Branch was desperately trying to initiate a high level, behind-the-scenes, diplomatic end run through the United Nations to extricate America from its nightmare predicament in Korea.

Truman's relieving General Douglas MacArthur of command and recalling him to Washington in April had triggered so much sound and fury among the political and military that the Senate finally felt called upon to make a full official inquiry into the facts surrounding the aging hero's recall.

No one in Washington was fooled about the underlying hypocrisy of such hearings. Typically, the Senate "MacArthur Hearings"—as this latest media circus was labeled by the press—quickly degenerated into the Mardi Gras buffoonery typical of the elected Washington political hierarchy. Attracting the customary enclave of pompous elected officials of both parties, this melodramatic witch hunt was hardly more than an opportunity for several narcissistic congressmen to grab a place in the history books for the veneration of their posterity. But, no matter the overall superficiality of these proceedings, General Omar Bradley flung a sobering pebble onto the surface, radiating waves of outrage on the complacent American public consciousness, when he testified before the committee on May 24, that the shamefully mismanaged war had already exacted the horrifying toll of 69,276 battle casualties with an additional 72,679 falling victim to nonbattle—frostbite, dysentery, trench foot, etc.—maladies.

With sobering and embarrassing testimony such as General Bradley's, the end result was that after almost a full year of suffering the daily media accounts of an endless litany of utter blundering by American military and political jesters, Truman and the JCS finally got the clear message the American public had become completely fed up with mishandling of Korea, regarding it as a barefaced exercise in futility and incompetence at the Executive level.

Whether or not it was Bradley's sobering wake-up call that actually turned the tide, his shocking testimony most likely did exert a strong subliminal influence on the sudden about-face in the American strategy in Korea which was taking place at the White House.

Most likely motivated by the newly-revised official JCS opinion that the *"Korean problem"* could not be *"...resolved by military action alone"* and, coupled with a strong negative groundswell of public opinion, the National Security Council responded on May 17 by issuing NSC-48/5, a major revision of its December 1949 Asian policy paper NSC-48 which pre-dated the so-called *"Korean problem"* by more than six months.

This new NSC-48/5 policy statement voiced several far-reaching changes to the original strategy for conducting the war in Korea. Expressed in simple terms, NSC-48/5 stated that the U.S. would no longer pursue the strategy of unifying Korea by military force; the achievement of the goal of unification would have to come through political influence. Secondly, it took the position that the White House was finally ready to negotiate a peace settlement provided Korea would be restored to its prewar dividing line at the 38th Parallel.

Thus, on June 1, 1951, the wheels were set in motion for a negotiated armistice when, at the prompting of the White House, UN Secretary-General Trygve Lie announced that a ceasefire near the 38th Parallel would satisfy the goals of the UN in Korea—provided the area was restored to peace and security.

The very next day, Secretary of State Dean Acheson confirmed before the "MacArthur Hearings" that the Allies' stance of a ceasefire near the 38th Parallel would indeed accomplish the Allied military goals in Korea.

With all current field intelligence indicating that the CCF were well aware that Allied Forces were in a favorable position to push the "stop" line much further north than the original north/south dividing line at Parallel 38, the powers in Washington already had covertly initiated overtures by the way of Moscow, but word came back from the Chinese Embassy in Moscow that Peking "...recognized no diplomatic relations with Washington."

Thus cavalierly rebuffed by the Chinese, the Secretary of State and the White House were forced to sit and cool their heels.

With few notable exceptions, it is almost axiomatic that the White House can keep no secrets from the military. Along the 38th Parallel, with rumors of a ceasefire running rampant at the front lines, many troops with only a short time left before becoming eligible for rotation home became understandably reluctant to take unnecessary risks. It was under this debilitating atmosphere of uncertainty that on June 3, Operation Piledriver officially kicked off from Line Kansas to Line Wyoming amidst rotten, rainy weather.

Harboring a seething resentment that he now was faced with actually being drafted into military service or being forced to enlist in the Army, Air Force or Navy, the first thing Monday morning, before he went to his job interview with Security Envelope, Collier stopped by the Army Recruiting Office on Campbell Avenue to see about rescheduling his appointment to take the Officer Candidate Test.

"Call ahead anytime you have a couple of hours. We'll test you," the recruiting sergeant told him, obviously fighting to hide his disappointment.

"Maybe I could still take it this morning, if I get free?" Collier asked hopefully.

"Maybe...come in and we'll see," the sergeant visibly brightened with the renewed hope that his prize pigeon had not flown the coop.

Housed in a low, white concrete-block building a short distance from the recruiting office in a quiet residential neighborhood near Jefferson High School, Security Envelope was located just a couple of streets off Campbell Avenue.

Collier's watch showed five minutes before 10AM when he pulled into the parking lot and reluctantly went inside.

"Mr. Crouse is expecting you," a young woman behind the reception counter greeted him. "Just follow me. I'll take you back."

Trying his best to muster an aura of enthusiasm, Collier dutifully followed her through the administrative offices, production plant and shipping docks of the small printing company to a narrow, white-walled studio with large windows at the rear of the plant.

"Mr. Crouse, this is Mr. Collier Ramsay," the woman introduced him to a lean man clad in gray flannel pants and white dress shirt with the collar loosed and cuffs turned up. The artist was perched on a high stool in front of a sturdy drawing table. The desk stood beneath a single skylight in front of two large windows at the center of the well-lit narrow room. The hawkish figure was bent intently over the work surface using a small brush in his left hand.

"Thank you, Eileen. Have a look around, Ramsay. I'll be with you in a minute, as soon as I finish this." Without glancing over at Collier, he dipped the brush in a bottle of black India drawing ink, automatically reshaping the point on a scrap of Bristol board at his right elbow.

"Sure, take your time," Collier muttered lamely, turning to examine a collection of neatly framed letterheads and logotypes on the walls around him. Among them, he was surprised to see the celebrated logos of several major national corporations, not to mention letterheads of two well-known New York banks. Leaning closer, it was hard for him to imagine that these designs were hand-lettered rather than typeset by a very good printer.

"Some of our more important clients," Crouse's voice roused him from his appreciation.

"Did you design all these logotypes? Do you have all these typefaces here in the plant?" Collier turned back to face him.

"We have a sizeable collection of typefaces. But, those logos are not typefaces...I hand-lettered all that stuff. Here"—he pointed to the piece on the drawing board—"take a look."

Collier walked across and looked down at the pristine letterhead design for a new car dealer in Richmond. Still glistening wet in spots, the entire letterhead occupied a space only about an inch high and three inches wide; incredibly Crouse had executed it at the actual size it would appear on a corporate letterhead.

"Unbelievable! Don Engel at RPI would never believe this." Collier gasped. "How long did it take you to complete this?"

"About two hours...I started last evening and finished after I got in about an hour ago."

"Unbelievable!" Collier shook his head. "It would take me a whole day at least, and I'd have to do it about ten times the size and have it reduced."

"Don't worry. I don't expect that you...or anyone else...can do this. Then they wouldn't need me." Crouse shrugged without changing expression.

"Well..." Collier began and shrugged, "so how come I'm here?"

"I've been farming all my illustrations out...an agency in Richmond, as a matter of fact. I can't draw anything worth two cents," the artist said.

"You're putting me on...aren't you?" It was hard for Collier to imagine anyone with such miraculous skills with a brush and ink not being able to draw anything he chose.

"No...not at all. I really don't have that kind of drawing talent. My animals and human figures are sad. For one thing, I don't have the background in anatomy. You learned anatomy as part of figure illustration at art school, didn't you?"

"Hm-m, I guess I never thought about that." Collier nodded thoughtfully. "So?...do you have much need for that kind of illustration? I'm not much good at pen-and-ink line drawing. I could put you on to a guy from school who is a whiz with brush and ink line drawing—you should just see his dry brush technique."

"Here's the portfolio you left a couple of weeks back. These samples look okay. I thought *you* were looking for work?" He handed Collier the manila folder with his samples. He had left the small portfolio of illustration samples including hand-lettered headlines and black-and-white wash drawings of a bacon package, a can of Pork and Beans and other grocery illustrations he'd done for the Kroger newspaper ads.

"Well sure...I am," he stammered. "But, compared to yours, my lettering is awful. Besides, I'm not really good at line drawing. I'm best at art for half-tone reproduction."

"There are passable scratchboard illustrations of a diamond ring and an alligator suitcase in that folder. Couldn't you make me a decent scratchboard of a Holstein milk cow about a half-inch high?" He picked up a yellowing magazine clipping of a spotted cow and extended it to Collier. "You need to make it more of a full side view with the cow facing to the right."

"Well...I guess I could give it a try." Glancing at the clipping, Collier's stomach did an excited flip as he began to visualize the challenge of doing a scratchboard drawing of an animal.

"Also, I think scratchboard might be perfect for some illustrations of buildings I need for corporate letterheads. If I gave you a good photo to work with, do you think you could do a scratchboard rendering of Shenandoah Life's new HQ building?"

"Well?...maybe. Scratchboard's tricky—it can be a bastard to work with."

"Okay, then. I need the cow first. Can you come back tomorrow morning about ten?"

"Are you kidding? I'm not sure I have any scratchboard in stock. Sherwin-Williams will probably have to order it. Even if I have the material, I'd need at least another day."

"Wednesday, then...I'm on deadline here. Forget the scratchboard. Look, it doesn't matter about the scratchboard if you don't have it. A decent line drawing will do just fine."

"Okay, I'll get right on it." Collier felt a drop of sweat trickle down the crack of his ass.

"Fine, I really am in a hurry for that spotted cow. Do that first and worry about the Shenandoah building later," Crouse grunted, turning back to the project on his board.

Momentarily, Collier hesitated, wondering if he'd said something to piss Crouse off.

"Was there something else?" the artist asked without looking up from his work.

"Why not go ahead and give me the photo of the Shenandoah Life building now? Maybe I'll find time to give that some attention, too."

"Sure." Crouse reached into a drawer in the small taboret beside his drawing table and located an 8x10 glossy of the building and handed it to him.

"Thanks." Collier placed the clipping of the cow and the glossy in the folder with his samples without even looking at either and made his exit without another word.

Leaving Security Envelope, Collier found Sixth Street and drove south until it dead-ended at the nearly-deserted parking lot at Highland Park. Parking beside the long steps up to the athletic playing fields, he cut the engine and sat there for a few moments staring despondently at the clipping of the cow and the 8x10 photo of the Shenandoah Life HQ. Remembering the nerve-wracking experience of doing the scratchboard drawings of the diamond ring and luggage as school assignments, a wave of anxiety washed over him. The simple truth was that it didn't matter whether he attempted to do the work on scratchboard or just brush and ink on plain, smooth, Strathmore Bristol Board; he was not very adept at doing either kind of line rendering. As a matter of fact, at art school on assignments requiring that he do meticulously close work—including any kind of hand lettering or using an inking pen—his hands shook so badly he could hardly do the work at all. It had taken him a full two weeks of late hours and god knows how much money in wasted scratchboard to complete the diamond ring and luggage assignments.

And, rendering a diamond ring and alligator suitcase was one thing, but a cow? On several occasions at school in Richmond, he'd tried drawing horses with little success. As for cows, it had never occurred to him to try to draw one—as best as he could remember, he didn't have a single image of a cow in his "swipe file."

He couldn't rightly say just how long he'd been sitting there wallowing in self-doubt before a shiny new station wagon pulled in beside him, and two young housewives with their colored nannies unloaded four toddlers and a couple of picnic baskets and started up the steps. Rousing from this pathetic funk of self-pity, Collier started the car and headed for his Aunt Blanche's county library in Salem to see if he could find a good picture book on cows.

As luck would have it, at the library, he quickly found several books with illustrations of cows. Within thirty minutes, he was headed home with, of all things, a children's picture book with a couple dozen good illustrations of Holstein cows in every imaginable pose and position.

Back in their apartment, Collier sat down with the book of cow drawings and quickly chose an illustration that seemed heaven-sent for his project. The image was about two-and-a-half inches high by four inches wide. Placing the book on his drawing table, he took a sheet of high-quality tracing paper and painstakingly traced the image. Then, turning the tracing over, he lightly covered the reverse side of the image by rubbing it with a broad-stroke graphite pencil—effectually transforming the tracing into its own carbon paper. Flipping the paper back over and carefully taping it firmly in place, he deftly transferred the traced image to the smooth surface of a large, scrap piece of expensive Strathmore drawing board.

When the transfer was complete, he took a finely-sharpened, Number 2 drawing pencil and lightly retouched the image, changing the position of the cow's tail and adding a scattering of delicate daisies to the pasture grass before he lightly retouched spots where the tracing was barely visible.

When he was satisfied with the pencil transfer, he went to the bathroom and brought back Emma's oval hand mirror and held the drawing up to make absolutely sure the perspective hadn't been distorted in the tracing process.

Perfecto!—a little trick he'd learned at school.

When he was certain the sketch was ready for inking, he selected delicate Number 2/0 and Number 0 Grumbacher, round-pointed, red sable watercolor brushes and took them into the kitchen and rinsed them under the cold water tap. When they were cleaned to his satisfaction, he carefully shaped the brushes to fine points by licking the ends with his tongue—another little professional secret he'd learned from his professors at RPI.

Returning to the drawing table, he carefully dipped the tip of one of the brushes into the ink bottle, reshaping it on the bottle's rim and shakily began practicing drawing lines on a sizeable scrap of cheap poster board, varying the pressure to change the thickness of the lines from wide to narrow as he allowed the brush point to describe arcs and curves. Finally, when his nervous tremors subsided to the point he felt sufficiently confident of his control of the brush, he carefully began to ink in the tracing of the Holstein cow mounted on the drawing board before him.

It was almost three o'clock in the afternoon when he leaned back and gave the drawing a final check in the hand-held vanity mirror.

Not bad!

As a matter of fact, for his first attempt, it was not bad at all.

He set the finished drawing aside, and immediately began transferring the tracing to a fresh piece of drawing board. This time the work went faster. By five o'clock, he had completed another rendering which he judged to be visibly better than the first. He found another 2/0 red sable brush that he used for touch-up work with retouch white and went to work. He was surprised at just how little touch-up the second rendering required. If the newspaper camera department reduced it to less than a half-inch high to fit Crouse's requirements, his imperfections would be virtually invisible to the naked eye.

Encouraged, he decided to call a halt to the project until he could take the completed renderings to the newspaper and have them reduced down to the required thumbnail size for final inspection.

At the newspaper, he was in luck. The nightshift supervisor took the images and told him to come back in an hour.

"Got your drawings right here. Turned out okay. Very professional," the night supervisor greeted him when he returned at seven.

The supervisor was right. Collier was more than pleased with the reductions. Both the original and the postage stamp-sized reduction looked very professional, indeed.

After a lengthy consultation about his brilliant concept how to convert the Shenandoah Life photograph for line rather than halftone reproduction, Collier left the 8x10 glossy with the night supervisor who told him to come back first thing in the morning.

Using the pay phone in the lobby, he called home to ask Emma if she wanted him to pick up some burgers for dinner.

No answer.

On the way back to the apartment, he stopped at the little Texas Tavern and bought a couple of burgers, but when he arrived home, Emma had left a note complaining that she had needed the car and finally had to call a friend for a ride to attend a seminar at Lewis-Gale Hospital. The note said she'd be late and not to wait up for her. Ravenous from working without eating, Collier wolfed down one of the greasy burgers, washing it down with a glass of icy-cold buttermilk from the fridge. When he'd finished, he left the other burger on the table, rinsed his glass and put it in the rack to dry.

The luminous hands on the alarm clock on the night table beside Emma's pillow glowed 9:25 when he fell exhausted into bed and turned out the light.

"Collier, get up! If you want to use the car today, you'll have to take me to work." Collier was aroused by Emma rudely shaking him. Blinking hard against the glare of her bedside lamp, he squinted at his watch.

6:06 AM.

"C'mon, now! I can't be late," Emma grouched and turned and left the room without so much as saying good morning.

Groggily, he rinsed under the shower and quickly dressed. When he walked into the kitchen, Emma had just rinsed her coffee cup and was placing it in the drain.

"Grab a cup and bring it with you. I can't be late for work," she ordered, impatiently.

Pouring a mug of coffee, he dutifully followed her out the door.

Sliding under the wheel, Collier had driven almost to the Roanoke city limit line before she spoke again.

"Where were you last night? What did you do all day yesterday?"

"Yesterday morning I had an appointment with the art director at Security Envelope. I spent the afternoon at my drawing desk doing an assignment he asked me to do. Last night I was at the newspaper getting some work done on the assignment so I could get it back to him this morning as he requested," hiding his resentment, he answered virtuously, recalling how she had nagged him to go see Security Envelope about a job.

"What kind of assignment?" she asked after a sobering moment.

"Here. See for yourself." Keeping a close eye on the road, he reached across and retrieved the manila clasp envelope from the back seat and switched on the dome light.

Suspiciously, she opened the clasp and examined the Photostats of the Holstein cow.

"You traced this from that book you had on the table beside your drawing board. Isn't that against the law or something?" It was more of an indictment than a question.

"Technically, you could argue the point. But commercial artists do it all the time. The trick is to make slight changes from the original so it really isn't a direct steal. Most commercial artists keep a "swipe file" of good illustrations of common objects, famous structures, domestic and wild animals, and various human figures including action poses and other miscellaneous for quick reference. I didn't have a cow—much less a Holstein—in my swipe file, so I went to Blanche's library and found that book. It was a stroke of luck, really. I altered the position of the tail and the cow's black-and-white markings in my drawing, so it isn't actually a copyright violation...beside that, my finished cut is less than a half-inch high. The original from the book is ten times bigger." He reached across and located the postage-sized reduction and put it on top.

She examined the image without further comment and was just replacing it in the envelope when he pulled in at the curb in front of her building at the VA. "Can you pick me up around half-past three?" she asked, gathering her purse and some papers.

"Sure thing. Have a great day," he said.

"You, too," she said and slid out of the car and was gone without offering him even so much as a good-bye peck on the cheek.

"So much for marriages made in heaven," Collier snorted half-aloud as he put the car in gear and headed for the newspaper offices at a fast clip—there were miles to go and work to do.

At *The Roanoke Times* offices, he was pleased to find that the night supervisor had completed his Photostats and left them with the receptionist. Looking them over, he was more than satisfied with the results. Back in the car, he headed straight for Security Envelope.

It was not quite eight when Collier pulled into a parking space at Security Envelope. He was pleased to see several cars in the lot and a light in Crouse's studio at the rear of the building. The entrance door was unlocked, but the lobby was unlit and the reception desk was not yet manned as Collier found his way back through the plant to Crouse's studio. When he entered, Crouse was perched on his stool as if he had spent the night working, intently applying his brush to the pristine Strathmore art board in front of him.

"What on earth are you doing here at this hour?" the artist grumbled without looking up from his work.

"I've got the Holstein drawing for you."

"No fooling? Bring it over so I can take a look," Crouse responded with genuine surprise.

Extracting the pristine, postage-stamp-sized illustration from the heavy manila envelope, Collier stepped forward and handed it to him.

Silently, Crouse examined the rendering under the magnifying glass attached to the arm of the fluorescent light clipped to his drawing table. He finally located an architect's scale and measured it.

"It's a hair over a half-inch. Under the glass, it still looks a bit shaky. You did this much larger and had it reduced. What if the client wanted to blow it back up for other presentations?" His look and tone of voice bordered upon a sneer.

"So...if it doesn't suit you, give it back."

Ignoring Collier's comment, Crouse placed the illustration in a drawer of his taboret.

"What about the Shenandoah Life drawing?" He looked at Collier expectantly.

"I have some ideas about that. I may have something for you tomorrow."

"I hope it's not as rough as this." Crouse muttered as he turned back to the work on the drawing table. "Make it tomorrow morning. I'm backed up on work I have to get out."

"Okay...I'll try," Collier mumbled and turned and left.

Back home before nine, Collier searched through the large, metal toolbox containing his supplies and found an aluminum mechanical inking pen and carefully cleaned it, scraping the dried India ink from the inside of the points before he took it into the kitchen and cleaned it more thoroughly under the faucet using a wet paper towel. When the pen was clean to his satisfaction, he returned to the living room, opened the points, and carefully sharpened them with a small whetstone. Then, using his T-square and masking tape, he set up a piece of smooth-surfaced Strathmore board on his drawing desk, careful to make sure the base of the board was secured at right angles to the edges of the drawing table before he went to work.

Screwing down the gap formed by the two sharpened prongs of the inking pen so it would produce what he estimated to be about a one-mil line, he then filled the hollow quill dropper built into the bottle's stopper and very shakily transferred a single drop of India ink into the tiny reservoir formed by the gap between the prongs of the mechanical drawing pen.

When at last he had nervously replaced the stopper without spilling any ink, he breathed an audible sigh of relief.

In Richmond, this kind of work had never been his strongest suit.

Pen in hand, anxiously he put his T-square in place and began slowly inking a line across the scrap of art board.

Not bad for the first try...still the line was somewhat heavier than he had hoped.

He made a slight adjustment to the tiny set screw and carefully drew the inking pen across the paper again, holding his breath as he watched the neat slender line flow from the device as it moved tautly across the page.

Better. Not bad...not bad at all!

Now he set seriously to work drawing one line about a sixteenth of an inch below the previous one until he had produced a block of some fifteen or sixteen precisely spaced lines spreading down the page for slightly more than an inch.

When he'd finished, Collier held the result in front of the mirror and breathed a satisfied sigh.

Sorting through the envelope, he removed one of the six Photostat negatives—a predominantly black-and-white image—of the original Shenandoah Life halftone glossy. Taking great care, he set it up with his T-square so that it was at right angles to the edge of the drawing board. Using a right triangle and a hard drawing pencil, he drew a light vertical line along the right-hand margin of the Photostat and, using a triangular architectural scale, he carefully marked off 1/16 inch increments down the line all the way to the bottom—at least a full half-inch below the edge of the Photostat image.

When he had finished this preparation, he went to the kitchen and recleaned the inking pen before returning to the living room to address the work at hand.

Refilling the pen, he tested and reset the width of the line on the same scrap of paper he'd used for practice. Satisfied, he took a deep breath and began inking lines across the actual Photostat negative.

This time, the work went faster and was virtually error free. When he had inked the final line at the bottom of the Photostat, the result was a negative image of the local life insurance company's HQ building, now rendered almost totally black by the overstriking of the tiny, neatly-inked lines. A quick check in the mirror reassured him the lines were perpendicular. He stood and stretched, well-pleased with the precision of his labor, trying to picture in his mind what the effect would be when he had the negative reversed and the image returned to the original presentation of black on white.

Setting the altered Photostat aside to dry, he went to empty his bladder and get the car keys.

When he returned and checked the drawing under the light, the ink had set. He carefully enclosed the finished drawing in a fold of tracing paper and placed his "masterpiece" in a file folder. With his heart in his throat and the masterpiece in hand, Collier headed for *The Roanoke Times* building downtown.

At the newspaper, he found the camera operator and explained what he wanted done, pleading that he needed a quick turn-around.

"I can have it for you by two, I think," the newspaper technician promised, intrigued by Collier's explanation of what he hoped the finished result would look like.

When he checked his watch in the lobby of the newspaper, Collier was surprised to find it was still not quite 11AM. Searching his mind for something to kill the time, his attention wandered to the latest headline about the conflict in Korea on the stack of morning papers on the reception counter. After a moment's consideration, he went to the phone booth in the corner of the lobby, found a nickel and dialed.

"I'm at the newspaper office just down the street. I wonder if I could take the Officer Candidate Test if I came right now?" Collier asked as soon as the Sergeant picked up the phone.

"Sure thing, come right on up," the Sergeant said without hesitation.

It was just before two when Collier, finished with the Army testing, walked the short distance back to the *Times* building.

"Judging from what you told me, I think you'll be quite pleased," the veteran technician told him, handing him a manila envelope.

"I hope you're right?" he stammered, fumbling to open the envelope. His mouth was so dry he had trouble speaking.

"Wow!" he exhaled, breathless with excitement and relief. The first glimpse of his project left him momentarily speechless.

Far exceeding his expectation, the resemblance to the glossy photograph had vanished entirely. There before his very eyes was an image of the Shenandoah Life HQ building looking for all the world as if it had been executed by one of the master artists who had rendered the finely-detailed engravings of the Lincoln Memorial or Jefferson's Monticello on familiar denominations of United States paper currency—similar to the work of one of the scratchboard geniuses rendering the fine jewelry and sterling silver ads in the *New Yorker* magazine.

The one-by-two-inch reduction was absolutely stunning, but, even at twice the size, the original itself was quite acceptable. Ecstatic over the result, Collier rushed to the car and drove straight to Security Envelope, anxious to show Crouse the finished product before he had to leave to pick up Emma.

"Well, good afternoon, Mr. Ramsay. Your timing is perfect," back at Security Envelope, the receptionist greeted him with a warm smile and unexpected news. "The agency people for the Mid-Atlantic Holstein Breeders Association were just here. They absolutely raved about your illustration of the cow...they particularly like the touch of having the cow standing in a field of daisies. They gave us a nice order for letterhead stationary and business cards. It was by far the biggest order we've ever had from them. They want exclusive rights to the image of the spotted cow to use on advertising and other promotions. Their agency folks indicated they may throw a lot more business our way."

"Well, that is unexpected news." Collier gave her a little wink. "I have some more work to show Crouse. If you don't mind, I'll just find my own way back."

Collier gave the receptionist a little wave and hurried past, wanting to go back to Crouse's studio unannounced.

"You were just here...what do you want now?" Crouse grumbled when he arrived and shot him a suspicious look.

"You said you're on a tight deadline. I've finished a line rendering of the Shenandoah Life building I thought you should check it out."

Collier removed a copy of the Photostat reduction.

"That's way too big. By the time I letter the corporate name and address around that, it would take a full one-fourth of the page," Crouse snorted.

"No, no...you letter right over my rendering of the HQ building—make it the central motif for the entire design. Give me that large scrap of tracing paper. See? Like this..." Using bold strokes of a soft pencil, he quickly superimposed the legend indicating a typeface similar to the corporate logo:

SHENANDOAH LIFE INSURANCE COMPANY
1234 Brambleton Avenue, SW
Roanoke, Virginia

When he'd finished, Collier tore off a small piece of masking tape and centered the tracing paper over the Photostat of his design and handed it to Crouse.

Crouse looked it over without comment before he finally put the work under the swing-arm-mounted magnifying glass attached to his drawing desk and examined it silently for perhaps the space of a full minute.

"Interesting. I may be able to use this...we'll see," Crouse shrugged. "By the way, we're using your spotted cow on those Holstein cow people's letterhead. I personally thought it was a little rough, but their Marketing/PR people seemed okay with it."

"Look Crouse, you can save your BS. That drawing was damn professional and you know it. You have no right to sell my work without my permission. You should've offered me a contract!" Collier blurted angrily before he could stop himself.

"Don't be foolish. Of course we're going pay you. I already sent Finance an order to cut a check for twenty-five bucks..."

"Call 'em and cancel. I won't sell that drawing to you," Collier snapped.

"Won't sell it? What's the matter with you? Twenty-five dollars is the going rate for a work that size in Roanoke." Crouse stopped what he was doing and turned to face him. Now his face showed some concern. "I guess since the dairy breeders are so pleased we might make it thirty-five..."

"It's not the price...it's the principle. In the first place, you weren't honest with me. Yesterday, you insinuated that my drawing was not up to your professional standards...then before I'd left the building—without offering me a contract or any other mention of payment—you had apparently already begun incorporating it into the association letterhead." Collier was absolutely livid now that the full impact of Crouse's deceit had become apparent.

"Well...ah...yesterday, you caught me at a bad time. I was up to my ears in deadlines and distracted. Last night when I took a closer look at your piece, I realized just how professional it really was. Now calm down. This engraving of the Shenandoah Life building is really professional. I like your idea of using it as a subtle background for the entire logo—I'll simply letter the company name and address right over it."

"That's not for sale either. I can't stop you from stealing my idea. Go ahead and get someone else to do a similar engraving for you."

"Whoa...just calm down, okay? I want you to come to work here with me. I had already decided to offer you the position of my assistant before you showed up with this Shenandoah Life piece. We'll start you at the new minimum wage—

seventy-five cents an hour. If things work out, I'll have them raise you to ninety cents after the first of the year. You can start tomorrow morning if that's okay."

"No thanks. I don't want to work for you," Collier replied without hesitation. "And, before I leave, I want both of my drawings back."

"Don't be a jackass. You can't have that cow drawing back. Clay's already sold it to those dairy people."

"Don't worry! I'll fix that. Before I leave here today, I'm going to see Clay and explain just why he can't use that drawing."

Security's president, Clay Moseley, was Emma's boss' son. The only male non-physician in the Moseley clan, he ran this very successful family-owned business. Collier liked Clay. Clay was a low handicap golfer and Collier had played with Clay on several occasions—the last time a few weeks back during the City-County tournament.

"Don't be a fool. Besides, Clay left about an hour ago to play golf in some weekend member-guest in Charlottesville. Why don't you just calm down? Working for me would be great experience for you—surely you've got enough sense to realize that."

"Don't patronize me, D.B. I know the experience would do me good, but you're a real pain in the ass. My life is too complicated already. Life's too short to spend time making myself miserable."

"Oh, come on. We'll get along okay. I promise," Crouse was fairly begging now.

It began to dawn on Collier that the man was under outside pressure to hire him.

Quickly putting two and two together, he wondered if perhaps it was Clay Moseley himself who had been impressed by the cow drawing—or maybe some sort of pressure had filtered all the way down from Emma's association with Dr. Simpkins Moseley, Sr.?

"Where is my drawing? I want it now," Collier persisted, determined to leave and never come back.

"I don't have it here. It's already gone out to the engraver," Crouse averted his eyes.

Collier saw the artist furtively glance in the direction of the door, most likely lying again. Turning to follow the man's gaze, he saw a heavy manila envelope in the Outbox on a small table by the door.

Collier quickly spun on his heel and picked up the package. It was clearly marked in heavy black marker: HOLSTEIN BREEDERS ASSOCIATION.

Without another word, he picked it up and headed out the door.

"Come back here," Crouse called frantically. "I'll call the law."

"Go ahead," Collier answered over his shoulder. "I'll call a lawyer while we wait."

"For chrissake, Ramsay, come back here. Be reasonable!" Crouse exclaimed as the faulty automatic-closing device let the door bang loudly shut behind Collier's retreating form.

Leaving the Security Envelope parking lot, Collier calculated he still had plenty of time to run by the recruiting office to check his Officer Candidate Test score before he headed for the VA to pick up Emma. Luckily, he found a space at the curb in front of the recruiter's building and he ran up the long stairway hoping to find the sergeant who had tested him.

Luck was on his side and the sergeant rose from behind his desk to greet him.

"Congratulations, you really blitzed the OCT. As a matter of fact, that's the highest score I've ever seen on that test. Sit down and let me sign you up."

"Not today...but it's good to know that I can enlist for OCS when I'm ready. I'll come back when we can talk about it. Right now, I'm late to pick up my wife from work," Collier thanked him and apologized for having to cut and run.

"Okay...don't wait too long. With the draft heating up to take married men, you never know when the enlistment rules regarding a fast track for OCS might be suspended," the sergeant warned him.

"Don't worry. I'll be back real soon...maybe tomorrow," Collier promised as he turned to leave.

Emma was late getting off work and was in a bitchy mood when she finally came out to the car.

"Take me home," she said, without looking him in the eye.

"What's the matter, Babe? Have a tough day?" Collier asked sympathetically. He knew Emma took her job much too seriously.

"The matter is not with me," she snapped.

"Oh?" he started. "What do you mean by that?"

"You know very well what I mean," she snapped back. "After all I did to get you that job offer at Security Envelope and you turned them down. You left them holding the bag with an important client who contracted to use that silly cow you plagiarized. You've got to give that silly drawing back to them."

"When hell freezes over!" Collier spat back angrily. "And, while we're on the subject, how dare you embarrass me by interfering in my professional life? Who do you think you are, God? I've never heard of such arrogance."

"Well, someone needs to take a hand. How long do you think I'm going to support you while you try to get work selling your dumb drawings?"

"Last time I looked, Lady, I made one-hundred-and-fifty bucks last month. That paid the rent, the phone and electricity bills."

"Hmpf! Big deal. I make almost twice as much...more when I work overtime."

"Emma, do you think I've forgotten you're squirreling a cool hundred a month into a Federal VA Credit Union account? Don't forget that I make it possible for you to do that with what I'm bringing in."

"Well, I'm doing it for our future. Besides, what's that got to do with you going to work for Security Envelope? They offered you a golden opportunity to get some valuable professional experience."

"I'd actually have to take a sizeable cut if I became D.B. Crouse's flunky on the Security Envelope payroll. At least Kroger pays me freelance rates for the extra illustrations and the hand lettering I do for their newspaper ads."

"But at Security Envelope, you wouldn't have to get all messy and covered with paint like you do when you run the silkscreen window banners. You come home looking and smelling like you've been working in a...a...sewer."

"So that's it. You're a snob. You should see Mr. Nobles over at his silkscreen studios on the other side of Catawba Mountain after he has worked all day screening the advertising cards his accounts display on the city busses. Forget it. I refuse to become Moseley's slave."

"Hmp-f, you're impossible!" she snorted, her face beet red with frustration. "I would have thought you'd appreciate what Dr. Moseley did to help you. He's willing to forgive you if you'll just let them use the stupid drawing of the cow. He even said that Clay would pay you double for the cow—and start you at ninety cents an hour to work as assistant to the artist. But I'd be embarrassed if you went to work there now...after the way you've acted."

"Don't worry. I'm not going to work for Security at any price," Collier retorted flatly.

"Beggars can't be choosers. What on earth's gotten in to you all of a sudden?" she turned in her seat, venting more anger and frustration. "I should have listened when my friends said you'd never amount to anything."

"Perhaps you should have," he replied, settling stoically behind the wheel.

In the car driving home, Emma's lack of respect for him settled between them like a funeral pall. Managing to avoid another confrontation with her the remainder of the evening, Collier finally went to sleep on the living room sofa before his watch showed ten.

The following morning, he rose early. Riding the city bus downtown to work, he thought it was just as well he had neglected to tell her about his visit to the Army Recruiting Office and his impressive score on the Army Officer Candidate test.

CHAPTER THIRTEEN

THE ROANOKE TIMES
Roanoke, Virginia, Tuesday, July 10, 1951
HISTORIC TALKS TO END WAR BEGIN AT KAESONG

————————

Negotiations May Last Weeks
By **Nate Polowetsky**
SEOUL, Tuesday, July 10 (AP) – High military officers of the Chinese-North Korean Reds and the United Nations today met in war-scarred Kaesong and opened historic talks aimed at ending the 54-week-old Korean war...

————————

THE ROANOKE TIMES
Roanoke, Virginia, Thursday, July 12, 1951
**ALLIES TAKE ACTION AFTER COMMUNISTS
BARRED ENTRY OF NEWSMEN TO KAESONG**
By **Phil Newson**
TOKYO, Thursday, July 12 (AP) – The United Nations broke off the Korean Armistice talks today.

The decision was made after the Communists halted a United Nations convoy carrying allied newsmen and service personnel to Kaesong for the historic talks...

————————

ON JUNE 23, 1951, Jacob Malik, the Deputy Foreign Minister of the USSR implied in a recorded radio broadcast in New York that China and North Korea would be willing to discuss terms of an Armistice to end the Korean War. With this long-awaited indication from Communist China that it also desired peace, President Truman directed General Matthew Ridgeway to arrange a conference with the North Korean commander.

Although Collier continued to help his uncle Ralph with the window banners and Kroger's advertising manager, Harvey Wirtz, was depending on him more than ever to help with the newspaper layouts, Emma remained on very chilly terms with her husband.

Their marital discord was momentarily put aside, however, when they went out to dinner with Gerry and Bill Deeds, Bruce and Jenny Bohon and Paul and Anita McKenzie to celebrate the news the North Koreans had agreed that peace negotiations would begin at a place called Kaesong on July 10, making the prospect of the draft calling married men into military service highly unlikely.

Having trouble sleeping and verging near the brink of nervous exhaustion, Emma still had not had a menstrual period in the almost three months since her tryst with Trey Moseley in Richmond. To further complicate the situation, since her return from Richmond, she had failed completely in her attempts to seduce Collier into having sex, reasoning that in the event Trey had gotten her PG, she wanted to make very certain Collier would have no reason to question his paternity.

It never occurred to Emma that Collier's indifference was of her own doing. To further undermine her underhanded scheme, it never entered her mind that it was totally out of character for her to initiate any interest in getting him into bed, or that Collier might not want to have sex with anyone who held him in such low regard. She never once considered her husband might have become quite fed up with her incessant harping about his lack of ambition. And, of course, she had no way of knowing Collier had been bedding their very willing, very desirable—not to mention almost insatiable—neighbor, Gerry Deeds, virtually daily during this time. Before self-absorbed Emma had considered any of this simple dynamic, the window of opportunity to make her shameful subterfuge successful had long-since passed.

Late in the evening, Thursday, July 12, Emma noticed a tiny spot of blood in her panties as she was changing into PJs for bed. In the wee hours of Friday morning, July 13, she came sharply awake, beset by waves of severe abdominal cramping, causing her to cry out in pain.

"What's wrong?" Instantly awake, Collier turned on a bedside lamp.

"I've got an awful tummy ache," she groaned, holding her belly in dire distress.

"Are you constipated?" It was a logical question. Emma was chronically constipated—lately the problem had grown even worse.

"No...I...don't think it's that," she moaned.

"Your period, maybe?" Collier ventured, tentatively. He was used to her experiencing severe menstrual cramps.

"Maybe..." she groaned, pulling back the covers to go for some aspirin.

"My God, Em!" Collier gasped as she pulled back the sheet. The crotch of her PJ bottoms was soaked with blood, and she was lying in a wide bright-red circle.

"Oh, Collie..."—she contorted violently in another wave of pain—"I didn't want to tell you, but I think I may be losing a baby," she wailed, leaving a bright-red smear of blood as she scooted her bottom nearer the side of the bed.

"C'mon, Hon, we've got to get you cleaned up and to the hospital." Collier rolled out of bed and quickly moved to her side to help her to the bathroom.

With his help, she managed to sit upright, finally scooting to the edge of the mattress and reaching her arms up to him. Taking a deep breath, she put her arm around his neck, allowing him to help her to the bathroom at the end of the hall. Once inside, she leaned against the lavatory while he stripped down her pajama bottoms, allowing her to step free of the awful, blood-soaked mess.

"Just leave them on the floor," he instructed, as he started the water in the tub and tested it. "This water's nice and warm. I'll steady you while you step inside the tub. Just stand still. I'll sponge the blood off of you."

"No...no! Let me. I can do it now. Soak that clean hand towel under the water. I'll wash myself," she protested, stepping into the tub, the pain momentarily subsiding.

"Alright. If you think you'll be okay for a minute"—reluctantly he agreed, handing her the damp towel—"I'll go back into the bedroom and slip on some clothes."

"Go ahead, get dressed...and Collier, call Lewis-Gale Emergency Room. Tell the ER supervisor I'm coming in and ask her to call Garrett Gooch. The number is in the front of the phonebook beside the phone."

Gooch was her OB-Gyn.

"I think I'd better get an ambulance." Collier turned to go back to phone.

"No...no. No sense in making a big fuss. Besides, an ambulance might take a week."

"Okay, okay Baby, I'll drive you," he soothed. "What do you want to wear?"

"My housecoat is in the closet. I'll need panties and a bra...bring an extra pair of panties."

"Okay, I'll be back as soon as I phone and dress," he called over his shoulder as he left.

As she steadied herself on the edge of the tub and sponged the blood from between her legs, she could hear him dialing the phone and giving instructions to someone at the hospital. She had just finished sponging off the blood and was toweling dry when Collier came back carrying several pairs of panties, a bra and her housecoat.

"Gooch is coming in—already on his way," he said, opening the medicine chest and running a small amount of water into the glass on the lavatory. Turning to face her, he extended his open hand with three Midol tablets. "Take these. Gooch said they might help the pain."

"Thanks." She nodded with a feeble smile.

"Can you get into these without my help?" he asked, pointing to the clothes.

"Yes...I can manage." She nodded, rummaging underneath the lavatory for Kotex and a sanitary belt.

"Okay...I'll grab a clean sheet from the linen closet to cover the car seat. Sit here. I'll be right back," he said, lowering the lid on the commode before he disappeared through the door.

By the time Collier came back with a folded sheet and some newspapers under his arm, she had finished fitting herself with the sanitary belt and Kotex and stepped into *two* pairs of panties as a hedge against further catastrophe. She stood as he helped her button the housecoat.

"Ready?" he asked, putting his arm around her waist.

"I hope so," she muttered between clenched teeth. She could feel the dampness already seeping into the sanitary pad and was tensing against the onset of another cramp.

Leaning heavily on him as they headed out without bothering to turn off the lights, they managed to make it to the car without further problems.

Thinking that Collier obviously had more concern for the car than getting her to the Emergency Room, she held her tongue as she watched resentfully as he carefully arranged a thick pad of old newspapers under the freshly-laundered bed sheet he had folded double for added protection. When he finished, she settled gingerly into the seat on the passenger side. Closing the door, Collier jogged around the car and wasted little time getting under way.

At this ungodly hour of the morning, there was no traffic in sight as he turned north on Franklin Road and let the car quickly accelerate.

In the closed car, the fetid scent of her blood was suddenly nauseating and she cranked down the passenger window as they passed beneath the railroad underpass at McClanahan Street, just before they crossed the Roanoke River Bridge.

"If you're pregnant, you have to be four months along. We haven't made love since the middle of March," Collier said, cranking down his window to let in more fresh air.

"You know how irregular my periods are. I had some spotting all along. Oh...oh, my God," she gasped, stiffening against the onset of another wave of cramping.

"Hold on, Babe, we're almost there." Collier patted her thigh reassuringly.

"What's your blood type, Mrs. Ramsay?" the triage nurse asked as they finally pulled under the portico at Lewis-Gale Hospital Emergency Entrance. Another nurse in blue scrubs and a colored nurses' aide helped her out of the car into a waiting wheelchair.

"O Positive," she replied, lips tightly pursed in pain as the scrub nurse covered her in blankets and led the way inside.

"Hold tight, Emma, everything is alright now." Ginger Lipscomb, the nurse in scrubs, squeezed her hand. Ginger was one of the smartest—and by far the prettiest—of Emma's classmates from their training days.

"How about your blood type, Sir, in case we need to give your wife a transfusion?" Emma heard Ginger ask Collier, as they were wheeling her inside.

"I'm O Positive, too," she heard Collier reply, just before the elevator doors swished shut.

A slatted pattern of warm, late-morning sunlight streamed through the Venetian blinds onto the apple-green wall of her hospital room, as Emma slowly came awake.

"How do you feel, Baby?" Collier asked, leaning anxiously over the foot of the bed.

"Like I was run over by a truck. What happened? The last thing I remember they were wheeling me onto the elevator." She tried hard to smile. Except for a vague soreness in her lower abdomen, she actually wasn't in any real pain, but she wasn't feeling exactly perky either.

"Gooch said you miscarried. He said the fetus looked to be about three months along...a boy, he said." He came around and squeezed her hand.

"Oh, Collie...I'm so sorry. I had no idea I was PG..." she said with a helpless look.

"I know. I didn't tell Gooch it would have had to have been at least month longer than that," Collier said.

"Poor Dear. Have you been here all night?" she quickly changed the subject, wanting to avoid a discussion about how long it had been since they had last had sex.

"No...after they took my blood for typing in case you needed a transfusion...after you finally settled down...I went home and shaved and showered. Gooch says you can probably come home tomorrow after lunch if you're feeling up to it. Your sister Anne is on her way, and your mom said she'd try to find someone to bring her to visit later. Gooch is still here in the hospital. He had another delivery come in. He promised he'd look in before he went to the office," Collier said, encouragingly.

"You're looking pretty good, considering the night you had," Garrett Gooch chirped with a wry smile when he came into the room an hour or so later. Anne and her mother had already come and gone. "How do you feel?"

"A little beat up, but not too bad." It was the truth. She really felt pretty good, but, recalling the severity of her cramping and all the blood, she was suddenly filled with concern. All at once overcome with anxiety, she dissolved into a flood of tears. "Garrett, will I be okay? I mean, *can* I have another baby?"

"There's no reason why not, as far as I can tell." Garrett smiled and squeezed her hand.

"Are you sure? What happened last night?" she persisted.

"Who knows? Sometimes these things happen for no apparent reason. But a uterine anomaly like a retroverted uterus might have had something to do with it...no way to tell, now." The doctor handed her a Kleenex. "Are you having any pain?"

"No, not really...a little sore...a little shaky, but otherwise, I feel alright," she said.

"Well enough to go home tomorrow, I should think?" The affable physician smiled.

"I'd rather go today. If Collier doesn't mind putting up with me," she said.

"I'll be fine if you're feeling strong enough," Collier replied seriously. "I'll go see about checking you out."

"Alright, then, I'll write your orders. You're free to go as soon as you like. Call my nurse and come by the office in about a week. I want to make sure everything is okay." The concerned gynecologist waited until Collier had disappeared down the hall before he turned back to her. "There something I should tell you now that Collier's gone."

"What's that?" She looked at him, wondering what was coming next.

"The aborted fetus was phenotype A Positive," he replied with an uncomfortable look.

"So?" she asked, completely oblivious to what he was trying to tell her.

"You and Collier are both O Positive. Does Collier know he wasn't the father?"

"Oh my God, no! He doesn't have a clue," she blushed, giving way to tears again. Quickly regaining self-control, she stammered, "It's not like you think...I'm a nervous wreck."

"Don't worry. I doubt anyone else picked up on the discrepancy. Your secret's safe with me."

"Oh, bless you, Garrett...I don't want to lose my marriage." She burst into tears again.

"Best get a hold of yourself...Collier will be coming right back." He handed her a box of hospital Kleenex and gave her hand a pat.

She wiped away her tears and blew her nose.

"Don't forget to call for an appointment. I have a suspicion your uterus may be retroverted...or prolapsed. I want to see you right away."

"Is that what caused me to abort the pregnancy?" she asked, anxious to understand.

"Could be...but I need to examine you in my office before I can be certain. Let's don't wait too long, alright?"

"Okay..." she nodded just as Collier came back with her former classmate, Ginger Lipscomb. Collier had her street clothes draped over his arm.

"Hi, Emma, you look fine considering what you've been through. If Collier will just step outside a minute, I'll help you get dressed," Ginger said, taking Emma's clothes from Collier.

Back home, Gerry and Bill Deeds hovered and fussed over her as soon as Collier wheeled into the driveway of the apartment complex. Gerry insisted on feeding them an early dinner. After dinner, Gerry washed the dishes and tucked Emma in before she and Bill bade them an early goodnight.

Stuffed with food and near exhaustion, it was still light outside when Emma drifted into a deep sleep.

It was already past nine the next morning when Collier came in to check on her.

"Hungry?" he asked, eyeing her with an anxious look.

"Not really, but I'd love some coffee if you have some made." She yawned and stretched.

"I have a fresh pot brewing...shouldn't be but a few minutes. How about some juice? I bought some fresh-squeezed just for you at the Mick-or-Mack down the street," Collier offered.

"That sounds good, but only a small glass. I'll get up and come in the kitchen. Give me a few minutes to wash my face," she told him. She was touched that he had gone to the trouble to go out and get real, fresh-squeezed orange juice.

"Don't dawdle. I have to go in to work for awhile. Gerry is going to look in on you while I'm gone," he said, heading back down the short hall.

Gerry was already sitting at the kitchen table when Emma walked into the kitchen to get her juice and coffee. Wearing a clingy, satiny kimono which didn't leave very much to the imagination, her buxom redhead neighbor had taken time to comb her hair and put on her face.

"How are you feeling?" Their friend from across the hall seemed right at home.

A girl could learn to hate a friend like that.

"Not too bad considering, I guess," she replied, not anxious to give up the extra attention due a patient recovering from a hospital emergency. "Would you like some coffee? Collier just brewed a fresh pot."

"Well, thanks, I believe I will," Gerry purred, stepping forward to accept a steaming ceramic mug from Collier.

"Have a seat and talk to me," Emma said, indicating a chair at the small table, "Collier was just on his way out the door."

"Yeah, I've gotta run." Collier nodded, as he turned to leave. When he opened the door, a delivery man from Jobe's Florist in Salem was standing there about to ring the bell.

"Here's a nice surprise," Collier said as he turned and handed Emma the florist box.

"Who on earth?..." Emma began, then looked up at Collier. "Did you send me these?"

"Not me, I'm sorry to say. Goodbye again, ladies, I really am running late." Blushing from embarrassment the flowers weren't from him, Collier ducked back out the door.

"Open them!" Gerry urged, when Collier had gone, "I'm fairly dying with curiosity."

Emma quickly untied the wrapping string, revealing a dozen, long-stemmed, crimson roses. When she took them from the box to put them in water, a tiny card fluttered to the floor.

"How odd!" Gerry said when she glanced at the handwritten inscription and extended the card to Emma.

The cryptic, plain white card read: O + O =A in the same way 1 + 2 = Fun and Games!

The card was unsigned.

CHAPTER FOURTEEN

THE ROANOKE TIMES
Roanoke, Virginia, Monday, September 24, 1951
HIGHEST POINT OF HEARTBREAK RIDGE TAKEN
By John Randolph

U.S. EIGHTH ARMY HEADQUARTERS, KOREA, Monday, September 24 (AP) – American infantrymen captured the tallest peak on "Heartbreak Ridge" in eastern Korea in a costly battle with bayonets and hand grenades...

500,000 MARRIED MEN COME UNDER DRAFT
WASHINGTON, Thursday, September 26 (AP) – President Truman today signed new draft regulations making half a million childless married men eligible for military service...

COLLIER'S JUBILATION AT THE NEWS of armistice talks in Korea and the reduction of the draft age to eighteen proved to be short-lived. Since the beginning of peace negotiations in mid-July, the newspapers had been filled with depressing news of walkouts and stalemates at Kaesong while the sounds of the combat over meaningless terrain echoed within earshot of the negotiators. It seemed incomprehensible to Collier that these self-important, high-ranking statesmen and military officers could indulge in such pettiness while completely ignoring the mounting toll of battlefield casualties at nearby places merely designated by the press as Hills 1059, 1100, 1120, and 1179.

There seemed to be no end to this empty sacrifice. Between August 17 and September 5, at a terrain feature nicknamed "Bloody Ridge," connecting Hills 900 and 983, the enemy suffered an estimated 15,653 casualties—including 4,000 dead. To Collier, it was difficult to call this purposeless combat a victory if it cost casualties of almost 3,000 American and 1,000 ROK soldiers. Now the daily news was filled with battle reports about another senseless piece of Korean real estate with the well-deserved descriptive, Heartbreak Ridge.

To make matters even worse, President Truman had signed into effect regulations removing the exemption for married men—the very thing Collier had counted upon as ironclad insurance he would remain outside the reach of the military draft.

Collier's frustration over the uncertainty of his draft status was further compounded by the humiliation of his abortive trial employment at Security Envelope to which he had finally agreed after Emma had driven him to the brink of divorce with her constant harping about her embarrassment at his refusal to give the Moseley family's generosity another try.

He truly had done his best to fit in at Security Envelope, but, from the beginning, it had been an exercise in futility. It hadn't been D.B. Crouse's fault that it didn't work out. Collier had known from the start that Security didn't have enough calls for his limited skills as an illustrator to keep him busy full-time. He had been little use to them otherwise. He was far too unsteady to emulate the tedious brush-and-ink technique which was Crouse's particular genius. They soon wound up at each other's throats when the impatient Crouse tried to teach him how to hand-letter with a sable brush at actual reproduction size.

Now that was ancient history.

More recently on the home front, news of Bill Deeds' sudden promotion and transfer to Dallas in mid-August left Collier with mixed emotions. While the regular orgiastic sex with Gerry had been exciting, the stress of maintaining the clandestine relationship with his next-door neighbor's wife had kept him on the brink of nervous exhaustion.

As if this hadn't been bother enough, Emma's Ford had developed a leak around the rear window, producing an ever-widening stain on the interior cloth of the cramped passenger compartment and an unpleasant moldy smell.

To celebrate their first anniversary, Collier negotiated a very good deal with the local Studebaker dealer to trade the lemon Ford. Without consulting Emma, he came home the evening of their anniversary driving a snazzy, brand-new, Canary Yellow Studebaker Champion Starlight Coupe—the sporty little coupe had been a dealer demonstrator with 529 miles on the odometer, coming complete with new car warranty.

"Close your eyes tight and don't peek," Collier said as he entered the apartment carrying a big, beribboned box.

After she reluctantly squeezed both eyes shut and let Collier lead her across the living room to the window overlooking the parking circle, Collier told her to open her eyes.

"What am I supposed to be looking at?" Emma blinked, not understanding Collier's childish game.

"What do you see?" Collier asked, a bit exasperated.

"Well...I'm not sure—can't you give me a hint?" Emma said, still puzzled and wondering what was in the fancy box.

"How do you like that sporty yellow car out there on the circle?" Collier asked.

"Oh my! Is it ours?"

"Happy anniversary, Babe. Put this on. We're going to Archie's Lobster House for dinner," Collier said, handing her the box containing a new cocktail dress.

Arriving back home from their anniversary dinner, the alienated couple finally got around to resuming relations in the bedroom. After Gerry Deeds, sex with Emma wasn't exactly fantasy fulfillment, but Collier had needs like any other normal, healthy, red-blooded, American male.

The following Sunday afternoon after they had resumed their intimacy, Collier was still lying beside Emma in the throes of a wonderful sexual afterglow when the phone rang and things had quickly gone to hell in a handbasket.

"Will you get that phone?" Emma murmured sleepily.

"Let it ring. If it's important, they'll call back," he resisted.

"Oh, Honey, please go get it. I can't stand to hear it ring," she had pleaded.

"C'mon, Babe, it'll stop in a minute. I don't want to talk to anyone right now," he murmured dreamily.

"Oh, Collier, you're so mean!" Emma protested as she rolled out of bed and padded out toward the kitchen. In his state of post-coital bliss, Collier was vaguely aware of her talking briefly on the phone before he felt her rudely shake him.

"Get up, Collier. That was Frank in Richmond. Daddy dropped dead about an hour ago. We have to go to the house so we can notify a list of people from daddy's toll-free company phone," Emma said with a curious lack of emotion.

Emma was the youngest of the Lowell siblings. Her sister, Anne, was two years older, and considered the prettiest, was always her daddy's favorite. A year older than Anne, her brother Frank was the youngest of the five males. During WWII, Frank had been a P-47 pilot in Europe with fifteen missions—but no confirmed kills—before the Germans surrendered. Once back home and out of the service, he had resumed his studies at Roanoke College to get his undergrad degree. Now a freshman at the Medical College of Virginia in Richmond, every time Frank's name came up, Emma had a nasty habit of reminding Collier he could have already been a doctor if he had continued on to MCV after finishing Bluefield instead of switching his major to art.

Collier had no love for Frank. Living at home while he attended Roanoke College to complete his undergraduate work, Frank was an irritating presence when Collier came home from Bluefield for his all-too-infrequent weekends with Emma. The truth was Collier had no love for any of her hard-boozing brothers—sisters either for that matter. Except for Jaynie in California, the rest of them were scattered all over the state and seemed to show up with amazing frequency on weekends to indulge in the favorite family pastime, drinking and playing cards.

While they both got dressed, Emma threw a few items into her overnight case and recited to Collier Frank's version of what had happened. Recently retired as Regional Manager of the C&P Telephone Company in Roanoke at age 62, Emma's father had taken Emma's mother to Portsmouth to visit L.E., Jr. who was manager of the telephone offices there. After leaving L.E., Jr. and Shasta, they had apparently stopped off for a few days with Frank on their way back to Salem. Arriving in Richmond at Frank's apartment, the senior Lowell had complained of fatigue and asked for an Alka-Seltzer. Before anyone realized he was in dire distress, the old tyrant had suddenly slumped over dead right there in Frank's living room.

Except for reciting those sketchy details, Emma had remained strangely silent until they were pulling into the driveway of the family homeplace.

"It's so strange. He's my father, but I never really loved him. He made Mama's life a living hell—mine, too," Emma intoned woodenly, finally breaking her silence. "I know it's an awful thing to say, but I really hated the miserable SOB. It's the saddest thing. Except for Mama, I don't really have much love for any of my family," she said, finally giving way to tears.

Once inside the house, Collier took over the thankless task of calling the long list of family and friends as Emma supplied them. By the time her brother Gene, his wife Frances, and their two daughters arrived from Fredericksburg late that evening, the list was reduced to less than a dozen former business associates and, as soon as he mixed himself a drink, Gene took over the phone.

The fourth oldest of her siblings and the second oldest male, Gene was on the downhill side of forty-five, and, like his father and older brother, was manager of the telephone company in Fredericksburg, Virginia. Also like their father, he and his other siblings of both genders were at least twenty pounds overweight, mostly around the middle. Collier guessed their Pickwickian potbellies bulging just below their ribcages were most likely due to cirrhotic livers in various degrees of development.

Gene's attractive wife, Frances, was the daughter of a former state senator and grew up in the horse country around Orange. About the same age, but completely unlike her florid, flabby hubby, Frances would be at least sixty before she ever looked a day past thirty-five. A regal, slender but heavy-breasted, country-club-bred, natural honey-blonde, Frances graduated Mary Washington and could make a simple white blouse and straight black skirt look as if she had just walked out of a chic New York boutique. Collier had lusted for her since the first time he had laid eyes on her when he was still a senior in high school.

Remembering the recent wake of the father of a college friend, Collier took the opportunity to enlist Gene's help in moving the big sofa away from the center of the large living room. They had just finished wrestling the ponderous settee aside when the cars began arriving one right after another in a steady stream, and Gene hurried outside to direct traffic onto the closely-mowed side yard.

Predictably and thankfully, among the early arrivals were members of Emma's mother's woman's clubs and church groups bearing mountains of food. Before a full hour had passed, the kitchen and dining room tables held enough fried chicken, ham, potato salad and deviled eggs, cakes, pies and banana pudding to feed a highway construction crew.

After completing the final phone call on Emma's list, Collier went into the kitchen, fixed himself a heaping plate of the ham biscuits, potato salad and banana pudding and slipped away from the crowded downstairs rooms to the spare front bedroom upstairs where Emma had directed him to stow their overnight luggage. When he had finished eating, he carefully placed his used paper plates and cup into the bedside trash can and lay down on the musty, well-used bedspread, staring into the gathering gloom at the passing traffic on the highway, trying to absorb the impact of Emma's father's death on the future of his marriage. He didn't know how long he had dozed when he came suddenly awake; someone was sitting beside him on the edge of the bed.

"I missed seeing you downstairs and came up to see if you were down for the night." In the darkness, an anonymous voice purred with a cultured feminine drawl accompanied by a subtle, perfumy female scent in the room.

"How long have I been asleep?" He stretched and yawned, not wanting to admit he didn't recognize the owner of the voice.

"Not that long...half-hour at the most," the anonymous female purred—her minty, slightly-alcoholic breath a faint whisper against his cheek. As his eyes rapidly became accustomed to the dark, Collier finally recognized the woman beside him as Frances, Gene's aristocratic wife.

"That's quite a bulge in your pants. You must have been having some very interesting dreams," Frances giggled.

Quickly coming more fully awake, he was now aware that his penis was painfully erect—a fact that was embarrassingly obvious in the reflected light from the passing cars on the highway.

"Sometimes that happens while men sleep," he stammered, ashamed to be caught like this, and realizing it was too late to camouflage his condition.

"Don't fret over it. It's the occasion. Surely you've noticed that wakes and funerals have a way of making people horny? If the men could still get it up, half of the people downstairs would be fucking their brains out...providing they had brains, of course."

Her unexpected use of coarse street talk took him completely by surprise. Collier was certain she'd had too much to drink. He'd grown accustomed to the rest of Emma's family's bawdy sense of humor, but the few years he'd known Frances had not prepared him for such uninhibited behavior from his quiet, well-mannered and proper sister-in-law.

"You're just making that up about funerals?" he said, sure she was putting him on.

"Not at all, but never mind. I hope you didn't mind my sitting here—and there's no need to be embarrassed about your hard-on. I have to confess, I've been sitting here resisting a great temptation to reach across and give that feisty cock of yours a little tweak."

Momentarily stunned to silence, finally he croaked, "You're kidding, right?"

"Not at all, I'm quite seris...seri-e-ous," she slurred the words. "I really wanted to give that thing a 'lil' ol' squeeze."

"Well...what stopped you?" He kidded, somewhat amused by her inebriated condition.

Before he could blink an eye, she was astride his thighs and fumbling with his fly, struggling to extract his swollen member from his jockey shorts.

"No...goddamn it, Frances, this is just plain nuts. You've got to stop," he said, losing his struggle to push her hands away.

"Oh, my..." she breathed as she finally managed to release the engorged length of him from his trousers. Taking his hand and roughly squeezing it to her breast, she leaned forward, teasing the end of his dick with long strokes of her tongue.

For such a slip of a woman, she was amazingly strong. No matter how he struggled, she refused to let him wrestle her off of him.

"Frances, you've got to get a grip on yourself. You've had way too much to drink. In case you've forgotten, I'm married to your husband's little sister," he scolded, somewhat less convincingly now.

"Why don't you just shut up and relax?"

Before he could stop her, she began stroking his testicles with both hands. She had hardly begun to stroke him before he began to come, erupting in what seemed a never-ending geyser, his semen spilling all over her hands and her skirt—and his clothes and the bedspread as well.

"Oh, jeez, I'm sorry, Frances. You took me by surprise. I usually have better control," he gasped, completely mortified by the suddenness of his ejaculation.

"Shush, silly. Just be quiet and stay put. Give me about ten minutes to get myself together. When you hear me go back downstairs, get up and go to the bathroom and make yourself presentable. By the way, after the funeral tomorrow, I'm going to stay over a few days to help out. Emma says you two are staying, too. I heard her tell her sister, Anne, that she's working graveyard—eleven 'til seven. I promise you I will let you make this up to me. I want a demonstration of this fabulous control," she added, then stood and padded off down the hall.

Collier waited in the dark until he heard her tiptoe lightly away. When he was sure she had time to make it downstairs, he went to the bathroom to remove the evidence and repair the damage to his clothes. After he had cleaned himself the best he could, he came back to the darkened bedroom, undressed and crawled into bed. Lying there looking out at the occasional late-night traffic, he made a solemn vow for the next few days he was going to volunteer for every little errand that would take him out of the house.

By noon the next day, however, his worry over the lurking presence of his predatory sister-in-law was all for nothing. Without so much as a word of farewell, after the funeral, Frances had a change of plans as she and her teenage girls went back to Fredericksburg.

If Collier had thought about it at all, he should have seen it coming. As if it were almost a foregone conclusion, with their father dead, the children had a meeting and Emma volunteered to move in with her mother. Passively, Collier resented the fact that Emma hadn't given much more than lip service about consulting him in the matter. Obviously, in her mind, she had lost all respect for him somewhere along the way during their first year of marriage. Yet privately, when the air had cleared, Collier had to admit—given the increasing uncertainty of his future with the military—moving in with Mrs. Lowell was not an all-around bad idea.

The decision that Emma move in with her mother was not entirely Emma's doing. Collier understood that during the meeting of the siblings shortly after the funeral, it was agreed upon that he and Emma would move into the old homeplace; while L.E., Jr. and Gene would return for a few days in the near future to inventory the estate and take care of probate, leaving the rest of them to pursue their own devices.

The inventory and probate went quickly enough. The bottom line was—except for the house, the fairly-new Olds sedan, the cabin and property on the other side of Fort Lewis mountain (all which were free of debt)—the selfish old bastard left Emma's mother scarcely enough to live on. So, it was quickly agreed by all that L.E., Jr. would buy the cabin from their mother to provide her with a small nest egg against hard times.

Even so, if it hadn't been for Collier taking Emma aside and insisting that her mother have the cabin and adjoining acreage officially appraised, the rest of the siblings would have let L.E., Jr. get away with grand theft from their very own mother.

Thankfully, Collier and Emma had had no trouble finding someone eager to take their lease at the popular Franklin Heights Apartments. By the first weekend in November, they had moved their paltry possessions and few pieces of furniture into the old homeplace.

With the possibility of his being drafted into the military now a looming reality, coincidental to their moving, Collier went to the Army recruiting sergeant and negotiated a deal for a deferred enlistment date of January 2, 1952, going through all the preliminary requirements of enlisting with the expressed purpose of going to Officer Candidate School. Although both Bo and Doyle had already refused the opportunity to take the OCT several weeks beforehand, the recruiters were more than delighted to extend the courtesy of offering the same negotiated enlistment to them—thus removing each of them from the shadow of being drafted and spending the holidays in some godforsaken Army camp.

CHAPTER FIFTEEN

VMI-VPI -Welcome Back For The 41ˢᵗ Year- VPI-VMI
THE ROANOKE TIMES
Roanoke, Virginia, Thanksgiving, November 22, 1951
WAR CASULTIES ARE OVER 100,000
Fourth Costliest War in American History

WASHINGTON, Nov. 21 (AP) - The American casualty toll in 16 months of battle in Korea passed the 100,000 mark today establishing the limited Asian conflict as the fourth costliest war in United States history.

THE MORNING PAPER CARRIED the latest depressing news from the Korean front that while the foppish, self-important peace negotiators wrangled over a 17-word sentence, U.S. troops were taking severe casualties during an assault on a nearby terrain feature dubbed Pork Chop Hill. With the date he had to report to the Army only a scant six weeks away, what had first seemed joyous news about the beginning of peace talks had quickly degenerated into a debacle as the parade of high-ranking military officers and politicians from Washington and Peking stalked in and out of the truce tents at Kaesong while they continued to sacrifice innocent lives in the senseless, bloody battle to hold meaningless high ground around Panmunjom.

Even as Collier sat contemplating the futility of the situation, wondering if this might well be his last Thanksgiving dinner at his mother's table, the latest senseless bloodbath was taking place at a craggy promontory designated Hill 255 on the military map, but christened Pork Chop Hill by the men who were fighting and dying there.

After a rather hurried meal, trying to put up a cheerful front, Collier gave his mother an appreciative hug and headed back to Mother Lowell's house to pick up Emma to take her to work. Obsessed with adding to her growing savings account, she had volunteered to work the holiday to earn incentive overtime pay.

When he arrived back at their new homeplace, Collier was not surprised to find most of the Lowell siblings already there to freeload off of Mother Lowell's full-course Thanksgiving dinner—a feast largely paid for with his and Emma's hard-earned funds. His stomach did a nervous flip when Emma's brother Gene and his adventuresome wife, Frances,·pulled in behind him. Trailing him inside the house, Frances lost little time elbowing her way through the large gathering of in-laws to give Collier a fierce hug.

"We're going to stay the weekend. I'm looking forward to finishing what we started." Planting a kiss hard on his mouth, she lost no time stating her intentions hoarsely in his ear.

Collier managed to extricate himself from his sister-in-law's overly-enthusiastic embrace as, grinning like an idiot, he stepped back pretending he was pleased to see everyone.

Seeking safe haven from the mob scene already setting up two card tables for an afternoon of bridge, Collier made his way upstairs to their bedroom where Emma was changing into her uniform for work.

"Don't get comfortable. I'm running late," Emma said, clamping a Kleenex between her lips before she pulled the starched, white uniform over her head, taking care not to mess her hair.

"Don't worry...I'm ready when you are," he said, crossing the room to the big Morris chair by the window. "Better wear your cape. It looks a lot like snow."

"Did Chuck tell you some woman called while you were eating dinner with your folks?" Emma asked as she located her heavy, uniform cape to protect her from the cold.

"Yeah...he told me. It's the woman I helped chaperone the girls to the football game."

"Oh? What would she want? You don't have much time left before you're leaving for the Army. You certainly can't be running around chaperoning any more bobbysoxers to football games," she complained, turning around to face him.

"Oh, it's probably about the cheap scarf I left in her car. And, don't worry. I'm not about to get suckered into that again. Besides, don't forget that I made that trip as a favor to your mom." He smiled a nasty smile as he got up and held her cape for her.

"Sure, I know, but just don't get yourself committed to anything between now and Christmas. We're already snowed under with party invitations. You'll have to make your goodbyes to our families and friends."

"Alright, I understand." Collier nodded and stepped aside, letting Emma precede him down the winding stairway. At the bottom of the stairs, Emma stopped to say hello to a newly-arrived cousin. In the kitchen the phone had started ringing again.

"I'll run get the car."

"Okay, I'll come right out. Pick me up in front," Emma called to his disappearing back.

"The Red Cross Bloodmobile is at the hospital today. Why don't you come in and give some blood?" Emma's voice brought him back to the moment as they entered the wide brick entranceway of the sprawling VA complex.

"I don't think so, not today," he demurred.

"Why not? With the war on, it's the patriotic thing to do," she persisted.

"Nobody can question my patriotism," he said, resenting her superciliousness. In just a few weeks he would be leaving for God-knows-where to do God-knew-what for his country.

"Oh, don't be so dramatic. Enlisting is just a cheap way of avoiding the military draft. If you're afraid of the needle, your secret's safe with me." She was being purposefully insulting. She knew damn well he had given blood many times before. With a concerted effort, he managed to hold his tongue, well-aware the spiteful bitch was trying hard to get his goat—a project he had come to recognize as her favorite pastime!

"Doesn't look as if they have many customers," he casually observed as they approached the entrance to Emma's ward on the far side of the complex; the large Bloodmobile truck was parked at the curb.

"Oh, they never draw blood in the mobile unit when they come here. They're set up inside the ward." Emma said. "Look, there's Ginger Lipscomb coming down the steps now—you remember Ginger? She was the best-looking girl in our nursing class."

"Yeah, I remember. Is she working for the Red Cross now?" Watching the shapely redhead approaching the car, if possible, the well-formed nurse looked even sexier now.

"No. Ginger still works at Lewis-Gale. Remember, she was working OB when I aborted. On some days off, she volunteers to work the Bloodmobile." Emma said. "Come on and get out and say hello. Don't let her think you're a snob."

"Sure, why not?" Unfolding himself from beneath the wheel, he walked around to the sidewalk to greet Emma's former classmate.

"You remember Collier from training at Lewis-Gale, Ginger?" Emma called to her ex-classmate as she stepped outside the car.

"Of course. We all had a crush on him. Emma tells me you're going into the Army right after the holidays. Maybe you'll run into our classmate, Lou Thacker. Lou's in San Antonio at Fort Sam Houston. You'll have to salute her; she's a Captain now." Ginger laughed.

"No fooling?" Collier couldn't help but smile. He remembered Lou as being sort of tomboyish. He'd always wondered if she had lesbian tendencies, but Emma assured him she did not. "I'd be honored to give Lou a snappy salute."

"I'm sure she'd really get a kick out of that." Ginger smiled. "If this thing in Korea continues much longer, I'm thinking seriously of joining up, myself."

"You're not leaving are you? As soon as I take report, I was going to let you take some blood," Emma changed the subject.

"Oh, no...we'll be here another hour at least. By the way, if you hurry, Trey Moseley's inside. He's coming here as part of his residency in January," Ginger informed Emma, then turned to Collier to explain. "Trey interned at Lewis-Gale a couple of summers back. Most of the girls in our class had a crush on him. He's movie-star good looking. By the way, Emma, Trey said he ran into you in Richmond, sometime back in April."

"Oh yes, he came to the convention banquet with his dad and mom. It'll be nice to see him again. I know his parents must be happy he'll be doing his NP rotation here," Emma remarked offhand. Collier understood NP was medical shorthand for Neuropsychiatric.

"Speak of the devil," Ginger nodded at a well-dressed, somewhat diminutive, male coming through the door.

"Trey, you remember Emma of course...have you met her husband, Collier?"

"Hi, Emma, long time no see. Hello, Ramsay. I've heard a lot about you." The pompous young physician nodded at Emma as he extended a hand to Collier.

"I'm afraid you have the advantage on me there," Collier replied, trying to maintain an even tone. He couldn't help but take an instant disliking to the man.

"Nothing bad, I assure you," the doctor spoke with a theatrical resonance. To Collier, his entire affect was phony and insincere.

"Emma tells me you've enlisted for Army Officer Training," Ginger interjected, sensing Collier's antagonism. "I certainly admire your patriotism."

"Well...I'm not sure it isn't all for nothing. I mean with the truce talks and everything, the fighting will soon be over." Collier resisted the praise, embarrassed that his strategy to avoid the draft would be construed as patriotism.

"Speaking of red-blooded patriotism, I just gave Ginger a pint of my all-American red blood. Why don't you slip inside and give some, too?" the abrasive Moseley crowed.

"I just gave a month or so ago. I really don't want to overdo it." Collier resented being put down in front of the women.

"It was more like six months...June, I think," Emma said accusingly, as if he were some kind of a coward.

"Oh, well, they get plenty of O-Positive, anyway," Collier defended, quite unnecessarily.

"A-Negative is a fairly rare genotype. It's in such short supply that I try to donate every month or so," Moseley sniffed and strutted toward the parking lot.

Watching him swagger off, Collier felt that he had just missed something important, but, for the life of him, he couldn't say just what.

CHAPTER SIXTEEN

THE ROANOKE TIMES
Roanoke, Virginia, Wednesday, January 2, 1952
REDS, UN WILL FREE CIVILIANS
CAUGHT IN WAR ASK ALL-FOR-ALL SWAP

MUNSAN, KOREA, Wednesday, January 2 (AP) Allied delegates today agreed to an "all-for-all' exchange of Korean War prisoners.

GROUND FIGHTING DULLER THAN USUAL

SEOUL, Wednesday, January 2 (AP) - The Korean ground fighting sagged into a first of the year lull Tuesday, much slower than the usual draining pace of the so-called "Twilight War."

FOR COLLIER AND FELLOW ENLISTEES, Bo Bohon and Doyle Pogue, reports of continued fighting contradicted by reports of the childish pomposity around the Korean negotiation tables hung over the holiday season like a storm cloud, taking most of the joy out of being allowed to spend Christmas and New Year's at home.

New Year's Day, Collier had leftover turkey sandwiches for lunch with his parents and spent the early afternoon listening to bowl games on the fancy Zenith Trans-Oceanic Radio for which Collier and Jim had scraped up the staggering sum of $124.95 to give their father for Christmas. From the way his father's face lit up, switching back and forth between broadcasts of the tight Florida-Tulsa Gator Bowl tussle, Alabama's rout of Syracuse in Miami's Orange Bowl, and the enjoyable one-sided Georgia Tech mauling of Ol' Miss in New Orleans, Collier was satisfied that the high-powered radio had been well-worth its exorbitant cost.

Emma had stayed at home with her mother, waiting until he showed up to take her to the Pogue's to watch the USC-Wisconsin Rose Bowl clash on Doyle's brand-new RCA 20-inch TV, which got a very snowy picture from WFMY-TV in Greensboro, North Carolina—about ninety miles from Roanoke. No matter how unreliable the reception, WFMY was the only TV reception available in the mountainous Roanoke area. As fascinated as he was to see the magic of TV again for one of the rare times since he had left Richmond, Collier was nervous about going into the military and unable to keep his mind on the game. Despite the closeness of the Southern Cal-Wisconsin Battle for the Roses, not even the gratuitous view of Marla's inner thighs diverted his mind from thoughts about the uncertain future. Despite the fact that Army recruiters had told them not to bring anything more than a shaving kit and some changes of underwear—which meant there was no real packing left to be done—as soon as the game was over, Collier and Emma said goodbye and headed home. When they got back home around ten, Collier went straight to bed while Emma stayed up to iron some uniforms.

Not surprisingly, Collier was still tossing and turning, wide awake when Emma came to bed around midnight.

"Collier? Are you still awake?" she whispered after she had undressed in the dark and climbed into bed.

"Uh-huh..." he muttered sullenly.

"I took a shower. Would you like to make love to me? It'll be a long time before we're together again." To his astonishment, she snuggled up against him and hugged his back.

What the hell? he mused. Shrugging inwardly, he rolled over to face her and lay there passively waiting for her to make a move. He'd just be damned if he'd show her the depth of his need.

To his surprise, she snuggled closer, cradling her right breast in her hand.

"Suck my nipple, Collier, please..."

He'd almost forgotten how much he had always enjoyed Emma's still rather maidenly body. Without a word, he took her nipple between his lips, pulling it hard inside his mouth.

"Let me have your finger," she breathed, expertly guiding his finger to her clitoris. In a moment, she was busy stroking his penis, already slick with a responding freshet of juices.

"Slow down. You'll make me come too soon," he gasped and gripped her wrist.

"Put it inside of me! Come when *you* want to—this night's all for you," she rolled on her back and spread her legs, opening herself wide to him. Guiding him into the tight opening of her vagina, she lifted her hips, pushing eagerly to take him in.

"Go, easy! I'll lose control." He gasped at the exquisite pleasure.

"Come on, give it to me," she inhaled sharply, "I want it all."

To Collier's delight, he felt her vagina slowly devouring the length of him. Before he could stop to rest, she was thrusting her hips with a grinding motion and he could feel himself teetering on the verge.

"Whoa...let me rest. I'll lose control," he pleaded, placing his hands against her hips.

"Forget control," she hissed, pumping even harder now. "Oh, my god, Collier, I think I'm going to come."

Pounding into her now with something akin to murderous rage, he tried to punish her. Responding to the steady stimulus of his constant grinding against her cervix, her breathing began to disintegrate into little broken gasps.

"Oh! Oh, God, yes!" she moaned as she raised her hips and began shuddering violently. "God, Collier, come inside me now."

"Isn't it ironic?" she whispered later in a sleepy voice, the moonlight-generated shadows of the naked tree branches painting a sensual chiaroscuro across her naked form.

"What's that?" he muttered, in his post-orgasmic, half-sleep state.

"I had to have my first-ever real orgasm the night before you're going to leave me for four months."

It was pitch dark in the room and the luminous dial on the bedside clock read 5:12 when Collier woke with a start. To his utter amazement, Emma's hand was on his prick.

"You want to do it again?" he whispered, experiencing a deliciously-wicked feeling of exhilaration for having this surprising control over her now. Recalling Grandpa Boyd's wry admonition when he was a teenager to avoid "cold collards and woke pussy," he wondered just what in hell had suddenly come over his erstwhile frigid wife?

"Do you think we could?" she inquired hopefully.

"I thought you'd never ask," he said, a renewed surge of power rising in his loins.

Following this miraculous lagniappe, Collier remained awake just long enough to thank a god he did not know or believe in for this totally unexpected blessing and to breathe a fervent prayer for strength to cope with his upcoming military ordeal. Then he slipped back into a fully-sated but uneasy sleep.

Collier was ill-prepared for the rude awakening awaiting him shortly after he met Bo and Doyle Wednesday morning at the recruiting office. As the sergeant checked the roster, he assigned each his permanent serial number. Collier's was RA 13415453, Bo's number ended with 54, and Doyle's with 55. The RA prefix, they soon found out, was for Regular Army because they had voluntarily enlisted. This distinguished them from their draftee companions who were assigned serial numbers with the prefix US. The sergeant had told them when they enlisted in November it was the Army's way of distinguishing between patriots and bums.

"Happy New Year and welcome to Uncle Sam's Army. Get in line, drop your pants, skin 'em back and milk 'em down. The medic needs to check your cute little weenies." A crusty sergeant wasted no time in introducing Collier, Bo, Doyle and the other twenty-odd raw recruits to the time-honored military vigilance against venereal disease—otherwise familiarly known as an old-fashioned "short arms inspection."

After spending most of the day undergoing more physical exams, listening to orientation lectures and viewing films, they were finally allowed to go home in the late afternoon. Following dispirited dinners with their families, they all said their goodbyes and rendezvoused at the N&W passenger station in Roanoke to board the train which was to transport them overnight to Washington. In the nation's capitol the following morning, they would transfer to another train to Laurel, Maryland—their ultimate destination: Fort Meade.

At Fort Meade, they would "process"—whatever that meant—before they were sent to Basic Training at installations elsewhere across the country.

Although Collier—Bo and Doyle, too—had booked Pullman roomettes so they could get a good night's sleep, Collier spent a rather restless night

The following morning during the two-hour layover at Union Station in Washington, he walked outside the historic railroad station and gazed out on the city with the Washington Monument rising in the middle-distance like a some tribute to a long-dead Roman emperor, and the Capitol Dome so close he could walk there in less time than it took to take a healthy piss. Reminiscing there in the morning chill, he recalled a certain Sunday afternoon he had ridden up from Richmond with Megan Hubbard—a fellow aspiring artist—while still a student at RPI. A talented sculptress, Megan had taken him on an unforgettable tour of the National Statuary Hall in the Capitol Building with a stopover at the National Gallery of Art. Fraught with erotic innuendo so thick he could have cut it with a knife, he had let the powerfully romantic opportunity pass unrealized. Finally, calling himself all kinds of a fool for the chances he had wasted in his life, Collier—with his buddies—boarded the Pennsylvania Railroad local to Philadelphia and New York for the short trip to Laurel, Maryland.

When they detrained at the Laurel station, they were greeted by a staff sergeant and four enlisted men who rounded up about twenty more recruits straggling off the train and directed them onto an Army bus to nearby Fort

Meade. At Meade, the lot of them were herded into a gymnasium, instructed to form a line and drop their pants while two medics poked at their genitals again.

"I think the Army is run by a bunch of queers," Bo said, disgustedly.

"If they don't turn some heat on, my teeny weenie will be so shrunk up they'll think I'm a girl," Collier shivered, standing in the cold.

Unhappy Collier's schoolboy humor elicited a titter from his disgruntled companions.

"Knock it off," the sergeant conducting the 'short-arms' barked. "In case you haven't figured it out, you're in the Army now."

"Did he say 'beat it off?'" some wise guy in the line behind them quipped.

"Put that energy into twenty push-ups, Wiseass," the sergeant said. "Step out here and count 'em out loud enough for us all to hear."

After they had suffered another humiliation of having their peckers examined and scrotums poked, they were directed back outside, into the cold, to a slow-moving line where they ultimately were fitted for shoes and boots and measured for and issued two of virtually every item of Army winter uniform and ancillary accouterments of clothing imaginable, from the heavy, cumbersome, blanket-like overcoat to baggy white undershorts.

"What size boot you wear, farmboy?"

"Uh? I don't know my boot size. I wear an eleven or eleven-and-a-half shoe, I think."

"In this man's Army, draftee's ain't allowed to think. Give him eleven-and-a-half," the snotty corporal told a PFC who reached into huge bins clearly marked 12 and handed Collier two pairs of boots and a pair of dress shoes.

"I'm not a draftee; I'm enlisted and, besides, these are size twelves..." Collier protested.

"Oh, God, *enlisted's* even worse!" The disagreeable corporal rolled his eyes heavenward. "Keep moving, Rookie, you're holding up the line."

When they had finished collecting their Army wardrobe, they were formed directly into another seemingly unending line where they were issued a pair of dog tags stamped with their names, blood types and serial numbers. Lugging a duffel bag full of boots and socks and uniforms and underwear, it was late morning when they were marched to a barracks with empty bunks, each holding a neat stack consisting of a clean mattress cover, sheets and a blanket.

"This may be home for the next few days. Pick a bunk and make it up. The latrine's out back," an indifferent corporal barked. "Meet me back in the street in fifteen minutes and we'll get some chow."

Following chow—consisting mainly of mashed potatoes and some sort of chicken hash—they were taken back to the barracks and given another fifteen minutes to finish making up their bunks. When they fell out into the street again, they were marched to a long, low building where each was given an eye and dental exam. From the dental chair, they were directed gauntlet-fashion between two lines of medical corpsmen gleefully sticking them with needles in both arms. Before they had barely begun, two recruits had passed out cold.

"Jeez! I think I must've been inoculated against every disease known to modern man. After that, I may never be able to pick up a fork to eat—much less an M-1 rifle," Doyle complained, gingerly rubbing both arms as they left.

"Not so loud," Bo whispered nervously and rubbed his arm. "They may have forgotten a few."

"Hang around the dayroom and barracks. Some of you will be traveling out of here first thing tomorrow morning," a sergeant told them before he marched them back to the mess hall at five o'clock and released them for the remainder of the evening.

After breakfast the following morning, true to the sergeant's word, a steady parade of NCOs ("Non-commissioned Officers" they'd learned the first morning in Roanoke)—including all ranks from Private E-1 to E-8 Master Sergeant—came in the barracks and read off the names of men, ordering them to fall out in the street with all their gear. One by one, the groups were loaded into trucks and carted off.

By half-past seven, with the barracks already half-empty, a sergeant came in with a list of names, including Collier and several other men, and marched them off to a nearby building to take some tests. To Collier's consternation, the first test they put in front of him was the Officer Candidate Test.

"The recruiting office in Roanoke already gave me this test twice," Collier protested to the nearest sergeant.

"This will make three then," the sergeant quipped. "You want to be an officer? This is a timed examination. You better get to work."

Collier had awakened feeling a trifle achy. When he swallowed, he had a scratchy throat—sure signs he was coming down with a cold. Stomach churning, Collier shrugged and opened up the test. It was quite difficult to read in the cavernous dim-lit room. To further compound his difficulties, the room—now filled with perhaps two-hundred recruits—was unbelievably cold.

"It would help a lot if they turned the heat up in here. It's so cold my hands are numb," Collier protested to the sergeant.

"It's proven that momma's boys like you score higher when they're not tested in overheated rooms." The crusty sergeant shrugged and laughed.

"Welcome to the freaking Army," the bespectacled recruit beside him whispered.

"Knock it off! No cheating," the rabbit-eared sergeant glanced suspiciously in their direction.

"Okay. Time! Close your test books. They will be collected by the monitors passing through the aisle. The following men will remain for further testing; the rest will report back to their barracks." While the OCT booklets were being collected, Collier's name was among a list of others called over the loud speakers with instructions to remain seated for additional testing. When he was finally sent back to the barracks just before noon, he had taken three or four additional tests.

"Those last were placement tests. They're probably looking for brain surgeons. There's always a shortage of brain surgeons. Brain surgeons make the best tank mechanics and dog-ass infantry," his bespectacled friend told him as they were marching back.

Chilled and exhausted as he was, Collier couldn't help but laugh.

Baked in giant pans, midday chow looked like chicken pot pie. There was peach cobbler for dessert. Suddenly ravenous, Collier filled his tray. When he had finished eating and was walking back to the barracks, he had to admit that, so far, the chow wasn't half-bad.

Back at the deserted barracks, Collier was relieved to see Bo's and Doyle's gear still resting beside their bunks, but there was no sign of either man. Momentarily, he considered looking for the dayroom, but the aching in his joints was getting worse, his nose was runny and his head was stopping up. Locating the latrine behind the barracks, he folded several layers of the thin GI toilet tissue to blow his nose. Taking a half-used roll of toilet paper back with him, Collier was shivering badly now from a chill. Grateful to be inside out of the cold, he flopped down on his bunk and pulled a blanket and his heavy Army overcoat over him, covering even his head. Almost instantly, he was sound asleep.

"Get up and get dressed. Meet me outside in five minutes." When Collier awoke in the pitch dark, a shadowy form holding a flashlight was shaking him.

"What time is it? What's going on?" Collier came groggily awake. His clothes were soaked with sweat and he ached in every joint.

"It's half-past four and you're on KP," the anonymous voice behind the flashlight said. "Better grab your poncho—it's pouring cats and dogs."

"No, get someone else...I'm too sick," Collier groaned and pulled his covers back over his head.

"You don't know what sick is, Mac, if you aren't downstairs in the street in five minutes. Better get a move on." Rudely ripping the blanket and overcoat completely off the bunk, the insistent PFC rudely raised his flashlight, shining it full in Collier's eyes.

"C'mon, man. I'm not kidding you. No way I can work today. I'm sick," Collier protested weakly.

"Look, your name's right here on this list, soldier," his tormentor growled, shining the flashlight on the paper. "Now, get up and get dressed. You can explain you're on your deathbed to the Mess Sergeant." The PFC gave him a dirty look and made his way down the line of bunks looking for the next unlucky victim.

In the dark, Collier located his shaving kit and shoved a bottle of Bayer aspirin into the pocket of his heavy overcoat before he located his rubber GI poncho. Making a hurried attempt to straighten up his bunk, he turned and stumbled his way in the dim reflections from the streetlight down the center between the rows of bunks, heading for the latrine to take a leak and shave.

Outside, the icy rain was coming down in sheets and the chilling blasts of wind seemed to cut right through the poncho and heavy overcoat. Seized with a fit of coughing, making a dash for the latrine, inside Collier hacked up a large glob of thick, greenish-yellow pus. His chest hurt terribly when he coughed. He located the Bayer aspirin bottle, shook out three tablets and swallowed them with a handful of water from the tap before he quickly shaved and brushed his teeth. When he finally braved the rain to make it back into the barracks, a collection of five other unhappy recruits were standing by the front door with the PFC who had wakened him.

"Okay. The prima donna's back. Hold your ponchos over your heads. Never mind trying to get into formation. Just follow me," the PFC instructed and opened the door a crack. "Stay close now. We're gonna double time in this goddamn rain."

Running the long two blocks in the driving rain to reach the mess hall, Collier thought his lungs would burst. When they finally made it under the lee of what passed for an entrance marquee, he was seized with another fit of coughing.

"Jesuschrist!" the PFC snorted, watching in disgust. "I'll tell the mess sergeant to take it easy on you."

"Uhm-m...thanks a lot," Collier nodded gratefully for the unexpected sympathy.

"Alright, stay with me in a group. We're going to go through the chow line and get breakfast before you have to report to work," the PFC instructed and ushered them inside. The sudden rush of warmth felt good to his aching joints, and the steamy air soothed his tortured lungs and throat.

Going through the line, Collier had the white-aproned KPs heap his tray with eggs and sausages and smothered two king-sized, golden-crusted biscuits with white gravy before he filled his coffee cup. *Feed a cold and starve a fever:* the childhood adage from his great-grandmother Argabright came back to him. He wasn't sure he had a fever, but he damn-well knew he had a cold.

"Collier! Collier Ramsay!" a voice called. He looked up to see Don Young, his old Bluefield Junior College roomie, coming across the large room, carrying an empty tray and cup toward the pass-through window leading back to the workers in the kitchen. Raised in southwest Roanoke county, Don had been his teammate at Andrew Lewis.

"Don...I see they got you, too." He set his tray down and went to shake his old friend's hand.

"Yeah...been here two days and had KP already. Thank God, I'm shipping out to Fort Benning for Basic today. After Basic, I'm hoping to be a PT instructor. I see they drafted you, too," Don laughed a hollow laugh.

"Well not exactly..." he said and told Don about enlisting for OCS.

"I looked into that, but they make you sign an indefinite commitment before they take you into a class. My wife didn't want me to take a chance on having to make the military a career."

"No...you're wrong, I'm sure. They told me I'd have to commit to three years when I'm accepted into an OCS class." Collier shook his head.

"Take my word. You'd better check it out," his former teammate warned, punching him familiarly on the shoulder. "Look, Collie, I've got to run. I've got to shower and pack my gear. Stay in touch." He turned and headed out.

"Good luck!" Watching him go, an icy seed of doubt was taking root in Collier's chest.

Despite his aches and the sorry condition of his lungs, Collier still mustered up a hearty appetite. His belly was full when they finally escorted him into the kitchen.

"Hang up that goddamn overcoat!" The cook pointed to a peg beside the back door and put him right to work mopping the floor. That done to the sergeant's satisfaction, an assistant led Collier back to a row of large metal sinks stacked full of huge, aluminum cooking pots and pans. The water was already steaming in the pair of the sinks farthest to his right.

"Scrape 'em here, and wash 'em here, and rinse 'em here." The assistant demonstrated by picking up a big square pan with a lot of egg sticking to it and scraping the residue into one of several large garbage cans in front of the sinks.

"Better use these gloves. You have to keep the water plenty hot. The main thing is to scrub out all the grease," the gruff assistant cautioned, testing the temperature of the water from the faucets and pointing to an assortment of stiff, wooden GI brushes on the ledge in back of the sinks.

Rolling up his sleeves, Collier donned the long rubber gloves and plunged his hand into the wash water, unprepared for the water's near-scalding heat.

"Judaspriest!" he gasped, pulling back his hand in pain. "This water's too freakin' hot."

"You'll get used to it soon enough," a nearby sergeant laughed. "Now, get to work. We start feeding the troops in a few minutes, and you're already way behind."

"You're crazy if you think you can order me to burn my hands. Here, test this and you'll see," Collier stood his ground.

The sergeant gave him a look and plunged his arm into the water up to his elbow.

"If anything, it should be a lot hotter to cut the grease, but I'll leave it this way until you get used to it. Now quit stalling and get to work." Dismissing his complaint, the sergeant snorted and walked away.

Reluctantly, Collier placed the pan the sergeant had scraped for demonstration into the water and started in to scrub. To his surprise, his hands and forearms quickly adjusted to the extreme temperature of the water. When he finished scrubbing the large vessel, he dunked it in the sink with the greenish rinse water where a fellow KP was waiting to pull it out and put it on a waiting cart. Taking great pains to get the utensils sparkling clean, in no time at all Collier had the drying cart full and it was being wheeled back toward the kitchen to the waiting cooks.

"Wait up!" Collier was about halfway through filling up a second cart when the sergeant wheeled the first cart back in.

"What's the matter?" Collier asked, wondering what the problem was.

"Check inside these freaking pots! You have to get them clean," the sergeant said, his voice dripping with disgust.

Collier took the pot and held it under the light. As hard as he tried he couldn't find a speck of food; it looked just fine to him.

"I don't understand—it looks okay to me." He handed it back to the sergeant, completely at a loss.

"Take off those gloves and run your finger around inside this rim. You're not getting out the grease."

Removing his gloves, Collier ran his fingers around the inside rim. The pot seemed fine to him.

"You've got to keep the freaking water hot." The sergeant began refilling the tub with steaming water. He nodded to the cart with the freshly-scrubbed pots. "You've got to scrub these out again. Get cracking now. We're running way behind."

Unable to feel any grease inside the pot, Collier turned back to the sink and started scrubbing again.

When he had scrubbed all the cooking vessels again, he signaled a cook who wheeled the cart back into the busy kitchen.

For the next few minutes, Collier held his breath as he set back to work. Now that his hands and forearms had grown somewhat inured to the superheated water, he was more careful to keep the water scalding hot. His throat was almost too raw to swallow now, and his chest rattled with congestion when he breathed. After about an hour, he located the bottle of aspirin and chewed several tablets, trying to ease the sandpaper feel of his throat. Slipping outside the kitchen door at intervals, he continued to spit up great globs of pus. In his weakened state, he had moved beyond exhaustion and had become an automaton. To his great relief, no more pots and pans came back. The morning hours drug slowly by.

Then, as they were just finishing with utensils from the breakfast serving, the soiled pots and pans from the noon mess started rolling in.

"Okay, take a load off. There's coffee and cake out in the mess hall." When he finished the last pot and pan from the midday meal, he was finally allowed to take a break.

"I'd just as soon skip the refreshments. I've got an awful cold and would like to go on back to the barracks and sack out for awhile," Collier told the new shift cook.

"Too bad, Mac, there's no time for that. My crew's already working to fix the evening meal." The white-hatted cook shook his head.

Collier was rendered speechless when he realized he wasn't being relieved.

The time passed as a blur of pots and pans, and it was almost eleven and pitch black outside when he was finally allowed to return to the barracks.

Wringing wet with sweat, aching from every joint and shaking violently, teeth chattering from the jog back in the icy rain, he gave his poncho a couple of shakes and hung up his filthy fatigues to dry. He considered going down the line to check with Bo and Doyle, but everyone seemed to be sound asleep; besides, he hardly had enough energy left to crawl into bed. Shivering now almost out of control he slipped into long johns and his only remaining set of fatigues. Then, pulling on his last pair of socks, he shrouded himself in a blanket and his heavy overcoat and dropped like a zombie onto the bed. All night long, Collier thought he would shake himself apart, lapsing back and forth, in and out of feverish dreams.

"Rise and shine, Mac. You lucky devil, you got the duty again. They must like you up at the big mess hall on the hill." It seemed to Collier he had hardly slept before the same PFC who had roused him the morning before was shaking him awake again.

"Look, man, you're going to have to pick on someone else. I'm lying in a pool of my own sweat from fever—I can't take another day up there," Collier groaned, covering up his head.

"Sorry, Mac. I don't make the list. You'll have to tell them yourself. Now rise and shine."

Before the PFC had moved two bunks down, Collier dozed off again.

"Goddammit, Mac, wake the fuck up. Bring your poncho. It's still pouring cats and dogs out there," the PFC growled, turning back to find that Collier hadn't moved.

"Look, man, I'm telling you, I'm sick. I can't do that again," Collier protested weakly.

"You're not in Kansas anymore, Mac. If you're not on the street inside ten minutes, the next light to shine on your face will be the MPs."

Fully awake now, Collier felt so rotten he momentarily considered waiting and taking his chances with the MPs. But, thoughtfully considering how refusing an order would look on the record of a candidate for OCS, he rolled off the bunk and quickly changed back into his stinking, still sweat-soaked, fatigues from the day before.

Shivering from head to toe, Collier shrugged into the heavy overcoat, retrieved his poncho from the foot of his bunk and headed for the latrine. Outside, his chest rattling with congestion, he hawked up what seemed like never-ending globs of thick phlegm. Then just like the previous morning, he located the little Bayer vial in his overcoat pocket, shook out three pills and took them with water from the faucet.

"About time, Mac. We're about to fucking drown out here," the unhappy PFC snarled when he saw Collier coming. Looking carefully around the assembled group, Collier couldn't find a single familiar face among the other poor bastards waiting in the driving rain.

"How come I'm the only one who has to go again?" he confronted the PFC when he realized he was the only man who had been in yesterday's detail.

"Everybody else is shipping out today. You're the only holdover of the bunch."

"How about Bohon and Pogue? You know where they're headed?" Collier asked.

"Bohon's headed for Oklahoma, I think. Pogue's leaving too. I ain't sure where, but it ain't Oklahoma. I'm sick'n'tired of this friggin' rain. C'mon now...let's double time." The PFC turned and broke into a trot.

Inside the steamy consolidated mess, they were joined by a couple dozen other bedraggled recruits as they replaced a group just coming off a long night of KP. Passing through the line, Collier filled his tray again, but now he ached so bad and felt so weak he only picked at his food.

"Soon as you're done, Ramsay, I want you back in the kitchen on pots and pans again." He looked up to see the familiar sergeant standing there.

"Look, Sir, I don't think I can do this again. I'm still coughing up gunk by the cupful. This crud is going to put me in the hospital with pneumonia if I don't get some rest," Collier pleaded. "Put your hand on my forehead. Any moron can tell I'm running a fever."

"Listen, Mac, you don't address NCOs as 'Sir,' and you best be careful who you're calling a moron. Now, finish your coffee and get your goldbricking ass back there. It was the Captain in charge of this here kitchen who told me to see if you were still here, so I could get you back on pots and pans. When he come by yesterday afternoon, he was real taken with how you rid them utensils of the grease."

"When does this captain come back around? If *you* won't let me go on sick call, maybe I can talk to him."

"Listen, Mac, don't be questioning my authority here. Do you want me to put you outside in the goddamn rain hosing out garbage cans? If I catch you whining to anyone else in this kitchen—or anywhere on this post—your sorry ass is in a sling." The sergeant turned on his heel and strode away without so much as another look.

"I think I heard somewhere the Army couldn't put you on KP more than two days a week. If you were on KP yesterday, then you're okay after today—until you get to Basic anyway," one of the other recruits sitting at the table remarked.

Doubting whether the recruit knew what he was talking about, Collier hung his coat and poncho on the hook by the back door, rolled up his sleeves and went to work.

It was after 2300 when Collier bundled into his overcoat, pulled his poncho over his head and slogged numbly back to the darkened barracks in the driving rain.

"*Now I lay me down to sleep, I pray the Lord my soul to keep. If I should die before I wake, I pray the Lord my soul to take...*" Collier began the only prayer he had ever learned before he paused, embarrassed by the dishonesty of his childish supplications. Then he started over. *"Hey, God, remember me? I know I haven't talked to you in awhile, but I'm sick and I'm scared. I guess I deserve this wake-up call for all the rotten things I've done. I know I've been unfaithful in my marriage, and I promise I won't ever...well at least, I promise I'll try not to ever. I am honestly sorry for weakness...my downright utter sorriness, God; I really don't want to be such a bad person. Please don't let me die like this...sick and alone. Please bless my brother Jim and take good care of him flying those airplanes...and bless my father and mother and Grandma Ramsay and Grandma Boyd and Aunt Blanche. Please bless everybody, God; we don't have a blessed clue what any of us are doing down here. And, oh yes, God, please bless Emma. But please, above all, God, get me off this round-robin KP duty before I die. In Jesus' name, Amen."* Collier couldn't remember the last time he had said his prayers. Why pray to a God you didn't believe in? But desperate times called for desperate measures and what was the harm. *"Please, God, forgive me for my miserable doubts, God; but, you made me weak like this...you should know what an utterly rotten specimen of manhood I really am."*

"Rise and shine, Mac. You're Lucky Pierre again." Collier blinked at the light in his eyes, hoping he was in a feverish delirium.

"Go 'way," he groaned. "They told me I'd served my time."

"Look, Mac, I'm not going to have this goddamn argument again. You're on the list, so get your ass in gear. And, by the way, bring your poncho. There ain't no signs of a let-up in this fucking monsoon."

"I'm telling you there's been a mistake. I was told that they can't make you serve more than two days KP in a week."

"Huh! I don't know who told you shit like that, but I promise you, here at Meade, we never heard of any pussy regulation like that."

"Just ask the mess sergeant when you get back. He'll bear me out." Collier groaned and turned over, pulling the blankets back over his head.

"Look, Mac, you got about ten minutes. Either get your lazy ass in gear or you can tell it to the MPs when they come to take you to the freaking stockade." He wheeled and disappeared into the dark, headed for the door.

Lying there considering his options, Collier finally resolved to plead his case with the mess sergeant. Still shivering from head to toe, he got up and headed for the latrine.

"Two-day limit on KP? Never heard of such a thing." The mess sergeant scowled when Collier confronted him as soon as he entered the Consolidated Mess.

"Look...put your hand on my forehead. I'm burning up with fever...I'm in no shape to work. I need to be in bed," Collier pleaded.

"Get off it, Mac. You don't know when you're well off. Better shut up and get back there to those pots and pans. If you don't quit making trouble, you're going to wind up outside on the back of an open two-and-a-half-ton truck in this shitty weather picking up garbage cans."

Despairing if he would last another hour—much less another day working with his lungs filled with pus and his body burning up with fever—Collier watched the apathetic sergeant go before he turned and shuffled disconsolately back to his steamy prison with the pots and pans.

Just like the driving rain—sometimes mixed with spitting snow and sleet—Collier's Dantesque phantasmagoria in the mess hall continued unabated over the next seven days. Each morning trapped in a nightmare of feverish delirium, Collier was roused off his sick bed to return to the seemingly boundless pile of crusty pots and pans.

At mid-morning on the tenth or eleventh day trapped in this surrealistic hell, he was outside in the rain clutching his poncho over his head, coughing up what seemed to be a never-ending reservoir of yellow-green mucous, when he was suddenly confronted by an officer wearing silver eagles on his epaulets.

"I'm Colonel McKinney. Is your name Ramsay, soldier?" the full-colonel asked.

"Yessir, I'm Collier Ramsay," Collier answered, wondering what was coming next.

"How many days have they had you here in this kitchen doing this, Private?" the colonel asked. The worried-looking, white-aproned assistant to the mess sergeant had joined him now.

"I'm not sure, Colonel McKinney. I've done it every day since the day after I got here." Collier paused to gather his wits, trying to remember the date of his arrival. "What's today, Sir? I've had KP since the fourth or the fifth, I'm pretty sure."

"Today is the fifteenth of January," the officer said. Giving Collier a closer look, he removed his dress gloves and pressed his right hand to Collier's forehead.

"This man is burning up." Turning to the mess NCO with disbelief, he asked, "You mean to say you've had this man here in this kitchen for eleven straight days without a break?"

"You'll have to ask the sergeant, but he's been here every day I have, Colonel," the assistant cook replied, adding lamely, "This was my weekend off."

"Ramsay, my car and driver are outside the main entrance. Get your coat and wait there for me in the car. I'll be right along."

Obediently, Collier got his coat and poncho and found a late-model, olive-drab Chevy sedan parked at the curb with the motor running.

For a while after that, time floated by like a dream. Collier vaguely remembered being driven to a building with a sign reading Post Dispensary No. 1 where the solicitous colonel escorted him through the back door and a captain in a white clinic coat took Collier's temperature, listened to his lungs and thumped his knuckles on his chest and back.

"Lower those filthy fatigue pants and bend over," the doctor ordered and stood aside while a corpsman stuck a large needle in his butt. He had no trouble remembering that because it hurt like hell.

"Take these—the directions are on the labels," the captain instructed, handing him a bottle of cherry-colored expectorant, a bottle of large white tablets marked Penicillin-G, and a bottle of APC tablets. The Army doctor wrote something on a prescription pad and handed it to him. "Don't lose this. First thing tomorrow morning, come back here and give it to the NCO in charge. He'll give you another shot of penicillin."

"I'm new on post and don't have a clue where I am. The only place I know how to find is Consolidated Mess Number One," Collier protested weakly.

"Don't worry, Ramsay. I'll send a driver...we'll see to it you get back here alright," Colonel McKinney interjected, taking him gently by the elbow. "Come on now, let's get you to bed."

Back at the barracks, the colonel and his driver accompanied Collier to his bunk, standing by while he stripped off the greasy, food-encrusted fatigues and shucked out of his filthy underwear. Reaching for what he thought were Collier's clean set of fatigues hanging behind his bunk, he discovered those were also soiled from Collier's marathon KP duty.

"Adams, take these and burn them," Colonel McKinney instructed the driver as he handed Collier a blanket to cover his nakedness.

"You'll have another set of fatigues before the sun goes down," the colonel assured him as he turned to leave. "Corporal Adams will pick you up around nine in the morning and take you back to the dispensary for your second shot. Do you need help getting to the showers?"

"No, thank you, Sir," Collier chattered, still shivering from the fever. "but if it's all the same to you, I think I'll sleep awhile first," he said, virtually collapsing onto the bunk, quickly covering himself with the pile of blankets he had borrowed from nearby beds.

"Alright, soldier. Take all the time you need to get well. When you're feeling fit enough, I need to talk to you before anyone else messes with your head. Just tell the NCO in the orderly room to contact Colonel McKinney at the Post IG. I've left explicit orders with Captain Sidwell, the company CO."

"Thank you, Sir. I think I'll be okay in a day or so if I can just get some sleep," Collier smiled and closed his eyes.

"Remember, just take your time. If anyone bothers you, tell them to see me. I promise there'll be hell to pay." The colonel reassured him and finally left.

Just as the colonel promised, the driver returned sometime that afternoon with two sets of brand new fatigues and new underwear. Sometime later on, Collier made it to the shower and slipped back in his bed, still much the worse for wear. After a rather restless night, the following morning, he recalled being taken back to the Dispensary and given another penicillin shot. Returned to the barracks by the colonel's driver, again he slept the clock around.

Sometime in the afternoon the day following his second penicillin shot, Collier draped his overcoat around his shoulders against the rain and chill and went to the latrine and took another long hot shower. Toweling off, he was relieved to find the congestion in his chest was better, but both cheeks of his ass hurt like hell.

Back inside the barracks to dress, he located the two brand-new sets of fatigues and clean underwear tucked neatly inside his duffel bag.

On the pillow of his bunk, he found a note:
Ramsay—As soon as you're back on your feet, report to the orderly room.
S/Sgt. Jacobs.

Screw that for now, Collier mused half-aloud as he headed out, opting to get some chow and another night's rest before he took on the Army again. The next morning when he awoke, his legs were still a bit wobbly, but he felt much better. Outside, a weak sun was trying to peek through the low-hanging clouds. After shaving and a shower, he reported to the orderly room.

"Ah, Ramsay, the Captain was just wondering when you'd decide to quit fucking off." Glancing up from an old-fashioned typewriter, the pimply-faced duty corporal sneered when Collier, dressed in his new fatigues, walked into the orderly room shortly after nine.

"Colonel McKinney said to give him a call when I was feeling better," Collier said, ignoring the corporal's insolence.

"Good morning, Ramsay. I'm Captain Sidwell—glad to see you're finally up and around." Collier looked up to see an overweight officer with a chest full of ribbons standing in the doorway behind the orderly's desk. "I'll call Colonel McKinney right away and tell him you're back to duty, but first let's have a little chat."

"Begging your pardon, Captain, but Colonel McKinney gave me instruction not to talk to anyone before he talked to me again. I think he'd appreciate it if you called him right away," Collier stood his ground.

"Look, Ramsay, I said I'd call McKinney. Now come on in here and sit down before I have you up for insubordination."

"I can just stay out here until the colonel arrives, Sir, if you don't mind."

"I do mind, Ramsay. Now quit being so suspicious and come on inside and sit right there." He stood aside and ushered Collier through the door, indicating a chair in front of his desk. "Can I have the corporal bring you a cup of coffee?"

"No, thank you, Sir" Collier said as he hesitantly took a seat.

"Alright, now." The captain took a seat behind his desk and leaned forward with a smile. "Are you feeling fit enough for duty then?"

"I'm sorry, Sir, before this goes any further, first call Colonel McKinney at the Post IG."

"What the devil's the matter with you? I just asked a simple question. You've had a rough few weeks. I'm only concerned about your health."

"I'm sorry, Sir. I'm just following the Colonel's orders. He said not to let anyone mess with my head before I reported to him. The Colonel was very clear about that."

"McKinney said he didn't want anyone messing with your head?"

"Those were his very words, Sir." Collier looked him straight in the eye. "I'd be grateful if you called him now."

"Well, sure...I understand. Get Colonel McKinney at the Post IG," Sidwell buzzed the corporal on the intercom, giving Collier a look of new respect. "You sure you won't have some coffee? This may take awhile."

"I'm sorry, Sir. I'm still not feeling up to snuff. I think it would be better if I went back to the barracks and lay back down until the Colonel gets here." Collier stood up and walked back out into the orderly room.

"Look, Ramsay, I don't know what you think you're up to. Just come back inside until I hear from McKinney. You're on thin ice with me." Sidwell was obviously nervous, trying his best to be intimidating.

"I'm sorry, Sir. This is nothing personal. I'm just following Colonel McKinney's orders. As soon as the orderly gets the colonel on the phone, you can take it up with him."

"You really are trying to be a smartass, aren't you, Ramsay? You think you've got my tail in a crack on this?"

"No, Sir, I don't know what you mean."

The flustered officer glared at him for a moment. Then he abruptly turned and strode back inside his office and closed the door.

Wondering what was going on, Collier stood there momentarily puzzled before he addressed the corporal again.

"Did I upset the captain? I don't understand."

"You might say the captain is not a happy man and a lot of his problems are all because of you," the corporal said without looking up from the typewriter.

"Because of me? What did I ever do to him?"

"Well...let's just say he should have intervened when they kept putting you on the KP roster. The Army has limits to how long an enlisted man can be made to perform certain extra duties—eleven days in a row on KP comes under the heading of cruel and unusual, I assure you. And this ain't the only time he's run afoul of the IG."

"What's IG stand for anyway?" Collier asked, feeling completely in the dark.

"You're kidding me, right?" the corporal said in disbelief. "You really don't know what a hornet's nest you've stirred up?"

"No, what hornet's nest and what's the IG?" he persisted, hating to be kept in the dark.

"IG is the Inspector General. Sort of the Army's way of making sure we all obey our own regulations. Keep up standards—play by the rules."

"I still don't understand. Who got this Inspector General office involved in my KP?"

"I assumed you did. You're telling me you don't know what the fuss is all about?"

"I really don't have a clue."

"Hmm-m, that's very interesting. Sounds to me like somebody has a real hard-on for Captain Sidwell. Or do you think the beef is with the mess sergeant up at Consolidated Mess Number One?"

Standing there, Collier thought he heard a jeep pull up outside. In a moment, a sergeant came through the door.

"McKinney at IG sent me," the IG Sergeant addressed the orderly. "We need to know if Ramsay is on shipping orders yet."

"So far, none today," the corporal said.

"Good." Nodding to the corporal, the IG Sergeant turned back to Collier.

"I take it you're Ramsay," he said. "Colonel McKinney wants you to come with me."

"You'll have to wait until I tell Captain Sidwell you're here," the corporal said and got up and started for the captain's door.

"Make it snappy! I'm running late," the sergeant called to the corporal's back.

"Captain Sidwell, the IG's here to pick up Ramsay. Do you need to have a word with him?" The corporal knocked perfunctorily and leaned inside the door.

The captain appeared in the doorway and waved his hand, "Take him, Sergeant. You're welcome to him."

"Colonel McKinney would like you to call him at the IG office, Sir—he said at your earliest convenience, Sir." The sergeant saluted smartly.

"Without delay, Sergeant, without delay," Sidwell growled as he returned the salute.

"First thing, we have to get you back to the Dispensary Number One to get an update on your health." Outside, the sergeant ushered him to the jeep, while the driver held the door for them to get inside.

At the dispensary, they were escorted back to the medical officer without delay.

"Okay, GI, you can put your shirt back on." When the physician had finished taking Collier's temperature and listening to his breath sounds with the stethoscope, he gave him another shot of penicillin and assured him he was going to live. In less than fifteen minutes, they were back in the jeep heading down the street.

"I'm dropping you at Post Service Club Number One. They have magazines, some books, some ping-pong tables and a snack bar there. Just make yourself at home. You're supposed to be on the clean-up detail, but I'll tell the NCO to leave you alone. Hardly anyone comes there until after evening chow anyway. Someone will pick you up and take you back to the barracks in time for evening mess," the sergeant told him as they pulled up to a large building.

"Look, I'm not sure what's going on. Why is the IG going to all this trouble for me?" Collier asked, still confused by the sudden attention.

"The IG stands for the office of the Army Inspector General. It's our duty to oversee the rights of individual soldiers—to see that you are being treated fairly. In your case, eleven consecutive days of KP constituted a major breach of authority. This was aggravated by your borderline pneumonia and the terrible weather conditions, which I might add, were obvious to all responsible. This is not the first time that raw recruits have been abused by being given excessive extra duty while waiting to be shipped out of here. We are trying to put a stop to this reprehensible practice and make sure it never happens again," the helpful IG sergeant explained.

Escorting him into the Service Club, the IG sergeant introduced him to the duty NCO and turned to leave. "Now, enjoy your day here. You'll be shipping out soon enough—relax and get some rest. I'll send someone back for you late this afternoon in time to make evening mess."

After the sergeant left, the duty NCO took Collier up on the balcony overlooking the gymnasium-sized main room which was arranged with tables and chairs, large ashtrays, checkers and chessboards, and an array of leather furniture. Chrome sand urns stood like sentinels on the floor beside every chair. Underneath the balcony overhang near the center of the main room, were a couple of ping-pong tables and a regulation pool table—balls neatly racked. Paddles and cue sticks were on the wall. From strategically-placed loudspeakers in the rafters, Jo Stafford sweetly sang, "...*see the pyramids along the Nile.*"

At the far end of the snack bar, two enlisted men were busy replenishing the soft drink boxes and setting up a fresh array of ready-packaged sandwiches and chips and an assortment of other snack food. On the wall behind the counter was the familiar, omnipresent, display of major brands of cigarettes. Off in one corner of the upper gallery, the young NCO led him to a cozy nook with a small grouping of furniture including an overstuffed leather chaise lounge. A copy of the *Washington Post* was folded neatly on an end table beside the chaise with a homey-looking floor lamp conveniently at hand.

"In case you're wondering, that *is* today's paper. Today's *Baltimore Sun* is already in the lounge downstairs. *The New York Times* and *The Wall Street Journal* will all be delivered within the hour. Just make yourself right at home. Nobody will bother you up here. The sergeant said to give you anything you like from the snack bar down there—that includes a pack of smokes if you need 'em. Anything you want is to be on the house," the affable PFC said and gave him a curious look.

Collier nodded, picked up the *Post* and idly checked the date. Thursday, January 18.

His senses reeled with shock. Was it possible he had been at Meade fifteen days?

"Is there a pay phone?" Collier asked. He needed to call Emma and his parents to let them know he was okay. They would be half-crazy with worry. Neither had heard a word from him in two whole weeks.

"There are three booths inside the front door. See down there just past the snack bar?" the PFC pointed over the balcony rail. "Do you need some change?"

"No. Thanks, anyway, I have change. I plan to call collect," he told the PFC. "Now, if it's okay with you, for the time being, I think I'll just sit here and catch up on the outside world."

"Sure...just ask if you need anything. I'll be around."

Watching the PFC disappear down the stairs, Collier sat on the chaise and turned on the reading lamp. Putting his feet up, he picked up the paper again, scooted around to make himself comfortable and leaned back to catch up on the news.

In practically no time at all, he was fast asleep.

"I hate to wake you. The sergeant said you'd been sick, but I wanted to make sure you're okay. It's almost thirteen-hundred hours. I thought you might want to get a bite of lunch." The PFC was standing there looking anxiously down at him.

"I guess I am still a little peaked," Collier stretched and yawned. He picked up the paper from where it had fallen across his lap and put it back together. "Lunch sounds good, but I think I better go find a phone and call home before I do anything else."

"Of course we'll accept the call," Emma's mother said when the operator told her the party was calling collect. When the operator put him through, she said, "Collier we've been worried sick. But, I hate to tell you Emma's already left for work."

"Well, I'm sorry I missed her. I can't call collect at the VA, but you can just tell her I'm still at Fort Meade—they haven't decided where they're sending me for Basic yet. Please get word to my folks. They'd never believe it—I've been washing pots and pans," he said, reassuring her he was all right but omitting any mention of how sick he'd been. "I feel sure I'll be shipping out of here any day. I'll call again as soon as I find out where they're sending me."

After he'd hung up the phone, Collier got a cup of coffee and a small package of Fig Newtons from the snack bar and carried them back upstairs. Wolfing down the cookies, he finished his coffee and browsed a nearby shelf of books. He was pleasantly surprised to find a dog-eared copy of Henry Miller's *Tropic of Cancer* which he had read when he was commuting by train home from Bluefield College. Like D.H. Lawrence's *Lady Chatterly's Lover*, Collier had found Henry Miller's coarse, plain-spoken prose liberating.

"You're looking better, I see. I heartily approve of your reading tastes." Shortly before 1700, Collier looked up to see IG Colonel McKinney emerging at the top of the stairs.

"I'm feeling much better, thanks." Sheepishly, he put Henry Miller back on the shelf.

"I was on my way home, anyway. I live off post in Laurel," the colonel shrugged. "Have you read *Tropic of Capricorn*?" In McKinney's new, dark-blue Buick convertible, they discussed Henry Miller until the Colonel dropped him off at Consolidated Mess No. 1. "You'll be going back to the Service Club tomorrow...one of my drivers will pick you up around oh-nine-hundred. Now, try to get a good night's rest."

Waking only twice to hack up purulence from his lungs, Collier rested fairly well. True to the colonel's word, Friday morning the IG driver arrived promptly at 0900 and drove him to the Service Club.

"The night crew scrubbed and waxed the floor down here last night after closing. Did you ever operate a rotary buffer?" the duty PFC asked as soon as he walked inside.

"No, but I guess I'm about to learn," Collier answered with an offhand shrug.

"I guess you're right...that is, if you think you're up to it. It's really not very hard," the PFC inquired apologetically.

"I'm fine...I really am." Collier smiled. "Let's go to work." After he got the hang of it, Collier found buffing the floor to be kind of fun. By 1100 hours, the dark-brown and tan checkered vinyl surface had a mirror shine.

"Not bad, for a rookie. Now get on back upstairs and read your dirty book." The PFC seemed well-pleased.

Reading and dozing and taking his pills, the day passed lazily by until 1650 hours when, to Collier's pleasant surprise, Colonel McKinney showed up to give him a lift again.

"I've got some news for you. You're on orders to leave tomorrow morning," the colonel confided as soon as they were in the car and underway.

"Oh? Where're they're sending me?" Collier held his breath, almost afraid to hear the news. He was far from feeling well again.

"Well, this is not for publication, but..." the Colonel hesitated, drawing in a breath before he continued, "...you're going to Camp Chaffee, Arkansas...but don't be alarmed. I doubt Chaffee's your final destination. Chaffee's usually just a sort of collecting and redistribution center."

"Where's this Chaffee? I never heard of it." From the Colonel's hesitant tone, Collier had an uneasy feeling he was being given the short end of the stick again.

"Chaffee's just outside Fort Smith—a small city just across the Arkansas River on the Oklahoma border."

"I'm not too sure I like the sound of that. My luck hasn't been running so good of late."

"Don't jump to conclusions. You're targeted for OCS. Chaffee's probably just a temporary thing. The Army's likely pooling you with a group to be sent somewhere else."

"I certainly hope you're right." Collier tried to smile.

"I'm pleased to have met you, Ramsay." When they reached his barracks, the colonel leaned across and offered his hand. "Take my advice and pack your gear tonight. They'll probably roust you out pretty early tomorrow. It may get very hectic in the morning."

"Thanks for everything, Colonel, I hope we meet again." Collier shook the colonel's hand and got out.

"The pleasure was mine, I assure you. I hope the next time we meet you're wearing gold lieutenant's bars. Take good care. I wish you the best of luck."

"Thanks. I need all the luck I can get." Collier smiled, then stood aside and watched the car until it turned the corner and was quickly out of sight.

When he was roused the following morning at 0430 hours, Collier was thankful he had taken the Colonel's advice and packed his gear the night before.

He had spent a miserable night, waking several times to rid his lungs of the awful crud. At exactly 0600, he was shivering in the pitch-black chill among a group of some thirty-odd recruits being loaded onto a commercial bus. Unable to get the slightest clue about their destination from the sergeant barking orders, the busload of disgruntled rookies was heading out of the main gate into the great unknown. Not wishing to compromise Colonel McKinney's confidence—and even more afraid that the information might somehow be in error—Collier kept their destination to himself, focusing on finding a good seat.

Collier had hardly begun to deal with the idea of a two- or three-day bus trip when it became light enough to see that they were traveling on Route 1 in a northerly direction. Within a half-hour, they passed a sign proclaiming "Welcome to Baltimore Friendship Airport." Ignoring a series of signs pointing to the main passenger terminal, the driver made his way around a group of nondescript hangars paralleling the main runway strips, finally passing through an open gate in a chain-link fence, stopping directly on the tarmac beside a taxiway.

"Okay, everybody off the bus. Smoke if you've got 'em. Looks like we're going to have a little wait," the burly sergeant barked, extracting a bag of Beech Nut chewing tobacco from the pocket of his heavy overcoat. "Stay close, now, and don't get separated from your gear. As soon as our plane gets here, we'll load right up and get you underway."

Suddenly confronted with the chilling idea of being marched into some Air Force transport like sheep to the slaughter and flown all the way to Arkansas set Collier's nerves on edge. His only previous experience with flying had been several years before when Charley Webber, his college roommate, had paid his fare for an impromptu weekend back home when they were still in college in Richmond. Aboard a recycled Piedmont Airlines WWII DC-3 at minimum altitude over the mountains between Lynchburg and Roanoke, Collier's maiden flight had been rather noisy and harrowing. That white-knuckle introduction to flying really hadn't invested Collier with a lot of confidence in commercial air travel. Recalling he had read in *The Roanoke Times* barely two weeks ago—just the day before he boarded the train for Fort Meade—that twenty-eight West Pointers had been killed when an Air Force transport slammed into an Arizona mountainside, was doing nothing to improve his confidence now.

And, as if his delicate emotional state wasn't bad enough, standing on the cracked tarmac outside a collection of disreputable-looking hangars with the temperature just a few degrees above freezing watching the busy parade of mostly commercial airplanes land and take off, the once-promising, rosy eastern horizon was gradually beginning to cloud over with an ominous bank of low-lying stratus clouds.

To further deepen his depressed state of mind, Collier had a violent coughing spell. Compounding this wretchedness, his throat was getting scratchy, too. Opening his duffel and rummaging through his shaving kit, Collier located the bottles of APC and Penicillin-G.

"I'm Private Ramsay, Sergeant. Can I go into that hangar there and see if I can find a faucet or a water fountain? I need water to take these prescription pills." Waving the hand holding the medicine vials, Collier pointed to the nearby corrugated-metal hangar bearing the rust-blemished legend, *Flying Tiger Line.*

"Forget it, Mac. You'll have to wait." Loading his jaws with chewing tobacco, the sergeant glared at him as if he'd asked permission to deflower his twelve-year-old daughter.

"But, Sarge, these are an Army prescription. I'm just getting over borderline pneumonia. I need to..." Collier began but the sergeant raised his beefy hand and cut him short.

"It's Sergeant, not Sarge! And forget it, Mac. If I let you wander off, in five minutes flat, I'd have thirty other wimps whining to go use the freaking water fountain." The sergeant crossed his arms across his chest as he spit a cloud of tobacco juice into the wind.

"But, Sergeant..." Collier protested, using the sleeve of his OD jacket to avoid the fine mist of brownish spit drifting back across his face.

"What part of 'no' don't you understand, Mac? You'll have to wait. They'll have something for you to drink on the plane."

"How much longer will we have to wait?" Collier asked, really aggravated now.

"Your guess is as good as mine. That goddamn airplane should have been here when we got here," the sergeant growled. "It's already about two hours late."

"Can I at least get my dress overcoat? I'm starting to get a chill." Their orders had specified Class A uniforms with the skimpy Eisenhower jackets for the trip.

"No. Everyone has to wear the specified uniform. An Army overcoat on a crowded airplane would be like tits on a boar hog. You won't need it where you're going, anyway."

"And just where is that?" Collier asked, hoping McKinney was wrong and he didn't have to fly halfway across the country to Arkansas.

"That's for me to know and you to find out. Now leave me the fuck alone," the sergeant snapped and turned his back, resuming his conversation with the driver.

Lugging his duffel back to rejoin the group, Collier's hands were growing numb and he had to shuffle from one foot to the other in his low-cut dress shoes, trying to maintain some feeling in his feet. Try as he might, Collier was helpless not to shiver in the damp cold.

"Nice guy—that sergeant." A nearby recruit overheard the exchange. "Say, man, you look like you're about to shake apart."

"Yeah, I'm getting over pneumonia." Collier nodded, fighting back a wracking cough.

After at least an hour shivering in the freezing, misty cold debating whether or not to disobey the sergeant, out of the corner of his eye, Collier's attention was diverted by a speck approaching low on the eastern horizon. Now, as the speck grew larger, unless his eyes deceived him, the military aircraft was trailing a plume of pale blue smoke from the outboard engine on the starboard wing. Before he could blink his eyes, Collier's attention was drawn to a tiny burst of flame licking the engine cowling of the approaching plane.

"Look out there at that B-17. It's trying to land with a starboard engine on fire," Collier shouted, pointing at the approaching plane. Almost at once, the air was split by the screaming sirens of a pair of fire trucks and a crash ambulance as they headed for what seemed destined to be a crash. To make matters even worse, it looked to Collier as if the lumbering old warbird was heading straight for where they stood.

Collier stood fast, watching fascinated as one of the fire trucks had already begun foaming the runway in the path of the rapidly descending plane. Riveted with morbid fascination, Collier breathed a sigh of relief as the doors under the wings swung open and the giant wheels slowly dropped securely into place. As if on cue, the foaming crew jumped back on the truck, heading hell-for-leather back down the strip. Keeping apace alongside the crippled B-17, they were already directing foam on the burning engine before the ancient bomber finally came to a halt, killing its engines with a grinding whine. The flames quickly winked out under the deluge of foam; within minutes a small tow tractor had hooked a cable to the bomber and—followed by one of the fire engines—towed the disabled airplane around a nearby hangar.

"Hey, look at this old war horse coming here," a nearby recruit called out, pointing to a twin-engine cargo plane putt-putting its way slowly toward them. The plane had apparently landed while they were preoccupied with the excitement.

"Okay, now, you men get your gear and form a single file up here." The tobacco-chewing sergeant had taken a position on the tarmac near where the plane finally stopped and killed its engines. In a less time than it took to tell about it, one of the pilots had opened the door and the ground crew wheeled over a ramp of boarding steps. Ramp securely in place, they pushed out a baggage cart and began collecting duffels from the men at the head of the line.

"Alright, listen up, everybody. Put your duffel bags on the cart as you board the airplane. Let's get a move on now. We're late enough already," the sergeant barked as he finally stepped aside to let the first man climb the ramp to the plane. Wasting no time, the stewardess accepted the roster from the sergeant and put it on her clipboard. As the men climbed the steps, she took a head count, checking off their names. When Collier neared the boarding steps, it gave him little comfort to see that here and there a rivet holding the aluminum skin was either missing or about to pop out of place.

"Can I have some water to take these pills?" Next to last in line, a very apprehensive Collier asked the stewardess as he finally stepped aboard the airplane.

"As soon as we're all seated, sir," the stewardess promised Collier water to take his pills.

Collier took the last seat on the aisle. He had scarcely made himself comfortable when the stewardess started down the center aisle, asking certain members of the group to exchange seats.

"We're going to have to move you, sir. Please come with me," the stewardess said when she reached his seat.

Following her back up toward the center of the plane, Collier took the seat she indicated on the aisle as his new seatmate gave him a distracted glance, settling deeper in the window seat.

"Have you forgotten my water, Ma'am? I really need to take these pills," Collier reminded her as he was settling in his new seat.

"If you'll just give me a minute, I'll be with you right away, sir." She nodded and followed the pilot back up the aisle to the cockpit door.

"Welcome to Flying Tiger Line—we're proud to have you aboard our flight. Please fasten your seatbelts, everyone. They're really pretty simple to use, but if you're having trouble, just raise your hand and I'll come help you out," she instructed as she started moving back down the aisle.

"Okay, now, one final thing," the harried stewardess said, moving back up to the front. "There's some bad weather coming our way and we might run into some bumpy air. In case any of you get airsick and absolutely have to throw up, check the pocket on the seat back in front of you. You'll find a paper bag like this." She held up a small, brown paper bag. "And, if any of you need them, I have some pills for motion sickness which can also help. It would be better to take them now. Before we taxi for takeoff, anybody need a Dramamine?" She held up a bottle of small tablets as a reflexive show of hands appeared throughout the plane, front to back.

"Good—better safe than sorry." The stewardess moved along the aisle, responding to the anxious show of hands.

When the stewardess had finished handing out the Dramamine, she poured Collier a tiny cup of water from a pitcher on a tray. Swallowing his medications, he leaned back and was asleep before the pilot began the takeoff run. It was not until sometime later he was rudely awakened by the impact of his head slamming hard against the back of the seat in front of him. Lightning was flashing all around them, and the booming thunder claps seemed to shake his very bones as the airplane was being tossed about so violently that Collier feared the turbulence might actually rip the wings right off. Looking out the window, they were bouncing through an overcast so impenetrable he could only get an occasional reassurance that the engine was still mounted on the wing. Collier tightened his seatbelt, holding fast to the arms of the seat until his knuckles turned a bluish white. Adding to his discomfort, the sounds of intermittent gagging and groaning reached his ears. Finally, the turbulence eased and the pilot managed to return the war-weary, converted cargo plane to more-or-less stable flight. Exhausted, he soon lapsed into an uneasy sleep.

"Tighten your seatbelts! We'll be landing at the Memphis Naval Air Station in a few minutes. Keep them fastened and remain in your seats. We'll only be on the ground long enough to take on fuel." Looking slightly the worse for wear, the stewardess was standing at his elbow shouting instructions over the engine noise of an airplane in descent.

"After we land, would it be too much trouble to get another cup of water? It's time to take my pills again," Collier asked before she turned to leave.

She nodded, reappearing as if by magic with his cup of water in hand.

"Your seatmate was getting queasy. I moved him closer to the toilet while you were asleep," she nodded at the empty window seat beside him. "Would you mind taking the window and letting me have your seat while we land?"

"No, Ma'am, not at all," he said, quickly unbuckling and slipping into the window seat.

"Nice landing," he breathed appreciatively, turning to the stewardess with some relief. She'd barely had time to buckle in before he felt the wheels smoothly kiss the runway.

"Captain Haywood flew these old birds across the Hump. They don't get much better than our Captain Tom." She smiled and winked as she undid her seatbelt and slipped out into the aisle. "Don't let anyone take my seat—it only takes a few minutes to refuel."

As she had predicted, Collier's watch showed 1952 when the co-pilot climbed back on board with the gas ticket in his hand. Collier was already dozing again when the stewardess slipped back into her seat and the plane lifted smoothly into the overcast. When he awoke again, it was pitch dark and the luminous dial on his watch glowed 2045. Steadily winking at him through the pea soup fog, the soft, red glow of the portside wingtip light told Collier they were flying completely blind. Dozing fitfully, he stirred awake as the familiar engine whine alerted him that they were again descending into the dark unknown.

"Is this Fort Smith?" Collier asked the stewardess in the seat beside him.

"Only a few minutes more. We've just begun our approach. Excuse me for a minute, I guess it's time to get this sorry bunch awake," she said, rising to slip into the aisle again.

When she left, Collier looked out of the window, anxious now to get a glimpse of good old terra firma again. At precisely 2159 hours, the airplane from hell finally broke through the overcast. Swallowing hard, Collier nearly choked when he found himself gazing almost eyeball-to-eyeball directly into a lighted kitchen window at a couple blissfully washing the dinner dishes. The old-fashioned Blue Willow pattern of the dinner plates stood out plain as day, the jut-jawed, rawboned man playfully snapping a dish towel at the woman's plump behind as she tried to dance aside.

Completely oblivious to Collier's considerable consternation at being hurled irrevocably toward the earth, the middle-aged farm couple couldn't possible have been more than fifty yards away. Before his sphincter had a chance to tighten with alarm at the perilous proximity of the farmhouse, there was a loud squeak of rubber hitting the concrete runway as the tired old C-46 touched heavily down and the pilot immediately started to brake. When the plane finally taxied up beside the hangar near the shabby terminal building, Collier grinned broadly at the stewardess and breathed a loud sigh of relief.

"My compliments to good ol' Captain Tom." Collier beamed as he unbuckled his belt and slowly stood and stretched.

Stepping out of the cabin, Collier was greeted by a blast of icy air. Descending the stairs, he trailed the straggling line of troops toward a beat-up Army bus, watching as their duffels were already being offloaded and stacked on of a pair of flat carts. Up ahead, a small detail of soldiers stood waiting to load their gear into the compartments beneath the bus. Almost at once, standing there in the night wind, he began shivering again as his chill quickly returned.

Leaving the Fort Smith airport, the bus was warm. In no time, Collier was deep asleep again. Awakened by the bus slowing to clear the guard shack at Camp Chaffee's main gate, his blissful slumber proved to be short-lived as the congestion in his lungs set him coughing again.

The skies had cleared, and in the bright moonlight, the entire Camp Chaffee landscape had a forbidding, desolate look. Less than a mile inside the gate, the driver turned off the paved main road onto a bare, dirt street leading between a forest of scraggly scrub pine and long rows of deserted barracks. Almost before Collier began to worry about what he had gotten himself into, the driver abruptly pulled to a stop in front of what looked to be a dimly-lit, wooden gymnasium.

"All out and get a move on. We don't want to take all night here. There ain't no heat inside this mausoleum," the unhappy corporal ordered.

Inside, the musty building was dimly lit and reeked of Clorox.

"Everybody form a single line along this here line." A shivering PFC shuffled them into formation as soon as they came through the doors.

"Alright, TEN-SHUN! Now, just listen up and follow orders. We've been waiting around three hours for your sorry asses...ah...for your plane to arrive." A grizzled staff sergeant glanced apologetically at the serious-faced, young captain standing close at hand with a stethoscope around his neck. The captain lowered his head to hide his faint smile.

"Okay, now just do as you're told, and as soon as we're finished here, we'll get you some hot chow and a place to sleep out of this friggin' cold. Now straighten up on this line right here," the sergeant quickly got back to the matter at hand, pointing to the faded sideline marker of a basketball court. "Alright, now, dress right and let's get a little space between you so we can get this over with. No, no, goddamn it. Don't you sad sacks even know *DRESS RIGHT, DRESS?*" the exasperated sergeant shouted in dismay as he stepped in with the corporal and slowly brought a semblance of order to the mass confusion standing in front of him.

"That's close enough, I guess," the disgruntled sergeant said when he finally gave up hope of ever forming a satisfactory military rank without prolonging the agony of being in the icy gym. "Now, loose your belts and drop your pants and underdrawers. You can just leave them around your ankles—you don't have to step all the way out of them."

Collier numbly fumbled with his belt and buttons until he stood shivering naked from the waist down in the sub-freezing cold.

"Turn your head that way and cough," the sergeant said a few minutes later as he rudely cupped Collier's scrotum in his icy palm and his gloved finger found his balls. At least he had taken the courtesy to wear a protective glove.

"Okay, Ramsay, pull your britches up. The captain would like you to step over there." As soon as he had finished checking Collier's private parts, the sergeant pointed to the officer with the stethoscope standing beneath the backboard at the far end of the gym.

"The sergeant said you wanted to see me, Sir?" Collier reported, still fumbling with the buckle on his GI belt.

"Oh, yeah, Ramsay. You can relax. We have orders from the...ah...from Meade to take your temperature, check your throat and listen to your chest. Open wide and let me take a look," the captain instructed and quickly flashed a little penlight down his throat and shoved a thermometer under his tongue. "Now pull up your shirt while I give your lungs a listen."

Unbuttoning his jacket and shirt and tugging them from his pants, Collier stood there dutifully waiting while the doctor put the icy stethoscope on his back and chest.

"Well, your throat is still a little red and your chest is full of gunk, but your temperature is only 100.4—nothing to write home about. Just to be on the safe side, I'm going to order you to remain in the barracks for another day and release you for '*light duty only*' for a couple of days after that," the captain said, writing something on the outside of the brown manila jacket attached to the clipboard in his hand.

"A couple of days after that? Am I staying here for Basic Training?" Collier asked, almost shaking apart again as he finished buttoning up his clothes.

"I really don't have any idea. If you have any signs of a relapse, report to sick call immediately. Now just go sit on that bench over there. I wish you the best of luck."

When the sergeant finished checking the last man, the new arrivals were loaded back onto the bus and driven a short way through a maze of buildings in a series of left- and right-hand turns. *Even if he wanted to go AWOL now, he would never be able to find his way out of here,* Collier mused as the driver finally pulled to a stop in front of a deserted-looking barracks.

"Find yourself a bunk and make it up. When you've finished, the chow hall is right up this street. You can't miss it. It's the one with all the lights. Get some hot chow and a good night's sleep," the corporal said as he herded them off the bus into the empty barracks. One by one, he tossed their duffels in a pile in the center of the room.

Without further delay, Collier found his duffel and pulled it to a bunk near the center of the room away from the door. Separating the mattress cover from the roll of freshly-laundered linen and blankets on his bunk, he got right to work making his bed. When he had finished, he borrowed two extra blankets from an empty bunk back and fell fully clothed onto the bunk and completely covered his head to shield himself from the glare of the bare bulbs filling the room with a garish glow. In no time at all, he had drifted into a dreamless sleep.

In the morning, a corporal rudely shook him awake. "Rise and shine, Mac, this ain't the Waldorf-Astoria. Dress in fatigue uniform, and go get some chow. A truck will pick you up outside at 0700 for work detail."

"Not me, corporal. There's some mistake. The doc said I should stay inside today. I'm recuperating from pneumonia."

"Tell it to the captain. The orderly room's out that door back there." The corporal nodded over his shoulder and left.

Surprised to find the water running hot in the latrine, Collier found a clean towel and quickly showered and shaved. Not sure when he would be able to get laundry done, he put on the same clothes he had slept in and headed for the orderly room.

"Save it, Mac. The captain ain't here today," the duty PFC said, almost before he began to plead his case.

"Well, let me speak to the officer in charge," Collier persisted, getting more frustrated by the minute.

"In a manner of fashion, you're speaking to him," the PFC replied. "My advice is to go get some chow while you still have time. Be there at 0700 when that truck comes to pick you up or there's going to be hell to pay."

Deciding an argument would be a waste of time, Collier found the mess hall and hurriedly stuffed down some oatmeal and a big serving of scrambled eggs with two biscuits smothered in thick, white gravy. Like the biscuits, much to his surprise, the rest of the chow was quite palatable.

"Look, I came here from Meade last night, and the doctor when we got here said I should stay inside and rest today." Dressed in fatigues and standing out front with the other recruit assigned to the crew, Collier began his protest as soon as a PFC pulled up in a truck to pick them up for the work detail.

"Sorry, Mac, don't waste your time with me. Make up your mind. I ain't got all day. Either get on board, or I'll send the MP death squad back for you." Too sick and discouraged to protest, Collier admitted defeat and swung his leg up over the tailgate. The driver climbed back in the cab and nearly threw them out of the truck as he carelessly released the clutch.

"Well, you gotta admit, it could be worse," a companion said after he had heard Collier's sad tale of woe and they discovered they had been assigned to pick up rations from a warehouse and to distribute them to various mess halls around the post.

About mid-morning, they passed a drill field where a Negro drill sergeant was counting cadence like the actor James Whitmore in the classic movie: *Battleground.*

"I don' know, but I been tol',"

Ol' Camp Swampy's a hell'uva hole,
Sound off!"
At the drill sergeant's command "Sound off," the company responded by shouting out cadence:
"One, two, three, four,
One, two"—*a pause of two beats*—"Threep, four!"

As much as Collier tried to fight his emotions, the sight and sound of the well-drilled colored soldiers stirred such a strong wave of patriotism in his chest

The detail wasn't taxing, and, to Collier's great relief, they finished their assigned duties in record time and were dropped off back at the barracks shortly after noontime chow.

"Take my advice and keep a low profile," the PFC driver advised as he pulled away.

That evening after chow, Collier discovered at least half their group had already shipped out while he was on work detail.

By the end of his twelfth day at "Camp Swampy"—which was just one of the many, less poetic euphemisms for Chaffee produced by the feverish brains of past soldiers condemned to be stationed here—only a handful of the survivors of their infamous Flying Tiger flight remained while new arrivals came and went like commuters rushing through Grand Central Station.

It was not until the end of his thirteenth day at Swamp Chaffee, he was finally delivered from the wilderness.

"Pack tonight. You and twenty of your buddies are leaving after morning chow. Wear Class A uniform for the trip." The company first sergeant gave him the welcome news when he came in from afternoon detail.

"Where to, Sergeant?" Collier asked and held his breath.

"Fort Sill, Oklahoma, Mac, but what do you care? Anywhere away from this godforsaken place would be good enough for me," the envious sergeant said with a bitter laugh.

Good enough, indeed, Collier mused. *Glory hallelujah, liberation day has come at last!*

CHAPTER SEVENTEEN

THE DAILY OKLAHOMAN
Oklahoma City, Oklahoma, Friday, February 1, 1952
CASUALTIES DROP, DRAFT QUOTA CUT
WASHINGTON, Jan. 31 (AP) - A sharp drop in the rate of casualties in Korea and an increase in enlistments has made it possible to cut originally planned draft quotas, Selective Service said Thursday.

THE ROANOKE TIMES
Roanoke, Virginia, Saturday, February 2, 1952
REDS TURN DOWN PROPOSAL
ON REPATRIATION OF CIVILIANS
MUNSAN, KOREA, Saturday, February 2 (AP) - The Reds hedged Friday on the question of behind-the-lines inspections during a Korean armistice and rejected flatly an Allied proposal to repatriate 600,000 civilians...

LOOKING AT A MUCH-USED Shell Oil highway map he found in the seatback pocket of the chartered Trailways, Collier judged it was about 150 miles due west from Fort Smith, Arkansas, to Oklahoma City. Except for dusty, little towns with picturesque names like Blackjack, Henryetta and Shawnee and, here and there, an occasional, pumping oil well scattered along the route, for the most part, the flat landscape was uninteresting and featureless. Following a stop at a Chicken in the Rough franchise in Oklahoma City where they were given lunch and allowed to use the restrooms, they were ordered back onto the bus which headed out through the center of the capital city, which, to Collier's amazement, actually had a pumping oil well on the lawn of the state capitol building. Consulting the highway map again, he found that Lawton—the town just outside the gates of historic Fort Sill where the renegade Apache Chief, Geronimo, was once held prisoner—lay another 100 miles in a general south-southwesterly direction. Still running a slight fever and suffering alternating sweats and chills during the unseasonably hot and deadly-boring bus ride, Collier perused a copy of *The Daily Oklahoman* he had recovered from a trash basket at the restaurant, passing the time by catching up on news of the outside world.

CASUALTIES DROP, DRAFT QUOTA CUT.

Contemplating the irony of the headline, Collier really couldn't decide whether to laugh or to cry. As if this news wasn't depressing enough, from what he could gather from other front-page articles, the parade of stuffed uniforms the UN called "negotiators" were still walking in and out of the Panmunjom peace talks like characters in some slapstick Three Stooges comedy.

Incredible! Here it was the second day of February, and there had been absolutely no progress in the negotiations since he had left Roanoke on January 2. Judging from the current casualty rate, he reckoned the corpses would still be piling up when he finished OCS. He wondered how many more men would have to die before he got his commission which—now he was finally on his way to Basic Training—would be sometime a little less than a year. From the looks of the morning headline, Eisenhower would be president by then. With the country having suffered four years under Harry Truman, the hapless Democrat intellectual, Adlai Stevenson, didn't stand a chance. One thing for certain, regardless who won the election, now more than ever Collier was determined nothing would deter him from winning his gold bars. He damn well had had his fill of being an enlisted man.

The bus finally stopped at the main gate on Fort Sill's Sheridan Road at dusk, taking on a sharply-dressed Negro corporal to guide the driver to their destination. Moving slowly into the reservation, Collier was heartened to see that in sharp contrast to Camp Chaffee, the streets inside the historic, permanent military reservation were paved, and the grounds around the rows of freshly-painted, buff-colored wood, stucco and solid, native-stone buildings were neatly-manicured. On his left, they passed a polo field complete with white-helmeted men in jodhpurs, busily swinging long mallets from the backs of glistening, well-groomed thoroughbreds. Beyond the polo match, the bus slowed as it approached a column of colored soldiers marching down the middle of the street ahead of them.

"AIN'T NO USE IN GOIN' HOME, JODY'S GOT YOUR GAL AND GONE. The strutting ebony sergeant sang out in a booming voice, followed by a two-beat interval attended the sound of thirty-odd, well-polished boots striking the surface of the pavement. "SOUND OFF!" The strutting sergeant demanded in an operatic bass worthy of Gershwin's 'Porgy':

"ONE, TWO!" the marching troops resounded.

"SOUND OFF!" their sergeant continued, maintaining the precisely-measured beat.

"THREE, FOUR!" the cadence count continued.

"NOW, COUNT IT ON DOWN," the sergeant exhorted with the fervor of an old-fashioned AME Holiness preacher.

"ONE, TWO, THREE, FOUR!"—a pause of two beats as boots slapped pavement—"ONE, TWO!—another two beats resounded the sound of marching feet—"THREE, FOUR!"

Just like a few days earlier when he first heard the rhythmic Jody chant at Camp Chaffee, Collier fought back a sudden welling of patriotism as their driver waited until the spit and polish formation of Negro soldiers executed a sharp "Column Right" into a side street.

"That's the Triple Nickel! The 555th Field Artillery Batallion—105 Howitzer outfit. The Nickel is the only all-colored battalion on the post—one of a few left in the Army, I think," their NCO guide proudly pointed out. "The Nickel got shit kicked out of 'em at Pusan Perimeter. That sergeant you heard calling cadence won the Bronze Star and also got a Purple Heart. There was a bucket full of medals handed out for that flap—most of 'em posthumously. The Nickels came to Korea from Hawaii just after the War started. They hardly arrived before they was overrun twice, losing all their howitzers and most of the crews during the big infantry bugouts at the pass north of Pongam in August 1950. Not many survivors lived to tell the tale."

"Sounds like you were there," someone up near the front spoke up.

"Not then. I landed September fifteen at Inchon to support the 'breakout,'" he replied.

When the column of soldiers finally cleared the traffic lane, the driver continued into the heart of the storied Artillery installation. On high ground to their right, the heat shimmered off the runway of a sizeable airfield with several big C-124 Globemasters parked among a scattering of other troop-carrying transports and a number of smaller light planes. In the middle-distance to their left, four rounded hills rose against the gathering dusk like stepping stones. About a half-mile past the airstrip, the driver down-shifted going up the long grade, finally pulling to a stop in front of a large concrete-block building which had all the earmarks of another gymnasium.

"Okay, everybody out. Let's get this over with so you can get settled in and have some chow," a master sergeant who could have stepped right out of a Norman Rockwell recruiting poster growled, as they were ordered inside. "Okay, don't just stand there...drop your pants and skin back those stubby little howitzers—you're in the Artillery now."

"I'm beginning to get the feeling the Army is more interested in my pecker than my girlfriend ever was," a bespectacled recruit beside Huck Finn grumbled.

"They've handled my dick more in the past four days than my girl friend has in the last twelve months," another agreed.

Collier nodded resentfully, suddenly seized with spasm of coughing. Turning away from the group, he hawked up a huge oyster and spit it into a Kleenex.

"My God, man, that's gross. Have you seen anyone about that cough?" the bespectacled recruit asked, nervously, attempting to cover his shrinking genitals with his hands.

"An Army doc saw me when I was at Meade. He gave me a couple of shots of penicillin and some Penicillin G tablets. But that was two weeks ago. The pills are long gone, but this damn congestion just keeps hanging on," Collier shrugged. Searching his pockets for a four-ounce bottle of over-the-counter cough syrup and a pocket tin of Bayer aspirin he had purchased at the PX at Chaffee, he glanced around, trying to locate a water fountain.

"I'm sure you can't help it. But if you have to cough again, please turn your head the other way." The bespectacled soldier shook his head in disgust and edged away.

The latest "short arms" groping over, the street lights glowed a soft yellow against the deep-purple twilight as Collier and his fellow recruits were ushered back on the bus as it continued up a long hill, turning left at last into a well-policed grouping of buildings fairly teeming with well-scrubbed young soldiers loitering on the steps and in the doorways. Passing a small PX and adjoining building housing a Service Club, here and there Collier observed these off-duty enlisted men tossing baseballs and horseshoes, throwing and kicking a new football, and other obviously off-duty activities. Finally, the driver made a sharp right turn and brought the bus to a halt just past the corner at an intersection bordering a well-kept group of barracks. In front of the corner barracks was a neatly-lettered sign:

FARTC

BATTERY A
2ND FIELD ARTILLERY TRAINING BATALLION
FORT SILL, OKLAHOMA

Taking full advantage of the unseasonably-warm weather, across the street a group of soldiers, wearing mostly tee-shirts over their fatigue pants, were playing a game of touch football on a block-long, well-lighted, but bare-dirt drill and athletic field. A sweaty, quite vocal game of basketball was in full swing on the far end of the field. When they pulled to a stop, Collier could see that they had been preceded by two other large busloads of trainees, still on their buses—impatiently waiting for Collier's group to join them.

"Okay, everybody out. Form four ranks of twenty-five men each on the street, here in front of the buses. We've got to take roll before we take care of getting you assigned a place to sleep. After that, we'll get you some hot chow." Sounding like he had a mouth full of grits, a corporal with a syrupy southern accent stuck his head in the door as soon as the bus came to a full stop.

"TEN-N-HUT! Give me your attention up here." After the group had formed a rather scraggly line in the street, the cornpone corporal attempted to get down to the business at hand. "Welcome to Battery A, Second Field Artillery...." Pausing and glaring at them until the shuffling and the whispered byplay stopped, the corporal waited a long moment before he cleared his throat and began again.

"Welcome to Battery A, Second Field Artillery Training Battalion, Fort Sill, Oklahoma. FART-CEE for short!" This weary attempt at humor was met with a nervous titter. "This will be your home for the next sixteen weeks. Battery A is under the command of Captain Ward. The First Sergeant is Master Sergeant Ellis. I am Corporal Dixon, a member of your training cadre. Now, will the following men answer loud and clear when I call your name and fall out and regroup over there with Corporal McGeoghan." Dixon pointed to a bespectacled, sharply-turned-out corporal standing several yards to his left. McGeoghan's boots—like Dixon's—shone like mirrors and his starched fatigues were nicely creased. On the lapels of both men's fatigues were garnet and black cloisonné emblems of the unit. Collier couldn't help but be impressed.

"Abbott!" Dixon began.

"Yo!" a muffled answer came from Collier's left as a lanky trainee broke ranks and moved over to where Corporal McGeoghan stood.

"Acton! Ambers! Baker! Beatty! Blevins! Carter! Carmine! Chambers! Chumbley! Daughtery!..." Hearing no response, Dixon looked up and called "Daughtery!"again,

"I'm Daughtery! Oh, yeah! Yo!" the embarrassed Daughtery finally answered.

Dixon shot him a look and went back to reading names. "Denton!..."

When he finished calling the names in the first part of the alphabet, Dixon looked up and said, "The rest of you will remain here in the second section with me. Now answer up.

"Madison!...Marr!..." Wasting little time in closing ranks, Dixon went down the roster calling out names of the remaining group of fifty.

"When I dismiss you, go find your duffel bag in that pile over there and stake out a bunk inside the barracks immediately behind me," Dixon instructed when he had completed taking roll. "No sense in fighting over bunks, they're pretty much all the same. Best save your energy for more important things—you'll need it soon enough, I promise you. Before you make up your sack, check the blankets and linen against the inventory sheet on the roll of linen and sign it. Give it to me when we assemble back out here at eighteen-forty-five hours—which is in exactly one-zero minutes. At that time, the entire battery will be marched down to get some chow. I'll point out the PX and Service Club Number 3 on the way to the Battalion Mess Hall. When you finish chow, report back here, and I'll show you how to make up your bed the way I expect to see it every morning when I escort Captain Ward through the barracks for inspection. After that, lights out is at ten-hundred hours. However, bed check isn't until after taps at eleven-hundred hours. Reveille is at zero-five-hundred hours. Any questions?" the corporal asked in his easygoing southern drawl.

"Where can we find a pay phone?" a trainee raised his hand and asked.

"There are some between here and the mess hall, a couple between the PX and the Service Club, on the same side of the street. There are more inside the Service Club. Okay, if there are no more questions, that'll do for now, but I strongly advise you to come back here at least long enough for me to show you how to make a bunk. After tonight, I expect to see those blankets stretched so tight they'll bounce a dime halfway to the barracks ceiling," Dixon drawled before he brought them sharply back to attention and bawled out, "FAW-LL-OUT!"

Momentarily watching the mass confusion as both his and McGeoghan's sections shuffled through the pile of duffels on the sidewalk, Dixon waited until Collier finally stepped in to claim the last remaining bag. Without a word, he followed Collier inside the barracks and stood watching the men as they claimed the remaining bunks downstairs. When he was satisfied everything was in order, the soft-spoken NCO turned on his heel and disappeared through a door into a private room occupying the left corner of the barracks by the front door. On the door was a neat wooden sign lettered: Cpl. Amos Dixon.

Big brother is watching you. Too tired to work up a good resentment at this final invasion of privacy, Collier dropped his duffel beside the nearest empty bunk, inventoried the pile of bed linen and blankets and signed the slip before heading back out to the street.

After chow, Collier returned to the barracks, and as sick and tired as he was, he tried to pay attention while Dixon showed them how to make a bed. As soon as the Corporal completed his competent demonstration, Collier stripped out of his uniform and tossed it on his bunk. Locating a clean set of fatigues for the next day, he hung them below the shelf at the foot of his sack. His watch showed 1035 as he located his shaving kit and headed for the showers. The dial glowed 1056 when he finally climbed into the sack and pulled the covers over his head.

If Collier and his new battery mates thought they would have Sunday off, they were in for a rude disappointment. True to Dixon's word, at 0500 Collier came wide awake at the sound of Reveille blasting through the large loudspeakers mounted strategically on metal posts throughout the FARTC area.

"Drop your cocks and grab your socks, Ladies. Fatigues are the uniform of the day. Roll call is at 0530 out in the street. Best get moving. We've got a busy day ahead." Before Collier had a chance to rub the sleep from his eyes, Corporal Amos Dixon came striding out of the door of his barracks room, growling like a bulldog on a short leash.

In the latrine, Collier coughed up some pus, but all-in-all he felt somewhat better than when he had gone to bed.

Following roll call and breakfast chow, the entire battery was formed in the street again and divided into four platoons of twenty-five men, which were immediately marched—a rather loose description of their scraggly, inept movement—to the drill field across the street where Corporals Dixon, McGeoghan and two other NCOs spent one full hour trying to teach them: Attention, Dress Right Dress, Right-, Left- and About Face, Parade Rest and At Ease. Following that, the next hour was devoted to trying to teach the simple exercise of marching together in cadence. Bothered by the steadily-growing discomfort from his congested lungs and his mounting impatience at having to do

Forward March, Column Right and Column Left over and over again, Collier became firmly convinced that his fellow recruits all had at least three left feet. He had serious doubts at the rate they were progressing, this bunch would ever get through Basic in just sixteen weeks! Finally, just when he thought his chest would burst from breathing Oklahoma dust, they were marched back across the street and dismissed in time to wash up for noontime chow.

Back from lunch, Collier had barely plopped on his bunk and was just dozing into a twilight state when Dixon rousted them into the street again for another two hours of close order drill. When they returned to the barracks, Collier had the beginnings of major-league blisters on both heels. Determined not to miss a single day of training, instead of collapsing on the sack, he slipped his boots back on and limped, painful blisters and all, to the PX to purchase large Band-aids, extra-wide adhesive tape, sterile gauze, peroxide and a vial of tincture of benzoin—the complete first-aid remedy for healing tender skin that he had learned from his basketball days. Returning to the barracks, he quickly tended his blisters and resumed setting up his footlocker according to the diagram he had roughly copied from the one Corporal Dixon had posted on the bulletin board.

"Are you Collier Ramsay, old sport?" A slightly undersized trainee in starched fatigues tapped him on the shoulder.

"Yeah, I'm Ramsay." Collier glanced up, wondering what was coming now.

"Excellent, old sport. I'm Charles Jones II, Lehigh College, Business Ad, Class of '51. You can call me Chip," the rather affected soldier introduced himself with an ill-concealed air of superiority and stuck out his hand. "I bunk upstairs. I'm headed for Officer Candidate School as soon as we get through this next sixteen weeks. Scuttlebutt has it you're also on the fast track for OCS, old sock?"

"Good to meet you, Jones. You're right. I have applied for OCS." Somewhat hesitantly, Collier shook his hand. It bothered him to think he might be stuck in OCS with the Ivy League Gatsby standing in front of him.

"Splendid, old sport, simply splendid! Our battery mates, Nat Reed, the big Indian-looking guy over there in the back bunk, and Herb Rudolph, the balding, pudgy one with the thick glasses on the bunk up there at the other end near Dixon's room, have both applied, too. Rudolph's a Temple grad," Jones confided, as if Temple University was a branch of the Philly jail. "But just between the two of us, judging from the Coke-bottle lenses in those glasses he has on, Rudolph won't make it to OCS."

Taking a closer look at the trainee Jones identified as Rudolph, Collier could readily see the pudgy soldier had a serious problem with his vision. The mere thought of taking another eye exam gave Collier a nervous twitch. Rather than take a chance back home on busting out on his application to OCS for poor eyesight, Collier had been cheating on the exam every time he took the test by committing the 20/20 line to memory. Besides suffering slight astigmatism, he actually read only 20/80 with his right eye and his left was only around 20/40—maybe 20/35 on a good day—which left him on shaky ground if he had to take the exam fair-and-square.

"Glad to meet you, Jones," Collier grunted, turning his attention back to his footlocker.

"Our other OCS applicant is Reed, the big Indian over there. Rudolph has been here on Post with me in a casual battery for the past three days, waiting for the rest of you to arrive. Rudolph is another Pennsylvania lad—Newtown Square, on the main line, just outside Philly. The big Indian is from Chicago. Reed came in on the bus with you. He isn't exactly a mental giant, but before the military draft caught up to him, he had a tryout as linebacker with the Chicago Bears." Jones ignored Collier's rather obvious hint that he wanted to be left alone.

"Hm-m, I remember him..." Glancing up, Collier recognized the gargantuan Reed as the man beside him at the short arms inspection when they first arrived on Post.

"No, wait, old sport, the shaving cream goes right here beside the shaving brush and razor—like this." Imperiously, Jones instructed Collier in the arrangement of his paraphernalia.

"Uhm-m thanks," Collier muttered resentfully, anxious to be left alone.

"Don't mention it, old sock. I took two years ROTC at college. Anytime you need help, just call on me." Jones nodded and went right on talking. "I never thought the draft would catch up to me. Can you believe it? My wife actually went into labor a few days after I reported to Indiantown Gap on the fourteenth of January. Charles the Third will be five months old before I ever get to hold him in my arms. Here I am halfway across the country, and I've never even seen my namesake. I see from your ring you're married, too," Jones rattled inanely on.

"Uhm-m." Collier nodded. "A year-and-a-half, but I don't have any kids and my wife's not PG. When the war started in Korea, I never thought the draft would ever get to me."

"It's a bitch alright, but at least you don't have kids. Well, see you around..." Jones nodded, moving up the aisle to where the owlish Rudolph sat sorting through his duffel bag.

"Okay, listen up, you men." Before Jones made it halfway to where Rudolph sat, Corporal Dixon walked out of the door of his room, carrying a large Campbell's Pork'n'Beans box, and began making an announcement. "Tonight you're going to get your first lesson on how to keep these barracks inspection ready. I have the distinct pleasure of inviting you to your first honest-to-god GI party." Collier watched as Dixon set the pasteboard carton on the floor inside the front door of the barracks, a trace of a smile playing at the corners of the corporal's mouth

"What kind of party? What's all this stuff for?" Edging closer, a rather naïve, eager-beaver trainee asked as he peered into the box at the pile of well-used, stiff-bristled GI brushes, two gallon-sized jugs of Clorox and at least a dozen bars of Grandma's good ol' lye soap—not to mention several large spray bottles of Windex.

"There are several large GI buckets in the closet by the latrine. Fill 'em with hot water, add a generous amount of Clorox, and you've got everything it takes to make a barracks floor clean enough to eat off. Grab a half-dozen rolls of good ol' GI toilet paper and this Windex will make those filthy windows shine, inside and out. The only thing missing is elbow grease. I'll give you three guesses who's going to supply that—the first two don't count." Dixon grinned.

"Do you mean we have to scrub the floor on our hands and knees?" The erstwhile pro football Indian from Chicago was obviously not at all enchanted with the idea.

"You're a fast learner, Reed." Standing there hands-on-hips, Dixon put Collier in mind of some Hollywood B-movie redneck prison guard lording over a crew of chain gang convicts.

Collier had been a non- participating witness to a GI Party during his recent tenure at Chaffee and understood full-well what Dixon had in mind. With a deep sigh of resignation, he shucked out of his fatigues, quickly sifted through his duffel and changed into the blue GI gym shorts Uncle Sam had issued him at Fort Meade. Thus stripped down for the work at hand, he padded shoeless to the latrine and filled two of the GI buckets with steaming water. Lugging the heavy pails into the room, he was reminded of the many mornings he and his brother Jim had made seemingly endless trips hauling similar five-gallon buckets of hog slop, feeding the nearly one-hundred-odd hogs his brother was raising for his 4-H project. Now, Collier wondered what he would have thought back then if he had known that someday he would be doing this. Idly, he speculated somewhat ironically if the Air Force had introduced his baby brother to GI parties.

"Okay, let's get busy or we'll be all night finishing this. Come on you guys— help me move these bunks out of the way." Collier set down the pails as he elbowed his way through his barracks mates. Picking up one end of the bed nearest the front door, he began clearing a space to scrub the floor. "

As the group reluctantly stirred to life and began pushing the bunks away, Collier opened a jug of Clorox and emptied half of its contents into each of the large buckets of hot water. When he finished, he proceeded to slosh both buckets of the steaming bleach-reinforced liquid across the floor. "Best fill these up again," he handed both buckets to a wide-eyed recruit and walked back over to the box containing Dixon's primitive cleaning tools. Choosing the newest of the GI brushes and removing the wrapper from a bar of the old-fashioned, brown lye soap, Collier moved directly to the front, right-hand corner of the barracks room. Without further ceremony, Collier fell to his knees and got down to the business of scrubbing floors.

"Well, what are you guys waiting for? I'm not going to do this by myself. Grab those brushes and let's get to work. Some of you get some toilet paper and Windex and clean windows—make 'em shine or you'll have to do them again. We'll be here all night unless Corporal Dixon is satisfied this place is ready for Captain Ward's inspection."

That broke the spell. Taking a cue from his example, one-by-one, the collection of reluctant soldiers joined Collier and got to work.

"Okay, now you guys take a break." After perhaps a half-hour of heavy scrubbing, Collier encouraged the others working beside him, as he stood and handed his brush to one of the stragglers idly watching.

When he finally stood and stretched and was pleased with the progress of his battery mates, Collier walked out back to the latrine to take a leak. Standing at the row of lavatories, Nat Reed, the pro-football prospect, was making a great show of drying his hands. The giant Indian left when Collier entered the room. Returning to the main barracks room, Collier glanced around, casually taking stock of those who were not afraid to work and the goof-offs who were just milling around. He didn't mind doing his share, but it never hurt for a guy to know who he could depend upon. Nat Reed had a bottle of Windex and was making a great show of cleaning window panes, but, as far as Collier could see, he was mostly goofing off.

"As soon as I finish this window, I'm going to get the mirrors in the latrine," Reed volunteered his martyrdom as Collier approached.

"You're going to have to go back over this. You can bet your butt Dixon won't put up with half-ass work." Collier pointed out areas where Reed had done a sloppy job.

"Look, Ramsay, tend to your own business. I saw you down on your knees, scrubbing your little heart out. Real gung-ho, but you're not fooling anyone. You're just trying to make brownie points with Dixon," the hulking, Geronimo look-alike snapped with a pugnacious sneer.

"You look, Reed, you'd better clean up your act. Fuck-offs will never make it here, much less in OCS," the words slipped out before Collier could control his anger.

"Who're you calling, 'Fuck-off'? You can't talk to me like that." Turning red as a beet, Reed stepped forward, balling his fists. Perhaps an inch over six feet, Reed was almost as tall as Collier, but outweighed him by at least thirty or forty pounds.

"Don't threaten me, you goldbrick. Go ahead and take your best shot, but I warn you, Reed, you'd better make it count. You'd better kill me if you do." Surprising even himself—but with a cold buffer of reason tempering the adrenaline rushing to his brain—Collier kept his hands down, as he quietly called Reed's bluff. While he wanted to avoid a fight, Collier calmly stood his ground.

Reed blinked, obviously surprised the smaller man was not backing down. "Oh, no. I get it now. You're trying to set me up. If I swing at you, I'll wind up in trouble and l-lose my ch-chance at OCS," stammering slightly, Reed stepped back and lowered his hands.

"Oh, no, Reed, I promise you it won't be like that. We can go out back. No one will see us there. You started this. Now let's go settle it once and for all. I don't want to live in the same barracks with something like this hanging over my head." Collier could scarcely believe this foolhardy show of bravado was rushing out of him.

"Well, alright...but not now. Not in broad daylight—I'll meet you later, after dark." Shuffling nervously, Reed made as if to leave, avoiding looking Collier in the eye.

"You're not afraid of being seen, Reed. You're not only a loudmouth goof-off—you're just plain chickenshit," Collier challenged as the truth began to dawn on him.

"Goddammit, Ramsay, that's enough! Back off now, before Dixon sees." Clearly, Reed wanted no part of him.

"Come on, you chickenshit. Let's go get this over with." Sensing triumph, Collier got in the coward's face.

"No goddammit, I'm not about to take a chance on you messing up my record," Reed muttered, looking desperately for a way to step past him now.

"Okay, Reed, run away and hide. You're worse than a just a goof-off—you're a bully and you're chickenshit. If you ever try to get by without pulling your share of the work again—or if I ever see you trying to push any of the other guys around—you're going to have to take me on. Next time there won't be any backing down. You understand?"

"You can't talk to me like that. I-I-I'll..." Reed's idle threats wilted in the empty air.

"You'll what, Reed? Come on; now's your chance. Let's get this done right now. I'm going to walk out that door. I'll wait out back at least long enough to smoke a cigarette." Collier wheeled and walked outside to the corner of the barracks, just out of sight of the orderly room. Lighting a Lucky, he checked his watch. When about fifteen minutes had passed, he walked over and snuffed the cigarette in the butt can by the back door and went back inside. The men were standing around in small groups now, hoping to see a fight.

"You're fucking crazy, Ramsay—you know that? I'm not about to risk losing my chance for OCS," Reed mumbled resentfully, standing on a chair, spraying Windex as if his life depended upon it.

"I may be crazy, Nat, but at least I'm not chickenshit." Collier sneered, knowing round one was his. Still?...he had a sinking feeling, chickenshit or not, he hadn't seen or heard the last of Reed.

"Just another day in paradise," Dixon quipped when he finally conceded they had done a passing job. After marching them to supper chow, he released them, free to use the PX, take in a movie, or visit the Service Club. Too tired and ailing to prowl around the area, as soon as Collier had stuffed his face, he waited in the long line to use one of the phone booths on the sidewalk outside the Service Club.

"I'm sorry, Collier, dear. Emma's gone to the picture show in Roanoke with some girl friends," Mother Lowell answered, her voice filled with disappointment for him.

"Well, I would have called sooner, but I haven't had the chance. Tell her I'll try to write a note tonight, but it might help speed things up if you would take down my new mail address." Waiting until his mother-in-law found a pencil, Collier dictated: "Pvt. Collier Ramsay, RA 13415453, Battery A, FARTC, Fort Sill, Oklahoma. Explain to Emma it's difficult to find time to use a pay phone, but I'll call back first chance I get."

"I'll be sure and tell her." his kind mother-in-law promised as he hung up the phone.

At 0500 on Monday, February 4, the myriad of large loudspeakers mounted on virtually every building and mast pole in the FARTC area reverberated the sound of Reveille throughout the huge Artillery Center. As soon as roll call was completed and announcements of duty rosters made, Dixon marched the battery across the street where—shoulder to shoulder—they advanced slowly, step-by-step, across the drill field policing it of discarded bits of field-stripped cigarettes, candy wrappers and all similar debris. After completing their first pass across the wide, smooth field and back again, they waited anxiously while Dixon, with MacGeoghan and several other NCOs, came behind them to inspect the thoroughness of their effort.

"Do you call this a 'Police Call?' Now, go back and get it right. This time I want to see your noses near the ground." Thoroughly chastened, Dixon sent them back to repeat the job. Twice.

Finally, after completing their third trip across, they reassembled and were marched back across the street to police their own area before they fell in to be marched to morning chow.

After breakfast, Collier spent time straightening his gear as the entire battery was sent in groups of ten to the battalion supply room to be issued combat packs, heavy canvas-covered canteens, bayonets with hard scabbards and the medical, mess, and ammo kits—all of which clipped into the small brass-grommets studded into the regulation combat web belt. Equipment issue completed, Dixon instructed them how and where to attach the canteens and other equipment to the belt before marching them off to a nearby classroom for a lecture on *Army Traditions, Values and Protocol* delivered by a pocket-sized, red-haired, freckled-faced spit-and-polish, corporal named Schnoedecker.

Having little trouble remaining alert to the end, Collier was not so much enthralled with the content of Schnoedecker's presentation, as he was impressed with the professional quality of the presenter and with his flawless use of the flip charts and other visual aids. After Schnoedecker wrapped up his lecture with a Q&A, Collier conceded to himself that the freckled corporal made as good a presentation as he had ever been privileged to attend.

Following the high-flown lecture on Army tradition, Dixon marched them to a nearby athletic field where they were required to take a fitness test, including push-ups, pull-ups, sit-ups and the running of an obstacle course with overhand ladders, rope climbs, scaling walls, a climbing tower and the like. At the end, they were timed in the 100-yard dash. Despite his congested lungs, Collier held his own, coming in second in his six-man heat, beating out the surprisingly fleet Reed by at least two yards with a final burst of speed.

Combat First Aid, Personal Hygiene in the Field, Map Reading, Compass Familiarization, Survival Skills. Over the several days that followed, the subject matter of the training became more and more oriented toward survival in combat and, for that reason—if no other—even more interesting. During the same period, they made two test runs over a Compass Course, one during broad daylight and another in the middle of the night. The vital nature of the subject matter notwithstanding, Collier couldn't help but admire the consistently high quality of the training.

"Privates Mears, Shanahan, Bullard and Maxey report up here to me," Dixon ordered at evening formation on Friday. "Take a good look at these men and listen up. These four men have been promoted to the temporary rank of Lance Corporal and will wear green armbands with corporal stripes on their left sleeves." Waiting until all four men were standing at Parade Rest in front of the Battery, Dixon held up a bright-green felt armband, with corporal stripes already sewn on, before passing one to each of the men he had named and continued speaking, "These Lance Corporals are responsible for seeing to the overall welfare of the men in their respective sections. If you have problems, you will take them to your Lance Corporal. They also have the responsibility of seeing to it that their sections keep the barracks and grounds inspection-ready and that the men under them perform all training duties at an acceptable level. The Lance Corporals will each answer to a Lance Sergeant. The Lance Sergeant will, in turn, report directly to me and Corporal McGeoghan and other cadre under Sergeant Ellis and Captain Ward. You will treat these five men with the same respect as permanent training cadre. Any questions?"

"Where...ah...who is this Lance Sergeant?" the question came from McGeoghan's section.

"He will be named and introduced to you at formation for evening chow," Dixon replied. "Any other questions?"

"You mean those guys will be able to order us around?" the question came from Nat Reed in the rank behind Collier.

"Within areas related to personal appearance, general deportment, performance of training, upkeep of the barracks area, and readiness for inspections—yes."

"How come those particular goof-offs were chosen?" the disgruntled Reed persisted.

"Because it is the opinion of members of the training cadre that these men have demonstrated exceptional performance and exemplary attitude during the first week of training. In the judgment of Captain Ward, they have all the qualifications necessary to assume the responsibility of leadership. In short, Private Reed, it is the observation of your cadre that these men are anything but 'goof-offs.' Anything else?" Although there was a low level of grumbling throughout the ranks as Dixon waited for them to settle down, no one spoke up again.

"Alright, we'll form again for evening mess in three-zero minutes. DIS-MISSED!" At Dixon's command the group fell out and scampered for the barracks on the double.

While the Lance Corporal selections came as a complete surprise to Collier, when he thought about it, he had to admit in the short span of several days, all four of the men selected had stood out and he couldn't quarrel with their selection. Still, he felt he had soldiered well. It particularly troubled him that as an applicant for OCS he hadn't measured up. Would this shortcoming seriously reflect on his application for officer training? As much as he hated to admit it, Collier felt close to tears. Yet, as he mulled it over in his mind, he took some small comfort that the other OCS applicants, Reed and Rudolph and Jones—particularly Jones who had ROTC at Lehigh—had been passed over, too. Feeling more unappreciated by the minute, Collier languished behind as all around him, his buddies were making a wild dash to rinse off a layer of drill field dust and check their mail before evening chow.

"Ramsay, I need to see you before you go in," Dixon called out as Collier shambled slowly toward the barracks behind the rest.

"Private Ramsay, reporting as ordered, Sir," saluting dispiritedly, Collier came to attention in front of Dixon

"Ramsay, you know better than to address NCOs as 'Sir.'" Dixon scowled.

"Yessir...I mean, yes, Corporal," Collier stammered, completely flustered now.

"Would you follow me? Captain Ward wants a word with you before you head for chow." Dixon wheeled, leading the way around the barracks. Pondering what trouble he had gotten himself into now, Collier glumly fell into step behind the corporal as Dixon led him back past the bulletin board to the separate structure housing the garage-sized orderly room.

"Corporal Dixon, reporting with Private Ramsay as ordered, Sir." Inside the orderly room, Dixon came smartly to attention and saluted Captain Ward who was waiting in the anteroom just outside his office door. First Sergeant Ellis and the pimply-faced company clerk working at a typewriter gave Ramsay a mildly curious once-over as Dixon reported in.

"Come in please, Corporal and close the door behind you," the Captain returned the salute, then led the way inside his office.

When they entered the small room, Dixon closed the door behind them and Collier stood at attention. As Collier tried to sort out what was going down, possibilities skittered around inside his head like chickens fighting over a handful of cracked corn. He was pretty sure he hadn't committed any major sins and now, all at once, he worried if he was about to hear bad news from home. Could his mother—or his dad—be seriously ill? Perhaps, even dead?

"Just stand at ease, Ramsay. Have you told him what this is all about, Corporal?" the Captain asked Dixon as soon as he had closed the door.

"No, Sir. I announced the appointment of the Lance Corporals at formation, but I thought you might want to break this to Ramsay yourself, Sir," Dixon said.

"Of course." Nodding, the Captain turned to Collier. "Ramsay, Corporal Dixon brought you here to inform you that we're appointing you Lance Sergeant for the entire Battery. Do you understand what that means?" The Captain paused to see if Collier understood.

"Well, sir...I...ah...Corporal Dixon told us we would answer to the Lance Corporals and the Lance Corporals would answer to a Lance Sergeant. So, I guess you're asking me if I want to be...to take charge of...of the entire battery?" Collier stuttered, afraid to believe his ears. Momentarily in a state of shock, Collier was almost as much relieved his fear he was about to hear some tragic news was unfounded as he was elated to hear his leadership potential had not been overlooked after all.

"Congratulations, you're now Lance Sergeant Ramsay." The Captain handed him a bright-green felt armband with sergeant stripes attached and stepped back. "This is a big responsibility. If you have any questions for me, ask them now. Otherwise, Corporal Dixon will fill you in on your duties and the chain of command."

"Thank you, Sir. I'm honored." Saluting, Collier accepted the armband and followed Dixon out of the orderly room. Outside, he turned to Dixon. "Corporal, I'm not really sure I want this lame duck promotion."

"What do you mean by lame duck?" Dixon stood momentarily flabbergasted.

"Well...I do appreciate the honor of being chosen, but the men resent being put under the control of somebody who really doesn't have any more actual standing in the Army than they do. When I put this armband on, I won't have a friend left in the battery. For the next fifteen weeks, I have to partner myself day after day with one or more of these men when we pair off for certain training. As far as reality is concerned, you're putting me into a no-win situation. Surely you can see what I mean?" Collier said, rather stubbornly.

"No. I don't see that at all. You applied for OCS. As a matter of fact, your OCT scores and aptitude testing show exceptional potential. It has always been axiomatic to the dynamic of command, that *familiarity breeds contempt*. Officer training isn't so much about winning friends; it's about leadership and inspiration. This will present you with an unprecedented opportunity to learn firsthand how to handle your relationships with the men you hold power over—but also have to live with. Leadership has always been about earning respect. That's the responsibility of command under the most testing conditions. I personally am expecting great things from you. Now put that armband on your left arm, Ramsay. I'm sure you won't let A Battery down." The well-spoken Corporal looked at him expectantly.

"Thank you, Corporal. I'll do my best." Collier shrugged, then slipped the armband up his arm, reminded of his great grandmother's admonition to be careful what he wished for.

"We might have known they'd give that armband to a big brownnose like you! Don't let that Mickey Mouse armband give you the idea you can push me around." When Collier walked into the barracks wearing the armband, Reed loudly jeered, calling attention to Collier's promotion.

"Listen, Nat," Collier walked directly over to Reed to set him straight. "I don't know what your problem is, but this armband comes off as easily as it goes on. If you have something personal to settle, just say the word and we can step outside anytime you say." Collier didn't really want to fight Reed, but if he were going to be a source of constant agitation, he wanted to get it over with, here and now.

"Oh, sure! Then when I whip your sorry ass, you'd have me before Captain Ward and I'd lose my chance for OCS," Reed protested, quickly backing down.

"Everyone in this room knows we've already had this conversation, Nat. No way I'd do that. As soon as we finish GI-ing the barracks, come find me. Let's go out back. No one will ever know but us,"

"Yeah, I know your kind. That's what you say now, but as soon as I whipped your ass, you'd go crying to Dixon." Reed was already moving away.

"Tell you what, Nat. Call your buddies Rizzo, Russo and Schepp over and I'll get Shields, Rudolph and Shanahan in on this. I'll give you my word in front of them. Then no matter what happens, we'll both avoid jeopardizing our applications to OCS," Collier offered, knowing Reed was more talk than action.

"Oh...no...you're just trying to set me up. Just stay off my case," Reed stammered, then turned to leave.

"Not so fast, Nat, you started this...might as well get it settled tonight for once and all." Collier motioned to Shanahan. "Hey, Jack, will you come over here a minute, please?"

When Shanahan walked over, Shields and Rudolph followed a few steps behind.

"Nat here thinks I'm picking on him, Jack. I'm offering to take off the armband and meet him outside tonight after we finish GI-ing the barracks," Collier filled Shanahan in.

"Look, I'm not going to fall for this—you guys are asshole buddies. You're just trying to set me up," Reed griped in a whiny voice, attempting to move around Collier.

The rest of the men edged even closer not wanting to miss what was going on.

"There's no setup involved here, and I'm not picking on you or anyone else. You're a loudmouth and a troublemaker, Nat. You've been goofing off every chance you get. From now on, you pull your weight just like everybody else. I'm not on your case, but I won't stand for goof-offs in this battery. The overall responsibility for A Battery's performance is on my shoulders now. If anybody isn't pulling his weight, it's my ass on the line."

"Why pick on me? I pull my weight," Reed protested, trying to step around Collier.

"That's just the point. You don't pull your weight. I watched you last Sunday, the first time we GI-ed this barracks down. That's going to change as of right now, understand?"

"See what I mean, you're already throwing your weight around." Reed stepped to his right, anxious to get past Collier.

"I'm not trying to throw anything around, Reed. I just want you and me to come to a simple understanding, here and now, and let that be the end of it. Captain Ward put this responsibility on me. I didn't ask for it and I'm not asking the men in this battery to do anything I won't do. Now, are we clear about that?" Collier moved back in front of Reed, blocking his way.

"Come on, you guys, settle this later. Being late for formation won't help the situation," Herb Rudolph called as he followed Larry Shields toward the door.

"Okay, you've made your point. Now let me by. You'll make me late for formation." Reed was very red-faced now.

"Come on, Collie, let's don't be late." Shanahan called, heading out the door. Outside in the battery street, the last of the stragglers were just falling in for chow.

"Okay, Reed, but I'm sick and tired of your chickenshit." With the battery forming outside, Collier let him pass and followed him out the door.

"Wait up, Ramsay!" Dixon caught Collier by the elbow as he came out of the door adjusting his helmet liner on his head. "As soon as this Battery is formed and Captain Ward announces your promotion, I want you to take command and march the men to chow."

"You what?" Collier nearly choked at the thought of trying to march the entire battery to the mess hall or, for that matter, anywhere at all. "Oh, no, Corporal, you can't be serious. I haven't had any more drill instruction than the rest of these clowns. As a matter of fact, some of them have had ROTC in school and are much better qualified than I am."

"Nothing to it. It's simple. I'll coach you. Now, let's get out there while the Captain announces your promotion.

"Oh, crap, Corporal, please don't make me do this now. Let me practice tomorrow at drill—at least give me a chance to prepare. You dumped this Lance Sergeant thing on me—why do you want me to make a fool of myself in front of the men even before I have a chance to earn their respect?"

"Look, Ramsay, it's only four or five blocks to the battalion mess hall...less than a quarter of a mile. If Captain Ward didn't think you could do it, he wouldn't have told me to turn them over to you. Don't worry so much. I'll prompt you. I'll be right beside you all the way. Get a move on now. Let's not keep the Captain waiting."

Guts churning, Collier stood before the formation and listened to the undercurrent of discontent as Captain Ward announced his promotion. He was so nervous just thinking about marching the battery, he almost missed hearing Dixon's command, "Lance Sergeant Ramsay, march this battery to the Mess Hall."

"Yes, Corporal," he saluted. Then, turning to face the waiting battery, he almost fell flat on his face when his feet tangled up, executing an awkward About Face.

"*Call them to Attention,*" Dixon coached him under his breath.

"*I know...*" Collier whispered back—trying hard to ignore the ripple of suppressed laughter at his clumsiness, he was certain his voice would fail him altogether.

"Ba-a-t-t-ery," Collier's voice cracked, wavering like a pre-pubertal choirboy before he managed to muster a measure of control and finish the command—"A-t-t-TEN-SHUN!" Momentarily paralyzed with nervousness, he stood there amazed as the battery struggled to assume a position of attention.

"*Now call out, 'Battery, Right Face,' then simply order, 'Forward March.' When the column nears the corner, begin the command, 'Column Left,' about four paces before you want to give the command of execution: 'March.'*" Dixon whispered again.

"*I know, I know,*" Collier muttered, gaining some small measure of control now.

"L-e-EFT,"—his voice grew a little stronger, letting the beginning of the command hang in the air a beat before he croaked—"**F-a-ACE!**" The sound was somewhere between a yelp and a scream. Watching with total disbelief, Collier felt a cautious swell of confidence as the scraggly battery clumsily executed the command.

"FO-R-R**WARD**,"—again he paused a beat—"**HARCH!**"

"*Not bad for a rookie! Now, wait until the column comes abreast of the FARTC sign before you begin your command for Column Left.*" Dixon said *sotto voce* as the battery lurched drunkenly for the corner.

Without turning his head, Collier nodded acknowledgement.

"COLY-**YUMN** LE-E-FT," he began the command as Dixon had coached—waiting until the lead man in the nearest file of the four-file formation cleared the corner of the street—before he bellowed, "**HARCH!**" It wasn't pretty, but—forgiving an occasional bumping together here and there—the still-green troops executed the turn with passable efficiency.

"'**March**', not '*Harch*', you showboat," Dixon struggled to hide the amusement in his voice.

As soon as the ragged column managed to negotiate the corner, Collier intuitively started counting cadence to get the column back in step and regain some semblance of a military formation. "Hup, Two, Thrip, Four, Hup, Tup, **Thrip, Fourp, HUP, TUP**"—recalling their drill instructor's rhythms, Collier paused two beats while their boots slapped the hard pavement twice—"**THRIP, FOURP.**"

"*My God, Ramsay, you're a goddamn natural!*" Dixon rasped with ill-concealed delight.

Ignoring Dixon—and wracking his brain as to how to restore the still-frazzled battery to marching order—it came back to Collier that their drill instructor made them count their own cadence.

"CO-O-**OUNT CAY-DENCE**,"—he paused a beat—"**COUNT!**" His voice was getting stronger with every syllable now.

"One, two, three, four. One, two, three, four. **One, two**,"—a pause while their boots slapped the pavement twice—"**three, four!**" The response began rather faint and hesitant, but grew stronger at the end.

"**YOU SOUND JUST LIKE A BUNCH OF PRISSY WACS.**" Disappointed by the weak response, Collier roared his frustration.

"*Careful, Lance Sergeant, we wouldn't want to insult our brave sisters at arms,*" Dixon cautioned in a whisper.

"Hup, Four, Hup Four, Yo' Left, YO' LEFT, YO' LEFT, YO' LEF, RIGHT, LEF!" Collier cautiously picked up the count. Recalling the Triple Nickel sergeant from the day they arrived on Post, the now almost-euphoric Collier was suddenly seized with inspiration.

"YOU HAD A GOOD HOME WHEN *YOU LEFT!*" Just like the old colored sergeant, he came down hard on '**You left!**'

"When you hear me chant '**YOU LEFT**,' give me back '**YOU'RE RIGHT**,'" he instructed, desperately hoping he wasn't about to get himself court-martialed. "Okay now, let's try it again. YOU HAD A GOOD HOME WHEN *YOU LEFT!*"

Holding his breath, Collier anxiously waited for the response.

"You're Right!" the answer was still rather weak and uncertain, but he detected a hint of life lurking there.

"Come on now, let me hear it! YOU HAD A GOOD HOME WHEN *YOU LEFT!*" he encouraged, picking up the chant again.

"**You're Right!**" the response was stronger now.

"That's a little better. Come on, A Battery, we can do better than that. YOU HAD A GOOD HOME WHEN *YOU LEFT!*"

"YOU'RE **RIGHT!**" the response was growing stronger with each attempt. The sharper trainees were catching on.

"JODY WAS THERE WHEN *YOU LEFT!*" Collier's voice resonated with renewed confidence as he felt himself taking command.

"**YOU'RE RIGHT!**" the response fairly exploded now.

"COME ON, *LADIES*. IS THAT THE BEST YOU CAN DO?" Collier urged stridently. "YOUR BABY WAS THERE WHEN *YOU LEFT!*"

"YOU'RE **RIGHT**," the response became somewhat tentative again.

"Oh, c'mon now, you sound like a bunch of titty-babies!" Collier challenged.

"At ease in there," Collier admonished the battery with scarcely-masked amusement edging his voice when a completely unmilitary ripple of laughter came floating back.

"*Titty-babies?*" Dixon whispered. Out of the corner of his eye, Collier watched the corporal roll his eyes with delight before he picked up the chant again.

"Come on, you sissies. Let's let everybody know A Battery is coming. JODY WAS THERE WHEN *YOU LEFT!*"

"**YOU'RE RIGHT!**" the response caused nearby windows to rattle.

"YOUR BABY WAS THERE WHEN **YOU LEFT...**"

"**YOU'RE RIGHT!**" Collier beamed with pride as the chorus resounded off every pane of glass in the FARTC compound.

"**AIN'T NO USE IN GOING HOME, JODY'S GOT YOUR GAL AND GONE... AIN'T NO USE IN GOING BACK, JODY'S GOT YOUR CADILLAC**"—he counted the slapping footfalls—"**SOUND OFF!**"

"ONE, TWO!" the men were also feeling the power now.

"**SOUND OFF!**"

"**THREE, FOUR!**" The electricity in the air made Collier's spirits soar. Moving more to the front of the column, he wheeled and theatrically started strutting backward like a drum major in a big-time college band.

"**NOW COUNT IT ON DOWN!**" he commanded with jubilation.

"**ONE, TWO, THREE, FOUR, ONE, TWO—THREE, FOUR!**" Incredibly, the battery was sounding, and looking, better every step of the way.

Totally caught up in the excitement of having these men responding to his command, Collier lost all thought that he was being observed until he caught a glimpse of Captain Ward standing on the far side of the street on the steps of the PX as he went strutting by. The Captain was talking to the Battalion CO and the two officers were grinning ear-to-ear.

Glancing nervously back at Dixon marching stride for stride just a couple of paces to his left elbow, Collier glimpsed the Corporal giving him an enthusiastic 'thumbs up.'

"*Don't forget you've still got to stop this train,*" Dixon said and winked. Now, when Collier looked up, the mess hall was just ahead.

"**BAT-T-TERY**"—Collier began the command as he saw the mess hall entrance looming with alarming speed—"**HALT!**"

Miraculously, the column came to a reasonably orderly standstill.

"**L-E-F-FT...FACE!...PAR-R-A-DE...REST!**" Drunk with this heady new authority, Collier checked his watch and addressed the expectant battery in front of him. "Alright now, don't forget we have a GI Party tonight. Report back to the barracks as soon as you finish chow. Anybody not present for the beginning of barracks cleaning at 0615 hours will be cleaning commodes with toothbrushes over the weekend. **BAT-T-ERY, FALL OUT!**"

Watching them disappear into the mess hall, Collier turned to Dixon and came to attention.

"Request permission to join the men for chow, Corporal!" Collier held back a grin.

"Don't pat yourself on the back too hard, Ramsay..." Dixon struggled to keep a straight face. "You've still got to figure out how to get that bunch to scrub the barracks tonight. Which reminds me, Ramsay, we're getting short on supplies. You'll need to take up a collection and send someone to the PX for Windex and Clorox if you expect to use it. If Captain Ward finds a single speck of dust tomorrow, you'll spend the entire weekend doing it over again."

"Yes, Corporal, I know," he replied, waiting expectantly for Dixon to dismiss him.

"Okay, now go get yourself a bite to eat." Dixon dismissed him.

"Thank you, Corporal." Collier saluted and headed inside for chow.

At supper chow, Collier was relieved to find—despite his fears the unwanted promotion would cost him the friendship of the few buddies he had—Larry Shields, Jack Shanahan and Herb Rudolph all invited him to join them at their table.

"No time like the present to start kissing the new Lance Sergeant's ass," Shanahan kidded as soon as he took a seat.

"Yeah, Lance Sergeant Ramsay, if you need anything like a cup of coffee, an extra dinner roll, just give me the word," Shields chimed in with a straight face.

"Cut that out or you'll all wind up cleaning commodes tonight," Collier threatened, stuffing his face with spaghetti and garlic bread.

"Would you like my dish of cobbler?" Herb Rudolph offered facetiously.

"Knock it off, you eight balls! With Nat Reed, Schepp and that gang of Dead End Kids from Brooklyn and Jersey goofing off, I'm going to need all the help my friends can give me when we GI the barracks tonight." Insecure in his new authority, Collier sobered, desperate to find support.

"What do you mean by: 'Friends?' You've got a lot to learn about the exercise of command, Lance Sergeant Ramsay. Haven't you heard? Familiarity breeds contempt!" Shanahan, an ex-cop from Savannah, Georgia, offered with a serious face.

"Yeah, you're on your own now, Lance Sergeant Brownnose," Rudolph interjected, poking a forkful of apple cobbler into his mouth.

"What's in it for us, Lance Sergeant, old buddy?" Shields got his two cents in. "If you've got so much pull with the brass, maybe you could swing us an off-post pass for Sunday?"

"Come on, guys, you know I can't do that." Looking from face to face, Collier pleaded for understanding.

"Why don't you lighten up, Ramsay? We're just kidding," Shields, a soft-spoken cowpuncher turned high-school teacher from Butte, Montana, relented. "We won't let you down. We'll make sure those cretins do their part."

Somewhat relieved, Collier finished cramming down his food and lit a Lucky as he slid his empty tray toward the waiting KPs and hurried back to the barracks to check the cleaning supplies. When he arrived, some of the men were already hanging around waiting to get started. Back toward the rear of the barracks, Rizzo and Russo were sitting on their bunks smoking, but making a mess, carelessly flicking ashes toward a nearby butt can.

"You, Russo and Rizzo, I'm glad I caught you." Momentarily letting their sloppy smoking habits go unaddressed, Collier fumbled in his pocket for his last five dollar bill. "Run up to the PX. We need four big jugs of Clorox bleach and two bottles of Windex. Be sure and get Clorox and Windex...no cheap substitutes."

"Would you just listen to the big shot, Lance Sergeant, throwing his weight around, Dominick?" Russo said, scattering ashes as he waved his hand in derision.

"Yeah, Ramsay, that phony armband don't mean jackshit to us," Rizzo said.

"If you aren't up and headed out that door in ten seconds, you'll regret you ever knew my name," Collier said, finally locating the rumpled bill and wondering what he would do if they refused.

"Aw, come on Sal. The big shot, Lance Sergeant, will have us court-martialed if we don't obey his orders."

"Russo, if you're trying to imitate some B-movie gangster, you're wasting your time on me. Now get moving before you find yourself in a world of trouble," Collier nodded at the door.

"This ain't over by a long shot, big shot, Ramsay, you'll see. Wait up, Dominick," Russo snubbed his cigarette in the palm of his hand and finally started out.

"Here take this," Collier smoothed the wrinkles on his last five bucks as he extended it toward Russo's disappearing backside. Seeing the money, Rizzo wheeled and started back.

"Here, gimme that; I'll take charge of the loot," Russo said, snatching the fiver out of Collier's hand before Rizzo reached him.

"Don't take all night, you guys, and don't forget to bring back my change and a cash register receipt," Collier shouted as they slammed out the door, heading down the steps.

The Dead End twins had no sooner left than Shields, Shanahan and Rudolph walked in, closely followed by Nat Reed who was busy bending Jake Schepp's ear. Another Dead End Kid from the Bronx, Schepp reminded Collier of a weird composite of the zoot-suited, weasel-faced Evil-eye Fleagle who could disintegrate Sherman tanks with his death-ray eyes and Fleagle's rustic counterpart, Joe Btfsplk, the hillbilly pariah with the unpronounceable name who walked around with a black cloud over his head bringing bad luck to everyone within range—both characters from Collier's favorite comic strip, Al Capp's *Lil' Abner*. Hands down, in Collier's estimation, Jake was the sloppiest trainee in the entire outfit. And, if his looks weren't bad enough, Schepp would run Nat Reed a close second for the title: "Biggest Goof-Off in the Battery."

"Come on, Schepp and Reed—get over here and help move these bunks." Bare-chested, Herb Rudolph had already stripped down to his baggy undershorts and was wrestling bunks out of the way, clearing a space to begin scrubbing the area by the front door.

"Come on, you guys! The best barracks is exempt from inspection next Saturday. Now, we don't have all night. I'll go get the hot water. Let's get busy on this floor," Shields said as he passed Reed, heading back toward the latrine. When Shields reappeared struggling under the weight of two five-gallon buckets of water, Schepp and Reed were still standing there, while Shanahan and a recruit named Jay Lawlor from Washington, DC—who had told Collier that back home he had been employed decoding intercepted radio transmission from Russia—had put on their gym shorts and were busy helping Rudolph.

"Come on, Reed, you, too, Schepp, take a brush." Shanahan extended each of the goldbrickers a brush and pointed to the box of supplies. "Grab a bar of that soap right there,"

"Whoa, not me! I'm a windows specialist." Reed refused the GI brush.

"No windows for you tonight, Reed. Everybody takes his turn scrubbing the floor. Besides, now that you bring up the subject of windows, I wound up having to go back over those windows you did last week," Shanahan said accusingly.

"Bullshit! Those windows were fine. Who made you boss, anyway? You're just kissing Ramsay's ass," Reed blustered, pushing up close to the shorter Shanahan.

"Did I hear someone take my name in vain?" Collier spoke up, anxious to defuse the fuss.

"I'm doing windows. Tell Shanahan he can't order me around," Reed wailed like a snot-nose kid.

"Leave Nat to me, Jack. I'll handle this." Collier nodded at Shanahan and waited until he moved back to join the group already on their hands and knees at the front of the barracks.

"No windows for you tonight, Nat. Get up there and grab a brush with the rest of 'em. I'm sick and tired of you not carrying your share of the load," Collier said, keeping his voice low.

"Look, Ramsay, if you think you're going to use that green armband to order me around, you got another think coming," Reed pushed up close and struck a belligerent pose.

"Quit stalling, Nat. You have to take your turn like everybody else. Now you and Schepp get on up there and get to work."

"To hell with that and to hell with that fucking armband," Reed said, not moving.

"I already told you, Nat, now get up there and get busy. I'm not going have you constantly whining, constantly testing me every time I turn around." Collier swallowed hard and stood his ground, his stomach hatching butterflies the size of pterodactyls.

"See what a chickenshit this phony is? He can't wipe his own ass without Dixon or Sergeant Ellis." Reed looked to Schepp. Rizzo and Russo had just returned from the PX with the cleaning supplies.

"I'm not afraid of you, Reed, but I'm not suicidal either. If Dixon catches us brawling, we'll both lose our chance for OCS," Collier said.

"I told you he was chickenshit," Reed persisted. Sensing Collier was backing down, he looked around for approval.

Now, recalling how Reed had chickened out a few nights ago left Collier confused. Suddenly, Reed didn't seem to be leaving him any way out.

"I've had enough of you, Reed. I'll settle this with you later, after dark behind the barracks, but not right now. Now, get on up front and get to work or I'm going to let you take your complaint to Dixon." Quite uneasy now, Collier turned to leave.

"See? I told you? See him run to Dixon. He's just plain chickenshit," Reed raised his voice and looked around the room. "Are you guys gonna let this chickenshit get away with this?"

"Come on, Nat. No sense in getting Dixon on our ass. Let Ramsay have his way for now. We heard him say he'd settle later. If he don't keep his word, everybody'll know what a chickenshit he really is. After it gets dark, we'll all go out back and watch you beat his brownnose ass." Rizzo warmed to the prospect of a brawl.

"No way this chickenshit will show. He's yellow through and through." Reed bumped Collier hard against the center support post as he turned and started to swagger away.

Now, Reed's bumping him was the final straw. Adrenaline rushing to his brain, Collier made up his mind he had to settle with the troublemaker, once and for all.

"Your buddies here heard me, Reed. Tonight—just as soon as it's dark—after we finish here, I'll come find you and we'll go out back."

"Okay, Chickenshit—I'll be waiting. Hand me that bottle of Windex and a rag. I'll get right on those windows." Reed mistakenly thought he had backed Collier down.

"Look, Reed, save your bullshit. Take this brush and get up there and start scrubbing floors." Collier took the brush from Shanahan and shoved it in Reed's hand.

"I told you, Chickenshit, I'm not scrubbing floors. I do windows like before." Reed carelessly flipped the brush back at him. It bounced off Collier's chest and clattered to the floor.

"Alright, Reed, let's go out back right now and get this over with. We'll see who's chickenshit." Collier turned, pointing to the door.

"No, no, hold up! Wait a minute, here. We have to wait 'til after dark. You just said so, yourself." Reed backed off a step, looking to his cronies for confirmation.

"Go on, Nat, don't let him bluff you," smelling blood, the gnomish Schepp egged him on.

"No, not in broad daylight. Don't you see? He wants to ruin my chances for OCS. He's trying to set me up." Reed stepped back a step.

"Now just look who's calling who Chickenshit." Collier stepped closer, adrenaline pumping faster now. It was all he could do to restrain himself from hitting the bastard flush on the chin.

"I'm not Chickenshit. I'm telling you, guys he's just trying to set me up." Reed turned back to Rizzo, Russo and Schepp. Most of the men up front had quit working and had edged closer to see what was going on; all of them were itching to see a good fight.

"Come on, Nat. You gonna' let him get away with calling you Chickenshit?" Schepp urged, hoping to shame Reed into taking Collier on.

"Aw, c'mon, Jake, you know I'm not chickenshit. Don't you see this brownnose bastard's just trying to get me in Dutch with Dixon. He's trying to set me up." Florid with frustration, Reed attempted to extricate himself without losing face.

"Bullshit! He's the one who'll be in trouble, Nat. We'll stand up for you. Come on, man, beat the crap out of the brownnose bastard. You can't just stand there and let a lightweight like Ramsay call you chickenshit to your face. Let's go out back right now and take the bastard down." The weasel-faced Schepp didn't want to let Reed weasel out now.

"Yeah, go ahead, Nat, don't let him push you around," Rizzo urged, his head bobbing up and down.

"I'll tell you what! Just for exercise, Rizzo, I'll take on you clowns first. I'm sick of all you chickenshits. Come on all of you, let's get this over with." Collier glared at Reed's cronies, ready now to take on the entire world.

"Whoa, why pick on me? Nat refused to scrub the floor." Schepp quickly bent and picked up the discarded brush.

"How about it Rizzo...Russo? You want some of me?" Collier challenged the entire group who had stopped work to see what was going down. "Anybody else? Get in line boys, now's the time."

"You're crazy, Ramsay. Why pick on us?" Now, Rizzo turned and pushed his way through the spectators to join the scrubbers. Russo and Schebb followed close behind.

"Alright, Reed, come on outside—it looks like it's just you and me." Collier brushed past Reed and headed out back.

"I'm not coming. Don't think I'm going to let you set me up." Reed was left standing alone, as the others turned away shaking their heads in disgust.

"You're a freaking coward, Reed. Admit it!" Collier wasn't about to let him get away again without testing him.

"The man is fucking crazy..." Reed complained to the turning backs, his face a study in humiliation.

"You're all talk, Reed. Either defend yourself or let these guys see what a blowhard you really are. I ask you guys—would you want a man beside you in combat with no more guts than Reed?" Collier was determined that Reed would put up or shut up. He wasn't about to spend the next sixteen weeks putting up with screw-ups like Reed.

"He's crazy, I'm telling you; Ramsay is really fucking nuts!" Reed protested weakly as he picked up a brush from the box and elbowed his way through the crowd of disappointed onlookers.

"Is that the best you can do, you chickenshit?" Collier called after him, his adrenaline rush slowly dissipating now.

"If you didn't have that Cub Scout armband, you wouldn't talk to me like that," Reed muttered under his breath seeking some measure of redemption.

Collier watched as, one-by-one, the men turned their backs on Reed and returned to work.

That night, the newly-made Lance Sergeant Collier Boyd Ramsay managed to remain awake long enough to include in his simple, heartfelt prayer a fervent plea for strength and courage. Collier wasn't quite ready to believe in miracles. Common sense told him he hadn't seen the last of his troubles from the Chicago Redskin and the Yankee Mob.

CHAPTER EIGHTEEN

THE ROANOKE TIMES
Roanoke, Virginia, Saturday, March 15, 1952
12 REDS KILLED IN CAMP CLASH

PUSAN, KOREA, Saturday, March 15 (UP) - Twelve Communist Prisoners of War were killed and 26 were injured in a new outbreak of violence last Thursday in a POW camp on Koje Island off the Korean coast, the Army announced today.

"THIS MORNING, IMMEDIATELY FOLLOWING INSPECTION, the Eagle will shit—any questions?" Dixon announced at the morning formation before he turned the battery over to Collier to march them to chow.

"What do you mean 'the Eagle will shit?'" asked Ringgold, a tow-headed, wheat farmer from Nebraska who, to Collier, looked for all the world as if he might be the first-born son of the unsmiling farm couple from the Grant Wood painting, *American Gothic*.

"That's Army lingo for payday. Those of you who have been in service long enough to have your pay record catch up with you will get paid this morning. Listen up now. These men report back here immediately following breakfast..." Dixon read off a list of names.

With less than a dollar in change in his fatigue pockets, Collier exhaled a big sigh of relief when he heard Dixon read his name. He had blown the last of the meager bankroll he had taken when he left home with the five bucks he had foolishly given Russo to buy Clorox and other supplies for their weekly GI Parties—now he was already another five bucks in hock to Shanahan. Army pay for a married Private E-1 with less than four months service was only a meager $50.00 per month; the Army sent the wife an allotment of $90.00. As much as he hated thinking about it, until Dixon's welcome announcement at morning formation, Collier had been resigned to having to telephone home after the morning inspection to ask his father to wire him a small loan to tide him over. No matter how hard up he might get, Collier would just be damned before he would call Emma to ask her to send him money.

Because of the intense pressure of the Basic Training schedule, coupled with his new responsibilities as Lance Sergeant, there had been little real opportunity for Collier to keep up with the day-to-day combat in Korea since he arrived at Sill. From what scarce information he could gather from perusing the several-days-old copies of *The Roanoke Times* his father had arranged to send him by mail—this and an occasional glimpse of the headlines from the local *Lawton-Constitution* and Oklahoma City's, *The Daily Oklahoman*—not a hell of a lot of progress was being made around the truce tables in Panmumjon. As if that wasn't depressing enough, now, polishing his brass and listening to one of several radios belonging to his barracks mates, it sounded like all hell had broken loose among the several thousand Communist POWs on an obscure pinpoint of land called Koje Island somewhere off Korea's southeastern coast near Pusan.

Regarding news of life in the everyday world, from what he gathered from these radios, he was vaguely aware not much change had taken place in the *Hit Parade* since New Year's Day. Lying on his bunk trying to work up the energy to take in *Texas Carnival*, the new Esther Williams movie showing at the Saturday matinee at the Post Theater just down the street, he gave little attention as the local DJ followed Kay Starr's hit record, *Wheel of Fortune,* with Johnnie Ray and The Four Lads wailing the vocal of a new song, *Cry.*

As for the new Esther Williams musical swimming extravaganza, he was ashamed to admit he had already seen the dumb flick just before he left home. Dating all the way back to 1944, when he had first laid eyes on the curvaceous, former Los Angeles swim champ in *Bathing Beauty,* her film debut, he had seen all of her movies because they usually featured sequences with diving. It didn't at all dampen Collier's enthusiasm that these frothy picture shows were filled with gazillions of sexy bathing beauties. He had cut his teeth on movies with Jon Hall and thrilled over any film or newsreel or magazine with pictures of fancy diving—simply because he had always fantasized becoming an Olympic springboard diver. As a kid growing up on the Roanoke River, he had become a local legend before turning twelve by diving off the top rail of the rusting, silver-painted, old iron bridge about a quarter-mile up-river from his daddy's house. And the diving instructor at the Red Cross National Aquatic School at Minnehaha Springs had been impressed with his potential on the springboard. According to the recent sports pages, at this very moment, his long-time hero, Miller Anderson, was being challenged in the three-meter springboard competition by a newcomer, David Browning, for top spot on the upcoming Olympic team. The incredible, pint-sized Korean-American, Dr. Sammy Lee, was still going strong and was almost a shoo-in to take the gold from the ten-meter platform. In 1948, Sammy had edged out the University of North Carolina head cheerleader, Norman Spear, to join Bruce Harlan and Miller Anderson on the U.S.A.'s three-meter springboard team. Most likely for the good of the team, the diminutive Asian was not competing in this Olympic springboard competition.

Among the women, nobody could touch Patty McCormick in either the springboard or platform events.

As for satisfying Collier's vicarious fantasies with regard to both bathing beauties and diving, the latest Esther Williams musical was a complete bust. Disappointingly, there weren't enough water scenes in the entire flick to fill a goldfish bowl—the movie consisted mostly of Esther trying to keep the aging, burlesque comedian, Red Skelton, out of trouble.

As far as Collier was concerned, Red Skelton was a total loser as a comedian. The only reason Collier was considering suffering through this tiresome film again was to sit there in the dark and lust over sexy Esther—who took up a lot of footage running around wearing skimpy bathing suits. The fluffy film also featured a hot new starlet, Paula Raymond, who really got Collier as horny as an old hound dog. Collier had first seen Paula Raymond two years before as Cary Grant's wife in *Crisis,* a really good Richard Brooks' movie about a brain surgeon on vacation with his wife in a small, Spanish-speaking country. Freudian or Oedipal or some such nonsense, Collier would be hard put to explain what it was about the young actress that was so attractive to him. It didn't matter, really. The simple fact remained from the first time he'd laid eyes on her, Paula Raymond really turned him on. Since then, he had seen every one of the six movies she had made even though most of her roles had been hardly more than the current "walk-on" in the new Esther Williams' flick which was hardly anything to write home about.

It didn't matter that her appearance was so brief a person would miss it altogether if he blinked, it gave Collier the beginning of a glass-etching hard-on, now, just thinking about catching another glimpse of the luscious Miss Paula Raymond.

After all, what was the harm in sublimating his growing resentments toward Emma? Over the full month-and-a-half he had been at Sill, he had written her at least twice every week.

So far, the selfish bitch had only written twice. That she was out running around somewhere virtually every time he called really chapped his ass. When he finally *had* reached her last evening after chow, she had hastily assured him she missed him and quickly brushed him off, protesting she was running late for some sort of dumb-ass nurses' meeting.

"Ramsay in here?" An abrasive voice intruded into Collier's brooding reverie.

"Who wants to know?" Collier responded absently.

"Captain Ward—he's our CO, in case you haven't heard."

"Corporal Jenkins?" Blinking hard against the backlit silhouette in the doorway, the voice sounded like the company clerk, but Collier wasn't entirely sure.

"You were expecting John Wayne?" the smartass Jenkins quipped. "Get a move on Ramsay. It's Saturday and our fearless Captain is anxious to get to the golf course."

"Lead the way. I'm right behind you," Collier grumbled as he grabbed his cunt cap, heading for the door.

"Glad I caught you, Ramsay! Hope I didn't take you away from anything important." When Collier rounded the bulletin board by the latrine, Captain Ward was waiting on the orderly room steps.

"Nothing that important, Sir," saluting smartly, Collier lied, purely hating himself for being the ass-kisser he had become.

"Good. Ramsay, I couldn't help but notice from your DD-1 that you were a commercial artist in civilian life." The Captain read from an open manila folder. "It says here you designed silkscreen posters and newspaper advertising—wasn't there a lot of hand-lettering involved?"

"Yessir, but lettering's definitely not my strongest suit," Collier protested, not liking the direction of this conversation at all.

"I'm sure you're being far too modest, Ramsay. Just look at this abominable signboard...it's a disgrace." The CO pointed to the shamefully amateurish, hand-lettered signboard listing the Battery Chain of Command, mounted beside the door to the Orderly Room. Captain Ward's name was prominently displayed at the top. "I'm sure you could do a better job than this."

It was impossible to argue. The amateurishly-lettered signboard looked like honorable-mention in a pre-school competition.

"Don't be too sure, Captain. You're giving me far too much credit here. I have no skills at sign painting. There's a big difference between using India ink on slick drawing board and applying enamel paint with stiff brushes on an enameled wooden surface like this sign board." Collier explained, trying his best to discourage his Commanding Officer.

"Save your excuses, Lance Sergeant. Certainly you can do a better job than this? Judaspriest, Ramsay, *anyone* could do a better job than this!" Clearly, the Captain was in no mood to quibble.

"But Sir, sign painting is not the same as doing lettering for advertising. I've never done anything even remotely like this before. I'm sure there must be a

professional sign shop on post. The FARTC sign out front is a first-class job."
Collier was no fool. He wanted no part of a project like this. He could just see
Ward bragging about his new sign at Battalion Officer's Call. Once word got out,
there would be no end to it. For the foreseeable future, his precious-little free
time would go to hell in a hand basket.

"I don't want some stenciled junk. I want better than that. Besides, there's a
waiting list at that Post sign shop longer than the promotion list to Major. I should
think you'd have more pride in your battery, Ramsay."

"But I do, Captain Ward. I'm trying to explain. I've never done anything
like this. I'm not at all sure I'm the best man for the job."

"We won't know until you give it a try. Now, will we? First Sergeant Ellis has
already secured a new sign board and has had three coats of white enamel sprayed
on it. I've instructed Sergeant Ellis and Corporal Dixon to make sure you have
time off to do a proper job. Come walk with me now down to Battalion. Here,
take this pass to leave the post. My wife's waiting in the parking lot to drive you
into Lawton to buy your supplies." The Captain wheeled, abruptly starting off in
the direction of Battalion HQ.

"You certainly took long enough. I was hoping for a swim." With the top
down on the shiny, yellow Chrysler convertible, the good-looking blonde waiting
in the parking lot at the rear of Battalion HQ was definitely not in the best of
moods.

"Meg, I'd like to present Lance Sergeant Collier Ramsay. Ramsay, this is my
wife, Megan. She'll drive you into Lawton to get your supplies." Ward's wife
scowled an inquisitive appraisal as the Captain continued speaking. "I'm running
late. After I golf with the visiting brass, the other wives are meeting us at 0630 at
the O Club for dinner—now please don't be late," Ward dismissed his wife with
an impatient wave and turned and walked over to where the Battalion CO was
waiting in his jeep.

"Calling you Lance Sergeant Ramsay is too much like dialogue from a bad
war movie. Do you have a first name?" The Captain's wife wrinkled her freckled
nose and frowned.

"Call me Collier, Ma'am." He waited for her to invite him to get in the car.

"Okay, Collier Ramsay, I'm Meg. Hop in." Leaning across the seat from
beneath the wheel, she unlocked the door on the passenger side. "I'm sure
you're just as anxious to get this over with as I am—after all, it *is* Saturday
afternoon."

Arriving at the paint store just off the town square in Lawton, Collier quickly
located a quart of black enamel paint before moving to the small combo art-and-
crafts section at the back of the store where he carefully selected an assortment of
square-tipped, stiffly-chiseled bristle brushes of various sizes and two pointed sable
brushes. Making his way back to the cash register up front, Collier picked up a
half-pint can of white enamel to use touching up the inevitable miscues of his
shaky hand.

"You didn't waste much time back there—you seem very sure of yourself,"
the captain's wife remarked as she tooled the big convertible out of the dusty,
lackluster business district, heading back to the Reservation.

"Just because I know what the job will require, doesn't mean I'm the best
man to do the work." He smiled and shrugged.

"Do I detect a bit of resentment here?" She shot him a questioning look.

"Frustration might be the better word, Ma'am. I tried to explain to the captain..." he began, but merely shrugged and left the half-finished thought hanging in mid-air.

Dropping him back at the Battalion parking lot, she smiled and said, "By the way, I guess you know that Paula Raymond, the hot new actress in the Esther Williams flick, is making a public promotional appearance before the movie tonight. It's most likely one of those Hollywood starlets 'giving-her-all-for-our-boys-in-the-service' things."

"You're not making fun are you? Is that really true?"

"Absolutely. Captain Ward and I are attending a cocktail party for her at the O Club before she makes her appearance at the picture show."

"Wow...that's really something! Thanks for cluing me in."

Dropping the paint and brushes by the orderly room, Collier headed for his bunk to take a nap. He intended to be well-rested and first in line at Post Theater No. 3 tonight.

Collier awoke to find he had overslept and missed supper chow altogether. Hurriedly showering and changing into a fresh uniform, he left the barracks and scurried down the street toward Post Theater No. 3, hoping desperately to beat the crowd. As he neared the theater in the gathering gloom, he was dismayed to see a long line backed up all the way past the Service Club almost to the PX. Resolutely refusing to be deterred by the waiting mob of people, Collier stoically took a place in line. After all he had suffered during the past ten weeks, he would just be damned if he were going to miss this once-in-a-lifetime opportunity to see the glamorous Miss Paula Raymond in the well-rounded flesh.

When he finally made it inside the theater, rather than having to stand in the back, he was forced to take a seat all the way down front. He'd hardly settled into the seat when a major stepped from behind the projection screen and walked to the front of the narrow stage where a corporal was adjusting the stand on a microphone. A hush fell over the boisterous crowd.

"Give me your attention, please," the major began, cautiously tapping the mike to see if his voice was getting out. When he was certain the mike was live, he unfolded a sheet of paper and began to read from his notes. "Tonight we are extremely fortunate to have the lovely Hollywood actress, Miss Paula Raymond, visiting us here at Fort Sill. A promising new star on the Hollywood scene, Miss Raymond has appeared in seven feature films since her debut in 1950 playing Cary Grant's wife in the motion picture, *Crisis*. Since then, Miss Raymond's career has blossomed into featured roles in seven major films: *Duchess of Idaho, Devils' Doorway, Grounds for Marriage, Inside Straight, The Tall Target,* tonight's feature, *Texas Carnival* and an upcoming film, *The Sellout*—costarring Walter Pidgeon with John Hodiak and Audrey Totter—which is scheduled for release later this year. In the feature musical you are about to see here tonight, Miss Raymond plays actor Keenan Wynn's sister—the girl Esther Williams is pretending to be. If that sounds complicated, when you see the picture, you will understand. Anyway, without further ado, it gives me great pleasure to introduce Miss Paula Raymond."

The major turned to his left and waited as a frumpish-looking female approached the mike from the right side of the stage. Wearing no make-up at all, the woman was dressed in baggy, badly-wrinkled camel-colored riding jodhpurs and a pale-blue checkered gingham western shirt. Her stringy, uncombed, shoulder-length, mousy-brown hair stuck out like the business end of a kitchen broom.

Hard put to understand just what was taking place, Collier assumed the frumpy female approaching center stage was a publicist or hairdresser or some similar flunky in Miss Raymond's entourage. When the major raised the woman's hand and announced, "Gentlemen, I give you Miss Paula Raymond," Collier couldn't believe his eyes and ears. Sitting in openmouthed-disbelief, Collier found it impossible to reconcile the drab, unkempt woman standing center stage not fifteen feet away with the glamorous screen image of his sexual fantasy, Paula Raymond. Like Collier, the crowd sat momentarily stunned before some polite soul midway in the small auditorium began to clap and the courteous ripple of applause was taken up by a scattering of the embarrassed crowd. As an awkward reflection of the expectant crowd's abject disbelief and disillusionment, almost as soon as it began, the applause quickly died down again.

"Thank you. I'm so thrilled to be here at Fort...Fort Sill, Oklahoma, tonight to bring greetings and heartfelt thanks to you true-life American heroes from all of your friends and admirers in Hollywood...." Collier barely heard the actress's words as he watched in utter disbelief.

"Miss Raymond is very sorry, but she will not be able to sign autographs..." When the actress had concluded her awkward speech, the major took her by the arm and promptly left the stage. Not really knowing how to deal with his utter disbelief and disillusionment, Collier remained in his seat and suffered through the film for about an hour waiting for his erstwhile fantasy-figure, Paula Raymond, to appear in her will-o'-the-wisp cameo. Her image disappearing from the screen almost before it had begun, as soon as the actress's brief walk-on was over, Collier quietly stood and left the theater, feeling cheated and depressed. Outside, he made his way to the Service Club and ordered a coke and a hot dog to make up for supper chow.

"Hi, Ram, I saw you come in the movie. Did you enjoy the show?" while Collier was eating, Chip Jones came over to say hello.

"Hey, Chip. That may well be the worst flick I ever saw," Collier grumbled, swallowing the last bite of hot dog. He hated the nickname, Ram, but a lot of the men called him that now.

"Yeah, it was a loser, alright,"—Chip agreed, continuing happily—"I left before it was done and came over here to call home. My wife's bringing our baby son here for Easter. Just four more weeks and I'll get my first look at my namesake. What do you think of that?"

"Chip, I know how much you want to see your baby son, but I don't think I'd brag too much about them coming here. You know the Army discourages trainees from bringing families out here while we're still in Basic," Collier reminded him.

"I know, Ram, but it's still a free country. They can't really stop my wife from coming—can they?" Chip asked, defensively. "Do you think they'll raise a stink?"

"Hey, man, I was just trying to offer some friendly advice," Collier countered as they walked along.

"You're right. I'll keep it quiet," Chip quickly agreed.

Back at the barracks, Collier lost no time undressing in the dark. Almost before he lay down and pulled the sheet and blanket over himself, he drifted into a restless, dream-filled sleep.

Some guy named Bohon came by last night asking for you," Shields informed him in the latrine the next morning as Collier was shaving. "He said to tell you he's in C Battery, just down the street."

With nothing more important to do on Sunday morning, Collier dressed in Class A uniform and headed to C Battery. The PFC on duty pointed out the barracks where Bo was billeted.

"Is Bohon around?" Collier asked a skinny GI perched on the side of his bed, still in his skivvies, stretching and yawning and rubbing sleep from his eyes.

"He left awhile ago, but it's still a little early for Chapel. On Sunday morning, he usually goes with some of the guys to the Service Club down the street to grab free coffee and donuts before Chapel services. Protestant services ain't 'til ten hundred hours. If you hurry, you might still catch him there."

"Well, I'll just be dad-burned," Bo said, grinning from ear to ear when he looked up and saw Collier walking toward him across the main room of the Service Club.

"The uniform looks good on you, but the Army hasn't improved your cussing very much." Collier embraced his old friend with a warm bear hug. Bo was wearing the green armband of a Lance Corporal.

"I leave the cussing to smart-aleck Lance Sergeants." Bo grinned, giving Collier's own green armband the once-over. "Looks like they been starving you. Don't you like the chow?"

"Truth is, I do like the chow, but I can't seem to get enough to make up for the way they run our asses off around this place." Collier shrugged, fairly beaming at his friend.

"C'mon over here, I want you to meet a couple pals of mine." Bo nodded toward a small group of soldiers standing against the far wall drinking coffee from paper cups and helping themselves from a table full of pastries. Overjoyed to see his friend from home, Collier followed along and shook hands with Bo's companions.

"How long have you been at Sill?" Collier asked, eyeing the sweet rolls and looking around for a coffee cup.

"I got here January fourteenth," Bo said. "We just finished our eighth week of Basic—Hell Week. Regular Basic is behind us now. We begin Survey and Metero tomorrow morning."

"We still have two more weeks of the regular Infantry Basic. We fire both the thirty-caliber air-cooled and the water-cooled machine guns and bazookas next week," Collier brought his buddy up to date.

"Not much to any of that. You get to toss hand grenades and go through the live-fire course the week after that. It's scary the first time—after that, it's really pretty much a joke. It's a real pain in the butt to crawl around on your belly and ass in all that dirt and mud."

"Are you telling me they fire blanks?" Collier asked, disappointed to think it was all a sham.

"Oh, heck no. The ammo's live alright. Even in daylight, you can see the tracers whizzing over your head. And every once in awhile you hear about one of those worn-out weapons throwing a wild round. But, truth is, they're so afraid someone is going to get hurt and ruin the Army's safety record, they don't leave much to chance," Bo shook his head and laughed.

"What is 'Metero,' anyway?" Collier asked, not much accustomed to Artillery jargon.

"Metero is short for meteorology. The Army's making us into weathermen," Bo laughed.

"I don't get it," Collier shook his head. "Where does that fit in with artillery?"

"The weather and atmospheric conditions have an important effect when you're trying to shoot a hundred-pound projectile through the air up to ten or more miles and land it within several feet of a specific target." Bo was surprised Collier didn't understand the connection.

"Pardon me all to hell for being so stupid," Collier said, embarrassed at his ignorance.

"Oh, lighten up, Collier. I didn't mean to sound like a know-it-all," Bo apologized.

"No problem, but while you're at it, how about telling me what Survey's got to do with anything?"

"Well, the entire system of aiming and firing guns toward unseen targets is based on information supplied from maps or by observers miles away from the guns themselves—the FDC...Fire Direction Center—controlling the guns depends on maps. This means the guns have to be set up at known—you know, *actually surveyed?*—locations so they can be aimed in identical directions. I'm not saying this very well, but it all boils down to using maps... coordinates...stuff like that. Anyway, I can't really explain it exactly, but you'll find out soon enough." Bo shrugged, frustrated he was having such a hard time expressing himself.

"I think I get it now," Collier reassured his friend who had actually done a better job of explaining than he realized.

"Good! It's really great to see you," Bo brightened.

"Great to see you, too. How'd you find out I was here, anyway?" Collier asked, wrapping two glazed donuts in a paper napkin and accepting a cup of coffee from the vaguely matronly, but quietly striking woman with a USO armband presiding over the pastry buffet.

"Jenny finally got a hold of Emma on the phone a couple of nights ago," Bo said, licking chocolate from his fingertips. "I call Jen at least twice a week from the phones outside the PX."

"Jenny had better luck than I've had. I haven't talked to Emma in a couple of weeks at least." Taking their food with them, Collier followed Bo across the room to a grouping of four overstuffed, burgundy-hued leather chairs forming a circle around a low table.

"Yeah. Jenny said she had trouble tracking Emma down. Jenny said they kept Emma pretty busy at the VA."

"I'm glad Jenny didn't give up. We probably would never have discovered we've been less than a hundred yards apart for six whole weeks and not a clue we were within a thousand miles of each other." Collier shook his head in wonder.

"Yeah—talk about a stroke of luck? The morning I left Meade, they put a bunch of us on a train to a hellhole called Camp Chaffee in Arkansas. From there, we rode a bus through Oklahoma City straight here. How come you were so long in getting here?" Bo asked.

"It's a long story. I'll stick to the highlights," Collier quickly brought Bo up to date.

"Well, I'll be here eight more weeks. It's good we finally wound up together again. By the way that nice USO lady over there is going to take a carload of us out to the Wichita Range right after Chapel—drive us all the way up Mount Scott in a shiny Cadillac. We'll get to see Lake Lawtonka and the buffalo herd. I'll bet she has room for one more."

"Well...I don't know. I've got work to catch up..." Collier hedged. Getting stuck on some Mickey Mouse tour of a bunch of rock-strewn hills was not exactly his idea of fun.

"I don't think we'll be gone that long. I'll ask her." Bo jumped up and walked over to where the rather proper-looking USO matron was just taking off her apron. After a brief exchange, she followed him back to where they sat.

"Miz Birdsong, this is my hometown buddy, Collier Ramsay. Tell him how long we'll be gone this afternoon," Bo introduced him to the somewhat older but borderline attractive USO volunteer. When he heard her name, he gave her a closer look. She wore no wedding ring and nothing about her features suggested she was of Indian blood.

"I plan to leave here at eleven hundred hours. I'm providing a picnic lunch. We should be back here sometime around fifteen hundred hours...three o'clock," the woman assured him. "I promise you, Mr. Ramsay, the view from Mount Scott is breathtaking. And at the Wildlife Preserve you can walk right up to the buffalo—it's becoming a fairly sizeable herd."

"C'mon, Collier? You don't have anything better to do," Bo urged eagerly.

"Okay, count me in. Real live American buffalo sound too good to miss. I'll be right back. I have to go make sure my pass covers being that far away from Post." Collier hurried off to check with the duty NCO at the orderly room.

Bo and two of his buddies were waiting by the curb with the USO volunteer when Collier returned. Since Collier's legs were longest, the others insisted Collier take the front seat when they all piled into the shiny, black Cadillac sedan.

"It's okay to smoke. I'm about to have one myself if one of you gentlemen will offer me a light," the USO matron told them as she closed the door. She had changed into a fringed and beaded buckskin skirt and the white, mannish-looking Western shirt tucked tightly into her waistband, accentuated her voluptuous hips and full-busted figure.

Letting the car roll smoothly forward as soon as the doors were closed, the Birdsong woman drove east from FARTC toward the gate at Sheridan Road. Once outside the reservation she turned north on Highway 62, the main thoroughfare to Oklahoma City. Collier had barely finished snubbing his Lucky in the ashtray when she abruptly slowed, swinging sharply left onto Highway 49. A few hundred yards past the intersection, the sign read: Mt. Scott 7 miles.

They had traveled only a mile or so before a series of four, smoothly-rounded hills rose up like stair-steps in the near-distance to their left. Alongside the paved road they were traveling, a lacy filigree of green willows traced the flow of a tranquil stream running along the base of the ridge of hills. As they drew closer and the formation became more clearly defined, Collier could see the four large mounds were quite dramatically sheared abruptly along their centerline, bisecting the spectacular geographic anomaly into a graduated series of sheer gray-granite cliffs.

"Those hills are the legendary Medicine Bluffs. It's easy to see the spectacular evidence of the ancient earthquake fault running right down their spine." The Birdsong woman pointed with fascination at the arresting formation. "At Sill they're known as: MB-One, Two, Three and Four. The earthquake fault makes up the watercourse of Medicine Creek, here, running along their base. Historically, Indian tribes from far and wide used this remarkable landmark as a sacred meeting ground. Geronimo, the famous Chiricahua Apache, is reputed to have leaped unharmed from the crest of the highest of those cliffs into this stream," their enthusiastic tour guide recited.

"I wasn't aware Oklahoma was part of Geronimo's stomping ground," Collier said.

"You're right. The Chiricahua Apache usually roamed more to the Southwest. The U.S. Cavalry chased Geronimo all over Texas, Arizona, New Mexico and Colorado. But when the old renegade was finally taken prisoner, he was held here at Sill in the old log jail. That ancient jail still stands on the Old Post. I suppose you're aware Geronimo is buried here at Sill?"

"Geronimo is buried here at Sill?" one of Bo's buddies expressed the group's surprise.

"Oh, yes. There's a lot of history buried here at Fort Sill. Quanah Parker—and Quanah's mother, Cynthia Parker, too—both are buried up on Chief's Knoll. Do you know who Quanah Parker was?"

"Seems like I read something somewhere—was he an Apache, too?" Collier racked his brain, trying to jog his memory.

"No, he was a half-breed Comanche. Quanah's mother, Cynthia Ann Parker, was taken captive as a child by a Comanche chief named Noconie—sometimes called Tah-con-ne-ah-pe-ah." Birdsong pronounced each syllable slowly. "Most modern history books call him Peta Nocona. Anyway, long story short, the young white girl, Cynthia Ann Parker became the bride of a Comanche chief and bore him the son named, Quanah. Quanah grew up Comanche and became their last great warrior Chief. Starving and ravaged in the futile, long-running war with the superior American Cavalry, Quanah finally surrendered his badly-decimated band at Fort Sill in June 1875. He soon was made Chief of the Reservation and learned English and became a judge. Quanah later became an important figure in helping Washington settle Indian affairs. We have a wonderful museum on the Post. When you get a chance, I recommend it strongly; Fort Sill played an important part in our country's history." The Birdsong woman enthused; then apologized. "I'm sorry...I guess I must sound like the local Chamber of Commerce."

"Not at all. That's really interesting. I'll try to make a point to visit the jail and those gravesites before I leave," Collier assured her, honestly impressed.

Past Medicine Bluffs, they traversed a rugged landscape characterized by wind-sculpted granite buttes. The scenery reminded Collier of old-time Western movies. In the approaching near-distance a rather low, but nonetheless dominating, rocky promontory rose out of the barren arroyos and small canyons.

"Is that Mount Scott, there up ahead?" Collier asked.

"That's right." Birdsong nodded.

"Doesn't look like much of a mountain," Collier blurted. Comparing the altogether unimpressive, half-mile high, rocky promontory ahead with the over five-thousand-foot elevation of Poor Mountain raising an imposing presence near his father's house near Salem, the approaching landmark looked more like a hill than a mountain.

"Mount Scott has an elevation of two-thousand, sixty-four feet above sea level—slightly higher than Mount Wall and Mount Sheridan in this same area. Even so, Mount Scott is actually only the second highest mountain in the Wichita Range. Officially, Mount Pinchot, in a restricted 'Special Use Area' a bit further to the west-northwest, is about a dozen feet taller," their tour guide said, somewhat offended.

"So that makes Mount Scott the second-highest peak in Oklahoma?" Collier deduced.

"No. Black Mesa up in the northwest corner of the Panhandle rises to four-thousand, nine-hundred-and-seventy-three—nearly five thousand—feet. Don't lose sight of the fact this is rather flat country down here, making the Wichita Range something of an incongruous land feature. While Mount Scott may be only half the elevation of Black Mesa, the view from up there is pretty spectacular," she continued with a perceptibly defensive tone.

"I'm sure it is. This country is just so different from where I'm from." Embarrassed, Collier lamely patronized, trying to avoid the impression he was belittling their gracious tour guide's rightful pride in her wild and craggy native Oklahoma landscape.

Ruefully, his apology came too late to mollify the insult. Momentarily, Ms. Birdsong fell silent, retreating into wounded feelings, but her sulk was short-lived. A short distance further along, she recovered, pointing out the entrance to Lake Lawtonka on the right hand side of the highway.

"If anyone needs to use a the restroom, the closest facility to Mt. Scott is just ahead, in the parking lot to the Lake Elmer Thomas picnic area—which, by the way, is where we'll eat our lunch," she warned, indicating the entrance to the approaching recreation area.

Assured her passengers were not in need of toilet facilities, at least for the short-term, Birdsong bypassed the entrance to the picnic area and turned the big car right, passing between a pair of sturdy gateposts with a sign advising the road up Mt. Scott opened and closed at 9:00.

"You're right. This is *absolutely* awe-inspiring," Collier gasped, as the narrow, circuitous road gradually spiraled its way upward around the rocky slopes toward the summit and the boundless, boulder-strewn, native-Southwestern, mixed-grass prairie spread before them unimpeded in every direction. Before the car had climbed halfway up the slope, Collier was more than willing to concede Hilda Birdsong's homespun pride was well invested—the view from Mount Scott was absolutely breathtaking!

"Go ahead and enjoy the view. We'll go back down and eat as soon as everyone is ready," their driver announced when they reached the flat, circular turnaround at the summit and she had parked the car. Spilling out of the backseat, Bo and his buddies wandered to an outcrop further to the northeast and stood overlooking the large expanse of Lake Lawtonka, trying to locate the Wildlife Refuge and the buffalo herd. Collier walked over to the nearby rim.

"Here take these glasses. Now look right down there..." Her wounded pride seemingly forgotten, Ms. Birdsong extended a pair of powerful military binoculars and moved around behind him. Her hips and lower torso brushed faintly against his backside as she leaned over his shoulder, pointing in a general southwesterly direction. "Medicine Bluffs are there...just past where Medicine Creek spills out of Lake Lawtonka. Can you make them out?"

"I'm not sure..." Searching the unfamiliar terrain spreading before him, Collier tried to ignore the distracting physical contact while he struggled to pick out a familiar landmark.

"Look down...where the road starts up the mountain?" Her breasts were touching now.

"Uh-m...I see the road, but ah-h..." he stammered. With her heavy bosom pressing against his back, he was having difficulty keeping his mind on the task at hand.

"That's Route 49. Now from the base of the mountain where the road jumps off Route 49, backtrack along the highway between the big lake to the left and the smaller lake to the right..." Both her breasts and hips were touching now.

"Okay...I see the road, but..."

"Look where Medicine Creek comes out of the large lake right below us, the creek bank is lined with willow and mesquite." Her breath was a minty zephyr against his cheek.

"Oh, I see the willows now!" he exclaimed, finally locating the creek and slowly tracing its path it as it moved back along the southern side of the narrow ribbon of highway.

"Good! Now, just follow that line of trees." He had been too long away from women. Her presence was impossible to ignore. Helpless to prevent it, his penis was growing hard.

"Oh, wow! I can actually see the earthquake fault. That is truly incredible," he gasped. Locating the shadowy line of the cliffs sharply delineating the northern face of the four little bluffs did little to distract his attention from the motion of her solid breasts. His penis had become a center pole inside the loose folds of his baggy GI undershorts.

"Alright, now just lower the glasses and follow my hand..."—her breasts moved against his shoulder blades as she leaned closer, exerting more pressure, urging him to pivot slowly to the right—"...there, see the water tower? That's Fort Sill. From there go a little left...see that sharp terrain feature? The pointy hill with a tiny concrete building on top?"

"Uh?...I'm not sure...I uh..." He could feel the pressure of her lower abdomen wriggling against his butt. Moving her left arm around his neck, both arms completely encircled him now. Gripping the heavy military binoculars with both hands, her weighty bosom settled against the tops of his shoulders at the base of his neck.

"There. Follow down my arm. See the sunlight glinting on the little blockhouse?" The pressure of her ample breasts and the faint essence of her bath soap with just a hint of talcum sent the blood draining from his brain.

"Uhm-m, I see it now! Looks like a miniature extinct volcano..." He nodded, finally locating the tiny blockhouse atop the completely treeless, almost perfect cone-shaped peak. With his penis as hard as the rock he stood upon, and with the nearest restroom at the base of this godforsaken hilltop, there was absolutely no place to hide a runaway erection. Leaning slightly forward, Collier twisted around trying to locate some temporary haven for adjusting his male parts in private. The unexpected shift in position dislodged the heavy binoculars from her grasp. At the very last instant, he lunged forward and caught them by the strap, narrowly avoiding the expensive field glasses plummeting over the side of the steep escarpment to the rocks below. When he straightened, she slyly averted her gaze from the tell-tale bulge in the crotch of his heavy, woolen uniform trousers.

"Here, take the glasses and put the strap around your neck before we lose them again." She stepped in close, brushing purposefully against the protrusion of his pecker. The unexpected contact was a jolt of lightning to his private parts. She left little doubt in his mind she knew exactly what she was doing. "Now, if you will direct the glasses to your left and drop down a little, you can see the HQ buildings on the Old Post. The old stone barracks and the log prison where Geronimo was held are all in the same vicinity. I'd be glad to take you some Saturday or Sunday...if you're interested and have the time."

"That's very generous of you. I'd like that; I just can't say for sure exactly when I'll have the opportunity. " he hedged. He felt certain her invitation included more than just a sightseeing tour and history lesson.

"I'm usually at the Service Club every Saturday after lunch. And every Sunday morning, you can always reach me that way. Guess we'd better find your buddies and have our picnic if we're going to get you back to Sill on time." Stepping back on the macadam parking circle to straighten her skirt, she glanced up and looked him in the eye as she carefully rearranged her blouse, stretching it tight against her breasts. In that sharply-etched instant, Collier understood that a contract of intimacy had taken place between them.

"I'll go round up the troops," he said as he turned and walked across the turnaround, trying to adjust his unruly anatomy back to some reasonable semblance of presentability.

Stuffed to the point of discomfort with fried chicken, potato salad and deviled eggs, it was with a mixture of regret and relief when shortly before 1500 hours, Collier helped police up around their picnic table in the Lake Elmer Thomas Recreation Area and repack Hilda's picnic basket. On the ride back to Sill, Collier struggled to resist looking at her, trying to bring his thoughts to bear on the week of training ahead.

"Can you just drop us back at the Service Club?" Bo asked as a young spit-and-polish guard saluted Hilda's big Caddy through the Sheridan Drive gate onto the military reservation.

"That's exactly where I was headed...unless, of course, any of you would like to take a quick tour of the Old Post," she offered. Intuitively, Collier understood the invitation was meant for him.

"Not today, thank you, Ma'am," Bo quickly declined after a hurried conference with his buddies in the back.

"I'm in no particular hurry. I'll take you up on that offer, Ma'am. I don't know when I'll get another chance to see the Post." Collier was helpless to resist finding out just what he was getting into.

"Wonderful...it shouldn't take us long at all..." Hilda Birdsong brightened, pulling up in front of the Service Club to drop off Bo and his buddies.

"Do you and your husband live in Lawton proper, Mrs. Birdsong?" Collier asked as soon the oversized Caddy started rolling again.

"My husband's no longer alive, but, yes, I live in town. Captain Birdsong was killed on Omaha Beach on D-Day," she replied, keeping her eyes straight ahead. "We had only been married a month before Alvin shipped overseas. He died a hero."

"Was he Artillery, Ma'am? Is that why you came back here to Sill?"

"Yes, Alvin was Artillery. My maiden name was Stewart—my great, great grandfather was a Cavalry Major under Colonel Ranald Mackensie, the officer who encouraged Quanah Parker to surrender his band. My father was a retired, full Colonel, Artillery. He was S-2 to the Post Commander when he retired—won a Silver Star in both World Wars. My brother was an Artillery Major. He was killed at Bastogne. Like any good Army brat, I was also in the military—a WAC lieutenant with the Judge Advocate General in the Pentagon. As the only surviving child, I came home to live here in Lawton with my mother after my daddy died. My mother passed away almost two years ago. Lawton isn't much to brag about, but I grew up here at Fort Sill. I love it here. I'm still inactive reserve and have privileges at the PX, and I'm welcome at the O Club." Suddenly nervous and apologetic, she glanced over at him. "I'm sorry. I didn't mean to bore you with my life story and family genealogy."

"Not at all, Ma'am. I can see now why you know so much of the local lore," Collier said, more than a bit impressed by her military background.

"Pay attention now; we're coming onto the Old Post...see those stone cavalry stables just ahead on the right? They were built by the first colored 'buffalo soldiers' who were camped here around 1869. Back then, our troops called the encampment 'Camp Wichita.' In those early days, the Indians called it 'the Soldier House at Medicine Bluffs'. This old stone house up ahead was originally built for the first commanding general, Brevet Major General Benjamin Grierson. They call it the 'Sherman House' because two Kiowa chiefs tried to assassinate him on the porch when General William Tecumseh Sherman traveled here in eighteen seventy-one in an attempt to bring a peaceful resolution to a series of Indian uprisings..." For the next thirty minutes, Collier allowed himself the pleasure of listening attractive older woman as she slowly tooled the big car through the narrow, almost deserted streets of the Old Post, pointing out an array of interesting sights, including the rustic log prison that once had held the legendary Geronimo as well as the original Old Post Chapel."

"Can we see Geronimo's grave?" Collier asked.

"Time passes by too quickly, I'm afraid. Geronimo's grave will have to wait. He and Quanah Parker are buried way out, across Highway Sixty-two." She looked at her expensive, yellow-gold wristwatch and made a wry face. "As much as I hate to say it, I guess we should be thinking about getting back. Perhaps you'll let me have an opportunity to take you out there some other day." She glanced shyly over at him as she turned the car and headed back in the opposite direction.

"I'd like that very much," he replied, wondering just what he was letting himself in for.

"I'll look forward to it." She smiled.

"I had a great time," Collier said when she pulled up in front of his barracks. It was almost dark and the street lights were already lit. He really hated to see her go.

"If you're free Saturday or Sunday afternoon, perhaps you'll let me complete our tour? One of the other volunteers can take the Mt. Scott outing. Here's my number, just in case you want to call me at home." She jotted a number on a personal calling card.

"In Basic, we never know what's coming next. I can't always be sure, but you can bet I'll make it if I possibly can." Collier slid out of the seat and closed the door.

After he watched the black Caddy disappear from view, Collier strolled the short block down to the dairy stand on the corner across from the drill field and wolfed down a couple of greasy hot dogs and a milkshake. Then—still on edge from the stimulating afternoon—he strolled dreamily back to the barracks and, using the reflected light from the street lights, readied his uniforms and equipment for the next day's training. When he finished, he lay down in the darkness and drifted into an exhausted and dreamless sleep, scheming of ways to see the widow Birdsong again at the earliest possible opportunity.

As sometimes happens, Collier had unwittingly prophesized his own unpredictable future. Due to the increased intensity of the schedule, he would not find time to see Hilda Birdsong again during that final frantic period of Infantry Basic. It was only by the most heroic of efforts he was able to reach her by phone to explain this sorry plight.

Ironically, however, Collier felt somewhat compensated for his frustration at not being able to keep his date with Hilda when—to his surprise and delight—during the final two weeks of Basic, the men of A Battery were afforded a serendipitous addition to their Weapons Familiarization. Having already qualified with the M-1 rifle, the standard issue of the Infantry, and the M-2 Carbine, the designated combat weapon for artillerymen, the men of A Battery were quite unexpectedly introduced to the army officer's longtime traditional sidearm—the trusty 1911 Colt .45 pistol. From old Humphrey Bogart and James Cagney gangster movies and from reading *I the Jury* and the other detective stories featuring Mickey Spillane's tough, sex-obsessed private eye, Mike Hammer, the Colt 45 automatic was a weapon Collier had fantasized about in his overactive, vicarious, boyish imagination for as long as he could remember.

Originally designed by John Moses Browning and initially produced by Colt, this classic pistol had served since WWI as the official military sidearm in the armies of several nations. After learning to field-strip and clean actual models of the classic handgun, Collier and his battery mates had been sorely disappointed when they had been forced to lie in the mud on their bellies, pelted by an unremitting freezing rain for an entire afternoon only to be handed a phony, CO_2-operated imitation of the real weapon and humiliated to qualify on a miniature, 1000-inch range (27 yards) with what was nothing more than a glorified BB gun. To further compound this indignity, among other rather unimaginative exercises being thrown at them was an altogether juvenile charade called "Buddy Movement" which was supposedly designed to familiarize them with teamwork in combat situations. It seemed to Collier a further sign that the cosmic forces were aligned against him when, through the abysmal luck of the draw, he found himself paired with his once and constant antagonist, Nat Reed. Inevitably, there was the infamous Confidence Course in a well-trodden area with rope climbs, steeplechase jumps, horizontal hand-over-hand ladders, and vertical walls to scale.

Sandwiched between this flood of last minute combat readiness training was a class on how to make a horseshoe-roll backpack—complete with extra clothing, entrenching tool, first aid-pouch, K-rations and the rest. The horseshoe roll, which was folded around the top and sides of the pack itself, consisted of a blanket tightly rolled inside a "shelter half"—Army lingo for half a pup tent. During A Battery's first overnight bivouac, it immediately became evident to Collier that the waterproof shelter half and lightweight poncho were among the most indispensable pieces of all of the indispensable array of their combat issue.

Also included in the final two weeks of Infantry Basic were classes on the basic artillery field radio, the ANGR-9—or "Angry-niner," as it was familiarly called. With the intricacies of the ANGR-9, they memorized "Able...Baker...Charlie..." and rest of the entire phonetic alphabet through "...Zebra". The communication instruction was followed by a middle-of-the-night Ten-Mile Forced March with an M-2 carbine and clips and a full-combat pack complete with horseshoe roll—a load approaching eighty pounds if weapons and ammo were included. The first march was quickly followed by the Night

Infiltration Course with exploding mortar rounds and live tracers whizzing overhead followed with machine gun rapidity by another exhausting night march—all field exercises with full pack. The second march was supposed to have been twenty-five miles, but, thanks be to another intervention of the cosmic forces, Captain Ward had been wearing new boots and had developed blisters, reducing the second ordeal to hardly more than fifteen miles! By the time the weary Battery marched back into the comfort of the barracks late that second Sunday evening, there was little doubt in Collier's mind that the entire seventy to seventy-five pounds of equipment and clothing represented a well-thought-out survival kit for the most hostile living conditions known to man.

Most of the training—such as Squad Defensive Live Fire, Physical Tests (it seemed there were always more physical tests) and Hand Grenade Training—was performed under actual conditions. The Live Fire Exercise on an Assault Course where targets—shaped and dressed like both enemy and friendly soldiers and civilians—popped up right in front of them, forcing instant decisions about whom to fire upon was as close to downright life-or-death as Collier ever hoped to encounter. When the smoke cleared on that particular Live Fire Exercise, the instructor informed Collier he had killed two of his own men. Thank god it was only an exercise!

The end result was that over the course of the weeks since February, Collier had acquired an amazing amount of knowledge about how to kill the enemy and stay alive to kill again.

"A BATTERY, EVERYBODY OUT IN THE STREET IN ZERO FIVE MINUTES IN COMBAT BOOTS WITH THE CONTENTS OF YOUR FOOTLOCKERS IN YOUR MATTRESS COVERS." On Monday, the 31ᵃ of March, the luminous dial on Collier's watch read 0218, as Dixon's strident voice dragged him up out of the dark abyss and he struggled groggily upright, trying to fathom who was disturbing his much-needed rest at this godawful hour. To further compound the insult, he had just come off a midnight stint of guard duty.

"Did that asshole say to put the contents of our footlockers in our mattress covers?" Up front across the aisle near the door, Herb Rudolph grumbled in sleepy disbelief.

Rubbing sleep from his eyes and blinking hard, Collier checked his watch again.

"That's what it sounded like," Shields replied, not at all happy to be roused in the middle of the night.

"Fuck Dixon and his silly shit; my head is killing me," Schebb grumbled from his bunk across the room. Like Rudolph, Schebb was notorious for his marathon weekend drinking bouts, resulting in killer hangovers on Monday mornings.

"A BA-A-T-T-ERY! FALL OUT IN THE STREET IN COMBAT BOOTS WITH THE CONTENTS OF YOUR FOOTLOCKERS IN YOUR MATTRESS COVERS IN ZERO FOUR MINUTES," Dixon intoned again.

"Okay, you guys, you heard the Corporal. Let's get a move on—unless you want to be up all night." Methodically stripping his bed, Collier silently he berated himself as he struggled to come fully awake. Barely two weeks had passed since Bo had warned him to expect something like this near the end of their first eight weeks of Basic. Throughout FARTC, the eighth week of Basic was known as Hell Week and this dreaded "mattress-cover-with-footlocker-contents" debacle had become something of a legend—widely known as the dreaded, near-legendary "HWC—Hell Week Clusterfuck."

I damn well should have known better, Collier bitterly admonished himself as he slipped into his combat boots and roughly stripped the sheets from his bunk, brusquely extracting the thin mattress out of its coarse muslin cover. Now that Hell Week had come and passed without A Battery having to undergo any extraordinary harassment—with the singular exception of the 25-mile forced night march in full combat pack—Collier had mistakenly assumed that they had been spared this particular indignity. *Never assume anything. If you do, you make an ass out of you and me,* Collier's father's wise counsel came floating up from his subconscious to haunt him.

"Come on, men. Strip your bunks and dump those footlockers into your fart sacks. Let's get moving out to the street." Fortunately, Collier had not locked his footlocker before he went to bed, and it was a simple matter to remove the top tray and slip the end of the mattress cover over the end of the open footlocker and dump its entire contents into the large cotton bag. Collier shouldered his bulky mattress cover and shouted orders to his barracks mates as he moved to the stairwell to check on the men upstairs.

"Check next door. Shanahan and I can take care of this end," Mears assured him, clomping down the steps in his skivvies, combat boots and helmet liner, his lumpy mattress cover slung over his shoulder. Satisfied that Shanahan and Mears had the situation well in hand, Collier ran next door to check on the squads in the other barracks.

"That took just over zero-one-five minutes. If we had been under enemy attack, you would have been overrun and left bleeding in a ditch." Dixon rolled his eyes in disgust when the mass confusion subsided and the bedraggled battery had assembled in the street. They presented a sorry sight standing in the chill night air in their drooping GI underwear.

"Now, fall back inside the barracks; put everything back in place. Go back to bed and get some sleep. Dismissed," Dixon finally ordered after having Collier put them through ten minutes of a comic, short-order drill doing left and right shoulder arms with their mattress covers.

"Pass the word. Forget putting your shit back together. Don't be too surprised if we do this again at least once more within the hour." Recalling what Bo had told him, Collier stood inside the door and warned his battery mates as they fell back inside. His advice proved to be dead on target. In exactly one hour and five minutes, Dixon roused them out again. This time they assembled in seven-and-a-half minutes—they had cut their time in half.

The second drill notwithstanding, Collier suspected Dixon's diabolical persecution was not over for the night, but it turned out he was in error. Even though the malevolent corporal did not roust them again that night, he might just as well have. Lying wide-eyed, poised for the next rude awakening, what pitiful little sleep Collier managed during the few remaining pre-dawn hours was restless, but not because of any tormenting dreams of Hilda Birdsong.

Eyes heavy-lidded with sex, Emma lay atop the badly-tangled sheets on the steel-framed cot in the unoccupied Resident Physician quarters at the VA hospital and watched Trey Moseley fasten the waistband of his expensive British golf slacks. That done, he adjusted his fancy silk rep tie and blew her a cavalier kiss, leaving her once again fairly screaming for sexual release.

It had been three full months since she had experienced her first-ever orgasm the night before Collier left for the Army. Although she had solemnly sworn never to let Trey Moseley bed her again, she had been helpless to resist his autocratic, overbearing demands. Tonight had been the tenth time she had given in to him in the three months since Collier left, and she purely hated herself for it. The guilt and self-loathing over her reprehensible behavior had become so debilitating to her mental and spiritual health it had seriously impaired her ability to reply to Collier's twice-weekly letters. It had been over two full weeks since she had written him.

Of course, her guilt was not the sole reason she hadn't answered Collier. There was also the overriding issue of his wanting her to come live with him in Oklahoma after he finished Basic Training in June. Emma firmly resolved not to give in to that bit of insanity. Here at home, with her top-paying job at the VA and taking care of her mother, she was able to live in comfort at the old homeplace—saving them the loss of her salary plus the outrageous expense of paying rent in an overcrowded Army town. Collier would just have to comprehend that it made no sense for her to give up her top-paying nursing job to be stuck friendless and alone in some rundown trailer in Oklahoma while he was up to his combat boots in Officer Training.

Tonight, she vowed she would write him before she went to bed.

CHAPTER NINETEEN

THE ROANOKE TIMES
Roanoke, Virginia, Sunday, April 13, 1952
EARLY ARMISTICE IN KOREA BELIEVED LIKELY

WASHINGTON, April 12, (AP) - Officials guiding truce negotiations in Korea said today that an armistice would be agreed on fairly soon, possibly by May 1.

THE DAILY OKLAHOMAN
Oklahoma City, Oklahoma, Sunday, April 13, 1952
CAUSE SOUGHT IN FATAL BLAZE

LAWTON, April 12 - Trained investigators late Saturday probed the smoking ruins of the Midland Hotel searching for cause of a fire which killed two persons here Saturday.

Mrs. Charles E. Jones III and her infant son, both of Chambers, Pa., were killed and four persons injured in the $100,000 fire which began about 6 a.m.

Mrs. Jones and her son were in Lawton to visit her husband, in officer's candidate school at Fort Sill. Jones, who had never seen his 10-weeks-old baby, rushed to the scene and had to be restrained from rushing into the burning building.

IN THE UNNERVING AFTERMATH of the Hell Week Clusterfuck, almost two full weeks passed before Collier and the men of A Battery could finally go to bed and rest easy. Although the training schedule was rugged and the weather had been unpredictable and uncooperative—sometimes even severe—time passed rather quickly during the final days of the regular Infantry Basic schedule. The first two weeks of April, the absorbing Fire Direction Center (FDC) training slipped by almost before Collier realized Easter weekend was nearly upon him.

"My wife and son are probably already on the ground at Will Rogers Field in Oklahoma City about now. She's taking a Greyhound to Lawton. They'll be checking in the Midland Hotel tonight—I called to make sure they're holding her a room," Chip Jones happily whispered to Collier as they sat eating supper chow on Good Friday.

"I hope you have a nice Easter with your family," Collier said rather insincerely. The truth was he had completely forgotten Chip had confided to him that his wife and baby son were planning to visit during training. Not that Collier was unsympathetic to the notion of a proud, new father wanting to see his first-born infant son. Collier fully understood that Uncle Sam had no real power to restrict families and friends from coming to Lawton. But in Collier's role as Lance Sergeant, Chip's open defiance of what amounted to a reasonable Army request left Collier with a sense of smoldering resentment that this fellow soldier had dumped his secret on him in the first place. In his need to share the anticipated joy of seeing his wife and son, Jones had unconsciously invested Collier with an unreasonable—and totally unwarranted—sense of complicity.

Resolved to let Chip Jones worry about his own problems, Collier quickly set aside his nagging recriminations and turned his thoughts back to his too-long-postponed plans to slip off for a romantic weekend with Hilda Birdsong. Somewhere in the Army codes, he was sure it was written that a man cannot live on K Rations, shit-on-a-shingle, and 105mm propellant alone. That he was married just be damned. He was really looking forward to spending the weekend alone with the Rubensesque Mrs. Birdsong. Unforeseen quirks in his training schedule had kept them apart too long. He had endured almost a full month of restless nights since he had felt the heat of those formidable breasts pressing into his back.

"Don't worry. As long as you still want to see me, I'll be waiting," Hilda had let him know in no uncertain terms that she was seriously smitten, the ensuing Saturday at Service Club No. 3 following that first Sunday together on Mount Scott. Collier had rushed in the Service Club wearing full field gear to apologetically cancel their plans because A Battery was heading out on a weekend bivouac.

Unfortunately, however, when Collier had said goodbye to her that Saturday, he had no way of knowing A Battery would be scheduled for yet another surprise forced march the very next weekend which also included another overnight bivouac. That second consecutive field exercise had been A Battery's introductory ARSOP—Artillery shorthand for Area Surveillance and Reconnaissance Operations. Although he found nothing exciting about having to straddle a slit trench to relieve his bowels and he certainly much preferred taking his meals in the civilized surroundings of the clean, well-lighted, battery mess hall, his fledgling ARSOP had been an uncomfortable, but informative experience. The bivouac had provided him the opportunity to help lay a complete battery of six 105mm howitzers—orienting the guns along a known compass setting, aligning them all to point in precisely the same direction—and actually fire the guns, taking turns with his fellow trainees performing their duties right along with the teams of regular Artillery cannoneers. He found it fascinating how the howitzer ammo came in two separate components—propellant and missle. The firing canister containing the primer and propellant had a string of seven, fist-sized, powder charges in silk bags—which left no ash—connected by a string which had to be cut according to Fire Direction Center's calculation of range, before being fitted with the proper projectile requested by the Forward Observer (FO). The Fire Missions came down from the FO—in this instance from Baker Battery—to FDC who used surveyed maps of the target area which usually included a plot for the location of the FO's Observation Post (OP).

"Fox Oboe Baker (Forward Observer Baker Battery), Fire Mission. Chinese Tank Convoy. From Blockhouse Signal Mountain, go left one hundred and down niner zero (presumably for the sake of clarity, the military preferred to use 'niner' instead of nine). Two rounds HEAT (High Explosive Anti-tank). Will adjust." During a two-day rotation on the OP, Collier thrilled as he watched the deadly process unfold. Receiving FOB's information, the FDC would plot a quick fix on their firing map, translate the range and direction into elevation and direction (compass azimuth) for Baker Battery gun crews to aim their guns and calculate the number of propellant charges required to send the deadly 29-lb. projectiles on a high arc to their destination, then transmit the data back to the firing battery. "Elevation one-two-five-niner, deflection zero-four-five, two rounds HEAT, Charge Five. Fire when ready." Within a span of only minutes, the battery commander would fire two rounds into the target area and call back to FO Baker: "Two rounds, on the way."

Locating the rounds bursting in the target area in front of him, FOB would call back a correction: "Right one-zero, drop three zero." FDC would then translate the adjustment to the guns as FOB continued to zero the battery in—attempting to get a tight bracket on the target with a minimum of adjustments from the guns. As soon as the guns had the target dead to rights (usually within 50 yards), FOB called in a final command to FDC, "Repeat range, twelve rounds HEAT, fire for effect." After the guns had fired for effect, the FOB would call in the result and either ask for additional fire or conclude the mission by a target assessment. "Chinese Convoy Disabled and Destroyed, Cease Fire, End of Mission."

Aside from observing this intriguing, multi-faceted Artillery by-play, both at the guns and the OP, to occupy himself on the OP, Collier filled time by locating and plotting to the nearest yard virtually every target on the range. Because of the obscure, often completely hidden, declivities in the rugged canyons and arroyos of the Oklahoma terrain, it became a fascinating pastime. During his brief time on the OP, Collier committed virtually every target to memory.

Although observing fire from the OP had been interesting, it had been particularly exciting to be down with the guns, shoving 105mm projectiles into the breech block opening as the gun crew simulated being overrun by the enemy tanks; quickly cranking down the tube and bore-sighting directly through the breech down the gleaming length of the tube, they had poured round after round of direct cannon fire on moving targets at point-blank range about two-hundred yards in front of them. One right after the other, as fast as Collier could shove the heavy projectiles in the breech and the number-two man could pull the firing lanyard, they fired at the moving target frames. Before the morning was over, they were scoring hit after hit. One thing for certain, if he ever had to repeat it in actual combat, Collier felt confident he would make the enemy suffer.

While Collier found firing the guns exciting, it had come with a price. Afterwards for several days he had suffered a distressing minor transitory hearing loss from the pounding his eardrums had taken with the cannon's roar. He first became aware of the disability when he found he was unable to hear the familiar chirping of the crickets that usually lulled him asleep. Even after the cricket sounds returned, he could still hear a faint, distracting ringing in his ear.

On the weekend following their final ARSOP, Hilda had sent word she was in bed with flu. Bad karma continued to dog them the next weekend when Collier's battery mates had been restricted because of academic deficiencies in their Fire Direction studies. Consequently, Collier and Hilda were denied the opportunity to spend any real time together during the ensuing four full weeks following their picnic on Mount Scott. Now, with Hilda fully recovered, Easter weekend approaching, and his schedule lightened, Collier was eagerly looking forward to a Saturday afternoon picnic at secluded spot Hilda knew out beyond Mount Scott.

Like the influenza gods, the fickle weather gods had other plans, however. On Good Friday, the morning temperature dipped a little below freezing, and although it warmed up to around 68 degrees in the afternoon, intermittent showers put a decided damper on the enthusiasm of the crowds for the annual pilgrimage to the celebrated Easter Pageant at the open Wichita amphitheater, and Hilda wisely opted to come up with Plan B.

"Just relax, Collier, Dear. Rest assured I am far more anxious to get you alone than you could ever want to see me." Hilda crooned on the phone Good

Friday, long-past pretending there was only a platonic interest on her part and intimating she planned a cozy weekend.

"I really don't care if we wind up in a deserted barn somewhere around Cache. I think I'll die if I can't see you again," Collier reassured her.

Collier spent a rather restless night fighting a recurring erection as he anticipated spending the Easter weekend alone with the sensual widow Birdsong. He had just dropped into fitful doze Saturday morning when a pair of MPs came stealthily into the barracks around 0645 with Captain Ward. Following a hushed conversation upstairs, they all drove hurriedly away with Chip Jones in an official olive-drab sedan.

After breakfast, his mind abuzz with worry that Chip Jones had stirred up a hornet's nest by bringing his wife to Lawton, Collier busied himself by preparing his gear for inspection and affixing brass to a fresh set of fatigues for Monday in preparation for attending the Firepower Demonstration at Signal Mountain OP. Staged for visiting generals and politicos, the Fire Power demo had been long-anticipated by A Battery and was rumored to include the first firing of the infamous 280mm Atomic Cannon.

Just before they were to fall out for Saturday Inspection, Dixon called Collier aside and gave Collier the sad news. "Chip Jones' wife and baby son were killed this morning in a hotel fire in downtown Lawton. Two sergeants from the Provost Marshall's office are coming to pick up his stuff. Have two of your Lance Corporals help you pack all his gear and personal effects and bring everything to the orderly room. Jones has been granted a hardship leave and won't be coming back to Battery A," Dixon ordered, shrugging helplessly with utter disbelief.

Reeling with shock, Collier explained to Mears and Shanahan what Dixon wanted and went along to help pack up Jones' belongings.

"I am sad to report a family tragedy that will result in A Battery losing one of its fine soldiers..." Captain Ward briefly informed the battery of the disastrous Midland Hotel fire at the rather desultory Saturday morning formation, concluding with the announcement, "I am canceling regular Saturday inspection. Enjoy your holiday as best you can."

"I guess you heard about the soldier's wife and baby dying in that hotel fire." On his way to meet Hilda in the FARTC Chapel parking lot at high noon, Collier bumped into Bo coming out of the PX.

"Uh-huh..." Collier nodded, amazed that the tragic news had spread so quickly.

"Isn't that the same guy you warned not to bring his wife here for Easter?" Bo persisted, falling in step beside him.

"Yeah..." Collier grunted. He had forgotten he had confided to Bo the conversation he'd had with Jones walking home from the PX almost a month ago.

"Well, it's a hard lesson, but you tried to warn him. It probably serves him right," Bo continued, field-stripping his cigarette into one of the butt cans in front of the PX.

"It's a hell of price to pay for wanting to see your wife and baby son," Collier spoke up, fighting a sudden, unexpected tear.

"Yeah...but there should be a lesson here," Bo persisted, taking no notice of Collier's distress. "Going through training is hard enough without being distracted by a wife and kid camped outside the Main Gate."

"Uhm-m," Collier grunted, turning his head to light a Lucky, using the opportunity to swipe away the spurious tear.

"Some of the guys in C Battery are catching the bus downtown to get a look at the hotel where she died. The Midland Hotel is that three-story building on the corner near the square..." Bo looked to Collier for confirmation.

"Yeah, I know the one. It reminds me of the old Hotel Fort Lewis on Main Street back in Salem," Collier concurred pensively.

"Can you believe anyone would want to go see a burned-out building?" Bo rolled his eyes in disgust.

"Oh well, it takes all kinds. I had a roommate in Richmond who chased ambulances hoping to see a fatal car wreck." Collier frowned, casting a doubtful eye at the horizon and a foreboding bank of low-hanging clouds.

"By the way my buddy, Wilson, in B Battery just got orders this morning," Bo said as Collier started walking away.

"Oh? Where to?" Collier stopped dead in his tracks, turning back to face him—afraid to hear the news.

"FECOM, where else?" Bo shrugged with a hollow laugh. Shorthand for Far East Command, FECOM almost certainly meant Korea.

"Geez...I'm sorry, man," Collier said with a sympathetic look. "If they don't get the Peace Talks settled, sooner or later, I guess we'll all wind up there."

"You've got at least awhile before you have to worry. With OCS, I mean. Maybe by the time you finish, the shooting will be over," Bo replied with mixed optimism and envy.

"Hell's bells, Bo, don't be so pessimistic. You haven't gotten orders yet. Besides, the fighting may be over before any of us get over there," Collier brightened, trying to cheer him up.

"Who knows? But I have a feeling I'm heading to FECOM," Bo replied, adding cheerily, "Whatever. Hey, I'm meeting Wilson at the PX. Want to join us for a soda—or a beer?"

"Give me a rain check, man. Right now, I got to run." Collier gave him a pat on the back and turned to leave, headed down the street toward the FARTC Chapel.

"Why are you headed to Chapel on Saturday morning?" Bo called to his retreating back.

"Got to see a man about a dog..." Collier waved and kept on going, breaking into a run as here and there giant intermittent drops of rain splashed a polka-dot pattern on the cracked sidewalk. As he rounded the corner, he whooshed a great sigh of relief when he caught view of Hilda's black Caddy parked behind the Chapel. The rain was just starting in earnest as he opened the car door and slid onto the wide bench seat beside her.

"Whew...at last! I was beginning to wonder if I'd ever see you again. Let's get the hell out of here." With unaccustomed exuberance, Collier slammed the door.

"I hate to say it, but it looks like our picnic at the lake is doomed." The rain was coming down by the bucketsful now.

"Do you get the feeling there's some plot against us?" Collier ruefully shook his head.

"Cheer up. Would you be terribly disappointed if we went to my house in Lawton? We could have our picnic in the comfort of my den?"

"That sounds like a plan." Collier nodded as she put the big car in gear.

"Did you hear about the hotel fire?" she asked as they left the Chapel parking lot.

"Yeah...the soldier who lost his wife and baby was in my battery," he said.

"Was he a close buddy of yours?" Hilda asked as they passed out the gate toward Lawton.

"No...not close, but like me, he enlisted to go to OCS."

"Do you have children, too?" The question was rather unexpected. His marriage had not come up during the brief time they'd had together.

"No, no kids."

"Not exactly a good time to bring up your marriage, but I couldn't help but wonder..." She looked over at him, somewhat apologetically.

"No need to apologize. My marriage is no secret and you certainly have every right to ask. Emma and I started dating in high school. It's a tired old story. I was the quarterback and she was a cheerleader...I became an artist. She's a registered nurse." He filled her in on the highlights. "It has not been a marriage made in Heaven. I hardly ever hear from her. She hasn't answered my letters in weeks. I have trouble reaching her by phone. "

"I take it there are no children on the way then?"

"We lost our only pregnancy..." He recounted Emma's unexpected miscarriage.

"I'm sorry..." she began.

"Don't be. I really don't want kids." The Caddy's wipers punctuated his speech with a rhythmic swish-swish against the hushed splatter of the driving rain. "Not now, anyway. With Emma, maybe not ever."

"In my opinion Emma doesn't deserve you."

"Don't waste your sympathy; I'm really no bargain." He frowned. They had entered the northern outskirts of Lawton. Just past the intersection with Fort Sill Boulevard, Hilda turned off of Cache Road onto Pershing Drive into a neighborhood of impressive, well-kept older homes. A large number of the dwellings had window air-conditioners—a few even had the box-like condensers for expensive, newfangled central systems.

"Don't sell yourself short." She flashed a brilliant smile.

"Does it bother you—that I'm married, I mean?"

"Only if it bothers you," she answered as they turned right and pulled into the drive of a large brick and redwood ranch-style house. Like the neighboring homes, the dwelling was sitting amidst large ornamental maples and oaks some distance back from the street on a spacious, neatly-manicured, corner lot. Modestly underscoring the affluence of the neighborhood, an outside condenser for central air-conditioning was screened behind a neatly-trimmed hedge of Japanese Yew.

"Then, don't give it another thought. I've been looking forward to seeing you again for almost a month now. I assure you I'm not looking for a cheap roll in the sack. I don't make a habit of indiscriminately sleeping around..." he awkwardly protested his sincerity.

"Good. This is home, sweet home. Let's forget the rest of the world and concentrate on us," she said as she pulled the Caddy into a double carport and cut the engine. "Grab our picnic basket and bring it inside while I unlock the door." Pushing the trunk release, she slid out of the car, dashing toward the door, trying to avoid the wind-whipped rain.

In just the few seconds it took to retrieve the basket and close the trunk lid, Collier was soaked to the skin by the time he followed her into the mudroom off the carport. Closing the door behind them, when he turned back, he was surprised to find a pretty, very young Indian girl standing there to hand him a dry towel and relieve him of the basket.

"Collier, this is my housekeeper, Opal Black Elk," Hilda introduced him as he followed the girl into the large, modern kitchen.

"Nice to meet you, Opal," Collier acknowledged the rather informal introduction, peering from underneath the towel.

"I'm happy to make your acquaintance, Sir." The girl stood smiling shyly as she waited quietly for Hilda to instruct her.

"You can go to your room, Opal. I'll call you if I need you later," Hilda dismissed the girl and she exited the kitchen by a door leading back into rear of the house.

"Opal's mother and sisters live at the Indian School. Since she graduated from high school, Opal lives here with me. There are three bedrooms and another kitchen on the far wing of the house—before Opal came, I rented the rooms to several young officers," Hilda explained as Collier struggled to remove his sodden uniform jacket.

"Oh, my, you're dripping wet. Come with me. Let's get you out of those dreadful clothes before you catch pneumonia." Hilda led him through a formal dining room, back through a formal living room into a spacious feminine bedroom on the far side of the house, opposite the door Opal had entered.

"Get out of those clothes and I'll put them in the laundry room to dry." She resumed her nervous chatter as she moved to her closet and came back carrying several coat hangers, an overlarge pink bath towel and a thick, white terrycloth bathrobe over her arm. Handing him the towel, she dropped the robe on the foot of the large bed. "Here, get out of those clothes, dry yourself and slip into this."

"Thanks..." he said, modestly waiting for her to leave to allow him to undress.

"Well? What are you waiting for? " she asked. "Get out of those soggy clothes before you catch a death of cold." Stepping around behind him, she began tugging the soggy uniform jacket from his shoulders. As soon as he had struggled out of the jacket, she hung it carefully on a coat hanger and hooked the hanger over the top of the door leading to the master bathroom. When she came back in the room, he was struggling to unloosen his soggy necktie. "Just stand still and let me..." she said, trying to help him.

"I can get it..." he grunted, tugging futilely at the wet knot.

"Quit. You're making it worse." Pushing his arms down to his side, she began worrying the stubborn knot. Hardly before he could protest again, she had unloosed the tie and was unbuttoning his shirt. The intimacy of the room and the act of her undressing him instantly caused his penis to struggle for release inside his newly-purchased Jockey shorts. Momentarily mortified, he moved to cover his embarrassing condition with his hands.

"Will you please just stand still a minute," she protested, lightly slapping his hands away.

Opening his mouth to object again, she stepped forward and planted her lips squarely on his, slipping her tongue inside before he could make another sound. Her tongue wantonly tasting him was like an electric current. Encircling his waist with her arms, she slipped her right hand beneath his buttocks, grinding her pudenda against his rock-hard organ.

"Let me get undressed. I want you inside me." After a moment, she stepped away and began pulling her dress over her head.

Watching hungrily as she tossed aside her expensive, pink-embroidered slip and reached behind herself to unhook the matching, well-filled brassiere—Collier wasted no time in stepping free of his Jockey briefs. Transfixed with lust, he watched as she finally stepped free of her panties and turned to face him. Without further hesitation, he led her to the bed and pushed her roughly back, burying his face in her luxuriant, sensuously aromatic pubic patch.

"Oh...ah-h-h-h!" she gasped, shuddering to release hardly before his tongue could find her center. Arching her back, she pushed hard against his mouth with a tiny frisson of after-pleasure as he continued to suck her little praline. "NO! No more, please. I can't stand it—it feels too...too good," Resisting the overwhelming pleasure, she grasped him by the ears, fighting weakly to push his head away. Within seconds, she gave in. Collapsing back on the bed, he pursued her and soon felt her responding again. Under the relentless licking of his tongue, she came once more before she finally rolled on top and straddled him, slowly guiding his throbbing penis inside her tight vagina. In the beginning throes of another orgasm, she leaned forward and stuck her tongue in his mouth again and began to ride him hard.

"What about birth control?" he gasped with effort.

"You worry too much...fuck me hard. Let's come together." Wriggling side to side to move him deeper inside her, she quieted his questions.

Beyond the point of no return now, Collier felt his life-essence gushing out of him like molten magma from some long-dormant volcano. When he fell back completely sated and they finally lay gasping, side-by-side on the big bed, the last thing he remembered was the sound of her contented breathing against his ear.

When Collier stirred again in the darkness, his watch glowed 0259 as he snuggled close against her deliciously-rounded derriere. Interlocked with his semi-erect organ resting between her legs, the texture of her pubic hair tickled the head of his overworked penis and he was amazed to find his ravaged organ slowly engorging with blood again.

"Uhm-m. Methinks I've let myself fall into the clutches of a sex maniac." She murmured with pleasure, wriggling hard against him until his penis was pushing into her moist center from behind.

"Get up on your knees and move over here to the edge of the mattress," when he felt her respond again, he got out of bed and coached her, taking her buttocks between his hands and adjusting her in a kneeling position on his side of the bed. Inside her again, he was surprised at the strength of her movement as she slammed her fleshy cheeks against him, answering him thrust for thrust. In no time at all they both came again.

"If you're trying to kill me, I think you've finally done it," she breathed in the sweaty darkness when they lay gasping with exhaustion.

"Don't worry—there's plenty of life left in you. It's me who is dead," Collier sighed, burying his face between her soft breasts.

"Excuses...excuses...excuses..." she whispered as he drifted off again.

When he stirred awake again his watch read 0815 hours and he was alone in bed. Through the skylight, he saw a hawk circling overhead against the grey, rain-sodden sky. Lying there, momentarily luxuriating in the memory of the past evening, he contemplated the pleasure of having her with him during the coming day ahead. Finally, he rolled out of bed and plodded across to the bathroom to empty his bladder. On the vanity beside the lavatory, he found a brand-new toothbrush and razor obviously placed there for him. Although his uniform was freshly ironed and hanging on the closet door, when he had brushed his teeth, shaved, and showered, Collier found a terry robe and made his way out to the kitchen. A tentative tour of the premises turned up no sign of life—the house was quiet as a mausoleum. The coffee pot on the kitchen counter showed no sign of recent use.

There was absolutely no sign of Hilda. A quick peek through the window revealed her car was missing.

Puzzled that she had made no mention of going to Easter services or the need to go out for any reason, he went back into the bedroom and was examining his freshly-pressed uniform when he found the note pinned to his necktie.

Collier—This has to be the Alpha and Omega of us. Last night was wonderful, but this can't go on. I'm heading out of town for awhile—at least until you have completed Basic. I'm sure you will understand. HB

Confused and depressed, Collier dressed and left the house walking as fast as he could, desperate to put the neighborhood behind him. He quickly found his way into the outskirts of downtown Lawton and caught the first bus back to base. When he got off near the FARTC Service Club, his watch showed 1125. The lateness of the hour meant Bo was probably already at the Chapel. It was just as well. As much as Collier liked his old friend, he was in no mood to talk to anyone—not at the moment at least. Desperately in need of a cup of coffee, he was hungry as a bear. Thinking back, he realized that he had not had a bite since breakfast the previous day, and it was now already too late for the custom Sunday breakfast at the battalion mess. Reluctantly, he climbed the steps to the Service Club in search of lifesaving sustenance. Inside, he found one of the regular USO ladies at the coffee urn handing out pastries.

After coffee and sweet rolls, still not at all in the mood for company Collier took a bus down to the Old Post and went to the Post Theater No. 1 for the first showing of *The Racket*, a crime thriller with Robert Mitchum, Lizabeth Scott and Robert Ryan. Still not feeling sociable, he ate candy bars and drank Cokes, and sat through two more showings, returning to the barracks after lights out at 2200 hours.

Monday morning, the news of the death of Chip Jones' wife and son settled over A Battery like a shroud. At morning formation, Captain Ward made a brief statement regretting the tragedy, but insensitively using the opportunity to remind the Battery of the Army's repeated admonitions against bringing their wives and/or sweethearts to the area while the Battery was still in Basic. Still crushed by Hilda's cruel rejection, Collier hated the entire Army system for being so insensitive to the humanity that drove their infernal machine.

After Police Call and chow, the Battery was loaded into deuce and a half trucks and transported to the Signal Mountain OP to observe the awesome firepower demonstration attended by a number of Washington and foreign bigwigs. By the time they returned, Chip Jones III's bunk had already been assigned to Private Jack Prine transferred in from a battery already finished training. From somewhere in Kentucky, Prine had been held back while he recovered from a bad ankle sprain incurred running the treacherous Confidence Course.

"Back to good old Preponderance over FORK and all that mumbo-jumbo." Tuesday morning, Collier was pleasantly surprised to discover that Prine seemed right at home in A Battery's new classroom curriculum in the altogether complicated operations of the Fire Direction Center. Using strange-looking, special protractors and slide rules right out of a science-fiction novel, through an unique process based on a target's location according to data received from the FO—and plotted relative to surveyed locations of the Observation Post (OP) and the actual guns—the FDC was able to compute direction and range to the target and spit out amazingly accurate firing data to the Battery. With the help of precalculated tables, corrections could be added for conditions such as a difference between target and howitzer altitudes, propellant temperature and atmospheric conditions—even the curvature and rotation of the <u>Earth</u>. All this information could be calculated manually. In most combat missions, some of these more esoteric, less important factors were arbitrarily omitted, sacrificing an inconsequential measure of pinpoint accuracy in the interest of speed.

All week long, Collier kept his antennae out to see what effect, if any, the death of Chip Jones' wife and baby had on battery morale. By Friday evening, Collier was satisfied to see that Prine was working well with Chip Jones III's former section mates. When he went to bed that evening, Collier experienced a transient, ruefully-ironic pang for Chip Jones before he drifted off to sleep praying Bo Bohon would be spared being sent to FECOM. By the following morning, the tragedy of the Midland Hotel had already become a dark footnote to the history of Battery A—another hammer stroke in the tempering of the protective armor of Collier Boyd Ramsay.

"Medical College of Virginia, Four-south. Ms. Graves speaking, how can I help you?"

"This is Emma Ramsay. I'm an RN at the Roanoke VA. May I speak to Dr. Moseley, please?" Emma asked the nurse on the line and held her breath. Trey had told her never to call.

"I'm sorry but Dr. Moseley is somewhere in the general vicinity of San Antonio, Texas. The Army finally tracked him down."

"Texas! I had no idea Uncle Sam was breathing down his neck!"

The miserable son of a bitch might have had the decency to tell me! Emma reacted mutely, thanked the nurse and hung up the phone.

Finally able to regain a semblance of control, she fumbled in her canvas tote and retrieved the small box of note paper she'd been carrying for several weeks to write Collier a long-overdue letter. After tearing two false starts into confetti, she finally finished jotting a short note and signed her name. Locating her checkbook, she wrote Collier a check and slipped it inside the envelope before she licked the flap and affixed a six-cent airmail postage stamp.

Feeling somewhat better now, she swiveled her chair around to examine the bookshelf behind her desk. Quickly locating *The American Hospital Directory*, a large volume listing fully-accredited major American hospitals, she quickly located the section listing hospitals in Lawton, Oklahoma.

CHAPTER TWENTY

THE ROANOKE TIMES
Roanoke, Virginia, Saturday, April 19, 1952
WAR PRISONER TALKS STARTED MAY
SETTLE ONE OF BIG ARMISTICE ISSUES

MUNSAN, KOREA, Saturday, April 19 (AP) – Allied and Communist negotiators today reopened secret Prisoner of War discussions that may settle one of the three major issues still blocking a Korean Armistice.

––––––––––

THE DAILY OKLAHOMAN
Oklahoma City, Oklahoma, Saturday, April 19, 1952
TRUMAN MAKES THREAT
TO KEEP CONGRESS ON JOB

WASHINGTON, Friday, April 18 (AP) – President Truman said today that if Congress balks at voting the money he thinks is needed for national defense, he will keep it at work all year, calling a special session every day if necessary.

––––––––––

THE DAILY OKLAHOMAN
Oklahoma City, Oklahoma, Saturday, April 19, 1952
AIRLINER SNAGS ON HILL, 29 DIE

LOS ANGELES, Friday, April 18 (AP) – A non-scheduled New York-Los Angeles airliner crashed and burned today in the Puente Hills, 25 miles from its destination, killing all 29 persons aboard.

––––––––––

FOR COLLIER, EASTER CAME and went without any word of progress emanating from the guarded media reports from the negotiating tables at Panmumjon. Back in Washington, business was as usual: "A tale filled with sound and fury, signifying nothing."

Carrying his AWOL bag into the Service Club for a cup of coffee, Collier's attention was drawn to a front page article in *The Daily Oklahoman* about the tragic crash of a non-scheduled airliner attempting to land at Los Angeles International airport in a dense early-morning fog. His thoughts flashed back to his recent white-knuckle flight from Baltimore to Camp Chaffee and he idly wondered if the plucky Flying Tigers stewardess had made good on her promise to quit flying. Likely not! Most humans were doomed to keep repeating their mistakes, he mused, sipping his coffee and trying to recall the perky stewardess's name.

"What's with the AWOL bag?" the USO volunteer inquired without real interest.

"I think I've finally lost all my marbles. I let myself get talked into hitchhiking to Dallas," Collier replied, his thoughts flashing back to the previous evening at the PX.

"You guys ought to go to Dallas tomorrow after inspection. It would be a shame to be this close and not get an eyeful of all them big-titted strippers before you leave Sill," Gerald Pollock, one of Herb Rudolph's drinking buddies, had advised a group of them over a final beer at "last call" last night. Pollock had just gotten back from 'The Big D' over Easter weekend and was full of embroidered tales about his success with a girl he'd picked up in a Dallas dancehall called the Cowgirl Corral.

"I'm ready," Rudolph said. "I'm horny. I'm ready to find a first-class whorehouse." With Herb's mainline Philly accent, the word came out sounding like whoo'erhouse.

"This girl was no whore," Pollock protested that his ability to attract women had come into question.

"Nothing wrong with going to a high-class whoo'erhouse. Saves time and is cheaper in the long run. Besides, you don't have to waste a lot of time talking to them," Rudolph defended. "Who wants to go to Dallas tomorrow?" Herb looked around the group, but no one spoke up.

"These guys are chickenshit. How about you, Ram?" Shaking his head with disgust, Rudolph had looked across at Collier.

"Not me, Herb..." Collier had seen enough of Rudolph's penchant for getting knee-walking drunk on PX beer.

"Oh, come on Ram—you never want to have any fun," Rudolph whined.

"Hitchhiking two-hundred miles isn't my idea of fun. What if we got stuck and couldn't make it back?" Collier was not enchanted with the possibility.

"No problem there. I had no trouble getting rides going and coming back," Pollock reassured them.

"C'mon, Ram, what do you say? We only got five more weeks. If we don't go now, we may not get another chance," Rudolph left no doubt he was serious about the project.

"Look, Herb, traveling over two-hundred miles just to spend one very-abbreviated night in Dallas is bad enough, but to try to hitchhike is absolutely insane. We'd probably get a ride out of town and wind up like Mears and Shields, stuck in some berg like Burkburnett," Collier protested. Several weekends back, Mears and Shields had struck out for Wichita Falls and gotten stuck in a little Podunk just on the Texas side of the Red River about halfway to Wichita Falls. A fairly good-sized town, Wichita Falls was about an hour south of Lawton. Collier could just see himself stuck in the middle of nowhere with Rudolph, and he certainly didn't fancy the idea of watching Rudolph drink himself into a stupor.

"You don't have to take a chance. Just ask the driver where he's headed before you get in," Pollock kept butting in.

"Sure, Ram, that's easy enough. That way we won't get stuck in the middle of nowhere," Herb refused to give in. "C'mon, Ram, what do you have to lose?"

"Well...we'd have to eat and find a place to stay. That'll cost a bunch in Dallas." Herb's idea of seeking the comfort of a prostitute was disgusting but compared to the prospect of moping around Lawton feeling sorry for himself, seeing Dallas did have a certain appeal.

"A bed at the Dallas Central Y only costs two bits a night, and it's right downtown," Pollock stuck his two-cents-worth in again.

"I'm not staying at any Y. I tried that once in Norfolk a couple of years back when I was a kid. When I turned down the bedspread, they hadn't changed the sheets. There was a puddle where some pervert had jerked off right in the middle of the bed." Collier shook his head.

"Forget the Y. Listen, Ram, I promise we'll find a decent hotel—maybe the Adolphus or the Baker even," Herb reeled off the names of two well-known hotels from a newspaper article about the Cotton Bowl game they had seen at the Service Club. "Louise sent me a bunch of cash. The hotel's on me. You can't say no to that."

Collier had to admit he liked Rudolph. College-educated, Rudolph could be good company when he hadn't had too many beers. Collier finally gave in and said "okay." Before he hit the sack, he carefully packed a clean shirt, a couple of sets of clean underwear, his poncho and his shaving kit in his compact AWOL bag. Already beset with serious misgivings, by the time he finally crawled into the sack, Collier pulled the covers over his head and prayed for rain. Given his sinful behavior over recent months, it came as no surprise that Saturday dawned bright and clear. Despite second thoughts, right after inspection Saturday morning, Collier gathered up his AWOL bag and picked up his pass from the orderly room.

"Wait up, Collier, where are you headed with that AWOL bag?" On his way to meet Herb at the bus stop near the PX, Collier ran into Bo standing on the steps of the Service Club.

"I got talked into trying to hitchhike to Dallas with Herb Rudolph. Want to tag along?"

"No, man, the first sergeant just gave me my orders. To tell you the truth, I'm not much in a mood for anything," Bo said, sending a small pebble skittering across the street with the toe of his boot.

"Where to?" From the look on Bo's face, Collier really didn't really have to ask.

"FECOM, where else?" Bo shrugged with resignation.

"Jeez, man, I'm sorry." Collier gave his friend an encouraging pat on the shoulder.

"Well, it isn't as if I expected anything else." Bo kicked at another stone and missed.

"When do you leave?" Collier couldn't think of anything else to say.

"I fly out of Lawton on Braniff to Tulsa on Saturday morning, May 10. From Tulsa, I fly Continental to Washington, DC. From there I take the train to Roanoke. I'll be home twenty-one days on what the Army calls 'Route Delay.' I'll fly out of Roanoke for Seattle on 31 May." Bo pulled a ticket folder from the inside of his blouse and handed it to Collier.

Briefly looking it over, Collier replaced the tickets in the folder and handed it back.

"Three weeks at home...could be worse, I guess." Feeling his friend's sense of disappointment, there was nothing left to say.

"I guess..." Bo took the folder and stuffed it back in the pocket of his blouse.

"There's Herb. I got to run—keep your chin up man." Collier tapped Bo lightly on the shoulder and headed for the bus stop, glad to have an excuse to get away.

Collier was still nursing self-recriminations for having agreed to the insanity of hitchhiking all the way to Dallas with Herb, when the friendly bus driver let Collier and Herb off at the main highway leading south from Lawton to Wichita Falls. The bus had hardly disappeared from view when the first car stopped and offered them a ride.

The roomy black, late-model Buick sedan was driven by an Air Force colonel with his wife who were originally from Philadelphia. Incredibly, they were heading all the way to Fort Worth. For homesick Herb this turned out to be something of old home week. Settling comfortably in the corner by the open window behind the wife with the pleasant warm breeze blowing in his face, Collier half-dozed, half-listened to the warm exchange between the sedan full of fugitives from the Philly area. Before they were halfway to Wichita Falls, the drone of conversation had lulled him to sleep. Except a stop for gas and to use the rest room at a filling station in Henrietta, Collier dozed off and on for most of the four hours it took them to reach to the outskirts of Fort Worth.

"Well, this is it. Take the next bus that says Dallas-Downtown," the affable colonel told them as he pulled up to a city bus stop in Fort Worth. "And don't do anything I wouldn't do."

The bus into Dallas only cost a dime. In less time than it took to smoke two Luckies and admire the parade of longhorn steers and well-stacked, healthy-looking women, the driver deposited them on Commerce Street within sight of the imposing older Adolphus and the newer Baker hotel.

"Let's check in and lose these AWOL bags," Herb urged as soon as the bus pulled away.

"I don't know. Those places look pretty ritzy, Herb. The Adolphus looks older—maybe it would be cheaper. That way we could save the bucks for a steak dinner at the best restaurant in town. Come on, let's ask that cop." Casting an eye at the Adolphus doorman assisting well-dressed guests arriving in a Lincoln Continental, Collier started toward the nearby policeman.

"Both the Adolphus and the Baker will set you back a minimum of ten bucks a night. If you're looking for a decent place to stay, try the Cotton Bowl Hotel. It's clean and air-conditioned and will only cost you a buck apiece and it's only a two-bit cab ride from here." the friendly cop on the corner drawled.

"Ever hear of the Cowgirl Corral?" Collier asked as the helpful cop flagged down a cab.

"Sure, it's a dump. You'll most likely wind up getting rolled. If you're looking for action, try a place called the Silver Spur. It ain't too far from the Cotton Bowl Hotel. Jack Ruby runs a decent place. Jack's girls are on the up and up."

Located on the older fringes of the downtown area, the Cotton Bowl Hotel turned out to be decent enough. At a buck a piece for the night, it was within the budget.

"Just in case we have to make a quick getaway." Herb winked at Collier as he paid the old man behind the desk for the room and waited for a receipt. "Can we get a bottle of good whiskey sent up to the room?" Herb asked as soon as he registered and was handed the key.

"Bourbon or blend?" the old man asked.

"You got Scotch?" Herb asked.

"Yeah, but we don't get much call for Scotch," the old man replied. "It's pretty expensive for this part of town."

"Scotch okay with you?" Herb glanced over at Collier.

"No booze for me. If I drink at all, I'll probably just stick with beer when we go out to eat." Collier shrugged. He was not about to waste any money on a bottle of booze for Herb.

"Do you have a fifth of J&B?" Herb turned back to the desk clerk.

"A fifth of J&B will set you back ten bucks..." the old man peered up from beneath a pair of shaggy eyebrows.

"Even in Dallas, ten is a little steep for that brand of Scotch. We're both headed for Korea. Where's your patriotism, old-timer?" Herb gave the old man a friendly grin.

"Eight's the best I can do—you'd have to pay six at the nearest package store and that's a dollar cab ride across town," the old man arbitrated.

"Okay, I'll take your word. Eight sounds okay." Herb conceded.

"Send up a bottle of club soda and some ice. You can keep the change old-timer." Herb peeled two fives off a hefty roll of bills when the old man returned from the storage room behind the desk with a bottle in a brown paper bag. The old man handed Herb the bag with the bottle, and they headed for the elevator.

The plainly-furnished room seemed clean enough. Collier undressed and hung his sweat-dampened shirt on a hanger in front of the window air-conditioner to dry and headed in to shower while Herb waited for the bellhop to bring him the soda and bucket of ice. By the time Collier had toweled dry and reentered the room, Herb had already downed two fingers of the Scotch mixed with soda and was pouring a refill over the recently-arrived ice.

"Man, oh man, this really hits the spot." Herb smacked his lips and extended the bottle to Collier. "C'mon, Ram, have a little drink on me. Cut some of the dust out of your lungs."

"Thanks, I think I'll pass. Time's a'wasting, Herb. It's already dark outside. If you're going to shower, get to it." Collier shook his head and began putting his uniform back on.

"Okay, don't get your ass into an uproar. Just take it easy, man. The evening's young and the night is long. Besides, if you're going with me, you need to take off that goddamn wedding ring." Herb advised as he mixed another drink and disappeared into the bath to shower.

Rather than argue about it, Collier slipped the ring off his finger and dropped it into his shaving kit. In less than a half-hour, Herb was dressed and ready to leave. He was working on his third drink as they headed out the door.

"Take us to the Shilver Sphur..." Quickly locating a cab at the stand on the corner, Herb's speech was already showing signs he had had a bit too much to drink.

"If you're looking for girls, I can take you to a better place," the driver said as they pulled away from the curb.

"Better how? I'm looking for easy pussy, man," Herb said, taking care not to slur his words.

"Bullshit, man, free pussy's the most expensive thing on earth—you'll wind up taking 'em to some joint and spending a ton of money. If you get too drunk, you might get rolled. I'll take you to a little hotel a few blocks from here where you can get your ashes dumped. The girls are clean and it'll only cost you five bucks. In a half-hour, you'll be walking a lot lighter and ready for a night on the town," the driver said, looking at Herb in the rearview mirror.

"Shounds good to me. How 'bout it, Ram?" Herb spoke up right away.

"No way—not for me. I'm starving. I haven't eaten since breakfast. Take us somewhere where we can get a first-class cut of meat that doesn't cost an arm and a leg," Collier told the driver. He wanted to get some food in Herb before he wound up too drunk to walk.

"Aw, shit, Ram, we can eat anytime. I came to Dallas to get my ashes hauled," Herb complained.

"You don't need me for that. Drop me off at a good restaurant, and then you're on your own." Collier held his ground.

"Driver, you heard the man. Take us where we can get a good steak. My buddy here is hungry. I got to feed him first or he'll be whining all night." Herb finally gave in.

"Okay, I know just the place," the driver shrugged. It was easy to see Collier was sober and not going to be talked into anything.

The restaurant was nothing fancy, but the thick sirloin covered the large platter and the home fries were not bad at all. Although he kept harping about needing to find a "whoo'er" and complaining about Collier being a wet blanket, Herb lost little time in attacking his meat and washing it down with two longneck bottles of local Lone Star beer. When the waitress brought their steaks, Collier finally relented and ordered a longneck bottle of Lone Star. Finally, stuffed to the eyeballs with steak and home fries, they ordered pecan pie and ice cream for dessert. The total bill came to just under six bucks.

"Here, Herb, leave the extra dollar for a tip." Collier handed Herb four singles as he stifled a healthy belch.

"Take us to the Silver Spur." Herb told the driver after hailing a passing cab.

"You guys must be new in town. I'd stay away from the Spur. Word has it the owner, Jack Ruby, is connected to the Chicago mob. I can take you to a better place if you're looking for women." Collier wondered if every driver in Dallas was pimping on the side.

"Just take us to the Silver Spur and spare us the scenic route," Collier spoke up. He'd heard the line in some old gangster movie.

"Okay, but don't say I didn't warn you," the offended driver sulked. Hardly before Collier could settle in the seat, the cab pulled to the curb in a rather rundown-looking neighborhood that reminded Collier of a painting by Edward Hopper. The only sign of life in the entire block of shoddy, old, red-brick warehouses and apartment buildings was a defective electric sign showing the pink neon outline of a half-naked girl. Underneath were neon letters blinking: G S G RL   I LS! NO   O V R. As the cab moved closer, Collier saw the sign was actually meant to read: GIRLS GIRLS GIRLS! NO COVER. Below the sporadically sputtering neon dancer, a theatrical display case held posters of several strippers wearing only G-Strings and Pasties.

"Well, here we are," the driver said. "It's not too late too change your mind."

"Thanks, anyway, but we might as well check the place out." Collier slipped the driver a buck and waved him on his way. When Collier turned, Herb had already wandered over to the open door and was examining the posters. Moths and a cloud of other insects were buzzing around a single bare bulb over the display case. Under the dirty, fly-specked glass, the sun-faded posters were billed: NOW PLAYING. Nowhere in sight was there anything to indicate the cabby had actually brought them to a place called the Silver Spur. Brushing aside a swarm of gnats, he peered up the steep flight of steps inside the open doorway. At the top of the long, ill-lit stairwell, all he could make out was a ceiling covered with cheap pink and blue crepe paper streamers and clusters of matching balloons attached to the water-stained Victorian molded-tin ceiling.

"What'cha think?" Herb asked, stepping back from examining the posters and looking curiously over Collier's shoulder up the long flight of stairs.

"Well...we're here. Might as well go up and take a look. Besides, this damn neighborhood gives me the creeps. It's kinda late to call back that cab." Collier lit a Lucky and shrugged and started up the steps with Herb following close behind. At the top they stopped and looked around.

Across the shadowy room near the far wall, three hard-bitten, rawboned-looking girls in cheap, tight-fitting evening dresses were sitting around a table. Through the haze, Collier could just make out a scattering of other girls at tables further back in the large smoke-filled room with two others standing at a jukebox about halfway down the wall on the left. At the far end of the room there was a small stage with a curtained backdrop where a buxom brunette in a G-string and tasseled, star-shaped pasties was finishing her strip routine. The accompanying combo of pianist, trumpet, clarinet, guitarist and drums playing a tired "bump and grind" were wearing cowboy shirts and looked like refugees from a cattle drive. The entire place reeked heavily of stale smoke, sweat and cheap perfume.

In the corner beside the stage, the two rest rooms had lighted Cowboys and Cowgirls signs over the doors. At an abbreviated bar along the right-hand wall, a clean-shaven, rather flamboyant man who Collier judged to be in his forties was chatting with a muscular bartender polishing a tray of beer mugs resting on the bar. Something right out of an old George Raft movie, the clean-shaven man combed his hair neatly back on both sides; parted in the middle, his hairline formed a pronounced widow's peak. The man wore an expensive-looking, well-tailored suit over a spotless white shirt with an off-white, silk-brocade necktie. Although he came off as somewhat flashy, the hawk-nosed Beau Brummell had a pleasant face with a prominent dimple in his rather long chin.

Pushing away from the bar, the expensively-dressed man ambled over and stuck out his hand. "I'm Jack Ruby—I run the place. I was Army Air Corps in the last one. I'm always glad to see our service men. Come on in and let me buy you a beer. Things will start to liven up any minute now. Let me introduce you to the girls."

Both Collier and Herb shook his hand and followed him to the table on the far wall where he introduced the three young women sitting there.

"Sit down, boys, and make yourself at home. Debbie Jean, bring me and these soldiers a bottle of Lone Star and bring something tall and cool for you ladies to drink. Tell Tony to put it on my tab." Herb caught Collier's eye and winked as the George Raft look-alike gave Debbie Jean's well-formed butt a familiar pat when the tall bottle-blonde headed toward the bar.

After a half-hour, Herb had already started on a third bottle of beer when the combo took a break. Ruby excused himself to talk to a pair of men who wandered in. Several other males in Western garb with their hair slicked back and cigarettes dangling from their lips had arrived and were already busy chatting up the girls at scattered tables around the room. Not wanting to lose out to the locals, Herb asked Debbie Jean to dance, apparently hoping to work up her interest for something more than dancing to the jukebox all night.

"Don't you want to dance, too?" Mary Lou, a bouncy little redhead with a perky butt and creamy breasts bulging out of a cheap, low-cut gown asked Collier as he nursed his second beer. Bored and tired, he was seriously considering leaving Herb and heading back to the hotel.

"Sure. Why not?" Collier put down his beer and let Mary Lou lead him to the floor.

"Where are you and your buddy staying?" the opportunistic redhead asked, melting easily into his arms.

"A place called the Cotton Bowl Hotel. It's not the Adolphus but it's not too shabby as hotels go," Collier said. The jukebox was playing the classic Artie Shaw rendition of *Star Dust*. With a couple of beers in him, Collier decided the big-titted redhead wouldn't be half-bad.

"Uh-m, the Cotton Bowl's okay. Mr. Ruby lived there awhile," Mary Lou murmured in his ear, insinuating a curvy thigh between his legs. She smelled good; her perfume was most-likely expensive. Looking up at him expectantly, she brazenly continued rubbing her thigh against his nether parts. Despite his resolve to resist her, he felt an old familiar tightening in his crotch as she aggressively pressed her body into his. He'd never been propositioned by a bar girl before, but he was pretty sure there would be a price tag on what was coming next.

"If you wanted a little fun, once in awhile Mr. Ruby doesn't mind if we leave a little early and go out on the town. Mr. Ruby owns a fancy place called the Bob Wills' Ranch House in a better part of Dallas. It's set up just like a regular club. You pay two bucks and they give you a card. Then you can buy regular drinks across the bar. They have strippers there, too. Sometimes, late at night, things get wild and they take it all off. A couple weekends back, some rich oilman's wife had too much to drink, stood up on her table and took off every last stitch." Mary Lou worked her thigh harder against his awakening genitalia.

"Sounds like fun," he agreed. She had his interest up and he was way past ready to get out of this sleazy joint.

"Maybe you and your buddy would like me and Debbie Jean to show you the town. It's kinda slow tonight. If you asked him nice and slipped him a couple of fives, I'm sure Mr. Ruby would let us leave early if he knows we're going to Bob Wills' Ranch House. I know a cab driver who'll take us for two bucks. They know me there. We'll get in free." Leaning back, she adjusted her low-cut dress, carelessly giving him a peek at the tops of her nipples.

The brazen little vixen was working him for all she was worth.

Tearing his gaze from the creamy tits spilling over the top of her dress, Collier turned and searched the dance floor, looking for Herb. He finally located him near the jukebox having an animated exchange with the owner, Jack Ruby. Before Collier could make a move in their direction, Ruby suddenly twisted Herb by the shoulders in an expert judo move and pinned him against the wall. Without a word, Collier left Mary Lou standing alone as he headed toward them on the run.

"What's the trouble here, Mr. Ruby?" Collier asked when he was a few feet away.

"Your buddy has a foul mouth." Ruby turned his head to Collier, still pinning Herb against the wall.

"I apologize for his behavior, Sir. He's had a few too many beers. If you'll call us a taxi, I'll get him out of here." With rising apprehension, Collier tried to ease the tension. Careful not to make a sudden move, Collier gently coaxed Ruby to release his hold on Herb.

"Tony, get a cab down front, pronto," Ruby called to the bartender and turned back to Collier. "Okay, soldier-boy, take this bum downstairs before I call the cops."

Seizing his inebriated companion firmly by the elbow, Collier quickly steered Rudolph toward the top of the stairs.

"Goddamnit, Ram, let me go." Herb struggled to break his hold on him. "Who's that two-bit hood think he is?"

"Shut up, Herb. That two-bit hood knows exactly who he is. Let's get the hell out of here." Holding him in a death grip, Collier growled hoarsely in Herb's ear.

"Who the fuck is that pimp calling scum? Who the fuck does he think he's messing with?" Outside on the sidewalk loudly cursing, Herb jerked free of Collier's grip. He was just tucking in his shirttail when the taxi came pulling up.

"Cotton Bowl Hotel," Collier told the driver when they were safely inside the cab.

"Fuck that. It's early yet. I want to find some action." Herb put up a howl.

"Well, suit yourself. Drop me at the Cotton Bowl. You're on your own, I'm not going to babysit your worthless drunken ass," Collier snapped.

"Oh, come on, man. I'm sorry, but it wasn't my fault. How was I to know the little whoo-er would get pissed when I asked her how much she wanted for a piece of her skinny ass?"

"Excuse me for butting in, but if you guys are looking for action, I can take you to a nice place across town—a regular, fancy nightclub where a better class of girls hang out," the driver interrupted.

"I'm not looking to go to another clip joint where some local, high-school dropout offers to give me a hand job for five bucks then tells me nice girls don't go all the way," Herb protested.

"That's not a problem. I can take you to a regular whore house if pussy's all you're looking for," the driver said.

"Are these girls safe? I mean I'm not looking for a dose of clap," Herb said, his interest piqued again.

"Sure. This place is the best in town." The driver twisted around, his arm rested on the seat back now.

"What do you say, Ram?" Herb looked to Collier hopefully. "I ain't been to a regular whoo-er house since the night I graduated high school. The cabby says these girls are clean."

"Look, Herb, I don't care what you do, but it'll be a cold day in hell before I pay a woman for sex. Besides, have you lost your mind? A prostitute is only as clean as her last customer. Ever think about that?"

"I got some rubbers with me. Come on, man. You can wait in the cab while I take care of business...then I'll go with you to this nightclub or anywhere you say. Everything's on me." Herb pulled the half-pint bottle out of his hip pocket and took a swig.

"Take him anywhere he wants to go, driver, but drop me at the Cotton Bowl," Collier repeated emphatically and turned back to Herb. "Go anywhere and do anything you like, but go easy on the booze—you've already had more than enough to drink. I'm warning you. If you get in trouble, don't call me to come rescue your sorry ass."

"Okay, after we drop your buddy at the Cotton Bowl, I'll take you to the best place in town," the driver turned and put the car in gear.

"How much they charge?" Herb asked after they were moving, a little hesitant now.

"Ten bucks for fifteen minutes. The Chicken Ranch charges fifteen," the driver said.

"The Chicken Ranch?" Collier asked, curious that a house of prostitution would have a name like that.

"Don't tell me you never heard of Miss Jessie Williams' Chicken Ranch. It's down south, in La Grange, a short ways outside Austin—about halfway between San Antone and Houston. In Texas, it's near about as famous as the Alamo. Past governors, state legislators, big-shot oilmen, visiting movie stars and football players...even local lawmen have all been regular customers of Miss Jessie's place."

"How far is La Grange? Can you take us there?" Herb took a little swig from the flask, perking up at the idea of going somewhere famous to get laid.

"Not tonight, man. Austin is over a hundred miles and La Grange is a good ways outside town. Look, forget The Chicken Ranch. I'll take you to a first-class place right here in Dallas. They have regular weekly medical check-ups just like the Chicken Ranch."

"Okay, lead on, my good man," Herb told the driver, then turned back to Collier. "Come on and ride with me, Ram. Don't cut out on me. You heard the man—fifteen minutes is all it takes," he was practically begging now. "Soon as I get my problem attended to, we can go to this fancy club the driver was talking about. It ain't costing you anything but time."

His irritation over Herb's run-in with the dance hall owner subsiding now, Collier reconsidered soberly. Glancing at his watch, it was not yet 2200 hours. Left alone in the shape he was in, there was really no telling what kind of trouble was awaiting his drunken buddy.

"Okay, you win. I'll come along, but if you don't lay off the booze, I'm calling a cab and going back to the hotel." Exhaling a big sigh, Collier finally gave in. He really wasn't in the mood for anymore of Herb's obnoxious behavior, but he wasn't sleepy and they had traveled over two-hundred miles to get here—might as well take a little walk on the wild side of life.

Given the go-ahead, the driver expertly tooled the taxi out of the section of rundown commercial buildings as it dissolved into a neighborhood of similarly rundown residences. Within what seemed to be only a couple of minutes, the driver slowed and pulled to the curb in front of a once-proud, sprawling old Victorian mansion.

"Okay, gents, this is it. Follow me and I'll introduce you to Madame De Luce. She runs a classy place. She'll see to it you get the best." The driver killed the engine, got out and came around the cab.

"Come on in with me, Ram. No sense in waiting out here alone." Herb turned back to Collier after he slid out of the cab.

"No thanks, I'll wait here. I'm telling you, Herb, I'm not about to have sex with a prostitute. Have fun, but please don't take all night."

"Come on in. At Madame De Luce's you aren't under any obligation to engage one of her girls. Local men drop around all the time just to pass the time of day with Miz De Luce. You can have a bottle of beer or a shot of whiskey on the house while you wait. You owe it to yourself to take a look at one of the few remaining old-time cathouses in the whole U. S. of A." The driver held open the door and peered in at Collier.

"Well, okay." Hesitantly, he relented, his curiosity quickly getting the best of him.

Following closely behind the driver and Herb, Collier climbed the short flight of wooden steps to a wide veranda where they stood waiting at the carved front door. The door was framed by an ornate, stained-glass-peacock fanlight overhead with matching sidelights. Reaching down, the cabbie gave the wrought-iron handle of the old-fashioned hand-operated door bell a vigorous twirl. In less than a heartbeat, the door was opened by a uniformed colored maid.

"Good evening, Vashti, I've brought two military gents to visit Ms. De Luce's place." Collier idly wondered if the comely, coffee-skinned girl had ever seen Butterfly McQueen in the role of her quixotic namesake in the Selznick classic western *Duel in the Sun.*

"Y'all step right in, Mr. Carl. You knows yo' customers always welcome here," the maid invited, moving aside to let them pass. Collier had an eerie feeling he had stepped inside the pages of a history book. Stepping across the threshold into the foyer of the authentic antebellum mansion, Collier noted the deep Chinese-red wall covering was the finest silk. The interior was furnished with priceless antiques his mother and Aunt Blanche would have gladly given their eyeteeth to own. Across the gracious entrance hall with curving stairways on either side, the maid held open one of the carved doors and ushered them back to an ornately-furnished sitting room where a half-dozen or more striking young women lounged about in semi-transparent nightgowns and negligees. Blinking hard to clear his head, he watched an older woman dressed in a floor-length ball gown of elegant ivory brocade detach herself from a group of three seductively-attired young women across the room and come gliding across the intricately-patterned, mosaic parquet hardwood floor like a grand dame, to greet them.

"Madame De Luce, at your service. What shall I call you gentlemen?" Oozing charm from the tips of her gloved fingers, the impeccably-mannered madam welcomed them.

"Just call me Herb, ma'am, and this is Ram," Rudolph answered in a nervous whisper.

"Vashti, bring these gentlemen some refreshment. What are you drinking? Whiskey, beer or coffee? What's your pleasure?" she asked politely.

"I'm drinking Scotch, Ma'am," Herb spoke up without hesitation.

"A Lone Star will do fine for me, Ma'am," Collier croaked, his mouth suddenly dry.

"Now, Mr. Herb and Mr. Ram, just follow me and I'll introduce you to the ladies." She turned and led them to the nearest group of girls, standing shyly smiling.

"Brenda, Molly, Sonja, June...this is Herb and his friend, Ram..." Like a puppy, Collier followed the madam as she went from girl to girl making introductions.

"Take your time, gentlemen. In case, Carl hasn't already acquainted you with our fees for services, our minimum here is ten dollars for the first quarter-hour and ten more for each quarter-hour thereafter, up to the first full hour. All night is two-hundred dollars flat, as long as you're out of here by noon. If you stay the night, we'll serve you coffee and a beignet in the morning before you leave." As Madame De Luce finished introducing them, Vashti arrived carrying their drinks on a pewter tray.

"Miz De Luce, Ma'am, thank you just the same, but I'm going to wait outside while Herb here...ah....avails himself of your services. I'll just pay you for my beer and wait in the cab with Carl," embarrassed, Collier protested, fishing in his hip pocket for his wallet.

"You'll do no such thing, dear boy. Just put that billfold back where it belongs and make yourself right at home and get to know our girls while Herb enjoys his trip upstairs," the self-possessed madam cooed and gave him a coquettish tweak on the cheek. She nodded toward a veritable harem of wholesome-looking, enormously attractive young women—some hardly more than school-age girls—lounging nonchalantly around a luxurious arrangement of boudoir chairs and an elegant ash-rose velvet settee near the center of the room.

"Excuse me, I see Vashti has some other guests. Why don't you just have a seat? The girls will entertain you while you wait." Madame De Luce turned and walked back across the room to greet a quartet of middle-aged men dressed in well-cut Western-style business suits.

"Sit here and tell us all about yourself," a petite brunette took Collier by the hand and pulled him to the settee. Her perky nipples and pubic triangle were clearly visible through the fabric of her diaphanous nightgown. Collier was dead certain she couldn't have been a day past sixteen.

"Well...ah...there's really not that much to tell..." Collier stammered and blushed neon red. He tried mightily to avert his eyes from the young girl's lush black pubic patch as she crossed her legs, exposing the ruffled, slightly-parted lips of her vulva and naked inner thigh. Twisting his head away to keep from staring, he found his nose less than two feet away from another pubic triangle—this one belonged to a flaming, natural redhead standing squarely in front of him, her satin negligee open from breast to crotch.

"You sure you won't change your mind?" the redhead teased, leaning forward to tickle him under the chin with her painted nails. This girl looked a year or two older than her companion, with absolutely mind-boggling breasts capped by huge pink nipples as round as silver dollar pancakes.

"No...I...mean, uh...yes, Ma'am, I'm sure," Collier stuttered, torn between ravishing the redhead right there on the settee in front of God and everybody or making a dash for the door.

"I don't mean to put you under any pressure or embarrass you, but don't you find us even mildly attractive? I mean, don't you like girls at all?" the brunette beside him on the settee, leaned forward, anxious to hear his answer.

"Oh, yes, Ma'am...I find you very attractive. It's just that...we'll I'm married. I love my wife." Desperate to extricate himself, he resorted to the first lie that popped into his mind.

"Oh, that's sweet. Someday, I hope to marry a man just like you," the third girl, a small-breasted, broad-hipped ash-blonde clad in a short, baby-doll gown, standing beside the redhead, interjected on his behalf.

"I'm not so sure you'd be saying that if you knew what was going through my mind," Collier laughed, relaxing a little now. "My...ah...machinery is on overload."

"Let me have a feel?" the flaming redhead teased. He flinched as her hands feinted a little move in the direction of his groin. Blushing an even deeper red, Collier crossed his legs, laughing an embarrassed laugh.

"Don't be so selfish," the redhead flirted. "Come upstairs with me and I'll pay Madame De Luce for you myself."

"You're just making fun of me." Collier blushed again.

"Fun or not—seriously that's a great idea." The redhead persisted, warming to the moment. "Come with us, and we'll all pay for you. Ever have a threesome, Mr. Ram?"

"No, Ma'am, I wish you'd quit kidding." Getting more uncomfortable by the minute, Collier had growing concern his captured penis might explode inside his Jockey shorts.

"She's not kidding. Come on, let's go upstairs. It's on the house." The blonde stepped forward and pushed her cute navel against his nose. He'd never before seen a real blonde so up-close and personal.

"Girls, I hate to break in on your conversation, but I'd like you to meet Les and Jim and Al. These gentlemen are from St. Louis and are looking for female companionship." Just at the verge of Collier giving in, Madame De Luce stepped in and saved the day.

Seizing the opportunity to escape, Collier stood and headed for the door.

"Too bad you're such a jerk. You missed all the fun," Herb said when he came back outside and was crawling back into Carl's waiting cab.

"You mean your buddy turned down all that easy pussy?" the driver, Carl, shot them a look of utter disbelief.

"He thinks he's too good to fuck a whoo-er," Herb sneered. "Too bad, those girls were really firsh class. I could use a dring. Let's go find this fancy nightclub you were talking about."

"Don't you think you've had enough for one night? Now that you've gotten your little problem taken care of, I was kind of hoping to go back and get some sleep," Collier said.

"We can always schleep. Take this goodytwoshoes back, Carl, and drop him off. Then we'll go have sh-ome real fun," Herb told the driver, obviously still more than a little in his cups.

"Okay, okay. Forget the hotel, I'll ride along," Collier conceded, worried Herb was likely to wind up in jail if left to his own devices.

"Where to then?" Carl asked then suggested, "There's always action at Bob Wills' Dance Club. It stays open until the wee hours."

"I heard Bob Wills' is owned by Jack Ruby. Isn't there a really first-class nightclub in town?" Collier asked, remembering what Mary Lou had told him back at the Silver Spur.

"Well, there is a fancy club called The Theater Lounge. It's not far from here in a ritzy part of town. I've taken visiting businessmen over there, and I've picked up a fare there once or twice, but I've never been inside. It has a dance band and a girl singer. No strippers or anything like that, but I understand it's a hangout for society broads and career girls on the prowl," Carl said not too enthusiastically.

"I'm crazy for career girls and I need another dring-g. Take ush there," Herb showed no sign of sobering up.

"Okay, let's go check it out," Carl eased the car away from the curb. As they left Madame De Luce's establishment, Collier was surprised to discover her place of business was located on the periphery of a neighborhood of older, apparently quite-respectable homes with well-established oaks and spacious, well-kept lawns. They quickly passed out of this comfortably-settled, upper-middleclass neighborhood into a snobbier, sparsely-populated area where stone and brick pillars and ornate gates barred the entrances to large estates protected by giant hedges or masonry walls. A few short blocks into this section, Carl turned right again between two, red-brick gateposts onto a tree-lined drive. One hundred yards in on the left, they passed a large parking area fairly overflowing with expensive cars and limos and partially screened by a giant privet hedge. Topping a slight rise, an altogether imposing structure appeared through the misty late-night air, silhouetted against a garish backdrop of floodlights. Complete with an overhanging backlit marquee displaying the name, THE THEATER LOUNGE, the nightclub occupied a building which, obviously, had formerly housed a large, commercial movie house.

"That'll be a buck-fifty, gents," Carl said as he pulled the taxi to a stop underneath the overhang of the marquee. A tuxedoed George Raft look-a-like held the door as they exited the cab.

Could it be possible that the gangster movie star's mother had been from Dallas?

"Keep the change." Herb leaned back in the front window and handed him a five.

"Thanks, gents. I'm going off duty at midnight, but I'm in no hurry to get home. I'll hang around awhile in case you need a ride back to town."

"Do you have a reservation, gentlemen?" the tuxedoed, muscle-bound attendant inquired in surprisingly cultured tones.

"No one told us we needed one," Collier spoke right up. "Are you overbooked?"

"If you'll just wait a moment, I'll consult the maître d'," the liveried cretinoid replied and walked a few steps over to another well-dressed goon, who could have been his twin, standing near the double doors guarding the entrance. Following a brief conversation, the cretinoid returned.

"The maître d' says we can set up a nice table for you on one of the middle terraces. The cover is usually ten dollars for non-members, but since you're servicemen, we're going to suspend the cover for you this evening. If you'll forgive me for taking the liberty, I should think you might want to show the maître d'—and his staff—some small token of appreciation for their generosities," the doorman said with a meaningful look at his outstretched palm.

"Herb, why don't you slip these nice gentleman a little show of our gratitude?" Not about to shell out his hard-earned pay for his comrade-in-arm's alcoholic debauchery, Collier gave Herb a dig with his elbow.

"*Mais oui, Monsieur!*" the still-boozy Herb peeled off a couple singles and handed them to the prissy Neanderthal and slipped another five into the *maître d's* outstretched palm as he ushered them into the well-appointed lobby, instructing the captain to seat them. No bumpkin, drunk or sober the mainline Philadelphian seemed to know his way around.

Once inside, it was even more apparent the building had formerly been a movie house. From either side of the lobby, a pair of main aisles led down the gently-sloping floor of the main auditorium to a postage-stamp dance floor and a small stage.

To offset the slanted floor of the former theater, the cavernous room had been ingeniously terraced into descending level sections to accommodate tables. Scattered throughout the high-ceilinged room, an efficient cadre of white dinner-jacketed wait staff was busily taking orders and balancing trays of food or drinks on upturned hands. Moving from table to table, several scantily-clad cigarette girls with plunging necklines and carrying little trays of smokes and candy mints suspended from frilly straps looped around their necks, prettily hawked their wares. As they followed the head waiter down the aisle, a nine-piece orchestra dressed in shiny tuxedos was just filing through a door beside the stage, obviously returning from an intermission. Complete with the cadre of George Raft look-alikes, Collier had the impression he was being escorted onto a New York or Chicago nightclub movie set.

"I hope you'll find this table to your liking, gentlemen." Gawking open-mouthed at the impressive setting, they followed the waiter to a small table which was quickly being set up on the widest-level dining tier about halfway down the sloping aisle, near the middle of the room.

"The Theater Lounge is operated as a private club, gentlemen. You can order almost any drink you like from our bar," the waiter informed them as soon as they were seated.

"Bring me a double Scosch," Herb tipped the waiter a pair of singles.

"Better go easy, Herb; we just got here," Collier whispered.

"Quit being sush a schtick in the mud," Herb slurred, a bit thick-tongued still.

"Might as well bring me two double Scoches. I'm thirsty as a Gila monster. While you're at it, better bring my preacher here a ginger ale." Herb winked at the waiter.

"Never mind my friend. I'll have a gin and tonic with a twist." Collier liked the looks of the place and was relaxing now. Lone Star tasted a lot like horse piss smelled, and he'd had his fill of beer.

"Just look around. The place is full of horny cunts," Herb said in a loud voice, before the waiter was barely out of earshot. Collier felt color creeping up his neck as two couples in evening wear seated at the table behind them looked around to locate the source of the coarse remark. Ignoring the disapproving stares, Collier carefully surveyed the room, acting as if he hadn't heard a word.

The well-dressed crowd appeared to be predominantly a mix of couples ranging from mid-twenties to late middle-age. However, as Herb had so astutely—however crudely—pointed out, seated at widely-separated tables placed around the room were a number of young, apparently-unescorted, women of late-college age—or slightly older—which Collier surmised were adventuresome and predatory young career girls, out on the town.

Wide-eyed, Collier watched as a pair of older, well-dressed gentlemen approached two of the young, unattached females seated at a nearby table. After a brief exchange, the youngish women rose and followed the men down the aisle to the dance floor.

"Did you get a load of that? This may be our lucky night," Herb enthused.

"Uh-huh." Collier grunted, with a warning clutch of apprehension in his gut. He had an uneasy feeling he might have trouble getting Herb out of here.

"Go ahead and bring me another one of these." Herb made quick work of both double Scotches as soon as the waiter brought their drinks. "How about you, Ram, might as well relax and have some fun?"

"No, I'm not ready yet," Collier declined a second round, but before the waiter could get away, Collier stopped him to inquire about the house rules. "I just saw a couple of men ask two unescorted girls to dance. Is that okay? I mean is there some sort of protocol?"

"Those gentlemen would have sent a note across to the ladies. Apparently, the ladies told them it was alright," the waiter explained, extracting from his pocket a small business-card bearing the legend, THE THEATER LOUNGE, engraved in small Helvetica type. "If you see an unescorted female you'd like to ask to dance, just write a note on the back of a little card like this and I'll deliver it for you. This enables us to maintain a proper decorum and respectability."

"Give me a card, I want to ask those two girls down front to dance," Herb said.

Reaching into the breast pocket of his dinner jacket, the waiter handed both Herb and Collier each a stack of several cards. With Herb already surveying the room with a lustful look, the waiter shot Collier a worried glance.

"See, Ram, the two down in front near the dance floor. Mine'sh wearing a pink-floweredy dress." Clumsily nudging Collier with his elbow, Herb almost knocked the pack of Luckies from his hand.

"Yeah, not bad," Collier grudgingly conceded.

"So what should we say on the card, if we wanted to ask the ladies to dance?" Collier asked the waiter. The system seemed harmless enough. A harmless dance or two with respectable women would slow Herb's heavy drinking, provide him a chance to sober up.

"Just ask them if you can buy them a drink and if they would like to dance," the waiter instructed and waited while Collier scribbled the note on the card.

When Collier handed him the card, the waiter stood momentarily waiting, before Herb handed Collier a dollar bill, "Don't be such a cheapskate, Ram. Give the man a tip."

Somewhat red-faced, Collier handed the single to the waiter and watched as he made his way down front to deliver the note. After a brief exchange, the girls looked up and gave them a little wave. The women turned back to the waiter and engaged him in a brief exchange. When they were finished speaking, the waiter started making his way back between the tables toward the kitchen. After a few minutes, the waiter reappeared bearing a bottle of what appeared to be Champagne with an ice bucket with a folding stand. With a towel over his left arm and with a lot of ceremony, the waiter proceeded to uncork and serve the Champagne. When the wine was poured, the two women lifted their glasses toward them in a silent toast before the waiter turned and started back up the aisle to where they sat.

"The young ladies send their thanks, but regret they cannot ask you to join them. They are waiting for someone, it seems. Too bad, gentlemen. By the way, I'll just add the twenty-five dollars for the Champagne to your tab."

"You'll fucking what?" Herb exploded, turning heads at several nearby tables.

"Please watch your language, sir. We won't tolerate vulgarity here," the waiter warned with a sharp, reproving tone.

"Just what kind of clip joint is this? You think we're going to stand still for this cheap swindle?" Herb pushed his chair back, glaring up at the waiter with obvious rage.

"Please keep your seat and lower your voice, sir," the waiter said, deadly serious now.

"Just who do you think you're fucking with?" Already started on his second Scotch, Herb was getting drunker and more belligerent by the minute.

"I've already warned you, Sir..." the waiter looked back toward the entrance for help.

"Just bring our bill and call us a cab. We'll meet you in the outer lobby," Collier tried to reassure the waiter, anxious to avoid a scene.

"We'll do no goddamn such thing. I want to see the manager. Get him here," Herb demanded, taking another drink and half-rising from his chair.

"Just keep your seat, Sir. I'll be right back," the waiter stood over Herb, waiting until he sat back down before finally turning to leave.

"They got some fucking nerve, trying to put one over on us like that!" Herb groused, more than a little drunk. "I suppose I'll never get that other drink now."

"Just calm down, Herb. I don't think we're going to get anywhere by making a fuss in a fancy place like this," Collier tried his best to defuse his anger.

"Don't tell me to calm down. I don't care where we are. We don't have to put up with shit like this," Herb continued to fret and fume.

"If you'll look over your right shoulder at the two gorillas headed our way, I wouldn't be too sure of that." Collier spied the waiter with a couple of tuxedoed NFL linebacker-types bearing down on them.

"Would you gentlemen please follow us? The manager will see you in his office," the waiter said, the gorillas standing at the ready on either side of him.

"What the fuck's going on here? What do you think you have to gain by these strong-arm tactics?" Herb exploded.

"Please keep it down, Sir. You're disturbing our other guests," the waiter quietly cautioned as his burly companions stepped in and took Herb by the shoulders, lifting all of his 200-plus pounds easily out of the chair. Before Herb could protest again, they stood him straight up and pivoted him around, forcefully hoisting him bodily up the aisle between them.

"Please just follow us, sir. Everything will be fine as soon as the management explains the situation to your friend." The waiter waited while Collier collected their overseas caps before they fell in behind the two bouncers hustling Herb through the disapproving crowd.

When they reached the lobby, their sullen entourage turned down a short hallway and entered an unmarked door opening into a small anteroom. As soon as the door closed behind them, the waiter knocked on the door to an inner office. After a moment, he entered with a muffled invitation from inside. After a couple of moments, the door opened and the waiter returned, followed by a rather intimidating figure close behind.

"I'm the manager here, and I apologize for this misunderstanding," the short balding man in evening clothes stepped into the antechamber and gave them a serious look.

"Is this your handwriting on this card?" The man extended a little white card under Herb's nose. He made no effort to offer a handshake or give his name.

"It's my buddy's here. He wrote the note," Herb said in a subdued voice, the gravity of the situation finally getting though to him now.

"Well, I think you gentlemen will agree that you plainly offered to buy the young ladies a drink. I understand that you thought the young ladies would return your generosity by favoring you with a dance, but your note indicates there were really no strings attached..."

"Those cunts and your waiter here knew full-well they were ripping us off. If you and your monkey-suited thugs think we were hicks and wouldn't put up a fuss, well, I've got news for you. As soon as I report this to the Military Police...uh-m-m, wait...oh, wow!..." Herb squeaked in distress as one of goons gave his arm a warning tweak.

"I must admit the young women may have taken unfair advantage of your generosity. And I understand your chagrin that Cray, here, didn't intervene."—he nodded toward the waiter—"So I'm going to make this one on the house, if you'll just give me these gentlemen's bill?" The manager held out his hand while the waiter fumbled for the bill.

As soon as the waiter handed him the bill, the manager tore the card in half. "Now, I think everyone in this room has had more than enough excitement for one evening. My staff will escort you both out front, and my personal driver will take you to your hotel. By the way, I'm sorry for our inhospitality, gentlemen, but just so there is no misunderstanding, please don't ever show your faces here again."

"If it's all the same to you, we'd rather take a cab back to town," Collier interrupted.

"It's not all the same to me. Now, follow these gentlemen. My car is waiting out front." Without a further word, the manager went back inside his office and quietly closed the door.

As soon as they were alone, the two goons strong-armed Herb outside and gently, but bodily, assisted him into the back of a dark-green, Lincoln sedan and waited for Collier to climb in the backseat beside him.

"Where to, gentlemen?" the driver asked before the gangster-types had closed the door.

"The Baker—downtown," Collier said, nudging Herb sharply with his elbow, praying he had sobered up enough to keep his mouth shut.

As soon as the driver let them out beneath the hotel's impressive marquee, Collier hustled Herb inside the Baker's lobby, breathing a sigh of relief as he watched the Lincoln speed away.

"Why the fuck did you tell'em to drop us here? I've still got a bottle and some mixer back in our room..." Herb immediately put up a howl.

"I didn't want them to know where we were actually staying, just in case they have a change of heart. Let's wait a few minutes to make sure the coast is clear, and we'll find ourselves a cab." Collier was feeling altogether paranoid now.

"I'm gonna find a phone and report thish to the MPs. The MPs'll put that clip joint off limish so fast it'll make that fancy club manager pish his pants." Herb protested drunkenly.

"Look, Herb, I don't think you want the MPs to see you in the shape you're in tonight. Come on now...it's almost 0100 hours. Let's see if we can find a cab and go back to our room. You can get another drink and I can get some sleep. We've got to hitchhike back to Sill in the morning. I've had enough trouble for one weekend. There's no way I'm going to miss bed check tomorrow night and add AWOL to my list."

"All of a sudden I'm not feeling sho good," Herb complained in the cab going back to the Cotton Bowl Hotel. "I need another dring."

At the hotel, Collier stood impatiently holding the elevator while Herb got a pitcher of ice from the night clerk—he still had a goodly part of the Scotch left upstairs.

"Look, Herb, if I were you, I'd lay off the booze. You've had enough for one night. Take the bed nearest the john if you're still feeling sick. I left a call with the desk clerk for 0700. I'm going to try to get some sleep," Collier advised, watching Herb pouring himself a drink from the half-empty bottle of J&B when they were safely inside their room. Quickly undressing, Collier carefully folded his clothes and put them on the top shelf of the little closet, preparing for a quick, morning getaway. He was fast asleep hardly before he clicked off the bedside lamp.

"This is your wake-up call for seven o'clock, Sir. Would you like me to call back in five minutes to make sure you're still awake?" the night clerk roused Collier from a disturbing dream about being held prisoner inside a tuxedo factory.

"No thanks. I'm awake," Collier said and put down the phone.

"Okay, Herb, rise and shine. Let's get our butts on the road," Collier called before he found the light switch. Almost before he began rubbing the sleep out of his eyes, Collier's nostrils were assailed by the nauseatingly-sour odor of puke which pervaded the entire room.

"Judaspriest! What the fuck?" Collier exploded after he turned on the lamp and surveyed the room. The room looked as if it had been struck by a garbage bomb. Herb's bed had been stripped and most of the bedclothes strewn into several little tangled piles between the window and the beds.

"Jesus Christ, man, turn off that fucking light," Herb was sprawled naked across the bare mattress of the adjoining bed with his forearms shielding his eyes. Everywhere Collier looked, puke-stained bath towels and washcloths were scattered across the floor, apparently used in futile attempts to clean up a half-dozen large pools of vomit at random points around the room.

"Jesus Christ yourself! Get up, Herb. We got to get out of here. We need to get our asses on the road." Trying desperately not to gag from the stench and trying to avoid looking too carefully at the ungodly disarray, Collier carefully tiptoed around the pools of puke and made his way to the closet to retrieve his clothes.

"Turn out the fucking light, I said...." Herb rolled over on his face.

"C'mon, goddamnit, Herb, get up and in the shower. While you dress, I'll try to find you some clean towels to dry your sorry ass." Collier quickly dressed, carefully retrieving his change and wallet from the bedside table. Sitting on his bed, reaching for his shoes he discovered both toes had been splashed with a vile green streaks of puke. When he turned to go in search of a wash cloth or anything clean enough to wipe off his shoes, Herb was still softly snoring—he had not moved an inch.

In the vomited-splashed bathroom, Collier miraculously found a half-used roll of toilet tissue still in the dispenser and used most of it to wipe the upchuck off his shoes. When he had finished the job, he went back and took a closer look at Herb.

Lying in what looked to be a pool of regurgitated gastric residue, here and there, Herb's hairy, naked body was spotted with splashes of half-dried puke. Distastefully assessing the task ahead, Collier surveyed the room and breathed a great sigh of relief when he saw his wasted companion's clothes safely piled on top of the dresser on the far side of the narrow room. Collier's relief was short-lived, however, when he negotiated his way through the war zone and made a closer inspection of Herb's discarded uniform. To his dismay, Herb's uniform had not completely escaped the ravage of his orgy of gastric distress. Mercifully, however, a closer inspection showed that the situation—both man and uniform—were not totally beyond repair. All he needed now was to get Herb in the shower and find enough clean towels to do the job.

"Get up, Herb. You've got to get cleaned up. We need to get out of here."

"Go 'way, man, I need to sleep," Herb grunted and limply waved his arm.

Looking for any solution to the problem of getting Herb into the shower and not at all willing to put up with any more of his crap, Collier spotted last night's ice pitcher sitting on the dresser top. The pitcher was still filled almost to the brim with mostly-melted ice.

"Desperate circumstances call for heroic measures," Collier recalled from some recent training lecture. In less than the time it takes to pull the pin and toss a grenade, he crossed the room, picked up the pitcher and emptied the entire contents full on Herb's snoring face.

"Oh, shit! Jesuschrist! Wha-da fuck?" Herb roused instantly, rolled off the mattress and came fully vertical, trying to get the ice water off his naked body with flailing hands.

"Get in the shower or I'll do it again," Collier ordered. "Come on, I'll start the water for you."

"Okay, okay," Herb followed reluctantly behind.

"Now, get in!" Collier ordered as soon as he had the water temperature adjusted. "I'm going to go see if I can scare up a clean towel to dry you off. If you're not ready to leave here in fifteen minutes, I'm leaving your sorry ass. You can make it back to Sill on your own." Collier wheeled and left the room. When he returned with an armful of towels he had discovered in a recently-vacated room, Collier found Herb still in the bathroom dripping from the shower, leaning over the wash basin with the dry heaves.

"Get away from the frigging sink. Puke in the damn commode!" Collier exclaimed disgustedly, as he handed Herb a towel "Dry your worthless ass off and let's get on the road."

"Oh, God, Ram, give me a break. I'll have to get better just to die," Herb straightened up and groaned.

"You got any clean shorts or a shirt in here?" As soon as Herb had dried off, Collier marched him back into the room and opened his AWOL bag.

"Yeah, if you'll just hand me that I'll find them." Herb nodded, somewhat subdued.

"Jeez, shouldn't we try to straighten up the room?" Herb groaned when they were finally ready to make their getaway.

"You can if you want to—personally I'm out of here," Collier said. He picked up his AWOL bag and turned, heading for the elevator.

Fortunately, when they exited the elevator in the lobby, the desk clerk was occupied with a group waiting to check out, so they went unnoticed out the door. At the corner, an empty cab was waiting and Collier wasted no time in climbing in.

"We're hitchhiking back to Wichita Falls, take us to the main road on the outskirts of town," Collier directed as soon as Herb was in the taxi and had closed the door.

"You're in luck. I just got a call to pick up a fare at Love Field. I'll only charge you half," the driver said as he pulled away from the curb.

Making good time speeding through the light Sunday morning traffic, in no time at all the runways of the sprawling commercial airport loomed ahead, shimmering through the morning heat-haze. At the airport entrance, the driver stopped where the road forked and let them out.

As soon as Herb got out of the cab, he stumbled into the nearby high, roadside grass and weeds and doubled over retching with dry heaves.

"Keep your money. This one's on me. You got your hands full with the basket case," the cabbie nodded toward Herb who was bent double, gagging in the weeds. "Take the left road—it goes into Denton. It's a college town. Should be some traffic out of there—parents and sweethearts heading back north from

-222-

visiting students for the weekend. Out of Denton, take Highway 81, north toward Bowie and Henrietta. That road takes you straight into Wichita Falls," the goodhearted cabbie advised.

"Time's a'wasting, Herb," Collier said and started walking after the taxi disappeared up the eastern fork of the road toward the airport. Looking back along the highway at the Dallas skyline, Collier wondered anxiously if the hotel clerk had already called the MPs who would be waiting for them when they arrived back at Sill.

"Hold up a minute...can't you see I'm dying here?" Herb turned with a plaintive look.

Trudging down the long hill in the morning heat, they had only walked about a mile with Herb stopping and gagging every hundred feet or so when they came to an access road marked Air Freight, leading into the western side of the big airport. After they crossed the access road, Collier stopped and set down his AWOL bag.

"What'ya stopping here for?" Herb protested, apparently feeling somewhat better now.

"As good a place as any. The driver said this is the main road north out of town. There may be some traffic coming out of the airport headed north to Denton. If we flag 'em here, it gives them a chance to pull over before they build up a good head of steam." Collier shrugged and lit a cigarette. He shaded his eyes against the sun, hoping to see a car coming their way.

After what seemed an eternity—but was probably was less than an hour— without sighting a single, solitary vehicle, a beat-up, sun-faded, rusty-red Chevy pickup truck pulled out of the airport, heading their way. When the driver passed, he slowed and gave them a quick once-over before he finally pulled to a full stop and gave his horn a little beep.

"Where ya' headed," the driver asked when they stood expectantly beside the truck.

"Fort Sill, Oklahoma...but Denton...Wichita Falls...anywhere along the way will do," Collier said as he looked in at the young, freckled-face boy at the wheel. Dressed in clean, but hard-worn jeans, and a western-style khaki shirt with the sleeves rolled up past his bony elbows, the skinny kid looked hardly more than fourteen or fifteen—hardly old enough to be driving a car, even with a learners' permit.

"Put your bags in the pickup bed and hop in. Wichita Falls is a fair piece out of my way. I can take you as far as Denton. I'm headed to Archer City, but it should be a sight easier to catch a ride to Wichita Falls in Denton. It's a college town. A lot of students live around Wichita Falls." The young cowboy reached across and released the door latch.

"Sounds good to me," Collier said and climbed in first, affording the still-slightly-aromatic Herb the seat nearest the open window.

"Call me Larry," the kid said after he had coaxed the old pickup's protesting gears into high and they were moving slowly north.

"Everybody calls me Ram. The walking wounded here beside me is Herb." Collier nodded at Herb who was already snoring, his forehead resting on his forearm in the rusty window frame.

"Y'all can smoke if you want to. If you can spare one, I wouldn't mind having a smoke myself."

"Sure thing," Collier pulled out his Luckies and held his Zippo while the boy got a light.

"You guys back from Korea?" the young cowboy asked, inhaling deeply from the cigarette. They were in open country now. Behind them, the skyline of Dallas was a hazy outline, vaporous through the morning heat.

"No...we're just finishing up our Basic Training—got about another month to go."

"I'd go in a heartbeat, but I don't turn sixteen 'til June third—got awhile yet before I even have to register for the draft. The war'll be over before the draft catches up to me. I got two more years of high school, but soon as I graduate, I'm leaving Archer City, Texas in my dust."

The beat-up Motorola car radio under the dash poured out the muted sound of Bob Wills and the Texas Playboys twanging out the mournful strains of *New San Antonio Rose*. Here and there along the desolate landscape, oil wells—their robotic mechanisms resembling bent old black men on hands and knees, demonically thrusting their genitals in and out—pumped obliviously in the blistering sun.

"Where's Archer City, anyway?" Collier asked, struggling valiantly to stay awake.

"About twenty miles south and west of Wichita Falls," the youth replied.

"Wichita Falls is only an hour away from Fort Sill. If Archer City is that close to Wichita, wouldn't we be better off if we just rode along with you?"

"No way. You'd never get a ride. Nobody comes through Archer City anymore—too far off the beaten path. There's only one traffic light in town. The only cafe is a greasy spoon. They even closed down the only picture show. About the only entertainment left is church socials and the local pool hall." Ticking off the town's deficiencies, the kid snorted in disgust.

"Isn't there another good-sized town between here and Wichita Falls?" Collier asked. "I'd like to make the most out of the ride with you, but I don't want to get stuck in this blazing sun out in the boonies with Herb in the shape he's in.

"Well, I guess I could take you on Three-eighty across to Decatur where it crosses Eighty-one, the main highway from Wichita to Fort Worth. You have to go that way anyway."

"How far is Decatur?"

"Twenty-five miles—give or take a mile." The kid slowed as they moved into the business district of a little town. "Come to think of it, I could take you up Eighty-one as far as Bowie. That would move you another sixty miles closer. It's not the way I usually go. But I could drop you in Bowie and cut across through Joy over to Archer City."

"I really don't want you to have to go out of your way. I was just trying to get directions," Collier apologized.

"Don't worry about it. It ain't really that much out of my way. The back road from Bowie to Archer City cuts through some lonely country, but it may be actually a mite shorter that way. That would take you another fifty or sixty miles closer. Bowie ain't much of a town, but it's that much closer to where you're going. Bowie is only about forty or fifty miles from Wichita Falls. Now that I think about it, you might even catch a ride with someone bypassing Wichita Falls altogether. Eighty-one forks there. Some folks go straight from Bowie to Lawton, through Temple and Walters on Eighty-two. I'll leave it up to you." The youngster shrugged. He had smoked the Lucky down until it almost burned his fingers; he took one final drag before snubbing it out in the overflowing ashtray beside the radio beneath the dash.

Sleep-deprived and sedated by the oven-like interior of the old truck, Collier—still pondering the quandary of whether to get out in Denton or go on to Bowie—lapsed slowly into a semi-somnambulant state.

"We're coming up on Denton now," the sound of the kid's voice over the hillbilly music and the drone of the engine roused Collier out of his half-dosing state. When he blinked and rubbed his eyes, a city-limits sign, Denton, Texas, Home of North Texas State College, loomed several hundred yards ahead. Inside the city limit sign, a fire hydrant and the beginning of a city sidewalk cutting a path through the roadside weeds, marked the outskirts of the little college town.

"Well? What's it's gonna be? You want to get out here or ride another hour to Bowie? It's up to you. It ain't none of my business, but I think your buddy could use the rest. Looks like he had a bad night. If I was you, I'd go on to Bowie," the kid advised.

"Yeah, Herb got a hold of some bad ice last night, if you know what I mean. You're right; he could use the rest. If you're sure we aren't putting you to too much trouble, Larry, I think I'll take you up on your offer to go on to Bowie," Collier said.

"It ain't really that much out of my way," the boy said, ogling a pair of long-legged co-eds walking in shorts along the sidewalk of the dusty, one-horse college town.

"How 'bout another cigarette?" When he pulled up at the intersection with U.S. 380 on the north side of town, Collier shook loose another Lucky Strike from the pack and offered it to the youth.

"Thanks a heap...don't mind if I do..." The youngster leaned forward and trapped the cigarette between his lips without taking his hands off the wheel.

"Don't mention it. I've got a couple extra packs in my AWOL bag I'll give you when you drop us in Bowie," he said, lighting both their smokes with his Zippo.

After he finished the cigarette and they were heading west through the godforsaken, sunbaked countryside, Collier slipped back into a fitful doze.

"You think you'll be going to Korea?" the kid asked, rousing him from his sleep again.

"Not right away. After I finish Basic the end of May, I'm scheduled to go to Officer training," Collier said, trying hard not to let the irritation at being waked show in his tone.

"How long is OCS, anyway—three months?" the youth persisted, just making idle conversation.

"Three months? I wish! Where you'd get the idea it only took three months to become an officer?" Collier struggled not to show he was offended.

"Well, the father of one of my high-school buddies was an officer in the last war—he called himself a 'Ninety-day Wonder.'"

"Oh, yeah, I've heard that expression, too. They were really more desperate for officers in World War Two than they are now, I guess. Nowadays, OCS takes twenty-two weeks—and that's not counting a week of orientation. Twenty-three weeks is only a week shy of a full six months," Collier pointed out.

"Well, I should think the war will be over by the time you get out of OCS," the kid said, trying to smooth over his misconception.

"Maybe. But a year ago, I thought it would already be over," Collier said.

"Yeah, I know. One of the guys ahead of me in high school joined up just after the war broke out. While he was in Basic Training, his best buddy stole his girl. When he came back on leave after Basic, he blacked his buddy's eye right on the street in the middle of town."

"Sounds like it served his buddy right." Collier laughed.

"Well, it really wasn't *all* his buddy's fault. The girl's parents are oil-rich. She's spoiled plumb rotten. She's made a play for every guy in town—even went swimming nekkid at a party in Wichita Falls." The lad shot him a questioning look to see if he got the picture.

"Yeah, I've met my share of rich-bitch daddy's-girls," Collier said.

"You got a girlfriend back home?" The kid obviously wanted to talk about women now.

"I'm married. My wife's a registered nurse. She finished training while I was still in college," Collier said, thinking the youngster would be impressed by the respectability of having a nurse for a wife.

"That's good, I guess. Two girls ahead of me in school are in nurses' training. The nursing students in Wichita are pretty fast, but I'm sure your wife's not at all like them."

"No...Emma's a good Episcopal girl."

Mulling that over for a moment, the teenager changed the subject. "Anyway, the guy who slugged his buddy is in Korea now—somewhere near where the truce talks are going on. He wrote his parents that he's got to stay another year before he can come home."

"*C'est le guerre!*" Collier shrugged.

"That sounds like French. What's it mean?" the kid looked at him, impressed.

"Too bad, but that's the way war is." Collier shrugged philosophically.

"Let me hear you say it again."

Collier repeated the simple French phrase and the kid parroted him several times until he got it right.

"*C'est le guerre!* Sort of French for 'tough shit.' Wait until I tell Ms. Galbraith, our French teacher at school." Laughing at his own joke, the kid repeated the phrase.

"I'm sure Ms. Galbraith will appreciate that," Collier quipped, not sure at all.

"Oh, she's okay. Yeah, *C'est le guerre!* That's war alright. Anyway, I hope they get the war over before you have to go," the kid gave him a sympathetic look and lapsed into thoughtful silence again.

"This is Bowie coming up. Sorry, I have to let you off, but my turnoff is just up ahead," the young man roused Collier awake.

He slowed and stopped the truck. Collier blinked and looked around. According to his watch, they had been driving for about another hour. Up ahead the road forked to the left which Collier recognized was generally west—the sun was already halfway to the horizon.

"Well, thanks. My buddy and I really appreciate the lift. My last name's Ramsay. Collier Boyd Ramsay. Look me up if you ever get around Roanoke, Virginia," Collier said and reached over to shake his hand.

"Larry Jeff McMurtry."—the kid offered his hand after he pulled over to the side of the road—"If you ever make it to Archer City, just ask for directions to the

McMurtry spread." Putting the truck in neutral, the boy pulled on the emergency brake and hopped out and came around the truck to help Herb out of the truck.

"Well, thanks again," Collier said, stretching his legs and arms, glad to have his feet on solid ground again.

"You don't really have to give me those cigarettes, Ram. I don't want to take your last pack." Now it became clear the kid had gotten out of the truck to make sure Collier hadn't forgotten his promise.

"Don't worry. I have plenty of smokes to get me back to Sill." Collier retrieved both AWOL bags from the truck bed and quickly found two extra packs of Luckies.

"Much obliged," their young benefactor pumped his hand again.

"Forget it. I really appreciate your going out of your way for us," Collier said.

"My pleasure. I hate to say anything, but the radio's been reporting bad storms and tornadoes all over, including Lawton and further south."—the teen said, pointing to a dark bank of clouds with high thunderheads rising to the north and west—"If I were you, I'd stay close around a gas station or some other sort of shelter right here in Bowie in case you get hit by a storm. We can get some god-awful, frog-strangler rain around here," he warned before he climbed back under the wheel and opened a pack of his newfound Luckies. He dug an old-fashioned kitchen match out of his shirt pocket and was lighting up before he put the truck in gear.

"Come on, Herb, it's time we hit the road again," Collier said as he gave the kid a goodbye wave.

Luck was with them. Eating a Hershey bar with a coke at a gas station in Denton, they found a young corporal heading back to Sill from a weekend with his sweetheart, a coed at the college. The sun was sinking low when their Samaritan dropped them off a scant two hours later in front of their barracks at good old FARTC back at Sill.

"I hope you won't tell anybody about last night," Herb said after they thanked the corporal and watched him drive away.

"Forget it, Herb. As far as I'm concerned, we had a good steak dinner and had a couple of beers. I never even heard of a man named Ruby or of a fancy club called The Theater Lounge. Come on, let's go grab a bite. Except for that Coca-Cola and the Hershey bar, we haven't eaten anything all day." Collier pointed to his watch. They still had time to make it to the battalion mess hall before it closed.

"Go ahead. I need sleep more than I need food," Herb declined Collier's suggestion and headed inside to crash.

"Put out that cigarette, Ramsay, and round up your Lance Corporals. Captain Ward just got word the entire area is under a tornado watch. We have to get the troops and the barracks ready in case we take a hit." Dixon grabbed him by the arm and stopped him, as Collier followed Herb inside to leave his AWOL bag before heading out to get some supper chow. Collier had little trouble locating the other three Lance Corporals. Within ten minutes, the battery was assembled in the street, nervously glancing up at a nasty-looking bank of black clouds to the northwest while Dixon briefed them on how the barracks windows should be lowered about one foot from the top and raised an equal distance from the bottom, theoretically to equalize pressure, preventing the barracks from imploding on itself in the event of a near-miss by a passing twister funnel.

"Make sure the carbine racks are secure and stow all small, heavy objects inside your footlockers. As soon as you're done, fall back out here—you have exactly five minutes," Dixon commanded as he dismissed the formation to go make preparations.

When the barracks windows were all adjusted and items stowed in footlockers, the battery nervously reassembled outside and listened while Dixon instructed them what to do if a funnel cloud were sighted.

"If a tornado is actually spotted on the Post, sirens will give us adequate warning with a long steady blast. Everybody should immediately seek refuge by lying flat in the drainage ditch around the drill field across the street. Now, fall out and stick close until the siren sounds the all clear," Dixon concluded his spiel.

"Wait a second, Corporal Dixon. How will we tell the difference between the actual tornado warning and the all clear?" a nervous trainee asked, eyeing the threatening sky with apprehension.

"The warning siren will be a continuous sound and the all clear will be a series of short blasts," Dixon replied.

"Can we go back inside the barracks if it rains?" Reed asked in a whiny voice.

"Not if the warning has sounded," Dixon snapped.

"You've got your poncho over your arm. Can I go back in and get *my* poncho?" Reed persisted.

"Okay, everybody go get your ponchos. One section at a time, but come straight back outside—don't mess around," Dixon agreed, staring off at the roiling clouds, more to hide his impatience with Reed than concern for the storm.

When the battery had filed back out with their ponchos, Collier took a seat on the barracks steps, lit a cigarette, opened his FDC manual and pretended to read, trying to put up a calm front. After about a half-hour, the sky opened up and dumped rain by the bucketsful with a brief fusillade of golf-ball-sized hail, driving them all back inside. Thankfully, the sudden storm was short-lived. Within less than a half-hour, the sky began to clear and the men slowly began to relax as Dixon ordered them back outside. The sun had fully set, street lights were on and minor outbreaks of horseplay were erupting into occasional laughter from the drill field across the street when the all clear finally sounded.

"Unless it rains hard during the night, just tell your Lance Corporals to leave the windows as they are until Reveille," Dixon instructed Collier and turned to go inside.

"Wait, Corporal, with all this tornado nonsense, we missed mail call," Reed called as he crossed the street.

"You're right. I forgot. Send someone to the orderly room, Ramsay. Make sure these men get their mail." Dixon instructed and disappeared inside his room.

Rather than send someone else, Collier went to pick up the mail himself. Sorting the envelopes alphabetically, he removed the only two envelopes addressed to him and gave the rest to the Lance Corporals to distribute among their men.

As much as it pained him to admit it, Collier's heart skipped a beat when he saw Emma's neat handwriting on one of the envelopes addressed to him. It had been close to a month since her last letter.

Thursday
April 17, 1952
My dearest darling:

I am missing you so much and feeling so very lonely without you. I have good news! I just found out that my brother, Chuck, and his wife are planning to move in with Mother and me next month. With someone here to look after Mother, I am going to write the Chief Nurses at both the Lawton and Fort Sill hospitals and see if they have a position available. If you can, try to look around and see if you can find us a cozy little love nest to rent.

I'm counting the days until May 25ᵗʰ. I just talked to Jenny and she told me Bo's airline ticket to Washington was going to cost around $136.50. I am enclosing a check for $137—go ahead and buy your airline ticket from Oklahoma City or Tulsa (or wherever) to Washington, DC. Send me the flight schedule, and I'll drive up to Washington and meet you there. We can take a day or so to drive back to Salem—it could be a second honeymoon.

I'm writing this at work, so I have to close. Take care my darling and hurry home. I love you with all my heart!

Your adoring wife,
Emma

Completely taken by surprise, Collier started over and reread the note. When he had reread it perhaps a half-dozen times, he refolded it, put it back in the envelope and sat there on his footlocker contemplating the irony of this sudden change of heart. After perhaps five minutes of mulling over the veritable truckload of nightmarish problems presented by the prospect of having fastidious Emma move out to Lawton, Collier headed out the door to find a phone.

"Emma, thank goodness I caught you home. I just got your letter. As much as I miss you, I have reconsidered. You simply cannot come out here while I'm in OCS. Trust me, it would be a disaster. OCS is like being in prison, except worse, and Lawton is a nightmare for an enlisted man's wife living alone..." he began and tried to describe what it would be like for her.

"Look, Darling, I know you have my best interest at heart, but I want to be out there where I can help you. At least we can see each other on weekends...don't you miss me? I'm half-crazy wanting to feel your arms wrapped around me."

"Of course I miss you, Emma, but you don't know how bad conditions are..." he continued, trying in vain to make her understand. After perhaps ten minutes or more engaged in what turned out to be an exercise in utter futility, Collier finally gave up trying to settle the question by long distance phone.

Back at the barracks, he went directly to the dayroom and drafted Emma a long, detailed letter describing the depressing prospects she would face living alone in Lawton. As much as he would like to believe his controlling wife had experienced some sort of miraculous epiphany, Collier Boyd Ramsay smelled a rat.

CHAPTER TWENTY-ONE

THE ROANOKE TIMES
Roanoke, Virginia, Monday, April 21, 1952
U.S. FLIERS DOWN SEVEN ENEMY MIGS

SEOUL, Monday, April 21 (AP) U.S. Sabre jet pilots reported they shot down seven Russian-built MIG-15s over North Korea today in an aerial dogfight that produced America's 11th jet ace.

––––––––––

THE DAILY OKLAHOMAN
Oklahoma City, Oklahoma, Monday, April 21, 1952
TORNADOES DIP IN SOUTHWEST
Two Counties Get Funnel Scare

Tornadoes tripped across southwestern Oklahoma Sunday and struck at least two points in Jackson and Beckham counties. A twister ripped across two farms three miles northwest of Sayre. Farm buildings were wrecked but no one was injured. Another funnel cut a path two miles long through pasture land 14 miles west of Altus near Duke. One-inch hail at Archer City, Texas brought scares to the Warika area...at midnight storms were still occurring. Lawton, Fort Sill, Ponca City, and Oklahoma City had more than a half-inch of rain.

––––––––––

THE DAILY OKLAHOMAN
Oklahoma City, Oklahoma, Monday, April 28, 1952
SECRECY TO VEIL TRUCE MEETINGS
BOTH SIDES AGREE TO BAR NEWSMEN

MUNSAN, KOREA, Saturday, April 28 (AP) – The top level Allied and Communist delegations met today on the Korean Armistice crisis—and agreed immediately to off-the-record talks.

––––––––––

DURING THE SMOKE BREAK at their first classroom session Monday morning 21 April, Dixon showed Collier a front-page article in *The Daily Oklahoman* about the previous evening's tornadoes and hail storms. The piece about the weather was given above-the-fold placement beside a prominently-featured front-page article—complete with two-column photo—bearing the headline: WILL ROGERS AIRPORT NOW HAS BUST OF ITS FAMOUS NAMESAKE. The photo was of S.N. Goldman, a wealthy, Oklahoma supermarket entrepreneur, gazing worshipfully at a very fine, bronze likeness of the great American humorist created by the famous deceased, Oklahoma sculptor, Jo Davidson. The article caught Collier's attention because he remembered seeing Davidson's famous, full-body sculpture of Will Rogers in the National Statuary Hall in the United States Capitol on one of his Sunday afternoon excursions to Washington while he was still studying art at RPI in Richmond. The article also served as a reminder to make an airline reservation to fly home.

Ironically, the only front-page mention of the war was a tiny bulletin headlined: U.S. FLIERS DOWN SEVEN ENEMY MIGS relegated to the extreme lower left hand corner of the page—there was absolutely no mention of the peace talks or Panmunjom. Idly Collier perused an article about yesterday's rash of tornadoes and the mention of a severe hail storm at Archer City, Texas, jumped out at him, reminding him of Larry Jeff "McSomething-or-other", the young cowboy who had given them a ride yesterday outside Love Field. When Collier went to look for Herb to see how he was feeling and to tell him the previous day's erstwhile knight in shining armor in the beat-up, Chevy pickup truck had most likely run into a bad hail storm before he made it back home to Archer City, Collier was informed the dashing "Philadelphia Whoo-erhopper" had already reported for Sick Call. By the time Herb rejoined the morning's training schedule, yesterday's hail storm in Archer City, Texas, had been preempted by more pressing issues.

Sheepishly, Herb avoided Collier for the next few days until Friday morning at formation when Dixon took them aside and told them they were both to report to the hospital on the Main Post for follow-ups on their OCS physicals.

"What do you think this is all about?" Herb asked on the post bus on the way to the hospital.

"Don't ask me." Collier shrugged, his gut churning with anxiety. Both he and Herb and Nat Reed had been examined head to toe barely more than a couple of weeks ago, and everything seemed all right.

"I think it's about my eyes," Herb said, nervously removing his thick, Coke-bottle-lens glasses to clean them. Herb's eyes had tested borderline when he had enlisted for OCS.

"I don't know. But if they want you to retake the exam, take my advice and memorize the twenty/twenty or twenty/twenty-five line on the chart when they first take you in before they begin the test. That's what I do. They always leave you in the room alone before the technician shows up. It's easy, Herb. The standard Snellen charts use only nine letters—C, D, E, F, L, O, P, T, and Z—and the twenty/twenty line is underlined with a thick red line," Collier confided.

It was true. Ironically, it had been the Army recruiting sergeant back in Roanoke who had taught him the trick. Collier suffered some astigmatism in his right eye and could just barely read 20/70 on his best day with that eye. Looking to earn another stripe on his sleeve, the recruiter had wanted to make sure his prize OCS applicant passed with flying colors.

It suddenly occurred to Collier they might be calling him back to check his eyes again. Uncorrected, Collier's left eye was a solid 20/25. Admission to OCS required the better eye correct to 20/20 with at least 20/100 vision in the other eye. Ordinarily, one would assume a 20/20 correction would be no problem for someone who could read 20/25 in his better eye, but the kicker was that Collier's better eye would not legitimately correct to 20/20. Due to some weird anomaly, his good eye would not correct at all. Exasperatingly, both eyes had some sort of odd, inverted-Y-shaped crystalline anomaly in the lens, and glasses would not correct either eye to a legitimate 20/20.

Until now, these minor defects had not been a problem. Collier's driver's license said he should wear glasses which—if you didn't count when he was doing close work at the drawing board—he almost never did. For that kind of work he used a special magnifying glass with tiny legs to hold it the proper distance above the work at hand.

"I don't think I can get by with memorizing the chart. All they have to do is look at these glasses. They'll know something's not right," Herb protested with a big sigh of resignation.

"Don't you correct to twenty/twenty in either eye?" Collier asked.

"Sure. Twenty/twenty in the right eye and twenty-thirty in the left," Herb said.

"Then, you've got no sweat. Twenty/twenty and twenty/one hundred will get you in," Collier reassured him.

"No fooling?" Herb brightened at the news.

"Scout's honor," Collier raised his hand in a mock salute.

"Rudolph, just follow the Private here. You're scheduled for an eye exam." As Herb had rightly predicted, when he reported to the Outpatient Desk upon arrival at the hospital, he was escorted directly to the Ophthalmology Clinic.

"Ramsay, you report to Otolaryngology. You're scheduled for a hearing test," the PFC at the appointment desk directed Collier as soon as Herb was on his way. "When you finish there, we need you back here. The eye clinic wants to see you, too."

Collier turned and walked slowly down the corridor. Both his ears and his eyes! The situation was even worse than he had imagined.

"I was just here a couple of weeks ago. Why do you need me back here again?" Collier protested as soon as the technician came out to usher him inside what appeared to be a soundproof testing room.

"I'm the new audiology technician. We need to recheck your hearing. There was some question about your previous test," the white coat said.

"What happened to the guy who tested me before?" Collier asked, put off by the new technician's superior attitude. Thinking back, Collier strongly suspected this might be connected to the transitory deafness and the lingering ringing in his ears following his stint as a cannoneer on the recent bivouac. He had casually mentioned the problem when he had been tested before.

"Corporal Rushing shipped to FECOM. Lucky SOB caught a cushy assignment at the hospital in Osaka." Rushing's white-coated replacement laughed. "I just got here from Walter Reed. I was fortunate enough to be in on the testing of a revolutionary new, Jap-made audiometer back there. The Japs are going to revolutionize audiometer testing—mark my words."

"This looks like the same machine I tested with before," Collier said, looking at the Rube Goldberg contraption on the table.

"I'm sure it is. But it gets the job done," the technician said, defensively. "Now, let's get on with business. Just stand here facing to your left, and cover your right ear with your hand like this." The medic positioned him behind a black line on the floor and showed him how to cover his ear. Moving to the far side of the tiny room, he said something that Collier couldn't quite understand.

"I'm sorry, I didn't catch that. Could you say it again?" Collier asked the technologist.

The man repeated what he'd said, but it still sounded garbled—indistinct.

"You'll have to speak louder, I've got my ear covered, remember?" Collier complained again.

"Can you hear me now," the technician asked, finally loud enough for Collier to hear.

"Yeah, loud and clear," Collier said.

"Alright, do an about-face and cover your other ear," the technologist instructed.

This time Collier only had to ask the medic to raise his voice once.

"Good. That'll be enough of that. Let's move to the table over there. Just take a seat in the chair against the far wall." The tech pointed to the table across the room. On a corner of the small table was the familiar black machine with the ungainly, round earphone attached by a long wire. The two chairs were arranged facing each other across a corner of the table with the machine placed between them. The graceless instrument reminded Collier of a phony stage prop right out of some low-budget, mad-scientist flick.

"This is an audiometer—it's designed to determine your range of hearing in all the high and low tones. If you'll just have a seat right there and pick up the earphone, we'll get started," the business-like clinician instructed, pointing to a chair.

"Yeah, I remember from the last time with the other guy," Collier muttered and took a seat. Picking up the earpiece, he nervously began untangling the wire connecting it to the machine. Replete with calibrated knurled knobs and a lighted dial, the instrument called up the memory of one of the old-time Halicrafter radios his childhood playmate, George Selwyn's, older brother, Robert, used to build from kits in the cluttered backroom of their daddy's old-fashioned, country store. "How come we don't get to use this new machine you told me about?"

"It's still experimental—what they call a prototype. It's most-likely several years away from production," the operator said, waiting for him to quit fiddling with the wire.

"So we're stuck here in the boonies with the WWI model—what is it, a tuning fork in a cracker box?" Not at all reassured by what was taking place, Collier finally lifted the earpiece ready to begin.

"Are you still hearing the ringing in your ears?" Ignoring Collier's sarcasm, the tech casually asked before Collier reluctantly put the earpiece to his ear. *So this was what the fuss was all about. He never should have confided to the first asshole about his temporary hearing loss.*

"No...that hasn't bothered me in a while," Collier lied, trying his best to look unconcerned.

"Good. Now, before we get started here, do you remember how this test works? When you hold the earpiece to your ear, I'll have the machine transmit a series of tones ranging from high-pitched sounds to sounds in the lower ranges. When I give you the signal to begin, the moment you begin hearing a tone in the earphones, push this button right here. As soon as you are no longer able to hear the tone, you push the button again. Are we clear on that?" the audiologist asked, fiddling with some dials and switches on the bulky, black box.

"Yeah, I remember," Collier muttered, trying desperately to keep his hands from shaking.

"Okay now, just relax. Why don't we do a trial run, just to make sure you're comfortable and understand how the instrument works. We want to get it right this time," the operator smiled encouragement.

He was right. There had been a problem with his first test a few weeks back.

During the practice run and during the ensuing tests of both ears, Collier tried hard to get some reaction to his performance by carefully observing the audiologist's body language and facial expressions. Finally, he gave up. *He hoped he never had to play poker with the SOB.* After what seemed forever but was probably less than a half-hour, the medic pushed back his chair and turned off the machine.

"Okay. All done. Unless you have another appointment in the hospital, you're free to go back to your battery."

"How'd I do?" Collier asked, adjusting his tie and blouse.

"Uhm-m...I don't evaluate—I just test. We live in a highly-specialized era—a medical officer will evaluate the results."

"Oh, come on, what about all the fancy training at Walter Reed you were telling me about? Certainly you have some idea whether I passed or failed?" Collier struggled to remain calm, but he was on the verge of losing patience.

"Relax. You're in no danger of getting a medical discharge for deafness, if that's what's worrying you." The operator laughed and shot him a thumbs-up.

Feeling somewhat relieved, Collier reported back at the reception desk where he was given a slip and sent to Ophthalmology. His anxiety somewhat assuaged by the smart-aleck audiologist's encouraging words, Collier nodded off into a light doze before he was finally summoned to the eye clinic.

"Just have a seat right there and put your chin in this cup," the white-coated Captain instructed, looking over Collier's medical records in the folder he carried.

There were no eye charts anywhere in view.

"Hm-m...let's do the left eye first." The Captain cut the examining room lights, took a seat facing Collier on the other side of the instrument, and flipped a lever shutting off the view through the right eyepiece.

Following the click of another switch, like magic an eye chart appeared on the wall in front of Collier.

"Read the smallest line you can see clearly," the examiner requested. It seemed to Collier that the man was trying hard not to yawn.

Squinting slightly and using his foreknowledge of the nine standard letters—a trick he'd learned from the Army recruiter in Roanoke—Collier rattled off "D...E...F...P...O...T...E ...C on the 20/20 line plainly underlined in red.

"Good...now...the other eye," the examiner closed off the left-eye opening and opened the right one, exposing the chart to his weaker eye.

"P...E...C...F...D," Collier surprised himself with how easy he could read the 20/40 line.

"Good...now let's see what we can do to correct that eye," the examiner said as he clicked a series of lens in the opening of the instrument. "Tell me when you can read the line underlined in red."

Having committed the 20/20 line to memory so he was able to fake being corrected to fulfill the requirement of a minimum 20/20 correction in the better eye, the rest of the exam went well. Before he left, he had chosen a pair of ugly flesh-colored plastic frames for a new pair of Army eyeglasses. Whistling softly, Collier made his escape feeling much relieved.

Momentarily reassured that he had nothing to worry about from a standpoint of qualifying for the OCS physical, Collier went back by the front reception desk to see if he could locate Herb before he caught a bus back to FARTC.

"Rudolph is still back in the eye clinic. If I were you, I wouldn't wait around," the NCO behind the reception desk advised.

"How'd it go?" Dixon asked as soon as Collier arrived back at the FARTC Area.

"Okay, I guess," Collier replied, still concerned about his eligibility for OCS.

"I wouldn't worry too much. The Army's hard up for Forward Observers in Korea. Over there, combat life expectancy for an FO is less than a week," Dixon winked.

"Huh?" Collier pretended not to hear the corporal.

"I said...life expectancy for a FO in Korea is less than a week,"

"Speak up." Collier leaned closer, turning his right ear toward Dixon.

"What's the matter with you, Ramsay? Have you gone deaf?" The corporal shot him a concerned look.

"Who left?" Collier leaned closer.

"Nobody left..."—Dixon raised his voice and leaned in toward Collier—"I asked if you'd gone deaf?"

"Looks like it. Starvation causes severe hearing loss, Corporal. If I don't get some chow before the mess hall closes, I'll probably be stone deaf before nightfall," Collier laughed, heading down the street.

Arriving late for noontime chow, Collier ate alone. Sitting idly mulling over the audiologist's pronouncement about his hearing test, it slowly began to dawn on him there might be a vast difference between hearing well enough to be allowed to stay in the Army and hearing well enough to gain admittance into OCS.

Running late, Collier had no time to fret over real or imagined questions about his hearing or his eyesight. Arriving back at the barracks, he saw to the loading of the battery into trucks to transport them to the Arbuckle Range for an exercise in Close Fire Observation. All Collier really knew about Arbuckle was that it was to the east across the main highway to Oklahoma City, vaguely somewhere out beyond the Indian School. As for Close Fire Observation, he was totally in the dark.

"Make sure all the men wear their steel pots." When Dixon added that bit of information, Collier forgot all about his anxiety over his hearing test. The only times he could recall having been required to wear his steel helmet over the plastic helmet liner was when the battery had been required to crawl under live machine-gun fire on the Infiltration Course and the time they fired howitzers on bivouac—and there had also been the time they actually tossed live grenades.

When the convoy rendezvoused at the destination of the afternoon exercise, Collier dismounted, surveying a curious collection of a dozen or more mammoth, grass-covered mounds approximately twenty feet high and perhaps a hundred feet long. Resembling burrows of some giant prehistoric moles, it quickly became apparent that the grassy mounds concealed and protected the backside of a number of heavily-reinforced, almost completely-buried concrete bunkers. On the far side—a scant fifty yards to the front of the bunkers—were a scattered collection of disabled tanks, military trucks and other brightly-painted pieces of out-dated military relics. Noting that the landscape close around the target area was scarred with impact craters, the reality of Close Fire Observation began to dawn on him.

"We're running late, Ramsay. This area will be under heavy artillery barrage in exactly two-zero minutes. We've got to move these trucks out of here before they're blasted all to hell. Have your Lance Corporals deploy their troops into the bunkers immediately. Make sure all personnel put their steel pots on and keep 'em on," Dixon ordered, tersely instructing Collier which sections should occupy each of the four bunkers spread before them.

"Listen up men. We have less than fifteen minutes to get the troops inside these bunkers with their steel pots on before all hell breaks loose." Collier summoned his Lance Corporals and quickly showed them which bunkers would house each section and explained that they were going to observe fire on the materiel targets barely fifty yards in front of them.

"Okay, Ramsay, you and I will take the bunker nearest the center of the range with Shanahan's section. McGeoghan, Schnoedecker and the new corporal, Wynne, will each go with his section." When the last of the men were safely underground, Collier returned to where Dixon stood watching the final truck disappeared around the line of bunkers, trailing a cloud of choking, Oklahoma prairie dust. As soon as Dixon dispatched the NCOs to their assigned squads, he turned and led Collier down the steps into the dank interior of the center bunker.

The interior of the bunker reminded Collier of a long, narrow, somewhat-damp, concrete coffin—the only opening was a constricted observation slit running almost the entire length of the front wall, overlooking the frontal target area. The narrow opening was barely wide enough to accommodate field glasses—or at most a BC Scope. Walking about halfway down the line, Collier elbowed his way through the clot of soldiers and peered out of the narrow slit.

"These bunkers are constructed of steel-reinforced concrete—the back wall is six-feet thick and there is at least twenty-five feet of good old Oklahoma sod piled on top of that. The front walls facing the target area are about half that thickness. In a very few minutes, those targets out in front of us will come under a barrage from a battery of eight-inch howitzers firing High Explosive Anti-Tank with impact fuses. Those of you who recall your weapons orientations, the eight-inch howitzer fires a projectile filled with two-hundred pounds of HEAT. When the first rounds start to explode, don't be surprised if a few fragments of shrapnel come zinging through the observation slit. You would be well-advised to keep your helmets on and your heads down. If you want to take a closer look, keep in mind it's hot enough to burn you. Don't be too quick to pick it up. In the entire history of the Artillery School, we have only had one man severely injured by shrapnel; we wouldn't want to spoil that record this afternoon. I also advise you to cover your ears with your hands—the racket you are about to hear is like nothing you've ever heard before," Dixon quickly instructed the men inside the bunker where Collier had deployed with Shanahan's section.

"KA-BOOMPH!" Collier was still standing staring through the slit when the first shattering round exploded a scant fifty yards in front of him. A piece of shrapnel came zinging close by his ear and bounced off the rear wall of the bunker, coming to rest by his boot.

Before Collier had time to cover his ears with his hands, the first blast was followed closely by an earthshaking "WHUUMPH!" as a short round landed directly on the backside of their bunker. For the next half-hour, the deafening cacophony continued non-stop with most of the rounds landing in the target zone right in front of the bunker. Without warning, the barrage ceased as abruptly as it had begun, and it became deathly quiet again. The assault stopped so unexpectedly it took Collier the better part of a full minute to realize he had been rendered temporarily deaf by the relentless assault on his eardrums. So much for Dixon's advice—his hands had been little help in shutting out the incredible noise.

"How many times have you been through the Close Fire exercise?" Collier asked Dixon that night back in the barracks area, before evening formation.

"Five or six—more, I guess," Dixon said.

"How do you stand it? Covering my ears with my hands didn't protect me much," Collier complained.

"I stuff my ears with good-sized wads of cotton and still cover them with my hands. McGeoghan and some of the others use rubber earplugs they get at the PX."

"In the future, I think it would be a good idea to warn the men to stuff cotton or something in their ears," Collier said. The residual ringing in his ears had almost stopped, but his hearing was far from returning to some semblance of normalcy.

"The whole idea is to give you rookies a feel for what combat is like. You're going to be an officer. Officers can't run around the battlefield with cotton in their ears." Dixon shrugged.

"Better than running around the battlefield deaf as a stone," Collier said.

Dixon gave him a funny look and walked away.

After the regular Friday-night GI party and A Battery's barracks were ready for Saturday morning inspection, Collier went to the PX and bought a set of earplugs. *Better late than never—almost any fool knew that.*

"Collier, over here...let me buy you a beer?" Coming out of the PX, Collier ran into Herb Rudolph drinking a bottle of Black Label in the canteen.

"Thanks, but I don't think so. I got to go shine my boots and shoes and my brass. Are you ready for Saturday inspection already?" He shot Herb a doubtful look.

"Ready as I'm going to be," Herb said and took a long pull from the bottle of beer.

"Guess you don't care that much about being restricted without a weekend pass."

"What makes you think I won't be ready for inspection? I always have before," Herb gave Collier a wounded look and put down the beer bottle.

"Sorry, Herb, you're right. You always have," Collier apologized. "By the way, I looked for you today before I left the hospital. They told me you were still in the eye clinic and not to wait around." He changed the subject, not wanting his friend to think he was preaching at him.

"I didn't have a chance to memorize the eye charts like you said. They really put me through the paces. But the good news is that both my eyes correct to twenty/twenty. Like you said, the minimum OCS requirement is one eye correcting to twenty-twenty. They even gave me new glasses. The guy said I can pick them up next week."

Collier stood there momentarily taken aback by the ironic twist of fate. As near blind as Herb was without glasses, Herb's vision still qualified for OCS while he, himself, might not even pass the exam on some dumb technicality regarding his inability to hear crickets chirping.

"Congratulations. That *is* good news," Collier said, forcing a smile.

"You're right. I guess I'd best be getting back. I've still got to polish my brass and shine my shoes." Herb stood and pushed back his chair. Without finishing his beer, he began walking toward the door.

On Friday, May 9, as soon as A Battery completed their weekly GI Party, Collier walked down to C Battery and found Bo Bohon sitting on his bunk, his duffle already packed. C Battery had officially completed their final week of Basic that afternoon. Now, less than two hours following supper chow, Bo's barracks was already practically deserted.

Bo had already affixed the artillery school badges on his epaulets and cunt cap—a traditional right of passage for completing training. When he saw Collier enter, Bo picked up a single sheet of paper from off his bunk. Grinning ear-to-ear, he shyly extended a printed, quasi-official, fill-in-the-blanks, Army document to Collier.

Headquarters
2d Field Artillery Training Battalion
4050 ASU
FORT SILL, OKLAHOMA
𝕷etter of 𝕮ommenbation

☆ ☆ ☆

Pvt-1 Bruce E. Bohon, RA 13415454 Btry "C"

1. YOU HAVE BEEN SELECTED AS THE OUTSTANDING TRAINEE OF YOUR BATTERY FOR THE WEEK ENDING 3 MAY 1952.

2. THIS WAS DETERMINED BY YOUR ACADEMIC STANDING, MILITARY BEARING, AND DEVOTION TO DUTY.

3. YOU POSSESS THE QUALITIES OF SELF IMPROVEMENT SO NECESSARY IN OUR ARMY TODAY.

4. I AM SURE YOU WILL MEET ALL FUTURE UNDERTAKINGS WITH THE SAME DETERMINATION AS YOU HAVE IN THE PAST.

9 May 1952

Joseph J. Holland

Commanding

Major

Arty

After reading it twice and turning it over in his hands to appreciate the document's importance, Collier handed it back, feeling a rush of admiration and respect, mixed with just a pang of envy.

"Way to go, Bo. This is quite an honor. Someday you can show this to your kids...and they can show their kids," he said, clapping his old friend on the shoulder. "I'm proud of you. You should be very proud of yourself.

"Yeah, I am, I guess. I never expected anything like this." Bo replied, the grin fading from his face. "The bad news is that I'm headed for FECOM. Twenty-one days of Route Delay before I ship straight to Japan. That only gives me about two-and-a-half weeks at home with Jenny and the folks. I just hope I live to have some kids."

"Jeez..." Collier blurted, searching for just the right words of encouragement before he continued. "Cheer up, man. They'll probably sign the truce before you get to Japan. C'mon, let's go to the Service Club. I'll buy you a Coke or a cup of Joe to celebrate your being named Trainee of the Century. It's going to be awful lonesome around here without your ugly face to cheer me up."

"Yeah, I'll miss you, too. I envy your being able to stay on here for another six months in OCS. Next time I see you, I guess I'll have to salute you. I never thought I'd say it, but I'm going to miss this place—now more than ever." Bo managed a wry grin as he stood and placed the commendation carefully inside an imitation-alligator stationary folio with his airline tickets and tucked the folio inside his AWOL bag.

Bo's remark about OCS struck a nerve, but Collier resisted confiding his anxiety about passing his most recent physical. Although Herb Rudolph had not officially been accepted to an OCS class, the first sergeant had already told Herb he would be staying at Sill after graduation—for the short term anyway. To date, Collier hadn't heard even that much about his own future.

Just thinking about it now, Collier's gubernaculum clenched as he considered the humiliating consequences of actually being turned down for OCS. Too much the realist, he realized even at this late date it was actually very possible he might already be listed on orders for FECOM with most of the rest of A Battery when they graduated in two weeks.

CHAPTER TWENTY-TWO

THE ROANOKE TIMES
Roanoke, Virginia, Saturday, May 17, 1952
LOVETT HOTLY DENIES UN
FORCES USE GAS WARFARE

WASHINGTON, Friday, May 17 (AP) - Secretary of Defense Lovett hotly denied today that UN forces employ germ and gas warfare in Korea and said that if the Communists themselves turn to such weapons they will wish they had never been born.

THE DAILY OKLAHOMAN
Oklahoma City, Oklahoma, Saturday, May 17, 1952
IKE IS SWEEPING OREGON PRIMARY

PORTLAND, Ore., Friday, May 16 (AP) - Gen. Dwight D. Eisenhower pulled away to a whopping lead in the first Republican returns of Oregon's presidential primary today.

The slow count of the long ballot also started Sen. Estes Kefauver of Tennessee on the way toward snapping up all 12 Democratic National Convention delegates.

ON WEDNESDAY, MAY 14, Emma received a phone call from Jenny Bohon reminding her that Bo was home on leave and had brought back some snapshots of Collier. She asked if Emma would like to meet them for breakfast at Norman's later in the week.

"Thanks, Jenny. I was going to call you, but I've been working overtime. I'd love to get together for breakfast. I'm practically dying to see Bo in his uniform. Norman's is fine, but Saturday is the earliest I can make it. Is that okay?" Emma asked, fairly bursting with curiosity to find out all she could about Fort Sill and Lawton.

She hadn't confirmed to Collier that she had followed through on her decision, but since her April 17th letter declaring she was returning with him to Oklahoma, she had already submitted a month's notice of her intention to leave the VA. She had also checked the VA system and found the nearest Veterans hospital was in Oklahoma City—about 100 miles north of Lawton. Since working that far away was clearly out of the question, she had subsequently written the chief of nurses at both Southwestern Hospital and Comanche County Memorial— the two private hospitals in Lawton, Oklahoma, inquiring about employment. She was confident that given her credentials she could probably have her choice of employment opportunities at the small-town Oklahoma hospitals. She had also written the head nurse at the post hospital at Fort Sill. Although Emma had yet to hear back from any of those hospitals, she was not particularly concerned. After all, it had scarcely been a month since she had written. If she didn't hear anything before Collier was due to arrive home on leave next week, she planned to phone them.

Wisely Emma had elected to work out her month's notice rather than waste her accrued leave for which the VA was obligated to pay her when she left. Every dime she added to their savings was important. She was fairly certain she couldn't expect to earn nearly as much working in some hick-town Oklahoma hospital. Even though Collier would be raised to E-5 while he was in OCS—which meant he would be receiving the lowest level of sergeant's pay—this amounted to only $145.24 plus $77.10, the basic allowance for quarters for married men with one dependent. The reality was this was a mere pittance compared to the more than $300 a month she would be bringing home even in Oklahoma.

Complicating her situation, shortly after Easter Sunday, she had begun having problems with her menstrual cycle. According to her calendar, she realized with concern that her period was already more than a week overdue. When she began cramping and spotting a few days later, she breathed a great sigh of relief, but her optimism proved to be short-lived. After a few days, the symptoms disappeared and she began having morning sickness almost immediately thereafter. On the verge of desperation, she called an old nursing classmate who had dropped out of training to have an abortion and afterwards gone back home to West Virginia and ultimately wound up working in the lab at a small hospital near White Sulphur Springs and confided her dilemma. The girl suggested she drive over to the sizeable C&O hospital in Clifton Forge the next morning and give a urine sample to a friend of hers in the lab there where they could discreetly perform a "frog test" off the official books.

The following morning, Emma drove to Clifton Forge to give the sample of her urine then returned home to sweat out the results. After a sleepless night, she received a call from the girl in the C&O lab informing her that the test was positive. She was definitely PG.

This left Emma in a state of absolute panic. However, after she calmed down and began thinking more-or-less clearly, she decided she needed to get in touch with Trey. His father was Chief of Staff at the VA and his snooty wife was the daughter of a prominent Virginia surgeon on the board at the Medical College of Virginia. If this came out, the SOB stood to lose just as much as she did—maybe even more. And, after all, the miserable little rapist was a physician and would most certainly know where to get this sticky problem resolved. Although Moseley left without so much as a goodbye and Emma had had no personal interest whatsoever about the insufferable SOB's whereabouts, in the twenty-four hours it had taken for the hormones in her urine to make a frog produce eggs, all that had changed.

Getting in touch with the bantam-rooster Don Juan proved easier than she had first imagined. Emma casually asked around at work if anyone on staff had heard from him and was surprised to find he had left a forwarding address with the personnel office when he processed out. According to hospital records, the midget Marquis de Sade had been temporarily assigned to the Medical Field Service School—MFSS—at Fort Sam Houston in San Antonio, Texas, for a brief introductory course in Military Protocol.

Brook Army Hospital at Fort Sam Houston was a hospital well-known to Emma—its legendary center for treating burns was often in the news. Despairing that MFSS or not, there was no way the Army—or even a Nazi concentration camp—could transform the sleaze bag, Moseley, into an officer and a gentleman as soon as Emma got home from work, she went to the telephone and called long-distance information for San Antonio, Texas. Even with information about his whereabouts, tracking Trey down was not easy. It took almost the rest of that day and half of the next to finally get him on the phone.

Captain Moseley was not thrilled to hear her news.

"There's no way you're going to lay this mess on me," the arrogant gutter rat blustered the moment she apprised him of their dilemma.

"Oh, no? You're A Positive. You're the genius—figure that out," she coolly replied.

"So-o...?"

"So? "Both Collier and I are O Negative." She replied coolly. "You're married, your father is my superior here at the VA, and your father-in-law is a celebrated gynecological surgeon. Do you want me to call and ask them to refer me to one of their hoity-toity, Famous-Families-of-Virginia surgeons to do a state-of-the-art, therapeutic D and C at MCV?"

Silence.

"You wouldn't dare..." he said at last, his tone demonstrably subdued.

Emma's continued silence was eloquent.

"Just what is it you expect from me?"

"Are you hard of hearing? I just told you I want a good medical abortion. Given my history of menstrual problems, I need a well-respected specialist to diagnose me as possible endometriosis or some related problem. I know you high-and-mighty Hippocratic guys stick together. With your connections, it should be no problem for you to locate a competent, gynecological surgeon—an old classmate or family friend—to come to your rescue and perform a D-and-C."

"Are you suggesting that I find a reputable surgeon to give you an abortion in a regular hospital?"

"That is *exactly* what I'm suggesting. You have until tomorrow morning at ten. If I haven't heard by then, I'll go to your father and tell him you couldn't get the job done." Emma gave him her number and hung up without another word.

Almost before she replaced the receiver on the hook, the phone began ringing again.

"Are you crazy?" He blustered as soon she picked up. "Even if I can find someone to do this, it's not like arranging a round of golf. It's going to take some time."

"I don't have time. My husband's due home in four weeks. Call me by ten in the morning, or I'll go straight to your precious daddy. If he won't help, I'll call your cutesy Junior League wife's daddy in Richmond. I don't think either one of them would like it, but I have a feeling one or the other will rush to my rescue." She hung up without waiting for an argument.

Luckily, her mother had gone to a meeting at the church because the phone began to ring incessantly the minute she disconnected and continued to ring for almost thirty minutes before it finally fell silent. As a result of nervous exhaustion from loss of sleep and anxiety, Emma fell into a deep slumber. Her bedside clock read 9:25 and it was dark outside when her mother roused her to tell her she was wanted on the phone, long distance.

"Look, I just wanted to make sure you had calmed down. I think I may have a solution to *your* problem worked out." Emma almost choked at Trey's patronizing referral to the unwanted pregnancy as being *her* problem. Clearly he refused to accept any responsibility in the matter.

"*My* problem? Listen, you creepy bastard, if you haven't arranged for me to have a medical D-and-C in a respectable hospital by tomorrow morning, you'll find out whose problem this really is. I had my daddy's former secretary at the phone company look up your snooty, society-surgeon father-in-law's unlisted number in Charles City County," she lied maliciously and hung up again.

When the phone rang again, this time a demonstrably more contrite Trey pleaded, "Look, goddammit, don't hang up on me again—I'm trying to tell you I've pretty much got this worked out, but you'll have to drive up to Pulaski tomorrow and probably stay overnight to make sure there are no complications. Can you arrange to do that?"

"Do I have a choice?" she asked and listened as he outlined his tentative arrangements with a former classmate at MCV who was now a practicing surgeon in the furniture-manufacturing town of Pulaski about sixty miles west of Roanoke.

"Alright. One of my nursing classmates lives in Pulaski. I'll call and check this guy out. If she says he's not a butcher or a drunk, I'll show up tomorrow morning and plan to spend the night."

"Great—it's set then. I'll call him back and get the ball rolling, so he can make arrangements for the OR tomorrow afternoon. I'll call you and confirm as soon as everything is set," Trey hung up before she had time to say okay.

Much relieved that help was on the way, Emma went back to sleep, but reawakened, doubled over with cramps, an hour or so later. Rolling out of bed to find some aspirin, she discovered her panties and the sheet were soaked in blood.

When Trey called back a little later to report arrangements were set in Pulaski, Emma gave him the good news, "Looks like you're off the hook. I just started cramping and flooding. Call your surgeon buddy and tell him Mother Nature has intervened."

"Goddamn you, do you know that I've compromised myself with a fellow physician over you? Do you have any idea what you've put me through?" he cursed and hung up the phone.

By the time her clock showed one in the morning, the worst of the cramps and heavy bleeding had subsided. At the end of three days, the bleeding had almost completely stopped; by the end of the week, Emma was back to her old self and looking forward to Collier coming home. This near-disastrous pregnancy fresh on her mind, Emma made an appointment with Garrett Gooch, to be fitted for a new diaphragm. With Collier in OCS and headed off to God-knew-where to do God-only-knew-what, she couldn't afford to be saddled with a kid. This was the second time she had lost a pregnancy—her mother had always told her: "The third time is charmed." It really didn't take a genius to understand three strikes were out in any league.

Rubbing the sleep out of her eyes, Emma yawned and stretched and sat up on the side of the bed. Locating a pencil on the night table, she ritualistically crossed off Thursday, May 15, on her bedside calendar. *Only eight more days before she would be at National Airport in Washington to greet Collier's plane.*

Wriggling into a pair of baggy shorts and shrugging into one of Collier's castoff shirts, she went downstairs to the kitchen, shook Rice Krispies into a bowl and busied herself by beginning a checklist of essentials she needed to pack into their sporty Studebaker coupe for their return to Oklahoma. By the time Emma rinsed her bowl, put it in the rack to dry, and headed upstairs to sort through her nurse's uniforms, she had almost managed to exorcise the troubling demons of Trey Moseley from her head.

CHAPTER TWENTY-THREE

THE ROANOKE TIMES
Roanoke, Virginia, Friday, May 23, 1952
ALLIES BLAST CENTER NEAR CAPITOL OF KOREA

SEOUL, Friday, May 23 (AP) Allied warplanes attacked and smashed the third Red supply base in two months, leaving in flaming ruin a huge storage center near the North Korean capitol of Pyongyang.

THE DAILY OKLAHOMAN
Oklahoma City, Oklahoma, Friday, May 23, 1952
STATE HAS EYES ON STORMY SKY

State residents scanned the skies for twisters late Thursday, but it appeared the second tornado warning in 24 hours for the state would pass without incident. The 10:40 p.m. tornado advisory warned of the possibility of a "tornado or two" in that part of the state east of a line from Wichita Falls, Texas to Miami, and west of a line from Fort Smith, Ark., to Hugo. The threat was expected to end by 4 a.m. Friday.

TRUCE TALKS TAKE THREE-DAY RECESS

MUNSAN, Korea, Friday, May 23 (AP) – Allied and Red negotiators today agreed to a three-day recess in the Korean armistice talks after a no-progress session.

NEWS FROM KOREA was not promising and it had been a full month since Collier's most recent hearing tests and eye exam, and he had still not heard a word whether or not he was going to be accepted for officer training. For that matter, neither had Herb Rudolph—but at least Herb knew he would be staying at Sill for the short-term at least. Of the three A Battery trainees who had applied, only the all-around fuck-up, Nat Reed, had actually received word he had been accepted into the July class at OCS. To think he might someday actually have to salute Reed was almost too intolerable to consider. What sin had prompted the cosmic forces to thrust upon him such a diabolical turn of destiny?

To further complicate his anxiety, Collier had not yet told Emma about this unsettling state of affairs. Each day for four long weeks he awoke expecting—*hoping, at least*—to receive confirmation he was headed for OCS. Dixon had assured Collier he would remain at Sill in a casual holding battery until he received a "yea" or "nay", but to Collier, that made little difference in his plight. He couldn't let Emma come all the way out to Oklahoma with him only to find he had been turned down and had been put on orders to FECOM?

All day Friday, the wind howled and the rain came down by the bucketsful, persuading Captain Ward to hold A Battery's final graduation exercise indoors at the nearby FARTC gym and recreation building. At the end of the brief exercises, with orders for a two-week leave and his airline ticket tucked safely inside his blouse, Collier pulled his poncho over his head and braved the elements long enough to grab a bite of chow before he headed back to the barracks to oversee the final inventory of returnable equipment from the men.

That done, he packed his own uniforms and other possessions into his duffel bag for storage in the supply room.

By mid-afternoon, his battery-mates had completed their final checklist to "Clear the Post" and were all packed. Despite periodic radio advisories for tornadoes in the area, most of them had weathered the elements and headed for the PX to make last-minute purchases, or have a final beer with their buddies or make their last farewells.

"Captain Ward wants all the windows lowered six-inches from the top and raised the same distance from the bottom just in case..." Around 0530, Dixon found Collier in the barracks doorway gazing anxiously at the troubled sky. Rounding up a handful of stragglers still hanging around, Collier saw to it the order was carried out despite the opening of the windows exposed the barracks to a goodly-amount of wind-driven rain and required they move the bunks toward the center of the room to ensure they would have dry beds to sleep on their final night.

By 1640, the sky had almost cleared and the sirens sounded at 1700, signifying the threatening weather had passed. Taking advantage of the "all-clear" to join Herb Rudolph and Nat Reed in lugging their heavy duffels, stuffed with most of their military possessions, down the street to the casual battery's supply room, when they returned to the barracks around dusk, Collier politely declined Herb's invitation to go into Lawton and get a decent meal. Exhausted, he was already in bed asleep when the strains of Taps sounded over the FARTC loudspeakers.

"Ramsay, wake up!" Collier drifted up to consciousness, being rudely shaken by Nat Reed. In the darkened barracks, the luminous hands of Collier's wristwatch showed 2250 hours.

"What the bloody hell! What's up, Nat?" Collier sat up in bed, groggily rubbing sleep from his eyes.

"Freaking Rudolph's gone nuts—if someone doesn't take a hand, he'll wind up in jail," Reed whispered hoarsely in his ear, not wanting to rouse the other sleeping men.

"Slow down...tell me what's going on," Collier whispered back, extricating himself from his blanket and planting his bare feet on the cool, wooden floor.

"Herb and I went into Lawton to get a steak, and he bought a pint of Scotch from the bootlegger in the alley behind the bank. He was okay until he started drinking the whiskey—then he started talking about going to the Midland Hotel and getting laid."

"The Midland? The Midland's no whorehouse. That's where Jones' wife and baby died. I don't understand—what's happened to get him in trouble with the cops?"

"The drunken bastard couldn't get the desk clerk to send a woman up, so he started to trash the room. When I left him, he was passed out cold, but the room looked like it had been hit by a battery of eight-inch howitzers firing for effect. When the hotel maid sees that room, they'll call the Post MPs, for sure. Come on, the taxi's waiting outside. I didn't pay him yet, so he isn't going anywhere."

As soon as Collier heard Reed say Herb had bought the Scotch, in the dark, Collier located the fresh khakis he'd laid out for tomorrow's flight back East. By the time Reed finished spilling out the rest of the story, Collier was fully dressed and tying his low-cut shoes.

"Come on, Nat. Let's get the asshole out of there." Fumbling in the dark to find his overseas cap, Collier headed toward the street.

"Whoa! No way! Not me." Reed didn't budge. "I'm staying right here. He's your buddy. You're on your own."

"With a friend like you, who needs enemies, Nat?" Collier stopped in his tracks and glared at Reed.

"Look, I got a cab and came and got you, didn't I? I'm not the bastard's keeper. I could have just let him clean up his own mess." Reed shrugged and stood his ground.

Turning it over in his head, in all fairness, Collier had to admit Reed had a point. "Okay, I'll take it from here. What room is he in? Do you have a key?"

"You don't need a key. Room three-o-four—right across from the elevator— the door isn't locked."

Wasting no more time with Reed, Collier hurried outside and climbed into the waiting cab. In Lawton, he had the driver let him out on the corner opposite the small Midland Hotel in a short block in the commercial district housing storefronts and a bank—around the opposite corner was a short street leading to a traditional Farmer's Market arcade encircling the small-town, central courthouse square.

Thankfully, for the moment at least, the sky had cleared and a bright silver sliver of the new moon was out.

"Here, take this and wait up there around the corner by the Square." Carefully tearing a ten-dollar bill down the middle, Collier handed the driver half and stuck the other half in the breast pocket of his khaki shirt. "Don't go anywhere. I'll give you my half after you take me back to Sill. I'll be a few minutes. I have to get my friend."

"Well, okay, I guess," the driver eyed the torn half-a-sawbuck. Even in Oklahoma City or Tulsa, ten bucks was a lot of cash.

Watching the taxi's taillights disappear around the corner heading toward the central Market Square, Collier slowly pirouetted 360 degrees, carefully surveying the empty streets. As far as Collier could see, there was not a soul in sight. He exhaled a heavy sigh of relief. The Sill MPs kept a tight reign on this dusty, little town. Keeping an ear sharply tuned for the sound of approaching vehicles of any kind, Collier walked swiftly down the row of business buildings and stopped just short of the dimly-lit, store-front-like entrance to the Midland and peered through the grimy, plate-glass window into the tiny hotel lobby. *Empty.* A yellowing No Vacancy sign hung in the middle of the door glass; *the night clerk was nowhere in sight.*

Careful not to make a sound, Collier slowly turned the doorknob on the glass-paneled door until it opened just a crack. Slipping his fingers up through the three-inch opening, he grasped the arm of the warning bell above the door, taking great care to prevent the clapper from making a sound. Inching carefully inside, Collier swung the bell-arm over the top of the door. Then, leaving the door ajar several inches, he tiptoed across the lobby and started up the stairs. Behind him, from the tiny apartment behind the front desk, he could hear soft, snoring sounds.

On the third floor, Collier had no trouble locating 304. Just as Reed had told him, the door was indeed not locked. Once inside, the dim, reflected illumination from the streetlight outside the window confirmed what Nat had said. The condition of the room reminded Collier of the photo of the tornado wreckage in Lawrence, Kansas he had seen on the front page of this morning's *Daily Oklahoman*. The headboard of the bed and nightstand lay splintered, their wreckage scattered about the room. The mattress had been pulled from the badly-bent metal framework of what had once been a bed frame, and Herb lay unconscious halfway in the bathroom on the floor. The damage was even worse than the wreckage Herb had left behind at the Cotton Bowl Hotel in Dallas.

Clearly, this man should never be allowed near alcohol.

Moving quietly across the room, collecting item by item, Collier gathered Herb's discarded clothes, finally locating a missing shoe underneath the mattress up against the far wall.

"Herb, Herb...wake up." Straddling Herb's torso and leaning down beside his ear, Collier shook him roughly. "C'mon, wake the fuck up. We've got to get out of here before the MPs throw your sorry ass in jail."

"Go way...The hotel's sending up a *who'er*..." Herb grunted and closed his eyes again.

Quickly locating the ice bucket on top of the writing desk, Collier walked back and flipped on the bathroom ceiling light. Without shaking Herb's inert form again, Collier started dribbling a stream of ice water in Herb's left ear.

"Jeez...goddamn! Whadda fugg?" Herb made a face, blinking wide awake. Rolling on his side, he raised his hands to shield himself from the glaring naked bulb.

"Get up damnit. C'mon, Herb, get dressed."

"Go away...let me sleep..."

Expressionless, Collier splashed another glassful of the ice water directly in his face. "Quit fucking around. Get up, Herb, and get dressed."

"C'mon, man...leave me alone," Protesting weakly, Rudolph struggled to roll back over, obviously still half-drunk. Collier splashed more water in his face, careful not to get too much on his disgusting buddy's underwear.

"Oh, shit, Collier...get off of me, man. Let me up." Pushing Collier angrily away, Herb managed to grab the edge of the commode and pull himself to a sitting position.

"Okay, Herb, I'm going to let you up. I have your clothes right here and I expect you to put them on without any argument. We need to get your worthless butt out of here before you wind up in the Post Stockade. I'm in no mood for your shit. Are we clear? Do you understand me or do you need another dose of this?" Collier looked him the eye, still holding the water pitcher over him.

"Uh-huh...I mean huh-uh. Goddamnit, Collier, don't pour anymore water. I'll get dressed. Just let me up." Rudolph raised his hands to protect himself, cringing at the threat of another splash of the icy liquid.

"Okay. Get up. Get dressed and be quick about it." Collier reached down and gave Herb a hand. As soon as the woozy Rudolph was on his feet, Collier reached across and handed him a clean towel. "Here, dry off, before you put these on." Gagging from the stink of vomit and stale alcohol, it was all Collier could do to keep from puking.

After Herb had dried himself as best as he could, Collier handed him his shirt and waited while Rudolph slipped it on and began fumbling with the buttons.

"Hold still, damnit. Let me." Collier brushed Herb's hand aside and took over the task. As soon as he finished with the buttons, he handed Herb his trousers and held his arm to steady him while he stepped in one leg at a time.

When Herb had tucked in his shirt and buckled his belt, Collier handed him his shoes. "Sit on the commode and put these on."

"Where are my socks?" Herb asked, taking a seat on the commode and looking back up at Collier with a drunken smirk.

"I could only find one—forget the socks! C'mon, Herb, quit fiddle-farting around. We need to get the hell out of here." Collier checked the pocket of Rudolph's khaki shirt and found a copy of his leave orders and his airplane ticket. "Where's your wallet, Herb?"

"Right here in my back pocket," Herb proudly fished the billfold out of his trousers pocket and flipped it open. It contained a single five-dollar bill and a pair of ones. "Jeezus—I had over a hundred in twenties when I left the Post. That frigging *who'er* the desk clerk sent up here stole my cash. Gimme the phone. I need to call that SOB."

"Forget the desk. You were passed out drunk, Herb—no telling where your cash is now."

"Forget my ass...I want to talk to the clerk downstairs. If he don't return my dough, I'll call the cops on this place," Herb howled.

"Okay, have it your way. Go ahead and call the cops. I sure as shit hope you have a good story about what happened to this room. Here are your orders and your ticket home. The plane leaves Oklahoma City in just under eight hours from now. The five bucks in your wallet will get you a cab back to the Post. I'll be seeing you, buddy. You're on your own." Handing him his orders and the airplane ticket, Collier started for the door.

"Aw, wait up, man. Don't leave me here like this. I just want to get my money back," Herb whined and began fumbling with his necktie, suddenly sober.

"Forget the money, Herb. And forget the freaking necktie—you can tie it in the taxi. I can't believe that after your drunken fiasco in Dallas, I still got up out of a warm bed in the middle of the night to come save your drunken ass again. If you want to take the cab back with me, bring that goddamn tie and come on right now." Waiting for Herb to pick his way around the wreckage, Collier located Herb's cunt cap on the shelf of the closet beside the door. Surveying the trashed room in the dim light from the bathroom, the damage was not really as bad as it had first appeared. Quickly rejecting any thoughts of trying to straighten up, Collier opened the door and stepped into the hall.

"Okay...okay...wait up, I'm coming..."

"Be quiet and stay close to me," Collier led him stealthily down the stairs and across the darkened lobby. The sound of snoring was louder now from the cubbyhole behind the front desk, as they slipped out, leaving the front door halfway open. Outside, the wind had come up again and it was blowing rain as they broke into a dogtrot to the waiting cab around the corner. Driving back to the Post, the wind was blowing so badly, the driver had trouble staying on the asphault.

"Tornado weather! The radio says there have been tornadoes all around us," the driver said, carefully negotiating around a massive tree limb blown across Sheridan Road, after they had passed inside the main gate.

"Just my luck," Collier muttered under his breath, anxiously searched the brooding starless sky. After all he'd been through for the past five months he hated to think the weather would cancel his flight.

Despite only getting a few hours of sleep, when he awoke Saturday morning, Collier was greatly relieved to see the blue sky and shining sun. If this weather held, it would be a great day for flying.

"I was just coming to get you. Thanks for saving my ass last night. I have a cab coming in thirty minutes." When he went to wake him the following morning, Collier was amazed to find Herb already dressed in a fresh set of khakis, ready to catch the airport bus.

CHAPTER TWENTY-FOUR

THE DAILY OKLAHOMAN
Oklahoma City, Oklahoma, Saturday, May 24, 1952
ALERT GOES OUT TO KOREA ALLIES

WASHINGTON, May 23, (AP) - The United States 10 days ago warned 16 United Nations countries with forces in Korea to be on guard against possible aggression in the Far East.

––––––––––

CROP, PROPERTY LOSS FROM
TWISTERS NEARS $3 MILLIONS

The weather bureau called off Oklahoma's third tornado alert in three days at midnight Friday after a jittery state tried to count the loss from hail, cloudbursts and tornadoes that struck Thursday and early Friday. Tornadoes destroyed five buildings at Fort Sill, doing damage totaling $250,000. Another small tornado demolished several small buildings in a three-block area of Lawton, doing about $150,000 damage. Another dipped briefly to destroy a barn in another part of town.

––––––––––

IN THE BEAT-UP DODGE TAXICAB riding into Lawton to catch the early bus to Will Rogers Airport just outside of Oklahoma City, Collier stared out the window in open disbelief. Overnight, a tornado had reduced sizeable structures to horrendous piles of rubble. The wind had exerted such force on the howitzer barns that some of the thick, steel tubes of the 8-inch howitzers appeared to have been actually twisted by the force of the tornado. Looking up at the almost cloudless sky, it gave Collier a passing shiver of uneasiness to think that this destruction had occurred only several hours before while he had been sleeping only a few blocks away.

It didn't help Collier's state of mind to be going home a lowly Private E-1 without knowing whether or not he would be attending OCS. Emma had been telling all her friends that she was returning with him as the wife of a future officer. She would never understand his present state of limbo.

Dozing fitfully against the morning sun on the ride from Lawton, Collier said goodbye to Herb as soon as the bus pulled to a stop in front of Will Rogers Airport. Pushing his way out of the bus, Herb took off on the dead run—barely in time to catch the flight which would eventually get him to Philadelphia. Inside the terminal, Collier stopped briefly to admire Jo Davidson's sculpted bust of Will Rogers before checking in at the ticket counter. After checking in, he went into the airport newsstand and paid thirty-five cents for the Signet paperback edition of Mickey Spillane's most-recent novel, *The Big Kill*—the fifth in the Mike Hammer series—before he bought a Hershey bar and walked over to the departure gate and took a seat on a deserted bench. Quickly engrossed in the hardboiled detective yarn, it seemed almost no time had passed before he heard the loudspeaker call his flight.

It was only a few minutes past 1100 hours when Collier slipped wearily into a window seat aboard the flight-weary DC-4. Despite his aversion to the thought of flying, he was fast asleep within seconds of buckling his seatbelt. Sleeping soundly through takeoff, Collier remained in a profound, coma-like sleep virtually all the way to Washington National Airport, waking only when the stewardess shook him to check his seatbelt in preparation for landing at an intermediate stop along the way. He gradually roused and finally became fully awake about a half-hour before their landing in Washington.

Walking across the tarmac to the terminal building at Washington National Airport, Collier experienced an unexpected clutch in his throat when he first caught sight of Emma standing just inside the gate. Collier had barely stepped inside the terminal when she rushed forward and hugged him fiercely around the neck, kissing him feverishly full on the mouth, both cheeks and his mouth again. He certainly couldn't recall Emma Lowell ever being so openly affectionate in public. The recent change of tone in her letters had hardly prepared him for such a public display of warmth.

When Emma finally eased her death grip, Collier stepped back and looked down at her, trying not to show surprise. He had to admit she looked quite winsome in her obviously-new, pink, cotton, shirtwaist dress. Emma's demonstrative welcome was so completely out of character for the rather introverted woman Collier remembered, he stood there in the midst of the deplaning passengers, shy as any schoolboy, momentarily ill at ease. It was almost as if he had just been greeted by a total stranger.

This new Emma was definitely going to take some getting used to.

"Oh, Collier, I've missed you so much—you'll never know. I'm never going to let you get away from me again."

"I...ah...I missed you too, Sweetheart. You...ah...you look really great—a sight for sore eyes," he stuttered, struggling to regain composure. Despite the apparent genuineness of Emma's newfound affection, Collier couldn't shake a nagging suspicion of her sudden change of heart.

"Do you have more luggage on the airplane?" Emma asked, nodding at the small AWOL bag in his hand.

"Nope. This is it. But I'm in dire need to find the nearest men's room. My bladder is about to pop," he said, looking anxiously around for a Men's Room sign.

"It's right this way," Emma said, steering him toward the concourse just beyond the gate.

Standing in line to take his turn at the crowded urinals, Collier attempted to order his confusing emotions and muddled thoughts. Despite all the lingering resentments for Emma's disrespect of him before he left home for the military—which made him strongly suspicious of this apparent sudden change of personality—he was a totally unprepared to find that he still found her attractive.

"Much better." Smiling with relief, Collier rejoined Emma in the concourse and looked around for the nearest exit sign. "Now, let's get out of here?"

Outside the terminal, a steady stream of taxis, hotel station wagons, limos and private vehicles of every description navigated around a huge traffic circle, dropping off and picking up passengers and their luggage underneath the wide, marquee-sheltered sidewalk. At the curb immediately in front of them, the liveried chauffeur of a long, black Rolls Royce—displaying a tiny diplomatic flag of some country or principality Collier did not recognize mounted on its headlights—was handing a uniformed Skycap the hand-tooled, wide-strapped leather luggage of a distinguished-looking black man and his mink-jacketed, natural-blonde, pure-Caucasian wife.

"That's disgusting. Sometimes I wonder what this world is coming to." Emma made a face. "The pedestrian crosswalk is down this way—see the parking area just across the traffic circle?" Emma pointed, steering Collier to their right.

"I can't believe you drove yourself up here in all this crazy traffic. Do you think you can get us back out of here?" Collier asked after they had dodged across the busy crosswalk.

"Don't be silly, Darling. I'm depending on you to get us out of this mess and drive back home. It took me all day yesterday just to drive to Fredericksburg. I spent the night with Gene and Frances and drove into Alexandria this morning. On the way, I had to drive through Quantico and Fort Belvoir. I was scared half to death." Approaching the sporty yellow Studebaker, Emma handed him the keys.

"No sweat." Collier tried his best to appear nonchalant, when in reality the prospect of driving in the big-city traffic left him sweaty-palmed. He had ridden past the heavily-trafficked airport intersection on a number of occasions with his former college roommate, Charley Webber, but they had never ventured inside the margins of National Airport. Truth be known, Collier had no earthly idea how find his way back to U.S. 1 South.

"The car looks good. You've done a great job of keeping it up." He held the door for her then circled around and put his AWOL bag behind the driver's seat. When he got in and closed the door, he adjusted the bench seat to accommodate his long legs while he refreshed his recollection of the instrument panel. Quickly reassured that he remembered where all the right buttons were, Collier turned the key and listened as the six-cylinder engine purred to life. "She still runs like a dream," he said, grinning like a kid who had rediscovered a long-lost toy.

"I've taken it back to the dealer for oil and lubrication every six weeks like clockwork—just like you said. As a matter of fact, I took it in Wednesday and had them give it a good going over. They assured me it's in great shape to make the trip to Lawton," she offered proudly. Coyly scooting closer, she leaned over and planted a deeply-probing kiss full on his mouth, squeezing the inside of his thigh just below the crotch. To his consternation, his only reaction was an almost imperceptible tightening in his gubernaculum—generated more by anxiety than lust.

"How do I get back to Route 1 through Alexandria?" Collier asked the parking attendant before they exited the lot.

"Just dive into that stream of traffic, then keep merging left and follow the signs. You can't miss it—this road dead-ends at U.S. 1." Nodding at the snarl of cars, the attendant handed back his change.

Without bothering to count the change or roll up the driver's window, Collier eased the car forward and stuck out his arm to signal as he immediately started to look for openings to merge into the madly-jockeying, bumper-to-bumper traffic. After a few hairy moments, Collier started to relax as other drivers grudgingly conceded him room to merge. Once they were on the main highway, Collier became more at ease as he passed the exit to Glebe Road and crossed the rickety, narrow bridge over the railroad tracks just before entering the historic Old Town section of Alexandria. Glebe Road, the bridge and the ancient red-brick buildings on King Street were familiar landmarks from the weekend excursions he had made with Charley Webber.

"Are you hungry?" Emma asked after they had finally passed through the business section of Alexandria and had entered the more sparsely settled residential section leading out of town.

"Sure, I could eat anytime you say," Collier said. In all the excitement, he had forgotten he hadn't had anything but a Hershey bar since the previous evening.

"I passed a nice-looking restaurant not far from here on the way up this morning. It's attached to a little motor lodge. If you're tired, we could get a room. I told your folks we'd probably take a couple of days to get back home." Emma hinted broadly, casually tracing the outline of his inner thigh with her index finger.

"I'm not particularly tired...I slept practically all the way from Oklahoma." It made him extremely anxious to think they might stop and get a room so soon.

"Well, I'm not suggesting we actually take a nap," she pouted coyly. Her fingers continuing the suggestive tic-tac-toe on the inner side of his thigh made him quite apprehensive.

"Uh? Oh, sure. Let's at least keep an eye out for a decent place to eat," he murmured.

"There...on the right...see down there at the bottom of the hill?" Emma exclaimed as they topped the long grade. In the valley about a quarter-mile ahead was a restaurant adjoining a collection of old-fashioned tourist cabins. Even from this distance, it was easy to see the restaurant enjoyed a busy patronage. Slowing where the roadway bottomed out and pulling into the crowded parking area, Collier noted a number of Fort Belvoir and Quantico stickers on the windows of the parked cars, indicating a vote of confidence from the local military. To his relief, the restaurant building and adjoining tourist court appeared neatly-kept and freshly-painted.

"Look, the vacancy sign on the motel office is lit. I know you have to be as tired as I am. When we finish eating, why don't we just get a room and stay here for the night?" Emma gave his thigh another enthusiastic tweak.

"We're just getting started. Let's eat and see how we feel. It might be better to make a few more miles so we don't have so far to drive tomorrow. I'm sure my folks are as anxious to see me as I am to have time alone with you." Patting her hand, Collier gave her a half-hearted smile. Still feeling absolutely no physical reaction to her bold advances, the thought of being alone in a hotel room with his libido out of commission brought Collier to the brink of desperation.

"Forget your folks. They can wait. I was thinking we could cut across Route 3 from Fredericksburg to Orange and over to Charlottesville or Waynesboro in the morning and take the Skyline Drive home. We could have another day, or even two, to ourselves—sort of a second honeymoon."

"Come on, let's eat—I'm starved. We can talk over lunch." He gave her hand a pat before he turned off the ignition and crawled out of the car.

"Come sit next to me?" She flirted coquettishly when they were shown to a booth and he moved to sit across the table opposite her.

"Well, sure. It's been so long. I had forgotten how beautiful you really are. I just wanted to be able to look at you." he lied, moving self-consciously around and sliding onto the bench beside her. Memories of her former aloofness and contempt for his work before he left to join the Army continued to roil inside him as his genitals remained as dead as the proverbial doornail.

"Here comes our waitress. Let's just order burgers to take out. You go next door and get a room. I'll order extra food and a couple pieces of apple pie. We may not feel like leaving the room for awhile."

"Okay...I'll be back in a minute. If they don't have a vacancy, I'm sure there are other places near Belvoir or Quantico," he agreed, slipping quickly out of the booth and heading for the door. Outside, he shambled reluctantly over to the office of the adjoining tourist cabins. Contrary to his original impression back at the top of the hill, even though they were recently painted, seen up close, the buildings were quite old—the wooden clapboards flaking from too many coats of cheap paint.

"Can I help you?" A wide-hipped matron with bushy eyebrows looked up and greeted Collier from behind the registration desk. The strong odor of bacon mixed with heavy, pine-scented cleaner told Collier that the woman likely occupied a small apartment through the door behind the registration counter.

"My wife and I would like a room." Collier ventured. Hotels and tourist cabins always made him feel like some shady character out of a sleazy pulp novel.

"Certainly, Sir. We have a very nice room ready for immediate check in. Two dollars a night...twelve dollars if you want it for the entire week. How many nights?" the woman asked, fumbling under the counter for a registration card.

"Just tonight," Collier said, approaching the registration desk.

"Two dollars and five cents tax—in advance. Please fill this out." Quickly filling in his name and address, he used his father's post office box in Salem which still appeared on his driver's permit. Scrawling "1951 Studebaker" on the line requesting Year and Make of automobile, he left the License Tag Number line blank. Opening his wallet, he counted out three singles and slid the card and money back to her when he had finished writing.

The woman looked it over then pushed the card back across the counter.

"I'll need your tag number. It's a Virginia law."

"The car is parked next door at the restaurant. I'll go look," he muttered, turning resentfully to go back outside.

"No...wait. It'll be okay. You can stop by later with the tag number," she called him back. "I'll just be a minute while I write a receipt." She pulled an old-fashioned receipt book from under the counter and began to write. When she finished, she handed him the carbon copy and counted out a half-dollar, a quarter and a two dimes in change from her cash drawer.

"I'll need a key," he said, impatient at having to remind her.

"Of course! I'm not used to working the front desk—our regular clerk is late," she apologized as she sorted through a drawer underneath the counter and found a room key attached to a diamond-shaped, wooden, hotel key tag. "You'll have to give me a quarter deposit for the key. It's fully refundable when you return the key at checkout."

"Sure." Collier nodded, handing back the quarter from the change she had given him.

"Number eleven—all the way at the end, on your left. It's quieter...more private back there," the woman said, taking the money and handing over the key.

"Thanks. By the way, can we order room service from the restaurant?" Collier asked before he turned to leave.

"I'm sorry, no." She peered out from under her bushy eyebrows. "There are no phones in the rooms, anyway. There's a phone booth outside the restaurant next door if you need to make a call."

"What time does the restaurant close?" He was surprised that his watch already showed 1730 hours. Since he boarded the plane early this morning in Oklahoma City, he had lost all track of time.

"Between eight and nine. They don't like to take orders past eight-thirty. After that, if you want food, you'll have to go out. There are several eateries and a drive-in burger joint up the road closer to Belvoir which stay open later—maybe as late as nine or ten. The diner near the main gate stays open all night."

"Well, thanks. You've been a lot of help." He gave her a smile and went out the door. When he rounded the corner of the building, Emma was already waiting beside the car holding a bag of takeout food. The brown paper sack was already showing greasy spots from the burgers.

"Any luck with a room?"

"Yeah...we're all set."

"Good. I'm ready for a little privacy...how about you?"

"Uhmm..." he nodded. "Here, I'll take that bag."

Emma handed him the bag of sandwiches. Collier accepted it gingerly, careful to keep from brushing the sleeve of his khakis against the oozing greasy spots. Moving around the car, he unlocked and held the door for Emma.

"Get in. Our cabin is all the way at the back."

Trudging around the back of the car, he opened the driver's door; depositing the bag of food on the back seat, then slid under the steering wheel and reluctantly started the engine. Putting the coupe into gear, he backed around, then headed down the line between the two rows of tourist cabins.

"Here we are," he announced, pulling into the parking space in front of Room 11. Cutting the engine, he got out of the car, retrieved his bag and the bag of sandwiches from behind the driver's seat before he walked around to open the passenger door.

"Is your suitcase in the trunk?" he asked.

"Oh, yeah, I almost forgot. We should take it in now, so you won't have to get dressed to come outside later on." She gave him a coy smile.

Dutifully, Collier went around and got her overnight bag out of the trunk before he escorted her up the rickety steps of the cottage.

The smallish room was about what he had expected. The furnishings had obviously been salvaged from low beginnings and had since seen long, hard use. The cheap, cracked linoleum floor was covered by what appeared to be a pseudo-oriental carpet and just inside the door was a ratty Morris chair that had seen better days. Flanked by two night tables holding dime-store lamps with yellowing paper shades, the standard-sized double bed had old-fashioned iron head- and footboards. The thin chenille bedspread had seen better days. A folding luggage rack was just inside a doorless closet area near the back wall beside the bathroom door.

A glance inside the bathroom revealed it had been recently redone in real ceramic tile, including the shower enclosure around the tub. Even the fixtures were new. The bathroom and shower enclosure were the only saving graces of the entire room.

Placing his bag on the desk while Emma—taking great care to fasten the flimsy security chain—closed and locked the door, Collier unfolded the luggage rack and deposited Emma's overnight bag on the frayed, canvas-webbing straps.

"Not exactly the Governor Tyler," he complained, referring to the elegant hotel in Radford where they had spent their wedding night.

"No, but the bathroom is a bit more civilized than our rather primitive room at Hemlock Haven Lodge at Hungry Mother Park. You were absolutely insatiable back then, remember? I could hardly walk or sit down, my bottom was so sore," she reminded him, recalling the rustic cabins at the State Park where they spent the rest of their orgiastic, two-week-long honeymoon.

"How could I forget," he murmured, his head filling with images of their sweaty, non-stop, animalistic rutting during those first two weeks of their marriage. They had made love night and day. Despite the fact she had been rubbed raw and bleeding, she never complained when he had awakened each morning with a throbbing hard-on. The vivid recollections of that erotic interlude triggered just a hint of arousal in his groin.

"Are you hungry?"

"Yes, but I'd like to get out of these clothes and freshen up. I'd like to take a quick shower, if it's alright with you? If you have to pee, go ahead." Emma blushed. She seemed suddenly shy now they were alone in a room with a bed.

"No, I'm fine. I went in the airport, remember? You go ahead and shower. As soon as you finish, I'd like to rinse off, too. It's been a long day," he said, loosening his tie and folding it carelessly over the back of the chair in front of the window. When he turned around, Emma had opened her little valise, and had removed the satin, ivory negligee she had worn on their honeymoon. She gave him a shy smile as she carefully smoothed it and placed it across the foot of the bed. Now, Collier watched hypnotically as she pulled her dress over her head and hung it carefully on a wooden hanger in the closet. When she had finished with the dress, she shrugged her slip over her head and stood before him in nothing but her panties and bra.

"Get out of those clothes. I'll only be a minute. One thing for sure, the Army's Saltpeter doesn't work on you," she giggled and ducked into the bathroom and closed the door. Glancing down, Collier smiled at the spreading circle of dampness around the impatient bulge in the crotch of his khaki trousers.

"Oh, Collier, Darling, yes...yes...yes!" Emma whispered in the pre-dawn darkness, shuddering once again in orgasmic ecstasy.

"Was it as good as our honeymoon?" Collier gasped, grateful he had been able to hold out long enough to survive yet another Herculean effort needed to grind Emma to a hard-won climax.

"Oh, Darling, much, much better. I was still faking back then. It took two-and-a-half years before you finally were able to show me what orgasm meant. What a twist of fate that I found out the night before you left to go in the Army," Emma murmured, completely unmindful of the sweaty, body-wrenching exercise it took to bringing her to orgasm for the third time since they had begun their marathon reunion the late afternoon before. "I hope it isn't too hard on you?"

"Not at all...if this is punishment, then throw me in the briar patch as often as you like, Miz Br'er Fox," he said, half-meaning it. Given their less-than-admirable sexual history, now being able to make her come with regularity really did do wonders for his ego—although he thought it well within the realm of possibility her newfound sexual liberation might kill him before they reached Salem and he saw his parents again.

"I'm sorry, Honey. Do my pubic hairs scratch you?" she said, mistakenly thinking his reference to the Uncle Remus folktale—Br'er Rabbit tricking Br'er

Fox into tossing him back into the sanctuary of the briar patch—referred to the texture of her pubic hair.

"No...no. I was referring to an old folk tale my Aunt Blanche used read to me when I was a kid. What I mean is that it's hardly punishment to make love to you. And, I purely love to see you come. Seeing you come, makes it better for me—complements my male ego. I don't enjoy feeling like I'm the one getting all the pleasure."

"Trust me, Darling. Your fragile male ego is safe and sound."

"That's comforting to know since I may well never be able to make love again."

"Idle threats will get you nowhere..." she murmured, kissing him passionately, playfully groping his poor, battered penis.

"Stop that. If you have all that energy this hour of the morning, what would you say to packing our bags and striking out for home? I hope you won't be too disappointed, but I think it would be a good idea to save our sightseeing on the Skyline Drive until we have more time."

"No, I agree. It was a selfish of me. After all, I'll have you all to myself when we start out for Oklahoma, and we only have a few days to spend with your parents and visit friends. By the way, Bo has to leave for Japan next week. He says he wants to see you before he leaves."

"Yeah, I'm anxious to see him, too. Come on, my insatiable nymphomaniac, let's get our clothes on and hit the road."

Consulting a highway map, Collier decided it would be best to continue straight through on U.S.1 to Richmond and pick up Route 60 through Bon Air, Cumberland and Buckingham Courthouse into Amherst. At Amherst, he picked up U.S. 460, skirting Lynchburg into Bedford, then on into Roanoke and Salem. Driving roads he could negotiate practically blindfolded from his college days, Collier made incredible time. Even after setting his watch ahead an hour to adjust to Eastern Time, the hands showed it was still almost an hour before high noon when he pulled into a filling station a few miles outside Roanoke and filled up the tank. After paying for the gas, he got change and went outside to the pay phone to call Bo.

"Collier, we've been hoping you'd call. Hold on, Bo's right here," Jenny answered.

"Where are you, man? Are you home?" Bo asked, anxiously.

"Almost. We're in Blue Ridge. Emma drove to D.C. yesterday to pick me up. We spent the night up there last night, but we got up before daylight and hit the road. We should be in Salem within the hour. When are you leaving? I want to see you before you go," Collier assured his friend.

"I fly to Chicago day after tomorrow; that's the twenty-fifth. I know you need to see your folks this afternoon, but can we have supper together tonight?" Bo asked, obviously pleased to hear Collier's voice.

"I don't know why not. I'll call you this afternoon and confirm," Collier said and hung up. He purely hated that Bo was being shipped to FECOM. He wanted to spend as much time with him as he could before he flew out. Now, Collier jiggled the receiver hook to signal the operator. When she came back on, he gave her his parent's number, smiling inwardly as he heard their phone begin to ring.

At slightly past 1330 hours, Collier finally turned off U.S.11 and crossed the familiar railroad tracks just past Logan's Barn Antiques at Glenvar, which had housed George Selwyn's daddy's general store back when he was still a kid.

"I know you must be starved," Lida greeted them when they finally pulled into the drive of his parents' home. His mother and father were waiting by the porch steps. Following his mother's obligatory smothering with hugs and kisses, Lida led Collier and Emma inside where a mouth-watering sandwich buffet awaited them on the kitchen table.

"Are you sure you're alright, Collier? You're nothing but skin and bones." After lunch, Collier walked the overgrown path across the pasture separating his parent's place from Grandma Boyd's rambling, white, frame farmhouse. Lana Texas Boyd began her doomsday cry before he had crossed the room to her familiar perch in the rocking chair beside the window. Behind her, the homemade bookshelves fairly groaned under the weight of his Aunt Blanche's extensive personal library. To Collier, those books represented the treasure trove of his childhood reading.

"It's all muscle. Don't worry, Grandma. I'm fine." Collier grinned as he bent to kiss her cheek, surprised at how she had aged; her pale-iris-blue eyes had taken on a weak and watery appearance. After answering his grandmother's questions for about a half-hour, Collier gave her a peck on her cheek and took his leave with a promise to return tomorrow.

"The papers are full of car wrecks. Don't go driving all over the county in that fancy car. Get some rest and stay home with Lida and Harry." His grandmother cautioned, a pessimist to the end.

"I will, Grandma," Collier lied and gave her a hug, long-since accustomed to promising the old worrywart anything she wanted to hear.

"You'd better listen, Collier," she called after him as he left.

Collier's watch showed almost 1600 when he walked through the kitchen door at the rear of his parents' house. As much as he wanted to take a nap, he sat at the kitchen table with Emma and his parents and chatted for awhile. When Emma finally excused herself to go upstairs to rest, Collier went to call Bo again.

"Hi, man. We'll treat for dinner if you want to go out somewhere. How 'bout Archie's Lobster House? Sky's the limit," Collier offered.

"Jenny says Archie's is fine with her. Come by here around nineteen-hundred, okay?" Bo said after a brief consultation with his wife.

"Okay, but it's Sunday. I had best call and get a reservation. Does a quarter-to-eight sound okay?" Collier asked, suddenly sick-to-death of using military time.

"Quarter-to-eight sounds fine with us. Go ahead and call. We'll see you then." Bo agreed. "By the way, I'll be wearing my khakis. My civvies don't fit so good anymore."

"I'll be in khakis, too. See you then." Collier returned the phone to the cradle.

Rejoining his folks at the kitchen table, Collier stretched and yawned. "I'm bushed. I flew all day yesterday and drove all this morning. It didn't help much that I didn't sleep well on that lumpy motel bed. Think I'll go up and try to grab a nap." Collier yawned and stretched again.

"Sure, go up and lie down with Emma. I laid out fresh towels on your bed." Lida reached out to squeeze his hand.

"Bo's leaving for Korea the day-after-tomorrow, and we're going to meet them for supper," he squeezed back, looking to his parents for consideration.

"Your father and I understand. Feel free to come and go as you please. We have plenty to eat and you're always welcome to eat here with us, but we understand if you want to go visit with friends."

"Thanks for putting up with us...I'm glad you understand," he said and headed up for a quick shower and a short nap.

Just past 1900 hours, Collier pulled up at the curb directly across from the Bohon's apartment over the tearoom on the corner of Main and Broad. Dodging the steady stream of Sunday-night traffic, Collier had hardly made it to the opposite curb when the door to the stairwell leading to the Bohon's apartment opened and Bo and Jenny appeared.

"Good to see you, man." Wearing freshly-pressed khakis, Bo stepped forward to shake his hand; grinning from ear to ear the longtime friends followed Collier back to the car. With Archie's Lobster House located out beyond the northeast boundary of the Roanoke city limits, the drive to took longer than Collier anticipated. When he finally found a parking place on the far edge of the parking lot and they had walked about the length of a football field to the entrance of the popular restaurant, a mob of people were lined up outside the door.

"Wait here with the girls, Bo. We have a reservation. I'll go find the *maitre d'*," Collier said, as he began elbowing his way politely through the overflow crowd.

"My name is Collier Ramsey. I made a reservation for a party of four." Once inside the foyer, he introduced himself to the hostess.

"Yes, sir, Mr. Ramsey, I have you right here on my sheet, but we're running a little behind. It shouldn't be more than twenty minutes or a half-hour," the hostess patronized.

"This is not acceptable. I want to see the *maitre d'*," Collier insisted.

"But sir, the maitre d' is busy. We're doing the best we can," she said as she checked her list and called a name from her list of reservations.

"Look, I came all the way from up near Shawsville, and my friend is shipping overseas to Korea tomorrow. We risked getting a speeding ticket in order to get here on time. If you won't seat us, I want to see the manager," Collier insisted.

At Collier's continued insistence, the unhappy woman disappeared inside the doors leading to the dining room. In less than a minute, she reappeared, followed by a middle-aged man wearing a tuxedo and an ugly scowl.

"I'm the manager, Sir, how can *we* help you?" The man was obviously not in a charitable mood.

"I had a reservation for a quarter-to-eight. I was here on time—that was almost fifteen minutes ago and my wife and friends are still waiting outside. Reservations used to mean something here. Has Archie's become so successful reservations don't mean anything anymore?" Collier was in no mood to be given the runaround.

"No, sir, it's not that at all. Our regular customers understand that turnaround is slower than usual on weekends. Sundays are always crowded and we've had a lot more drop-ins than usual from our motel tonight." The abrasive manager shrugged.

"Motel drop-ins, go hang. Look here, my name is Collier Ramsey. I made a reservation for seven-forty-five. My friend is leaving tomorrow for Korea, and we have our wives with us. This will be the last dinner we'll have with our wives for a long time. Don't you care that soldiers are sleeping in the rain and mud in Korea to keep your loved ones safe and sound while you are home snug in a warm bed, sleeping with your wife?" Collier raised his voice to make certain everyone inside the crowded foyer could hear.

"Of course we care, sir. And we have your name right here. We're doing the best we can." The embarassed manager turned beet-red at having his patriotism and integrity challenged in a foyer full of people.

"I always thought Archie's was as good as their word. If you're taking drop-ins ahead of someone who called ahead and was given a specific time the restaurant would be ready to serve him, then I consider your establishment guilty of bad faith. The dining room staff at Hotel Roanoke would never treat their guests this way," Collier persisted, incensed at the cavalier disregard for his reservation.

"If you'll go get the rest of your party and just wait here a moment, Sir, I'll see what I can do." Anxious to extract himself from this embarrassment, the manager turned and disappeared inside. By the time Collier had summoned Emma and the Bohons to join him, the hostess was waiting with a stack of the impressive, imitation-leather-bound menu cards.

"Right this way, Mr. Ramsey." She whisked them quickly inside and seated them at a well-located table, near the rear of the large dining room.

"This is a very special occasion. I insist we drink a toast to friendship and good luck." Over Emma's and the Bohons' feeble protests that they didn't drink alcohol, as soon as they were seated, Collier ordered a bottle of the best New York champagne. In no time at all, the wine steward had set up a tableside ice bucket with four champagne glasses and uncorked the champagne.

"Well, here we are. We mustn't let all this rude behavior spoil a perfectly good dinner and a wonderful evening with old friends. Let's drink to Bo, our hero and our good friend. May God keep you safe and sound and send you back to Jenny and the rest of us with a chest full of ribbons in all good speed." As soon as the waiter had poured the wine and his unsophisticated table companions' nervous laughter had died down, Collier raised his glass in a toast.

"I'll drink to that," Emma raised her glass and took a little sip as Bo and Jenny shyly followed suit, leery of the alcohol.

"O-oo, the bubbles tickle your nose, kinda like Alka Seltzer," Jenny tittered nervously, replacing her glass on the table.

They all laughed at her observation. After a few tentative sips, none of them really wanted to finish their wine. Not wanting to waste perfectly good champagne, Collier asked the waiter to take the ice bucket with the remaining wine with their compliments to a young couple sitting across the room. With the waiter hovering over them, waiting to take their dinner orders, Emma nudged Collier and whispered, "Look, there's Alden Scott at that table over to our left. And look who's with him—Courtland Spotts. The last I heard from my sister, Anne, Alden and Courtland were both going to VMI."

Turning his head discreetly, Collier spotted Alden Scott at the nearby table with their former high-school classmate, Courtland Spotts. Alden Scott—"Scotty"—and Emma's next oldest sister had been an item for awhile at Andrew Lewis. He was wearing an Air Force uniform, and Gus Spotts was in Army pinks. Both were wearing the gold bars of second lieutenants.

"Don't you want to go over and say hello?" Emma asked.

"No. They're both officers. They'll be ill-at-ease to be seen with the likes of miserable Private E-2s like us," Collier said, feeling a pang of envy and humiliation. First thing tomorrow morning, he resolved to call Fort Sill to see if there were any news on his status for OCS.

By the time their food was served, they had all forgotten the unpleasantness of getting seated. For dessert, Collier suggested that everyone order Archie's celebrated pecan pie, topped with a scoop of vanilla ice cream.

"Put your wallet back in your pocket, Bo. This check's on me," Collier insisted when the waiter give him the check. When he looked at the tab, Collier swallowed hard. The total came to $29.51, including four bucks for the champagne and the four desserts. Although he rarely carried more than twenty dollars in his pocket, fortunately Collier had left home with a little over fifty dollars in his billfold to be certain he had more than enough to play host for the evening. Leaving six dollars on the table for a tip, he settled the bill with the cashier at the door.

Back in Salem, Collier and Emma got out of the car to make their goodbyes. Collier gave Bo a solemn handshake and Emma gave both Bo and Jenny a warm hug. They stood there on the sidewalk and waited until their friends had started up the steps to their apartment before getting back in the car.

"I know how you feel about drinking. I hope you didn't mind my ordering the champagne and picking up the check. After all, Bo is heading off to war," Collier said as they pulled away from the curb.

"Well, it's a little late to apologize. I saw you leave twenty-percent for a tip. Get over your delusions of grandeur. You can't afford to be such a showoff. Don't forget, I'm leaving a well-paying job to go back out there with you," Emma admonished.

"Look, Emma, that money was mine—earned with a lot of sweat and even a little blood. And, while we're on that subject, I've been scraping by on a little over twenty-five bucks every payday while the Army has been sending you my allotment check for fifty dollars a month. And, just to set the record straight, nobody asked you to go with me back to Sill. As a matter of fact, I called you a month ago and tried my level best to talk you out of it. Remember?"

"I remember no such thing," she fired back.

"Oh, come on now. I even sat down and wrote you a long letter. I'm sure you remember that."

"I thought you loved me..." her voice wavered pitifully.

In the greenish glow of the dash lights, Collier saw her open her purse, fumbling for a Kleenex. Sensing the conversation was about to dissolve into histrionics, Collier bit his tongue and made no reply.

"After yesterday and last night, I thought you were happy I'm going back with you," she sniffed and blew her nose.

"I'm certainly happy to be back home, and I'm certainly happy to be making love to you again, but I've tried to warn you that Lawton, Oklahoma, is going to be a rude awakening for you. It is absolutely nothing like Salem, Virginia. What's going to happen when you get out there and can't find work and discover what I've been telling you about that little Army town is true? I'll most likely already be in OCS and you'll be crying to come back home."

"It won't happen, I promise. All I want is to be with you. Don't you love me anymore?" She sniffled and blew her nose again.

Refusing to dignify her age-old feminine ploy of reducing all spousal differences to a shower of tears and the question of affection, wisely, Collier made no response. At his parent's house his folks had long-since gone up to bed, but had left a table lamp burning in the living room. Locking the door, Collier waited while Emma went up and turned on a bedside lamp in their bedroom before he switched off the light and followed her up the stairs. Carefully avoiding watching while Emma flaunted her nakedness changing into her nightgown, he quickly went about the business of undressing and hanging up his khakis. After she donned her robe and headed for the bathroom, Collier—wearing only an Army tee-shirt and his Jockey shorts—slipped into bed and drifted off to sleep without turning out the light. When he awoke sometime later, the silver moonlight was streaming through the window across from his side of the bed and Emma had snuggled up close to him in the dark. She had pulled up his tee shirt and her fingers were playing lightly over the hair on his chest.

"Are you awake?" she breathed in the semi-darkness.

"Uhm-m..." he muttered grudgingly, wanting to ignore the urgent messages her busy fingers were sending to his overly-responsive loins.

"I'm sorry I was such a pill," Emma whispered, her breasts warm against his back.

"It's okay. You were right. I should have consulted you before I ordered the champagne," he acknowledged, his penis already hardening inside the tight restraint of his Jockey briefs.

"Do you love me?" she sighed, hunching her pudenda brazenly against his buttocks.

"Of course," he murmured. Turning in the bed, he kissed her wetly, pressing his body tight against the length of her.

"Be quiet or we'll wake your folks," she giggled softly as she sat up and began pulling her nightgown over her head.

The following morning, they drove into Salem where Collier dropped Emma off at Mick-or-Mack supermarket to pick up some groceries for his mom. Not at all interested in pushing a grocery cart, Collier walked down Main Street to the post office to get the mail from his father's box. He had only made it about halfway down the block past the Presbyterian Church on the corner—which stood across Main from the stately St. Paul's Episcopal where he and Emma were married—before he ran almost headlong into Guy Spruhan, Sr., his former high-school coach.

"Well, well...who have we here? I guess the Army will take almost anybody nowadays," Collier's former coach muttered, the ever-present Camel cigarette clamped tightly between the thumb and forefinger of his left hand which twitched erratically with a pronounced alcoholic tremor which had earned him the nickname, 'Shakey'. While Collier was still in high school, Shakey was considered rather reprehensible for sending his pre-teen, grade-school daughter—pulling her little red wagon full of empty beer bottles—to the nearest beer emporium beside the Salem Theater. Her wagon-load replenished, she would wend her way back home, happy to do her daddy's dirty work. Over the years, it was little wonder that Guy Spruhan, Sr. had become well-known as "a man of the broth"—the Irish euphemism for a man with a prodigious thirst.

"Hi, Coach, nice to see you, too. How're you getting along as a gentleman of leisure?" With an illustrious history as coach at VMI, but long past his prime when he had come to coach at Collier's high school, the ancient coach had been involuntarily retired, again, a couple of years back.

"I was okay until a second ago," Shakey said, favoring Collier with a dark scowl.

"How are Gus and Jack these days?" Ignoring the old man's slight, Collier inquired pleasantly after the coach's sons. Passable athletes, both young Spruhans had played all sports ahead of Collier in high school.

"They're fine. They're both married now." Coughing, the old coach hacked up a glob of phlegm and spit into the street. Blowing his blue-veined, W.C. Fields nose into a red-bandana handkerchief, he lit another Camel off the butt of the one he had already burned close down to the stub.

"Yeah, me too," Collier replied offhandedly, anxious to be moving on.

"Where's your brother? I heard he was in pilot training," the coach asked, suddenly interested. Collier's brother had always been the coach's pet.

"You heard right. Jim's flying B-25s out in Enid, Oklahoma..." Collier filled him in on his brother's Air Force training.

"You know, it's too bad Jimmy didn't have your physique. He was always twice the athlete you were."

Suddenly revisited with long-submerged resentments, Collier was sorely tempted to remind him that, as Jim's football coach, he had been responsible for ruining his brother's right knee—not giving him time to heal properly before returning him to play. To his credit, Collier managed to hold his tongue. It was pointless to confront the old boozer about ancient history now.

"I'll tell Jimmy you asked about him, Coach." Ignoring his former coach's boorish effrontery, Collier nodded, pushing on past before the pathetic figure could pursue the conversation.

That afternoon after grocery shopping, Collier drove into Roanoke and visited his Grandmother Ramsey. She was expecting him, and as soon as he gave her a big hug and seated himself at the kitchen table, she went to the refrigerator and produced a huge mixing bowl filled with thick and creamy bread pudding. When he said goodbye a little over an hour later, Collier was stuffed so full of pudding he had to slip the Studebaker seat back to give himself room to drive back to Salem.

The next few days drifted by with Collier trying to dissuade Emma from packing bulky pots and pans and various household items such as bed linens and brooms and assorted mundane junk readily purchasable at the PX once they made it to Lawton. After several heated arguments failed to prevail against her logic-tight brain, he finally gave up and concentrated on packing a few items of his civilian clothing—a pair of jeans, two pairs of golf slacks, several golf shirts, a dress shirt and his best sport coat with a pair of penny loafers and his well-worn golf shoes. He also resurrected a disreputable Sears & Roebuck golf bag from his father's basement to transport his clubs.

One Saturday afternoon back in mid-May when he'd had time on his hands, Collier had ventured to the Main Post to investigate the Fort Sill Golf Club. A friendly corporal who worked in the golf shop had been good enough to take him on a tour of the course. Collier had been pleasantly surprised to discover that the Golf Club—a recent addition to the old post's amenities—was a full eighteen holes. Designed in 1946, the course was heavily wooded—the back nine winding through a lush, parkland setting quite rare for southwestern Oklahoma. Collier had been enchanted to find that Medicine Creek meandered through the entire back nine and the course played something over sixty-five-hundred yards from the championship markers. Scattered among the native burr oaks, numerous types of exotic nut trees lined the fairways, and bouncing merrily along in a beat-up truck, the enthusiastic corporal pointed out some apparently-significant historical sites.

Collier had been particularly surprised when the young NCO told him that memberships were quite affordable and open to all military personnel regardless of rank. Amazed that even a lowly E-1 enlisted man could acquire a membership on a monthly basis and play on equal footing with Officers and NCOs—a rare instance of democratic equality in the well-defined military hierarchy—he paid the nominal fee for a quarterly membership and resolved to take full advantage when he got back to Oklahoma. Looking at the ratty bag as he stuffed it in the trunk of the Studebaker, one of the first things on his list of things to do when he returned to Fort Sill was to plunk down twenty-five bucks for a brand-new 10-inch round, leather, touring-pro golf bag he'd had his eye on in the Fort Sill pro shop.

On a trip into Salem to do errands for his mother, Collier used a sidewalk phone booth near the Mick-or-Mack and called the orderly room of the Casual Battery where he would report when they arrived back to Sill. He was sorely disappointed when he was told that there was still no news about his application for OCS. Fishing in his wallet, Collier located the scrap of paper with Herb Rudolph's phone number in Newtown Square, Pennsylvania. He idly shuffled the stack of coins on the phone-booth shelf as he waited for the long distance operator to put him through.

"I'm glad you called, but I haven't heard a word," Herb told him when he came on the line. Chatting for a minute or two, they agreed to meet at the Post Guest Quarters on the following Monday when they both arrived back at Sill. Herb was bringing Louise back with him, a prospect which offered Emma the comfort of having a girlfriend in the area while Collier was occupied with his military duties—whatever they turned out to be. When the long distance operator came back on the line to inform him his three minutes were up and he would have to deposit more money, Collier promptly said goodbye and replaced the phone on the cradle.

CHAPTER TWENTY-FIVE

THE ROANOKE TIMES
Roanoke, Virginia, Friday, June 6, 1952
IKE SAYS HE WILL END KOREAN WAR
ABILENE, Kan, Thursday, June 5 (UP) - Gen. Dwight D. Eisenhower
Thursday effectively answered the charge he wouldn't reveal what he
stands for in his campaign for the Republican nomination by declaring
on issues ranging from civil rights, federal aid to education, farm price
support, socialized medicine and ending the war in Korea.

UN TROOPS ASSAULT DUG-IN COMMUNISTS
SEOUL, Korea, Friday, June 6 (AP) - United Nations raiders assaulted
dug-in North Koreans on the mountainous eastern Korean front
Thursday and drew a mortar and artillery barrage.

BRIGHT AND EARLY Friday morning, June 6, Collier finished his coffee,
pushed aside the morning paper, and went outside to cram the last of Emma's
boxes and suitcases into the backseat of the Studebaker, already jammed to the
ceiling with household implements. When he had jammed the last of her
superfluous junk inside, Collier turned to give his parents a farewell hug.

Finally in the car and moving around the circle heading out of his father's
driveway, Emma suddenly screamed, "Wait, Collier, stop the car, I almost
forgot."

"Judas Priest, what the devil's wrong, now?" Collier asked, wondering how he
could possibly cram another item into the little coupe.

"Wait right here. I'll only be a sec," she said as she opened the car door.
His parents stood agape by the steps, watching with curiosity as Emma ran up the
steps and into the house. When she came back out, she was carrying an old-
fashioned, quart-size, wide-mouth, glass Ball canning jar.

"What the hell is the canning jar for? We can buy canning jars at any store
when we get to Lawton..." he began, but she quickly hushed him.

"I'm sick and tired of having to beg you to stop to use the bathroom. If you
won't stop when I have to go, I'll just squat right here in the car and pee in this,"
she said, leaning forward and slipping the jar securely beneath her seat.

"Look, Honey, I assure you that won't be necessary. Just let me know when
you first start to feel the urge, and I'll start looking for a nice place with clean
restrooms, I promise," Collier reassured her sincerely. Trying to imagine the idea
of Emma urinating into the opening of the glass canning jar in the confines of a
fast-moving car was more than he could bear.

Driving steadily west on U.S. 11—the Lee Highway—for the first three hours,
Collier retraced the route they had taken on their honeymoon at the lodge at
Hungry Mother State Park. When they had finally passed through the one- and
two-stoplight towns of Radford, Dublin, Pulaski, and Wytheville and were
approaching the little town of Marion, Emma asked wistfully. "Do you think we
have time to drop by Hemlock Haven for lunch?"

"No way, Honey, we've got to put some miles behind us. If we're going to make it to Lawton sometime Sunday, we need to make it at least to Nashville before we stop for the night."

"Alright...but it seems a shame. We're so close and we've never been back there, you know?" She gazed pensively at the cedar-dotted rolling hills of the passing Southwestern Virginia countryside.

In downtown Bristol, they laughed as they drove down State Street which was boldly marked "Virginia" on one side and "Tennessee" on the other side of the center line. Continuing on U.S. 11, they drove west through Johnson City, Bull's Gap, Morristown and Strawberry Plains as they traversed the limestone capped "Rocky Top" mountains toward Knoxville.

After they finally made it out of the mountains, Collier took the truck bypass west around Knoxville. When they were back on the main highway at Farragut, Collier was discouraged when he saw a road sign indicating they still had nearly 200 miles to travel before they reached Nashville. At the rate they were going, it would take at least three more hours to make it that far, and the hands on his watch already confirmed it was well-past 1800 hours. Although Collier had refrained from saying anything to Emma, squinting directly into the setting sun was making him very sleepy. Despite keeping the radio volume unusually loud, Collier had been having difficulty just staying awake.

"I think I've about had enough driving for today. Keep your eye out for a likely-looking place to spend the night—something with air conditioning and a nice restaurant nearby," he instructed Emma.

Continuing on several miles past Knoxville, they eventually came to a crossroads where the highway split with U.S. 11, turning sharply left as it swung south toward Chattanoga. U.S. 70 continued straight ahead, but there was no sign to indicate where it led. Pulling to the side of the highway, Collier consulted the unfolded road map before he figured out the right-hand fork led directly to Nashville. After driving another hour, they still had not passed a likely-looking place to spend the night. Just when Collier thought he could not drive another mile, they found a homey local eatery near the courthouse in the sparsely-populated town of Crossville. Ordering the blue-plate special of chicken-fried steak, mashed potatoes with carrots and garden peas, they both devoured the food with ravenous appetites and ordered slices of hot, homemade apple pie for dessert.

"Is there a nice tourist court with air-conditioning nearby?" Collier asked the waitress as she handed him the check.

"I went to a movie in Knoxville last year that was air-conditioned—it was really nice. There are tourist cabins just up the street on the way out of town, but the nearest air-conditioning is most likely Nashville," she said, sadly shaking her head at the outrageous notion.

It was almost 1100 hours when Collier pulled into the tourist court on the western outskirts of Crossville. The twin rows of ancient tourist cabins were faintly reminiscent of the ones they had stayed in the week before, just outside Washington. The friendly waitress had called ahead and the proprietor was waiting at the office door to register them. Collier paid the white-haired man $1.50 in advance.

"Number twenty-five is the last cabin on the left. I'll need another fifty-cents deposit for the key...it's refundable when you return the key in the morning," the old man said.

"Don't worry about the refund. We plan to be back on the road quite early. We'll leave the key in the room," Collier assured him and headed back to the car.

Grabbing his shaving kit and Emma's overnight bag, Collier unlocked the door and returned to the car to help Emma inside. Stepping inside the room, they were met by a blast of stale hot air; the room had obviously not been aired for several days, at least. While Emma headed in to take a cool shower, Collier busied himself opening the one small window and placing the adjustable window screen into the opening to keep out the bugs. A full fifteen minutes later when Emma came out of the bathroom, Collier was lying completely clothed on the bed fast asleep. Taking great care not to wake him, Emma turned out the lamp before she collapsed exhausted on her side of the hotel bed.

When Collier awoke in the dark, his watch glowed 0529. Feeling a bit frazzled, he located his shaving kit and closed the bathroom door before he turned on the light and got under the shower which quickly went cold. In the heat of the stuffy tourist cabin, the unheated water felt good on his skin. To save time and human energy, while he was still under the tepid shower, Collier lathered his face and scraped off his stubble. Although this was an exercise to which he had grown somewhat accustomed from the overnight bivouacs in Basic Training, he stepped out of the shower with his face feeling a trifle raw. Locating the fresh pair of Jockey shorts he had placed inside his toilet kit, he quickly dressed in the dark.

"Wake up, Honey, and get your things together. We've got a long way to drive and appointments to keep." Collier gently shook Emma awake as he walked back across the room and turned on the light in the bath.

The bedside Big Ben alarm clock showed a few minutes past six when Collier left Emma to her early-morning ablutions and located a nearby filling station to top off their gas tank from an antiquated gas pump with a large glass cylinder at the top. To operate the pump, the attendant had to fill the cylindrical glass reservoir by working a manual lever at the base of the outmoded pump before he could insert the hose and start filling their car. He checked the oil stick and was delighted to find the Studebaker had not used a drop of oil. Filling up the radiator from a heavy cast-aluminum water can, Collier carefully replaced the vacuum top, closed the car's hood and drove back to the motor court.

"Are these alright? I'm tired of suffering in this heat," Emma asked when he returned to the room. She was dressed in a white tee-shirt and tight tennis shorts.

"You look just fine. C'mon, I'm starved. I just hope those folk at that nice restaurant up on the courthouse square are open."

As it turned out, it was a wise decision to eat breakfast before they left Crossville. After almost six hours of hard driving, Collier's watch showed 1259 hours when they finally pulled in for lunch in Dickson on the western side of Nashville. According to the car's odometer, it had taken them nearly six hours to traverse a mere 200 miles; however, the good news was if the map was correct, it now seemed all of the mountainous terrain lay behind them. Once they had finally reached the high Tennessee plateau an hour or so past Knoxville, the Studebaker had fairly zipped along in overdrive at 55 to 60 mph.

Except for delays at several sections of U.S. 70 being repaired or widened to four lanes, Collier was able to keep the car in overdrive, maintaining a goodly pace most of the rest of the way to Memphis. However, at 1635 hours—just after they crossed the long bridge over the Mississippi into West Memphis, Arkansas— their luck ran out.

Across the Mississippi Bridge on the Arkansas side of the big muddy river, the smooth, concrete, Tennessee highway suddenly turned into a deeply-pitted, badly-eroded, narrow two-lane strip of a crumbling material which might have once been passed off by Arkansas highway contractors as asphalt. A rusting highway marker indicated Little Rock was only an enticing 135 miles ahead. After the well-cared-for highways in Virginia and Tennessee, this nightmarish goat track they found themselves on followed along badly-kept fence lines, frequently making sharp, right-angle turns where the fences delineated the boundaries of rundown farms hardly bigger than residential city building lots. They had barely gone two miles along the zigzag obstacle course of ruts and potholes when they came up behind a traffic jam of four tractor-trailer rigs backed up behind a local farmer pulling a homemade trailer full of hogs, chugging along at barely ten miles an hour.

"Let me see the Arkansas map," Collier requested impatiently, holding out his hand while keeping a wary eye on the brake lights of a big oil-tanker in the slow-moving convoy ahead.

Opening the glove box, Emma passed across the Arkansas highway map Collier had picked up at their last gas stop in Memphis. Unfolding the new map, Collier carefully refolded it until it displayed the area of Arkansas which approximated their current location.

"Look, Honey. See here, just up ahead, U.S. 79 splits off U.S. 70 and bypasses Little Rock through Pine Bluff a little to the south. The mileage to Pine Bluff looks almost the same. On the other side of Pine Bluff, we can pick up 70 again about fifty miles west of Little Rock at Hot Springs. If these truckers continue straight on 70 toward Little Rock, let's take the southern route." Collier handed the map back to Emma.

"Well...I can't tell much by looking at the map. The two roads look the same except the one to Little Rock is red and the road through Pine Bluff is blue. They both seem to be major highways. I don't know anything at all about Arkansas. Pine Bluff certainly doesn't look as big as Little Rock, but it still looks to be a sizeable town." Emma shook her head uncertainly.

"If the road looks okay when we get to the turnoff, what do we have to lose? It's bad enough having to make a right-angle turn every quarter-mile, but anything beats having to follow these trucks for a hundred-and-thirty-five miles in this insufferable heat all the way to Little Rock at ten miles an hour," Collier grumbled, peering anxiously into the setting sun at the slow-moving convoy ahead.

Another fifteen minutes of driving at a snail's pace brought them to the turnoff to U.S 79. The sign read: Little Rock 129 miles, Pine Bluff 128 miles. When the creeping convoy of trucks ahead continued on U.S. 70 to Little Rock, Collier turned left on U.S. 79. Although the road now still zigzagged along the fence rows, there was almost no traffic as they passed through acre after acre of rice paddies, the full-grown rice stalks glowing a iridescent bright yellow-green against the setting sunlight.

On U.S. 79, they were able to make better speed for the next eight or ten miles until they came up behind an aromatic farm truck full of pigs. Fortunately, this time at the first wide place in the road, the farmer pulled over to let them pass. The trip continued virtually uninterrupted for the next hour-and-a-half, and, although the roadbed was still full of pot holes big enough to swallow a small car, its overall condition had improved slightly. The air perceptibly cooled after they began to climb out of the rice fields up through the pine- and hardwood-forested foothills. With the sky rapidly growing darker now, Collier switched his headlights on.

"There's no way we're going to stop here! We'll spend the night in Hot Springs," entering Pine Bluff, Emma declared, after carefully studying their options on the map.

As it turned out, there wasn't any inducement to stop in Pine Bluff, anyway. The entire town had closed down tight for the night. Past the courthouse square, they came upon the Pine Bluff Tourist Court, a rustic-looking establishment with buildings tackily veneered to look like rough-hewn log cabins. Despite the outside sign being turned off, a dim light shone through the curtained windows of the office with a single bulb burning outside and a dim VACANCY sign hanging wistfully in the glass-paned door.

"Keep driving," Emma commanded resolutely, when Collier slowed to take a closer look. "Let's get out of here."

From Pine Bluff, the road wound through the mountains to the little crossroads of Sheridan and continued through similar communities of on the eastern slopes of the Ouachita Range before finally connecting with U.S. 70 just east of Hot Springs. As they grew closer to Hot Springs, the surface of the road proved to be in slightly better repair, and they made it into the outskirts of the celebrated resort slightly after 2130 hours. Just outside the city limits, the road widened and became East Grand Avenue. Compared to the ghostly quiet of Pine Bluff, the outskirts of the bustling, celebrated, resort, once notorious for its private, high-stakes gambling clubs, was lit with signs advertising a variety of luxury hotels and spas, with an added abundance of less-pretentious tourist accommodations.

"Looks like we'll have no trouble finding a place to stay, but it's probably going to cost an arm and a leg. Notice how many of these snooty places use the newfangled term 'motel'? Whatever happened to good old American 'tourist cabins' and 'motor courts?' " Collier grumbled.

"Motel, schmotel, let's find a place to eat. Pull into that little restaurant up ahead. I'm starved." Emma pointed to a likely-looking establishment with a red neon sign blinking 'All-night Diner'. After giving the place an appraising look, Collier turned in when he saw the crowded parking lot was filled with cars displaying local license plates. Emma's choice of restaurants proved to be fortuitous. The home-style fare wasn't fancy, but it was tasty and filling and the prices were quite reasonable. When they finished eating, Collier asked the waitress how far it was to Lawton, Oklahoma, as she handed him the check.

"I don't know 'bout Oklahoma, 'ceptin' it takes a couple of hours to Mena— that's right near the state line. Howard, do you know how far Lawton, Oklahoma is from Mena?" anxious to help, the waitress asked the night cook.

"I don't rightly know where Lawton is. How 'bout you, John? You ever hear of Lawton, Oklahoma?" the cook asked a white-haired man at the far end of the counter. He was dressed in a coat and tie, but his suit had seen better days.

"Best I can recall it's somewhere south of Oklahoma City, near the Texas border," the older man replied.

"How far to Oklahoma City?" the cook asked the white-haired man.

"Beats hell out of me." The older man ruefully shook his head.

"If you're heading to Fort Sill, I just left there. It's right at three-hundred miles from here. You still got a full day of hard driving in front of you." Their accommodating informant was a young staff sergeant, in khakis with a chest full of ribbons, who had just stepped inside the door.

"Judas Priest! Three hundred miles? What's the best way to go from here?" Collier asked, crestfallen they still had that far to travel.

"Here, I got a map"—the young soldier unfolded a Texaco map from his hip pocket and quickly traced the route with his forefinger—"there isn't any easy way out of Arkansas. The only half-decent road is U.S. 270—that takes you over to Mount Ida, up through Fort Smith. From Fort Smith, you take 64 across to Sallisaw and pick up 69 at Checotah and rejoin 270 down here at McAlester...from there just follow the signs into Ada over to Paul's Valley and on into Lawton."

"Why go all the way up to Fort Smith when you can take this Route 88 just past Mount Ida into Mena and on into Oklahoma? It looks like it would save a lot of driving." Collier pointed to the place where 270 started turning north toward Fort Smith. He dimly recalled the bus ride from Fort Smith to Lawton back in February. As sick as he had been back then, his memory of that trip was something of a blur, except he remembered it was a tedious all-day ride.

"I don't know. See the broken lines on the map? That road is not hardtop. It may be okay, but that trail is likely to be deserted—no filling stations, certainly no telephones, probably not that many houses. Why take the chance? It's hard enough traveling through these Arkansas mountains on the so-called main highways—such as they are," the sergeant reminded him.

"You've got a point there," Collier conceded and jotted down the highway numbers on a paper napkin. He thanked the sergeant and returned his map before he paid the check. Outside, when they got back on Grand Avenue, Collier slowed as they approached The Arkansas Traveler Motor Court. Both the Vacancy and Air-conditioned signs were lit.

"Air-conditioned...I haven't slept in an air-conditioned hotel since I was in Richmond a few months back," Emma said wistfully. Even in the mountains and late at night, the heat remained oppressive.

"Let's go for it," Collier readily agreed.

"Two-fifty in advance," the tired-looking, middle-aged woman behind the desk said with a 'take-it-or-leave-it' look.

Removing a handful of loose bills from his trouser pocket, Collier grudgingly counted out three singles and handed them across the desk.

"Fill this out while I get your change." The woman slid a registration card across in front of him and handed back two quarters.

Dreading spending another second in such smothering heat, Collier quickly filled out the registration card, savoring the promise of sleeping in an honest-to-God, air-conditioned room. Without glancing at the registration, the woman handed him a key.

Inside their room, the refrigerated air from a noisy window unit washed over them. By 2300 hours, Emma had showered and had fallen into a troubled sleep.

Reluctantly dragging his aching, travel-weary bones out of the bed and into the shower at 0545, Collier was pleasantly surprised that Emma made no protest when he awakened her. Dressing quickly, they revisited the same cafe for breakfast. By 0700, the temperature was already near eighty degrees when Collier pulled into a Texaco filling station on West Grand Avenue out by the airport. While the attendant pumped the gas, Collier helped himself to a road map of Arkansas-Louisiana, Mississippi, and East Texas-Oklahoma and carefully surveyed the route ahead, trying to get a firm picture of the best route to take them across the remaining mountains into Oklahoma on the first grueling leg of the remaining 300 miles to Lawton.

At the early hour on Sunday morning, traffic on the twisting mountain road was almost non-existent, and Emma adjusted her little travel pillow and quickly fell asleep. His attention focused on negotiating the badly-eroded and aptly-named pig-trail—the perfect description for U.S. 270, Collier lapsed into an anxious preoccupation with the uncertain status of his OCS application and how he could break the news to Emma if he found that he had been turned down. Lost in this unsettling reverie, Collier had lost all perception of time and distance when, a few miles west of Mount Ida, he spotted a roadside sign up ahead: U.S. 270, FORT SMITH - 96 miles. A hundred yards or so beyond the larger sign, a second, smaller, sign read: Arkansas State Road 88, MENA - 22 Miles with an arrow pointing to the left.

Beyond the second sign, Collier quickly spotted the tempting turnoff to the shortcut a couple-hundred yards ahead.

When he drew nearly abreast of Arkansas State Road 88, as far as Collier could see—before it disappeared around a sharp curve—the side road was paved with an asphalt surface at least as serviceable as U.S. 270. On impulse, he eased onto the shoulder and rechecked his road map. According to the map, Arkansas 88 looked pretty much a straight shot into Mena. But the broken-line legend on the map indicated the route was a "Semi-surfaced, hard-surfaced road." A further notation explained: *"Apt to be dusty when dry, muddy when wet."* Obviously, this meant that most of the road was graveled, not blacktop.

Without a cloud in the sky, the arithmetic was simple. The road signs clearly showed that Arkansas 88 cut 70-odd miles from U.S. 270 which went 80 miles further north before finally turning west, just south of Fort Smith. Moreover, the map showed that he could probably save at least another 50-60 miles after he crossed the Arkansas line by taking secondary roads, from Mena into Oklahoma, which offered almost a straight shot into McAlester.

Discouraged by the thought of the extra miles, impulsively Collier turned onto Arkansas 88 and moved cautiously ahead.

Although Collier had to admit he was not all surprised, he was more than a little disappointed to find the black-top only lasted for less than a mile before it turned into a thinly-graveled surface. On the other hand, the road was at least as wide as U.S. 270 and, so far, the going seemed easy enough. After traveling another two or three miles, caution overtook him again when he encountered the rusting hulk of a farm truck resting halfway down the steep embankment.

As he crept cautiously along, the road got narrower and the drop-off down the mountain more precipitous. After what seemed an eternity, they eventually came upon a group of houses near a tiny, white, clapboard church bearing a sign: Mountainfork Baptist Church. Consulting the car's odometer, he calculated he had negotiated a scant 13 white-knuckle miles. Ruefully, a glance at his wristwatch told him the ordeal had taken almost a full hour. The map indicated 17 more miles to Mena. He gritted his teeth: *Nothing left to do but forge ahead.*

Although the road was not perceptibly better, Collier had grown accustomed to driving on the rough, graveled surface and was now making slightly better time. Almost another hour passed when the road suddenly became hard-surfaced with blacktop and he slowed to read a little sign.

MENA, ARKANSAS
Birthplace of T. TEXAS TYLER
Songwriter and performer of the song "A Deck of Cards"

With the perceptible slowing of the car, Emma stirred awake and stretched and yawned.   "Have you ever heard of T. Texas Tyler?" she asked as she sat up straight and read the sign.

"Sure. He's the guy who did that corny record about the young soldier during WWII in North Africa who was threatened with court martial for spreading out his deck of playing cards while the chaplain was holding religious services. It's really more a recitation than a song..."

"Oh, yes, I've heard it. Wasn't it sort of country?" Emma yawned again and fluffed her pillow.

"Uhm-m...sort of corny anyway." Collier nodded. "But country or corny or not, that one record probably made him rich...and got his name on that sign back there." Collier laughed.

"I have to pee real bad, Honey. Hurry and find a nice place to pull over." Emma looked anxiously down the tree-lined street.

At the center of the rustic village, Collier pulled into what appeared to be the only filling station in town. Much to his surprise, the establishment was open. While Emma went to use the Ladies Room, Collier told the attendant to fill his tank.

"Do you have a pay phone?" Collier asked, watching the attendant pump the lever.

"We don't have no pay phones in Mena. You can use the phone on the wall beside the register inside. Give the crank a couple of turns, then give the operator the number you want to call. Just ask her to give you the time and charges. You can pay me when you're done."

"Okay, thanks." Collier nodded and went inside and hesitantly took the ear piece off the hook and gave the handle on the side of the box a hard crank. When the operator came on the line, he gave her the number for the orderly room at Fort Sill. Several minutes passed before he heard a ringing on the other end.

"This is Ramsey. I'm still on the road. Have I received any orders yet?" Collier asked the duty NCO and held his breath.

"Yeah—they finally got here. You're to report to OCS on the seventh of July. Your orders are on the captain's desk," the corporal told him.

"How about Herb Rudolph?" Collier asked, breathing a silent prayer.

"Rudolph ain't going to OCS, but he is staying here at Sill. He got assigned to FARTC as cadre." Collier's heart sank as he listened to the corporal deliver the disappointing news.

"Does Herb know it yet?"

"Yeah, he got here late last night. He and his wife are at the Guest Quarters on Post."

"Okay, thanks. If you see Herb, tell him I should be arriving in Lawton sometime this afternoon." Collier said goodbye and hung up. He hated that Herb didn't make it, but knowing he finally had been assigned an OCS class was like having the Rock of Gibraltar lifted from his back.

Chapter Twenty-six

AFTER THEY LEFT MENA, ARKANSAS, and Collier resumed negotiating the treacherous dirt road through the western elevations of the Ouachita Mountains, the morning temperatures still hovered in the refreshingly-cool high-70s, and Emma had little trouble going back to sleep. When they finally stopped in Ada, Oklahoma around noon for gas and a cold Coca-Cola, the late-morning temperature had risen well into the 90s, which made going back to sleep virtually impossible. By the time they reached Lawton, Emma was nervously considering resorting to the wide-mouth Bell canning jar to relieve her swollen bladder.

The tired, decades-old, bank building in downtown Lawton looked to Emma as if it might be waiting to be robbed by the notorious Bonnie Parker and Clyde Barrow, as the incongruous, modern electric clock over the entrance scrolled, blinking: SUNDAY....JUNE 8....2:59PM....TEMP 102....SUNDAY.... Along the sidewalk in the center of the town, an Indian family strolled in beaded-buckskin regalia, all four members—dad, mom, brother and baby sister—licking fast-melting ice-cream cones. At the end of the second block, Collier turned right onto Fort Sill Boulevard and drove up to the main gate and pulled into the information center at the right-hand side of the gate. After a few minutes, he came back holding a temporary pass for their car.

Following Fort Sill Boulevard past familiar fenced areas filled with artillery pieces and at least two motor pools before passing by row after row of barracks, they finally turned on a street marked Quinette Road and pulled to a stop in front of a plain, wooden structure which had obviously been converted from a regular Army barracks. The neat military sign in front read: Guest Quarters.

"I have to find the ladies room quick." Emma got out of the car and headed up the walk.

Waiting inside in the common sitting room, the slightly-pudgy soldier with a receding hairline stepped forward and presented himself without waiting for Collier to introduce him. "I'm Herb Rudolph. Louise will be back any minute.

She called about an ad for an air-conditioned apartment that sounded too good to be true and went to take a look."

"Collier speaks highly of you, Herb."—Emma shook his hand—"I don't want to appear to be rude, but I desperately need to find the nearest powder room."

By the time she had freshened up and rejoined the two men, they were engaged in an animated conversation about Collier's acceptance in OCS. Not wanting to interrupt, Emma took a seat, picked up a copy of *The Daily Oklahoman* and scanned an article about Ike's campaign promises to bring peace in Korea.

She had barely started reading when Herb exclaimed, "Here's Louise now." Lowering the newspaper, Emma watched as a trifle overweight, blonde woman came bouncing through the door.

"You're not going to believe this place. It's partially furnished, and the woman's only asking a hundred-thirty a month...it has two big bedrooms...we could split the cost. We have to hurry. The woman would only promise to hold it for an hour." Without introduction or preamble, Louise Rudolph started babbling breathlessly in her high-pitched voice about the fabulous, furnished apartment she had just seen in Lawton. Before Emma knew quite what was going on, she and Collier were back in the Studebaker following Herb's Nash Ambassador.

Passing out through the gate at Fort Sill Boulevard, they had only traveled a short distance when Herb turned right onto Cache Road. After another couple of blocks, he turned left onto 16th Street into an impressively-affluent, tree-filled neighborhood of spacious older homes. A couple more turns and they pulled into the driveway of a rambling, ranch-style house.

"This is way out of our league. This is where the officers live," Collier protested as they followed Herb into the drive.

"Half of one-thirty is only sixty-five...remember you get a pay raise when you start OCS?" Emma reminded, surprised at his reaction. It wasn't at all like Collier to be so chintzy about money.

"Well, yeah. But a buck sergeant's pay, including the dependent's allotment is barely two hundred. That doesn't leave a lot to live on." He avoided looking her in the eye.

"I'm a registered nurse, remember? I'm going to find a job. Come on, let's at least go look. After all, you wouldn't want me living in a slum." Emma opened the door and got out of the car, trying to catch up with Herb and Louise. To her chagrin, Collier lagged reluctantly behind.

"Collier, will you please hurry up..." she called back over her shoulder.

"Go ahead. I'll catch up. It's too damn hot to hurry," Collier grumbled and waved her on.

Emma finally caught up to the Rudolphs at the door.

"Hilda Birdsong, this is Emma Ramsey," Louise made a hasty introduction. "Emma and her husband, Collier, would be sharing the apartment if we take it."

"I'm pleased to meet you. Go in and look around—take your time. I'll wait outside and make sure your husband finds you." The woman smiled, turning back to wait for Collier.

"Thank you. Oh, this is really lovely..." Emma squealed, heading to catch the Rudolphs.

The entrance door opened directly into a sparsely-furnished, combination kitchen, dining, and living area. Off of this multi-purpose room, two doors opened to separate bedrooms connected by doors to a spacious common bath. Although the house was comfortably air-conditioned with a central unit, both bedrooms were rather small and unfurnished and not at all well-lit — illuminated only by high, narrow windows on the outside walls. The common bathroom was more than adequate with a good-sized tub and shower with sliding-glass doors which seemed to work okay. Immediately, Emma's warning flags went up as she contemplated having to share the bathroom with anyone but Collier.

"Well? I like it. What do you think?" Louise asked her as she finished inspecting the second of the two bedrooms.

"Uhm-m...I'm not sure. I'd like a chance to compare..." Emma shrugged.

"We like it. It's not far from the post and convenient to the bus," Louise insisted.

"Uhm-m-m?...I don't know. What about furniture? Beds for the bedrooms? Are you just going to sleep on the floor? And what about night tables and a lamp and chairs? We'll need those, too," Emma replied, resisting the feeling that Louise was trying to bulldoze her into making an ill-considered decision.

"I have a brand-new mattress for one bedroom. You can find another mattress, a pair of box springs and cheap bed frames and the other pieces at the used-furniture place downtown. In the meantime, one of you can bring my mattress in and sleep on the floor. There is china, flatware and cooking utensils in the kitchen cabinets. Of course, you have to supply your own towels and bed linens." When Emma turned around, the Birdsong woman had followed them in and was standing right behind her. Collier was still nowhere in sight.

"Linens are not a problem. I have my own," Emma said.

"We do, too. You can have that mattress. Herb and I will get our own bed downtown," Louise spoke up. She clearly wanted to rent the apartment.

"Uhmm...I'm not sure. Did you see my husband? I need to get his opinion," Emma asked the lady of the house.

"He went back to get his cigarettes from the car—he said he'd be right in."

"I have to wait 'til Collier sees it before we make up our minds." Emma looked to Herb and Louise for understanding.

"Well, go get him. We haven't got all day." Louise sniffed impatiently.

"Well, speak of the devil." Herb nodded as Collier shambled through the door.

"Come back here, Collier, and take a look. Herb and Louise want to go ahead and take this place." Emma took Collier's hand and pulled him toward the bedroom to the right of the bathroom door.

"I thought the place was furnished. Where's the bed?" Collier asked immediately, glancing around the bare room.

"Mrs. Birdsong says she has one mattress, but one of us will have to buy another. She says she doesn't have bedsprings or bed frames. If we don't want to sleep on the floor, we'll both have to find springs and frames in town." Emma gave Collier an anxious look.

"Tell you what I'll do. Go to the used furniture store on the Square near the movie house and pick out another mattress and two bedsprings and frames—and get a couple of cheap night tables, too. I'll call them and pay the cost. After all, I'll need the stuff for future tenants. My housekeeper's brother, Moses Black Elk, has a truck. If you hurry, Moses Black Elk can round up some boys from the Indian School and have whatever you pick out delivered this afternoon. I pay all utilities, but you'll have to have the phone transferred to your name...work it out between yourselves. " The lady of the house made the offer virtually irresistible.

"Well, come on. What are we waiting for? We can't beat a deal like that." Louise clapped her hands and headed for the door with Herb in tow.

"Wait up, not so fast. Collier hasn't a chance to tell me what he thinks."

"Well...the place looks okay to me. After all, I'll be cooped up in OCS most of the time. But it would ease my mind to know you're living with friends...and you can't beat the neighborhood. This is a first-class section of town—mostly doctors, lawyers, business professionals and high-ranking military officers who live off-post. Can we afford it? How much are we talking about?" Collier frowned.

"One-thirty a month—your half is sixty-five," Louise interrupted before Emma had a chance to answer.

"We were paying almost fifty back at Franklin Heights—but we were both working. Don't forget, even with your allotment, I'll still only be drawing a little over one-twenty a month," Collier reminded.

"That's not a problem. I'm going to start looking for a job tomorrow, first thing," Emma assured him. "I like the idea of living in this highly-respectable neighborhood. Most likely, I'll have to take a job working third shift to begin with, and I don't want to be driving home in the dead of night through a rough section of town."

"I know the head nurse at the local hospital. An experienced registered nurse like you shouldn't have trouble finding work." The Birdsong person spoke up again. With the prospect of the couples renting her vacant apartment, she was already taking a proprietary interest.

"What sort of lease do we have to sign?" Collier asked the woman.

"I'd expect you to sign a commitment to at least ninety days," the woman said.

"That's reasonable enough. As a matter of fact, we'd probably like the agreement to give us the option to renew," Collier said, thoughtfully.

"I'm okay with that," the homeowner agreed.

"Okay, what are we waiting for?" Collier took Emma by the hand and headed for the door.

Collier had little trouble finding a parking space near the used-furniture store and they all got right to the task at hand. By the time they finished picking out the pieces they wanted, Moses Black Elk had arrived with a dilapidated truck and a husky teenage Indian helper and had already started loading the truck.

"Tell your bosslady we are going to get some supper and we'll be right along," handing him a ten-dollar bill, Collier instructed Moses Black Elk. After he left, the four of them walked down the street to a nearby café. When they had finished eating and arrived back at their new apartment, Moses Black Elk was already setting up the beds. Shortly afterward, the Birdsong woman showed up with a lease agreement and ballpoint pen in hand.

With Indian handymen hard at work, within an hour, Emma had helped Collier move their meager possessions from the car and had already made their bed. Closing tight the outside door, the air-conditioning felt good.

"Flip you to see who goes first for the shower," Collier offered to the Rudolphs.

"I think you should let us go first. Herb has to report at FARTC at the crack of dawn," Louise said. Emma bit her tongue to keep from reminding her that *they* had driven all day in the broiling Oklahoma sun. Providentially, Emma was rescued from venting her resentment when the Birdsong woman reentered unannounced through the door connecting their new apartment with the main house.

"I didn't intend to come in without knocking, but you can see I had my hands full. Let me set this down on the table. Welcome to your new home," their new landlady said cheerfully. She was carrying a steaming, fresh-baked apple pie and a quart of vanilla ice cream.

Watching their landlady leave, Emma grudgingly admitted despite her well-rounded fanny, Hilda Birdsong was a handsome woman. Picking daintily at the pie and ice cream, Emma idly wondered if her own derriere would start to spread as she aged. Too tired to care, she helped Louise wash the dishes and store the remaining food. After Louise left the room, Emma called her mother back in Salem to give her their new address and phone number.

"I almost forget to tell you, dear, but a Major Moseley called from Texas. He said he was an old friend from the VA and was trying to track you down. I told him you had gone back to Fort Sill with Collier. He wanted to know how to get in touch with you, but I told him I hadn't heard from you since you left here. He said he'd call back later."

"Whatever you do, Mother, don't give him my address or phone number."

"Well, I won't, dear...but he seemed so nice."

"Oh, he's nice enough I guess, but I just don't want to stay in touch with him. Trust me, I have my reasons. Goodnight, Mother, I'm dead tired and need to sleep now."

"Alright, dear. Write me when you have the chance."

Collier was already asleep when Emma climbed into bed and lay there in the dark beside him with confusing images of Trey Moseley dancing in the darkened theater of her mind. Just before she dropped into fretful oblivion, Emma wondered sleepily how the Birdsong woman knew she was a nurse.

BOOK TWO

CHAPTER TWENTY-SEVEN

THE DAILY OKLAHOMAN
Oklahoma City, Oklahoma, Thursday, June 11, 1952
KOJE MASSACRE BY REDS BARED

KOJE ISLAND, Korea, June 11 - (AP) - The still bleeding bodies of eight North Korean prisoners of war murdered by hard-core Reds were dug up Wednesday from a rubble-covered wall in Compound 77.

THE ROANOKE TIMES
Roanoke, Virginia, Friday, June 12, 1952
BLOODIEST BATTLE OF THE YEAR RAGING

SEOUL, Thursday, June 12 - (AP) - Allied raiders, supported by planes and tanks, struck again today against Chinese positions on the Western Korean Front on a scale that probably will mark this week as the bloodiest thus far of 1952.

THE DAILY OKLAHOMAN
Oklahoma City, Oklahoma, Thursday, June 26, 1952
BRITISH OFFICIAL LASHES AT ATLEE ON YALU CHARGE

LONDON, June 25 - (AP) - Former Prime Minister Atlee charged Wednesday the big American bombing of Yalu power plants in Korea carried the "conditions of total war" to Red China and endangered chances of an armistice.

THE DAILY OKLAHOMAN
Oklahoma City, Oklahoma, Monday, June 30, 1952
BALDY'S MUDDY, BLOODY
By Jim Becker

A WESTERN FRONT OUTPOST, Korea, June 29 - (AP) - Blood dripped steadily from the three litters. It seeped through the canvas and dripped like a leaky faucet into pools of rain water, turning them pink. Strapped to the litters under rain-soaked blankets were the bodies of three soldiers...

A column of infantrymen—grimy, unshaved, mud-soaked—plodded down the steep, slimy path leading to Old Baldy, a round, bare hill where an allied outpost had fought off a series of hammer-like communist blows.

THE DAILY OKLAHOMAN
Oklahoma City, Oklahoma, Friday, July 4, 1952
90-PLUS WEATHER ON TAP FOR HOLIDAY

The mercury went up to a high of 93 degrees in Oklahoma City Thursday at 3 p.m. The low was recorded at 7 a.m. at 71 degrees. The forecast calls for more of the same over the weekend holiday.

SEOUL, KOREA, Monday, July 7 (AP) – Communist troops fighting from heavily fortified bunkers hurled back an armor-supported Allied raiding column which knifed into Red lines in the outskirts of Panmunjon shortly before midnight...

THE DAILY OKLAHOMAN'S WEATHER FORECASTS of temperatures in the low 90s had gotten to be something of a joke around Lawton and Fort Sill. For the nearly three weeks since June 9 when Collier and Emma first arrived on Post, the daytime highs had exceeded 100 degrees every day.

With time on his hands until he reported to OCS on July 7, Collier had begun reading Edna Ferber's new novel, *Giant*, which—beginning in the June issue—was being serialized in *The Ladies Home Journal* and was scheduled for publication by Doubleday in November. Aside from being a fascinating history of the "new Texas" with a thinly-disguised, scathing caricature of the wildly-flamboyant oil wildcatter, Glenn McCarthy, this new Ferber saga took on the important social issues of discrimination and exploitation of Texas's large Mexican population by Texas land barons and their newly-oil-rich counterparts in the socially-inept Texas white aristocracy. So far as Collier had progressed in reading the serialization, Ms. Ferber's new book promised to be a bold and telling indictment of the ongoing perpetuation of economic enslavement of large populations of poor, largely ethnic Americans—proof of a sort that in America, money made the economically advantaged more equal than equal.

Although Collier felt prepared for the upcoming grind of OCS, he still made daily lists and checked them endlessly. Just before he graduated Basic Training at FARTC, he had talked to a recently-busted-out OCS candidate who had told him horror tales about changing uniforms six or seven times a day in a training regimen that required even fatigue uniforms to be lightly starched and sharply pressed. The ex-candidate advised Collier to have at least seven extra sets of fatigues and four extra sets of dress uniforms in order to have a minimum of three, freshly-laundered changes of uniforms every day. Although Collier fervently hoped some of these tales were pure bullshit, he took advantage of his remaining free time to make a visit to the Post Quartermaster and purchase an additional three complete sets of both fatigues and dress khakis plus two shiny-new pairs of regulation combat boots, which he planned to use strictly for daily inspection.

On Emma's trips into town to shop and make application for work at the local hospital—accompanied by Hilda Birdsong, which made Collier extremely nervous—Emma had found a local woman who took in sewing, specializing in altering uniforms. The seamstress was not only a wizard at alterations, but was also expert in attaching military insignia to uniforms, conforming precisely to OCS regulations. With little time to waste, Collier and Emma took all of Collier's uniforms, old and new, to the seamstress with a bag full of newly-purchased insignia to be sewn in place. When they picked up the completed alterations, they were pleasantly surprised to find that the efficient seamstress had taken the entire lot to a laundry-and-dry-cleaning establishment specializing in starching and pressing uniforms to comply with the most rigid military standards.

Also as part of his preparation, Collier purchased several sets of a costly new kind of brass insignia which did not require the constant, time-consuming polishing with a Brasso cloth as did the easily-tarnished Quartermaster-issue brass issued during his processing at Fort Meade.

With all this preparation completed, Collier packed his remaining gear and moved out of the Casual Battery barracks into their new apartment at Hilda Birdsong's house in Lawton—which proved to be something of a disappointment. With daytime temperatures soaring over 100 degrees, Hilda's antiquated, grossly-overworked air-conditioner proved pretty much unequal to the task. While by early morning the apartment would have moderated to a quite-tolerable mid-70 degrees, by bedtime, the temperature would climb back to nearly 80 which—despite their wives' grumblings—Herb and Collier knew from recent experience was actually like a gift from heaven.

Lying in the darkness in bed at night in their oven-like bedroom with a newly-purchased electric fan recirculating hot air over them, Collier tried not to consider what it was going to be like returning to barracks living when he entered OCS the coming week.

When Emma went to put in her application for work at the local hospital, she had quite fortuitously found two days work doing private duty with the dying matriarch of a wealthy local family. In self-defense in her absence, Collier took the opportunity to invest 35 cents in the matinee double-feature at the air-conditioned Lawton movie house which was as refreshingly cool as the large, walk-in meat locker at his Uncle Ferris Saunders' butcher shop at the Roanoke City Market.

> *Dear Collier,*
> *I don't really know exactly where I am. All I know is that it took us four days marching all day to get here from where we landed. Our troop carriers landed us at least a mile from shore in mud so deep it almost sucked the soles from our boots. I've never been so scared in my life. I could see bullets splashing in the mud beside me as we made our way to firm ground in a small city. From there, it took us a full-morning's march to make it to Seoul which looked totally destroyed...the destruction everywhere is unbelievable...*

Tuesday, July 1, Collier received a brief note from Bo describing his landing on Korean soil.

With what Collier recalled of magazine and television pictures of MacArthur's famous landing at Inchon Harbor, Collier was certain Bo's unit had been put ashore at low tide in the same area. To imagine slogging knee-deep in mud with bullets landing all around you, gave Collier cause for serious self-examination. Would he make a good officer? Could he lead men bravely into the face of enemy fire?

Emma's patient died Thursday, July 3 leaving her free to enjoy the July Fourth Holiday. To celebrate Independence Day, Friday morning, Hilda Birdsong talked Collier and Emma and the Rudolphs into joining her for an old-fashioned, Fourth-of-July picnic at a delightfully secluded—and surprisingly uncrowded—private swimming beach on Lake Lawtonka, out past Medicine Creek at the base of Mt. Scott.

The lake water was crystal clear and surprisingly refreshing. With their blankets spread under a shady overhang of water oaks, cottonwoods and willows lining a meandering tributary of Medicine Creek, the picnic proved to be an all-around success, not to mention a welcome relief from the heat in town.

Lying on a blanket in the shade of an enormous water oak, eyeballing from beneath hooded eyelids the sensual posturings of curvaceous, young females in their skimpy bathing suits, Collier found it necessary to go into the water to adjust his anatomy in order to conceal an embarrassing erection. When Emma caught him at it the second time, she tugged him into the lake. Swimming into the lee of the wooden diving raft, she pulled the crotch of her two-piece suit aside and brazenly fucked him right there in the water within sight of at least a dozen people. The thrilling conceit of their audacious coupling was so overpowering they both reached climax in less time than it took to think about it. Later, back on the blanket, Collier caught Emma looking at him with an open expression of complete adoration as she contemplated the outrageous impudence of their erotic escapade.

Perhaps a half-hour had passed with Emma and Louise taking the sun, and Herb snoring quietly in the shade, when Hilda shook Collier from his post-coital stupor and asked if he minded accompanying her to the country store at Meers to replenish their ice.

"Not at all." Suspicious of Hilda's intentions, but afraid a refusal would rouse unnecessary attention, Collier followed her dutifully to the car.

Collier's suspicions were quickly confirmed. They had only traveled up Route 49 a short distance past the road leading up Mount Scott, when Hilda pulled the Caddy off into a dirt side road and parked under a thick grove of willows and cottonwoods. Leaving the motor running to afford the benefit of the Fleetwood's custom air-conditioning, she pushed back the seat, leaned across and kissed him hungrily on the mouth.

"I saw what you and Emma were doing in the water behind the diving raft. How do you think that made me feel? Are you trying to drive me crazy?" Hilda breathed hotly in his ear when she finally came up for air.

"I...ah...uhm-m..." Collier sputtered, trying hard to collect his wits.

"And, while we're on the subject, what on earth were you thinking when you persuaded your wife and friends to rent my apartment? Don't you know how much it hurts me to lie in bed alone knowing you're fucking that sexy young wife of yours just on the other side of my bedroom wall?" Her breath was coming in short raspy sounds.

Still speechless, Collier watched wide-eyed, as she pulled down the straps of her one-piece bathing suit and wriggled it down over her hips and knees, letting it fall to the richly-carpeted floorboards. In less than a heartbeat, she turned to him bare-ass naked, shoving him roughly by the shoulders back across the wide bench seat. Staring open-mouthed up at her cantaloupe breasts with their rosy silver-dollar-pancake nipples, like a fly in a web, he watched as she scrambled to her knees behind the steering wheel, leaned over him and started pulling down his swimming trunks. Before he could mount a protest—as if he actually wanted to—she had freed his rock-hard dick and was riding him like some sex-crazed broncobuster from an old Frederick Remington painting.

"Goddamn, it Hilda...have you lost your mind? I don't have any protection...are you wearing your diaphragm?" He blurted, on the verge of coming to orgasm.

"Forget the diaphragm...oh, my god..." she gasped as he felt her begin to shudder in tiny waterfalls of ecstasy as he erupted inside her. Despite his protests, she continued to ride him until her head finally collapsed upon his chest. Lying there in a dreamy state of post-orgasmic ecstacy with the muted sound of Hank Williams' twangy voice singing "...your cheating heart will make you weep..." drifting from the Fleetwood radio, Collier idly reflected upon the French expression *la petite morte*—"the little death," which the French so appropriately employed to describe the orgasm.

"Hilda...my god, how long have we been gone? Emma...Herb and Louise...they're not stupid. They'll know we've been up to something. We've still got to go out to Meers for ice." When his head began to clear, Collier made an attempt to arouse Hilda from her languor and push her upright.

"Relax. We've been gone less than three-quarters of an hour. I already have an extra bag of ice in the insulated chest in the trunk," she sighed with deep contentment, not at all in a hurry to release his still-semi-turgid penis from the pulsing confinement of her vagina. In a moment, she sat upright and began a slow, rhythmic movement against him, quickly building into another orgasm.

"Follow me." When she had finished ravishing him for the second time, Hilda opened the door and motioned him to follow her along a narrow path through the trees to the bank of the small stream. Wading into the waist-deep pool, they quickly rinsed their bodies of the evidence of their coupling. By the time they had slipped into their swim suits and were headed back down 49 toward Lake Lawtonka to rejoin the others, the fancy car's air-conditioning had blown them almost completely dry.

"Oh, Honey, I didn't mean to be so rough on you." That night in the shower, Emma crooned as she lovingly rubbed some scented body lotion on the irritated surface of Collier's abused penis.

"It's alright," Collier said, watching with amazement as his battered penis began to swell again.

Slightly sunburned from spending almost the entire weekend in the relatively cool water of Lake Lawtonka, when he arose and went to urinate on Monday morning, Collier could barely stand to touch his penis. Yet, as sore as his poor member might be, he still dreaded the thought of enforced celibacy during the next eight weeks, restricted to the confines of OCS.

At 0840 hours, he kissed Emma goodbye when she dropped him off at the OCS reception area. Lugging his well-stuffed duffel to a growing pile of similarly bulging bags, Collier left it with the others. Lighting a Lucky, he ambled over to join the group of perhaps fifty or sixty eager candidates. His heart sank contemplating having to spend the next six months undergoing the grueling OCS regimen with this bunch of overgrown Eagle Scouts. He had hardly time to introduce himself when a grizzled sergeant walked out on the tiny stoop of the converted barracks building and motioned them all inside.

"At ease! Smoke if you've got 'em. Sit on the floor if you want to—unless you prefer to stand. Now tone it down and let me have your attention up here." Inside the sweltering, seemingly-airless room, the sergeant quickly quieted the expectant buzz. In addition to the sergeant, standing against the rear wall, was a group of three officers—a captain and two first lieutenants—and another master sergeant. Standing at parade rest on a small platform with a lectern situated against the far wall, all five were outfitted in impeccably-starched khakis with bright-red tabs on their epaulets. Each of these stonefaced gargoyles was wearing a chest-full of battle ribbons.

Unsmiling, the Captain stepped to the lectern and spoke in a well-moderated, but clear and commanding voice, "Welcome to Easy Battery, Class Three-zero of Fort Sill's Artillery Officer Candidate School. I am Captain Jesse W. Whitley, your Tactical Battery Commander. To my right is Tactical Lieutenant Frank Robinson, and on his right is your Tactical Lieutenant, William Suit."

As Whitley made the introductions, each officer took a half-step forward and saluted. After Lieutenant Suit stepped back in place, Captain Whitley continued with the introductions of the Master Sergeants. "To my far left is your Tactical Master Sergeant, William Grubbs, and on my immediate left is Tactical Master Sergeant, Jacob Ernst." Both sergeants followed the same protocol as their commissioned officers, stepping slightly forward and saluting before they stepped back.

"Again welcome, gentlemen, and congratulations for being selected for Officer Candidate Training. On behalf of my Tac Staff, I want to assure you we are honored to be serving with you and look forward to watching your progress over the next twenty-two weeks here at Fort Sill OCS. Wthout further preamble, Lieutenants Robinson and Suit and I will turn you over to Sergeants Grubbs and Ernst. I wish you all success." Whitley saluted again and nodded to his officers as they all did a smart about face and left the room through a door at the rear of the room.

"Alright, give me your attention up here," Master Sergeant Grubbs growled as soon as the officers left the room. As if by some magical transformation, the heat-bedraggled, ragtag collection of would-be artillery officers stiffened, somehow aware there would be no nonsense in the presence of this battle-seasoned duo. "Knowing full well you are of very limited ability to understand plain English and certain you have limited capacity to remember anything at all, my name is Master Sergeant William Grubbs. It will be my unfortunate duty to play nursemaid to the Alpha Section of Easy Battery, Artillery OCS Class Three-zero. My able counterpart, Master Sergeant Jacob Ernst, will be in charge of Baker Section. In all fairness, it is my duty to inform you the average attrition rate in this school is sixty-seven percent—that means only one out of three make it through. Look around you carefully. If, through some foul oversight of our Almighty Maker, you should make it through this next twenty-two weeks to become an officer, the candidate on your left and the candidate on your right will not be with you. Make no mistake, from this moment forward, it is not only my—and Sergeant Ernst's—sworn duty to oversee your training and performance, it is our dedication...and our fervent wish...to make sure none of you pathetic excuses for soldiers graduate from this school. It is completely distasteful to both of us to think the day might come when we would have to salute any one of you." He stopped speaking and let his steely gaze wander around the room to make certain he was completely understood. When the sergeant's icy stare briefly locked eyeball-to-eyeball with his, Collier was determined not to let the bastard stare him down. In that electric instant, Collier was certain he had become a marked man.

"Now, there are certain things about Officer Candidate Training you must understand. Despite the seeming impossibility of the task, we here are determined to make gentlemen of you all. From this moment forward, you will be severely reprimanded and duly assessed demerits for using any foul language or curse words. While we probably will tolerate and overlook an occasional 'doggone' or 'darn', you would be well advised to forget them all. We are seasoned combat veterans whose hearing is not always the best and sometimes we might misunderstand. Any Tac Staff member or Upperclassman hearing any of you utter off-color language of any kind unworthy of an officer of the United States Army will immediately assess you with fifteen demerits—automatically depriving you of your weekend pass. And you are on your honor as a future officer and gentleman to report your own crimes and misdemeanors and accordingly be duty-bound to assess yourself for these violations."

For the better part of the next hour, Collier stood with sweat running down the crack of his ass while the pair of mossback sergeants took turns trying to convince the lot of them that they would be better off to resign the first thing tomorrow morning before they all busted out tomorrow night. Finally, they were ordered outside and marched—carrying their duffels—about halfway up the main street where they were dismissed under the watchful eye of a group of predatory Redbird upperclassmen who were to be the first of a succession of demanding, supercilious—if not downright malicious—martinets overseeing their torture for the next eighteen weeks. Eighteen weeks being the magical—most certainly unattainable—period of time one had to survive in this diabolical hellhole in order to have one's mind twisted enough to be afforded the privilege of wearing the red tabs of a Redbird upperclassman. As soon as they were assigned to a barracks, the Redbirds in charge had them count off by "twos" before they were ordered to fall into the barracks, where the "twos"—including Collier—were instructed to haul their duffels upstairs and choose a "cubicle."

"As soon as you choose a cubicle, put your duffels on your beds, and open all the windows, top and bottom—we need to get some air circulating up there." The Redbird in charge sent them up the steps.

Upstairs, Collier and his new barracks-mates found the familiar open space of the regulation Army barracks sub-divided into two-bed cubicles using freestanding partitions made of unpainted two-by-fours and pre-finished sheetrock panels resembling crude approximations of homemade Oriental screens. Except for the cubicle divisions, the only other difference between this barracks and the one he'd lived in at FARTC was a lowered ceiling using cheap fiberboard ceiling tiles. The Redbird had not overstated the need to circulate some air; the upstairs sleeping area was as hot as a Death Valley crematorium. Even after opening all the windows, the barracks fairly reeked of *eau de combat boot.*

"I'm Joe Rollins. The Redbird told me I should bunk with you?" After opening the window, Collier turned to find a stocky, compact Negro, who barely came up to his chin, standing beside the righthand bunk. The slightly-balding soldier was already graying at the temples of his close-cropped, nappy-headed hairline and looked several years older. Two prominent front gold teeth lit Rollins' grin.

"I'm Collier Ramsay. Good to meet you Rollins. Welcome to the slaughterhouse." Collier stuck out his hand. Despite his bemusement at being assigned what was most likely Class Three-zero's only black man for his cubicle mate, for the first time since he'd left home this morning, Collier allowed himself to smile.

"Where're you from Rollins?" Collier asked as the new arrival seated himself on his footlocker and opened up his duffel.

"If you mean where in the Army, I just got back from Korea two weeks ago. I spent almost a year in the vicinity of Old Baldy in a one-o-five howitzer battery before I got sent back here to OCS. Past two weeks, I been home on leave in little town named Bluffton next door to the South Carolina-Georgia line. It's right across the river from Savannah."

"Well, welcome to our little country club, Rollins...or should I call you Joe?"

"Either way...but Joe is fine," the serious pocket-sized soldier replied.

"Call me Collier. Rollins and Collier—sounds like a vaudeville team." Collier chuckled.

"If you don't mind my asking, where you from...before the Army, I mean." Rollins was unwinding an olive-drab GI towel encasing the shiniest pair of genuine Corcoran combat boots Collier had ever seen.

"Virginia...near Roanoke," Collier answered as his eyes fairly bugged out of his head, watching Rollins extract a second pair of towel-wrapped Corcorans, placing both pairs carefully on top of his unmade bunk. Both pairs were laced in neat ladder rows.

"Okay candidates, let's get to work and make this place fit for human habitation." Collier and his new cubicle-mate had barely begun to unpack and organize their space when their newly-assigned team of Redbirds ordered them down on their knees and supplied the entire barracks with the all-too-familiar wherewithal of GI buckets, brushes, lye soap and bleach.

"It looks like we've come full circle, Ram." When Collier stripped out of his khakis and dropped to the floor in tee shirt and gym shorts, he was literally flabbergasted to find Nat Reed, his old nemesis from FARTC Basic, at his elbow.

"I'm glad we both made it, Nat," Collier said with a big grin. "But I've got an uneasy feeling we're in for a rough ride."

They had no sooner finished GI-ing the barracks floor when they were ordered outside and double-timed to a nearby supply room where they were issued new helmet liners with fancy orange and yellow stripes around the lower rim, a muslin mattress cover and two sheets, complete with a pillowcase chocked full of paperback military manuals of varying sizes covering every protocol, procedure, piece of equipment and weapon known to God and man. These manuals—they were soon informed by their Redbird tormentors—were to be sized, left to right in descending order on the shelf mounted on the wall above their hanging uniforms at the head of their beds.

All this transpired before noon "mess" (an officer candidate never referred to his meals as chow). Upon double-timing back from mess, the Redbirds assigned to Collier's section were waiting to provide instruction on how to hang their uniforms in a prescribed order with sleeves neatly overlapping on the hanging rod beneath the bookshelf. This instruction completed, one of them opened a footlocker and proceded to set up a precisely-defined display of shaving and toilet items neatly arranged on the removable top tray. In the storage space below the tray, underwear and socks were smartly folded and laid out in the prescribed order for inspection.

"Your cubicles will be kept inspection-ready at all times." The Redbird glanced from face to face to see he was clearly understood.

"You mean all times except after duty hours?" another of Collier's new battery mates asked for clarification.

"You should get your hearing checked, Candidate. I mean at *all* times.'"

Wisely, the candidate made no further comment.

"From what I've been told about our daily routine, that won't be near enough uniforms on the hanging rod or underwear and socks to keep up with the frequent changes we'll be required to make. Are we allowed to add more uniforms to fit our needs?" referring to the rather limited quantities displayed on the examples, a second perplexed candidate asked.

"Use your ingenuity, Candidate." Slapping a pristine pair of white gloves against his open palm, the Redbird named Armstrong informed the disheartened fledgling candidate.

"But where?...and how?...I don't understand," the flabbergasted candidate stammered.

"Be resourceful, Candidate. And while we're on the subject, the first thing a combat soldier should know is that his life depends as much on keeping his feet in good shape as it does on keeping his weapon clean. When you entered the Army you all were issued two pairs of combat boots. While in OCS, each day you will alternate wearing them. To make certain you are not cutting corners by using one pair for display while wearing the other for duty, in OCS we lace one pair of boots with crossed lacing and the other should be laced in an ascending row of parallel bars...you know, like rungs on a ladder." With practiced hands, Armstrong deftly relaced the nearest pair of crossed-laced boots. "On odd days of the calendar, you will wear the cross-laced boots and display these parallel-laced boots. You switch boots for display on even-calendar days. Now, if there are no other questions, this barracks is expected to be inspection-ready by 0600 hours tomorrow morning, and it will be kept that way twenty-four hours a day. Of course, Sergeant Grubbs has already told you all candidates are restricted to the OCS area for the first eight weeks. As you will notice, there is a Sign-out Card fixed to the outer standard of the dividing partition beside your bunk. Anytime you leave the barracks area, you will slide your button opposite the location where you plan to be." Armstrong pointed to a slender card pre-printed with a variety of destinations: HQ, PX, STUDY HALL, LIBRARY, CHAPEL, including spaces for TRAINING/DUTY and OFF POST. The card had a regular shirt button which could be freely moved to indicate any of the printed locations by sliding it along a vertical track formed by two threads attached to the top and bottom of the card.

"Beginning immediately, you and your barracks are subject to constant inspection—routinely this barracks will be inspected at least three times each day," Armstrong continued. "You will be allowed ten demerits each week in order to earn a full weekend pass. A full pass is defined as being from after noontime mess twelve-hundred hours Saturday until twenty-hundred hours Sunday night. Candidates receiving over ten demerits, but less than thirteen, will be restricted to the barracks area Saturday. Over twelve demerits and you'll not only be restricted, but you will also be required to join your fellow goof-off candidates double-timing the trail up MB-4 on Saturday afternoon. If you receive over fourteen demerits, you will be restricted to the barracks area for the entire weekend and be required to march up MB-4 both Saturday and Sunday afternoon." Armstrong paused. "And, that reminds me. Just so everyone will know the pleasure of ascending MB-4, you all will make the march this coming Sunday, right after noon mess. A word of caution—and this applies immediately: You are all advised to drink plenty of water and take salt tablets several times a day. The salt helps the body retain fluid. In this low humidity your sweat evaporates immediately and you don't realize how much body fluid you're losing. A soldier can become dehydrated without realizing it. Dehydration can cause heat stroke. Heat stroke can kill. Now...are there any other questions?"

"What's MB-4?" a fresh-faced candidate in front of Collier asked.

"See those four, pretty little round hills?" Armstrong pointed out the window in Collier's cubicle at MB-1, -2, -3 and -4 rising like giant stepping stones in the middle-distance.

"Doesn't look so tough to me. What's so bad about that?" the candidate rattled on.

"Nothing really—it's probably about five miles roundtrip to the top and back and MB-4 rises only to an elevation of about fifteen-hundred feet. In the early days, I'm told the summit of MB-4 was a favorite picnic outing for military and even civilian families. I don't imagine you'll see many picnickers up there this Sunday though. And, after this Sunday, you may think twice about whether you want to go back. Any more *intelligent* questions?"

"Sir, Candidate Nordby, Sir." A slender, blond Nordic type raised his hand.

"What is it, Nordby?" Armstrong asked.

"Did I understand that we're restricted for the first eight weeks? Do you mean restricted to the Post?" Nordby asked, unbelieving they could not leave the immediate OCS area.

"I mean you are restricted to the OCS area—that includes the mess hall, the PX, the laundry, the tailor and barber shop. Under no circumstances can you wander around the Post without a pass for the first eight weeks. Am I clearly understood?" Armstrong looked around as the full impact of his pronouncement sank in.

"Alright, quit standing around. You've got a lot to do." Although Collier was certain he wasn't the only one with a swarm of questions buzzing around inside his head, he bit his tongue as Armstrong ordered them to work, then pivoted sharply on his heel and disappeared down the steps.

"Did I say something wrong?" Nordby asked the group when the upperclassman was gone.

"Don't worry, Nordby. Armstrong has a heart of gold. He's probably just having his period. Either that or his hemorrhoids are bothering him again," Collier wisecracked as the group broke up to resume putting their cubicles in order.

"Did you hear the Redbird explain about alternating lacing on our boots?" Collier asked Rollins.

"Yeah. I heard him alright." Rollins nodded and immediately set to unlacing one pair of boots, carefully relacing them with a brand-new pair of laces in crossed-laced style. When he finished, he glanced curiously over at Collier. "Roanoke, Virginia, eh? Say, man, you sure you're gonna be okay with this?"

"What's that supposed to mean?" Unpacking his gear, Collier looked back at Rollins, a little surprised by his candor.

"Well...you know...my being black and all. Say, Man, the trial and execution of the Martinsville Seven was in Virginia. How do you feel about Malcolm X and the Black Power movement—stuff like that?"

"Look, Joe, that kind of stuff may mean something on the outside, but there's a war going on. We're all soldiers here. In here, that race stuff doesn't mean a thing to me."

"Well...that may be all well and good, but, just the same, I hope you don't think you have to buddy-up with me outside. You know, at the PX or in town, things like that. My guess is Oklahoma is every bit as redneck as Mississippi or Alabama...or Virginia, for that matter."

"Why would I not want to buy you a beer in town? Or go to a movie, maybe. Unless of course you're afraid I'd ruin your reputation."

"Oh, no. You know I didn't mean it like that. Besides, where you been? They don't serve Niggers or Mexicans in bars in Texas or Oklahoma. They don't let us in movies either."

"Okay, then we'll do our drinking at the PX and go to movies on Post—we get the best movies quicker here, anyway. But, come on, Joe. Lighten up. Let's forget all this nonsense. We're classmates...bunkmates...buddies, right? And, just for your information, I don't like the word Nigger, no matter who uses it." Collier warmly clasped Rollins on the bicep with his hand.

"Huh?" Rollins was rendered momentarily speechless.

Then, Collier stepped back a pace and regarded his new cubicle mate with a serious face. "That is, of course, unless a lynch mob of these local rednecks shows up. Then, Joe, it's every man for himself."

Totally flabbergasted, his cubicle mate's jaw dropped in an open-mouthed expression of utter shock.

"Come on, Joe, lighten up. I'm no redneck bigot. I had a colored nurse— they called them 'mammies' when I was a kid. Aunt Sally, my mammy's mother, was my mother's mammy. Aunt Sally and Uncle George and their kin were originally slaves of my great, great granddaddy before 'the war of northern aggression.' After the war, my great, great granddaddy deeded Uncle George and Aunt Sally the land and their cabins. When my mama grew up, our families were warmest of friends. When I was a kid, we used to go see Aunt Sally and Uncle George and their kids and grandkids sometimes on Sunday after church. We're all in this world together, man. Besides, if you're really worried about your reputation, after our first eight-weeks restriction, I won't be doing a lot of socializing with you guys on weekends. I have a wife in town." Collier finally had to laugh.

"Well, I didn't mean..." while he was listening, Rollons had already finished relacing his boots, hanging his uniforms and was earnestly engaged in setting up his footlocker. In the interim, Collier had barely completed emptying the contents of his duffel on his bunk.

"Slow down, Joe...you're making me look bad." All at once, Collier wasn't sure he could stand comparison with a perfectionist of Rollins' caliber.

"Best shape up, Candidate, or you'll be dripping a trail of your sweat up MB4." Joe gave Collier a sly wink and continued work.

When he had finished organizing his footlocker and hanging his clothes, Collier sat on his footlocker polishing his boots, assessing his barracks mates as they occupied themselves with similar tasks at hand. Except for Rollins and candidates George Barker and Dudley Von Gruenigen—veteran sergeants who appeared to be nearer his age—Collier's original assessment that he was several years older than most of his classmates seemed to be confirmed.

"Easy Battery, zero-five minutes." When Collier heard the the final warning countdown for evening mess formation, he checked his watch with grave consternation. Already 1630 hours and he still had miles to go before he could even think about sleep.

As soon as Easy Battery fell out and was properly assembled, Tactical Battery Commander Captain Jesse Whitley barked in an authoritative voice, "Battery, At Ease. Candidate Allen Daw, drive yourself up here, front and center."

OCS operated under an entirely new terminology and set of rules. Collier had already observed from the Tac Staff and Redbirds that in OCS "At Ease" really meant "Parade Rest" and "Drive" meant "March" and—even more-importantly—"March" always meant "double time." Candidates never walked anywhere in OCS.

Standing there in their first formation, Collier and the rest of the battery watched as a candidate from the other section took a quick step backward out of the line, executed a sharp Right Face and double-timed in back of the formation, up through the aisle between the two sections and came to a stop at attention about two-paces directly in front of the Tactical Battery Commander.

"Sir, Candidate Daw reporting as ordered, Sir." Daw saluted, holding the salute until Captain Whitley returned it.

"About face" Whitley commanded and when Daw was facing the Battery, "You may stand At Ease."

"It gives me pleasure to announce that Candidate Allen Daw has been chosen at random to serve as first Acting Battery Commander of Easy Battery. As you may recall from Sergeant Grubbs' and Ernst's orientation, this battery will be run by you, the candidates, while you are here. Each week, new candidates will be appointed to function in the various command roles ranging from Acting Battery Commander on down to Acting Section NCOs. Like the other designated weekly appointees for this, the first week of training, Candidate Daw will wear this insignia for the remainder of the week. You will give him the same military courtesy and respect as you would a regular officer of the same rank."

Whitley stepped forward and fastened a felt armband with a large felt facsimile of captains' bars around Daw's right bicep. As soon as Daw adjusted the armband in place, Whitley handed Daw a piece of paper which Collier assumed was a roster of the other candidates who would fill out the initial command complement. This done, Whitley stepped back and saluted Daw. "Take charge of your Battery, Battery Commander Daw. Call up your Exec and have him name this week's appointees to Easy Battery's new Acting Command Staff."

Sweat dripping down his spine, Collier—and he assumed most of the rest of the other ninety-nine candidates—stood with tightened sphincter waiting while Daw accepted the roster from Captain Whitley.

"Candidate Owen Farrar, drive yourself up here, front and center," reading off of the roster sheet, Daw called out in a voice cracking slightly under the strain,

It was not until the entire list of Acting Candidate officers and NCOs had been named that Collier finally was able to relax. He knew his turn was coming. It was only a matter of time, but, he had dodged a bullet for this week at least.

Following evening mess, Collier managed to sort and arrange the pile of manuals on his shelf in smooth descending order. When the task was completed, in a stroke of sheer inspiration, he took a well-sharpened No. 2 pencil and inscribed in descending order 1 to 59 each manual with a tiny, virtually microscopic, number at the base of the spine. Watching with open-mouthed admiration, Rollins sharpened his own pencil and followed suit. That frustrating, time-consuming chore complete, Collier turned to the task of putting the mattress cover on and making his bed. Then with his cubicle-mate's help—Rollins was a born soldier and a natural-born organizer—Collier finally managed to put his side of the cubicle in some kind of rudimentary state of 'Inspection readiness.'

Finally collapsing exhausted on his bunk sometime shortly after midnight, too tired to be apprehensive, Collier had little trouble in going to sleep.

"Easy Battery, one-zero minutes," the Candidate First Sergeant Dudley Von Gruenigen roused Collier awake just before 0500 hours. Marching double time to the parade field in shorts and tee-shirt for thirty minutes of morning Physical Training in the grayish pre-dawn light, Collier noted the thermometer mounted outside the mess hall already read 91 degrees.

By the time the battery had double-timed back to the battery area and Rollins had stripped naked and was heading for the shower, Von Gruenigen was already calling, "Easy Battery, one five minutes..."

That Collier managed to wriggle his still-sweaty, post-shower body into fatigue uniform and scramble back out to morning mess formation with all his buttons buttoned and his shoe laces tied bordered on the order of a downright miracle.

As good fortune would have it, the morning was spent at a nearby howitzer park for artillery weapons familiarization—a litany of nomenclature Collier already knew by heart.

"That thermometer must be broken...that can't possibly be right," as Easy Battery filed single file into the mess hall for noonday chow, a candidate with 'Tate,' printed on his nametag gasped in outright disbelief when he glimpsed the column of mercury standing at 105 degrees on the thermometer mounted beside the mess hall door.

"That thermometer's not broken...welcome to Fort Sill," the sweaty mess sergeant in a grease-stained apron quipped, standing by the door in the hope of catching a breath of air. Despite the oppressive heat and the complaining groans of their fellow candidates about the food, both Collier and Rollins ate a hearty lunch washed down with at least a quart of strong, sugar-laden iced tea.

"What's this five demerits for 'Broken lumber under the bed?'" Back in the barracks, Rollins yelped when Acting Section Leader Archer Barber Des Cognets—a rather self-important Bostonian—passed around the daily gig sheet.

Upon close examination, Rollins found a sliver from the end of a well-chewed toothpick lying beneath his bed.

"One demerit for 'Rope on blanket...'" Collier sucked in a sharp breath of relief when he found he had incurred only a single demerit by his name as Rollins passed the sheet to him. Picking up a nearly-microscopic filament of khaki thread on the foot of his bed, he had to laugh.

"Easy Battery, one-zero minutes," Acting First Sergeant Von Gruenigen called from the assembly area as Collier—to avoid messing up his 'demeritless' cubicle, but not about to waste a single second of the few minutes remaining before he had to fall out for a tedious afternoon at the motor pool to begin their two-week Motors instruction—stretched his lanky form on the well-scrubbed floor beside his bed, using his helmet liner as a pillow.

A scant half-hour later, waiting patiently behind about two-dozen men to take his turn climbing over the tailgate of a two-and-a-half-ton prime mover, Collier watched in horror as the candidate immediately in front of him placed his hand over the tailgate and slipped awkwardly to the ground as he raised his right foot attempting get traction to swing himself aboard. The young soldier's wedding ring caught the tip of the hook on the heavy safety chain and, right before Collier's eyes, the weight of the soldier's fall amputated his ring finger as clean as if it had undergone a surgeon's knife.

As shocked as he was, reflexively Collier had the presence to step aside to avoid being splattered by the gushing spray of blood. Then quickly loosing his belt to use as a tourniquet, he called loudly for someone to hand him a bandage from their SOP web belt pouch to staunch the bleeding. As soon as he was able to control the flow of blood, Collier searched the graveled parking area for the amputated digit. Locating it almost immediately, he picked it up, rinsed it with water from his canteen, and wrapped it in his handkerchief waiting for the medics with an ambulance. Watching Collier place the severed finger in the handkerchief, one of the candidates beside him fainted dead away.

"Can you get me two changes of PT shorts and at least two more tee shirts? I'll need them right away," Collier asked Emma that night after evening mess when she met him in the parking lot behind the PX, directly across from the mess hall. Despite low humidity drying his body prespiration, his sweat-soaked gym shorts and tee shirts worn that morning had been still soggy when Collier removed them from his laundry bag to don for afternoon PT. Collier overheard the Redbird Armstrong threatening another candidate suffering the same problem, with demerits for wearing an unfit uniform as they were double-timing to the PT field.

"They make you wear fresh uniforms even for PT?" Emma asked, flabbergasted the system could be so incredibly Mickey Mouse.

"They do indeed," Collier said, more depressed than aggravated. "You think that's bad, we have to GI the damn barracks again tonight." Hardly before he had uttered the profanity, he felt a twinge of guilt for violating the OCS code. Could it be true this insidious, childish brainwashing was already taking a toll on his brain?

"That's absurd. They're just trying to get your goat."

"Well, they're doing a pretty good imitation of that so far." Collier scowled, ruefully shaking his head. "The whole idea is to get your goat. The dropout rate is out of sight. Dropouts exceed bust outs for poor performance, poor grades and the like. The average class of one hundred only graduates about thirty-three."

"Well...at least they've made you clean up your language. Give me a kiss. I got to go. See you tomorrow night, same time, same station?" she said, leaning across to give him a good-bye peck.

"I'll be right here," he said as he turned to open the door, then he hesitated and began to worry his wedding band off his finger.

"Just what do you think you're doing?" Emma asked, with a puzzled look.

"Here take this and put it in a safe place. I just saw a guy lose his ring finger this morning and I'm not ready to be called 'nine-finger Ramsay'." Handing her the ring, he recounted the incident of the candidate slipping as he attempted to get into the deuce-and-a-half.

"I'll keep it in my jewelry box," she said and gave him another peck as he left the car.

"This floor looks like a pigpen," Collier had no soooner arrived back at the barracks, when the sadistic Redbird, Armstrong, was malevolently organizing another GI party. Emma had hit it on the head: Mickey Mouse! The utter malice of the act irked Collier to the edge of rage.

"Lights out in three-zero minutes," barely an hour after the GI party was completed to Armstrong's satisfaction, Des Cognets warned they had little time left for tasks requiring light. Stuck between the rock and the hard place, Collier tried to decide whether to finish shining the boots he had just taken off or to spend the time reading over the Tech Manual for the Electrical System on the GMC two-and-a-half ton which was just so much gobbledygook to him. Since keeping the big trucks running might save his life someday—he opted in favor of trying to figure out how to troubleshoot the 'sparkplugless' ignition on the new GMC prime-movers—after all, he could always shine his boots in the light in the stairwell which—due to fire regulations—was left burning all night.

Putting the finishing touches on his boots just before midnight, Collier tumbled into bed exhausted.

"Easy Battery, three-zero minutes," when Von Gruenigen gave his first call at 0500 hours, Collier rushed downstairs with toilet kit and towel. Careful not to cut himself, but hurrying to make room for the waiting line of fellow candidates, he shaved while under the shower.

Returning to the barracks forty-five minutes later, dripping with sweat from morning calisthenics, Collier stripped as he dashed inside the barracks door and rinsed under the shower—this time with the water running full cold—before he bounded up the steps three at a time to change into fatigue uniform to begin the training day. Using both of his 'duty towels' to dry himself, he was still damp with perspiration as he struggled into his fatigues.

Gathering up the previous day's fatigues to put them in his canvas AWOL bag for surreptitious safekeeping away from the eyes of Armstrong and the other prying Redbirds, Collier was astonished to find the entire uniform was caked white with dried perspiration. Both pants and blouse were so stiff with salt he was sure they could stand alone if he leaned them against the wall.

Gathering the salt-caked fatigues from the previous day's wear and his sweat-soaked PT shorts and tee and Jockey shorts, he rolled them into a bundle and stuffed them into the AWOL bag with his toilet kit. With all this 'non-tolerated,' yet highly-essential contraband under his arm, he headed downstairs and dashed across the street and placed them just inside a long, unoccupied, old-fashioned, WWII barracks tent set upon a sturdy wooden base. Inside was a veritable mountain of similar bags and bundles of contraband.

Collier thanked his lucky stars he had purchased the extra sets of uniforms during the week prior to entering OCS. The implied dishonesty of a system predicated upon the myth that whiskers shaved themselves and uniforms stayed perpetually inspection-ready left him feeling as if he were walking a tightrope of razor wire across the Grand Canyon.

"Due to the danger of heat exhaustion or heat stroke resulting from the extreme temperatures of the current heat wave, until further notice, the practice of double-timing to and from classroom training outside the immediate OCS area has been temporarily suspended," Candidate Battery Commander Daw announced at morning formation. Going into breakfast, the thermometer by the messhall door already showed 89 degrees. Over breakfast, Collier scanned a front-page article in *The Daily Oklahoman* predicting daytime highs in Oklahoma City in the upper 90s with a chance of showers. He shook his head, wondering if the official Oklahoma weather bureau was aware the daytime highs here at Sill had been over 100 for the past several days without a drop of rain.

Thank the big Redbird in the sky for small favors, Collier mused acrimoniously.

"Take that extra stuff to the tent across the street," returning to make a final inspection before formation, Collier advised Rollins who was just finishing putting his side of the cubicle in inspection order.

"Easy Battery, zero five minutes," outside in the battery street, the Acting First Sergeant called out the final warning.

"No time. Besides, I have a better idea," Rollins grunted, lugging his extra laundry bag to the small study space at the top of the stairwell. Standing on a folding chair beside the study table, Joe reached above him and displaced one of the moveable ceiling tiles. Quickly cramming his bundle of contraband into the opening, Rollins replaced the tile. Stepping from the chair, he took out his handkerchief and wiped away any possible trace of his boot prints from the shiny surface of the chair and carefully realigned it with the study table.

"I guess that'll have to do. Come on, let's go." Rollins winked as he grabbed his Motors manual and headed for the steps.

At the sprawling central motor pool for their morning Motors training, Collier and his battery mates resented Daw's not granting permission to strip down to tee shirts as did the regular motor pool personnel. But—thank the Cosmic Architect for small favors—the motor pool staff had set up several giant electric fans to help move the suffocating, fetid, gasoline- and grease- and exhaust-saturated air around inside the oven-like, corrugated-metal structure housing the service bays.

Even though they marched at a regular pace back from "Motors" to partake of noontime mess, when Collier arrived back at the barracks after lunch, he found his fatigues were again soaked with sweat, and he took the opportunity to change.

"This is really chicken...ah...feathers," Des Cognets exclaimed in dismay, stopping just short of uttering a forbidden epithet when he saw the demerit sheet.

"What's wrong?" Farrar, several cubicles down on the far side asked.

"I got five demerits for 'Whispering Commands.'" Des Cognets waved his demerit sheet in disgust. "Just wait until I see that sadist Armstrong."

"Best just keep it to yourself. Complaining is only going to make it worse," Rollins suggested with good intention.

Des Cognets gave him a withering look and handed him the demerit sheet.

"Two for 'Sahara Dunes Behind Footlocker'," Rollins read his sheet and sadly shook his head.

When Joe passed the demerit sheet on to him, Collier was totally disbelieving to find he had not been assessed a single demerit—to ensure there was no mix-up, there was a zero in the slot beside his name. His total remained at one.

As good a soldier as Joe Rollins was, Joe's total now stood at seven and it was only Tuesday.

Unreal as it seemed to him that his two-day demerit total remained at only one, it didn't relieve Collier's foreboding sense of impending doom to see the capricious inequities and sinister highhandedness in the distribution of demerits. Anyone could see Rollins was a "soldier's soldier," sharp as the crease on Eisenhower's famous jacket sleeve. What kind of system were they caught up in? Instead of remembering how it felt when they were subject to such malicious harassment, Redbirds were a diabolical, vicious, and malevolent bunch. Wondering when the other shoe would drop on him, Collier passed along the demerit sheet to Ettinger in the next cubicle.

Recalling the optimistic forecast for showers in the morning *The Daily Oklahoman* he had read in the mess hall at breakfast, all afternoon, under the unrelenting sun at an outdoor classroom listening to lectures on Field Sanitation, Collier kept searching the high, virtually cloudless sky for some hope of rain. But rain was not to come. Collier could not recall ever seeing such high cloudless skies. Looking out across the sun-scorched, Oklahoma landscape Collier recalled images from the movie of Steinbeck's *The Grapes of Wrath.*

Struggling to stay awake sitting outside in permanent bleachers built under a tree listening to classes on Field Sanitation, surreptitiously Collier had thumbed a July 5 issue of *New Yorker* magazine secreted under the notepad on his clipboard. Glancing over and dismissing a story entitled *The Cure* by John Cheever on Page 18, Collier flipped slowly through the pages browsing advertising illustrations until he came to page 43 where a pretty good scratchboard rendering of a bottle of Booth's House of Lords gin caught his eye. While he admired the artist's skill, the flair and execution of the illustration really didn't give offer much inspiration. As his reverie drifted back over his struggles to build a career as a commercial artist, he wondered what being away from the drawing board two years would do to his talent.

If indeed he had a talent to begin with.

Although they marched to and from the outdoor classroom to the rendezvous area where they boarded two-and-a-half-ton trucks for the trip back to the barracks area, in the southwestern Oklahoma low humidity, Collier had hardly been aware he had broken a sweat until he had shucked out of his sweat-soaked fatigues to change for the proscribed half-hour of PT before supper. He was utterly flabbergasted to find the fresh set of fatigues he had changed into following lunch was already impregnated with salt. How could he have possibly sweated so much just sitting on a bench all afternoon listening to some corporal talk about the virtues of Lister bags for cooling drinking water and how soldiers had been shitting in slit trench latrines since the dawn of history? Sardonically, Collier made a mental note not to dig a slit trench latrine above a stream, lest runoff seepage contaminate any source of desperately-vital drinking water.

At supper chow, the thermometer by the mess hall door showed 105—unchanged since lunchtime and virtually the same as the seemingly neverending sequence of days before.

"I can't believe the salt in these uniforms...I hope you're taking plenty of salt tablets and drinking a lot of fluids." Emma shook her head in dismay in the PX parking lot, as Collier handed over his soiled fatigues in a spare laundry bag.

"Trust me. I'm gobbling salt like a herd of cattle. If anything, I'm really concerned I might be taking too much." He gave her a serious look.

"Don't worry about that. The body only uses what it needs and excretes the rest through our urine and through the lungs and, of course, through perspiration." She giggled.

"That's good to know," Collier said, glancing warily at his wristwatch. It was a little earlier than the day before. He was surprised to see he still had almost ten minutes to spare.

"By the way, I've been called for an interview at the Post hospital tomorrow morning at eight A.M.," Emma said, trying to appear offhand.

"That's great. I'm sure you're excited, but don't set yourself up for disappointment. I imagine they have a waiting list," he tried to express enthusiasm, but he was too tired to exhibit much feeling about anything at all.

"Don't worry...I'm not counting my chickens. I called the supervisor at Lawton Hospital, and she said they may have another private duty case in a day or so."

"Every little bit helps. How're things going between you and Louise?" Collier wanted to include their landlady, Hilda Birdsong, in this casual inquiry, but was afraid he might betray a hint of guilty, unhealthy interest.

"Louise is fine. She worked at the Post Office back home and thinks she may get on part-time here."

"That sounds great. I know that would help them a lot. Look, Honey, I guess I better run along. No telling what the chickenshit bastards have in store for us tonight." The thought of returning to the whimsy of their Redbird tormentors was almost more than he could bear.

"Collier! You know how I hate that coarse expression. Besides, I thought you were forbidden to use such language."

"Report me to the language police. I hate this chickenshit place anyway," dreading another day of this totally unrealistic training, he snorted in a sudden fit of anguish.

"Calm down, Collier! What's come over you?"

"Sorry...two days of this Howdy Doody crap and I'm ready to hang it up. At least, in Basic, they treated us like grown men."

"Well...it's entirely up to you." She gave him a probing look. "What would happen if you did resign? Would you stay here? Would they send you over to FARTC with Herb?"

"Not likely. Candidates who resign or bust out here usually go straight to FECOM. But, Korea can't be much worse than this. At least in Korea they treat you like men."

"You're just tired. You'll feel better tomorrow. Don't let them get your goat."

"Easy for you to say...you have no idea. Doesn't it register on you why we have to change uniforms six or seven times a day? Enough of this, anyway, I've got to get back to the zoo." He leaned across and gave her a resentful goodbye peck on the lips. Watching her drive the little Studebaker out of the PX parking lot, he felt an overwhelming pang of jealousy for her freedom. Only two days in and he was already sick to death of this regimented insanity. He wondered what she would say if she knew that half of the previous night and periodically all day long he had been obsessing on the idea of handing in his resignation. As ashamed as he was to admit it, the only thing that had kept him from quitting was the fact he had never quit anything in his life—that and the absolute refusal to let the big dumb Indian, Nat Reed, get the best of him.

"Move out, Candidate, unless you're looking to dock yourself five demerits?" trotting back to the barracks, a Redbird who sounded a lot like Armstrong hailed him from the obscuring glare of the setting sun.

"Sir, Candidate Ramsay, Sir. Yessir." he answered the shadowy form, picking up his pace. There was no letting up. The sneaky bastards were everywhere.

"Easy Battery, one-zero minutes," shortly after midnight, Von Gruenigen's voice insinuated itself into Collier's sweaty, fitful sleep.

"Collier! Come on, get up." When he opened his eyes, Rollins was rudely shaking him.

"What?" Collier sat up and rubbed his eyes. My god, he felt like hell!

"Get dressed. We've got to fall out in the company street," Rollins said, already dressed in fresh fatigues.

"Able section present or accounted for! Baker section present or accounted for..." the Candidate section chiefs were reporting as Rollins with a few other tardy arrivals elbowed their way into formation just as Acting Battery Commander Daw was taking report. As soon as Daw turned and reported "Easy Battery, all present and accounted for," Tac Lieutenant Robinson stepped forward and whispered something in Daw's ear. Daw nodded and stepped forward and whispered in Von Gruenigen's ear. Von Gruenigen nodded and Daw did an about face and returned to his usual position.

"First Sergeant, take command of the battery," Daw ordered and Von Gruenigen saluted as soon as they were back in place.

"At my command, you will fall back inside and report back out here in zero-five minutes with your military manuals in your pillowcase. You have zero-five minutes. That is all. Easy Battery, Dis-s-smissed!" Von Gruenigen ordered as soon as Daw turned the battery over to him.

Back inside, pulling the row of military manuals he had spent so much time arranging by descending size for inspection, Collier cursed under his breath as he dumped them into his pillowcase and headed back outside in the mad scramble.

For the next fifteen minutes, they stood there at attention until the section leaders checked their pillowcases and reported everything in order.

"When I dismiss you, you will fall back inside. Your manuals will be back on the shelf ready for inspection when you report to go to Motors class tomorrow morning. That is all. Easy Battery, dis-s-missed!"

Quickly conceding the impossibility of putting the manuals back to "inspection readiness" in the dark, the battery crawled back in bed, resigned to the necessity of rising an hour early in order to complete the frustrating task.

"Get up...you still have to put your manuals back on the shelf." Shaken awake the next morning by Rollins at 0500, Collier seriously weighed the consequences of handing in his resignation before the first class of the morning—it would certainly save him a lot of unnecessary aggravation. Still groggy from losing sleep and under the duress of the "manual crisis", he decided to wait until after breakfast, at least. After completing the irritating chore of replacing his manuals on the shelf in inspection order, Rollins asked him a question about the Waukesha engine, and Collier's thoughts momentarily turned away from ideas of resigning as he was reminded of the upcoming test in Motors class.

Marching to Motors after breakfast, Collier berated himself for having failed to resign before allowing himself to suffer one more morning of the humiliation and hardship—torture really—as he firmly resolved to suck it up, go ahead, resign and get it over with when they came back for lunch. Then, back in the barracks to change uniforms before noontime chow, Collier breathed a sigh of relief when the gig sheet was passed around and he saw he had dodged another bullet. Incredibly, he had slipped by another day without a single additional demerit.

On the mess hall bulletin board, he scanned the headlines about the bloody fighting on some godforsaken piece of worthless real estate called Old Baldy. Today there was no mention of Chorwon per se, but his thoughts turned to Bo and he breathed a silent prayer to a Creator in whom he didn't really believe to keep his old friend safe from harm. Momentarily relieved he had managed to survive yet another day without incurring the wrath of the upperclassmen, and somewhat sobered by the headlines about renewed fighting in Korea, marching back to Motors class, he decided his resignation could wait at least one more night. At a subliminal level, Collier understood the thing that really prevented him from resigning was the idea of quitting was somehow worse than the idea of suffering another twenty-four hours of this Mickey Mouse chickenshit.

Actually, his fear of combat in Korea was nothing compared to his fear of having to face his father.

Collier loved his dad and hated to think of disappointing him. From the time Collier was just a boy, he remembered Cocky preaching, "Quitters are losers...never be a quitter."

So, for the moment, at least, Collier decided to stick it out one more night; he could always quit first thing tomorrow morning. The following morning, agonizing between his desire to quit and his pride for never quitting anything—if you didn't count piano lessons—he had gone through the motions of readying his cubicle for inspection and was headed out to the morning formation trying to build up resolve to hand in his resignation when fate almost took the decision out of his hands. Running with reckless abandon to avoid being late for breakfast formation, Collier slipped on a pebble and took a nasty, ass-over-elbow spill on the concrete walk outside the barracks, landing squarely on his butt. The solid trauma to his tailbone had left him wincing in pain each time he took a step.

"Here, Ramsay, lean on me. Come on over and sit here on the barracks steps." Tac Lieutenant Robinson had witnessed the incident and rushed to his aid.

"Sir, I'm okay, Sir."

"That was a nasty bump. You best let a medic take a look." Against Collier's embarrassed protests, Robinson insisted Collier report immediately to Sick Call, concerned he might have suffered some serious damage to his spine or hip. To cover his own and the Army's ass, the young medic at the nearby Post Dispensary sent him by the regular Post bus to be X-rayed at the Post Hospital.

Waiting for over an hour in radiology, Collier scanned the *The Daily Oklahoman* for news of the raging battle for Old Baldy. For a war that should have been over a full twelve months ago, it seemed criminal to be sacrificing good American lives for a worthless dunghill on the barren, war-ravaged Korean landscape—to further compound the travesty, the papers said the fighting was actually near the truce tents at Panmunjon. The heat wave was getting almost as much space on the front page as the war. It came as no news to Collier that the weather bureau was predicting temperatures in the mid-90s for Oklahoma City through the coming weekend, yet there was no mention of the scorching daily highs of 105 (and likely higher) they were currently suffering here at Sill. It seemed ironic that—of all the weekends of the entire year—it would most likely be under record high temperatures when he and his luckless battery-mates would have to make the dreaded forced Saturday afternoon trek across the near-mythic, ever-ascending slopes of MB-1, -2, -3 all the way to the top of MB-4 in full field pack.

After wasting the most of the morning, the radiologist at the Hospital told Collier he saw no evidence of serious injury to the spine or hip and sent him back to duty. Catching another Post bus back to the motor pool in time to rejoin his classmates before Motors class was over, Collier managed to avoid having to make up an absence which might have put him in later jeopardy of being sent back to another class.

Sitting on his butt all morning at the dispensary, and in the air-conditioned X-ray department of the Post Hospital, not to mention riding on a Post bus with all the windows open, Collier had scarcely broken a sweat. Yet, far-fetched as it seemed, when he returned to the barracks from the motor pool for noon chow, he again found his uniform was caked with salt. Unbelievably, he and most of his classmates were forced to change uniforms again before they returned to Motors for the afternoon session. With the huge fans blowing a minor hurricane directly on him, working all afternoon under the hood of a two-and-a-half-ton prime mover inside the metal buildings of the motor pool kept Collier a trifle damp with sweat. Head abuzz with newfound confusion about pistons, cylinders, transmissions, differentials, solenoids, distributors, blah, blah, blah...ad infinitum, after marching back to the barracks to lay out his evening uniform and change for PT, once more his fatigues were stiff with salt.

The evening schedule called for class-A khakis for a two-hour study hall following supper chow; showering after PT, Collier was already damp again and sweat was beginning to show through the fabric of his starched khakis before he finished buttoning his blouse.

When he showed up in the parking lot behind the PX with his salt-caked laundry during the fifteen-minute break between evening chow and study hall, Collier was disappointed to find Herb and Louise waiting with the freshly-laundered uniforms Emma had taken from him the evening before.

"Emma said to say she's sorry, but she was called to take a private case at the hospital in Lawton. We're going to try to fill in for her the next few days," Louise explained.

"Well, I really appreciate your taking the time. There's no way a guy can make it without fresh laundry every day," Collier expressed his deep appreciation, suddenly aware how completely surreal OCS was and just how vulnerable and dependent he was upon outside help. Having to suffer two wasted hours sitting in his perspiration-soaked khakis in the upstairs of an oven-like classroom building during the entirely unnecessary and deadly-boring study hall did little to improve his attitude. Then, as if things weren't already bad enough, when they finally returned to the barracks after study hall, they found there had been a surprise inspection after evening chow. Collier found his manuals scattered in disarray on his bed.

"What's this?" Collier asked as, to his utter dismay, Joe handed him the demerit sheets for the second time that day.

"*Improper display of manuals,*" neatly inscribed on Collier's sheet, the outrageously spurious offense had been assessed a whopping five demerits. The notation hit him like a sledgehammer blow to his gut. Wracking his brain trying to fathom the real—or imagined?—shortcomings in the careful way he had restored his manuals to their prescribed position on the shelf above his bed, for the life of him Collier could not imagine what he could have possibly done wrong. In less than six hours time, his previously admirable total of one demerit had skyrocketed to an intimidating total of six black marks—and it was only Wednesday. These bullshit games were clearly out of hand! Seething with shock and resentment, Collier firmly resolved he was resigning first thing tomorrow morning as he numbly began restoring his manuals to their "inspection-ready" on the shelf. The proverbial straw had finally broken *this* camel's back!

But somehow morning came and went again as—his manuals resentfully replaced and realigned—Collier marched sullenly off to suffer the malevolent and completely spurious indignities for yet one more wretched day.

Herb and Louise were waiting again that evening in the PX parking lot. "Emma says to tell you, 'hi.' She thinks the case she's on will last a few more days." Louise told him as she accepted the tightly folded bundle of sweat- and salt-soaked clothing he passed through the window of the big sedan and handed out the lightly-starched and pressed items of uniform and underwear he had given them the previous evening.

"Thanks a million for bailing me out again. I'd really be up the creek if I didn't have someone to take care of my laundry. Give Emma my love and tell her I'll see her when her case is over," Collier remarked distractedly, his mind already on the hundred-and-one other things he had to do before he finally got to sleep around midnight.

The last two days of the training week went by without anything remarkable happening.

Still standing at six demerits Friday afternoon when they returned from Motor class, Collier's total remained unchanged. Although they were automatically restricted for the first two months, six demerits was well below ten, the magic number granting freedom of a weekend pass after they had completed their first eight weeks.

Their first Saturday inspection was everything Collier had imagined, yet, all things considered, much less. In just five days, he was beginning to comprehend in OCS almost everything was some sort of nightmarish make believe—like walking around in a Salvadore Dali painting. The whole system was cosmetic. Like a Hollywood movie set, OCS was mostly a façade...a false front...window-dressing!

Following Saturday morning inspection and noontime chow, the Redbirds offered the battery a choice of going up MB-4 that afternoon or waiting until Sunday morning at 0900, and accompanying the main group. Although the temperature was still hovering around 105, tomorrow's forecast offered little hope of relief.

"Eat light, Joe; in this heat this won't be a walk in the park," Collier advised his cubicle mate after they had wisely decided it made more sense to volunteer to go that afternoon and get MB-4 behind them. Then, they could have all day Sunday to relax and rest. Hurrying back to the barracks after chow, they busily assembled the required full horseshoe packs.

"Use your head; nobody will check your pack," Rollins urged Collier to cheat as he ingeniously stuffed his pack with wads of tissue paper he took from his inspection-ready Corcoran boots beside the bed.

"You're probably smart to do that, Joe, but it's dishonest. Besides, I'd hate to think what the Redbirds would do if they decide to check your pack."

"Bull-puckey! Ever hear of this thing called American ingenuity? That sadist Armstrong suggested it himself. A good soldier has to always look for an edge." Rollins rolled his eyes at Collier's holier-than-thou Pollyanna attitude and kept right on stuffing tissue in his pack.

With a gung-ho group of slightly more than two-dozen candidates from Easy Battery assembled with perhaps a hundred-fifty others—including those in the more-senior batteries who had to make the hike because of excessive demerits—Collier and Joe left the assembly area at 1430. The outward march to the base of

MB-1—the first and smallest of the quartet of stair-step-like, smoothly-rounded historical landmarks—took only about 30 minutes in the unrelenting afternoon sun. Even before they had begun the actual ascent, the entire entourage was already sopping wet with sweat. Yet, typically, in the desert-like absence of humidity, their uniforms were drying fast leaving light tracings of salt residue outlining the areas of evaporating perspiration.

"Okay, take ten...smoke if you got 'em. It would be a good idea to take a couple of salt tablets. We've got salt and extra water over here at the truck," sensibly, Armstrong, the Redbird in charge, ordered a break before the group started the actual climb.

"Come on, Joe. Let's take a couple of salt pills," Collier headed for the truck.

"I took two tablets back at the barracks. Too much salt'll make you sick." Refusing more salt, Joe followed along and gulped down several canteen cups of water.

"Joe, you've lost a lot of water in this heat...your body needs to replace the salt."

"Too much salt is bad for you," Steadfastly, Rollins rejected Collier's advice.

"Okay, field-strip those butts and let's head out," the lead Redbird ordered when the well-needed ten-minutes had elapsed.

When they reached the summit of MB-1, the lead Redbird called another halt and led them to the brink of the spectacular and dizzying precipice where some ancient cosmic accident had bisected all four of the pleasantly-rounded hills. At this point, the drop was perhaps only a little more than 100 feet. The stark granite cliffs stretched around this first curve of Medicine Creek, disappearing several hundred yards ahead around a sharp bend where the next slope up MB-2 began. On the far side of Medicine Creek, Route 49 followed a path along the lush line of mesquite, cottonwoods and willows tracing the outline of the creek bank. From this height, it was easy to locate the almost invisible turnoff toward the creek at the foot of MB-4 where Hilda Birdsong had practically raped him a few Sundays back.

On beyond, well-past the summit of MB-4, he could see Lake Lawtonka and the little side road winding around Mount Scott. It was absolutely breathtaking to look along the line of sheer cliffs running almost dead center, bisecting the line of four hills as if some celestial force had chopped them down the middle with a gigantic cleaver. Even to the most unschooled it was easy to deduct this was caused by a cataclysmic settling of a prehistoric earthquake fault. Although at this initial vantage point on MB-1, the drop was probably only slightly over 100 feet— staring almost straight down made Collier somewhat queasy. Concerned he might be getting a bit dehydrated, Collier swallowed two salt tablets, washing them down with a few frugal gulps of water from his canteen.

"Better take some salt, Joe," Collier advised as they were prepared to resume their trek up the trail.

"If you hadn't stuffed all that field gear in your pack, you wouldn't need that stuff," the pigheaded Rollins took a large swig of water, but steadfastly refused the salt.

By the time they had reached the summit of MB-2, several of their party had already shucked out of their packs and tossed them beside the path, planning to retrieve them on the way back down. By the time the expedition puffed to a halt at the highest point on MB-3, more than one-third of the hundred-fifty-plus candidates had strewn their packs along the trail.

"Best keep our packs on, Joe, or something tells me we'll be sorry." Collier stopped Rollins from following the example of the less circumspect of the marchers, sensing their Redbird overseers were taking notes.

Although the remainder of the trek to the summit of MB-4 measured only a few hundred yards, in the 105-degree heat and under the unrelenting sun, it took nearly a half-hour to traverse the final leg of the ever-ascending, seemingly never-ending path. Finally attaining the summit of MB-4, Collier looked back on a long line of stragglers still struggling to catch up. At least a couple dozen had actually fallen out and were sitting at various points along the trail with their heads between their knees—a few were bent double, throwing up their toenails by the side of the route.

"Okay, take fifteen. Shuck out of those packs and take a load off. Smoke if you got 'em—if you don't, don't try to bum off me. The topographical elevation here at the summit is approximately fifteen-hundred-feet above sea level. The actual height of the cliff at this point is around three-hundred-feet. If you want to take another peek over the edge of the cliff, use caution. Go very slow—the slope down to the edge is steeper than it looks. For those of you who haven't heard, legend has it Geronimo, the famous renegade Apache, once jumped from here to escape capture by the cavalry." Standing at the highest elevation of MB4, the ranking Redbird pointed to the brink of the forbidding precipice a couple-dozen paces to his right.

"Come on, Joe, I don't ever plan to come back up here—might as well take a look." Slipping his pack off his shoulders, Collier lit a Lucky before he moved gingerly down what appeared to be a rather gently-descending slope toward the edge of the cliff.

"That's Mount Scott, right there," Collier waved his hand in the direction of the dominating land feature slightly to the north and west.

"Oh, shit!" Joe yelped behind him as he stumbled over a loose stone. Abruptly knocked off-balance, Collier took the force of Joe's full weight, miraculously managing to right himself and steady Joe as they tottered dangerously near the brink of the dizzying escarpment.

"Judas priest! Be careful, Joe! You about gave me a freaking heart attack!" Collier gasped, sharply sucking in his breath.

"Oh, jeezie, Ram," Rollins panted, bending at the waist with his hands braced upon his knees. Staring wide-eyed down between his dusty Corcoran boots at Medicine Creek some 300 feet below, Collier could have sworn that just for a moment, his ebon-skinned cubiclemate blanched nearly snow white.

"Here, Joe, take my hand. Let's get back on more solid footing." Collier reached out and securely grasped his hand, then started inching his way back up the deceptively-sharp slope. Glancing nervously back toward the dizzying brink of the precipice, Rollins was obviously in distress. When they finally reached the safety of the relatively-flat hillcrest, Joe abruptly freed his hand from Collier's grip, moved a few steps away and began vomiting.

Suddenly aware just how close Joe had come to plunging them both to certain death, Collier felt his knees turn to jelly and he slowly sat down in the grass. When he finally regained some measure of composure, Collier stood and took a couple more salt pills before he turned his attention back to his suffering companion.

"Better take these, Joe. Wash 'em down with this." Joe's nausea apparently passed, Collier handed his shaken cubicle mate two salt tablets and offered him a drink from his own canteen. Still reeling from his brush with disaster, this time Joe made no objection.

"Okay, let's saddle back up and head back down." The Redbird in charge began waving the expedition to their feet.

When Joe turned to retrieve his discarded pack, a Redbird was holding it out to him.

"We wouldn't want to forget this, Candidate." The upperclassman handed the shaken Rollins his paper-stuffed pack, but gave no hint he was aware of Joe's subterfuge.

Eager now to get their ordeal over with, Collier directed Joe to follow the Redbird who had already started back down the trail, rounding up stragglers. Even with the stragglers stopping to identify their abandoned packs and other assorted equipment as they moved along the trail, they made much better time going down. Miraculously, Rollins made it all the way back to the barracks without throwing up again.

Back in his cubicle toweling off after a refreshing shower, Collier stared out the window at Medicine Bluffs rising silently in the middle-distance. Absently tossing his towel on the bed, Collier stepped into fresh underdrawers, preparing to dress for evening chow, and made a solemn vow he would resign before he was ever forced to go up MB-4 again.

Following supper, the mess hall thermometer showed 103 as Collier made his customary trip back to the barracks to pick up his dirty uniforms. With Emma working private duty at the hospital in downtown Lawton, Collier expected to find Herb and Louise, but he was pleasantly surprised when he found Emma waiting when he reached the lot behind the PX.

"Just wait 'til you hear my good news," Emma enthused before Collier could even say, hello.

"Oh? What's going on?" Collier asked, resentful Emma showed no interest or sympathy for his having to suffering the malevolent indignities of this diabolical torture chamber.

"I've gotten a temporary slot at the hospital on Post. I start tomorrow—aren't you proud of me?" she chirped.

"Congratulations," Collier grunted, his voice edged with wounded feelings.

"Uhm-m, thank you, darling. But there's going to be a slight hitch, I'm afraid," Emma babbled on, completely insensitive to Collier's trials and tribulations.

"Oh? What's that?" Collier asked, his interest revived somewhat.

"I'll be working evenings and won't be able to be your main laundrywoman anymore. Herb and Louise say they don't mind doing it once in awhile..."

"Don't worry about it. I have plenty of extra uniforms. I'll start sending with the regular laundry just like the other guys," he grumbled, unaccustomed to the role of martyr.

"I'm sorry, Honey. Sure you don't mind?"

"Neah. If it works for the other guys, it will surely work for me. Besides, I'm thinking seriously about quitting this chickenshit, anyway..." He let the thought trail off, hating himself for having become such a pathetic bellyacher.

"Well... that's up to you of course. I'm sorry, you're so miserable, Honey. Now, let me go. I've got to run. I'm meeting Hilda and Louise at Post Theater

Number One for a movie." She patted his hand as if he had just announced he was going to change brands of shaving cream.

Watching the taillights of the Studebaker disappear down the street, Collier felt a wave of resentment rising in his chest, hating her for being able to come and go, flitting about with the freedom of a bird. Ever since the self-centered bitch had greeted him so all lovey-dovey at Washington airport, he had wondered how long it would be before the real Emma showed up.

Driving away from the PX, Emma glanced resentfully in the rearview mirror at her husband standing in the parking lot holding her delivery of freshly-laundered uniforms. It would be just like the whiny jerk to make good on his threat to quit OCS just when her physician-acquaintance and sometimes lover, Trey Moseley, had managed to pull a few strings all the way from Brooke Army Hospital to help her get on at the Post hospital.

Well, just let Collier quit if he couldn't stand the pressure; she had come to like living here, Emma mused resentfully. If she managed to elevate herself to permanent employee status at the Post hospital and Collier actually quit OCS and they sent him overseas, she might just stay on right here in Lawton, Oklahoma. Trey Moseley had called a few nights back and hinted he might wangle a three-day TDY to fly into Sill over Labor Day weekend for some sort of trumped-up medical consult. It troubled her to admit she had sort of led Moseley on, letting him believe she would be glad to see him—but then, after all, he *had* gotten her this great new job.

What really disturbed Emma the most was merely talking to Moseley had called up such a powerful wave of conflicted sexual feelings when she actually couldn't stand the thought of him. To her credit, she had been civil to the cocky little womanizer, but she felt guilty she hadn't bothered to inform Moseley that Collier's mandatory OCS restriction ended that weekend and she and Collier were meeting Collier's brother, Jim, in Oklahoma City.

Well, if Trey did actually show up here, it would serve him right that she was going out of town. She didn't want to see him, anyway—or did she?

CHAPTER TWENTY-EIGHT

THE DAILY OKLAHOMAN
Oklahoma City, Oklahoma, Friday, August 1, 1952
**KOREAN WAR ISN'T POLICE ACTION,
ONE-MILLIONTH DRAFTEE DECLARES**
DETROIT, Thursday, July 31 (AP) – A young man just out of college
became the Army's one-millionth draftee of the Korean War today.

THE DAILY OKLAHOMAN
Oklahoma City, Oklahoma, Friday, August 1, 1952
CHINESE DRIVEN OFF 'OLD BALDY'
SEOUL, Korea, Friday, August 1 (AP) – Allied troops in a bloody
bayonet battle drove Chinese Communists off the crest of Old Baldy on
the Western Korean Front.

THE ROANOKE TIMES
Roanoke, Virginia, Saturday, August 30, 1952
NORTH KOREAN CAPITAL BLASTED IN RECORD BLOW
By MILO FARNETI
SEOUL, Saturday, August 30 (AP) – Allied warplanes blasted the North
Korean capital of Pyongyang from dawn to dark Friday with a record
number of 1403 sorties for the 26-month-old war...

FOLLOWING THEIR ARDUOUS, NEAR-DISASTROUS foray up MB-4, on
Monday, July 14, Easy Battery was thrust back into their studies on the intricacies
of military motors with an introduction to the inner workings of the combustion
engine.

At mail call, Collier received a second note from Bo Bohon indicating that he
was at an unnamed outpost a few-days march northeast from the port of Inchon.
When news of the first battle for Old Baldy came on June 26, the radio reports
said that Old Baldy was located about 80 miles northeast of Seoul, not very far
from a place called Chorwan. With plenty of time on his hands waiting for his
OCS class to begin, Collier went to the post library and found a military map of
the area. According to the map, Inchon was a short distance westsouthwest of
Seoul, just west of Yongdongpo. Collier found Chorwan just above the 38th
parallel—a little over 100 miles north of Seoul and about 80 miles east of the
truce-talk tents in Panmunjon. The combat map showed Chorwan was at the
western base point of an area known as the Iron Triangle. Now that he was
actually counting down the days until December 13, when he supposedly would
graduate OCS, it gave Collier some restless nights wondering what it would
actually be like to be in combat and worrying if Bo were out of harm's way.

On Thursday, July 17, Collier read news reports that the second battle for
Old Baldy had begun. The next morning, a radio in the barracks reported that
the Filipino battalion holding the infamous Korean land feature known as the
Alligator Jaws since early spring had been relieved by the United States 2nd
Infantry Division. Senses dulled from the non-stop training and the relentless

-307-

heat, Collier—and most of his battery-mates—were outraged to think that those "peace negotiators" were walking in and out of the truce-talk tents, disrupting the negotiations over petty differences in trivial protocol, while good men like Bo were fighting and dying in the nearby hills over worthless pieces of Korean real estate.

Back from the motor pool for noontime mess when the final demerit sheets for the week were passed around, both Collier and Joe were greatly relieved to find that the weekly scoresheet for their trangressions remained in single digits—comfortably less than the damning twelve demerits which would have demanded they make another trip to the summit of MB-4.

Saturday morning, July 19, dawned bright and hot. Despite the daily weather reports in *The Daily Oklahoman* predicting a daily high reaching *only* into the upper 90s, by the time Collier finished breakfast, the unrelenting heatwave in this godforsaken southwestern corner of Oklahoma already registered 97 on the mess hall thermometer. Jogging back to the barracks, Collier was driven by feelings of impending doom. He still had a list of last-second preparations to make for the Saturday morning inspection beginning inside the barracks and ending outside, standing in formation under the broiling, mid-morning sun. He was already perspiring torrents. Just imagining the effects of this tidal wave of sweat on his freshly-laundered, sharply-pressed Class-A Khakis was enough to give his ulcer's ulcer an ulcer.

Collier had risen an hour early to gather his stash of contraband possessions into a rubberized laundry bag and stow it across the street in the abandoned barracks tent. Now—after he double-checked his cubicle to make certain every item was in its appointed place—he stripped naked and sponged himself with rubbing alcohol before he put on clean underwear and directed his attention to making sure his appearance would be as inspection-ready as humanly possible.

Rollins, on the other hand, was frantically assembling his contraband items into a jumbled collection of dirty uniforms, shoeshine equipment, toilet kit and paper grocery bags stuffed with all manner of junk. When he finished collecting this clutter, he piled the entire collection of loose items inside of a pair of soiled fatigue blouses and tied them into two separate bundles. Standing on his footlocker, he loosened the nearest ceiling tile and jammed both bundles and the trio of brown paper bags up inside the space between the rafters. Making certain the unsightly contraband was safely out of view, Joe carefully replaced the tile, stepped down and neatly dusted his bootprints from the pristine surface of his footlocker using a scrap of folded toiletpaper which he stuffed into a trouser pocket before reopening his footlocker for inspection.

"Standby! Here they come!" Joe had hardly straightened when the lookout from downstairs section called up the stairwell before scuttling back to his own cubicle.

"Atten-hut!" Carefully taking their prescribed places to the left of their footlockers, Collier and his barracks mates came to rigid attention when Candidate Battery Commander Daw led the team of Redbirds into the sweltering barracks.

By the time the inspection entourage finished downstairs and reached Collier's cubicle, a raging torrent of sweat was flowing into the crack of his ass and running down his leg into his socks. The Redbird Armstrong came to a halt in front of him, gave him a scathing look up and down starting at his haircut and ending at the toes of his shoes. After he had given Collier a careful personal scrutiny, Armstrong glanced into his footlocker and gave his side of the cubicle a withering glance before he moved to Rollins' side.

"What's your name, Candidate?" Armstrong asked.

"Sir, Candidate Rollins, Sir."

"Have you ever actually worn either pair of these boots, Candidate?" Armstrong asked, knowing full-well the gleaming Corcorans were merely for show.

"Sir, yes, Sir. Both pair, Sir," Rollins lied with great sincerity.

"You use this shoeshine kit to keep these Corcorans shined like this?"

Collier's sphincter tightened, knowing full-well the shoeshine kits and toilet articles—like the pristine white towels they were displayed upon for inspection—had never been used for anything but show.

"Sir, no, Sir."

"Where's the shoeshine kit you used to polish these Corcorans?" Armstrong bore in, ready for the kill.

"Sir, all used up, Sir. I threw it in last night's trash."

Afraid to move his head, but helpless not to peek, Collier watched the exchange between his cubicle mate and the Redbird inquisitor out of the corners of his eyes. After a long moment, Armstrong did a right face and made as if to move on to the next cubicle. After taking a single stride, he stopped dead in his tracks and turned to face Rollins again.

"Did you ever wonder what was up there behind those ceiling tiles, Candidate Rollins?"

"Sir, I beg your pardon, Sir?" Much like the previous Saturday when he nearly stumbled over Geronimo's cliff at MB-4, Rollins' ebon face blanched almost pasty white.

"Are you hard of hearing, Candidate Rollins?"

"Sir, no, Sir."

"Well, answer my question. Have you even wondered what might be up inside those ceiling tiles?" Armstrong asked, his voice as cold as a northwind.

"Sir, I assumed some rafters and electric wiring was up there, Sir." Admirably, Rollins tone betrayed no hint of insubordination.

"A logical assumption, Candidate Rollins. But do you know what happens when we assume something is true, Candidate Rollins?" Armstrong asked, his voice taking a less intimidating tone.

"Sir, no, Sir." To his credit, Rollins' tone remained clear and strong.

"We are in danger of making an A-S-S out of U and ME. Do you understand, Candidate Rollins."

"Sir, yes, Sir."

"Well, Candidate Rollins, what do you think we should do about that?"

"Sir, about what, Sir?"

"About assuming rafters and electric wires are the only thing behind those ceiling tiles, Candidate Rollins, that's what."

"Sir, I don't understand, Sir."

"Are you trying to make an ASS out of U and ME, Candidate Rollins?"

"Sir, oh, no, Sir."

"Well, what are you waiting for, Candidate Rollins? Close that footlocker and step up there and see what you can find."

"Sir, yes, Sir." Rollins saluted, before he slowly turned and bent to close the lid of his footlocker. Stepping up on the closed lid, he pushed aside the ceiling tile and made a show of probing around the shadowy recesses with his hand. "I can't feel anything up here, Sir. I imagine the wires run more to the center, down the line of lights."

"Candidate Ramsay, fetch me the chair from your desk."

"Sir, yes, Sir." Moving swiftly between the bunks, Collier came back with the chair.

"Step down, Candidate Rollins; let's put this chair up there. It will afford us a closer look."

"Sir, yes, Sir." Rollins stepped aside, pretending full cooperation in the enterprise.

"Put the chair on the footlocker, Candidate Rollins." Armstrong took the chair from Ramsay and placed it squarely in front of Joe.

Joe took great pains in arranging the chair so the legs rested solidly on the surface of the footlocker. Then he stepped aside and waited.

"Well? What are you waiting for, Candidate Rollins. Climb up there and take a better look. The rest of your battery mates are anxious to know there is absolutely nothing up there. Candidate Ramsay, will you be so good as to hold the chair steady so your cubiclemate won't fall?" Armstrong motioned Collier to step forward and take hold of the back of the chair.

Reluctantly, Joe climbed up on the chair and, knowing he had been caught, began extracting the bundles of contraband clothes and gear, handing them down, one by one.

"Well, that is a surprise. I wonder who these might belong to, Candidate Rollins?"

"Sir, they appear to belong to me, Sir," Rollins replied and hung his head when he had stepped down and stood watching as Armstrong examined a shirt to read the stitched-in nametag of its owner.

"It would seem so, Candidate Rollins; it would certainly seem so. Do you have any idea just how these items might have gotten themselves up there, Candidate Rollins?"

"Sir, I put them up there, Sir."

"A clear offense. So what do you think an appropriate punishment should be, Candidate Rollins?"

"Sir, offense, Sir?" Rollins was determined to play the innocent to the end.

"I'm warning you, Rollins, don't put me on. Insubordination is a dismissal offense."

"Sir, I would never be insubordinate, Sir." Dark circles of sweat had appeared at Rollins' armpits.

"What sort of punishment do you think is appropriate here, Candidate Rollins?"

"Sir, punishment, Sir? I don't understand."

"This seems a rather serious infraction to me—wouldn't you agree, Candidate Rollins?"

"Sir, an infraction of what, Sir? I don't recall any regulation about the use of the ceiling space, Sir. Where do you suppose I might look that up?"

Caught completely offguard, Armstrong was momentarily speechless.

"Make that ten demerits for standing inspection with an armful of dirty uniforms and other contraband," Armstrong ordered the candidate following with the demerit sheet.

"Candidate Daw, Candidate Rollins will report for the march up MB-4 both this afternoon and again tomorrow morning."

"Sir, yes, Sir," Battery Commander Daw replied as he followed the entourage of upperclassmen to the next cubicle down the line.

"I'm sorry, Joe. I hate to say it, but I have a feeling one of our classmates ratted you out," Collier commiserated when they had returned from lunch and Rollins was donning his fatigues to make the trip up MB-4.

"I know. I'm used to it. They act like they don't care if Mann and me are black, but most of 'em—even some of the TAC staff—really hate the idea of a black man being an officer. They can't help it. They been brought up that way." Rollins shook his head. A Negro candidate in the other barracks, Charles Mann, had been a late arrival, put back from Class 29 because of a sprained ankle.

"Yeah, but they don't represent the entire class. You can't let a few rednecks get your goat." As ashamed as he was to admit it, Collier had heard more than one of his bigoted classmates make snide remarks about the Army's token "niggers."

"Don't worry. It'll take more than a few white trash to get me to resign." Rollins picked up his pack—this time filled with the appropriate gear—and left with a resolute stride.

"He should have had better sense," Emma responded that evening when Collier recounted Rollins' misfortune.

"But we all have to hide our stuff. Every morning when we leave the barracks, we hide our dirty uniforms, the actual toilet kit we use, extra food...all evidence we actually live there."

"They are just trying to test your ingenuity, I guess," Emma shrugged.

"The entire program is dishonest—a total sham. It really isn't fair," Collier grumbled. It really pissed him off Emma couldn't see the dishonesty of it all.

"By the way, the head nurse at Post hospital called me to come back for a second interview tomorrow. If I can't make it, I'll see if Herb and Louise can meet you with your laundry," Emma said, pecking him on the cheek.

Thoroughly indoctrinated into the world of ignition systems and power trains, Easy battery's education in the mysteries of engines finally culminated with a hectic, overnight motor march on Thursday and Friday, July 24-25.

During the remaining days of July, Collier received no further word from Bo.

On Monday, July 28, Easy Battery became the first battery in the history of OCS to be allowed to sing while marching in formation to and from their scheduled routine.

"Get this battery in step, Candidate Shoemaker," Tac Lieutenant Robinson growled.

Shoemaker—who had succeeded Ettinger who, in turn had succeeded Daw, as Candidate Battery Commander—was struggling to get the battery in step as they began marching back to the OCS area following an afternoon in an ovenlike classroom, struggling to stay awake during a series of mind-numbing lectures on the inner workings of hand-held radios. Trying to remedy the situation, Collier, serving as Candidate First Sergeant, began calling out in what amounted to a comparative undertone, "Yo' lef, yo' lef, yo' lef, rye, lef..."

Collier's low-key cadence visibly improved Easy Battery's appearance as they marched along Sheridan Road. Still well outside the OCS area, one of the candidates in the ranks whispered to Collier, "Do you know any of the Jody Chant?"

"AIN'T NO USE IN GOING HOME, JODY'S GOT YO' GAL AND GONE..." Eager to find some relief from the deadly sameness of their routine, Collier shouted out the chant without further engcouragement, before glancing sheepishly over to Shoemaker for a reaction.

Caught completely by surprise, Shoemaker looked to Tactical Sergeant Grubbs who glanced anxiously to Tac Lieutenant Robinson marching alongside the battery on the sidewalk. Robinson shrugged, then grinned and nodded at Shoemaker.

Shoemaker caught the nod and shot Collier a quick thumbs up. "Keep it up."

"SOUND OFF," Collier shouted joyously at his newfound sense of freedom from the boring OCS SOP.

"One, two, three, four. One, two, three, four...One, two...three four," The battery of already highly-seasoned soldiers picked up the chant.

"I don't know, but I been told..." Collier moved to the front to encourage his fellow candidates.

"I don't know, but I been told..." Easy Battery responded with resounding enthusiasm.

"Oklahoma's a *heck* of a hole..." Collier was careful to keep his language clean.

"I don't know, but I believe, I'll be home by Christmas Eve..." The rest of the way back to the barracks, Collier and the battery kept up their lively Jody chorus.

Marching into the OCS compound, personnel from other batteries stopped and stared at this flagrant sacrilege. Once inside the OCS compound, Collier noticed Captain Whitley and Lieutenant Suit standing on the steps of the OCS HQ building taking it all in. When Collier looked over to Lieutenant Robinson, thinking to warn him they were being observed, Robinson nodded he had already seen them and indicated it was time to tone it down.

"Lieutenant Robinson says to call the Jody Cadence on the way to chow." Shoe whispered the surprising instruction to Collier when the battery fell in for evening mess. Apparently Captain Whitley had been favorably impressed with the visible improvement in Easy Battery's esprit. From that afternoon forward, Easy Battery became known as "The Singing Battery." Although there were periodic attempts at competition from companion batteries, none ever became a serious threat.

Depending on the source of the evaluation, it was a toss-up as to whether or not their course in Motors had been an abject failure or a resounding success. Daytime temperatures still relentlessly hovering over 100 degrees, the days blurred into weeks as the second battle for Old Baldy came and went. Collier was too exhausted and disheartened by his own plight to notice when the third battle for the bloody hill began on August 1. With headlines full of Eisenhower's promises to end the war—that coupled with the pressures of training—all of the news of Korea seemed moot and remote as the sweaty training moved on to courses designed to make it clear that artillery must shoot, move and communicate.

By August 1, the nightmarish motor march was long forgotten as Easy Battery began to explore the intricasies of Military Law and the Uniform Code of Military Justice. That lofty course of enlightenment was intermingled with practical classes in airborne operations as they were introduced to something called ABSOP involving the mysteries of determining center of gravity, how to tie a wonderous assortment of seaman's knots and how to load and tie down artillery, miscellaneous heavy equipment and their prime movers (military lingo for vehicles) in the bowels of a large cargo plane. This was quickly followed by two weeks of communications studies in which they were taught the mysteries of AN/GRC-9 two-way military radios, otherwise affectionately known as "Angry-Niners 619 and 610." Most of this training Collier had already had in Basic, but now that it was gradually dawning on him that these courses might someday save his life, it never hurt to review.

"Drive yourself over here, Candidate. Suck in that monstrous gut...screw in your chin...give me ten pushups..." In between classes, Collier and his classmates were fair game for the constant childish chickenshit from the Redbird upperclassmen. Every evening, Collier told Emma he was sick and tired of the emptyheaded foolishness. He was sorry, but FECOM or not, he was handing in his resignation the first thing the next morning. Yet every morning, for pride's sake—or whatever reason—he opted to tough it out another day.

"Jim called. He got your letter about meeting us in Oklahoma City Labor Day weekend. He says he will go ahead and book two rooms at the Biltmore Hotel, if that's okay with us." Emma was in a good mood when she met Collier on Sunday, August 24, in the PX lot after supper. Much anticipated as their "Liberation Day," the upcoming holiday marked the end of Easy Battery's eighth week of training. It was hard to believe, but in just six-and-a-half more days, the Singing Battery would be eligible for a weekend pass beginning at high noon Saturday and not ending until 8 PM Monday, giving them a full extra day for their first weekend of freedom.

"A full weekend in a first-class hotel—the luxury of clean percale sheets, a tile shower, sweet-smelling towels and breakfast in bed. Sounds great to me. I'm game. How about you?"

"Probably cost an arm and a leg, but it will be worth every dime. We can treat it like a second honeymoon." Emma reached across and squeezed the inside of his thigh.

"Call Jim and tell him to make the reservations. You can be packed and meet me right here at high noon Saturday. It will only take us a couple or three hours to make it to Oklahoma City." Collier reached across and tweaked her in response.

The remaining days before Saturday, Collier and his battery mates burned midnight oil giving extra attention to making the barracks and their daily uniforms ready for the scrutiny of the Redbirds and Tac Staff, not wanting to incur unnecessary demerits which would threaten their much-anticipated freedom. Thursday's gig sheet had only two demerits beside Collier's name. That night when he said his prayers, he remembered to breathe a final word of thanks.

Over breakfast, Friday, August 29, Collier briefly perused the headlines about the renewed, all-out air attack on the North Korean capital, fleetingly hoping this tactic might speed up the peace negotiations at Panmumjon. Tired of false heroes, he flipped through the pages looking to find what was playing at the movies in Oklahoma City; tomorrow afternoon this time, he would be on his way to civilization for the weekend, at least.

Or so he had believed.

"Ten demerits for 'Non-payment of Golf Club Dues;' jeez, Collie, what's this all about?" In the barracks to change into a fresh uniform, Friday, before noon mess, Joe Rollins asked with a frown, passing the gig sheet to Collier.

"Don't ask me. I didn't know you played golf, Joe." Collier reached for the sheet to take a look at the record of his own sins. As of yesterday afternoon, he had been a virtual shoo-in for a full weekend pass.

"No, no, not me, Collie. The ten gigs for 'Non-payment of Golf Club dues' are yours," Joe corrected.

"Ten demerits for 'Non-payment of Golf Club Dues'? Is this some kind of joke?" Collier looked down at the sheet, not believing his eyes at the damning notation which doomed his much-anticipated trip to Oklahoma City.

Immediately, Collier deduced the whole thing was some idiotic Army screw-up. The offense listed against him was for some completely spurious, certainly misplaced and ridiculous offense related to "dues" to a "club" which did not actually offer official memberships. He had never even played golf in Oklahoma—he barely knew how to find the Golf Club. Reflexively reaching into the hip pocket of his khakis, Collier retrieved his wallet and extracted a neatly-folded, but rather sweat-stained, square of paper. Carefully unfolding the paper so as not to damage its slightly stuck-together condition, Collier opened the paper and immediately felt a rush of relief. Beneath an official document heading for THE FORT SILL GOLF CLUB, the document had an official sub-heading RECEIPT OF PAYMENT FOR SERVICES AND GOODS. Beneath these headings was a section for the NAME and ADDRESS of the beneficiary of said "Services and Goods" and below that the sheet was lined like a ledger underneath headings for DATE, DESCRIPTION OF SERVICE OR PURCHASE and AMOUNT. Below the AMOUNT column at the bottom far-righthand corner of the page was a space for TOTAL.

There, right in front of him, inscribed in the blurry ink from a ballpoint pen, were appropriate notations to the fact that Pvt. Collier Boyd Ramsey, RA 13415453, A Battery, FARTC, Fort Sill, Oklahoma had on 17 May 1952 paid a total of $6.00 for Full Greens Fee Privileges through 17 August 1952. It was duly signed by Corporal Randy Something-or-Another, Asst. Club Professional—the last name was sweat-smeared, totally illegible.

Carefully reexamining his vindication to make absolutely certain of his ground, Collier dashed headlong down the stairs into the battery street, making straight for Lieutenant Robinson.

"Sir, Candidate Ramsay, Sir. Permission to speak to Lieutenant Robinson before the battery is formed...Sir," breathlessly, Collier reported to the Candidate Executive Officer Flood. "Please, Flood, there's been a gross snafu on my demerit sheet."

Reluctantly, Flood turned to Robinson who had overheard and nodded assent.

"Sir, Candidate Ramsay, Sir. Permission to discuss the demerit sheet," Collier reported to Lieutenant Robinson, just as the Candidate First Sergeant was announcing 'Easy Battery, zero five minutes.'

"At ease, Ramsay, what about the demerit sheet?" Robinson returned his salute.

"Sir, Candidate Ramsay, Sir. I believe the ten demerits I received on today's gig sheet are in gross error, Sir..." Collier went on to make his case that the Post Golf Club did not really have members *per se*, but operated on the basis of daily greens fees. He produced the sweat-stained receipt for payment of greens fee through August 17, pointing out it was dated May 17. "So, you see, Sir, this clearly states that I paid for 'Greens Fee Privileges.' It doesn't say anything about Club Membership."

"Well...I don't know, Candidate. I don't play golf. You can be excused from standing inspection tomorrow morning while you go straighten this out. When you're done, report back to me in the HQ building, and I'll make a ruling on whether the offense is valid. Until tomorrow morning, the offense stands." Robinson remained unmoved by Collier's facile explanation.

"Oh, Collier, how could you be so stupid? Does this mean our weekend with Jim in Oklahoma City is completely ruined?" Emma protested in utter exasperation that evening in the parking lot behind the PX.

"But it's all a stupid Army mistake. I didn't join their stupid club. I merely paid for greens fees three months in advance. I'll get it all straightened out first thing tomorrow morning. Can you meet me here at 0800 and give me a lift to the Golf Club?"

"Oh, honey, I can't. I have an eight o'clock appointment to get my hair fixed. You don't want to take me to meet Jim in Oklahoma City looking like a wreck, do you?"

"Well, if I can't straighten this out..." he began and stopped, not wanting to admit to even the barest possibility of guilt. "If I don't get this cleared up, I'll be restricted to the Battery area until 0800 Sunday morning, so it won't make much difference how you look."

"Oh, Collier, how could you? You better get this thing cleared up. I won't have my weekend completely ruined." She ground the car into gear and screeched out of the parking lot.

Sick to death of her selfish, self-centeredness, Collier was glad to see her leave.

After an almost sleepless night, at 0730 hours Collier walked directly from the mess hall and reported to OCS HQ where he was given a pass to travel to the Golf Club. When he boarded the regular Post bus traveling in the direction of the Old Post, he flashed the driver his pass. It was necessary for OCS underclassmen to be able to show official permission to be at large on the Post during duty hours.

At the Golf Club, after paying his green fees up through the month of September, Collier waited for a copy of the receipt and asked to see the Club officer, Major Roger Martin.

"Major, Sir, I've got a problem here..." he began and explained his quandary, ending with a plea for understanding and, most of all, a little creative help. "If you could see your way clear to jot a note to my CO explaining that your receipts do not carry an explanation that paying greens fees in advance obligate the player to an ongoing relationship requiring a formal resignation at such time that the player no longer wishes to continue to play golf, it would be greatly appreciated."

"I'll be glad to oblige, Candidate Ramsay, but instinct tells me that you shouldn't get your hopes up. Now, what's your CO's name and rank?" Major Martin took down Captain Whitley's name and quickly jotted a note on a sheet of Golf Club stationary. Before he folded it and placed it in an envelope, he showed it to Collier for his approval. "Does this satisfy your request?"

"Yes, Sir. Thank you very much, Sir." Collier said, waiting for the Major to dismiss him.

"You're very welcome and good luck. By the way, Candidate, what's your handicap?" the Major asked as he returned Collier's salute.

"I haven't been posting scores, Sir. But, at the moment, my handicap off the golf course is the U.S. Army and a self-centered wife," Collier said.

"I know the feeling," the Major said, as Collier hurried out to catch a returning bus.

"Sir, Candidate Ramsay, Sir. Permission to see Lieutenant Robinson, Sir," Back at OCS HQ, Collier reported to First Sergeant Desmond and handed him the envelope with Major Martin's note. Contrary to Army protocol, in OCS, the entire Tac Staff—NCOs included—were entitled to be addressed as 'Sir.' When Desmond took the envelope over to Robinson's desk, the Lieutenant opened it and glanced at the note. Then he looked up and motioned Collier to approach his desk.

"Sir, Candidate Ramsay reporting, Sir...I've taken care of my Golf Club dues. As you can see from Major Martin's note, there was a misunderstanding about my obligation. I was not aware I had to make official resignation to end my relationship with the Golf Club." He held a sharp salute and waited.

"Stand at ease. I'll need to confer with Captain Whitley." Robinson returned his salute, pushed back his chair, carried the note across the busy room and handed it to the Tactical Battery Commander who had been observing the entire exchange.

Following a brief whispered conversation between the two officers, Robinson walked back over. "Captain Whitley will see you now."

"Sir, Candidate Ramsay, thank you, Sir." Collier saluted and moved directly to Captain Whitley's desk. "Sir, Candidate Ramsay, reporting as ordered, Sir." Collier stood at attention waiting for Captain Whitley to look up from Major Martin's note which was resting at the center of his uncluttered military desk.

Collier continued to hold his brace and salute as, with great deliberation, Captain Whitley continued to ignore his presence. Finally, after what seemed ages, but was probably no more than a minute, Whitley slowly raised his head and gave Collier a withering look before he returned his salute.

"I shouldn't have to waste my time with this, Candidate Ramsay. What's your story? I'm warning you, it better be good." Whitley still hadn't offered him permission to stand at ease.

"Sir, Candidate Ramsay, no excuse, Sir. This was clearly a misunderstanding which, as you can see by Major Martin's letter, I have settled to the satisfaction of the Golf Club. The entire thing was the result of the Army failing to make the terms of my obligation clear to me. I assumed I understood but never thought to ask..." Collier began and made a rational, if not eloquent, presentation of his case. When he finished, he concluded, "I hope you will take into consideration my academic standing and my exemplary record of low demerits and erase these demerits from my record. My wife and I have plans to meet my brother this afternoon in Oklahoma City. My brother is undergoing pilot training in B-25s at Youngblood Field in Enid. We have reservations at the Biltmore and have been looking forward to this weekend for quite awhile."

"Candidate Ramsay, no matter how well he performs, an officer always meets his financial obligations. The offense stands. You will be restricted to the Battery area until 0800 tomorrow morning. It's unfortunate your wife and brother have to suffer for your failure to perform your duty. Any questions?"

"Sir, Candidate Ramsay, No Sir." Fairly seething with rage and his heart plummeting into his shoe tops, Collier saluted and waited to be dismissed.

"That is all. Report back to Lieutenant Robinson." Whitley returned the salute and Collier executed an About Face and turned to leave.

"Hold up a moment, Candidate Ramsay. Drive yourself back here. I have something else I feel the need to tell you."

"Sir, Candidate Ramsay, Sir." Collier returned to Whitley's desk and reported again.

"I think you should know, Candidate Ramsay, it is has been reported to me that you exhibit an attitude of confidence to which you have no legal claim."

"Sir, Candidate Ramsay, Sir. I don't understand, Sir?"

"A pity, Candidate. For the sake of your future, I hope you won't waste too much time figuring it out. You're dismissed."

"Candidate Ramsay, drive yourself up here...," to add insult to injury, Taft—in his first morning as Candidate First Sergeant—ordered Collier to report "front and center" as Easy Battery stood in formation following Saturday morning inspection.

"Sir, Candidate Ramsay, yes, Sir." Collier reported, wondering what else could possibly happen.

"Candidate Ramsay, Tactical Lieutenant Robinson wants you to address this battery for five minutes on the subject of "An Officer's Responsibility to Meet His Financial Obligations." Any questions?" Candidate First Sergeant Taft whispered.

"Sir, Candidate Ramsay, no, Sir." Collier saluted, then asked in a matching whisper, "Does he mean now?"

"Yes. He *definitely* means now." Candidate First Sergeant Taft left no room for doubt.

Over Taft's shoulder, Collier saw Captain Whitley, standing ramrod straight behind the new Candidate Battery Commander Hundley and Tactical Lieutenant Robinson. When Collier momentarily locked eyes with Whitley, the Captain's mouth twisted into a malevolent grin.

"Tactical Lieutenant Robinson has asked me to address this battery on the subject of 'An Officer's Responsibility to Meet His Financial Obligations,' an area in which I have recent firsthand experience. Some lessons are hard come by, but in my experience those lessons which are accompanied with some discomfort or pain are the lessons that best define a man's character..." Collier began, struggling to maintain self-control.

"I'm sorry, Emma, but the bastard, Whitley, wouldn't give an inch. When I got back from settling the Golf Club dues, he told me the offense would stand and dismissed me without so much as a 'howdy-do.' But, cheer up, Honey. The good news is we can still leave tomorrow morning at 0800. With luck, we could be in Oklahoma City in time to meet Jim for a late brunch..." following Saturday inspection, Collier sheepishly confessed to Emma who was waiting with the engine running in the PX parking lot, freshly-coiffed and with her bags packed. Wisely, he withheld recounting Whitley's cryptic remarks and the added mortification of having to make a stupid speech to the entire battery.

"Sometimes I can't believe just how utterly hopeless you really are, Collier Boyd Ramsay. Get out of this car. You are a complete waste of my time," Emma sniffed disdainfully. She scratched off and left him standing in the parking lot, without so much as a goodbye wave.

All afternoon and evening, Collier tried to call Emma, but couldn't reach her. He was too embarrassed to call the Rudolphs to ask if they had seen her. When he finally went to bed, the only positive thing he could say about the beginning of his first weekend following Class 30's mandatory eight-week restriction was the good luck he hadn't been assessed enough demerits to force him to make a dreaded march back up MB-4.

Infuriated that Collier had spoiled her plans for an idyllic weekend in Oklahoma City, Emma drove directly to the Post hospital. Heading straight to a phone in the nearly-deserted nursing office, she dialed a number she had jotted on the back of an envelope. The party on the other end picked up on the first ring.

"Trey, I'm glad I caught you. There has been a slight change in plans. My dumb husband got himself restricted until tomorrow morning. It looks like I can get away this afternoon after all. Would it be okay if I came over and visited for awhile?"

"It would be better than okay. I'll leave the door open while I jump in the shower."

CHAPTER TWENTY-NINE

THE ROANOKE TIMES
Roanoke, Virginia, Tuesday, September 2, 1952
NAVY MAKES IT ONE-TWO SMASH

SEOUL, Tuesday, September 2 (AP) – The Navy Monday followed up its massive bombing raids at Siberia's doorstep, with smashing blows by air and sea at the Korean port of Chongjin.

The one-two smash, which carried the war to within view of Russian guards on the Siberia-Korea frontier, was by far the biggest all-Navy show of the Korean War...

The pilots who worked over Chongjin had carried out the daring raids of the morning on the synthetic oil refinery at Aoji, just eight miles west of the Siberian border...

* * * *

Largest Navy Show of War

The Navy said a record 338 sorties of individual flights were hurled against the three targets...

THE DAILY OKLAHOMAN
Oklahoma City, Oklahoma, Wednesday, September 3, 1952
SMALLER DEFENSE BUDGET FORECAST

WASHINGTON, Tuesday, September 2 (AP) – Secretary of Defense Lovett said today the armed forces may not ask for as much money in the next fiscal year as was given them in the current year.

WASTING NOT ONE PRECIOUS SECOND of his cruelly-delayed "Liberation Day," Sunday morning, Collier was already in the PX parking lot and waiting to leave on the stroke of 0800 hours.

As soon as Emma pulled up, she slid into the passenger seat as Collier replaced her under the wheel. Collier's foot jammed the accelerator pedal to the floorboards as he headed for Oklahoma City in the Sunday-morning traffic. The odometer indicated a little over 100 miles and his wristwatch showed 0952 hours when he pulled to a stop in front of the marquee of the towering Biltmore hotel.

Located on the southeast corner of Sheridan and Harvey at the heart of the bustling old cattle-and-oil metropolis, the Biltmore hotel was a venerable Oklahoma landmark. Whether true or not (both the 1931 First National Center and 1931 Ramsey Tower were officially listed as 33 stories), when it opened in 1932 at twenty-six stories, the impressively-ornate Biltmore was claimed to be the tallest building in Oklahoma. And, with more desireable rooms going for the outrageously exorbitant price of $4.00 per night at the height of the Great Depression, it certainly had to be the most expensive. Arriving at the stately hotel in time to enjoy Sunday brunch with Jim in the impressive hotel dining room, afterward, Collier and Emma retired immediately to their room—ostensibly to take a refreshing nap. Hardly before they closed the door, Emma was pulling her dress over her head, heading for the shower where Collier joined her and began soaping every inch of her glowing skin.

"Did you put your diaphragm in before...?"

"Forget the diaphragm..." dewy-fresh from the shower, Emma put her fingers to his lips to shush his question as they immediately fell on the bed and became entangled in what seemed to Collier the most powerful, completely uninhibited lovemaking of their entire married life.

Afterward, lightly snoring on the bed in a sensual stupor, Collier was oblivious as Emma—much anticipating a return engagement of their erotic afternoon, but now anxiously counting on her fingers the date of her last period—silently berated herself for foolishly forgetting to take similar precautions during her orgiastic reunion with Trey Moseley the previous afternoon and evening. Tiptoeing into the bathroom with her travel kit, she inserted her diaphragm before she showered and climbed back into bed. Snuggling against the well-conditioned body of her sleeping husband, she sighed contentedly, unconcerned she might be trying to close the proverbial barn door after the horse had already gotten out.

"I'm in the lobby. Is Emma ready to go window shopping? Our movie starts in thirty minutes," Jim roused them out of their nap a few minutes past noon. Over brunch, Collier and Jim had agreed to take in the latest John Wayne movie playing just down the street while Emma browsed the chic downtown shops.

"Go ahead to the movie. You need to spend some time with Jim. After you shower off, I think I'll run a tub and soak before I go shopping," Emma urged Collier to join his brother.

"We haven't told our folks yet, but Hitch and I are getting married in Enid immediately following my graduation. She is going to ask Emma to be her Maid of Honor and I'm counting on you being Best Man." Jim broke the news to Collier over a game of straight pool in a nearby downtown billiard parlor after they had left the John Wayne movie early. Enduring an hour of tiresome saloon brawls with breaking mirrors and chairs was enough; they both agreed if you'd seen one John Wayne film, you'd pretty much seen them all.

"Well, congratulations, Brother. How do you think Mom will take it? Last I heard from Dad, they're planning to come to Lawton for my graduation on December thirteen. We plan to drive both cars up to Enid in time to see you get your bars and wings on the sixteenth." Caught completely off guard, Collier did his level best to show enthusiasm. Betty Hitchcock was Catholic. The dyed-in-the-wool Baptist, Lida Ramsay, became semi-hysterical anytime the subject of Jim marrying Hitch came up.

Truth be known, Collier had serious reservations about Jim marrying Hitch, but it didn't have anything to do with her being Catholic. From the first time he'd met Hitch when Jim was still attending Roanoke College, Collier felt a subtle antipathy. In this regard, he understood his feelings had a lot to do with Hitch's overtly abrasive Yankee personality. The oddly-matched couple had been mostly apart since Jim had left Roanoke College. It was Collier's not-so-humble opinion that one of the major reasons the relationship had lasted this long was that it fed on Jim's resentment of Lida's obsession with Hitch's Catholicism, fueled and kept alive by the axiom: "Absence makes the heart grow fonder."

"That's Mom's problem. Lida or no Lida, we're getting married. Hitch's folks are driving out from New York." Jim glanced over his shoulder at Collier and shrugged before he turned back to the table and called, "six ball in the cross-corner!" as he deftly executed the difficult bank shot. Judging from the quality of his pool game, Collier surmised his brother hadn't been spending all his time flying airplanes.

"Don't be such a pessimist. It may be a marriage made in heaven. I wish them all the best. Let's take a shower together. We still have two hours before dinner." Emma was in a romantic mood when Collier rejoined her later in their room.

That evening, Jim insisted that they let him take them to the Cattlemen's Cafe, a popular local restaurant. Taking a cab through the suburbs, they all marveled at the grotesque—but nevertheless ubiquitous—oil rigs pumping tirelessly on the front lawns and backyards of the houses they passed.

"How long have these wells been pumping?" Collier asked the taxi driver.

"The first Oklahoma oil strike, the famous Nellie Johnstone Number One, was in 1897 near Bartlesville, about forty miles north of Tulsa. That old gusher put Oklahoma on the map. I guess when you come right down to it, the old Nellie J changed the whole dang world. They've built a scale model of the original rig up there to mark the spot. If you go up that way, you should drive over and take a look," the driver enthused, delighted at the opportunity to talk about a celebrated history which made instant millionaires of hardscrabble ranchers.

"Bartlesville? I thought Tulsa was the 'Oil Capital of the World?'" Collier asked, somewhat confused.

"Well...that's true, but the Tulsa field wasn't discovered 'til nineteen aught-one at Red Fork nearby to Tulsa. Back then, Tulsa was just a trading settlement with a general store and about two-hundred people, more or less. The famous Glenn Pool field was discovered in aught-five, and the reserves were so big they had to build storage tanks to store all of the crude pumping out of the ground. Overnight, Tulsa mushroomed from a wide place in the road into a boomtown." The driver glanced back over his shoulder to see if they were properly impressed.

"So, some of these wells we're passing have been here since around 1905?" Collier asked.

"No, no. Oklahoma City remained pretty much a cattle town until 1928 when the Discovery Well came in," the driver corrected. "Wasn't until most a year later the Wilcox zone was discovered when the Mary Sudik Number One blew wild for over eleven days—blew oil clear into downtown. I reckon that gusher was about the most publicized oil well in history. Remember driving by the State Capitol Building?" the driver asked, his voice brimming enthusiam. "There's an oil well pumping right across the street that was drilled on a slant to a spot directly beneath the Capitol Building. The Oklahoma City field is still one of the most productive oil and gas fields in the world."

"No wonder these folk have wells pumping in their front yards." Collier smiled.

"There's a marker where Discovery Well was and I could show you where Mary Sudik Number One was, too. It's only about a mile-and-a-half from the Discovery Well. I'd only charge you five bucks for the side trip. Wouldn't be more than twenty or thirty minutes out of your way," the driver glanced hopefully in the rearview mirror.

"Oil, schmoil, who cares! I'm starved. How far is this restaurant, anyway?" Emma interrupted, effectively ending the driver's running history about famous oil wells.

"That would be interesting, but the lady's hungry," Collier said, "We don't have time this trip; maybe some other time."

"Is Tinker Field anywhere near here?" Jim asked. Tinker Field was a fairly well-known Army Air Base during WWII.

"Tinker's a little southeast from downtown. Your restaurant is more southwest." In the rearview mirror, the driver gave Jim's cadet insignia the once-over. "You gonna be assigned to Tinker when you get your wings?"

"Not that I know of, but you never can tell. One of my instructors up at Vance was stationed there during World War Two," Jim shrugged. They had left the residential areas and were now driving through what looked to be a large area of stockyards.

"Well, here we are. That's the Cattlemen's up ahead on the right," the driver announced as he slowed the cab and pulled into the crowded parking lot of a rather seedy-looking restaurant. Much to Collier's disappointment, the Cattlemen's was located smackdab in the middle of a sprawling spider-web of railheads abruptly ending in a confusion of cattle-filled stock pens.

"This doesn't look or smell very appetizing to me." Emma wrinkled her nose at the aroma of cattle dung hanging heavily in the superheated early September air.

"You should get a whiff after we've had some rain," the driver snorted.

"Why on earth would they put a restaurant here?" Emma whined.

"To feed the hungry cowboys and cattlemen—cowboys got to eat Ma'am. The Cattlemen Cafe was opened in 1910...the same year this new 'Stockyard City' was opened. It's changed hands over the years, but the Cattlemen's Cafe's been the best place for steaks in Oklahoma City—probably the best steak place in the whole Southwest—ever since. The last time it changed hands was in 1945 when old Hank Fry lost it in a craps game at the Biltmore hotel to the present owner Percy Wade."

"Isn't there some other, more respectable place?" Emma started to protest even before the driver turned off the engine.

"Look, Emma, the driver can take you and Collier back to the hotel dining room if you'd rather eat somewhere else, but I'm going to eat here. The Cattlemen's Cafe is an authentic American landmark. Several presidents, famous politicians, movie stars like John Wayne, Gene Autry, Randolph Scott—well-known people from all over the world come here for these steaks." Obviously displeased with Emma's complaining, Jim handed the driver a ten-dollar bill and opened the door.

"Don't be silly, Brother. We're coming. Come on, Emma, you act as if you never sniffed a little cowshit before." Laughing, Collier dismounted and helped his wife out of the opposite side of the cab.

The homespun interior of the Cattlemen was something like stepping into a popular highway truck stop. Against one wall, there was a diner-like counter where several cowboy types sat on stools, picking their teeth, patting their bellies and belching with satisfaction; against the opposite wall were maroon-colored leather booths. Hanging everywhere were framed vintage photos of the surrounding stockyards dating all the way back to 1910. Included among the pictures were a number of exterior and interior shots of the eatery, with rather artless pencil sketches of the previous owner, Hank Fry, alongside the current proprietor, Percy Wade, and most of the celebrities mentioned by the taxi driver, providing a visual history of both restaurant and the glorious days when cattle and cowboys were kings in the old West.

"What can I get you, Hon?" a skinny waitress with a Shirley Temple mop of copper curls and a toothpick between her teeth, asked as soon as they were seated in a well-worn leather booth in the main dining room.

"Don't we get to see a menu?" Emma sniffed disdainfully.

"Right by your elbow...see there between the sugar dispenser and the catsup, Hon," the rawboned waitress smiled evenly, refusing to be insulted by the likes of the prissy bitch in front of her. "Mostly all you get is steak here—best you ever sunk a tooth in. If you're really hungry, get the T-Bone."

"Do you have *filet mignon?*" Emma asked.

"Best you ever tasted—full eight ounces, melt in your mouth. We can also serve a smaller filet with bacon...take your choice. What y'all want to drink, Hon?" The waitress continued to hold the little pad close to her concave chest, the longsuffering smile pasted to her lips.

"I'll have iced tea," Emma said.

"Same for me," Collier echoed, still looking at the menu. He was hungry enough to eat a whole cow.

"Are you as dry in here as the rest of the state?" Jim asked, hoping to find a drink with more hair on its chest.

"I guess I might find some real honest-to-god booze for you, Hon. You want it mixed with ginger ale?" the waitress winked mischievously.

"If you got Scotch whiskey, I'll just take about two fingers straight—in a water glass. If it's bourbon or blend, some ginger ale on the side would be fine." Jim winked back.

By the time the waitress returned with their drinks, Collier and his brother were ready to order their steaks. Not surprisingly to Collier, his brother ordered the T-Bone and Emma ordered the small *filet mignon*. As hungry as he was, Collier ordered the strip sirloin. The menu said the strip was a center cut. To Collier, that promised a better likelihood of natural tenderness. From the downhome look of the place—and even though their advertising proclaimed their steaks were "USDA Choice and Prime"—Collier assumed these cowboys had never heard about aging cow meat. When their steaks were served, however, he was absolutely flabbergasted to find the beef had been aged to perfection. His sirloin was the best steak he had ever eaten.

"What do you think of the Peace Talks? In my opinion, the entire thing is like some sort of obscene comic opera—all those pompous bastards dressed up in their phony dress uniforms and parading back and forth for the photographers. They ought to send the lot of the 'so-called' negotiators into combat. Why didn't the UN declare a 'ceasefire' at the beginning, when they first went to the tables? Those clowns are waltzing in and out of the negotiation tents while good men are dying almost within earshot of Panmunjom," Jim complained rather soberly in the taxi going back to the Biltmore. Over dinner at the Cattlemen's Cafe, Jim had put away a sizeable amount of Scotch. Collier was amazed his baby brother's speech showed no sign of inebriation.

"I couldn't agree more. Why do we let them get by with it? Truth be told, I wonder just how many of our congressmen and other government officials have sons in the military," Collier echoed his brother's righteous indignation.

Looking out the window at the Oklahoma City skyline, Jim sniffed at an expensive cigar he had purchased back at the Cattlemen's. Pensively rolling it between his fingers, he respectfully refrained from lighting it in the cab. "Why do we let Truman and the do-nothing politicians get by with any of this? I love this country as much as any man, but we supposedly agreed to end the war over a year ago—we're supposed to be ironing out the details of how to split up the real estate. Why do we have to continue the killing?" his brother asked.

"As far as I'm concerned, it's criminal. For all we know, Bruce Bohon and hundreds of others may be lying dead or wounded while those empty-headed diplomats are sitting around the truce tents complaining over the lack of proper laundry service and ice for their dinner cocktails. What's the bloody point?" Adrenaline rising, Collier voiced all the frustrations he had held in check since January, all during Basic and especially now he was in officer training. Collier was no coward, but he hated to think about the good men being betrayed while the country's so-called "fearless leaders" used brave men as pawns in a meaningless chess game to determine where some mythical line would be drawn on the map. Back at Sill, he couldn't allow himself to verbalize any criticism of the White House or Congress—after all, he aspired to become an officer and officers shouldn't question the wisdom of their commanding officers.

"Ease up, Brud," Jim squeezed his shoulder. "To those assholes in Washington and Moscow and Peking, war is just some sort of surreal freaking game. Human lives mean nothing, to clowns like Truman and Atcheson and Churchill. It's always been this way. Surely as long as these peace negotiations have dragged on, they can't go on much longer."

"Don't be so certain. I wouldn't be at all surprised to find myself in Korea in combat before the end of January. We just got news that Lieutenant Kit Hathaway, one of our original upper classmen, was severely wounded last week at Old Baldy. Kit graduated OCS the first week in August. That was scarcely a month ago," Collier said with a slight shiver.

"Don't be so melodramatic. You still have three-and-a-half months to go. The stupid war should be over by then," Emma sniffed.

"I hope you're right," Jim said and turned back to the approaching skyline.

Saying their goodbyes with promises of a reunion in Enid following Collier's graduation in mid-December, Collier and Emma watched Jim begin the long drive back to Enid after breakfast on Labor Day morning. As soon as his brother's car disappeared around the corner, Collier went to the hotel desk and requested a late checkout. Putting the Do Not Disturb sign on their doorknob and slipping the security chain into the slot, Collier turned to find Emma already spread-eagle naked on the bed.

Back at Sill at the formation Tuesday morning, still walking around in a rosy haze of sensual afterglow, once again Collier was abruptly ordered to report to the front of the battery.

"Tactical Battery Commander Whitley requests you enlighten our fellow candidates on 'The Duties of a Lance Jack in Paris, France.' You have zero-five minutes," Candidate First Sergeant Taft whispered when Collier drove himself sharply front and center.

"What's a Lance Jack?" Collier whispered back, holding his smart salute and trying desperately not to shit his pants.

"I don't have a clue what a Lance Jack is. You're on your own, Candidate," the Candidate First Sergeant whispered, returning Collier's salute.

Fully resigning himself to being the victim of Whitley's twisted sense of humor, without the slightest notion what on earth a Lance Jack might be, Collier executed a sharp about face.

"Easy Battery, give me your attention up here. It has just been brought to my attention that this battery is sadly lacking in knowledge of the vital subject of the duties of a Lance Jack in Paris, France..." With a surreptitious glance at his watch, Collier began improvising a nonsensical dissertation. Only after the minute hand on his watch was a full three-zero seconds past the five minute mark did he allow himself to conclude the whimsical speech, "...so you see, the main duty of a Lance Jack in Paris, France, is to see to it that the moral sanctity of officers of our glorious military does not become a senseless casualty transversing the treacherous mine fields of the *Folies Bergere* or die in the trenches at *Place Pigalle*." When he finished, Collier saluted and requested permission to return to ranks. Behind Taft, Collier saw that Captain Whitley and Lieutenants Robinson and Suit had all turned their faces away to conceal their amusement.

Waiting for the morning announcements, Collier slowly came to an awareness of an almost mystical change. Miraculously, since the consciousness-raising—near heart-attack-producing—incident of the ten demerits for the "Non-payment of Golf Club Dues," his gig sheet had been relatively free of major deficiencies. Collier wondered if they were cutting him some slack because of his age. Turning this curious realization over in his mind, Von Gruenigen and Collins were older by at least a couple years, and he was not aware the powers that be were taking it easy on them. Perhaps the easing of pressures was because of his outstanding performances in the classroom—and on the OP. Had the Tac Staff instructed the Redbirds to cut him some slack?. One thing for certain, these welcome dispensations had nothing to do with exemplary soldiering.

"I don't know but I believe, I'll be home by Christmas Eve..." in what now had become Easy Battery SOP, Collier took control of calling cadence as the "Singing Battery" marched to breakfast. Gradually infused with a benign sense of enlightenment over the past two months, he had slowly become aware that a good bit of his natural resentment for the childish, toy-soldier OCS harassment had dissipated. Now, in a kind of "white-light" or "burning bush" experience, it occurred to him, as he called the Jody cadence, to wonder if becoming the focus of Captain Whitley's hazing might actually represent some sort of mystical rite of passage. Protected by sublime ignorance, had he somehow been elevated to a sort of special status?

In the mess hall, washing down a huge breakfast of oatmeal with raisins and brown sugar and a large helping of powdered scrambled eggs with link sausages and French toast with a giant mug of GI coffee, Collier glanced soberly around at a number of relatively new faces, suddenly sobered that during the crucible first eight weeks of training, Easy Battery had already lost at least thirty—maybe even as many as forty—more than a third of their original number. As fast as the washouts and dropout's bunks came vacant, they had been replaced with candidates from Baker, Charlie and Dog batteries who had been put back for lost training due to sickness or injury or a few who were put back for classroom deficiencies. Beginning their breakthrough ninth week, Collier realized that those who still remained had somehow survived a kind of mystical gauntlet. Examining himself in the mirror the first morning back from his thoroughly liberating weekend in Oklahoma City, it was as if—like the fabled Alice—he had stepped back through some magic looking glass. Whatever had transpired, his outlook had miraculously taken on an entirely different perspective. Incredibly, the once-rebellious Collier Boyd Ramsay no longer wanted to run up the white flag.

That evening following study hall, Easy Battery held an informal meeting and formed committees to oversee such necessary areas as Honor Code, Policies and Standards (which dealt with establishing uniformity in SOP), Activities (planning social activities, God willing) and even appointing a five-man Staff for putting together a Class Book. Accepting time was fast slipping away, Wells, a former newspaperman, immediately accepted chairmanship of the Class Book Committee, and, although it meant he would have to give up most of his coveted, all-too-brief stress-relieving late-afternoon sessions on the PT field punting a football or shooting baskets with Reed, Collier resignedly accepted the responsibility of handling the layout design and producing original art and hand-lettering for the book's Section Headers.

Without realizing it, other subtle changes in Collier's perspective were taking place. By virtue of an outstanding score on his Motors test—a subject quite foreign and intimidating to him in the beginning—Collier realized that he had grown more confident he could actually stick it out. Like the first time he witnessed the sunrise from the summit of Sharp Top back home at the Twin Peaks of Otter, it suddenly dawned on him he had discovered a completely new sense of himself.

He was now determined to become an officer in the U.S. Army.

Because—unlike most of the others in Easy Battery—a great number of the principles were already familiar to him from having undergone Artillery Basic and FDC training at FARTC, Collier found himself looking forward to the daunting mysteries of Gunnery which began the first day of their ninth week of training. Carrying their newly-issued, white cloth bags, jam-packed with strange instruments called GSTs and GFTs, along with a curious assortment of maps, slide rules, triangles, protractors, and other odds and ends, the lads of Easy were marched to a nearby group of classrooms identified by neatly-lettered, wooden signs on the doors bearing the inscription: GUNNERY, 1ST WEEK.

The mind-bending, knee-weakening intricacies of Gunnery included an array of courses delving into the principals of calculus, physics, chemistry, and astronomy, plus an intimidating dose of trigonometry, which Collier had skipped in high school, then struggled with—actually floundered in—at Bluefield College. At Bluefield, he would have gladly dropped trig had not his pre-med curriculum required he that take it. Ultimately, Collier was given an entirely gratuitous—totally dishonest, actually—C-minus from the young professor, mainly because he was Captain and high-scorer on the freshman basketball team.

"FB, FDC, OP, OF, GST, GFT, Preponderance, Fork, Meteorology, and Survey, it's all gobbledygook to me," Joe Rollins echoed the plaintive chorus of his bewildered classmates in study hall during the middle of the first week of Easy Battery's baptism to Gunnery.

In the spirit of Class 30's watchword, "Cooperate and graduate," Collier undertook to tutor Rollins and Nat Reed. Fresh from Artillery Basic training at FARTC, Nat was doing okay on the OP, but struggling with the mathmatical intricacies of the classroom.

From the beginning, slowly but surely, this rude and daunting initiation into the more complicated inner workings of Field Artillery began to take its toll on the men of Easy Battery. By the beginning of the second week of Gunnery—Class 30's tenth week overall—four candidates had already been put back two weeks to

Fox Battery, to give them a second chance to demonstrate competency in this essential core curriculum. Two more were given their outright walking papers.

To add to this stress, Collier—along with several other classmates—had received letters from home saying that mysterious strangers in dark suits had been skulking about making inquiries about them. Collier became particularly anxious when he learned that his second cousins had told his mother a pair of well-dressed gentlemen had been asking questions around Bluefield, and his old RPI classmate, Walt Davies, had written a note telling him the same thing was happening in Richmond around the Franklin Street campus of RPI.

During Easy's second week in Gunnery, a Candidate named Charles Drake showed up on Monday when they came back for lunch. A wispy, whitish blond with albino eyebrows, looking to be several years older and totally out of place, Drake's hard-used uniforms clearly showed that he had been a master sergeant as he moved his gear into the space two cubicles down from Collier and Rollins recently vacated by Candidate Roger Smith, who, already busted back from Dog Battery, had voluntarily resigned after only two days of Gunnery lectures.

The newly-arrived Candidate Drake proved to be about as forthcoming on the subject of Charles Drake as a wooden cigar-store Indian. From the precious little anybody could get out of him, he was a veteran of a storied, old-timey, wheel-mounted, mule-drawn, 75mm mountain artillery outfit in Colorado which had distinguished itself in the Italian Alps during WWII. Ostensibly, Drake had been sent to Sill to upgrade the TO&E of his highly-specialized battalion with the addition of another combat-experienced commissioned officer, while brushing up on the latest in modern Gunnery techniques in the bargain. Then, just when the men of Easy were getting accustomed to having the taciturn combat veteran in their ranks, at the end of his second week, Drake simply vanished—disappeared just as suddenly and mysteriously as he had appeared. As if the stress brought on by the grind of Gunnery classes and Drake's enigmatic will-o-the-wisp appearance and disappearance weren't enough to worry about, toward the end of the second week in Gunnery, the Tactical Battery Commander, Captain Jesse W. Whitley, called Nordby, McAdams, Lowell and Etnire aside and handed them a perfumed envelope, formally engraved with the legend: **Oklahoma College For Women, Chickasha, Oklahoma**. Inside the envelope was an engraved invitation requesting the presence of Class 30 at a semi-formal, fall dinner-dance on their campus the following Saturday night from 2000 hours until 2400 hours.

"Begging your pardon, sir, I think we may have a potential problem here?" Standing nearby with Collier and several others, Candidate Exec, Bob Glendening, spoke up immediately.

"A formal dance with real-live college girls? What could possibly be the problem with that?" Nordby, who was from South Dakota, objected with a vociferous howl.

"Hold up a second. What are we talking about here, Candidate Glendening?" Captain Whitley raised his hand. Something in Glendening's tone of voice put him immediately on guard.

"Sir, I'm from Oklahoma City, Sir, and I used to date a girl from Oklahoma College for Women. What about Rollins and Mann? Oklahoma College for Women is for white girls. They have admitted a few Indian girls, but mostly OCW is as white as driven snow." In B Section's barracks next door to Collier, Glendening's cubicle mate, Charles Mann from Georgia, was Easy Battery's second Negro Candidate, recently put back from Dog Battery.

"See here, gentlemen, we're not applying for admission. May I remind you that both individually and collectively the U.S. Army is color blind," Captain Whitley arbitrarily brushed aside the notion anyone might discriminate against a future officer of the Army because of race.

"Okay. What about it? Any other objections to accepting the invitation?" Etnire looked at Norby, McAdams, Lowell and Glendening.

Standing just within earshot, Collier heard the entire exchange. However well-intended, he seriously doubted Captain Whitley's naïve assumption that the lily-white faculty and student body of the woman's college would welcome Rollins and Mann with open arms. Surely Whitley was aware that, beneath the surface, a goodly number—at least more than half—of the ninety-eight white members of Class 30 were also—and not-so-secretly—prejudiced against Negroes. More than once Collier had openly rebuked his more bigoted classmates when he overheard them openly referring to both Rollins and Mann as "niggers" or "spades" or "darkies" behind their backs. Moreover, Collier was dead certain Rollins and Mann weren't completely oblivious to their classmates' prejudice against their race.

No one spoke up. If the members of the Activities Committee doubted Captain Whitley's reassurance that Rollins and Mann would be welcome, their objections remained unspoken.

"It's settled then," Etnire announced with finality. "Where is this oasis of femininity?"

"Chickasha is about fifty miles north, on the main route to Oklahoma City. The trip takes approximately an hour each way. Busses have been reserved to arrive here at 1830 hours. Dress khaki uniform. The entire Battery will attend. There will be no exceptions," Candidate Battery Commander, 'Sal' Salamone, announced Easy Battery's plans to attend the OCW dinner-dance at the next formation.

"What about married men whose wives are here in Lawton? Are our wives invited?" Bert Hancock raised his hand, saving Collier and Flood, along with several others, from having to ask the same question.

"Sorry, but wives are not invited. We are not going to quibble over such details. Tell your wives this is a function of Army Military Etiquette Instruction. Married or single, individually and collectively, Easy Battery will attend as one man. There will be no exceptions." Captain Whitley stepped forward and made himself crystal clear.

"I hear that you're going to a dance at some woman's college and I'm not invited." When Emma met him in the PX lot that evening, Collier discovered that the wives' grapevine had already done its work.

"We don't have a choice—it comes under the umbrella of our Military Etiquette Instruction," Collier parroted Captain Whitley' advice.

"Military hanky-panky, if you ask me. We wives won't stand for this. Bert Hancock's wife, Ellie, says it is the same as suborning adultery." Emma pounded her fist on the steering wheel for emphasis. Ellie Hancock was forever spouting legal terms; her father was a hotshot Tulsa lawyer. "We're going to go as a group and take this to the Post Commandant."

"Look, Emma, I don't like this anymore than you do, but it's part of the drill. You can't fight the U.S. Army. Might as well give in and accept it. Taking this silliness to Colonel Burrill won't help," Collier endeavored to sooth her indignation, but she screeched the Studebaker off in a huff.

Over the next ten days, Emma and the other wives gradually calmed down, accepting the trip to Chickasha as just another blazing fascine in their collective martyrdom as "Joan at the stake." Fortuitously for Collier, as far as Emma was concerned, the issue was quickly resolved; by the time the night of the dance rolled around, she was scheduled to work second shift.

In the disquieting matter of Joe Rollins' and Charlie Mann's being made to feel as welcome as their fellows, before the battery boarded the two large Army busses for the trip to Chickasha on the appointed Saturday, Easy Battery's official chaperones, Lieutenants Robinson and Suit and their wives—splendidly attired in dress uniforms and floor-length ball gowns—secretly enlisted Collier, Dudley Von Gruenigen, George Barker, Brewster Robertson, a former high-school classmate, Jim Miller and several others of their more racially-unbiased classmates to stick close to these dark-skinned brothers-in-arms to insure that they felt included. According to this carefully-worked-out plan of action, Collier and Von Gruenigen and their co-conspirators seated themselves with Rollins and Mann near the center of the bus so they would be neither conspicuous by being among the first, nor stand out as being the last to step off of the bus.

Alighting from the vehicle in front of a large building at the woman's college a few minutes before 2000 hours, the two bus-loads of starched and polished khaki-clad soldiers were immediately greeted by an enthusiastic contingent of carefully-coiffed, surprisingly-attractive young women in rather jejune and unstylish—albeit obviously expensive and blushingly-daring—evening gowns, who ushered them into a large ballroom where a sumptuous buffet loaded with a cornucopia of fancy, catered food stood as mute testimony to Oklahoma's recent bonanza of instant oil-rich millionaires.

"My name is Thelma Ray Faulkner. You can call me Thelma. I'm a junior here." A pretty, rather outgoing, brown-haired girl walked across and introduced herself as Collier entered the spacious hall.

"I'm Collier Ramsay. May I present Joe Rollins, Charlie Mann and Dudley Von Gruenigen—you can call him Von—this is John Garrett and George Barker." Collier shook her hand as he introduced a group of his classmates according to the best military ettiquette.

"I'm pleased to meet you all. Now, hurry and get in the buffet line. The band starts at nine." Taking Collier by the elbow, Thelma steered them toward the buffet line. After they had loaded their plates with food and were seated at a large round table covered with a snowy-white table cloth and matching linen napkins, Thelma introduced them to her schoolmates: senior Betty Jean Brannan and sophomores, Mo Anderson, Betty Remy and Ann Marie Hooper. They had hardly begun eating before Von Gruenigen had Thelma engaged in a deep conversation about the fascinating intricacies of the field artillery.

When he looked up from his food, Collier saw a pretty, dark-haired coed looking directly at him. Caught staring, the girl blushed and lowered her head with a shy smile. Certain the last thing on earth he needed was to be pushed onto a dance floor with a harem of outrageously-nubile, depressingly-respectable daddy's girls. As soon as he finished eating, Collier politely excused himself and wandered quietly down a dimly-lit corridor looking to find a place to smoke. Outside, he quickly located the fresh pack of Luckies he had stashed in the top of his socks just above his shoetops to keep the lines of his uniform looking neat and trim. Expertly peeling back the tinfoil, he shook loose a cigarette and gazed up at the star-filled sky. Idly fishing his Zippo from his trouser pocket, Collier lit the cigarette. Inhaling the mellow smoke deep into his chest, he searched the night sky for the Big Dipper, reflecting upon how quickly he had matured since college and trying to remember what young college girls talked about, anyway. Scarely two brief years out of RPI and he had to admit he didn't have a clue.

"My name is Loyce Willett. It's spelled L-O-Y-C-E not L-O-I-S. I don't supposed you'd let me have a drag off that before you put it out?" Collier was just before snubbing out the cigarette when the dark-auburn-tressed women touched him lightly on the shoulder.

"Sure, but here..."—he held out the pack to her—"Why not have one all to yourself." Flicking his Zippo to flame and trying not to be obvious, he gave his intruder a closer look. Up close, she looked a trifle older than her schoolmates.

"No thank you, really." She brushed aside the offered cigarette. "I'd really prefer to have a little puff on yours. I'm a Phys Ed major and shouldn't be setting a bad example." She smiled nervously, reaching for the glowing butt. Quickly putting the cigarette stub to her lips she drew intensely, inhaling two or three times in quick succession, each time pulling the smoke deep in her lungs.

"Thanks a lot. I needed that. Now I better run...they'll be looking for me. I'll see you back inside." She handed back what remained of the cigarette stub and left as quickly as she had come.

Watching Loyce Willett's trim backside disappear through the door, Collier carefully field-stripped the butt, scattering the remaining tobacco shreds into the light breeze. With the small square of tinfoil he had torn from the pack, he rolled the remaining fragments of foil and paper into a tiny ball about the size of a small marble before he went inside looking for the nearest trash receptacle. Making his way back toward the lighted doorway of the ballroom, Collier's eyes adjusted, and he was distracted by a large, gilt-framed portrait of a striking Indian girl dressed in fringed and beaded buckskin, sitting by a rushing waterfall.

"Te Ata, our most distinguished alumnus," a female voice behind him interrupted his reverie. "OCW's major claim to fame."

Collier turned to find a noticeably-older blonde dressed in a striking black-satin evening gown. In her hand, she held an almost empty paper cup.

"Te Ata? Sorry, I never heard of her. She certainly is beautiful. Just what was her claim to fame?"

"Te Ata was a storyteller and a singer. After she graduated from here in 1919, she went to New York and began a stage career. From there, she studied acting at Carnegie Institute in Pittsburgh and later at Columbia University back in New York. Te Ata became famous for her one-woman show built around the songs, legends and cultures of the Indians. She was a favorite of Franklin Delano and Eleanor Roosevelt and was often their guest at the White House. She was also invited to perform before the King and Queen of England. In the early nineteen-thirties, she married Clyde Fisher, the director of the Hayden Planetarium. Doctor Fisher was quite a bit older and they lived in New York City until his death about twelve years ago."

"Judging from her outfit, I assume Te Ata was an Indian. I thought the Oklahoma College for Women only accepted Caucasians?" Collier asked, puzzled by the contradiction.

"Whites...not specifically Caucasians," his volunteer historian explained. "In Oklahoma, Indians are considered to be white. Negroes are non-whites. Please understand, I personally, am not bigoted, but I have a feeling our faculty and at least some of our girls are uncomfortable your officers brought along two black men."

"Our CO says the U.S. Army is color blind. My classmates will soon be officers leading soldiers in bloody combat to defend your comfortable way of life," Collier bristled, a rush of indignation rising in his chest.

"Well, that may be true, but I wouldn't encourage your Negro classmates to ask the girls to dance. This is a school for very proper, young women who only dance with first-class gentlemen." She gave him a knowing look.

"Joe Rollins and Charlie Mann are about to become officers in the United States Army. They both will be first-class gentlemen by act of the United States Congress."

"I didn't mean to offend you, but, let's face it, outside of the military, in the South and a good part of the rest of the country, Negroes still aren't welcome in restaurants and still have to ride in the back of the bus. Here at OCW, we may be a little slow moving into the twentieth century, but we aren't exactly stuck in the dark ages. For instance, as of this semester, the "for women only" restriction will no longer be in effect. The Oklahoma State Regents just passed a ruling allowing men students with certain qualifications."

"Lucky men..." Collier replied with raised eyebrows. "This may come as a shock to your delicate ladies, but we did not come here entirely as volunteers. I can assure you of that."

Catching his not-so-subtle sarcasm, the buxom blonde reddened and lowered her head.

"I'm sorry. I really didn't mean that the way it sounded. I'm Collier Ramsay, by the way." His flare of temper quickly cooling, Collier offered his hand to ease the affront.

"I'm AnnaBelle Lee. Just call me AnnaBelle." The woman smiled and shook his hand.

"So nice to meet you, AnnaBelle. Please forgive my rudeness. I'm feeling a little like a leaf in a cosmic windstorm at the moment." He nodded at the photograph. "Now tell me all about your distinguished Indian princess, Te Ata, here."

"Te Ata was her tribal name. Her white-man's name was Mary Frances Thompson. Te Ata's father, Thomas Benjamin Thompson, was a Chickasaw. She was from over around Tishomingo, about fifty or sixty miles south and east of here. Tishomingo is near Ardmore. Ardmore is Gene Autry country—everyone knows who he is. Te Ata's mother, Alberta Freund, was a white woman—daughter of a Texas sharecropper. Te Ata's father was an important member of the Chickasaw tribe; her grandfather was a tribal chief."

"How do you spell Te Ata? I'm from Salem, Virginia. Back home, my Aunt Blanche Pedneau is county librarian. Aunt Blanche attended summer school at Columbia University back in the thirties. I'll bet anything she's heard all about this famous Indian actress." Collier took a cheap imitation of a Reynolds ball-point pen out of his shirt pocket and carefully wrote down the spelling on the mimeographed souvenir dance program he had been given when they arrived.

"I would be surprised if she didn't. To our students, Te Ata is practically a goddess."

"Your students? Are you on the faculty here?" Although she appeared a trifle older than the rest of the students, it had not occurred to Collier she might actually be on the teaching staff.

"I am a teacher, but not here. I just graduated OCW this spring in Elementary Education. I was a little late in finally getting a degree. I served two years in the Navy just out of high school. When I got out of the service, I studied awhile at the University of Tulsa and UCLA. After that, I worked in Tokyo and actually taught English at Tokyo University before I came back here in 1950 to get my teaching degree. Several of my former classmates told me they were inviting a group of young Army officers to this dance. It's not that often OCW has a bunch of eligible men on campus. It sounded intriguing, but now I'm here, I feel more like a chaperone than a co-ed. Even you mistook me for an instructor."

"It's not that you look older exactly, you...ah...you appear more sophisticated."

"You're rather full of it, you know? And while we're on the subject of age, you also look older than your buddies. I'm not exactly ancient, but most of your classmates look a trifle young for me." Her laugh was musical as she gave him a knowing look.

"You're right about my classsmates. Except for me and Von Gruenigen—and the two black men—most of them are barely twenty-one. I really don't know how old Von is, but judging from his World War Two combat ribbons, I'd guess he's at least a year or two older than I am. I'll be twenty-four in January. I'm married. My wife is a nurse at the Post hospital."

"Twenty-one may be about the right age for my recent classmates, but that would be robbing the cradle for me."

"Oh, don't act so blasé. You may have been in the Navy and traveled around some, but you hardly look like you're shopping for a cemetery lot."

"You're too kind—a real Virginia gentleman."

"I'm not being kind...you can trust me on that Miss AnnaBelle Lee. I like your name. My father had a sister named Annabelle. I'm sure I'm not the first to tell you the famous Virginia writer, Edgar Allan Poe, wrote a sad poem about a woman named Annabel Lee?"

"Not the first or the last. By actual count, you are number nine-hundred thousand, nine-ninety-nine. I hear it all the time. I like some of Poe's work. But I'm not that crazy about my name. I taught some young soldiers at the University in Tokyo. Other than a lot of bawdy limericks and dirty songs, I don't remember them as being that much interested in poetry. I don't exactly see you as being a reader of poetry," she teased.

"My mother loved poetry and she worshipped Poe. She read Poe to me and my younger brother before we started school. Poe attended Mr. Jefferson's University—the University of Virginia. We studied him all the way through grammar school, high school and college."

"Your mother must be something of a romantic. Collier is an unusual name. You're the first male—the first person actually—named Collier I ever heard of."

"It got me in a lot of fights as a kid. In high school and college, I was something of a jock. No one paid much attention to my name. By then most everybody called me 'Ram.'"

"After college, what did you do in civilian life?"

"I was a commercial artist. I worked for a big grocery chain—you might say I was sort of a Michelangelo of bean cans and bacon packages."

"Being an artist is a pretty long way from killing people with artillery fire. We just got over one war. When are we going to learn how to settle out differences without killing each other? A boy I taught in Japan has been in Korea over a year now, dodging bullets while all the stuffed shirts have been in the truce tents. All this time while those pompous, jackass generals have been dickering over dotting their Is and crossing their Ts, good men have been fighting and dying over nothing. When is this insanity going to stop?" It was an impassioned speech, and she looked at him intently; just for a moment Collier thought she might burst into tears.

"Not in our lifetime, I'm afraid. For some reason or another, we seem destined to keep repeating the same mistake, all in the name of glory. That's enough about the stupid war. I hear the music starting up. Would you care to dance?"

"Sure, why not? I'm not much of a dancer really, but I'd better get back to the others. I don't want my Tac officers to think I'm antisocial."

"I'm not exactly Cyd Charisse, myself." She laughed. "Before we trip the light fantastic, come with me. It'll only take a minute or two. My ex-roommate lives next door in Sparks. We have some homemade brandy to spike this punch—guaranteed to make you dance like Fred Astaire."

"Thanks, I think I'll skip the brandy. I'm not much of a drinker. I'll meet you back in the ballroom. We have two Tac officers and their wives riding herd on us. A married man caught sneaking into a girl's dorm would not exactly be considered conduct befitting an officer and a gentleman."

"Okay, soldier boy...can't blame a girl for trying. You go join the others. I'll be right along." Snapping off a mock salute, she turned and headed for the door.

Inside the ballroom, the lights were dimmed and the buffet had been cleared. As Collier entered, the small orchestra was playing a half-passable rendition of Artie Shaw's arrangement of *Moonglow*. Across the room, Von and Garrett were standing with Rollins and Mann talking to a group of young coeds. After a minute, Von and Garrett escorted two of the coeds out onto the dance floor in front of the small dance orchestra. As soon as the dancers left the group, the other two coeds abruptly turned their backs on the two black men and walked away. Clearly embarrassed, Joe and Charlie made their way to a group of chairs lining the wall and took a seat, trying their best to act as if nothing out of the ordinary had transpired.

"Here I am. Is your offer to dance still good?" Before he could decide whether or not to go across to say hello to his affronted classmates, AnnaBelle reappeared like magic. Now, her paper cup was brimming almost to the rim.

"Sure thing." Collier waited while she entrusted her cup to a busty brunette at a nearby table before he led her onto the dance floor where a half-dozen of his more intrepid classmates were already tripping the light fantastic with pretty young partners.

If he had been apprehensive about dancing with this stranger, Collier's apprehension quickly disappeared. The worldly AnnaBelle fairly melted into his arms, fitting her body suggestively into his and following him step for step, almost without missing a single beat. Painfully aware of her pudendum brushing a sensual rhythm against him beneath the silken fabric, he responded instantly with an uncontrollable, highly-predictable physical reaction.

"Please forgive me, but I have to powder my nose." As soon as the dance was over, Collier politely excused himself, heading for the restroom to wipe the telltale flow of his juices from his undershorts before they started soaking through into the relatively thin khaki uniform.

When he returned, the opportunistic elder Lothario, Von, had zeroed in on the fair AnnaBelle. Not particularly anxious to have to go through all the repair work again, Collier glanced over to where Joe Rollins and Charles Mann sat alone in a far corner of the ballroom. Given the controversy over last year's trial and execution of the Martinsville Seven and the recent advent of Malcolm X and the Black Power movement, it suddenly occurred to Collier to wonder what would be the reaction at the Pentagon and in the White House war room if *Stars & Stripes* ran a photo of a pair of colored soldiers as wallflowers at this snobby girl's-school dance.

Understandably, but not surprisingly, Joe Rollins and Charlie Mann remained anchored to their chairs, not about to risk humiliation again. From time to time during the remainder of the evening, Collier stopped and chatted with his classmates, inquiring if he might get them some punch and on two occasions inducing them to go with him outside for a smoke.

Predictably, as the night progressed, the only time he saw Joe and Charlie dancing they were with their OCS chaperones, Louanna Robinson and Joyce Suit. Uncomfortable that his Tac officers were neglecting their attractive wives—and at the same time satisfying the best traditions of military protocol—Collier took inspiration from seeing these gracious women dancing with his shunned classmates and danced one dance each with both Louanna and Joyce.

Drifting from place to place, chatting with his classmates and occasionally slipping outside to grab a smoke, the remainder of the evening Collier carefully avoided dancing with any of the snobbish college women. Around 2330 hours, when he finally got around to looking for AnnaBelle again to ask for a final dance, she was nowhere to be found.

On their bus home, both Rollins and Mann—with a number of others—were already lightly snoring before the bus had cleared the city limits of Chickasha.

"I saw you dancing with the fair Miss AnnaBelle Lee. She's a looker—a real armful." Collier made light conversation with Von in the seat beside him, trying to keep awake.

"She's an armful alright. I got her phone number. I'd like to see her again," Von smiled dreamily. Pulling his overseas cap low over his eyes, his older classmate promptly slouched down in the seat, effectively avoiding further comment.

When the busses finally deposited the men of Easy back at Sill just after midnight, Collier was able to hitch a ride into Lawton with Bert Hancock whose wife rented a room in a private home near Hilda Birdsong's place. Slipping quietly inside their bedroom, Collier undressed in the darkness and slipped into bed buck naked. Snuggling close to Emma's warm, nicely-rounded backside, his erection was already full-sprung and at the ready.

"Go away. Don't come in here wanting to take all the horny fantasies you got from rubbing bellies with those college girls out on me," Emma whispered, edging coquettishly away.

"It's wasn't like that. The entire evening was a bore. There is nothing on this earth as boring as a bunch of silly college girls."

"Don't lie to me, Collier Ramsay."

"I missed you terribly."

"Uh-huh. I can tell." Emma reached behind her and squeezed his rock-hard prick.

Collier wiggled closer to let her get a better grip.

During mid-morning on the first day of the third week of Gunnery, Collier paid little attention when a nondescript NCO walked into their classroom where the instructor—a professorial-appearing Major—was quite miraculously making the mysteries of trigonometry come crystal clear. Unnoticed, the NCO tapped Joe Rollins on the shoulder, whispering quietly in his ear.

Although Collier paid little attention at the moment, it should have been significant to him that Joe—sitting in the row immediately in front of Collier—had gathered up his classroom materials and stuffed them in his bulky white muslin bag before he got up and followed the anonymous corporal out of the room. By the time Easy Battery returned to the barracks for noon chow, Collier had taken little note of the curious incident until he approached his cubicle and discovered that Joe Rollins' side of the cubicle had been stripped completely clean. Nothing was left to indicate the darkly-complected soldier—or anyone else—had ever occupied the space.

Immediately, everyone assumed Rollins—a model soldier, but struggling with academic difficulties—had simply been put back two weeks to join Fox Battery which was just beginning their first week of Gunnery. It was a logical assumption. Although academic deficiencies were much-dreaded and to be avoided at any cost, it was not uncommon that slower, but otherwise deserving, candidates were given the benefit of repeating the mathematically and technically convoluted Gunnery courses rather than losing the promise of them making good line officers. It was a practical solution. After all, wasn't the Artillery attempting to train competent combat officers, not convert soldiers to college professors? Joe Rollins would not have been the first man in Easy Battery to feel the sting of being put back two weeks for academic deficiencies.

Before nightfall, however, the rumor mill could provide no word of Joe Rollins' presence anywhere in OCS. By the time Saturday morning rolled around, all that remained of the candidate was the hilarious anecdote about his contraband possessions spilling out of the ceiling above his bunk during that infamous Saturday morning inspection almost eleven weeks before. While it remained largely unspoken, the question of his disappearance being related to his race hung in the air like the vaporous miasma of a sun-ripening corpse.

Although he personally missed having Joe around, his absence burdened Collier with the additional responsibility of keeping the entire cubicle inspection-ready by himself. Even so, Collier managed to get through the first four weeks of the complex theoretical and academic side of Gunnery with minimal demerits and without missing a single problem on the final test.

Toward the latter part of this period, Easy battery had begun spending most of their afternoons engaged in Service Practice. Service Practice was Artillery nomenclature for actually observing and adjusting fire from the vantage points of the assorted OPs on the numerous stark, arroyo-eroded artillery ranges scattered throughout the rugged Wichita and Arbuckle sectors of the historic fort. Afternoon after afternoon under the blistering sun, sitting with his section-mates on the canvas slings of their folding wooden camp stools with powerful Zeiss 10x50 military binoculars at the ready, Collier would watch as 105mm, 155mm, and sometimes even 8-inch howitzer, batteries fired the daily missions that he and his fellow classmates called in on their field radios.

"Candidate Garrett, fire mission." The instructor would summon the next candidate to bring his camp stool and take the hot seat before assigning the next fire mission, "From Blockhouse Signal Mountain, go left one-hundred, then down five-zero. You will find a mass of bright-red-painted materiel (actually this particular target was the twisted hulk of a decommissioned WWII half-track prime mover). This red-painted materiel marks a rendezvous area of six Russian-built Chinese tanks. Able Battery has exactly one-zero minutes to fire for effect, three rounds HE (High Explosive) for destruction."

Using the measuring reticule etched on the left lens of the binoculars to estimate actual location on the ground, the designated candidate FO (in this case, Garrett) would nervously call down his approximation of the target location to FDC. "Fox Oboe Able, Fire Mission. (Fox Oboe Able was military shorthand for 'Forward Observer, Able Battery.') From Base Point, go left six-zero, drop five-zero. (Base Point represented a prominent landmark with surveyed data at FDC—Fire Direction Center.) Six stationary enemy tanks. Two rounds HE, will adjust."

Upon receiving the Fire Mission from FO Able, FDC would plot the location, and—through a complicated system of mathematical black magic including factoring in wind direction and speed and atmospheric pressure—would rapidly compute the firing data, calling the numbers down to the battery, "Able battery, fire mission. Deflection two-five-niner (deflection was the number of compass degrees clockwise from zero degrees at true north), elevation zero-three-eight (elevation represented the number of feet above an established baseline altitude above sea level for the geographic area). Six enemy tanks. Two rounds HE, charge four (105mm ammo came packed with seven powder charges in individual silk bags connected by a string), fuse quick (Fuse Quick exploded upon impact.). Will adjust."

"Roger, FDC. Deflection one-niner-zero, elevation zero-three-eight. Shell HE, charge four, fuse quick..." Able Battery's radio operator would reconfirm the deflection and elevation before passing the vital data to the guns.

"Deflection one-niner-zero, elevation zero-three-eight. Shell HE, charge four, fuse quick..." the Lieutenant in charge of the gun crew would pass along the information to the crew chief who oversaw the data being translated into the aiming mechanisms of the guns.

Operating with practiced efficiency, as soon as the gun crew finished aiming the guns and cutting the charges (replacing four of the seven, silk, powder bags back in the casing—the gun crew swiftly moved the unused bags to a burning pit located safely out of the firing area), the designated crew member then screwed the appropriate fuse into the threaded-opening at the business-end of the bullet-shaped projectile. This completed, he passed the projectile to a crewman who seated the missile into the casing containing the charges and passed it to the appropriate teammate who rammed it into the breech.

As soon as the assembled missile was seated, the crew chief slammed the breech block closed. This completed in just a matter of seconds, the number-two cannoneer tapped the crew-chief on the helmet and called out, "Deflection one-niner-zero, elevation zero-three-eight. Shell HE, charge four, fuse quick...Ready, number one." (Or number two, et cetera, depending upon which of Able battery's six howitzers was actually being fired.)

"Ready, number one and two..." The moment the Lieutenant acknowledged the guns were ready, the battery commander gave the order, "Fire," and the crew chiefs would pull the firing lanyards and the howitzers would erupt with a near-deafening Boom, sending the deadly projectiles into space.

This done, the radioman would report, "Fox Oboe Able. Two rounds HE, fuse quick, on the way!" The gun crew would spring into immediate action clearing the spent shell from the breech and swabbing out the bore with a special ramrod, readying the howitzer for the next adjustment or the next mission.

"On the way!" When FDC radioed the information back to the OP to FO Able, all eyes went immediately to the general area on the eastern slope of Signal Mountain, anxiously searching to locate the two tell-tale incoming bursts of orange flame and gray-white smoke.

"Right three-zero, add three-zero..." Upon seeing the rounds hit too far left and slightly below the bright-red-painted materiel, FO Able would call back to FDC attempting to narrow the bracket on the target as quickly as possible.

Using this correction, the guns would fire two more rounds with amazing speed.

"Drop one-zero, add zero-five. Six guns, three rounds HEAT (High Explosive Anti-tank) for effect." When FO Able finally narrowed the bracket to the point the adjusting rounds exploded within twenty yards of the target both horizontally and vertically (in real-life combat, the tanks would most likely have begun to move) he would call in a final adjustment and order the battery to 'Fire for effect.' The overall objectives were accuracy and speed. In real combat, the success of the Field Artillery depended upon the FOs ability to make quick and accurate adjustments and bring the final fury of the guns onto the target before the enemy had time to escape.

Surprisingly, even to himself, Collier Ramsay easily became the standout at Service Practice among his peers. It hadn't hurt that he had already experienced more than a few hours during Basic at FARTC on these same OPs watching experienced FOs zero in on many of the very same targets. With his nimble mind and the photographic eye of a trained artist—not to mention the hand-eye coordination of a long-range basketball sharpshooter—it seemed unremarkable to Collier he would take to adjusting artillery fire across this complexly-sculpted, rugged piece of southwestern Oklahoma geography.

Arriving back in the OCS area from Service Practice, each afternoon the candidates passed around the grade sheets for the day's missions, just like they passed around the daily demerit sheets. Traditionally, gunnery instructors on the OPs had always awarded only two basic grades for firing missions during Service Practice: S for Satisfactory and U for Unsatisfactory. That all changed when Easy Battery's Candidate Collier Boyd Ramsay arrived upon the scene. On the days Collier was given fire missions, the grade sheets started showing up with notations of 'E for Excellent' by his name. Overnight, in all things pertaining to Gunnery, Collier Boyd Ramsay had become something of a prodigy in the eyes of his instructors, his classmates, the OCS Tactical Staff and eventually the hierarchy of the Artillery School whose main job was to send topflight FOs to Korea.

In Collier's mind, this was just the kind of distinction he hoped would equalize his less-than-brilliant performance in the realm of soldierly proficiency. In an atmosphere where delivering destruction to the target was the primary goal, it never occurred to him that these skilled performances might eventually work against him.

While his extraordinary skill on the range had been much-admired—even celebrated—among virtually all of his earlier Service Practice instructors (most of whom who were Korean combat veterans) for whatever reason, Collier eventually found himself a "target for destruction" for a misanthropic Gunnery Instructor appropriately nicknamed "Unsatisfactory Hal." Unlike most of the Service Practice instructors, Captain Harold 'Hal' Sweeny had no actual combat experience in either WWII or Korea.

Dating from the very first fire mission assigned to Collier by Captain Sweeny, it became obvious to Collier's classmates that Unsatisfactory Hal was out to make sure that Easy Battery's star gunnery student would finally mess up and spoil his unbroken record of never receiving a dreaded "U". Day after day, the titanic battle between instructor and pupil became the focus of interest as Easy Battery entered the fifth week of gunnery in what was, overall, the thirteenth week of training. Morning or afternoon on both Signal Mountain and Arbuckle ranges, Captain Hal would always save the final mission of the day for Collier and assign him seemingly impossible targets. Some were so close to the edge of "range limits" that many of the Range Safety Officers in the gunnery school pool were verging on the brink of stomach ulcers lest they be assigned to ride herd on the diabolical targets Unsatisfactory Hal always saved for Candidate Collier Ramsey.

Although he was well-aware of the sinister spider web he found himself caught up in, Collier actually looked forward to the rivalry between himself and Captain Sweeny. Unblinking, day after day, Collier continued to perform with an unbroken record of exemplary performances on the OP. Inevitably, of course, Sweeny held all the cards in this titanic struggle; clearly it was a game which, sooner or later, Collier was destined to lose.

On that fateful afternoon, the October sun had already dipped well below the canyon rim on a completely unfamiliar range several miles out beyond Signal mountain when Captain Hal finally called Collier and assigned him what the malevolent, diabolical instructor knew was the perfect—*the impossible*—target.

From the moment Collier's section arrived at the unfamiliar OP, Collier had immediately begun trying to prepare himself for what he instinctively intuited would provide Unsatisfactory Hal his best effort to assign him an impossible target—ultimately bringing Collier his first "U." While his classmates struggled to fire unfamiliar targets on this rugged new range which resembled something closely akin to the Dakota Badlands, Collier began eyeballing the landscape, methodically comparing it to his topographical firing map, familiarizing himself with the exotic, unfamiliar—virtually unfathomable—maze of eroded ridges and hidden canyon floors spreading in front of them. When Collier finally felt comfortable he had located and plotted the most difficult—sometimes almost invisible and nearly impossible—targets lurking on both the near and peripheral rims of the wasteland of sandstone canyons and buttes reticulated with arid stream beds between, he immediately set about looking for the more unknowable, the least obvious and most impossible, possibilities that might excite the diabolical imagination of his nemesis to bring about his downfall.

Collier had long since completed his exhaustive survey and the two-and-a-half-ton prime mover had already been waiting for a full half-hour to take them back to the Fort when Unsatisfactory Hal delivered to Collier what he was certain was his *coup de grace*.

"Candidate Ramsay, Fire mission." The devious instructor's voice fairly oozed malevolent triumph and anticipation as he called Collier to bring his stool to the OP. "From the bright blue-painted materiel at the foot of the small domed mesa in the foreground, two hundred yards below and five-zero yards right of the BP, go up five-hundred and left five-hundred and you will find a dull mustard-colored mass of materiel resembling a gasoline tanker. Mobile Communist Fire Direction Trailer, HE for destruction."

True to his evil cunning, Sweeny had waited until the area was completely backlit by the setting sun and the shadowy landscape had become almost too dim to clearly see the nearer targets, much less targets out on the very edge of range limits.

Even before Unsatisfactory Hal had finished delivering the order, with remarkable intuition, Collier's had already placed an unerring finger on the spot on his firing map which marked the target. In the left margin of the official topographical map he had already penciled in the coordinates locating this virtually inaccessible target to the nearest yard.

While caution told him that in order to play the cat and mouse game with an instructor clearly out to get him, he should proceed by the book and call down for adjusting fire, beginning at a point within several hundred yards of the difficult target, he knew from looking at the precipitous contours on the map that he ran a considerable risk of the rounds being lost from view in the horrendous maze of tiny canyons which surrounded the distant target. Already, several of his classmates had been done in by this same frustrating situation this afternoon.

Why take a chance when he already had the target zeroed in? What would he do in a real combat situation?

Without further hesitation, Collier quickly made up his mind.

"Fox Oboe Able, fire mission. Coordinates: three, four, seven, one, seven. Niner, eight, four, two, three." Collier calmly called in the target's coordinates to the nearest yard and continued, "Motorized enemy Fire Direction Center, Shell HE, fuse quick." Pausing just a beat to emphasize the certainty of his decision, he continued in a cold, deliberate voice, "Battery two rounds. Fire for effect."

"Ceasefire...ceasefire..." Veins bulging at his forehead and his face neon red, Captain Sweeny jumped off his campstool, shouting in the phone to FDC.

Although Collier had correctly identified the target and called in the perfect mission, ironically, it was his own virtuosity—and arrogance—which brought about his downfall.

"What's the matter, Hal?" Major Mortensen, who had accompanied Sweeny to the OP to observe the afternoon's session, stood up and asked with some concern.

"Ordering the battery to FFE without establishing a bracket on the target is taking a foolish, completely unnecessary risk of wasting rounds," Sweeny blustered.

"But, Hal, according to my map, your Candidate nailed it. Let them fire the mission. I want to see him blow that piece of materiel right off the map." Mortensen shrugged, not understanding that Sweeny was realizing a triumph in his personal crusade to spoil Collier's unblemished record on the OP.

"That's beside the point. We're trying to teach these men how to observe fire in combat. They well could be observing fire on Outpost Kelly by Christmas Eve."

"But, Hal, think about it. *That is the point.* Trying to adjust fire in that maze of barrancas has already resulted in several exercises in futility in other fire missions this afternoon. This FO has just done a remarkable job of saving rounds by pinpointing a difficult target to the nearest yard. Give the man credit for an outstanding mission—a job well done. In my opinion, Candidate Ramsay deserves an 'S'...with a notation that he demonstrated excellent judgment," Mortensen persisted.

"Begging you pardon, Major Mortensen, the Unsatisfactory stands." Ignoring the Major, Captain Sweeny uncapped a red pen and noted a big fat red 'U' beside Collier's name on his clipboard.

"Alright now, men, pack up. We need to get moving. We'll be late for mess," Sweeny called to the class as he placed the clipboard and pen inside his bag and bent to fold his camp stool.

That evening, Collier—seething with resentment for such cavalier treatment—was ordered to report to Tactical Battery Commander Whitley before Easy Battery fell out for formation. He found Whitley waiting just outside the barracks at the foot of the steps.

"Stand at ease, Candidate Ramsay. I just wanted to have a private word with you regarding your performance on the OP this afternoon. Major Mortensen is a personal friend and told me all about Captain Sweeny ruining your exemplary record on the range. I have had a word with Captain Sweeny, and he has agreed he was hasty in his decision to award a 'U' for your performance today and has amended your grade to 'Satisfactory.' With Major Mortensen's recommendation, I have personally told Lieutenant Robinson to make a notation that you showed excellent initiative and excellent judgment—not to mention, a lot of guts—in going directly to FFE without wasting rounds trying to adjust fire in that impossible terrain."

"Thank you, sir." Collier momentarily forgot the protocol of first identifying himself before addressing a superior.

"Keep up the good work, Ramsay. That is all...you're dismissed." Whitley returned Collier's salute, started to leave, then hesitated.

"Hold up, Ramsay, I'd like one more word."

Almost up the steps and about to reenter the barracks, Collier wheeled and saluted again. "Sir, Candidate Ramsay, yes Sir."

"Are you familiar with Greek mythology, Ramsay?"

"Sir, Candidate Ramsay, Sir. A bit, Sir."

"Have you ever heard the story about of Icarus, Candidate?"

"Sir, Candidate Ramsay, yes Sir."

"Remember what I told you about affecting an air of self-confidence to which you have no legitimate claim?"

"Sir, Candidate Ramsay, I remember sir," Collier replied, holding his breath, wondering what was coming next.

"Keep up the good work, Ramsay." Whitley returned Collier's salute and left without further word.

CHAPTER THIRTY

THE DAILY OKLAHOMAN
Oklahoma City, Oklahoma, Thursday, October 9, 1952
IKE SAYS ENEMY SWINDLED ALLIES FOR MORE TIME
SAN FRANCISCO, Wednesday, October 8 (AP) - Gen. Dwight D.
Eisenhower blistered the Truman administration's foreign policy tonight,
and declared that the truce talks in Korea were a "Soviet trap."

––––––––––––

THE DAILY OKLAHOMAN
Oklahoma City, Oklahoma, Friday, October 10, 1952
TRUCE DEADLOCK LOOKS HOPELESS
WASHINGTON, Thursday, October 9 (AP) - The administration now
sees no way out of the Korean truce deadlock, barring an unexpected
switch in communist strategy concerning repatriation, informed sources
said Thursday.

––––––––––

THE ROANOKE TIMES
Roanoke, Virginia, Friday, October 11, 1952
RED APPROACH TO CONTESTED MOUNTAIN CUT
SEOUL, KOREA, Saturday, October 11 (AP) - Sturdy South Korean
infantrymen today cut off the northern approach to strategic White
Horse Mountain and almost surrounded the Reds clinging to the crest,
an Allied frontline officer said.

––––––––––––

NEWSPAPER HEADLINES HERALDING DEPRESSING NEWS that the
truce talks at Panmunjom had ground to a complete halt were further
disheartening with the report of the death of the former Easy Battery Redbird,
Lieutenant Charles Armstrong, during late September fighting for a land feature
called Outpost Kelly. This was quickly followed by the tragic news of another
Redbird, Dalton Maxey, becoming a battle casualty in the bloody struggle for
White Horse Mountain in early October, casting a pall over the men of the
'Singing Battery.' Battles for places with names like Bunker Hill, T-Bone, The
Hook, Sniper Ridge, The Punchbowl, Luke's Castle, and other pieces of battle-
scarred real estate flickered across the front pages of the newspapers, side by side
with articles about the futility of the peace negotiations. Hardly before they had
time to philosophize upon the obscene contradiction of the war machine laying
waste their comrades while a parade of foppish negotiators sauntered
nonchalantly in and out of the truce tents at Panmunjom, the first full week in
October, Easy Battery—themselves preoccupied with such trivialities as the
presentability of their dress uniforms and the shine on their boots—enjoyed a brief
respite from the intricacies of Gunnery as they were abruptly introduced to the
subject of Combined Arms.
   Taking to the field in a week-long series of RSOPs, Collier and his classmates
were forced to perform in the roles of battery commanders, execs, scouts, FOs,
chiefs of sections and artillerymen as, like surrealistic chess pieces, they moved
their howitzers in and out of new positions, simulating combat.

When they returned to their barracks at the end of the second week in October, looking forward to resuming the final four weeks of Gunnery, the men of Easy Battery were caught up in a chaotic, seemingly-unnecessary, reorganization of the entire Artillery OCS. At reveille formation Saturday morning, October 11, completely without preamble they received the word there would be no Saturday inspection and that all weekend passes had been cancelled.

"When Candidate First Sergeant Tate dismisses you, you will fall back inside and immediately begin moving all of your belongings—footlockers and beds included—into the street in front of the barracks behind you," Tactical Lieutenant Robinson, instructed, then turned the battery back over to Tate.

"What about our training manuals and textbooks and Gunnery bags? Should we change into fatigues?" asked Archer Barber Des Cognets in his unmistakable Boston accent.

"Everything comes outside except the cubicle partitions. Strip the barracks clean. And, yes, it would be advisable to change into fatigue or PT uniform," Candidate Tate announced after a hurried consultation with Lieutenant Robinson. "Easy Battery, dis-missed!"

"What the devil is this all about?" Momentarily frozen into inactivity by Robinson's strange announcement, the men of Easy Battery milled about outside the barracks muttering questions in a state of utter confusion.

"Alright, you heard the Lieutenant, let's get busy. We've got a lot of work to do and we're burning daylight." Candidate First Sergeant Tate waded into the confused ranks, urging them inside to get to the task at hand.

By 1000 hours the street behind them was filled with footlockers, bunks piled high with uniforms and manuals, FDC paraphernalia, boots and shoes and M2 carbines and god-only-knew what else. All day long, the OCS area swarmed like an anthill as the entire organization engaged in a chaotic party game of musical barracks. Taking time out only to eat, by nightfall Saturday, some semblance of order was restored to the outside areas as the candidates continued to bring some sense of military respectability to their new barracks. Their labors continued all day Sunday. By the time the dust had cleared Sunday evening, Collier and his classmates found that Easy Battery had now become How Battery. Of course this had no effect on where they stood in the precisely-ordered twenty-two weeks curriculum, as they continued on target for their scheduled December graduation on December 13. Exactly what the benefit this reorganization brought about was never exactly clear in the minds of Collier and his classmates, but, by the time Monday morning rolled around and they resumed training exactly where their former identity as Easy Battery left off on Friday afternoon, it was not something anyone in the newly-named How Battery wasted a lot of time trying to figure out.

CHAPTER THIRTY-ONE

THE DAILY OKLAHOMAN
Oklahoma City, Oklahoma, Sunday, October 12, 1952
CREST OF KOREA HILL IS TOO HOT

SEOUL, KOREA, Sunday, October 12 (AP) – South Korean soldiers slashed to the top of shell-pocked White Horse Mountain this morning but pulled back from the crest shortly before noon under savage Red artillery and mortar pounding.

THE DAILY OKLAHOMAN
Oklahoma City, Oklahoma, Monday, October 13, 1952
SOUTH KOREANS CHOP OFF REDS ATTACKING HILL

SEOUL, Monday, October 13 (AP) – South Korean troops crouched behind speedily built make-shift barriers on the crest of White Horse Mountain, hurled back several weakening Chinese Red attacks last night and early today.

SINCE THE WEEKEND PRIOR to Easy Battery's week-long Combined Arms exercises in the field when Collier had made an offhand remark about her not having a period since their Labor Day holiday in Oklahoma City, Emma's tummy had been in knots with anxiety that she might actually be pregnant.

Following the battery's return from their week of ARSOPs, she had been secretly relieved when Collier had been restricted to the Post while his battery moved their possessions to a new barracks. After suffering what seemed a lifetime of restless nights worrying, Emma went directly to the Post hospital early Monday morning and headed straight for the office of her friend, Agnes Kowalsky, in the clinical laboratory.

"Hi, Agnes, what do you hear from Stan? Has he left Korea yet?" Emma asked cheerfully.

"Haven't heard a word for over a week now, Emma. I keep waiting for the phone to ring. What brings you here so early?" Frowning, Agnes looked up from the front page of *The Daily Oklahoman* with the headlines about the fighting over White Horse Mountain.

"I know you'll be glad to get him back. The waiting must be hard," Emma empathized.

"You can say that again." Agnes nodded and gave her a puzzled look. "What's up? Are you working days now?"

"No. I need a favor. I wondered if you could run a pregnancy test on me?"

"Well, of course. How long since your last period?"

"Probably six weeks...maybe a few days more." Emma felt a trifle foolish that she hadn't worked out the exact arithmetic before she came to the hospital.

"Well, I'm not busy. Take this down the hall and bring me back some pee." Agnes handed Emma a specimen cup.

"How long will it take?" When Emma returned, she handed Agnes the cup.

"Call or come by anytime tomorrow. I should have your report early in the morning. Be sure and ask for me. I'm doing this off the book...strictly QT."

"Thanks bunches, Agnes, I really appreciate this. I'll be in early tomorrow. I hope you hear from Stan soon." Emma turned and headed out the door.

Busying herself with polishing her white nursing shoes and starching and ironing her nursing caps, Emma had pushed the anxiety over her possible pregnancy to the back of her consciousness by the time she reported back to the Post hospital for her evening shift. Thankfully, her shift in the Post-op Recovery Room was shorthanded and she had no time to worry about the test until she remembered to set her alarm early when she tiptoed into her bedroom just after midnight and fell into bed.

"Well, the frog died. You're definitely PG. Congratulations, I guess. Who's your OBG?" Agnes greeted her with the news as soon as Emma walked into her office Tuesday morning.

"Thanks, Agnes. I don't have an OB. Frankly, I never planned on this." Although Emma couldn't say she was surprised that she was pregnant, she hadn't actually given the consequences much thought. "Can you recommend someone on the hospital staff?"

"Most of the staff use Colonel Snow. I know his nurse. Want me to give her a call and get you in?" Agnes spoke right up, reaching for the phone.

"Sure, why not?" Taken off guard, Emma had no reason to postpone the inevitable.

"Hi, Lauren. I've got one our nurses here who just found out she's PG—about six weeks along she thinks..." Emma stood transfixed as Agnes dialed an in-house number and spoke to someone on the other end of the line.

"Can you come in this morning—like right now?" Agnes moved the instrument from her mouth and covered the mouthpiece as she looked to Emma for an answer.

"Sure, why not?" Emma glanced at her watch and shrugged. She had the entire morning free, might as well get it over with.

"She says yes, Lauren. Her name is Emma Ramsay. I'll send her right up and thanks a lot." Agnes hung up the phone and jotted a name on the back of a lab slip.

"Colonel Snow's nurse's name is Lauren Sellers. Take the elevator up to second and turn left. OBGyn is all the way to the end of the corridor. Good luck." Agnes handed her the slip with a smile.

"Thanks, Agnes. I owe you," Emma said, trying her best to return her smile.

"You're right about having a prolapsed uterus. I hate to be the bearer of bad news, but I'd be remiss if I didn't warn you that it would be a miracle if your uterus flipped and you carried this pregnancy to term. Otherwise, the outlook is good. Except for your retroverted uterus, you are in exceptionally good health. The spontaneous abortion should occur very soon—certainly before the end of the first trimester. It could happen any day now. Considering your good physical condition, at this stage it won't amount to much more than a heavy menstrual period." Following his examination, the kindly Colonel Snow wasted no words informing Emma of what he considered was a pessimistic prognosis.

Struggling to conceal her relief, Emma thanked the fatherly physician and left his office trying mightily to keep a straight face; she wanted to shout "Hallelujah" to the lone buzzard circling high over HQ flagpole as she made her way to the parking lot. She hoped she wouldn't have to wait too much longer before she was rid of this nightmarish pregnancy. She didn't trust the myth that lightning never struck the same place twice. The guilt of the damning possibility that for the second time, Trey Moseley, not Collier, had been the sperm donor who had kept her sweaty-palmed ever since she missed her September menstrual period. Now at least she wouldn't have to worry about having to break the unhappy news to Collier. At this particular moment in their less-than-perfect marital history, she wholeheartedly shared Collier's unwavering prejudice against having children, not for a few more years anyway. Now—if the learned Doctors Snow and Gooch were correct about her retroverted uterus—maybe never and that suited Emma just fine.

CHAPTER THIRTY-TWO

THE DAILY OKLAHOMAN
Oklahoma City, Oklahoma, Friday, October 31, 1952
FIERY, DUST-CHOKED STATE DUE NO REST
Warm, dry and dusty Oklahoma will continue to be just that Friday, with
southwest winds and temperatures ranging from 75 to 82 in the south
and west.

THE ROANOKE TIMES
Roanoke, Virginia, Saturday, November 8, 1952
HEAVY ATTACK AIMED AGAINST ENEMY FORCE
SEOUL, Saturday, December 8 (AP) – Allied artillery thundered on the
central Korean front again today in a continuing massive barrage aimed
at smashing the Chinese infantrymen's best pal, his own big guns...
The Chinese guns had blocked determined assaults by South Korean
troops to recapture Triangle Hill. The South Koreans still held nearby
Sniper Ridge northeast of the communications hub of Kumhwa.

THE DAILY OKLAHOMAN
Oklahoma City, Oklahoma, Sunday, November 9, 1952
HOPES FOR RAIN GAIN STRENGTH
Drought-parched Oklahoma was promised light rain and showers
Sunday as a cold front moved toward the state.

THE DAILY OKLAHOMAN
Oklahoma City, Oklahoma, Tuesday, November 11, 1952
CHURCHILL BLASTS SOVIETS ON KOREA
LONDON, Monday, November 10 (AP) – Prime Minister Winston
Churchill Monday night accused Russia of blocking peace in Korea in an
attempt to scatter the strength of the free world.

AS INCREDIBLE AS IT SEEMED to those who lived through it, from July 7,
through October 29, the men of Easy—now How—Battery suffered through
unrelenting daytime temperatures averaging above 100 degrees. To make matters
worse, not a single drop of rain fell in the Lawton/Fort Sill area during this entire
three-month period. As day after rainless day under the broiling sun brought no
relief, memories of the Oklahoma Dust Bowl and the motion picture of John
Steinbeck's *The Grapes of Wrath,* edged into Collier's subconscious. Both the
novel and movie had been filled with garish images of the dust storms which had
transformed the once-verdant Oklahoma farmland into a veritable desert.
    Early Wednesday morning, October 29, a scant three days before they were
to begin their momentous eighteenth week of training—their final week as lowly
underclassmen—a strange-looking cloudbank loomed on the margins of the
northwest horizon as How Battery marched to training films on military courtesy
and protocol and etiquette. When they emerged from the classroom building a

little over an hour later, the ominous cloudbank had moved higher in the sky which had begun taking on a strange bluish hue—even the sun appeared as an eerie, weak, pale-lilac disk and the air itself had a kind of grittiness.

"As you can see for yourselves, the area is threatened by a rapidly-approaching dust storm. We are suspending classes for the day so you can take appropriate measures to button up your barracks to keep out the dust. Form ranks outside and march back to your battery area. It would be a good idea to wet a handkerchief and hold it over your mouth and nose," the instructor said.

"Stuff the carbine muzzles with cleaning patches," Tac Sergeant Ernst advised when they arrived back at the barracks area, but not even the movie of Steinbeck's novel had prepared Collier for what was coming. The rest of the day and the following day became a nightmare. No matter how tightly they closed the windows and doors and stuffed the sills with sheets, blankets, tee shirts and assorted other material, the nearly-invisible microscopic dust insinuated itself in through unseen cracks and openings until the interior of the barracks was blanketed with a talcum-like residue.

When they awoke on Saturday morning, from what little fretful sleep they had been able to manage, the men of How Battery were relieved to find that the air had miraculously cleared; the same storm that choked the air with dust had taken with it a significant measure of the deep layer of powdered topsoil which had plagued them for weeks. That they were excused from their final official Saturday inspection as underclassmen was little compensation for having to spend the entire weekend trying to rid their barracks and all of their possessions of the fine talcum-like residue of the storm.

Although the press of cleaning up the mess prevented Collier from spending the entire weekend in town, shut safely inside the well-constructed brick and masonry womb of Hilda Birdsong's house, Emma and the Rudolphs fared much better. Emma, much to Collier's chagrin, had to work the weekend and was little help.

"I'm pregnant—about two-and-a-half months now. I had hoped I wouldn't have to tell you this at all, but now I don't think I should wait any longer. The baby is due sometime around the last of April or the first week in May. It obviously happened in Oklahoma City over Labor Day." Emma waited until after their Saturday evening dinner marking the end of How Battery's eighteenth week celebrating the newly-awarded red tabs on Collier's epaulets to break the news of his impending fatherhood.

"But...I...uh...I didn't think you could carry a pregnancy!" Recalling her spontaneous abortion in Roanoke, initially Collier was more surprised than distressed at the news.

"I know. I would have told you sooner, but Colonel Snow, my OBG at the hospital, kept insisting that my prolapsed uterus wouldn't support a pregnancy. He virtually assured me I would abort within the first two months. Well, it turns out he—and Garrett Gooch—were both wrong. Through some miracle—or curse—about two weeks ago, my so-called prolapsed uterus flipped into a normal position and now Colonel Snow says the pregnancy looks fine. Like it or not you're going to be a father."

"Well, if he was wrong once, he could be wrong again," Collier offered, hopefully.

"Don't bet on it. Female intuition tells me we are going to become parents, like it or not."

"Big daddy, Ramsay" or "I never would have guessed you had it in you?" and "You sure you didn't have some help?" By noon Saturday, November 8, following his first inspection of a junior battery as an upperclassman Red Bird, Collier had already become the object of unmerciful kidding from his mostly-bachelor How Battery classmates as word of Emma's pregnancy had quickly gotten around. On the other hand, Bert Hancock and several others of his married classmates whose wives were also expecting gave him a heartfelt thumbs up and clasped him around the shoulders.

Monday morning, proudly wearing the new Red Tabs on his epaulets and listening absently to his classmates discussing the bloody battles around Sniper Ridge and Triangle Hill, Collier was puzzled when Sergeant Grubbs came over to his table in the mess hall and whispered in his ear, "Soon as you're done eating, Ramsay, drive yourself over to HQ and report to Captain Whitley. Don't waste time. I don't want to have to send you out to Arbuckle Range in a jeep,"

"At ease, Ramsay. Pull up a seat." When Collier arrived at the orderly room, Captain Whitley returned his salute and pointed to the metal folding chair in front of his desk.

Holding his fatigue cap in his lap, Collier sat down and waited heart in throat. Surely Whitley wasn't going to bust him out at this late date.

"Congratulations on winning your Tabs. And congratulations on your wife's pregnancy," Whitley eased his mind hardly before Collier had settled into the olive-drab metal folding chair.

"Thank you, Sir, but how did you know my wife is pregnant?" Collier blurted, both impressed and flabbergasted.

"You should know by now that word travels fast around here. It is true, isn't it?" Grinning like the Cheshire Cat, his usually stone-faced CO leaned back in his handsome leather chair, the singular decorous concession to the austere furniture in the plain wooden barracks office space. Whitley obviously was enjoying the puzzled look on Collier's face.

"Yes, Sir, it is true, Sir. Emma is due around the end of April or the first week in May," Collier replied, still wondering what this interview was all about.

"Not exactly a well-timed event, Ramsay. Given the circumstances of your rapidly-approaching graduation and the current demand on us here at Sill to send as many of our graduates directly to FECOM as fast as possible, I would think that might have given you some concern." Whitley's smirk disappeared as his voice took on a more serious tone.

"No, Sir. I mean, yes, Sir...I mean I agree, Sir. Not well-planned—in fact you could say it was not planned at all," Collier admitted sheepishly.

"I sincerely hope that is not a reflection on our training and discipline here at the Artillery school." Whitley raised his eyebrows, reflecting concern.

"No, Sir. I mean...I...No excuse, Sir," Collier stuttered, trying to extricate himself.

"Never mind, Ramsay. I do understand these things can happen."

"Sir, yes, Sir." Worrying the sweatband of his fatigue cap round and round between his hands, Collier fretted, not knowing what was coming next.

"Well, this just may be your lucky day. As it happens, your timing might not have been as bad as it seems. You're in luck. I want to offer you a reprieve—a chance to remain stateside at least until April—maybe even until May when your baby is due. But May is seven months off...and I can't guarantee you'll still be in the country that long."

"I don't understand, Sir. Just what are we talking about?" Collier straightened and leaned forward in the metal chair, thoroughly confused.

"The Pentagon has sent us a levy for a small number of Artillery officer candidates to be commissioned in the Medical Service Corps. It seems the Medics are losing almost as many—maybe even more—Assistant Battalion Surgeons in Korea as the Artillery is losing FOs. Both are about the same rate as the Infantry is losing Platoon Leaders. We're asking for volunteers. These volunteer officers will be sent to San Antonio the first week in January for three-months training at the Medical Field Service School at Fort Sam Houston before they receive further assignment. But let's face it; this is not a free pass. After completing MFSS, if the truce still hasn't been signed, these officers will most likely go directly to FECOM—straight to the front unless I miss my guess. Anyway, I'm offering you the opportunity to transfer to MSC and go to MFSS in San Antonio. The next class at MFSS starts in mid-January and runs until mid-March."

"Well...I don't know, sir. I feel like I would make a first-class Artillery officer. With all due respect, sir, when it comes to Gunnery, I think I'm among the top in my class." Stunned by the offer, Collier wondered if this were a reflection on the Army's confidence in his ability to serve in a combat arm.

"I can't argue, Ramsay. You *are* among the top of your class. You can't imagine how hard it is for me to let you get away from us. The Artillery needs men of your caliber. But so do the Medics. It has also been pointed out to me by HQ, that you had two-years college pre-med."

"Yes, sir, but that was just heavy in Biology and Chemistry. It really didn't have much to do with medicine *per se*," Collier protested. "Pardon me, sir, but I don't know what to say...what to think, really. After almost five months—a year really, counting Basic—of preparation and dedication to become an Artillery officer this sudden change in my future prospects is coming at me a little too fast."

"I understand, Ramsay. I'm sure you want to discuss this with your wife. But, time is of the essence. You can give me your answer first thing tomorrow morning. I will give your other five classmates the same opportunity." Whitley stood up to signify the interview was at an end.

"Who are the others, sir, or is it out of line to ask?"

"Well, not out of line to ask, but for the moment, at least, I think that should be classified until those men have had the opportunity to make a choice."

"Yes, sir. Of course, sir." Collier saluted and waited to be dismissed.

"By the way, Ramsay, I think I should warn you that offering you a choice now doesn't mean that the Army won't order your transfer anyway if you refuse." Captain Whitley returned the salute, already shuffling through a small stack of folders on his desk.

"What did Whitley want with you?" Bob Skyar asked, passing him coming up the stairs.

"Sorry, Bob, I'm not at liberty to say." Collier grinned as it suddenly dawned on him that Skyar's wife was pregnant too.

Walking back to the barracks—as a newly-annointed Redbird, he was permitted to walk at a normal pace—contemplating the crucible experience, it suddenly occurred to Collier that miraculously, over the past ten months, the Army had actually transformed him from an overgrown, irresponsible, boy into full-grown manhood. Now, sooner than he cared to ponder, he would have a child of his own to rear. He only hoped he could be half the man his father was.

Reporting back in time to accompany the battery to an OP on Arbuckle Range where they were adjusting the fire of an 8-inch howitzer battery, Collier was assigned to back up Lieutenant Les Standiford, a young Range Safety Officer, newly-graduated from VMI and very nervous about having the responsibility of double-checking behind FDC to make sure all plots were within range limits. For this morning's service practice, the Safety Officer was set up on a portable folding wooden field table just to the left of the OP. Most likely the uninitiated young Range Safety Officer would have had a nervous breakdown if he'd known he was virtually on his own as, all morning long, Collier's head was abuzz with conflicting thoughts about Captain Whitley's offer to transfer to MSC.

Who else among his classmates were being offered the opportunity to transfer to MSC? Skyar's wife was pregnant and Flood and Hancock's wives were expecting, too. Barker's wife had already presented him a son. Would they be offered the same proposition? As far as Collier could tell, Barker, Skyar, Flood and Hancock all seemed to be competent in Gunnery. Were they—and he—being chosen because they were in some unknown way deemed deficient to the rest of their classmates as prospective Artillery officers? Should he phone Emma at lunch to break the news and talk this over? His gut told him Emma would have already heard it through the wives' grapevine before he saw her tonight at the PX. Of course, it all boiled down to the fact he probably didn't really have a choice. Emma would jump at the possibility he might be able to be stateside when the baby came. Besides, the fact that he would be graduated from MFSS as an Assistant Battalion Surgeon would appeal to her as a nurse. She was already looking forward to going back to Roanoke so that Garrett Gooch could deliver the baby at Lewis-Gale.

"This target is only three-hundred yards inside range limits. Metero says the wind is gusting up to twenty miles per hour out of the northwest. Looks pretty chancy to me. What do you think, Ramsay?" Collier was brought back to reality as Standiford nudged him to take a closer look at the FDC plot of the latest target called down from the OP.

As Safety Officer, Standiford stood to forfeit $100 for every round out of safety limits.

"Uhm-m? You're probably right. It's cutting it pretty close. No sense in taking a chance." Collier agreed, taking a closer—actually his first—look at Standiford's plot on the chart.

"Ceasefire," Standiford called over the phone.

"Ceasefire, hell, Standiford! That plot is a good three hundred yards inside of limits," Captain Gerrard, the veteran Gunnery instructor, hollered indignantly across from the OP to their left. A rather roughshod, former-Texas-sharecropper-sergeant from nearby Denton, Gerrard had been commissioned in the field at Normandy. Fiercely proud, he was a damn fine Artilleryman who had learned his gunnery the same way he had earned his silver railroad tracks—the hard way! What Gerrard lacked in spit and polish, he made up for with soldierly acumen.

"Yes, sir, I know. But the wind has come up to twenty knots out of the northeast. No telling what could happen to artillery rounds at that extreme distance from the guns," Standiford defended his judgment. After all, if the rounds drifted outside safety limits, it was his ass on the line.

"We're not talking badminton shuttlecocks here, Lieutenant. We're firing eight-inch howitzers back there. Those projectiles are almost as heavy as a jeep," Gerrard chided the rookie Safety Officer.

What Gerrard said about the size and weight of 8-inch projectiles was true. All morning long, they had watched the sky, catching an occasional opportunity to pick up one of the ponderous rounds in flight, actually able to track it visually to its target.

"Well, sir, that may be, but I still think we're taking a big chance. Do you see that squatter's shack and chicken coop just outside range limits? I saw the squatter tending to his chickens earlier this morning. In winds like these, we certainly shouldn't be taking a chance, firing rounds out there that close to human life."

The squatter's shack and chicken coop were familiar landmarks on Arbuckle Range—they had been there for as long as anyone could remember. The structures were makeshift constructions using scrap pieces of plywood and odd bits of discarded lumber and chicken wire.

"Listen, Lieutenant, that damn squatter has been repeatedly warned to get off that land. He's been out there long enough to know he is on the edge of an artillery range. If a wayward round hasn't wiped him off the face of the earth before now, these 8-inch howitzers certainly aren't going to do it this morning. By my calculations, those shacks are at least another two-hundred yards outside range limits," Gerrard persisted.

"I don't like it, sir. With the wind, conditions are way too iffy," Standiford protested.

"Nonsense! FDC has the benefit of updated meteorology. Hell's bells, Standiford, quit being such a goddamn ninny. Go ahead and let them fire two rounds at the initial plot. It will be interesting for these future FOs to see what effect the wind has. If the initial rounds are too close to limits, *then* we can always call the mission off," Gerrard kept insisting.

"I'm sorry, Sir. In my judgment this mission is dangerous. I'm calling it off," Standiford raised the field phone to his mouth and pushed the "Talk" button.

"Wait up. If a round lands out of limits, I'll pay your fine myself. These men here are your witnesses." Even though Gerrard knew Standiford's plot of the squatter's shack was correct and the young lieutenant was being properly judicious, he challenged the young Range Officer like some roughneck bully showing off to his poolhall pals.

"Begging your pardon, Captain Gerrard, the money is nothing compared to the Boards of Inquiry if these rounds drift out of limits, sir. If that happens, I'm afraid not even General Harper can let me off the hook," Standiford reminded Gerrard unnecessarily. Major General A.M. Harper was the current Commandant.

"Don't be so dramatic and don't let these men see what a coward you really are, Lieutenant. After all, the plot *is* within limits, isn't it?" Gerrard was downright insulting now.

"Well, alright, Sir." Much against his better judgment, Standiford pushed the Talk button and told FDC, "Disregard the Ceasefire—go ahead and fire two rounds. Will adjust."

Within a matter of seconds, the booming sound of two 8-inch howitzers echoed ominously from the gun placements about a mile behind the OP. Shading his eyes, Collier looked skyward hoping to pick up the flight of the ponderous 8-inch projectiles and visually track them to their destination. Catching the whirring sound of the overhead artillery, Collier had no luck picking the rounds up visually.

"Holy shit!" Standiford gasped as, right before the eyes of everyone on the OP, the ramshackle chicken coop and squatter's shack disintegrated into a cloud of dust.

When Collier rushed to the BC Scope to get a better look, lumber and chicken feathers filled the air.

"Ceasefire, end of mission," Captain Gerrard lowered his glasses, grabbed the field phone and called down to FDC. Handing the phone back to Standiford, he nudged Collier aside from the BC Scope to take a closer look.

"Here, Lieutenant..." He hastily jotted an IOU for $200 on a page he tore out of his little field notebook.

Passing the IOU to the young lieutenant, Gerrard turned to the men on the OP. "Stow your field glasses, fold the tripod and pack up the BC Scope. That's quite enough excitement for one day."

Riding back to the Post, Collier's thoughts were filled with the confused feelings that he had most likely just fired his last mission as an Artillery FO and he had just been given a reprieve from going straight to FECOM right after New Year's Day. If his luck held, he might even be around to see his firstborn son—intuitively, Collier was confident the baby would be a boy—before heading off to war.

THE DAILY OKLAHOMAN
Oklahoma City, Oklahoma, Friday, December 12, 1952
PRESIDENT SNEERS AT IKE, MACARTHUR

WASHINGTON, December 11 (AP) - President Truman today denounced President-elect Dwight D. Eisehower's trip to Korea as a piece of demagoguery and said he doubted that Gen. Douglas MacArthur has any new solution to the Korean War.

THE ROANOKE TIMES
Roanoke, Virginia, Saturday, December 13, 1952
EISENHOWER PUZZLED OVER TRUMAN'S ATTACK

HONOLULU, Saturday, December 13 (AP) - President-elect Dwight D. Eisenhower is shocked and puzzled by President Truman's blast at his trip to Korea it was learned today, but is determined not to become involved in any public wrangle with the President...

THE DAILY OKLAHOMAN
Oklahoma City, Oklahoma, Tuesday, December 16, 1952
LOVELY LANA SINGLE AGAIN

CARSON CITY, Nev., December 15 - Blonde beauty Lana Turner flew into Nevada Monday for a quick divorce and then went back to work in Hollywood.

THE RADIO DEEJAY GAVE THE TEMPERATURE as 29 degrees as Friday, December 12, dawned bright and clear. With a predicted high around 60, the weatherman promised a perfect afternoon for viewing the graduation parade.

"Welcome to Lawton, Oklahoma. I was getting worried about you. It's good to see your smiling faces at last." When Cocky and Lida pulled their sedan into the carport at Hilda Birdsong's place around mid-afternoon, Emma—who had been keeping a watchful eye out for the better part of two hours—ran outside to greet them with hugs and kisses. "Do you need to use the powder room? I hate to rush you, but if we're going to see Collier before his class's graduation parade, we need to get a move on."

"I'm fine. I went when we stopped for gas outside of Elgin," Lida assured her.

"We both did. Lead on," Cocky said, "I'll follow."

"Come on Lida, you ride with me and we can catch each other up on the news," Emma said.

"I simply cannot believe a good Baptist son of mine could be marrying a Catholic." By the time Emma opened the car door for her mother-in-law, Lida was already whining about Jimmy's upcoming wedding.

"How Battery, CSMO. For-ward, harch." Collier's eyes brimmed with emotion as Candidate Battery Commander Kelly brought the Battery to Closed Station Marching Order, and, dressed in winter dress OD flannels, the men of How

Battery stepped off as one man just as the Post band struck up the strains of the Washington Post March.

"Eyes right...pre-e-e-sent arms..." Passing the reviewing stand for the final time, the one-hundred, ramrod-straight young men snapped their heads smartly to the right as a single unit, bringing hands to the right eyebrow in a sharp salute.

"I don't know, but I been tol', How/Easy Battery is solid gold, SOUND OFF..." Violating all military SOP covering the maintenance of proper decorum, immediately upon passing the reviewing stand, Collier shouted forth improvised lines of the Jody Chant.

"ONE TWO," the battery responded with a Cadence Count that echoed from Signal Mountain to MB-4. Following the cadence count, the Singing Battery burst into the lyric of a song they had composed to be sung to the tune of *The Marine Hymn*.

> *"From blockhouse Signal Mountain*
> *To the house on MB-4,*
> *We have double-timed around the world*
> *A dozen times or more.*
> *From the messhall to the battery,*
> *To the classrooms on the hill,*
> *You can hear the songs of How/Easy,*
> *The Pride of old Fort Sill."*

The battery continued singing until they marched into the assembly area beyond the reviewing stand and were dismissed.

"Hi, Mom—Dad, it's great to see you." As soon as the Battery was dismissed, Collier joined Emma and his parents in the grassy parking area behind the reviewing stand.

"Oh, Collier, we're so happy. Emma gave us the wonderful news." Lida's eyes brimmed with emotion—elated far more by the prospect of becoming a grandmother than for pride in seeing her son become an officer in the Army.

Following this brief, teary reunion, his father and mother followed Collier and Emma to the Post Guest Quarters to check in and grab a brief rest before going to the Officers' Club for the long-awaited graduation party. As soon as he had helped his father unload their luggage, Collier hurried Emma back to the car, intent upon making it to the Military Police office on Sheridan Road to get a bright yellow "O" for "Officer" decal for the windshield of their car. From there, they drove to the apartment in Lawton where Emma changed into an ivory-colored satin cocktail dress, and Collier donned his custom-tailored "Pinks and Greens", officer's dress uniform for the very first time. Worn with a khaki shirt and a dark olive tie, "Pinks" described the rich khaki-beige trousers and "Greens" was for the deep forest-green color of the contrasting blouse (military for jacket) which hung rakishly to mid-thigh. He had already meticulously attached his sparkling-new, gold Second Lieutenant's bars and the MSC Caduceus insignia which represented his new branch of service. His expensive new low-cut dress shoes were polished to inspection-ready perfection.

"You are stunning, my dear—truly beautiful. The officer and his lady made a grand entrance—can't you just see us on the Sunday society page of The Lawton Constitution..." Collier bowed and made a broad sweeping gesture with his arm.

"You cut a handsome figure, Collier, even if I am prejudiced. You look as if you were born to be an officer." Emma stood back and admired him in the resplendent new uniform.

Although Collier and Emma and his parents drank only the fruity punch containing no alcohol, the celebration in the O Club ballroom quickly became a rather noisy, quite-animated mob scene. Overflowing wives, girlfriends, parents and TAC officers, along with other high-ranking military dignitaries, overjoyed with a sense of release from six-long months of unbearable pressure, the spacious room was already pleasantly aglow from the virtually-unlimited supply of beer and liquor from the adjoining bar before the party officially got underway.

The celebration continued unabated following the formal dinner and speeches. Throughout the course of the evening, Collier managed to introduce his parents and Emma to TAC lieutenants Robinson and Suit and TAC sergeants Ernst and Grubbs and their wives. It was not until later, toward the end of the evening, however, he found an opportunity to present Captain Whitley to his father.

"Harry Milton Ramsay, I would like to present Captain Jesse W. Whitley, our Tactical Battery Commander. Captain Whitley, Sir, this is my father," Collier introduced them, hoping he followed the proper military form of introduction and address from his recent course in Military Protocol and Etiquette.

"I am honored to meet you, Mr. Ramsay, Sir. You can be very proud of your son." Whitley stepped forward and shook his father's meaty hand. Collier exhaled a covert sigh of relief that Cocky had on a new white shirt and had cleaned and trimmed his fingernails for the occasion.

"Excuse me, just for a moment, Sir, I want to say goodbye to George Barker and his wife—they're leaving. They want to get an early start tomorrow morning. It's a long drive back to Atlanta." Collier seized upon an excuse to avoid the embarrassment of having to listen to the perfunctory exchange between the two men and headed across the room to catch Barker.

When he returned a short time later, Collier could hardly believe his ears when he overheard Captain Whitley telling his father, "Mr. Ramsay, you should be very proud of Collier. In my position, it is unmilitary to play favorites, and I certainly couldn't afford to have this repeated, Sir, but it is my opinion that your son is by far the most intelligent and, all-round, the finest soldier of this entire class. I know he was quite torn between wanting to remain in the Artillery and taking the opportunity to be commissioned in the Medics to provide the chance he might still be in the States when his wife gives birth. I think he may be entertaining some foolish notion that he took a coward's way. Rest assured your son is no weakling—far from it. From the beginning, he steadfastly refused to let us break him of his innate, unshakeable belief in himself which originally my staff and I mistakenly perceived as an altogether unwarranted sense of arrogance. We were wrong, Sir. Lieutenant Collier Ramsay has the sort of self-confidence I believe will take him anywhere he chooses to go. I would feel honored to have your son at my side in combat; he is going to be a fine leader among men."

Although the thermometer dipped to around freezing overnight, Saturday dawned fair and crisp, with a predicted high around 60. A picture-perfect day for graduation.

Before entering the pre-graduation ceremony breakfast back at the O Club with Emma and his parents, his father took him aside and repeated the conversation Collier had overheard the previous evening. "Your Captain Whitley told me not to tell, but he said he would feel honored to serve with you in combat. He told me you were the all-around best soldier in your class."

"That was nice of him, Dad, but don't you imagine he may give that speech to all the fathers and mothers?" Collier blushed, pleased his father had been taken in by Whitley's bullshit.

"He told me not to tell you. He said you'd say just what you did. Come on, I'm starved—let's find the women and eat." Beaming with pride, his father clasped him warmly around the shoulder as they headed inside.

Thankfully, at the graduation ceremony, the speeches were short and to the point. In practically no time at all, Collier found himself crossing the stage at Post Theater Number 1, as—in that dreaded, cross-handed maneuver everyone dreads the impossibility of—he accepted the rolled, beribboned certificate of his commission to Second Lieutenant in the Army of the United States of America with his left hand and saluted the Commandant, Colonel J. R. Burrill, with his right.

"I remember back in July when you told us during first-day Orientation it was your dedication you wouldn't live to see the day you would have to salute me. I'm glad I proved you wrong." Descending the narrow steps on the left of the stage, Collier returned the sharp salutes of both Sergeants Grubb and Ernst as he handed each man a crisp bill in keeping with the venerable tradition for young officers receiving their first salutes from an NCO..

"It's a pleasure, Lieutenant Ramsay, Sir," they responded in unison, grinning from ear-to-ear. Because "Ramsay" was far down in the alphabetical order of the graduating officers, in their left hands, both of the crusty sergeants already grasped a fistful of crisp one-dollar bills.

"Come on, folks, let's get out of here." Collier quickly rounded up Emma and his parents. Most of his farewells having already been said at the O Club the previous evening and at this morning's graduation breakfast—and with all his gear packed and waiting for Army-shipping to his parent's address—Collier felt absolutely no further need to return to the OCS area following the graduation ceremony. With Emma and his folks firmly under control, he steered them toward the parking lot and headed back toward town. Passing through the Sheridan Road gate, it was all he could do to keep from grinning when his bright new yellow "O" decal earned the respectful salutes of the guards.

Back in their Lawton apartment, the domestically-inclined Louise Rudolph had prepared a mouth-watering sandwich buffet—complete with homemade apple pie.

"Dig in everybody. I'm going to get out of this uniform." Collier disappeared into the bedroom and lost little time in changing into civvies as, for the first time in almost six months, he was finally able to relax. Wolfing down several sandwiches and an oversized slab of apple pie with ice cream, Collier excused himself, retreated into the bedroom and collapsed on the bed and fell immediately into a deep sleep, totally oblivious as Emma busied herself sorting out items she needed to pack for their long trek to Enid for Jim's graduation and marriage to Hitch immediately following receiving his wings and bars.

"Enid is only a half-day drive from Lawton. It makes no sense to drive here early and incur the expense of several extra days in the overpriced Youngblood Hotel." With his graduation scheduled for Friday, December 19—a full six days away—Jim had advised them he would be up to his eyeballs flying right up to the very last day. Collier and Emma and his parents all agreed that it was only prudent to remain in Lawton until the following Thursday before embarking to Enid. Collier strongly suspected Jim wanted to keep Lida away from Hitch's Catholic mother as long as possible; Collier was already more than a little tired of his mother's constant carping about Jim marrying a Catholic.

"Why don't we do some sightseeing?" Collier suggested. The extra days in Lawton offered a perfect opportunity to show his folks around and perhaps difuse some of the tension.

"That's a great idea. We can show your folks around the fort, and we could go see the Wichita Wildlife Range," Emma chimed in, excited as much for herself as for her in-laws. Other than one Sunday afternoon excursion to the top of Mount Scott late in June before Collier began OCS, she had been afforded no other opportunity to explore the wilds of the Wildlife Refuge out beyond Wichita Mountain Range. Hilda Birdsong had told her to be sure to to see the Holy City of the Wichitas and the free-ranging herd of buffalo on the Wildlife Refuge. The bison herd was reputed to be the largest in America—maybe the largest in the world.

"If we have time, I'd like to see the Holy City of the Wichitas where they hold the Easter Pageant?" As if she were reading Emma's mind, Lida spoke up right away. A famous local landmark, The Holy City of the Wichitas was a manmade reconstruction—featuring a natural amphitheater—built as the setting for what was advertised as "The longest-running Easter passion play in America." With some attention in magazines and big-city newspapers, over recent years, The Holy City of the Wichitas was rapidly becoming a minor tourist destination.

Rummaging in her purse for a Chamber of Commerce brochure, Lida read aloud, "*The Holy City started as an Easter Passion Play in the Wichita mountains in 1926. The impetus behind both the pageant and city was the late Reverend Anthony Mark Wallock. He was born in 1890 in Austria. He immigrated to the United States with his parents at two years of age. After completing ministerial studies at the Garret Biblical Institute, Wallock served at several churches before coming to Lawton as pastor of the First Congregational Church. In 1926, he took his Sunday school class up a mountain where a tableau of the Resurrection was presented. The popularity of this service led it to become an annual event. In 1927, the service became nonsectarian, and was referred to by the Lawton Constitution as "Oklahoma's Oberammergau."*

"What's 'Ober-whatever' mean?" Lida held her place with her finger and glanced over at Collier.

"*Oberammergau* is the town in Bavaria that's famous for the Passion Play," Collier said, secretly pleased that Hilda had explained this to him when they were planning their infamous picnic outing that had been rained out.

"Uhm-m." Lida nodded and continued reading, "*Each year the Passion Play expanded its cast and worshipers. In 1930, it attracted 6,000 people. By 1931, the congregation has swelled to 15,000 with 150 cast members, and by 1934, 40,000 worshipers came. Because of the event's popularity, it received a grant of $94,000 from "federal funds [that were] unconditionally set aside for the Wichita Mountains Easter Pageant." The first buildings were completed by the Federal Works Progress Administration (WPA); they included walls and gateway to Jerusalem, Calvary's Mount, the Temple Court, Pilate's Judgment Hall, Watch Towers, Garden of Gethsemane, dressing rooms and rock shrines. A ceremony to dedicate the Holy City was held in 1935, when the cast for Easter Sunrise*

Service had grown to 1,200, which included an "a capella" choir, and Knights Templar from all over the state..."

"Okay, Lida, that's enough." His father raised his hand then turned to Collier. "If it's not too far and the weather stays good, do you suppose we could find time to take a ride out there? It might make a nice Sunday afternoon trip. We could all fit in my new sedan." Cocky looked over at Collier expectantly.

"Sure, why not? We could take sandwiches and have a picnic somewhere. If we left around mid-morning, we could go up Mount Scott first before we eat lunch. There are picnic spots with tables at the Park campgrounds out that way," Collier agreed.

The all-day picnic excursion to Mount Scott and the Wichita Wildlife Range quickly escalated into a major project. Emma and Lida made a list and went off to the Post Commissary to do the shopping.

Sunday dawned bright and clear. Collier—unaccustomed to the opportunity to sleep late—awoke promptly at 0530 hours in time to see the pale-orange blush of dawn through the high, narrow bedroom window as it was already beginning to chase the stars from the deep indigo night. At the horizon, an expanding area of electric-blue heralded the coming of a perfect day. Quietly rolling out of bed, Collier shrugged into his robe and padded into the kitchen, thinking to get the paper and start the coffee pot which Emma had readied before they went to bed. He was not surprised to find his father already up and raring to go. Lida was curled up on the livingroom sofa.

"Good morning, Son. I loaded the picnic basket and thermoses into the car. Looks like we'll have a fine day for sightseeing," his father greeted him cheerily from across the kitchen where he stood at the gas range, carefully attending a large skillet of frying bacon. "I'm not quite ready to cook the eggs. Have a cup of coffee and then let's call the girls. We've got a busy day ahead."

"We're going to have sunshine, but it's going to be pretty chilly." Going to the door to retrieve *The Daily Oklahoman*, Collier checked the weather before heading for the coffee pot. As predicted, the thermometer mounted outside the kitchen window read 23 degrees.

"Looks like we're going to have a sunny day," Lida enthused as she made her entrance. Ever the fashion plate, Lida was wearing tweed slacks and an Irish knit turtleneck—over her forearm she carried a navy-blue Eton blazer.

"That blazer will feel good outside. But we'll also need to take warmer coats. It'll be breezy on top of Mount Scott and the predicted high is in the upper forties—fifty at the most," Collier warned them.

"We girls can ride in the back seat. Mr. Ramsay, you ride in front with Collier," Emma took charge of the seating arrangements when they went out. Since Collier was familiar with the area, it was already decided the night before that he should drive.

"Looks like God took a giant meat cleaver and sliced them right down the middle." His mother echoed almost the same reaction Collier had the first time he had laid eyes on the spectacular grey-granite cliffs of Medicine Bluffs rising sharply above the willow- and mesquite-lined banks of Medicine Creek.

"This rugged terrain puts me in mind of some old cowboy movie," his father said, peering intently on the boulder-strewn landscape as they approached Mount Scott.

"This is Mount Scott up ahead." Collier slowed as they rounded a curve and the dominating rocky land feature loomed before them, rising abruptly out of the much lower surrounding hills.

"How high is Mount Scott?" his father asked.

"Twenty-four hundred and sixty-something—give or take a foot or two. About eighteen or twenty miles north and west of here, there's another mountain, which is supposed to be a few feet higher. I forget the name," Collier parroted the wealth of local lore Hilda had imparted when she had first brought him here with Bo and his buddies during their Basic at FARTC.

"Sticking up right out of the plain, these so-called mountains make a scenic landscape, but they would hardly qualify as hills back home." Cocky laughed.

"Breathtaking, simply breathtaking..." his mother kept repeating from the back seat as they wound their way back down Mount Scott shortly after noon. They had spent about an hour taking in the surrounding countryside from the mountaintop.

"It's beautiful alright..." Collier mumbled a tight-lipped assent, suddenly alarmed by the unexpected softness of the brake pedal. The fully-loaded sedan was quickly gathering speed as they started down the narrow spiral road. Frantically—fighting not to betray the sudden gnawing fear in his belly—he pumped the brake pedal with little or no response. To compound his rising anxiety, Collier was sure he detected a faint smell of burning rubber which told him the overworked brake pads were running hot and were rapidly losing hold. Wasting little time, Collier quickly depressed the clutch and downshifted into second gear. Slowly releasing the clutch again, he let the transmission buffer the insistent pull of gravity against the dead weight of the heavy automobile. Instantly, the car began to slow perceptibly. Collier slowly let out his breath as he felt the vehicle respond back to his control. However, only when they finally wound down to the bottom of the steep, circuitous grade and had coasted to stop at the intersection of Route 49, did he dare shift back into third.

Making certain there was no approaching traffic from either direction, Collier edged slowly onto 49 heading west toward the roaming grounds of the Wildlife Refuge, covertly testing the overheated brake pads as they went along. After perhaps a mile, he exhaled a sigh of relief when he found the pads had sufficiently cooled and were taking firm hold again. They had only traveled a short distance further on when they encountered a simple highway sign: US Wild Life Reserve. Just beyond the sign, the highway passed beneath a hulking primitive, rectangular, stone-masonry arch with the legend: WICHITA NATIONAL FOREST & GAME PRESERVE.

Lida resumed reading from the brochure, "*In 1901, President McKinley set aside these mountains as a Federal Forest Reserve. In 1905, Teddy Roosevelt renamed it as a Game Preserve. Wantonly slaughtered by both cowboys and Indians and commercial hunters, the 1800s saw a wholesale slaughter of the American Bison—the buffalo—which once estimated at sixty-million in the wild had been the most prolific large wild animal on the face of the planet. Out of these vast herds of American Bison originally roaming the plains, by 1900, there were estimated to be only one-thousand still alive. In 1907, fifteen American Bison—buffalo—were donated by, of all places, the New York Zoological Society. Now that herd has grown to such a size it is maintained at around six-hundred head by selling off the excess numbers at an annual sale. Longhorn cattle, elk and wild turkey were added as time went by. In addition to preserving these historic, traditional wildlife, the establishment of this Refuge also preserves a rare and unique geological feature from North America's not-so-distant, but quickly-disappearing past—a remnant 'mixed grass prairie.' The Wichita, a spacious 59,000-acre land area, is sort of an island, where original primitive grasslands were spared destruction because the land was literally 'too rocky to plow.'*

"The sign says the Holy City is up ahead on the right," Collier interjected as he slowed and prepared to turn. The brakes seemed okay again, but he resolved to have them checked.

Teeth chattering against the numbing chill, after patiently observing Emma and his parents' hour-long exploration of the site of the famous Easter Passion Play—an altogether disappointing assemblage of crudely-designed and constructed rock buildings which, however earnest, portrayed a rather unimaginative vision of early Jerusalem—Collier finally rounded up his sightseers, hoping to catch a glimpse of the elusive buffalo while it was still light. Several miles past the Visitor Center and Quanah Parker Lake, they were driving through a grassy pastureland when they came upon a large, prairie dog village.

"The little devils are certainly not afraid of us. For them, this is home sweet home." Collier chuckled watching the antics of the busy little creatures.

"Look up ahead on the left there are buffalo! Quick, get the camera, Lida! Pull up, Collier. Let's get a closer look," Cocky exclaimed excitedly, pointing through the windshield.

"Here. I already wound it to the next picture. We're near the end of the roll...number six or seven. Make every shot count." Lida handed him the boxy Kodak Brownie and began searching in her purse for another of the eight-exposure rolls.

Edging slowly to the side of the narrow road, Collier parked on the margin of the grassy turf as everyone spilled out of the car, headed for the herd of sixty or seventy of the massive, shaggy animals peacefully grazing a hundred yards away.

"Wait up! Don't get too close. Buffalo are very unpredictable and not to be trusted. We passed a sign a few miles back, warning that buffalo were very temperamental and could be dangerous," Collier warned, but, surprisingly, the buffalo completely ignored them.

"Want to try to and find some Texas longhorns or maybe spot a wild turkey?" Collier asked. His father had finished off the remaining three exposures on the roll and was reloading the camera.

"Forget the cows. Let's go back," Emma chattered, pulling her light jacket close around her. "It's getting dark and I'm about to freeze. Who wants to see a turkey or a dumb old cow, anyway?"

While his dad and mom made no protest, Collier thought he saw a look of disappointment cross his father's face as they all piled in the car for the journey back to town. Driving slowly along, Collier discreetly tested the brakes and was much relieved to find they seemed to be working fine again.

Monday dawned fair and cold with a predicted warming to around 50 degrees.

"These pads are okay, Lieutenant," the sergeant in charge of the Motor Pool said, wiping the dirt from his hands on a greasy rag as one of his crew began replacing the wheels and tightening the lugs. While Lida helped Emma gather her travel clothes for packing for their odyssey to Enid and the ensuing long trek back to Virginia for Christmas, Collier spent most of Monday morning on Post shipping some final odds and ends back home and, just to be on the safe side, he had stopped by the Motor Pool and asked the sergeant to pull the wheels on his father's car to reassure him the brake pads were safe to drive.

"I had no idea there was so much history here," his mother remarked Tuesday morning, as Collier drove his parents on a tour of the Old Post, including the historic old log jail, the ancient cavalry stables, and Geronimo's grave. With time on their hands, following a leisurely brunch at the O club, they all bundled up against the chilly, breezy day and ventured downtown to catch the matinee of *High Noon* with Gary Cooper and Grace Kelly.

Wednesday morning dawned cold and gray. Looking for the complete weather forecast in *The Daily Oklahoman,* Collier saw where Lana Turner was getting divorced again—this time from millionaire entrepreneur and sportsman, Dan Topping. She had been previously married to band leader, Artie Shaw, and had had much-publicized affairs with movie leading men, Victor Mature, Tyrone Power and Fernando Lamas.

"I hope she took him good. Damn stuffed-shirt Topping wasn't man enough to hold a woman like that," Cocky sniffed when Collier pointed out the article. Dan Topping was part-owner and president of the New York Yankees baseball team, and Cocky had a big thing for Lana Turner, and, besides, he was a died-in-the-wool Red Sox and Dodgers fan.

Thursday, Lida helped Emma give the house a superficial cleaning—they had given Opal Black Elk money to give the place a thorough cleaning after they were gone. Not wanting to take a chance on being pressed into janitorial service, Collier took his dad to see an Artillery Firepower Demonstration at Signal Mountain Range.

"Awesome...unbelievable. I loaded powder in artillery shells during the First World War, but that seemed so remote. Now I have a better understanding about the result of what I was doing. I can only imagine how you must feel when you're controlling the direction of such power..." In hushed tones, his father talked about the powerful display of killing machinery all the way back into Lawton.

"Yeah, it's a serious responsibility, alright. I feel kinda like I'm a deserter— taking my commission in MSC and wasting all my training. I don't like to brag, but I got to be pretty damn good at that Artillery stuff, you know?"

"You don't need to tell me. Captain Whitley told me you were the best in the class. But he also said you were needed more in the Medics. A man should go where he is needed most."

"I just hope you both are right." Collier gripped the steering wheel hard as he turned into the drive at Hilda's place. Seeing the artillery demo left a feeling of emptiness in his chest.

With all of their household goods either packed and shipped or given to Herb and Louise, Collier and Emma and his parents packed their remaining possessions into their respective cars and with Collier leading the way, headed back through town to take the main highway northeast to Chickasha. At Chickasha, they picked up Highway 81 which led directly north through the tiny towns of Minco, El Reno, Kingfisher and Bison—all the way into Enid. With chilly stops in Okarche and Hennesey for gas and use of the restrooms, the drive took a little over three hours. Just south of the town of Bison, the mist started freezing on the windshield, and Collier fervently prayed the light rain would not turn the roads to ice.

On the map, Enid appeared to be about the size of Lawton. Originally the location had been a watering hole on the Old Chisholm Trail. A jumping-off spot for the famous Cherokee Strip Land Run in 1893, according to local lore, the town got its name when some high-spirited cowhands turned a homemade chuckwagon sign reading "DINE" backwards and upside down. In his artist's eye, Collier could visualize the image produced by such a prank and admitted the apochryphal tale might contain more truth than baloney.

Finding Vance Air Force Base and the Youngblood Hotel proved to be no problem. After traversing mile after mile through the wheat-fields of the north Oklahoma flatlands under the chilly, misting, brooding overcast, they had just passed a sign reading Enid 5 mi. when the ghostly outline of what Collier first assumed must be a gigantic grain elevator seemed to emerge out of the bleak winter landscape. As the mist-shrouded form gradually took shape, Collier saw the giant YOUNGBLOOD sign on top.

"That must be Vance Air Force Base." Almost simultaneous with their arresting first view of the monolithic hotel projecting above the small city skyline, Emma called attention to a formation of three B-25s which swooped almost directly over the car and landed on the airstrip of the sizeable military installation to their left.

Formerly Enid Air Force Base, in 1949, Vance AFB was renamed for hometown hero, WWII B-24 pilot, Lt. Colonel Leon Robert Vance, who was posthumously awarded the Congressional Medal of Honor when the search for his plane was abandoned after his plane disappeared over the North Atlantic in 1944 enroute to England from a sortie over Germany. Rolling down the driverside window, Collier waved and pointed excitedly to his father following closely behind. In his rearview mirror, Collier saw Cocky flash his headlights in acknowledgment.

"Well, I never! You would think that out of common courtesy they could have waited for me to go along." Checking in at the Youngblood, Lida was exasperated to find that Elizabeth and Ben Hitchcock—who had already arrived earlier in the week with Betty—had left a note at the Registration Desk saying they were out meeting with the Chaplain at Vance Air Force Base to go over plans for the wedding ceremony.

"Harry Ramsay, I want you to take me out to that flying field this very minute. I don't want that Catholic bitch forcing my son to say a mass or sign away the rights to my grandchildren...or any such thing like that," Lida demanded immediately upon reading the note.

"Just calm down, Mother," Collier said. "I believe your precious Emily Post says the bride is in charge of the wedding."

"Don't tell me to calm down. I won't have any son of mine being taken into slavery to their stupid Pope."

"Oh, you must be the Ramsays. I'm Beth Hitchcock. This is my husband, Ben. Of course, you already know Betty." Before Lida could open her mouth to speak again, Beth Hitchcock walked off the elevator, followed by her husband and Lida's soon-to-be daughter-in-law.

"I'm glad we caught you in time. If it's alright, I'd like to go with you when you meet with the Chaplain who is going to perform tomorrow's ceremony," Lida interjected after the brief babble of introductions and small talk were concluded.

"Oh, my, I'm sorry, Lida. I left that note yesterday and completely forgot to have the desk clerk tear it up," Beth Hitchcock smiled, sweetly apologetic. "I didn't get your RSVP before we left Hempstead, but I assume you got my letter about tonight's rehearsal. Afterwards, we want everyone to join us for a rehearsal dinner at the Officers' club out at Vance."

"We'd be delighted...and I assume Jim told you we're inviting everyone to a dinner here at the hotel tomorrow night after the graduation ceremony and the wedding." Lida returned Beth's frozen smile—a stranger would have assumed the two women were lifelong friends.

"Then it's settled. You'd better go ahead and get checked in. We'll need to leave a little early to get your car cleared to get on the base." Beth Hitchcock clearly wanted to leave no doubt she was in charge of the show.

"Oh, don't you look handsome in your uniform." Collier's wristwatch showed a little past 1800 hours when Lida wrapped her arms around Jim in the foyer of the Vance AFB Chapel. Since their own car was loaded to the tops of the windows with household possessions, he and Emma had hitched a ride with his parents. It made no sense to have to clear both cars onto the military installation.

"This is Major O'Reilly. The Major is the Catholic Chaplain here on Base," Jim introduced them to the gnomish little priest.

"A pleasure to meet you, Major," Lida offered her hand with a crocodile smile.

After some false starts and self-conscious beginnings, the wedding rehearsal went off quite well. Following the brief—less than an hour-long—run-through, the entire wedding party, including Chaplain O'Reilly, repaired to a private room in the Officers' Club for drinks and the rehearsal dinner.

At the bar to get drinks, Jim confided to Collier some optimistic news, "The fates seem to be smiling on us. Looks like we may be able to see each other in Texas. After Christmas, I'm going to Perrin Air Force Base for B-26 transition. Perrin's between Sherman and Dennison just north of Dallas—probably no more than a half-day drive to San Antonio."

When they were all seated, Collier assumed it was a sardonic turn of fate that Lida was seated beside the priest at the opposite end of the table. Earlier, Collier had noted that the Irish clergyman was already showing signs he'd had a bit too much to drink. Dismissing the cosmic irony of the thirsty little Catholic chaplain being stuck with a Southern-Baptist teetotaler as his dinner partner and feeling a trifle sorry for his mother's plight, Collier gave his full attention to the mouth-watering, blood-rare cut of rib roast on his plate. Later, as the dinner party was breaking up and they were taking their leave of Jim and the Chaplain to drive back into town, it appeared that Lida and Father O'Reilly had become the best of friends. His intention to question his mother on the drive back to the Youngblood became secondary to his concern for the condition of the roads when, upon emerging from the Officers' Club, they were confronted with what appeared to be the beginnings of a sleet storm.

"We're used to driving in this stuff—just follow us," Ben Hitchcock offered solicitously.

"Who do they think they are, bossing us around?" Lida muttered resentfully.

"Forget it, Lida. Ben is just trying to be nice. All Yankees think Southerners have never driven in snow and sleet," Cocky chided good-naturedly on the way to the parking lot. "I just hope this doesn't amount to much. I'd like to be on the road at the crack of daylight Saturday morning."

"Freezing rain, sleet and occasional snow ending tomorrow morning...overnight low at Vance AFB will be around 27...noontime temperature Friday is expected to be near 40 degrees with a low temperature Saturday morning near forty..." Cocky tuned in a local radio station as soon as they started rolling.

When Collier awoke Friday morning, the click-click-click of sleet pellets were beating a steady rhythm on the windowpane; tiptoeing to the window, the cityscape and countryside beyond was a fairyland of snow and ice. Although the sky remained foreboding, by noon the temperature had risen a few degrees into the mid-30s, and most of the light snow and the ice covering the power lines and trees had disappeared. Fortunately, the rain and sleet had stopped almost completely and the roads were clear by the time they piled into Cocky's sedan, heading for Jim's graduation at the Base.

Standing in the lobby of the Base Theater following the ceremony, Jim stood grinning ear-to-ear as Lida and Cocky pinned the gleaming, new gold bars on his epaulets and Hitch attached the silver wings above the left-hand pocket of his blouse. As soon as the job was completed, with the Hitchcocks leading the way, they all hurried to the nearby Base Chapel to witness Jim and Hitch exchange their vows. Standing beside his brother at the altar, it was all Collier could do to keep from laughing out loud when he saw a Protestant chaplain accompanying Father O'Reilly as he entered to perform the ceremony. Collier turned and caught a glimpse of Lida sitting smugly on the front pew. When she saw him looking, Lida gave him a smile of angelic innocence.

It was still spitting snow as they pulled their cars from the curb just before daylight the following morning, heading for the highway leading to Tulsa where they planned to swing south, down through Fort Smith into Little Rock. They had already made it past Tulsa by late morning, and the temperature was still in the thirties, but the mixed rain and sleet had stopped and the highways were clear. Passing through Fort Smith in the early afternoon, there was still some daylight left when they drove into Little Rock. When Collier led his father past the Capital building in the gathering gloom, it was gaily bedecked with Christmas lights. Wanting to avoid city traffic the following morning, Collier drove on through the downtown section into the eastern outskirts of the city. Much to Collier's surprise, they came upon a first-class motel right across the highway from a huge restaurant specializing in fried catfish—his father's favorite food.

"I'm in heaven," his father said, rubbing his belly as they left the restaurant an hour later heading back across the highway to the motel and bed. "What time should we leave tomorrow?"

"There's a TV Motel on the Nashville bypass. Driving distance is about the same as today—a little further maybe. After we get to Memphis, the Tennessee roads are good. If we leave early enough, we might make it to that motel in time to see some of the Rams and the Lions game." Los Angeles and Detroit were playing for the National Conference title in Detroit. The winner would play Cleveland for the NFL championship the Sunday following Christmas Day.

"You're your daddy's boy, alright." A sports fan to the bitter end, Cocky clasped Collier affectionately around the shoulder and gave him a wide grin.

Although both women would have put up a howl had they known why they were being pulled from their warm beds so early, neither did much complaining the following morning when Collier and his dad hustled them into the automobiles. They arrived at the Mississippi Bridge at Memphis just before noon. Once past Memphis, they stopped at a homey café in the town of Arlington for an old-fashioned, after-church, Sunday "dinner" of fried chicken with mashed potatoes, green beans and homemade yeast rolls. After filling up with gas, they were able to breeze along at speeds of 60 mph or better on the smooth concrete Tennessee highways and made it to the truck bypass on the outskirts of Nashville just before 1500 hours. Following the trail of billboards, they had little trouble finding the TV Motel.

"Why are we stopping? It's barely mid-afternoon," Emma roused from a peaceful doze.

"Have you forgotten? You're three-and-a-half months along and have a finicky uterus. We've been on the road for nine hours. Besides, I'm dog-tired. For the last two hours, I've been fighting to stay awake. We all need some rest." The very picture of the worried husband and expectant father, Collier's voice expressed grave concern.

"Well, I'll be darned! This is a nice surprise. I'll go tell Dad to turn his TV on," Collier exclaimed theatrically, after they had checked in adjoining rooms and he turned on the television.

"My finicky uterus, huh? Do you expect me to rest with that thing blaring?" Emma howled when Collier "accidentally" discovered the football game was on the television set in their room.

"Come on, Sweetheart. I've been driving for three days and need a break. Besides, it's the playoffs. I'll turn down the sound," he contritely pleaded.

"Okay, you overgrown bad boys can see your precious football game in this room. I'll go next door with Lida." Leaving the door ajar for Cocky, Emma left the room.

"I got to hand it to you; we can't beat a deal like this!" Collier's father rubbed his hands together as he closed the door, his eyes already glued to the TV. The Detroit stadium was blanketed in a cloud of fog and both the Lions and Rams had already scored.

Still stuffed with fried chicken and white gravy, and half-exhausted from driving, both men were dozing fitfully before halftime and both were snoring by the time the game was over. Collier finally awoke just in time to see that Detroit had out-dueled LA, 31 to 21.

In bed early after Collier and Cocky brought back a bag of hamburgers from a nearby greasy spoon, Collier drifted into a sound sleep watching episode eight of the much-talked-about TV documentary series, *Victory at Sea*.

Sometime after midnight, he roused to the hiss of static on the snow-filled TV screen.

"Looks like a great day for a drive. Emma and I made it almost to Nashville the first night coming out to Lawton." Collier conferred with his dad the following morning, loading their cars in the pre-dawn darkness.

"It's about a ten-hour haul to Salem if we go straight through. The girls are anxious to get home with a few days to shop before Christmas—maybe they wouldn't mind the long drive." Cocky offered, looking to Collier for a reaction.

"I don't know. I'll have to leave it up to Emma. She's pregnant and, besides, we're gonna lose an hour passing out of Central Time." Collier could scarcely believe he was hearing his own voice expressing fatherly concern. Parenthood had never exactly been high on his list in his grand scheme of things; besides, he still hadn't made up his own mind how he felt about becoming a father.

"Let's get going. We don't have to decide yet. I'll have to see how I feel after we've made it to Bristol, if that's okay?" Emma replied grouchily, when Collier broached the question in the still-darkened motel parking lot. Climbing into the car, she pulled her mother's hand-crocheted afghan over herself and curled into a semi-fetal position with her head resting on her traveling pillow against Collier's right thigh. The muted metronomic "thump-thump" of the closely-spaced dividers in the endless concrete ribbon of Tennessee highway had already lulled Emma fast asleep when Collier saw the rotating beacon lights of the Nashville airport on his right. A short time later there was a sign pointing the way to Andrew Jackson's much-celebrated mansion, The Hermitage, as they came into the sleeping little town of Lebanon.

"Where are we? What time is it?" Emma roused and stretched and asked, looking at the unfamiliar highway.

"It's exactly twelve-fifty-nine. We're right on schedule. Are you hungry? Bristol's just up ahead." Surprisingly, they had traversed the nearly 300 miles in just under six hours.

"I feel okay. Let's get lunch in Abingdon and just go on home," Emma said, looking at the map when they were driving down the main drag of Bristol.

In Abingdon, they decided to buy sandwiches and eat them on the road. It was just before sunset when, near exhaustion, they made it into the Ramsay driveway. With Christmas Eve only two days away, everyone was more than glad to be off the road. Leaving most of their luggage in the automobiles, the road-weary travelers sat around the kitchen table quietly reminiscing about the trip while Cocky fried up thick slices of country ham to make his greasy ham-and-egg sandwiches.

"Goodnight Emma, goodnight son—it's great to have you back home." After they had eaten and washed up the dishes, his parents bid them a weary goodnight and headed up the stairs.

Later, incongruously wide awake lying in the darkness looking at the moonlight streaming through the window, Collier listened as a long coal train click-clicked its way along the Virginian Railroad tracks across the river. Feeling, more than hearing, Emma's regular breaths, he wondered what it would be like now that he was going to have a son of his own. If only he could be half the man his father was.

Never for a moment did it occur to Lieutenant Collier Boyd Ramsay that the fetus inside Emma's womb might be a girl.

CHAPTER THIRTY-FOUR

Merry Christmas
THE TIMES-REGISTER
Salem, Virginia, Friday, December 26, 1952
Y&T HOLDS ANNUAL CHRISTMAS PARTY FOR YOUNGSTERS

On last Saturday, December 20, the Salem division of the Yale & Town Manufacturing Company held its annual Christmas Party for children of employees.

THE ROANOKE TIMES
Roanoke, Virginia, Monday, December 29, 1952
DETROIT DUMPS CLEVELAND FOR PRO GRID CROWN

CLEVELAND, Ohio, Sunday, December 28 (AP) – The younger Detroit Lions smashed through a veteran Cleveland Browns team today for two touchdowns and a field goal to win 17-7 and cop their first professional football championship in 17 years.

THE ROANOKE TIMES
Roanoke,-Virginia, Wednesday, December 31, 1952
EXCEPT FOR THOSE AT FRONT, GIS TO STAY LONGER

TOKYO, Wednesday, December 31 (UP) – American soldiers in Korea except those at front line, will have to put in more time before they can be sent home, General Mark Clark's Far East Command Headquarters announced today...

San Antonio Express
San Antonio, Texas, Friday, January 2, 1953
29-YEAR-OLD 'HILLBILLIES KING' DIES

OAK HILL, W.Va., January 1 (AP) – Hank Williams, singer and composer called the "King of Hillbillies" by his followers, died today in his automobile on his way to fill an engagement in Ohio.

MONDAY MORNING AFTER DRIVING EMMA and his mother into Roanoke—Emma to see Garrett Gooch, her OBGyn, and Lida to do some last-minute Christmas shopping—Collier seized the opportunity to visit Grandma Ramsey. Parking in front of the well-loved, well-lived-in old house at 1712 Moorman Road, he entered without knocking. The moment he entered, Collier's olfactory senses were beset with the seductive redolence of baking fruitcake mixed with a faint aromatic whiff of evergreen. He stopped long enough to peek into the front living room. The traditional Christmas tree was lavishly decorated by a half-century-long accumulation of mismatched Christmas tree lights and blown-glass ornaments, its tinsel-roped lacy cedar branches burdened to the point of breaking. Underneath was a mound of gaily-wrapped presents.

Turning back to the entrance foyer, Collier moved along the wide, dark center hall, passing the bedroom on the left where his cancer-ridden aunt, Annabelle, had spent her last days. Just beyond, a narrow passageway opened into the spacious, high-ceilinged kitchen.

As he expected, Ocie Ellen Ramsay was sitting at the round pedestal kitchen table stirring fruitcake batter in an oversized heavy stoneware mixing bowl.

"Collie! What a nice surprise! Don't you look handsome in your uniform! Stand back and let me get a good look at you," the old woman exclaimed with delight. Beneath an iron-grey helmet of hair pulled tightly back into a bun, her softly-lined face broke into a huge smile. "What have they done to you, child? You're skinny as a rail."

"I've missed your cooking, Grandma. Maybe you can fatten me up while I'm here." Collier bent and gave his grandmother an awkward hug and a big wet kiss on the forehead.

"If you've already had breakfast, you can start right now. Look in the Frigidaire—the big bowl on the bottom shelf."

"Let me guess. Banana pudding, right or wrong?"

"You're right. I made it last night just for you. Eat it all. I'll make more and some custard for Christmas Day." Beaming rays of pure love up at him, his grandmother continued to stir the thick, fruitcake batter.

"How many fruitcakes are you making this year, Grandma?" Collier asked. The homemade shelves on the wall between the Frigidaire and the pantry were loaded with fruitcakes—each cake carefully wrapped inside a dishtowel, kept perfectly moist surrounded by slices of Starke's juicy Red Delicious apples.

Crowded with large mixing bowls brimming over with the goodies (meats) from black walnuts, pecans, English Walnuts, nigger-toes (Brazil nuts), and almonds arranged alongside bowls of candied fruit—Maraschino cherries (red and green), citron and candied orange and lemon peel and other candied fruit Collier couldn't name—the roomy, circular, wooden, pedestal kitchen table served as a veritable production line for his grandmother's fruitcake factory. The nuts were ordered in bulk in large burlap bags by Collier's father from a merchant friend of Collier's uncle, Ferris Saunders, who operated a butcher stall inside the City Market Square, beneath the upstairs gymnasium/auditorium. Packaged in cellophane-wrapped packages, the candied fruit came from the same supplier. Every November, immediately following Halloween, Cocky would load his car with burlap bags of nuts and distribute them among his sisters and his brother, James, to be cracked and have the goodies extracted. No distribution of the packaged candied fruit was necessary as Collier's aunts chopped them into small pieces as, from time to time, they dropped in on the baking process which stretched out over December. So much were the fruitcakes looked forward to by those lucky enough to receive one, there was hardly ever a complaint from the grandchildren who were pressed into service cracking and picking nuts.

Collier could remember cracking shells and picking the goodies from the seemingly endless supply of nuts—the paper-shelled pecans were easy, but the nigger toe shells were hard as granite. Over the years, the nut cracking had become sort of an art form, and Collier and his brother, Little Jim—to distinguish him from Big Jim, their father's brother—had developed a sort of competition to see who could extract the most of the goodies undamaged from the shell.

"Who cracks and picks the nuts, Grandma, now that most of my cousins are grown and gone?" Collier asked, reaching into the new refrigerator for the bowl of banana pudding.

"I still have plenty of volunteers. With a family our size, there's always a new generation to take their place." His grandmother smiled.

"Just don't let any of my young, whippersnapper cousins get too fond of banana pudding, Grandma," Collier had already removed the earthenware bowl and found a large soup bowl in the cabinet. Sitting there spooning the soup bowl full of pudding, Collier wondered soberly if this would be his last Christmas sitting across from his grandmother at this table.

"What would you say, Grandma, if I told you that Emma and I are going to have baby—it's due in May?" Collier broke the news as he swallowed a mouthful of pudding.

"I'd say it was way past time. Come give me another hug." The old woman fairly beamed.

"You know the odds are on our having a boy. There's only been one female child born to my father and my two uncles," Collier said.

"Well, don't bet too heavily on that. Your father only had two brothers and seven sisters. You just might have a little girl," his grandmother said.

"Either way will be okay," Collier said with more conviction than he felt.

"Your Aunt Jackie is pregnant too. I think she's due about the same time as Emma." His grandma beamed at the idea of the coming grandbabies. "Have you thought about a name?"

"Not really. What do you think we should name a boy, Grandma?" Sitting there stuffing his face full of banana pudding, Collier passed the next thirty minutes with his grandmother, speculating on their choice for her coming grandson's name.

On the way out of his grandmother's house, Collier paused to use the telephone in the nook beneath the stairs and called Jenny Bohon. "Jenny, I'm glad I caught you home. We just got in from Oklahoma last night. What do you hear from Bo?" He quickly caught her up on the news about Emma's pregnancy and about his orders to go to San Antonio.

"I'm happy you'll be able to stay in the States for a few more months. Maybe you'll still be around when Emma has the baby. Bo's old employer, Yale and Town, had a Christmas party Saturday night and everybody asked about him. This will be our first Christmas apart..." Jenny's voice cracked and she stopped speaking altogether for a moment, trying to pull herself together. "Bo says it has gotten really cold over there but they have to be very careful about building fires, especially at night..." When she finally was able to speak again, Jenny brought him up to date. "The last time I heard from him—about a week ago—he wrote asking for thick hunting socks and some really good, fur-lined gloves. I sent him both last week, but there's no way they'll get there by Christmas. I'm really glad to hear Emma is in a family way. When do you have to leave for San Antonio? How long will you be there?"

"We'll leave on the thirtieth. We'll have to find a place to live before I start school on January twelfth. There are at least five...maybe six...military bases around San Antonio. Finding a place probably won't be easy."

"Will I see you before you go?"

"Probably not. All of Emma's brothers and sisters are starting to come in to her mother's house for a big, family gathering—it's already taking on the signs of their annual non-stop card-playing, liquor-drinking, Christmas debacle. Emma and I are staying up at Dad's and Mother's. Jim and Hitch may be coming from New Orleans in time for Christmas, but they have plenty of room," Collier explained apologetically.

"By the way, have you seen or heard from Marla Pogue—do you know where Doyle wound up?" Collier changed the subject. The simple truth was that he wasn't anxious to see Jenny face-to-face—just talking to her on the phone made him feel guilty enough about being in the States while Bo was facing God-knew-what horrors on the front lines in Korea.

"I ran into to Marla on the street in Salem awhile back. Doyle wound up working in Supply—the Quartermaster Corps. I think she said he's somewhere in Japan..." Jenny went on talking, not wanting to let him go.

When he finally hung up the phone, Collier drove downtown and parked on upper Jefferson Street in front of his father's office building. Walking across the wide expanse of railroad tracks at the Jefferson Street crossing, Collier went into the business district intent on some last-minute shopping. Leaving Davidson's men's shop where he bought his dad a couple of good dress shirts, Collier was pulling his spiffy Army trench coat tightly around himself against the cold wind knifing up Jefferson Street when he looked diagonally across the busy thoroughfare just in time to see an elderly black man exit the state ABC store with a quart-sized bottle of spirits tightly wrapped inside the ubiquitous brown bag. Before Collier could shout a warning of their impending collision, two well-dressed men exited the store busily engaged in conversation; not looking where they were going, the men crashed headlong into the old gentleman. In the blink of an eyelash, the old man's precious bottle of Christmas spirits went crashing onto the sidewalk.

"Why don't you watch where you're going, you old fool? You've splashed that cheap rotgut all over us," one of the men blustered angrily.

"I'se sorry, sir. I...ah..." the crestfallen black man apologized out of sheer habit.

"You really owe me to have my pants cleaned," the obnoxious man continued arrogantly.

Watching his broken dreams spreading in an ever-widening circle around the brown bag at his feet, the old man just stood there mutely, watching the men go. In his entire life, Collier could not ever recall seeing such a look of despair haunting a human face.

"Merry Christmas, sir." Carefully picking his way across the street through heavy traffic, Collier swiftly gained the old man's side and handed him a ten-dollar bill.

"Oh, thank you, Suh, but I can't take this..." Standing there looking at the money, the old man stuttered, trying to find words to express the look of surprised-gratitude on his face.

"You honor me by taking it, sir. Merry Christmas, sir. I hope nineteen-fifty-three is our best New Year ever." Collier snapped the old gentleman a smart salute and left.

Hurrying back down Jefferson with his packages, Collier stopped at the First National Bank and purchased five-hundred-dollars in American Express Travelers Checks, withdrawing several hundred more in cash. When he left, he turned west on Campbell Avenue and briskly walked the long block to Henry Street and S.H. Hieronimus department store to see what they had to offer in the way of new television sets. Roanoke's first television station, WSLS-TV, had gone on the air on December 11, and Collier had seen a full-page spread for Admiral TVs in yesterday's *Roanoke Times*; Admiral was advertising 17-inch table models for $199. The trip to Hieronimus proved to be a waste of time. The least expensive models which appeared to be even minimally acceptable were the newer 21-inch console models which started at nearly $300. Collier had thought he might talk to Jim about chipping in and getting his dad a set as sort of a combo Christmas/Birthday present—Cocky's birthday was in March—but, with the baby coming, he could ill-afford that kind of money at the moment. Leaving Hieronimus disappointed, he hurried back down Campbell with his collar turned up against the chill and found Emma and Lida standing inside the cozy warmth of the S&W Cafeteria.

"You're late...what's in the packages?" the women asked, curiosity getting the best of them.

"For me to know and you to find out. Let's eat, I'm starved..." Collier laughed and went over to check his packages with the girl at the coat-check room.

"Garrett Gooch says it's okay to travel if I don't let myself get overtired. He also said I can work as long as I feel like it—but he thinks I should take it easy after March, my seventh month. I went ahead and bought two maternity nursing uniforms. The Director of Nurses at Fort Sill gave me a letter of recommendation to the Director of Nurses at Brooke Army Hospital at Fort Sam."

"I'm glad Garrett says it's okay for you come with me to Texas, but I don't think you should rush right out and get a job when we get there. It'll be time enough to think about that after we get there," Collier patted her hand.

To everyone's delight, Jim and Hitch rolled in Tuesday afternoon, a day early, for Christmas Eve. The following afternoon, Collier and Jim drove to Mother Lowell's to pick up the large box of Christmas presents Emma and Collier had bought at the Post PX and had shipped from Fort Sill. All the way back to their parents' house, Jim and Collier chuckled over the anticipated look on their father's face when he opened the box with the big Zenith Transoceanic Radio they had chipped in on to give him for Christmas so he could listen to his late-night baseball games and other sporting events from far-off places like Cincinnati and St. Louis. Christmas morning, it was a toss-up who was delighted the most with their Christmas present—Cocky with his brand-new radio or Emma with a folding Trimble baby bed.

"This is exactly like the one I had for Collier and Jimmy. I wouldn't have traded it for anything in the world," Lida explained. Painted a soft yellow and featuring large panels of screen wire, the fancy bed was sort of a combination crib and playpen.

No one laughed when Collier quipped, "It looks like a fancy rabbit pen."

With promises to get together later, after they both were settled in Texas, Jim and Hitch made their goodbyes just after breakfast on Christmas day, headed for Hitch's parents' home at Hempstead, Long Island. The few remaining days flew by as Collier and Emma spent their time running back and forth between his parents' place and Mother Lowell's where most of Emma's brothers and one sister were still holed up in their non-stop bridge and drinking marathon. Although Emma's hormonal sister-in-law, Frances, kept angling to get him alone, Collier successfully managed to avoid more than superficial contact with her before Emma's brother, Gene, finally rounded her and their daughters up and headed the family back to Fredericksburg late Sunday afternoon.

On Monday, Collier drove his father to the Hotel Roanoke so they could watch the telecast of the NFL Championship on Roanoke's newly-inaugurated pioneer TV station, WSLS-TV. The Detroit Lions' quarterback, Bobby Layne—with running back, Doak Walker—put on an offensive show, humbling the favored Cleveland Browns 17-7 in Cleveland's own backyard.

"I'm very proud of you, son. I hope you always know that," his father spoke the words softly in the darkness of the car driving back home after the game. "I know I shouldn't get my hopes up, but I'm about to pee my pants, hoping Emma is going to give you a son. Not that we won't love a granddaughter just as much...I mean...well, you know what I mean."

"I know, Dad. Let's just hope Emma isn't making a foolish mistake going with me to San Antonio. Quite frankly, I don't feel at all good about it, but she won't listen to reason."

"I know...just take care of her and get her back here safe and sound in time to have the baby at Lewis-Gale," his dad said as they pulled into the driveway of the homeplace.

With much hugging and some tears from the women, Collier and Emma headed out late Tuesday morning, December 30th, hoping to make the 350 miles to Chattanooga by nightfall. Their luck was good and the roads were surprisingly lightly traveled. Swinging south on U.S. 27 west of Knoxville, Collier followed the trail of "See Rock City" and "See Ruby Falls" signs painted on an endless assortment of barn roofs and other farm outbuildings, and they finally checked into the Rock City Motor Court just at dusk. The restaurant had been crowded with fans wearing gold and black for the Georgia Tech Yellow Jackets and the deep, almost brown, Maroon, and White colors of the Mississippi State Bulldogs—upcoming opponents in the time-honored Sugar Bowl. Somewhat revived by a supper of chicken-fried steak with brown gravy and biscuits, they drove up Lookout Mountain to catch the stunning view of Chattanooga, with just a blush of pale peach separating the western horizon from the stars and the lights of the small city twinkling below.

Back in the room studying the Texaco road map, Collier estimated New Orleans to be around 500 miles. If they got up early, they could spend New Year's Eve in the French Quarter. Without confiding this plan to Emma, after a long, hot shower, he left a wake-up call for 0600, and crawled exhausted into bed beside his sleeping wife.

"Damn! Wake up, Honey! It's already fifteen minutes past six. We need to be getting on the road." The following morning, Collier bounced out of bed, unhappy that he had overslept. Rushing into the bathroom, he quickly shaved while Emma took her time getting out of bed.

"Are you okay?" Collier asked, coming out of the bathroom, just as Emma was coming in.

"Uhm-m, I think so. I feel like I could sleep a week, but I'm hungry enough to eat an elephant." Rubbing sleep from her eyes, she slipped into the tiny bath and closed the door.

Quickly dressing in his winter ODs—which he had hung in the bathroom in hopes of restoring some measure of presentability—Collier gathered up their discarded underwear and socks from the previous day and put them into the brown-paper motel laundry bag and took them out to the car. When he came back inside, Emma had finished dressing.

"Let's go get some breakfast before you check us out. I may have to come back here to use the bathroom. I drank at least a quart of prune juice the last two days before we left home."

"Okay." Long-since resigned to Emma's lifelong curse of chronic constipation, Collier nodded, trying to hide his frustration. There were slightly over 500 miles of bad road ahead if they were going to make New Orleans by nightfall.

"Might as well skip going back to the room. I'm sure I couldn't go, even if I tried," Emma told him with a wan smile and a shrug after their hurried breakfast.

Collier's watch showed 0730 hours when he pulled out of the motel parking lot into the busy traffic of US 11, heading south. They had barely cleared the southwestern outskirts of Chattanooga from their rearview mirror before Emma curled into the fetal position on the wide front seat with her cheek resting on his thigh and fell fast asleep.

"Collier, I think I need to stop. Find a place quick, I can't wait..." Just as they were coming into Fort Payne almost an hour later, Emma suddenly sat bolt upright. Collier quickly spotted a fairly new, clean-looking Shell station and pulled under the overhang beside the gas pumps. Hardly before they stopped rolling, Emma was out of the car and headed for the Ladies Room.

"Better?" Collier asked when she returned about fifteen minutes later. He had topped off the gas tank, used the Men's restroom, and moved the car to a parking area outside the door marked "Ladies Room." His watch now showed almost 0900 hours, and they had only traveled fifty miles. At this rate, he calculated it would take at least nine more hours to make it to New Orleans—unless the prune juice continued to interrupt their journey.

"A little...but not nearly enough, I'm afraid." Climbing back in the car, Emma showed a tight-lipped smile. Curling up, she was fast asleep again before they cleared Fort Payne. She didn't stir to life again until they had negotiated the heavy traffic around the outskirts of Birmingham. The dominating statue of Vulcan, the Roman and Greek God of Fire and the Forge, on the rugged mountaintop overlooking the smoking steel furnaces, offered mute testimony to the blue-collar city's well-deserved reputation as the "Pittsburg of the South."

It was almost two o'clock by the time they entered the outskirts of Tuscaloosa, passing the campus of the University of Alabama. The ancient brick-arched buildings on the venerable quadrangle put Collier in mind of Washington and Lee University back home in Lexington, Virginia, also the home of VMI.

"I'm some better now, thank goodness," Emma reassured him after he stopped again for her to use the Ladies facilities at a rather elegant Shell station on the southern outskirts of the campus. By the time they were back on US 11, Collier's watch showed 1429 hours and the late-afternoon sun was already peeking through the windshield just below the lowered sun visor on Emma's side of the car. Traffic picked up south of Tuscaloosa, and they had the rotten luck to get behind a virtually endless line of commercial trailer trucks, no doubt heading to the Port of New Orleans.

"Let's stop and grab a bite, maybe give these trailer trucks a chance to clear the road," Collier suggested after they had finally crawled their way into Meridian. A clock on a bank showed almost five o'clock civilian time. It was already showing signs of getting dark.

Just as Collier predicted, they made excellent time over the now-nearly-deserted highway. When they rolled into Hattiesburg, Collier's watch showed 1852 hours and the announcer on WWL said the station was coming up on the seven o'clock news.

"That looks like a nice place just up ahead," Emma said, pointing to a neat, little, white-clapboard, colonial-looking motor court.

"Are you tired? If you don't think it would hurt your pregnancy, it just occurred to me that we could probably make New Orleans in less than two hours. You wouldn't believe Canal Street at midnight on New Year's Eve. I mean I really wouldn't want to take any unnecessary chances, but you really have slept most of the day, anyway."

"Two hours? I really think we should stop now. We can see New Orleans tomorrow morning. My tummy is acting funny again. We've been on the road almost ten hours. Let's stop at this place...it looks nice. I really should be taking it easy on our baby."

"Okay...we'll stop. This place looks respectable enough." Reluctantly, Collier let the car glide to a stop in front of the motel office. Ten hours was really a lot of time on the road for a woman in her delicate condition. To tell the honest-to-god truth, he was getting pretty frazzled himself.

"Hold on...I'll be right back." Collier patted her gently on the thigh and got out of the car and walked inside.

"Good evening, sir..." Before he could ask about a room, a white-haired gentleman looked up from the registration desk and shook his head.

"Didn't you see the No Vacancy sign? We're full. The whole town is full. I doubt there's an empty room within a hundred miles. Which way you heading, anyway?"

"South...New Orleans, then west to Houston and San Antonio. Surely there must a decent place to sleep between here and New Orleans." Collier had a sudden empty feeling in his gut.

"I wouldn't bet on it. It's New Year's Eve, and the Sugar Bowl is tomorrow—Mississippi State and Georgia Tech. I've even had several people stop in tonight traveling north out of New Orleans toward Birmingham and Huntsville. They said they saw nothing but No Vacancy signs along the road between here and New Orleans. My advice is to stay out of New Orleans and head west at Slidell." The old man had spread out a map and pointed out the route. Any fool could see that they would be after midnight if they had to make it all the way to Baton Rouge.

"You don't think we might find anything at all around Picayune or Slidell...maybe a bed-and-breakfast or a little fly-by-night motor court around Slidell? I have business in New Orleans," Collier lied, looking hopefully at the map.

"Not likely. My guess is you're more likely to find some little mom-and-pop motel or maybe a small bed-and-breakfast closer to the outskirts of New Orleans than in Picayune or Slidell. And, there's always Metarie and Kenner out near the airport—La Place is just west of there."

"Well, thanks for the information, anyway." Collier sadly shook his head and left.

"I hate to tell you this..." Collier began and gave Emma the discouraging news, neglecting to tell her what the old man said about going through Baton Rouge instead of New Orleans.

Putting the car in gear, Collier pulled back onto the highway. "I'm sure we can find a small bed-and-breakfast or some mom'n'pop motel on the outskirts of New Orleans," Collier did his best to sound cheerful.

"If we find something before we get to New Orleans, let's stop. No reason we have to make it all the way to New Orleans. Any place with a bed and a shower will be fine. It doesn't have to be fancy...just a place we can spend the night in a clean bed."

South of Hattiesburg, US 11 became a tree-lined tunnel through the cypress-forested, swampy, bayou country landscape, as the Studebaker's high-beam headlights bored through the lily-choked waterways on both sides of the highway. After about twenty minutes, Emma curled up on the seat and fell fast asleep again.

After crossing the Pearl River—at a tiny town aptly named Pearl River—the traffic began to pick up a bit. Passing through Slidell, the only motor court Collier saw was completely dark with a No Vacancy sign sputtering above the office door. As they started across the northern margin of Pontchartrain, the traffic thickened even more. Although he hated having to slow down, with nothing but water on both sides of the car and traveling this late at night, it gave him a feeling of increased security to have the company of fellow travelers. Curled on the seat beside him, Emma continued snoring lightly. The sky ahead began to take on a definite glow as they moved ever-closer to the outskirts of New Orleans.

"My tummy's hurting bad now—where are we?" Emma sat up and looked around.

Where US 11 had joined US 90 a few miles back, the highway had widened into a broad thoroughfare and they were entering the outskirts of the city. Glancing at his watch under the reflection of a passing truck headlight, Collier saw the time was 2159—almost ten o'clock.

"We're just coming into New Orleans. Do you need to stop at a filling station, or should we try to find a place to spend the night?"

"Keep going, I think I can wait awhile." Emma said.

"It's just as well," Collier looked around with apprehension. Just like the ones they'd passed in Picayune and Slidell, all of the motor courts were dark with No Vacancy signs. To make matters even worse, on both sides of the wide boulevard, all of the gas stations and restaurants were closed tighter than a drum. With the city speed limit reduced to 45 mph, it was five or ten more minutes before they saw the beacon lights of the Lakefront Airport coming up on the left. On their right, a sign proclaimed: LAKEFRONT AIRPORT—The Air Hub of the Americas. A short distance beyond the airport, all signs pointed left to downtown New Orleans. In the near-distance, the brightly-lit downtown area was ablaze—the ambient light formed a rosy dome reflected against the smoke and river haze. In his mind's eye, Collier imagined the mists rising off the big muddy river flowing lazily through the heart of the city.

"Oh, Collier, Honey, we have to stop soon. I've started cramping again. I can't hold it much longer," Emma moaned in obvious distress.

Two blocks before they reached Canal Street leading directly into the heart of the city, there was a small army of police with flashlights blocking all traffic from turning to the left.

"What's the trouble, officer?" Collier rolled his window down and asked the nearest cop, when they were forced to stop for the backed-up traffic ahead.

"Typical New Year's Eve—Canal Street is closed. Downtown New Orleans is just one big bumper-to-bumper parking lot since five o'clock tonight. Happens every year—fools just abandon their cars and hit the bars." The officer shrugged and laughed.

"Is there a filling station open nearby? My wife needs to use the Ladies room real bad."

"I'm not sure. There should be some all-night stations up ahead."

"How about motels or any kind of lodging? We've been traveling since morning. We need a place to spend the night."

"There are a lot of motor courts up ahead, but I doubt you'll find a vacancy until after you pass through Kenner," the kindly policeman apologized.

"How far is it to Kenner—what's it like on west of the city?" Collier asked; the traffic had started inching forward again.

"There are a lot of places to stay on both sides of this highway—but it's New Year's Eve—Sugar Bowl. Lot's of luck, Lieutenant..." the cop called with a laugh, as the slow-moving line of traffic began to move on past.

"Oh, Honey, I can't wait much longer. I'm afraid I'll mess my pants," Emma moaned.

"Hold on, Babe, I'm doing the best I can." Collier looked desperately on both sides of the street—for the next two-dozen blocks, everything was closed up tight.

"Oh, God, Collier, it's too late. I've messed myself," Emma suddenly cried in distress.

"Should I pull off into one of these gas stations or closed-down motor courts?" Collier was at a complete loss what to do.

"No...just keep on looking for a place—it's too late now." She was quietly sobbing with her head leaning against the window, a perfect picture of abject despair.

"Look! I think that place is open up ahead." Collier pointed to a cheap Vacancy sign on the left in the next block. Several of the bulbs were missing, but it was unmistakably lit. When he turned in and parked and tried the door he found it locked. Desperately, he rattled the knob and pounded on the wooden door.

"Hold your horses...I'm coming," he finally heard a voice from inside. In a moment, the door opened a crack and a mulatto woman peeked out and inquired, "You looking for a room?"

"Yes...I'll take the very best room you have."

"Got just one lef'. It'll be five dollah, in advance," the woman said, giving Collier a suspicious look.

"I'll take it...here's the five. Give me the key. My wife's pregnant and we've been traveling all day."

"Jes' you hold on a minute whilst I gets the key...." In a minute she was back. "I mos' forgot...there'll be another dollah for a deposit on the key." She stood her ground and waited.

"Here..." he handed her a dollar bill and took the key. Affixed with thick cotton twine to a crude, hand-carved wooden tag, the key was to an old-fashioned keyhole lock.

"Which room is four?" Looking around, he saw a group of rundown wooden cabins to the right behind the shabby office.

"All the way in the back. Easy to find. The numba's is on the dos. You can park back there. Check out is noontime, no late checkouts." Before he could ask for extra towels, the woman had already closed the door.

Wasting no time in moving the car, Collier went around and held the door for Emma who was still sniveling softly. She followed close behind as he walked up on the rickety porch and unlocked the door. Fumbling on the wall, he finally located the switch which turned on a single bare electric bulb, in the center of the tiny room, hanging in front of an iron, potbellied, wood-fired stove.

"Oh, my God!" When she saw the room, Emma let out an anguished wail.

Against the lefthand wall the ancient iron bed had once had a coat of white paint. The bed was made up with a pale-green chenille bedspread with a small ragged-edged hole near the footboard on the far side. Off of the back wall, there was a small bathroom with a commode, lavatory and cheap, tin shower stall.

"Come on, I'm sure we can find a better place than this." Encircling her with his arm, Collier urged Emma back toward the door.

"No. Wait. Get my overnight bag. At least let me change out of this filthy underwear. I can grab a shower at least." Emma headed for the bathroom while Collier went back to the car.

"Oh...Collie the water's cold as...as-s...i-i-ce...' When he made it back from the car with her overnight bag, Emma had already stripped and was vigorously scrubbing herself with a tiny bar of motel soap.

"I'll see if I can make a fire in this stove," Collier called in through the plastic curtain, "at least it would warm things up."

"Okay...but first hand me a towel." Emma said, turning off the shower and pulling back the curtain.

"Jesus...you call this a towel?" Collier handed her two towels—hardly bigger than hand towels—he found lying on the top of the commode tank. Scarcely bigger than large washcloths, the towels were barely thicker than dime-store dishtowels.

"There's some kindling, but no paper to start a fire." Collier complained, looking around the shabby room. Aware of the strong, residual odor of cheap perfume masking the nauseating scent of body odor; the room was as redolent with the stink of human sweat as any atheletic locker room he'd ever been in.

On the wall above the bed, there was a faded picture of a black, jazz-trumpet player in a cheap, dime-store frame. It slowly dawned on Collier they had taken lodging in a place for colored people. Anxiously glancing over to see if this had occurred to Emma, he exhaled a sigh of relief. In her extreme fatigue, Emma seemed blissfully unaware they had landed in a colored motel—thank God for small favors, for the moment at least.

"Forget the fire—I'd be afraid the place would burn to the ground anyway. There apparently aren't any blankets. Go get our topcoats out of the car..." Emma instructed, turning back the corner of the bed. She had changed into clean underwear, put on a fresh cotton blouse and a pair of woolen slacks. Now she was pulling a sweater on over that.

"You mean you want to stay here?" Collier was taken by surprise.

"What's the alternative? You're too tired to drive another mile. I don't know about you, but I've had about all of this day I can stand." Emma shrugged. "Hurry back before I collapse."

"Happy New Year, by the way." Emma gave him a hug and a tender kiss on the mouth, when he came back from the car with their coats.

"Happy Nineteen Fifty-three." The hands on his Elgin showed 0011 hours as he helped her crawl atop the lumpy mattress, instinctively leaving the chenille bedspread in place.

"Lie down and I'll cover you." Collier spread their topcoats over Emma who was already shivering atop the flimsy chenille spread. Snuggling up against her warm backside in the dark, soon he was almost as snug as a polar bear with a cub.

"Wake up, Honey. Let's get on the road." In the diffused sunlight streaming through the unwashed window by the door, Collier's watch showed twenty-minutes past eight when Emma roused him from a bad dream in which he was sleeping on a prison cot fairly crawling with bugs. Already up and fully-dressed, Emma was just coming out of the makeshift bathroom.

Outside in the bright morning light, looking around the sleazy neighborhood, Collier hurried Emma into the car and continued on US 90, heading west. By unspoken agreement, Collier did not begin to look for a place to stop for coffee or breakfast until they had negotiated the spidery Huey Long Bridge and had made it safely to a respectable-looking café in the township of Mimosa Park, a few miles west of New Orleans. After they had eaten, Emma curled up on the seat beside him and slept as Collier followed U.S. 90 west through Houma, Morgan City, New Iberia, Lafayette, Crowley and Lake Charles.

Just before 1400 hours, the stench of oil and gasoline permeated the car as they were finally crossing the Sabine River into Texas at Orange, a busy port clogged with oil tanker ships.

"Welcome to Texas!" Collier announced, rousing Emma from her fetal position on the seat beside him. "As soon as we get past this stench, let's find a place to eat."

"Where are we?" Emma sat up and rubbed her eyes.

"Orange, Texas."

"Orange, Texas? Do they grow oranges in Texas? It doesn't smell like oranges to me."

"Yeah, they grow oranges in Texas, but I'm not sure about around here." The water beneath the bridge looked greasy.

"How far to San Antonio?" Emma yawned, blinking against the afternoon sunlight.

Coming off the ramp on the Texas side of the Sabine Bridge a road sign proclaimed:
Port Arthur 22
Beaumont 25
Houston 103.

Making a quick calculation, Collier said, "Three-hundred miles, give or take a few. Houston's only a couple of hours. We've already been on the road six hours. I thought we might find a place to stay in Houston and have an easy drive into San Antonio tomorrow morning."

"That sounds fine to me. I'm dying for a shower—I feel dirty from sleeping in that awful place last night."

By the time they pulled up to the office of a well-kept motor court with the Vacancy sign lit, the sun was a mere rosy glow on the western horizon. After checking in and freshening up a bit, they walked across the parking lot to an adjoining restaurant. The restaurant clock showed 1820 when, stuffed to the eyeballs with chicken-fried steak and mashed potatoes, they walked back to the room. Within thirty minutes by the clock, they both had showered and were fast asleep.

"Are you awake?" Emma whispered in the dark.

"Yeah."

"What time is it?" Emma never wore her watch to bed.

"O-five-twenty-one," The Army had Collier thoroughly habituated to military time.

"How far is San Antonio?"

"Pretty close to three-hundred miles." Collier had looked at the map last night just before he turned out the light.

"I'll never go back to sleep. We've only got a week before you have to report for duty, and we have to find a place to live. Let's get on the road." Without giving him a chance to protest, Emma reached across and turned on the bedside lamp.

The drive across the desert-like Texas landscape seemed stretch out forever, but in the sparse, early-morning traffic, Collier was able to maintain a healthy average of more than 60 mph on the desolate, incredibly flat south-Texas stretch of US 90. Passing through the occasional farm town, they sporadically encountered rundown ranch houses, an isolated, pumping oil well and a few longhorn cattle.

"*The time is ten o'clock and the temperature in downtown San Antonio is sixty-eight degrees on this beautiful Friday, the second day of January in the year of our Lord, nineteen-fifty-three. You are tuned to WAOI, San Antonio in the great state of Texas at 1200 on your AM Radio dial. This is just in over the news wire. Known as the 'King of the Hillbillies', country singer, Hank Williams, was found dead in his Cadillac automobile just outside the town of Oak Hill, West Virginia this morning...*" About halfway to San Antonio at a hardscrabble town called Schulenburg, the Houston radio station faded, and Collier fiddled with the dial until he found a clear channel station. After he read the news of Hank Williams' death, the disk jockey announced in a deep Texas drawl, "To honor his passing, here's the great singer-songwriter, Hank Williams, singing his own composition, *Your Cheating Heart...*"

"Are we going to have to listen to that noise for the next three months?" Emma groaned.

Just before noon, Collier began to see a substantial number of low-flying military aircraft and, soon after, the stunted skyline of San Antonio rose up from across the prairie in the middle-distance, shimmering through the noonday haze like a mirage. As if right on cue, the WOAI disk jockey announced, "By special request from a senorita named Carmelita, here's Kosse, Texas' own Jim-Bob Wills and his Texas Playboys with their rendition of *San Antonio Rose...*"

"*Lips so sweet and tender, like petals falling apart. Speak once a - gain of my love, my own. Broken song, empty words I know still live in my heart all a - lone. For that moonlit pass by the Alamo, and Rose, my Rose of San Antone...*" Collier smiled, singing softly along. Emma was going to have to get used to a lot of things in the Sovereign State of Texas and this twangy, folksy, Texas fiddle music was high on the list.

"Wake up Emma! We're coming into San Antonio."

Blinking against the midday glare, Emma sat erect and stretched, rubbing the sleep from her eyes as they entered the outskirts of the historic city. With U.S. 90 metamorphosing into East Commerce street, almost before Collier realized what was taking place, they had moved into the very heart of the downtown area of San Antonio, a sharply-defined two- or three-block area dominated by Joske's—a large, modern-looking department store which was literally wrapped around a large Catholic church.

"Look Collier—the Alamo!" Hardly before Collier had time for more than a passing glimpse, he had driven past the miniature park fronting the unimposing, grey fortress-like Spanish mission. To Texans—and most other Americans—the ancient mission represented the Bunker Hill and Valley Forge of Texas independence, attaining an ironic historic infamy as the death place of legendary Texas heroes, Davy Crockett, Jim Bowie and Colonel William Travis.

"Let's get out and look around. I saw some restaurants. We could get some lunch and find a city map. We need to locate Fort Sam," Collier suggested. Circling the heart of the downtown business area, he finally found a parking space and they entered a nearby eatery.

"One-hundred-twenty-five for one-bedroom!" Emma exclaimed over a bowl of soup at a downtown restaurant featuring mostly Tex-Mex fare. "Typical military town! Gouging our poor soldiers and pilots for all the market will allow." Emma grumbled, discouraged by the Apartments for Rent ads in the classified section of the *San Antonio Express*. With an eye to finding a location as near to Fort Sam Houston as possible, she had circled several of the ads.

"As soon as we finish lunch, let's drive out near Fort Sam and see if we can find a nice affordable motel to spend the night. I can get cleaned up and we can go on Post and maybe get some help finding suitable housing," Collier suggested, cleaning up his plate of refried beans while he waited for the check.

Heading north out of the business district, Alamo Plaza quickly became Broadway, a wide thoroughfare running along the eastern edge of the seemingly-endless Brackenridge Park. With golfers enjoying the Texas sunshine in short sleeve shirts, Collier immediately recognized the pine-forested golf course as the venue for the Texas Open Golf Tournament which would be coming up soon in February. Near the northern boundary of Brackenridge Park, they followed street signs and had little trouble finding Fort Sam Houston. Inside the main gate, Collier pulled into the Information Center and got a map, asking the NCO directions to the HQ building for the Medical Field Service School and Brooke Army Hospital—since 1946, more properly Brooke Army Medical Center.

"Alamo Heights and Terrell Hills are best for officers if you're lucky enough to find something in either place." At MFSS HQ, a polite, civilian female employee gave them a list of local rental agencies specializing in furnished apartments for married personnel. She also called and made them a reservation at the Alamo Court, a motel on New Braunfels Avenue, just outside of the main gate. When she hung up the phone, she offered a final word of advice. "Welcome to Fort Sam Houston and San Antonio. You're new here and will likely want to see the historic downtown area with the Alamo and the Governor's Palace—and our best off-Post movie theater is also downtown—but let me caution you not to venture downtown after dark alone. Because it would dishonor the local law enforcement and the San Antonio city government, the Army has traditionally refrained from officially declaring the area 'Off Limits' after dark, but Post MPs patrol the area after 1700 hours and all commanders have been instructed to warn their personnel it's not really safe to be alone downtown at night."

"She's not exactly a spokesperson for the local Chamber of Commerce," Emma laughed as they left.

"No, but remembering the graffiti and vandalized buildings, I'm not surprised the Army is taking steps to keep the troops out of trouble."

"Before we leave the Post, would you mind driving me over to Brooke Army Hospital. I want to make an appointment to see the Director of Nursing."

"Sure. I need to locate the hospital anyway," Collier agreed, glad that Emma was thinking about working—for awhile, at least. She would be bored to death sitting at home all day with nothing to do.

"Guess what. They're hard up for part-time nurses. I think I can pretty much write my own ticket." Emma came out of the Brooke Army Hospital nursing office in less than ten minutes, clutching a sheaf of application forms in her hand.

"Well...that's good, I guess," Collier hestitantly conceded.

"You'll never guess who I ran into," she teased.

"Who?" he asked, his interest piqued.

"Remember my redheaded classmate, Ginger Lipscomb? It ought to be against the law what she does to an Army officer's uniform." There was hint of jealousy in Emma's tone.

"Hmm-m." Collier murmured—no red-blooded American male could forget Ginger.

"Ginger let Lou Thacker talk her into joining theArmy. She's just finishing MFSS and is being assigned somewhere back in Virginia—near Richmond, I believe she said."

Although the adobe Spanish façade with faux-wooden beams sticking out near the roof line seemed something of a caricature, the Alamo Court turned out to be a welcome refuge after three grueling days on the road. The best and most surprising thing of all was there were telephones in each room connected to a switchboard in the office.

"I'm calling about your ad for an apartment..." Before Collier finished bringing in their overnight bags, Emma was already busy on the phone.

"Don't get undressed, we have three places to look at," Emma stopped the nearly exhausted Collier as he finished bringing in their stuff—he had already begun to loosen his tie. Anxious to find more permanent lodging, he reknotted his tie and followed Emma out to the car.

"Let's look at these two in Terrell Hills first. They're closest to Fort Sam," Emma directed Collier up New Braunfels to the less-expensive of the two listings. Just north of Brackenridge Park, the wooded parkland with giant pine trees had virtually disappeared, giving way to the incursion of dwarfish and twisted native live oak.

"Drive on...surely we can do better than this," Emma directed when they located the first address. The neighborhood looked to be quite respectable, but as might be expected, the cheaper of the two rentals was, at best, barely borderline acceptable.

The second listing in Terrell Hills was an apartment occupying the converted second story of a singularly-unimpressive, green clapboard house. A spidery, L-shaped wooden stairs led to the narrow apartment entrance stoop which was superimposed over a section of the front porch roof—both the stairs and stoop had a sturdy rail to guard against falling.

"What's next? I think we can find something without steep steps..." Collier patted Emma's abdomen with a concerned reference to her delicate condition.

"Well, maybe, but did you see that nice little shopping strip and supermarket at the bottom of the hill? This location is the best of those we have to choose from. As long as we're here, let's at least take a peek." Emma signaled him to pull in and park.

Grudgingly, but dutifully, Collier got out and walked with her up the short flight of stone steps to the wide front porch of the lower apartment and rang the bell.

"Yes, I sometimes rent for three months. Many of my tenants have been at Fort Sam for training. Go up and take a look around." The woman who answered the door greeted them and handed over the key.

To Collier's surprise, Emma experienced no serious difficulty climbing the steps. They both were pleasantly impressed with the homey atmosphere of the airy upstairs flat. With large windows looking out over the city from all directions in the combination living/dining/kitchen area and an overlarge double bed in the spacious, airy bedroom, all-in-all, the apartment appeared to be quite livable. On its right-hand wall, the kitchen contained a tiny, two-burner gas cooking stove with an oven, a full-sized refrigerator and a sink. The kitchen area was separated from the living room by a cheap chrome and Formica-topped dinette table. The living area consisted of a floral chintz-covered couch which pulled out into a sleeping sofa, two stuffed, straight-backed chairs, a coffee table and a lamp table with lamp at the left-hand end of the sofa, separating it from a chair near their bedroom door. Despite its plainness, the apartment had an overriding atmosphere of cleanliness and sense of livability.

"I like it. What do *you* think?" Emma turned to Collier after she had taken a second careful tour of the layout and they were preparing to leave.

"I still have serious reservations about you having to climb all those steps." Collier cautioned, looking almost straight down on their Studebaker in the parking area below.

"The exercise will do us both good. Besides, with all these windows, I think we can stay fairly comfortable in this heat," Emma reminded him.

"Can we afford ninety a month? And does that include lights and water?" Collier questioned, still wondering if they were making a mistake coming to a decision after only seeing this one place.

"You're an officer now. Our take-home is over three-hundred if you include the extra eighty-five-fifty Quarters Allowance. Besides, I don't think I'll have any trouble finding work at the Post hospital."

"Uhm-m, but you're not working now. Back at Sill, you were bringing in three-hundred on your own. Between the two of us, we were taking home almost five-hundred a month."

"Don't worry so much. You may be going overseas in three months. Besides, we have money in the bank." Emma pointed out. She had clearly fallen in love with this place.

"Well, okay, if you think we should. Let's go ask about the water and lights. Maybe we can negotiate," Collier agreed. Privately, he liked the place almost as much as Emma. The convenience of the little shopping center and the proximity to the public golf course at Brackenridge Park had not escaped him.

"Water and lights run less than thirty a month. Both are billed to me—you pay me when you pay the rent. I'll take a check for two months rent plus utilities in advance, but you'll have to give me a deposit of one-hundred in cash to seal the deal. I'll refund your deposit when you leave, providing you leave the place in as good a condition as you find it now," the owner said in a take-it-or-leave-it tone.

"Will you take American Express Travelers Checks?" Collier asked. He was running low on folding money.

"I'm sorry, I'd rather not," she said, unblinking.

"Okay, I can give a hundred now, I guess." Carefully watching Collier grudgingly count out the deposit of five twenty-dollar bills, she signed the receipt *Mrs. M. F. Hamblin.* "You may call me Margot. My husband, Martin Hamblin, was a B-29 pilot in the Pacific in WWII. We retired here in 1950, after he served his final tour at Brooks Field. Martin died of a sudden heart attack last year. He was only fifty-five." Despite her nondescript cotton housedress and her hair pulled severely back into a bun, the woman looked at least ten-years younger than fifty-five.

"This door is to the interior stairway." She pointed to the door in the far corner of the bedroom. "I keep it locked from the inside and have the only key. Since I had the upstairs kitchen put in, I had the door installed so I could rent the upstairs out as an apartment."

"I couldn't help but notice the picture on the television screen in your living room. Is local TV reception that good all the time?" Emma asked their new landlady when they were back downstairs and she was getting them an extra key.

"Oh, yes. Ask anyone; WOAI reception is quite dependable up here in Terrell Hills."

"Wait here. No sense in our hauling this junk around." With the keys to their new apartment in hand, Collier began unloading their possessions and hauling them up the steps an armful at a time while Emma waited by the car. After depositing the final armful of mostly household goods on the dinette table in the kitchen, his watch showed 1625 and the sun was sinking fast over the western horizon. Looking over the collection of mundane household goods he had lugged up the steps, Collier grudgingly admitted that he was glad Emma had saved them the trouble of having to spend the evening at the commissary or local grocery store.

"Did you see the picture on the television set in her living room?" Emma asked Collier as soon as they were headed back to the Alamo Court.

"Yeah. It was really sharp...best I've ever seen," Collier agreed, hoping Emma might be persuaded to splurge for a TV set.

"You know Roanoke has its own channel now?" Emma continued tentatively.

"I know. Are you thinking that we ought to get a television set?" he asked, trying to sound offhand.

"Well, even if I can find part-time work now, I won't be able to work after a couple more months or so. At best, if I want to keep the car, it's going to be a pain driving you onto the Post at some ungodly hour in the mornings—then coming back again to get you in the afternoons. That means I'm going to be stuck here at home a lot. I just thought we might try to find a cheap television. It would help me fill the time. The Army will ship it back to your folks' house, in case they send you overseas when you finish here in March."

"Okay, after we eat, we'll ask around about local television stores."

"We bought our TV at Joske's Appliance Store on Broadway. Joske's is the biggest department store in town," the waitress at the little restaurant beside the Alamo Court told them when they asked where to buy a TV. "Joske's is close by, at the shopping strip near Pershing across from one of the northern entrances into

Brackenridge Park. From here, go back south on New Braunfel's and take a left on Pershing—it's the first through-street past the entrance to San Antonio Country Club. It's only a couple of streets over to Broadway. When you come to Broadway, take a left—you can't miss the shopping strip on the left across from the park."

"How late do they stay open?" Emma asked.

"Oh, it's Friday night. I think they're open at least until seven—maybe later. This is a military town."

"I'm not tired. Pay the check. Let's go have a look around," Emma said, gathering up her purse.

Revitalized from his dinner of chicken-fried steak and home-fried potatoes, Collier had an easy time finding his way across Pershing to the shopping strip on Broadway. With its lights blazing inside and an array of 17- and 21-inch TVs in the window all showing the local news, Joske's appliance store was still open, just as the waitress predicted.

"Look, they're a Magnavox dealer," Emma enthused, spotting the Magnavox logo in the store window. Back home, they both had been favorably impressed with Bill and Gerry Deeds' elegant Magnavox radio and record changer.

"Whoa...let's don't go overboard. Magnavox specializes in consoles with fancy cabinetry. Mrs. Hamblin's set was an RCA table model and we both were impressed with the picture—an inexpensive table model makes more sense if we're going to be moving around," Collier reminded Emma.

"I'm not going overboard, but as long as we're going to splurge, we might as well get the best. You know your daddy always says it pays to buy quality—and he's the chintziest shopper around."

"Okay, okay...we don't have to buy anything tonight, anyway. It won't hurt to have a look." Collier turned off the ignition and went around to open the car door.

"Oh, Collier, just look at that set back there—it's head and shoulders better than the rest." Emma pointed to the remarkably clear picture on a set—sitting among a group of several 21-inch table-model sets with rabbit-ear antennas.

"It certainly stands out alright," Collier agreed. Placed among five other table-models, the set with the clearly better image was displayed on a wide, carpet-covered bench. Unlike the companion sets in the group, its cabinet was constructed of a rich, walnut-stained wood.

"No wonder it's head-and-shoulders better. You might know it's a Magnavox." Emma shook her head, noting the $399 price tag. The other sets grouped around it were between one-hundred and one-hundred-fifty dollars less.

"The main store downtown sold out this model before Christmas. This Magnavox is the last table model we have in either store," the balding clerk with a bushy, drooping cowboy moustache said. "Our new models are coming in. I'll mark this one down fifty dollars if you want to take it now."

"We'll have to get a table to set it on. Maybe we should look at the console models before we decide," Emma said, remembering the new apartment was devoid of tables of a suitable size.

"You don't have to have a table for the Magnavox, Ma'am. It comes with its own set of matching legs that screw directly into the base. With these attached, it makes a chic, very stylish, console." The eager salesman lifted the carpet covering and pulled a set of four nicely-turned legs with heavy brass screws projecting from the larger end and brushed-brass ferrule footings capping their base from a hidden shelf. Locating a dog-eared Magnavox circular from the clutter on his clipboard, the salesman showed them a picture of the set standing alone, legs attached.

"Oh Collier, that looks very classy. Let's take it," Emma exclaimed, clapping her hands together in delight.

"Can you deliver it tomorrow?" Collier spoke up without further consulting Emma.

"Where do you live? Tomorrow's Saturday...besides, we only deliver out of town once a week."

"On Garrity, just off of New Braunfels in Terrell Hills. Actually, it's not far from here," Collier said. "We'll take it if you can deliver tomorrow before noon."

"Okay, I think I can have my boys deliver it before nine. But Saturday's payday—I'll need 'em back here by ten," the salesman said.

"You got a deal if you'll take American Express Travelers Checks." Collier held his breath waiting for an answer.

"Tell you what. The Alamo Heights branch of the Broadway Bank opens at eight tomorrow morning. They'll cash travelers checks. I'll hold this until you can get the cash."

"Okay...I can do that. I need to open a local checking account, anyway." It was true, Collier reasoned, they would need a local bank if they were going to be in San Antonio another ninety days, and they were already running low on cash.

When they left the store, Emma was beside herself with anticipation. "I'm too excited to go to sleep. Let's go to that grocery off New Braunfels and lay in some supplies. That way we can check out of the Alamo Court early in the morning, go to the bank and get the necessary cash and get our new TV delivered. We can be watching TV before I fix your first lunch in our new home. Tomorrow's Saturday. I wonder if Channel Four carries *Your Show of Shows*...and Ed Sullivan's *Toast of the Town* on Sunday night?"

Up early, Collier easily found the Alamo Heights branch of the Broadway Bank and converted all their travelers checks to cash. Back at Joske's Appliance Store by nine, they completed the deal, and after watching two Mexican handymen load their new TV onto the store's pickup truck, they led the Joske's driver back to their new apartment and anxiously watched the workmen wrestle the heavy television up the spidery steps, standing by as they screwed the four walnut legs into the base and set it on the floor.

When they plugged it into the wall outlet, turned on the switch, adjusted the built-in rabbit ears and the near-perfect picture of an old Hopalong Cassidy western quickly appeared on the large screen, Collier finally let out his breath.

"Gracias, senor, gracias, gracias..." the obviously startled driver said when Collier walked them back to the truck and handed them a five-dollar bill to split as a tip. Watching them drive away, Collier had the distinct feeling that Mexicans weren't used to such democratic treatment in the Sovereign State of Texas.

By the time Collier climbed back up to the apartment, Emma had pulled up a padded easy chair and was watching Hoppy chase a gang of rustlers or bank robbers across the plain.

"I saw a driving range out near Brackenridge Park. If you don't mind, I think I'll go hit some golf balls. I'll be back in time for lunch." Collier waved goodbye as he grabbed his clubs and headed for the car.

CHAPTER THIRTY-FIVE

San Antonio Express
San Antonio, Texas, Monday, January 3, 1953
U.N. HURLS BACK NEW RED DRIVES
SEOUL, Saturday, January 3 (AP) – Allied defenders fighting in 10 degree below Zero weather—coldest of the Korean winter—drove back about 175 Chinese Reds who attacked the highest peak on Sniper Ridge in predawn darkness today.

San Antonio Express
San Antonio, Texas, Sunday, January 25, 1953
ALLIED JETS SHOOT DOWN FOUR MIGS
SEOUL, Korea, Saturday, January 24 (AP) – Sabre jets shot down four Red MIGs and damaged nine more Friday in the fourth day of raging air combat near the Manchurian border, the Air Force said.

FIRST THING MONDAY MORNING, Collier dropped Emma at Brooke Army Medical Center, so she could talk to the Nursing Office about part-time duty while he headed to the Post PX to buy a copy of the January 5th issue of the weekly *ArmyTimes*. Since receiving his commission in mid-December, every Monday Collier had religiously checked the advance listing of orders for all officers headed to FECOM and other destinations which the *ArmyTimes* posted—routinely publishing orders six months (most often even farther) in advance—and updated each week from the Pentagon.

ArmyTimes in hand, Collier went to The Pit—a combination pub, coffee and sandwich shop frequented mainly by transient officers—bought a cup of coffee, found a table and opened the military newspaper, carefully running his finger down the extensive list of second lieutenants on the weekly list of orders. When he reached the bottom of the list, he went back to the beginning and repeated his search, not wanting to take any chances on overlooking his name among the fine print. Finding no orders posted for Second Lieutenant Collier Boyd Ramsay, he let out a sigh—he could breathe easier for another week at least.

Checking back at Brooke Army Medical Center he found Emma in the coffee shop thumbing through the January 5th issue of *Time* magazine with a rather heavy-handed, signature Boris Chaliapin cover portrait of Elizabeth II, painted against a motif of a rose blossom.

"Collier! I just ran into Bert and Ellie Hancock. They want to go downtown and have lunch and see *The Greatest Show on Earth*. I hear it's a great movie," Emma said as soon as she spotted him coming through the door.

"What time's the show? Remember what the woman said about not being downtown after dark?"

"Here come Ellie and Bert now. We can ask them about show times," Emma stood as the Hancocks walked into the coffee shop.

"First show's at three. Most movies last two hours or less. That would put us out around five. It's just getting dark about then, so we should be alright," Bert reassured them.

"Come on, we can all pile into our car," Collier agreed. He had read good reviews of DeMilles' latest extravaganza and was really anxious to see the show.

Arriving in the downtown plaza area around noon, Collier found a parking place about two blocks from the movie theater, and they lunched at the same restaurant at which Emma and Collier had eaten the day they first arrived. After lunch, they strolled the downtown area, admiring the Governor's Palace. Collier was fascinated by the wide variations of architecture dating from the Alamo, which had been completed by the Spanish Empire during the 1700s as a combination mission and fortification to be used to educate the native Indians. Among other historic buildings were the red-brick Bexar County Courthouse and the somber gray-granite façade of the Municipal Plaza Building.

To make sure they would get a seat before the movie started, they ambled over to the movie house and were not surprised to find a line of people already waiting at the box office. Waiting in line, Collier noted the pedestrians in the downtown area—most of obviously Mexican descent—outnumbered their well-scrubbed Caucasian counterparts in white business shirts at least two-to-one.

Once the motion picture started, Collier lost all track of time. With the exception of a scene where Cornel Wilde, as Sebastian, the trapeze flyer, misses his catcher and falls and it is plainly evident he lands on a cushioned mat poorly disguised as the sawdust of the circus floor and at another dramatic moment when the circus boss, Charleton Heston, needs a transfusion and there is an entirely misunderstood emphasis on the rarity of AB Rh-Negative blood, Collier could find little to criticize about the thoroughly-entertaining film.

"We should have remembered Cecile B. DeMille never makes a run-of-the-mill, two-hour movie," Ellie Hancock remarked as they walked out of the movie theater. The clock in the lobby showed slightly past 1740 hours, and it was already quite dark outside.

"I'm completely turned around. Do you remember where you parked?" Bert Hancock asked.

"Sure. It's just around the corner and down that way about two blocks. You stay with the girls while I go get the car," Collier assured him. He had volunteered to drive because he already knew the way.

"Let Bert go with you, Collier. Remember what the woman at MFSS headquarters told us about being downtown after dark?" Emma grabbed Collier by the elbow and stopped him from leaving alone.

"Don't be absurd. I'm a grown man. It's hardly a couple of blocks. Bert needs to stay here with you girls. I'll be back before you know it." Collier shook free and left at a brisk pace.

If Collier had felt secure standing in front of the lighted theater entrance that feeling quickly left him as he turned the corner. Except for a single street light at least two blocks away, the apparently-deserted street was quickly enveloped in a mantle of complete darkness. If he had left with a sense of optimism, it quickly turned to anxiety.

"*Venga! No le permiten consiguir legos.*" The Mexican voices sounded extremely close at hand. He couldn't understand the words, but there was an unmistakable sense of urgency in their tone. Without further debate, Collier broke into a dead run, straining every muscle to reach the sanctuary of his car. As he ran, he desperately searched his pants pockets until his fingers finally locked around his car keys. When he reached the Studebaker, his outstretched key found the tiny lock as if it were guided by some cosmically-directed homing device. Without a wasted movement, he slid into the car, hit the lock button on the door-window frame, and managed to start the car just as he saw the shadowy forms bearing down on him in the mirror on the driver's door. Slamming the gearshift lever into Low, he let out the clutch and launched the vehicle forward with a screech of burning rubber just as the nearest pursuer put his hand on the door handle. The sudden forward movement of the car dislodged his would-be assailant and sent him cartwheeling like some grotesque rag doll into the inky darkness.

At the end of the block, Collier slowed just enough to turn right toward the beckoning lights of the Plaza, barely braking to slide into the next intersection and turn right again toward the lights of the movie theater a short distance ahead.

"My God! What would you have done if they had caught you?" Emma gasped when Collier told them what happened.

"I don't want to think about it, but I can tell you one thing. This is our last trip to downtown San Antonio after dark." Collier laughed nervously, already feeling his knees go weak from the subsiding adrenalin reaction.

Later, with Emma snoring lightly in the dark beside him, Collier—still shuddering from his close encounter—was moved to recite his ritual childhood prayer for the first time since the nightmare experience exactly one year before at Fort Meade when he had walking pneumonia and had been at the mercy of the sadists who kept putting him on KP.

"Let's go out to eat. I'm hungry as a bear." The following afternoon when Collier returned from playing golf, the memory of the incident had faded.

"The nursing office at Brooke called about an hour ago. They want me to take a post-op case tomorrow morning. You weren't here, and I didn't want to get off to a bad start, so I told them I would. I have to report at 0630. I hope you don't mind taking me in," Emma looked up from ironing the wrinkles out of a uniform she had packed before they left Fort Sill.

"Well, no, if you're sure it's okay, I don't mind at all. Let's go to the O Club for dinner and celebrate."

"No...I'd rather not. Let's make it an early evening. I'll have to get up by 0500. I haven't worked for a month, and I'm PG—I need to get some rest. If you'll go to the store and pick up some things, I'll cook bacon-and-egg sandwiches and we'll watch TV."

"Okay...an evening in might do us both some good. Make a list, and I'll go to the market as soon as I shower." He leaned across the ironing board and gave her an obligatory kiss before he headed for the shower.

For the remainder of the week, Emma's first case at the short-handed hospital quickly evolved into a series of post-op cases continuing over the weekend. Monday morning after he dropped her off, Collier went to the O Club to grab a bite of breakfast before he reported for his first day at MFSS. After spending most of the rest of the morning in orientations and acquiring a required list of manuals and textbooks on a range of subjects including Human Anatomy, Medical Terminology, First Aid, and an illustrated handbook for performing various lifesaving, battlefield surgeries—which left him feeling more than a little bit anxious—just before 1400 hours, Collier, Bert Hancock, Skyar and Flood from Class 30 at Sill, with several other eager-beaver second looeys fresh out of OCS at Benning, were told to report immediately to a Major Moseley at the quadrangle.

"Listen up, you men. I wouldn't be asking you to do this if it weren't important. If you will direct your attention directly behind me, you will see about two-hundred Medical and Dental officers—along with a few members of a special group of graduate students in Hospital Administration from Baylor University. These highly-skilled professionals are waiting to be taught military courtesy and short-order drill. They need to learn how to wear the uniform and how to salute and march and, in general, how to act enough like officers in the Army to command respect from the men they'll serve with." Major Moseley, a pocket-sized, rather Napoleonic medical officer, wearing expensive special built-up elevator shoes, quickly filled them in when they arrived in a ragged group at the edge of the quadrangle.

"You expect us to teach those misfits short-order drill?" The bantam-rooster major's announcement brought a protest from a recent grad from Benning OCS.

"That is correct!" Moseley snapped. "Now, there are exactly twenty of you. Count off by twos, with ones and twos pairing off as two-man teams. I'll go over and split that herd of esteemed Army officers into ten groups of about twenty. Each two-man team will take a group to a spot away from the others and teach them how to wear the uniform, form ranks, salute, how to march and the rest of the basics. You will meet your groups every afternoon here at 1400 hours for the next two weeks. I expect you will make them into soldiers. Now form ranks and count off."

Not at all happy at being saddled with the assignment, Collier joined his compatriots as they formed into a squad and went about the business of pairing off.

"My name is John Henry Pewter. I just graduated Infantry OCS at Benning," Collier's new partner introduced himself. Standing several inches shorter than Collier in his sharply pressed khakis, whatever Pewter lacked in stature, he more than made up for with his spit-and-polish military dress and bearing.

"Collier Ramsay. I just graduated OCS at Fort Sill, Oklahoma," Collier replied and shook Pewter's outstretched hand.

"Are you up for this?" Pewter sadly shook his head.

"Do we have a choice?" Collier shrugged, as Moseley called them back to attention.

"Okay, men, form back into four equal ranks. I'll march you over...we'll divide that herd into smaller groups, and I'll introduce you to your new charges. Now, Fall-in. I wish you the very best of luck." As soon as they were assembled into a squad-like group, the major marched them forward to the milling herd dressed in the guise of Army officers.

"Atten-shun! Give me your attention up here." Moseley called the ragtag mob to attention and explained what he'd already told Collier and the other junior officers. After what resembled a scene in a kindergarten schoolyard, Moseley managed to finally get the docs and dentists and administrators to form ranks so he could divide them into ten groups of twenty—the final three groups numbered twenty-one. Thus prepared—Moseley methodically marched Collier and the other newly-appointed drill instructors down the line, dropping off a two-man team in front of each of the newly-formed groups.

"Okay, please quiet down and stand at ease while we get acquainted. I am Lieutenant Collier Ramsay, and this is my partner, Lieutenant John Henry Pewter," Collier handled the introductions to the rather bedraggled formation of fourteen doctors and a half-dozen dentists after he and Pewter had half-marched, half-herded them to an uncrowded area on a far-corner of the quadrangle.

"Look, Lieutenant 'Whatever-your-name-is', I am a cardiologist—a heart specialist. It's bad enough that the Federal government saw fit to tear me away from my practice in Allentown, Pennsylvania, and ship me here to be assigned to god-knows-where to check hemorrhoids and treat a lot of gonorrhea, but I don't have any intention of listening to some second looey who's still wet behind the ears tell me, a major, how to salute and march." A slightly-graying, jut-jawed Major whose nametag read, *Smithson*, and who looked to be in his mid-thirties, immediately stepped forward to set the record straight.

"I assure you that Lieutenant Pewter and I both will be glad to exclude any of you who are already competent in military courtesy and the rudiments of drill from this unnecessary exercise. As a matter of fact, Major Smithson, I'll turn the group over to you, and you can begin by stepping out here and instructing your fellow officers in the proper way to affix your military brass. But first, allow me, if you will, to point out that the placement of your caduceus insignia on your collar is all wrong, and the gold oak leaves on your epaulets are upside down."

"Don't be a smart-ass with me Lieutenant. I'm your superior here. I won't tolerate insubordination."

"And, I won't salute any clown who doesn't know how to dress himself—who can't even make a proper display of his branch of service or his rank." Collier stepped forward and confronted the self-important major eyeball-to-eyeball.

"I won't be treated this way. I demand to talk to your superior officer," Smithson persisted, a blush of bright red spreading up from his badly-wrinkled collar.

"Pewter, go get Major Moseley. Any other of you officers who feel your competence in all matters military is beyond reproach, step over here and form a single rank behind me. I'm sure the Army has made some mistake in subjecting you to this demeaning activity. We'll get Major Moseley over here and you *prima donnas* can straighten *him* out."

Collier waited a full minute, but not one of the others stepped forward.

"Okay, Lieutenant Pewter, will you escort Major Smithson, here, over to report to Major Moseley.

"Before you go, Major, would you like for me to help you become more presentable? I'm sure you want to look less a clown before you plead your case." Collier stepped in front of Smithson and looked him up and down.

"Okay...okay! Look, you made your point. I admit I could stand to learn a thing or two about how to dress and all that soldier protocol. Not any of us are happy to be drafted into the Army. I'm sorry I took it out on you. Show me how to wear my insignia. I really don't want to go around looking like a burlesque comic."

"The lieutenant can show you how to fix your insignia, George, but he can't work miracles—not even Jesus Christ himself could keep *you* from looking like a clown." A major in the rank behind the cardiologist eased the tension, eliciting a good belly laugh from the other officers in formation.

"Okay, okay...let's keep it down. We wouldn't want Major Moseley to think we were having too much fun. Now, if you'll just stand at ease and gather around Lieutenant Pewter and me, we'll show you how to attach your insignia and give you tips on tying a military tie and how to align your buckles and even some hints on how to keep your shoes and brass looking sharp." Collier motioned them to form a loose circle while he and Pewter moved from man to man, adjusting their insignia with a running dialogue about how to maintain proper military dress. When they had everyone looking halfway presentable, they formed their charges into a squad of four ranks and began to teach them Right, Left and About Face. When it appeared most of them were getting the hang of these simple maneuvers, Collier and Pewter marched them for a bit trying to teach them to execute passable Column Lefts and Column Rights. If Collier had thought the raw recruits in A Battery at FARTC had two left feet when it came to learning to do simple Left and Right Face with all the rest of the basics of drill, he was ill-prepared for dealing with this ragged-ass bunch, all ranked Captain or Major, plus a lone silver-leafed Light Colonel—another heart surgeon—thrown in for good measure.

Fortunately, Collier had no scheduled classes following this extracurricular assignment. With orders to rendezvous again the next day at the same time, Collier and Pewter dismissed their charges at 1500 hours, which worked out perfectly for Collier to pick Emma up when she got off duty.

"The hospital asked me if I would work this coming weekend, and I said I would. I hope it's okay. I have three days off before I go back. I thought it would give you a chance to play some golf," Emma offered anxiously, hoping he wouldn't be upset with her.

"Sure...just as long as you're feeling okay. I think you should find an OBG to keep an eye on you while we're here. You need to do that right away."

"I already made an appointment with one of the Army OBs for Thursday. I'll check it out with him. How was your first day at school?"

"You wouldn't believe..." As he told her about the sawed-off Major Moseley drafting him and his fellow OCS grads as baby-sitter drill instructors, Collier never noticed the apprehensive look on Emma's face.

A little overwhelmed at first, Collier quickly settled into a daunting schedule of classes running a gamut of Medical Terminology, Basic Human Anatomy, First Aid, Field Sanitation, and Epidemiology. These included a steady stream of brutally-graphic movies illustrating horrible diseases and others depicting gory, step-by-step, surgical procedures which engendered nightmare fantasies about having to perform bloody amputations or some other equally heroic procedure on some godforsaken battlefield.

While the idea of performing lifesaving surgery brought him to the edge of panic, Collier welcomed the introduction to Medical Terminology as it made reading for the other courses immeasurably easier. His mother had made him take two years of Latin in high school, insisting that the English language had it roots in Latin. From the very first day in Medical Terminology class, Lida's infinite wisdom came clear to him when the instructor passed out a several-page-long list of medical roots and stems and prefixes and suffixes—most of which were readily recognizable as being from the Latin—with orders that they be committed to memory. Although Collier had never really liked having to memorize lists and such, it didn't take a genius to understand that these magic bits and pieces of language held the keys to the mysterious jargon of medicine. Evenings at home, Emma would drill him by asking him to supply the appropriate root or stem for a common medical word in current use. When he took the test at the end of the second week, Collier was the only one in the class who earned a perfect score.

Like his comrades in this crash course of becoming *bona fide* Assistant Battalion Surgeons, it didn't take Collier long to realize that the Army was dead serious in its mission to prepare him to assume the full responsibilities of an actual physician in both regular deployment behind the lines and in combat situations. The all-too-realistic teaching films on emergency battlefield procedures were quite graphic and—although sometimes performed in a clean, well-lighted hospital OR—were absolutely authentic, with meticulous attention to details like how to locate, clamp, and tie-off major blood vessels each step of the way before completing an amputation of a major limb or some equally-daunting, lifesaving surgery. During classes in rooms designed for instruction on the dissection of human cadavers, they were required to perform actual dissections of large, laboratory animal specimens until the use of a scalpel became virtually second nature.

Owing to almost daily instruction in actually performing venipunctures to start intravenous (IV) plasma and whole blood transfusions and for giving morphine injections, Collier's arms and hands quickly became human pin cushions, resulting in a mottled mass of ugly bluish-green subcutaneous hematomas.

After his class had completed the two-week-long extracurricular assignment of teaching the incoming doctors, dentists and pharmacists to dress and behave like officers, Collier took advantage of his free time to go back into the classroom to review the films on surgery over and over again.

Time passed quickly the first two weeks and Collier had lost all track of time.

"Happy Birthday, Honey." At the crack of dawn Sunday, January 25th, Emma kissed him awake and handed him a cup of steaming coffee and several packages containing a set of fancy hand-knitted golf club head covers and an expensive full-fingered, doeskin-soft, right-hand golf glove. Aware that he could exchange it later, he didn't embarrass her by telling her the glove was for left-handed players.

"It looks like you might have a good day for golf. We'll go out to dinner tonight and celebrate," Emma told Collier in the car as he was driving her to work.

As it turned out, the weather turned bad as a front moved in. Disgruntled, Collier headed home, determined to catch up on much-needed sleep. When he pulled into the little cul-de-sac parking area fronting their apartment, he took no particular notice of a shiny, new Buick sedan parked in front of the Hamblin house.

"Long time, no see, stranger." He couldn't believe his eyes and ears when he saw Gerry Deeds in all her voluptuous glory standing right in front of him as he stepped out of the car. Without preamble, she stepped forward and wrapped him in a death grip and kissed him full on the mouth. Her serpent tongue insinuating its way between his lips, rendered him weak-kneed with raw sexual hunger. For an instant Collier thought he might actually come in his undershorts.

"My God, Gerry, you're a sight for sore eyes. Where's Bill? What are you doing in town?" Finally able to come up for air, Collier's questions erupted in rapid-fire order.

"We just got in late last night. We're staying in a motel off Broadway, back toward town. At the moment, Bill's on the morning plane to Mexico City—we may be moving there, for awhile at least. Where's Emma? Aren't you going to invite me in?"

"Emma's working at the Army hospital. I go pick her up at three. She'll be surprised to see you. She's pregnant...about five months. Sure come on up...that's us at the top of the steps." He gently extricated himself from Gerry's embrace and—still trying to catch his breath—gently turned her to face the stairs.

"I assume we're alone." Inside their apartment, Gerry turned and securely turned the dead-bolt lock behind them before she handed him her coat and followed him like a shadow as he hung it on the old-fashioned coat tree beside the door.

"No one here but us chickens," he said, nervously contemplating the erotic possibilities and weighing the dangers of being here alone with this former lover—a real-live nymphomaniac if such a creature ever existed. When he turned back, Gerry pasted the full-length of her sensuous form against him again, and her ravenous tongue took up just where it had left off. In his too-long-deprived condition, the erotic rush was almost more than he could bear.

"Where's the bed? Or do you want to take me on the kitchen table? Frankly, with what I have in mind, I don't think that table would stand the strain. C'mon, what are we waiting for?" Pulling away, Gerry took him by the hand, urging him toward the half-open bedroom door. Before they were barely inside the bedroom, she had already pulled her one-piece dress over her head and tossed it with reckless abandon on the little chair beside the bed. She had on panties, but was wearing no bra.

"Ever since we left Roanoke, I've dreamed about this moment night and day. Get naked! I want to look at you," she ordered, stepping out of the plain-white panties. Now, feet apart and her pelvis tilted arrogantly forward, she stood stark naked before him in all her melon-breasted, fiery-red-pubic-patched magnificence. Before Collier could make a move, she had already dropped to her knees and was fumbling with his belt buckle. Transfixed with lust, he watched as she freed his organ and took it full into her mouth.

"Wait...I can't stand much of that..." Collier protested weakly as he roughly pushed her back a step, while he finished removing his clothes.

"Oh, Baby, just look at you! I want you to give it all to me—empty yourself inside of me. After that, I'll suck you completely dry. Let me grab a towel. I don't think Emma would be too happy finding a puddle of my juices in her bed." Collier watched spellbound as she walked to the bathroom to locate a bath towel. When she came back, she carefully spread it on the bed. Placing herself on the towel, she lay back on the pillow with her legs wide apart, inviting him. "Oh, Baby, it's been way too long..." her voice husky with lust, he wasted no time mounting and entering her.

"Oh, god, Gerry, I'm sorry I can't hold out, I'm gonna come. Emma's been pregnant since September—it's been too long since I've had sex with anyone." He felt himself coming almost before he had barely begun to enter her.

"Don't hold back—give it all to me. I'm already coming myself just from thinking about it." It was the truth. Collier could already feel the walls of her vagina contracting as his stored-up reservoir of semen began erupting into her.

"Wake up, Collier, you've got to go get Emma, and I've got to get out of here," Collier had long-since lost count of how many times and how many ways the red-haired nympho had ravished him—or he had ravished her—when she shook him rudely awake from a deep sleep brought on by sheer post-coital exhaustion.

Stretching and rubbing his eyes, Gerry was standing beside the bed fully dressed.

"Oh, Gerry! Today's my birthday. I think I died and went to heaven," he murmured and reached for her, but she stepped back just beyond his reach.

"No, more—you've got to get a move on. Remember, not a word to Emma that I'm in town. Go out and enjoy your birthday celebration, and I'll show up here again tomorrow afternoon around four and you can act surprised." She kissed him lightly and left without another word.

"Surprise!..." True to her word, Gerry knocked on their apartment door the next afternoon barely ten minutes after Collier had brought Emma home from work. Looking over Emma's shoulder as the two women embraced, Gerry give Collier a slow, sly wink.

Spirits buoyed by the happy reunion with their friend from home, Emma insisted that they take Gerry back to the O Club for dinner.

"My motel is not too far from here. Can you sneak away tomorrow at lunch? Bill may be back in another day or two," Gerry whispered the name of her motel across the table at the O Club when Emma excused herself to go to the powder room.

"I'll do the best I can...I'll call if I can't make it." Collier felt the blood running to his crotch as he undressed her in his mind.

"I best be getting back. I'll call tomorrow afternoon..." When they returned to the apartment, Gerry declined coming in for a nightcap and left with a promise to get together again the following evening.

"I'm beat...I need to get some rest," Emma said, heading straight to bed. She was having second thoughts about working. Pregnancy hadn't helped her constipation and her hemorrhoids were worse.

"I'll be in in a minute. We have a quiz tomorrow. I need to look over some notes," Collier said, relieved to have an opportunity to let his erection subside.

"We'll have to put our plans on hold. Bill came back early. Thank God he called from the Mexico City airport this morning," Gerry gave him the bad news the next day at noon, as soon as she picked up the phone. "He said to ask if you two would be our guests for dinner."

"Dinner sounds fine, but I'll have to ask Emma how she feels. To say I'm disappointed I won't have you in bed again is the understatement of the year," Collier told her, not really knowing if it was the truth or a lie. Part of him wanted to run like hell, the other half was half-crazy to have her naked in his arms again.

"It's too bad we don't have longer to go over old times, but we have to fly back to Mexico City first thing tomorrow. Gerry needs to find us a place to live. The company wants me to locate there for the next six months, at least," Bill explained at dinner that evening. It was obvious he was looking forward to showing Gerry around the ancient Mexican capital.

The next day, Emma had to attend a nursing in-service after she got off duty. As soon as he finished his morning schedule of classes, Collier left Fort Sam early, intending to catch a recuperative siesta. Arriving home about half-past noon, he had already begun undressing when he was interrupted by a light rapping on the door. When Collier opened the door, Margot Hamblin was waiting on the threshold.

"Lieutenant Ramsay, I saw your car. You're home early—I hope nothing's wrong."

"No, no, Ms. Hamblin. I got some unexpected free time, and Emma has to stay a little late at Brooke this afternoon. I've been working pretty hard lately. I thought I'd take the opportunity to catch a nap before I have to go back and pick up Emma." Collier had already shrugged out of his khaki shirt and the tail of his tee shirt was hanging over his uniform trousers.

"I'm glad I caught you alone. May I come in for a minute? There's something you and I need to talk about." Without waiting for an answer, she stepped inside and closed the door.

"I...I'm not sure I understand, Ma'am—is there a problem about our rent?" Collier stammered, stepping back a step. Taken quite off-guard by such unexpectedly insistent behavior, he was at a total loss to comprehend.

"It's nothing like that, Lieutenant...ah, may I call you Collier? I wish you'd call me Margot. This is awkward, but I thought we ought to discuss the fact that redheaded woman was with you alone in your apartment almost all day Sunday, while your poor wife was at work."

"I...uh...Gerry is an old friend of Emma's and mine. We haven't seen her or her husband, Bill in over a year. Her visit was quite a surprise." Stammering and trying to gather his wits, Collier felt his face turning red with guilt.

"Don't bother to protest your innocence. I could hear quite a lot of your conversation and, ah, the other sounds of your...ah...activities while she was visiting you. I'm sure your poor pregnant wife would be upset to hear the details of that." Stepping closer, she followed his retreat step for step.

"I...uh...so? I'm not sure what you're getting at? Are you telling me you want me to vacate your premises?"

"No, no, not that. *That* shouldn't be necessary at all. As a matter of fact, I just thought since you are home alone a lot and since your wife is pregnant, well...we—you and I—might come to a better understanding. I may be a widow, but I'm not all that old, you know?" The aggressive woman stepped forward before he could take another backward step. Reaching out she took both his hands and placed them firmly on her breasts. Her modest breasts were firm, but warm and softly-yielding—the overly-large nipples were already rigid to his touch.

"Wait...I...ah...Mrs. Hamblin...Margot, I think you...we...should think twice before we start anything like this..." His mouth gone dry, Collier was at a loss to form coherent speech.

"What's the matter? Certainly I can't be all that bad to look at." Before he could pull his hands away, she leaned forward and kissed him wetly on the mouth.

The exotic contradiction of her overriding respectability and her unexpected, blatant wantonness left him weak-kneed, rendering him helpless to resist as he opened his lips. When they finally broke apart to catch their breaths, she reached behind her and locked the door. Taking him firmly by the hand, she led him into the bedroom and stood by the bed fumbling with the zipper at the waist of her dress.

Losing little time stepping free of his freshly-pressed khaki uniform trousers before his sudden flow of pre-ejaculate soaked through his undershorts, Collier hurriedly folded them over the back of the bedside chair. "Get undressed. I'll be right back. I need to find a towel," he directed, heading for the bathroom.

By the time he reentered the room, she had pulled her wispy frock over her head and draped it across the chair on top of his pants. Now, she was standing in a pale-blue pair of panties and tiny matching bandeau bra.

"Do you think my undies are sexy? They came all the way from Paris, France."

"I like your undies fine, but I want to see you naked. Right now!" He spread the towel across the bedspread. When he turned back to help her undress, she had already slipped out of the bandeau and was stepping out of her panties. Tossing her undies on the bedside chair, when she turned back to him, Collier saw that she had taken a razor and carefully trimmed her pubic hair into a coquettish heart-shaped motif.

"Let me help you. I want to see you naked, too." She bent to help him step free of his rapidly-dampening undershorts, cupping his scrotum in her right hand, lifting his balls to get a better view.

"Goodness gracious, you're so wet!" she exclaimed, touching the end of his penis with the tip of her finger, lightly smearing the pearly drops of his pre-coital juices around the turgid, purple glans.

"Bend over with your elbows on the edge of the mattress," he ordered, turning her around to face the bed. Dutifully, she obeyed, as he urged her feet apart and entered her vagina from behind.

"I've always hoped this secret passageway would come in handy," Margot Hamblin said, later on as Collier came back from taking a shower. His watch showed 1600 hours and he was already running late to pick up Emma.

Hurriedly dressing, Collier watched as his surprising landlady gathered up her clothes and unlocked the unused door in the corner of the room leading to her apartment downstairs. "Be sure and put the towel in the laundry basket. I made sure we didn't leave any other evidence." She blew him a kiss as she disappeared down the inside stairway still naked with her dress and undies in a small bundle, pulling the door tightly closed behind her. Collier quickly dressed in golf clothes and headed for the door.

Torn between going back to check to see if Margot had indeed removed all the evidence of their orgy and having to explain to Emma why he was late, Collier raced down the spidery outside steps two-at-a-time. Scratching out of the parking area, Collier caught sight of her standing naked at her living room curtains blowing him a kiss.

"Judas H. Priest," he wondered, "just what in hell have I gotten myself into now?"

CHAPTER THIRTY-SIX

San Antonio Express
San Antonio, Texas, Saturday, February 14, 1953
GEN. VAN FLEET FAVORS USING A-ARTILLERY

HONOLULU, Saturday, February 13 (UP) – General James A. Van Fleet feels that atomic artillery could be used to advantage by the United Nations in Korea as long as as the present military deadlock lasts, his aide said Friday.

San Antonio Express
San Antonio, Texas, Saturday, February 14, 1953
BURKEMO LENGTHENS LEAD IN TEXAS OPEN
By DICK PEEBLES
Sports Editor

Taking up where he left off Thursday stocky Walter Burkemo of Franklin, Mich., continued Friday to treat par like it was a punching bag and he was Rocky Marciano.

The blond husky who had never won a major golf tournament fired a sizzling 33-32—65 for a 36-hole total of 127 and a three stroke lead at the halfway mark of the 72-hole Texas Open at Brackenridge Park municipal course.

EACH MONDAY THROUGH THE END OF JANUARY and the first two weeks of February, Collier continued to meticulously search the most-recent published orders in the weekly *ArmyTimes*. To his relief, there was still nothing under his name. On Monday afternoon, February 2, parked outside Brooke Medical Center waiting for Emma to get off from work, Collier flipped through the current issue of *Time* with the Artzybasheff portrait of Studebaker head honcho, Harold S. Vance, superimposed against a backdrop of Raymond Loewy's design sketches for the new 1953 Commander Starlight Coupe. Collier had already seen prototypes of Loewy's sporty new models in the Jarrett-Chewning showroom in downtown Roanoke when he was home over Christmas. No doubt about it, the new Studebaker was one hell of a fine-looking automobile.

"Have you heard from your brother and Hitch?" Emma asked as soon as he helped her in the car and came around and slid under the steering wheel. Collier had been hoping that his brother and Hitch were coming to visit later in the week to attend the Texas Open Golf Tournament.

The last they had heard, Jim was still uncertain whether or not he could get away from B-26 training at Perrin AFB long enough to make it worthwhile to drive. The distance was about 300 miles.

"I'm going to try to call him as soon as we get home," Collier said. He really was hoping Jim and Hitch were going to make it. He had just read in Sunday's *Express-News* there was going to be a special Pro-Am at the exclusive Oak Hills Country Club northwest of town on Wednesday, the day before the big tournament began. Collier had driven by Oak Hills going to and coming from the rugged "hill country" terrain of Camp Bullis where he attended such field exercises as how to set up, take down and move the tents and equipment for a MASH unit—Army shorthand for Mobile Army Surgical Hospital. They had an overnight encampment there two weeks back. Meandering through a picturesque, hilly-landscape of twisted live oaks, designed in the early 1920s by the famous golf architect, A.W. Tillinghast, the venerable Oak Hills golf course promised a true aesthetic experience. With the likes of Sam Snead, Lloyd Mangrum, Julius Boros and Cary Middlecoff in the field, Collier was hoping to surprise Jim by taking him to this smaller, more intimate event.

"We're coming. My CO is a golfer and gave me a weekend pass. I don't have to fly again until next Monday. Hitch and I are leaving leaving here tomorrow morning at daylight. With any luck at all, we should be in San Antonio tomorrow in plenty of time for the cocktail hour," Jim gave Collier the happy news as soon as he was summoned to the orderly room to return Collier's call.

"I'm sure Jim and Hitch are going to want to have a drink or two while they're here—I hope you don't mind." Collier turned to Emma as soon as he hung up the phone.

"No. I'm used to it, just as long as it doesn't get out of hand." She rolled her eyes, reminding Collier how it was with her family. "Get some fresh sheets out of the linen closet and give me a hand making up this pull-out bed."

"Were going to get pretty tired of each other before he leaves on Sunday," Collier remarked resignedly as he surveyed the room and the reality of his brother's visit started to sink in. With the pressure of MFSS and the extra daily commutes to get Emma back and forth from work, it was the first time he had really given the idea of Jim's visit any serious consideration. With only a well-worn sleeping-sofa as part of the sitting-room furniture, their apartment was cozy enough for the two of them, but it was not at all intended for the entertaining of overnight guests.

The following morning, Collier hurried home early after his scheduled classes to make certain everything was in readiness for his brother's visit. Much to his surprise, just past 1300 hours, Collier stood at a window and watched Jim's Studebaker pull up beside his own car, parked at the curb below.

"Need any help, Brud?" Standing in the front door, Collier called and waved.

"No. Everything's under control. We're traveling light." Grinning ear-to-ear, Jim looked up and waved back as he and Hitch started to climb the steps. Carrying a Kraft-paper grocery bag in one hand and a dark-blue AWOL bag in the other, his brother made his way up the steep steps behind Hitch.

"You're looking great Hitch. Did you have any trouble finding us?" Collier gave his sister-in-law an awkward hug and an air kiss before he clasped his brother around the shoulder.

"No trouble at all. Where's Emma?" Jim's breath exuded the sweetish odor of alcohol.

"She's still at work. I have to go get her in a few minutes. Let me help you with your stuff."

"Well...maybe we need to talk about that? I brought some beer. I wasn't sure how Emma would feel about it. Will it be a problem, do you think?" Jim asked as he sat his bag on the floor just inside the door.

"No...it's okay. Give it here—I'll put it in the fridge." Collier transferred the half-dozen beers into the refrigerator.

"Would you join me? I need to cut the dust out of my throat." His brother winked as he rescued a pair of longneck bottles of Pearl beer from the fridge before Collier closed the door.

"No thanks. Sit down and relax. I have a little surprise in store." Collier poured himself a glass of half-flat coke from a quart-sized bottle in the fridge and went to retrieve the newspaper article about tomorrows' Oak Hills Pro-Am. "Actually, this will be better for spectators than the Open itself. The galleries will consist of mostly club members. The Open has already sold several thousand five-dollar books of tickets for the entire event. I already have two books for us. They gave the military a dollar off the regular ticket price."

"Sounds like Oak Hills is some snooty private club. Are you sure the public will be admitted?"

"I'm sure. I called the pro. They're charging a buck for an admission tag."

"Why don't you two go in the bedroom and stretch out on our bed and catch a little rest while I go get Emma. That way you can catch a second wind before we go out to dinner."

"No way. Hitch can rest if she wants to. If you don't mind, I'll ride along. I'd like to get a look at Fort Sam Houston and see some of ol' San Antone." Chug-a-lugging his beer, Jim followed Collier to the door.

"I'll give you a quick look at Brackenridge Park. That's where they'll be playing the Open." Riding down Broadway, Collier purposefully continued south a few blocks past the turnoff to Fort Sam. Except for the pro practice rounds, the neatly-manicured golf course had been closed to the public for several weeks in preparation to host the big event.

"It's hard to believe this golf course is open for public play." Jim shook his head in awe as they drove by the picturesque, pine-lined fairways.

"So far, San Antonio has been perfect for winter golf. We had a light snowfall one Saturday morning a few weeks back, but by the time I had finished grocery shopping, the sun had melted off the snow and the temperature was in the seventies." Collier laughed.

"You're looking dashing, as usual. I have taken the whole weekend off. I know Collier has already made plans to go out to some country club tomorrow afternoon, but did he tell you we plan for the four of us to tour the Alamo tomorrow morning at nine? Neither Collier nor I have been inside," Emma greeted her well-tanned sister- and brother-in-law.

"Sounds like fun. It would be anti-Texas...anti-American really...to come to San Antone and not see the Alamo." Collier was a little surprised to look in the rearview mirror and see his brother seemed actually enthused at the idea of walking around some crumbling old church.

"There's the Alamo." Collier nodded as they drove by the next morning looking for a parking place.

"This entire tiny one-square city block is called *La Villita*. In Spanish, it means either a small village—like in senorita, the '*ita*' suffix attaches a meaning of smallness—or it is sometimes used to mean a small house. Of course in this case, it means village—or actually a settlement. Usually 'casa' is the better word for house. Including the Alamo mission and fortification, *La Villita* was the original site of the first settlement—it hardly encompassed more than this one, small, solitary square block—this is the true heart of downtown San Antonio," Emma attempted to explain the size of the original site of the Alamo and its fortifications.

"Well...I must admit I'm glad you made me come." It was barely past 1100 hours by the time they made it back to the car. Not someone generally given to being herded around, Collier was pleasantly surprised by how much he enjoyed the tour of the Alamo. He was completely amazed by how quickly the time had gone by.

"I know you're anxious to get out to your golf tournament. What do you say you drop Betty and me off at the apartment? I have some stuff for sandwiches. I'll fix you a quick bite of lunch before you leave. You can take Jim's car and leave our car for Betty and me. We may do a little sightseeing and shopping later on."

After grabbing a sandwich as they were turning into Oak Hill Country Club just before 1300, Collier was somewhat apprehensive when he saw the long line of automobiles parked in the grass on both sides of the lane at least a quarter-mile before he saw the main club house ahead, overlooking the old club's signature oak-tree-lined fairways.

"Crap, Brud, just pull over and park. We'll walk the rest of the way. I hope we're not too late to catch up with Sam Snead," Collier said, tying the laces on his golf shoes. *The Express* had not published pairings and starting times for this extracurricular pro-am. Collier had assumed the private country club would not be teeing off until late morning since pro-ams were always intended to be more of a social affair than they were golf events.

"You gentlemen will need a ticket. That will be one-dollar please." A man with an Oak Hill Country Club emblem embroidered on the upper left breast of his black Alpaca cardigan stepped out of the crowd encircling one of the two greens adjacent to the clubhouse and produced a stack of ticket-tags.

"Are we too late to catch Sam Snead?" Collier asked, not sure he wanted to shell out a buck to see the lesser-known pros in the field.

"It's your lucky day. That's Snead's foursome walking up to hit their second shots, right down there on number-nine fairway," the wizened Texan said, pointing beyond the clubhouse.

As the old man had told them, the foursome of Snead and Lloyd Mangrum, the dapper pro with the Errol Flynn mustache, and their amateur partners were just hitting their second shots to the ninth green near the old, Spanish-style clubhouse.

"Fore!" someone shouted as Collier and Jim arrived just in time to see Lloyd Mangrum launch a low-flying approach rocketing toward the flag on the elevated ninth green. "Fore left!" the cry was echoed again, just as the plummeting golf ball stuck the green looking for all the world as if it would ricochet into the gallery. All around them spectators ducked, folding their arms to protect their heads.

"Twock!" the ball hit the green a scant twenty-feet in front of Collier, took a little hop straight up and came to a screeching halt not fifteen feet from the flag.

"My God, have you ever seen anyone hit a short iron that low?" Jim whispered in Collier's ear.

"I know. All these guys hit the ball like they are playing with a bag full of three irons." Collier had barely gotten the words out of his mouth when another cry of "Fore" went up as Snead hit a low-flying shot straight at the flagstick. Incredibly, the ball struck the green about ten feet in back of the hole, and, instead of ricocheting over the gallery into the side of the clubhouse, the little white pellet backed up to within four or five feet of the hole."

As it turned out, the afternoon was memorable. The gallery was able to walk right along in the fairway with Snead and Mangrum and their amateur partners, listening as the garrulous pros regaled their small gallery with a running dialogue about their salad days on the pro circuit—sleeping in their beat-up automobiles and subsisting on bread and canned Pork'n'Beans.

"Sam, I'm surprised at you trying to lead these poor folk astray. Ben Hogan told me all about those rusty old tomato cans full of money you got buried in your backyard back in Virginia," Mangrum replied.

"Lloyd, don't believe all that stuff that Hogan says about me," Sam said. "Hogan hardly knows I'm alive. The only thing Ben ever said to me was, 'I believe you're away, Sam.'"

The banter continued until they walked off the eighteenth green into the clubhouse in the late afternoon.

The following morning, Collier and Jim had trouble finding parking. By the time they arrived at the Brackenridge Park course to catch the opening round of the Texas Open, Snead's foursome were just putting out on number one. On number two tee—a 200-yard par three—Collier and Jim were flabbergasted to find that the teeing areas at Brackenridge were woven, rubberized-fiber driving range mats, resembling oversized ordinary doormats available in most hardware stores. Collier watched in open-mouthed awe as Snead took out a pocketknife and whittled a wooden tee down to half-size and wedged it firmly between the elements of the woven mat, then put his golf ball on it and hit it as if it were an ordinary everyday occurrence on the tour. To their amazement, Snead's ball hit the green about ten feet past the pin and backed up a foot or two.

Dutch Harrison, stepped up behind him and hit one inside of Snead's ball, resting in the shadow of the pin.

"Why didn't you tell me you were serious, Dutch? I would have hit mine closer if I knew you were really trying," Snead drawled as they stepped off the tee, walking toward the green.

Over the first two days, Collier and Jim were privileged to witness an amazing demonstration of golf from a Nordic-looking unknown from Michigan named Walter Burkemo who shot 62 and 65 on the rather short but narrow, pine-tree-lined golf course which only measured about 6700 yards from the back tees. Incredibly, by the time the sun set Saturday night, Burkemo had been replaced as the leader by an unknown hometown favorite, Tony Holguin, who held out on Sunday to finally win his first official tour victory, pocketing a first-place check for $2000. Having a local boy take home the winner's share of the attractive $10,000 purse was a fitting touch to an exciting event. Lloyd Mangrum and Dutch Harrison played well, finishing in the money with $415 and $320 respectively, but, all things considered, Collier's hero and Brackenridge course record-holder, Slammin' Sam Snead, made a lackadaisical showing, finishing well back in the pack.

"Two-thousand bucks ain't bad for a week's work, Brud. I think I'm going to take golf a lot more seriously from now on," Collier told Jim after they had driven home from the golf course Sunday afternoon.

"If you learn to hit those quail-high wedges, let me know. With those guys, it's like throwing darts. It was really great. Thanks for everything," Jim said as he gave Emma a hug late Sunday afternoon and carried his and Hitch's bags down the steps to his car.

"Take good care and be safe driving back," Collier and Emma called as they gave his brother and Hitch farewell hugs and watched them drive away.

"Would you mind if I lie down for awhile? I'm feeling a bit tired. Don't let me sleep too long. I want to watch Ed Sullivan tonight," Emma said when Collier came back inside.

"Not at all, go ahead. I'm going to watch the news. I'll get you up on time." Collier poured himself a Coke and went over to turn the television on.

Lying on the bed, Emma stared wide-eyed into the gathering gloom, reflecting on her meetings with Trey Moseley over the past two afternoons.

"Don't try to lay that on me," the arrogant little jerk had whined, referring to her pregnant condition when she bumped into him in the Post Commissary one morning last week quite by accident.

"I pray to God it's not yours, but truth be told it very well might be," Emma told him she had apparently conceived over Labor Day weekend when they had slept together during his abortive visit to Fort Sill.

"Why didn't you let me know? I might have arranged to have it taken care of like the last time," Moseley whined, looking furtively around. Then, looking for privacy, they moved their conversation outside in the parking lot.

"My OB at Sill told me that with my uterine retroversion there was no way I would carry a fetus beyond the first trimester. Garrett Gooch had told me the same thing back home. Everyone was taken by surprise when my uterus suddenly flipped into normal position around the ninth or tenth week—nobody more than me." Emma wrestled her heavy bag of groceries into the trunk of the car. Typically, the cavalier Moseley made no offer to help.

"I might see you in Roanoke in the spring. I confess I have a morbid curiosity to see who your baby looks like." Moseley sneered. Now she regretted she had told him she was going back home to stay with her mother until the baby came. She wanted to have her own OBG, Garrett Gooch, deliver her firstborn child.

"Don't you dare show your face around my baby," she had warned the self-styled Casanova standing in the parking lot, but the arrogant bastard had only laughed.

CHAPTER THIRTY-SEVEN

San Antonio Express
San Antonio, Texas, Monday, March 2, 1953
BIG RED ATTACK SMASHED BACK
SEOUL, Korea, Monday, March 2 (AP) - Chinese Reds hurled their
biggest attack in a month - 750 men - against the Allied lines last night
but got nowhere.

San Antonio Express
San Antonio, Texas, Friday, March 6, 1953
JOSEPH STALIN DIES
LONDON, Friday, March 6 (AP) - Joseph Stalin died Thursday night
behind the six-foot-thick walls of the Moscow's Kremlin.

THE ROANOKE TIMES
Roanoke, Virginia, Saturday, March 14, 1953
**SKY FIGHTING STRESSED AS MUD,
SNOW SLOW LAND ACTION IN KOREA**
SEOUL, Saturday, March 14 (AP) - Paced by a new top-ranked jet ace
who bagged his 13th, Saberjet pilots claimed a kill of six Russian-built
MIG-15 jets near the Manchurian border in flaming Friday-the-13th sky
battles.

THE FINAL TWO WEEKS OF FEBRUARY, Collier and his classmates spent
mostly in field exercises with experienced Medical Corpsmen out in the dusty,
dwarf-oak-forested, hill country of the Camp Bullis Military Reservation,
experiencing firsthand the setting up of Battalion Aid Stations and MASH units,
negotiating compass courses through unfamiliar landscapes in the wee hours of
the night, and other assorted scenarios to approximate the hardships of combat in
a foreign terrain. As if he needed added incentive to learn as much as he could
about fending for himself and men who might come under his future command,
Collier addressed his studies with a renewed seriousness as word of the stepped-
up spring offensives around Old Baldy, Pork Chop and T-Bone Hills, White
Horse Hill and the Upper and Lower Alligator Jaws dominated the headlines of
the *Express* and were reported by major network TV newscasters such as John
Cameron Swayze of NBC's nightly *Camel News Caravan* and CBS's *Douglas
Edwards and the Nightly News.*
   "*God bless Bo Bohon and all of those brave soldiers in Korea and keep
them safe...*" Collier prayed every night now, ending his prayer with pleas for the
safety of all the men in those exotic places with colorful names, undergoing who-
knew-what sort of horrors. As best he could figure out, Bo was located
somewhere in the general area of the recent combat, and it had been several
months since he had gotten word of his safety.
   Every morning just after class, Collier checked the list of future orders on the
HQ bulletin board, hoping to see his name on orders on a posting—domestic or

foreign—any place other than FECOM. And every Monday regular as clockwork, Collier continued to check the *ArmyTimes* for advance listings of future officer postings. Finally, in mid-February, several of his classmates' names showed up in the *ArmyTimes*, listed as headed straight for FECOM—where else?—immediately upon graduating MFSS. Several other names he recognized were heading for Germany. But with regards to FECOM or EUCOM, his name was still not on either list.

The final Friday morning in February, checking the postings of orders on the HQ bulletin board, *voila,* right before his eyes, the name Second Lieutenant Collier Boyd Ramsay, O1936991 was on the list to report to Company B, 6th Medical Training Batallion, MRTC (Medical Replacement Training Center), Camp Pickett, Virginia, Monday, 23 March 1953. One line below his name was a similar posting for Second Lieutenant John Henry Pewter, except that Pewter was to report to Company A. Scanning down the list, Skyer, Flood, Johnson, Battaglia, along with Brewster Milton Robertson—his former high-school classmate who had also been an OCS classmate at Sill—and Paul Golden Price who had graduated OCS with Pewter at Fort Benning were among a list of his other MFSS classmates who were going to various companies at MRTC at Pickett.

Mentally doing the arithmetic, Collier determined 23 March would give him exactly ten days after his graduation from MFSS to get Emma back to Roanoke before he reported for duty at the infamous Medical Replacement Training Center at Camp Pickett, which he knew through the grapevine was out in the boonies somewhere between Petersburg and Lynchburg, Virginia.

Collier regretted he wouldn't have an opportunity to tell Emma the good news until she returned from Austin late Sunday evening. Emma was leaving for Austin straight from work with a group of professional colleagues to attend a weekend nursing seminar. The thought of greeting her with the news of orders stationing him less than two hours drive from home just in time for her to get settled in before their baby arrived was almost too good to be true. He still was having trouble believing his stroke of luck.

And, guiltily, Collier had to admit that he had been looking forward to Emma being away for the weekend. He certainly had not tried to avoid Margot Hamblin—*au contraire,* Collier had actually hoped to create other opportunities to see his sensuous landlady—however, for whatever reason, Collier had not had the pleasure of being alone with her again since their first time together. As a matter of fact, thinking about it on his way home with a mimeograph copy of his new orders, he couldn't recall having seen their erotic landlady around since their memorable escapade, and that had been exactly four weeks and three days ago— *not that anyone was counting.* Much to his disappointment, when Collier arrived back at the apartment, Margot's car was nowhere in sight. Hoping Margot would show up later on, and still feeling quite pleased the Army was not sending him straight to Korea following his graduation, Collier climbed the steps to the apartment, thinking he had time to play a leisurely nine holes of golf.

Placing his shiny new leather briefcase on the coffee table, he moved into the bedroom and stopped cold in his tracks when he saw Margot Hamblin spread-eagle buck naked upon the bed.

"It might be a good idea to go back and lock the door," she winked and laughed at his openmouthed surprise. "When you come back, get naked and lie down right here. This time, I want to get on top."

When he returned from locking the door, Collier quickly stripped and lay down on his back and watched as she mounted his jutting phallus and began riding him like a bucking bronco. In less than the time it takes to count to sixty, she was coming to her first orgasm. After that, she briefly rested before she went back to fucking him with abandon. He lost count of the number of her orgasms as the count soared and he began worrying what his folks would think when they found out he was an adulterer who had been fucked to death by a real live nymphomaniac.

When she finally collapsed sometime later, Collier rolled on top and began slowly pumping in and out of her in long, rhythmic strokes. When he started to come, she was building to the crescendo of yet another orgasm. Gasping and shuddering in little frissons of orgasmic release, moments later they both finally collapsed exhausted.

Collier was roused from near-catatonic exhaustion as Margot gasped, "Oh, my, I can't believe your staying power. Could I interest you in standing at stud for my bridge club?"

"Did you ever hear the fable of the Golden Goose?" Collier teased.

"I can't believe I've neglected to take advantage of you for a month. I can't bear to let you leave San Antonio without having you again at least one more time. I'll be looking for the opportunity every day from now on to ravish you." Departing through the door to her private stairway, she blew him a kiss and was gone.

"A gang of us are driving down to Nuevo Laredo this afternoon—want to tag along?" John Henry Pewter asked him Saturday morning over coffee in the "Snakepit," an on-Post snackbar.

"Nuevo Laredo? You mean Mexico?" Collier asked. From time-to-time, he had considered the idea of going to Mexico, but with Emma pregnant, the notion hadn't seemed very practical.

"Sure, Mexico—where else?" Pewter replied, annoyed Collier should be so ignorant.

"How far is it?" Collier asked. With Emma in Austin, if the trip were not too long, what was to prevent him driving down there?

"A-hundred-fifty miles, more or less—straight down U.S. 81. Chuck Edmond and C.W. Omahundre are both taking their cars. We'll split the gas. Omahundre has been down twice before. We're going to park in Laredo and walk across the bridge. I can ask Omahundre if we have room for one more. Are you interested?"

"Well...I really hadn't thought about it, but my wife is out of town for the weekend." Collier's mind was going mile-a-minute. He had really wanted to go into Mexico. Collier was particularly interested in seeing a bullfight, and he had seen the romantic bullfighting posters in the *Villita* in downtown San Antone advertising corridas at the *Plaza de Toro* in *Nuevo Laredo*. A hundred-fifty miles was scarcely more than a three-hour drive at the very most. He could take his own car. If he left after morning classes, he could be there and across the border by 1600 hours at the very latest. "Where and when are you meeting?"

"The Pit at 1300 hours. Omahundre says that will put us there by no later than 1700."

"Okay. But if I go, I'm going to take my own car. I'm married and my wife's pregnant. I probably won't want to stay down there as long as some of you single guys." This was the nicest way Collier could think to say he didn't want to be at the whim of a bunch of drunks.

"It's a free country. Besides, an extra car is a good thing. I might want to leave early myself. Maybe I could bum a ride back with you." A clean-cut kid who had been teaching English Lit at a small liberal arts college in Ohio when the draft caught up to him, John Henry Pewter was Collier's age. Despite the open look of small-town Ohio naivety on his face, Pewter was half-smart at the very least. Of all his MFSS classmates—including Hancock, Flood, Skyar and the rest from Sill—Collier liked Pewter best of those who would be reporting to the Medical Basic Training Center at Camp Pickett, Virginia.

"I'll be glad to give anyone a lift back, providing I can find them without scouring the back alleys of Nuevo Laredo. If I decide to go, I'll be at the Pit at 1300 hours."

Except that it was a boring drive and Omahundre turned out to be an over-cautious driver who rarely exceeded 60 mph. True to Omahundre's word, they arrived in the small border city of Laredo at 1630 hours and he led them to the parking lot of a small Baptist church within walking distance to a bridge leading across the Rio Grande.

"Omahundre wants to take us to see a live sex show. Omahundre says there are donkeys fucking young senoritas. He says we've never seen anything like what goes on over here." Collier shrugged, pretending disgust. He had read about the live sex shows with donkeys, but never really believed the stories were true. Collier was ashamed to admit it even to himself, but he couldn't help but be more than a little curious about such aberrant sexual behavior.

"Omahundre says the place is fairly crawling with gonorrhea..." The sun was sinking low on the western horizon and Pewter babbled excitedly as Collier followed Omahundre and the others across the bridge onto the main drag of the dusty town. Swarming with military men from virtually every branch of service, both sides of the street were lined with bars, and—from the moment they crossed into Mexico—the air had taken on a strongly-fecal smell.

"Anybody hungry?" Omahundre asked the group as they walked deeper into the town. "I hesitate to mention it now, but it's probably no accident that you won't see many stray dogs hanging around south of the border. But don't worry. I can take you to a place where you can trust the food."

When nobody admitted to being hungry, Omahundre laughed.

"Okay," Omahundre said, pointing to a large café on the far right hand corner of a busy intersection up ahead. "If you want to come back and eat later on, this large cantina up here on the corner is an alright place."

"Remember this cantina," Collier told John Henry Pewter when they reached the major intersection. "If you want to go back early, check back here at 2300 sharp to see if I'm ready to go back to San Antone."

"Okay, I'll keep that in mind," Pewter said, eyeing a group of malnourished prostitutes with pitifully-scrawny boobs barely peeking above their low-cut Mexican blouses.

"Alright, just to get everybody in the proper mood, I'm gonna take you to a live sex show before you get too drunk to remember it. Those who are interested follow me. Those who are not, you're on your own. Remember where we parked the cars. We rendezvous for the trip back to San Antone no later than 0300 hours." Omahundre turned right at the next corner and led the group of ten young officers down a narrow, unpaved and muddy alleyway.

Looking around him as they moved deeper into the squalor of the crowded barrio, Collier was glad to be in the company of the rest. He resolved to get back on the main drag just as soon as they took in the sex show.

"Here—one buck American. Give the senor your money and get a move on—the show is about to begin." Omahundre herded them all inside a part adobe/part wooden building which had seen better days.

Inside, Collier found a rickety seat two rows from the small stage. The badly-worn, molded plywood seats were obviously rescued from some old movie theater. Even in the dim light, the stage, with a cheap red-velvet curtain was plainly visible and everything in the room had seen better days. Before the curtain opened, a fat Mexican man in a dirty shirt with buttons missing moved through the audience offering to sell a variety of pornographic photographic postcards featuring young women engaged in unbelievable acts of sexual congress both with each other and with a small burro or donkey.

When the curtain finally opened, there were two women of indeterminate age, one skinny and one rather fleshy, standing on stage on each side of a thin mattress pad. With little preamble, they began kissing and disrobing each other and were soon on the mattress entangled in what looked to be a human pretzel, performing what the French called 'soixante-neuf'—sixty-nine. As revulsed as the entire scene made him feel, the unabashed raw sex was intensely arousing. Following what was intended to pass for both women reaching intense orgasms, the fat Mexican impresario led a small burro onto the stage. Then, to Collier's unbelieving eyes, the women took turns having sexual congress with the donkey. Incredible as it seemed, the donkey seemed to be an enthusiastic partner.

The depraved, disgusting tableau filled Collier with a strong sense of revulsion, bordering on the verge of nausea when just before the curtain closed, their act culminated with both women putting—or pretending to put—their mouths around the end of the donkey's dick. Outside, it was all Collier could do to keep from slipping between the buildings and throwing up.

"I don't like this neighborhood. I'm going back to the main drag. Remember, if you want a ride back early, meet me at the big cantina at 2300 sharp," Collier told Pewter, before he left the others.

Wandering the much-better-lighted main part of the seedily-Americanized, little business district, Collier had completely lost interest in the faux-cantinas and the cheap native silver and leather and blanket and pottery shops. By the time 2300 rolled around, he was verging on the edge of starvation

Resentfully—but dutifully—he paced back and forth until 2315 before he finally gave up on Pewter and headed back across the bridge. Locating an all-night Tex-Mex diner on the American side near where he had parked, Collier wolfed down a plain American cheeseburger washed down with a long-neck bottle of Pearl beer before he got in his car to head back up the long desolate highway. He was almost back to Artesia Wells when the nausea overtook him. His mind flashing back on the image of the Mexican prostitutes putting their mouths around the grotesquely-glistening, red donkey penis, Collier pulled to the side of the road and threw up his toenails into the Texas sagebrush under the star-filled sky. When he finally felt well enough to drive again, he discovered he had been under the watchful eye of a moth-eaten, yellow hound dog, warily lurking at the edge of the car's headlight beams. When it crossed his mind that this one mangy cur at least twenty-five miles north of Laredo was the first stray dog he had seen in either Nuevo Laredo or back on the American side of the Rio Grande, he threw up in the sagebrush again. When the nausea finally left him, still feeling a bit queasy, Collier got back in the car and started north again, the aftertaste of greasy hamburger still sour in his mouth.

Collier's watch read 0259 under the street lamp when he finally pulled to the curb in front of the pale-green house in Terrell Hills. Thinking about what Omahundre had told them about the absence of dogs in Mexican towns, he ran up the stairs two-at-a-time, unlocked his door and barely made it inside to the commode before he tossed his toenails again.

"Let me give you some hair of the dog..." cringing over the bartender's choice of words and feeling as if he would have to get better just to die, at the O Club for breakfast the next morning, Collier, much against his better judgment, took the bartender's advice and let him stir a generous jigger of Hennessey Five Star Cognac into his well-sugared coffee.

"You ever think about practicing medicine?" Collier asked the bartender before he had half-finished sipping the miraculous brew.

"Yeah, but I wouldn't like the clientele. I'm much more at home with a bunch of drunks," the bartender winked.

"Give me a refill," Collier ordered, hoping a second drink might heal him enough to play a round of golf before Emma returned from Austin. The golf would help kill the time and the fresh air might help restore him to health. He wanted to be in fine fettle so he could take Emma out to dinner to celebrate his orders to Camp Pickett.

Collier could hardly wait to see the look on her face when he gave her the news.

CHAPTER THIRTY-EIGHT

THE ROANOKE TIMES
Roanoke, Virginia, Wednesday, March 25, 1953
MASSIVE FIGHTING RAGES FOR STRATEGIC 'OLD BALDY'

SEOUL, Wednesday, March 25 (AP) - American Seventh Division troops counterattacked at dawn today under heavy Communist shelling in a renewed drive to win back the key bastion of Old Baldy guarding the main invasion route into South Korea.

****

1,000 Red Casualties

Crashing artillery barrages and the flow of battle across the shell-stripped crest of Old Baldy made it impossible to estimate the toll there in the first 36 hours of fighting. But officers at the front estimated that the Chinese had suffered more than 1,000 casualties in the early fighting on the wings—at T-Bone and Pork Chop hills to the west and Whitehorse Mountain and Upper and Lower Alligator Jaw

---

THE ROANOKE TIMES
Roanoke, Virginia, Thursday, March 26, 1953
AMERICANS LOSE STRATEGIC PEAK

SEOUL, Thursday, March 26 (AP) - U.S. Seventh Division troops completely abandoned the strategic peak of Old Baldy on the main invasion route to Seoul early today after three days of bitter fighting.

NEWS OF STALIN'S DEATH ON MARCH 5TH brought a momentary ripple of hope for the Peace Talks at Panmumjon—which quickly died down when it became obvious the infamous dictator's death was not going to have any effect on the war. Following the perfunctory graduation exercises at MFSS on Friday, March 13, Collier and Emma went back to their apartment and packed and loaded the last of their possessions for the trip back to Roanoke. Mindful that Emma was halfway through her sixth month of pregnancy, but anxious to make it to Shreveport their first night, before bedding down Friday, they left their keys with a note listing their forwarding address at Collier's father's P.O. Box in Salem in an envelope on the kitchen table. After a fitful sleep, they rose early, took a final look around and headed north on U.S. 81 toward Austin shortly before dawn on Saturday. Passing the spectacular 300-foot University of Texas Tower and the nearby Texas Capitol Building—with its unabashed copy of Thornton's ornate Capitol dome in Washington—just after sun-up, they encountered light traffic all the way north to Round Rock where they turned east on U.S 79. According to plan, they made it to Shreveport in time to find a first-class place to spend the night. Rising before dawn again Sunday, they continued to enjoy relatively light traffic all the way to Chattanooga where they checked into the same motel in which they had stayed on the trip to San Antonio. Overtired from two days of hard traveling, Collier overslept and they were late leaving Chattanooga on Monday morning.

"How are you feeling?" Collier asked as they entered the outskirts of Bristol just before 1500 hours Monday afternoon—they had spent the entire day driving through the mountains. "It's just three o'clock and we only have a little more than 100 miles left into Roanoke."

"I'm fine...it would be foolish to stop now," Emma said. "Find a place for me to pee and I'll go back to sleep."

Pulling into a new-looking Shell station, while Emma used the restroom, Collier filled up the tank and called his folks. With Emma sleeping curled up on the seat beside him, just before 1800 hours, Collier pulled into his parent's drive where Lida had dinner already on the table.

The next few days were spent getting Emma comfortably settled into her mother's home. With plans to commute back and forth on weekends as often as his schedule would allow, Collier kissed Emma goodbye Sunday morning, March 22, just before noon and headed the Studebaker east out of Roanoke on the Lynchburg Turnpike toward Blackstone and Camp Pickett. If he had been in an optimistic mood when he left home, his optimism quickly evaporated when he arrived on the outskirts of the shabby little town of Blackstone just before 0300. Stopping at the guard shack at Pickett's main gate, he got directions to the MRTC and found the OD at HQ building.

"You can sack in a temporary room at our so-called "Transient BOQ" tonight. Just pick any empty room. We'll assign you a permanent room after you report to Major Boyce tomorrow morning. Unless you're going to be there to watch over it, if I were you, I'd lock my extra gear in the car until you can get quarters in the permanent BOQ and can put a lock on the door. By the way, Lieutenant John Henry Pewter checked in earlier and said to tell you if he wasn't at the Transient BOQ, you could find him at the Officers' Club. The BOQ is straight down this road about a half-mile on the left. There's a sign...you can't miss it. The O Club is just past the BOQ, another half-mile on the left across from the Post movie theater."

"I presume I can get dinner at the Officers' club."

"Kitchen's closed Sunday nights, but the bar's open. You want food, you'll have to go off the Post."

"What's the best restaurant Blackstone has to offer?"

"There are only a couple of greasy spoons in town, and I wouldn't recommend either one to my worst enemy. If you're really hungry, it would be worth your while to drive into Petersburg and go to the O Club at Fort Lee—it's only about a thirty minute drive from here."

Collier's depression deepened when he pulled into the parking area of what the OD called the Transient BOQ which was housed in an ubiquitous Army wood-frame barracks building much like the ones he had lived in in Basic and OCS at Sill. Inside, however, he found the building had been finished with crude pine lumber and divided into small private rooms in deference to its occupants of officer rank. The interior walls were bare, unpainted wood, and while he couldn't find it by rubbing his finger across the window sill, he had a peculiar feeling there was a gritty, microscopic layer of dust overlaying everything. Staking his claim on the first empty room he found with fresh sheets and blankets folded on top of the unmade bed, Collier exited the room and wedged his newly-minted calling card engraved with the simple legend *Lieutenant Collier Boyd Ramsay* in a crack in the firmly-closed, but ill-fitting, door.

"Yo, Pewter," Collier went down the hall calling his buddy's name without an answer. Coming back he opened doors until he found Pewter's gear in the room across the hall from the room he had chosen. Leaving a note, he headed out to find the O Club.

Echoing the overall atmosphere of neglect exuded by the reactivated WWII training camp, the exterior appearance of Camp Pickett's "so-called" Officers' club was little better than the sorry buildings Collier had encountered at Camp Chaffee. Although it was still really nothing to write home about, at least the interior décor was a decided improvement.

"Pewter. They told me you were already here." Collier made straight for his friend when he saw him sitting on a stool at the bar. "When did you arrive in this military paradise?"

"Actually, I flew into Richmond yesterday and caught a bus here this morning. This hellhole is a disaster for a man without a car."

"I can see that. Anyway, I'm here now. My wife's back in Roanoke at her mother's place. She has the use of her mother's car, so I have my trusty Studebaker for commuting back and forth on weekends. What are you planning to do about chow?"

"I was just before walking across the street to the PX and loading up on some cheese-and-peanut butter crackers and cookies and Hershey bars."

"Well, having a stash of a few snacks on hand sounds like a good idea, but the OD said the dining room is open Sundays at the Officers' club at Fort Lee. Petersburg's less than an hour's drive from here. I went to college in Richmond. Petersburg is a nice town. What have we got to lose? Let's go check it out. I'm sure we can find at least a hamburger somewhere in case we strike out at the O Club."

"Sure, why not? I'm up for anything."

"I never got a chance to tell you, but I waited fifteen minutes for you that night at that big cantina in Nuevo Laredo. I worried that I might have missed you somehow," Collier told Pewter as he returned the guard's sharp salute, driving through the east gate on Morgan Road. The salute was one of the first signs of real soldiering he had seen since arriving this afternoon.

"I'm sorry. I really appreciate it...I hope you didn't wait too long." Pewter gave him an anxious look.

"Neah. After fifteen minutes, I hauled ass back across the river.

"By the way, that reminds me...what did you think of those senoritas and the donkey show?" Pewter asked with a shy grin.

"The donkey show was one of those things a Catholic man might tell his priest about on his deathbed. Personally, I'll go to my grave denying I ever enjoyed such a depraved event." Collier laughed. Thinking over what he said, he added, "If you're Catholic, no slur intended."

"Me Catholic? No, I'm an Ohio Methodist—probably just as bad. But, to tell the truth, I haven't spent much time in church lately."

"Same here—except in my case, I'm Virginia Baptist which is probably worse than Catholic—certainly worse than Methodist, Ohio or any other brand. My parents dragged me kicking and screaming to a little Baptist church until I finally rebelled when I was eleven." Collier laughed and told Pewter about the look on Lida's face the night he walked out on his Tenderfoot Badge.

"I didn't play sports, but I was a Life Scout. The Scouts are not so bad," John Henry Pewter replied somewhat defensively.

"Listen...don't misunderstand. I got nothing against the Scouts. Some good, some bad, like anything else I guess," Collier lied. No sense in getting off to a bad start by hurting the feelings of his rather naïve comrade-in-arms.

"Yeah...just like anything else, I guess." Pewter nodded philosophically.

"I might have stayed if they had given merit badges for Playing Sports or Chasing Pussy—what do you think your old troop leader would have said about that Donkey show?" Impressed by his own humor, Collier laughed out loud.

"I think he might have enjoyed it. Our troop leader was our assistant pastor until the regular preacher caught him in bed with his fifteen-year-old daughter. Even that might have been swept under the rug, if one of the elders hadn't caught the sneaky devil in the choir loft with his wife," Pewter returned Collier's cynicism, tit-for-tat.

"Listen, half of what little sex I got when I was in high school and even of college age, I got from the foxy daughters of the pillars of the community. I'm sure you've a few stories of your own."

"Uhm-m..." Pewter murmured what Collier took for an assent then fell suddenly silent.

"What did I say? Did I strike a nerve or something? Was it about screwing the daughters of church-goers?" Obviously, something he'd said had offended his companion.

"No—nothing like that. Well...I mean...it's just that I haven't had much success with women. Truth be told, I went to Nuevo Laredo hoping to change that, but when I saw those Mexican prostitutes, I decided it was better to remain a virgin than come back with a dose of clap or worse."

"You're kidding, right? I mean you're not still a...a virgin?"

A virgin at twenty-three or twenty-four? Collier was certain Pewter was putting him on.

"No...I mean yeah. I mean I'm not kidding. I didn't even date much in high school or in college—practically not at all."

Collier shot Pewter a quick appraising glance in the reflected headlights of a car behind them.

"Hey, look, I'm not a homo, if that's what you're thinking. I grew up in a small town where everyone's life was an open book. The only girls who were...were...ah...free with their favors were from the wrong side of the tracks," Pewter stammered self-consciously when he caught Collier's look. "I hope you won't spread this around."

"Don't worry, pal. Your secret's safe with me. As a matter of fact, I just decided that I am going to dedicate myself to fixing your unhealthy condition. We can't have an officer in Uncle Sam's Army running around with his ashes un-hauled. It's not only unhealthy; it's downright un-American."

"Well, now look...I don't...ah..." Pewter didn't seem overly appreciative of Collier's sudden interest in his sexual credentials.

"Relax, Pewter. This ain't going to hurt a bit. I promise I'll deliver your virginity to some maiden of good social standing—it will be a shining moment for the both of you."

"Look, you can stop fooling around. I know you're putting me on."

"Trust me. I'm not fooling, my good man. From this moment on, I won't rest until we remedy your debilitating condition. Do you carry prophylactics with you? A Scout is always prepared." Warming to the idea of this unholy crusade, Collier chuckled at his own humor.

"C'mon...quit playing with me. I'm sure I'm not the only virgin shavetail in this man's Army," Pewter complained, more than a little pissed at Collier's cavalier sense of humor.

"I am not playing. On my word as an officer and a gentleman, I assure you I am not. I am as serious as brain cancer. We're going to get you laid, or my name's not Collier Boyd Ramsay. Well, do you or don't you carry any rubbers on your person?"

"No...I would never stoop to that. Do you walk around with prophylactics in your wallet?"

"No, but I'm married. I'm not looking to get laid. But, now that you mention it, it occurs to me that nubile maidens usually travel in pairs. I might have to sacrifice my marital fidelity in order to consummate your sexual initiation. I best get us both some rubbers at the first drug store we come to." A street sign read Washington Street as they were coming into the outskirts of Petersburg and Collier slowed when he saw a sputtering Rexall Drug Store sign in the block ahead. Pulling up to the curb, the fly-specked store's window was overcrowded with Geritol, 666 Tonic, Vicks Vaporub and other banners promoting patent medicines and greasy hair pomade. They were clearly in a black neighborhood. "Wait here, I'll be right back," Collier left the motor running and went inside the store.

Emerged from the drug store a few minutes later, Collier handed his flabbergasted companion a slender, red matchbook-size package of Trojans. "Here, put this package of three's in your pocket. Make sure you keep it where you won't run a chance of accidentally pulling it out in public reaching for your cigarettes."

"Thanks. How much do I owe you?" Pewter wriggled his slender wallet from his hip pocket, wedging the thin package of condoms in-between a healthy sheaf of folding money.

"Be careful not to leave them against the outside of your wallet where their outline will show through when you take it out. It wouldn't make a very good impression if you had your wallet out to give the CO's wife a calling card," Collier advised somewhat tongue-in-cheek as Pewter replaced the slim leather folio in his hip pocket.

"Oh, God, I never thought of that. Where do you put them to keep them out of sight?" Pewter asked, not yet accustomed to his newfound role as a modern-day Don Juan.

"Don't worry. They're okay where you have them for the time being. Let's find the Fort Lee Officers' club and see if we can get a big juicy steak. No red-blooded pussy hound should go hunting for a prospective piece of tail on an empty stomach."

"I wish you'd quit using that term. Wanting to experience sex with a woman doesn't necessarily make me a pussy hound. Besides, you haven't answered my question. Did you come over here for sex when you in college in Richmond? Do you know where a respectable whorehouse is?" Clearly excited over the idea of actually being with a woman, Pewter was torn between maintaining a semblance of respectability and the exciting prospect of standing at the threshold of losing his virginity.

"Whorehouse, John Henry? I wouldn't have a clue where the local cathouses are. In Richmond, I lived right on the edge of the red-light district, but I've never paid for sex in my life. What's more, I don't intend to start now. Why rent a cow when you're already swimming in milk? Besides, I already promised you we are going to find you a genuine debutante...at the very least, an ex-sorority girl."

"Look, you aren't fooling me. Even if we find someplace where I can meet respectable women, they're not just waiting around to fall into bed with me." Pewter resented Collier poking fun at him.

"Is that anyway for a graduate of Benning OCS to talk? At Sill, they trained us to be fearless leaders of men into the perils of mortal combat. Besides, you're putting a sordid slant on this. You were an English teacher. Have you read anything about the Holy Crusades?"

"Surely you're not trying to put a noble face on your trying to get me laid?"

"Don't you get it yet? That's it, Pewter. That's *exactly* what I'm trying to make you understand. We are on a mission of mercy."

"I don't want to be thought of as a charity case."

"Surely you're not so selfish Pewter that all you think about is yourself? Think of the poor women—the suffering. We are knights in shining armor. Ours is a noble quest to find these poor damsels in distress and let some sunshine into their lonely lives."

"There you go, playing with me again. Just because you're not a virgin doesn't give you the right to think I'm inferior to you."

"Whoa, Pewter, hold on just a minute. I'm going to a lot of trouble here. You're riding in my automobile on my gas and will be using rubbers...ah...prophylactics...that I paid for out of my own pocket. This crusade to rid you of the cancer of your virginity, restore the honor of young, Red-blooded American Manhood...not to mention the integrity of the entire Officer Corps of the United States Army,...I am unselfishly undertaking as a holy cause. As of this evening we are Knights Templar in quest of the holiest of holy grails—the lonely, sexually-deprived vessels of American maidenhood. After all, by virtue of the U.S. Army Medical Corps, we are now members of the Hippocratic fraternity, sworn to stamp out suffering and pain."

"Ramsay, you are so full of crap your eyes are turning brown. I really don't mind the idea of finding some high-class whorehouse. Can't we at least just ask around?"

"Oh, ye of little faith! For the time being relax. First, we have to feed the driver of this noble chariot a steak."

Driving into Petersburg, Collier found signs directing them to Fort Lee without difficulty. Just outside the entrance, a sign proclaimed: Home of the Quartermaster Corp. Passing through the main gate, the guard gave them directions to the Officers' club. In sharp contrast to the shoddy, reactivated-from-mothballs condition of the wooden WWII buildings flaking paint in post-card-sized patches back on the Camp Pickett reservation, Fort Lee had a solid sense of permanence marked by freshly-painted barracks, with warehouses and maintenance sheds reminiscent of Fort Sill and Fort Sam Houston. Even more imposing than its impressive façade, on the interior, the Officers' Club was warmly-welcoming. Tastefully wallpapered walls contrasted with the soft, polished sheen of immaculate wooden paneling.

Arriving well-before the dining room stopped serving at 2100 hours, they found the bar and both ordered tall pilsners of draft beer which they carried to a lounge area with tables and overstuffed leather chairs. Much to Collier's disappointment, there were no unattached females of any age or description to provide targets of opportunity for their holy quest.

"I'm starved. Let's find a table in the dining room before I succumb to malnutrition." —Collier picked up his half-empty glass of rapidly-warming beer and nodded toward the entrance of the dining room. He hoped the absence of unattached females was a reflection on the early hour or perhaps just because Sunday was a slow night.

Almost an hour passed before Collier, well-stuffed with mouth-watering prime rib eye steak, led Pewter back to the lounge. Except for four field-grade officers and their wives occupying two tables and an attractive young matron looking to be in her early-thirties who was accompanied by a pretty girl in her early-twenties seated at a round table in the corner by a window, the bar remained virtually devoid of people.

"Did the CO die or is Sunday always like this?" without preamble, Collier walked over and addressed the older of the two women as if he were greeting a long-lost, childhood friend.

"You must be new on Post. Tomorrow's a duty day." The older woman smiled a non-committal smile.

"We're not stationed here. We're at Pickett, just down the road," Collier said. "I'm Collier Ramsay. My fellow officer is John Henry Pewter. We both just arrived today from Fort Sam Houston in San Antonio, Texas. Perhaps you ladies would allow us to buy you a drink?"

"That's awfully kind, Lieutenant Ramsay, but we were just about to leave. Julie, dear, would you ask Herbie to call us a cab?" Smiling pleasantly, the older of the two women addressed her younger companion, gathering up her purse as if to leave.

"No need to take a cab. Permit us to offer you a ride home. We probably should be heading back anyway." Bowing low, Collier offered his assistance with a sweeping gesture of his hand.

"Well...that's very kind of you." She glanced over to her younger companion, then gave both of them a closer look. "Taxis are hard to find in Petersburg on Sunday night. If it's not too much trouble, we'll take you up on that offer. I'm Cathy Rush and this is my daughter, Julie Moore. My first husband, Colonel Andrew Moore, was Julie's father—unfortunately poor Andy resides in Arlington now."

"Pull up here on the left," Cathy Rush directed a short time later as Collier approached an older, two-story, white clapboard house on a respectable-looking street lined with large overhanging trees. Upon leaving Fort Lee, they had crossed a river and driven perhaps two or three miles into the suburban township of Colonial Heights. Collier carefully noted the route, well aware he would have to find his way back to Route 460 if he didn't want to spend half the night wandering around Petersburg.

"It's early. If you'd like to come in, I can make you a cup of coffee. It might help keep you awake for the drive back to Blackstone," Cathy offered when Collier pulled to the curb.

"Sure, that sounds good to me." Without consulting Pewter, Collier turned off the ignition and walked around to open the passenger door. After assisting Cathy to the curb, he offered his hand to help Julie climb out of the cramped back seat. Collier caught view of a delightful expanse of inner thigh and just a glimpse of the crotch of peach-tinted panties with what appeared to be little blue flowers on them. When Julie caught him looking, she smiled and lowered her eyes. Secretly, Collier intuited that if Pewter played his cards right, this was going to be his lucky night.

"Welcome to our humble abode. My grandfather...Julie's great-grandfather...built this house just before World War One. Our family has lived here since 1914. I live downstairs. The door at the far end of the porch is the *private* entrance to Julie's upstairs apartment. Julie, dear, why don't you take John Henry up and show him your cute little cubbyhole." Although it came off innocently enough, Cathy obviously wanted to let them both know her daughter lived separate and apart and was clearly on own.

"Follow me, Lieutenant. I think my mother's telling us they want to be alone." Julie took Pewter's hand and led him down the long porch.

"Come help me fix the coffee...or would you prefer a beer?" Cathy asked as soon as she saw Julie and John Henry disappear inside the other door. Without waiting for an answer, she led Collier through the door, into a large sitting room and down a wide hall leading into the kitchen at the back of the house.

"Coffee sounds great." Collier murmured, appreciating the view of her nicely-curved backside.

"Have a seat. This will only take a minute." His hostess indicated a grouping of chairs around an oval maple dinette table and went over and turned on a florescent light above the cooking eyes of an electric range. Collier sat and watched appreciatively as she moved about measuring coffee into a pot and putting the pot on the stove to perk. Watching her move about the kitchen in her simple black cocktail sheath, he idly wondered what she'd do if he encircled his arms around her from the rear and nuzzled the brunette curls at the nape of her neck—maybe even give the lobe of her ear a sociable nip.

"Would you like to see the rest of this place I call home?" Adjusting the temperature controls of the stove, she turned back to him and took his hand.

"The main bathroom is right here inside my bedroom door. For company, there's another little powder room with a commode and lavatory right down the hall nearer the living room," she recited as she led him inside the darkened bedroom. Before he could think to make a comment—and while he was still trying to rethink his next move—she turned to face him and moved into his arms as easy as if they had known each other forever. Scarcely before Collier knew quite what was happening, his hostess eagerly pulled his mouth down to hers. This was clearly a no-nonsense woman. The urgency of her movements left no doubt she wanted him to take her to bed. Encircling his right hand beneath her buttocks, as she pushed her pudendum against the instant swelling in his loins, using his left hand, he began pulling her blouse from her skirt. Deftly she reached behind her and unsnapped the clasp of her bra, releasing the solid masses of her overripe matronly breasts to his caresses. Beneath his fingertips and his lips and tongue, the large nipples came quickly erect.

When they finally broke apart, she led him around to the other side of the double bed, snapped on a tiny bedside lamp with a ruffled, pink translucent shade and began to pull off the rest of her clothes.

"You are one true force of nature in the bedroom, Lieutenant Collier Ramsay. I hope Julie and John Henry hit it off half as well..." Cathy Rush said, an indeterminate time later, making little circles in the fine line of hair leading from his navel to his penis.

"I hope so, too. I know it's hard to believe at his age, but Pewter's still a virgin..." Lying in the soft light filtering down the hall from the living room and suspended in a state of erotic afterglow, Collier confided Pewter's embarrassing condition.

"Don't worry. Julie can be something of a wanton hussy at times. If your buddy, John Henry, is really a cherry, I'm not sure we shouldn't go up and rescue him." Cathy laughed.

"I really hate to leave, but tomorrow will be a long day. I have to report to a new assignment." Collier gave her hand a squeeze as he got up and started to dress. Being a Knights Templar was not such a bad deal, Collier reflected pleasantly in the aura of sexual afterglow. "I wonder what's keeping them?" Almost a full hour had passed since Collier had told Cathy about Pewter's virginity.

"You told me he was a cherry. I rather imagine Julie has opened him to a veritable fairyland of carnal delights," Cathy murmured dreamily, snuggling up beside Collier on the front porch steps in the pleasant early-spring breeze.

"Well, I'm sure Pewter is in capable hands, but I really would appreciate it if you'd see if you can get him moving. As much as I hate to go, we need to get back to Pickett. We both have to report to our new CO tomorrow morning," Collier reminded her as he helped her to her feet and waited for her to rescue John Henry from a fate better than death.

"Well, how did it go?" Collier asked Pewter as they were crossing the bridge back into Petersburg, heading back to Blackstone.

"I had a great time. Julie teaches English literature at the high school. We have quite a lot in common. We talked about F. Scott Fitzgerald and Ernest Hemingway." Pewter was slouched down in the seat with a silly grin on his face.

"Forget the Hemingway and Fitzgerald stuff. How does it feel now you're no longer a virgin?" Collier persisted impatiently.

"Oh, come on Ramsay; Julie's not that kind of girl. Besides, she would never do anything like that with her mother downstairs in the rooms just below her." Pewter sat up straight, indignant at Collier's suggestion of impropriety.

"Not what kind of girl? What do you think Julie's mother and I were doing for the past three hours—playing tic-tac-toe? Do you think those two were at the Officers' club looking for a third and fourth for bridge?"

"Collier, just who do you think you're fooling? You two weren't having sex—not with her daughter right up upstairs?"

"Pewter, I cannot believe you spent two hours alone talking about Hemingway and Fitzgerald with that poor sex-starved girl. Didn't you kiss her or feel her up...or anything?"

"No. It wasn't like that. She's a nice girl. She teaches school."

"John Henry Pewter, that poor girl was dying for a good screwing. I can't believe you just walked away and left her suffering!"

"You've got a dirty mind, Collier. Besides, I don't believe you had sex with her mother."

"Pewter, I hereby officially resign as your sexual tour guide. It's a good thing I didn't take you to a whorehouse. You couldn't even make out in a whorehouse with a handful of hundred-dollar bills. No wonder you're a cherry."

"Hold on, Ramsay. You don't understand."

"You're right about that, John Henry. I really don't have a clue."

They drove on without speaking for awhile with Collier seething over John Henry's utter hopeless naïveté.

"Quick Ramsay, pull over. I think I'm gonna puke," Pewter spoke up suddenly, rolling his window down.

Pulling the Studebaker to the shoulder, Collier watched while Pewter quickly opened the door, stepped into the night and started puking his guts out into the roadside weeds.

"Are you okay, now?" Collier asked when Pewter finally got back in and closed the door.

"Yeah. I think so. I'm just not that much used to drinking alcohol, I guess. I never have more than one beer—two at most," Pewter confessed.

"Happens to the best of us," Collier sympathized, thinking how wrong he'd been in his assessment of Pewter's urbanity just because he hailed from the Midwest and had graduated Miami University—the Miami in Ohio. Collier realized if he had bothered to put two and two together, Pewter's downright lack of sophistication went hand-in-hand with his virginity approaching the ripe old age of twenty-four.

"Have you got any chewing gum?" Pewter asked, wiping his mouth and forehead on his handkerchief.

"Sure. Here, help yourself." Lifting his hips, Collier located an almost full pack of Beemon's Cinnamon-flavored gum in the left-hand pocket of his trousers.

"God, Ramsay, I'm sorry about that. I like the taste of beer and I like some of those fancy cocktails, but I guess I need to go easy with the drinking. I'm just not used to it." Pewter mumbled, stuffing several sticks of gum in his mouth and tossing the empty paper wrappers out the window into the summer night.

"Let's get back to the girl. What happened?" After what her mother had told him, Collier found it impossible to believe Pewter had failed to score.

"She did try to kiss me once or twice, but I think she was just being nice..." Pewter finally admitted.

"Just being nice? Did she kiss you like your sister?"

"I don't have a sister...but now that you mention it, I don't think sisters kiss brothers like that."

"Like what, John Henry?" Collier couldn't believe he was having this conversation.

"She kissed with her mouth wide open. I don't think she's had much experience at kissing."

"And I suppose you have?" Collier's voice oozed sarcasm.

Pewter fell silent for the better part of several minutes before he asked, "Do you really think Julie wanted me to...ah...you know, take her to bed?"

"I don't just think it, Pewter—it's a damn fact. Her mother was laughing about her daughter's healthy sexual appetites."

"You didn't tell Cathy I was a virgin, did you?"

"No..." Collier lied, "but I guarantee she not only knows you're a virgin now, but she also knows you're a dumb jerk."

"I'm sorry, Collier. I really think I should go to a whorehouse. You wouldn't enter the Olympic freestyle without first taking swimming lessons, would you?"

"You may have a point there," Collier said and lapsed into brooding silence until he bid Pewter a terse goodnight at the transient BOQ.

"Soon as you're dressed, let's go find some breakfast before we report to Major Boyce," Collier suggested the following morning while they were shaving in the community latrine at their temporary billet.

"I hope you won't tell anyone about last night..." Pewter began self-consciously, glancing nervously around to make certain they were alone.

"Don't worry; nobody would believe me if I did." Collier laughed, rinsing his razor before he stepped across and turned on the shower.

"We're glad to have you both here in the Sixth Medical Training Battalion of the Medical Replacement Training Center. Sharp young officers right out of OCS with the ins and outs of Basic Training fresh in their minds are just what we need," Major Boyce welcomed them to his command, then directed them to report directly to the COs of their respective training companies.

"Lieutenant Collier Ramsay, reporting as ordered, sir," Collier saluted Captain Rodolph Mullins, his new CO, in the orderly room of Company B.

"Relax and have a seat, Ramsay. It's good to have you on board. Just give me a minute...I'm short-handed and have to get this morning report out to Battalion." The tan, weathered, coal-black-haired Captain with a close crew-cut returned Collier's salute and motioned toward a folding metal GI chair which was the only other chair in the room.

Warily assessing his new CO, Collier glanced around the bare interior of the room with plain pine-paneled walls. A stiff studio photo of a plain-looking woman with two small children—a boy and a girl—in a cheap, dime-store frame sat on the Captain's desk. Beside it was another, somewhat faded, photo of a small group of coal miners standing outside the entrance to a mine with their lunch pails in their hands. At the front of the group of miners was a young man who bore a remarkable resemblance to the man behind the desk.

Attached to the metal button on the right-hand pocket of his new CO's sharply-pressed fatigue blouse was a neatly-printed leather-encased nametag: Captain Mullins. Above the opposite pocket on the left-hand side, Mullins wore several rows of combat ribbons including the Purple Heart with two oak-leaf clusters, a Bronze Star with a cluster denoting he'd been twice cited for bravery, an Army Commendation Ribbon with two clusters, the WWII Victory Medal, the European Campaign Medal with two battle stars, the National Defense Medal, Korean Service Medal with three battle stars and an arrowhead device for the Inchon Landing and the UN Service Medal. Also, there was a good conduct ribbon with two knots on the accompanying knot device which indicated he had served several tours as an enlisted man. This was confirmed by a framed certificate hanging on the wall behind the desk commemorating the battlefield promotion of Staff Sergeant Rodolph Mullins to Second Lieutenant during the battle of St. Lo following the D-Day landing at Omaha Beach.

"Have someone run this report over to Major Boyce at HQ, Fred." Captain Mullins stood and handed a young Staff Sergeant the morning report before he remembered Collier was sitting there. "Forgive me, Lieutenant Ramsay. This is Sergeant Fred Alley. Sergeant Alley is our First Sergeant—he runs the whole show."

"Glad to meet you, Sergeant." Collier stood and returned the Sergeant's salute.

"Looking forward to serving with you, Lieutenant Ramsay." The Sergeant awkwardly saluted again, closing the door behind him when he left the room.

"When we're alone, or at the club, Lieutenant—anytime we're out of earshot of the enlisted personnel—call me Randy. Do they call you Collier or is there some nickname you prefer?" The captain leaned back in his chair and smiled a friendly smile.

"I've been called a lot of things, but Collier is probably best." Collier smiled, trying hard to relax.

"I see you're from Roanoke. Janie and I drive right through there when we go back home for a visit. We're from Kentucky...near Hazard. Ever been up in those cricks and hills?"

"Yes, Sir. I played basketball at Pikeville when I was at Bluefield College. They gave us quite a lesson..." Collier was recounting the drubbing he and his Bluefield teammates had taken at the hands of the Pikeville Junior College team when the phone rang on Mullin's desk.

"Mullins here..." the captain's voice was all business answering the call. He listened for a minute or so before he grunted, "Thanks, Charlene. I'll take care of it from here..." and replaced the phone back on the cradle.

When he hung up, Mullins turned deadly serious. His voice and choice of words didn't sound like any Kentucky coal miner Collier had ever met. "Look, Collier, I hate to dump something like this on you hardly before we've gotten acquainted, but we've got something of a problem here."

"What's up?" Collier held his breath, not knowing what to expect.

"I don't know what they told you up at headquarters, but we are very shorthanded here. TOE calls for a First Lieutenant XO"—XO was military shorthand for Executive Officer—"and Second or First Lieutenant Platoon Leaders for all three platoons of these raw trainees. On paper, each platoon consists of three nine-man squads of recruits with a platoon sergeant for each platoon—that's a total TOE of thirty men. Up until your arrival this morning, I've only had two Lieutenants to assume the responsibilities of four junior officers. You make three, so that still leaves us one man short with not much hope of getting anybody else before these men complete their sixteen-weeks of Basic the middle of May." Mullins hesitated, pulled out a pack of Philip Morris and offered Collier one.

"No thanks, those things give my throat a fit," Collier declined as he produced and lit a Lucky from a pack tucked inside the top of his sock underneath his trousers. Inhaling a deep drag from the cigarette, he replaced the pack and carefully lowered his pants leg back over his hiding place.

"So? If you're saying I'll have to command two platoons, Sir? That's okay with me."

"No...that's not exactly what I'm driving at—although that might happen sooner than I'd like to think. To get to the point, the other Platoon Leader and, coincidentally, also our XO, is Lieutenant Jack Scarborough. Jack is a Korean veteran—he has a Bronze Star with a cluster. He was a first lieutenant when I got here nine months ago and with his exemplary war record he should be in line for a captaincy, but he's had some personal problems and was reduced in rank to Second Lieutenant about a month ago for showing up at Battalion Officers Call with alcohol on his breath. Since then his drinking problem has gotten worse. Up until now we—the first sergeant and I—and Lieutenant Carnes, have managed to cover for him..." Mullins carefully brushed the long ash from his Chesterfield into an ashtray made from the base of an artillery shell before he looked back at Collier again.

"Well...you can depend on me. Just tell me what you want me to do. I'll help Scarborough anyway I can." Collier wasn't sure exactly what was coming next, but he was anxious to reassure Mullins of his willingness to serve.

"I appreciate your loyalty, Collier. That was Jack's wife, Charlene, on the phone. I know you're a stranger to Blackstone, but we've been looking all over for Jack the entire weekend, with no luck. I found him Friday night in a local dive out off Kenbridge highway and took him home. Charlene had gotten him in pretty good shape by yesterday morning when she left for work at the local telephone office. When she came home last night, he was gone again. According to the bartender at the O Club, he stopped in there and had a couple of double Bloody Marys, but left without taking the Sunday Brunch Buffet. No one has seen him since. I want you to go off Post and track him down. I hate to do it, but this time when you find him call me. I'm going to have the MPs take him to the stockade and lock him up."

"Yessir. Where do you want me to start looking?" Collier stood and snubbed his cigarette in the artillery casing ashtray on Mullins' desk.

"Here's a map of Blackstone. Hazel Baker, Jack's current girlfriend and main drinking partner lives right about here on Hungarytown Road." Mullins motioned for Collier to take a look at the map. "If he isn't there, but Hazel's at home, she may can give you some clue where else to look."

"What's the number of her house?" Collier asked, tracing with his forefinger a route through Blackstone out Old Nottoway Road past College Road two blocks, to the left-hand turnoff at Hungarytown Road.

"It's not exactly Country Club acres out there. They don't have house numbers out that way. After you turn south off Nottoway Road, it's a good mile or mile-and-a-half to her house. You'll have to start looking at the mailboxes. Remember the name Hazel Baker—it's on the box. I've been out there a time or two already, myself. Here, take this map."

"Wish me luck." Collier folded the map and headed for the door.

Finding Hungarytown Road was easy enough, but finding Hazel Baker's mailbox was a different matter altogether. On his first and second pass through, Collier missed seeing it because the mailbox had been knocked askew and was teetering low into a clump of weeds and honeysuckle. To further frustrate his search, Hazel's rundown shack had cardboard replacing more than a few broken windowpanes and the yard was overgrown with weeds with a battered Ford pickup truck up on cinderblocks with its wheels missing and he initially dismissed the possibility that an Army officer's girl friend could be living in such a disreputable shanty.

When he finally realized he had actually been going around in circles, passing by the address, he pulled into the weed-choked driveway. As he drew near the falling-down shanty, he caught view of a mud-spattered, red Ford convertible which matched the description Rodolph Mullins had given him of Scarborough's car. Collier turned off the engine and lit a Lucky to steady his nerves before he exited the car and went up to the door and knocked. Collier wasn't much of a praying man, but he hoped Scarborough wasn't a fighting drunk.

"Are you the doctor? I hope it's not too late?" A frowsy-looking bottle blonde with a half-inch of dark-brown roots showing where her hair was haphazardly parted answered the door clutching a badly-stained, raw-silk Japanese Kimono, frayed at both cuffs and hem and riddled with ugly cigarette burns. Even from an arm's length away, her breath was positively flammable.

Reflexively, Collier dropped his Lucky and squashed it under his heel.

"I'm not a doctor, ma'am. What's the problem here?" Looking over her shoulder down the end of the short center hallway, Collier could see a man's naked shins and feet protruding through the grillwork of an old-fashioned iron bed. The floor of the center hall was littered with trash and garbage—empty cigarette packs, takeout food wrappers, even a discarded Kotex box rested on the floor outside the door to the bathroom, halfway down the passageway. What appeared to be at least a carload or more of empty whiskey bottles and beer cans and longneck beer bottles littered the furniture and floor of the smallish front room. Flung carelessly across a chair with one of the springs sticking through the stuffing of the backrest in the far corner beside a window of the front room, were the pants and blouse of an Army OD uniform with rather scruffy gold Lieutenant's bars attached to the collar. Collier had little difficulty making out the name SCARBOROUGH on the leather-encased name tag on the pocket of the blouse.

"Oh, please help me...help him. Come back here and take a look. I found him this way when I woke up. He's so gray and cold, and I can't get any response from him. I called a doctor. He should be on the way," the near-naked blonde grabbed Collier's hand and yanked him through the door, tugging him down the short, narrow hallway to the bedroom at the rear.

"For godsake Ma'am, get a blanket...something...let's cover him up." Collier ordered sharply as he entered the room, assessing the situation in a glance. From the light snoring sounds coming from the filthy bed, Collier was instantly relieved that Jack Scarborough was far from being a corpse. Respectably endowed and completely nude, lying spread-eagle on his back on the bed, Scarborough's semi-erect penis—complete with a scrap of toilet tissue adhered to the glans—was waving casually at half-mast. Beneath his body, the sheet was stained dark-brown and yellow—the overpowering odor of urine and feces permeating the air. Between the near wall and the bed was a small trash can overflowing brownish-smeared toilet paper with which someone had tried to clean the shit and god-knew-what-else off the bed.

"You said a doctor is on the way? How long ago did you call?" Collier asked, reaching down to take Scarborough's pulse, searching his brain, trying to formulate a plan. If Scarborough wasn't in some sort of medical crisis, the drunken bastard was already in enough trouble without getting a civilian involved.

"Unh?...I called over an hour ago. His nurse said she would try to reach him at the Infirmary at Farmville State Teachers College. He's the school doctor I think."

A good forty-five minutes drive, Farmville was at least twenty-five miles down 460, all the way past Crewe and Burkeville. Coming down 460 yesterday, Collier had passed right by the campus of the well-known girl's school—they called it Longwood now. His high school teammates, Hunter Miller, Ballard Wood and Bung McClung had played their college football just down the road a few miles south of Farmville at Hampton Sydney.

"An hour ago? What did you tell his nurse?"

"I told her it was an emergency...a man was dying. I gave her my address."

"Did you give her Scarborough's name?"

"No...I think I might have said it was an officer from the Post, but I'm sure I didn't mention Jack's name."

"Thank God for small favors," Collier murmured to himself as he scanned the room, but saw no telephone. "Where's the telephone?"

"In the front room." She led him back, tiptoeing through the obstacle course of scattered bottles and cans into the front room. In the far corner next to the ruptured chair holding the OD uniform, there was a folding aluminum lawn chair. Between the two chairs the telephone rested upon an upended orange crate. On the floor beside the crate, lay the tattered and discolored, pamphlet-sized C&P phone book for Blackstone, Nottoway, Crewe, and Burkeville open to the page listing the number for Dr. E.A. Bennett. The only number for Dr. Bennett was on Church Street. Apparently, the good physician had his office in his home. Collier picked up the phone, dialed the number and waited, hoping he wasn't too late to divert the doctor from a wild goose chase.

"Doctor Bennett's office..." the woman's voice called to Collier's mind a kindly grandmother from a Norman Rockwell painting.

"Yes, Ma'am, I'm calling to cancel an emergency call...I hope it's not too late..." Collier told as soon as she came on the line.

"Thank you for calling back. The lady didn't leave a phone number. Doctor Bennett wanted to tell her to call the Fire Department or the Police in Blackstone for help transporting him to the hospital on Post at Pickett—the doctor had to go out in the country to deliver a baby..." the grandmotherly woman prattled on.

"Yes, Ma'am...thank you, Ma'am. Everything's alright now, Ma'am..." Collier interrupted as politely and kindly as he could, then he pushed the disconnect button before he dialed the Post telephone exchange operator and asked to be put through to Randy Mullins.

"Relax. I found him, but it's going to take some doing to get him sobered up. I may be not be back until sometime this afternoon," Collier filled Mullins in as soon as he picked up the phone. "Unless you insist, I'm not going to call the MPs or get the Army involved in any way."

"That's fine with me. I don't really want to make a fuss," Randy agreed as Collier heard him gently put the phone back on the cradle.

"I don't understand...we've got to get Jack to a doctor. Who are *you*, anyway?" She stood there in front him clutching her kimono closed across her scrawny bosom while it gaped wide open below, exposing her peroxide-bleached pubic patch.

"The name's Ramsay, Ma'am. I'm an officer from Jack's outfit. We've got to get Jack sober and out of here. If his CO has his way, Jack will wind up in an Army jail. Now, Ma'am, can you please find something else to cover yourself?" Collier turned to the little open closet and started rifling through the hangers looking for a decent robe. Finally, he handed her a quilted housecoat and headed for the kitchen looking for something that would hold water. Finding a rusty bucket beside the back door, he filled it brimming full with water from the sink faucet and marched back to the bedroom and sloshed the entire contents full into Scarborough's open-mouthed, snoring face.

"Oooh...she-e-it! What the fuck!...goddamn!" the naked scarecrow sat bolt upright, coughing and spewing the ice-cold well water in all directions.

"Scarborough, get your filthy, sorry, drunken ass out of bed and into the shower. I'm trying to keep you out of the Post Stockade." Collier held onto the bucket in case he needed a handy weapon and stepped out of range of a sudden counterattack.

"Who the fug-g...the fuck are you?" the sputtering figure on the bed leaned back on his elbows trying to squint through the two red-rimmed slits that passed for his eyes.

"Name's Ramsay. I'm the new platoon leader. Look, Jack, Randy's really pissed this time. He told me to call the MPs and have them take you to the Post Stockade. Get up and get in the shower. We've got to get you sobered up enough to take you home to sleep it off. Now that Randy knows I've found you, I think he might cool off a bit."

"Fuck that. I'm not going home." Scarborough belched and reached down and scratched his balls before he fell back on the sodden mattress and closed his eyes again.

Without further protest, Collier promptly went back into the kitchen, refilled the bucket, marched back into the room and delivered it to Scarborough again in the face, full-force.

"God-d-damn, ma-a-n-n. I'm going to fucking kill your sorry ass!" Sputtering to a sitting position, Scarborough looked wildly around for something to use as a weapon to carry out his threat.

"In the shape you're in, you couldn't kill a day-old kitten. Get up if you don't want another dose of this." Collier turned and headed back to the kitchen.

"Okay, okay wait. Don't do that again. I give up, goddamn it. I've had enough. I'm getting up." When Collier came back with the bucket, Scarborough had managed to come to sitting position on the side of the bed.

"Look, Captain, I've got him up. There's no percentage in getting the MPs in on this. I'll take him home. Can't we find someone to babysit him while he has a chance to sober up? I think he needs medical help..." While Scarborough was in the shower, Collier called Mullins again to keep him up to date.

"Okay...I know a local cop who owes me a favor. Cliff Blackwell's a gorilla—big and tough enough to make Jack behave. I'll call Jack's wife and tell her you're coming. I'll have Cliff waiting there to meet you when you make it to Jack's house. Come on back here as soon as you get Scarborough home." Randy gave Collier directions to Scarborough's house in town.

When Collier finally got back to the Post, Randy told him HQ had assigned him a room in the permanent BOQ and he spent the rest of the afternoon moving his gear and settling in his new quarters. Since Pewter was without transportation, Collier volunteered to lend his hapless friend a hand in moving, too. The so-called permanent BOQ turned out to be somewhat better than the Transient quarters, but neither were anything to stop traffic and brag about.

"You've got to be kidding..." Pewter said when Collier recounted his adventures over dinner at the Post Officers' club.

"C'mon, Collier, have an after-dinner brandy on me," They were standing at the door to the lounge and John Henry tried to steer him back to the bar after they had finished in the dining room.

"No thanks, John Henry. You've got a short memory. We've both had enough alcohol over the past few days to last us for the rest of my life. Tomorrow's a duty day. If you want a ride back to the BOQ with me, come on. I'm heading straight for bed."

"Judaspriest, Ramsay, it's only a little past 1900. It's way too early to go to bed," Pewter protested.

"Sorry, John Henry, I'm bushed. I'm going back, crawl into bed and read awhile before I turn out the light. If you want a ride with me, come on. I'm leaving now."

"Don't worry about a ride. Stay and have a drink with me. I'll drop you at the BOQ when we leave." An attractive woman in civilian clothes who appeared to be in her late-twenties had walked up behind them. Collier had noticed her in the dining room taking dinner alone.

"I'm Collier Ramsay. This is John Henry Pewter. We're both assigned to MRTC training Medical Corpsmen. We just arrived Sunday from Fort Sam." Presented with a godsent target of opportunity to consummate Pewter's carnal initiation, Collier wasted no time in making an introduction.

"I'm pleased to meet you. I'm Fanny Burke. I'm a DAC—Department of the Army Civilian—working in Medical Records at the Post Hospital. My father's in the Diplomatic Corps. He's currently in Germany. My mom and I have a house in Blackstone. She usually eats dinner here with me, but she has a cold and stayed at home tonight. I was just going to have an after-dinner brandy. Please join me. You wouldn't want a lady to have to drink alone." The affable young woman stepped forward and shook hands. "I'll have a Brandy Alexander, Joey. What are you gentlemen drinking?"

"How could we refuse such a nice invitation? I'll have what the lady is having, Joey," Collier addressed the bartender.

"An Alexander will be alright, I guess," Pewter muttered rather reluctantly.

When the bartender finished making the drinks, Collier signed the tab and followed Fanny Burke and John Henry to a table in the far corner of the lounge.

"Here's to the Devil! He's going to have his hands full now that old Joe Stalin is down there shoveling brimstone," Collier raised a toast. On the corner of the small, round table was the March 16 issue of *Time* magazine with Boris Artzybasheff's portrait of the recently-deceased Russian leader rendered in halftones of gray.

"I'll drink to that." Fanny Burke raised her glass, exposing quite a bit of the smooth inner surface of her thighs as she took a seat at the table.

"I just hope Russia under Molotov isn't worse," John Henry reflected soberly, blushing self-consciously and averting his eyes from the gratuitous display of feminine flesh. Ill at ease because she made no effort to shift her position, John Henry picked up the magazine and briefly thumbed through the pages before he placed it back on the table.

"I hope you'll forgive me, I need to find a phone and call my wife," Collier set his glass on the table. He had already called Emma before dinner from the pay phone booth outside Battalion HQ. As soon as Collier rounded the corner and was out of sight, he diverted into the Men's Room and took a leak. After he washed his hands and straightened his tie in the mirror, he headed back to the bar.

"I'm leaving John Henry in your good hands, Miss Burke. See you in the morning, John Henry." Before John Henry could protest, Collier bowed to the lady and left.

At the BOQ, Collier quickly undressed, carefully hung his uniform on hangers, slipped into bed and turned out the light.

Sometime later Collier roused out of his exhausted slumber long enough to hear Pewter enter the BOQ and tiptoe softly down the hall. The luminous hands on Collier's watch showed twenty-five minutes before midnight. Pulling the covers under his chin, he drifted back to sleep, wondering if indeed Pewter had gotten lucky.

"Let's eat at the O Club. That woman, Fanny Burke, kept me up drinking Brandy Alexanders until almost midnight and I'm not anxious for anyone to see me looking like this," Pewter complained he didn't want to be seen at the regular mess hall the next morning in the parking lot. It was only 0600, and they didn't have to report for duty until 0730 hours.

"I take it she gave you a ride back here when you left the club?" Collier asked. Pewter really didn't look nearly as bad as he apparently felt.

"Yeah. I got the distinct feeling she wants me to ask her out."

"What's wrong with that, John Henry? The woman sounded intelligent and she looked pretty good to me," Collier said, exasperated at Pewter's naïveté.

"Well, I don't like aggressive females. I'd like to be the one calling the shots." Pewter protested.

"John Henry, if that woman...any woman...waits for you to take charge, you're going to die a virgin."

"What makes you think you're such an expert, anyway?" Pewter asked, offended by Collier's air of superiority.

"Which one of us is the virgin here?" Collier pointed out, losing patience with his badly hungover friend.

John Paul merely glared at him and changed the subject. "I hope it's cool this morning. My company is going to the range to qualify with the M-1. I'm sweating already. Captain Miller says I have to march with the trainees. He and the other lieutenant are riding in a jeep."

"Quit avoiding the question, John Henry. What's wrong with Fanny Burke? She said she graduated college and seemed to be very pleasant company. What are you looking for, Elizabeth Taylor? The woman may not be Elizabeth Taylor, but she is quite a dish by any standard—she certainly has an outstanding pair of tits."

"I'll thank you to leave Elizabeth Taylor's tits out of this," Pewter snapped. He had a big thing for Elizabeth Taylor. Her new movie *The Girl Who Had Everything* was coming to the Post Theater across from the O Club in a couple of weeks.

"Well...if you're waiting for Marilyn Monroe, then, I wish you luck. Anyway, I'm glad I don't have to march to the range this morning. My company is scheduled for familiarization with the M-1 later this week. Which reminds me, I have to brush up on field stripping an M-1. We didn't spend much time on the M-1 in OCS. The M-2 Carbine was the Artilleryman's weapon. I'm surprised that Medical Corpsmen are given weapons training, anyway. I thought the Geneva Convention forbade Medics to carry weapons?" Collier reflected, surprised at curriculum which constituted a contradiction in the international rules of war.

"I'm going to ask my CO, too. It's not very clear to me." Pewter was relieved at the opportunity to divert the conversation away from his virginity.

"Since when did Medics carry weapons?" At the orderly room, Collier asked Randy.

"We include weapons training during the first eight weeks of Infantry Basic. It's true that Combat Medics don't carry weapons, but sometime around 1948 or '49, the Geneva Convention was amended to clarify the Medical Corpsmen's right and duty to defend himself and his wounded if he should come under fire. Trust me, they throw away the rule book in war. Find Fred and ask him to get you an M-1 from the supply room. While you're at it and have the time, go ahead and brush up on the M-2 Carbine and Colt 45, too..." Randy Mullins agreed it would be a good idea to refamiliarize himself with the standard Army side arms. "While you're at it, ask Fred to give you lesson plans for some of the Combat First Aid courses. Go sit in on Sergeant Alley's classes every chance you get. He's a good instructor and you can get a feel for how to make an effective presentation." The mention of classroom presentations brought an Collier's an uneasy feeling. Public speaking had not exactly been his strong point in OCS.

"Yessir!" Collier saluted and turned to leave.

"No problem, Lieutenant, we can do it right now, if you have time," Sergeant Alley readily agreed to refamiliarize him with the weapons. In practically no time at all, Collier had field stripped and reassembled both the Colt 45 automatic pistol and the M-2 Carbine several times, quickly recalling the step-by-step method he had been taught in Basic and OCS. When he felt comfortable he could do it again with no difficulty, he tackled the M-1 rifle which took considerable more time because only one brief session had been given during OCS.

"I was Artillery and the M-1 is new to me. Would you mind walking me through the routine the trainees have to go through in close order drill and presenting the rifle for inspection?" Collier asked Alley after he felt sure he could assemble and reassemble the weapon with reasonable competence.

"Sure. It's basically the same as you learned with the M2 Carbine. First you have to adjust the sling..." Alley began and coached him as he clumsily familiarized himself by performing the drill maneuvers with the heavy rifle.

"Not bad, Lieutenant, I think you've got it down pat," After about a half-hour, Alley gave him a thumbs up for his effort.

"How much does this monster weigh, anyway?" Collier asked, hefting the heavy rifle from one hand to the other, surprised at how it compared to the smaller M2 Carbine.

"Nine-a-half pounds, Lieutenant," Alley grinned. "That's a real man's piece. That baby saved my life more than once—and the lives of thousands of good men."

"I know that's true, but I can assure you of one thing, Sergeant: for my money, I'll take the M-2. This damn thing weighs a ton and pulling back that bolt is not for sissies," Collier held the weapon in front of him in the manner required for inspection. With some effort he thumbed the powerful bolt open into the locked position.

"It takes a bit of getting used to..." Alley conceded.

"I guess the whole issue is moot. Didn't medics wear white armbands in Korea?" Collier asked.

"Not so's you could notice, Lieutenant. Those red crosses just made a better target for the Gooks." Alley's mouth screwed into a wry grin. "First thing a Corpsman latches onto is a weapon. I carried an M-1 myself. It's more accurate at a distance."

"That may be true, but don't underestimate the Carbine—I qualified Expert at 200 yards."

"Okay, suit yourself. In combat, it's easier for a Corpsman to come by an M-1, but you're an officer. Assistant Battalion Surgeons can latch onto a variety of weapons around the Aid Station.

"What are we telling these trainees about carrying weapons?"

"Well, basically we have to go by the book and tell 'em about the Geneva Convention—then, unofficially we tell 'em the truth. In case you haven't noticed, these men are the bottom of the draft pool—damn near '4-Fs', most of 'em. It's a crime that the Army is drafting them in the first place. It makes me ashamed of the system."

"Oh, come on, Alley, aren't you being too hard on these men?"

"Wait until you've spent a few days with them, sir. You'll see I'm telling you straight. It's a crime to send these poor cripples into combat. You'll see."

"So we're telling them that it's okay for a Medic to bear arms?"

"Not exactly. We're telling them that the Gooks are as likely to shoot them as look at them, and they should take all precautions to protect their asses and the asses of their wounded. I hope you never have to face it, Lieutenant, but the Chinks and North Koreans don't see war as some bloody cricket match."

"Well...forewarned is forearmed. Thanks for the refresher course. If I wind up in Korea, first thing I'll do is find myself an M-2 and a Colt 45. Now, how about finding me those freaking lesson plans?" Collier handed back the heavy rifle.

When they returned to the orderly room, Mullins was just about to leave.

"I'm going up to HQ to see Major Boyce. Apparently as soon as he sobered up enough to drive, Jack Scarborough took off again. I can't get his wife, Charlene, on the phone and no one seems to know where to find him. He's already been reduced in rank. It's a shame to see him wind up his combat record in total disgrace. Hang around here until I get back. We'll need to talk," Mullins confided as he went out the door, striding purposefully toward the street.

Before Mullins was barely out of sight, the company clerk stuck his head in the door and pointed to the phone "It's the Virginia Highway Patrol, sir. They're asking for Captain Mullins, but they said they would talk to you."

"Lieutenant Ramsay, sir, this is Captain Rowell of the Virginia Highway Patrol. I'm calling from the Appomattox Barracks, west of you beyond Farmville." The patrol captain said as soon as Collier identified himself. "We have a man here whose ID says he is First Lieutenant Jack Scarborough, Executive Officer of your company. He asked me to speak to your CO, Captain Mullins?"

"We have a Lieutenant Jack Scarborough. What's the problem, Captain? Maybe I can help?" Collier replied cautiously.

"One of our patrolmen found Lieutenant Scarborough dressed in civvies and passed out cold in a red Ford convertible, parked beside Route 460, just west of Prospect this morning around seven o'clock. The ID in his wallet and the title papers in the car's glove box, confirm the car is his. When we revived him, he was totally incoherent, drunk as a skunk. As a former MP Officer in the last war, I really don't want to bring charges against him—besides, he wasn't actually driving so we can't honestly charge him with a moving violation. We were hoping you could send someone to come pick him up..." the policeman offered hopefully.

"Thanks for your consideration, Captain. I'm sure we can send someone right away. Give me your phone number and I'll call you right back." Collier thanked the policeman and took down the number.

"Randy, we've found Jack..." As soon as Collier hung up, he called Battalion, got Mullins on the phone and gave him the news.

"Hold on a minute..." Mullins said. Collier heard a muffled sound as Randy placed his hand over the speaker of his phone. After a few seconds, Mullins came back on the line, "Stay put, I'll be right there and we'll try to figure something out."

Replacing the phone on the cradle, Collier walked over to the window and saw Mullins walk out of HQ and start down the hill at a half-trot.

"The Major says not to involve the MPs. I sent someone to relieve Carnes from his classroom lecture—it's the last scheduled class of the day. We can't take a jeep or a car from the motor pool; there would be too many questions and this is the Army—there's always the paperwork. Carnes doesn't have a car. Jaynie took our car to Petersburg to shop at the commissary at Fort Lee. I hate to ask, but would you mind using your car to drive us to Appomattox to pick Jack up?"

"No...I don't mind at all," Collier quickly volunteered.

Driving west on 460, Randy filled Collier in, "In Korea, Scarborough was a good soldier. Like me, he was commissioned from sergeant to second lieutenant during the First Battle for Old Baldy last year, the end of June. He was also awarded a Bronze Star. Also, a lot like me, he's from the Kentucky coalfields right up the crick from where I grew up. Jack was promoted again to first lieutenant and awarded a cluster for his Bronze Star after the Fourth Battle for Old Baldy in mid-September. I recommended him for promotion to captain when he got here in November. He was almost a shoo-in to make it as soon as he had a year in grade. I don't want to lay all his troubles on his wife, but Charlene is a real looker, too bad she's a tramp. When Jack came home, he found out she had been making the rounds of the beer joints in Harlan and Hazard while he was in Korea—probably slept with every no-good coal miner's son who'd buy her a beer. Still, he stuck with her and brought her here. Hardly before he reported for duty, he caught her in bed with a mechanic from the local Ford dealership. Next thing he knew, he was finding her shacked up drunk with every Tom, Dick and Harry store clerk, truck driver and farmer's son in Nottaway County. Finally, he gave up chasing around looking for her until she came home Christmas week and gave him the clap. I managed to get them both treated with penicillin as 'urethritis non-venereal' in Petersburg by a civilian doc. That's when Jack started drinking with her to keep her at home. That worked for about a week. Shortly after New Year's she took off again. This time Jack bumped into the slut you met the other day in a local joint. Within less than a month, he was on the sauce as bad or worse than Charlene ever was. You've already seen where he wound up. It's all I've been able to do to keep him out of the Stockade. This is the last straw. If he's lucky, Major Boyce will endorse his request to resign the military under honorable conditions."

"He's in the back sleeping it off. Been out like a light since Corporal Brady brought him in." Upon their arrival at the Appomattox Highway Patrol Barracks, Captain Rowell escorted them back through the front offices of the facility along a hall, briefly repeating what he'd told Collier about finding Scarborough passed out, parked along the highway. When they entered a room at the rear of the building and turned on the light, Scarborough was sprawled on a single metal bed, still passed out cold.

"I really appreciate your discrimination here..." Randy began and briefly thanked the policeman. "Now, what do I need to sign? We'll get him out of here."

"Nothing to sign, Captain. He had pulled completely off the highway and really wasn't violating any law. Follow me and we'll see if we can rouse him and get him on his way. I presume one of you will drive his car back to Pickett?"

"Oh...yeah. I'll take him in back in the Ford," Randy nodded to the policeman and turned to Collier. "If you don't mind, you can follow us to make sure we don't break down in that piece of junk?"

"No Sir, I don't mind," Collier agreed.

With the help of two burly highway patrolmen supporting Scarborough on each side, they half-walked, half-carried him down the hall and out into the parking lot behind the barracks. When they reached the mud-splattered red convertible, Captain Rowell produced the keys and unlocked the passenger-side door, holding it open while his two patrolmen poured the still-limp Scarborough onto the back bench seat.

Back on the highway in heavy late-afternoon traffic, Randy kept Scarborough's Ford just under fifty-five all the way back to Blackstone. Collier pulled in and parked at the curb when they pulled up in front of a modest, gray clapboard house a few blocks off the main drag leading into town. The two of them managed to wrestle the still-limp form out of the car, up on the porch, half-carrying, half-dragging him down the center hall of the rundown shotgun house onto the iron bed in the back bedroom.

"Can you watch him while I see if the phone works?" Randy asked as soon as they dumped Scarborough's corpse-like body onto the bed.

"Sure." Collier nodded, moving a step closer to the bed.

"Okay, I called Major Boyce and filled him in. You can go on back to the Post. Cliff Blackwell is sending over an off-duty deputy to baby-sit Jack until tomorrow morning. Thanks for your help. I hope you'll keep this under your hat." Randy beamed gratitude for action above and beyond the call of duty.

"Keep what under my hat?" Collier laughed and winked.

"I'm missing you very much. What kind of day did you have?" An hour later, feeling somewhat revived by a hot shower and change of uniform, Collier called Emma from the phone booth inside the entrance foyer at the BOQ.

"I went shopping for baby things with your mother. She bought the baby a lot of clothes. For her sake, I hope it's a little girl." Emma laughed.

"Well...I'm not surprised. I know Lida loves Jim and me, but I'm sure she always hoped one or both of us would have been girls..." Collier said, suddenly aware he really was hoping for a son. And, deep in his heart, Collier knew his dad was hoping for a grandson.

"Are you coming home this weekend?" Emma asked.

"No, I couldn't leave Saturday until after inspection. Besides, it's been awhile since I was in Basic. I have too much catching up and settling in to do," he replied.

"I'm disappointed of course, but it's just as well. Some of the girls have asked me to play bridge Saturday night. It's been a long time since we've gotten together. It'll be a lot of fun."

"Good..." he went on chatting about mundane things for a few minutes before he finally interjected, "Look, I hate to go, but I'm at a public phone and there are other people waiting," he lied.

"Will you call tomorrow about the same time?" she asked reluctant to say goodbye.

"I'm not sure. Everything is so new, and we're short one officer here, and I have to use a public payphone. I don't like to use the phone booths in the battalion area. They're too public, besides the phones outside the Service Club should be kept available for the troops. That means I have to use the phone either here at the BOQ or at the O Club," he equivocated, not wanting to establish a habit of nightly phone calls.

"Are you going to call tomorrow night or not?" Emma was getting angry now.

"I can't promise. So let's just forget tomorrow night and Thursday I'll be going over to the Mullins' for dinner. So why not let's leave it that I'll call again Friday night?" he suggested, hoping to calm her down.

"I don't know why you can't find time to call your wife. Does your commanding officer know that we're expecting our firstborn child? Don't those Army people have any children of their own? I can't take laxatives and my hemorrhoids are worse," Emma interrupted, her voice rising near the edge of hysteria now.

"Please, Emma, just calm down. I'm brand new here, and I tried to explain that we're shorthanded. I've already been here two days and haven't even found time to spend with my troops. I'm not even sure what tomorrow's training schedule is like..." he tried to make her understand.

"Have you told them about my retroverted uterus...do they understand I'm in my seventh month?"

"Yes, Emma, I have explained to my CO all about that and he assures me that Major Boyce will grant me an immediate VOCO the minute you call after your water breaks. But I've been trying to explain to you that we're in a real bind here for adequate officer personnel. I can't go whining for special privileges." He did his best to keep the frustration out of his voice. "I'll call again Friday night around 1800 hours—that's six o'clock civilian time. In the meantime, let's both try to figure out a schedule of maybe twice-a-week calls—maybe Tuesday and Thursday or Friday. The weekends I have to stay here, I'll call both Saturday and Sunday unless we have the troops in the field," he did his best to calm her down.

"Twice a week! Is that all you care about your poor pregnant wife and unborn son?" *Now, the baby had magically changed gender in utero!*

"Look, Emma, be fair. We're not the only Army couple who is expecting a baby. I imagine I have several poor draftees right here in the company whose wives are expecting. Do you think they get a chance to go home weekends?" he pleaded, trying to restore an air of calm.

"Don't treat me like a child. You know that's not the same thing...and what's VOCO anyway?" she asked, her voice somewhat calmer now.

"VOCO is military shorthand for Verbal Order of the Commanding Officer. And, no, it's not the same thing as being an enlisted man. I went through the hell of Basic and OCS so I can enjoy the privilege of coming home on occasion during this wonderful time in our life. But I have a duty to perform. I have to share responsibility with my fellow officers. Surely you can understand?" He lowered his voice, hoping to ease the tension in their exchange.

"Oh, Collier, I do understand...but I don't like it. Look, I have to go now. I see some of the girls coming up the drive. I'll talk to you Friday around six. Kisses and hugs!" Cutting short the call, she abruptly hung up the phone.

So much for our cavalier expectant father's lack of responsibility, Collier breathed half-aloud as he replaced the receiver on the cradle.

When he arrived at the O Club a short time later, Collier found John Henry at a small table in the corner of the lounge, having a drink with Fanny Burke. Fanny was wearing a rather form-fitting knit dress. Something told Collier she was not planning to go to church.

"Let me have a draft beer, please," Collier ordered when he walked into the bar. Wade Carnes was sitting on a barstool nursing a beer and chatting up the bartender, Joey Glascock, who was an off-duty corpsman working at the Post Hospital.

"Say, Ramsay, I'm a little short and have a hot date later tonight. Can you spare me a twenty until the eagle shits?"

"Sorry, Lieutenant, I'm a little short myself." Collier was taken aback by Carnes' unseemly request. There was an unwritten rule about borrowing money in the officer corps—particularly from officers junior in rank.

"No problem. Never hurts to ask." Carnes scowled. "At least you could offer to buy me a beer."

"Sure thing. Joey pull Lieutenant Carnes another glass, and put it on my tab," Collier tried to maintain a display of equanimity. It was worth the price of a beer to get rid of Carnes.

"Did you and Sir Galahad Mullins rescue the fair-haired boy again?" Carnes asked with a sneer after the bartender brought him a beer.

"What are you talking about, Lieutenant Carnes?" Collier asked innocently, remembering Randy's instruction to keep Scarborough's latest misadventure on the QT.

"Don't act innocent with me, Ramsay..." Carnes began, but Collier raised his finger to his lips and gave the loudmouth Carnes a sign to button his lip.

"I'm tired, Lieutenant. Let's take one of those chairs in the corner," Collier said, moving across to a grouping of over-stuffed leather easy chairs across the room.

"Why all the mystery? The whole Post knows Charlene's gone again and Jack hauled ass out the main gate in that fucking Ford, looking for her this morning before daylight. Alley told me about the call from the Virginia Highway Patrol. My God, man, everybody here knows Jack Scarborough is a fucking drunk." Carnes shrugged derisively as he took a seat.

"Don't you think it's rather bad form to demean a fellow officer in front of enlisted men or civilians? I'm sure Randy Mullins and Major Boyce would not take kindly to hearing you were bad-mouthing one of the Battalion's officers in the O Club...or anywhere else for that matter." Collier nodded toward Joey behind the bar, then flicked his eyes in the direction of Fanny Burke sitting up near the door with John Henry.

"Bad form? You sound like some fucking Ivy League queer. Look, Ramsay, I don't need you to tell me how to behave. Do you call Mullins and Scarborough officers? Those ex-sergeants stick together; they both were commissioned from the ranks," Carnes sneered, carelessly scattering ashes on the table as he stubbed his cigarette in an ashtray. It was easy to see that he'd already had too much to drink.

"Have it your way, but when Mullins comes on Post tomorrow morning and finds out you've been gossiping company business around in public, I wouldn't look for an endorsement to Captain when your turn comes up." Collier knew Carnes had already been passed over at least once and three strikes were out in any man's Army.

"Two days here and you're already sucking up to Mullins? I should have known you were just an ass-kissing Boy Scout."

"Whatever suits you, but I was just trying to be helpful. If I were you, Lieutenant, I'd be more circumspect. I'm not the only pair of ears around." Collier raised his eyebrows knowingly as he took a tentative sip of his beer.

"If you can't spot me a twenty, how about a ten?" Carnes glowered resentfully.

"Sorry, Lieutenant, I'm near about as broke as you." Collier shrugged.

Was the man so socially-retarded he was totally oblivious his cavalier behavior rendered him persona non grata?

"Well, no sense in hanging around here," Carnes suddenly stood and walked across to where John Henry and Fanny were sitting, without bothering to thank Collier for the beer.

"I wonder if I could see you a moment out in the foyer, Lieutenant. I have a personal matter I'd like to discuss," Carnes interrupted Pewter's private *tête-a-tête* with Fanny without so much as a howdy-do.

Collier sat and watched helplessly as John Henry excused himself and followed Carnes outside the room. Collier wanted desperately to warn Pewter what was coming, but there was no way to stop it now. In less than a minute—certainly no more than two—John Henry came back inside the lounge folding a thin sheaf of bills back into his billfold and tucking the billfold into the hip pocket of his trousers. Suddenly depressed, Collier took one more sip of beer before he set the half-empty pilsner on the table then stood and walked across and left a dollar on the bar for Joey. Nodding goodnight to Pewter and Fanny, Collier headed for the parking lot.

"Hey, I'm glad I caught you. You've got a car—how about a lift into town? Save me a two-dollar cab ride." Carnes stepped out of the shadows of the tattered canvas entrance marquee as Collier walked outside the club.

"Sorry, Wade, maybe some other time, but I'm too tired tonight. I'm way past ready to hit the sack..." Collier politely declined.

"Listen, I might be able to fix you up with some local pussy. My Blackstone regular has a good-looking friend," Carnes persisted in an insolent tone.

"I appreciate the offer, but I'm a married man. Goodnight, Lieutenant. See you in the morning." Offended by Carnes' temerity, Collier kept right on walking without so much as a backward glance.

"Goodnight...*you stuck up SOB*..." Carnes growled resentfully, appending the concluding epithet under his breath, not intended for Collier to hear.

Arriving back at the BOQ, Collier considered briefly calling Randy at home to warn him word was already out about their trip to Appomattox to rescue Scarborough. When he realized how late it was, he decided that morning would be soon enough to bring his CO up to date.

Over breakfast chow, the Wednesday morning paper reported heavy fighting for a series of strategic Korean hills with picturesque names like Old Baldy, T-Bone, Pork Chop, Whitehorse Mountain, Upper and Lower Alligator Jaws and Outpost Vegas and Collier shuddered to think Bo might be caught up in that bloody mess just before he was due to rotate back home. Mullins was waiting in his office when Collier reported back from breakfast, stuffed with pancakes. He filled his CO in on Carnes spreading gossip about Scarborough.

"I've already had Cliff Blackwell's men deliver Scarborough to Major Boyce. Jack'll be well on his way to becoming a full-fledged civilian again before noon chow unless I miss my guess. With any luck, Scarborough will be home helping the Army pack up his possessions before retreat," Mullins quickly brought him up-to-date. "And, Collier, don't worry too much about Carnes. Wade can be something of a malcontent. By the way, Carnes has a bad habit of borrowing money and forgetting to pay it back. He probably owes a few bucks to half of the junior officers on the Post."

Collier started to tell his CO about Carnes' attempt to hit him up for a loan last night at the club, but stopped when he recalled Carnes accusing him of kissing Randy's ass. When he left to oversee his company's reveille formation, he made a mental note to warn Pewter about Carnes' reputation of being a deadbeat.

As his eyes traveled up and down the ranks of raw recruits during the morning formation, Collier was reminded of the substandard state of their physical condition and the sorry future outlook for the caliber of replacement corpsmen in the ranks of the Army Medical Corps. Not only were these poor misfits marginal 4-Fs, but some of them were borderline cripples and spastics.

Later on, after breakfast, when Collier followed his drill instructor, Corporal Farrell, to observe him putting the third platoon through their paces in short-order drill, he stood by aghast as he watched Taylor Jarvis, a particularly inept recruit from Georgia, struggle in vain to pull back and lock the bolt of his M-1 rifle to execute the command: 'Inspection Arms.'

"Have you seen this man, Jarvis? Has anyone told you about him?" Collier asked Randy Mullins at noon in the Battalion Mess.

"Yeah, I've seen him. And, yes, his condition has been brought to my attention. Jarvis is just one of a long line of physically-impaired recruits which represent what the draft boards are sending us these days. We can't play favorites. We can't coddle these borderline cripples. What do you suggest we do about it?" Mullins looked up questioningly from under bushy black eyebrows as he shoved a forkful of green beans into his mouth, washing them down with a swallow of coffee from an oversize Army cup.

"Well...I think Battalion should know about this. Can't we complain to the draft board? How can we certify a man like Jarvis ready for combat? Don't we have some way...any way...to send him home?" Collier was appalled at Mullin's casual acceptance of a clearly unacceptable situation.

"Ease off, Lieutenant. You just got here. Jarvis is by no means the worst of the lot. We have two men in this current bunch missing more than one finger on the same hand and one with a badly-deformed left foot. They all seem to be keeping up with the rest of the company—even a little ahead of some of the luckier ones with all their fingers and toes."

"Are you saying, we have to just stand by and let the Army send men like Jarvis—and these others—into situations where the welfare of fellow soldiers, the welfare of the Army, are endangered by their physical deficiencies? In all good conscience, I don't see how I can do that."

"I don't think you have much choice, Lieutenant," Randy's voice went flat. "In the past, I—and some others among my fellow officers—have tried to send some of the worst cases back to civilian life, but ,believe me, it is probably easier to get the Army to air-condition all the barracks or issue well-scrubbed, clap-free, sorority girls to soldiers on weekend pass."

"Are you saying it's not possible? Or are you telling me it just isn't worth the extra paperwork?" Collier tried to maintain a non-accusatory tone, but he saw Mullins stiffen as he heard the questions.

"I think what I'm saying is a little of both. I've given my best effort in the past to get some of the worst of these cases an honorable medical discharge and been refused even before it got out of Division level. Not a single case made it all the way to the desk of an authority who could make it happen. I'm not one to waste effort on exercises of futility," Mullins took a more conciliatory tone.

"But, Sir, it's criminal what the draft boards are sending us. I wonder how many Congressmen's sons have been drafted—or volunteered or for duty?" Taking a cue from the sudden defensiveness in his CO's body language, Collier reverted to the formal term of address expected from a junior officer.

"Whoa, Lieutenant, you're really skating on thin ice now. As officers in the United States Army, we are at the disposal of the Executive and Legislative Branches." Mullins gave Collier a steely stare; clearly the usually friendly Captain didn't want to pursue the issue.

Although Collier had a world of respect for Mullins—and he didn't exactly consider himself a crusader—in Collier's book, to knowingly put incompetent soldiers in danger of harming themselves or their fellow soldiers was tantamount to dereliction of duty. It was Collier's opinion that dereliction of duty not only constituted a court martial offense, but the offense also exhibited a breech of ethics and exhibited a total lack of personal integrity. He decided to let the subject drop for the moment, but he firmly resolved to quietly explore the administrative avenues open to him to bring about Jarvis' return to civilian status.

"I want to check my mail..." Losing all appetite for the noontime meal, Collier excused himself. Democratically refusing an overeager KP's offer to scrape his tray into the garbage, he performed the soldierly task himself. Reflexively adjusting the visor of his fatigue cap the required two-knuckles above his eyebrow line, he made his way out of the mess hall still bothered by his abrasive encounter with his CO. Stopping to consider if he had time to go by the PX for a candy bar, he was approached by a rather emaciated scarecrow of a soldier.

"Can I have a minute, Lieutenant Ramsay...ah, Collier? Remember me?" the Ichabod Crane look-a-like saluted, nervously addressing Collier in a familiar tone.

"Uhm-m...I'm not sure..." Collier gave the skinny apparition a closer look. The rather forward recruit looked familiar, but for the moment Collier couldn't come up with a name.

"It's Al Stump, Collier...ah, uh...Lieutenant...Sir. It's me, Ram, your brother Jimmy's old classmate from Andrew Lewis and Roanoke College. Remember?" The man pleaded now, growing more anxious by the second.

"Judas Priest, Al. I'm sorry I didn't recognize you. No one told me you were here." Collier did a doubletake as he recognized his brother's old fraternity brother. Intelligent and personable, Al had been a Baptist Orphanage boy. While Collier was away at college, Lida and Harry had practically adopted him. "You look like death warmed over, man. Are you sick?"

"Well...yeah, I have had a run of bad luck. I wound up in the hospital with pneumonia shortly after I got here in November. Then, right after I returned to duty after Christmas, I developed a hernia which kept getting worse and they finally sent me back to the hospital for surgery. After a couple of weeks on the post-surgical ward, they sent me home on three weeks of recuperation leave. I'm right down the street in Company C. We're in our twelfth week of Basic—the third week of training in the medical part of Basic."

"Damn, talk about a run of rotten luck. For godsake, Al, relax. We're old friends." Collier smiled as he reached over and put his hands on Al's shoulders.

Al had remained stiffly at attention, not sure how much familiarity he should assume in public with an officer.

"Well, ah...thanks. It seems so odd having to salute you. Don't get me wrong. I mean I'm not used to talking directly to officers." Al grinned shyly as he relaxed a bit. "This won't get you in trouble, will it?"

"Neah—not at all. But we can't openly fraternize on Post—in or out of uniform. We might have a coke in the PX. But we can't go to a movie or shoot baskets at the gym or anything like that. If you don't have wheels, I could give you a ride back to Roanoke some weekend when we both are free." Collier wracked his brain trying to figure out the complicated protocol regarding fraternization with enlisted personnel. His thoughts flashed back a year, vividly recalling just how lonely and intimidating Basic training could be.

"I'm off most weekends after Saturday inspection. A ride to Roanoke for a weekend at home would be great," his brother's old classmate's face lit up like a white phosphorous flare.

"It's a deal. I'll come find you later. It's far easier for me to make the contacts," he said.

"That would be great. Don't forget. I've got to run. We're going to the firing range this afternoon." Al came to attention and snapped him a sharp salute.

"I won't forget. Just don't fret if I don't make it around for a few days. I just got here this week and won't be going home for a week or two." Collier returned his friend's salute with a broad wink.

"I'll be looking for you." Al turned and took off on the dead run.

Watching the skinny figure double-timing down the company street, Collier resolved to call his parents and to write Jim with the news. Even if he couldn't exactly take Al under his protective wing, his family would be happy to learn Al had a sympathetic friend on this godforsaken outpost.

CHAPTER THIRTY-NINE

THE ROANOKE TIMES
Roanoke, Virginia, Monday, April 13, 1953
HOGAN WINS MASTERS TITLE ON RECORD 274
By HUGH FULLERTON, JR.

AUGUSTA, Ga., April 12 (AP) – Ben Hogan, the little man who has made golf a science instead of a game, won his second Masters Tournament today and broke the tournament record with a 72-hole score of 274.

––––––––––

RISING EARLY SO HE COULD MARCH ALONGSIDE THE COMPANY on the five-mile trek, Collier spent all day Wednesday with the company at the rifle range. Making certain his actions weren't obvious, he roamed up and down the firing line occasionally offering advice and encouragement, all the while making a careful assessment of Taylor Jarvis and the other physically-handicapped trainees with regard to their ability to perform at a level consistent with the more physically-able recruits in the company. Collier was appalled to discover that many of the men who had no outright crippling physical anomalies were such sad specimens of manhood that they really had no business in the military—not even the non-combatant Medical Corps.

It tore the heart right out of Collier to watch Taylor Jarvis have to use both hands in his struggle to pull the bolt back to cock his M-1 rifle. He would liked to film these travesties of the country's draft board so he could show them to the Congress—and to Eisenhower? What would Ike say if *Pathé* and/or *Movietone* newsreels screened this blatant insult to the public trust in the movie houses across the country.

So much for the myth of the superiority of the American war machine.

When he finally dismissed the weary company back at the barracks area, Collier headed to the BOQ more determined than ever he was going to find a way to return poor Taylor Jarvis to civilian life with an *honorable* medical discharge. Observing the sorry assortment of physical misfits at the range today had been the final straw. Freeing Taylor Jarvis had now become a holy crusade.

Arriving late for dinner at the O Club, Collier's mood brightened momentarily when he found Pewter in the lounge deep in conversation with Fanny Burke. Miss Burke was looking better all the time.

"Come join us." Pewter waved him over. Collier nodded as he went to the bar and asked Joey to pull him a glass of beer.

"I'm bushed. How was your day?" Collier asked trying to make conversation as he took a seat at their table. While standing at the bar he had picked up the new edition of the *ArmyTimes* and was idly flipping through the pages, scanning the latest list of published orders.

"I can save you the trouble. I already looked. We're not on the list. That means we're safe until October at least," Pewter said, reminding Collier unnecessarily that overseas orders were usually—but not always—published at least six months in advance.

"There goes your chance to win the Medal of Honor," Collier winked at Fanny, who returned his wink with a sly smile.

"I think I'll head on back. I'm dead on my feet and tomorrow's another killing day," Collier said, suddenly exhausted.

"I'd like a ride back to the BOQ," John Henry spoke up as Collier got to his feet to leave. He said goodnight to Fanny and quickly fell in behind Collier as he headed for the parking lot. It also seemed obvious that John Henry had made no progress in that direction. It was no wonder John Henry was still a virgin at twenty-four. The man was hopeless—an utter disgrace to himself, the United States Army and to his fellow countrymen.

Classroom training, drill, PT, infiltration course, field exercises, the confidence course, overnight bivouac, and the weapons ranges; Collier's schedule was jam-packed with the dawn-to-dusk duties of overseeing the functions of putting the company through the rigorous schedule of Basic Training.

Lately he had become obsessed with the widespread, flagrant draft board violations regarding the physical capablilty of the men they were drafting to serve in the military. Now, he was spending virtually every minute of his spare time researching the complicated and complex formal procedures involved in getting a *bona fide* medical discharge for Taylor Jarvis—despite the fact that leaving the military was clearly against the physically-handicapped soldier's wishes.

"But I don't want to get out of the Army. I'm already working to improve the strength in my hands. Bring me an M-1. I'll show you. I've already learned to pull open the bolt," the unhappy recruit protested. It soon became evident to Collier that being drafted into the Army represented the high point in the life of this youth who probably had spent his life up until now being the butt of his schoolmates' and fellow-workers' ridicule.

"But, Jarvis, you don't understand. The government never should have drafted you in the first place. What will you do in combat? You aren't physically able to keep up with your platoon in our field marches over this flat Virginia terrain. How do you expect to keep up with your outfit climbing over the rugged Korean mountain slopes? You can't complete the confidence course. You have yet to do one successful chin-up on the bar. To certify you as fit and send you to a combat outfit would not only put you—but would also put your fellow-soldiers— at grave risk," Collier tried to reason with him.

"Couldn't you assign me to a supply unit or an aide station...anything? I do okay in things like that," the eager misfit pleaded, his heart about to break.

"Jarvis, I only wish I could transplant your courage and enthusiasm into the rest of this goof-off outfit, but I can't in good conscience let the Army keep you in the military." Collier remained firm, despite his understanding of the soldier's need to cling to the only glimpse of manhood and self-esteem he had ever had.

"Neither Major Boyce nor I am happy you insist on going through with this charade. I told you that I, and some of the other company commanders, have tried to get medical discharges for other trainees—some worse off than Jarvis, even—and the process is just too burdensome...too complicated really. Don't forget you are questioning the integrity of the local draft board system. That opens up a political can of worms no one would ever get the lid back on," Randy protested when Collier asked if he could take Taylor Jarvis to the base hospital for a complete physical to support his request for the physically-impaired recruit's release from duty.

"I'm not afraid to take on Jarvis's draft board. My daddy served on the local draft board during World War Two. As for politics, my father has had a longtime affiliation with the infamous Virginia 'Byrd Machine.' If push comes to shove, I might even get my father to contact the Congressmen from Jarvis's home district in Georgia."

"For godsake, Ramsay, you can't be serious. Back off. Leave your daddy and politics out of this—it's overkill. We're soldiers. According to the Constitution, we're at the service of the President—our Commander-in-Chief. At our level, politics and the military are like oil and water. I've already talked to Major Boyce. Go ahead and get Jarvis a physical at the hospital. Both the Major and I will endorse your request if Jarvis's physical comes back judging him unfit for duty. But let that be the end of it. Now will you please get out of here?" Randy gave in.

"What's going on down there? Will I see you again before our baby comes?" Emma's whining increased every time he called. While his conflicting dread of impending fatherhood continued, Collier felt guilty that he hadn't been able to get away.

"Of course. I'm doing the best I can, but we're short one officer and I had to pull OD last weekend. I'll try to come Saturday after next...providing something doesn't come up here to prevent it." Finally, Collier agreed to drive back to Roanoke on April 18 following Saturday inspection. He had already been gone nearly three weeks. On the positive side of the ledger, *The Army Times* still had not published any orders sending him, or John Henry, to FECOM—or, for that matter, EURCOM either. With every passing day, the outlook seemed better and better that neither he nor Pewter would be sent overseas.

"Collier, you poor boy, you're skinny as a rail. The Army must be starving you to death." Emma's corpulent mother was of the same school as his Grandma Boyd when it came to feeding her menfolk. After wolfing down two, Dagwood-sized double-decker sandwiches, Collier made small talk while Emma's mother put away the food and cleaned up the mess. Finally, he excused himself and went up to bed.

In the morning, he had no memory of Emma coming to bed, as he had overslept and the women had left for church. Leaving a note reminding Emma he was going to visit his folks awhile and would be back to say "goodbye" shortly after lunch, Collier headed out.

"Your mom and dad just got back from Sunday School. They wanted to say goodbye, so they didn't stay for preaching. They're inside fixing us some sandwiches to take with us." At his parent's house, Collier found Al sitting on the porch with his AWOL bag packed, reading the Sunday *Roanoke Times*.

"Next time you come home, I wish you'd go to church with us," Lida said when Collier walked into the kitchen. Harry was just wrapping the last of a half-dozen big ham-and-cheese and chicken-and-cheese sandwiches in wax paper, preparing to stuff them in a brown paper bag with two man-sized slices of pecan pie.

"Well, maybe. But you know Emma is always after me to go to church with her. I can't please everyone," Collier hedged, not wanting to make a commitment.

"We saw Jenny Bohon at Sunday School. She said Bo was scheduled to leave Korea around the first of June. She expected him home by the middle of the month," his father interjected before his mother could start an argument about religion. Lida was overly-concerned about his immortal soul.

"Well, that is good news. Thanks for the sandwiches. Al and I will make quick work of them. Army chow's okay, but there's nothing like your homemade Dagwood sandwiches. I'm sorry, but we've got to run. I've got to get Al back to his outfit before his pass runs out." Collier gave his dad a tap on the shoulder and his mother a kiss and a hug.

By the time he arrived back at Mother Lowell's, it was already past 1300 hours, and Collier left Al sitting in the car while he went in to say goodbye to Emma.

"My, God, Collier, you only just got here." Emma was not in a happy mood.

"Be fair, Emma. Did you expect me to just sit here and twiddle my thumbs while you and your mother went off to church?" Collier stood his ground.

"We were only gone a little over an hour," Emma pouted, not in a reasonable mood. "Why don't you invite your brother's friend in? At least you can stay and chat for a few minutes. It's almost May. Our baby's due...it could come almost anytime now. Will I see you again before the baby comes?"

"Look, I'm sorry, Babe. I'm running late. I've got a lot to do when I get back to Pickett. I'm not certain when I'll get back home. Could be next week or not at all, depends on my CO's need for me. I'm low man on the totem pole. I'll call tonight after I get back. It was wonderful being home, even for such a short time." Giving her a hug and a kiss, Collier headed to the car before she could protest again.

Monday morning, Collier had a cadre NCO take Taylor Jarvis to the post hospital for a complete physical after he had flunked his second repeat of the standard PT test. Not only couldn't the poor devil do a chin-up on the bar, he couldn't do even one sit-up; Jarvis' performance on the confidence course continued to be so abysmal the cadre were actually afraid he might badly hurt himself.

When the perfunctory medical report came back Wednesday morning certifying Jarvis for duty, Collier headed out to the hospital with blood in his eye.

"This man can't even do one push-up...he can't pull back the bolt of his rifle with one hand; even with his glasses he's borderline legally blind. How can you certify him fit for duty?" Not unlike the recent inductees he had taught to drill in San Antonio, the young physician was a Captain, most likely a draftee from some cushy urban practice.

"Well, I have no choice. His heart and lungs are okay, and he really doesn't have any measurable neurological anomalies we can find," the young Medical Officer stammered. He was somewhat intimidated that his judgment was being questioned by a real-live soldier, no matter his junior as an officer.

"Begging your pardon, Captain. I am this man's platoon leader. As a commissioned officer sworn to uphold the Constitution of the United States of America, I cannot in good conscience certify this man for duty. Did you or any Medical Officer with a *bona fide* M.D. personally examine this man?" Keeping in mind his Grandpa Boyd's pithy advice, '*You can catch more flies with sugar than you can with shit,*' Collier tried his best to keep the anger out of his voice.

"Well, I listened to his chest and..." the young Captain began, but Collier interrupted.

"Certainly, as a Medical Officer, you must be aghast at the condition of the human misfits the draft boards are sending us? Do you understand that I'm putting through the paperwork for a medical discharge for this recruit? My father is a big-time, mad-dog, Byrd Democrat and fairly frothing at the mouth because

Ike won the election. If Jarvis' discharge doesn't go through, I'm going to write my congressman and stir up all kinds of stink. You better be ready to answer to your CO why all this shit came down on him."

"Well, look now, you can't just come in here and badger me into changing my medical opinion like that...I...ah..."

"Okay, don't say I didn't give you a chance. By the way, my battalion CO is aware of the purpose of my visit here and who I came to see," Collier lied glibly. "I have nothing against you personally, Sir, and I appreciate what you're up against. It's the draft board's fault, but they won't take the heat. I only hope you're ready when the shit hits the fan. Thank you for your time, Captain. Have a good day...unless you've made other plans..." Oozing contempt, Collier's voice bordered close to insubordination as he saluted and started off without waiting for his salute to be returned.

"Wait up, Lieutenant...can we go into my office? Tell me what I need to do..." The Captain suddenly changed his tune, almost pleading now.

That afternoon, following his regular duties overseeing A Company's training, Collier showed the amended medical report to Randy, requesting permission to hand-carry it to Battalion to 'unofficially' bring it to the attention of Major Boyce before initiating the formal paperwork requesting an honorable medical discharge for Private Taylor Jarvis as being physically unsuitable for military duty.

"You know I don't like this. Why do you always want to rock the boat?" Randy said, handing back the amended medical report following a cursory look.

"Because it's the right thing to do, Randy—it's really just as simple as that," Collier said as his unhappy CO handed back the folder containing the papers.

"You know I had to tell Major Boyce. He's not happy about this. He likes you. I like you. Both the Major and I have been using our influence to keep you out of the pipeline to FECOM. Is this the way you want to thank us?"

"You know better than that. This is about integrity and good conscience. I cannot sleep well knowing we might send Taylor Jarvis into a combat situation. Frankly, it pisses me off to think those smug bastards on the draft board back in Georgia would send someone like Jarvis to the Army. If I thought I could find the clout to raise a public stink about this, I'd send copies of this medical with an anonymous letter to *The Washington Post* and *The New York Times* in tomorrow's mail."

"Now look..." Randy began, coming quickly to a standing position behind his desk.

"Don't worry. I'm not a crusader...at least not *that* much of a crusader." Collier held up his hand.

"Thank God for that, at least!" A look of relief passed over Mullin's face as he sat back down.

Collier stood there waiting, uncertain was coming next. The situation was bad enough as it was, he didn't want to keep Major Boyce waiting.

"Alright, get on out of here; don't keep Boyce waiting." Randy finally waved him out.

"The Major is expecting you." At HQ, the First Sergeant ushered Collier toward the door to Boyce's office. Walking along, the First Sergeant whispered, "Don't be too long with this. The major's wife has been calling every fifteen minutes. They are expected at the Colonel's house for cocktails. They are going to the O Club at Fort Lee for dinner."

"You know you have the entire MRTC command upset. For both our sakes, I don't suppose I can talk you out of this?" The Major returned Collier's salute and took the folder containing Jarvis' amended physical without opening it.

"No, Sir. Frankly, Sir, I don't know why everyone is so upset. It's the right thing to do. To tell the truth, Jarvis is only the tip of the iceberg in this mess."

"For godsake, Lieutenant, don't tell me you're thinking of doing this again for some of the other men?"

"No, Sir, I am mightily ashamed to say I'm not. But I should. In my company alone, there are at least two men missing fingers on their trigger hands. My friends among the junior officers in the other companies report cases of their own just as bad or worse. How can the Army justify this unacceptable shoddiness in the induction process?"

"If it gives you any comfort, Lieutenant, all of my company commanders have raised this question many times and have made the same requests, and I have bucked those upstairs with my endorsement without results. Draft boards are strictly a civilian function. That means strictly political. When it comes to politics, no one in the Pentagon wants to rock the boat."

The statement was rhetorical; Collier continued to look the major in the eye.

"If I might be so bold to ask, what do you plan to do if this crusade on Private Jarvis' behalf fizzles out somewhere along the chain of command?"

"I hope that doesn't happen, Sir."

"Randy Mullins says you have made copies of all of this. He says you threatened to take it to the Washington and New York papers. Do you know that copying official military documents is a court martial offense? Besides that sounds a lot like blackmail to me." Boyce looked him directly in the eye, trying his best to stare him down.

Collier returned the Major's stare with an open look. Finally, the Major dropped his gaze to the folder on the desk in front of him. "If I endorse this, then do I have your word this is the end of your war with the draft system?" Major Boyce opened the folder and took out his fountain pen.

"Yes, Sir. If Jarvis receives an honorable medical right away, you have my word," Collier agreed, fervently hoping his voice wouldn't betray his sense of relief.

"Also, I hope you haven't seen fit to talk too much about this with Lieutenant Pewter or Skyar or any of the other junior officers in the Battalion. I wouldn't want this to become some sort of sacred crusade." The Major's fountain pen remained uncapped.

"No, Sir. There has been some occasional talk about the shocking physical anomalies that are passing the draft board physicals, but I haven't mentioned my efforts to send Jarvis home with anyone outside of Captain Mullins. As you already know, he discouraged me, but wouldn't actually forbid me to try to get Jarvis released. Pewter is my friend, but he knows nothing about my efforts on Jarvis' behalf. As for Carnes, he's in A company, but we aren't confidants. Besides..."—Collier added sheepishly, a blush creeping up his neck—"I didn't want to risk giving them the same idea and reducing my chances of succeeding on Jarvis' behalf."

"Alright, I'll sign and send it on tonight." Trying mightily to conceal his smile at Collier's confession, Boyce lowered his head and uncapped his pen.

"Thank you, Sir." Collier snapped to attention and saluted, waiting to be dismissed.

"One more thing, Ramsay. Have you read much from Ralph Waldo Emerson?"

"No, sir, I'm not much of an intellectual. Except for required reading in college, I'm afraid most of my reading is limited to fiction. Why do you ask?" Collier asked, still waiting for Boyce to return his salute.

"Emerson once advised, *'Always do what you're afraid to do.'* My instructor taught me that at VMI, and I always thought it was good advice for a young officer faced with the daunting responsibility of leading men. Just between the two of us, I feel compelled to tell you Captain Mullins and I both admire your courage in seeing this through. It takes a lot of guts for a young officer to buck the system." Boyce tested his fountain pen on a scrap of paper and endorsed Collier's request for Taylor Jarvis' honorable medical discharge from active duty. When he finished, he recapped his pen and replaced it in the inside pocket of his Eisenhower jacket. That done, he finally returned Collier's salute.

"Hop in." Leaving the HQ parking lot, Collier pulled to the edge of the street and picked up Pewter and Carnes, trudging along MRTC Road toward the BOQ.

"Have you seen the latest *Army Times?*" Pewter asked as soon as he and Carnes were in the car. He was holding a copy of the April 25 issue of the tabloid paper in his hand.

"No...am I in there? Are you telling me I have orders to FECOM?" Collier croaked, his stomach suddenly filled with butterflies the size of C-124s.

"No, not you. Me. And Flood and Skyar and Battaglia and several more who came here with us from San Antone. I...we...leave Pickett in June for twenty-one days leave before we have to report to Fort Lewis, Washington for shipping to Yokohama." Pewter tried mightily to keep the disappointment out of his voice. They both had been almost positive the Pentagon had passed over them.

"You sure I'm not in there, too?" Collier couldn't believe all of his fellow MFSS grads were being shipped overseas and not him.

"I'm sure. Congratulations." Pewter said, struggling to keep his voice light. He had unfolded the newspaper and was looking for the right page.

"How about Robertson? Or Paul Golden Price? Were they on the list?" Brewster Robertson was another Fort Sill OCS classmate and Price had graduated Benning OCS. They both were fellow MFSS grads who had come here on the same orders which brought them all to Pickett.

"Yes, here's Price. But, Robertson isn't on the list," Pewter said. He had located the page and handed the tabloid to Collier so he could see for himself.

"Have you eaten supper, yet?" Collier asked after he had confirmed for himself that he was not on the Orders list. Curiously, he felt left out; yet, at the same time, he felt relieved. Now all signs pointed to his staying in the States, but he knew he wasn't completely out of the woods.

"Yeah, I had a bite at Battalion mess. Liver and onions, not my favorite," Pewter said, making an awful face in the rearview mirror.

"Me either. I'm going to clean up and head for the O Club. Why don't you come along? A ribeye steak sounds good to me," Carnes volunteered.

"Not me," Pewter said. Lately Pewter had been studiously avoiding the O Club. Fanny Burke had been breathing hot and heavy down his neck, trying to get him to take her out.

"Count me out. I'm too tired. I may just have cheese and crackers in my room." Hardly able to contain his excitement over Boyce endorsing Jarvis' papers for medical discharge, Collier pulled into the BOQ parking lot and lagged behind until Carnes disappeared through the door.

"It's early. I really don't have any intention of eating cheese and crackers. I just wanted to get away from Carnes. As soon as we shower and change, let's motor into the O Club at Fort Lee for a couple of beers and a decent meal. It'll help ease the pain of your orders to FECOM." Collier gave Pewter and little pat on the shoulder.

"Sounds good to me. We can celebrate your dodging the bullet—kill two birds with one stone. I'll be ready in three-zero minutes," Pewter said, heading for his room.

At Fort Lee, there was no sign of Cathy and Julie Rush in either the dining room or the bar. Over dinner, Collier caught a glimpse of Major Boyce and Colonel Miller with their wives across the dining room. So much for hope of a chance encounter with a potential target for Pewter's defloration; it certainly wouldn't do for Major Boyce and the Colonel to see him, a married man with a pregnant wife at home, trying to pick up loose females in the Fort Lee Officers' club.

"I've got a hellacious day tomorrow. I don't want to spend half the night cruising beer joints in Colonial Heights looking for some boozy sluts. Let's call it an early night and go home," Collier said after they had finished eating an exceptional steak.

"It's fine with me," Pewter readily agreed.

"We got another problem off the Post. This time it's not Scarborough." Randy hit him with the news the first thing when he walked into the company orderly room Wednesday morning. "Charles Sullivan, one of the trainees, is AWOL. He wasn't here for last night's bed check. You might know he's one of those Seventh Day Adventist or Jehovah's Witness COs." At Pickett, CO was military shorthand for Conscientious Objectors, as well as Commanding Officer. "It's bad enough we have to try to teach these self-styled Pacifists they might have to bear arms—even kill. Word has it among Sullivan's barracks' mates his wife followed him here and is living somewhere just outside of town. We've got to try to find this eight-ball before the MPs get involved and he winds up a suicide in the Post Stockade." Randy's eyes rolled heavenward at the thought.

"Do any of his buddies know where this house is?" Collier asked, dreading he was elected to go on another wild goose chase.

"Yeah, one of Sullivan's bunkmates, Quentin Thomas's, wife is living in the same house with Sullivan's wife. Dadgum it! We warn 'em not to let their wives come here. Why won't they listen?" Randy exploded.

"No sense in cussing...just give me directions how to find the place. We're wasting time." Collier struggled to keep a straight face, Randy almost never swore or used strong language of any kind.

"Get with Alley. He'll fill you in. I guess I'd better call Major Boyce and put him on alert. If you run into trouble, give me a call." His disgruntled CO was already picking up the phone.

Driving down Blackstone's main drag, using notes he made from talking with Sergeant Alley, Collier checked street signs until he found 8th Street, then turned right toward West Entrance Road. At the fifth intersection he turned right again at Ridge Road into an area of rundown houses and followed the badly-paved road which quickly petered out, leaving him traveling on a mostly-uninhabited, narrow two-lane. After his odometer showed he had traveled almost a mile, the road took a sharp turn almost due south and he slowed as he approached a pair of rusty RFD mailboxes marking the entrance to a lane, again on the right. Standing about a hundred yards off the road in a field of tangled, unmown weeds, was a dilapidated cinderblock house with large patches of shingles missing from its roof and the small front stoop sagging sharply to the left, supported against falling completely down by a stack of broken cinderblocks. With cardboard taped over several broken window panes, this sad relic had never been more than borderline livable, and now it tottered on the brink of complete collapse. Cautiously, Collier turned in and found a place to turn the Studebaker around so he could make a fast getaway if the situation turned ugly.

"If you're looking for Charlie-Earl and Gladdie, they ain't here," wearing a cheap, badly-worn blue-chenille bathrobe which spoke volumes about a young life marked by all kinds of luck—mostly bad—a sleepy-eyed, young colored girl with two badly-discolored, rotten front teeth, cautiously pulled and scraped open the front door, sagging from one broken hinge.

"Where are they? I need to find Private Sullivan before he winds up in more trouble than he is already in."

"I swore I wouldn't tell, but I hope you can catch him and talk some sense into him. Gladdie's knocked up, and Charlie-Earl says he's taking her home to West Virginia. Irma Thomas, the other girl, took them into Blackstone to catch the bus. I tried to tell 'em they were making a big mistake, but they wouldn't listen." Old long before her time, the young black woman crossed her arms in a pose of self-righteous indignation.

"How long have they been gone? What kind of car does Mrs. Thomas drive?" Collier asked. It was already past 0930. He wanted to catch up to the misguided couple before he wound up having to call Trailways or Greyhound and have them stop the bus.

"Not more'n a half-hour. Irma drives a light-blue 1949 Ford with South Carolina plates—the right taillight missing. They weren't in no particular hurry. The bus don't leave 'til ten." The woman probed the missing spaces around her rotten front teeth with her tongue.

Pulling to the curb in front of the one-horse bus station beside the town sundry drugstore, Collier relaxed when he saw the blue Ford with the broken taillight parked several doors down the street. He quickly left his car, walked the half-block back to the bus station and went inside. The place smelled faintly of human sweat and cigarette smoke mixed with the odor of a pine-scented cleaning solvent, underscoring a pervasive and resigned air of ultimate decay. Without having to look, Collier was certain the walls of the restroom were decorated with hand-penned graffiti, mostly of an obscene and pornographic nature. With a small barred ticket window on the far wall, the tiny waiting room had a half-dozen heavy oak benches with brass spittoons placed conveniently at each end. Collier exhaled a long sigh of relief when he saw the soldier he recognized as Sullivan standing with two women beside a bench near the center of the waiting room. When they looked up and saw him, one of the women detached herself from Sullivan and the other woman and, eyes averted, hurried past him out the door leading to the street. Collier was certain the woman was Irma Thomas, Quentin Thomas's wife.

"Take it easy, Sullivan. I'm not here to cause you trouble. Besides, there's no place in this godforsaken county to run and hide," Collier soothed the harried young soldier who was attired in his military khaki trousers with a cheap, white dress shirt carelessly stuffed into the tops of his pants.

"Stop...I've got a gun," Sullivan warned dramatically and Collier pulled up short when he saw the man's right hand was holding something under a raincoat draped across his arm.

"Don't be a fool, Sullivan. Trust me; I'll wait until you put your wife on the bus. Then we'll go back to the Company. Use your head. Four more weeks in Basic won't be nearly half as bad as three years in the Post Stockade." Out of the corner of his eye, Collier saw the big Greyhound pulling into the boarding lot behind the station.

"You'll never take me alive," the desperate soldier's voice trembled with false bravado, but Collier could see the defeated man was weighing the consequences of what he'd said.

"Don't be a fool. What good will you do your wife and baby, if you kill yourself?"

Sullivan's shoulders slumped, as the realization he was in a no-win situation hit home.

"Come on, man. My wife is pregnant, too. She's back home in Roanoke. Our baby's due next month," Collier held out his hand for the gun.

"Will you let me wait 'til Gladdie's on the bus?" Sullivan looked down at the skinny woman with the swollen belly sitting on the bench.

"Sure...I'll even give her eating money for the trip," Collier glanced down at what looked like a grease-stained bag of food sitting beside the woman's handbag on the bench.

"He's right, Charlie-Earl. Take the deal before you wind up messing up our lives." The young woman's face brightened at his offer. She gave him a hopeful look.

"You sure?" Sullivan gave his self-righteous wife a pleading look.

"Sure, I'm sure. What good will it do either of us if you wind up in jail?"

A story as old as Adam and Eve—the woman always putting the blame on the man.

"Okay, Sullivan, let's have the gun before I change my mind." Collier took a step forward and extended his hand.

"I ain't really got no gun. I ain't that big a fool." Sullivan blushed, unfolding the raincoat from his arm.

"You're not nearly as smart as you think. You threatened me by saying you had a gun. These folk here are witnesses. That alone is enough to send you away for awhile." Collier nodded at several waiting passengers sitting on nearby benches. He was teetering near the end of his patience; this shit-for-brains redneck was very hard to feel sorry for.

"That's your word against mine. Besides I ain't really AWOL. I'm just late getting back from a pass." The feckless trainee was clutching at straws.

"Come on, Sullivan. Today's Wednesday. You've been back from weekend pass for two days already. Give it up, soldier. Sit down here and say goodbye to your wife. Where were you...where is *she*...going, by the way?" He asked.

"Beckley. We live in Crab Orchard, a couple of miles south of town. We change busses in Roanoke and Bluefield. It's a twelve-hour trip altogether. I took the very same route coming down," the dull-eyed young woman, interjected, anxious to be part of the equation.

"Give me one of those tickets, and I'll see if I can't get your money back," Collier took one of the tickets from Sullivan's reluctant grasp and started toward the ticket window across the small waiting room.

He had only taken a few steps in the direction of the ticket window, when he noticed the magazine stand adjoining the ticket office. He stopped, turned back to face them and asked the woman, "While I'm at it, what kind of candy do you like? I'll get you a couple of candy bars and a banana or an apple to eat on the bus. Can I get you a magazine or a book to read?"

"I'd like a Payday bar and a Hershey with Almonds, if that ain't too much. I ain't particularly fond of apples or bananas...or any other fruit, so don't waste your money on any of that. If they've got the new issue of *Photoplay* or *True Romances*, I'll take either one. What I'd really like is a pack of Chesterfields and some Wrigley's gum. Don't waste your money on none of them boring books." The woman rolled her eyes at the thought of actually reading a book. Upon closer examination, her lipstick was slightly smeared and she reeked of cheap perfume. Wearing a castoff print dress several sizes too large for her as a maternity dress which could have walked right off the pages of a WWII-vintage Montgomery Ward catalog, on her feet, she wore a pair of dirty-white, off-brand, high-top tennis shoes.

The old man at the ticket window frowned as wordlessly he reluctantly counted out the money for the refund. Moving across to the magazine stand, Collier selected three Payday bars and three Hershey's with Almonds, several packets of cheese-and-peanut butter crackers, a couple packets of chocolate cookies, a pack of Wrigley's Juicy Fruit chewing gum and a pack of Chesterfield cigarettes. As a final gesture, he picked up the latest issue of Photoplay magazine before he paid the gum-chewing woman behind the counter with money from his own pocket. He waited while she rang up the sale and put the items in a Kraft paper bag. He came back across the room and handed the empty-headed, slack-jawed young female the bag.

"Here, this should more than cover your meals until you get back to Beckley." Collier peeled a twenty from the small fold of paper money he carried in his pocket.

Then he turned to Sullivan and handed him the money for the ticket refund. To their credit—and very much to Collier's surprise—they both thanked him.

"Never mind thanking me, just thank your lucky stars I'm cutting you a break. If I find out you've spread the word about this to the rest of the company, I promise you'll regret it the rest of your life," Collier warned them somewhat sheepishly, more than a little embarrassed to be playing the role of Good Samaritan when he rightfully should be sending the feebleminded jerk to the Post Stockade. Dreading the bus might be running late, Collier took a seat on the bench across from the parting couple and prepared to wait.

He had hardly seated himself when he was pleasantly surprised to see a Greyhound motor coach pulling into the parking lot out back of the building. The squawky loudspeaker announced the arrival of the Richmond to Roanoke Greyhound with a caution that the bus would be departing as soon as it had unloaded and loaded luggage of the arriving and departing passengers. The announcer made it clear the bus would not be dallying overlong at the station.

"Okay, you heard the man; we best be getting your wife on the bus," Collier arose and hurried the couple out to the boarding area and waited while they said their goodbyes. When she was finally aboard, Collier allowed Sullivan to wait and wave a final farewell as the bus pulled out of the lot.

"Okay, Sullivan, let's head back to our home-sweet-home. You can change back into uniform and have noon chow before you rejoin your buddies in the classroom after lunch." Collier herded the glum recruit out to the Studebaker parked nearby. On the drive back, Collier quizzed Sullivan about Quentin Thomas's wife, the third woman who had been sharing the shack with Gladdie and Irma.

"Her name is Savannah Mae Jones. She's the wife of Cordell Jones, one of them niggers in Company B. I'm sure glad we ain't got that problem to contend with in Company A," Sullivan made a face; obviously he had a low opinion of Negroes. Collier ignored the remark. He had no intention of engaging this borderline mentally-retarded hillbilly on the issue of white supremacy.

"I just got back. Sullivan is in his barracks getting into uniform. Make sure he rejoins the company after chow," Collier told Alley as he walked into Randy's office to give him a full report.

"We're lucky. I caught them just in time. I could still be out on 460 halfway to Lynchburg trying to catch that bus," Collier said, quickly bringing his CO up to date, but leaving out the part about buying the wife snacks and giving her money for food.

"Isn't Private Thomas' wife still out there at that shack? Don't you think somebody ought to go send *her* back to wherever she came from?" Randy asked.

"I don't know how we can do that. Unfortunately, it's still a free country. She can do what she wants. We can't make her leave." Collier shook his head.

"Who is the other woman? You said there were three," Randy asked, concerned their troubles were not over in this matter.

Collier repeated Sullivan's information about the wife of the Negro in Pewter's outfit next door, repeating Sullivan's remark about being glad there were no coloreds in their outfit.

"Well, I can't say I hold that against him. We've got enough trouble trying to make soldiers out of these trailer-trash whites. Okay, that's enough excitement for one day; let's get back to work." Randy shrugged, turning back to the report on the desk in front of him. Deciding that telling Randy about the respect he had for his black cubiclemates in OCS would serve no useful purpose, Collier quietly excused himself and headed out to grab a bite of lunch at Battalion Mess.

"I have good news and bad news," Randy greeted Collier as he walked into his office just before 0600 hours. He had planned to ask Randy if he wanted to join him for breakfast in the Battalion mess. The look on his CO's face alerted Collier that the bad news was worse than the good news was going to be good.

"Bad news, first," Collier said, bracing braced himself.

"Charles Sullivan is gone again. Quentin Thomas's wife said Sullivan's wife went back to West Virginia and came back yesterday driving a beat-up Ford. Her stupid husband missed bed check last night. This time, when we find him, he's going to Post Stockade." Randy tried to remain calm, but from his expression, Collier knew he was serious.

"Okay. What's the good news...or do I have to wait until we find Sullivan and lock him up?" Collier asked, hoping to lighten the tension in the room.

"Stop being such a smartass. The good news is your request for Taylor Jarvis's medical discharge came through. We can let him go as soon as we make sure he has transportation back to Bumfuck, Georgia." Randy's leathery face broke into a smile.

"His daddy said if the discharge came through, the family would come and pick him up. I have the family phone number right here." Collier located the number at the bottom of the stack of papers on his clipboard.

"Okay. I guess we should call him over and give him the good news. He can start packing his gear and we can process him to clear the Post anytime. But, in the meantime, we gotta find Sullivan. We never should have cut him a break in the first place. I think we best just call the MPs and turn him over to them. His cretinoid wife has a car. No telling where they are by now."

"I have a hunch, at this early hour, Private Charles Sullivan is still logging Zs. He's about as lazy as he is dumb. Why don't I just jump in my car and go check in town? It may save the Army the trouble of a wild goose chase."

"Okay. But if he isn't there, don't waste time trying to track him down. That's what the MPs are for. Be back here before 0900. Carnes called in sick." Randy made a face. Collier felt certain Carnes had a hangover. Although he was ashamed to admit it even to himself, when he searched the latest orders in *The ArmyTimes*, Collier kept an eye out for Carnes' name, hoping to see that the asshole was shipping out.

"I'm glad I found you, Sullivan. Hop in." Approaching the shack Sullivan's wife had been sharing with Thomas's wife and the other woman, miracle of miracles, Collier encountered Sullivan walking disconsolately along the country road dressed for duty.

"Please don't hand me over to the MPs, Lieutenant Ramsay, sir. I told my wife to head back to West Virginia this morning. I was coming back to the Post as fast as I could." The downhearted soldier gave him a desperate look.

"Relax, Sullivan. It's all I can do not to plant a kiss on your stupid forehead. I'll take you straight to the mess hall. We both could use some chow." Collier was forced to laugh when he saw the surprised look on Sullivan's face. Clearly the man was sure he had suddenly gone stark raving mad.

After returning Sullivan to duty, Collier stopped by the BOQ before he went back to MRTC and found Carnes' waiting. "I saw you pull up. Can I borrow your car for about an hour this morning while you're with the troops? I have to go to town to take care of some important personal business," Carnes request took Collier by such surprise he really couldn't think of a reason to refuse. Silently berating himself for giving in, while he waited for Carnes to get his gear and lock his room, Collier jotted down the mileage on the odometer on the back of a calling card and slipped it inside the pocket of his blouse.

"The tank is full. I filled it up this morning. Park it in the HQ lot when you bring it back. Don't be late. I want it back by lunch time to go into town," Collier lied. Watching the oily lieutenant drive off in his car, Collier had a sharp pang of ill-boding and regret, but the feelings quickly dissipated as he was caught up in the morning's activities running the company through yet another strenuous encounter with the Confidence Course.

After lunch, any concerns about his car were overshadowed by Collier's anxiety at having to deliver his first classroom lecture on "Sucking Chest Wounds." Considering that the tired soldiers had full bellies and were always fighting to stay awake in after-lunch classroom sessions, the lecture went okay. Thank God he had found a good, 25-minute, training film on the subject. The film was filled with graphic images of actual combat wounds with an accompanying loud soundtrack—all of which helped rescue him from his ineptitude and inexperience as a classroom presenter. Following a desultory, post-lecture Q & A, Collier dismissed the class and gathered his materials, heading back to the orderly room.

"Where's your car?" John Henry asked.

"Damned if I know!" Collier exclaimed when he realized that the Studebaker was nowhere in sight. After a moment, it dawned on him that he had loaned the car to Carnes. But that had been this morning—seven or eight hours ago. At the time Carnes took it, he had assured him he would only need it for an hour or so.

"Has anyone seen my car—or heard from Carnes?" Collier asked both the CQ in the company orderly room and the duty sergeant at Battalion.

"I can assure you your car has not been outside my window all day. I remember wondering this afternoon if you might have taken it off Post on some errand." Major Boyce overheard the exchange with Battalion Duty NCO and volunteered the information as he was leaving Battalion HQ for the day. Collier's regular parking spot was clearly visible just underneath the Battalion CO's window, an unlucky quirk of fate which irked Collier no end, since he found it impossible to sneak away from the MRTC area during duty hours without the Major taking notice.

"Have you called the gatehouse yet? They keep a detailed record of all vehicles coming on or off the Post," Boyce suggested and pointed to the phone on the desk.

"I hadn't thought that far ahead. Thank you, Sir." Collier picked up the phone and dialed. When the duty sergeant at the gate came on the line he checked the log. "We have a notation of Carnes taking the car out this morning, but there is no record of him bringing the car back on Post," the duty sergeant said.

"Call the other gate at West Entrance Road, just in case," the Major suggested after Collier hung up.

Collier dialed West Entrance gatehouse with no luck. Except for the single exit entry of his leaving this morning, neither gatehouse had seen any more of Carnes or the car all day. After calls to the BOQ and the O Club failed to locate anyone who had seen or heard from the missing Carnes, Collier left word at both the company and the BOQ, and he and John Henry hitched a ride with a passing officer from D company and went to the O Club, ordered a beer and entered the dining room. The clock over the bar showed 1925 hours. Carnes had kept his car all day. Collier couldn't decide whether he was more worried than he was highly pissed.

"Did Wade pay you back the money he borrowed yet?" Collier asked Pewter, more than a little frustrated over Carnes failure to return his car.

"No, as a matter of fact, he hasn't. We've been so busy, I haven't had time to give it much thought." Pewter frowned.

"I wanted to warn you. Randy Mullins told me not to loan Wade money. He has a bad reputation for not remembering his debts," Collier said, sipping on his beer.

"You think you should call the town cops or the Virginia Highway Patrol to check and see if there have been any accidents?" Pewter asked.

"Wouldn't hurt, I guess. While I'm at it, I'll call the MPs, too. Just in case." Collier took his beer and headed for the bar.

"No luck. I guess I should be relieved that my car hasn't been wrecked." When he came back a few minutes later Collier brought Pewter a fresh beer and sat down and shook his head. "I should be ashamed to admit it, but I'm getting so pissed at Wade, I don't really care whether he might have been hurt in an accident."

"Don't feel bad. Wade definitely isn't exactly Mr. Congeniality," Pewter said as he thanked Collier for the beer.

"Well, long time—no see." So preoccupied with anxiety over his missing car, Collier had not considered they might find Fanny Burke in the lounge after dinner.

"Hello, Fanny. Yeah, it has been awhile. How have you been?" Collier asked, distractedly. He left Pewter talking to Fanny and headed for the phone sitting idle at the far end of the bar.

"Still no luck," Collier said as he rejoined Pewter and Fanny who had taken seats at a table in the lounge.

"Fanny says she thought she saw your Studebaker parked in front of a local beer joint on the outskirts of town as she came back on Post tonight," Pewter informed Collier as he approached their table.

"Are you sure it was my car? Nowadays, there are a lot of Studebakers around," Collier asked, holding his breath, trying not to get his hopes up.

"I'm not positive, but I think it's worth checking out. I went to high school with the owner of that joint. I'll give him a call. There's a local directory up on the bar." Fanny had already risen and was heading toward the bar.

"Wait. If you call, just ask your friend if Wade's still there. If he is, I don't want him to know we're on to him. I'll get a cab to take me out there. I certainly don't want Wade Carnes driving my car if he's been drinking all afternoon." Collier followed Fanny toward the phone.

"Don't be silly. If Carnes is still out there, I'll take you. No need to call a cab." Fanny was already thumbing through the book. "Here it is," she grunted. In no time she had dialed a number and was speaking in low tones to someone on the other end.

"I was right. Carnes has been there all afternoon with some local floozy. My friend says to hurry; he'll hold Wade there as long as he can if he tries to leave. Come on, my car's parked outside." She nodded toward the door.

Sure enough when Fanny pulled into the parking lot of the roadside joint which had once been a filling station, Collier was relieved to find his Studebaker at the far side of the wooden structure, sitting off to itself.

"Wait up. I'll go inside with you to get the keys," Pewter said, not sure if Carnes would make a scene when Collier confronted him.

"I'm not going inside. I have an extra set of keys. First, let me make sure the car is okay." Collier headed straight to the car, slowly circling it, examining it for dents or scratches. It only took a few seconds for both men to ascertain that the car was apparently unscathed on the outside.

"Do you want to ride back with me or Fanny?"

"You," John Henry answered without hesitation; he was clearly gun-shy when it came to being alone with Fanny.

"Okay, wait here while I go thank Fanny. I'm going back to the BOQ. Should I tell Fanny you're coming back to the O Club?"

"No. I'll go back to the BOQ with you," Pewter said. He waited until Collier had thanked Fanny, before he crawled into the passenger's seat. When Collier started the car and turned on the headlights, the lights on the instrument panel showed the needle on the Fuel indicator was sitting close to Empty. A quick glance at the odometer showed the car had been driven 259 miles since Carnes had taken it that morning.

"Aren't you going to tell Wade you're taking the car?" Pewter laughed, considering the consequences of Carnes coming outside to find the borrowed car gone.

"Fuck Wade Carnes!" Collier gratefully patted the steering wheel as he pulled out on 460, following Fanny's car back toward the east gate of the Post.

"What did Fanny say? Is she going back to the O Club?" Pewter asked. John Henry clearly had developed a fly and spider, love-hate, fascination for the predatory Fanny.

"Yeah, but first she's going to follow us while I park my car out of sight in the hospital parking lot and give us a lift back to the BOQ. It's early yet. After that, she said she thought she'd go back and wait awhile at the O Club. She doesn't want to miss the show if Carnes shows up wondering what happened to the Studebaker. Too bad we can't be flies on the wall. I can hardly wait to hear what Wade is going to say when he finally has to tell me he lost my car." Collier laughed out loud, contemplating the seriousness of Carnes' predicament.

"On second thought, suddenly I'm not all that tired. I think I'll just ride to the Club with Fanny. If he shows up, I'm anxious to see what Carnes has to say for himself. I'm sure he'll be out of his mind, wondering what happened to the car." Pewter laughed out loud.

When he had parked the car at the hospital and Fanny had dropped him back at the BOQ, Collier bid Fanny and Pewter goodnight and went to his room and stripped out of his duty uniform. After a long, hot shower, he fell, exhausted, into bed.

"He didn't mention my missing car?" Collier asked John Henry the next morning shortly after 0600, walking along MRTC Road toward the Battalion mess for an early breakfast. It seemed incredible to Collier that Carnes had shown no sign of concern when he finally showed up at the O Club the previous evening. Apparently, he had taken a taxi back from town when he left the beer joint and discovered Collier's car missing.

"Not a word. As far as Fanny and I could tell, you would have thought he didn't have a care in the world. It's a darn good thing he didn't have your car to drive. He was pretty unsteady on his feet." Pewter gave Collier a knowing look.

"Well I can hardly wait to see what he has to say about my car when he shows up for duty this morning—if he shows up for duty. He may not have the balls," Collier mused aloud, considering Carnes' disreputable reputation.

"Good morning. It's a beautiful day." Holding a copy of the day's training schedule, Carnes greeted Collier when he walked in the orderly room at 0745 from breakfast at Battalion mess. Carnes seemed remarkably unperturbed.

"Good morning, Wade." Holding his breath waiting to see what Carnes had to say about the car, Collier went over to his mail tray and began sorting through the usual stack of memos, bulletins, and various Army communications. After a few minutes, Carnes walked inside to his desk without saying another word.

"Wait up, Wade. I need my car. Where did you park it, if I might be so bold as to ask?" Infuriated by Carnes' act of innocent nonchalance, Collier could wait no longer before he confronted the dispicable SOB.

"Your car?" Wade shrugged in exaggerated innocence. "I left your car in the Battalion parking lot when I brought it back yesterday morning just like you said. It only took me an hour to complete my errand in town." Carnes' look was worthy of an Academy Award.

"Save your lies for someone else, Wade. The staff at Battalion said the car never showed up back there all day."

"Oh, that's ridiculous. Those miserable goof-offs are lying to protect their sorry asses. Check the gate on MRTC road. They keep a log of every vehicle going and coming on and off the Post. They'll have a record of my leaving and coming back." Carnes shrugged again, determined to defend his innocence to the bitter end.

"I've already checked, Wade. The only notation in their log is when you left yesterday morning heading off the Post. There's no record of your coming back on Post," Collier confronted him.

"I can't believe they would fail to log my return, but I have to admit I never pay attention to whether or not the guard on duty makes a notation on the sheet. It's not my responsibility to oversee Post security." Carnes' voice showed contempt, but not a lot of concern.

"Well, it's your responsibility to return my car to me. You said you'd leave the keys with First Sergeant Alley. He said he didn't see you all day yesterday. Where did you leave the keys?" Collier was having difficulty remaining calm.

"Oh...yeah. I guess I did forget to leave the keys. I was feeling sort of punk. I called in sick and it slipped my mind. Here are the keys, anyway." Carnes reached into his trouser pocket and handed back the ring with the spare key. Unaware that he was digging himself deeper into his own devious artifice, Carnes continued to show no outward sign of concern.

"You must have made a speedy recovery," Collier said.

"Why? What do you mean by that?" Carnes said, suddenly on guard.

"Where were you last night around eighteen-hundred hours?" Collier asked, boring in.

"Uhm-m? I'm not sure. The BOQ I guess. I stayed in bed most all day. Finally went to the O Club last night to grab a burger and a beer. Ask your buddy Pewter. He can tell you about what time I showed up there." Sensing Collier knew something he wasn't telling him, Carnes was showing signs of nervousness now.

"You weren't at the BOQ. Unless you were playing possum and wouldn't answer your door."

"Well...I'm not sure. I may have gone to the PX for some aspirin or something. I was feeling kinda rough. I made it to the O Club later on. The dining room was closed. I don't know what time it was." Carnes continued to hedge.

"Yeah, Pewter told me you showed up last night after twenty-two hundred."

"Uhm-m. Well, I don't know what to tell you about your car. If I were you, I'd report it stolen to the MPs." Carnes shrugged.

"Last time I saw it, you were in it and driving down MRTC road. The last record of anyone driving it is on the log at the guard house on MRTC Road. If anyone reports it stolen, I think it should be you." Collier said.

"Not me. It's your car. I brought it back." Carnes was getting defensive now.

"You have no proof of that."

"Well...I...ah. I want to talk to those assholes at the Gate where I came back in."

"That's a waste of time, Wade. Why don't you just tell me the truth. What did you do with my car? Witnesses at the O Club say you were pretty sloshed last night. Did you park it somewhere and forget where you left it? Is it wrecked in some ditch somewhere?"

"Look, lay off me about that car. I brought it back and left it in HQ parking lot. End of story."

"Okay, then I guess that leaves me no choice but to have to call the MPs and the law in town and report you stole it." Collier walked over and picked up the phone on the company clerk's desk.

"Report I stole it? Just wait a cotton-picking minute!" Carnes yelped.

"You heard me, Wade. You're the last one who had it and the record clearly shows you took it off Post and failed to bring it back. What do you think the MPs will make of that?"

"Look, you can't frame me for losing your goddamn car. I won't stand still for that." Carnes blustered.

"I don't think you have much choice, Wade. Now come clean, where's my car?"

"Look, Ramsay, I already told you. I brought your car back and left it at Battalion like you said. I gave you your keys. End of story."

"You know, Wade, you're such a liar and a deadbeat, I hate even standing in the same room with you. I'm not going on with this little game. I have my car. I found it just outside Blackstone last night and drove it back on Post myself. You had that car all day and put two-hundred-fifty-nine miles on it. Where in hell did you take it, anyway?" Suddenly tired of the entire charade, Collier decided to quit sparing and fire for effect.

"You mean you found your car in Blackstone last night? Two-hundred and fifty-nine miles? Well, I certainly don't know anything about that."

"Come on, Wade, you gotta do better than that. You took my car off Post yesterday morning and it didn't come back. I have an airtight case. Now are you going to come clean or not? Do you want me to let the MPs ask the questions?" Collier was running out of patience. When he began the confrontation, he had thought only to get an admission of the truth from the miserable SOB, but now he was beginning to consider the idea of bringing charges against the lying bastard.

"Oh. Well, I guess I did have it, alright. I was afraid to tell you it got stolen while I was parked in Blackstone yesterday. I just kept hoping it would turn up. From the mileage you say it was driven, it looks like some kids must have taken it joyriding."

"Come on, Wade, quit lying. Give it up. We—Pewter and Fanny and I—saw you in that joint sucking down beer with some floozy when we found the car parked outside last night. I got witnesses. I've got you dead to rights."

"You're mistaken. I was in the BOQ all evening until I went to the O Club later on looking to get a beer and a burger. Ask your asshole buddy, Pewter. He was there with Fanny Burke, that stuck-up Blackstone bitch who works at the hospital."

"Oh, I know you were at the O Club. They already told me. It just so happens that those two were with me earlier when we spotted my car at that dive outside Blackstone. They both saw you in that joint before I drove my car back on Post. Look here, Wade, you—or someone you know—drove my car a total of

259 miles after I handed you the keys yesterday morning, thinking you were going to town and coming straight back here. That car was in your possession last night just after dinner time at that sleazy beer joint. I think you owe me an explanation...and also an apology for standing here lying like a cur," Collier said evenly, trying to hold back his rising anger.

"Carnes, I need you to take this paperwork up to Major Boyce at Battalion. Wait 'til he signs it and bring it back here to me. And don't' dawdle." When Collier looked up, Randy Mullins was framed in the doorway of his office holding a large, brown envelope.

"Yessir, right away." Obviously grateful for the opportunity to get off the hot seat, Carnes took the envelope and headed out the door.

"Come inside a minute, Collier, and close the door. We need to talk," Mullins said and went back inside his office. Collier followed, closed the door behind them and stood at Parade Rest in front of Mullin's desk, uncertain as to what his CO had on his mind.

"Pull up that chair and take a load off. I couldn't help but hear your conversation with Wade Carnes. There's something I think you should know." Mullins picked up a pack of Chesterfields, extending them in Collier's direction. Collier shook his head and pulled out a pack of Luckies and lit one of his own.

"What's that, Sir?" Collier exhaled the first drag of the Lucky. He was aware Mullins and Carnes had a history of service together that went back a ways, but he was not in a forgiving mood.

"Carnes is reluctant to tell you about his activities yesterday because they involve a very personal situation which is embarrassing, not only to him, but also involves someone very close to him." Randy gave him a searching look before he continued.

"So?..." Collier's voice dripped sarcasm, not at all in a forgiving mood.

"So? So, do you want to hear this or do you want to be a smartass?"

"Look, Randy...ah...Sir...that deadbeat borrowed my car under false pretenses yesterday morning using the excuse he was going to run an errand into town. Then he kept it all day, running up two-hundred-fifty-some odd miles on the odometer. If I hadn't stumbled onto the fact it was parked outside of Fred's beer joint last night and gone out there and driven it back on Post myself, there's no telling where the car—or your fine Lieutenant Wade Carnes—would be this morning." The words came ripping out like machine gun fire.

"Okay, okay. I gathered that was the case and I'm not trying to excuse the man. Wade is not exactly well-thought of..."

"Well-thought of! The man is a godd... Wade Carnes is a gosh-darned deadbeat and a liar." Collier stopped short of cursing. Randy Mullins was not given to profanity and didn't tolerate its use in others.

"Just calm down, Ramsay. I'm not trying to argue that Carnes is a shining example of what an officer in the Army should be. But we can't always judge the world in black and white."

Taking another deep drag on his cigarette, Collier made no reply.

"I don't intend to excuse him, but Carnes took your automobile to Richmond yesterday morning, to Saint Luke's Hospital. He went to give blood to make up for transfusions that had already been given to a patient there. Those original transfusions actually saved a woman's life."

"Gave blood to a patient in Richmond? Who is this woman anyway? I thought Carnes was from somewhere up in...ah...the coal fields, somewhere near your neck of the woods?" Collier was having a hard time connecting Carnes with such a redeeming act.

"That's right. Wade grew up in Harlan. I guess you have a right to know. The woman was Beverly Scarborough—Jack's wife. Beverly is Carnes' first cousin on his mama's side."

"Beverly Scarborough? I thought they went back to Kentucky several weeks ago." Now, Collier was thoroughly confused.

"No. She...they...didn't go back to Kentucky. As a matter of fact, this is all quite in confidence, but Jack is in a private sanitarium for alcoholics in Richmond."

"Oh...but what happened to Beverly? I don't understand." Collier's thoughts were buzzing around inside his head like a swarm of bees.

"If you have to know, Beverly almost bled to death from a botched abortion. I don't know much about the details, but apparently she was in her fourth month—much too far along for even a respectable surgeon to perform." Mullins sadly shook his head and stubbed out his cigarette.

"Well? Why did Carnes keep the car all day..." Collier let the question trail off, trying to put himself in Carnes' shoes.

"Carnes is Carnes. Don't waste time trying to figure that out. Besides, what would you have said yesterday morning if he had asked you to borrow your car so he could go to Richmond to give a transfusion?" Randy spread his hands on his desk and gave Collier a knowing look.

"I get your point." Thinking it over, Collier shrugged.

"I'd appreciate your not telling Wade you're on to him. He doesn't know I know. Jaynie's cousin back home told her what was going on."

"Your secret's safe. But, now what do I say to Wade?" Collier's anger bubbled up again.

"Why not just tell him not to ask you for any favors ever again and let it go at that. Why beat a dead horse? There are always going to be the Carneses in this world. We might as well write them under the heading of: Lessons learned the hard way." Randy leaned back in his chair, assuming a contemplative pose.

"I'm not in a very philosophical mood. It's hard for me to see Carnes as some sort of saint. That deadbeat SOB owes everyone on Post but me. He owes Pewter twenty bucks."

"So? What the hell? Don't lend him any more money or cars. Some of our best lessons are learned the hard way. Surely you must know that by now. Why don't you head out and join the cadre marching the company to the Confidence Course? Give you the chance to cool off a bit before you run into Carnes again." Randy stood and waved him out the door, then called to his back before he left the room. "Wait. Major Boyce wants to see both of us at HQ at zero-niner-forty-five hours. I'll send the HQ Jeep to the Confidence Course to fetch you."

"Major Boyce? Do you have any idea what that's all about?" Collier asked. He didn't like the sound of being summoned to HQ. The only thing he could think of that Boyce might possibly want to talk to him about was his request for a Medical Discharge for Taylor Jarvis.

"The Major didn't say. But look out for that Jeep. I'll send it a little early. I don't want to be one second late with Boyce." Randy gave him a knowing look.

Too late to march alongside the company, when Collier arrived at the Confidence Course, a sister company from MRTC had arrived ahead of them and their lieutenant had already started his training cadre running the trainees through the obstacles. The men from B Company stood At Ease waiting their turn at the entrance to the Course. A hundred yards or so down the collecting area at the entrance to the course, an OD-painted staff car was parked. The Lieutenant Colonel standing beside it occupied himself looking through a powerful pair of field glasses at the troops running the various manmade obstacles on the difficult course.

"Collier Ramsay, Baker Company." Collier didn't recognize the other lieutenant or the enlisted cadre ahead of them and walked just inside the entrance to the Course to introduce himself. Instead of saluting, Collier merely extended his hand.

"Bob Shane, Dog Company. Just down the block. I've only been here a week," his counterpart said, shaking Collier's hand. Then he added, "The last of our men are about to start. Your men won't have to wait very long."

"Thanks. Who's the brass in the staff car?" Collier nodded in the direction of the light colonel with the binoculars.

"I don't have a clue. His driver brought him here about fifteen minutes ago. Some sort of official observer from the look of him. My guess would be that he may be from the IG's office," Shane observed.

"You may be right. Best be on our Ps & Qs." Collier winked and checked his fatigues to make certain his blouse was buttoned properly.

"Yeah, right," Shane grinned, reflexively following Collier's example. "Nice meeting you, Ramsay. Go ahead and tell your staff they can start their men through anytime they're ready. Dog Company is already coming out the other side."

"Thanks. See you around." This time Collier saluted and Shane returned the salute, both self-conscious that they might be under the scrutiny of the mysterious colonel. But when Collier looked back again, the colonel had gotten back into the staff car and his driver was pulling out of the parking area.

Mullins was as good as his word. The Jeep arrived at the entrance to the Confidence Course at 0915 and Randy was waiting at the foot of the steps leading up to Major Boyce's office when Collier arrived back at HQ. Collier felt a wave of apprehension rising in his gut. The OD Chevy staff car was parked in the Visitor slot underneath Boyce's office window.

"Come in, Captain Mullins...Lieutenant Ramsay. I would like to introduce you to Colonel Baxter Luce. The colonel drove down last night from *Washington*." Major Boyce stepped forward, ushered them into his office and introduced the officer Collier had seen earlier at the Confidence Course. The insignia on the collar of his meticulously-starched fatigues was a fancy gold sword and fasces crossed and also wreathed in gold metal—the impressive insignia of the Office of the Army's Inspector General Division.

"Have a seat, gentlemen, and smoke if you like. Before we get started, can I have Sergeant Gentry get anyone coffee or a soda?" Boyce asked, pointing to a small circle of straight-back chairs arranged in the center of the room. The effect was intended to be relaxing and friendly, but Major Boyce was obviously up tight.

"I'll have coffee...black," the no-nonsense Colonel said.

"Sounds good. I'll have the same," Randy agreed, trying his best to seem at ease.

"I'll have a Coke if you have it," Collier chimed in. He knew Sergeant Gentry kept a well-stocked cooler of soft drinks always at the ready and his throat was suddenly dry. His sphincter had also screwed down to pinhole-size.

They all hung back until the Colonel had moved inside the circle of chairs and taken a seat, placing his slender briefcase on the table. Randy waited, following Boyce as he took the chair beside the colonel. Collier followed and took the seat beside Randy, directly across from the unsmiling IG colonel.

"Let's get right down to business. I'll turn the floor over to Colonel Luce. He has to drive back to Washington immediately after lunch," Boyce began after the coffee and Coke had been served and the NCOs had politely backed out of the room. Collier looked away when he caught the colonel glaring directly in his direction, focusing instead on a shower of dust motes filtering through a bright ray of sunlight on the back of the colonel's slick-shaven head. When Collier finally got the courage to look back to the colonel, he had taken a manila folder from his briefcase and was in the process of spreading it open in front of him.

"Yesterday morning about this time, my superiors at the Pentagon called me and a few other high-ranking staff officers in to discuss this request for a medical discharge for one of your trainees, a Private Taylor Jarvis. Your name—your signature, actually—is prominently displayed as being the initiating officer, Lieutenant Ramsay. Is that correct?" Wasting no time in getting to the case at hand, Colonel Luce held up a thin sheaf of papers Collier assumed was a copy of his request for Jarvis' medical discharge.

"It is, Sir. I mean, I am the initiating officer in this action. If you're here to question the validity of this action, I suggest we get Private Taylor Jarvis up here so you can meet him and see his physical condition for yourself," Collier replied, his voice dripping self-righteous sincerity.

"Hold on, Lieutenant, give me a chance to explain before you get your ammo wet. This isn't really about blocking your request to relieve Private Jarvis from active duty; it's much more far-reaching than that."

"I don't quite understand, Sir." Now Collier was completely confused. If this bad-ass Colonel wasn't here to block Jarvis's medical discharge, then why had he driven all the way down from the Pentagon? What was this freaking inquisition all about?

"Perhaps I should have explained. At the beginning, your request would most likely never have come under the scrutiny of the Pentagon—most certainly not this promptly, anyway—had it not been brought to our attention by a Congressman, actually a senior...very senior...United States Senator. He was quite upset. Now you can see why I was sent down here with such dispatch."

Collier watched as Randy Mullins and Major Boyce nodded as if they were in complete understanding. Did that mean he was right in his assessment the Colonel was here to block Jarvis's release from duty?

"No, Sir, Colonel Luce, I'm thoroughly confused. Are you saying that the U.S. Senate is pressuring the Army to block my request for Taylor Jarvis's discharge?" Collier felt his anger rising. Who did these high and mighty bastards think they were?

"No, not that. I assure you my compatriots and superiors at the Pentagon are eager to see Private Jarvis returned safely home as a civilian in good standing with a bona fide Medical Discharge. Our cause for concern, the reason for the high-ranking Senator's cause for concern, is that this incident goes no farther. There have already been requests to several congressmen from some of Jarvis's fellow trainees with similar physical...uh...anomalies to intervene on their behalves. We want to take steps to stop this mass uprising before we are under the curl of a tidal wave of public and political scrutiny questioning the policy of lowering the usual physical requirements to draft borderline draftees into the Medical Corps. Can't you see what a Pandora's Box that would open up?" The Colonel leaned forward pugnaciously.

"So? What are you saying? You're here to make sure these men don't contact their congressmen back home?" Before he had begun his crusade to get Jarvis out of the military, Collier told Randy he was considering using his father's longtime political affiliation with the Byrd Machine to contact their own Congressmen from the district back home on Jarvis's behalf. But Randy had advised him it was overkill.

"No, Lieutenant, of course not. This is a free country. Being in the military doesn't take away our constitutional rights. I just want to find out what your plans are now that you've opened up this can of worms." The Colonel picked up the folder and gave it a significant look.

"Although, frankly, I am ashamed to admit I'm not going to, I have no plans to intervene on the behalf of any other of these poor devils. God help me—God help us all," Collier said.

"I'm much relieved to hear that, Lieutenant. If there is nothing else then, we have no further business here." Colonel Luce replaced the papers in the folder and the folder in his briefcase and stood erect.

"That's all, Ramsay. You're free to return to the company. Wait around, I want to have a word with you when I get back." Randy looked to Boyce for a tacit agreement, before he waved Collier out the door.

Collier stood and saluted and waited until each of the brass returned his salute. Leaving the room, he could feel the tension in the air. These men were actually afraid of him.

"Taylor Jarvis' folks are up at HQ with Major Boyce. They're here to take Jarvis back to Georgia. For his sake, I think you should take Jarvis up there to meet them. Maybe take them all to lunch before we see him off. That boy is heartbroken about having to leave the Army. Too bad we don't have more that feel that way," Randy said when he returned to the orderly room.

"I'll go get him. He asked if he could wear his uniform, this one last time. I told him it was okay." Collier looked to Mullins for approval and he nodded.

It was all Collier could do not to break down and bawl when he finally waved goodbye to Taylor Jarvis and his family as they drove away shortly after lunch. The physically-impaired recruit had struggled mightily not to show his disappointment when Collier finally gave him a hug and watched him climb under the steering wheel of the family station wagon. His father let him take the wheel as a token of confidence—a loving father's gesture to restore his son's failing self-esteem.

CHAPTER FORTY

THE ROANOKE TIMES
Roanoke, Virginia, Tuesday, May 3, 1953
WARSHIPS RIP INTO ENEMY'S COAST TOWNS
SEOUL, Tuesday, May 5 (AP) - Six United States warships ripped
Communist lines with heavy shell fire Monday around the Korean East
Coast towns of Kojo and Kosong. Marine fliers from the carrier Bataan
in the Yellow Sea plowed up the west coast with bombs.

Vol. 9, No. 124   Tuesday, May 5, 1953
HEMINGWAY, AP WRITER WIN PULITZER PRIZES
NEW YORK, May 5 (AP) - The Pulitzer Prize for fiction for 1953 was
awarded to Ernest Hemingway today for his "The Old Man and the
Sea."

* * * * *

THE WHITEVILLE (N.C.) News Reporter and the Tabor City (N.C.)
Tribune shared the award for meritorious public service for campaigns
against the Ku Klux Klan which resulted in the conviction of more than
100 Klansman, INS reported. They are the first weekly newspapers ever
to earn the Pulitzer prize.

REDS' THAILAND DRIVE ADDING NEW THREAT
HANOI, Indochina, May 5 (UP) - Vietminh Communist invaders
stabbed towards the Thailand (Siam) border today adding a new threat
to Franco-Loatian defenders already battling against the Reds in the
Indochina state of Laos.

MARKING THE BEGINNING of Emma's ninth month, May Day—Friday, May
1—came and went without any signs of the baby coming. Tuesday, May 5, dawned
bright and clear, bringing Collier renewed dedication to the holy crusade of
ridding John Henry Pewter of his unwholesome virginity before his naïve
compatriot left Pickett in early June for a three-week route-delay furlough at home
in Ohio prior to shipping out for FECOM.

Although it meant Collier would most likely remain stateside for the duration
of his Army commitment to enjoy his rapidly-approaching fatherhood, Collier
found it difficult to feel good about being passed over for assignment to FECOM.
News of renewed fighting in Korea only served to heighten his sense of guilt for
being excluded from accompanying Pewter and his other fellow officers to Korea.

Then to further deepen Collier's sense of discontent, there were the morning
headlines about Hemingway winning the coveted Pulitzer Prize for—of all things—
The Old Man and the Sea.

"I cannot believe they gave Hemingway the prize for that dumb story.
What's the freaking modern literary world coming to, anyway?" Collier grumbled

to Pewter over breakfast in the Battalion Mess. Pewter—who had studied English and American Literature at a small Ohio liberal arts college—ventured no opinion about the Pulitzer.

"Lieutenant Ramsay, Sir, Captain Mullins wants you back at the orderly room right away. He said it's important." One of the trainees rushed over and saluted, all out of breath.

"Your father called. Your wife is in labor at Lewis-Gale Hospital in Roanoke," Randy told him, reading the name of the hospital from a scrap of paper on his desk. "I already called Major Boyce and you are officially on three-day VOCO; that plus the upcoming weekend will give you five days. Be back here Monday. Get moving man; maybe you can make it to Roanoke before you're officially a daddy. Call me later after the dust settles, and don't come back here without cigars for all the officers in the MRTC."

"Well...I..." rendered speechless by the news, Collier stood frozen in his tracks. VOCO was Army lingo for Verbal Orders of the Commanding Officer.

"Well, what? Don't just stand there—get moving man. And don't forget to check your gas tank. You sure don't want to run out of gas in the boonies somewhere between Lynchburg and Bedford. Don't forget. Call me later. You've got my home number."

"I already filled the tank. Thanks for the VOCO. I'll call you later," Collier said as he wheeled and headed for the door. Breaking speed laws all the way to Roanoke, Collier's head was filled with melodramatic images of being greeted with the news that Emma and their baby had died of some horrible medical complication...or the baby being born with an unspeakable disfigurement...or the baby being stillborn...or...? The tragic scenarios ran on like Previews of Coming Attractions in the macabre movie theater of his mind.

Parking in a No-Parking Zone, Collier rushed up the steps of the old hospital, two at a time. "My wife's having a baby...where's the delivery room?"

"Two-South," the Pink-lady volunteer told him, grinning ear-to-ear as she watched Collier run for the elevator.

"You're just in time." On Two-South, Garrett Gooch greeted Collier coming down the hall from Emma's room. "Emma and the baby are fine. Congratulations, it's a boy!"

"Hi, Honey, come over and meet your son." Emma smiled wanly from the bed, as the tiny form nestled in the crook of her arm, wrapped in a blue hospital receiving blanket, stretched and made the ugliest face Collier had ever seen in his life. Upon closer inspection, the baby was as red as a tomato and as wrinkled as any prune the new father had ever seen.

"It looks awfully red and wrinkled. Is it okay?" It crossed Collier's mind that the leathery-looking creature lying in Emma's arms might have an Indian father—or maybe even be of Negroid descent. He was certain the tiny infant was the homeliest baby he had ever laid eyes upon.

"He's fine. He's perfect. He's been here less than an hour. Don't pay any attention to the redness. He's a little jaundiced, that's all—a lot of newborns are. The redness and yellow tinge in his eyes will clear up right away—his little eyes will be white and his skin will be nice and pink and smooth before too long. Wash your hands in the bathroom...then come let him hold your finger—he's got a grip like a wrestler," Emma said, placing her forefinger in the baby's tiny palm, watching his tiny fingers wrap around.

"He's awful skinny and wrinkled...are you sure he's alright?"

"Quit worrying. He's fine. Take my word for it. He's healthy as a horse." Emma laughed at Collier's concern. "Go wash your hands and you can hold him for a little while."

"I'll wash my hands, but I don't think I'd better hold him just yet. He looks awful small." Collier disappeared into the bathroom to wash his hands.

"Come here and get a closer look. See his little dimple? He has the Ramsay chin. He's going to be the spitting image of you." Emma raised up on her elbow and touched the tiny infant on the point of his chin. Sure enough, the baby had a pronounced dimple, but for the life of him, Collier couldn't see any family resemblance. Anxiously, he unwrapped the receiving blanket and took a quick peek to make sure the baby was normal in all respects.

"By the way, your Aunt Jackie is in the room just down the hall. She had a boy yesterday."

"No fooling?" Collier shook his head in disbelief. He hadn't been aware that Jackie was even pregnant.

"No fooling. But I've got disappointing news. They have already named their son Kim." Kim had been one of their top two choices for a name—no matter if the baby were a boy or a girl.

"Oh, well, where does that leave us?" Collier searched his brain trying to remember their choices of baby names, but his brain wasn't working at all at the moment.

"We agreed to stick to Celtic names, remember? You were always partial to names that started with K. I brought the list from the baby magazine. It's in the pocket of that diaper bag." Emma nodded toward a padded canvas bag resting on a chair across the room.

When Collier walked over and extracted the much-worn, dog-eared magazine, it was already open to two facing pages listing names for boys. He flipped it to locate the Ks on the second page and started reading.

"Well?..." Emma prompted. "Read me the Ks."

"Kane, Karsten, Keene, Keegan..." he began and read down the list, "...Kelly, Kenneth, Ken, Kent, Kenton...Kerry....Kevin..."

"How about Kyle? Kyle was our second choice if the baby was a boy," Emma reminded him.

"Yeah, Kyle sounds okay to me. I think I like Kyle better than Kim for a boy anyway. Kyle Boyd Ramsay has a nice ring. How's that sound to you?"

"Sounds fine. I can already see it on the posters when he runs for President." Emma laughed.

"He won't be running for President—he'll be too honest and have too much self-respect to be a politician." Collier hadn't really thought much about their baby's future, but he certainly didn't want a politician in the family. No matter what his son wanted to do with his life, he hoped he had the self-respect that came with a strong sense of personal integrity.

"Well, maybe. I hope he wants to be a doctor or a dentist. It would be a shame to waste his brains." Although she didn't come right out and say she hoped the baby wouldn't grow up to be an artist, she made her meaning clear.

"Flowers for Emma Ramsay?" A young candy-striper came in carrying a vase of flowers.

"Oh, how lovely," Emma enthused. "Put them on the chest. Give me the card, Collier. Who are they from?"

The candy-striper stopped to let Collier remove the card.

"Best wishes—this time I hope you got the right genotype," Collier read the inscription aloud. "That's a strange comment...but it's not signed," he said as he made his way over to the bed to hand it to Emma.

"Oh well, the flowers are lovely. They're probably from one of my nursing friends. Whoever sent them will be calling to ask if they got here—you can bet on that. Put the card in the drawer of the night table. I'll have to send thank-you notes." Emma glanced at the card again before she handed it back to him.

"By the way, I got a call from Ginger Lipscomb just before you got here. Remember my old nursing classmate Ginger? She's an Army nurse now. We ran into her at Fort Sam Houston," Emma said as she shifted the sleeping baby in the crook of her arm.

"Sure, I remember Ginger. Wasn't she being sent somewhere in Virginia when she left Fort Sam?" Collier nodded, not wanting to show unusual interest.

"She's up near Washington—Fort Belvoir, I believe she said. She said to tell you hello and congratulate you on being able to stay in the States. She's being sent to Japan, by the way. Believe it or not, she's thrilled to be going overseas. I told her I give thanks every night that you don't have to go anywhere any farther away from Roanoke than you already are." Emma gave Collier's hand a squeeze when she handed him the card.

"Well...me too." He felt a twinge of guilt that Pewter and Skyer and Flood and his other classmates—and now even Ginger Lipscomb—were being shipped to the war zone while he stayed at home. It wasn't that he didn't appreciate his good fortune or that he didn't care about his wife and newborn son, but he had trained to be an officer to lead men in combat. Now he would never be able to find out for sure whether or not he had the right stuff.

"You need to call my mother and your folks and give them the news. They'll be coming to take little Kyle back to the nursery soon. I need to rest. I feel like I've been run over by a truck. As soon as they take the baby to the nursery, why don't you run up to see your folks? Bring your folks back this afternoon. I'll feel more like company by then," Emma said.

"Okay. Time's up. We need to get this big boy back to the nursery." Emma had scarcely finished speaking, when a nurse pushed a rolling bassinet into the room and put the baby in the cart. As she left she said, "I'll bring him back for a feeding in two hours. Family and friends can view the babies through the nursery window from 6 to 8 P.M."

"How're you feeling? Can I get you anything?" Collier attempted small talk, but hospitals and sickrooms always made him ill-at-ease.

"Give me a kiss and get on out of here. You can come back later this afternoon." Smiling weakly, Emma shooed him out of the room.

After he called his folks, Collier called Mother Lowell and gave her the news; then he phoned Randy Mullins back at Pickett.

"It's a boy, Kyle Boyd Ramsay. Six-pounds-eight-ounces, twenty-three inches long. I think I got me a future basketball All-American," Collier told Mullins as soon as he picked up the phone, adding, "Will you let Lieutenant Pewter know?"

"Sure, I'll pass the word at Battalion Officers Call. Don't come back here without cigars for me and Major Boyce. If you know what's good for you, you'll bring enough to pass them around to the officers at HQ and our sister companies, too. Better not bring any of those cheap two-for-a-nickel cigars, it's not too late to have you shipped to FECOM," Randy laughingly admonished before he hung up.

Heading downtown to the cigar store, Collier waved away the clerk's offering of cheap cigars with "It's A Boy" printed in blue on the cellophane wrappers and purchased three boxes of the store's finest hand-wrapped Tampa cigars.

With twice- and three-times-a-day visits to the hospital the next four days, finally Collier helped the nurse's aides load Emma and little Kyle Boyd Ramsay in the car just before noon on Saturday morning. When they arrived at Mother Lowell's at half-past twelve, Emma found her older sister, Anne, waiting to help bring the baby inside to a gathering of about dozen of her family and a few close girlfriends. The rest of the afternoon, Collier made several trips into town to purchase baby items from the pharmacy and made a trip to the supermarket to pick up grocery items to feed the hungry throng who were now playing Canasta around the large dining room table. The rest of the time, Collier did his best to stay out of the way.

"How are things going?" Around 1600 hours, while Emma was giving little Kyle a bottle of formula, Collier slipped upstairs and called Randy Mullins at home.

"Things are fine. I brought Emma and the baby home today. I just wanted to let you know I'll be back tomorrow night," Collier volunteered.

"Good. We're shorthanded. I know you hate to leave your wife and newborn son, but I'll try to see to it you can leave early next Saturday. It's really not that far to drive to Roanoke," Randy said, apologetically.

"Have a cigar. Take two if you like." Collier found Pewter in his room at the BOQ when he arrived back at Pickett late Sunday.

"Thanks, and congratulations, Daddy." Pewter grinned. "Man, I'm glad you're back. It's been too quiet around here the past few days. I miss going into Fort Lee. Fanny Burke is getting on my nerves," Pewter said.

"Not tonight, John Henry. I'm bushed. If you want to take chow with the troops, that's okay. I still don't see why you don't like Fanny Burke. She certainly has the hots for you. You could do a lot worse."

"That one would want to get on top."

"So, what's wrong with that, John Henry?"

"Well...you know what I mean. I don't like pushy women. I want the woman to know I'm in charge."

"Look, John Henry. I'm going to the O Club and have a good dinner. I'll protect you from Fanny Burke if she's there. By the time you find a woman or a girl who will put up with your unlayable ways, John Henry, you'll be too old to get it up." Collier shook his head.

"Have a cigar, Sir, and keep this box to pass around to Battalion officers and at Post HQ." Monday morning, Collier stopped by Battalion and offered Major Boyce a cigar, leaving one of the three boxes for distribution among the higher ranking echelons. As soon as he left HQ, he stopped in at each of the sister companies, presenting cigars to all the officers, passing others around to the principal NCOs.

"A massive tornado slashed through downtown Waco, Texas, today killing at least one-hundred-fourteen people and injuring an estimated five-hundred to one-thousand more. More than eight-hundred homes, hundreds of businesses, and countless automobiles were destroyed or severely damaged. Losses have been estimated upwards to forty-million dollars. The tornado is said to be the deadliest

in Texas history..." Collier listened with extreme anxiety to the WRAL announcer on his car radio that afternoon enroute to Petersburg for dinner at the Fort Lee O Club.

"My brother Jim is taking pilot training somewhere in Central Texas; do you have any idea where Waco is?" Collier asked Pewter, suddenly filled with anxiety for his brother's safety.

"Not really. If you have a phone number, you could call him when we get to Fort Lee," Pewter suggested.

"No...I don't have a number. I guess my parents know how to reach him by phone, but I wouldn't want to call and worry them unnecessarily," Collier replied thoughtfully.

"You could just call your parents to say hello. If there were any news, they probably would have heard," Pewter replied, thinking the situation through.

"Good idea," Collier replied. When they arrived at the O Club at Fort Lee, he headed for the phone.

"Your brother called late this afternoon. He didn't want us to worry about the tornadoes. Waco is south of Dallas. Jim's at Perrin Air Force Base, just north of Dallas—that's a good distance from Waco. But the main reason he called, I'm sorry to say, is he just got orders sending his outfit to Japan and, most likely, on to Korea. He and Hitch are coming home for two weeks sometime in early June," Collier's father passed on the good news and bad news.

"Your brother will be getting to Japan about the same time I—and Skyer and Flood and the rest of us—will. Who knows? Maybe I can look him up when I get to Korea—if he goes to Korea. You could send me his address," Pewter observed after Collier hung up the phone and told him the news about his brother's orders.

Lingering in the lounge after dinner, over an after-dinner brandy, Collier—depressed over hearing about Jim's orders to FECOM—rather dispiritedly passed out cigars to the regulars with whom he had come to have a speaking acquaintance, warming to their good-natured kidding and corny jokes about his new fatherhood. Finally, after an hour or so of this superficial banter, he apologetically told Pewter to drink up, he was ready to go back to Pickett and get some much-needed rest. Pewter made no protest. Sensing Collier was in no mood for idle banter, Pewter pretended to nap on the drive back to Blackstone. Tooling the car swiftly through the moonless countryside in reflective silence, Collier had them both safely back at the BOQ shortly after 2130 hours.

"Anybody seen this week's *ArmyTimes*?" The following morning Collier asked when he walked into the orderly room. He was still uneasy about his name not being included on the same orders with Pewter and the list of other second lieutenants, representing virtually all of their classmates who had come with them from MFSS. That he was the only one of the group remaining here at MRTC just didn't make good sense.

"Forget the *ArmyTimes*, Ramsay. Come in and close the door." Something about Randy Mullins's voice gave Collier an uneasy feeling.

"What's up?" Collier asked, his mind racing ahead, wondering if he had missed something important on the training schedule or perhaps there were repercussions from the Pentagon about Jarvis' medical discharge.

"Have a seat and smoke if you want one," Randy began as he walked around to the other side of his desk and picked up a single piece of paper. "I hate to have to drop this in your lap, particularly just when you became a father and everything..."

"Drop what? What's that paper?" Collier asked, looking at the paper in Mullins' hand, becoming more anxious by the second.

"The orders sending your buddies to FECOM—Yokohoma as it reads on here." Randy waved the paper as if he could read it from across the room.

"So? What's that got to do with me?" Collier wondered what he was missing here.

"That's just it. The *ArmyTimes* screwed up and left your name off the list they published on April twenty-fourth."

"Yeah. I already know. We talked about this last week, remember Captain?"

"No. Well, I mean, yeah, I do remember, but that's not what I'm telling you. You *are* on those orders. Major Boyce called me last night at home. The orders came down this weekend. Your name is right here with the rest of them." Randy stepped around the desk and handed Collier the orders, pointing out the appropriate line.

*To AFFE, Yokohoma, 2ⁿᵈ Lts., from Cp. Pickett—J.G. Johnson, D.A. Pacitti, P.E. Pitts..J.H. Pewter...T.W. Flood...*Collier's eyes skipped across the page until the typewritten letters ***C.B. Ramsay***...jumped at him right off the page.

Momentarily speechless, Collier carefully reread the orders. There was no mistake. They were all leaving Pickett on June 6 with travel delay. The orders had them reporting to POE (Port of Embarkation), Fort Lewis, Washington on 29 June 1953.

"Jeez...I don't quite know what to say..." Collier looked at the orders, looking back to Randy again in shock and utter dismay.

"Needless to say, I'm sorry, Collier—for more reasons than one. I will miss you around here. You are a fine officer. I want you to know I'm sending you out of here with a six on your Efficiency Report. You're pretty much assured of being promoted to First Lieutenant as soon as you hit Korean soil," Randy said lamely.

Seven was the highest number on the numerically-based Army Officer Efficiency Report system (OER), but in reality, unless the officer (he or she) had won a Silver Star or the CMOH with a handful of Purple Hearts, a "Six" was the highest recommendation an officer could ordinarily expect to get. A "Six" was like hanging the moon. In everyday language, it translated to being put at the very top of the promotion list for an officer's branch of service, a quantum leap ahead of other officers with the same time in grade. As for being promoted to First Lieutenant within thirty days after landing on Korean soil, that had pretty much become SOP; Collier assumed this would continue as long as there was a war going on.

"Thank you, Sir."

"The company is in the classroom all morning, if you want some time to call home with the news. As a matter of fact, I have some business at HQ. You can use my phone if you like." Randy picked up his overseas cap and stood aside.

"I really appreciate the offer, Sir, but it's too early to be calling home. I think I'll go get breakfast before I call. I need some time to collect my wits." Collier stood to leave.

"Take your time. But take my advice and don't put off calling your wife too long. It'll make it easier if you give her time to sort things out."

"Don't worry. I'll call this morning right after breakfast. Give her time to tend to the baby and eat breakfast...you know, things like that." Collier nodded and left the room, his orders in his hand.

"I'm sorry, Collie. I really am. But, on the bright side, at least we're on the same orders. We might even be assigned to the same outfit overseas," Pewter said at Battalion Mess when Collier gave him the news.

"That's true," Collier brightened. He had been so preoccupied with how he was going to break the news to Emma, he hadn't thought about much else.

"Cheer up, man. Your brother is going over about the same time as we are. Could be you'll be close enough to see each other while you're overseas." Pewter grinned encouragingly, and slapped Collier on the back.

"You're right again. I'll call Jim tonight and give him the '*good news*,'" Collier said with good-natured sarcasm.

"I'm sorry to have to lay this on you, Babe. I hate it just as much as you do..." there was little he could say to console Emma. Predictably, she bawled and ranted protests verging near the edge of hysterics when he gave her the news. Finally, he gave up and said goodbye.

With the company winding down the final curriculum of Basic the last three weeks of May and with Randy seeing to it he had Saturday afternoon and Sunday off to go home to be with Emma and little Kyle, the first week of June rolled around before Collier had much time to brood. As a sort of farewell tribute to their last night at Pickett, Collier took Pewter to the Fort Lee O Club for dinner the last official night of their stateside assignment. The following morning, he took Pewter to make their final stops to "Clear the Post," before he dropped his friend at the bus station in Blackstone to catch a bus into Richmond.

"See you in Chicago." Pewter shook his hand outside the bus station. They would be meeting at Midway airport and taking the same flight to Seattle in three weeks.

"Have a great leave, but don't waste your virginity on some silly high-school girl back home," Collier kidded, pretty sure Pewter wouldn't even shake hands with a female during the next three weeks.

"Your brother just called. He and Hitch pulled in last night. He's got two weeks before he has to report to Reno and wants to know if we can go to the Beach next week for a couple of days. I can get Anne to keep little Kyle...please, Honey, let's go. It would be like a second honeymoon," Emma greeted him as soon as he walked through the door.

"Well...that sounds like fun. I'm game if we can work it out." Collier shrugged. It would be great seeing his brother again. A few days at Virginia Beach might take some of the edge off of such gloomy circumstances.

"Jenny, what do you hear from Bo?" Attending church at the old Fort Lewis Baptist to please his mother, Collier ran into Jenny Bohon after services in the parking lot. The last he'd heard, Bo was scheduled to ship home from Korea around the first of June.

"I haven't heard a thing. I'm on pins and needles. I keep hoping he'll call and tell me he's on his way," Jenny said. "I don't think I could stand it if anything happened to him now."

"Don't worry. Unless I miss my guess, he'll be calling you from somewhere in California any day. Tell him I'm sorry I missed seeing him, but tell him I'm glad he's home. Tell him Jimmy and I are on our way over there." Collier gave Jenny a reassuring hug.

A little before sunup on Tuesday morning, the two couples piled into Collier and Emma's Studebaker headed for the Beach. Laughing, joking and singing all the way around Petersburg, finally, one-by-one, Collier's passengers drifted off to sleep cruising smoothly along in light mid-week traffic on 460. Collier himself was having trouble staying alert when he was suddenly roused fully conscious by the sound of a siren close at hand. When he checked his rearview mirror, a highway patrolmen was close behind with red-lights flashing, blinking his headlights to signal Collier to pull to the shoulder. Glancing guiltily down, the speedometer needle held steady on 86 mph. Slowing, Collier pulled to the shoulder of the highway and waited until the patrolman got out and approached the car.

"Oh, shit." Jim said, fully awake now by the siren.

"Let me see your license and registration, please?" The stern-looking patrolman asked politely through the rolled down window on the driver's side.

"Yessir...I have them right here." Collier included his military ID with the license and registration. He had never been stopped before, but he knew enough to give himself every advantage. His head was filled with horror stories he'd heard about speeders being hauled before local Justices of the Peace and being thrown into jail until they could pay exorbitant fines.

"Do you know how fast you were going?" The cop looked inside at Emma and Jim and Hitch rubbing sleep from their eyes.

"Yessir. When I heard your siren, my speedometer read eighty-six." No sense in lying about it. The cop had him dead-to-rights.

"You folks coming from Roanoke?" the stern officer asked non-committally, looking over the registration papers, driver's license and military ID.

"Yessir...Salem, actually." Collier amended.

"Where are you going in such a hurry?" The cop continued to look them over.

"Virginia Beach. That's my brother, James, and his wife in the back. He's a lieutenant—a pilot—in the Air Force. We're both on leave before going to Korea. He ships out next week and I leave Roanoke for Seattle to ship to Korea on the twenty-fifth," Collier said, his heart pounding in his chest.

"Do you have your orders with you?" clearly the crusty Patrolman had heard his share of sad stories in his day.

"Yessir. As a matter of fact, I have my orders in my baggage in the trunk. Would you like to see them, Sir?" Collier reached for the keys to shut off the engine.

"Hold on. That won't be necessary. I'm going to let you go, but I'm going to call ahead to the barracks. If you're pulled over again for speeding—or any other traffic violation—I'm going to tell them to throw the book at you. Now slow down and enjoy your vacation at the beach." The patrolman handed back Collier's papers and tipped his hat. "Good luck overseas."

"Time passes too fast when you're having fun," Emma mused ruefully Friday on the way back from Virginia Beach where even the sporadically overcast weather had not put a damper on their fun.

Tuesday morning, Jim put Hitch on a plane to New York City where she would live with her folks in Hempstead on Long Island while Jim served overseas. Having to drive three-quarters of the way back across country, Jim left on Thursday, the second week of June, heading to Reno, Nevada, for Survival School before his outfit shipped through Frisco to Hawaii and Japan.

"What do you hear from Bo?" On Friday, the twelfth of June, Collier called Jenny Bohon after his dad had told him Jenny said Bo's rotation home from Korea had been delayed because his replacement hadn't arrived.

"His last letter was May 25. He was packed and ready to leave. He was expecting his replacement any day," Jenny said, on the verge of tears.

"Leave it to the Army! Give 'em a chance and they could mess up a solar eclipse!" Collier commiserated.

Although Collier knew he would most likely be put on a troopship in Seattle for the crossing to Japan, a slow sense of dread began building inside him at the prospect of having to fly from Roanoke to Chicago—where he would meet John Henry—and then on to Seattle, by way of Denver. It did little to help his frame of mind when, Thursday night, June 18, he saw a breaking bulletin on the late TV news about a disastrous military air crash involving troops somewhere near Tokyo. Called the "worst air disaster in the history of aviation," the crash had occurred at Tachikawa Air Base in Japan when an engine fire caused a C-124 Globemaster to go down shortly after takeoff, killing all 129 aboard—including the six crew members and 123 soldiers being flown to Korea. The brief Associated Press account said the military and Douglas Aircraft, the aircraft's manufacturer, had immediately grounded all Globemasters to determine the cause of the crash.

Although he tried his best to shake off his sense of impending doom, the news of the crash did nothing to improve Collier's brooding state of mind and his sense of impending disaster. The remaining days of his leave, he spent his time trying rather unsuccessfully to appreciate the joys of fatherhood during the daytime and—completely ignoring Garrett Gooch's six-week post-natal moratorium on intercourse—trying to fuck his brains out at night.

The night before his leave-taking, after a quiet dinner with his parents in the kitchen, Collier went upstairs and finished packing his B-4 bag and carried it down to the living room in readiness for the trip to Woodrum Field to catch the next morning's 1100 A. M. Piedmont flight to Chicago. His father was still up and sitting on the porch.

"Here's a little something to tide you over. A little extra cash never hurts, particularly when you're away from home." His father pressed a fold of five twenties in his hand.

"I can't take this, Dad," Collier started to protest, but his father pushed his hand away when he tried to give the money back.

"Don't be a fool. I know you're tight on cash..." his father squeezed his shoulder when Collier bent to give him an awkward hug. His father was right about his being short on money. The hundred brought his travel money up to a grand total of just under three-hundred bucks; god-only-knew when the Eagle would shit again.

For Collier, the following morning went by in slow-motion, as if he were walking around in a dream. At the airport, he gave his parents a hug, kissed Emma and the baby and boarded the Piedmont Airlines DC-3, stowed his AWOL bag above the seats and took a seat by the window. Fastening his seat belt, he glanced around the travel-worn interior of the travel-weary old DC-3. Now, looking out the window at Harry, Lida, Emma and the six-week-old baby in her arms, standing by the heavy-woven-wire fence waving goodbye—in that single, clear instant, Collier Boyd Ramsay was visited by the certain insight none of them would never see him alive again.

In that moment, all the anxieties over how he would perform in combat, along with all fear of being wounded or killed, left him and he experienced a sense of unworldly calm—almost. Making a solemn vow to the Cosmic forces that he would never again be unfaithful to his wife, Collier gave his family a final wave, tightened his canvas seat belt and looked around for the Emergency Exits as he was filled with a melodramatic sense of impending doom.

CHAPTER FORTY-ONE

The Roanoke World-News
Roanoke, Virginia, Thursday Afternoon, June 25, 1953
RHEE DEMANDS FIGHT TO DEATH
SEOUL, June 25 (Thursday) – (AP) – "We want to fight until death," President Syngman Rhee shouted Thursday to screaming hundreds of thousands demonstrating against a truce on this third anniversary of the Korean war.

LIFE
JUNE 29, 1953
Life on the Newsfronts of the World:
Worst Air Crash

One rain-filled afternoon last week a giant Air Force C-124 Globemaster lifted off the runway at Tachikawa airport near Tokyo and disappeared into the murk. The tower heard one brief radio message from the plane: "One engine dead; returning for G.C.A. landing." A few minutes later, in a flat spin, the C-124 crashed into a muddy farm field northeast of the airport. There were no survivors: the plane carried to death 129 persons, seven members of the crew and 122 servicemen returning to their units in Korea after leave in Japan. It was—by a margin of 42 deaths—the world's worst disaster in the history of aviation.

-1-

BREATHING SOMEWHAT EASIER when he deplaned at Washington National Airport, Collier entered the terminal with a renewed sense of well-being. But his respite from his deeply-ingrained fear of flying was short-lived as he had only a short layover before he had to board a four-engine American Airlines DC-4 for the continuing flight to Chicago Midway airport where he was to meet Pewter. Uncle Sugar—the GIs nickname for Uncle Sam—had booked them both out of Chicago Midway on the same flight through Denver into Seattle-Tacoma airport. Late leaving Washington National, therefore late arriving Chicago Midway, Collier had to run down the long concourse to make his connecting flight. Crossing the tarmac to board the United Airlines Super-Constellation, Collier climbed the boarding stairs with only minutes to spare. Before he selected a seat, he searched the boarded passengers looking for Pewter with no luck.

Up until that moment, his fear had been that he would miss the plane and Pewter would be forced to go on to Seattle without him. Now just the opposite was true. With no choice but to remain on board and continue on to Fort Lewis, Collier placed his AWOL bag on the overhead rack and took the aisle seat over the wing near the front of the plane on a row that had an adjoining empty seat, just in case Pewter made the flight.

"No...sorry. Another officer and I are traveling to the Far East Theater together on Government orders," he explained to other boarding passengers as he guarded the empty seat beside him, anxiously searching the faces of the remaining boarding passengers. Finally when there had been no boarding passengers for at least several minutes, his spirits sank as there still was no sign of Pewter.

"Looks like your buddy is a no-show," the stewardess said as she came by reminding the passengers to fasten their seatbelts. Up front, Collier saw the second stewardess making preparations to close the door. While he wasn't exactly rendered panic-stricken by the thought of continuing on to Seattle without Pewter, it was all Collier could do not to leave the plane and go back and wait for Pewter and take a later flight.

"Wow...my flight out of Columbus was late. I thought I was going to miss this plane for sure." When Collier looked up from fastening his seatbelt, Pewter was standing in the aisle waiting for him to give him room to slip into the window seat.

"To tell the truth, I'd given up on you. I was going to wait in the airport in Seattle until you caught up to me so we could report to Fort Lewis together."

Greatly relieved that Pewter had made the flight, Collier ignored the annoying drone of the big engines just outside their window as he quickly lapsed into a fitful sleep, rousing on and off into short periods of wakefulness long enough to marvel at how the sleek aircraft was literally racing the setting sun to the western horizon as they sped around the curve of the earth.

"I don't see how you could sleep like that with all the racket from the engines," Pewter complained when Collier finally roused awake for their short stop at Denver.

"This brochure says Mount Rainier is located in a large park outside Seattle. At 14,410 feet Rainier is the highest peak in the Cascade Range. Rainier may be visible from the airport. It says here that from various locations around the park you can see four other Cascade volcanoes: Mount St. Helens, Mount Adams, Mount Baker, and Glacier Peak. On a clear day, you can see the tip of Mount Hood, in northern Oregon, from Paradise Meadows." For a short time after they left Denver, Collier studied a travel brochure about the Pacific-Northwest area surrounding Seattle, before he yawned and drifted back to sleep, trying to imagine how it would be to be confronted by a mountain almost four times as high as Poor Mountain or the twin Peaks of Otter back home in Virginia.

"Please secure your seat belts; we'll be making our approach to Seattle-Tacoma." The pretty stewardess shook Collier awake. In the distance far below he could see the lights of a city.

"Come on, let's get a rental car. We've got four days before we have to report. Might as well take a look at Seattle and the great northwest," John Henry enthused as they walked across the tarmac into the modern terminal building.

"Look, John Henry. I hate to remind you, but I'm married and have a child. I'm on a limited budget. I've squirreled away a few bucks in case we get to spend some time in Tokyo, but I don't want to waste my stash on sightseeing in Seattle," Collier resisted.

"Don't worry. I'll pay for the car, you can be chauffeur. After all the miles we logged in your car at Pickett going into Petersburg and Richmond and Farmville, I owe you, anyway." Pewter said, extracting a roll of lettuce big enough to choke a full-grown hippopotamus.

"That's fair enough, but, if I were you, I'd save some of that for Tokyo. Even if we strike out here, when we get to Japan, you can go to one of those fancy

Geisha houses. The Japanese women are schooled in the arts of pleasing men. They take their customers to bathe together in large communal pools." Just thinking about a pool full of naked, brown-skinned Japanese girls brought a frisson of excitement to Collier's loins.

By the time they both collected their B-4 bags and picked up a rental car, the sun had already set and the first stars were twinkling in the indigo night.

Deciding they were both too tired to drive the remaining twenty or thirty-odd miles south to Tacoma and Fort Lewis and chance being unable to find a motel with a vacancy, Collier located the highway leading to Fort Lewis and pulled into the first respectable-looking motel with a vacancy sign lit and registered for a room with two double beds.

Parking outside the room, Collier opened the trunk and stood aside while Pewter rummaged around in his B-4 for his toilet kit. Hauling out his AWOL bag containing his own toilet kit, Collier locked the rental car and followed John Henry to the door. Inside the room, Collier took a quick hot shower while Pewter fiddled around trying to adjust the TV. Brushing his teeth, Collier turned down the bed nearest the bathroom and fell asleep with Pewter stretched out on the other bed watching *Gangbusters* or *Dragnet* or some other cop show Collier was too exhausted to care about.

The next morning, Collier overslept. It was nearly 0800 Pacific time—almost 1100 back East—when he came awake and rubbed the sleep out of his eyes. Rolling quietly out of bed, Collier brushed his teeth and dressed without waking Pewter and went outside. The parking lot was shrouded in dense fog as he walked to the office and took a complimentary copy of the *Seattle Post-Intelligencer* from the desk.

"Don't worry. This ground fog will burn off when the sun gets a little higher. The forecast is for a beautiful day. It was eighty-six degrees in Anchorage, Alaska, yesterday," the clerk advised him cheerily, as if good weather in Alaska were some kind of local omen.

Filling two paper coffee cups from a glass Silex pot on an electric warming plate in the tiny office lobby, Collier stirred cream and sugar into one, leaving the other one black—then he headed back across the parking lot to wake Pewter.

"Get up, John Henry, and get dressed. Here's some coffee—two sugars and cream. Let's head out and find some breakfast...I'm hungry as a horse." Collier shook the sleeping Pewter.

Grudgingly, Pewter pulled back the covers and crawled out of bed while Collier took a seat at a small round table by the front window. Unfolding the copy of the *Seattle Post-Intelligencer*, he idly scanned the headlines for news of the war.

"What's the weather like?" Pewter asked, coming out of the bathroom.

"It was foggy when I got the coffee and newspaper, but the forecast is for 'Sunny and Warm.' It was eighty-six degrees in Anchorage, Alaska, yesterday," Collier answered without looking up from the paper. "It might be a good day for sightseeing. Today's only Thursday. We don't have to report until the twenty-ninth—that's Monday, I think."

"Yeah. That gives us four days to look around Seattle. Today is the third anniversary of the North Korean invasion of Seoul. Any news from the peace talks?" Pewter had started dressing.

"No news from Panmunjon, but Syngman Rhee gave a big anniversary speech in Seoul exhorting the crowd to 'Fight to the death.'"

"Easy to say, when someone else is doing most of the fighting for you. Are we checking out of here?" Pewter had finished tying his tie and was ready to leave.

"Yeah. No sense in paying three bucks a night when we can stay in the transient BOQ at Fort Lewis practically free." Collier folded the paper and grabbed his AWOL bag.

True to the desk clerk's word, the fog had begun to lift by the time they checked out of the motel and had eaten breakfast. Checking for directions with the waiter in the restaurant, they paid their check and Collier got under the wheel of the rental car and turned onto the highway heading in the direction of Fort Lewis.

"We're heading almost due south. The waiter said if the fog lifts, we may be able to see Mount Rainier, which will be generally to the southeast. That will be on our left. Keep a sharp eye out as soon as we clear this line of trees." Driving along the highway, Collier kept glancing out of the driver-side window, but the terrain rose sharply on both sides of the highway for the first few miles, and the area was heavily forested with tall evergreens

"No views of your big mountain in this pea soup," Pewter said, glancing at the fog-veiled treetops as they rode along.

"Well...don't give up. The waiter seemed pretty sure we would be able to see Rainier from the highway," Collier said, concentrating on safely negotiating the broken patches of fog.

Finally, as they broke out of the worst of the fog, Collier chanced a glance out of the corner of his eye and was totally unprepared to see the goddamnedest mountain he had ever seen in his life, looming so close it appeared to be on the verge of falling over on top of them.

"Holy shit!" Pewter gasped. "Stop the car."

Completely awed, Collier found a wide place on the shoulder of the highway and pulled over and they both got out of the car.

"Holy shit is right," Collier agreed, standing by the side of the road gawking almost straight up into the sky. Poor Mountain or the Twin Peaks of Otter or McAfee's Knob and all the rest of the higher peaks in the Blue Ridge chain back home—which had always been rather inspiring sights to Collier—were mere pimples on the ass of Pan, the Greek mountain diety, compared to this unbelievable hulk of stone and ice towering above them.

Finally, after kicking themselves for not having a camera to capture this astounding image, they got back in the car and drove the remaining ten miles until they crossed into the boundaries of the Fort Lewis military reservation.

"When we find the gate, turn in. We have to report Monday. Might as well go check into the transient BOQ and have a look around," Pewter suggested.

Collier nodded, still unable to take his eyes away from the colossal mountain towering over them.

"Turn in here," Pewter said when he spotted the main gate. Still having trouble keeping his eyes off of the mountain, Collier turned in and parked at a small structure marked by a sign: Welcome Center—Information.

Inside the modest Welcome Center, a freckled-faced WAC corporal examined the registration papers of the rental car, issued Collier a sticker granting temporary access to the Post and gave him instruction how to find the transient BOQ.

"Is that Mount Rainier across the highway?" Collier asked before they left.

"Yes. Quite a sight isn't it? I'm from the Adirondacks in upstate New York. I've been here over a year and I still can't get used to it," the young WAC said, shaking her head in awe.

"Maybe we can walk over to the foot of it some morning before we leave and take a closer look," Collier remarked to Pewter as they turned to leave.

The young corporal covered her mouth with her hand to suppress a laugh.

"Just how far is it to the base of that rock?" Collier asked sheepishly, realizing the mountain must be farther than it looked.

"Forty or fifty miles at least. You can drive it in about an hour." The young woman grinned.

Still sneaking occasional peeks at the looming prescence of Rainier, Collier had no trouble following the signs to the HQ Building of the Replacement Center.

"If you check in now, we might have room on a troopship leaving Seattle tomorrow afternoon. Weather's good this time of year. Junior officers occupy little staterooms—twelve bunks to a stateroom. It's a little cramped, but the food is out of this world. Takes twelve or thirteen days around the Great Circle route," the sergeant at the Replacement Center said.

"What's plan B?" Collier asked. He liked the idea of going by ship, but he had hoped to see a little of Seattle and Tacoma—maybe even drive down to Olympia—if they had enough time before they had to ship out. It also had not escaped him that a city the size of Seattle must certainly provide opportunities for Pewter to meet some eager young debs just waiting to help divest a clean-cut young Army officer of his burdensome virginity.

"There are flights out of Sea/Tac about two or three times a week—sometimes more often than that. The Army has contracted with Pan American and Northwest OrientAirways for champagne service on their luxurious, double-decked Boeing B-377 Stratocruisers. Flights take about twenty-four hours—they land in Anchorage and Shemya in the Aleutians for refueling. Four or five charming stewardesses to wait on you hand and foot....how can you beat a deal like that?" The sergeant rolled his eyes in mock ecstasy, imagining the possibilities.

"When's the next ship?" Collier asked. He wasn't at all enchanted with the idea of flying anywhere, much less flying around the Artic Circle, even if in the summertime.

The sergeant consulted the typewritten sheet in front of him. "We don't have another ship until the end of next week."

"Forget the ship. When's the next flight?" Pewter spoke up, much to Collier's chagrin.

"The next flight is Sunday, the twenty-eighth." The sergeant checked his list.

"Forget Sunday...our orders say we aren't due until Monday. C'mon John Henry, let's get a room at the BOQ and talk this over." Grabbing Pewter firmly by the elbow, Collier steered him toward the door.

The transient BOQ was nothing to write home about, but the price was right. After they checked in and deposited their bags in their rooms, Collier drove them around the Fort until they located the O Club. That accomplished, he headed out the gate and down the road to Olympia, Washington, still gawking at the surreal spectacle of Mount Rainier looming over them.

Peopled mainly with matronly window-shoppers, Olympia proved to be a disappointment for Collier, still hoping to find fertile territory in his crusade to deflower Pewter before they left the States. After they had a pleasant lunch in a nice café—Collier ordered Shrimp Louis which turned out to be a cupful of the tiniest shrimp he'd ever seen dumped on top of a bowl of shredded iceberg lettuce and covered with what looked to him to be French Dressing for which he really had no great affection—they decided to head back up the highway to try their luck back in Tacoma and Seattle.

After a quick look at Tacoma, they eventually moved on to spend the evening cruising cocktail bars in downtown Seattle before Collier finally gave up in disgust. It wasn't as if they hadn't met a number of attractive single women—mostly secretaries and shop girls having an after-work drink, and most certainly looking to meet men. Most of these nubile prospects were open to an offer of a free cocktail from a pair of young Army officers. The problem was John Henry.

Pewter was an absolute dodo when it came to making small talk with women.

During the course of the evening, they bought drinks for at least six or eight pairs of attractive females who thanked them for the drinks before quickly moving to more interesting possibilities.

"Try to talk about something other than the weather and the scenery, John Henry. And don't simply tell women how nice they look—if you want to compliment them, tell them they remind you of Marilyn Monroe or Elizabeth Taylor or Ingrid Bergman or some other sexy movie actress. Ask them about themselves. Trust me, John Henry, women never get tired of talking about themselves," Collier advised, but Pewter was not a promising student. Friday and Saturday evening proved to be repeats of their first foray—John Henry was absolutely hopeless when it came to women.

"Let's just ask one of the old timers at the Fort about the local whorehouses. I'm looking to have sex. I'm not looking for a wife." John Henry obviously had no interest in the excitement of the hunt.

At the O Club, the bar was crowded with officers who had just flown in from Tokyo—most of them returning after a year or more in Korea. The room was full of ribald stories about the Geisha houses in Japan, mostly Yokohama and Tokyo.

"Stick to the traditional places. Except for drinks and dinner at the R&R hotels, stay away from the modern American-looking places," a captain with a chest full of ribbons, including the Bronze Star and a Purple Heart, advised as he held a beer in one hand and threw a dart just out of the bullseye with the other.

A first lieutenant spoke up, "Yeah, the *Kenno-tenobi* is the best place. Ask anyone who's been there. They treat you like a king. The mama-san will greet you and ask you to remove your shoes. The whole place has straw mats on the floor. The mama-san will give you a pair of slippers before they take you into a little dressing room where you exchange your uniform for a silk kimono. Then they take you into a little sitting room and bring you a little cup of warm sake—rice wine—before they start to bring the women out. Go easy on the sake. That stuff will knock you for a loop."

"What do you mean, bring the women out?" another lieutenant asked, all ears now that the subject was sex.

"They seat you in a little room overlooking a tiny courtyard while they present the girls. They bring them in groups of around seven or eight..." the captain with the darts said, describing the process of how to pick out a partner for the night. He added, "Never choose a girl from the first couple of groups."

"Seven or eight? What's wrong with the first two groups? I don't understand." Pewter asked, confused.

"Nothing probably. It's just sort of traditional you never choose a girl from the first couple of groups. Anytime after the second group, pick any girl who turns you on," the lieutenant said.

"How much are we talking about for a quickie?" Pewter asked, clearly enthralled by the subject.

"Stay away from 'quickie houses'. You'll likely wind up with a dose. At the old-style places like the *Kenno-tenobi*, you pay about twenty-dollars American. That's something like six-thousand yen at the exchange rate of three hundred yen to one dollar American. That includes all the amenities like the baths and a massage—you can tip your girl when you leave if you like," the young lieutenant said.

"Begging the lieutenant's pardon, I don't know anything about the *Kenno-tenobi*, but I can certainly tell you that the absolute best hotel in the whole country is the old resort Hotel Fujiya at the base of Mount Fuji." This time it was a major at the end of the bar speaking.

"How far from Tokyo—or Yokohama?" Collier asked. He expected their time to be limited while in Japan.

"Hakone's about an hour by train. Hell's bells, on a clear day you can see Mount Fuji from downtown Tokyo," the major spoke up again, not wanting a captain and a lieutenant to steal his thunder. He pronounced Hakone: Hyuh´-cone-ee.

"How much do you tip? And how about Korea? How are the women there?" Collier asked.

"Forget the whores in Korea. There are a lot of strange venereal diseases in Korea. Granuloma for one—I knew a guy whose dick damn-near rotted right off. The Korean women look more like Aleuts—you know, Indians or Eskimos—compared to our Caucasian women here in the Northwest. Among Orientals, the Japanese women are prettier with more delicate features—their faces are like little painted flowers." The lieutenant looked around to see if he had made his point.

Pewter glanced at Collier and raised his eyebrows.

"So what about VD in Tokyo...or Yokohama? Are you saying there isn't any clap or syphilis or granuloma inguinale...or anything like that in Japan?" Collier asked, totally dismissing such an obvious exaggeration. He recognized granuloma inguinale as one of the diseases they were warned about at MFSS at Fort Sam. He particularly remembered granuloma because of the horrific color slides that their unblushing instructor had shown them.

"Well, sure. There's a lot of VD all over Japan. But at first class places like the *Kenno-tenobi*, the girls are checked daily by a physician. If an American comes down with something, the Japanese authorities close the place right down." The captain spoke up now, clearly tired of the lieutenant hogging the spotlight.

"How do you spell *Kenno-tenobi*?" Collier had added the spelling to the other names of places on the back of a calling card. If he were going to get John Henry laid before they went to Korea, Tokyo was his last chance.

Orders posted on the bulletin board had them reporting at 0400 hours the following morning with a list of thirty-five or forty other officers, about twenty-five of which were second or first lieutenants and the rest captains and a single major and none above that rank. When they asked the NCO inside why such an ungodly hour, he told them they were scheduled to fly out of Sea/Tac airport the following morning at 0600 hours and it would take at least an hour to process and be transported by military bus.

"Don't you have a ship going this week?" Collier asked, panicked at the thought of flying across open water for almost a full day and a night.

"Sorry, the next ship, the *Marine Phoenix*, isn't due back in port for at least a week." The NCO shrugged.

"Oh, shit," Collier said when they were outside again.

"What's the matter? A few minutes ago, you were chomping at the bit." Pewter shot him a curious look.

"I purely hate the thought of flying. Do you know we land in Anchorage, Alaska, and Shemya, a little rock way out in the Aleutian Islands, to refuel. After that stop, do you have any freaking idea how long we'll be in the air?" Collier asked, his voice heavy with downright dread.

"Not really—quite awhile, I guess." Pewter shrugged. "But those Boeing Stratocruisers are double-deckers; we'll have plenty of room to move around. You remember what we were told about flying on those fancy airplanes with good-looking stewardesses and champagne service." John Henry fairly beamed with anticipation.

"Have you been reading the newspapers or watching TV?" Collier asked, suddenly recalling the news of the Globemaster crash near Tokyo less than two weeks ago.

"Why?" John Henry had no idea what Collier was talking about.

"Did you read about that Globemaster crash in Japan ten or twelve days ago? Globemasters are double-deckers, too," Collier said, trying to make his point. "Airplanes that big were never intended to fly."

"Nonsense. One crash does not make a case against flying. Commercial aviation is safer than driving in your car." Pewter dismissed the idea with a wave.

"Yeah, tell that to the wives and parents of those one-hundred-twenty-nine GIs," Collier whined.

Spending most of the morning packing and doing last-minute shopping for toilet articles, a goodly supply of Hershey and Payday bars and cigarettes at the Post Exchange, Collier called his folks mid-afternoon to bring them up to date on his travel schedule.

"Take good care, son. We'll pray for you," his dad said when they picked up on separate phones. Trying not to show their concern, they both wished him a safe trip.

"Don't drink any of that Champagne. If the plane goes down over water, you'll be too drunk to swim," his mother warned before she hung up.

When he phoned Emma, he called collect on her mother's phone at no cost—a special consideration to the widows of former Chesapeake and Potomac phone company execs.

"Your son is growing like a weed. I'll send pictures as soon as I get the film developed. Anne took some shots with color film," Emma promised.

When he said goodbye to Emma and hung up the phone, Collier was left with a peculiar feeling of emptiness, almost a total absence of emotion. It was almost as if he given himself an interim divorce.

"Here I am again, God. about to get on an airplane. If I should die before I return home to my parents and wife and little son who doesn't even know me—please take care of them and keep them safe from harm. And, God, please keep my brother, Jim, safe and get Bo Bohon back home to Jenny...and...Grandma

Ramsay...and..." That night when he said his prayers, Collier tried not to miss blessing anyone of importance in his life. He fell asleep before he had halfway completed the list.

2.

HAVING SHOWERED THE NIGHT BEFORE, Collier and Pewter both quickly shaved, dressed and were waiting with their B-4 and AWOL bags in front of the BOQ at 0355 hours with the others the next morning when the bus pulled to the curb. Overhead, the cloudless sky was filled with stars, promising a perfect day to begin the daunting flight.

"Alright, you men, I am Major Arlen Richards. I am in command for this flight. Please give me your attention, answer to your name, and board the bus as I call roll: Aaron, Adams..." a major with quartermaster insignia on his lapels stepped off the bus and began calling names from a roster he had attached to a clipboard. Collier took note that a half-dozen or more captains, most of them medical officers, had joined their group. When everyone was accounted for and aboard the bus, the driver rudely clashed the tired old bus in gear and they headed out.

"This is right out of some eerie Poe short story," Collier remarked to Pewter, trying to fight off his feelings of impending doom when they disembarked the bus and were being herded across the virtually-deserted interior of the marble-veneered Sea/Tac terminal. The surreal setting reminded him of an ancient mausoleum as they followed the major to a door in the corner of the cavernous room with its soaring window-wall overlooking the taxiways leading out to the runways. On the tarmac directly beneath them, a sleek, silver-skinned giant airliner was a beehive of activity, being serviced by a busy ground crew.

"A Boeing 377 Stratocruiser. That's what I call going in style," one of the other "second johns" from Pickett, remarked trying to muster some measure of enthusiasm.

"That's the same plane we called the C-97 Stratofreighter, when I was in OCS at Benning. Down there, we called them 'Pregnant Hippopotomi,'" Pewter laughed.

"Alright, at ease everyone! I am Major Arlen Richards, and, as you were told back at Fort Lewis before we boarded the bus, I am in command until we arrive in Tokyo. Answer your name when I call it." They had barely assembled in front of a pair of black double doors when the overanxious Major called the roll again. Like a mother hen with her first brood, the Major obviously didn't relish the prospect of having to explain the loss of a second lieutenant to a United States Army court martial board.

Richards was still calling the roll when the flight crew including a pilot, copilot, navigator, flight engineer and six drop-dead-gorgeous stewardesses silently and—given the early hour—somewhat sullenly excused their way through the milling assemblage of sleepy-eyed Army lieutenants and captains, making their way down to board the plane.

"Welcome aboard our Pan American Airways Boeing 'Strato-Clipper' special charter service for Haneda Airport serving Tokyo, Japan. My name is Sheila. I'm the chief stewardess in charge. We have a total complement of six stewardesses aboard—that's one for every six passengers on this flight. Powered by four 3500 hp, four-bladed Pratt and Whitney R-4360-B6 Wasp 28-cylinder radial engines, this airplane is one of the most modern, most comfortable, and most reliable commercial aircraft in long-haul service. As you will readily see, the Boeing 377 Stratocruiser aircraft comfortably seats sixty-three in its extra-wide passenger cabin. Some of the seats can and will be made up into sleeping berths during the long flight. You will also find there is a circular staircase leading down to our lower-deck beverage lounge. We are well-stocked to serve you delicious snacks, complete in-flight meals and round-the-clock beverage service including unlimited Champagne both in the main cabin as well as the beverage lounge. Please feel free to take any seat that is unoccupied. FAA regulations require you to fasten your seat belts on take-offs and landings. We are prepared to depart as soon as you are all on board and seated. Our stewardesses will begin taking orders for beverages immediately," the Chief stewardess stood just inside the boarding doorway reciting her spiel into the PA mike like a carnival pitchman as she directed traffic into the spacious cabin which, to Collier, looked more the size of a railroad passenger car than an airplane.

"Let's go up front. There are plenty of empty seats up there," Pewter started toward the forward section, but Collier grabbed his arm and pulled him back.

"Whoa! Remember coming out from Chicago? We don't want to deal with all that engine noise. Let's sit over here, across from the stairway down to the lounge." Inside the boarding doorway, Collier led Pewter directly across the aisle to seats underneath the lighted Emergency Exit sign.

To ease his anxiety, Collier idly extracted a copy of the June 29 issue of *Life* magazine from the pocket on the seatback in front of him, briefly lusting over the long legs of dancer/actress Cyd Charisse on the reddish-pink cover before he idly thumbed through the pages until his eyes focused on a blurb about the disastrous air crash of the giant C124 Globemaster troop carrier aircraft at Tachikawa AFB just outside Tokyo.

Frozen with anxiety, Collier sat silent and rigid while the giant plane taxied across the runways to the run-up blocks and revved up the four powerful Pratt and Whitneys. Before he found the presence to breathe a prayer, the plane was lumbering forward, slowly gathering speed. The 'bump, bump, bump' of the giant tires gone slightly square from sitting overnight shouldering the massive weight on the cooling tarmac, sounded for all the world as if they were rolling on four flat tires. Just when Collier was certain they would never make it off the ground, miraculously, the aircraft lifted off the runway, straining to attain altitude. Almost before he could unclench his fist, the experienced captain had started to turn out of the pattern and the winking lights of the sleepy city of Seattle were disappearing beneath the plane.

Collier had barely begun to thank his guardian angel for allowing them to get safely airborne when he drifted into an exhausted sleep.

"Ramsay, Ramsay, wake up! Something's wrong." Collier came groggily to his senses with Pewter shaking him rudely awake.

"Huh? What's up?" Collier came alert and rubbed his eyes.

"An engine on the other side of the plane just quit." Pewter leaned across and pointed out through a window two rows ahead of them, on the opposite side of the aisle, immediately past the entrance to the spiral stairway to the lounge.

"No shit!" Collier's sphincter tightened when he saw the four-bladed prop on the outboard port engine was no longer turning.

"Don't worry; these babies are designed with a redundancy safety factor." Collier shrugged, attempting to show an air of confidence when he turned back to Pewter.

Inside, it was all he could do not to shit his pants as he felt the captain slowly bank the plane into a gentle turn into the starboard side of the giant aircraft. Gathering his wits, trying to assess the seriousness of their situation, as far as Collier could tell, for the moment, they did not seem to be losing altitude.

"This is Captain Tabor from the flight deck. As those of you who are awake may have just noticed, we've lost power in the outboard portside engine. Please do not be alarmed. This aircraft is designed to fly on three engines...even two if the need arises. We're turning back to Sea/Tac and should be landing in approximately forty-five minutes. We've already radioed Sea/Tac tower and requested Pan American to provide a back-up aircraft and crew. In the meantime, the bar is still open. We're sorry for the inconvenience. Enjoy your flight." The pilot attempted to reassure them the situation was under control.

"Jeezie, do you really think we'll have to ditch?" Pewter stared down at the moon reflecting off of the darkly-mercurial surface of the vast expanse of the Pacific below.

"Relax, John Henry, the pilot and crew look to me like family men. Remember, they are on this airplane, too. Let's have a Bloody Mary—no time to worry about things like your mother's family's history of alcoholism." Collier gave Pewter's forearm a reassuring squeeze and leaned out into the aisle looking to flag down the nearest stewardess.

What the hell? If he got out of this alive, it would make a great tale to tell his grandkids.

"Please fasten your seatbelts. Captain Taylor says the Sea/Tac tower has given us an emergency clearance to land straight in and we're about fifteen minutes from touch down." Collier had drunk only half of his Bloody Mary when the Chief Stewardess came down the aisle checking seat belts.

To his great relief, almost before Collier had begun to formulate a credible plan of action in the event they went into the drink, the lights of Seattle appeared below and the captain brought the crippled airplane in to a perfect landing.

The entire melodrama transpiring in less than two hours, when they reentered the terminal at Sea/Tac, it was just beginning to get light outside.

They had been in the terminal a full thirty minutes before Major Richards came back to the group and gave them the news. "Give me your attention, please. Pan American is sending a replacement airplane, but it is going to take a few hours while they locate suitable equipment and ferry it here. Your luggage will be transferred to the new airplane when it arrives. Feel free to circulate around the terminal, but keep checking back with me. I won't be hard to find." Out the windows, the sun was just beginning to rise. It looked to Collier like the beginning of a long, boring day.

"Come on, Pewter, looks like we're going to be here for awhile. Sleeping on benches in airport terminals is conduct unbecoming an officer; let's go find someplace we can at least sit comfortably and stretch out." Grumbling at their unhappy plight, Collier made a beeline toward a relatively deserted-looking sitting area on the far side of the lobby out of the mainstream of terminal traffic. Rescuing an orphaned wooden chair leaning against a nearby marble column to serve as a footrest, Collier used his canvas AWOL bag as a pillow and made himself as comfortable as possible, given the unforgiving rigidity of the hard plastic.

Collier's wristwatch showed 0752 just before he drifted back into a sound sleep.

"Wake up Ramsay...you too, Pewter; Major Richards wants us to go down and have our picture taken with some movie stars." The hands of Collier's watch pointed to 1111 as their fellow-traveler, Paul Golden Price, shook both Collier and Pewter rudely awake.

"What's up?" Collier asked groggily, slowly coming to his senses.

"Major Richards asked me to round up everyone I could. There are some movie actors coming in and their publicity people want us to pose with them for pictures. Can't you just see the headline: 'Actors Salute Brave Young Lions Heading To The Combat Zone,'" Price's voice clearly resonated excitement.

"Oh, get the hell out of here. You're putting me on," Collier protested. After the aborted morning flight, he was in no mood to become the butt of anybody's joke.

"No joke, Lieutenant. Follow me if you want to send the folks back home your picture with some honest-to-god movie stars." Without Collier's knowledge, Major Richards had come up behind him.

"Come on, Collier; we might as well go see what's going down. I've never even seen a real movie star up close." Pewter grabbed onto Collier's arm, urging him to get up.

"Who are these so-called movie stars anyway? The Three Stooges? Roy Rogers and Trigger? Oliver and Hardy?" Collier complained.

"When did you get to be so particular? Movie stars are movie stars. Besides, what better do you have to do—sleep in that seat all day? Come on, Ramsay; don't be such a jerk," Pewter said, tugging Collier's arm.

"Okay, Major, bring your men and follow us." Accompanied by about a dozen of their stranded group—the aloof, higher-ranking Medical Officers had disdainfully declined—Collier and John Henry shambled doubtfully along as the Major and the well-pressed Hollywood duo led them through the double doors marked: Private Aviation.

"You might know Paul Golden Price and Brewster Robertson would be up front." John Henry nudged Collier as they spotted their buddies from Pickett leading the way down the stairs.

Emerging into the late-morning sunlight, Collier blinked and looked around at the collection of private aircraft parked nearby on the apron, including a four-engine DC-4 with the corporate logo of a company Collier had never heard of and several DC-3s—one bearing the name of an Alaskan Charter service. Three smaller single-engine planes were parked nearby, further to the north. Looking ahead to their group gathered at the gate in the chain-link fence, Collier saw the pin-striped Hollywood types pointing to a rather nondescript unmarked DC-3 taxiing across the tarmac toward them.

"That's them," one of the Hollywood suits said as a ground crew attendant in orange coveralls directed the much-traveled DC-3 to a parking area on the tarmac immediately in front of them and signaled the pilot to cut his engines.

"That old crate looks more Air Lower Slobovia than Air Hollywood," Collier muttered under his breath, embarrassed at the star-struck naivety of the group. "If they're trying to remain incognito, they're doing a great job of it." The oil-and-grime-spattered airplane's motors had barely wheezed to a stop and the props had scarcely stopped spinning when two more of the ground crew in bright-orange coveralls rolled a moveable stairway in place beneath the DC-3's door. Squinting against the midday sun, Collier waited with ill-concealed skepticism for the door to open revealing the identity of the alleged "movie stars." After what seemed the better part of five to ten minutes, the door finally swung open and a neatly-uniformed stewardess stepped out and stood aside, waiting at the top of the moveable stairway. In a moment, the first of the passengers appeared and started down the steps.

"Robert Mitchum!" Pewter gasped, loud enough to attract disapproving attention from the rest of their group as the first of the DC-3's passengers moved down the ramp, striding imperiously across the tarmac. "Is that enough movie star to suit you?"

"Who's that with Mitchum?" an unidentified member of their group wondered aloud. The swaggering movie star was accompanied by two anonymous companions.

"Maybe they're his parole officers," Collier quipped *sotto voce* to Pewter, referring to Mitchum's notorious history of arrests for marijuana and determined not to appear overly impressed. Mitchum had a knack for playing tough guys and losers with hearts of gold. Lately the tough-guy actor had been keeping some pretty impressive company on the silver screen. Collier had particularly enjoyed Mitchum's recent appearance in the big studio western *The Lusty Men*, with the serious actress, Susan Hayward.

"Stand aside," one of the studio goons motioned for the clot of bystanders around the gate to give Mitchum room as, heavy-lidded with his trademark sneer, the actor elbowed his way toward them. Pushing aggressively through the crowd of open-mouthed young officers, another of the studio muscle men joined them to help escort the actor into the terminal. As Mitchum passed close by, Collier was surprised to see the actor looked to be as well-built as he actually appeared on the silver screen. *Hooray for Hollywood!*

"What's going on? I thought these jerks were going to take our pictures with the movie stars..." up front by the gate, Collier heard one of his group complain as he watched Mitchum disappear into the crowd, headed toward the terminal.

"Just keep your shirt on, Lieutenant. Bob Mitchum's only part of the group. We're saving the best for last!" One of the Hollywood types snorted impatiently, pointing back to the airplane. Following the press agent's gaze, Collier spotted Rory Calhoun, a fairly well-known cowboy actor, just starting down the rolling stairs, accompanied by a pretty, young Latin-looking woman.

"Who's that?" Pewter asked, as the tall, good-looking actor with the curvaceous young woman came toward them; Calhoun was wearing a plain Western shirt without a tie.

"Rory Calhoun. He plays mostly supporting roles in westerns and gangster movies. Over the last few years, he's been slowly making his way up the ladder in Hollywood. Just last year, he played opposite Susan Hayward in *With a Song in My Heart*." Collier didn't mention to Pewter that he had seen Calhoun's most recent horse opera, *The Silver Whip*, a trite melodrama with Dale Robertson and a newcomer, Robert Wagner, about a struggling stage coach line. Now, all at once, it clicked in Collier's mind that both Mitchum and Calhoun had been in recent movies starring Susan Hayward; could it actually be that the sexy redhead was on that plane?

"Who's the babe with Calhoun?" Pewter whispered as the handsome cowboy actor and the good-looking, well-stacked brunette threaded their way through the crowd.

"Lita Baron—she's his wife," Collier whispered back. He had seen a picture of Calhoun and his attractive wife in a movie magazine Emma's sister had been reading back home.

"She looks Mexican...or South American, maybe," Pewter whispered as they approached.

"She was born in Spain," Collier whispered back, recalling the information he had gleaned from Emma's sister's issue of *Photoplay* or *Modern Screen*.

"Excuse us, please." Calhoun smiled shyly as he and his pretty wife pushed through the crowd to the doors into the terminal and disappeared unescorted up the stairwell. Just a shade under six-two, Collier was not accustomed to being in the company of taller men and Calhoun towered at least a couple inches over him. At least six-four or better in his stocking feet, Calhoun looked every inch the movie hero. Privately, Collier was pleased to see the movie cameras and fan magazines had not exaggerated the actor's height. Up close, Lita Baron was even prettier than her pictures in the magazines. Seen beside her towering husband, she was quite tall for a female—a very sexy Spanish Amazon. None of the Hollywood publicity men made a move to accompany the ruggedly-handsome actor and his impressive wife as they quietly made their way through the waiting group.

"Listen up, now! You, you, you, you and these three men right here follow me. The rest of you remain back here inside the gate for a group picture when our star gets off the plane." Scarcely before Collier could wonder what was taking place, the head man of the Hollywood publicity crew pointed out Price and Robertson—along with Collier, Pewter and four or five others of the group just behind them—and led them across the tarmac to the foot of the moveable stairway leading up to where the stewardess stood waiting expectantly at the plane's doorway.

"You two, come up the steps with me." The bossier of the two pinstripes pointed to Price and Robertson and led them up the steps, directing them to stand one at each side of the plane's open doorway. When he came back down, he said, "The rest of you wait with Claude right here."

Shading his eyes and peering up into the dimly-lighted interior of the plane, Collier's attention was drawn to a shadowy flurry of activity. As he watched mezmerized, two rather burly George Raft look-alikes wearing black shirts and white ties with double-breasted, pin-striped gangster suits and carrying shiny, 4 x 5 Speed Graphic press cameras stepped outside the plane. The brassy duo stood at the top of the ramp with cameras raised and strobe lights blazing as a stunning blonde in a brilliant, aquamarine jersey sheath stepped to the doorway of the plane. Cameras momentarily lowered, the dazzling blonde stood smiling as the lead PR man carefully posed Robertson at her left elbow and Price at her right, with their free arms encircled behind her waist.

"Who is the babe?" the obviously ingenuous young lieutenant beside Pewter gasped.

"Are you kidding me? Where have you been hiding?" Pewter asked.

"What do you mean?" the open-mouthed young lieutenant asked, still in the dark.

"That's Marilyn Monroe, you idiot!" A less charitable member of their group saved Pewter the trouble of answering.

At the top of the rolling stairway, the Speed Graphics were flashing as the PR photographers directed Price and Robertson to move in even closer.

Never send boys to do the work of men, Collier snorted under his breath, scarcely able to believe they were having trouble getting his oafish compatriots to snuggle closer to Marilyn Monroe.

Finally satisfied they had done their job, the photographers at the top moved to the bottom of the stairway and snapped shots of Monroe and her two grinning companions as they attempted to walk down the narrow stairway three abreast, bumping intimately at the hip. When the threesome finally made their way to the bottom of the stairs, Collier and John Henry, along with the rest of the select group, were arranged around the eye-catching beauty while the photographers went about their work.

After perhaps ten minutes of the photo shoot, a protective pair of matronly-looking female attendants from the plane stepped in and escorted the charismatic actress across the tarmac toward the entrance to the stairs leading to the terminal lobby. Collier, with Pewter right at his elbow, followed so close behind that Collier was afraid he might step on the four-inch heels of the actress's matching aquamarine satin pumps—so close, in fact, that Collier was becoming half-intoxicated from inhaling the scent of freshly-showered female the alluring actress left in her wake. Entranced with pure lust, Collier watched the sensual ripples of the voluptuous starlet's exquisitely-molded curves as they moved beneath the thin, jersey fabric of the clinging dress. Seen full-on, her nipples were well-defined—even the seductive outline of her pubic triangle left little to Collier's imagination. Now, he could absolutely verify to the folks back home that the actress's claims she wore no undergarments—including panties—were undisputedly true.

"Wait a minute, please," Marilyn purred in her slightly breathless voice and brushed aside the hands of her two matronly companions. "I want to tell these nice soldiers I'm coming to Korea right after we finish shooting in Canada. Sometime around September, I would imagine. I hope I see you all there." She waved and blew them all a kiss before she allowed her overly-solicitous attendants to whisk her out of sight into an elevator.

The excitement over, for the next couple of hours, Collier and Pewter and their group moved aimlessly around the terminal lobby, waiting fruitlessly for further word concerning the status of a Pan Am replacement plane.

"Hey guys, Robert Mitchum is upstairs at the bar in the Eagle's Nest Lounge. What say we go up and have a beer?" Shortly after 1400 hours, Robertson came rushing over to where Collier sat with a dozen of so of their frustrated companions.

"Come on, Collier, I'll buy the beer." Pewter stood and gave Collier's sleeve a tug.

"Sure, why not? Grab your bag and we'll stash 'em in a coin locker." Collier unzipped his AWOL bag and shoved the paperback he'd been reading inside.

"Here, put your bag in here," Collier pushed his AWOL bag inside a locker in the large bank of coin-operated storage lockers on the wall near the stairway to the cocktail lounge.

As advertised, Robert Mitchum was leaning against the bar at the top of the stairs rather boorishly giving the attractive, young, female bartender a hard road to travel over the way she had mixed his drink. It was easy see that Mitchum had had at least one too many and the frustrated bartender was on the verge of tears.

Further back in the lounge area beyond the bar, a group of a dozen or more of their fellow officers were already crowded around several tables they had pushed together. The number of empty beer bottles on the table gave stark evidence they were past caring about the status of the missing Pan Am replacement plane.

"Grab yourselves one of those chairs and join us," Paul Golden Price beckoned them over, pointing to several empty chairs at a table across the aisle.

"We've been sitting here for the past half-hour listening to the rotten SOB give that poor, young bartender a hard time. It's kind of hard to miss the jerk," someone across the table remarked. Collier looked back over his shoulder at Mitchum standing at the bar, generally creating a loud, completely unnecessary, nuisance over the 'proper way to make a Martini.'

"I'm Rory Calhoun. I was on the plane from Hollywood with Marilyn Monroe. We're flying up to Canada to make a movie. Our press people tell me you guys are going to Korea and are waiting for a plane. Lita and I were in Korea with the USO last Christmas. I don't want to impose, but I thought you might let me sit in with you awhile and buy a couple rounds." When Collier looked up, the tall actor was standing in the aisle at his elbow.

"That's nice of you, Mr. Calhoun. Pull up one of those chairs," Robertson stood to scoot his chair around the table to make room. When Calhoun was seated, he ordered a round of drinks for everyone. While they were waiting for the drinks, he explained they were en route to Edmonton, Canada where they were going on location to nearby Banff and Jasper National Parks to film a movie entitled *River of No Return*. Calhoun was particularly proud that the film was being directed by the international Hollywood icon, Otto Preminger. He obviously felt that being in such high-powered company was an important milestone in his struggle to escape being typecast in cowboy and gangster films.

"I envy you. Count yourself fortunate to be able to give something back to this country. I know that no one in his right mind wants to get shot at or bombed, but I tried to join the military during World War Two—they turned me down because I had a record. You're lucky. I really do envy you." Calhoun reflected sincerely.

An uneasy lull settled over the table. No one sitting at the table was prepared to hear a movie star make such an open confession of a criminal past.

"You mean ah...a criminal record?" one of the captains asked, certain the famous movie star couldn't be talking about being in jail.

"Yeah. As a kid I got sent up for stealing cars. I served three years in Reno, Oklahoma, when I was still just a teen. I'm sorry to say our laws frown on taking convicted felons in the military. Of course, at the time, that probably wouldn't have altered my course as a budding career criminal. One thing for sure, I never want to risk going to jail again." Calhoun laughed self-consciously. He seemed to be a genuinely shy and unassuming man.

"THROW THIS GODDAMN THING OUT. DO YOU REALLY EXPECT ME TO DRINK SHIT LIKE THIS?" The sound of Robert Mitchum loudly cursing the waitress interrupted the small talk around the table. All eyes turned toward the bar as Mitchum pushed himself away. Slopping the contents of his glass on the bartender, the actor headed toward the stairs, trying hard not to stagger.

"If you're leaving now, Mr. Mitchum, please come back and pay your check..." Verging near the edge of tears, the humiliated young bartender called him back.

"You don't expect me to actually pay for shit like that?" Stumbling against the barstools, Mitchum continued lurching drunkenly for the stairs.

Shocked at seeing such an inexcusable display of bad manners from a well-known movie star, no one at the table spoke.

"There, ladies and gentlemen, goes the famous movie star, Robert Mitchum, in all his glory," Calhoun stood with a sweeping gesture, dramatically mocking Mitchum to everyone in the lounge. "Don't worry, Bob I'll take care of your tab."

"Fuck you, Calhoun, you goddamn jailbird," Mitchum stopped and stared back drunkenly, before resuming his stagger toward the steps.

"Takes on to know one, Bob. By the way, I'll leave a ten for your tip. You can pay me when you sober up." Pushing aside his chair, Calhoun moved swiftly to the bar to settle Mitchum's check. When Calhoun came back to the table, the pretty bartender was laughing at something Calhoun said, proudly holding up a wine list he had autographed for her.

"Don't be too hard on Mitchum; he's had a rough day." Following an awkward moment, the conversation started up again as Calhoun told a funny story about Mitchum showing up that morning at the Los Angeles airport with a horrible hangover, only to discover he was too early for the airport bars to be open in order for him to get a "little hair of the dog." The talk went on that way for awhile until, inevitably, someone told the latest off-color joke. From that point on, the empty beer bottles kept piling up faster than the young cocktail waitress could clear them away to make room for refills.

"Rory, our plane ees ready." Collier looked up to see Lita Baron, Calhoun's striking wife, standing beside his chair.

"Sorry, guys, I gotta go. I think our agent is signing Lita and me on for a USO tour of Korea in the fall...maybe I'll see you there. I wish you luck. This should be enough to cover our check and leave a generous tip." Pushing back his chair, he peeled off several twenties plus a ten. "You're lucky. You only have to face the Chinese Communists in Korea; I have to spend the next three months with Bob Mitchum in the Canadian wilderness." He winked broadly, flashing a brilliant Hollywood smile.

"Come on guys, let's go find Richards and see what's going on with getting us another plane." Collier pushed back his chair. As much as he dreaded flying, he knew they still had long hours of flight ahead of them, and he was past ready for getting back in the air.

"I was just coming to find you. We finally have a replacement airplane. Gather your gear and meet me back at the door we came through this morning. Don't waste time. We've been delayed long enough." The anxious Major was about to start up the steps to the cocktail lounge when he encountered the group coming down.

Retrieving their bags from the coin-operated storage lockers, Collier and Pewter quickly made their way to a window overlooking the tarmac, anxious to see their waiting replacement plane. The only airplane in sight was a disreputable, oil- and dirt-smeared DC-4 that looked for all the world like it was headed for the scrap heap.

"It must not have landed yet," Pewter offered.

"Unfortunately, I have a sinking feeling it has," Collier said as he made out the weather-faded logo: Pan American Airways across the fuselage of the DC-4 above the window row.

"Surely that's not our plane?" Price and Robertson, Marilyn Monroe's newfound-celebrity twins chorused in open-mouthed disbelief.

"If you're speaking of the four-engine Pan Am, I'm afraid it is," Major Richards came walking up.

"But, Major Richards, Sir, what happened to the Army's contract to fly us 'Champagne Service with hot- and cold-running stewardesses'?" One of their group wailed.

"Isn't there something you can do? They certainly can't expect us to fly on that," an older captain with the caduceus insignia of a medical officer protested loudly.

"Sorry, Captain. It's axiomatic. In an operation of any size, you have to expect a few losses." Richards flashed an unhappy grin.

When Collier reached the tarmac, the DC-4 looked even more decrepit than when first viewed from the terminal window. As he made his way up the boarding stairs, he nervously noted missing rivets in the aircraft's aluminum skin—it was impossible to imagine this airplane having ever been shiny and new.

"Jesus Christ on roller skates! The freaking Army must be out of its mind if they expect us to fly all the way to Tokyo on this frigging wreck." What little remnant of optimism Collier had left totally vanished when he mounted the steps just behind Pewter and entered through the aircraft's oversize cargo door. Except that a canvas sling bench ran the length of both sides of the poorly lit gutted aluminum-ribbed interior of the old cargo aircraft, the work-worn cabin reminded Collier of the interior of one of the dirty railroad boxcars in which he had often worked during his Christmas vacation jobs unloading the heavy holiday flow of mail, at the N&W passenger station in Roanoke.

"Might as well save your bitching—this is it. Find yourself a seat and make yourselves comfortable. I hope you ate a good lunch. All we have on board is K-rations. The good news is we do have both cold and hot water aboard in these big containers"—Richards pointed to the pair of large aluminum containers—"so you can mix the coffee and cocoa. There is also a generous supply of paper cups. But, please do not—I repeat do not—use the limited hot water to warm the meat can selection from the K-Rations."

Collier hesitated and looked around, flabbergasted they faced well over twenty hours on board this wreck.

"There are GI blankets stacked on both benches at the rear of the cabin— there should be more than enough to go around. If you can sleep, do so by all means. It would go a long way in helping to minimize the discomfort of this trip." Collier listened while their fearless leader gave them more depressing news.

"This is your pilot, Captain Graves...on behalf of Pan Am, I want to apologize for your inconveniences today. Welcome aboard the first leg of our flight along the Great Circle Route from Seattle-Tacoma to Elmendorf Air Force Base in Anchorage, Alaska. Elmendorf is a distance of about fifteen-hundred air miles north and slightly west of here in the Alaska Daylight Time zone which is in Greenwich Mean Time Zone Minus Eight. For your orientation it is currently fifteen hundred twenty-three hours here. Seattle is on Pacific Daylight Time in GMT Minus Seven. Before we land at Elmendorf set your watches back one hour. At our normal cruising speed of slightly over two-hundred miles per hour, and fighting a slight headwind, we estimate an elapsed flying time of about seven hours. There is a box of sandwiches and hot coffee up near the front of the cabin. There is also a supply of K-Rations. We expect to have good weather all the way in to Elmendorf where we will have a layover of approximately two hours for you to enjoy a hot meal. We will have a crew change there and will refuel the airplane for the second leg of your flight into Shemya Air Force Base in the Aleutian Islands..." the bored pilot's voice came over the intercom sounding like just another day in the office.

"Can you believe they're giving us fucking K-Rations instead of steak and Champagne?" one of the Medical captains up near the front said in disgust.

Collier sincerely hoped he would not get hungry enough to resort to eating K-Rations on this trip. In his limited experience, the M cans should all be labeled "Instant Heartburn."

"Quit bitching," Major Richards reminded them impatiently. "At least you're not being shot at. We could be wet and sleeping in the mud somewhere on Pork Chop Hill."

"Come on, Pewter; let's grab ourselves some of those blankets before they're all gone," Collier pushed through the disgruntled members of the group who had boarded before them and headed for the pile of OD GI blankets at the front of the cabin where several cases of the all-too-familiar olive drab packages of K-Rations were pushed against the bulkhead by the head. Selecting three of the blankets, he moved back by the large cargo door to the canvas bucket-seat bench on the right side of the cabin, unfolded two of the blankets and spread them across two sections of the metal-pipe framing which divided both benches into long rows of single-section seats. Placing his AWOL bag for a pillow at the end of the improvised pallet of blankets, without removing his shoes, he lay down on the blanket-bed and was asleep before the captain came back on the intercom instructing them to fasten their seatbelts for takeoff.

"This is the first officer from the cockpit. Please fasten your seatbelts and stow all loose items underneath the seats. We are beginning our approach to Elmendorf Air Force Base in Anchorage, Alaska. Turn back your watches. The local time is ten minutes past midnight, Alaska Daylight Time. Also let me remind you that this time of year, the sun orbits the horizon without actually setting. While daylight is not exactly sunlit in the sense we are accustomed to in more southern latitudes, being this far north this time of year, Anchorage has almost twenty-four hours of functional daylight. You will see the effect is like living in a perpetual sunset or, if you prefer, sunrise. Hence the expression: 'Land of the midnight sun.'" Collier awoke to the sound of the pilot's voice over the intercom. Through the window in the bulkhead opposite him where Pewter was just coming awake and rubbing his eyes, Collier saw a clear, but strangely-lit dark-amber-colored sky which gave off an eerie unworldly appearance of being neither day or night. Riding low on the horizon through the thick layers of the earth's heavy atmosphere, the sun appeared to radiate a sort of surreal starburst halo—reminding Collier of artist Chesley Bonestell's fanciful illustrations of Moonscapes and Marscapes he'd seen in magazines.

"Pay attention where you come into the terminal when we deplane. We will all rendezvous back at that same door in two hours. It is exactly eleven twenty-nine hours now, Alaskan Daylight Time—don't forget to set your watches." Major Richards was right at home in the role of mother hen. His concern about them getting lost was ill-founded, however. The terminal at Elmendorf was a large, no-frills, hanger-type building that would have impressed any visiting congressman, worried about the military wasting money.

"Gentlemen, the men's latrine is over to your right. When you've taken care of business, come back here, and I will take you to get some hot chow." They were met at the door by a staff sergeant who waited until they had used the latrine. As soon as they were reassembled, he escorted them across the cavernous waiting area and led them across the tarmac to a military mess-hall-style dining facility. The chow was surprisingly good, and Collier stuffed himself full of home-fried steak—which was surprisingly tender and smothered in a rich, brown gravy—and mashed potatoes with Brussels sprouts, a rarity in Army mess halls back home. After he had polished off a heaping serving of apple cobbler and was scraping his tray over a garbage can at the clean-up area, Collier asked a cook in immaculate kitchen whites wearing a blousey white chef's hat with sergeant's chevrons pinned to the whites, "Do you guys always eat this good?"

"Tonight is just average, Sir. We try to make a tour up here as pleasant as we can." The smiling mess sergeant beamed with pride.

"I can't believe it's no colder than this—and it's well past midnight." Walking around outside after eating chow, Collier was surprised at how pleasant the temperature was this time of the early-morning hours. The thermometer on a metal Coca-Cola plaque nailed to the wall outside the door to the terminal parking area indicated a moderate 59 degrees.

"You forget, the sun never sets up here this time of year, so there is no cooling during what we consider night hours back in the States," one of the KPs on smoke break reminded him.

Inside the rudimentary terminal, both Collier and Pewter bought some postcards with pictures of the weird amber sky of the "Land of the Midnight Sun" and some with pictures of totem poles. Purchasing accompanying postage stamps, they mailed the cards to the folks back home.

"Okay, we're all here. Let's head out," After Major Richards took roll, he led the way back to the waiting plane.

"This is Captain Monohan. On behalf of Pan Am and your new crew, I want to welcome you back aboard for the second leg of the Great Circle Route from Elmendorf AFB to Shemya AFB, a distance of about twelve-hundred air miles. At a normal cruising speed of slightly over two-hundred miles per hour, and fighting a slight headwind, we estimate an elapsed flying time of about seven hours."—the over-zealous Captain sounded like a phonograph record—"Shemya is on Hawaii-Aleutian GMT MinusTen which means we have to set our watches back two hours before we land. We are going to run into a front about an hour out and will be flying in soupy weather all the way," as the pilot delivered the bad news over the intercom, Collier moved his watch back to 0035 and, ignoring the uncomfortable pipe separators, stretched out on his improvised bed as soon as they were airborne and went right back to sleep.

Pewter was still sleeping when Collier awoke and saw they were still flying in a soup. About fifty percent of the time, the solid bank of clouds was so thick it obscured the outboard engines from his view. Groggy and stiff from lying on the wooden cargo deck, Collier pulled himself erect, shook and refolded the blankets and spread them back on the bucket-seat bench.

His mouth dry and tasting like yesterday's possum droppings, Collier reflexively rubbed his fingertips across his two-day stubble. He was certain he smelled like a stable hand and he felt as if he had been wearing the same damned uniform for a month, at least.

Unfortunately, there was nothing to do about washing up now; there was no running water in the lavatory in the head. Grabbing his AWOL bag he located the compact, leather zipper bag containing the Sunbeam electric razor he had received as a Christmas gift from his folks. Recalling an electrical outlet up front on the bulkhead by the door to the head, Collier extracted the Sunbeam and made his way, rib-by-aluminum-rib, to the front of the cabin.

Locating the electrical plug-in, Collier unzipped the leather bag and took out the razor. He crossed his fingers, held his breath and plugged in the razor cord. To his complete amazement anything might actually still work in this decrepit, outmoded aircraft, when he switched the razor on, it buzzed to life. Standing there in the narrow passageway, running the shaver across his face and looking out of the porthole window, Collier stared numbly into the dense cloud bank which had enveloped them in a gray cocoon since takeoff from Elmendorf.

"Shemya approach control, this is Pan Am Seven-two. Estimate twenty miles out, over..." After a few minutes, Collier was jolted out of his reverie by the first officer's voice in the cockpit.

There were some popping sounds and a loud hum of static before a voice came back, "We read you, Pan Am..."

"Roger. Pan Am is approaching Shemya and maintaining five thousand. What's your weather?"

More static...

"Roger...Shemya has radar contact. We're currently reporting four hundred, with one mile visibility with rain. Shemya altimeter is two nine point seven nine and the wind is two-eighty at ten..."

"Roger that, Shemya."

Anxiously listening to the exchange, Collier continued moving the electric shaver over his jaw line, checking behind with his fingertips to make sure the surface was becoming smooth. Except for the buzz of his electric razor and the sound of the engines, there was silence for what seemed an eternity.

"Continue present heading and descend to nineteen-hundred feet. Stay with me for your approach..." Collier could see the pilot and the first officer exchanging words, but except for static, there was nothing more from Shemya on the cockpit speakers for the next several minutes.

"Shemya, this is Pan Am Seven-two; we're at nineteen hundred."

"Roger Pan Am. Turn to heading three-twenty and descend to eleven hundred."

"Pan Am Seven-two descending to eleven hundred and turning to heading three-two-zero."

Fascinated, Collier unplugged his razor and watched the pilot and first officer as they prepared the plane for landing.

"Okay, Pan Am Seven-Two, we have you coming on course. Prepare to start your descent for landing...we have you approaching the glide path. Start your descent at four-hundred feet per minute now. No need to acknowledge further transmissions."

Collier watched as the Captain picked up a hand mike and his voice came over the intercom, "Attention in the cabin, we are making our approach into Shemya Air Force Base where we will refuel and have our last hot meal before we begin the final leg across the Pacific into Tokyo. Please find a seat and buckle up."

Over the whine of the engines, Collier heard the landing gear going down. Then he felt—more than heard—the heavy gear locking into place.

"I'm showing six hundred and still nothing, Shemya."

"Come left two degrees now, Pan Am, and correct your rate of descent...you're slipping below the glide path.

Collier felt the aircraft yaw slightly to the left and straighten up again.

Standing there just behind the flight crew, Collier was momentarily transfixed—totally fascinated they were flying blind in a pea-soup fog trying to hit a desolate, miniscule, hunk of rock in the middle of the Pacific Ocean, two-thousand miles away from the Alaska mainland. At this point, he was too traumatized by the unending series of disasters already plaguing this doomsday flight to feel anything but curiosity for what was coming next.

Absently winding the razor cord into a tight coil, he put the razor back into the supple leather travel case. There were no flight attendants aboard to order them around this miserable airplane and he felt no particular hurry to find his seat.

"We have you at five hundred, Pan Am. You're looking good. We've turned on all our lights. You should be breaking through this stuff anytime now."

Collier stared hard out the window trying to find a break in the solid cocoon of fog. Now he was conscious of the fact the sound of the engines had changed— the pilot was struggling to control their altitude.

"Oh, shit!" Collier's head snapped sharply to the right when he heard the captain curse. Through the cockpit windshield, Collier saw the island appearing like a ghostly-apparition through a misty-web of grasping fingers of fog. They had finally broken through the overcast, and, through tendrils of low-hanging clouds, Collier could see they were only a matter of seconds away from crashing into the edge of the bleak, rocky coastline. To their left, was the beckoning runway running almost halfway down the westernmost—now the easternmost, since they were heading to the Orient—margin of the island. The runway was plenty long, but the plane was dangerously low. The problem was the plane was more than several hundred yards too far right. If the pilot didn't make a miraculous correction to their left, they were going to land in the arctic water. Collier had a sinking feeling that even if the pilot was able to make a correction to avoid going into the drink this late in the instrument descent, they would almost certainly crash into the craggy cliffs or on the rocky surface of the rugged island. If he had to make a choice, Collier hoped the pilot would opt to ditch in the water. Except that it appeared to be pock-marked with a variety of ragtag buildings and a variety of storage tanks—most likely fuel and ammo dumps—to Collier's eye the partly grassed-over terrain looked like the surface of an English moor much like a brooding illustration from Sir Conan Doyle's *Hound of the Baskervilles*. It didn't take a genius to figure out there was absolutely no place to crash land a plane as big as the one they were on.

"Pull up...pull up, Pan Am...repeat, pull up..." the Shemya controller's strident commands came through the radio, but, even as he felt the engines take on a sudden burst of power, Collier was certain the commands were too late as their ancient bird floundered and settled even closer toward the tops of the spray-capped waves. Just when it seemed certain they were going into the ocean and the rocks, the war-weary aircraft began to slowly climb—four engines straining—into the beginning of a wide turn.

"Do you wish to declare an emergency, Pan Am?" the Shemya tower asked

"That would be an affirmative, you stupid asshole..." the last was barely audible as the pilot breathed into the mike, completely occupied with the controls.

"Okay, you're cleared to circle, Pan Am, if you can stay clear of the clouds...and you're still cleared to land..." the embarrassed Shemya controller ignored the insult.

"No shit, Shemya..." In the righthand seat, the copilot was busy flipping switches and pulling levers.

Judging from the sudden dead air, Collier had a sneaking suspicion the first officer's mike was live. The silence continued as the valiant old warbird labored in a wide bank.

"Missed the approach and on the go," the copilot's voice came back on as he labored over the controls.

"Roger, Pan Am, climb on runway heading...cleared to eleven-hundred feet. Turn right out of five hundred to a heading of one two zero and report reaching eleven-hundred feet," Shemya control came back.

"Roger, Shemya. We'd like to try another approach," the copilot answered.

"Okay, Pan Am. That was a close one. Our weather is pretty poor, but you're our only customer right now."

Nothing but static and engine sounds as the pilots struggled to bring the plane around.

"Eleven hundred. Heading one two zero degrees, Shemya," after several minutes, Collier heard the copilot come back on.

"Roger. Pan Am. We're below minimums again, currently. Hold at the Shemya beacon, standard pattern with three-minute legs approved. If you wish, report established in the holding pattern."

"Thanks, Shemya. Won't be able to hold long as fuel is going to be a problem. We had some pretty strong head winds coming over."

Several minutes passed before Collier heard the copilot come back on, "Pan Am Seven-Two established in the holding pattern. What's your weather, Shemya?"

"Latest weather is one-hundred feet and half mile with fog and light rain, Pan Am. What are your intentions?" Shemya answered tersely.

"We really need to get this bird on the ground soon, so we'd like to make another approach and take a look, even though you're below minimums," the Pan Am copilot replied.

"That's affirmative, Pan Am Seven-Two. We have you on radar outbound on a heading of one-four-zero in the holding pattern. After thirty seconds, turn inbound to a heading of three-two-zero and prepare for landing. Report wheels down and locked."

"Roger, Shemya. We are ready for landing and showing three green," the copilot answered.

"We can't afford to miss again, so let me know when you see something. I'm going to fly it in," Collier heard the captain tell the copilot as he felt the drafty old airplane start to come around.

"Okay, Skipper," the copilot replied. "Understand you'll keep her coming."

"Start your rate of descent now, Pan Am. You're on course and on the glide path four-and-one-half miles from touchdown. No need for further response. You are cleared to land. Now come left two degrees...still on glide path...looking good....

Standing just outside the cockpit, Collier listened, frozen with anticipation, waiting for the next transmission.

"On course. On glide path approaching minimums...take over and land visually," Shemya control came back.

Realizing they were about to land on that jagged rock pile again, Collier walked himself back to his seat, holding on to the aluminum ribs of the fuselage for dear life, as he heard the copilot say, "Got the rabbit in sight dead ahead, Skip."

Barely making it to the rear of the airplane and buckling in his seat, Collier felt the airplane kiss the runway with scarcely a screech of tires. His fists clenched tight on the aluminum frame of the bucket seat, Collier held his breath—waiting for the crash, but the roll-out and taxi in was completely uneventful.

Deplaning, the passengers were greeted by a howling gale. Glad to be on solid ground, Collier, and his fellow passengers—who remained blissfully unaware of the drama having taken place during their near-disastrous approach—followed a young, apple-cheeked corporal to a school bus painted in weather-faded OD. Before the bus was underway, the fog rolled back in and the bleak landscape was enveloped again in an impenetrable gray shroud.

"Judas priest, I'm glad this mess lifted in time for us to come in VFR," Collier remarked to the young bus driver, shivering as much from the frigid drop in temperature as from the sudden realization of the caliber of the disaster they had just narrowly avoided came over him. He had learned the flying jargon VFR—Visual Flight Rules—from his brother Jim.

"Oh, we have this all the time. Our tower would have guided your pilot in as safe as a baby in its mother's arms," the young driver remarked offhand.

Collier smiled but remained silent, fervently hoping the control tower was already busy recalibrating their radar and ILS—Instrument Landing System—or whatever they had to do to take care of business to prevent this from happening again.

Transported from the refueling area adjacent to the runway along a narrow, twisting road on the inland side of the runway, the bus passed through several sporadic, small collections of Quonset huts and other, somewhat bedraggled, ghostly wooden buildings resembling the barracks at Fort Sill. Although the buildings seemed unfit for habitation in Collier's opinion, there were men moving in and out. The fog, however, prevented a clear image of the settlement on the bleak outpost. The bus finally pulled up in front of a larger—though still wooden and corrugated metal—military-looking building at the end of a spidery, wooden-railed, planked walkway bridging the swamp-grass-covered rocky expanse from the parking area.

"Everybody out. This is our Cordon Bleu gourmet mess hall," the young driver quipped, pulling the handle opening the door.

Inside the rudimentary mess hall, Collier made straight for the latrine, took off his shirt and set to washing up. When he had done the best he could, he dried on the shirt and donned a spare from his AWOL bag. Not exactly a new man, but until he could find a place and the time to take a good, hot shower, this repair job would have to do. As an afterthought, he brushed his teeth, trying to rid his mouth of the taste of a very bad day; then he confiscated a roll of GI toilet paper and stuck it in his AWOL bag—a hedge against a mid-flight bowel crisis.

Probably because he was so glad to have escaped a horrible death, the chow—it was breakfast time on this desolate rock—seemed even better than at Elmendorf. On his way back out of the mess hall, Collier swiped a regular ceramic coffee cup to avoid having to drink from the cheap paper cups Pan Am had supplied.

"You want to be court-martialed for stealing government property?" Major Richards asked when he saw Collier grab the toilet paper and cup.

"You'd better be careful, Major. You may want to be on my good side if you have a call of nature before we arrive in Japan," Collier said, risking the fact that Richards was a little short on sense of humor, but almost certain he would never see the Quartermaster major after they arrived in Japan.

Surprisingly, Richards laughed.

"A tour on Shemya is only twelve months—it's more than long enough. The Army tries to see to it we have all the latest movies and plenty to read—all the latest magazines and books." the apple-cheeked bus driver answered Collier's questions about duty on the island, on the way back to the airplane.

"It's almost July and it feels like winter back in Virginia—the wind makes it even worse. Is it always this bad?" Collier persisted.

"This is as good as it gets, believe me. If they ever give the world an enema, they'll put the catheter here," the young driver said earnestly. He was barreling along the narrow road in a thick fog that reduced his vision to practically nothing.

"How can you see in this shit? Aren't you afraid you'll meet some oncoming traffic?" One of Collier's compatriots asked the question troubling everyone on the bus.

"Neah! Except for snow removal equipment, this is practically the only vehicle operational on this freaking place." Their young driver laughed maniacally.

"Well, just the same, I wish you'd slow down," Major Richards, who was sitting across the aisle on the seats nearest the front door, spoke up.

"I'm sorry, sir. I didn't mean to alarm you," the driver apologized, but as far as Collier could tell he didn't slow down that much.

"How about extra duty? Do you have to pull KP and guard duty way out here?" Collier asked, trying to get his mind away from the fear of being in a head-on crash. He couldn't visualize what soldiering on this godforsaken rock would be like.

"It's pretty much the same as the States except when we arrive on base we are assigned a partner for suicide watch." The driver said completely straight-faced.

"For what?" A chorus of the men behind Collier who had been listening asked in horror.

"Just kidding. Sirs. We have to keep our sense of humor, or we'd all be Section Eights before the end of the first month." The cherub-faced driver laughed at his own joke.

At the airstrip, the peasoup fog was so thick Collier could barely make out the plane less than twenty-five yards away. Bounding out of the bus and heading for the boarding steps, as intimidating as it was to contemplate reboarding the C-54 for a takeoff in this nightmarish weather, Collier had no trouble reconciling the dismal prospect of staying on Shemya against the promise of finally arriving in Japan.

"This is Captain Monohan from the flight deck; welcome back aboard. I hope you enjoyed the hot meal and the opportunity to stretch your legs. Please buckle up for our final leg to Haneda Airport serving Tokyo. The flying distance is approximately two thousand miles. At our normal cruising speed of two hundred twenty-five miles an hour, our estimated time in the air will be something just over ten hours—depending on winds aloft. In case you're still confused by the change in time zones, the time is now exactly ten-hundred-eleven hours—repeat that is one-zero-one-one hours Hawaiian-Aleutian which is GMT Minus Ten. We left Seattle on Tuesday, June 30, at around fifteen-thirty hours Pacific Daylight Time. Counting about five or six hours in layovers plus total flying time of around sixteen hours, it is now very late in the first day of July in the year of our Lord nineteen-hundred and fifty-three. For those of you who are unfamiliar with world travel, we will be crossing the International Dateline a few hours out of Shemya. Traveling east, the date is one day earlier on the other side of the International Dateline. So, although we will be in the air approximately half a day, when we arrive in Tokyo it will be tomorrow, July Second, GMT Plus Nine. The difference between GMT Minus Ten and GMT Plus Nine is seventeen hours. If we're in the air twelve hours, we should arrive Tokyo tomorrow—which will still be today—around seventeen hundred hours. If you're confused, maybe some of your buddies can help you figure it out. We will fly at an altitude of five thousand feet. Thanks to the Air Force on Shemya, you will find several large bags of sandwiches and a large box of delicious fried chicken, just like your mother made, to keep you from starving on the way to Tokyo. Also, don't forget we still have the K-Rations aboard. Once we are in the air, I suggest you make yourselves as comfortable as possible—this is going to be a rather long flight." The intercom crackled Monohan's cheery message.

"Just another day in the wild blue yonder," Pewter quipped and buckled up.

"Not much blue about it that I can see," Collier griped.

"Just another day in the wild gray yonder then," Pewter grinned.

"You know where you can put your wild gray yonder," Collier snapped, not at all amused as he set to rearranging his pallet of blankets.

Just one more time, God. Let me get to Tokyo safely, and I swear I'll never fly again, Collier buckled up and breathed a silent promise to the God who didn't know him.

The pilot wasted no time in running up the engines and taxiing out to the end of the runway in the fog which was still so thick that Collier could barely make out the outboard engines. Without delay, the plane wheeled around and started down the runway. Before Collier had time to work up a full-fledged nervous breakdown, they were in the air again.

When the ancient warbird finally reached altitude, Collier unbuckled and spread his lengthy form on his pallet on the cabin floor. Belly full and adrenalin subsiding, he quickly fell asleep. When he awoke, the sky was clear and he could see the broad expanse of the Pacific stretching endlessly below. Going to the head to take a leak, he came back and rearranged his pallet and stretched back out. He dozed fitfully for about an hour longer before he finally came fully awake again.

Thirsty after his long nap, Collier found the ceramic cup he had purloined from the mess hall on Shemya and made his way slowly to the front where the coffee and water urns were sitting beside a huge Great Northern Toilet Tissue carton heaped to overflowing with pieces of golden-fried chicken. Reaching across and taking a paper napkin from a stack beside the box, he plucked out a drumstick and bit into it, realizing almost instantly that there was something dreadfully amiss.

"Judas Priest!" Collier gasped, looking down at the drumstick at the raw, red, blood oozing from where he'd taken the bite. He stopped chewing instantly and spit the mouthful of bloody chicken into the outsized Kotex Sanitary Napkin shipping carton put on board to act as a trash container. Rare steak was okay, but he had always insisted on his chicken and pork cooked well done. When he'd finished spitting out as much of the distasteful meat as possible, he rinsed his mouth with water from one of the urns, rushed to the head and spit into the commode, fighting back a strong urge to vomit.

By the time Collier retraced his steps to the cabin, in his brief absence his flight-mates had taken note of his experience with the raw chicken and had made a run on the small box of sandwiches which was completely empty now.

"Too bad. Women and children to the lifeboats, but it's every man for himself." Major Richards, sadly shook his head—in his hand he jealously guarded a pair of sandwiches.

"In an operation this size, you have to expect a few losses," Collier repeated the Major's maxim of logistics and shrugged. He really didn't care about the sandwiches. He'd lost his appetite, anyway.

"Don't worry. I saw what happened, and I got a couple of sandwiches for us while you were in the head, before our honorable fellows were cleaning them out," Pewter reassured him when he returned to his bucket seat.

"Thanks for looking out for us, John Henry. And don't worry about it being enough. I have about a dozen candy bars in my AWOL bag, in case we need a little something to tide us over." Collier winked and settled himself for the long flight ahead.

"This is the flight deck. If you will look out your windows on either side you will see we are rapidly approaching the coastline of Japan. We are about fifty miles south of Tokyo and Haneda Airport and will be flying rather low over the countryside on our approach to Haneda," after what seemed an eternity, but was more like five or six hours, the captain came over the intercom, continuing in a monotone, "As I tried to explain back in Shemya, we have crossed the International Dateline passing through a number of time zones. Tokyo is on Greenwich Mean Time Plus Nine. The day is now Thursday, July second. Set your watches gentlemen—on my mark the time will be 1331."

All up and down the line of bucket-seat benches, the passengers in the airplane readied the stems of their watches expectantly waiting for the pilot's command.

"Mark!" Hearing the command, Collier, like the rest of the weary officers aboard set his watch and started to gather his belongings and straighten his appearance as best he could.

After he had finished gathering his gear, Collier went to the window and looked out. The rich, emerald-green, Japanese countryside stretched before him like a picture book. Checker-boarded and crosshatched everywhere by rice paddies and punctuated by a number of small, conical mountains rising out of the plain like so many tiny green fairy breasts, below them were scattered houses surrounded by cultivated farms. Back home in Virginia, these pretty little mountains would be considered to be more like pointy little hills. There was not a wasted inch of land anywhere the eye could see; most of the little mountains were terraced all the way to the top by rice paddies. The pilot had descended to a lower altitude and now the picturesque panorama seemed to be whizzing underneath them at a dizzying rate.

"Up ahead on our left, you will see see the low skyline of Tokyo." Sure enough, when he looked, the Tokyo skyline was shimmering like a mirage through the low-lying heat haze. "Haneda Airport control reports an expected high today of ninety-five, but inside the city, the temperature will go up to over the one-hundred mark. Now, if you look further to the left, you can catch a view of the almost picture-perfect, snow-white cone of Fujiyama—not Mount Fujiyama. In Japanese, 'yama' means 'mountain. So when you say 'Mount Fujiyama' you would be saying 'Mount Fuji Mountain.' In that regard, the Japanese usually call the volcano 'Fujisan,' but 'Fujiyama,' or 'Mount Fuji' is standard in English—just be aware that either will sound foreign to native Japanese."

Looking to his left, Collier sucked in his breath when, just as the pilot told them, he saw the majestic, incredibly-beautiful, snowcapped cone rising above the green landscape. At the lower altitude, Collier now became uncomfortably aware of the increasing temperature inside the cabin. Sweat was popping out all over his body as the inside of the old cargo plane was rapidly becoming an oven.

"Please take your seats and buckle up. We are beginning our approach to Haneda Airport. Although, officially, Japan is still under rule of the United States military government under command of General Douglas MacArthur, essentially, the Japanese have been allowed to resume their normal lifestyle and the pursuit of restoring their manufacturing and consumer businesses to a pre-World War Two economy. The point is that you will have to clear Japanese Customs at Haneda before they release you to the United States Army for processing—it's SOP. The good news is if you are lucky enough to have some time here before being shipped somewhere else, Tokyo is a thriving, bustling beehive of activity during the daytime. The Japanese are notorious for their ability to reproduce goods and technology. If you are in the market for a good camera, I recommend you consider a Japanese-manufactured Canon or Nikon. Both cameras use thirty-five millimeter film—the color film is developed as positive and returned in thirty-five millimeter slides—but you can have negatives made, if you prefer to have snapshot prints. The Canon is a replica of the world-famous Leica, manufactured in Germany by a guy named Leitz who literally invented thirty-five millimeter photography. The Nikon is the Japanese version of the German-made Zeiss Ikon Contax which essentially was inspired by and modeled after the Leica. But, get this, the Japanese lenses are considered to be at least equal—if not superior—to their German-made counterparts." The pilot was clearly a camera buff but Collier tuned out the boring monologue, worried now about yet another landing.

When he felt the wheels go down and lock, Collier took his seat and was looking for the seatbelt when the copilot came back on the intercom. The long Pacific crossing nearing its end, the chatty captain was obviously enjoying himself.

"Thank you for being the guests of Pan American Airways. Be careful not to get carried away in Tokyo. After dark—with all the bars and so-called Geisha houses and thousands of your fellow GIs rotating from Korea every six months or so on R and R—it is literally Sodom and Gomorrah. Have fun, but not too much fun—the city is swarming with military and civilian police."

Collier had barely pulled his seatbelt tight when he felt the airplane settle and touch down on the runway, as the captain reversed the pitch of the propeller blades and rolled to a stop. Collier watched out of the nearest window as the pilot guided them across the taxiway to the group of white masonry buildings making up the Haneda air terminal on the far side of the field.

BOOK THREE

CHAPTER FORTY-TWO

THE ROANOKE TIMES
Roanoke, Virginia, Thursday, July 2, 1953
RHEE'S ANSWER GIVEN TO ENVOY
Eisenhower Pledge Reported Refused

SEOUL, Thursday, July 2 (AP) – President Eisenhower's truce envoy talked in private with South Korean President Syngman Rhee for nearly two hours today after receiving Rhee's answer to last-minute American concessions intended to win Rhee's support of a truce in Korea.

A reliable source said their discussions are in a temporary stalemate but continuing.

A letter outlining Rhee's latest position on the all-but-signed armistice agreement drafted by U.N. Command and Communist truce teams at Panmumjom was given to Assistant Secretary of State Walter S. Robertson last night or early this morning. Its contents have not been made public, but a reliable source said Rhee last night repeated to Robertson that South Korea cannot accept President Eisenhower's pledge that the U.S. will work for peaceful unification of Korea unless there is concrete assurance on how such unification could be achieved.

Vol. 9, No. 186   Monday, July 6, 1953
CONTINUED HEAVY RAINS
SLOW ATTLEFRONT ACTION

HQ, EIGHTH ARMY, July 6 (Pac. S&S) – Scattered patrol clashes and weak Chinese probes against central front positions made up the lightest day's fighting in Korea for the month of July.

* * * * *

Mechanical Failure, Human
Error Blamed in C-124 Disaster

TOKYO, July 6 (Pac. S&S) – Scattered patrol clashes and weak Chinese probes against central front positions made up the lightest day's fighting in Korea for the month of July.

1.

COLLIER'S UNIFORM WAS DRENCHED IN SWEAT when he emerged from the door of the flight-weary DC-4 at Tokyo's Haneda airport, and the oppressive heat hit him like a blast from an open-hearth steel furnace. Standing there blinking against the strong sunlight as he started down the rolling boarding stairs, he exhaled a deep sigh of relief as he suddenly realized that he had somehow survived another harrowing flight in an airplane. When he was finally standing flatfooted on *terra firma*, contemplating the full import of the miracle, he resisted an almost irresistible desire to fall to his knees and kiss the tarmac. Before he had time to take a step in the direction of the terminal, his senses were assaulted by a pervasive, near-sickening odor which, combined with the heat, momentarily pushed him to the verge of nausea. Following the initial shock, however, he was able to gain control over this queasiness and trudge resignedly toward the entrance to the terminal building across the parking apron. Above the terminal doors was a banner bearing the legend, "Welcome to Japan", in English with 日本にようこそ—what Collier assumed were the corresponding Japanese characters—displayed underneath in bright red.

"Okay, don't stand there gawking. Let's get in out of this heat. We have to process through Japanese Customs before we can board the buses to Camp Drake." Major Richards stood at the bottom of the steps, herding their entourage across the oil-stained tarmac into Customs where the pitifully inadequate air-conditioning did little more than move the hot, fetid, air around with virtually no effect on lowering the oppressive temperature. It was easy to see how the Japs had lost the war.

Astutely noting that his travel companions were being shuffled through Customs only to be herded back outside to a waiting Army bus, and intelligent enough to know that as bad as the heat was inside the terminal, it had to be even worse outside on the bus, Collier found the nearest wooden bench and plopped down to wait his turn.

By the time they finished inspection by the Japanese Customs authorities and were finally allowed to pass through the gates, officially entering onto Japanese soil, Collier's watch read 1559—adjusted to Tokyo time according to their pilot.

Last to finish processing Customs, Collier folded a substantial wad of Japanese Yen and deposited the small handful of coins called Sen and Rin plus an additional bundle of paper Military Script—representing his last one hundred and fifty American greenbacks—into his pants pocket and followed Pewter out the door. The thin fold of one hundred and twenty-five bucks in paper Military Script consisted of five singles, two fives, a ten and five twenty-dollar bills. By comparison, the remaining twenty-five American dollars exchanged for the colorful Japanese Yen notes made up a sizeable roll. Despite the doubtful luxury of the over-worked Japanese air-conditioning, Collier's uniform was still damp with sweat when he and John Henry walked over and boarded the Army bus. Moving directly down the aisle, Collier led the way to a pair of empty seats near the rear.

"Grab the window on that side and open it to give us a breath of air when this relic starts moving," Collier advised Pewter, taking the window opposite, immediately opening it as wide as it would go.

Major Richards—accompanied by the young captain who had greeted them when they arrived at Haneda—boarded the bus behind Collier and Pewter and the driver closed the door.

"I am Captain Andrews. Welcome to Tokyo, Japan. We will be taking you to Camp Drake, a large repel-depot on the outskirts of the city. Answer when you hear your name. Aaron, Adams, Bailey..." even before the driver closed the door, the young officer started taking roll. "Repel-depot" was military shorthand for replacement depot; Collier knew Camp Drake was the processing center for virtually all personnel arriving and departing FECOM.

They had hardly left the Haneda parking lot heading into Tokyo when Collier became enthralled with the constant flow of Japanese riding bikes and running at a half-trot in both directions along the side of the highway through a series of outlying villages. No one walked. They all seemed to be in a big hurry to get where they were going.

"Quick, John Henry, come here and get a load of this," Collier called across to Pewter who had his head stuck halfway out of the opposite window. To Collier's amazement, they were fast approaching what appeared to be an elderly woman pedaling a bike, while balancing a full-sized Smith-Corona electric typewriter atop her head. Watching the amazing sight recede from view, Collier silently resolved to buy a good 35mm camera when and if he could afford the expense.

"Alright, everyone give me your attention up here. We're approaching the Camp Drake Replacement Depot. When you get off the bus, follow Captain Andrews directly inside the Reception Center. I know you're tired and hungry, but you will have to attend a short orientation before we can assign you a bed and feed you, so let's get this over with," Major Richards informed them as they passed by an unmanned guardhouse and pulled to a stop in front of a sprawling, three-story building looking more like a factory than a military barracks. Inside, they were herded into a close, airless room where Captain Andrews quickly took roll and left the room. Exhausted and utterly depleted by the oppressive heat, Collier half-dozed before Andrews came back into the room and introduced them to a master sergeant whose name Collier failed to catch.

"Welcome to Japan; welcome to Camp Drake. Camp Drake serves as the main Army Replacement Center for troops going into and coming out of the Korean Theater. As I am sure you are already aware, the news from Korea is both good and bad. Word of a final agreement is expected almost any day—actually almost any minute—now. On the other hand, the Chinese forces are making a senseless, last-ditch effort to try to gain more ground and effectively alter the final DMZ..." the sergeant droned on about Camp Drake as Collier fought to stay awake. "Your duffels are being stored in the room next door and will be available to you with proper ID...orders will be posted daily by 0700 hours on the bulletin board just outside that door...if your name is not on shipping orders, you are free to go into Tokyo VOCO and do some sightseeing. Buses run every half-hour on the street outside the gate you entered. The fare is only a few Japanese Rin—about a dime American." Jerking in and out of a doze, Collier caught intermittent snatches of the spiel. "If you're looking for a good place to have a drink and hear some music without being taken to the cleaners, try the O Club here on the base or the Roof Garden atop the transient officers billet at the Yuraku building..." The sergeant continued with a reminder about routine SOP. "Orders are posted daily on the bulletin board just outside this room and you are required to check the posted orders each and every day..." Collier dozed fitfully, catching a snippet here and there. "You are free to leave the base VOCO as soon I answer your questions. Do not forget to check the bulletin board. If you fail to show up for a posted shipment, you will be treated as AWOL..." The sergeant wound down his speech. "If there are no further questions, that's it. Welcome to Japan and good luck during your tour in the Far East Command. Follow the corporal outside the door and he will show you to the mess hall where you can get some hot chow. After you eat, come back here. Upstairs is the barracks area. Feel free to choose any bunk with fresh bedding rolled up on top of the mattress. We apologize you have to make your own bed. You should have no problem locating the showers and latrines. While you are here, I urge you to visit our O Club. The cuisine is superb and, at only twenty-five cents military script, the drinks are strong and cheap. There is a dance band and a first-rate floor show each and every night. Again, welcome to Japan." The Sergeant came to attention, saluted and stepped aside.

They followed the corporal outside and down the street to a large open mess. Curiously, Collier was still not very hungry, but not knowing when his next meal might be, he forced himself to eat, careful to avoid anything that looked or smelled like chicken.

"Come on. Let's go stake out a bunk and crash," Pewter said when they had finished eating.

Having no clear sense of how they had gotten there, Collier followed John Henry back to the huge, hangar-like barracks building. Passing by the office where they had listened to the sergeant, they climbed the stairs to the vast barracks area above.

"Judas priest, there must be at least a thousand bunks!" Pewter gasped.

Letting his eyes gradually adjust to the dark, Collier finally said, "Follow me. There's safety in numbers. Let's take a bunk over in the middle of that bunch of sleeping men."

"Wherever you say. All I want to do is crash." Pewter followed dutifully behind.

"Okay, right here is good enough." When they had negotiated their way across to an area where several hundred sleeping bodies lay on bunks near the middle of the room, Collier stopped, and set down his AWOL bag at the end of one of a pair of empty bunks which had mattresses rolled neatly at the head, with mattress covers, sheets, and a blanket folded into a neat stack on the pillow on top.

As tired as he was, Collier unrolled the mattress in place, wrestled on the fresh mattress cover, and quickly put on the sheets. When he had finished making his bed, Collier stripped out of his sweaty clothes, picked up his AWOL bag and headed for the brightly-lit latrine and shower area on the far side of the large room.

"You tlake tlowel? You like to buy nice Zori sandal?" Inside the latrine, the enterprising Japanese attendant offered them clean towels from a large stack and showed them a pair of curious-looking, blue-rubber sandals ingeniously designed to stay on the feet by slipping a sort of Y-shaped thong between the first two toes. From the looks of the soles, the sandals appeared to be made from recycled auto tires.

"Aren't you too tired to shave?" Pewter whined, exasperated that Collier would take the time to shave after all they had been through.

"I'm too tired to think, but I do know one thing for sure. I want to get out of here in the morning and head into Tokyo before some sergeant herds me onto a truck and ships me off to Korea. You heard what the guy said, VOCO until our names appear on orders." As bone-tired as he was, Collier took his time and shaved, careful not to cut himself. Pewter found his shaving kit and meekly followed suit. When they both finished shaving and brushed their teeth, each went in and took long, hot showers.

"See you in the morning. If you want to go into Tokyo, I'm going to get up before the crack of dawn and find that bus. I want to shuck this place like a bad habit."

"Sure, if you think it's okay," Pewter answered tentatively as Collier spread out on the bunk, pulling the blanket over his head to shut out the world.

"Wake up, Collier. Wake up." When Collier opened his eyes in the dark, Pewter was shaking him.

"What's going on?" Collier came groggily awake, trying to figure out just where he was.

"Shh-h...listen! They're calling our name..." Pewter whispered. He was lying flat on his bunk with his head barely visible under the blanket a bare yard away from Collier's face.

"You're dreaming, John Henry. For chrissake, go back to sleep." Collier was not at all happy to be roused awake before he had hardly gotten to sleep.

"Listen...hear that?" Pewter whispered again as a voice blared over the intercom reading a list of names.

"*The following officers will report downstairs to the orderly room in thirty minutes. Listen carefully as I read the names. Abel, Alexander...Ackerman, Robert...*" Sure enough, the voice on the bitch box started reciting a long list of names. Collier struggled to stay awake long enough for the voice to get past the Os when, sure enough he heard, "*Pewter, John!...*"

Senses alerted now, Collier waited a few minutes longer before he heard the words "*Ramsay, Collier*" come blaring into the room.

"Do you believe me now?" John Henry whispered, his eyes barely visible, peering owl-like from under the blanket.

"Okay. I heard him. Go on down there if you want to. I'm staying right here and going back to sleep. If anyone asks, I went into Tokyo. The sergeant said we could go into Tokyo tonight if we felt like it. He said to be sure and check the list every morning, and according to my time clock, morning doesn't end until eleven hundred fifty-nine hours. If I have to go to Korea in the shape I'm in, someone is going to have to take me on a stretcher," Collier grumbled and promptly went back to sleep.

"Collier, wake up. I knew we should have answered that roll call. Look down the row—they're coming after us." When Collier awoke, Pewter was reaching across and shaking him again. Now, blinking hard into the darkness, Collier saw the shadowy figures of two men with a flashlight and a clipboard making their way down the line of bunks toward them, checking each occupant against their list. As far as Collier could see, they were having little or no success finding anyone on their roster.

"Keep still and cover your head, John Henry. Pretend to be asleep. They'll get to me first. Let me handle this." Collier whispered and ducked back under the blanket, peeping through a crack as he watched the two men inexorably make their way toward them.

"Come on, wake up. Can't you hear the intercom?" one of the voices shook his foot and growled.

"Whadda fugg?" Collier raised his head and blinked, clearly annoyed.

"Are you listening to the intercom? If your name's on the list, you have to report...." A shadowy figure behind the flashlight shined it directly into Collier's eyes.

"Get that fucking light out of my eyes you simple shit before I shove it so far up your ass it will light up your eyes! My buddy here and I just got off a plane at Tachikawa from Kimpo. We're shipping stateside from here in a few days! Neither of us has slept in a bed in four months—not since our last fucking R&R!" Collier growled, raising up aggressively in bed.

"Oh, Jeezie, I'm sorry, sir. We're trying to locate officers on orders to ship out to Kimpo tonight. You and your fellow officer have a safe trip back home." The shadow moved the light out of his eyes and quickly moved further down the aisle.

"If they come back and ask us for ID, we're going to get court-martialed," Pewter whispered when the two NCOs had drifted far enough away to be safely out of earshot.

"You worry too much. Go back to sleep. Those jerks just made up my mind. I'm going to grab another couple hours before the sun comes up, then head out for Tokyo first thing tomorrow before anyone can stop me," Collier whispered back.

"The following officers will report to the orderly room..." the voice reciting the names over the bitch box sounded like a broken record as Collier slipped back into the oblivion of sleep.

"Wake up, John Henry. Let's get the hell out of here before someone puts us on an airplane to Korea." Collier shook Pewter awake at 0529 hours. He was guardedly pleased to find the voice on the intercom had fallen silent, for the moment at least.

"I'm not sure we should be doing this," Pewter said, clearly shook up after hearing his name read well into the wee hours of the morning.

"Suit yourself, John Henry. What's the difference between us going now and those smart guys we came in here with who left to see the sights last night?" Collier pointed out the logic in his current plans.

"The difference is since we didn't go in with them, we know they were planning to ship our asses out this morning if we had reported downstairs last night when they were paging us. Also you lied to those NCOs. Having knowledge before the fact is dishonest. It's a matter of personal integrity," Pewter protested the obvious.

"Well, I'll leave you to your honor then. Go ahead to Korea. If no one stops me, I'm going into Tokyo. I'll be back as soon as I run out of money—which shouldn't be too long." Collier quietly began stuffing his toilet kit and other scattered belongings into his AWOL bag. Following Collier's example, Pewter followed him to the latrine to finish his preparations. Having just shaved only a few hours before, both men splashed water on their faces, brushed their teeth and dressed. AWOL bags in hand, they set out down the stairs. Warily tip-toeing past the windowed wall of the orderly room and taking great pains not to wake the corporal sleeping on a folding cot inside, they made it safely past and out the door—careful not to let it slam behind them. Outside, it was just getting light as across the way a long line of enlisted men in full combat packs were boarding a waiting caravan of buses, most likely headed for a troopship at Yokohama. A scant hundred yards to their left, Collier could see a small, deserted guard house standing at the center of the wide opening in the high chain-link fence. There were no patrolling guards or MPs anywhere in sight to pose a problem making their getaway.

"Come on, John Henry. Before we leave, we might as well save our money and get some chow." The inspiration seized him when he spotted a line forming outside the mess hall where they had been taken last evening following their orientation speech.

With patches and insignia clearly showing they were not from any outfit indigenous to FECOM, Collier was afraid they might be recognized as transients on their way to Korea, but to his utter wonderment they strolled into the mess hall and went through the serving line without so much as a glance or question from anyone. "Apparently Drake is such a military melting pot, no one pays any attention to the appropriateness of any of the daily denizens being here," Collier observed to John Henry as they left the mess hall heading for the street to see if they could find a bus heading into Tokyo.

Outside the gate, Collier became suddenly aware of the squalor and atmosphere of decay in the outskirts of the huge city. The nearest group of buildings were prominently anchored by a rundown, western-style, granite bank building adjoined by what appeared to be a residence, and a wooden shop or perhaps a market of some sort. Except for advertising signs in exotic Japanese hieroglyphics, they could have been on Main in Blackstone or any street in any down-at-the-heels country town in the South. Even at the early hour, already the street was bustling with activity, and there were more than a dozen Japanese civilians—mostly men in Western business attire—already waiting for the bus. Standing there in the early-morning light taking it all in, it slowly entered Collier's consciousness that he was already becoming somewhat acclimated to the fecal odor pervasive in the atmosphere.

"Do you speak English? How much is the fare into downtown Tokyo? Do you know the Yuraku building?" As soon as they climbed aboard the bus, Collier asked the bus driver, stupidly emulating a Hollywood version of some shipwrecked sailor trying to communicate with South Sea natives.

"The fare is ten rin to the Yuraku. I will go right by there. It takes almost an hour to get into the city from here. Take the two seats directly behind me. I'll alert you when we get close." The bus driver spoke perfect English, without a trace of Japanese or foreign inflection.

"What's your name? Where did you learn to speak English? You sound just like an American," Collier asked, pleased to find someone with whom they could communicate.

"My name is Hideaki Tanaka. I *am* an American. I grew up in California, near San Francisco. My parents both graduated from San Francisco State College. They had become naturalized U.S. citizens and were working as interpreters for a travel agency when Pearl Harbor took place. Like hundreds of Americans of Japanese descent, my parents and I were interned at Heart Mountain Relocation Center near Cody, Wyoming. My father volunteered for the U.S. Army in nineteen forty-two and died at Normandy Beach on D-Day. My mother died of cancer at Heart Mountain in nineteen-hundred-and-forty-five before the first bomb was dropped on Hiroshima. I was more-or-less adopted by friends of my parents after my mother died and I returned to Japan with them several years ago. Like most of the Japanese-Americans, we all—my parents as well as my adoptive parents—lost all property as the result of their internment. Anti-Japanese feelings were running high, so I came back to Japan with them. I still live with them here in Tokyo. I take night courses at Tokyo University. They own a neighborhood grocery back there outside Camp Drake where you caught the bus." The driver recounted his personal history without apparent bitterness.

Riding along taking in the scenery, Collier was appalled at the glut of traffic. On the trip from Haneda airport the preceding afternoon, he had noted that the automobiles were of both European and American manufacture—with a number of the taxi drivers preferring the undersized French Renault sedans. The buildings in the suburban areas were a curious mixture of mostly wooden residences of traditional Japanese architecture with paper windows, and shops and marketplaces which were indigenous Japanese-style buildings, side-by-side with more Western—more American-looking—buildings of concrete and masonry with modern glass windows.

Defying what seemed to be almost certain death, people—men, women and children of all ages and wearing all manner of dress both Western as well as Oriental—fairly clogged the middle of the street. Seemingly oblivious to what seemed to Collier almost certain disaster, the bus driver never slowed as the throng parted—in the same way the Red Sea parted for Moses—at just the last instant as the lumbering vehicle seemed certain to crush them underneath its wheels.

After riding for the better part of an hour, the setting began to evolve from this curiously-picturesque, quasi-Oriental/quasi-modern setting to a more Westernized cityscape. The closer they approached the center of the city, the more modern and American the architecture appeared.

"We are approaching the Ginza—the shopping district, with neighboring office buildings on all sides—the heart of Tokyo. On your left, the moat and the high stone wall protect the Imperial City, the home of our Emperor—who, I'm certain you already know, is currently Michinomiya Hirohito." The driver had become their self-appointed tour guide as they neared the end of a high rock wall bordering a wide moat. The wall was surmounted by an ancient Japanese structure with a pagoda-like roofline.

"If you will look to your left at the line of buildings running beside the moat as it parallels the avenue, you can see a classic, six- or seven-story square granite building with all the antennas on the roof. That's the Dai Ichi Building. General MacArthur had his headquarters on the fifth floor."

Following the driver's directions, Collier had little difficulty spotting the building with the antennas rising from the roof.

"The Ginza—Tokyo's equivalent to New York's Fifth Avenue—is just beyond the wide thoroughfare. You can always orientate yourself by that large, earth-globe sign atop the building just inside the Ginza. In addition to the department stores and boutiques, the area also has a number of sophisticated night clubs. Most of the shops and stores are open at night; with all the exotic electric signs, the Ginza is really spectacular after dark," the driver continued as they turned at the corner moving subtly away from the heart of the commercial districts.

"Stay on the bus when I stop up here to let these people off. Most of them are going into the Ginza to begin the business day." The driver pulled to the curb a block or so ahead and opened the door to let the passengers depart. As soon as the last passenger had exited the bus he pulled back into traffic. After perhaps a half-mile, they turned off the boulevard into a less-congested area with large trees along park-like boulevards.

"Up ahead, we're approaching Frank Lloyd Wright's famous earthquake-proof building, the beautiful Imperial Hotel. Legend has it that on the very day of its grand opening, one of the most devastating earthquakes in recorded history struck Tokyo and Yokohama, killing tens of thousands of people and reducing both cities to rubble. Miraculously, the much-publicized Imperial Hotel survived almost intact, suffering only minimal damage." The driver slowed the bus as they approached the grounds of the famous landmark hotel fronted by a large reflecting pool.

"Tell me, Hideaki, where is the absolute best Geisha house in Tokyo?" Collier asked, lowering his voice although the bus was completely empty.

"That depends on what you mean by Geisha. Do you mean our traditional Japanese Geishas who are trained in the classical arts of entertainment, or are you looking for sex?" Hideaki asked quite matter of factly.

"Is there a difference? I thought Geishas were trained to please men," Collier replied, clearly embarrassed now. Someone else had made the distinction back at Fort Lewis if his memory served him well, but he had paid no attention then.

"Traditional Japanese Geisha's are not prostitutes. The prostitutes are mis-named Geishas by the American soldiers who don't understand Japanese tradition. In Japanese, we call prostitution: *Mizu Shōbai*: 'the water trade.' *Mizu shōbai* is the traditional euphemism for the night-time entertainment business in Japan provided by so-called 'geisha' bars and nightclubs. Is that what you're looking for?" Hideaki asked.

"Yes...tell me where to find the absolute best place—give me the name in case we go looking in a taxicab," Collier asked, wanting to come up with a specific destination. He was more determined than ever to get John Henry laid. He would never forgive himself if a fellow officer died, in combat, a virgin.

"There are several I would recommend. Do you prefer a traditional Japanese place or a more Western-style hotel?" The question took Collier momentarily aback; he had not given any thought to the idea they might have a choice.

"I'd want a place more on the order of a traditional Japanese place. It brings a more...ah...more romantic image to my mind," John Henry chimed in.

"Then the absolute best place is the *Kinno-tenobi*, an old-style hotel in a quiet Japanese residential area. The *Kinno-tenobi* has the traditional baths and has a reputation for always having an endless supply of beautiful, young girls from the country. It costs only something like six-thousand yen—twenty dollars American. I have been saving my yen to go there myself," Hideaki said with a shy laugh.

"How do we find this place? Would most of the taxi drivers know how to get there?" Collier asked.

"I would think most experienced cab drivers know the *Kinno-tenobi*. But don't worry. I'll write down the address when I let you off at the Yuraku. That way you can give them the actual street address," Hideaki reassured them.

"Someone told us that first-class Geisha houses offer their...ah...patrons a choice of women and bring them out in waves—you know groups—for inspection before you make your selection. Is there any truth to that?" Collier asked.

"*Ahso*. The better places offer you a choice of more than just a few girls. Usually you pay when you enter—that is to prevent what you call 'window shopping' back in the States. Then you are escorted to a dressing area where you trade your clothes for a kimono before you are taken into a sitting area. In the sitting area, you will be offered sake—the traditional rice wine—while the women are presented for appreciation and selection in groups of five or six or more. From there, it becomes a matter of personal taste. When you see a girl who particularly appeals to you, you make your choice and she will escort you to your room. At the *Kinno-tenobi*, the fee covers the entire night. The night is yours for your pleasure—you don't have to leave until the next morning," Hideaki reaffirmed in general what they had heard back at Fort Lewis.

"What time the next morning? Do they serve breakfast?" Pewter asked; clearly Hideaki had his attention.

"You will be served tea and oranges and sake and rice cakes in your room during your stay, but it is considered polite to leave sometime well before noon the following morning," their informative tour guide replied.

"How about the traditional communal Japanese baths—you know—where everyone bathes together? Does this *Kinno-tenobi* place have them?" Pewter asked.

"Oh, yes. In Japan, the bath is something of a social custom." Hideaki chuckled.

"What time does this *Kinno-tenobe* open for business?" Pewter asked, his interest clearly aroused.

"They never close. It's open around the clock."

Passing the Imperial Hotel, they emerged into an area populated by a number of Western-styled high-rise buildings.

"This is the Yuraku Building on the left on the far corner of the next intersection," Hideaki said as the trees thinned out a bit and a rather tall building came into view.

When they pulled to the curb beside the Yuraku, Hideaki wrote a name and address on a little slip of paper. "Here is the name and address of the *Kinno-tenobi*. I'm sure you won't be disappointed."

"Thanks and good luck with your studies at the university," Collier said as he took the slip of paper, handed Hideaki two dollars in appreciation for his informative tour and followed Pewter out of the bus.

One of several similar buildings which had been commandeered for use as transient billets for officers coming and going in and out of Tokyo, the Yuraku was a seven-story building that had been converted from an office building to a hotel during the post-WWII American occupation.

When they entered the Yuraku, the aloof DAC behind the registration desk informed them coolly. "The roof garden is closed mornings, Sir—it opens for lunch at noon and stays open until zero two-hundred in the morning. You can get breakfast in our restaurant through the door across the lobby in the far corner."

"How much are rooms?" Collier asked, suddenly interested in the possibility of having a place to spend the night rather than going back to Drake and risk being shipped to Korea before he had had a chance to blow his money on a final fling before he had to chance going to war.

"One dollar—five for seven nights, sir. Do you want to engage a room?" the DAC asked.

"Maybe. Do you have a room with two beds? My buddy and I can share— we're just looking for place to hang our hat while we see the sights." Collier tried not to seem overanxious.

"Yessir. You're in luck. We have several doubles vacant at the moment," the DAC clerk offered, waiting expectantly.

"Good. I assume the rooms have locks on their doors. We need a place to leave our stuff." Collier nodded at his AWOL bag.

"Of course the rooms have locks." The DAC seemed offended that Collier could insinuate otherwise.

"Wait a minute. Let's talk this over. Why do we want a room here? I thought we were going to the...ah...the place Hideaki told us about." Perplexed at Collier's sudden whim, Pewter tugged at Collier's sleeve, pulling him a few feet back from the desk out of the DAC's earshot.

"A room here will give us a base of operations—we don't want to lug these freaking AWOL bags around everywhere we go. I'm beginning to feel like it's attached to me by an umbilical." Collier held the bag up for emphasis and added. "Don't sweat it, John Henry. I'll pay the buck."

"Oh no, it's not the buck...I'll split it with you," Pewter said.

"Good, we'll take one of the rooms with two beds," Collier said, peeling off a one-dollar bill in military script and handing it to the DAC.

"Both of you sign the register, please." The young woman took the money, pushing a clipboard in Collier's direction. Without further ado, Collier and John Henry both signed in, accepted keys to a room on the third floor, and walked across the lobby to the elevator.

"It's still a couple hours before noon, John Henry. I suggest we catch up on a few Zs before we head out to get you laid." Locking the door behind them, Collier dropped his AWOL bag on the floor, disrobed, folded his khakis, then sprawled across the bed and went sound asleep.

"I'm hungry enough to eat a horse," Collier observed as, refreshed from their naps, he and Pewter stepped off the elevator into the bright sunshine at the Yuraku's roof-garden restaurant a few minutes past high noon. Seated around a scattered handful of the umbrella-topped tables, a number of captains and higher-ranking, field-grade officers were already drinking cocktails while the tuxedo-outfitted, eleven-piece, Japanese dance band played the Guy Lomdardo arrangement of *Charmaine*, note-for-note.

Taking a table across the wide expanse of the roof-garden club, Collier accepted a menu and inquired of the tuxedo-clad waiter, "What's your best Japanese beer?"

"Either Asahi or Nippon—depends on your personal taste, Sir," the waiter replied with polite equanimity.

"Bring us one of each and we'll make up our minds," Pewter solved the problem with diplomacy.

"Damn, both taste pretty good. Here. Give them a try. See which one you want." After Pewter had sampled both, he passed the bottles across the table for Collier's approval.

"I'll take the Asahi, but both are really good." Collier smacked his lips in serious appreciation, then passed the bottle of Nippon back to Pewter.

When the waiter returned, they both ordered club sandwiches and sat there sipping beer, enjoying the orchestra and the spectacular view of Tokyo.

"As soon as we've finished lunch, we'll find a taxi and go to the *Kinno-tenobi*. Today's your lucky day, Pewter-san." Already feeling a bit euphoric from the beer, Collier raised his Asahi in a mock toast.

"Do you know how to find the *Kinno-tenobi*?" Collier asked the taxi driver they flagged to the curb outside the Yuraku.

"*Kinno-tenobi*? *Iie*. What is *Kinno-tenobi*?" the driver asked with a heavy Japanese accent.

"It's a hotel. Do you know this address?" Collier read the directions Hideaki had written on the back of the calling card.

"*Ahso*. You get in. I take you to *Kinno-tenobi*. Twenty dorrah, American."

"We give you five dollars. If you take us directly there without scaring us to death, we may give you a tip when we get there." Collier had heard some Korean veterans back at Sill talk about bargaining with the Japanese cab drivers and merchants—the same applied to the Koreans he was told.

"Ten dorrah—too far to go for five." The driver counter-offered.

"Make it seven and we'll still consider a tip if you get us there safely and in good time," Collier looked at the expression on Pewter's face and grinned.

"*Ahso*...get in." The driver reached behind him and opened the door of the tiny Renault. They had barely closed the door before the driver was barreling headlong down the wide street directly into an impenetrable sea of people which amazingly always seemed to part, just at the last moment. Vehicles approaching from the opposite direction were driving with the same seemingly-reckless disregard for human life.

"Slow down. We're not in that big a hurry," Collier told the driver, on the verge of a heart attack.

"*Ahso*..." the driver's head bobbed up and down, as, if anything, he sped up.

Turning his attention away from the unnerving game of automobile brinksmanship, Collier tried to enjoy the panorama of the world's most populous city. According to the booklet, Tokyo had twenty-five residents per square foot. He had read in a brochure, coming over on the plane, that the Japanese were vigorously promoting birth control and had legalized abortion to keep from populating themselves right out of a homeland.

"*Ahso...Kinno-tenobi.*" The wizened Japanese driver suddenly pulled to the curb in front of a rambling Japanese residence, perched above the street among some pines.

"You wait here while I make sure this is the right place," Collier told Pewter getting out of the taxi and going to the front entrance of the building to verify they were at the right address.

After a brief exchange with the kimono-clad Japanese woman answering the door, Collier returned to the cab and gave Pewter a big thumbs-up. "Jackpot, John Henry! Pay the man."

"We owe you seven. Just keep the whole ten." Pewter paid the taxi driver. When they had watched the cab disappearing around the corner, Collier led the way up a long, gentle flight of stone steps leading to the entrance.

"I owe you from all the trips to Fort Lee when we were at Pickett. This is all on me." Standing at the door to the *Kinno-tenobi* waiting, Pewter pulled out a sizeable roll of yen.

"*Koh-NEE-cheewah. Wah-TAHK-sheewah Fumiko, dehss.* Welcome to the *Kinno-tenobi*, gentlemen. My name is Fumiko." The Japanese woman who welcomed them was dressed in an elegant, richly-embroidered kimono with a wide sash.

"We...ah...we were told we could find...ah...the...ah...company of young women at this place," John Henry stuttered nervously.

"*Ahso*, you were told correctly. You have come to the right place. That will be twenty-five American dollars in your military currency. If you prefer to pay in Japanese currency it will come to nine-thousand yen."

"How come we have to pay more if we pay in your country's currency?" Collier protested, although Pewter had volunteered to pay.

"Your money is more stable than the yen. You can choose either way." Their hostess waited patiently for them to decide.

"I have more in military script than yen," Pewter said, counting out two twentys and two fives.

As soon as Fumiko collected her fees for services, she welcomed them inside, stopping them just beyond the richly-carved door and asking them to remove their shoes.

"Thank you, gentlemen, please put these on and follow me." She gave them both doe-soft cloth and rice straw *Zori* slippers to wear and beckoned them to step onto the floor which was entirely covered with the traditional *tatami* mats made of rice straw. Following her up a short series of wide steps, she showed them each into a curtained private cubicle at the top of the stairs.

"Take off your uniforms and put on the kimonos you will find hanging inside. When you are finished changing, bring your uniforms back out here to me." She held aside the curtains and waited for them to enter the changing rooms.

When he finished disrobing, except for his Jockeys, Collier shrugged into the black silk kimono hanging in the cubicle—the kimono was really more like a short, loosely-fitting American dressing gown. Transferring his wallet with his ID and his cash into a large pocket in the robe, Collier folded his khakis over his forearm and stepped outside and handed them to Fumiko.

John Henry joined him almost immediately, also holding his wallet and handing over his clothes. From the telltale ridges underneath the silken fabric, Collier could tell that Pewter was still wearing his GI undershorts underneath.

Fumiko gave a quick clap of her hands and, astonishingly, a young serving girl appeared. After Fumiko instructed her in Japanese, the girl took their uniforms and disappeared behind a screen.

"Follow me, gentlemen." She led them another step up and guided them down a short passageway, seating them on a bench in a large three-walled room. The fourth side was open, overlooking a courtyard with a tiny brook trickling across smooth white river rocks through a perfectly-manicured, miniature Japanese garden.

They were no sooner seated than Fumiko clapped her hands again and a pair of lovely, kimono-clad girls appeared, each bearing trays with a spirit lamp, a porcelain flask and a shallow porcelain cup—the time-honored set-up for serving sake.

"Would it be considered rude if I didn't drink the sake? I had a Nippon beer for lunch, and I'm not much of a drinking man," Pewter asked, artlessly unmindful of the ritual traditions.

"Not at all. Just leave it there and say '*arrigato*,'" Fumiko advised, bowing to the girls, dismissing them. Collier looked at the two women admiringly, wondering if they were among the girls available for more personal services.

"If you are ready now, I will introduce you to our girls and you can make your choice. The sooner you choose, the longer you will have to enjoy the pleasure of her company," Fumiko reminded them.

"Bring them on," Pewter said, euphoric with rising carnal anticipation.

"*Ahso...*" Fumiko turned and disappeared behind a bamboo-and-paper screen.

"Remember what Hideaki said. Don't choose from the first wave..." Collier's whisper faded to breathlessness as Fumiko led a parade of eight perfect, petite, doll-like, kimono-clad girls from behind the Oriental screen into the room. The girls stepped up onto the platform facing the bench Collier and Pewter occupied and stood there smiling expectantly.

"These are our most beautiful and talented girls. Take your time and make your choice," Fumiko urged and stepped to one side while Collier and Pewter gave the girls a closer inspection.

"They don't seem to have much in the way of bosoms. How old do you think they are?" Collier whispered low enough for only John Henry to hear, seriously concerned at how young these so-called 'women' appeared to be.

"I have no idea. I'm sure they are all over legal age. I really like the shortest one on the left end. If I don't find someone I like as well on the second or third wave, can I ask what's-her-face to bring that one back to me?" John Henry asked, his whisper heavy with sexual anticipation.

"I don't know. You're on your own," Collier said. He was having trouble finding any among this first group who turned him on.

"Are these all you have?" Collier asked. "We'd like to see some more before we make up our minds."

"No. We have others. I show you." Fumiko clapped her hands and the girls turned and started to march back toward the bamboo screen.

"Wait. I want that one, the girl at the head of the line," John Henry said abruptly.

"Emiko!..." Fumiko spoke a few words in Japanese and the girl turned and returned to where she had been standing before.

"This is Emiko-san. She will escort you to a room; please follow her. Your clothes are being cleaned and ironed. They will be brought to you before you are ready to leave." Fumiko bowed low and indicated to Pewter that he should follow the doll-like girl standing before him.

"I'd rather wait until my friend has made his choice. We'd like rooms close together, if that's alright with you?" Pewter hesitated, not wanting to get too far separated from Collier.

"That is perfectly agreeable with me. But you needn't wait. When Collier-san has chosen, I'll put him in a room adjoining yours," Fumiko reassured Pewter, but he shook his head.

"No...If it's all the same to you, I'd prefer to wait. I'd like to see who Collier-san chooses." Clearly Pewter was leery of being separated and left alone.

"*Ah so desu ka.* I don't mind. Here are the girls now, for Collier-san's pleasure." She bowed and turned as another group of seven young women came from behind the bamboo and paper screen.

This time Collier's eyes immediately went to a girl head and shoulders taller near the middle of the line. She was slightly more well-endowed than the rest. When they finally were standing in front of him, seen up close, Collier was both appalled and aroused to see how very young the taller girl appeared—clearly several years younger than her companions, this slender flower appeared hardly more than twelve or thirteen. Struggling not to betray his excitement over the prospect of possessing such exotic, forbidden fruit, to be polite, Collier waited until they all stood expectantly for his inspection as he pretended to appreciate each of them separately.

"They are all so lovely; it's difficult to choose," Collier said to Fumiko, "but I choose the tallest girl, there in the middle of the line."

"Keiko, stay here with Collier-san," Fumiko ordered politely, then dismissed the others in Japanese.

"Come with me, Collier-san," the slender Keiko stepped forward and bowed, then turned and followed Emiko who was leading John Henry back along a corridor of polished, light-colored wood with matching regular Western-styled hinged doors instead of traditional Japanese sliding shoji panels.

At the very end of the long corridor, Emiko stopped in front of the last door, and opened it, stepping aside and waiting for Pewter to enter.

"This room is ours," Keiko said to Collier in English, opening the last door on the right, cross-corner from the room Pewter and Emiko had entered.

"Well, see you later. Check out is before noon, but when you're finished, knock on the door. I'll be ready to leave anytime you say," Collier said to John Henry, certain his virginal friend was shaking in his boots.

"Okay...see you later..." John Henry flashed an uncertain smile and disappeared behind the closing door. Collier heard a distinctive click of the bolt sliding in place as soon as the door was completely shut.

"After you, Keiko-san." Collier turned to the tall child/woman, insisting that she precede him into the room. When they both were inside, she closed the shoji panel, pulling it firmly shut.

When his eyes slowly adjusted to the soft light filtering through the mulberry-bark paper panels along the upper part of the exterior wall, Collier could see that the room was entirely, and neatly, functional with the only furniture being a small bed and a small table with two chairs. On the table was a porcelain decanter and two matching sake cups.

"Let me help you with your clothes, Collier-san," Keiko said pushing up close to him and starting to fumble with the sash of his kimono. She exuded a faint bouquet of orange blossoms.

"No, you first. Here, let me." He pushed her gently back and unloosened the obi—the wide sash—of her more traditional kimono. When he finished, he slipped the silken garment from her shoulders and helped her step free. Seen in the soft filtered light, this slender girl/woman was a brownish-ivory figurine. Standing naked before him well-muscled in a soft, quietly feminine way, her rich brown skin virtually flawless, she was incredibly beautiful. He had expected to see only buds where her breasts blossomed, but, to his surprise, her breasts, like the rest of her body, were solid and well-formed.

"How old are you?" Collier asked, perplexed that he had mistakenly taken her for a teenager.

"Nineteen...why do you ask? Am I too old for you? Did you want a younger girl?" she asked, obviously wounded and perplexed. Her English was good, but with a definite accent.

"Oh no, nothing like that. I was just curious, that's all. All of you girls seem so young to me," he said and added, "You look like painted porcelain dolls."

"Here. Let me take your kimono, Collier-san." Keiko resumed loosening his kimono, inviting him to step out of it.

"Oh, why you not take off your underwear?" She looked at him with a pouting look.

"I'm just shy, I guess. Most Americans are not accustomed to disrobing in the company of other people." Glancing self-consciously down at his Jockeys, Collier realized that even though he was standing in front of a beautiful naked woman who was inviting him to have his way with her, embarrassingly, his trusty member—which only moments ago had been slowly engorging with blood in erotic anticipation—was definitely, and embarrassingly, no longer erect.

Had something physical gone suddenly, and dreadfully, wrong with him?

"Let Keiko take off underwear. Then come lie down here on bed with me." She quickly knelt in front of him and began slowly tugging at the waistband of his Jockey briefs. Feeling none of the familiar rush of blood to his genitals accompanied by the pleasant heat and heaviness which always came with erotic stimulation, Collier was too embarrassed to look down. He knew full-well his penis was still as shriveled as a little worm.

"You come lie down with me—it will soon be alright." The beautiful naked young female tugged him by the hand, leading him toward the bed.

"You lay down first. I want to look at you. I've just gotten back from the war and I need to unwind. Do you understand what I'm saying?" He lied, desperately searching for a justification—or an explanation—as much for himself as for her.

Obediently, she stretched out on the far side of the bed and lay there with her hands folded across her firm, high-sitting breasts, the brownish-pink circles of her aureoles and her nipples peeking through her fingers.

Nothing.

As erotically attractive as she should have seemed to him, Collier still felt no reaction.

"You come here beside Keiko, Collier-san. I will make you forget all about war. I will make you forget all about Korea." She rolled up on her near elbow and beckoned him with her right hand. Without a word, Collier moved to the bed and stretched out on his right side, the full length of his body running along beside her. On impulse, he leaned closer and brushed his lips across her right nipple and watched the rubbery flesh contract.

"No...wait. Let me help you relax—we have all night and it's not even dark outside." She pushed him back and urged him to turn onto his stomach, straddling him across his thighs just below the buttocks. When he had made himself comfortable, she began slowly massaging his neck and shoulders and slowly eased her fingers on down, kneading his back. When her fingers finally worked their way to the top of his buttocks, he felt her pull the cheeks of his ass apart, sensuously massaging his anus and his testicles. Her slender fingers gently tracing a circle around his sphincter only produced the slightest suggestion of heaviness to his loins.

Her fingers gently working his muscles, still slightly sore from the brutal punishment of the long flight, Collier drifted off to sleep. When he awoke with a start, Keiko was lying beside him, her arm resting across his buttocks.

"You very tired, Collier-san. The muscles of your back are very tight. Come, Keiko will take you to a nice, warm bath." Keiko urged him off the bed. As soon as her feet hit the floor, she handed him his robe. Shrugging into her own kimono, she led him outside and along the hallway down a short stairway into a large, steamy room containing two traditional Japanese baths which were really like small swimming pools with wide steps leading down into them. In the bath furthermost from the door stood a man and a buxom Japanese girl in all their naked glory.

"*Konbanwa,*" Keiko greeted the couple, stepping out of her kimono and hanging it on a wooden peg behind a low bench against the wall.

"Let me take your kimono, Collier-san. The bath will do you good," Keiko said, reaching out for his robe which, much against his will, Collier let her take.

Keiko led him down into the nearest bath which was more warm than hot. Stooping so the water covered his privates, Collier shed his shyness and felt himself relax. But even with Keiko bumping playfully against him, being immersed in the warm water did nothing to revive a spark in his curiously—and most annoyingly—dead genitalia.

Keiko finally led him out of the bath and dried him off giving particular attention to rubbing his genitals before she dried herself and handed him his robe.

When they returned to the room, Collier noted that while they had been in the baths, his clothes had been returned nicely pressed and hanging on a hanger.

"Come get back on the bed with me. I will make you happy now." Quickly slipping out of her kimono, Keiko urged him back to bed. Collier followed hopefully.

Unfortunately, despite her artful erotic manipulations nothing happened to relieve Collier's embarrassing inability to perform. Finally, he got up and went into the small bathroom and took a leak. It was incredible. He had actually been naked with this sexy Japanese girl for an entire afternoon and nothing had happened. At the tender age of twenty-four, his dick had finally become just a waterspout.

"Look, I'm sorry, Keiko-san; it's just no use. It's not your fault. I'm going to get dressed now and leave. I've paid for all night, and I'm going to leave you something more in appreciation for all the extra effort on my behalf. You can take the rest of the night off and just relax." Collier went across and started putting on his shirt.

"Oh, no, Collier-san. It's alright...you mustn't leave. You are just tired and sad from the war. Please don't leave. You give up too soon." Keiko jumped up from the bed and tried to keep him from buttoning his shirt. Clearly, the girl was quite distressed.

"Please don't take this personally—I mean it has nothing to do with you, Keiko-san. You are lovely—quite attractive...ah...pleasing to my eyes." Collier firmly removed her hands from interfering and continued dressing by stepping into his trousers. When he finished zipping up, he suddenly realized that he couldn't leave without telling John Henry. When he thought about it, he felt guilty at leaving naïve Pewter alone with a naked woman all afternoon long—poor guy was probably going out of his mind.

"I'll be right back, Keiko. I'm going next door to tell my buddy that I'm going to leave,"

He wanted to tell John Henry he was ready to head back to the Yuraku.

"No...it's not polite to disturb them..." Keiko said, trying to no avail to prevent him from leaving the room.

"John Henry—are you in there? It's me, Collier..." Stepping into the hall, Collier tapped lightly on the door to Pewter's room and waited, anticipating his buddy's reaction to being rescued from the post-coital blahs.

No sound, nothing but silence.

"John Henry, open the door. I'm getting ready to leave." After waiting for what seemed much too long without even the slightest sound of movement behind the door, Collier knocked again.

Finally, the shoji-style door slid open just a crack, and Collier could just make out the eyes, nose and mouth of Emiko in the light filtering over his shoulder from the lights in the hallway.

"Pewter-san say he not ready to leave; you go away, he find you later," the girl said.

"John Henry? Are you okay? I'm getting ready to go back to the Yuraku. I'll wait while you get dressed, but don't take too long. I'm hungry and want something to eat." Collier laughed inwardly, contemplating Pewter's reaction to no longer being a virgin when they were reunited back outside.

"You wait..." the almond eyes retreated from the crack in the door. Impatient at the game of cat and mouse between himself and a Japanese whore, Collier seized the opportunity to widen the opening in the door, trying to follow the girl into the room.

"No, you wait. I'll bring John Henry to you. He say not come in the room." The feisty Japanese girl stood her ground.

"Hey, Buddy. What's up?" When Collier looked over the girl's shoulder, Pewter was standing behind Emiko with a stupid grin on his face. To Collier's alarm, he looked as if he had been drugged.

"I'm ready to go back to the Yuraku. Get dressed. I'll wait for you. I'm in the room next door," Collier said, now more than a little concerned for his friend's well-being.

"Jeez, Collier, we just got here. I'm not ready to leave quite yet. We got all night. Relax and stay awhile." John Henry grinned stupidly. In the reflected light from the hall Collier saw his pint-sized friend's outsize dick was as vertical as the Washington Monument and standing almost as tall.

"No way, John Henry. I'm out of here. Take your time; I'll see you back at the Yuraku later. Don't be all night. Don't forget we need to go check the shipping orders back at Camp Drake in the morning. We don't want to wind up being court-martialed for desertion." Collier waited, thinking John Henry would change his mind, rather than be left here all alone.

"Okay, buddy. I'll see you back at the Yuraku in plenty of time to make it back out to Drake in the morning. Take care. Come back here, Emiko, and get back on the bed." Without another word, Pewter turned and disappeared back into the shadows of the room.

"Your friend, John Henry, he no want to leave. Why don't you stay? Keiko make you all well again; you just wait and see." Keiko pleaded when Collier returned to the room. From the distress in her voice, Collier realized he had insulted her. The Japanese were a proud people. According to their code, he suddenly realized he was causing her to "lose face."

"Look, Keiko, this is not your fault. You are a very lovely and desirable woman. You really are very beautiful. Believe me, the problem is with me. It has nothing to do with you." Collier finished dressing and retrieved his shoes, ready to change into them when he got back to the street exit.

When he reached the door and turned back, Keiko had retreated into the shadows and was sitting forlornly on the bed. On impulse he went back to her, pulling the fold of military script out of his pocket.

"Here, Keiko, take this. Thanks for all you did—you are really a lovely girl. It really isn't your fault..." He let the words die on his lips. Shocked and more than a little humiliated, by his failure to perform, he folded two ten-dollar bills of military script into her hand. Glancing over his shoulder as he softly closed the door, he saw she was lying on the bed in the fetal position with her back to him. He couldn't be sure, but he thought he heard her softly sobbing. Collier left without speaking further, knowing full-well he had already protested far too much.

Outside on the front stoop, he put his shoes back on, leaving the slippers by the entrance door. Still bothered by his puzzling failure to muster an erection under the stimulation of the masterful massage and expert erotic manipulation of the sensual Keiko, he walked down the street to the busy thoroughfare where he hailed the first cab that came along and told the driver to take him to the Yuraku— he had quite enough of whorehouses to last him all his life.

"Can you take me to the Imperial Hotel instead of the Yuraku?" They had only gone a few blocks when Collier changed his mind, suddenly feeling better he had had the good sense to get out of there. The night was young. It would be a shame to waste the golden opportunity to be able to tell the folks back home he had visited the world-famous hotel.

"*Ahso.* I tlake you to the Implelial. Is not far, not a probrum." The gnomish little Jap struggled with his pronunciation.

Riding through this exotic city at night, somewhat restored by his long restful nap, Keiko's magic massage and the warm sensual bath, he was now feeling less humiliated by the minute. It was understandable that he had not been sexually responsive at the *Kinno-tenobi.* After all, the idea of paying for sex was a contradiction to his whole philosophy about the male-female equation in the cosmic scheme of things. For him, the romance of the chase had always been everything. If all he wanted to do was get his rocks off, he could masturbate any time he chose.

"Here is Implelial Hotlel. Twlenty dorrah, prease." The driver pulled up in front of the ornate entranceway and stuck his hand out. Recalling his recent cab ride to the *Kinno-tenobi,* Collier realized the driver was trying to cheat him. From what little he had already seen, the ritual of haggling over money seemed to be *de rigueur* in occupied Japan.

"Twenty is too much. Here's a five." Going through the bargaining process again, Collier quickly settled for seven bucks, paid the man and departed the cab. After the little Renault had driven away, Collier turned and looked around. He was standing under a cedar-framed *porte cochere* of what seemed to be far too small a building to possibly be the celebrated earthquake-proof Imperial Hotel, the near-mythic *piece de resistance* of the iconoclastic, Frank Lloyd Wright.

Deciding to walk back around the reflecting pool to the entrance of the stone-paved driveway to get a better, more comprehensive view, Collier's original sense of disappointment, that the famous building seemed so undersized, melted when he took in the brilliant integration of stone and wood and space from the more distant perspective. Combining the most elegant features of Mayan and art deco architecture, Wright's masterwork of structural design was executed in a fascinating collage of highly-porous, greenish volcanic rock with pierced terra cotta grillwork and yellow brick. Great slabs of cast cement, mimicking the Gargoylian-like forms of scarabs, turtles and peacocks, embellished both interior and exterior wall surfaces. Standing literally awestruck in the presence of such overpowering genius, after perhaps ten minutes of drinking in the intricate beauty, Collier strolled back under the portico and walked inside the lobby. Although magnificently-appointed, the atrium and the lobby instantly returned him to the original sense of smallness. However, this disappointing comparison of size and space quickly disappeared under the spell of Wright's genius with window pane and furniture design, along with other brilliant accouterments.

Wandering around attempting to take it all in, turquoise and beige carpets of native American Indian designs, woven in Peking, pointed the way through innumerable oddly-geometrical nooks and crannies. A maze of narrow, mysterious-looking, low-ceilinged, cave-like passageways led into airy lobbies and ballrooms with ceilings hand-painted in peacock designs and shimmering with gold leaf—it gave Collier shivers of excitement just to walk the same space in this magnificent structure which had housed and entertained movie stars, royalty, heads of state, and millionaires from every part of the world.

Pausing before the show-windows of the commercial shops in the small lower arcade, Collier admired impressive displays of Mikimoto pearls and Noritake china. Back home, the same pristine, single twenty-odd-inch strand of Mikimoto pearls priced here for $100 dollars would have set him back $1000, at the very least. The very same $100 dollars would buy Emma—and his mother, too—a complete twelve-place setting of Noritake china including expert packing and shipping back home to the States in sturdy wooden crates.

Canon and Nikon cameras of the latest model were in the same price range. All of these luxuries plus coveted items such as top-of-the-line American golf clubs were even cheaper, he was told, if purchased in the military PX at Drake. Idly browsing the display windows lusting over such bargain luxury items, he felt a sharp pang of regret that he had not been able to bring more money with him when he had left home.

After leisurely exploring the premises for the better part of an hour, Collier walked back out into the warm night and had the major domo hail him a cab which transported him back to the Yuraku. Heading directly for the elevator, he went to the Yuraku's roof-garden restaurant and ordered a Vodka Collins and a rib-eye steak, blood rare, with a baked potato and sour cream, green beans and apple pie a la mode—his all-time favorite feast. When his food was served, he dug in with gusto.

"Where's your sidekick?" Robertson, Skyar, McIntyre, Flood and Price stopped by the table just as he finished his last bite of pie.

"He's sightseeing, going to meet me here." Collier generalized, not about to tell them Pewter was at a Japanese whorehouse getting his brains fucked out.

"In case you don't know, we have it on good authority we don't have to be so particular about checking back with Camp Drake right away. They have a daily flow of ships and airplanes bringing replacements in—if you don't show up tomorrow morning they move you up on the orders and call your name the next day. Our advisor told us to stay until our money runs out. There's plenty of other guys on the list to keep them busy," Price confided.

Collier nodded offhandedly, resolved to go back down to the desk when Pewter got back and tell the girl they were staying a couple more days at least.

Sipping the lemonade-tasting Collins and enjoying the large dance orchestra playing Guy Lombardo arrangements of all the latest popular American songs, Collier marveled at the exotic setting overlooking the large city with the Ginza shopping district in the middle-distance, ablaze with colored light. Finally stuffed to the eyeballs with the superb fare and a bit mellow from his second Collins, he became aware the Tuxedo-clad vocal quartet was crooning a haunting Oriental-sounding melody with a refrain which sounded something like "*Shee-an-nona-yo-doo, shee-an-nona-yo-doo, yo...*"

"What are those words they're singing? What do they mean?" quite enchanted by the haunting song, Collier asked the nearest waiter.

"*Shina No Yoru....S-H-I-N-A N-O Y-O-R-U...*" after slowly pronouncing the words, the waiter spelled them in Japanese. "In American, it means 'China Nights.' It's the number one song in Japan."

"Give them this and ask them to do it again, for me," Collier handed the waiter a dollar for himself and a five dollar bill for the band leader.

"The leader said to thank you and tell you that they will do the song again later, after they take their break," the waiter reported when he came back.

"Okay...I'm not going anywhere," Collier muttered, trying to hide his chagrin that the band leader had taken his money and not immediately played the song again.

Sitting there in the romantic setting overlooking the bright, colorfully-lit skyline of the Ginza, with the better part of two strongly-mixed Vodka Collins under his belt, Collier's was suddenly overtaken by a powerful wave of melodramatic melancholy. Convinced he would soon be tragically killed in combat, his thoughts kept reflecting morbidly back on his completely unexpected, confusing and disturbing impotence with Keiko. No matter how hard he tried to rationalize his failure to perform as being a simple result of his prejudice against seeking the services of a prostitute, he still couldn't help feeling humiliated. To further compound his mortification, he had stooped to lying to Keiko about being a combat veteran in excusing his inability to perform.

The reason for his malfunction was all too complicated to puzzle out—but, still, his disturbing, unexpected impotence nagged at the edge of his consciousness. He wondered if he ought to find a doctor and get a check up. That was absurd, he dismissed the idea out of hand. There was nothing physically wrong with him. Hadn't he had been in championship shape back in Seattle? And that was only a few days ago. The problem was that he was simply a man of refined sensibility, not at all inspired by the crass, commercial setting of a Japanese whorehouse.

Besides, wasn't the purpose of their visit to the *Kinno-tenobi* for Pewter, not for him?

And, in that regard, he could certainly take credit for a job well done. Leaning back and looking up at the stars, Collier took great satisfaction in the knowledge that Pewter was no longer a virgin. He couldn't help but laugh out loud, just thinking back over all his misadventures leading up to the culmination of his crusade to effect the defloration of his naïve friend. If Collier lived to be a hundred-and-ten, he would never forget the sight of John Henry standing in that doorway with a glorious hard-on, pulling the not-so-unwilling Emiko back to bed.

Sitting there, his self-doubts multiplying with each and every sip of the potent Collins—he was now on his third, or was this his fourth?—Collier sank deeper and deeper into a morass of worry and self-doubt. Not only had he been unable to raise a hard-on, his libido had been as non-responsive as a cadaver on a mortuary slab.

"Collier Ramsay, I can't believe it's really you." Collier looked up to find Emma's nursing classmate, Ginger Lipscomb, standing beside the table. It should really have been against military regulations to put a figure like hers in an Army uniform.

"Ginger! My God, girl, you are a sight for sore eyes. Have a seat. Let me buy you a drink. You can bring me up to date." Collier stood and pulled out a chair.

"I can't now. I'm late. I'm staying at Army Hall. Give me a call if you're going to be in town for a day or two. I'd love to talk old times." Ginger leaned close and gave him a kiss full on the lips before she stepped back, gave him an apologetic look and headed for the elevator. About halfway to the elevator, she stopped, turned around, came back and kissed him hard on the lips again. "I really mean it. Call me, Collier. We've wasted far too much time already."

Watching her leave, Collier whiffed just the faintest suggestion of expensive perfume mixed with heady, woman scent. Still tasting her lipstick, he shook his head, trying to make sense of her totally unexpected outburst. As if in some eerie answer to his recent doubts about his failing manhood, he suddenly realized Ginger's kiss had sent blood rushing into his loins.

Doctor Frankenstein! It's alive...it's alive!

Looking around for the waiter, Collier caught sight of a group of three quite-attractive American or British women getting off the elevator and surveying the crowded rooftop searching for an empty table. All morbid obsessions about his physical problems vanished in the heady scent of Ginger Lipscomb's wake, Collier appreciated the latent eroticism of the three women as they made their way across the terrace.

Suddenly euphoric to realize his neurotic preoccupations about his failed manhood were rooted in his self-fulfilling imagination—and taking courage at the diminution of his inhibitions from the alcohol—Collier rose from his chair and addressed the approaching trio of attractive females with a gentlemanly bow of respect, "Perhaps I could offer you ladies a seat at my table...and a drink."

"Well, thank you, Sir. I do declare, ladies, chivalry is still alive, after all," the honey-blonde said, blatantly flirtatious, immediately pulling out the nearest chair and taking a seat. After a slight hesitation, her two companions, a wheat-blonde and a tallish, but slightly hippy, natural brunette, faintly-reminiscent of the movie actress, Jeanne Crain, sat down.

"I'm Collier Ramsay, at your service, Ladies. What's your pleasure?" Collier sat back down and waved a waiter over.

"Cuba Libre," the two blondes ordered rum and coke in unison.

"What is that you're drinking, Lieutenant?" the slender brunette asked Collier.

"Vodka Collins, Ma'am," Collier replied.

"Vodka Collins? I don't think I've ever heard of that," the Jeanne Crain look-a-like mused aloud. Wearing a simple, form-hugging, pale sea green cheongsan—most likely made of local silk—she was really a knockout.

"Here...try a sip?" Collier pulled out the drinking straw, turned it upside down in the tall, frosted Collins glass and passed it across to her.

"Uhm-m, this tastes like lemonade. Alright, I'll have one of these." The brunette took another sip and handed Collier back his glass. Keeping eye contact, he took a sip without flipping the straw again—a gesture of implied intimacy he'd seen in some old movie.

"While we're waiting for our drinks, perhaps you ladies would be so kind to tell me your names and what on earth are nice American girls doing in Tokyo, halfway around the world?" Collier looked them over carefully. They were all quite attractive, but, without any makeup except a little lipstick, the taller brunette was the least eye-catching of the trio.

"I'm Janet...this is Dorothy and this is Madison," the smaller of the pair of blondes made the introductions.

The Jeanne Crain look-a-like was Madison.

"I don't recall seeing you here before," the taller blonde, Dorothy, said.

Momentarily, Collier considered giving them a song and dance about being on R&R, but thought better of it. Telling the truth saved having to remember all the lies. Besides, these girls were most likely looking for someone to take them on the town, and his funds were running too low to go jousting windmills. "I'm on orders for Korea. I'm only here for a day or so. I'm billeted here at the Yuraku."

"Where are you from, Lieutenant Ramsay? Back home in the States, I mean," Janet, the more petite of the two blondes asked.

"Roanoke, Virginia. How about you ladies?" Collier shifted the conversation back to the women, not really in the mood for *Twenty Questions*.

"I'm from Ohio, Dorothy is from Iowa and Madison is from West-by-God-Virginia," the talkative Janet filled him in.

"Do you mind if we ask your lovely companions to dance?" An eager-beaver young naval aviator and his two companions resplendent in dress whites approached the table.

"Not at all...if the ladies are interested..." Collier replied, trying not to sound resentful. The cheapskate bastards had been sitting there all evening dancing with women at other tables around the terrace—too chintzy to pick up the check for their drinks.

"I'm sorry, but I promised my dances all to Collier," Madison spoke up. Rising, she took Collier's hand, abruptly tugging him out of his chair, taking him completely by surprise.

"My pleasure." Surprised, Collier stood and followed her as she threaded her way to the tiny dance floor in front of the bandstand. Watching the undulations of her ample derrière and thinking she was even better looking than he had originally appreciated, Collier suppressed an encouraging stirring in his nether parts.

"I hope you didn't mind?" the brunette murmured in Collier's ear as soon as they were dancing.

"Not at all. I was trying to get up my nerve to ask you, anyway," Collier breathed in her ear. Her breasts and thighs moved seductively against him.

"I've been to Roanoke. I went to college in Staunton. I graduated from Mary Baldwin in forty-nine," she volunteered, making idle conversation.

"I know Mary Baldwin—some of the girls in my high school class went there," Collier said, a trifle out of breath. It made him very edgy dancing with this attractive single female halfway around the globe far from the prying eyes of home.

"Can you recall their names? They may have been classmates." She kept him at a very chaste distance, only occasionally brushing belly-to-belly, thigh-to-thigh.

"I'd have to think about that. We were class of forty-six—that was seven years ago," he hedged. His earlier concerns about impotence could definitely be put behind him.

"I was class of forty-six at Dunbar High in Charleston. You're a good dancer...I love the music, don't you?"

"Uhmm-m..." Collier murmured assent.

"In Japanese, the name of this song is *Shina No Yoru*—the GIs all call it 'She Ain't Got No Yo-yo.' I hate it that they would make fun of such a lovely song..." she murmured, pressing closer, swaying in time with the music.

"Uhm-m..." not trusting his voice now, he nodded agreement.

"It means China Nights. The song is very popular over here. I've been meaning to find a record to mail back home."

"I should get one, too..." He was certain she must be dazzled by his brilliant repartee.

"How long do you have before you have to leave for Korea?" When the song finally ended, she stepped back a step, making no indication she wanted to return to the table.

"I'm not sure. When we arrived at Drake late yesterday, we were given VOCO to come into Tokyo with no specific instruction when to report back. Looks like the Army must have a large backlog of junior officers waiting shipment to Korea. I think the whole idea is to get as many troops as possible there before the truce is signed, because we will be, more or less, limited to that number afterwards. I know they only allowed us to convert a maximum of three-hundred dollars to military script when we processed through customs. I get the general impression the military doesn't count on us coming back to Camp Drake until most of our money is gone. After that, the way they're handling shipment orders, it could be the day after we report back. It doesn't really matter, I guess. It looks like they will finally sign the truce most any day now." He shrugged.

"Don't hold your breath. I've been in MacArthur's Tokyo headquarters for over a year. That's what they've been saying almost everyday I've been here." She looked up at him, frowning disgust for having to suffer such fools. When she reached up to touch her hair, he noticed a heavy male college ring on a chain around her neck.

"Oh, well, when the Chinese discover I have arrived, they'll sign right away, I'm sure..." He let the words trail off, embarrassed that one dance could render him so completely moronic.

"Look, please don't be offended, but I don't like being up here with all these young flyboys and other hotshots asking me to dance. Forgive me, but I'm going to just quietly take the elevator back downstairs and go back to my little hidey-hole at Army Hall. Please apologize to my girlfriends for me, and please don't take it personally—I hope you understand." Unexpectedly, she stepped back and reached out her hand to wave goodbye.

"Well...sure. I'm sorry to see you leave...I enjoyed the dance. I thoroughly agree with everything you said about the song," he stammered, crestfallen to see her leave.

"I enjoyed the dance, too...I really did. And I do love the music, but, if I hung around this zoo, we wouldn't have a moment's peace, anyway." She pleaded for understanding.

"Isn't there some other place—away from the American military?" he asked, grasping at straws. "I really enjoyed our conversation."

"Well...I...uh...there is little Japanese teahouse I like. It's near here and off the beaten path, but you would probably be sorry. I'm not very good company, I'm afraid." She hesitated, apparently not in all that much of a hurry to run away to Army Hall.

"Trust me, I won't be sorry. My next stop is Korea. I'm not exactly the life of the party, myself, these days. Just give me a minute while I settle the check." He extracted the roll of military script from his trousers' pocket.

"Okay, I'll wait for you in the lobby. Tell Janet and Dorothy I'll see them in the morning—or whenever," she said, heading for the elevator.

"IT WAS VERY NICE TO HAVE MET YOU, LADIES. Your friend, Madison, asked me to tell you that she was going home. I'm afraid I'm turning in, too. I've got a busy day tomorrow." Back at the table Collier delivered Madison's message; then he settled the check and excused himself.

"Wait up a second." Janet, the petite blonde caught up to him at the elevator. "If you're taking Madison somewhere to a quieter place, Lieutenant, I hope you have a pleasant evening. It might help you both if you knew tonight is the first time she's been out for an evening's entertainment since she got news her fiancé—a Naval carrier pilot—was shot down over Korea, almost a year ago. For a long time, we worried she might be suicidal. We were all beginning to wonder if she would ever quit grieving and finally let his memory go." Janet sadly shook her head.

"I'm sorry to hear that, but I'm glad your friend is finally getting over her fiancé's death," Collier replied as he turned and stepped into the elevator. "Goodnight, again, it was very nice to have met you and your friends."

On the elevator going down Collier had second thoughts about hooking up with a woman who probably needed a psychiatrist. It wasn't too late. He could just explain to her that he was tired, then go on back to his room and catch up on some much-needed rest.

His ego and his better judgment were at war. Even though he had definitely felt the old familiar heaviness in his loins dancing with this attractive female, the trauma of his failure with Keiko a scant two-hours ago still nagged him. What if he actually had become suddenly impotent? To hell with common sense—he would be probably be in Korea by this time Monday night, anyway.

"Are you sure you want to do this? You might as well understand I'm not going to wind up in bed with you, if that's what you're thinking. It's not too late to change your mind." Most likely also beset with second thoughts, Madison warned him as soon as he walked up to her, waiting in the lobby near the door.

"Trust me. Just some company and quiet conversation is all you'll get from me, Scout's honor!" Collier made a pathetic attempt at the traditional Boy Scout's high sign.

"You might as well save all that Boy Scout sincerity, Lieutenant Ramsey. The MPs might get you for impersonating a Scout." She laughed. The woman was no dummy, but then it didn't really take a genius to figure out what he had on his mind.

"C'mon, lady, quit worrying so much about your precious maidenhood. I said you're safe; can't you take 'yes' for an answer?"

"Okay, come on, let's get out of here," she conceded reluctantly, still not all that convinced. "The place I have in mind is really not that far. We can walk if you feel up to a little stroll." She gave him a questioning look and turned to leave.

"A stroll is fine with me. After thirty hours on a DC-4 with bucket seats, a little walk would do me good." Collier offered his arm as she led him toward the door.

Outside the Yuraku, she steered him along the tree-lined street away from the rosy glow of the Ginza. Between the overhanging limbs of the sheltering trees, Collier caught glimpses of a star-filled sky. Now that the sun had gone down, the temperature had dropped a little, but he was certain it still hovered near the nineties—the humidity seemed even higher, if that was possible. Before they had covered half a city block, his entire body was damp with sweat.

"Here we are." Just when he was about to suggest they flag down a taxi, she led him to the entrance of an unimposing little Japanese tea house. Inside they were greeted by a kimono-clad mama-san who—seen against the authentic Japanese backdrop—might have decorated the pages of *National Geographic*.

"*Ahso, Madison-san.* It's been too long since we've seen you here," the tiny mama-san warmly welcomed Madison.

"*Konbanwa, Moreko-san.* I'm very glad to see you again. You're right. It has been too long. Allow me to present my friend, Collier-san. We are looking for something to drink and a quiet corner where we can talk." When Madison presented him to Moreko-san, the ageless Oriental proprietress made a polite bow.

"Come. I show you." The woman led them to a cozy cubicle in the back of the tearoom which was furnished with a round table just big enough for two chairs.

"I think I'll have sake tonight, Moreko-san," Madison ordered without waiting to be asked.

"I'll have the same," Collier said, not caring what he ordered. He had no intention of drinking very much.

"You said you were from West Virginia—whereabouts?" Collier asked as soon as Moreko-san left to get their drinks, trying to get on a more comfortable footing.

"Dunbar—it's just west of Charleston. If I have my way, I'm never going back." She sniffed and wrinkled her nose.

"I know where Dunbar is. What's wrong with Dunbar? As West Virginia goes, Charleston isn't all that bad," he ventured diplomatically. After all, this woman probably still had family back there.

"Maybe not to you, but you didn't have to live there. You've never seen the bad roads and the squalor of the coal-camps." She frowned, remembering.

"Whoa...you assume too much. I went to school at Bluefield College and played basketball against some nice little colleges all up through the state," he generalized, not wanting to disparage the hardworking people of the coal-mining state. "Do you come from a long line of West Virginians?" he blurted, puzzled that her apparent erudition contrasted with such an unsophisticated blue-collar background.

"Heavens no! I was born in Wilmington, Delaware. We moved to Dunbar when I was twelve. My daddy was a corporate physician for Dupont—but his family roots were on the southwestern border between Virginia and West Virginia. Believe me, moving from Delaware to West Virginia was quite traumatic for this twelve-year-old girl." She raised her eyebrows expressively just as their Japanese hostess brought a tray through the door.

"Be clahful; is vlely hot," Moreko said, placing a spirit lamp with two porcelain flasks of sake and matching saucers in front of them.

"*Arrigato, Moreko-san.*" Madison smiled her appreciation.

"*Do itashimashite.* Can I get you anything else, Madison-san?" Moreko asked, bowing politely.

"*Iie.*"—To Collier, Madison's reply sounded like 'No.'—"That will be all for now."

Nodding politely, Madison watched the woman leave.

"I guess 'No' is 'No' in any language." Collier laughed. "But what does '*do-ee eetashi-maash-ee*' mean?" Collier asked, impressed by her easy use of the language.

"*Arrigato* is 'Thank you' and *do itashimashite* is 'You're welcome.'"

"Do you understand—and speak—Japanese," Collier asked, impressed she already seemed to know the language.

"*Sukoshi.* That means a small amount in Japanese."

"*Sukoshi...*" Collier tried the word.

"Very good, Lieutenant. You get an A."

"How do the Japanese say a lot?" Collier tried to hide his leer.

"*Takusan.*" She said, pouring some sake in her cup.

"Sounds to me like you're almost fluent." He said, impressed.

"Oh, no! Not nearly as fluent as I'd like. The Japanese speak English so well it kills our motivation. I work on the sixth floor of the Dai-ichi building in General MacArthur's old headquarters. We have a lot of daily contact with the Japanese—some of it can't help but rub off on you." She shrugged prettily. Trying valiantly to avert his eyes from staring, Collier eyed the sensual outline of the swell of her breasts against the clingy fabric of her *cheongsam*.

"So how come a nice Mary Baldwin girl like you winds up halfway around the world?" Collier regretted the question hardly before he had finished blurting out the words. Distracted by his lascivious fascination with the form-fitting dress, he recalled too late what her friend back at the hotel had told him about Madison's fiancée's tragic death.

"It's a long story. Let's change the subject, shall we? I'd much rather hear about you. You're from Roanoke and played basketball at Bluefield—so what did you study at Bluefield?" If he had touched a nerve about her sweetheart's death, she really didn't seem to be all that upset.

"I took pre-med at Bluefield, but transferred to RPI in Richmond and studied commercial art. I was an advertising artist when the Army caught up to me."

"Were you ROTC or did your daddy have a lot of political pull? How did you wind up with a commission?" Her question was borderline insulting, but he let it pass. His gubernaculum clenched, dreading the inevitable question about his marital status.

To lie or not to lie? That was the real question.

"Neither. I had a college exemption after World War Two and was already twenty-one by the time the North Koreans invaded Seoul. When war broke out, the Selective Service Commission was drafting eighteen-year-olds. I was almost twenty-three before they ran out of high school kids and the draft finally caught up to me. When that finally happened, rather than be drafted and wind up a private in the Infantry—or maybe even be put in the Navy or Marines—I enlisted in the Army to go to Officer Candidate School. The Army is famous for making truck drivers out of college professors. I was a commercial artist, so naturally I wound up in the Artillery in Oklahoma." He laughed.

"So what have you got against the Navy or the Marines?" she asked guardedly.

"I'm prone to get seasick and besides, I really don't like all those silly buttons on the uniforms." Remembering her fiancé was a Navy flier, he kept his answer light. "It's odd though; growing up, I always rooted for Navy in the annual Army-Navy football game."

"Why would you care about the Army-Navy game?" She looked at him suspiciously.

"My father is a world-class sports fan. My brother and I grew up to love all sports—it was our way of life, I guess. I played quarterback in high school before I hurt my back. The Army-Navy game has always been a major event in the world of football. My dad took us to Philly in 1946 to see Doc Blanchard and Glenn Davis play their final game against Navy. Navy was a three-touchdown underdog and was behind twenty-one to nothing when a midshipman fullback, Lynn Chewning, a 1945 all-Southern Conference selection at VMI who had transferred to Annapolis, literally took over the game, scoring three touchdowns. Sadly, Navy failed to convert the extra points. So, in the final minutes, trailing eighteen to twenty-one, Navy got the ball back and Chewning marched them down to the Army one-yard line when time ran out. It was quite a thrill, but that wouldn't interest you."

"Why not? Can't a girl like football, too?"

"Well...I didn't mean to sound so superior...it's just that not a lot of women care that much about sports," he apologized, not exactly sure how he had gotten himself into this exchange in the first place.

"If you went to Artillery school, how on earth did you wind up in the Medical Service Corps?" Abruptly changing the subject, she reached across and considered the serpent-entwined caduceus on his MSC insignia.

"When my OCS class was ready to graduate, it seems the Army was losing more Assistant Battalion Surgeons in Korea than they were Artillery officers, so Uncle Sam sent down a levy to transfer about a dozen of my class to MSC. I was pre-Med at Bluefield College. Go figure! I really hated not being able to stay in the artillery," he said.

"What's wrong with the Medical Corps? My father was a Medical Officer during WWII. Got a medal and came back home a hero. He was wounded in the South Pacific. With his legs full of shrapnel, it was too hard on him to go back to private practice as a GP in a small town outside of Baltimore. That's why he took the job with Dupont in Wilmington, Delaware. Thank God I was already twelve when he took the promotion to head up the Dupont medical staff at the Dunbar plants. I only had to be there for a little over four years before I graduated high school and went off to Mary Baldwin. I know it hurt my mother, but I spent most of my school holidays visiting my classmates and with summer schools at UVA in Charlottesville. I managed to graduate in just three years. My roommate's father was a career-Congressman in Washington, the standing chairman of some important military procurement committee. He got us both cushy Department of the Army Civilian—DAC—jobs in the Pentagon. After a year, I jumped at the chance to come here and work with other DACs at MacArthur's Headquarters. It's a damn shame what Truman did to MacArthur. It's a damn shame what Truman has done to kill all our fine young men. Harry Truman could have ended this war two years ago. How come Truman and his Joint Chiefs of Staff didn't insist the UN demand a ceasefire while these so-called peace talks were going on? We've been suffering useless slaughter now for two years for nothing—absolutely no reason." Clearly passionate about her hatred of Truman and the obscene travesty at Panmunjom, her voice rose almost to a howl.

"Well, it finally looks like they are going to get it settled now," Collier ventured tentatively, not wanting to add to her agitation.

"Two years too late and some thirty-thousand good American boys dead while those stuffed-shirt SOBs have been walking in and out of the truce tents at Panmumjon complaining about not having enough ice to make a decent martini..." Looking up somewhat sheepishly, she let her words trail off. "Sorry about that. I guess I get rather wound up sometimes."

"No need to apologize to me. Some of my OCS classmates are dead—and a lot of guys I grew up with and played ball with and against are dead or wounded—my college teammate lost his right foot, and he was planning to become a college basketball coach. One of the guys I enlisted with has spent over a year over there on Heartbreak Ridge. He was scheduled to rotate home a month ago—I hope he made it back..." Collier stopped and bit his tongue, coming dangerously close to letting it slip that both he and Bo had wives waiting for them at home.

"Drink your sake before it gets cold." She picked up one of the porcelain flasks, poured her saucer-like cup full and took a sip.

Following her example, Collier filled his own cup and took a more tentative sip. The taste was sweetish, a little too much like wine to suit his taste.

"You have to get used to it," she said, noting his frown.

"I guess I'm just not sophisticated enough to appreciate all this culture. I'm really not that much of a drinker, anyway," he confessed with a sheepish laugh.

"Me either. But I do like sake. It's much better than beer. A good Mary Baldwin and Hollins girl wouldn't be caught dead drinking beer." She lifted her little sake saucer, crooking her pinkie finger like a snooty matron. "Give it another try. It sort of grows on you."

"Okay, if you say so..." He picked up his saucer and took another sip. This time it didn't seem quite as sweet, but he was not optimistic it was a taste he was likely to acquire.

"Would you prefer we have Mureko bring some tea?" She asked, concerned he was enduring the sake for her benefit.

"Don't be silly...and don't give up on me so easily. I can be corrupted." He protested without considering his choice of words. Catching too late the double-entendre in his offhand remark, he watched her face to see if she misunderstood his meaning.

"I'll bet you can." She laughed. He got the distinct feeling that nothing much got by this girl.

"Where do you live? Does the government provide you DAC women housing?" He changed the subject, wondering where they might go to continue the evening if things escalated to a more agreeable footing.

"I live at Army Hall. It's an American-style building used for billeting DACs and military officers, very much like the Yuraku. The top three floors are for women—the lower floors are exclusively male. Some of the other DACs have similar billets at Sanno Hall, the Shiba Park Hotel and the Tokyo Kaikan. The accommodations are adequate, but they are like living in a dorm at school—more like a convent, really. No opportunity to have a private social life—not like you would think in a city as wide open as Tokyo. As we sit here at this moment, within a five-mile radius there are at least ten-thousand red-blooded American troops getting drunk as skunks and foisting their adulterous pent-up libidos on hapless young Japanese country girls forced into prostitution by so-called 'Honorable' Business Men. Lucky you; you get to have sake with a hypocritical

Baptist college girl from West-by-God-Virginia." She averted her eyes as she emptied her saucer of sake.

Collier sipped his sake without comment, wondering if too much sake was causing this intense young woman to go maudlin on him.

"Have you done any sightseeing? Been to any of the honky-tonks on the Ginza? They are really jumping this time of night." She suddenly brightened and her mood seemed to lift.

"No...well I did stop off at the Imperial Hotel earlier tonight. I poked around inside for awhile before I came back to the Yuraku," he confided, omitting his side trip with John Henry.

"You must see the Ginza before you leave Tokyo. It's really fabulous by any standard—the Japanese equivalent of Times Square and Broadway." Her spirits had lifted. She seemed genuinely enthusiastic now.

"I'm not sure yet if I'll have time—I'm on day-to-day notice of shipping out of here." He hated to be reminded. He hoped John Henry was already back at the Yuraku by now.

"Would you like to see the Ginza tonight—I mean right now? We could stroll like the Japanese couples do in the evening. It's not far. It's been quite awhile since I've been over there, myself," she offered, seemingly genuinely eager to be his tour guide.

"Sure, why not? I'm up to it if you are." With her sudden change in mood, he seized at the opportunity to spend more time with her—who knew what adventures the evening might bring his way?

"Come on. Let's go. We'll take a taxi. It's really further than I care to walk in this ungodly heat." She pushed back her chair and turned discreetly away, poking her fingers into the neckline of her dress. When her fingers came back out, they were clutching a fold of military script.

"Oh, no, no! Don't! I'll pay. Just tell me how much to leave?" he said, realizing she was about to pay the check.

"Don't be silly. Tonight's on me." Madison extracted a single dollar bill from her wad of cash and left it on the table.

Outside they had no trouble flagging down a taxi.

"*Ginza!*" Madison told the driver, who sped away hardly before they had closed the door.

"*Asoko ni Ginza ga arimásu...*" In only a matter of a few minutes, the driver pulled to the curb at the edge of a broad avenue ablaze with neon lights.

"*Arrigato,*" Madison replied. Again, before Collier could out-fumble her, she pressed a bill into the driver's outstretched hand.

"Please let me pay for something..."

"Come on; time's a'wasting," she stifled his protest. Opening the door of the cab, she led him to the curb and they were immediately enveloped by a sea of people. The driver had dropped them in a section of the Ginza heavily-populated with strip joints, theaters, and other establishments offering various exotic diversions for GIs rotating back for R&R. As noisy as it was with music blaring from the many nightclubs, they pushed their way further through the glut of half-drunken soldiers and sailors. After a time, the sea of uniforms began to thin and Collier and Madison emerged from the theater district. Now the preponderance of military personnel was replaced by ordinary-looking Japanese couples—some in native kimonos—window-shopping along an avenue dominated by large department stores and other smaller shops.

"Wow! Just take a look at that TV set...I've never seen such good reception." Collier stopped dead in his tracks in front of a department store with a TV set showing a swimming meet. The picture was incredibly sharp, far better than any he'd seen back in the States.

"Yes. It is amazingly good, considering the newness of it. Actually, there's not much television available here yet—the Japanese only started manufacturing TV sets and broadcasting this year," Madison explained as she pulled Collier away from the TV and began to stroll again.

"What in hell?" Collier muttered half-aloud as he chanced to glance into the window display of a tiny shop and did a double-take. His eyes fairly popped out of his head when he saw a brazen display of what appeared to be life-size rubber vaginas and penises lying in the window. Averting his eyes, he hoped Madison hadn't seen the tastelessly-conspicuous display.

Too late! She had already caught him gawking.

"I'm told those items were standard issue to the Japanese Army stationed on remote islands in the Pacific during World War Two. They are sort of barracks humor around the Dai Ichi building—you men are an adolescent bunch when it comes to sex." She laughed at his obvious discomfiture.

"Don't count me among that locker-room mentality. I certainly have to admit this display shows an air of sophistication I haven't seen back home. But, as long as we're on the subject, I can't imagine ever being that hard up." Collier said. He didn't want her to know such a public display of items for masturbation really made him uncomfortable.

"You never know how hard up you'll get in Korea...one of these might come in handy," she teased, obviously sensing his discomfort.

"Well, what's good for the goose..." he began, then bit his tongue to keep from making an obscene observation about the penises appealing to her priggish sister DACS and the hundreds of American and UN military women scattered throughout Japan.

"Go ahead and finish the thought. I think you're too chicken to say it out loud." She laughed, reading his mind.

"I prefer not to go there. Besides, women are the more fortunate gender when it comes to sex. There's no reason you ladies would ever have to do without."

"I beg your pardon! Just what do you mean by that?" She stopped dead in her tracks, not at all sure she hadn't been insulted.

"Nothing personal. But don't pretend to be so naïve. With all the horny men around slobbering to find release, even a fairly homely girl can take her pick any time she wants."

"Oh...well you might have a point, but I think you're exaggerating," she said seriously, obviously not having given the subject that much thought.

"I'm not exaggerating in the least. A good-looking dish like you and your friends back at the Yuraku can almost have your pick of men. Don't put me on. Surely you know that? You even warned me tonight that you weren't going to wind up in bed with me. So you must have assumed I wanted to go to bed with you."

"Well, over here, I admit it's different than back home. American women are in short supply. With all the military, even we homely girls get a lot of attention. Besides, I really didn't think you were...ah...attracted to me that way."

"Don't apologize. It's not necessary. But now that the subject has come up, I certainly find you quite attractive...but I...uh..." Leaving the thought unfinished, he resumed walking again.

"Wait. Finish what you were going to say." She tugged his arm, pulling him to a stop, whirling him to face her.

"Please. I'm sorry...let's change the subject. I was thoroughly enjoying the company. I...I don't want to ruin a perfectly lovely evening," he protested, stumbling over the words.

"I'm enjoying the evening, too. Don't worry; I'm not trying to mess things up. Finish telling me what you think of me." She gave him a curious look.

"There's nothing more. I think you are a very desirable woman. But that doesn't mean I'm some caveman who wants to drag you behind the nearest bush and rape you." Collier held his breath. He didn't have the slightest notion how he had gotten into this, but he was afraid it was ruining the promising beginning of what seemed to be an otherwise beautiful evening.

"I never took you for a caveman. Are you suggesting it's more your style to take me to a dreamy old Japanese hotel at the foot of Fujisan and make tender, but passionate, love to me—like the dashing hero in some Jane Austen romance?"

"Well—if you insist on making fun of me, yes, that is exactly what I meant— but I'm quite happy to just have your company here on the Ginza. I find it very pleasant to stroll with you like this."

"Me, too. But I've walked enough in this heat; let's go back." She smiled and squeezed his hand before they turned around and began walking again.

Not wanting the evening to come to an end so soon, Collier slowed the pace, racking his brain for some place to go or something to do. "Look, I don't want to let you go so soon. Isn't there some place we can go and just talk, maybe hear some quiet music...you know some nice air-conditioned spot where genteel couples go?"

"I do. If you don't have to check back at Drake tomorrow, we could catch the Bullet train down to Miyanoshita in the Hakone area at the base of Fujiama. It's a trifle expensive, but there is a fantastic old hotel there. After all, we're civilized adults. We could share a room without having to uh...you know? Without pawing each other and tearing at each other's clothes, couldn't we?"

"Sure. I have no problem with the idea of a platonic evening together. But it seems a bit heroic—not to mention expensive. There must be some place closer that would be more accessible."

"But, that's not the point. Think about the adventure. Tomorrow is July Fourth. I never figured you for a 'stick-in-the-mud.'" Her lower lip poked out in an irresistible "little-girl" pout.

"Well...the truth is my buddies tell me we actually don't have to check back with Drake tomorrow. They're pretty disorganized out there. With ship- and planeloads of new replacements arriving from the States almost daily, they are pretty loose about enforcing reporting back. It's embarrassing, but I've already told you, my real problem is I am quite short on cash. Fourth of July or not, what you're talking about sounds way beyond my means."

"Oh, don't worry about the money. The trip's on me. I've been pretty much a recluse for over a year; I'm pretty flush right now. It's Friday. It's only a little over an hour by train. If nothing else, you owe it to yourself to take a ride on the Japanese railway system. They are reputed to be the most efficient in the world."

"Well, I admit I'm tempted. The idea sounds intriguing. Back in the States, my father has worked for the Norfolk and Western railroad his entire life. Before I left home, he told me about the Japanese railroads and said to take a train ride if I could. He would really get a kick out of it if I told him I had ridden a train over here," Collier said, slowly warming to the idea.

"I'm not sure I'm flattered you like the idea of a train ride better than spending time with me, but I'm not going to complain. If you want to take a train down there and spend the night, the entire trip's on me. It's much cooler there and Fujiyama is absolutely breathtaking any time of year." Clearly, she was gaining enthusiasm for the idea.

"Alright!" he agreed, caught up in her excitement. "But could we stop back at the Yuraku so I can leave a note for my buddy? Besides, I want to pick up my AWOL bag—I'll need a change of clothes."

"Okay, fair enough. Let's find a taxi. I'll stay in the car while you run into the Yuraku, Then we'll whiz by Army Hall so I can pick up a change of unmentionables, my nightie and my toothbrush. *Takushi! Takushi!*" She shouted, waving her arms frantically at a passing cab.

At the Yuraku, disappointed he couldn't locate Pewter either on the Roof Garden or in their room, Collier left a note on the bed. *J.H. I'm taking the train to see Mount Fuji, back tomorrow afternoon. Don't worry about reporting back to Drake tomorrow. I checked around and we won't be in any trouble if we stay in Tokyo for another day or two at the very least.* On the way out, he told the clerk at the front desk that he wanted to keep the room for at least two more days and paid her in advance.

Seven stories high, Army Hall was similar in appearance to the Yuraku. Waiting in the little Renault taxi while Madison went in to gather her belongings, Collier fretted when he realized he had lapsed back into the same strange, erotic dead zone he had experienced at the *Kinno-tenobi* with Keiko. What had come over him? How could he, Collier Boyd Ramsay, ravager of women, suddenly go cold-stone-dead sitting here contemplating erotic fantasies of spending the night with such an overpoweringly attractive female?

Back in the taxi with her overnight case and an oversized leather drawstring purse, Madison babbled something in Japanese to the driver and they started out again.

"Does '*uhki dozo*' mean '*take us to the train station?*'" Collier asked, as the driver whizzed along, dodging in and out of the *kamikaze* traffic still quite congested at only a quarter-to-nine on Friday night.

"That's right! Literally '*uhki dozo*' means '*train station, please.*'" She nodded. "You're catching on fast."

"Is it spelled U-K-I D-O-Z-O, just like it sounds?" Collier was impressed that Madison seemed so fluent after only a little over a year in the country.

"No. '*Uhki*' is really spelled E-K-I. *Dozo* is spelled just the way it sounds," Madison explained.

"The E in Eki is pronounced UH? But they say '*E'miko*' and '*E'igakan?*'"— the taxi driver who had taken him from the Kinno-tenobi back to the Yuraku had told him that '*eigakan*' was Japanese for 'movie theater'—"How do you know when an *E* is not an *E*?" Suddenly learning Japanese was not turning out to be so easy as he had first thought.

"I'm not sure about the rules. What I've picked up is from actually living here and the necessity of communicating just to get around. It's really not as complicated as it sounds," Madison assured him as they pulled up in front of the railroad station.

"If you grew up riding trains, you're in for a treat. Before the war, the Japanese were legendary for their railroad system. Originally, this old station was much larger and the domes were of Russian influence. We pretty much destroyed the entire upper story and the domes when we fire-bombed Tokyo and other major cities to the ground during the late forties. Under MacArthur's occupation the Japanese have been able to reestablish their excellent railroad system to almost pre-war levels of efficiency. They pride themselves their trains run on time to almost the minute. They run on a twenty-minute schedule. We better hurry to the platform or we'll wind up having to kill twenty precious minutes waiting for the next train." Madison urged him into the mob as she came back from the ticket window with their tickets in hand. Just as she predicted, they had barely reached the platform when the electric train came speeding into the station, braking smoothly to a stop.

The outdated, almost antique, turn-of-the century American décor of the passenger car was in glaring contrast with the railroad's reputation for efficiency. The green-velvet-plush of the seat upholstery called up sharp images of his boyhood when he and Jim had ridden the local train thirteen miles into Roanoke almost every Saturday so he could take his dreaded piano lessons and his mother could go shopping. Out of politeness, Collier made no comment.

"I'm wondering if we shouldn't have called ahead for a reservation. Aren't you worried we might not be able to find a room?" Collier asked, suddenly concerned they were operating on hardly more than a sophomoric whim.

"Don't worry. I'm way ahead of you. We're all set. I called back at Army Hall. Just wait until you see this hotel. You're not going to believe this place." Madison grinned like a mischievous child.

Once outside the blaze of lights of suburban Tokyo, the surrounding countryside was swathed in a deep-purple mantle of night. Collier was only able to catch an occasional glimpse of yellowish lantern-shine as they passed an isolated farmhouse and a quick, warm blur of light as they sped through a small town or village along the way.

"*Miyanoshita! Miyanoshita!...*" the conductor called, moving through the coach.

"This is us—we're here," Madison said hardly before the train ground to a halt.

Outside the provincial station, a nostalgic, early-1930s-vintage bus—complete with chrome headlamps mounted on the front fenders and spare tire mounted just beneath the driver's window—was waiting for them at the curb.

"*Fujiya-san?*" Madison inquired of the driver.

"*Ahso...*" The driver nodded, assisting them both on board the rickety vehicle.

Aboard the bus and seated with the half-dozen other passengers who had disembarked the same train, the driver closed the door with an old-fashioned hand lever and got underway, following the narrow, twisting cobblestone road as it wound its way between the houses of the tiny village, passing by a series of what appeared to be cozy inns dotting the hillside along the way.

"Get ready. When we round this next curve, we'll be able to catch a look at the mountain. It's only visible for a few seconds as we pass between two hills."

"Oh...my...God!" Collier gasped as they rounded the curve, and, in the near-distance, the perfect, snow-capped cone of Fujiyama rose out of the plain in the ghostly moonlight. Truly breathtaking, in the same way Mount Rainier imposed a sense of sheer dominance of the landscape, in its symmetrical perfection, Fujiyama imparted a mystical sense of quiet majesty. In much the same way, the ancient inns along the route in the Hakone area possessed almost an artificial, picture-postcard perfection, when they arrived a few minutes later, perched on a hillside, the Fujiya hotel itself was something right out of a coffee-table book.

Depositing his passengers at wooden entrance to the ancient hotel, the bus continued around the circular cul-de-sac, chugging back down the grade toward the Miyanoshita station. Handing the waiting light-blue-uniformed bellmen their luggage, Collier followed Madison into the entrance foyer and up the steps to the Hotel Fujiya's lobby. The abbreviated entrance anteroom was located at the bottom of the hillside as the progression of the hotel's ancient buildings flowed up the natural slopes and terraces. From this rather perfunctory foyer, a wide stairway with exotic, heavily-lacquered, bright-red, Oriental banister rails led up to the lobby, itself, with its imposing registration desk against the wall across the spacious, high-ceilinged antechamber.

As they entered the lobby, Collier was enthralled at the simple elegance of the interior. Exuding a quiet refinement, the décor achieved an awe-inspiring sense of grandeur. Although the Japanese architecture, itself, was basically post-and-beam—with the darkly-stained, circular vertical posts formed from what obviously had once been massive trees—the interior was an interesting melding of Western pragmatism with a strong Oriental flavor, incorporating ornately-carved Oriental woodwork intermingled with the occasional *shoji* and *fusama* panels. Some of the windows were overlaid with darkly-lacquered, lacy, wooden Japanese filigree. Instead of the traditional *tatami*, the floors were covered with thick, lushly-woven western-style carpeting. This concession to Western decor was underscored by the use of modern American chairs with Oriental tables in the lobby-sitting-area to the left of the registration desk. The sitting area and lounge to the left of the entrance stairs were furnished with low, lime-green, upholstered easy chairs and reading tables and decorated with massive Oriental vases and oversized pottery containing bonsai trees.

"Wait here and hold onto this for me while I go check us in." Preceding their fellow passengers who were still waiting for the bellmen to help them with their luggage, Madison handed Collier her Samsonite and walked over and rang a simple bell resting on the registration desk.

Like magic, a young female clerk appeared from behind a screen, flipped through a stack of cards and, after a brief, but obviously heated discussion, registered Madison.

"Come on. We're good to go. Just follow me." Registration complete, Madison returned and led the way. Following dutifully behind the bellman with their bags, Collier gawked up at the soaring *shoji* screens rising all the way to the ceiling behind the first landing where a stairway at the far-back, left-hand corner of the lobby curved around, rising to the next floor. Walking along the wide corridor at the top of the stairs, the doors to the rooms—unlike those at the *Kinno-tenobi*—were hung Western-style on hinges rather than using sliding Japanese *shoji* or *fusama* panels.

When they reached the floor above, the bellman efficiently led them to their room and ushered them inside. "Welcome to our humble abode, Collier-san."

"*Arrigato,*" the bellman bowed and left as soon as Madison tipped him.

The bed and furnishings in the suite were a tasteful blending of the best of Japanese and Western décor. To Collier's immediate puzzlement, there was only one bed in sight and it was not over-generously wide.

"Well? Aren't you going to say something?" Madison looked at him for a reaction.

"This is truly fabulous. It's sort of a Japanese version of the fabled Greenbrier resort back home in West Virginia." Exhausted as he was from lack of sleep—but still puzzling over the lack of another bed—Collier was impressed.

"I asked them to send up some Asaihi beer, some sake and some snacks to nibble on when I checked in. I'd like to take a shower and freshen up—would you mind terribly if I go first?" Seated on one of several boudoir chairs in the alcove by the large picture window, Madison was already slipping out of her shoes. The chair's pale sea-foam green upholstery fabric matched the silk duvet on the bed.

"Not at all...ladies first," Collier bowed, plopping down in a chair across the room and removing his own shoes. Loosening his belt and tie, he unbuttoned the collar of his shirt and pulled the shirttail out. Then, scooting forward and putting his feet up on the edge of the bed, hardly before he knew what was happening, he dropped off into an exhausted doze.

"Your turn." Madison roused him awake as she came out of the bathroom dressed in a short-length silk kimono, briskly toweling her hair. As groggy as he was, he was pretty sure she didn't have a stitch on underneath the flimsy robe.

"Uhm-m, thanks." He stood and stretched and yawned. "Did you bring the kimono with you? I'm traveling light, I'm afraid—no need for fancy dressing gowns in the combat zone."

"The kimono comes with the room. There's another one in the bathroom. I think that's our beer and other stuff, now." She nodded toward the tapping sound at the door. "I'll take care of the room service and send your khakis to the laundry. You run along and get your shower."

In the luxurious bathroom, Collier wasted no time stripping out of his sweaty uniform. Locating his toilet kit, he gave himself a much-needed shave. That done, he brushed his teeth. Adjusting the shower to run as hot as he could stand it, he stepped under the soothing spray, soaping luxuriously with the recently-used bar of what looked to be pure Castille soap Madison had left in the soap dish. Absently soaping the length of his penis some of his tired-anxiety lifted as he felt his recalcitrant—recently downright undependable—organ tingling signs of life again. Although he fully intended to respect his benefactor's request that there be no messing around, all the same it was comforting to know he was once again capable of playing the rogue—if and when the need arose.

"*She ain't got no yoyo...*" chuckling and humming softly the GI's irreverent version of the haunting Japanese song, he rinsed off, turned off the hot spray, and stepped outside the tub, toweling himself dry with a sweet-smelling pure white cotton towel. When he had thoroughly dried himself, he went back to the lavatory and brushed his teeth again, swishing his mouth out from a tiny-bottle of mouthwash his mother had given him as a going-away present.

Just as Madison had told him, he found a matching silk kimono hanging from a bamboo hook. Stepping into his last fresh pair of Jockey briefs from his AWOL duffel, he stuffed his soiled underwear into a paper hotel laundry bag, carefully folded his discarded uniform over his forearm, and took a final look around.

"Well, here goes nothing." Breathing ceilingward this melodramatically prayerful line from some old Gary Cooper or Humphrey Bogart movie, he inhaled a deep breath and stepped back into the bedroom.

"Amazing what a shower can do. You look positively revitalized." Madison beamed when she saw him.

"I feel better, anyway," he grunted grudgingly.

"Have some sake or an ice-cold Asahi. I promise it will make a new man out of you." Madison was sitting in a chair pulled up to the room service tray with an ice tub containing several bottles of beer resting on the luggage table at the foot of the bed.

"Thanks, I hope you're right." Collier walked over and took a beer from the fancy ice tub. Passing up the food, he pulled up a matching chair. Perched across from him with one long leg folded underneath her on the chair seat—the other poking shamelessly from underneath her skimpy robe—Madison was exposing a lot more of her anatomy than he really cared to see if he had any hope of keeping his promise to behave himself.

"So, now are you glad you came?" Madison asked.

"I really wouldn't have missed this for the world. My dad will get a big kick out of hearing I actually rode a Japanese train. And this old hotel is something right out of a picture book." He struggled to keep steady eye contact, but the seductive exposure of the vast expanse of her outer thighs kept diverting his attention. If he had been worried about his manhood before, his anxiety had been for nothing, as he felt the old-familiar reaction.

"I hate to be a wet blanket, but I could use a little shut-eye. Is that the only bed?" Out of exasperation, he stood and walked over to the picture window.

"Yes...I apologize."

"Couldn't we call for a rollaway?"

"I asked at the desk—rollaways aren't available."

"Okay...look, as tired as I am, would it be alright if I use the duvet and make a pallet on the floor." Looking at the thin Oriental rugs overlaying the unrelenting marble floor and thinking back to his recent flight to hell, this was déjà vu.

"Not so fast. When you were in school, did you ever read about the Pilgrim's bundling boards?" Watching as she carelessly shifted her legs underneath her, carelessly retucking the wispy kimono around her naked thighs, caused Collier to turn away. With his back turned, at least her voice seemed disengaged from the maddening frustration of his rebellious sexuality.

"Bundling boards? I'm not sure I remember," he hedged. Surely she didn't expect they would sleep in that same bed with some sort of barrier between them? If he was lying in the same narrow bed with her half-in, half-out of that tissue-thin negligee, there wasn't enough snow on the cone of that ancient volcano to keep his rampant testosterone in check. As intriguing as this escapade originally had seemed to him, he was beginning to suspect he'd made a terrible mistake.

"Look...I apologize for not being able to get us a room with two beds. When I called for reservations, they told me they could give us a rollaway, but when we arrived, because of the overload of married GIs in the occupation forces celebrating Independence Day holiday with their kids, they ran out of rollaways. I argued and pleaded with the desk clerk, but to no avail. We're grown up.

Certainly we can work something out. If anyone sleeps on the floor, it will be me."

"Oh, no! You know I wouldn't think of letting you do that. *I'll* make the pallet on the carpet using the duvet from the bed. The carpet provides some padding. On the way flying over here, I had to sleep on the bare floor of the airplane with only a couple of thin GI wool blankets to make my pallet; compared to that, a pallet made with that duvet will be a luxury."

"Don't be absurd. I wouldn't hear of it," she protested before he'd scarcely finished speaking. "All this is silly. We're mature, civilized and responsible adults. This bed is plenty wide enough. Certainly we can both sleep there in relative comfort without getting in each other's way?"

"Look, I appreciate the offer, but these Japanese beds are not nearly as wide as American beds. Back in the States, this bed would be considered hardly larger than twin-size." It was ironic. She had made him promise to behave and now she was trying to talk him into sleeping with her on this narrow bed—it was all he could do not to laugh out loud.

"Quit being so hard to get along with. That bed may be a little cramped for two, but it's ridiculous to have one of us sleeping on the floor. Do I have bad breath or something? Are you afraid of me?"

"No, I'm certainly not afraid of you—and you certainly don't have bad breath." Her insistence on bed-sharing had suddenly grown from an anthill to a mountain the size of Fujiyama.

"Well, okay. So? What about it?" She leaned forward, clearly exasperated.

"Alright. We can give it a try, I guess. Worst case is that I wind up sleeping on the floor if we get in each other's way."

"Okay, it's settled then," she gloated.

Br'er Rabbit was right back in the briarpatch! Considering his solemn promise to behave and looking at her sitting there in the tissue-thin kimono apparently completely nude underneath, he sincerely hoped she'd brought an old-fashioned nightie to wear to bed.

"Okay. I just hope you know what you're letting yourself in for..." He let the thought trail off. He really wasn't anxious to talk her back into letting him sleep on that marble floor.

"It's settled as far as I'm concerned. By the way, I know it's a little late to be telling you this, but I'm told by my roommates that I snore." She giggled, trying to hide her embarrassment by taking a tentative sip of sake.

"The same has been said of me. I suggest you go to sleep first, so you won't have to put up with that." He smiled mischievously. Their conversation was beginning to take on all the characteristics of a couple on their honeymoon.

"So, you've been here before? Is it a favorite haunt of yours?" he ventured, not wanting to get back on the subject of sleeping arrangements.

"Yes, but it is not a haunt. I came just once—Fourth of July, exactly one year ago. I was enchanted with the hotel and the scenery, but the trip ended badly and I never really got over it—at least not until tonight, I guess. When I met you back at the Yuraku, I decided tonight might be the perfect time to chase some ghosts."

"Well, I hope it's working out..." Now she had moved across the room and was staring out the window onto the chiaroscuro patterns of moonlight on the outline of the Oriental roofs of the adjacent buildings. Her face had a pensive look.

"It is. I'm glad you're here to keep me company—I'm not brave enough to chase my ghosts alone."

"We all have ghosts, I guess..." Her angst had become a little heavy-handed now.

"No second thoughts?" She walked back and took a sip from her sake cup.

"No. Not if you're enjoying it?" He eyed the bed, tentatively.

"I'm having the time of my life, so far." She finished off the sake and poured it full again.

"I'm glad." He meant it. She still had a haunted look. He hoped she wasn't going to get bombed. Nothing worse than a maudlin drunk.

"Tell me all about yourself. You were a jockstrap and an artist. That seems quite a stretch when I think about it." She changed the subject as she took another sip of sake.

"Seems perfectly normal to me. I'm not some freak." He shrugged good-naturedly.

"Oh, I didn't mean to imply you were. It's just that the combination of he-man with artistic inclinations is not along conventional lines."

"You're right about that. Believe me, I took some kidding along the way." He laughed out loud, just thinking back on it. "But enough of me. Just what is it you did in Washington?"

"I was a spy—a cryptologist. I decoded Russian and Chinese diplomatic transmissions for a hush-hush agency reporting to the Pentagon and State Department. I got to be quite good at it, believe it or not. In Washington, I studied under some former members of Herbert O. Yardley's famous American Black Chamber—the celebrated code-breakers who broke the Japanese code in the early nineteen twenties."

"Never heard of them."

"Well, Yardley wrote a famous book about it: *The American Black Chamber*. It got a lot of attention back in the early thirties."

"I'll try to find a copy, first chance I get." He meant it—spy stuff fascinated him.

"If you're serious, I'll loan you a copy when we get back to Tokyo. There are a couple of copies lying around our offices."

"I am definitely serious. That kind of thing really interests me. Are you still doing stuff like that over here now?"

"Yeah. Over here, we intercept military transmissions from the Chinese and Russians and decode them. Next time you go by the Dai Ichi building, look at the antennae on the roof. Except that I have to report to a dumb-ass, G-2 colonel who wouldn't know how to use an Orphan Annie secret-decoder ring, I am the person in charge of our entire Far East cryptology operation. Not bad for a debutante from Dunbar, West Virginia, don't you think?"

"I'm impressed. I was in Army Basic with a guy named Jay Lawlor who said he worked in cryptology in Washington. Have you ever run into him, by any chance?"

"Sure...Jay worked under me for awhile. I hated to lose him, but he bumped heads with a fairly highly-placed, stuffed shirt in the Pentagon, and we had to fire him. It caused quite a stir in certain circles. Jay had earned very high security clearances, and for a time, there was some talk going around that it would be better all around if he had a fatal accident."

"You mean kill him? You're putting me on, right?" He searched her face for sincerity.

"I'm about as serious as Eisenhower is about golf. Are you really that naïve?" She shot him a closer look.

"Well, yes, I guess I am, at that." He blushed.

"Trust me there was some scary stuff going on in Washington back then—for that matter, there still is. DC is a scary place. There's even some scary stuff going on over here right in the Dai Ichi building where I work."

"Oh? And just what do you mean by scary stuff?"

"You really don't want to know. Let's change the subject. Have another beer and tell me about your love life. Surely you have a girlfriend back home."

"I'm an officer and a gentleman. A gentleman doesn't tell. Besides, it's getting rather late. I really do need to catch some shuteye. Would you mind terribly if I crawled up on that bed and logged a few hours-worth of serious ZZZs?" He pointed to his watch which showed a few minutes past 0100 hours.

"No, not at all. As a matter of fact, as soon as I brush my teeth, I'm going to join you. I could use some sleep myself." She put down her cup and went into the bathroom. When she came back, she walked across the room, removed and folded the duvet and turned down the bed. Walking back across to place the folded duvet on one of the Victorian chairs in the alcove, she returned and asked, "Which side do you sleep on?"

"Doesn't matter. Soldiers sleep alone." He caught himself just in time. In his extreme fatigue, he had been about to say he preferred the right-hand side, nearest the door—the side he always slept on back home with Emma."

"So do single girls, but if it's all the same to you, I'd prefer to take the left-hand side nearest the telephone. I'm supposed to have the holiday off, but I had to call the OD at Headquarters and leave the number here. I'm chief cryptologist. I'm always on call."

"That suits me fine, but I'm embarrassed to confess I don't sleep in PJs. All I have is my underwear. For modesty's sake, I'll wait until I get under the cover, before I take off the robe."

"Don't let that bother you. I didn't bring any PJs either. I'm going to sleep in this robe." Blushing prettily, she gathered the abbreviated kimono around her and tightened the sash. Then she crawled into bed and pulled the covers up to her neck. "Come on to bed, so I can turn off the light."

"It's okay; go ahead and turn it off. I want to brush my teeth. I can find my way in the dark." Draining the remaining drops of beer, he put the empty bottle back on the tray, went into the bathroom and brushed his teeth again. When he reentered the bedroom, she still had not turned off the Japanese shoji lamp on her night table.

"Crawl in bed, silly. I won't peek." She waited for him to crawl under the covers and take off the robe. Averting her eyes when he rolled over and placed the robe on the chair beside the bed, she finally switched off the light.

"Thanks again for bringing me here. I really do appreciate it. I'll see you in the morning. Goodnight and pleasant dreams," he murmured drowsily, already half-asleep before his head hit the pillow.

When he awoke in the darkness sometime later he tried to hold onto an intensely-erotic dream of Ginger Lipscomb and it took him a moment to remember where he was. As the events of the evening came back to him, he remembered crawling into bed, but he didn't remember hearing Madison say goodnight. Lying there, letting his eyes adjust to the semi-darkness of the reflected moonlight coming through the window, he came slowly aware that Madison's slender form was so close beside him he could feel the heat of her body. Then he realized she was lying there, softly sobbing.

"Madison? What's the matter? Is my snoring keeping you awake?"

"No, I'll be alright. I...I had a bad dream," she snuffled between soft intakes of breath. "I apologize. I didn't mean to wake you."

"I'm sorry. If you want to turn on the light, it's quite alright with me."

"No, no. Go back to sleep. I'm okay. I really am." She meant to reassure him, but her soft snuffling continued.

"Want to talk about it?" He resisted reaching over, feeling helpless to console her.

"No. Please go back to sleep. This is embarrassing enough without letting you see me such a mess."

"Oh, don't give me that. There's nothing to be embarrassed about. Everyone has an occasional case of the 'night horrors.' I've had them once or twice myself."

After perhaps several minutes, he heard her blow her nose and felt—more than saw—her fluff her pillow against the headboard and pull herself to a half-sitting position in the bed.

"Better now?" he inquired softly. Now his eyes were fully adjusted and he could see her clearly propped up against the pillows, dabbing a Kleenex at her eyes.

"Uhm-m, I really am. I feel silly that I made such a fuss."

"Quit apologizing and tell me about the dream. It's just a dream. Dreams never killed anyone." He laughed what he hoped was a reassuring laugh.

"I guess not. But, I might as well confess. I wasn't crying over some silly dream." She reached for another Kleenex and blew her nose again.

"What's the matter then? Tell me what's bothering you? Are you homesick?"

"Homesick?" Her sobbing had subsided for the moment. "It's not that. I really do love it here in Japan.

"Well? Tell me what the hell's got you so upset. I don't understand." He had forgotten just how exasperating women could be.

"Oh...it's nothing really. Those ghosts I mentioned earlier tonight...they came back to haunt me. I'm not as over all that as I thought I was, I guess."

"Ghosts? You mean your fiancé—the naval pilot?" He might have known. Before he left the Yuraku, her friends had tried to warn him.

"Yes. I never should have come back here so soon. I thought I was over it."

"Well, tell me what happened. Why did you break up with this guy?"

"That's just it...I didn't exactly break up with him. It was more the other way around. He told me there was someone else. A so-called friend of mine. He'd been seeing her all along."

"Oh, boy. Sounds like you're well-rid of him. He's certainly not worth crying over."

"But, you don't understand. I was glad that he broke it off. I didn't know about his affair with my friend, but he was an egotistical jerk and I was tired of him. I was going to break it off, anyway, and he saved me the grief." She laughed a dry laugh.

"So-o?...why all the tears?" Now Collier was at a complete loss to understand.

"He said some things that hurt me and I fired back at him. I made some very personal remarks about his abilities as a man. He had a very fragile ego. It upset him very much."

"Good for you—served him right. Why feel bad about that? The jerk deserved what he got."

"Well?...he went back to Tokyo and accused my girlfriend of ridiculing him behind his back—he made quite a scene with her."

"So? With friends like that, who needs enemies?" Now Collier was even more at a loss to understand what all the recriminations were about.

"I know you're right. But he left her in near hysterics, a nervous wreck. I wrote him another, even nastier, note, after he went back aboard his carrier less than two weeks from the night he left me here. Not long afterwards, he was shot down in flames over Korea, my curses still ringing in his ears." she sobbed, bursting forth a fresh shower of tears.

"Don't cry. Come here." Collier rolled closer, pulling her to his chest.

"Oh, God, life's such a mess..." She hugged him tight. In no time at all her sobs quieted and she dropped off asleep, snoring lightly in his ear.

"Oh, my. I must be squashing you half to death," she murmured a few moments later as she jerked back awake, rousing Collier from a fitful doze. She made no immediate effort to extricate herself from their inadvertent embrace.

"No...I don't mind...you were fine. I'm glad you finally got some sleep." He waited for her to roll off of him. Sleeping with her lying pressed against him, his erotic dream of Ginger had returned and his penis had become as hard as steel. The inopportune bulge was pressing into her thigh, not far from the naked vee of her crotch.

"Thanks for putting up with my maudlin hysterics," she said, raising her head from his chest.

"Don't be silly. I'm glad I was here for you." He held his breath, still waiting for her to roll off of him.

"I can tell." She giggled, snuggling her lower body suggestively against the growing bulge in his Jockey briefs.

"Look, I can't help it. I am human you know?" He was getting irritated now. One thing he always hated was a 'common tease.' Besides, his hard-on was response to his dream of Ginger.

"Don't apologize. I hereby release you from your promise. I think your friend down there has found a home." Her open mouth found his, cutting short his protest as she reached down, trying to slip her hand down inside the waistband of his undershorts.

"Slip out of your underwear; your juices have made them soaking wet," she urged.

Without protest, he lifted his hips, helping her slip his Jockeys down, finally kicking free altogether.

"Not any wetter than you," he whispered back, his fingers gently peeling open the petals of her flower, his index finger slipping easily inside her center.

"Wait! We'll never be able to sleep on these sheets afterwards. Let me get a towel to put under us." She rolled off of him, padded into the bathroom and came back with several fresh towels, depositing all but one on the blanket bench at the foot of the bed.

"There. Now come here; let's take up where we left off." Spreading one of the towels carefully on the center of the bed, she positioned her ample backside squarely in the middle of the towel and beckoned him to resume his position on the bed beside her. He rose to his knees, anxious to taste her.

"Don't! We're both wet enough. I want you in me...now! You can do all that later, if you still want to." She pulled him back down on top, carefully guiding him inside her. "Go slow," she cautioned. As lubricated as they both were, her opening was extremely small and tight. It was almost more than he could stand, trying to keep from coming before he fully entered her. Finally through some miracle, he was at last inside her, feeling the warmth of her clinging tightly to the pulsing length of him.

"Hold up just a second." He breathed heavily, trying to regain control. "Give me a moment...ah...this feels too good. I don't want to come too soon." He stopped her from moving against him. Momentarily suspended by a tenuous thread of self-control, he hovered just at the brink of orgasm.

"Go ahead and come. Don't worry about me. I always get right to the brink, but I've never been able to actually have a true orgasm. From all the magazines I read, it's not that unusual with women."

"That's baloney. Trouble is most men don't take the time to give their women pleasure. Just lie still and relax." He rolled over on his back and pulled her astride of him, sliding down on the bed until his face was buried in the wetness of her bush.

"Oh, please...you don't have to worry about me..." she protested weakly as he slowly began licking her, taking great care to torture her clitoris with the tip of his tongue.

"Hush! Don't talk so much..." He came up for a breath of air and went back to what he was doing.

Madison moaned, pushing hard against his open mouth, losing herself in the rhythm of his licking tongue.

"Oh, my god!...oh, m-y-y god!" After an interminable time, suddenly she stiffened. Digging her fingernails into his shoulders, she began to shudder in violent, successive waterfalls of ecstasy. When the first wave of her orgasmic contractions had subsided, she made as if to move off of him, but he held her fast, resuming the gentle nibbling on her clitoris.

"Stop! I can't stand anymore right now..." she moaned, her efforts to pull back quickly growing fainter. Soon, she started to respond again. In hardly any time at all, she shuddered to climax again.

"What are you trying to do to me?" she gasped when he finally let her move off his face and lie on her back beside him, still shuddering in tiny frissons of pleasure.

"Didn't you like it?" he said, trying to suppress any hint of egotism from his voice.

"You know damn well I loved it. Now let me make you come. I want you inside of me." Impetuously she rolled back across his chest, kissing him passionately. Pulling herself into position astride his thighs, she slowly reimpaled herself onto the length of him. Moving her hips up and down his thrusting organ, she quickly became caught up in her own pleasure again as she guided both his hands to cup her breasts, tweaking her erect nipples with her fingertips, increasing the urgency in time with the frenzied rhythm of her hips.

"Come on inside me. Oh, please...hurry, hurry...oh please come with me..." she gasped with mounting pleasure.

"I don't want to come inside you—we shouldn't take the chance..." he protested, still reluctant to withdraw until the very last instant.

"Oh, please come inside me. It's alright, I'm safe...my cycle's past," she gasped, urging him as she built to the brink of another orgasm. "Oh, my god...please come inside me NOW!" her cries were lost in another tidal wave of pleasure.

Finally, unable to hold back any longer, Collier felt geysers of his semen emptying deep inside her. Too late to worry now.

"I think you have killed me, Collier Ramsay. You've made a total slave of me!" Madison gasped when she finally caught her breath. She had rolled off him and was lying on her back staring at the ceiling in the darkness in a posture of complete submission.

"You're wrong. No more slavery for you. I just freed you from the bondage of yourself. Now, I think it would be a good idea for both of us to get some sleep."

"Yes, master," she sniggered like a teenager, wriggling closer, pulling the sheet over them.

When he awoke again—lightly snoring and still snuggling sensuously against him—Madison had thrown her arm across his chest.

As tender as it might be from her ferocious ravaging, his still-throbbing penis was standing proudly at full attention. For the moment, he couldn't recall feeling so completely male—so completely confident of his manhood. The kaleidoscopic montage of images of his fiasco with the Geisha whore, Keiko, and the resulting trauma about his troubling balky libido the previous evening at the *Kinno-tenobi* had faded into a distant memory now—relegated to some hidden wellspring of future nightmares in the Stygian recesses of his own, over-populated secret purgatory of self-doubts.

Pulling Madison closer, he went back to sleep.

When he came awake again, the early morning sunlight was streaming through the window over the rooftops of the adjacent buildings and Madison was kneeling beside him, his erection in her mouth.

"Wait! I don't want to come that way, not now," he protested mildly, trying to pull himself away from her busy attentions as he felt himself on the verge of coming again.

"Why not? What's fair is fair." She pulled back, smiling.

"Look, Madison, there's something you have to understand. When it comes to sex, women have it all over us poor men. You women can always perform—after an all-too-limited number of orgasms, we underprivileged males have to wait while nature recycles our exhausted libidos. If you want some more attention from your old soldier down there, you'll have to back off and let him set his own pace."

"But you're hard as a rock. You may be a better man than you give yourself credit," she argued, reluctant to give up her attention.

"I appreciate your confidence and your admiration, but let's not waste all that enthusiasm on me alone. Come up here. If I'm going to come again, I want you to come with me." He reached for her hand, urging her to mount him again.

"Easy...I'm sore—go very slow..." she cautioned as she carefully lowered herself on him again. In hardly any time at all, she had thrown caution to the wind as—despite her tenderness—she abandoned herself to her pleasure. When she finally reached orgasm, he also came again. Finally they lay side-by-side in utter orgasmic collapse.

"Let's try the baths. Here at the Fujiya they are fed by natural, warm mineral springs—most likely heated by the same subterranean lava pools that once fired the volcano." When they had revived enough, at Madison's insistence, Collier put on his robe and accompanied her down to the baths which consisted of two twenty-by-twenty-foot square pools in a high-ceilinged chamber deep in the bowels of the hotel.

"You've created a wanton hussy. I never thought I'd risk being seen naked before strangers," she said, suddenly taking new courage at finding they had the baths to themselves. More than a bit apprehensive about parading naked before strangers again, Collier carelessly folded his robe on the bench-like table beside the pool and stepped into the warm pool. Madison quickly followed his example, came over and hugged his back and groped his genitals, realizing they had the entire baths to themselves. Soon their innocent, childlike cavorting and splashing became more sensual, with nipping and groping each other's nakedness. Inevitably, it was only a matter of time before these erotic games escalated to the point where Collier found himself embarrassingly turgid again.

"We can't take the elevator back up with you poking out like a pup-tent. Come here, Lieutenant; let's sit on the steps. I'll take care of that problem in no time at all." Madison giggled and led him to the steps and straddled him.

"My god, woman, you've become insatiable..." Collier breathed into her ear as she slowly moved her hips, sliding the full length of him almost out of her before she slowly lowered herself back down his rigid shaft.

"Oh my, I think I'm going to come again..." she breathed just as he reached a point where the pleasure seemed no longer bearable.

"*Ohayo!*"

"*Gozaimasu...*"

The unexpected sound of a male—quickly echoed by a cheery female—voice nearly gave them both heart attacks as greatly flustered Madison slid off him, immediately slipping to the lower steps to hide her nakedness from the older Japanese couple who were accompanied by two teenage daughters.

"*Ohayo...*" Madison finally managed when she regained some semblance of composure.

"*Ohayo...*" Collier blushed and returned the salutation, wondering just how much their unexpected company had witnessed.

"As soon as you lose your erection, let's get out of here," Madison whispered tersely in his ear.

"Trust me, my erection is no longer a problem." Collier laughed as he stood and held out his hand to help her up the steps.

Back in their room, they got in the shower together.

"That family just scared me out of my wits." Madison chuckled over her embarrassment of being caught *en flagrante*.

"I probably won't get another erection for a hundred years," Collier echoed her good-natured disquiet at the mortifying encounter.

"I wouldn't bet on that if I were you." Reaching between his legs, Madison began gently soaping his genitals. Under her insistent stimulation, Collier felt himself becoming fully erect again.

"Just let it ring..." Madison gasped in response to the ringing phone, a full half-hour later, riding him hard, building to another soul-shattering orgasm. The woman was insatiable.

"What's up?" Collier asked, lying in a state of post-coital exhaustion beside her as she finally got around to calling the desk to inquire about the calls she had neglected to answer.

"I might have known I couldn't escape, not even for a stolen weekend. We've been intercepting a flurry of coded exchanges between Russia and the Chinese Communist high command. My staff at headquarters suspects they relate to the final negotiations at Panmunjom. They're worried the Chinese are trying to sabotage the truce."

"But, why would they want to do that at this late stage?"

"Who knows? They've done nothing but stall and mess around for two whole years—since both sides went to the negotiating table in July of 1951. This all sort of fits in with reports they have increased their artillery and mortar bombardment in areas around Chorwan over the last several days—there are reports of possible troop build-ups. There's more than a little concern they might try a last-minute attack in a desperate attempt to push the line south, back below the thirty-eighth parallel. They need me back at the Dai Ichi building, ASAP. I'm sorry, but all good things must come to an end." Reluctantly, Madison rolled out of bed and started putting her things back in the overnight bag. "It shouldn't take long. We can meet again, later."

Two hours later, Collier reluctantly bid her goodbye as they sped across Tokyo in a taxi. "I'll be right here at the Yuraku when you're able to break free. Whatever the case, please call me. I want to see you again before I go back to Drake and let them ship me over."

"Don't worry. It shouldn't take long. I'll call the first chance I get to break loose. I'm not going to let you get away without seeing you again." She took an official-looking card out of her purse and scrawled something on it before she pressed it into his hand as he exited the cab in front of the Yuraku. "Don't go back to Drake until you hear from me. I think I might just be in love with you." She kissed him deeply and pushed him out of the taxi.

Standing amidst a teeming throng of Sunday afternoon strollers, many carrying gaily-colored parasols protecting them from the relentless sun, Collier watched regretfully until her taxi finally disappeared amid the careening jumble of cars and buses. The card she had given him was embossed with the official seal of the American Occupation Headquarters at the Dai Ichi building. The address line listed a telephone number—most likely an exchange board. Beside the telephone number, she had scrawled "Ext. 25" in pencil underneath.

"I'm sorry, there's been no word from Lieutenant Pewter—you don't have any messages from anyone, sir," the pretty WAC corporal behind the desk informed him, attempting to conceal a lurid paperback romance beneath the jumble of papers on her desk.

"Thanks, Corporal. I'll be in my room for awhile. I'll let you know when...or if...I go back out." Collier took the elevator to his floor and fell exhausted on the bed, the woven-bamboo blades of the Japanese ceiling fan slowly recirculating the fetid air above his head.

Collier's watch showed 1925 hours when the Yuraku's bellman knocked on the door and shoved Madison's message under it.

I'm sorry, but I'm stuck here and won't be able to get away tonight. I'll get back to you tomorrow morning when things have eased up a bit. Don't go back to Drake until you hear from me.
Anata Ga Suki,
Madison.

What kind of mess had he gotten himself into now? Collier wondered as he reread the note. He really did want to see her again, but he didn't want to get too serious. What would Madison have to say when she found out he was married and had a baby son back home? Awake now and not wanting to try to go back to sleep in the airless room, Collier took a cold shower, dressed and caught the elevator up to the Roof Garden. As he might have expected given the holiday weekend, the place was jammed with uniformed servicemen along with a plentiful gathering of females.

"Pull up a seat and have a drink." Bob Skyar waved him over to a large, round table near the low wall delineating the edge of the rooftop where Skyar, Flood, Price, Battaglia and Robertson were seated with a quintet of doll-faced Japanese women, obviously enjoying themselves.

"I saw you last night, but I haven't seen you around today. Have you been back out to Drake?" Flood asked as soon as Collier snagged an empty chair and ordered a Vodka Collins.

"Neah. I was up late. I found a bed and sacked out all afternoon." Collier shrugged, intentionally non-committal.

"Where's Pewter? I thought you two were joined at the hip," Robertson quipped sarcastically. Robertson was married and not a hell of a lot of fun in this crowd of horny bachelors.

"Oh, Pewter's sightseeing. He'll be along sooner or later. Speaking of Camp Drake, has anyone heard anything about when we should be reporting back?" Collier asked, half-afraid to hear the truth.

"Last report was from McIntyre. He went out there this morning to check on things. Mac said they were shipping replacements by the planeloads every day from Tachikawa. He said about half of the guys on our flight over were still being posted for shipment, the others' names had been scratched through, which meant they most likely just gave up and went back because they had spent all their cash here on booze and Geishas."

"Uhm-m..." Collier nodded. Thinking about the still-absent Pewter, he was suddenly forced to consider his own diminishing funds. He had already spent almost half of his military script, and he really didn't have anything to show for it. Yesterday, wandering the shops in the lower passageways of the Imperial Hotel, he had thought he might have enough to buy a Canon or Nikon camera before he finally went back to Drake and let them ship him to Korea. He was already running too low to do that now. If he sent her the money, he hoped Madison might be willing to buy one for him after he was able to save back a few extra bucks in Korea.

Thinking of Madison, he reached into his shirt pocket and extracted her note, hoping one of the Japanese women would translate the Japanese words she had written there.

"*Ahso, Collier-san. 'Anata ga suki'* is like 'I like you *very* much.'" A girl named Yoko sitting at the table looked at the note, trying to translate it for him.

"In this country '*Anata ga suki*' is a very strong expression of affection. '*Aishiteru*' which literally means 'I love you,' is rarely used in Japan—except perhaps in the lyrics of a popular long song. Over here we use '*Anata ga suki*' or sometimes '*dai suki*,' they both mean about the same. I think this woman likes you very much Collier-san. Do you feel the same?"

"She's a very nice lady." He nodded, wanting to change the subject. He had asked for a simple translation, not advice for the lovelorn...or more likely a warning of portending doom.

"I think this lady is thinking you are more than merely '*nice*.'" The Japanese girl giggled and blushed.

Typically, the drinks at the Yuraku were quite muscular. As the evening wore on toward 2000 hours and the number of Vodka Collins mounted up, thinking back over last night at the Fujiya, he reflected on every old war movie he'd every seen where married men had fallen for women they had met under the stress of war. He wasn't ready to admit he had fallen in love. *What the hell, he didn't even know the meaning of the word.* But, one thing he did know for sure— he'd give almost anything if he could have Madison naked in his arms just one more time. *C'est le guere!* He raised his glass in a silent toast, sinking deeper into his mood of melancholy.

"Save my place. I'll be right back." Collier excused himself and took the elevator to the lobby and persuaded the WAC corporal on the desk to put him through to Madison's number at FECOM headquarters.

"I'm sorry; that extension doesn't answer. Can I take a number and ask them to return your call?" the switchboard operator at the Dai Ichi building asked when the call went through.

"No, thank you. I'll try back later," Collier replied and hung up the phone.

Back on the Roof Garden feeling the buzz from all the drinking in the heat of the Tokyo night, Collier judiciously declined another drink and went back down to his room, undressed and carefully hung up his uniform. Leaving the light on to prevent the room from spinning in the dark, he lay down on the bed and promptly passed out. When he roused from his alcoholic meltdown, his watch showed 0529. Taking a cold shower to clear his throbbing head, he toweled off, put back on the same underwear and jotted a note to Pewter that he was going out to Drake to check on the status of their orders. Leaving the note on the pillow of Pewter's bed, Collier dressed and went down to the lobby to find the nearest bus out to Drake.

It turned out that buses to Camp Drake stopped on the corner in front of the Yuraku every twenty minutes and—despite the hopeless glut of the Japanese traffic—ran like clockwork, nearly as punctual as the Japanese trains. At the early hour in the gray pre-dawn light, the bus was already two-thirds full of half-dozing, alcohol-soaked servicemen in varying states of disarray and Japanese civilians going to their daily jobs. Making his way to a window seat at the rear, Collier made himself comfortable and promptly dropped off to sleep.

Even this early in the morning, the trip took the better part of an hour. Getting off the bus at the same gate from which he and Pewter had left scarcely forty-eight hours before, he cautiously made his way back to the orderly room of the barracks building, sidled up to a group of Second Johns crowded around the bulletin board and took a quick look at the daily orders posted there. He found his and Pewter's names still there, but now they were buried somewhere near the middle of the list that was crosshatched with pencil lines through names of men

Collier assumed had already been shipped to Korea. At least four or five were names he recognized as being on their flight from Sea-Tac. Notable, along with his and Pewter's names, the names of Skyar, Flood and the others he had seen drinking at the Yuraku last night still remained unscratched through, and the order had been sloppily updated at the top to specify a shipment for that very afternoon at 1300 hours.

Collier quietly turned around and left.

Outside, he headed across to the open mess and had a monumental breakfast on Uncle Sam, overriding protests from his queasy stomach. When he left the mess hall, he found the PX and purchased a package of three Jockey briefs with matching tee shirts. On a whim, he bought an engraved Japanese silver case for his Zippo before he caught another bus back into town. Passing by the University, Collier was again impressed at how busy the Japanese seemed, moving always at a half-trot. Except at night strolling on the Ginza, no one in Tokyo ever seemed to move at a normal walking pace. Entering the busy business section of the sprawling city, he caught a fleeting glimpse of the celebrated futuristic Japanese monorail electric train, hanging by skyhooks from the cantilevered single rail. It imparted the appearance of belonging in a *Buck Rogers* or *Flash Gordon* comic book.

Back at the Yuraku there was still no sign of Pewter.

The WAC corporal on duty at the reception desk could find no listing for *Kenno-tenobi* in the phone directory. Resisting the urge to try to get a taxi driver to take him back there—after all, after almost two whole days and nights, he couldn't imagine Pewter still being there—Collier undressed and went back to bed.

When he awoke again, it was mid-afternoon. The new WAC private first class at the desk said a woman had called for him and left a message she would call back.

Still no word from Pewter.

Instructing the WAC PFC to send someone to fetch him from the Roof Garden if he should get another call, Collier headed for the elevator. Periodically all afternoon and evening, Collier called the Dai Ichi switchboard, but got no answer from Madison's extension.

"If you will give me the party's name, perhaps I can track her to another extension," the Dai Ichi operator offered.

"Thanks, but that isn't necessary," Collier declined. Earlier, he had already thought to try to reach her at Army Hall, then hung up at the last second because he was too embarrassed to tell the switchboard he didn't know Madison's last name.

Finally, just before 2300 hours Collier decided to give up his vigil. Paying his bar bill, he tipped the waiter and headed back downstairs.

"The lady just called again and said to tell you she was sorry she kept missing you, but she would try to come by here on her way to work sometime before zero-eight-thirty hours in the morning," the WAC PFC informed him with a sympathetic frown.

Still no word from Pewter.

Suppressing a consuming urge to go outside and scream in frustration, Collier thanked the PFC and went upstairs to his room, undressed and flopped down on the bed. This time he turned off the light and gave way to near nervous exhaustion.

Awake again and dressed before 0700 hours, Collier went down to keep a vigil in the lobby for Madison.

Ten-hundred hours came and went and still no Madison—no Pewter either. When he called the Dai Ichi switchboard, he received no answer at extension twenty-five. Calling one last time just before noon, Collier finally left a message with the switchboard for "Madison at extension twenty-five" that he was checking out of the Yuraku, reporting back to Camp Drake.

"If anyone asks for Collier Ramsay, tell them I've gone back to Camp Drake." Collier handed the duty WAC an envelope with a short note to Madison with his APO address, went upstairs and packed his possessions in his AWOL bag and caught a bus back out to Camp Drake. Wandering through the gate and into the barracks building in the mid-afternoon heat, no one paid him any attention as he climbed the stairs to the second level, selected an empty bunk in the cavernous room and—stripping to Jockey briefs and tee shirt—he folded his khakis neatly over the iron bunk frame. Using his AWOL bag for a pillow to insure it was still in his possession when he awoke, he took a nap. When he awoke from another erotic dream of Ginger Lipscomb, he was damp with sweat and had to wait a few minutes for his erection to subside. Carrying his khakis and stuffing his shoes into the AWOL bag, he went to the latrine and entrusted his possessions to the Japanese attendant while he refreshed himself with a cold shower. Out of the shower and toweled dry, he put on his khakis and made his way downstairs.

Asking directions in the orderly room, he found the O Club to be within walking distance and headed in the direction of the only air-conditioned sanctuary he could think of. Just as he had hoped, when he entered the O Club, he was greeted by a blast of artic air—the first he'd felt since night before last at the Fujiya.

Checking his AWOL bag with the Japanese girl in the cloakroom just outside the main dining room, Collier noted on the coatroom counter the headlines on the latest *Stars and Stripes* heralded the news that the Commies were amassing troops and raining artillery and mortars on Heartbreak Ridge east of the Iron Triangle and Chorwon in apparent preparation for last minute attacks. The news dispatches suggested since the final negotiations would likely settle on using the MLR—the Main Line of Resistance—as the final line of demarcation for the peace settlement. The CCF were going to try to move the MLR as far south as possible before the truce was finally signed which, for days now, was promised to be a matter of only hours away.

Judas priest! Those bastards were still fighting over there. Collier sobered.

The O Club dining room at Drake compared favorably with a night club in Chicago or New York. Somewhat similar to the Roof Garden at the Yuraku, there was a small stage and dance floor at one end of the dining room where a full fifteen-piece orchestra was playing Glenn Miller and Guy Lombardo arrangements of nostalgic standards mixed with songs on the current Hit Parade. It came as a rather pleasant surprise that he had hardly been seated at a ringside table when a pretty, doll-like Japanese vocalist stepped to the mike and warbled a haunting rendition of China Nights—*Shina No Yoru*—which didn't do a lot to lift his depression from not being able to see Madison again or his mounting concern for the whereabouts of Pewter.

Wasting no more time on such futile reflections, Collier ordered and polished off a blood-rare, six-ounce filet mignon. Stuffed and feeling somewhat better and still holding out faint hope that John Henry would come strolling up at any moment, Collier settled back to enjoy the music for the rest of the evening. The festive crowd at the O Club was still going strong when he finally paid his tab and headed back to the barracks building at 2230 hours.

"I'm Lieutenant Collier Ramsay. I just got back from VOCO in Tokyo and see I'm posted on orders for Korea. When am I due to ship out?" he asked, knowing full well the answer.

"Ramsay? Oh, yeah. I've got you right here." The fresh-faced duty NCO found his name and wrote it down on a sheet of paper alongside a list of other names. "The uniform is combat fatigue. Report here at zero-six-hundred with field pack containing your personal toilet stuff, extra underwear, socks and an extra set of combat boots. There won't be a lot of time in the morning before we load the bus. I suggest you find a helmet liner and steel pot to fit you tonight—and don't forget an entrenching tool; it might come in handy. There are plenty of empty combat packs in the room containing your duffel bags, on your right back down the hall. Soon as you're packed, I suggest you catch some sleep."

Collier had no trouble locating the room where they had left the duffels. Now, neatly arranged alphabetically, Collier quickly located his overstuffed bag among the stacks awaiting their owners to show up for shipment to Korea. Using the key he kept on the chain with his dog tags, he unlocked the heavy padlock and extracted two carefully-folded fatigue uniforms, extra socks and both pairs of boots from the top of the bag. Sorting out the soiled items from his AWOL bag, he stuffed them inside the duffel before he refolded the top flaps and locked the carrying strap back into place. He sorted through a large bin of brand-new helmet liners and found one that fit him without too much adjustment of the inner-liner tapes. Finding a companion steel pot to suit him was no problem. He selected one with enough scars and scratches on its dull-OD-painted surface to look as if it had already won the war. Wearing the helmet liner and pot, he carefully sorted through the pile of canteens and entrenching tools and carried the unwieldy pile of equipment upstairs to find a place to spend his last night in the relative safety of the civilized world.

Locating a bunk on the fringes of a large area of sleeping men, their combat packs at the heads of their bunks, Collier made up his sack. Then, still carrying the equipment, he went to the latrine to brush his teeth and thoroughly wash out the canteen with scalding water. When he came back, it took him perhaps thirty minutes to assemble his pack. Finally satisfied that he was ready to move out on momentary notice, he climbed under the top sheet and closed his eyes for what would probably be his last time to sleep between real sheets until god-knew-when.

*Now I lay me down to sleep...*Searching his brain to remember the last time he had prayed, Collier began the silent mantra of his childhood prayer for the first time in at least a week. *Look, God, I can understand why you might have given up on me, but they say you're a forgiving God...please forgive me for being unfaithful to Emma...and please bless Emma and little Kyle...*he recited the tedious litany of family members eligible for blessings, painfully aware he was the one most in need. *Please, God, bless Madison...ah...I don't even know her last name. And please forgive me for letting Madison believe I am single...please bless her and keep her safe and help her to find a decent man who will be good to her...and please, God, bless my brother, Jim, and keep him safe and away from here until the shooting has stopped in Korea. Please bless Pewter. Keep him safe from harm. And, please, God, please let the fighting come to an end where I am going tomorrow. Above all, please help me to do my duty, and please don't let* *me show how afraid I am in front of the men I am supposed to lead. And, last but not least, please let Bo already be safely home to Jenny. In Jesus' name...Amen.*

"Collier, wake up."

"What?" Collier roused in the dark, confused as to where he was.

"Wake up, man. It's me, John Henry. Why didn't you wait for me?" Collier came groggily awake in the dark with Pewter leaning over him, rudely shaking his shoulders.

"Goddamnit, John Henry, where the fuck have you been?"

"You know where I've been, Collier. Why'd you go off and leave me?" Pewter seemed angry.

"Pewter, do you have any idea what day this is?"

"Sure...it's Monday, six July."

"What day was it when I left you at the *Kenno-tenobi*—or can you remember back that far?"

"It was Friday, the third—don't be such a smartass."

"Smartass? Look, John Henry, I stayed as long as I could. I'm almost out of cash."

"Yeah...I know. Me too. Fumiko kicked me out of the *Kinno-tenobi* until I could come back here and get some more cash. What's left of my stash is in my duffel in that room downstairs." Pewter put his AWOL bag on the floor and sat down on the empty bunk beside him. "By the way, the WAC corporal at the Yuraku said to give you this." He pulled a wrinkled envelope from his hip pocket and handed it across. The envelope bore the seal of the Far East Command with an address in the Dai Ichi building. Flipping the bedsheet aside, Collier came to a sitting position before he opened the envelope and read the hastily-scrawled note inside.

"I'm sorry I haven't been able to make it back to you. Intelligence reports from agents behind North Korean lines say many of the Chinese have contracted—and are dying from a mysterious illness—Korean Hemorrhagic Fever—which is said to result in bleeding from the eyes, nose, mouth and skin. Our health officers here at HQ are pretty sure it is not related to the plague, but there have been recent reports of cases in American troops who are being sent to a certain MASH for treatment and study. Please try to stay in Japan as long as you can. Intelligence also indicates the CCF may be gathering their forces for a final push before the truce is signed—which may take as long as another month. As soon as I can get away, I will come out to Drake and find you. Keep a low profile. Hang out during the day at the post movie theater and in the evening at the Officers' club. I really miss you.

Anata ga suki,

Madison.

"What's that all about? Are you in some kind of trouble?" Pewter asked after Collier had reread the note and put it back in the envelope.

"Neah. Nothing to worry about. It's a note from a girl I met the night I left you at the *Kenno-tenobi*—which, by the way, was a good three days ago now."

"Well...I know...but you don't understand. If you only knew how...how good Emiko was to me...*for* me. Judas priest, Collier, I never dreamed sex could be so fandamntastic." Eyes glazed over, Pewter stared off into the distance, remembering.

"Well...at least I'm glad for that. You won't have to risk dying a virgin in the combat zone."

"I can't hardly stand to think about going over there and having to do without." Pewter sat up straight, a look of sheer desperation crossing his face.

"Well, you haven't shipped over yet. Don't let anyone know you're here. You can hang around for another day or two until your funds run out."

"Well, so can you. I've got enough for a couple more days for the both of us. Get out of bed and get dressed. The buses run all night." Pewter brightened at the thought.

"Too late for me, buddy. I've already reported in and am scheduled for shipment right after chow in the morning. The CQ said the buses will be waiting to take us to Tachikawa as soon as we get back from the mess hall."

"Oh, what the hell, they'll never miss you. You've seen how it is around this zoo."

"I don't want to take a chance. Besides, it's different now. I've already reported in. Go get your cash and get out of here before someone puts an arm on you, John Henry. Might as well enjoy what little time you have left." Collier reread Madison's note and stuffed it into a side pocket on his combat pack. "I'll see you in Korea. It won't be hard to find you—there just aren't that many MSC slots in the combat zone. Now, I need to get some sleep; zero-four-hundred will come soon enough as it is." He gave John Henry a friendly tap on the shoulder and got back in bed.

"Well...I hate to let you go like this..." John Henry began, but Collier cut him off.

"Quit stalling, John Henry. Get the hell out of here. Your turn is coming soon enough."

As soon as Pewter turned and started down the line of bunks toward the stairs, Collier turned his back, pulled the sheet over his head and went back to sleep.

"It's zero-four-fifty-five, Collier. Wake up. Let's go find some chow, before we have to catch that bus." Pewter was whispering in his ear when Collier came awake again.

"Are you crazy? I thought you were going back into town." Collier rubbed his eyes. Pewter was dressed in fatigues and his combat pack was lying on the bunk beside the one Collier slept in.

"What the hell? I decided I have to go sooner or later. I'd rather go with you. Maybe we'll be able to stick together over there." Pewter sat on the adjoining cot, waiting for him to get dressed.

Fully outfitted in fatigues with combat packs, they were marched to get breakfast chow, still in the pre-dawn darkness. Miracle of miracles, the buses were fully loaded by 0600 hours and pulled out single file into the heavy morning traffic for Tachikawa, right on time.

Predictably, even at the early hour, the horrific glut of Japanese civilian traffic was stop-and-go. Their bus was the last of six, and, by the time the buses pulled to a stop at the edge of the tarmac at Tachikawa Air Force Base at just before 0815, there was already a ragged single file of combat-loaded enlisted men and officers stretching the length of a football field to the yawning, opened double-doors of a giant Globemaster C-124 parked on the edge of the runway.

Collier's gut did a flip. The behemoth aircraft in front of them was a carbon copy of the very same aircraft which had crashed off the end of this very same runway on 18 June—less than three weeks ago! That crash killed all 129 aboard—the worst crash in the history of aviation. All the news reports he had read indicated the military had grounded their entire fleet of C-124s pending investigation of that crash. How could it be possible they were flying on the very same type of airplane when the wreckage of that disaster was most likely still being probed?

"Hey! Isn't this the same type of airplane that crashed here a couple of weeks back?" Collier stopped a passing airman from the ground crew servicing the plane.

"Yeah. I was standing right here when I saw that baby auger in. I knew everyone of the crew. I'll never get over it. It was horrible. Could have been worse though, there were only one-hundred-twenty-nine aboard, including crew—fully-loaded, these babies will hold two-hundred-six troops with full combat packs." The ground crewman took off his cap and wiped the sweat from his brow.

"I read in *Life* magazine the Air Force had grounded all these planes pending an investigation." No matter how hard Collier tried to keep the edge of panic from showing in his voice, the statement was an accusation.

"Yeah. Officially, they are already grounded, but there's still a war on. I think tomorrow or the next day will be the last day we'll be flying these boxcars for awhile. This old baby is going to make this final trip to Kimpo today, then nothing else for awhile. It's a shame. One crash and they ground the entire fleet. And all this so soon after they were grounded the end of last year for fuel tank leaks—they were only cleared to fly again since February." The airman looked fondly at the big plane and shook his head regretfully.

"Kimpo? Is that near Seoul?"

"Yeah—right across the Han River bridge, just south of Seoul. I've made the trip a couple of times myself, just for the ride. Qualifies me to wear two Korean Service Ribbons."

"How far? How long does it take—one way?"

"Kimpo is roughly seven-hundred air miles—about three-and-a-half or four hours flying time. This old gal is powered by four of those big Pratt and Whitney's—twenty-five-thousand horsepower apiece—she'll top out at over three hundred MPH if you're talking ground speed."

Seven hundred air miles away from civilization. God only knew how many miles away from home. Who would have thought that in less than four hours he would actually wind up in a godforsaken place like Korea?

"That's pretty impressive for a plane that big," Collier croaked hoarsely—his mouth too dry from abject fear to work up a good spit.

"Look, have a good flight, Lieutenant, and keep your head down when you get to K-fourteen. I heard on Armed Forces Radio this morning the damn Chinks are getting ready to mount a last-minute offensive before the truce is signed." The airman put his cap back on and continued ambling toward the boarding plane. Numbly watching him walk away, Collier took a final drag off the

Lucky he was smoking and field-stripped the butt, scattering the shredded tobacco to the wind as the boarding line of troops were about to cross beyond a sign: NO SMOKING BEYOND THIS POINT. A hundred yards to their left across the tarmac, a busy crew of Army nurses and medics were unloading litters carrying wounded from an OD-painted C-47. The wounded coming off the C-47 all were hooked up to IV fluids—mute evidence of the seriousness of the situation awaiting them in Korea.

"Is what you said to that airman true? Did that Globemaster crash right here—off the end of this runway? Are all of these airplanes actually supposed to be grounded?" Pewter asked him, watching the airman walk away.

"Yeah...it's true enough about the crash—but apparently the Globemaster fleet hasn't officially been grounded yet," Collier croaked. Trying to blink away the premonition of his death, a ghostly apparition of his obituary in *The Roanoke Times* flashed before Collier's eyes.

Collier Boyd Ramsay, 2ⁿᵈ Lieutenant, U.S. Army

Lieutenant Collier Boyd Ramsay died on Monday, July 6, 1953, a victim of the worst air disaster in the history of modern aviation, killing 206 combat-loaded troops plus 7 crew as it crashed on takeoff from Tachikawa Air Force Base just outside Tokyo, Japan. Ramsay is survived by his wife, the former Emma Lowell, and infant son, Kyle, of Salem, his parents, Mr. and Mrs. Harry Milton Ramsay, also of Salem, and a brother, Air Force Lieutenant James Harris Ramsay, who is also stationed in the Far East Command...

Just behind them, burly former OCS classmate Tom Flood, one of their fellow-passengers on the flight from Seattle, asked, "How can they be flying this goddamn thing when the order is already been published grounding the entire fleet tomorrow?"

No one volunteered a reply, and Collier just shook his head.

By the time Collier and Pewter climbed up the perforated metal ramp and struggled up the stairs to the second level of seats, the mammoth aircraft was filled almost to overflowing.

"How many did that airman say this thing holds?" Paul Golden Price, who had climbed aboard just ahead of them, asked as he was buckling himself in.

"Two-hundred-six combat troops, fully-loaded with combat packs." Collier parroted what the airman had said. "I tried to do a head count when we first got here and came up with one-hundred-eighty-nine the first time and one-ninety-one when I took another count. At any rate, we're not actually overloaded—for whatever that's worth," Collier said as he took the window seat opposite Pewter, trying in vain to make himself comfortable with the awkward combat pack complete with entrenching tool strapped to his back.

"I'm sorry. We're going to have a short delay while they load some equipment in the cargo bay," the pilot announced over the intercom. "For what little comfort it will afford, we're going to leave the front bay doors open so you can catch a breath of air in this heat."

Much to the irritation of everyone, they were forced to sit and wait almost another hour before a parade of two-and-a-half-ton, six-by-six prime movers pulled away and he heard the whirring sound of the cargo bay doors winding shut.

"If you ask me, we should be on a troopship. Nothing this big was ever intended to fly," apparently almost as apprehensive as Collier, an anonymous lieutenant a few seats down from him complained.

Holding his breath and clenching his hands tightly around the edge of the bucket seat frame, Collier braced himself for the inevitable crash, helpless not to look out the window as the pilot of the giant aircraft ran up its huge Pratt and Whitney engines and finally let the airplane begin lumbering down the cracked concrete strip. Then, finally and amazingly, just when it seemed the plane had run out of runway, the awkward giant lifted slowly off the runway, and Collier watched with macabre fascination as the tangled wreckage of their recently-ill-fated sister ship flashed by underneath them, so close he could almost touch it with his hand. Checking his watch just as they became airborne, Collier was surprised it was already a few minutes past noon.

Due to his extreme discomfort sitting in the canvas bucket sling with a pack on his back, Collier had little trouble staying awake for the first hour of the flight as he caught a heart-tugging glimpse of the snow-capped Fujiyama out the corner of his eye shortly after takeoff. Flying at an unusually low altitude, they passed over the picturesque quilt-scape of the Japanese countryside. Within a few short minutes after they finally left the Japanese mainland and were flying low over the Sea of Japan, Collier finally drifted off to sleep. When he awoke again, they were approaching land and his watch showed 1350 hours.

Collier's appraisal that they were making final preparation to land at Kimpo proved to be correct. The pilot came on the intercom just before the plane started to gradually lose altitude, hopefully in preparation for landing. "Welcome to Korea—and as of right now—still a war zone. I'm sure you noticed we have been maintaining an altitude of only a little over two thousand feet which was okay until we crossed into Korean airspace where the favorite pastime of former Communist troops who have become reintegrated into the indigenous population are taking potshots at passing airplanes with the tons of abandoned military weapons lying around in the bushes. So far we've managed to escape any major damage. We'll be landing in about half-an-hour. I seriously advise you to keep your steel pots on at least until the truce is signed. Only three weeks ago, a whole squadron of Bedcheck Charlies flying small Russian biplanes like the Polikarpov PO-2s bombed a big petroleum dump near Inchon only a few miles east of Seoul. Then, just last week, our lads shot down two Bedcheck Charlies about twenty miles south, at Suwon. Kimpo security was breached several nights ago by a party of several guerillas who killed a ROK soldier on guard detail and stole some automatic weapons. My guess is that there will be attacks by these lingering diehards for sometime, even after the truce is signed. Now buckle up...and...on behalf of our crew, we wish you luck."

Collier's watch showed 1510 hours when the captain finally lowered the wheels and began the final approach to Kimpo running along what Collier guessed was the wide, shallow bed of the Han River just south of Seoul. When they landed, the monstrous aircraft settled as gently as a feather onto the runway surface of steel mats laid on top of the bare soil. It was just past 1600 when they finally were herded into a rather loose formation in front of what passed for a terminal building with a glass-enclosed control tower on top. Overhead, the sky was filled with a steady stream of helicopters marked with the Red Cross emblems of the Medical Corps and carrying wounded on litters affixed to their landing skids as they landed near a pair of med evac airplanes.

"Look at that, will ya." Pewter pointed to a pair of corpsmen rushing a litter toward the open bay of a DC-4 with an Army nurse running alongside, holding high a plastic bag of plasma with an IV tube running into the arm of the wounded GI on the stretcher.

"So much for rumors of truce, John Henry," Collier muttered, looking off into the distance to a steady line of ambulances arriving from across the river.

"Yeah..." Pewter mumbled dreamily. "You know I just realized that I fucked myself right through the Fourth of July."

CHAPTER FORTY-THREE

Vol. 9, No. 187   Tuesday, July 7, 1953

CHINESE ATTACK IN MUD, RAIN, TO LASH PORKCHOP, ARROWHEAD

SEOUL, July 7 (Pac. S&S) – Heavy rains failed to hold down fighting yesterday and this morning as the intensity of the battles from the west-central to the east-central front increased.

One of the largest enemy-initiated actions was against the 7th Division Yanks on Outpost Porkchop...

THE ROANOKE TIMES
Roanoke, Virginia, Tuesday, July 7, 1953
OVER 2,000 REDS STORM U.S., KOREAN OUTPOSTS

SEOUL, Tuesday, July 7 (AP) – More than 2,000 Chinese Reds stormed through ankle-deep mud and a curtain of fire today in American outposts on the western Korean Front....

One assault—against Pork Chop Hill was the first Chinese blow against an American Division in nearly three weeks....

The other attack was against Republic of Korea (ROK) forces near Arrowhead Ridge east of Porkchop.
* * * * *

Both actions raged through the predawn darkness and were continuing in a driving rain after daybreak.

Vol. 9, No. 190   Friday, July 10, 1953

CHINESE THROW SUICIDE WAVES IN FUTILE ATTEMPT AT U.N. LINES

TOKYO, July 9 (UP) – Chinese Communists hurled new attacks on the flaming western front early today and sent 1,500 men in suicidal waves against an eastern front position called Kim Il Sung ridge.
* * * * *

Reds Hit Seoul Route Defenses

TOKYO, July 10 (UP) – Chinese attacks crushed into two South Korean outposts on Korea's western front early today in the Communists' stubborn drive to crack Allied defenses guarding the Chorwan valley invasion route to Seoul.

One outpost east of Arrowhead ridge was overrun but tough ROK 2d Division troops knocked back the assault on a position west of Arrowhead.

SEOUL, Friday, July 10 (AP) – Blazing artillery duels today carried into the fourth day the battles for two Allied held hills in western Korea 40 to 45 miles north of Seoul.

As of midnight last night, the Reds—attacking in rotation with 1,000-man forces against each position—still held small gains on ridges leading to the crests of American-defended Porkchop Hill and Arrowhead Ridge, defended by South Koreans.

———

1.

LOOKING AROUND IN ALL DIRECTIONS, what Collier could see of Kimpo Air Base consisted of a jumble of wooden buildings and corrugated-metal Quonset huts, their weathered OD paint badly flaking—plus a veritable forest of canvas-covered, wooden-sided tent-huts. Outside these crude tent-huts, enlisted men in shorts, made from cutoff fatigues, moved randomly about—some tossing baseballs, footballs and basketballs back and forth, while round and about a few strummed guitars and played harmonicas while others were pitching horseshoes, and some were just sitting or sprawled flat on blankets on the ground soaking up the sun.

Here and there, like some mad artist run amok, a few of the buildings—along with occasional wooden fences and signposts and garbage cans—had been painted a bright Air Force Blue. Nearby, a large collection of deuce-and-a-halves, three-quarter-tons and Jeeps stood idle inside a fenced-off area fronted by a sign designating the area as the Kimpo Motor Pool.

A bit further down the street, another neatly-painted sign heralded the proprietorship of the 335th Fighter-Interceptor Squadron. Across the runway in the near-middle-distance, an imposing mountain rose out of the river plain.

While they were standing there a flight of Sabre Jets took off in a roar. Seen against the backdrop of the mountain, their sleek fuselages girded with a bright-yellow band edged in black and their high tailfins echoing the same motif, it was a stirring sight, causing chills to run up his spine.

"What's the name of that mountain?" Collier asked a passing airman.

"I don't know if it has a Korean name. See the nipple on the top? We call it the Witch's Tit." Collier smiled at the young airman's seriousness.

Collier's watch showed 1632 when the three-quarter-ton Dodge weapons carrier carrying all six of their group of MSC officers finally moved out, passing a rather large sign which read:

U.S. ARMY, ASCOM AREA COMMAND, R&R DETACHMENT,
U.S. ARMY QUARTERMASTER GROUP KOREA.

Watching the sign disappear from view as they entered a deeply-rutted muddy road, he was visited by a strong feeling that he would never live to see that sign welcoming him to Kimpo on his way back to Japan on his first R&R. Revisited by the same premonition of impending doom he had experienced when he had boarded the Piedmont DC-3 in Roanoke barely over a week before, in that moment, he resigned himself to the certainty he would not live to see the lovely Madison of the no-last-name again.

The truck had scarcely begun bumping over the much-traveled road running along the wide, shallow, sandbar-filled river Collier had seen on their approach to Kimpo, before they passed an intersection to a side road with signs pointing the way south to Suwon. Just past this intersection, they climbed a high, curving approach along the wide riverbed and abruptly made a sharp left-hand, right-angle turn onto a rickety, jerry-rigged, temporary wooden bridge across the wide stream. Just before their truck moved onto the uneven, wood-planked surface of the bridge, a sign confirmed Collier's assumption they were crossing the Han River. On the northern, downhill side of the bridge, the road turned right, continuing west along the Han. According to frequent crudely-hand-painted signs along the route, it didn't take long to see they were on their way toward Seoul. Passing through the war-ravaged outskirts to the city, Collier was revulsed by the sight of a Korean toddler squatting beside a hut, shitting through a wide-slit running from the crotch to the ankles of his raggedy trousers—no hint of toilet paper anywhere in sight. It immediately came clear why the pervasive, putrid, fecal stink seemed ten times more powerful now than he had first experienced in Japan.

Sitting near the tailgate on one of the folding benches running along the interior sidewalls of the weapons carrier with the side-flaps rolled up to let in air, Collier realized that the edge of the weather front had already moved over them, obscuring the Witch's Tit with rain as he felt the first large drops hit him in the face. Collier quickly helped his companions roll down the canvas side flaps just as the deluge hit them full-force. Within a short time, they entered into an area of completely-gutted ruins marking what had once been the outskirts of a city. Collier was fairly certain they were now entering Seoul. After perhaps another ten minutes, the driver slowed and entered a pair of gateposts marking the beginning of a masonry-walled compound which had been reconstructed from brick obviously rescued from the rubble of the mass destruction all around them. The muddy, unpaved drive led down into a bowl-like central area, where the truck pulled to a stop in front of a wooden barracks building.

"Welcome to Seoul, South Korea gentlemen. This compound is just down the road from Eighth Army Headquarters—which also serves as HQ for the Eighth Army Surgeon who will be making your duty assignments within a day or so, maybe less for some of you, depending upon the current circumstances of the officers you are to replace. Let's get out of this rain. Find an empty bunk and make yourselves comfortable. Your duffels will be arriving shortly, but I suggest you don't unpack because you will not be staying here overlong," a burly sergeant informed them in a gravelly voice as soon as they had all climbed down from the truck.

Running for shelter from the driving rain, Collier glanced around, taking in the scattered array of wooden barracks alongside some smaller outbuildings constructed of the omnipresent resurrected brick. Despite all the news photos he had seen, the scene was so completely surreal Collier felt as if he were experiencing a dream.

"Were those ruins we just came past Seoul?" someone asked.

"Yeah...you are now in the southern outskirts of Seoul. A little way up the road, there is the old Korean gate marking the official entrance to the city. You'll see it before you've been here very long. Take my advice and stay away from the local women. There's a lot of strange VD going around. Eat your dick right off—penicillin don't even faze some of it." The sergeant grinned a malevolent grin.

"Charming chap," someone muttered.

"If you need anything, I'll be in the orderly room over there." The sergeant pointed to a small, brick building. Spitting a jet of tobacco juice into the mud, he turned on his heels and left on the dead run.

"Come on. Let's find an empty sack and crash." Pewter tugged at Collier's sleeve and led the way inside the barracks. As wet as it was on the outside, the interior of the barracks was hot and airless. Locating a pair of bunks near the door on the off chance they might catch a wayward breeze at night, Collier and Pewter unrolled the mattresses and bedding and went to work making up their beds. Soon they were both passed out dead asleep.

"Come on and load up; the colonel says to take you down the road and feed you some home-cooked chow. You'll be on K-Rations soon enough." Collier's watch showed 1735 hours when the sergeant stuck his head in the door and roused them awake. Outside, the same three-quarter-ton truck that had brought them from Kimpo was waiting with the motor running—what passed for remaining daylight was diminishing fast in the driving rain.

By the time they finished eating and were deposited back inside the compound, it was pitch dark and there was no sign of letup in the incessant rain as great rivers of run-off cascaded down the slopes of the bowl-shaped compound, pooling in a temporary lake at its lowest point. Although Collier noted that the brick orderly room and the nearby latrine with the shower room were lit with bare electric bulbs—and he could hear a gasoline generator running somewhere nearby—there was no electricity in the barracks building where they had to sleep. Forced to rely on light from several Coleman kerosene lanterns they found near the door, someone in their group produced a deck of cards and organized a poker game using wooden matches for chips. Finally around midnight, Collier folded his last hand, went to bed about even and drifted off listening to the incessant pounding of the rain on the roof.

The entire next day came and went like a slow-motion sequence in a movie. Except for their trips in the three-quarter-ton truck to the large mess hall in the Eighth Army compound, they had nothing much to occupy themselves in the monsoon-like rain except to read or play cards. Having had the foresight to pick up a pulp paperback edition of Richard Prather's most-recent Shell Scott detective novel at the PX newsstand at Camp Drake, Collier settled himself on his bunk and read, periodically dozing for short naps when he grew weary of Prather's entertaining, tongue-in-cheek prose.

Shortly following evening chow, Collier finally gave up trying to read. Turning his back to the light from the single Coleman lantern, he decided to wait until he found out where he was being assigned before he wrote Emma or his parents. Breathing a long, silent prayer asking a God-unknown to bless everyone he knew or had ever heard of, and asking for strength and courage to acquit himself with dignity, pleading forgiveness for his many peccadilloes and infidelities and, finally, asking for divine intervention in finding out the last name of Madison, so that he might write her to inform her that he thought he might be truly in love with her, he drifted off to a restless sleep.

On Wednesday morning, 8 July, there was a break in the rain but it was short-lived, resuming with what seemed increased fury after perhaps an hour.

Shortly after the driver brought them back from breakfast, a pimply-faced private stuck his head inside the door. "Lieutenant John Henry Pewter, the Sarge wants you in the orderly room."

When he returned a few minutes later, fighting hard to maintain an unflappable front, John Henry began gathering up his gear and stuffing it inside his pack. "Well, I guess I'll see you later. I've been assigned to the Forty-eighth MASH. They told me it's at someplace named Camp Mosier, near a town called Uijongbu."–John Henry pronounced the word WEE-JONG-BOO–"From what the Sergeant said, it's not too awful far from here, just a short ride north of Seoul."

As soon as he finished packing, Pewter shook hands all around and climbed into a waiting Jeep. Collier waved and stood watching until the Jeep had climbed the hill and finally disappeared from view in the driving monsoon, then went back inside and laid down on his bunk, pulling a pillow over his head.

All day long Collier watched as, one-by-one, his fellow junior officers were called to the orderly room, only to come back and pack up and leave for various assignments. Like Pewter, some were assigned to MASH units, another to a collecting station near Chorwon in the Iron Triangle and another to the Eleventh Evac Hospital in Wonju, a remote town a little south and west of Seoul.

"You've got the place to yourself tonight. We're due for another shipment of replacements tomorrow." When the Jeep driver pulled up to take him to chow that evening, Collier found himself alone–the sole remaining officer of the original half-dozen who had left Seattle with him a scant week before.

"Wake up, Lieutenant. Pack your gear. The Eighth Army Surgeon wants you PDQ." A PFC Collier didn't recognize was shaking him by the shoulder and shining a light in his face.

"What time is it, anyway? What's this all about?" Collier grumbled, not happy to be roused out of a sound sleep.

"It's just before twenty-one-hundred hours." The PFC stood holding the big Coleman lantern so Collier could see to dress and gather up his gear.

"Lieutenant Ramsay, reporting, Sir..." At the Eighth Army Surgeon's office at HQ compound, Collier was escorted directly to the office of the Exec and told to go right in. His watch showed 2125.

"Stand at ease Ramsay and come around here. I've got a little job for you tonight. I see you went through Artillery OCS. I hope you can still read a map." The Exec, Colonel Bailey, looked up from a sheaf of military maps he had in front of him on his desk.

"Yessir. I'm pretty good with maps." Uncertain what was going on, Collier moved around the desk.

"I don't know if you've heard, but after two long years in the truce tents, that ranting, wide-eyed Korean lunatic, Syngman Rhee, has managed to start up the war again just when we're within hours of signing the truce."

"No, Sir. I've heard nothing about that." Collier felt the bottom drop out of his stomach.

"Yeah. The last week in June, the negotiators at Panmunjom reached a tentative ceasefire agreement, but that nut Rhee refused to sign and gave a speech saying South Korea wanted to fight to the death–or some-such drivel. Now the Chinese have decided to retake Hill two-five-five with the official truce only hours away. General Taylor is convinced this is just the Chinks' way of saying we need to keep Rhee under control. What a mess." Colonel Bailey put his finger on a land feature on the topo map on the desk in front of him.

"Yessir—sounds like a mess right enough." Collier had a sinking suspicion that this was leading to something he wanted no part of.

"See here where the elevation is marked two-five-five? See the way the land feature is shaped? I'm sure you've heard of Pork Chop Hill." The colonel looked up at him for agreement.

"Yessir. About everybody who can read has heard of Pork Chop Hill." Collier bent and gave the map a closer look. "What makes it so important now, Sir? I mean now that the end of the fighting is in sight?"

"Nothing. That's just it. Human life means nothing to the Chinks. The Chinks are just making a goddamn nuisance of themselves, and it's costing us good American lives. We've been fighting to hold that worthless piece of rock for two whole days now and already lost almost a full company of men whose families were planning to welcome them home."

"So? What about the map?" Collier asked, pretty sure he didn't want to know what this empty dialogue about the futility of war was really all about.

"As I just said, at dusk, day before yesterday, on six July, right about here, the Chinks—blowing bugles and beating drums—swarmed up Pork Chop Hill—Hill Two-five-five—in overwhelming force, overrunning the summit in an all-out surprise attack. The Chinese were so numerous that forces of the Seventeenth Regiment ran out of ammo trying to repulse the attack and were forced to retreat to positions below the summit." The colonel pointed to a nearby terrain feature marked with the elevation 200. "By the time we reinforced our numbers and were resupplied with ammo, an undetermined number of the Chinese had taken up positions on at least part of the crest. Last night, we launched counterattacks, but we couldn't keep them down or retake our positions. The Commies made a new push to keep the hill, forcing the Seventh Division to again reinforce. Parts of four companies have defended Pork Chop under a firestorm of artillery from both sides. This morning the rain temporarily ended allowing us to withdraw the original defenders. Fresh troops from the Second Battalion of the Seventeenth counter-attacked and re-took the hill, setting up a night defensive perimeter. But the Chinks have numbers already up there. They're not about to give up. It's a bloody mess." The colonel looked at him for understanding, his finger still in place on Hill 255.

"Yessir, Colonel Bailey. It sounds like bloody hell." Collier agreed lamely—wondering if the colonel was trying to tell him the U.S. Army was looking for him to storm the hill singlehandedly.

"I hate to have to do this. Particularly when you have just arrived in the combat zone expecting to hear the war had ended any second now, but there are countless wounded up there unattended by competent medical attention. In the confusion of battle, an Aid Station on the forward slope was overrun leaving the Battalion Surgeon, his MSC and at least one corpsman stranded. They were able to radio back with an Angry-niner they found in the bunker of the Artillery FO. At least two of them are wounded—both with leg wounds which render them helpless to help themselves, much less any of the other wounded. There is an area big enough for an H-forty-seven chopper to land, and they have arranged to identify themselves with flashlight codes beginning at twenty-three hundred hours tonight. Now that the Chinks have retreated below the forward crest, both sides have suspended—or at least lessened—mortar and fire artillery for the time being.

Our troops will not resume bombardment until after zero-one-hundred hours tomorrow morning which gives you and the chopper a two-hour window of opportunity." The colonel looked up at him to see if he understood.

"Opportunity? For what?" Collier croaked.

"Opportunity to rescue the doc and his MSC and the corpsman, of course, and evacuate them by chopper."

"Huh?" Collier grunted with apprehension as the reality of what the colonel was proposing dawned on him.

"Look, Lieutenant, you will be taking an experienced medical corpsman with you. Sergeant Williams volunteered for the mission—the wounded medic is a former buddy of his. Williams is a former footballer from Auburn. Williams is a hoss. He'll be a big help in loading the litters on the chopper." The Colonel looked up expecting an indication of appreciation.

"Look, Colonel, I'm sure you know I have no actual combat experience. I just got here and have no idea what that terrain is like—much less what it will be like at night..." Collier began, but the colonel held up his hand to stop his protest.

"Don't worry about that. Sergeant Williams is already here. He's been on Pork Chop. He knows the terrain. He can brief you before you leave. We have a Bell Sioux chopper standing by right outside. It has covered litter racks to give protection against the rain and is already loaded with a full-combat medical pack, including plasma bags and plenty of morphine syrettes—the whole ball of wax..." the colonel continued with growing enthusiasm.

"Wait up, Sir. Isn't the Bell Sioux the chopper with the goldfish bubble? Besides the wounded medics already on litters, there must be god-only-knows how many other wounded on top of that hill. How can we justify evacuating those medics first and how can we all get back off in one chopper?" Collier recalled dozing through a class on helicopter evacuation at MFSS at Fort Sam. He vaguely remembered the bare-bones chopper was equipped with two racks for carrying litters, one on each side of the cockpit bubble. Under the goldfish bubble, he didn't recall there being much room for anything else save one or maybe two passengers and the pilot himself. That meant either overloading the chopper or the pilot having to make a return trip for either him or the volunteer, Williams.

"That's an affirmative, Lieutenant. The Forty-seven-D Bell is the one with the goldfish bubble—the workhorse of combat medical evacuation. Warrant Officer Yates has already flown in and out of Pork Chop on multiple missions," the colonel affirmed.

"But, begging your pardon, Colonel, the Sioux will only transport two litters, plus two ambulatory or semi-ambulatory personnel under the bubble with the pilot. That leaves at least one of us without a ride back." Collier had the distinct feeling he wasn't giving anyone in the room any information they didn't already have.

"Don't worry, Lieutenant. Warrant Officer Yates is confident he can squeeze three in the cockpit with him. The trip back to the Battalion Aid Station is only a matter of minutes. If he has time to make a return trip, the bombardment is lifted until zero-one-hundred. We have a window of opportunity of over two hours. Besides, there is some chance one or more of the three wounded up there may already be dead." The colonel gave him a reproving look for daring to question the well-thought-out logistics of his plan.

"Now, here's two copies of the topographic map. One is clearly marked with your landing site, the last-known position of the wounded, along with the last-known positions of our troops. Commit that to memory. The topo chart you'll take with you obviously can't have our positions on it in the unlikely case you fall into enemy hands. Now, come with me and I'll introduce you to Yates and Williams. You have a lot of planning to do before twenty-two-thirty hours." The colonel handed him both a marked and unmarked copy of the topographic terrain map.

Glancing at his watch, Collier saw it was already twenty-one-thirty-seven as he reluctantly followed the Colonel through the door.

"Lieutenant Collier Ramsay, may I present your chopper pilot, Chief Warrant Officer Reilly Yates, and your able-bodied point man, Sergeant Sandy Williams. Private Arnold Shaw, here, is from Able Company, Seventeenth Infantry. He was the last medic off the summit this morning before the Second Battalion counterattack and the monsoon started back up. As you can see, he has volunteered to brief us despite his wounds." In the adjoining room, the Colonel introduced Collier to a scarecrow of a warrant officer and to a hulking Staff Sergeant—who stood at least six-feet-four, weighed around two-hundred and looked like he could play wide receiver for the Washington Redskins. With them was an enlisted corpsman with his right arm in a sling. They all glanced up from a copy of the same topographical map the colonel had just handed him and grunted recognition.

"Pull up that chair and sit down, Lieutenant, and let's all listen to what Shaw here can tell us about the current situation up on Pork Chop as he goes over this map with us. We're going to have to plan this thing down to the last detail, and we're going to have to have all the luck we can get if we're going to have any chance of pulling it off," the Colonel said.

"Please help yourselves to the brownies. I had them sent over from the officers' mess." Bailey grinned like a fool. On the table beside the topo maps was a plate of what appeared to be fresh-baked brownies.

"Okay, Shaw, tell us all what happened and what the situation was when you left," Colonel Bailey prompted the wounded man.

"It started sometime on Monday morning. The Gooks started up on their loudspeakers. They said they were coming up and would take no prisoners—warning us to surrender or we were all going to die. We could see a lot of movement at the base of the hill in their sector, but, except for this incessant ranting, nothing much happened all day until about time it started to get dark. That's when they started coming. It looked like a whole division—they looked like ants swarming up that slope. I know we medics are not supposed to carry weapons, but we all do. I grabbed my carbine and started firing right beside a fifty-caliber machine gun emplacement. At first it was like shooting fish in a barrel. If we hadn't run out of ammo, we could have killed a gazillion gooks. They kept on coming as if nothing was happening. Before we knew it, they were right on top of us and we were down to what few grenades we had left. Finally, we were down to rifle butts, bayonets, knives—whatever we could find. Some guys were even throwing rocks. I was swinging a piece of lumber from one of the bunkers until it got blown...or knocked...out of my hand. I thank the powers-that-be I had time enough to find my body armor...I'll never laugh at that idea again." The heroic medic paused to adjust his arm in the sling.

Collier suppressed a shudder, thinking how often he—and his OCS classmates—had pooh-poohed the sissy idea of wearing body armor.

"They pushed us right back down the hill. Then Baker and what was left of George Company showed up, but that didn't even slow 'em down. We were no match for them numbers. They pushed us right off Pork Chop like we weren't even there. Then reinforcements showed up in these APCs and we pushed them back off again."

"Armored personnel carriers?" Collier asked, trying to make sure he followed what Shaw was talking about.

"M-Thirty-nines and some T-eighteens. The M-Thirty-nines are open-topped. Over and above their crew, they transport and deliver ten infantrymen to the combat zone—safe from fire," Williams volunteered. Vaguely Collier recalled being given engine familiarization and being allowed to drive an M-39 over open terrain during an ARSOP exercise in OCS. Like tanks, basically they were track-propelled—actually WWII Hellcat tank destroyers with the gun turrets removed. Customarily, they were used more for hauling ammo and supplies than transporting troops.

"So who's controlling the summit now?" Collier asked, thoroughly confused. He opened his notebook, prepared to take notes. After all, it looked as if his life were about to be put on the line.

"We were when I left by APC today around fourteen-hundred hours," Shaw spoke up again.

"We? Meaning Companies Able and Baker of the Seventeenth Infantry?"

"Yes, Sir. And, like I said, what was left of George Company came up and joined us—they were only a handful by the time they reached the crest. They had taken a pretty hard hit."

"So? How many men did you leave up there? Two hundred?" Collier asked.

"No way! Are you kidding? Less than two-dozen riflemen and two medics were left unwounded in Able Company, but reinforcements were supposedly on the way." Shaw shook his head sadly.

"Who's in command up there?" Collier asked, noting the number on his pad. The simple arithmetic of the American losses was chilling.

"First Lieutenant Shea. He was the Exec before the CO got killed. I never saw such a man—an honest-to-God superman if there ever was one. Yesterday, with only his rifle, he personally rallied nearly a squad from what few we had left, and took out a Gook machine gun emplacement practically by hisself. When I left, he was still all over the place, fighting off the Chinks—promising everybody reinforcements were on the way. The Gooks hit us eight or nine separate times that night. Finally pushed us back to our alternate CP on the south slope—we lost at least half of our front positions. Talk about heroes. 'The Old Man,' Sergeant Hovey, was killed sometime that first night. Hovey was in his forties. He was gonna retire when he got back home. He used to tell us stories about the liberation of Nazi death camps in World War Two. He fought like a wild man."

"A damn shame..." Collier shook his head.

"Yeah. I'm damn lucky to be alive." Still somewhat in a state of shock, Shaw shook his head.

"So, altogether, how many able-bodied men were up there when you got off?" Collier persisted.

"Not many, but General Taylor withdrew them all this morning, anyway," the Colonel said.

"So have they already been reinforced?" Collier asked Bailey, certain they had or else they wouldn't be planning this mission.

"Best I know, Able, Baker and George were withdrawn right after Shaw, here, was evacuated. The Second Battalion counter-attacked this morning and retook the summit. I am assured we still hold it now." Bailey nodded.

"Okay, Shaw, let's look at the terrain—bring me up to speed." Collier took a seat and placed the topographic chart in front of him. Unmistakably, the outline of Hill 255 traced the shape of a Pork Chop on the topo map—two distinct fingers of high ground, one marked 'Brinson,' on the left, and an unnamed finger beyond, off of the other side of the slope, before dropping precipitously to the valley floor.

North across the valley were the distinctive land features the GIs had dubbed T-Bone and the Alligator Jaws, with Arrowhead and White Horse Hill even further north across the dotted double line that marked the course of the Yokkok-ch'on river.

For the better part of the next fifteen minutes, the wounded corpsman went over the terrain map while Collier asked questions and made notations directly on the map.

"Here's where the three of them are stranded—just above this temporary chopper landing zone right below the summit." The sergeant pointed to the right-hand-most of two projecting fingers of high ground. Collier had no trouble locating the isolated postage-stamp-sized flat land-feature clearly delineated by the separation of the topographical lines on the map.

"See this narrow ravine running from the landing zone in the defilade of this sharp ridge up to this small OP at the top? The chopper landing zone is right about here. The wounded are in a bunker nearby, just up the slope at the top of this little ravine." He had no difficulty in identifying the flat landing area adjacent to where the lines converged into a sharp V delineating the ravine leading up to an outcropping that had been used as the OP for the Artillery FO. Obviously, the OP also had served as a temporary forward Aid Station during the first two days of the fierce battle. Both areas were on Brinson finger, below the crest of Hill 255 in an area most likely swarming with bloodthirsty Gooks just waiting to mount another assault on the summit.

Visualizing the utter impossibility of the mission, Collier felt a cold trickle of sweat run down his spine. His gut felt as if he had swallowed a bag of wooly-worms.

"Well then, Lieutenant, do you understand the lay of the land?" Bailey roused him from his chilly reverie.

"Yeah, I can see the lay of the land alright. Shaw, have you actually walked this terrain? How far down the ravine is it from these wounded to the chopper? Is this defilade plenty wide enough to carry a litter safely down?"

"I estimate twenty or twenty-five yards, give or take a yard. And, yeah, it's plenty wide enough to get a litter down. But it's going to be slow going. That terrain is not exactly a Sunday stroll in the park, Sir." Shaw shot him a meaningful look.

"I've never actually been down to this OP, but I've negotiated plenty of similar terrain." The burly Williams spoke up. "You look strong enough to me, Lieutenant. The two of us should be able to handle moving a litter twenty-five yards through almost any terrain. The problem is going to be time. Even given the cover of this rain, that chopper is not going to be exactly invisible to the Gooks," Williams cautioned.

"So, how much payload will your chopper carry, Mr. Yates?" Collier doubted that Yates weighed 140 soaking wet, and the last time Collier weighed, he was down to around 150. He figured Williams for a solid 200 pounds. Hastily doing the arithmetic, Collier calculated a total of 500 pounds.

"Don't worry; it can carry the three of us and two litters, no sweat—I've done it several hundred times already." Yates sucked on his cigarillo and shrugged.

"Do you think you can find that pinpoint of terrain in this lousy weather at night?" Collier challenged the wooden-faced chopper pilot.

"Don't worry about the mule; load the wagon," the unflappable chopper pilot replied, impassively snubbing out the smelly stump of a cigarillo and reaching for his second brownie.

"How about supplies? We'll need at least two combat medic packs." Looking around the room, Collier saw nothing that fit the description of a fully-equipped combat medic's pack.

"We have three already loaded in the chopper. One for you, one for Sergeant Williams and a spare for the chopper just in case you have to leave yours behind. You're going to have your hands full moving the wounded down that rocky rift." Bailey grimaced as if his hemorrhoids were bothering him.

"I need to see one of those packs. Williams and I both should familiarize ourselves with their contents—don't forget we'll be operating in pitch black in this frigging rain. It's going to be black as a mausoleum out there."

"I'm way ahead of you," Bailey boasted like a kid looking for an A on his report card. "I already have one made up in my office for that very purpose." He walked out of the room and returned in a moment with an OD backpack slightly smaller than a regular combat pack. It was marked with a medic's red-cross emblem stenciled on its canvas surface.

Wasting no time, Collier undid the straps and, with Williams, looked inside, checking and committing to memory the location of the sterile, combat bandage packs, rolls of heavy gauze, adhesive tape, sulfa powder and tablets, several vials of penicillin and some penicillin tablets, and the ever-needed staple, quarter-grain morphine Syrettes with the long, plastic covers keeping the needles sterile and, last but not least, several web-belt tourniquets—just in case of life-threatening hemorrhaging. When both he and Williams were satisfied they could find what they needed without unnecessarily using a flashlight, Collier pushed the demo pack aside and looked across the table at Yates. "How long will it take to get there?"

"Forty-five minutes—at most an hour—depending on visibility and how long it takes to locate them—*if* we locate them." The wizened pilot spoke without taking the cigarillo from the corner of his mouth.

Looking at the clock on the wall, Collier saw that the minute hand was already easing past the number twelve—marking the time as straight-up 2200 hours.

"What time does our artillery lift?" Collier looked across at Bailey.

"Precisely twenty-two-forty-five. We have General Taylor's solemn word on that." Bailey held up his hand in an approximation of the Boy Scout salute.

"Okay, we better get moving. I guess I'm as ready as I'll ever be." Collier heard his own voice as if he were in a dream. "If there are no further questions of Colonel Bailey or Private Shaw, let's saddle up and get on with this."

"No question for me. I'm ready. Let's go. We'll need all the time we can get while the artillery's lifted." Williams stood and pulled his poncho over his head, waiting for Yates to lead the way.

"You heard the man. We're wasting time. Let's get the fuck out of here." CWO Yates pushed back his chair, snubbing out his cigarillo in the top of an empty K-Ration can.

"Wait up. We're forgetting something. We each want a Colt .45 automatic with a couple of extra clips for each and also M-2 carbines with a half-dozen extra thirty-round clips. That'll be a total of eight clips. And we'll both need dependable flashlights—with new batteries." Collier made his requirements clear.

"What? I don't have any extra weapons handy. We can't hold up this mission. Now get on that helicopter," Bailey blustered.

"You'd better come up with those weapons quick, Colonel, or this mission is not going to make." Collier stared Bailey in the eye and stood his ground.

"Alright...let me see what I've got in the weapons room." Bailey gave up trying to stare Collier down and turned and left the room. In less than a couple of minutes, he was back with a corporal who held the M-2 Carbines cradled in his arms, each already fully-loaded with a curving fifteen-round clip. Two flashlights and a pair of Colt .45 handguns with extra clips for all of the weapons were slung over his shoulder in a canvas musette bag.

Stepping forward and taking the musette bag, Collier checked the flashlights and handed Williams one. Extracting both pistols, he strapped on the regular-issue leather holster of one and handed the other to Williams. When he had the holster belt comfortably adjusted, he tied the holster down, wrapping the dangling pair of rawhide laces around his thigh so that the butt of the pistol hung just at the heel of his right hand when it hung naturally at his side. Then he smoothly lifted his hand, unsnapping and lifting the holster flap, pulling the weapon from the holster in one deftly-executed motion. Inserting a clip into the empty handle, he slid the barrel back to jack a round into the chamber then slid the mechanism back again, opening the breech to make sure the round was properly seated. Giving him an appreciative look, Williams followed his example.

While Williams was adjusting his holster and jacking a round into the chamber of the Colt, Collier turned his attention to the carbines. Taking both rifles from the corporal, he checked them both to make sure the banana clips were securely seated before he placed one aside on the table. Pulling back the bolt of the one he still held, he jacked a round into the chamber then slid back the bolt and checked to make certain the mechanism was properly operating. Holstering his Colt, Williams gave Collier an admiring nod and did the same with the other carbine.

Still in a trancelike state, Collier removed his flashlight from his pocket, shrugged his own poncho over his head and followed the chopper pilot out of the room, down the short hall and out the back door where the chopper stood waiting in the heavy downpour like some futuristic dragonfly. Standing on the back stoop, Collier flicked the switch of the flashlight and was rewarded with a sharp, narrow beam of light cutting through the driving rain. Williams nodded as he tested his own light, replacing it beneath the poncho.

"Hold up." Collier spread his arms, holding back Williams and the CWO while he cocked his sidearm, stepped out into the rain and fired a round at a sharp angle upward into the falling rain. Quickly holstering the Colt, he pointed the carbine into the air and squeezed off two rounds.

Without waiting for instruction, Williams stepped forward and checked both his weapons in the same way.

"Just to make sure we don't shoot our pilot by accident." When Williams finished firing, Collier advised the Sergeant to put both his handgun and the carbine on safety.

"Alright, Mister Yates, let's go." Collier stood aside for the pilot to lead the way. Without hesitation, Yates went down the short flight of steps with a bound, splashing across the muddy courtyard to the chopper, Collier and Williams close upon his heels.

"Wait! Show me how the straps and covers on these litter racks work. When we get up there we won't have time to waste." Collier halted Yates outside the chopper, and with Williams at his side, they stood watching while the pilot quickly demonstrated the simple mechanisms that opened and secured the clear, curving Plexiglas covers providing shelter over the litter racks. When Collier was fairly comfortable that both he and Williams could operate the covers without unnecessary delay, he nodded to the CWO, motioning Williams to follow him and the pilot into the bubble cockpit.

By the time they had seated themselves and secured the over-the-shoulder harnesses, the pilot had the rotors slowly grinding into motion. Before Collier was fully accustomed to the chopper's eggbeater rhythm, they had risen at a dizzying rate with the lights and rooftops of the Eighth Army Compound rapidly disappearing in the rain which was swirling in fitful sheets around them.

Flying nose tilted slightly down, the tiny chopper drove through the rainy night as Collier was taken completely by surprise as brightly lit Seoul appeared, stretched out below them to their left. He was even more surprised at how quickly the lights disappeared as they passed over the relatively flat Han River basin around the South Korean capital. When the last of the lights had disappeared over the horizon behind them, they were swallowed in total darkness, a cold mist from the constant driving rain blowing through the open side ports of the plastic canopy.

"Twenty-two forty-one. We should be almost there." Collier tapped Williams on the shoulder to show him the luminescent dial on his watch. Collier had hardly spoken when Yates leaned around the edge of his seat and pointed animatedly down and to the front. Straining to see in the pitch black night and driving rain, at first Collier couldn't make out a thing. Suddenly, Collier caught a tiny flash of light which—just as quickly as it flashed on—was gone again. Alert now, Collier stuck his arm through the sling of his carbine, picked up one of the First Aid Combat packs, handed the other to Williams as he slipped his left arm under the carrying strap. Unholstering the forty-five, he held it at the ready with the safety still on but the sliding mechanism comfortably under his thumb. There was a slight change in the speed of the rotors as the angle of the chopper banked sharply right and the bottom dropped out of Collier's stomach as the frail whirlybird began to drop like a greased anvil into the black abyss.

Then, just like on a roller-coaster, the whirlybird righted itself and seemed to stop on a dime when another fleeting flash of light sparkled through the wind-driven rain bubbles on their Plexiglas—not two-dozen yards off their starboard. Incredibly, the source of the flicker of light seemed above them now, but before Collier had the opportunity to equate that odd fact with his memory of the terrain on the topographic maps, he felt a slight bump as the chopper settled as light as a feather to a landing in the inky void. Feeling strangely detached, Collier suppressed a sudden urge to laugh out loud as his mind wandered back to all the advice he'd heard in Basic and OCS about keeping a tight asshole to avoid the embarrassment of shitting his pants in combat. For the moment, that was the very least of his worries. He felt quite certain, if through some miracle he survived this night, he wouldn't be able to shit for at least a month.

"Stay low, Lieutenant, remember the blades—I'm keeping them running for a quick getaway. The little defile leading up there is straight ahead. Use your peripheral vision—it will help your eyes adjust in the dark. And be careful. This postage-stamp outcrop drops off at least four-hundred-feet straight down on either side and to our rear. Good luck..." Yates voice was an echo above the whirring of the chopper blades and the pelting of the driving rain as Collier sucked a deep gulp of air into his lungs, undid his harness straps, thumbed the safety off on his handgun, and stepped out onto the skid. Scarcely able to see his hand in front of his face, the moment he felt his feet hit solid ground, Collier released the strap that held the canvas litters. The folded litter wedged awkwardly between his left elbow and his with the medical pack uncomfortably bouncing against his back, Collier struck out at a half-trot, bent low to avoid decapitation by the whirling blades. Remembering what Yates had said about using his peripheral vision, he was instantly rewarded by picking up out of the corners of his eyes the dark crevice marking the beginning of the ravine a scant dozen paces straight ahead.

"It's steeper than I figured. Stay close and be careful of your footing," Collier gasped over his shoulder as started the steep ascent struggling with the awkwardness of the pack and one of the litters. He made himself slow his rapid breathing which he recognized resulted more from the adrenaline reaction than from the effort of the short dash across the rock-strewn landing shelf. Halfway up the defilade, Williams prodded him from behind to get his attention and put his forefinger to his lips and pointed above them, cautioning they should stay as quiet as possible as they were surrounded on all sides by a reinforced battalion of bloodthirsty Chinks.

Thankfully, the scramble up the narrow ravine proved to be somewhat shorter than Collier had anticipated from looking at the topo map. When they neared the top, Collier crouched low and slowed his pace, taking cover behind a pointed, egg-shaped boulder rising out of the floor of the declivity, not wanting to blunder into an ambush.

Rewarded now by the use of peripheral vision, he carefully surveyed the flat, eagle's-nest-sized OP with the rocky escarpment rising sharply behind it to the summit of Pork Chop. The clearing itself was really not much bigger than his parent's living room back home. Fortunately, the area was clear of large boulders or trees or other concealment for enemy forces. As his eyes became accustomed to the light in the driving rain, Collier made out the shadowy shapes of at least two uniformed figures huddled under an small outcropping of rock near the bottom of a near-vertical path rising to the top of Pork Chop Hill a scant hundred yards above them.

Letting his gaze slide up the cliff-like escarpment, he felt fairly sure there were no places to hide directly above them. Wasting no time, Collier quickly moved across the small space, dropping the carbine and litter on the ground beside him as he fell to a kneeling position beside the huddled form of the nearest soldier who had a white-painted lieutenant's bar on his steel pot. The soldier lying beside the lieutenant had the shredded remnant of a red cross medic insignia on his helmet. From the closer vantage point, Collier made out the form of a third soldier lying behind them in a small declivity, his steel pot pulled over his face to shield him from the rain.

"Thank, God...I never expected to see a friendly face again..." the lieutenant raised up on his elbow and greeted Collier as Williams dropped his litter and carbine, taking a kneeling position beside the other two forms huddled motionless to their left.

"Shut up and show me exactly where you're wounded." Collier bent over the young officer and went to work.

The wounded MSC pointed to his legs and the legs of his semi-conscious corpsman. Using bayonets to tighten them, both men had homemade tourniquets fashioned from their web belts twisted tightly around their upper thighs just below the groin.

"How long since these tourniquets were put on?" His night vision now almost fully-functioning, Collier could see the two men with the tourniquets had each suffered gaping shrapnel wounds both above and below the knee.

"I don't know exactly. Several hours at least. I've loosened them a little every so often to provide some blood supply. Last time I loosened them, we both were getting some blood to the wounded areas." The wounded lieutenant grimaced in pain as he spoke.

"How's your guy?" Collier turned to Williams, wondering if the corpsman was still alive.

"He's unresponsive, but I get a steady pulse." Williams said.

"Is that the FO?" Collier asked the MSC, indicating the inert third body huddled close against the base of the vertical slope. "Is he alive?"

"Yeah...I haven't been able to get him awake. He's not bleeding. But he was breathing the last time I looked," the MSC replied and shook his head.

"Okay, no more talk. Let's get to work." Collier reached beside him and began unfolding the canvas litter.

"Take Tolliver first. I'm okay, for now." The MSC nodded toward his unconscious corpsman.

"Okay, let's get at it." Collier finished spreading the litter open and, taking care not to damage the wounded corpsman's ravaged lower legs, he grasped him underneath both legs at mid-thigh and motioned for Williams to take hold underneath the shoulders. Signaling their readiness with their eyes, both men lifted the body onto the stretcher.

"Hang on, we'll be back," Collier assured the Lieutenant and nodded at Williams. Placing their carbines alongside the corpsman, they quickly grasped the handles and headed back into the mouth of the ravine toward the waiting chopper, careful to lift the stretcher high as they negotiated their way around the egg-shaped boulder guarding the upper entrance to the thumbnail-sized outcrop.

Going back down was more difficult, complicated now by the bulk of the stretcher with the dead weight of the wounded medic on it. When they finally reached the landing zone, they moved directly to the left-hand side of the idling chopper. Setting aside their carbines, they carefully secured the litter to the rack on the chopper's landing skids.

As soon as the stretcher was secure, without a word, Collier and Williams picked up their carbines and headed silently back across the shelf up the cut. Pausing momentarily behind the egg-shaped boulder to scout the upper slope for enemy, both men dashed back across the clearing and dropped their carbines beside the remaining canvas litter.

"Take the FO. He must have head trauma. I can wait," the lieutenant said when they arrived back at his side and unfolded the litter.

"Relax, Lieutenant. We don't have time to waste." Collier signaled Williams to grab the lieutenant beneath the shoulders as they swiftly transferred him to the stretcher in much the same way they had the wounded medic. When they lifted the litter, Collier was gratified to find the weight of the Lieutenant seemed noticeably less than that of his corpsman.

Moving into the mouth of the narrow rift, a tinny pinging sound jingled off Collier's helmet as if someone on the top of Pork Chop had loosed a pebble down the slope. Not bothering to stop and look, he swiftly led the way back down the defilade where they quickly secured the stretcher to the chopper's opposite litter rack.

"Stay here. I'll go get the other guy. If he's alive, I can bring him fireman's carry. Get in the chopper so you can help load him inside when I get back." Collier ordered Williams to enter the chopper, wheeled and started back.

"But Yates says we can only carry two..." Williams protest was lost in the whirring noise of the chopper blades and the howling monsoon as Collier headed back up the narrow cleft still carrying his carbine.

This time, when he reached the granite egg, Collier barely bothered to scout the area as, keeping low, he rushed across the miniscule OP and dropped to one knee beside the inert form against the far cliff. Grasping the victim with his right hand just above the knees and his left hand under the upper rib cage, Collier reached for his carbine and gathered himself.

"Uht-t!" Grunting against the expected exertion, Collier executed a mighty heave, lifting with his legs like a weightlifter as he swung the limp body over his left shoulder in a fireman's carry, with the victim's head hanging down across his back. Surprised he had succeeded so easily, Collier renewed his hold around the victim's dangling thighs and, still gripping his carbine tightly, he headed back down the narrow draw, slowing his stride to negotiate the obstructing boulder, careful not trip under the burden of the dead weight.

"Here. Take him and strap him in." At the chopper, Collier leaned inside the opening of the Plexiglas and helped Williams strap the victim in the remaining empty seat.

"One of you is going to have to stay. This bird won't carry the extra weight. I'll come back as soon as I can." Yates shouted above the noise.

"Okay...go...Go...GO!..." still clutching his carbine, Collier stepped off the skid and headed back away from the whirling chopper blades before Williams, still busy trying to secure the unconscious soldier in the seat straps, could object. By the time Collier made it back across the small landing zone and looked back, the whirlybird had already risen off the pad and was rotating swiftly away from the ledge. He watched with mixed feelings of accomplishment and utter lonliness as Williams peered anxiously down at him through the stygian blackness and driving rain.

As soon as the chopper disappeared from view, Collier moved back up the mouth of the narrow draw, cautiously taking a position behind the sentinel boulder to make sure their presence hadn't been discovered by the Gooks. As best as Collier could tell in the howling monsoon there was nothing moving on the OP itself. Letting his gaze move upward, he scouted the steep path zigzagging down the slope from the top of Pork Chop for any sign of an enemy patrol.

The luminous dial on his watch showed 2315; the entire operation had only taken a half-hour. Crouching behind the boulder with the rain pouring off his steel helmet as he anxiously watched the steep path down the hill, the mathematics of his precarious situation began to take shape inside his head.

Forty-five minutes each way to take the wounded back and return—a total flying time of an hour and thirty minutes. With another fifteen minutes to take the wounded off the chopper—the total would be, at the very least, a minimum of one hour forty five minutes. The cold, hard truth of the simple arithmetic was that Yates would more than likely run out of time. No matter how experienced the veteran chopper pilot was, he simply could not possibly make it back before the ceasefire lifted. The topo map of this godforsaken rocky finger had clearly shown that the only way down was a sheer drop of several hundred feet—most likely more. The only other path led up the cliff and taking a chance on sneaking through a teeming horde of murderous Gooks salivating for his blood. The odds of pulling that off were "little" and "none."

He was freaking stuck.

The chilling futility of his predicament beat a steady mantra into his consciousness, keeping an unholy rhythm with the driving rain bouncing off his steel helmet.

Yates said he would be back. Trying to erase all negativity from his thoughts, Collier attempted to make himself comfortable, wedged between the wall of the rift and the protecting granite boulder guarding the entrance to the OP; at least this gave him a vantage point in the event the enemy had heard the chopper and came down to investigate.

"*Chiksunggi...*" Collier snapped instantly alert as the sound of the Korean voice came drifting down through the rain from somewhere above. Adrenaline pumping, he strained his ears trying to pick up the voice again over the noise of the rain beating against his steel pot.

Nothing.

In all this stress, had he started hearing things?

From somewhere deep in his subconscious, Collier recalled a lecture in OCS about the differences in the South Korean, North Korean, and Chinese languages. As best as he could remember, "*chiksunggi*" was North Korean for "helicopter." He remembered the instructor saying that the North Koreans preferred using their native words for modern technology while the South Koreans would incorporate a sort of Japanese-American "pidgin English" version of such inventions. The comparisons the instructor had used were the North Koreans saying "*rogumgi*" for "tape recorder" and "*chiksunggi*" for "helicopter," whereas South Koreans would say "*teipa rakoda*" and "*helrikoptyuh*."

Fighting against dozing off as his adrenalin subsided, Collier anxiously checked his watch again—1242. Eighteen minutes left before the shit hit the fan again. He lifted his face to catch a sobering splash of the incessant rain. He couldn't afford to doze—it was the best way he knew to wake up dead.

"*Chiksunggi...*" Collier blinked alert as he caught the word again. The guttural, excited Korean voices carried through the rain now, as clear as a bell.

Anxiously scanning the steep path descending the escarpment, Collier now made out the shadowy forms of two men midway up the path slowly picking their way down the slope toward him. Slowly...silently...he thumbed back the safety mechanism on his carbine. Remembering that he had fired off two rounds back at HQ, he breathed a silent prayer the weapon hadn't jammed as they were sometimes reported to do when fired in the fully-automatic mode.

Chop, chop, chop... Were his ears deceiving him or could that really be the sound of an approaching chopper somewhere behind him through the rain?

He slowly retrieved his flashlight from under his poncho and pointed it back toward the chopper sounds, blinking two razor-sharp needles of light into the void of rain and darkness.

"*Chiksunggi! Chiksunggi!...*" the urgently-spoken words rang clear from above him in the darkness. Lifting his eyes, he could see the two forms scrambling to speed their descent down the slippery path.

Chop, chop, chop, chop... Growing louder, the steady beat of the helicopter blades was no illusion now. Frantically, Collier blinked the pencil beam of his flashlight again several times, a lump of desperation rising in his throat. Rapidly shifting position, Collier turned back and cradled the stock of the carbine in his right hand atop the rounded rock. Taking hasty aim at the nearest of the two forms scrambling down the path, he squeezed off a round and watched as a flinty spark kicked off the granite surface just over the head of the nearest Gook. Hastily adjusting his aim, Collier squeezed the trigger again—this time holding the trigger down taking advantage of the fully-automatic mode to fire off a staccato burst of three.

"*Aiee-ee-e!...*" Through the murk, Collier heard a scream as he saw the nearest of the two Gooks stiffen and fall back against the slope. There was an answering flash as his companion squeezed off a burst of rounds pinging and whizzing as they wildly ricocheted off the rock defilade around Collier's head.

Chop, chop, chop, chop, chop... The sound of Yates' whirlybird chittered closer behind him now. Firing off two more bursts, the firing pin clicked on empty. Quickly replacing the magazine, Collier lowered his head and peeked back around the side of the stony barricade. Now, far above the Gook who had returned his fire, there were more Chinks pouring over the top, swarming like ants down the path.

Raising his carbine, Collier took careful aim and fired off another burst of six.

"Aieee-ee! Uht-ah-h-h...uh!" He heard the screams as several of the topmost group of Gooks tumbled into space, landing with heavy thumps in the OP not fifteen feet in front of him. Before he could raise the barrel and fire a second burst from the new magazine, Collier was inundated in a hail of fire which missed him only by a hair.

Leaning to his right, he spread out prone and aimed his carbine back up the slope from the opposite side of the rock. The lone Chink near the bottom was reloading his automatic rifle as Collier took dead aim and shot him in the upper body, squeezing off a single shot. The enemy soldier stiffened, then collapsed, sliding and tumbling down the path and coming to rest on a ledge about ten feet above the OP. Taking careful aim again, Collier delivered the crumpled form a *coup de grace* squarely in the face. It was a calculating, cold-blooded act of rage that brought an unexpected, almost orgasmic, rush of purest pleasure.

Looking quickly back up the slope, the fresh horde of Chinks were scrambling down the path with alarming speed. Collier squeezed off the remaining burst of six or seven and watched fascinated as more of the shadowy forms stiffened and fell. Pulling two fresh magazines from under his poncho, he deftly replaced the empty magazine. Firing off another burst, Collier blindly swiveled on his belly like a crab, half-crawling, half-sliding back down the ravine around the final granite outcropping screening the chopper landing zone. In the shelter of the last defilade, he rose to a crouch and made a mad dash down the slope, blinking his light for all he was worth. He was rewarded by the miraculous whirling flashes of the chopper blades descending like the rustling wings of a settling pheasant through the murk.

"Move out. The whole freaking Gook Army's hot on my ass..." Collier dove through the opening of the Plexiglas, shouting instruction to Yates before the skids ever touched the ground.

"I know. I could see the flashes coming in. Great shooting. You sent at least a dozen of the slant-eyed bastards straight to Chinese hell. Hold tight! We're getting the fuck out of here..." Yates shouted, pulling the control back toward his chest and to his right, lifting the chopper back and around as they started falling into Stygian space.

A hail of bullets rattled against the Plexiglas canopy and the spidery aluminum framework as the chopper pulled sharply up and away. Leaning forward, Collier stuck his carbine out the opening in the Plexiglas bubble and fired a departing burst. Dropping like a brick into the void of night and swirling rain, Collier watched as the flashes from the Chinese weapons quickly faded and finally disappeared.

As soon as they were safely away, Yates leaned around to make sure Collier was no worse for wear. "Are you hit?"

"Neah. I'm fine...okay...good to go..." Collier replied, struggling to keep the tremor out of his voice as the adrenaline subsided. Carefully replacing the spent magazine in the carbine, he placed the weapon on the deck, jerking his hands back when they came in brief contact with the overheated barrel. Slipping his hands under his thighs, Collier sat on them to keep from shaking apart as the adrenaline reaction set in full force. Finally, as the adrenaline quickly left him, he gave way to wracking sobs of sheer relief.

2.

They had barely traveled a mile when Collier heard a familiar chirring sound—like wind blowing through dry leaves—which he immediately recognized from his days at Sill as artillery rounds passing overhead. These were followed by the "boom, boom, boom" and pale orange flashes through the inky rain as both friendly and enemy forces resumed their assault on Pork Chop right on time.

"Where did you take Williams and the wounded?" Collier finally asked when he could no longer hear or see the artillery. Reasonably certain the worst of his adrenalin overload had passed, he surreptitiously wiped away the evidence of his tears on the sleeves of his fatigues.

"The One-two-one Evac Hospital. I'm taking you there, too—it's near Yongdongpo, a couple of miles south of the Han River Bridge, just a short hop from here," Yates told him as the first reflections from lights of Seoul showed above the rim of the horizon. It seemed like hours had passed but Collier's watch showed 0052. Less than an hour had passed since his miraculous escape.

"Well, okay...I guess. Why the change?" His trembling had almost subsided and his voice was nearly normal now.

"Not sure, but I think you will be staying there...at least for awhile. They are getting almost all of the severe, life-threatening wounded from Pork Chop and Heartbreak Ridge," Yates attempted to put some sense into Collier's new assignment. "Be grateful. At the One-two-one, even the enlisted can sleep on a regular bed with sheets. Officers are billeted in Quonsets. In my opinion, the One-two-one is the best deal an MSC can get in the combat zone."

"Well, thanks for the heads up. After tonight, I'm ready for some peace and quiet," Collier said, placing his hands back underneath his buttocks to quiet his trembling which was threatening to start all over again.

"See that long line of headlights below?" Yates pointed down to a traffic jam crossing the Han River Bridge, extending south all the way past where the military highway took a sharp left toward Suwon.

"Yeah...what's going on?" Collier leaned forward and shouted in Yates ear, to make himself heard.

"Ambulances. All hell's busting loose north across the MLR, from Pork Chop to Arsenal and Eerie...and Alligator Jaws up across the Yokkok-ch'on to Arrowhead—even Heartbreak is taking a pounding from mortar and artillery fire. The fucking Chinks are a purely-mean bunch of muthafuckers." Yates shook his head.

"Are they all headed to the same place we're going?" Collier couldn't quite get his mind around the enormity of the situation. This last-resort fighting made no sense with the actual truce so near at hand.

"You got it. See that lighted chopper pad? That's the One-two-one just up ahead." Yates said, pointing down through the driving rain at the brightly-lit white chopper pad about a half-mile ahead bisected by a red cross. The seemingly endless line of headlights beneath them ended where the lead vehicles were turning into the gates of a large compound of sizeable masonry buildings below. "Bird Colonel Spaulding's CO and Major Hoffstetter is XO. You'll answer to Major Hoffstetter, he's a pussycat; the troops all call him 'Dad'."

Inside the well-defined, tightly-fenced and well-lit enclosure, a prominent succession of four, formidable brick buildings rose up the hill less than a hundred yards from where they were going to land. Each of these buildings had once been three stories high, but now the top story of all four were empty shells, ravaged by bombs or artillery. Scattered all around the main buildings were separate outbuildings, some made of brick, some wood, which, seen from above, had restored roofs, showing no evidence of the pounding they must have taken. A row of six or seven Quonsets stood at right angles along a narrow street separating them from the fourth and topmost of the dominant main masonry buildings.

Picking up his carbine, Collier thumbed the safety to the "on" position as they settled onto the pad and he prepared to depart the chopper. A Jeep with its canvas top up was approaching through the rain.

"Thanks for the lift," Collier said, trying to keep the emotion from his voice as he reached forward and clasped the heroic chopper pilot by the shoulder.

"It has been a distinct pleasure to make your acquaintance, Lieutenant. That was about as ballsy performance as I've seen...and I've been around the block. I'm honored to have given you a ride." A warm glow of pride spread through Collier's chest that the heroic, but impassive, chopper pilot would pay him such a compliment.

"Thanks, Mr. Yates, but you've got it wrong...you're the real hero in my book."

"Get out of here." In the rain and darkness, Collier imagined he saw the wizened pilot blush. "Now, take care—and don't let them put you to work tonight. They are on overload trying to take care of all the wounded, and it looks like it will be going on for awhile yet. They have two first lieutenants here who will be fighting over you as a replacement. But tell Hoffstetter to cut you some slack tonight. Insist on finding a bed and grab some rest before they shove you in the breech."

"Okay, but I'm not sure I can tell a major what I will and won't do." Collier laughed.

"My guess is that Hoffstetter already has heard what happened tonight up on that finger of the Chop. He's going to cut you some slack before he puts you to work—you won't be good to him or anyone else if you wind up with exhaustion. Anyway, good luck."

"Thanks...and good luck to you." Collier said, making ready to leave.

"By the way, I have a couple of old buddies here— CWOs Flood and Grey. Soon as you're settled in and the shooting stops, look 'em up and tell 'em Floyd Yates said 'hello.' See ya around, I'm sure."

"You can count on it...and thanks again. Stop back by after I'm settled and I'll buy you a drink." Collier said, stepping out into the rain toward the waiting Jeep.

"Major Hoffstetter said to bring you straight to his office—he's our Exec. You can put that weapon in the back." The private offered to take the carbine, but Collier jerked it back and held on tight. Approaching the closest of the main brick buildings at the center of the fenced compound, through the driving rain, Collier could see a large, sheltering marquee projecting out over the short flight of steps leading to what obviously was the main entrance to the series of four dominant buildings rising like stair steps up the hill in front of them.

"Sergeant Major Henderson is waiting right inside—he'll take you to Major Hoffstetter." The private reached across and rotated the catch on the canvas door of the covered Jeep.

"What's your name, soldier?" Peering back at the Jeep driver, Collier asked, struggling to swallow a sudden flair of resentment as he prepared to step out under the shelter of the marquee.

"Uh-h...Private Boulware...ah, uh...Sir!" At least now the careless private had presence enough to understand that his ass was in deep shit.

"Thanks for the ride, Boulware. You can be sure you'll be seeing me around." Collier wheeled and started up the steps without bothering to close the door, forcing the private to put the Jeep in neutral and stretch across to grasp the handle and pull it closed.

Inside the double entrance doors was a narrow landing which served as a waiting foyer for anyone waiting for transportation to arrive. From this narrow foyer, another three steps led up to a second pair of doors leading into the main reception area or lobby.

In better days, the lobby would have been impressive by any standard. However, as remarkable a job as had been done to reconstruct the building under wartime conditions, evidence of the destruction of bombing and shelling in an area that had been bitterly fought over nearly a half-dozen times was everywhere. Bearing silent witness to the destruction was the crude diagonal lumber that made up the ceiling, apparently doing double-duty as the floor of the next level of the once four-story building.

"Welcome to the One-twenty-first Evac, Lieutenant Ramsay. I'm Sergeant Major Henderson—the First Sergeant. Major Hoffstetter is expecting you if you will follow me." The burly, slightly-rumpled old soldier at the top of the steps stood at an insolent excuse for attention, his hand casually pointing to his right brow in what was intended to pass for a salute.

"Pleased to make you acquaintance, Sergeant." Collier returned the salute in the proper fashion. "Take me to the Major." After what he had just been through, Collier made little effort to conceal his displeasure at the Sergeant's insolent demeanor.

"I'll take your weapon, Lieutenant. It's SOP here at the One-two-one." The Sergeant reached out his hand.

"I'll just hold on to this for the time being, Sergeant. If you care to argue, bring Major Hoffstetter out here." Collier stood his ground.

"Uh-m-m, I'm sure that won't be necessary, Lieutenant." Henderson took a closer look at Collier's grimy fatigues and steel pot and thought better of making a scene. "If you will just follow me."

"This is Lieutenant Ramsay, Sir." Henderson led him directly through a medium-sized anteroom with several desks past a glass partition separating the area into two rooms. Passing by the inner area—which held a desk with a nameplate emblazoned M/Sgt. Ansel Henderson—they entered a somewhat pretentiously-oversized office with "Major Edward Hoffstetter, Executive Officer" neatly lettered on the door. The major sat behind an impressive wooden executive desk worthy of the Pentagon.

"I'm pleased to welcome you to the One-two-one, Ramsay. Come in and take a load off." Hoffstetter returned Collier's salute and turned back to the formidable sergeant. "That will be all tonight, Sergeant—I'll see you first thing tomorrow." Hoffstetter dismissed the sergeant amiably.

"I am already aware that you just had a pretty harrowing experience up on the Chop. I was up in Receiving about an hour ago when Williams brought in those three wounded medics from the Seventeeth Regiment. That was a remarkable thing you did—I'm glad you made it back. I don't know if you've been told, but Eighth Army Surgeon has assigned you here to us. I have two lieutenants in my command who have been waiting for a replacement for over a month now. For tonight, I'm going to sleep on it. I'm not exactly sure which one I'm going to let go first."

"Yessir." Making no move to put down the carbine or pull his poncho over his head, Collier remained standing beside an empty chair. To his left was a door with "Colonel Augustus F. Spaulding, U.S. Army Medical Corps, Commanding Officer" lettered on it in gold.

"At any rate, making your assignment will be my last official act." The friendly senior officer made no reference to the carbine or the Colt .45 automatic whose holster was now protruding outside Collier's poncho. "My own replacement, Lieutenant Colonel Harold Scroggs, is already sleeping in his room in the Field Grade Officers Quarters up at the top of the hill along the forward boundary of the compound. We will finish the process of turning over my duties to him late tomorrow morning in time for me to catch an afternoon flight to Tachikawa. I hope to be on my way back to the states via Hawaii no later than day after tomorrow—which now, by the way, will be—the tenth—Friday. I will make sure you meet Colonel Scroggs before I leave, no matter whether I assign you to Major Smith over in Supply or up front here as Adjutant."

"Did you say Adjutant, Sir?" Collier croaked. "I thought TO and E for an Evac Hospital called for at least the rank of Captain to serve as Adjutant."

"That's right, Lieutenant. I know what TO and E calls for, but there's still a war on over here, or haven't you heard?" The Major shot him an exasperated look.

"Yessir...it just surprises me that you would even consider putting a green Second John in such a responsible position."

"Lieutenant, I know for a fact that yesterday, up on the Chop, there were at least two First Lieutenants, recently promoted from Second Lieutenant with less than ninety days in Korea, who were made temporary Company Commanders of their Infantry outfits when their COs became untimely casualties. War is a hell of a finishing school, Lieutenant. I have already told Henderson to put in the paper work for your promotion to First Lieutenant before I leave here tomorrow. I've been in the Reserve since World War Two when I was called back to active duty last year. I was promoted to Captain before I was shipped over here. I was Exec at a front-line MASH for about two months before I was transferred down here and given the reserve commission of Major. I immediately applied for Regular Army. If I get it and can keep my rank, I'm going to stay in—might as well make the military a career now. Counting my reserve time, I'll only have less than eleven years to serve before I'm eligible to retire with twenty. Enough of this chit-chat. I know you must be exhausted. Are you hungry? We keep a skeleton crew in the hospital dining room and food service round the clock."

"No sir, I'm really too beat to eat. A shower might be nice, but all I really want right now is a bed." Remembering the endless line of ambulances streaming down the narrow road from the Han River Bridge, Collier figured the quicker he found a hiding place, the better his chances of getting a good night's sleep.

"Okay, follow me. You can have both a shower and a bed. It's up to you. I'll take you to your permanent billet. It's on my way. You'll find the showers are right out back of your Quonset hut. One advantage of being here is even though we have our own generators to supply the OR, we are also connected to the Seoul city electric power system and—as undependable as the Korean power often is—between the two electric power sources, we almost always have the basic comforts of home: hot water and electric lights." The Major stood, walked around the desk, retrieved his poncho, which had been spread drying across two metal folding chairs, and slipped it over his head. Motioning Collier to precede him out the door and leaving the lights burning, Hoffstetter then led him past Sergeant Major Henderson's desk and into the hall. Crossing the hall, they exited through a single door which opened directly outside into the area between the first two of the four main buildings.

"Follow me; we can stay out of this monsoon until we reach the topmost building. After that, it's only a quick dash across the street and a few huts down to your new home-sweet-home." Sticking close to the wall, Hoffstetter led the way to the stairs and started up. At the top landing, he opened the door and waited for Collier to enter into the second building. Looking back down from this vantage point, Collier could make out the silhouette of twisted steel window frames and crumbling brick walls.

Inside the second of the buildings, the wide corridor was lined with a double row of litters and smelled strongly of fresh blood. Under the yellowish light from the bare ceiling bulbs, Collier could see a group of several corpsmen moving from litter to litter, trying to give what comfort they could provide. Just in front of him, a grandly-mustached blond lieutenant about his age, wearing a black-cloth armband with the white felt cutout letters, AOD, attached, was bent over a litter holding a soldier with what appeared to be a massive head wound, listening to his heart sounds with a stethoscope. After a moment, the moustachioed young officer stood and summoned one of the corpsmen several litters up ahead.

"He's gone. Pull him out of line and take him to the morgue." The AOD had already moved to the next litter and was bending over with his stethoscope before he finished speaking.

"That's Lieutenant Graves, from our attached Laboratory unit—they provide our microbiology and pathology services. With the MASH units up to their eyeballs in wounded and getting first priority on qualified Assistant Battalion Surgeons, we're shorthanded on our TO and E for Administrative Officers. Here, we all take turns at Administrative Officer of the Day; your rotation will come up about every eight or nine days. Everybody has to help out. Fortunately, after this week, you won't have many nights like this. But, for the moment, thanks to that senile old fart, Syngman Rhee's, big mouth, all hell has broken loose up north again. We have these critically wounded lining our corridors all the way up the hill—last count was around seventy-four, with more in those ambulances stacked up the Suwon highway all the way back to the Han River Bridge. We try to perform medical triage and take the wounded to surgery on a need-to-operate, lifesaving basis. But take a look around you; in an operation of this magnitude, how do you decide who's on first? And they tell me there's no end in sight."

Completely aghast at the sight of a soldier just ahead with his left arm splintered and dangling by the threads of tendons, lying carelessly across his chest and another with a gaping head wound exposing glistening, grayish, brain tissue, Collier was rendered momentarily speechless.

Thank God, at least he wouldn't have to pull AOD tonight.

Navigating their way up a second flight of stairs between buildings Two and Three, they were greeted by another double line of wounded on litters in the corridor—Collier hadn't attempted to keep a count, but he felt quite certain Hoffstetters' estimate of over seventy waiting pre-ops was not overstated.

"On our left is our Quarantine Unit—we've started to take the most virulent cases of Korean Hemorrhagic Fever from the Forty-eighth MASH since we have the Laboratory Section here." As they passed through Building Four, Hoffstetter pointed offhandedly to a large Off Limits to Unauthorized Personnel sign standing at the entrance to a closed unit. The mention of the illness sent a chill up Collier's spine as he recalled Madison's warning note before he left Tokyo.

Passing out by way of the ambulance entrance at Receiving at the rear of Building Four, the litters were coming in a steady stream when Hoffstetter paused to brief him before they stepped outside into the pouring rain.

"This is the last building. There is a line of six Quonset huts just across the street. The first five huts running down from our right are nurses quarters. The end one to the extreme left just before you start down the hill to the guard gate is The Broken Drum, where—including our two Chief Warrant Officers—all of our administrative officers below the rank of major are billeted. Out back of Quonset row, behind the showers and latrine is the Chicken Coop, a euphemism for the long tar-paper-covered building housing the field grade officers," he explained, adjusting his poncho. "I had Cha, the Korean houseboy, make up a bed for you. Cha is his family name. His given name is Dong. Formally he is Cha Dong. In Korea the family name is given first—we all call him Cha. When Rock Costigan and Chuck Lohr ship home, you can pick another bed. But for tonight, I didn't think you'd be very choosy. Cha's still up and waiting for you. He'll help you with anything you need. We're glad to have you aboard, Ramsay. Goodnight, I'll see you in the morning for chow—say around zero-six-hundred hours." Hoffstetter clapped him on the back and pushed him out the door into the rain, hastily pointing him to the left, down the line of six Quonset huts.

THE BROKEN DRUM—You Can't Beat It! Approaching the final Quonset through the driving rain, Collier made out a yellow and brown, hand-carved, wooden sign in the shape of a snare drum mounted beside the door. Suspended underneath the snare drum motif, a ladder-work of eight nameplates making up a directory of the current residents hung in descending order of their rank.

Inside the Quonset, Collier was surprised to find the first ten-foot section had been converted into a sort of parlor with padded benches lining the walled partition separating the parlor from the sleeping quarters further back. The floor was carpeted in cheap loop carpeting in a ghastly shade of lime-green. Immediately inside the entrance door were several metal folding chairs with matching red cushions on their seats. Dangling through the lowered ceiling made of twisted crepe paper streamers stapled to the bulkheads in a crisscross lattice work, to his right was a tiny ruby light fixture in the shape of an Oriental paper lantern. Across the tacky, wistfully-homey sitting area, a doorway consisting of a curtain fashioned from the same fabric used to cover the cushions on the benches separated the privacy of the sleeping quarters. As tired as he was, Collier couldn't help but smile as he pushed through the curtained doorway. In the garish red glow from the light fixture, the overall effect was that of the waiting room of a down-at-the-heels New Orleans cathouse.

Inside the sleeping area, the only light came from a single bare bulb hanging from the high, curved ceiling near the back door of the hut. The rather narrow sleeping section consisted of a center aisle between two rows of metal-framed GI bunks. Most of the hut's occupants had upended salvaged wooden K-ration or ammo cases to serve as make-do bedside tables which held cheap electric reading lamps with paper shades. At the extreme rear of the billet, a young Korean stood waiting beside the last bunk at far end of the lefthand row of beds. As Collier tiptoed quietly toward him, he noticed the Korean boy had made the bed with crisp white sheets and pillowcase and was holding several snow-white towels folded over his forearm.

"Ahso rhootenant, Crollier Ramsay, this is Cha, numblah hana housebloy, Bloken Dlum," the diminutive Korean greeted him in a respectful whisper when he finally reached the side of the bed. Collier recognized the word "*hana*" as being Korean for the number one. Collier was somewhat surprised the houseboy had used "*hana*." Somewhere in one of their orientations on the Korean language, Collier recalled being told Koreans used the Japanese expression "ichiban" meaning number one to express the concept of being the best, of greatest importance, or greatest beauty or efficiency in terms of the numbers one to ten.

"I'm pleased to meet you, Cha. Thank you for making up my bed. Where are the showers and the latrine? I'd like to take a shower before I lay my head on these nice clean sheets."

"Ahso, rhootenant...latleene and schlowah are light oultslide..." Having some difficulty translating the eager houseboy's Japanese-influenced English pronunciations with the mixed up Rs and Ls, Collier followed him to the back door and peered outside at the shadowy outlines of two outbuildings not more than two dozen steps away in the driving rain.

Wasting no time, but taking care that the safety was on, Collier carefully propped the carbine against the wall using the makeshift night table for support. Pulling his dripping poncho over his head, Collier undid the leather holster thongs from around his right thigh, unfastened the web belt and placed the leather-holstered Colt handgun on the table top. This done, he sat on a metal folding chair and began to unlace and pull off his grimy, mud-caked boots in preparation of shucking out of his filthy fatigues.

"You give clothes to Cha. I fix good as new for you when you wake up." Collier's ear was already tuning out the extra Ls and Rs, readily deciphering the houseboy's heavy accent.

"Thanks, Cha, you get that stuff clean before I wake up and you will be number *ichiban* houseboy, alright. Now give me those towels, and let me hit the showers." Collier took the towels and, wearing only his poncho, headed for the door.

Back from the shower—which, surprisingly, was hot to the point of being almost scalding—Collier turned out the light and was asleep almost before his head his the pillow.

"Get up Ramsay and get dressed. It's zero-five-forty-five. I will be back in five minutes to take you down to the Officers Mess for a first-class breakfast. I'll introduce you to a few of our other officers before we put you to work." Hoffstetter stood over him in the semi-darkness.

Rubbing his eyes, Collier reluctantly pulled back the sheet and swung his legs over the side of the bunk, peering into the gloom for his missing underwear and fatigues.

"Cha had your duds washed and pressed. They're right there on the chair. I'll be back in five minutes. You can carry the poncho. It looks like the monsoon has lifted for the time being." Pointing to the chair, the major turned and walked out the back door.

Scarcely awake and trying hard to replay in his head the incredible events of the previous evening, Collier's eyes slowly adjusted to the half-light as he began to put on his freshly-laundered uniform. No doubt about it, Cha was number *hana* houseboy—number *hana* in Collier's book at least.

By the time Hoffstetter came back, Collier was fully dressed and was just picking up the web belt to put on the Colt handgun.

"Carry the belt with the forty-five in your hand and bring along the carbine, too. As of today, we're still officially in the combat zone, but if dotty old Syngman Rhee will behave, the truce is due to be signed any day now. It is extremely unlikely that anyone will need to carry weapons here in our compound again. I'll have Major Smith in Supply give you a receipt. He'll take good care of your pistol and carbine," Hoffstetter instructed.

It was getting lighter by the second as Collier followed Hoffstetter outside down the line of six adjoining Quonset huts with name placards like The Hen Party. Like The Broken Drum sign beside their male officer hut, the nurses' billets had corresponding directories with the names of their occupant nurses, mostly captains and first lieutenants, listed on the directories dangling by their doors.

At the end of Quonset row, the dirt street turned sharply right and started down the hill.

"In the low building on our left, just past the NCO mess, is our attached Laboratory Section." Hoffstetter pointed out the points of interest as they walked along." "They do the more exotic lab work and some pathology for most of the MASH units, too. Their CO, Major Robotham, answers to me and to the Chief of Medicine and the Eighth Army Surgeon. It sounds confusing, but it works okay."

Past the building housing the Lab, a long row of low one-story, shed-like buildings paralleled the lightly-rutted street, ending just past the street running in front of the main building and leading around to the guard house at the entrance to the barbed-wire-enclosed compound. Up ahead in the area beyond the row of sheds, a Quonset with a sign identifying it as The Laundry stood in the open area adjoining the large motor pool to the left of the chopper landing pad. About fifty yards beyond The Laundry was a low, rectangular, wooden building painted white with half a Quonset jury-rigged to its left-hand side, forming a slightly off-center T.

As they approached the building, Collier saw a rather apologetic sign by the entrance door identifying it as the OFFICERS' MESS.

"After you..." Major Hoffstetter stood aside and held the screen door, ushering Collier into the small foyer. "Our cocktail lounge is in the Quonset to the left"—Hoffstetter indicated a pair of double doors chained shut and padlocked—"Don't mind the locks and chains. Major Smith is Club officer. The bar is open for business and doing a land-office trade every day, Sundays included, promptly at seventeen-hundred hours. We have several Japanese slot machines and a jukebox Smitty had sent over from Tokyo—with all the latest Hit Parade and a bunch of oldies like Glen Miller and Artie Shaw. I'll buy you a drink this afternoon if I'm still around—which I sincerely hope I'm not. Come with me, and let's go through the line before the nurses hit like a tidal wave. Not counting our Chief of Nursing Services, Major Olsen, we usually have around forty, depending on how many are being replaced in the Eighth Army area. Our own TO and E calls for thirty. We act as the Rep'l-Depot for Eighth Army Director of Nurses who hangs out over in Seoul at Eighth Army Medical Headquarters. At night, our little lounge is quite popular with young infantry and artillery officers and some of the flyboys from across the river at Kimpo. They are all looking to score with the nurses. War is hell—you'll see when you meet our lineup of Florence Nightingales. We have no trouble getting volunteers from the states—as a matter of fact, there's a waiting list."

"I beg your pardon?" Collier was not quite following the Major's line of thought.

"Most nurses over here were not in great demand as date material back home, but over here, they are 'the only game in town'...if you get my drift?"

"Uhm-m, I see what you mean." Collier nodded as they entered the Officers' Mess and he caught view of a pair of nurses, decidedly less than homecoming queen-candidates, sitting across the dining area smoking cigarettes and sipping coffee.

After they had passed through the chow line and he had filled his tray, Collier followed Hoffstetter to a large table where a sizeable collection of senior officers— captains and several majors—were in various stages of finishing their breakfasts and sipping from coffee cups.

"Gentlemen, I'd like for you to meet Lieutenant Collier Ramsay..." Hoffstetter started in introducing Major Greenberg, Chief of Surgery; Major Hughes, Chief of Medicine; Major Halpern, an ophthalmologist; Captain Mutch, a gastroenterologist-internist; Captain Junius Howell, an otolaryngologist; Major Honeycutt, the hospital Chaplain; and Major Smith, aka "Smitty," Chief of Supply.

"Is this going to be Rock's replacement? Rock has seniority over Lohr." The cagey Major Smith lost no time in putting his bid in for having Collier assigned to him.

"Maybe...but for the time being, I'm sending him up to Greenberg to help process the wounded from the Chop...and now, the Triangle—the Gook artillery has gone crazy since Syngman Rhee released all those prisoners and went on Korean radio to say he was going to keep fighting until the ROKs reunited Korea. Last I heard, we had almost eighty pre-ops lined up and more coming in the back door." Hoffstetter motioned for Collier to take a seat beside him at the end of the table near the window.

Taking a seat, Collier poked idly at his food. He had lost his appetite when Hoffstetter announced that he was sending him up to process the never-ending parade of horribly wounded he had seen last night when he first arrived.

"If you're ready, Lieutenant, just come with me." When he finished his coffee, Major Greenberg stood and waited for Collier. Without saying goodbye, Collier followed the Major out of the door.

"The idea is to identify the dead and pull them out of the line. If, in the process, you're able to identify some of the wounded whose need for surgery is more acute—more life-saving-dependent—than others, you can move them ahead in line. But don't waste a lot of time trying to differentiate those. They are all going to die soon enough if we don't get them in the OR and out of here on a plane from Kimpo to Japan," Greenberg explained as they walked up the hill and entered the hospital. Inside, Greenberg led him past a big OR with a pile of arms and legs and body parts in the corner on a bloody sheet. Somewhat surprised that the gory sight did not cause him to gag, Collier saw that the team of surgeons and nurses manning five tables simultaneously were scrubbing out of OD-painted five-gallon cans suspended from the walls over wash tubs serving as sinks.

Beyond the OR, they passed through areas Collier took to be Post-op Recovery and Intensive Care.

"Major Olsen, meet Lieutenant Ramsay. Get him a stethoscope, show him the ropes and put him to work." Moving into Intensive Care, Greenberg introduced Collier to a blonde nurse in freshly-laundered, sharply creased combat fatigues covered with a white apron from the OR. In sharp contrast to the homely nurses he had seen in the Officers Mess, Olsen was not at all bad looking.

"My pleasure, Major." Although he didn't salute, Collier paid appropriate respect.

"Glad you're here, Lieutenant. Take this stethoscope and follow me." The impassive Chief of Nurses handed him a stethoscope and led him toward a door dividing Recovery from the other side of the building. The snug fit of the Major's sharply-pressed fatigues, gave unintended notice there was a lot of woman inside.

"Do we still have the three men who came in on a chopper from Pork Chop last night, Major?" Collier asked—following the Chief Nurse along the center corridor out a door and into the enclosed, windowed passageway connecting building Two with building Three.

"The unconscious one we sent directly over to Kimpo and flew him out last night. The other two with shrapnel wounds in their legs were patched up last night. We sent them to Kimpo to be evacuated to Japan before daylight as soon as they were stabilized. Are you the MSC who Riley Yates flew onto Pork Chop to rescue them?" Olsen stopped short and gave him an appreciative look.

"Yes'm. Me and a medic named Williams. I'm glad to hear they're okay." Collier blushed.

"Thanks to you. That was quite a heroic thing you did. I'll buy you a drink when we get through this nightmare the Chinese have put us in right now." Olsen pushed through a door and stepped into the center passageway connecting the buildings. The floor was lined with a double row of litters. A few stretchers ahead of them on their right, Graves, the lieutenant from the Lab section he had met late last night with the AOD armband was bent over checking life signs with his stethoscope of a patient suffering what appeared to be a hastily-bandaged, sucking chest wound. Two pair of corpsmen were following close behind him.

Sucking chest wound. Collier heaved a sigh of relief, when he saw almost all of the wounded had terse descriptions of their injuries scrawled with an ink marker directly on their dressings—in some cases, the terse diagnoses were scrawled directly on the skin if there were large exposed areas of naked flesh.

"This one's gone," the AOD, Graves, said, motioning with a jerk of his head for two of the corpsmen to pull the litter out of line and move the next one up. Bending and checking the dog tags of the dead soldier, Graves jotted the soldier's name and serial number on a cardboard tag with a string attached.

"Tag him and put him in the morgue," Graves told the second pair of corpsmen trailing them. He instructed the other pair to move the other litters to keep the line tight and moving.

Collier watched with morbid fascination as a corpsman took the little cardboard tag and fastened it to the corpse's big toe. With the help of his companion, they picked up the litter and moved about ten feet ahead, turning into the door of what appeared to be a small section of a Quonset which opened off the corridor connecting building Two with building Three. A sign over the door identified the Quonset section as The Morgue. On closer inspection, Collier could see The Morgue had a small, electric refrigeration unit attached with a standby gasoline generator in case of a power failure.

"Billy, I'd like to introduce Lieutenant Collier Ramsay. Ramsay, this is our chief lab tech, Billy Graves." Olsen made the rather informal introduction.

"We had a passing introduction early this morning, I think. I've lost all track of time." Wearing surgical gloves, Graves withheld the offer of a handshake.

"Yeah, we met about six hours ago..." Collier murmured awkwardly. He was not at all anxious to begin monitoring life signs among the human carnage lying on the floor in front of him.

"Billy, how about showing Lieutenant Ramsay the routine? As soon as he gets the hang of it, you can go get some sleep. If we need you back here later, I'll send someone to get you." Olsen handed Collier a pair of surgical gloves, gave them both a smile and left.

"Well...nothing much to show. All I'm doing is checking for heartbeat, assessing life signs and the severity and gravity of their wounds. The idea is to move those with the more immediately life-threatening injuries ahead for surgery. There is a Medical Officer up closer to the OR assessing them and making final decisions. Most of them will go directly to Kimpo for air evac to Japan as soon as they are out of surgery and stabilized." Graves handed Collier the stethoscope.

"I'll start right here..." Heart pounding, Collier pulled on the gloves, put the earpieces into his ears and bent over the next litter.

He was rewarded with the sound of a steady pulse.

"Good luck. I'll see you later," Collier nodded absently as Graves peeled off his gloves and took off like a scalded dog. Motivated by the utter desperation—and near-futility—of the depressing situation, Collier immediately became immersed in the task at hand.

"Was Graves here all night without relief?" watching Graves disappear through the door, Collier asked the corpsmen helping him.

"Well?...every few hours a nurse or a doctor came, letting him take a coffee break. Except for that, he's been here round the clock since Tuesday morning," the nearest corpsman volunteered.

"Judaspriest! You mean he's been here forty-eight hours without relief?" Collier exploded as he contemplated the sobering situation.

"That's affirmative. The shit has definitely hit the fan..." the second corpsman volunteered the obvious.

"How about you? Have you guys had any relief?" although he didn't think he remembered the current cadre of corpsman being here last night when he came in, Collier asked, afraid to hear the answer.

"Oh, yeah, we've had relief. We're eight hours on, eight hours off. Not so bad when you can go lie down for awhile or go outside and walk it off." To underscore his point, the corpsman stood from crouching beside a litter and flexed his cramping legs.

"I'm glad at least someone gets relief...come here...move this one up to the head of the line," Collier instructed when he looked up from a young soldier with his left arm blown completely away and a bloody combat dressing covering a sucking chest wound. Incredibly, the young soldier was still alive.

"My God, how long has this poor soul been lying here?" Perhaps two hours later, Collier had reached the halfway-point in the double line of litters as he knelt, staring with disbelief at the maggots crawling all over a gangrenous wound in the wounded man's right leg just above the ankle. Taking a pair of bandage scissors he had commandeered from a passing nurse, he quickly cut away the upper part of the trousers of the wounded soldier's fatigues and found a web-belt tourniquet tightly cutting off his lower circulation just above the knee. He lost no time loosening the belt, but was horrified to find little responding blood-flow restored to the lower limb. Collier felt certain the soldier would lose the lower leg if, indeed, they were able to save his life.

"Listen up. One of you corpsmen go back down this line and check every last leg or arm wound for tourniquets—somebody missed this one, and it is probably going to cause a man to unnecessarily lose his lower leg. That is if we aren't too late to save his life."

Watching one of the medics start back checking for possible missed tourniquets, Collier shook his head that such a dereliction of responsibility could have occurred.

Shortly after noon, Major Olsen appeared with a faintly horsey-looking nurse to relieve him long enough to wolf down some coffee and a sandwich from the patient mess on the second floor. By 1245, he was back at work with no sign of a let-up in the never-ending parade of ambulances and choppers bringing in new cases from Pork Chop and the Triangle.

Just after 1500, moving robotically in his exhausted, trance-like state to hold the stethoscope to the chest of the occupant of the next litter, Collier suddenly found himself staring at what looked for all the world like the spitting image of the

dirt- and blood-smeared face of his old OCS nemesis, Captain Hal Sweeny—
"Unsatisfactory Hal." Blinking hard to make certain he wasn't hallucinating from
sheer exhaustion, Collier did a doubletake then quickly checked the wounded
soldier's dogtags. Sure enough, the man was Hal Sweeny in the flesh—or what was
left of him.

"Shrapnel wounds chest & abdomen"—nearly obliterated by blood and dirt,
the legend had been hastily scrawled on the gory bandage on Sweeny's chest as
Collier—suddenly revived by the shock of seeing his old adversary lying near death
right in front of him—shakily placed the stethoscope on Sweeny's chest.

Sweeny's pulse was weak and thready, and his breath came in shallow gasps.

"Here, quick, grab the end of this litter. We need to move this man to the
OR immediately," Collier summoned the team of corpsmen following close
behind and followed as they moved the stretcher forward, placing it at the head of
the waiting line outside the Operating Room nearby. As Collier turned to move
away, Sweeny opened his eyes and flashed him a tired look of recognition and
gratitude. Assured he had done all he could do to help the helpless colleague
who had taught him and his classmates at Sill so much about the deadly nuances
of adjusting artillery fire, Collier immediately returned to his place in the rapidly-
building line of wounded with a somewhat renewed sense of how many lives were
depending on him.

As the leaden hours slipped by, the number of dead mounted as they began
stacking corpses on top of corpses inside the refrigerated Quonset hut. Around
1930 hours, Olsen sent another nurse to relieve him—just long enough to grab a
snack and some coffee and come directly back to work.

"Have you seen Hoffstetter since this morning?" Collier asked Olsen as he
polished off his coffee and stood to go back to work. Beyond exhaustion now, he
wondered when Hoffstetter would be sending him relief.

"Hoffstetter is history. He turned operations over to Scroggs and headed for
Kimpo. I heard from one of the ambulance drivers that he caught a DC-4 to
Tokyo, but I got news for you, Lieutenant. That was yesterday." Olsen related.

"Yesterday?" Collier was certain he misunderstood.

"Yeah, Lieutenant, yester-fucking-day. You've been so busy playing good
Samaritan, you haven't noticed you worked the clock around." The brassy Olsen
smiled, tight-lipped.

"Jeez...no frigging wonder I'm a zombie." Collier stood and tried to stretch,
having trouble comprehending he had actually lost a day.

"If Hoffstetter's gone, where's the new Exec? What's his name, I forget?"
Collier finally asked, trying to recall the name of Hoffstetter's replacement.

"Light Colonel Harold Scroggs, MSC. Last I saw Scroggs was after dinner.
He was heading for the Chicken Coop." Olsen shook her head in sympathy.
Hoffstetter had already explained to Collier the Chicken Coop was a euphemism
for the long, tar-paper covered building behind Quonset Row which housed the
field grade officers—the rank of major and above.

"Okay, then, who's pulling AOD?" Collier asked, suddenly confronted by
the reality he had lost an entire day in the numbing fatigue of dealing with this
fucking insane nightmare.

"Major Smith is AOD," Olsen replied. "But don't get your hopes up. You
won't see Smitty near these pre-ops if that's what you have on your mind."

"Who do I look to for relief then?" Collier asked in quiet desperation, not
sure he could stand on his own two feet, much less go back up there to attend the

stretcher cases. Suddenly considering the enormity of the situation, he was beset by the certain feeling there was no relief for him in sight, not at least in his immediate future, and he was already well beyond keeling over from sheer exhaustion.

"I'm not sure. Who sent you up here in the first place, anyway?"

"Hoffstetter...but he turned me over to Greenberg to bring me up here Thursday morning right after breakfast chow."

"Well, Greenberg is Chief of Surgery. Don't look for any help there. Down here, the docs are elitists—the closest any of our docs have been to a battalion aid station is a MASH, and we have only a couple of those. At battalion, you MSCs may be Assistant Battalion Surgeons, but down here, our prima donna docs don't have anything to do with MSCs—except maybe to bug Smitty and his motor pool officer, Rock Costigan, to let them use a Jeep to go into Seoul to the Eighth Air Force O Club for drinks and dinner. Also, Smitty is in charge of our so-called Officers Mess and our little Quonset social-club attachment—the docs kiss his ass shamelessly when they want to buy booze for a party in one of the nurses' huts."

"Speaking of Costigan, how about him? Doesn't he take his turn up here?" Collier asked hopefully.

"Theorectically, I guess he should, but I've never seen him around when there's a big flap up north. He sometimes comes around when we're having trouble with the generators or lights in the OR or other things related to Supply. He was a Fireman back home in Bumscrew, Gee-A., which translated to his being the Assistant Battalion Surgeon in his local National Guard outfit—which, for your edification, translates here into being practically good for nada relating to medicine, including basic First Aid. Frankly, I would hate to think my life would depend on Rock giving me artificial respiration. About the only mouth-to-mouth he has given since he got here twelve months ago, is to Maureen Wingfield, an aging, Clara Barton-wannabe, and a couple of her Red Cross princess predecessors who unfortunately are quartered with me in the lady's wing of The Chicken Coop."

"I take it Rock is hell with the ladies, then?" Collier looked up with complete disinterest, too tired to really care about petty. estrogen-fueled jealousy.

"He thinks he is. And Maureen Wingfield and her sisters—not to mention my horny, somewhat-less-than-beautiful nurses—are so hard up, she...they...don't give a damn he's married and has about a half-dozen kids in diapers back home."

"Oh, well. There shouldn't be a shortage of replacements to keep the ladies happy when Rock gets his ticket home. How about Chuck Lohr? Is he on the rotation to help out up here?" Collier was desperate to find out whom he could turn to for help.

"Chuck is a short-timer, too. Besides, he's Spaulding's favorite—kisses the senile old CO's ass shamelessly." Olsen took the last sip of her coffee and pushed back her chair to leave.

"Who else around here can help me out? I'm about to fall flat on my face, Major."

"There's Flood and Gray and the junior officers from the Laboratory section, but you're the new guy on the block and you're stuck for now, I'm afraid."

"But Judaspriest, Major, I've been at this practically non-stop since before zero-nine-hundred Thursday morning—that's going on two whole days and nights, now. Not to mention night before last...two nights now, I guess...I was up on Pork Chop Hill dodging Chinese bullets, I need...I deserve...some freaking rest."

"I was here off-and-on all night the last three nights, and I've been on most of both of the last two days, too, Lieutenant. Go see the Chaplain—or someone else who gives a shit." Olsen fired back over her shoulder as she walked away. "While you're feeling sorry for yourself, there are a bunch of guys up there dying on litters. Their lives are depending on you...on me and my nurses...on Greenberg and his surgeons...on all of us. Quit fucking whining and get back to work."

Burning from the plainspoken Chief of Nurses' caustic observation, Collier meekly followed her out the door, trudging reluctantly back to the ever-increasing line of badly-wounded pre-ops waiting in the adjoining corridor.

"*I've been doing triage continuously since 0900 yesterday morning. Can you send me some relief?*" Desperate now and not at all deterred from seeking help, Collier jotted a note to Major Smith and gave it to one of the fresh corpsmen who were being relieved with fresh bodies every four hours right on time.

Despite the corpsman's assurances he had delivered the note directly to Major Smith, midnight came and went without Collier hearing back from his request.

Sometime around daylight, Collier had to tie a tag on the toe of one of his instructors from MFSS in San Antonio—a freckled-face kid who had taught them how to start IVs in combat. Counting one of the Redbirds from his early days at OCS who was staring lifeless—his head blown halfway off—when Collier reached him early in his stint at this grisly chore, this made the third man Collier recognized from previous stateside duty assignments. Two of the three were dead—that was assuming Sweeny survived. This insanity was getting way too fucking real for him.

With Truman and Ike and all those strutting peacocks snoring in their beds back home in Washington and nearby at Panmunjom only a twenty-minute chopper ride from here, where was the glory and honor in all this fucking, senseless sacrifice?

"Good morning, Lieutenant, sorry I haven't been able to get up here before now, but the Sergeant of the Guard had a little excitement on the back of the compound, and, on top of everything else, the OR has kept us pretty busy down in Supply—those boys in Surgery have their hands full up there tonight." Finally around 0315, Major Smith came wandering up and tapped Collier on the shoulder just as he finished tagging his thirty-second dead soldier since he had come on twenty-eight hours before.

"Better late than never. Collier stripped off his surgical gloves and offered the major a Lucky. The Major declined with a wave of his hand and lit his own cigarette—a Chesterfield.

"Don't bet on it. I hate to tell you, but I don't have anyone to send up here at the moment; I'm sorry. Hold on until morning, and maybe we can designate some relief at the CO's Officer's Call after breakfast chow. Now, I've got to run. There have been some breeches of the fence. We think some of the villagers are trying to steal food and gas from the motor pool. Keep up the good work...good night and good luck." Major Smith walked away with a wave of his hand, the glowing ember from his cigarette describing an arc against the dark backdrop of the outside door.

"Good morning, Lieutenant. I'm Harold Scroggs, the new Exec." Collier's watch showed 0610 when he looked up through blurry eyes at the spit-and-polish light colonel, standing above him in fresh-ironed fatigues, offering to shake his hand. "I'm told we should get you some relief up here."

"Yessir. I'm Lieutenant Collier Ramsay, Sir. Major Hoffstetter said you were here. I've been here since just after midnight Thursday morning, July ninth. I got here the same day you did—I think it is going on three days ago now." Collier said, still astraddle a litter which held a soldier with an ugly shoulder wound exposing at least two-inches of the naked humorous below the juncture with the collar bones. Collier jammed two morphine syrettes into the flesh of the tricep before duck-walking forward to the next litter. Unfortunately, despite the bad crack in the neck of the humorous, the shoulder wound would just have to wait its turn. Fortunately, the soldier's vitals were good. "I hope you're here to tell me my relief is on its way."

"You mean you haven't been relieved at all? I was told we were sending you relief two days ago at my first officers call."

"I'm still here, Sir. I've had sporadic breathers to grab a bite to eat and take a leak, but no one to replace me—and the wounded just keep coming in. I haven't had time to even think of shitting in three days." Collier nodded, too exhausted to even consider saluting. He'd lost count of how many dead he had tagged for the morgue when the total reached over seventy and he had no idea how long ago that had been. Remembering back to the Officers Call to which the Colonel was referring, Collier recalled he had already been at this ghastly duty for sixty or seventy hours now, at the very least.

"Come on, Lieutenant, surely you must be exaggerating..." the Colonel began, but let his words trail off as he took a closer look at Collier's zombie-like appearance.

"No, Sir. I've lost count of the litters that have come in, but the number who have died before surgery is well over seventy now." Collier stared him in the eye accusingly.

"I'm not surprised by that, Lieutenant. After all, we've already admitted and processed well over three-hundred since Wednesday morning, seven July when the flap on Pork Chop began. Today is Sunday, twelve July. The American casualty count of wounded evacuated from Pork Chop Hill alone looks to be astronomical...some guess it may wind up being nearly a thousand. And, given the nature of what we do, we're getting more than our share of those—but I guess I don't have to tell you, of all people, that."

"No, Sir, but I've already been here for three days—close to seventy-two hours without anything like what could qualify as relief. If you can't find me relief, I'm walking out of here within the hour. You can put me in the stockade; at least I won't die of exhaustion there."

"Well, now, Lieutenant, I don't know if I like to hear talk like that."

"I'm sorry, Sir. Like it or not, get me some relief...Sir...or you're going to have a one-man mutiny. Besides, even in wartime, the IG is still around to see justice is done. Ask Major Olsen; she can be my star witness at my court martial."

Scroggs stared at him in momentary disbelief before a look of understanding that Collier was in dead earnest slowly came into his eyes.

"Okay, I get your message loud and clear. Hang on for fifteen minutes, Ramsay—half-hour at most. I'll see what I can do about relieving you." Seeing a budding administrative clusterfuck hatching before his eyes, the career-minded Scroggs reassured him, turned on his well-polished bootheels and walked briskly away.

"I'm Rock Costigan. Major Smith says to tell you you're relieved." In less than fifteen minutes from the time Scroggs walked away, a swarthy-looking lieutenant in sharply-pressed fatigues, ill-mannerly picking his teeth, tapped Collier impudently on the shoulder.

"Thanks...do you understand what's going on here...what you have to...?" Collier began, but Costigan cut him off.

"Sure thing. This ain't my first rodeo, Cowboy. I've been here twelve months, three weeks and four fucking days." Costigan snarled, declining to take the blood-smeared stethoscope and the pack of stringed, cardboard tags from Collier's outstretched hand.

"Rots of ruck, Buffalo Bill," Collier muttered through gritted teeth, straightening, he turned his back and walked quickly down the corridor toward building Four, anticipating the untold luxury of a hot shower and welcoming thoughts of slipping into around-the-clock unconsciousness.

Finally crawling between the sheets mid-morning Sunday, freshly-showered and scoured free from all the gore and grime, he nearly slept the clock around.

"Colonel Scroggs told me to report to you, Major," Collier said, as he saluted the weary-looking Major Smith in the Supply office on Monday morning, 13 July, after ravenously devouring a mountainous tray of breakfast. Astonishingly, both his duffel and his AWOL bag had been delivered to him by an enlisted man in a Jeep, and he was wearing socks without holes in them for a welcome change. Just as miraculously, if not more so, a package of three letters from Emma and one from his parents arrived simultaneously with the duffel. Emma's most recent letter dated June 30 stated that she had seen Jenny Bohon in the Mick-or-Mack in Salem and she said her last letter from Bo was dated June 21, and he was expecting to be leaving Korea any day.

"Good morning, Ramsay. I hope you're in better shape than when I saw you last. By the way, if I were you, I'd avoid any unnecessary confrontation with Rock Costigan. He's convinced you're the cause of his having to pull duty screening pre-ops. And, incidentally, the good news is that Rock just got shipping orders this morning. Now that Scroggs has officially assigned you to me as Costigan's replacement, he's packed and chomping at the bit, raring to head for Kimpo." Major Smith took the half-burned cigarette dangling from the corner of his mouth and knocked the ashes into an ashtray made from a cutoff artillery casing. "I've got all the papers to transfer his properties to you—shouldn't take but a minute or two."

"Whoa, Major. What kind of property inventories are we talking here? This sounds like a railroad job to me..." Collier looked at the rather daunting stack of papers in the Major's hand.

"Mostly motor pool—as my assistant, your main responsibility will be as Motor Officer. Those trucks and Jeeps out there will be all yours. You're about to become the most popular guy inside the compound." Major Smith looked up with a sly grin.

"I'm not sure I'm looking forward to that." Collier didn't bother to return the smile.

"Looking forward or not, let's get this fucking deal over with. I've got a Jeep and driver outside," Rock spoke up from behind him. The antsy lieutenant had entered without Collier knowing.

"Look, Lieutenant Costigan, I appreciate your wanting to get out of here, but if you expect me to sign for that Motor Pool without doing a vehicle-by-vehicle walk through, you've got another think coming." Collier turned and faced the blustering, red-faced Lieutenant. He fully appreciated the fact that Costigan had served a year here and deserved to leave for home, but he wasn't about to be pressured into signing for anything he couldn't validate. *Once your name is on the paper, it's your ass that is on the line.* Collier remembered quite well being taught in OCS not to sign for anything you couldn't see, touch, taste and/or shoot or drive.

"Look, Ramsay, just go ahead and sign. I'll vouch for it all being here. Besides we're officially still at war. What we can't locate, we'll write off as a combat loss." Major Smith slid the stack of papers and a pen across his desk toward Collier.

"I'm sorry, Major Smith, but if you're so certain about this inventory, then you sign for it now and I'll inventory it with you later today after Costigan is gone. I can sign for it then." Collier glanced over the several sheets of paper listing miscellaneous deuce-and-a-half trucks, three-quarter-ton weapons carriers, Jeeps, military ambulances and a number of other specialty vehicles, portable generators and various trailers the Major was trying to push off on him.

"Go ahead and sign, Smitty. I got a Jeep and driver outside waiting to take me to Kimpo. I got a flight to catch." Costigan brightened at Collier's suggestion, but Major Smith leaned across the desk and glared at Collier for having the ballsy-impertinence to question his word.

"Okay, okay...slide them back over here," the kindly major seemed much less kindly now as he reluctantly scrawled his name on the dotted lines of the several military inventory sheets.

"Thanks, Smitty. I'll send you a postcard," Rock came around the desk and gave the older man a hug before he bolted for the door.

"Charlie, get somebody in back to come mind the desk and you meet us outside. We're going to inventory the motor pool," the major gruffly ordered the corporal on the front desk. "Okay, Ramsay, come with me. Let's get this over with." The major snatched up the sheaf of papers and put them on a clipboard—clearly he was not a happy man.

At the motor pool, it quickly became evident there were more than a few glaring discrepancies to the inventory sheets which the Major duly noted, changing the numbers where appropriate. The process became quite drawn out when Collier insisted that the Motors sergeant produce the Trip Tickets for vehicles he assured Collier and Smitty were signed out by drivers and would be returned later in the day. By the time they had gotten three-quarters of the way through the long list of vehicles and miscellaneous equipment and taken a break for lunch, the Major, wilted by the oppressive heat and high humidity and somewhat chastised by the glaring discrepancies in the inventory—yet glad to finally be putting the bogus inventory right—had softened his attitude.

"Okay, gentlemen, that's enough for today. Let's save this final sheet for tomorrow. I have to go open the O Club or we'll have mutiny on our hands." With the shadows growing long and the tedious project clearly projecting they would have to return in the morning to finish up, the Major suggested they call a halt in the proceedings.

"Let me see that last page, Charlie." Collier took the clipboard from the major's clerk and gave it a cursory once-over to ascertain that other than ambulances and trucks the final sheet did not contain any significant items of equipment like choppers or aircraft. When he was satisfied there were no surprises on the final sheet, he handed back the clipboard and shrugged. "To hell with coming back tomorrow. I'll sign off when we get back to Supply."

"Good. I'm glad to get that over with," the Major smiled, visibly relieved. Walking back around in front of the hospital from the motor pool, as they approached Smitty's office in the Supply Room, the major waved Collier away, pointing up the hill to Quonset Row. "Go check your mail and wash up. Meet me down at the bar in about three-zero minutes. I'll buy us both a drink. As Assistant Supply Officer, you're now officially the Assistant Club Officer. Don't worry about the motor pool: if we run into any serious discrepancies, we can always survey them as war losses."

Back at The Broken Drum, the efficient houseboy, Cha, had made Collier's bed, leaving everything shipshape. Incredibly, Collier's fatigues from the previous day had been washed, ironed and were neatly folded on the metal chair beside his bunk. On his pillow, Collier found a set of freshly-laundered, sweet-smelling towels. Stripping to his Jockeys, Collier wrapped a towel around his waist, picked up another and stepped outside; then, suddenly aware he hadn't had a bowel movement in several days, he bypassed the shower building and went directly to the outhouse. Paying solemn tribute to the democratic principle that all men were created equal when it came to possessing assholes and being rather full of shit, the imposingly-long, eight-holer facility served both junior and senior officers equally.

Choosing a toilet-hole near the center of the insufferably hot enclosure, Collier placed his towels on the wide, bench-like platform and raised the lid and took a seat. Selecting a recent issue of *Life* magazine from the nearest stack of reasonably-current, stateside reading materials which were conveniently placed between the toilets to enrich the purely philosophical experience of a satisfying dump, Collier tuned out the incessant drone—of both propeller- and jet-driven aircraft landing with regularity across the Han at Kimpo—as he started thumbing the pages of a months-old issue of *McCalls* (most likely purloined from one of the nurse's huts) admiring the scantily clad, almost nude, pictures of young females in their underwear as he waited hopefully to begin the long-overdue process of evacuating his bowels.

He had been sitting there for perhaps ten minutes without significant results when Lieutenant Colonel "Walter" Reed, the new Assistant Eighth Army Surgeon fresh from stateside, walked in. Although he was officially second in command to the asshole Colonel Bailey in the Eight Army Compound back in Seoul, because he was a highly-qualified thoracic surgeon stateside, back at Brooke Army Hospital, Reed had managed to get himself billeted in the Chicken Coop with the 121st's field-grade officers out back of Quonset Row. A good-natured dude, he suffered the inevitable nickname "Walter" with good humor.

"Good evening, Ramsay. Mind if I join you?" The affable and distinguished career medical officer asked deferentially, clearly recognizing the democratic principles of nature.

"Please make yourself right at home, Colonel." Collier nodded respectfully, immediately resuming admiring the intellectually-uplifting ads for brassieres and panty-girdles.

"Thank you," the distinguished-looking colonel murmured as he selected a hole one space down from Collier, dropped his pants, raised the lid and promptly took a seat and cut loose one of the most sonorous farts, Collier could ever remember hearing.

"I beg your pardon." The dignified officer blushed a bright beet-red; then, befitting his exalted rank and station, he picked up a recent edition of *The New Yorker* magazine from the stack between them and began to engage in much the same intellectual pursuit as Collier.

Perhaps five minutes passed when—above the customary drone of air traffic—Collier's ears perked up as he became aware of what he strongly suspected was the putt-putt sound of an ancient biplane engine approaching from a distance, north over Seoul. Listening more intently now as the sound of the outmoded rotary cylinder engine grew closer, he stiffened as he heard the dull, but quite unmistakable, sound of a small explosion.

Beside Collier, the Colonel turned to face him as they both suspected the same conclusion.

"Bedcheck Charlie?" Collier asked.

"Bedcheck Charlie," Colonel Reed concurred, almost simultaneously.

Not particularly alarmed by the far-off sound of the old airplane—with the intermittent and somewhat muffled *Whump!... Whump!* of the hand-dropped, twenty-five-pound bombs—Collier and the Colonel exchanged largely-amused, however increasingly-frequent glances, as the sounds of the lone-eagle marauding antique biplane grew slowly closer.

WHOOMPH!

The loud, unexpected and alarmingly-forceful concussion blew open the lids on the surrounding six empty holes of the eight-holer outhouse, as Collier reflexively hit the concrete Johnny-house floor, buck naked, his Jockey briefs around his ankles.

After what seemed an indeterminable wait, but was probably not more than a minute at most, Collier listened while the "putt-putt" of the prop-driven airplane continued in the near-distance in the vicinity of Kimpo AFB, before it finally occurred to him what had really happened—one of the pilots from the new Sabrejet squadron across the river had been showing off, and the rather powerful, window-rattling, toilet-lid raising concussion had been the result of his having broken the sound barrier, a not infrequent occurrence in the area.

As the realization slowly dawned on him, Collier raised his head to find he was staring directly into the sheepish face of Colonel Reed who was spread-eagle on the floor directly opposite him with his pants bunched around his ankles.

Gathering his fatigue trousers about his thighs with his left hand, the dignified Colonel got up off the floor, resumed his seat on the eight-holer with studied decorum and went calmly back to studying the lingerie ads in *The New Yorker* magazine which had never left his hand.

Recalling the recent success of the two Navy F4U Corsairs in downing two Bedcheck Charlies on July third, just three days before he arrived in Korea, Collier, too resumed his position on the toilet as he listened with interest while a flight of prop-driven Mustang fighters took off from Kimpo and started buzzing the area, obstensibly in pursuit of the fading sound of Charlie. With the sounds finally fading, Collier's long-overdue bowels finally came to life and he lost interest in the air drama across the river. Mission accomplished at last, Collier put aside a particularly-engrossing illustration of a busty young thing in the latest undergarments, wiped his ass, pulled up his Jockeys and turned to head for the shower.

"Lieutenant, Ramsay." The dignified colonel looked up from his *New Yorker* as Collier prepared to leave.

"Yessir." Pausing in mid-stride, Collier looked back expectantly.

"If you don't tell anyone about this, you can certainly bet I won't." The distinguished surgeon's face was inscrutable.

"My lips are sealed, Colonel." Collier saluted smartly and left without another word.

CHAPTER FORTY-FOUR

The Roanoke World-News
Roanoke, Virginia, Wednesday, July 15, 1953
ALLIES HALT CHINESE DRIVE TO SMASH LINE
Curtain of Fire From Big Guns, Rain Stall Foe

SEOUL, Wednesday, July 15 (AP) – Rain, ROKs, and roaring big guns checked the raging Chinese offensive on the Korean East-Central Front today after it had smashed miles inside Allied territory.

By 3 p.m. (1 a.m., EST, Wednesday) it was apparent at U. S. Eighth Army Headquarters that the Communist drive on the 20-mile sector had stalled—at least for the moment.

STARS AND STRIPES

UNOFFICIAL PUBLICATION OF UNITED STATES FORCES, FAR EAST

Vol. 9, No. 207   Monday, July 27, 1953

TRUCE

SIGNED

FIGHTING ENDS TONIGHT
By S/Sgt. Bob McNeill

PANMUNJON, July 27 (Pac. S&S) – Truce delegates this morning quietly wound up their two years of peace-waging and rang down the curtain on the 37-month-old shooting war in Korea.

THE ROANOKE TIMES
Roanoke, Virginia, Monday, July 27, 1953
KOREAN TRUCE SIGNED
ARMISTICE SIGNED 10AM—CEASEFIRE 10PM

PANMUNJON, Monday, July 27 (AP) – UN Command and Communist senior truce delegates signed the long-awaited Korean armistice in a crisp 10-minute ceremony halting three years and one month of undeclared war..

GRANDMA COLLIER'S TRITE OLD SAYING, "It's always quietest just before the storm," was the last thing on Lieutenant Collier Boyd Ramsay's mind Tuesday morning, 14 July, as he slogged down the muddy street to attend officer's call, holding his poncho over his head to protect him from the seemingly-ceaseless monsoon. He had no way of knowing, by the dawn the following day, the adage, "It never rains but it pours" would have been infinitely more fitting as—to the complete surprise of everyone—the ambulances began arriving through the ceaseless downpour with wholesale numbers of wounded from the senseless firestorm of Chinese artillery (and mortars) taking place near the Iron Triangle and further east, around Chorwon near Heartbreak and Bloody Ridge.

Scarcely three days had passed since word had come down that the Eighth Army commander, General Matthew Taylor, had ordered 7th Infantry commander, General Arthur G. Trudeau, to abandon Pork Chop Hill during the daylight hours Saturday, 11 July. That news had come with mixed emotions from all sides. The bottom line, however, was with the truce so close at hand, it made no sense to sacrifice more good American lives for the purpose of salvaging a few-hundred yards of worthless real estate.

With this news fresh on their minds, there was a general air of relief among the 121st's officers sitting at Officer's Call in Colonel Scroggs' office when Chief of Surgery, Greenberg, reported the last of the backlog of seriously wounded from the recent flap on the Chop had finally been cleared. To everyone's gratification, well-over 150 American soldiers had been patched up and airlifted to Japan by the previous morning, 13 July, and things were more or less back to business-as-usual at the 121st, as all day long Tuesday, practically every radio in the compound was hopefully tuned to Far East Armed Forces Radio for news from nearby Panmunjom about the impending truce. Although there was no word a final resolution had been reached, by the end of duty hours that evening, there was a general atmosphere of celebration and congratulatory rounds of drinks all-around during the evening at the half a Quonset hut the 121st's officers affectionately referred to as the "Officers' Lounge." When Major Smith finally shooed everyone out of the club around midnight—bribing them to go quietly by giving one of the nurses complimentary fifths of both vodka and Scotch to make sure they had enough booze to continue the party—there was general agreement to continue the celebration at "The Hen Party," one of the five nurses' Quonset hut billets up on Quonset Row.

"Go ahead with the others. I'll close up here," Major Smith pushed Collier toward the door where the merrymakers were making a noisy exodus.

"I don't mind staying and helping you close, Smitty. I'm really not anxious to party," Collier countered sincerely; he'd had more than enough celebrating for one night.

"No. I'm serious. I want you to go with them—for awhile at least. I'm worried about Flood. He's been on the wagon for several months until tonight, and he's already had a few too many. I'd appreciate you going up there and seeing if you can get Mister Gray to talk Flood into laying off the booze for the rest of the night."

"Well...I don't know..." Collier had noticed Flood was feeling no pain, but recalling his nightmare experience with Herb Rudolph both in Dallas and back at

Lawton last June at the end of Basic still too deeply etched in his consciousness, he was not anxious to get involved with Flood, much less become further embroiled in what seemed destined to become an all-night drunk.

"Just for awhile, please. You'll being doing me...and Flood...a big favor. Just try to get Mister Gray involved—they're buddies. Gray has looked out for Flood many times in the past. Take this to the nurses; they'll need it before the night is over." The Major handed him a fifth of I.W. Harper bourbon and practically pushed him out the door.

By the time Collier arrived at The Hen Party, the record-player was blasting out Glenn Miller's *In the Mood*, loud enough to wake the dead, as the celebration was continuing full-swing. One of the more sober of the nursing contingent was already at the back door of the hut, trying to placate the Director of Nurses, Major Olsen. Finally, Olsen pushed her way into the center of the hut and got everyone's attention. "I'm giving you fair warning. If you don't get the noise down to a dull roar, you're going to wind up with Colonel Spaulding on one of his infamous Seventh-Day-Adventist warpaths, and nobody wants that to happen."

Apparently this argument struck a nerve. At the mention of Spaulding's name, the group quieted perceptibly.

After Major Olsen politely declined a chorus of invitations to join the party, the nurse to whom she had been talking went over and turned the volume on the phonograph down a few clicks, firmly explaining to the chorus of protesters, "I can assure you we don't want Colonel Spaulding walking through that door. The last time that happened, it took almost six months for him to relent and withdraw his ban on partying on Quonset Row."

"Here...do something with this." Collier handed the fifth of I.W. Harper to the nurse setting up a makeshift bar on a stack of three Army footlockers at the foot of the nearest bunk. Straightening up, Collier surveyed the interior of the Quonset hut filled with a kaleidoscopic blur of feminine undergarments drying on coat-hangers, hanging from nails and hooks and practically everything else a girl could find on which to hang a hanger. Walking in, he had brushed beneath and through a sensual gauntlet of these feminine unmentionables. The combination of the visual-tactile stimulus of the silken undies with the overwhelming sensuality of the permeating collective body scent of six nubile women melding with the aroma of god-only-knew how many various perfumes, produced the warning symptoms of an erection coming on if he didn't take immediate evasive action.

Wasting little time, Collier located WOJG Carl Gray. "Smitty's worried about Mister Flood. He asked me to ask you if you'd help me keep an eye on him."

"Look, I'm tired of playing nursemaid for Flood. I know what's going to happen. He's been behaving himself for too long. Tonight he's hell-bent on tying on a rip-snorting drunk."

"Well, that's what the Major is afraid of. He said we should try to get him to go sleep it off before it gets out of hand."

"It's already out of hand. Look, he's already in his 'lampshade phase.'"

"What do you mean 'lampshade phase'?" Collier was completely at a loss.

"When Flood approaches his limit, he starts putting lampshades and trashcans...even women's underwear on his head. See there, he's got a lampshade on his head right now." Gray pointed across the narrow room, and sure enough, Flood was carrying on a lively conversation with one of the heavy-featured nurses, modeling a frilly lampshade on his head. "C'mon. We need to move in closer. This is the beginning of the end and we don't want him to hurt himself."

"What do you mean 'hurt himself'?"

"I know the signs. Flood's going to fall flat on his face any second now." Gray grabbed Collier by the elbow and practically dragged him across to where Flood was playing Douglas Fairbanks, Jr., using a curtain rod as a sword. Before they could reach the well-oiled CWO, Collier watched in utter disbelief as Flood's eyes rolled back in his head. Then he stiffened and pitched face-forward onto the floor between two bunks like one of the granite steles at Stonehenge, out cold as an Eskimo's dick.

"My god, somebody help me. He may be hurt bad." Collier quickly dropped to his knees beside Flood's inert form. Judging from the impossible angle of the Chief Warrant Officer's right elbow jutting from beneath his limp torso, Collier was afraid what he would find. With one of the nurses to help him examine the fallen man, Collier was much relieved and totally flabbergasted to discover the CWO had sustained almost no discernible injuries.

"I can't believe it. He's got to be the luckiest SOB on earth." Collier breathed a big sigh of relief.

"You've got a lot to learn." The nurse beside him hiccupped. "Don't you know you can't hurt a drunk?"

"Come on, Gray; round up some help; let's get him out of here." Collier turned to Gray, standing over Flood looking down with disgust.

"Leave me the fugg alone..." Unexpectedly, Flood raised up on one elbow, suddenly alive again.

"You stay right where you are, Flood. Gray is going to help me get you to the hut and get you to bed." Collier firmly reassured the fallen alcoholic.

"You can go fuck yourself, Lieutenant, Sir. I'm going to stay right here. There's a party going on." Flood had pulled himself to his knees and was trying to stagger fully upright.

"Come on now, Mister Flood, give it up. You've had enough. You just passed out cold. It's time to call it quits." Collier twisted around, anxiously trying to find Gray to help him.

"There's nothing wrong with me. I fucking tripped. Now somebody get me another drink. VO and ginger..." The drunken warrant officer pulled himself up by grasping the edge of the bunk frame.

"C'mon, Flood, you've had enough..." Collier reached out to help him to his feet.

"Get your fuc...you're stinking hands off of me, Lieutenant." Flood violently jerked his arm from Collier's helping grasp.

"Okay, Mister Flood. I was just trying to help. I'll see you all in the morning." Collier stepped back, contemplating the situation. Recalling Herb Rudolph's drunken behavior in Dallas and Lawton, he was not about to be sucked into jousting windmills.

"Robert...I think you'd better listen to the lieutenant. It's getting late, and you've had enough to drink..." a nearby nurse offered friendly advice.

"Jesus...why doesn't everybody tend to their own business? I'm okay. The war's over, and I'm just trying to relax." Flood finally stood erect, brushing mostly-imaginary dust off of the front of his fatigues and angrily brushing aside Collier's outstretched hand.

"Have it your way..." Collier began, but let the overture of conciliation die on his lips as he stepped back and considered the impossibility of reasoning with a drunk.

Not wanting to leave the impression he was disgusted with the mounting general state of inebriation in the hut, Collier nodded pleasantly at various nurses and doctors then moved to the footlocker bar and mixed himself a light Vodka Collins. Drink in hand and looking for an early opportunity to leave, he moved to the fringe of a discussion between a group of docs and nurses and idly listened to snatches of conversation.

"I hear we admitted some Korean Hemorrhagic Fever this week..." a medical officer Collier couldn't recall having seen before was asking a nurse he also didn't recognize.

"We admitted five cases already. Apparently, now the Forty-eighth MASH is sending them all to us." The nurse carelessly stirred her drink with her finger. My god, Pewter was at the 48th.

"The literature now refers to it as Hantaan Virus. The concentration of cases occur up north in Hantaan River Valley, near the confluence of the Hant'an and Imjin rivers..." a second, slightly-effeminate physician near Collier spoke up. Collier vaguely recognized the man as having been in the OR during his nightmare marathon experience tending to the carnage from Pork Chop Hill.

"Hantaan smantaan mumbo jumbo. Call it anything you like, but it's Hemorrhagic Fever, pure and simple. You ought to see these patients bleed from the eyes, nose, mouth and around the fingernails," a hatchet-faced, slender, slightly-older nurse—with her hair pulled back in a bun like the woman in Grant Wood's painting *American Gothic*—sniffed and took a hefty swallow of the amber liquid in her glass.

"My nursing buddy up at the Forty-eighth MASH told me it starts like a bad case of the flu." The first nurse pulled her finger out of her drink, sucked it absently and stuck it back in again.

"It makes me nervous having something as scary as this so near the general population." The medical captain Collier had recognized from the OR spoke up as he unwrapped a cigar and licked it from end to end, finally swirling it in and out of his mouth. Watching the enjoyment on the young doctor's face, Collier made a firm resolve not to get caught in the shower alone with him.

"As far as the etiologists can determine, KHF is not airborne. There is no evidence...no pattern...of patient-to-patient spread." Colonel Reed, the Assistant to the Eighth Army Surgeon had sidled up beside Collier and was standing at his elbow.

"It's obviously viral. It won't grow anything when we smear it on an agar plate," Billy Graves, the bushy-blond handlebar-mustachioed tech from the lab, volunteered.

"What's the onset like?" a young nurse who had edged up on the far side of the group asked.

"Just like a bad case of flu. Severe malaise, weakness, prostration, fever, nausea—we're talking about severe retching and uncontrollable vomiting, food revulsion, difficulty in retaining even liquids...headaches, ocular problems with redness and severely-swollen eyelids..."—the American Gothic lookalike paused to drop her cigarette butt into a nearby empty cup, then continued her long-winded recitation—"...redness of the skin around the face, neck, and upper torso. These blotches are an external indication of far-more-serious, widespread, internal capillary leaks. Blood pressure can drop into the danger zone if the patient doesn't rally. That's usually the beginning of the end. There is a profuse and bloody outpouring of urine in the terminal phase." American Gothic finished her recitation of the symptoms and bummed a cigarette from the nurse beside her.

"Early recognition and hospitalization is tantamount to recover. Danger of secondary bacterial infection is high because of the patient's overall debilitation." Doctor Reed added his two-cents-worth.

"Anybody worth their stethoscope can tell this nightmare isn't just the ordinary flu." The first nurse pulled her finger out of her glass and sucked it again.

"Are we talking epidemic here?" An anonymous male voice spoke up from the far side of the circle.

"There were eight-hundred-twenty-seven cases year before last in fifty-one. Eight-fifty-five last year. So far this year, we've reported slightly less than a hundred cases, but, historically the peak months are October through December when the Korean winter sets in." Apparently Billy Graves was the resident epidemiologist, too.

Bothered by the vivid descriptions of an exotic indigenous disease he had never heard of which was now being treated just across the street in the Isolation Unit, Collier turned away. Glancing at his watch, he was surprised to see it was already 0122 hours. There were going to be a bunch of hung-over nurses and doctors, not to mention several frazzled administrative officers—most likely including himself—when the sun came up in less than five hours. Hastily draining his drink, he politely elbowed his way through the crowd, heading directly for the door.

"Do you have to leave, Lieutenant? The party's hardly started," a faintly equine-faced nurse, who would have benefited significantly by wearing two-size-larger fatigues to cover her ballooning corpulence, followed him into the improvised separate entrance foyer. She gave a meaningful coy glance at Greenberg, the Chief of Surgery, and an OR nurse snuggling in a dark corner, the doctor's skilled hands deftly unbuttoning the blouse of the nurse's fatigues. The plain, gold wedding band on the Chief of Surgery's busy left hand caught the light from the single electric bulb hanging just inside the door.

The heavily-perfumed essence of the nurse who had followed him out of the party was beginning to reactivate Collier's earlier stirrings of a hard-on, and he was sorely tempted to give in to her invitation—unless he grossly misinterpreted all the signs, her body language told him she was fairly dying to have him, or any available hard dick, to fuck her flat.

"Yeah. I'm sorry, but I gotta go. I'm beat. Tomorrow's going to be another killer day, and I've got more work than I can handle." Collier apologized, located his still-dripping poncho and danced quickly out the door. It was hard enough just trying to do his duty and keep his wits about him without having some silly wallflower from Fargo, North—or was it South?—Dakota, hanging around, tugging his sleeve, expecting him to scratch her itching libido every time he turned around.

Without so much as "good-night" and without looking back, Collier pulled his poncho over his head and took off at a dogtrot into the never-ending monsoon which had started up full-force again, hellbent for the door to The Broken Drum about fifty yards up the muddy street. Safely inside, he shook the rain off the poncho, pushed through the curtains and made his way back to the sanctuary of his bunk. Wasting little time, he stripped out of his damp fatigues and climbed into bed. Plumping his pillow with his fist, he closed his eyes and tried to shut out the world.

No use! He snorted silently in disgust after at least thirty minutes of trying to drift off to sleep, unable to ignore the throbbing erection which had sprung to life a tempting few doors back up the godforsaken, muddy street.

Over time, slowly but surely, his erection subsided as the erotic images of silken lingerie segued back to the chilling details of the discussion of the outbreak of Korean Hemorrhagic Fever. Lying there in the dark, the horrors of the insidious disease began to take charge of his overactive imagination. His throat really had been feeling scratchy all day; Collier's stomach clenched with fear, and he felt himself breaking into a cold sweat as images of bloody eyeballs and gore-oozing fingernails danced behind his swollen eyelids. Finally, somewhere between images of his corpse-like body being carried to the morgue still alive and being slid into a cremating furnace, he slipped into an uneasy sleep.

The fear-filled dream unfolded behind Collier's tightly-clenched eyelids in slow motion like the Daliesque sequences from the Hitchcock film, *Spellbound.* In his nightmare, he was back up on Brinson's finger on Pork Chop Hill, fighting a horde of Gooks as they came swarming down the steep escarpment like ants in the greenish-darkness. Just as he was about to squeeze off the shot killing the closest Chink, his carbine jammed and the weapon metamorphosed in his hands into one of the bloody amputated arms he had seen stacked on the bloody sheet in a corner of the OR. He had just begun swinging the amputated limb at the horde of greenish Gooks when the dream again metamorphosed. Now he was in a hospital ward looking into a cracked mirror at his own image, blood oozing from his eyeballs, nose, ears, mouth and fingernails.

"Huh!" Collier came awake with a start—trembling from the horror of the all-too-realistic nightmare. When his agitation finally subsided, feeling altogether foolish, he fumbled in the darkness until he located his tiny, battery-operated penlight on the make-do bedside lamp table and examined his face and fingernails in the small shaving mirror from his toilet kit.

Nothing. No open sores, no rash. Normal as blueberry pie. He breathed a sigh. The freaking dream had seemed all too believable. He had to get a grip.

Still trembling, he turned out the light and pulled the covers back beneath his chin.

Lying in the dark, his throat really did feel a little scratchy. Just before sleep took him again, he sheepishly resolved to keep a close eye on his symptoms—a man couldn't be too careful. It would be the final irony that his obituary in *The Roanoke Times* would state he had died of some embarrassing disease rather than the stupid war.

"Wake up, Ramsay. The shit has hit the fan again. The fucking Gook artillery and mortars are apparently preparing for another assault, this time somewhere near Chorwon—they have been pounding the area around the Punchbowl with everything they've got . The Forty-sixth MASH just called, and they're dispatching a regular circus parade of ambulances filled with seriously wounded. Major Smith wants you in Supply. We need all hands on duty when the wounded arrive." Collier rudely awoke to the shadowy form of Lieutenant Chuck Lohr—the longsuffering Adjutant still waiting for a much-overdue replacement to free him for rotation home—standing over him. In the dark,

Collier's watch glowed 0448. Grudgingly, but without complaint, he climbed out of bed and began pulling on his fatigues.

Another night without adequate rest...sooner or later, there had to be a freaking end to this. Although it was bad enough with a steady stream of choppers and ambulances arriving all morning long, this time, the carnage from the senseless—nonetheless costly and relentless—last-ditch Chink artillery conflagration in the northeastern sector around Chorwon, Heartbreak Ridge and the Punch Bowl thankfully proved to be somewhat less than the previous week's flap at Pork Chop Hill.

"Greenberg needs endotrachial tubes in the OR. A Navy nurse, Captain Rose Tibideaux, is waiting at the chopper strip to escort you to the USS Repose anchored in Inchon Harbor. They're going to lend us some tubes and other stuff. Get over there and get back here as quickly as you can—lives are depending on you." Smitty pushed Collier out the door sometime just after daylight.

"Hop in. I'm Rose Tibideaux from the Repose. This is Chief Warrant Officer Yates." At the chopper strip, Collier found a surprisingly-pretty Navy Lieutenant Junior Grade—the equivalent of an Army First Lieutenant—with her unblemished, snow-white Navy uniform setting off her light-chocolate-colored skin, waiting with CWO Yates in the same chopper that had rescued him from the finger of Pork Chop a week ago.

"Pleased to meet you, Lieutenant Tibideaux. Mister Yates and I already know each other." Collier shook the attractive nurse's hand and shot Yates a wide grin as he climbed into the chopper and strapped himself in.

Collier had surveyed the village of Daibongdong and the surrounding area from the bombed-out shell of the third story of Building Four one morning several days back, and he vaguely remembered flying back across the Han River the night Yates rescued him from the Chop, but that had been at night and in the driving rain. Now, in broad daylight, he watched, fascinated, as the chopper quickly rose almost vertically to perhaps 500 feet and the countryside unfolded swiftly below him as they struck out WNW toward Yongdongpo and Inchon with Kimpo's network of runways spreading out just across the wide-trickle of the Han.

It seemed they had scarcely gotten airborne when the outskirts of Inchon loomed ahead with the mudflats of the infamous harbor stretching before them in the distance.

"There she is. We just got back from Japan. We're already loaded almost to capacity—we can carry seven-hundred-fifty wounded if we jam them to her gunwales, but we've already taken on almost five-hundred from this latest flap, and it looks like we've got the worst of it behind us. The young nurse nudged him with her elbow, proudly pointing out through the forward windshield of the bubble canopy. At the mouth of the harbor, sitting right on the periphery of the mudflats, Collier could see the superstructure with the red cross emblem on the white-painted sides of the USS Repose. "We're going to sail as soon as we take on another hundred or so. We take them to Japan and come right back again...takes a little over a week if we are in a hurry to get back here. We were just outfitted with the new helicopter pad back in March...makes a world of difference now we don't have to wait on tides and boats."

Collier watched with his hands tightly clenched on the sides of the seat as Yates lowered their whirlybird as softly as a dandelion parachute onto the white- and red-painted chopper pad.

"Come on in and I'll show you around," the overeager nurse invited as soon as they were solidly on the deck.

"Thanks, but give me a raincheck. I need to get those tubes back to Greenberg as fast as I can." Collier reminded the well-meaning nurse.

"Of course. When we get back from Japan, I'll come over and get you. You can have dinner aboard and spend the night. We know how to show you a good time," she said, not at all aware her casually-chosen words might be misunderstood.

"Sounds good to me. Now, let's go find those endotrachial tubes." Collier prodded gently.

"I don't think we'll have to go looking. Here comes Lieutenant Commander Rowe, our Exec now—looks like he already has what we came for." Looking in the direction she was pointing, Collier saw a white-uniformed officer approaching across the pad with a rather large bundle wrapped in snow-white linen, apparently fresh from the autoclave.

"Tell Greenberg to keep these. I have enough for this trip, and we'll get some more in a few days when we dock in Japan." The efficient-looking officer ducked under the idling chopper blades and handed the bundle through the opening in the Plexiglas canopy.

"Thanks, I'll tell him. I hate to have to beg and run, but we really need this stuff back at the One-two-one...I know you understand." Accepting the rather large bundle as soon as the officer stuck his head into the bubble cockpit, Collier nodded and motioned the Navy nurse back from the idling blades of the whirlybird.

"Let's get out of here." Collier told Yates as soon as both doctor and nurse had cleared the chopper pad.

"Lucky you went to Inchon. The Eighth Army G-Three came looking for a thousand-gallon, water tanker truck while you were gone." Smitty casually remarked when Collier came back to Supply after delivering the endotrachial tubes to the OR.

"What's that got to do with me?" Collier asked, confused.

"Since Rock Costage left, you're Motors Officer, remember?" Smitty said, looking up from a stack of paperwork.

"I don't remember seeing anything resembling a water tanker truck." Collier said, trying to recall his walk-through inventory of the Motor Pool.

"I don't guess you do. We don't have anything remotely like it here." The Major pulled out his Zippo, trying to light his well-chewed cigar stump. The Zippo had a fancy, engraved Sterling silver case similar to the one Collier had bought in the PX at Camp Drake.

"I don't get it. Why is it good I wasn't here?"

"You signed for it. As far as Eighth Army G-Three, you are the proud owner of a one-thousand-gallon water truck." Smitty shrugged.

"No shit! There must be some mistake. I never signed for anything like that." Before the protest had barely escaped his lips, Collier felt a sinking feeling in his gut, recalling that in the press of other business, he had signed the final sheet of the Motor Pool inventory without giving it a close examination.

"You signed alright. I found it right here in the file. You'll find it right on top, if you care to take a look?" Smitty picked up a folder, extending it in Collier's direction.

GMC M222 Truck, Water Tank, 2 ½ ton, 6x6 (TM 9-8024). It was there alright, plain as day. And his own signature jumped out at him from the bottom of the page.

Judaspriest! He'd be a long time dead before he ever finished paying for a piece of equipment like that at inflated Army prices—the Pentagon was notorious for the exorbitant prices they paid military contractors, an outrageously-irresponsible exercise of the "Good-old-boy System."

"Did you tell him I signed for that without having time to complete my inventory? My god, Smitty, there must be some way to get out of this." Collier's mouth was so dry he had trouble speaking.

"Don't sweat it. That Water Tanker has been missing since way before I was here. A long succession of incoming new Motor Officers kept on signing for it, resolving to survey it off the books as a 'combat loss,' but, ironically, in the press of combat, no one has ever gotten around to it. That's probably why the G-Three was here today. He's a short-timer. My guess is he's just covering his own ass as best as he can. That water truck is most likely low on his list of things to worry about. Besides, I took him down to the club and bought him a drink—two or three as a matter of fact. I doubt we'll see him back here again." The Major winked a sly wink.

In his dream that night, Collier was before a court martial trying to explain how he lost an entire factory-assembly-line of GMC water-tanker trucks; then the dream abruptly changed to the setting of a military prison where he was swinging a sledge hammer, busting up large rocks. Mercifully, he woke with a start and spent the rest of the night in dreamless slumber.

Still, the first thing next morning, he grabbed the inventory sheet listing the 1000-gal GMC M222 and headed for the Motor Pool to make sure the other items on the sheet were present or accounted for.

"Lieutenant Ramsay, Major Olsen says for you to come to Recovery. There's a patient who's asking for you," a surgical tech stuck his head inside the Supply Room office door, mid-morning Thursday, 16 July. After two days of the nightmarish firestorm in preparation for the totally-uncalled-for and completely-senseless Commie push in the northeastern sector, there had been little let-up in the constant flow of wounded coming in on a seemingly-endless stream of ambulances and choppers from the front.

"You sent for me?" Collier asked, a trifle out of breath from running up the long, spidery flight of stairs between Building One and Two. Major Olsen was waiting just outside the Recovery room.

"Come in here." She nodded toward Recovery. "There's a young sergeant came in here by chopper last night who's been asking for you. Says a friend of yours was wounded two days ago near Heartbreak Ridge." Major Olsen led him inside Recovery to a bed where a soldier with both legs in casts was sitting up, trying to take nourishment from a ward attendant.

"This is Lieutenant Ramsay, Sergeant Miles," Olsen introduced him and stepped aside.

"Good to meet you, Sergeant. Sorry it has to be under these circumstances..." Collier offered lamely, not at all sure what this was all about.

"It could be worse, Lieutenant." The young sergeant essayed a wan smile. "Bo Bohon, a friend of yours, is in my outfit. Bohon and me was buddies. We landed at Inchon together and was assigned the Eight-two-one-niner Army Unit, a free-floating metero unit with the Second Division. He was hit same day as me—

Tuesday, July Fourteen—up on Heartbreak. Actually, he was wounded twice. The fucking..."—the sergeant blushed, pausing when he remembered Major Olsen was standing there—"'Scuse me, Ma'am..."—he continued, finding a more polite adjective—"...the freaking Gooks started cutting loose with every mortar and artillery piece they had...on the eighth—last Wednesday. They was hitting us with about a thousand rounds every six hours. Bohon took a bunch of small-fragment hits all over with shrapnel, mainly in his arms and hand. They had us surrounded so we couldn't get him out—couldn't none of us get out—so we had to let him lie on the litter waiting for the Infantry to break us out. Then, he got hit again really bad on Tuesday the fourteenth. His right arm was blown almost clean off. It would take a miracle to save that arm. Somebody lifted him like a baby and put him on the front seat of a truck and we got him off that hill. They zipped him in a body bag and strapped him on a chopper. Last I saw of him, that chopper was hightailing at treetop level for the Forty-sixth MASH. I hate to be the one to give you such bad news, but I thought you'd want to know." The sergeant stopped talking and let the attendant adjust his pillow.

"I really appreciate it. I'll try to get through to the Forty-sixth right away and see about him. If I find out anything, and you're still here, I'll let you know." Collier squeezed the Sergeant's hand, but got no response—he was already fast asleep.

"Bayonet...ring me through to Bandit..." Collier went straight back to Supply and started in the long, frustrating process of going through a countless series of exchanges of the primitive military telephone system to reach the 46th MASH.

"This is the Forty-sixth MASH. How can we help you?" Eventually, a male voice answered loud and fairly clear, considering the static on the rudimentary military telephone network.

"This is Lieutenant Collier Ramsay at the One-two-one Evac. I need to check on a patient who was evacuated by chopper from Heartbreak Ridge on Tuesday..." Collier started in and asked for information about Bo's condition.

"Wait one, and I'll transfer you to Receiving..." the switchboard operator at the 46th MASH answered and began ringing him through.

"Yeah...we started him on plasma and put him on a plane out of K-Thirty-eight to Osaka. He was alive, but I don't have much hope for that right arm. We stopped the bleeding and he still had what was left of the pieces when he left here. They gave him a Purple Heart, but I don't know what good they think that will do him in the shape he was in. It would take more than all the king's horses to put that Humpty-Dumpty arm back together again, if you get my drift." The war-weary female voice on the other end of the line searched desperately to find humor in the macabre.

"Do you mean he won't make it?" Collier asked, afraid to hear the answer.

"Oh, no, I don't mean any such thing. If we get 'em here still breathing, there's better than a ninety percent chance they'll make it back home alive." The fiercely proud voice fired back before she hung up, insulted he had the temerity to suggest such a thing.

All day long, Collier agonized over the news about Bo, with Osaka out of touch by phone or radio except through high command outlets at HQ in Seoul—which was clearly out of the question—there was no way to get further news of Bo's fate. There was nothing left to do but write Emma the distressing news and have her call Jenny to find out how he was doing—a wholly unsatisfactory course of action, since, from all reports, Bo could already be dead. As soon as he got off duty and showered, Collier sat down and, with more than a little trepidation, wrote Emma a long-overdue letter, bringing her up to date, including the distressing news of Bo's wounding.

Catching a late supper, Collier arrived in the crowded Quonset lounge filled with overworked, nearly-exhausted doctors and nurses reeling from several days of dealing with the unspeakable horrors of the entirely spurious, non-stop Gook artillery barrages and various senseless infantry assaults in the northeast sector, apparently trying to push the line further south before the truce was signed. From the buzz of alcohol-fueled conviviality and the vacant stares in their eyes, the denizens of the One-two-one were just beginning to achieve their customary off-duty state of alcoholic nirvana.

Captain Donovan—"Wild Bill" as he was called behind his back—the CO of the hospital complement, buttonholed Collier as he approached the bar.

"I thought you might want to know Scroggs submitted a commendation today for your heroics up on Pork Chop. And he put through all of the papers for your promotion to First Lieutenant. Also, your file arrived from Japan. I'm impressed, Lieutenant. You have straight 'sixes' on your efficiency reports."— Collier was surprised; an efficiency rating of six represented exemplary performance of duty and was highly unusual—"Has it ever occurred to you to go Regular Army? Reserve or RA either way, you'll be stuck here for a year. You're already twenty-four. You'll be twenty-six by the time your three-year commitment is up. The truce is going to be signed any day now. You're married and have a kid back home. Regular Army is a fine career. You could go RA, do your year in Korea, then volunteer for Japan and have your wife and kid sent over if you sign on for a two-year tour. Your wife would enjoy living in Japan with a houseboy, a maid, a nanny and a gardener. She'd live like a queen. Just in case you want to think it over, I brought you these." Donovan handed him an envelope containing the application papers for Regular Army Commission.

"Thanks for telling me about the commendation. I really didn't expect it. I've already submitted a recommendation for the DSC for the chopper pilot Yates. And thanks for the word on my Efficiency Reports. And thanks for the vote of confidence, Captain Donovan. I've already given some thought to going RA. You're right. It's not a bad life. I could do a lot worse in civilian life." Collier nodded. "I'll look these over and give it serious thought tonight. But I've had a hell of a day, and that's too much to think about right now. Right now, what I need most is a stiff drink."

"Okay, but don't put this off. You've just had a commendation for bravery; the timing will never be better. C'mon, I'll buy you that drink." Donovan steered him to the bar.

"Thanks for the endotrachial tubes today. What did you think of the USS Repose?" Collier had just gotten a drink in hand when Greenberg approached with a word of appreciation.

"To tell the truth, I didn't have time to take a look. But Lieutenant Tibideaux invited me back for a visit if things ever get back to our customary SNAFU around here again," Collier replied, remembering the shapely, coffee-skinned Florence Nightingale in Navy whites.

"Oh? You're not looking to change your luck?" Greenberg stepped back a half-step, flashing a lascivious grin.

"Change my luck?" Collier knew full-well what the Chief of Surgery was driving at, but had no intention of dignifying such abhorrent sexual and racial intimations.

"Don't play dumb. I know what you southern boys say about coon-ass." Greenberg winked.

"Coon-ass?" Collier had heard the expression before and had a vague recollection it had something to do with colored people—something related to Cajuns or New Orleans. He seemed to remember hearing the term in 1948 when he and Jim had gone to New Orleans to see the Sugar Bowl game.

"Come on, Ramsay, don't try to play dumb with me. You're not blind are you? Tibideaux is colored—what you Virginia boys call a high yellow. She's from some bayou around New Orleans. Cajun folk call 'em coon-ass down there." Greenberg's grin twisted into an ugly sneer.

"Well, that's interesting. Red, white and blue or purple polka dots, she's a damn fine-looking woman," Collier said without further comment and prepared to walk away. Such blatant bigotry and lewd sexual innuendoes from this superior officer made him extremely uncomfortable. It was particularly troubling to hear this trashy talk coming from such a talented surgeon—and a Harvard man at that.

"Did you ever see such a fine, calypgian ass." Greenberg leered.

"Calypgian? I'm afraid I'm not following you, Captain," Collier said, not anxious to pursue the conversation. He searched the room, desperately looking for somebody to rescue him.

"Calypgian. You know...the peculiar low curve of the spine resulting in that peculiar high shelf formed at the top of the buttocks. You see it mostly in nigger bitches from the West Indies. My roommate at Harvard was from Jamaica—he educated me about those hot-blooded, high-assed bitches. Looks like those fancy, white-uniformed SOBs in the U.S. Navy have lowered their professional standards. Well, like I said, Lieutenant, you're fixing to change your luck." Greenberg laughed a nasty laugh.

"I'm sure the Major is only kidding. I'm married and have an infant son back home." Collier tried to cut the arrogant Chief of Surgery dead. He had seen him at several parties in the nursing quarters making out with one of his scrub nurses.

"War is hell, Lieutenant. All the rules are suspended over here. Eat, drink and be merry for tomorrow you may die." With his lip curved in an ugly sneer, Greenberg raised his nearly-empty glass and elbowed his way back toward the bar.

"Hey, Lieutenant, have the iron lungs gotten here yet?" from across the crowded room, Major Hughes, the Chief of Medicine, called to Collier who was edging away from Greenberg, trying to put as much distance as he could between himself and the disgusting Chief of Surgery.

"What iron lungs? First I've heard of it. I just got back from borrowing endotracheal tubes from the Repose." Collier looked to Smitty behind the bar, hoping he could clue him in.

"We admitted two cases of polio this morning from over in the eastern sector, and the pipeline has it we will be getting another one before the shift changes tonight. Both our cases are showing signs of becoming bulbar. Major Olsen and I are holding an Inservice on Polio...with particular reference to bulbar...over in the dining room in exactly fifteen minutes, if you care to sit in. I recommend you attend. The Eighth Army Surgeon's office tells me there was a minor epidemic last summer. Looks like we may be about to have another one on our hands. Seems like the indigenous population is pretty much immune—most likely because they have traditionally fertilized their agriculture with human feces since before written history and have undergone some sort of self-inoculation. Anyway, this particular strain of the virus is quite virulent to our troops and seems to go quickly into the bulbar form of the disease. We're trying to round up all the iron lungs we can find. How are we doing with that, Smitty?" Hughes turned to Major Smith who had come out from behind the bar.

"The two lungs from the Eleventh Evac should be here any minute. We've located two more in Osaka and have 'em on standby to be flown over at a moment's notice—I'm just waiting for Major Olsen to give the go-ahead." The serious-faced Supply Officer replied.

"I'd like to sit in on the Polio Inservice if it's okay with you, Smitty," Collier asked.

"Sure thing. I'm going, too. I have a feeling we could be in for a rough time. Go ahead, Major, lead the way." Smitty turned back to Hughes and pointed to the door leading across the enclosed breezeway to the dining room.

"I'm sure word is out that we admitted two cases of polio today. Judging from the history of the minor epidemic which started about this same time last summer, the Korean strain of polio is a particular virulent strain to our military—with an unusually high percent of the cases going quickly into the bulbar form." Major Hughes began the Inservice lecture and continued, "Bulbar polio occurs when the polio virus infiltrates nerves within the bulbar region of the brain stem."—he had sketched a remarkably good diagram of the brain on the blackboard and pointed to the brain stem at the top of the spinal column at the base of the brain—"Thankfully, in the normal population in the U.S., bulbar polio comprises only about two percent of cases of paralytic polio..."

Collier sat on the edge of his seat in rapt attention as Hughes explained how the cerebral cortex is connected to the brain stem and how the destruction of these nerves weakens the muscles supplied by the cranial nerves—particularly the Glossopharyngeal Nerve which partially controls swallowing and functions in the throat, tongue movement and taste. Also vulnerable is the Vagus Nerve which sends signals to the heart, intestines, and lungs—and the Accessory Nerve which controls upper neck movement.

"So you see, with the adverse effect on swallowing, secretions of mucus can build up in the airway causing suffocation..." Hughes droned on, listing more serious, but not exactly life-threatening sequelae including facial weakness caused by destruction of the trigeminal nerve and facial nerve. "Among other things, the Trigeminal Nerve innervates the cheeks, tear ducts, gums, and muscles of the face, and its impairment results in double vision, difficulty in chewing, and abnormal respiratory rate, depth, and rhythm—which may lead to respiratory arrest." Hughes paused dramatically to see if he were impressing the group with the seriousness of the situation before he delivered the final summation. "Pulmonary edema and shock are also possible, and may be fatal. Any questions?"

"When will the iron lungs get here?" A momentary pregnant silence was followed by a steady buzz of anxious questions from the group.

The Poliomyelitis Inservice session proved to be the "quiet before the storm" as, slowly-but-surely, the number of admissions with polio started to build. Before the beginning of the following week, the first Polio patient—a young Marine lieutenant from Virginia near Roanoke—quickly worsened into bulbar complications and died before the staff could get the iron lungs into operation. During this period, suspected Polio patients had been moved from a regular ward in Building Three into Building Four to a newly-established Isolation Unit across the corridor from the KHF Isolation Unit in preparation for the fast-developing outbreak.

Suddenly the One-two-one was faced with not only the KHF outbreak, but also threatened with a full-scaled epidemic of bulbar polio. By the time the staff—including Collier and Major Smith—were trained to operate and maintain the initial pair of iron lungs, the two remaining iron lungs on Korean soil were already on their way and four more had been rounded up and were being flown into Kimpo from Osaka.

It was at this precarious juncture the following week on Wednesday, 22 July, the Korean electricity began acting up and for several days and nights on end, the nursing staff, including Collier—and even Major Smith—were constantly being summoned from their appointed duties or rousted out of a sound sleep to rush up to the Polio Isolation unit to hand-operate the iron lungs until the Korean electricity blinked back on again.

Finally, on Friday, 24 July, two days before truce would finally be signed, the Korean power source in Seoul seemed to right itself, and, after duty hours, Collier went to the O-Club bar and had a double Rum Collins before he sat down to a satisfactory dinner, then trudged off up the hill to shower and get some much-needed rest. But, running so long on the raw-nerved edge of exhaustion, sleep wouldn't come.

Lying alone in the darkness of The Broken Drum, his heartbeat and breathing increased and he became sharply aware he was experiencing some scratchiness of his throat with an attending stiffness of his neck.

Polio? Lying frozen with fear he was suddenly seized by the sensation that his eye sockets were swollen and his body was beginning to itch.

KHF!

Finally, after what seemed a lifetime, but was probably less than a minute, he crawled out of bed, turned on the light and looked into the mirror.

No rash. No edematous eyeballs. No physical anomalies that he could see.

Too early to show symptoms, he reasoned, arguing with himself that he should go find Major Hughes and report his desperate situation before it was too late and he endangered other vulnerable, innocent members of the staff.

Lying there numb with terror and debating a course of action, he drifted back to sleep.

Saturday morning, Collier awoke at the sound of roosters crowing in the village across the fence. Terrified by what he might see, he got out of bed and quickly examined himself in the mirror. No bleeding from the eyeballs...or fingernails! No blotchy skin. He breathed a sigh of relief that—despite a lingering scratchiness of the throat and a slight stiffness of his neck—he apparently was as healthy as that damn-fool chicken across the barbwire fence.

"Collier, thank goodness. I hoped I'd find you here. The opportunity came up so fast I had no way to let you know I was coming. It's great to see you again." Shortly after 0800, Collier had just returned from his ritual checking of the outside light bulbs and had reported to Scroggs that he could tell Colonel Spaulding all 222 were in good working order, when he looked up from his desk and saw Ginger Lipscomb standing there big as life.

"My god, Ginger, what on earth are you doing here?" The apparition of the lovely redhead standing in front of him in Army battle fatigue uniform left him almost speechless.

"Ever since I missed spending time with you in Tokyo, I've been kicking myself. An opportunity came up last night to hitch a ride over with a nurse friend who was delivering a shipment of two iron lungs and I jumped at the chance. What time do you get off duty? I have to fly back tomorrow before noon. I had to switch weekends off with another nurse." She looked doubtfully around at the virtually-deserted administrative offices. In one of the divided glassed-in cubicles off the entrance foyer, Master Sergeant Henderson was briefing Otis Owen about Colonel Spaulding's latest suggestions for the fireplace project in the officers' mess. Behind him, seated behind the massive desk in his office guarding Spaulding's inner sanctum, Harold Scroggs was the only other officer personnel present on Saturday morning.

"I'm not actually *on* duty—as Adjutant, I'm never really *off* duty. I'll ask my Exec, he's in his office now." Collier peered in at Scroggs with a hopeful look.

"If you don't have to pull AOD, you can take the weekend. I'll see you at Officers' Call Monday." Scroggs had been eavesdropping and spoke up before Collier could make a formal request. He smiled out at Ginger, acknowledging her arrival with a casual wave.

"Thank you, Sir." Collier replied, turning back to Ginger with a smile.

"Is there any way we could find someplace where we can be alone...to...talk?" She looked doubtfully around, obviously hoping to find a place where they could find some semblance of privacy.

"Well...I..." He wracked his brain trying to come up with a place. Other than retreating to the tiny anteroom at The Broken Drum, he had never thought about a need for any kind of privacy before. That could hardly be considered private, since his bunkmates were constantly coming in and out in a steady stream. Almost any unoccupied room where they could be alone would do. Although over the years he often fantasized ravishing Ginger Lipscomb, Collier was certain Emma's classmate from their nurse's training days at Lewis-Gale had no romantic interest in him.

"Begging your pardon, Lieutenant, I keep a small house in the village you can use. Nobody would bother you there," Sergeant Owens spoke up.

"Ah...that's very nice of you, Sergeant...I ah?..." Officially the village was off limits to the 121st's personnel, an order which was widely ignored by both officers and enlisted men. Only the nurses avoided going there for obvious reasons relating to the fact a significant number of the 121st's males were actually rumored—with just cause—to maintain houses for Korean sweethearts they kept there.

Collier snuck a peek over his shoulder to see if Scroggs had overheard and saw the Exec had discreetly closed his door.

"Okay, Sergeant. We'll take you up on your offer. How do we find this place?" Collier turned back to Owens.

"I need to go give my Korean labor force their work orders. I'll meet you at the gate in ten minutes, if that's alright with you. I promise I won't keep you waiting long." Otis turned and headed out the door.

"Come walk with me, I want to pick up my kit with my toothbrush before we leave. You can get a quick look at our hospital along the way." Collier picked up Ginger's oversized purse—a copy of a western saddlebag in OD canvas—and steered her out the door and up the steps toward Building Two. After they had made their way up through all four buildings and Collier had picked up his toilet kit and stuffed it in his AWOL bag, he guided her down the back way to the gate just as Otis Owens was coming up the street in front of the main building.

Collier was pleasantly surprised to discover the sergeant's house was just inside the outer boundary of the village, less than fifty yards across the main Suwon highway.

"There's sandwich stuff from the hospital mess in this ice box—and also beer. And, there's plenty of liquor in this cabinet. Help yourself. There are toilet facilities and a place to wash up behind that screen. If you need anything else, just ring this bell. My moose will be near at hand to get you most anything you need." Obviously impressed by Ginger—usually toothless except when in the presence of visiting brass or facing close scrutiny from stuffy superior officers like Colonels Scroggs and Spaulding, the crusty Sergeant displayed his full set of sparkling GI dentures—Owens quickly left Collier and Ginger sitting on the doorstep loosening the laces on their combat boots before they entered his well-cared-for house.

With its Japanese-influenced *titami* (rice mat) floor covering, the tiny Korean house was scrupulously clean. Except for the ice box and liquor cabinet and a low table—and the ubiquitous large mattress-like sleeping *futon* resting on the *titami* surface near the center of the room—there were no other furnishings in the tiny house. A large decorated Oriental screen hid the areas Collier assumed held rudimentary toilet facilities. Across the room was a second screen which he imagined screened off the simple kitchen area which usually consisted of a cutting board and a small charcoal-fired Japanese hibachi grill. Vaguely, Collier understood that influenced by the half-century-long occupation and enslavement by the Japanese, the architecture and furnishings were steeped in traditions which went back before written history.

"Come here, I'm fairly dying for a hug..." Ginger stepped close, wrapped her arms around him, and pasted the entire length of her body close against his as soon as they were alone. The thin cotton fabric of her summer fatigues did practically nothing to moderate the unnerving impact of her solid breasts and her lower pubic area pushing against him. When she finally eased her enthusiastic embrace, she leaned her head back then kissed him fiercely on the mouth. Her lips were slightly parted, but she made no overt attempt to insert her tongue between his lips, yet she left him with little doubt she would have welcomed his escalation of the kiss if he had chosen to seize the opportunity.

"You've lost a little weight, but it looks good off you," she said when she stepped back and looked him up and down. Although she seemed to take no notice of the swelling in his crotch, the beginning of his enlarging member was already embarrassingly manifest and made him extremely ill-at-ease. After she leaned in and kissed him warmly, but chastely again, in a graceful cross-legged maneuver she lowered herself to a sitting position, pulling him down beside her on the comfortable futon. "Does your Sergeant keep a Korean housekeeper or was he referring to his sweetheart as his *moose?*"

"His sweetheart, I'm sure. Over here 'moose' is GI gutter slang for '*museme*'—it's the Japanese word for a young woman of...of easy virtue." Collier smiled.

"Do you keep a moose?" The question took him completely off guard. Searching her face, he found it impossible to tell whether or not she was serious.

"You're kidding, of course," he gave her a searching look.

"Uhm-m...maybe..." Her green eyes twinkled, searching his face for truth. After a long moment, she cleared her throat and asked. "What do you hear from Emma?"

"I don't hear from her much at all. I write two or three times a week. I've only heard from her three times since I left home the end of June. She says the baby is colicky...she complains he's taking all her time."

"I can hardly believe you're parents now. In training, Emma never really seemed like the mother type to me." Ginger ventured, idly looking around the simple, but rather exotic, room.

"Uhm-m...I have trouble believing it myself..." he let the words trail off, not at all happy to be on the subject of his uneasy fatherhood. "

"Do you have a picture of the baby? I'd love to see him. If he favors his papa, he must be a good-looking baby."

"Yeah...my Mom sent me a picture just last week. But, I don't think you'll find much resemblance to me...of course it's hard to tell from baby pictures..." He fished in the hip pocket of his fatigues and brought out his wallet. The recent Kodak color close-up of Emma holding baby Kyle was remarkably clear. No matter how often and how hard he studied the face of the ten-week-old infant in Emma's arms, Collier could find no family resemblance. There was no dimpled chin or button nose, no likeness to the either the Ramsays or the Boyds. Without further comment he removed the snapshot and handed it over. "She...we...named him Kyle."

"Kyle is a nice name." Ginger took a long look at the photo and handed it back. "I wouldn't worry about the resemblance. With babies this young I've always suspected those who see unmistakable family traits were mostly doting, overeager grandmothers and aunts."

"I guess you're right. But, it bothers me that I don't feel a stronger...ah...affection for the...the baby." He almost said "kid," a demeaning trashy word he had always hated. "I guess I just wasn't ready for fatherhood. To tell the truth, when I found out Emma was PG, I was still having trouble believing the miraculous turnaround in her feelings for me. The first two-and-a-half years of our marriage, she didn't like me very much." Collier took a fleeting look at the snapshot and stuck it back in his wallet. "I should have seen it coming back in college. Everything changed between us when I decided to switch majors from Pre-med and go to Richmond to study commercial art at Richmond Professional Institute."

"Hm-m..." Ginger eyed him questioningly. "Aren't you imagining things?"

"Not at all. We started going together our junior year in high school. All I cared about was playing ball. She was the first girl I ever dated. You know the old story: High school quarterback marries the head cheerleader—they wake up one morning several years later with an innocent baby or two and find out they don't like each other. It's a tired old story: The American Dream."

"I knew you and Emma had a lot of spats and falling outs when she was still in training and you were in college, but so did everyone who was going steady back in those days. Besides, aren't all marriages pretty rocky at the beginning? Come on, now? You're just imagining things."

"No. I'm being quite realistic, actually. The truth is, I was really kind of 'Peck's bad boy' in high school. I was a dreamer. Then after high school, I went from wanting to be a coach, to taking pre-med, to studying art. It's no wonder Emma really never thought I would amount to much. I think most women see men as raw material anyway; they marry with the idea of making their husbands into something worthwhile—sort of the Pygmalion concept in reverse. You know the old saying: Behind every successful man is a strong woman. I'm sure Emma thought I had some potential...she's already trying to talk me into going back to medical school on the GI Bill when I get home."

"Oh, come on. You had a good job as an artist. I'm sure she must have been proud of you."

"Are you kidding? Right before I enlisted in the Army, she was pushing me to take a job selling paint supplies. I can't really say I blame her for being pretty disgusted with me when I was going through OCS. I kept threatening to quit. Still?...one thing she should have known, I've never been a quitter. After I was commissioned, her attitude toward me changed a little...but I'm certain that had a lot to do with her getting PG. Also, I think she liked telling her brothers and sisters and all our friends back home I was an officer..." Collier stopped in mid-sentence, surprised these resentments had come floating up out of his subconscious. He'd almost blurted that the only thing that had kept him from asking Emma for a divorce had been her surprise pregnancy...it was difficult to think about leaving her with the baby. Standing there looking at Ginger, the idea he still might divorce Emma when he got back home took on renewed relevance.

"Oh, you don't really mean that. I...and most of Emma's nursing classmates...always thought you were quite a catch. Do you remember encouraging me when I showed you one of my pitiful attempts at painting? I knew you were just being kind."

"Yeah, I remember. Your drawings weren't all that bad...they were quite good, really." Being here alone with this girl...this woman...who had haunted his romantic fantasies since college days left him almost tongue-tied.

"Uhm-m?...now you're just being nice." She blushed, idly tracing a little circular pattern on the surface of his thigh with her forefinger. Her innocent finger movements did nothing to ease the growing feelings of schoolboy awkwardness inside him.

"Are you hungry?" he asked, folding away the snapshot and stuffing the wallet back inside his pocket. His watch showed almost straight up noon.

"Not really...we grabbed breakfast at Kimpo while we were waiting for the truck to transport the respirators over here. If you don't think I'm too depraved, I think I'd like a drink. If your Sergeant has some tomato juice, a healthy double Bloody Mary sounds real good to me."

"A Bloody Mary sounds good. Let me look in that cooler. No telling what Otis has in this little hideaway..." Collier walked across the futon on his knees to the ice box and peeked in. "Well, I wish you'd look. It's our lucky day." He held up a can of Campbell's V-8.

"Wonderful. I actually prefer V-8 to regular tomato juice. Can I help?" Ginger brightened eager for a drink.

"No need. I don't see a strainer. I hope you don't mind a little ice in your drink?" He asked as he went to work. There were large Old-fashioned glasses on a shelf behind the cabinet and a tray of GI silverware, complete with a long-handled ice tea spoon. Shielding her from his movements, he slugged an extra muscular dollop of Smirnoff into her glass; in practically no time he had finished concocting two Bloody Marys. "Here...try this..." he pivoted on his knees and handed her the glass with the heavier dose of vodka. Out of respect for the Sergeant's property, he had taken care to wrap the bottoms of the glasses with large paper napkins, most likely commandeered from the enlisted mess across the street.

"Whoa! Are you trying to get me drunk?" She took several swallows of the extra potent drink and ran her tongue around her lips. "I should warn you I sometimes get wild when I have too much to drink."

"Well...we're private here and there's plenty of vodka where that came from..." He took a tentative sip from his own glass which he had mixed with a lighter touch.

"This may be the best Bloody Mary I've ever had. Here, fix us both refills and then come back over here. We've got a lot of catching up to do..." she finished off the drink in a couple of gulps and handed back the glass before he had a chance to make himself comfortable again.

Setting his sweating, soggy napkin-wrapped glass carefully on the *tatami* mat, Collier again knee-walked across the futon and put together another Bloody Mary in Ginger's empty glass—this time he was more judicious with the booze. When he scooted back and handed her the glass, she took a tentative sip before she set her glass beside his alongside the futon. She made no mention that he had hardly touched his own drink. When she turned back, she pulled him close and kissed him hard, this time forcing her tongue between his lips, wantonly exploring his mouth. After what seemed an eternity of this hungry exploration, she pushed him flat on his back and spread herself on top of him crushing his poor engorging penis inside the confines of his Jockey briefs. It was impossible to tell the difference between the pleasure and the pain as she immediately began to unbutton his blouse.

"Don't move..." she breathed, when he reached to help her with his blouse. Redirecting the effort of his hands he began unbuttoning her fatigue blouse in return. He had only half-finished the task, when she lowered her face upon his chest and started nibbling his nipples, a sensation which he found so unbearably erotic he thought he just might come right there in his Jockey's without further stimulation.

"Stop...I want you naked..." He pushed her back and resumed fumbling with her buttons.

"Here...let me..." She pushed away his hands again and quickly pulled her half-unbuttoned blouse over her head. Tossing the garment on the floor, she reached behind herself and unsnapped her bra, releasing a pair of the most sensual rose-tipped breasts he'd ever imagined. He'd barely had a glimpse of her lovely bosom when she twisted slightly and lowered her right nipple into his mouth.

TAP, TAP...TAP...TAP! The knocking came from just outside. "LIEUTENANT RAMSAY, EXCUSE ME, SIR, MAJOR OLSEN NEEDS YOU BACK ACROSS THE STREET—SHE SAYS TO TELL YOU STAT! THE KOREAN POWER HAS GONE OFF AGAIN AND WE NEED ALL HANDS TO PUMP THE RESPIRATORS." One of the corpsmen from the isolation ward was outside, shouting through the *shoji* door.

"Oh, shit! You might know something like this would happen..." Collier cursed, sitting erect and fumbling with his buttons. "Just hold on here and finish your drink. This never really takes that long..." He grabbed his cap and crawled on his knees toward the door reaching for his boots.

"No...wait. I'm coming with you. I don't want to stay here alone." Ginger gulped down the rest of her drink and followed close behind.

As it turned out, her decision not to stay was a wise one. The Korean power flickered off and on all night and the only time they were able to be together was when Collier was able to accompany her to the officers' mess for dinner. After they had eaten, he left her under the care of Smitty in the lounge. When Smitty closed the O club just before midnight, Major Olsen sent word to bring her up to the hospital where she provided Ginger with the opportunity to take a hot shower, and gave her the use of a private room in Chicken Coop reserved for visiting brass.

"I might have known something like this would happen. I'm sorry..." nearly exhausted from hand-operating an iron lung most of the night, Collier apologized as he drove Ginger to Kimpo in a jeep the next morning after breakfast to catch her airplane back to Tachikawa.

"Don't be silly. It was not your fault. I hope you're not sorry we very nearly became lovers..."

"I'm only sorry we couldn't finish what we started—if you only knew how long I've had a...a secret crush on you. I hope you aren't sorry. I'll be coming back to Tokyo around the end of October. I'd like to think we can spend my R&R together," Collier offered hopefully.

"I'll count the days..." Ginger said, hugging him and kissing him passionately before she turned and walked inside the wooden terminal building, trying not to be obvious as she wiped the wayward flow of tears from her eyes.

Standing with his fellow officers in the courtyard out back of Quonset Lounge, Monday night, July 27, Collier stared into the star-filled sky as tick-by-tick, the luminous minute-hand of his watch finally moved to point straight up to 2200 hours—ten o'clock.

After a moment of expectant silence, a chorus of cheers erupted all around him.

"Thank, God, peace at last!" Major Olsen fairly shouted as on the far side of the compound at the foot of the hill, the enlisted men started blowing party horns, whistles, bugles and beating a steady riot of celebration on any piece of metal that would make a noise. Across the fence in the village, the Koreans were lighting strings of firecrackers, while further down the road toward Suwon, there were answering streaks of skyrockets blooming across the sky beneath the gibbous moon which looked like a giant orange pumpkin rising in the east.

"I've been looking for you. I just got back from Tokyo. A woman on the staff of the Far East Headquarters command in the Dai Ichi Building gave me this to deliver to you. She says she's a friend of yours." Colonel Reed, the Assistant Eighth Army Surgeon, came over and handed Collier an envelope bearing his name and the hand-written legend "Photo: Please Do Not Bend" printed across the lower left-hand corner.

"Thanks. I'm obliged. She's a friend." Careful not to bend it, Collier took the envelope without looking inside and slipped it into the shirt pocket of his fatigues. All around them, the rowdy celebrants were slowly dispersing, heading excitedly up the hill to continue celebrating the ceasefire at the nurses' huts on Quonset Row.

When he had finished helping Smitty straighten up the O-Club bar, Collier bypassed the noisy celebration at The Hen Party and continued directly to The Broken Drum. Being constantly summoned to the Polio Isolation Unit to hand-operate the iron lungs when the exasperating Korean electricity failed, Collier had kept a watchful eye on his physical symptoms. He had been suffering a stiff neck and a scratchy throat off and on for over a week now, and for the past several days, he had been bothered by a nagging case of diarrhea.

Since Ginger's surprise visit, the 121ˢᵗ had already admitted three more cases of polio—with all three of the patients suffering from the more virulent bulbar form of the disease. Polio was thought to be transmitted from feces through poor personal hygiene. Korea was a filthy place. They had also admitted two cases of KHF. While rationally he was pretty certain he was not infected with either KHF or Polio, Collier vigilantly (but secretly, to avoid being considered hypochondriacal by his fellow staff members) monitored his temperature frequently throughout the day, meticulously scrubbing his hands at every opportunity.

With the entire staff either celebrating a few huts down at The Hen Party or returning to their duty stations in the hospital, Collier found The Broken Drum deserted. Heading directly to his bunk, he removed the envelope from his shirt pocket and lovingly examined it under the light of the single electric bulb. Neatly hand-printed on the upper left-hand corner of the envelope was the name Madison Argabright bearing the return address: Eighth Army HQ Section, Dai Ichi Building, Tokyo, Japan. Inside was a snapshot of Madison posed full-height against the backdrop of a modest sign which read: Army Hall. She was wearing a simple Oriental cheongsam which seductively modeled her voluptuous figure. Across the back of the photo was written in a flowing feminine script: *I think about you often. As you can see, I tracked you down and have your address. I can hardly wait until you come back to Tokyo on R&R. I have been snowed under, but will write a long letter in the next few days. Anata ga suki, Madison.*

Argabright! Collier suddenly became aware of the unusual but familiar family name on the front of the envelope. Argabright was his Grandma Collier's maiden name. Like most of the Collier clan, his Grandma's branch of the Argabright family was from around Bluefield and Princeton, West Virginia. Now Collier recalled Madison saying her father was from somewhere in southern West Virginia, along the Virginia border.

My god! Could Madison be his distant kin?

Retrieving his box of writing paper and envelopes from the homemade footlocker Otis Owens' indigenous labor crew had fashioned for him in the shop behind Supply, Collier jotted a pair of quick notes to his Aunt Blanche and his Grandma Collier, casually asking if they recalled having a physician cousin on the Argabright side of the family with a daughter about his age named Madison. Smiling wryly, he sealed both envelopes and took another loving look at the photo trying to find a family resemblance.

It really was a small world, after all.

Placing the envelopes on the top of his footlocker, he shook three APC out of the bottle on his bedside lamp table and washed them down with a swallow of the remaining dregs of the Rum Collins he had carried with him when he left the Club.

Rereading Madison's note, the line about R&R jumped out at him. He had just promised to spend his R&R with Ginger. What had he gotten himself into now? A trivial matter of incest was nothing compared to being in love—or lust—with two beautiful women at the same time.

Not feeling sleepy, he decided to walk back down Quonset Row to inspect his renovation project involving the bombed shell of an extremely large wing—

really one very large room—attached to the end of Building Four, just at the eastern corner where the street started down the hill. With the truce now firmly in place and with new cases of KHF and polio slowing somewhat, Collier had obtained permission from Scroggs and enlisted Sergeant Otis Cook's indigenous labor force to re-roof the empty shell and convert the space into fancy new quarters for his fellow administrative officers currently billeted in The Broken Drum.

The ingenious Korean carpenters, using mostly rudimentary tools fashioned from the metal of empty aviation fuel cans and artillery casings, had already finished putting the roof back on the space, and had—at Collier's instruction—partitioned the entire compact wing into two separate rooms. The larger room was to be a spacious, semi-barracks-style, sleeping quarters for eight which would be subdivided by movable privacy partitions, inspired by Collier's memory of OCS at Sill. The remaining, somewhat narrower, social room which ran down the side of the building bordering the street down the hill between the biological and pathological lab and the main hospital would have a fancy bar. The design of the bar was the inspiration of Sergeant Owens. Underneath the wide countertop, the bar was fronted with corrugated, translucent, milky-green plastic material designed to be used as windows for Quonset huts. underneath the counter top of the bar were shelves. This space was also wired for single-bulb electric light receptacles so the lights shown through the translucent plastic of the bar when the ceiling lights were turned down low. Behind the bar was shelving for liquor bottles and glasses brought over from Japan. The bar with the adjoining large party room beyond promised to make one hell of a party space. Best of all, the location was further from the Chicken Coop than The Hen Party which reduced the prospect of Colonel Spaulding's periodic puritanical intrusions. He could already anticipate the fast-approaching grand opening event of The Broken Drum reincarnated. Poking around now with his flashlight inside the sleeping quarters, Collier took particular pride in the labor crew's progress on what was to be his own private cubicle.

After perhaps an hour, he finally began feeling tired and walked slowly back to the Quonset quarters. Standing by his bed looking down at the photo of Madison, suddenly the words Army Hall jumped out at him.

Ginger also lived at Army Hall.

His throat tightening and his gut churning from renewed anxiety, Collier gargled a large mouthful of Listerine and headed for the eight-holer latrine, the nagging diarrhea cramping his overworked lower bowel again.

CHAPTER FORTY-FIVE

STARS AND STRIPES
UNOFFICIAL PUBLICATION OF UNITED STATES FORCES, FAR EAST

Vol. 9, No. 245   Thursday, September 3, 1953
U.N.C. ASSURES REDS ALL PRISONERS RETURN

PANMUNJOM, Sept. 3 (Pac. S&S) - The U.N.C. today assured the Communists that all Red PWs would be returned, thus easing tension on both sides.

THE ROANOKE TIMES
Roanoke, Virginia, Thursday, September 4, 1953
DEAN RETURNS FROM CAPTIVITY

PANMUNJON, Friday, September 4 (AP) - Major General William F. Dean was returned to the allied side today after three years of Communist captivity...

STARS AND STRIPES
UNOFFICIAL PUBLICATION OF UNITED STATES FORCES, FAR EAST

Vol. 9, No. 244   Tuesday, September 22, 1953
Red Lands MIG Near Seoul
By S/Sgt. Bob McNeill

SEOUL, Sept. 21 (Pac. S&S) - A Russian-built MIG flown by a Communist pilot landed at Kimpo airfield, 15 miles west of Seoul, at 9:24 this morning, Fifth Air Force announced.

TUESDAY, 28 JULY, the day after the truce was signed, Collier was called into Scroggs' office and told, "Get a Jeep and drive over to the main PX in Yongdongpo. The previously-scheduled Inventory Officer has rotated stateside and you're replacing him."

Recalling his one experience as inventory officer back at Pickett, Collier secured a Jeep from the motor pool and headed out the gate, dreading the next several days. At the main PX in Yongdongpo, he was met by the PX Officer, Captain Junior Laneaux, who introduced himself then introduced a pair of unlucky inventory officers, an Infantry Second Lieutenant Case and another Second John named Pope.

"Follow me inside, gentlemen. Lieutenant Colonel Martin Brewer, from the Eighth Army G-Three's office would like a word with you before we get underway." Captain Laneaux led them inside the PX. Carefully hanging a prominent CLOSED FOR INVENTORY sign on the entrance door, he locked the door behind them.

"It is a distinct pleasure to meet you gentlemen. I'm Colonel Martin Brewer, from Eighth Army HQ Supply. Since Lieutenant Ramsay is substituting for Captain Bert James who originally was to have been in charge, he will officially go on record as the officer in charge of this inventory. To show our appreciation for your services in performing this inventory, our first order of business is to offer each of you an opportunity to purchase any item in our inventory before we get started—and that, by the way, includes some extremely hard to get 'waiting list only' items such as Nikon and Canon cameras, a few extremely hard-to-get sets of 'pro shop only' golf clubs and the more-sought-after patterns of Noritake China." The light colonel made a sweeping gesture at the glass-enclosed showcases around the interior of the large PX.

"That's extremely thoughtful of you sir," the infantry lieutenant grunted enthusiastically and walked across to a case of cameras to look them over.

"Thank you all the same for the generous opportunity, but unfortunately, Colonel Brewer, Sir, I'm afraid I couldn't buy a roll of film until my next pay day." Collier wryly shook his head, then asked. "I can't help but wonder if I might be able to get you to set aside a Canon camera and also have a complete set of Noritake china shipped back home to my wife—and defer the order until next payday?"

"I assure you that would be our pleasure, Lieutenant. Captain Laneaux, will you make a note to set aside one Canon Four-S-Two and a twelve-place setting of Noritake china?" Colonel Brewer directed the PX Officer then turned back to Collier. "Before you leave, you can pick out the Noritake pattern of your choice, Lieutenant."

"Thank you, Sir." Collier nodded appreciation as he followed the Colonel back to the section containing cameras, slide projectors, binoculars and other luxury items of Japanese and German manufacture, ready to get down to the business at hand.

"Any questions before we begin?" The colonel gave Collier the current inventory sheets for that particular section of the large PX.

"No sir, I've done this before back at Pickett." Collier took the sheets, moved to the glass display counters and quickly got to work.

Toward the end of the day, Collier alerted the colonel to several major discrepancies he had discovered in the inventory. "I hate to bother you, Colonel, but I can't seem to find a number of expensive cameras, some binoculars, several expensive sets of registered name-brand golf clubs, a significant number of cases of popular brands of cigarettes and some other items."

"Oh, yes. I should have told you. There were some items purchased since the most recent in-store inventory. I'm familiar with them. I have the sales slips back at headquarters. Go ahead and check them off. I'll personally vouch that they are documented as being purchased and accounted for." The suave colonel flashed Collier a reassuring smile.

"That's okay, Colonel Brewer. You can bring those sales slips with you tomorrow. I couldn't certify them as sold without seeing those sales sheets personally, Sir." Collier was taken aback that this senior officer would suggest that he be a party to such shoddy accounting. On the Korean black market, the cigarettes alone were worth a small fortune.

"Oh, don't be so fussy, Lieutenant. I'd have to go all the back into Seoul tonight. Just take my word. That should be good enough. We'll just keep it between gentlemen. Besides, we're still in a combat zone here. I don't like to drive after dark." The Colonel gave him a friendly pat on the shoulder.

"Nothing personal, Sir, but I'd prefer to wait until I see the paperwork. Just a matter of personal responsibility, Sir...I'm sure you understand." Collier was flabbergasted that the Colonel could suggest he be a party to such casual inventory procedures.

"It is nothing personal, Lieutenant. I fully appreciate your high standards of integrity and am not at all surprised. Your Colonel Scroggs told me he gave you papers for application for Regular Army status just a few days ago. You have a brilliant record. But, as a future career officer, I'm sure you wouldn't want to show disrespect for a superior officer, now would you? It's getting late and I'm getting thirsty. Just initial these fucking items as being here and let's get on with this." The smile had faded from the colonel's face.

"Well...all right, Sir. I didn't mean disrespect..." Intimidated by the senior officer's unexpected outburst, Collier reluctantly initialed the missing items on the inventory sheet and went back to work.

Working well past the usual time for mess at the 121ˢᵗ, the colonel took them all into Seoul to the Air Force Officers' club for dinner. Totally out of time and place and in sharp contrast with the nearby South Korean Capitol Building which close-up showed the ravages of war, Collier was totally unprepared to see such an ostentatious display of luxury and elegance sitting in the middle of wholesale destruction and human squalor.

"This is incredible!" the two other lieutenants remarked in unison, completely awestruck.

"Yes, I come here often. It helps me forget the sadness and destruction of the war." The colonel beamed, as if the place was his personal property. "Almost all of the furnishings and supplies are flown over here from Japan, some all the way from the States."

"I wonder how many hours of R&R were cancelled to make planes available to ship all this stuff from Japan?" Collier remarked to no one in particular.

"You have my table ready, Claude?" Frowning, the Colonel ignored Collier as he led the way, following close behind the Korean maitre-d.

Following the first day's minor clash of rank and ego, to Collier's great relief, the next morning the inventory process moved smoothly along. Collier was amazed to find they had finished and had signed off on all the inventory sheets for the large area PX by mid-afternoon the third day.

"If you'll wait around a few minutes, Captain Laneaux and I will discuss the matter of your camera and china, Lieutenant," Colonel Brewer instructed Collier as he turned to escort the other two inventory officers to the door. Collier waited as the Colonel and the PX officer thanked his fellow officers, bid them farewell and turned back to where he stood waiting.

"Come back to Captain Laneaux's office with me, Lieutenant, I have a little present for you." If the colonel harbored any leftover resentment for their earlier encounter, Collier could find no evidence of it now. When he followed the two senior officers into the PX office, on the desk was a brand-new Canon IVS₂, complete with leather carrying case, sitting beside the newly-opened cartons it had arrived in, shipped directly from the factory in Japan.

"Oh, I'm sorry, Sir. I wasn't kidding. I'm practically dead broke. I'll have to wait until payday." Collier was embarrassed by the misunderstanding.

"Oh, no, you don't understand. This is a gift. It's customary that the PX officer show proper appreciation to head of the inventory team. We've already given smaller tokens to the other members. This is special. You were designated as the responsible officer of the team," the suave colonel reassured him.

"Well...I don't know. No one told me to expect anything like this..." Collier hesitated, certain he was being bribed.

"Believe me, Lieutenant, it's all on the up-and-up. Ask your Colonel Scroggs when you get back to the One-two-one." The colonel obviously was feeling a little testy now.

"Well. Thank you, Sir. Frankly, I'm overwhelmed. I don't know quite what to say..." Collier sputtered, realizing he was caught in an impasse. Moreover, to tell the truth, he really wanted that camera. Priced in the PX at $135, but costing somewhere in the neighborhood of $400 back in the States, the Canon IVS₂ far exceeded Collier's expectation of being able to purchase a decent camera. His ambition had been to settle for something far less expensive. He was hoping to afford something on the order of the newest 35mm American Argus C-4 with a 3.5 lens which was something less than fifty bucks at overseas PX prices, or, at the very best, a Zeiss Ikon Contessa with a Tessar Opton 2.8/45 lens with Synchro Compur and lightmeter which would run a trifle less than a hundred dollars over here—if he was lucky enough to be able to find either one.

"A simple 'thank you' is quite enough, Lieutenant. Now, if you'll choose the pattern you like and fill out these papers, we'll ship the twelve place setting of Noritake to your wife. Then take your new camera and let's all get out of here."

Feeling compromised but caught in an impossible situation, Collier quickly chose a simple, plain-gold-banded pattern from the Noritake catalog, wrote down Emma's shipping address, thanked the colonel again and headed for the door. Back home, the twelve-place setting of Noritake would run at least $500 dollars in Roanoke.

"Wait up, Lieutenant. If you hadn't considered it before, I can put you on to an easy way to improve your finances while you're stuck in this godawful place." The Colonel followed him out to where his Jeep was parked.

"I'm not sure what you mean, Sir?" Collier asked, anxious to get far away from the corrupt officer without further delay.

"I know a discreet, respectable moneychanger who'll give seven-hundred-fifty hwan for an American greenback. The new official rate is only three-hundred-ten." The Colonel idly inspected an imaginary blemish on his boots.

"It's illegal to have American greenbacks, Colonel. It's a court-martial offense if you're found to have them in the Far East Command. I exchanged what few I had at the Tokyo airport for military script when I arrived back in July." Scarcely able to believe he was having this conversation with such a high-ranking officer, Collier turned away, carefully placing the new Canon camera with the booklets and boxes it came with on the floorboards of the Jeep.

"Don't be so naïve, Lieutenant. Some of your respected doctor buddies and countless other officers and enlisted men are building nice little nest eggs for themselves back home. I'll be dropping by your Officer's lounge from time to time. Keep this conversation in mind if you happen to run across any loose greenbacks floating around the One-two-one. Thanks again for all your good work. Drive safely, now. Next time I need an Inventory Officer, I'll be in touch." The Colonel stepped back and waved as Collier drove swiftly out of the parking lot, heading east back toward Seoul.

Coincidental with his third wedding anniversary, on the fourth of August, Collier was transferred from being Motor Officer under Major Smith and reassigned to replace Chuck Lohr as Adjutant. Chuck was long past due for rotation home. Now, as newly-appointed Adjutant, virtually overnight, Colonel Scroggs—at the bidding of the obsessive-compulsive Augustus Spaulding—transformed Collier's previously simple life into a hellish mockery, filled with inconsequential busy work. Not the least of these highly obsessive chores was checking all electric light bulbs throughout the entire compound every morning before Officers Call and initiating a major project of having Otis Owens' Korean Labor force construct a massive stone fireplace in the officers' mess.

Within a week, almost entirely one wall of the officers' mess building had been torn out and replaced with canvas tarps to keep the elements out as the giant fireplace began taking shape. By the end of this same period, Collier was prepared to give a blood oath that, including all bulbs lighting the outside stairwells, there were exactly 222 outside light bulbs.

As if that weren't bad enough, to further complicate his life, throughout August, cases of both KHF and Polio continued to trickle in at a rate just steady enough to keep the 121ˢᵗ Staff on edge, as they feared a full-blown epidemic of either or both diseases. The Polio admissions continued to be almost one-hundred percent bulbar, requiring Collier to make frequent trips to Isolation to hand-operate the iron lungs. Despite the constant reassurances from Major Hughes, Captain Mutch, and Major Olsen, and practically the entire medical staff—including Billy Graves and his buddies at the Laboratory—and despite the constant self-administered, self-conscious lectures to himself to *"Get a fucking grip,"* Collier's malignant hypochondriacal symptoms—including an annoying, low-grade diarrhea—continued to plague him.

Every morning when he awoke, against all rational self-castration, Collier massaged his stiff neck, shamefacedly examined his image in the mirror for skin lesions, and gargled salt water while asking of his reflection in the shaving mirror, "What new disease will we die from today?" This ritual completed, he showered, shaved and dressed and, with his chest filled with a numbing, unnamed dread, walked out whistling bravely with his head held high to do his duty, waiting for the first cramping of his lower bowel.

To compound his budding hypochondria, over coffee call one morning Collier overheard a conversation between Major Hughes and Captain Mutch about a recent admission of a young GI with cancer of the throat.

"Was he a smoker?" Hughes had asked.

"Yeah. He smoked like a chimney," Captain Mutch had answered.

"I'm not surprised. These damn things don't do anybody any good. I'm going to quit as soon as I get back to the States." Major Hughes took a final drag on his cigarette, grinding it out in one of several ashtrays on the table.

"While you're at it, you might as well get circumcised or, better still, just give up sex and ice cream, and booze, too, as long as we're on the subject—then you'll probably live forever."

"What's being circumcised got to do with anything?" Collier croaked, suddenly confronted with these new, entirely unsuspected, dangers to his health. He had been circumcised, but it never occurred to him it had anything to do with longevity. He had been a heavy smoker—three packs a day—since high school. Was it too late to change his ways?

"Outside of throat and lung cancer, one of the most common cancers is carcinoma of the penis in uncircumcised young males," Hughes spoke up.

"Are you serious about ice cream and alcohol being bad for you?" Collier suddenly experienced a sinking feeling in his gut. He hadn't had any ice cream lately, but he was drinking every night except Monday—designated as his self-imposed "alcohol-free health night." Practically all of the medical staff officers and nurses were observing this disingenuous routine.

"Sure, all milk products, including ice cream and cheese are loaded with cholesterol and booze is fairly loaded with triglycerides—both are fatty substances that clog the arteries," Captain Mutch chimed in.

"Uh...really?" Collier nodded and swallowed hard. He loved milk and cheese. He hadn't realized it until now, but it had been a hidden blessing that fresh milk was not available in the combat zone. His mind reeling with the added burden of these newly-acquired hazards to his health, Collier put out his cigarette, excused himself and went directly to the privacy of The Broken Drum to examine his penis for any signs of malignancy. That same day he traded his stock of luxuriantly flavorful Lucky Strike for the virtually tasteless new Micronite-filtered Kents which substantially reduced the tar and other contaminants in the smoke.

Rationally, Collier understood that his hypochondriacal preoccupations were wholly imaginary. But it made no difference. Despite his enlightened self-understanding, despite all his Socratic objectivity, he had become a frigging, walking-talking head case, heading straight for a Section Eight. The only thing that saved him was that he understood, at a purely rational level, his symptoms were mostly imaginary, generated by unhealthy preoccupations with his physical health exacerbated by his conviction that he would die here in this godforsaken land. To his everlasting credit, but not to his benefit, however, Collier was able to carry off his charade of mental health and remain highly functional, with both Scroggs and Spaulding giving him top endorsements on his application for an RA commission.

Although he had written Madison immediately after receiving her photograph, reassuring her of his adoration, Collier had made no mention of the possible distant relationships between their family trees, nor had he confessed that he was married with an infant son back in the states. On Friday, August 14, he received an answer to his letter to his Aunt Blanche inquiring about his southern West Virginia relations.

"...in answer to your question about our relation to a physician named Argabright, we do indeed have a first cousin named Bessie Argabright from just outside Princeton, W. Va. who has a son named Winston Argabright who is a doctor. We wrote Aunt Lolly and she says Winston has a daughter named Madison. The last time she heard, Winston's girl was working in Washington with the government...."

After reading the letter twice, Collier folded it carefully and, not at all sure how he felt about this latest, bizarre twist of fate, walked numbly down to the O Club and ordered a Rum Collins to help him process the thoughts and emotions bouncing around inside his skull like a string of firecrackers. The best he could figure, Winston Agrabright would be his second cousin. Would that make Madison his second cousin, too? Collier wracked his brain; he'd never really been exactly sure how to sort out Mendelian Laws of Inheritance.

Of one thing he was certain: he and Madison were guilty of some degree of incest, but he was pretty sure their relationship was just barely distant enough to allow them to be legally married if that occasion ever arose. Still, children born between such close kin were in danger of being mentally deficient and afflicted with unspeakable anomalies. He had recalled having heard all manner of horror stories from his parents about such things while growing up. He wished that he had paid more attention to Mr. Steele in eighth-grade science class.

Should he write Madison and tell her about their kinship? How would she react?

Would it end all chances of ever having her in his arms again?

To hell with all this guilt. He hadn't even told her about Emma and the baby. He would just wait and let her find out for herself.

Speaking of Emma and little Kyle, he had just gotten a letter from Ginger Lipscomb, saying that she was still at Army Hall in Tokyo looking forward to his first R&R, which she now hoped would be before she shipped home sometime in early November. She had included a photo of herself in a two-piece bathing suit. Collier placed the snapshot on his bedside table beside photos of Emma and Madison. Taking his stationary out of his footlocker, he dashed off a note to Ginger thanking her for the picture and assuring her that he was counting the days until he came to Tokyo in November. When he finished writing the note, he picked up the two photos of Ginger and Madison and momentarily fantasized going back to Tokyo and being sexually ravaged by them both.

Was this the same man who had been offended by Colonel Brewer's overtures about dealing greenbacks on the Korean black market? What kind of man was he, anyway, to have such a convenient sliding scale of morals and integrity? Could it be he was some sort of modern-day Don Juan or Marquis de Sade? Pondering the intriguing question walking down the hill to the Officers Mess, Collier whistled off-key as he allowed his reveries to return to his recent encounters with both women.

From the beginning of Operation Big Switch, the hospital had received a steady stream of repatriated prisoners who required immediate—but transitory—medical attention before being flown on to Japan or Okinawa for shipment home or for further stateside recuperation. The U.N. had assigned Alex McGrory to the 121ˢᵗ as an interpreter during Big Switch, but Collier had not actually observed any of the Aussie's considerable language talents put into action. Accompanied almost everywhere he went by a newly-attached and rather attractive Australian Red Cross woman named Flossie Rowell, almost every night during Big Switch, Alex and Flossie would get half-in-a-bag on gin and tonic and wind up doing the Japanese Coal-miner's Dance—or at least so they said.

The pleasant company of Alex and Flossie notwithstanding, for Collier, Operation Big Switch had climaxed early at the 121ˢᵗ with the ostentatious ceremony surrounding the repatriation of General William Dean on August 4, which was orchestrated with much pomp and circumstance on a spur-of-the-moment, makeshift parade ground that Collier had improvised with the help of Otis Owen's Korean labor force.

As resentful as it had made him to have overseen most of the work and then to have been relegated to the rear rank of the hospital staff, Collier silently suffered this ignominy as he watched while General Dean was helped down out of the giant Huey whirlybird, escorted by Generals Maxwell Taylor and General Arthur Trudeau looking as important in all their dress finery with acres of battle ribbons as a foppishly-costumed chorus in some Gilbert and Sullivan operetta.

Then, just at the most dramatic moment, an official Korean limousine came rolling right onto the chopper strip before pulling to a stop and depositing Syngham Rhee.

To Collier's surprise and relief, the ceremony was brief. Keeping strictly to Army protocol, Trudeau introduced General Taylor, who acknowledged President Rhee, but did not allow the obstreperous Korean dignitary an opportunity to address the gathering until he had given a short, concise, carefully-worded—the Army still hadn't exactly decided whether Dean was to be treated like a hero or a blundering idiot—welcome home to General Dean. After Taylor had had his brief say, he introduced Rhee, with a private aside to advise the aged, semi-senile Korean President to "keep it short" out of consideration for General Dean's debilitated physical condition.

After the ceremony, a number of the media followed Dean and his entourage of high brass, and watched while he climbed the stairway to the VIP ward in Building Two. Much to Colonel Augustus Spaulding's—as well as the Eighth Army Surgeon's—everlasting chagrin, the 121ˢᵗ Evac was not allowed to oversee Dean's immediate medical attention. As soon as the short check of his vitals by Major Hughes and Captain Mutch was concluded, Dean was whisked back into the chopper and lifted off, connecting with a waiting plane at Kimpo to speed him out of Korea as fast as humanly possible.

That afternoon following General Dean's departure, still plagued by persistent pain and stiffness in his neck, Collier allowed himself to be examined and X-Rayed by Captain Alonzo "Hoot" Gibson, a board-certified Canadian oral surgeon.

"I couldn't help but hear the kidding you've been taking about your stiff neck and throat pain. Have you had your teeth looked at lately?" At breakfast one morning a few days back, Gibson approached Collier about the on-going problem with his neck. Gibson had enlisted in the American Army on the promise of being able to gather experience performing complicated surgical repairs on combat-related facial injuries, only to be frustrated to find the Army Medical Corps' private fraternity had black-balled him from the OR in favor of surgeons with bona fide American medical degrees but who weren't nearly as qualified with specialized experience in the field.

"No. I had a dental exam back at Pickett in the spring. I don't think there's a problem with my teeth. Besides, it seems unlikely that *both* sides would be affected if I had an abscessed tooth." Collier tried to dismiss the idea that his problem was even remotely related to his teeth.

"Oh, I'm not suggesting you have a dental infection *per se.* But your symptoms are strongly suggestive of impacted molars—you know...your wisdom teeth?" Hoot explained.

"Impacted? I'm not sure I understand." Collier was confused.

"A large percent of the normal population have three sets of the large chewing teeth—they are properly known as their first, second and third molars. The third molars which are farthest back, behind the second molars, usually don't come in until the person is in their late teens or early twenties. Usually a person has four of these "wisdom" teeth located top and bottom and, if there is room and they are properly aligned, they simply push their way through and take their place without a problem. But often there is a problem with lacking enough space or the location or angle of the unemerged wisdom teeth, and they are blocked from coming in. This sometimes occurs and the patient is never aware of the latent, unemerged wisdom teeth. It really wouldn't hurt to come by my office upstairs and let me X-Ray your jaws," Hoot explained.

"Well...maybe. I'm pretty busy. I'll think about it, though." Collier hesitated, not at all convinced.

"Okay...come by anytime. It will only take a minute."

"Alright...I'll come first chance I get. You're right. This pain is driving me nuts." Collier told the older clinician as they walked up toward the main buildings from the mess.

All morning long, hope blossomed in Collier's chest as he replayed over and over the oral surgeon's possible diagnosis for his pain and suffering. Finally, just before lunch, he slipped away and made his way up to the rear of the surgical suite to Gibson's office.

"Come in, Collier, I'm just finishing up. Mildred, will you take Lieutenant Ramsay back and X-Ray his jaw on both sides? We need to see what's going on with this man's wisdom teeth," glancing up from suturing inside a patient's mouth, the genial oral surgeon instructed his surgical assistant without pausing from his work.

Dutifully Collier followed the dental assistant back and submitted while she made a complete set of X-Rays of both his jaws.

"I was right. This is the real physical reason for the pain in your jaws and neck. See right here. Your third molars are severely impacted top and bottom on both sides. We can take care of that little problem in no time at all. You'll hardly know you've been in the chair." Pointing to the X-rays on the light board a half-hour later, the oral surgeon beamed at the prospect of getting right to work.

"Well...I'm not sure when I can make the time...I...er...how long will it take for each tooth?" Collier was taken aback at the idea of having his teeth pulled.

"A little over an hour...no more than two. I've done plenty of these. Come in just before lunchtime tomorrow morning. I'll get those troublemakers out. Afterwards, you can take a nap and we'll go down for a little drink at the O Club after work. I promise—no sweat. Come on now, let's go get some lunch and we can talk it over." The enthusiastic specialist rubbed his hands together in anticipation.

"Will you do the uppers first? Or one side first?" Or will you just do four separate extractions?" Collier asked as they walked down toward the officers' mess, still reeling from the sudden turn of events.

"Oh, might as well get it over with. No sense in stretching it out. I'm going to do both sides, upper and lower—all four molars in one session. Don't worry. The trauma and post-op sequelae should be something less than a tonsillectomy," the oral surgeon reassured him.

"A tonsillectomy?" Collier had had his tonsils out when he was six and—other than his nightmarish memories of his induction under the ether anesthetic, he could remember very little about it. Trying hard not to obsess on the idea of undergoing this kind of procedure in such a primitive place, he asked. "Are you going to put me under ether?"

"No, no. I'll do it under local. You won't feel any pain. It'll all be over before you know it." Gibson said, passing through the lunch line, filling his tray to overflowing. Collier had lost his appetite thinking about his upcoming ordeal.

All afternoon, Collier tried to think up some reason to postpone the unexpected surgery, but could come up with no legitimate reason. That evening, his already finicky appetite suffered even more, and by 2100 hours, he was more than a little drunk on Vodka Collins in the O Club lounge. Wisely, he paid his tab, made it up the hill without making a spectacle of himself and fell on the bed in a half-drunken stupor. Gratefully, his alcoholic coma quickly became a deep gentle sleep.

Surprisingly, the next morning, he awoke feeling not that much the worse for wear.

The time between waking and time for his surgery sped by. Almost before he knew it, he had climbed the steps up to Gibson's cubbyhole in Building Two.

Robotically, he moved into the dental chair and submitted to the first pricks of the needle which began the numbing process.

"Is that Novocaine?" Collier asked when Hoot had completed the injections.

"No. Xylocaine. It's only been out about four or five years, and it's light years better than Novocaine. It's mixed with epinephrine which helps control the bleeding and also perpetuates the duration of the Xylocaine," Hoot assured him as he bent close over him, injecting the anesthetic deep into his tissue both above and below the jawline. While they waited for the anesthetic to take effect, Collier idly surveyed the array of surgical instruments on the tray in front of him and was astonished to see a hammer and a small chisel lying among the other instruments.

"What's the hammer for?" Collier asked. His jaw was growing rapidly numb and his tongue felt twice its normal size.

"Oh...we're probably going to have to chisel the molar roots away from the jawbones. It's not a problem. I do it all the time." The oral surgeon had donned a mask, but from the sound of his voice, Collier was sure he was smiling with malevolent glee.

Sure enough, before the procedure was over, Gibson had hammered and chiseled away at both sides of his mouth, removing the impacted jaw teeth in several pieces.

"Okay...all done. That wasn't so bad, now was it?" Including the jarring, hammering and chiseling away at his jawbones on both sides, top and bottom, the complete procedure had dragged on for almost three hours by the time the experienced oral surgeon had completed the suturing and removed his mask. "Try to keep your jaws clamped down tight on the sponges I placed inside the cavities to help stop the bleeding. Take these extra sponges and replace them after several hours. The anesthetic will start to wear off soon, and I'm going to give you fifty APC and a couple dozen of these one-eighth-grain codeine pills to ease your discomfort. My guess is that you'll take a nap and feel like coming down to the club later for a nightcap. Don't be afraid to take the codeine. It will help you sleep tonight. At any rate, I sleep in the hut next door if you need me." The oral surgeon seemed unconcerned, but he was quite solicitous of Collier's well-being.

True to Gibson's prediction, the pain began to creep through within two hours after Collier went to The Broken Drum to lie down, but fortunately he drifted off to sleep. In less than an hour from the time he woke from his nap, the pain bordered on being excruciating, quickly escalating to the point where it was almost unbearable—a completely unexpected situation for Collier who had always tolerated pain better than most of his teammates, and most certainly far better than his mother and even Emma who were constantly plagued by "killing" headaches.

Determined to ignore the pain, he took three more APC. After trying to tolerate the situation for the better part of an hour—by then he was pacing up and down the aisles between the bunks in the sleeping area of The Broken Drum, squeezing and unsqueezing his fists and kicking the furniture, anything to divert attention from his distress—he solemnly vowed never to minimize the suffering of others. Finally when he could endure the pain no longer, Collier took three more APC tablets with one of the tiny 1/8 grain codeine pills, but after waiting thirty minutes expecting relief, as far as he could tell, the medication had no effect at all.

Suffering for another hour, he took two more codeine, but he might as well have taken peppermint lifesavers as far as any effect in relieving his pain.

Shamelessly, he was sobbing like a baby now.

As dusk approached, Warrant Officers Gray and Flood came back from chow. Rather than let them see him blubbering like a ninny, he walked out back along the tin-can spangled fence between the latrine and the Chicken Coop—anything to distract his attention from the unrelenting throbbing in his jaw and ears.

"I'm sorry to have to bother you, Doc, but I can't stand this any longer. I'm no sissy, but I've already taken a half-dozen of the damned codeine and God knows how many APC." Shortly before 2000 hours, Collier finally gave in and went next door, greatly relieved to find Gibson sitting on his bunk in his skivvies writing a letter.

"Jesus, Collier, I'm sorry. Why did you wait so long? Come with me to my office. I have some morphine locked in a cabinet there." Gibson dropped his pen and slipped on his fatigue pants, leading the way across the street to the hospital.

In Gibson's office, Collier gulped down two morphine pills and accepted a little vial containing about a dozen more. At last, just before 2300 hours, Collier felt the effect of the heavy dose of morphine kick in, but still it only served to dull the pain, reducing it to the level of a dull, persistent throb.

Thankfully, by mid-morning the following day, the pain had subsided to a manageable level. By evening, Collier felt comfortable enough to go to evening chow where the friendly mess sergeant fixed him a steaming cup of chicken broth. Declining Smitty's invitation to have a drink, Collier slowly made his way back up the hill, falling exhausted on his bed.

At 0251, he roused wide awake, his lower jaw on both sides throbbing once again in excruciating pain. Collier fumbled around for his bedside flashlight, and quickly took two morphine pills. By 0345, he felt some minor effect of the morphine kicking in, but he was getting no real measure of relief. To add to his discomfort, he was now aware that both sides of his face had ballooned into lumps the size of small oranges. Not about to risk suffering through another agonizing episode like the previous afternoon and evening, he pulled on his pants and headed next door to rouse Gibson.

"Jesuschrist! You've got dry sockets on both sides. I can't remember when I've had a patient who has had such rotten luck." Gibson shook his head apologetically when Collier roused him out of a sound sleep, pointing the beam of his flashlight at his face.

"You mean they've abscessed on top of everything else?" Collier moaned.

"No. Not an abscess. Dry socket is not an infection, so don't worry about septicemia or anything like that." Hoot tried to ease his mind, but Collier was in no mood to receive a PhD on dental surgery as he went back to the Drum next door to tough it out the rest of the night.

All the following two days, Collier continued to prowl the hut, his fists clenched against the pain which no longer responded well to even double-doses of morphine. On the third night, he thankfully drifted off to sleep and woke the following morning with the pain a mere shadow of the previously excruciating level and the swelling visibly reduced.

The pain and swelling rapidly subsiding over the next day, by the end of the week, Collier returned to full duty. The good news was that he no longer suffered the irksome stiffness in his neck, and his neurotic preoccupation with his health had taken on a different perspective.

"Okay, now old sock, what do we want to die from today?" Now, on friendlier terms with his hypochondria, every morning when he arose, Collier winked wryly at his reflection in the shaving mirror.

On 7 September, the next letter from Madison arrived, it was dated August 19.

"...I just found out from my father that he is second cousin to your mother...I hope you don't mind that we are guilty of incest, because I can hardly wait to do it again...

Vacillating between whether or not he should confess his marital status to Madison, by Saturday, 12 September—after four full evenings and countless discarded attempts—Collier finally managed to finish his reply.

"I can hardly wait to continue our incest... " Seeing no reason to confess having a wife and baby son waiting back home, Collier answered Madison's letter, shamefully rationalizing: " *What the hell? Misery is optional.*" If he were lucky, he would fuck himself to death on his first R&R back at the Fujiya hotel with his kissing cousin, and he would die happy without having to suffer the anguish that a confession of his marriage was sure to bring.

Perhaps, if he were *truly* lucky—he allowed himself to be seduced by the erotic fantasy—Madison would prove to be a truly "liberated woman", a wanton hedonist who could care less if he were married or not. Besides, the secret of Emma and Kyle was nothing compared to his problem of how to keep Ginger and Madison secret from each other. Perhaps he could split his R&R. Use half to meet Madison at the Fujiya, then, under the guise of having to return to Korea, find another place to rendezvous with Ginger. After all, he was halfway around the world from civilization and family or anyone else who could possibly keep tabs on him.

All's fair in lust and war.

Just at dawn Monday morning, 14 September, there was a cloudburst and thunderstorm which literally sent a tidal wave of water rushing down the hill between the main hospital and its ancillary buildings across the dirt street, temporarily flooding these low-lying structures, including the NCO Mess, the enlisted men's 1-2-3 Club, and the building housing the Clinical Laboratory unit—fortunately leaving the hospital itself and the nearly-completed renovation of the wing housing the new quarters of The Broken Drum high and dry. Smitty's crew of indigenous Korean laborers had just finished hosing out the resulting silt and muck from those unfortunate buildings with highly-pressurized fire hoses when Colonel Martin Brewer—the corrupt Eighth Army G-3 who had bribed him to sign for the fraudulent inventory at the Yongdongpo PX—came pulling up in his Jeep in front of the hospital unannounced.

"Good morning, Lieutenant Ramsey, please tell Hal I'm here," the colonel greeted him brusquely, cavalierly referring to Scroggs by his nickname which Collier knew his stuffy boss-man hated.

"Send him in," Colonel Scroggs directed with an annoyed look, obviously having heard Brewer's highhanded entrance through the open door to his office, an expedient against the relentless oppressive summer heat.

"Good morning, Hal. I hate to hit you with this so early on a Monday, but it's been over six weeks since the truce was signed, and I need to reconcile some major discrepancies in the inventory of major equipment..." Collier barely heard Brewer state his mission before Scroggs got up and closed the door.

"Lieutenant Ramsay, come in here, please, and close the door." Less than fifteen minutes had passed when Scroggs opened the door and summoned Collier inside where Spaulding and Brewer sat staring at him in an accusatory way.

"What can you tell me about this missing GMC M-two-twenty-two water tanker truck?" Colonel Spaulding glared at Collier as if he had personally sold the vehicle in question to the Chinks on the black market.

"I'm afraid I don't know anything about any water tanker truck, sir," Collier replied, completely at a loss to follow the Colonel's line of thought.

"You signed for it when you took over the motor pool from Lieutenant Costage—certainly it must have been there when you made your inventory. You couldn't possibly have missed anything as big as a one-thousand-gallon water tanker truck...or could you?" Brewer's voice oozed an insulting tone.

"I can't imagine how, Sir. But as I recall Costage was way past due for rotation home and in a hurry and I remember being pressured...ah...urged...by Major Smith to go ahead and sign so Costage could catch his plane at Kimpo." Collier spread his hands, pleading for understanding.

"Look, Colonel Scroggs says Major Smith has gone up to the 38ᵗʰ MASH and I don't have all day here. Come with me, Lieutenant, and let's go check the motor pool. I need to resolve this right away." Brewer stood, nodding toward the door.

Fifteen minutes walking through the two-dozen or more vehicles with an added quarter-hour to check the separate files for each vehicle currently assigned to the compound revealed the 121st had at one time or another actually had the vehicle in question, but there was no record of the vehicle being around beyond October 3, 1952. Incredibly, the vehicle had been missing for almost a year without being noticed by Major Smith, his immediate predecessor, or Rock Costage, or any of the constantly rotating motor pool personnel.

"Looks like your ass is in a crack, Lieutenant. Providing they don't send you to Leavenworth, you're going to be an old man by the time they take the cost of that water tanker from your pay," the malevolent Colonel gloated as they walked back up the steps from the Motor Pool to the street in front of the main building.

"But, Colonel, I was assured any discrepancies in the inventory would be surveyed under the heading of 'war loss,'" Collier protested weakly, practically sweating blood.

"Who told you that? It's not so easy to write off gross negligence in the military. Besides we are at peace now." Brewer persisted, malevolently.

"Are you serious, Colonel? Or are you just exercising your natural rottenness?" After suffering the week of pure hell with his jaws, Collier was in no mood to be taken for a fool and he certainly wasn't going to let this corrupt bastard get away with charging him for this loss without a fight.

"I'm serious as a heart attack, Lieutenant. You'd better be careful of your tone. I'll add insubordination to the charges."

"Then we may wind up as cellmates, Colonel." Collier stopped dead in his tracks on the street at the foot of the front steps as he confronted the smirking senior officer.

"And, just what do you mean by that?" Brewer snarled indignantly.

"Well, when I suggest the IG look into your financial affairs, I wonder how you are going to hide the fortune you've been making, buying cigarettes for a dollar a carton and selling them in Seoul for ten bucks...not to mention all the money you've been making black-marketing greenbacks for Korean *hwan*, then converting *hwan* to military script. It should be easy to check your bank accounts back home in the states. Certainly, a close investigation would uncover a trail of stateside bank deposits and investments a mile wide—and I imagine once they start to dig, there might be some more interesting facets to your extracurricular life which would prove embarrassing to explain," Collier fired back without thinking of the consequences as the prospect of his endangered future flashed before his eyes.

"What! How dare you. Why...I will...I'll..." Brewer stammered, blustering at Collier's audacity and impudence.

"You'll what, Colonel Brewer, *Sir*?" Collier challenged, realizing now it was 'advantage Ramsay.' The gauntlet was in the colonel's court.

"Look, Lieutenant, surely you must know I was only kidding. Of course I'll see to it the discrepancies of the motor pool inventory are surveyed as a war loss. You certainly don't think the Army has the time, personnel or resources to pursue all the missing materiel left in the aftermath of this bloody war?" The colonel straightened, trying to regain his poise.

"I certainly hope not, *Sir*—for the sake of *both* our careers." Collier shrugged, waiting impassively.

"Please tell Scroggs not to worry...the matter of the inventory is resolved. I'll be on my way." The disgruntled colonel spit in the sand and started toward his vehicle.

"I should think it would be better for both of us if you told the colonel yourself, Colonel. After all, it's only a matter of simple courtesy...not to mention being proper protocol." Collier stared the spiteful bastard down.

"You're right, of course." Averting Collier's stare, Brewer turned and started back up the steps, pausing to look back when he reached the top. "If I were you, Lieutenant, I wouldn't press my luck." The arrogant Colonel clearly wanted to leave with the upper hand.

"That's good advice coming from a man who has one helluva lot more to lose than a mere shavetail, Colonel." Collier moved to follow him inside to Scroggs' office, wisely not trusting the oily bastard as far as he could see him.

After Brewer had cleared the air about the missing water tanker, Collier walked out with him, watching the livid Colonel silently crank his Jeep.

His throat still scratchy and jaws and neck hurting again, as soon as the arrogant G-3 colonel left, Collier headed for officer coffee call at the mess hall looking for Major Sammy Lee, the newly-arrived ear, nose and throat doctor. Still obsessing on the idea he might have cancer as the result of heavy smoking, Collier resolved to ask Lee to examine his throat. Up until now, Collier had resisted taking his problem to Junius Howell, the resident staff otolaryngologist who repeatedly made subtle remarks needling Collier about his neurotic tendencies. As far as Collier was concerned, the self-nominated prima donna, Howell—whose twin brother was a plastic surgeon...or dermatologist...or some other kind of esoteric specialist on the Faculty of the Bowman Gray School of Medicine back home in Winston-Salem, North Carolina who was supposed to have written a famous textbook—had summarily written Collier off as being hypochondriac and couldn't be trusted to have his best interest at heart.

To Collier, Dr. Sammy Lee promised to be a different species of Homo sapiens, altogether. Two-time Olympic Gold Medal winner from the ten-meter tower, the diminutive (the top of Lee's head barely came up to Collier's shoulder), American-born Korean physician was one of Collier's heroes. The previous week at an informal cocktail reception to welcome new officers aboard, Collier had cornered Lee and, adolescently-sycophantic, spilled out his pathetic boyhood ambitions to become a diver.

"My name is Collier Ramsay, Major Lee. I doubt you remember, but we met when you arrived. I'm adjutant here..." Collier waited until the pocket-sized medical officer had finished his coffee and was walking toward the door before he approached him about his problem.

"Sure, I remember, Lieutenant. You're the former springboard diver, right?" Lee stopped and smiled up at him.

"Yes, Sir, I always wanted to be a diver..." Collier was relieved the celebrity athlete seemed so readily approachable.

"I've been meaning to look you up, Lieutenant," Lee began to Collier's surprise.

"Please call me Collier, Sir." Collier interjected.

"Okay, if you'll call me Sammy. Walk back the hospital with me. What's on your mind?" Collier was surprised at the famous officer's casual friendliness.

"Thank you...ah...Sammy," Collier stammered, then blurted, "I've been having some problems with my throat, Sir, I wondered if you might take a look at it?"

"Sure...how long has this been going on?" The undersized Korean looked up sympathetically as they walked along.

Pouring out a capsule history of the KHF and polio outbreaks and the ensuing, embarrassing beginning of his persistent hypochondria, Collier finished with, "So you see, I really do understand this is most likely all part of some insidiously neurotic preoccupation on my part, but I think it might help me shake the damn thing if I were examined by a competent specialist who told me all this was the product of my overactive imagination. I can't go to Major Howell...he makes fun of me."

"Well, I see nothing funny about it. Come with me right now. I'll check you over before I start seeing today's assortment of goldbricks looking to get out of duty." The empathetic specialist steered him past the main entrance toward Admissions and the Outpatient Clinic across from the guard gate where Julius Howell had assigned him to take morning Sick Call ever since his arrival.

"Have a seat." In his office in the Outpatient Clinic, Lee was all business as he seated Collier in an adjustable examining chair and cranked him back to almost a prone position.

Shrugging into a freshly-starched clinic coat, the diminutive physician adjusted the leather headband of the stock-in-trade head-mirror on his forehead to make certain it would catch the reflection of the light.

"Just relax and open your mouth very wide and try not to gag...I lost two mirrors this week already from having them bit in two and swallowed..." Moving to Collier's side, Sammy Lee joked as he warmed a mirror similar to a dentist's mirror over the alcohol flame of an Etna lamp and got down to work.

Opening as wide as he could as Lee poked the mirror seemingly halfway down his esophagus, Collier struggled mightily not to gag. Surprisingly, the exam was over almost before it had begun.

"Ah ha! I think I've found your problem. Do you want the good news or bad news first?" Lee asked, cranking the chair to an upright position as he pushed back the head band with the mirror and moved aside the bright overhead light.

"The bad news...might as well get it over with." Collier said, preparing to hear the worst.

"You have a lump the size of a golf ball in your larynx," Lee replied, busying himself putting his used instruments back in a small sterilizing tray.

"Is it operable? I mean...I..." Collier stuttered, paralyzed with fear.

"It's operable. I can take it out." The surgeon gave him a serious look.

"Is it malignant, do you think?" Collier felt himself grow faint with fear.

"Not to worry. Looks like a ball of female pubic hair." The impish little Korean grinned.

"Uh...you mean?...I...ah..." Collier sputtered, finding it hard to laugh as he slowly realized the physician was reassuring him that he had found nothing wrong.

"As far as I can see your, throat is fine. If your symptoms worsen, don't hesitate to let me know. I'll keep a close eye on you. Now, let's get down to some serious business." Sammy adjusted Collier's chair to an upright position.

"Okay...what's on your mind, Doctor?"

"Sammy, remember?"

"Okay, Sammy." Collier had a feeling he was being had.

"You're adjutant of this joint. How hard would it be to get our hands on some bed sheets...without signing your life away?"

"Bed sheets?" Collier was not sure he'd understood.

"Yeah. You know, regular hospital bed sheets? As far as I can find out, except for MASH units, we're the only other place in the combat zone that has sheets." Sammy Lee leaned forward seriously.

"Well...I should be able to liberate some sheets...a few...how many are we talking about?" Collier replied guardedly, not having a clue where this curious request was going.

"Oh...four...six maybe, with some...a few...pillowcases, if they're available, too." Sammy waited anxiously for a reply.

"If I may be bold to ask, why am I going to pursue this peculiar midnight requisition?" Collier asked, still not sure how far he was going with this.

"Well, I'm not thinking of forming a Korean branch of the KKK if that's what's worrying you. I've been treating a major in the engineer outfit up the road—about a mile, back toward Seoul—for a chronic sinus condition. They are throwing a big going-away party for their CO and want to do it up right with white table cloths...get the picture?" Sammy smiled.

"Engineers, huh? What do they have to trade?" In the combat zone, a good officer was always on the lookout for the opportunity to lay his hands on something hard to get—Engineers could get their hands on a lot of stuff, like lumber and nails.

"How does a boxcar load of cement sound?" Sammy asked, trying hard to hide his enthusiasm.

"A boxcar of cement? How much cement does a boxcar hold? How much cement can we have for the sheets—I should think we would need to ask for a truckload at least. Sheets are hard to come by." Collier enthused, a two-and-a-half-ton, six-by-six truck full of cement would come in handy for a lot of things.

"I'm not talking about a measly truckload. I'm talking about the whole boxcar full."

"The whole boxcar? My God, Sammy, what the hell will we do with a boxcar load of cement?" The idea was overwhelming. He wasn't an engineer. He didn't have the foggiest notion how much concrete a boxcar load of cement would produce.

"How about a swimming pool, for starters? There's plenty of empty space in this compound...a nice, twenty-by-forty pool would look good—in the empty lot just beyond Supply between the laundry and the officers' mess. As hot as it is, it would do wonders for morale."

"Jeesus, Sammy, a whole boxcar full of cement—Spaulding will about shit." Collier tried to envision their CO's reaction. The old fart had been bugging Scroggs about laying some cement sidewalks after Otis Owen finished the stone fireplace on the ramshackle officers mess.

"Just think of the brownie points. You can do a lot with that much cement." The ENT physician encouraged.

"I know. I guess we could tell him the swimming pool would be good therapy for our patients—a sort of an adjunct to rehab. And he's been complaining about the muddy walkways around the Chicken Coop." Collier's mind raced ahead, envisioning a myriad of far-ranging uses for a full boxcar-load of cement.

"Now you're talking. Go see Spaulding right now before those engineers find another source for sheets." Lee urged as he stood and shoved Collier toward the door.

"That's a real coup, Lieutenant. Tell Smitty I said to give you all the sheets you want. Don't let that cement get away from you," Spaulding enthused when Collier gave him the news. Visualizing inviting visiting dignitaries and superior officers for a swim, and the thought of having sidewalks around the mud-plagued compound was enough to send the phlegmatic, old colonel into the throes of acquisition-crazed ecstasy.

"Call your contact in the engineers and ask him how many trucks and men we should send to transport the cement." Collier made straight for Sammy Lee with the news.

"I already discussed it with them. If I deliver the sheets this morning, they will deliver the cement this afternoon." Sammy could hardly contain himself at the idea of having the wherewithal to build a swimming pool.

By mid-afternoon, a long column of two-and-a-half-ton, six-by-six, cement-loaded military trucks showed up at the gate, and Major Smith and Sergeant Owens directed them to some empty sheds behind Supply where they had the Korean laborers stack the veritable mountain of cement bags.

Sammy Lee lost no time in putting his scheme to work. When Collier walked down to breakfast the following morning, he could hardly believe his eyes when he saw Sammy Lee directing Otis Owen and his indigenous workforce as they staked the outline for excavating a swimming pool.

"Would you like to drive me over to Seoul this morning around ten o'clock?" At breakfast the next morning, Sammy Lee invited Collier to go with him where he was giving a diving exhibition by command performance of President Syngman Rhee who had invited a contingent of Korean government officials, plus a crowd of hand-chosen dignitaries.

"Judaspriest, Sammy, you just got here. How come you're already giving an exhibition for Syngman Rhee?" Collier was impressed.

"Following the Russo-Japanese War in the early 1900's, Syngman Rhee and my father both left Korea in exile to escape the Japanese. First they went to Hawaii in 1905 and in 1907 they emmigrated from Hawaii to California where I grew up. Rhee and my father were like brothers. My father died trying to get Syngman elected to the Korean presidency. Colonel Spaulding sent me over the other day to check him for a chronic ear infection, and Uncle Syngmam insisted I put on a diving exhibition," Sammy explained

"Have you taken a good look at Seoul? Where in hell are you going to put on a diving exhibition around here?" Collier asked, passing around the traffic circle at the impressive centuries-old Southgate to the city, ornately decorated with traditional oriental motifs.

On a recent trip into the ravaged city, Smitty had pointed out that Seoul still retained two gates of the ancient wall that once surrounded it, plus three imperial palaces—the Gyeongbok Palace, built in 1394 by the first monarch of the Choson dynasty; the Changdeok Palace (1405-1412), containing many valuable relics; and the Deoksu Palace (1593), which housed the National Museum and Art Gallery. Also, near the center of the city, Smitty had shown Collier a huge bronze bell that was cast in 1468. Now, driving down the central boulevard leading directly to the Capitol building, all around them, the buildings were gutted hollow from aerial bombing and artillery during the several times the capital city had changed hands during the three long years of war. Passing a shop filled with brass plates and candle holders and trays and a variety of other ornaments made from discarded artillery casings, here and there Collier noted the neat piles of brick and rubble. Along the streets were many armless or legless or sightless Korean adults and children giving mute evidence of the terrible carnage.

To Collier the ghoulish cityscape looked surreal, like a Hollywood back lot set for a WWII combat film.

"I know it's hard to imagine a swimming pool in the middle of all this devastation, but Uncle Syngham said all the bombardiers must have been sportsmen because they bombed everything but the Olympic diving pool. I've already seen the stadium. You won't believe this place could exist in the middle of all this destruction."

Sammy was right. When they arrived at the stadium site, Collier was completely flabbergasted to find a full-fledged, Olympic-sized pool with a regulation ten-meter tower and three-meter springboard sitting in the heart of the ruins. Going with Sammy to inspect the diving tower, Collier climbed the steps to the springboard and was amazed to find the board was a brand-new regulation springboard manufactured in the States. A laminated wooden model, the board had a state-of-the-art abrasive non-slip sandpaper-like coating on the surface. Collier had read about such equipment, but had never seen a board like this close up—not even at the regulation pool in Byrd Park in Richmond which had an impressive metal diving board.

For whatever reason, the water in the pool was murky to the point of looking stagnant and polluted, as if it might have come out of a nearby rice paddy, but Collier didn't say anything. He didn't want to offend their proud Korean hosts who, obviously, had gone to a great deal of trouble to pump in such a sizeable amount of water from somewhere.

"Don't worry about the looks of the water. It came from the city waterworks and has been treated and chlorinated." Lee turned and walked to the steps leading to the dressing rooms underneath the pool. "Come on, let's get this show on the road; follow me."

"Come on, Collier, why not dive with me from the springboard?" In the dressing room, Sammy tossed him a pair of racing trunks and tried to coax him into joining him in the exhibition.

"You've got to be kidding, Sammy. No way am I going to make a fool of myself in front of all these people." Collier shook his head vehemently. Even if he had been in shape and had been diving recently, he knew he was far outclassed by a two-time Olympic champ.

"Chicken! I think all this business about you ever having been a diver was just a pile of bull manure," Sammy kidded, but Collier just ignored him.

"Jeezie, Sammy, would you just get a load of this!" On the way back up to the pool, Collier stopped by the open door to a storage room containing at least a dozen brand-new 16-foot-long laminated springboards just like the one on the 3-meter tower stacked against the wall.

"Looks like the Koreans are serious about my helping train their divers," Sammy laughed. "Come on; let's give them a show."

When they emerged back beside the pool, Collier followed and stood by as Sammy walked around the side of the diving tank and talked with a scattering of early-arriving Korean spectators.

"Collier, come here a minute, I want you to meet an old friend." Sammy had been chatting with the early-arrivals for perhaps ten minutes when he called Collier to join him.

"Suh Yon-Bok, I would like to present my fellow officer, Lieutenant Collier Ramsay. My old friend, Suh Yon-Bok, won the Boston Marathon in nineteen-forty-seven. Suh Yon-Bok says he is still running and may run in the next Olympics if South Korea fields a team," Sammy introduced Collier to an ageless-looking, wiry little Korean who was several inches taller than the diver.

Collier shook hands with the noted Korean athlete then turned, looking up at the gathering crowd waiting for the arrival of their aging President. When Rhee showed up and took his seat right on time, Sammy went over and had a few words with the well-recognized, world-renown figure. After a few minutes, Sammy looked up into the grandstand and called out something in Korean to the crowd. As a result, a woman in the audience stood up and—at Sammy's urging—moved over to sit in the section with the Korean President. When the shy woman was seated, Sammy directed a photographer to take their picture.

"A relative on my mother's side. She'll be a neighborhood hero when they see her picture sitting with Uncle Syngham." Sammy waved and smiled. The sometimes ill-humored President waved back in a gesture of happy familiarity.

For the next hour, Collier stood awestruck at the poolside ladder underneath the diving towers waiting with an armful of towels, as he watched his hero—now at the advanced age of thirty-four—put on an unbelievable display of the dazzling skills that had made him two-time Olympic champion. Starting on the 3-meter board, the compact Korean diver ran through the entire series of basic required dives in all five categories: front dive with front approach, back dive with back approach, inward dive with inward approach, reverse dive with forward approach (what the kids back home called a gainer), and a twisting dive.

"How about reverse dive with a half-twist in the full layout position? It's my favorite of all the dives," Collier asked when Sammy climbed out of the pool after executing a double-twisting inward two-and-a-half somersault from the springboard, now looking to climb up to the ten-meter tower. Properly executed, the half-twisting reverse dive in full layout position was one of the most graceful dives to watch. Stepping off a full-front approach, the diver soared high above the front end of the board laid out in the classic swan-dive position with his feet projected outward from the board, then, at the apex of his dive, the diver slowly rotates his head toward his left shoulder, almost imperceptibly dropping his left arm poolward as his body, still in the swan dive position follows back down by the tip of the board to enter the water like a knife.

"I'll try. I haven't done that one in awhile, though. I concentrate more on the multiple somersaults in the tuck position. They show better for a runt like me." Sammy chuckled as he climbed back up to the 3-meter board, measured off the approach, obviously trying to visualize the dive in his mind; then, without making any additional preparation, he stepped off the approach and launched himself off the end of the board, reaching an incredible height and executing the dive almost flawlessly, entering the murky water with hardly a ripple.

"How's that?" the proud, elfin Olympic champ asked with a sly grin as he climbed out of the pool.

"Frigging incredible, you absolutely nailed it!" Collier congratulated as he handed Lee a towel.

From that point on, Sammy's exhibition consisted of a spectacular display of twisting somersault dives from the ten-meter tower: single- and double-twisting one-and-a-half, two-and-a-half somersaults from the required forward, back, inward, and reverse positions. As his *piece de resistance*, Lee executed a breathtaking, forward three-and-a-half in the tucked position—the dive he invented, clinching the 1952 Olympic Gold Medal for himself. Although most of these dazzling acrobatics were performed in the tucked and open-pike position which lacked the grace of the full layout position, to Collier, a former-wannabe diver, the exhibition was utterly breathtaking.

"My wife, Roz, is coming to Japan, and I've arranged to be able to meet her there and spend almost a week. Is there anything I can get for you?" Sammy said on the way back through Seoul returning to the hospital.

"Gee, Sammy, that's great you'll get to see your wife. But I can't think of anything." Collier resisted the idea of asking Sammy to deliver a note to Madison or Ginger.

"You know, I have an idea. During World War Two, the Japanese Army issued these rubber vaginas to their troops stationed for long stretches on the remote Pacific Islands. These things were sort of hot water bags and could be filled with warm water to enhance their...ah... utility. They used these gadgets to relieve their unresolved sexual appetites. Well, anyway, you can still actually buy them on the Ginza in Tokyo—I saw some in a shop window last month on my way over here. I've been thinking while I'm in Tokyo we...you and I...might invest in a bunch of these rubber pussies and maybe even a few rubber penises for all these horny, homely nurses. We could rent them out—fifty-fifty partners—what do you say?"

"You're kidding, right?" Collier shot him a suspicious look.

"Hmm-m? Maybe it isn't such a good idea at that." Sammy's eyes twinkled as he changed the subject back to his upcoming trip to see his wife.

With the new pool rigidly off-limits over the weekend to allow the concrete to cure, late Sunday night, Otis hooked up a long series of hoses and began to fill the pool.

"The staff is after me to put on a little diving exhibition at the opening party for our new pool tomorrow morning. Can you get us a Jeep? I know where we can get us a darn-good diving board—they'll never miss it." Sammy approached Collier at breakfast Monday morning.

"Judaspriest, Sammy, where in hell do you think you're going to mount a diving board? Do you think you can work something out with Otis Owen and get his Korean workers to devise a one-meter fulcrum?" Collier asked. He knew exactly where Sammy was headed to get the diving board.

"Not necessary. We'll just figure out some way to mount the board directly on the side of the pool. That shouldn't be a problem."

"But, Sammy, the sides of that pool are only about a foot above the water line. What kind of dives can you possibly hope to execute from that height?" Collier cautioned, thinking his friend was setting himself up for a bitter disappointment.

"Oh, don't worry about the height. I can do 'em all—except, of course, the three-and-a-half. Now, let's go find Sergeant Owen. We need to get that diving board." The cocky little Korean athlete urged Collier toward the door.

When they arrived in Seoul at the swimming pool, a pair of Korean men were waiting to put the brand-new diving board in their three-quarter-ton utility vehicle. Mounting the diving board directly on the side wall of the pool proved to be easy enough for Otis' ingenious Korean workers. But, just as Collier had predicted, the tip of the board was less than a yard above the water when it was bolted into place. When Sammy tested it, the tip of the board actually slapped the surface of the water when he worked it hard—fortunately it did not actually dip beneath the water's surface, impeding the necessary rebound, and Collier was amazed at how much lift the compact midget diver was able to generate. At the apex of his lift, Sammy was at least six—maybe eight—feet above the board. Without further preamble, Sammy turned his back to the water, lifted his arms, flexed his knees in the beginning of a routine standing approach and launched himself into the air, tucked into a tight ball, spinning with blinding speed as he reached full altitude, then straightened and came back down by the tip of the board, stretched straight out into the full-entry position before he knifed into the water almost without a splash.

"Pretty good lift, don't you think?" The amazing diver winked and rubbed the towel across his head after he hoisted himself over the rough concrete side of the pool.

"Jeeze, Sammy, how many revolutions was that?" Collier still couldn't believe his eyes.

"Only two and a half—I'll never make three at this height with the tip of the board deadened by slapping the water." He laughed at Collier's stunned look.

Standing watching the current Olympic champ run through a dazzling routine of dives off the poolside-mounted springboard, if Collier had been concerned about the next-morning's exhibition, all doubt was now erased. The following morning, Sammy gave two exhibitions—one for the patients and the second for the staff—both were to rousing ovations with resulting encores.

Afterward the exhibition—largely due to the time he was spending overseeing the final stages of the renovation of the luxurious, new quarters for The Broken Drum and making plans for a grand-opening party there—except for an occasional session of after-hours ping-pong in the patient lounge where, playing about even, they waged an ongoing all-out war, Collier saw less and less of Sammy in the days that followed.

One of the Red Cross women had discovered a first-class guitar-player and singer, "Smiley"—a nice-looking, young Air Force sergeant at Kimpo Air Force Base across the river whose real name was Jimmie Rodgers, the same as the old-time "Blue Yodeler"—who had been coming once or twice a week in the evenings to entertain the patients up in the patient lounge in Building Four. After lights out, Colonel Reed, the Assistant to the Eighth Army Surgeon, had been bringing Smiley to the late-night parties at The Hen House where Collier often wound up leading a half-drunk sing-a-long among the docs and nurses and all the usual administrative partygoers. Colonel Reed particularly liked it when Collier led a Weavers-type sing-a-long of Burl Ives' popular folk tune, *On Top of Old Smokey*, and Collier had readily agreed with Colonel Reed that Smiley should be invited to the gala unveiling of the new The Broken Drum.

Friday, September 18, the night of the grand opening of their new billet, Collier wound up on top of the bar leading the half-drunken assemblage in chorus after chorus of *Old Smokey* and *Blue Tail Fly* and *Foggy-Foggy Dew* and a medley of Hank Williams' cheating lover songs until the good-natured guitarist, Smiley Rodgers, finally pleaded he would be AWOL if he didn't get back to Kimpo in time for morning formation, and left in the wee hours of the morning.

"Grab a Jeep and let's go over to Kimpo." Colonel Scroggs greeted Collier as he came through the door Monday morning, 21 September. The hospital staff had spent a busy weekend treating nearly a dozen GIs suffering methyl-alcohol poisoning from drinking some ersatz American Haig and Haig Scotch and I.W. Harper bourbon whiskey they had purchased on the black market—which turned out to be wood alcohol. The ingenious, enterprising Korean bootleggers were quite adept at heating the bottom of commercial liquor bottles, inserting a large needle through the softened glass and extracting the good liquor which they replaced with home-distilled methyl (wood) alcohol before reheating and resealing the glass. Methyl alcohol poisoning was sometimes fatal; these unlucky GIs were fortunate to the extent that all of them would live, despite the touch-and-go circumstance of a pair who might be facing a future of methyl-alcohol blindness.

"What's going on at Kimpo, Colonel?" Collier asked. He couldn't recall seeing the usually taciturn Harold Scroggs so excited.

"A North Korean pilot named No Kum-Sok has just flown his MIG-15 fighter plane into Kimpo. He wants to turn over his top-secret Russian fighter to our Air Force and ask for political asylum. Run get my Jeep from the Motor Pool." Scroggs was already past Collier, heading for the front door.

By the time they got to Kimpo, the base was buzzing with MPs. As hard as they tried, they couldn't get near the hangar where the Air Force ground crews had pushed the near-legendary, supersonic jet fighter away from public view. On the runways across the way, a constant stream of jet fighters were taking off and landing as the Air Force was taking no chances the NKCA or the Chinese—or even the Russians—might attempt to destroy the top-secret jet fighter plane, rather than let it fall into American hands.

By mid-afternoon, Scroggs had exhausted every avenue of influence he could think of to get a peek inside the hangar—with no results. Finally around 1445, they headed home, excited by such a dramatic turn of events, but sorely disappointed.

When they got back to the 121 that evening, Collier found a letter from Madison waiting with his mail.

"I just received your letter and am sorry you are having so much trouble with your wisdom teeth. Because I unexpectedly found myself pregnant with your child last week, I took the liberty of using my influence with Eighth Army HQ personnel section and discovered you neglected to tell me you were married and had a son back in Virginia. Looking back on our brief time together and the passion that sprang up between us, I guess I understand why you didn't tell me...please know I do love you and want you to know that I forgive you, but, no matter how I feel about you, I cannot, in good conscience, continue to be involved with a married man. Of course, I have already had a discrete abortion at a Japanese clinic. When (if) you come to Tokyo on R&R in November, please don't try to contact me. It's in the best interest of both of us we never meet again..."

Mentally and physically exhausted, Collier walked out back of the Chicken Coop, leaned on the beer-can-laden barbed-wire enclosure and bawled like a baby.

The following morning, still somewhat depressed, Collier read in the *Stars & Stripes* that the defector Communist pilot, No Kum-Sok, had been oblivious to an American standing offer of an $100,000 reward for a MIG-15. The paper later reported that test flights conducted at Okinawa and in the United States revealed the MIG-15 was not supersonic after all, which went a long way toward explaining why the American pilots were so effective in shooting them down.

After reading the most recent *Stars & Stripes* account of the MIG-defection, Collier decided to venture down to his office and check through the mounting pile of paperwork accumulated during his recuperation. Idly sorting the assorted bulletins and orders which filtered down daily from Eighth Army HQ, he came across a curiously-worded, highly ambiguous Army communiqué which seemed to imply—after careful reading for at least the third time—that all "reserve" officers, called to active duty after the beginning of hostilities on June 26, 1950, were eligible for release from active duty at the end of their two-years of active duty.

"What's the date of your commission?" Captain Donovan asked when Collier walked down to the hospital staff CO's office and showed him the rather enigmatic and confusing document.

"Thirteen December Fifty-two...but I went on active duty two January fifty-two. I'll have two years on active duty in three-and-a-half months on two January fifty-four." Collier argued.

"Yeah, but this relates specifically to commissioned officers. You haven't even completed nine months since you got your commission. You sure as hell don't think Uncle Sugar is going to waste all that money spent on giving you a commission, do you?" Donovan snorted and handed him back the papers.

Discouraged, Collier took the paper back to The Broken Drum and read it and reread it a dozen times, at least, weighing his conflicting ambitions of: One: Becoming a career officer in the Regular Army and spending another year in Korea, then signing on for two more years in Japan where he had planned to pursue his affair with Madison unimpeded by prudish civilian stateside convention—he most likely would have wound up asking Emma for a divorce—against his current option Number Two: The seductive scenario of returning stateside and resuming civilian life as an artist back home away from all this ruin, disease, human suffering and miserable, depressing squalor.

What the hell? Hope of continuing his interrupted relationship with Ginger was tenuous at best—she was rotating stateside in November. If he became RA, stuck it out here for another nine months, then rotated to Japan and divorced Emma, Madison would forgive him. Even if Donovan was right and he didn't qualify, what did he have to lose?

Finally, late that evening, with nothing better to occupy his time, he went down to his office and—using his awkward hunt-and-peck, two-finger typing method—carefully filled out the military form requesting his release from active duty pursuant to the recent difficult-to-translate Department of Army communiqué to which he referred by its official number. Without any real hope in his heart for success, he walked it slowly down the deserted hall and dropped the form into Donovan's In-Box.

"Bayonet, put me through to Bullfrog..." Back in his office, Collier picked up the phone and went through the tedious process of calling John Henry at the 48th MASH. Lucky to find him awake and near the phone, Collier excitedly told him about the communiqué.

"Your Captain Donovan is right. There's no way that bulletin applies to us." Pewter reacted immediately.

"Maybe," Collier conceded, then continued, "But, what do I...what do you...what do we...have to lose?" He argued, disappointed at Pewter's response.

"Well...nothing...except our dignity when we get a letter from the Pentagon telling us we should learn to read before we go wasting the Army's time," Pewter chided.

"Okay, forget it. Have it your way, Pewter. I'll send you picture postcards when my ship arrives in Seattle or San Francisco in January," Collier fired back.

"Okay, okay. Don't get your ass up in the air. I'll see if I can find the bulletin or directive or whatever and give it a look." Still skeptical that the communiqué applied to either one of them, Collier's old compadre was quick to humor him.

"Suit yourself." Collier sniffed disdainfully. "Not to change the subject, but why don't you come down to visit? I'm fixing to throw a big party to christen the new quarters for administrative officers. Booze, music, dancing girls...you name it." Collier told him about his project to reincarnate The Broken Drum.

"It's hard for me to get a vehicle here. You're adjutant at your place. Why don't you get a Jeep sometime soon and drive up here to visit?" Pewter asked before they broke off the call.

"Soon...I promise." Collier hung up and trudged disconsolately up the hill to bed.

"Good news and bad news," Scroggs greeted Collier as he came in before Officers Call the following morning.

"Bad news first for me always, Colonel," Collier replied disinterestedly—it was far too early to playing games. "Your recommendations for the Medal of Honor for Yates and Williams were turned down."

"What!" Collier looked sharply up from digging through the pile of routine bulletins in the In-box on his desk. "With your permission, sir, I'm going to buck that recommendation right back through channels this very morning. Both of those men are genuine heroes. Right up there with Alvin York and Audie Murphy, in my book."

"Cool off, Ramsay. You haven't heard the good news yet." Scroggs looked at him with a twinkle.

"Okay, give me the good news, and then I'm going to start raising hell with Eighth Army about the commendations for Yates and Williams."

"Thanks to you, both men have been awarded the Silver Star," Scroggs replied, waiting to get a reaction.

"Shit! Can't we buck this back, Colonel? They both deserve at least the DSC. You read my commendation." Collier looked to Scroggs knowing full-well he might as well count his lucky blessings that Yates and Williams had been awarded anything.

"Yes, I not only read your commendation, I interviewed both CWO Yates and Sergeant Williams when I submitted my recommendation that you receive the Medal of Honor—which, judging from the Silver Stars for these two, bodes well that at least a Silver Star is in your immediate future."

"It's a dishonest system, Colonel. Both those men deserved at least a DSC...and I really could give a rat's ass about a medal for myself. I'm no hero. Those men volunteered—the Army didn't give me a choice." Collier protested, but Scroggs raised his hand to cut him off.

"Save it, Ramsay. Just be satisfied. The Silver Star is not exactly chopped liver. Besides, you'll be pleased to know that you have been invited to Eighth Army HQ tomorrow afternoon to present these men their medals at a special retreat parade."

"Thank you, Colonel...I guess I had better ask Cha to get my dress khakis pressed..." Collier said trying not to show his disappointment and chagrin.

CHAPTER FORTY-SIX

THE ROANOKE TIMES
Roanoke, Virginia, Thursday, October 29, 1953
REDS BLAMED FOR DEATH OF 6,113 U.S. PRISONERS

29,815 REPORTED STILL MISSING

WASHINGTON, October 28, (AP) - The Army made public tonight a grisly story of Communist atrocities in the Korean War, reporting that probably 6,113 Americans died in the blood bath.

In what the Secretary of the Army Stevens called a "cold blooded program of murder and torture," 29,815 persons are estimated to have lost their lives.

STARS AND STRIPES
UNOFFICIAL PUBLICATION OF UNITED STATES FORCES, FAR EAST

Vol. 9, No. 301   Thursday, October 29, 1953
**U.N. SAYS RUSSIA TOOK
DIRECT ROLE IN KOREAN WAR**

PANMUNJOM, Korea. October 28, (AP) - The U.N. Command today charged Russia had directly participated in the Korean War with planes, tanks, guns and munitions.

TRUE TO HIS WORD, Collier commandeered a Jeep the following Sunday afternoon and found his way onto the military bypass around Seoul a few miles north to the 48th MASH. The 48th—which now, like most of the similar Mobile Surgical Hospital units, had become more or less permanently established during the several months following the signing of the truce at Panmunjom—was set up as a conglomerate arrangement of tent and Quonset units.

"Great to see you." When Collier arrived, Pewter was waiting to greet him at the door of one of the Quonset huts. After a quick tour of the unit and a brief introduction to his CO, a surgeon from a small town in the Florida panhandle, Pewter led him down the road to a nearby Korean village. It took Collier by complete surprise to find Pewter had actually taken a house in the village and was living with a "Korean Wife." Doing his best to conceal his surprise during the course of the two hours he visited with him and his newfound lady friend—who was not exactly a likely contender for Miss South Korea in the upcoming Miss Universe Competition—Collier had to laugh out loud on his way back, trying to beat the military curfew of darkness as he ruminated over how hard it had been to finally accomplish the loss of his buddy's virginity. Now he had a live-in Korean "moose"—go figure?

Over the next two weeks following the surgical extraction of his wisdom teeth, Collier's symptoms of a stiff neck and sore throat—however real or imagined—rapidly improved. Lately, he found himself going through almost entire days without even thinking about KHF or polio or throat cancer. In fact his mental health had improved so much that his ritual of waking up each morning and confronting his image in the shaving mirror with the neurotic question, "Well, what new disease do we want to die from today, old sock?" had become something of a personal joke.

The surgery had not relieved him of his neurotic proclivities entirely, however. Much to his disgust, he still walked around harboring a subconscious fear that he would die of some unknown exotic malady. The inevitable consequence of this deeply-ingrained psychosomatic mindset was that now he was plagued by a somewhat chronic, low-grade diarrhea which had led him lately to the subliminal suspicion he might actually have leukemia. To divest himself of this new neurotic fixation, he secretly prevailed upon Billy at the lab to run a CBC which came back as normal as a bacon for breakfast or a piss-hard upon waking up in the morning.

Finding his blood count was normal was a big relief, but diarrhea is diarrhea and shitting one's drawers is real enough no matter what the etiology. So he suffered along in silence, more and more isolating himself from the morning officer's coffee call to avoid the abrasive derision of several of the highly superior members of the medical staff, not the least of which was Sammy Lee's smart-aleck cohort, the self-proclaimed hotshot otolaryngologist, Junius Howell. To replace the loss of greatly-missed, social contact evenings after chow, more and more, Collier avoided going into the Quonset Bar, accepting instead offers from some of his NCO friends to join them for a drink at the NCO club. He greatly enjoyed the level of respect these pragmatic, down-to-earth enlisted men showed him, and he especially enjoyed the refreshing atmosphere of complete unpretentiousness.

"Let's take a ride up to Uijongbu and take a look at the country." One sunny day during his post-surgical recovery period, he had taken Major Smith up on the unexpected invitation to accompany him on a purely pleasure jaunt. They had wandered for almost the entire day on back roads through the country, turning eastward from the battle-scarred mountains in the Uijongbu corridor to follow meandering trails barely wide enough to accommodate their Jeep. Their tour was a kaleidoscopic whirl which Collier attempted to chronicle with his new Canon camera. He shot such picturesque scenes as Korean women harvesting and washing huge quantities of large, white, parsley-like vegetables by a stream, Korean women washing clothes in another stream, an old papasan with a white beard carrying an unbelievably-massive load of hay on one of the ever-present A-Frames (which allowed the primitive Koreans to become their own beasts of burden), a man with a pony, a group of kids driving an ox cart with wheels taken from a war-ravaged Jeep, and, finally, a woman carrying a huge bundle with a small infant on her hip. Up beyond Uijongbu, they lucked upon the edge of the South Korean National Forest—or at least *some* Korean forest—which was something of an anomaly in this countryside where trees were mostly scrubby, more like bushes than full-fledged trees. Somehow, miraculously, by dead reckoning and intuition they managed to find themselves back on one of the main military highways in the late afternoon and made their way back through the abject ruins of Seoul past the old landmark railroad station, finally crossing the Han River Bridge at Yongdongpo in time for supper chow back at the 121st.

"Bayonet connect me with Bullfrog. Bullfrog hook me up with Barbwire...Barbwire put me through to Molehill...Molehill get me ..." Suffering the exhausting ignominy of being transferred from switchboard-to-switchboard, down the long line to K-9 switchboard outside of Pusan, incredibly, Collier was finally able to reach his brother Jim on 3 October, to wish him a happy birthday. Although their conversation was marred by static over the primitive long-distance phone wires, the reunion was a happy one. Collier asked his brother why he didn't fly himself up to Kimpo the following Friday, 9 October, to join him in the gala housewarming party for the new—lavishly improved and expanded—version of The Broken Drum.

"When pigs fly." His brother laughed at Collier's naïve belief he could just take off and fly a B-26 around Korea like a private pleasure craft.

The very next morning, Collier's pleasure at reaching his brother by phone was further enhanced when he found Herb Rudolph—his old buddy from Basic training who, with his wife Louise, had become his and Emma's housemates when they leased the big apartment from the sensuous Hilda Birdsong back at Lawton—waiting outside the officers' mess for him after breakfast. Herb was wearing Staff Sergeant stripes with a single rocker underneath.

"Herb, you old reprobate, how long have you been in Korea? Where are you stationed?" Clasping him warmly around the shoulders, Collier hit his old friend with a rapid-fire barrage of questions, before he laughed and added. "Congratulations on making sergeant. Corporal Dixon back at FARTC would shit his pants if he saw you wearing those stripes."

It turned out that Herb had actually arrived in Korea back in January, six full months before Collier finally landed at Kimpo the first week in July. The bespectacled suburban Philadelphian had been stationed right across the river at Eighth Army HQ in Seoul all this time and had finally located Collier just last week when Louise wrote Herb that Emma had brought her up to date.

"I'll come back first chance I get," Herb waved goodbye after Collier had invited him in for a cup of coffee in his office which—except for the occasional presence of CWO Gray who was AOD—they had enjoyed all to themselves, being as it was Saturday morning.

Too frazzled to protest the insistence of both the Chief of Medicine, Major Hughes and gastroenterologist, Captain Mutch, at coffee call on Wednesday, 14 October, Collier allowed himself to be sent to the clinical lab to have a stool culture made with swabs from his colon to check for intestinal organisms, such as amoebic dysentery, which might explain his long-running chronic diarrhea that had become alarmingly severe over the weekend. As part of their work-up—and because they agreed it would do their over-reactive patient a world of good to get away from daily stress—they decided to admit him that night to the unoccupied VIP ward (it was really a large room with six beds and a fancy portable toilet) in Building Two so they could give him a complete physical work-up in the hospital the following day.

"*Wake for morning in the bowl of night, has flung the stone that sets the stars to flight. And the Hunter of the East has caught the Sultan's turret in his noose of light.*" Just before sunrise Thursday morning, Collier came slowly to wakefulness to the sound of a sonorous voice quoting poetry. Momentarily confused as to his whereabouts, he peeked through slitted-eyelids at the shadowy, rather tall silhouette of a man outlined against the pre-dawn light streaming through the backdrop of the plastic-coated chicken-wire covered, bomb-twisted, metal window frame on the wall across the room.

After a moment, the shadowy form moved and disappeared behind a portable screen and Collier heard the unmistakable sound of a man pissing into a toilet followed by the boom of an all-time prize-winning fart.

Slowly, Collier remembered he was in bed in his own hospital as he recalled checking into the VIP room with the private, portable toilet Major Smith had had his indigenous Korean labor force install when Korean President Syngman Rhee had been admitted, a week or so after the truce was signed, to undergo treatment for the flare-up of a chronic ear infection. Later, during Big Switch, Collier had watched while General Ridgeway's G2 had whisked General William F. Dean off to the privacy of this VIP room adjacent to the General Medical Ward. The outside stairs leading up from the street had been cordoned off with a military guard until Dean could undergo a brief medical examination before he was transported by staff car to nearby Kimpo airfield across the Han River for transport to a hospital in Japan.

Typical of Colonel Harold Scrogg's military mindset, when he learned General Dean was going to be coming through the 121, he had Smitty paint the toilet olive drab—he had even considered adding a white general's star on the side, until Collier and Major Smith had both subtly discouraged this as overkill.

Now, watching the shadowy form shake the residual drops from his penis and turn to leave the privacy-screened toilet area, Collier—still struggling to clear his sleep-drugged brain—made no sound and did not stir a muscle, wondering about the identity of this world-class farter who had been surreptitiously admitted sometime during the early hours of the morning.

Lying quietly feigning sleep, slowly the events of the previous evening—when Major Hughes decided to admit him to the medical ward—returned to Collier's consciousness. Hughes wanted to determine if his chronic diarrhea were merely a psychosomatic manifestation of stress or perhaps, whether, he had contracted some of the myriad of exotic—or even ordinary, garden-variety, quite-treatable—intestinal organisms floating around among this primitive, god-forsaken civilization which still depended upon human feces for fertilization of its rice paddies and vegetable gardens. Since the truce was signed on July 27, the 121ˢᵗ had become the collecting pool for a veritable textbook of enigmatic, nightmarish exotic diseases striking down healthy young American soldiers without warning—not the least of which were the recent disturbing cases of Korean Hemorrhagic Fever and sporadic bulbar polio cases still being admitted several times weekly to their small isolation ward on the far end of the floor in the building up the hill.

In the cold light of day and in his secret heart-of-hearts, Collier was embarrassed to admit he could have given into a weakness of character exacerbated by an unreasonable conviction he would die in this place, truly the rectal orifice of the earth. To his everlasting humiliation, he admitted to himself he had most likely fallen victim to the very same, runaway hypochondria which was running almost epidemic among frontline soldiers with far too much time on their hands now the truce was signed. Thinking back, he could trace the wellspring of his malignant, hypochondriacal preoccupations to the major outbreak of bulbar polio among U.S. soldiers early in August. Before the siege abated a few weeks ago almost as suddenly as it began, the sudden outbreak of that particularly virulent strain of polio had laid low a total of eight American GIs, resulting in the emergency airlift of every iron lung in the entire Far East Command being shipped to the 121. Lying there in the VIP ward, Collier's mind drifted back to the touch-and-go nights and days of having to depend upon standby, back-up, gas-operated, electric generators because the Korean electricity was anything but reliable—except to be relied upon to abruptly blink off for various lengths of time, varying from minutes to hours, almost every day. At one time or another during this white-knuckle period, the entire medical and administrative staff had taken turns manually pumping iron lungs to keep these unfortunate victims alive until they could be evacuated to Japan.

Although polio crisis had abated somewhat within a matter of a few weeks, during that hectic time, the first cases of Hemorrhagic Fever had begun to show up, followed by a litany of other arcane entities described only on the back pages of the medical books. By now convinced he was destined to die from one or the other of this mounting list of nightmarish maladies, the only thing saving him from becoming a bona fide psycho case was that he fully understood the root of his problem resided solely in his head. Unfortunately however, while at a purely objective level Collier recognized he had fallen prey to this unhealthy neurotic preoccupation, he still couldn't completely shake the subtle effect it had upon his fragile mental health.

Thinking back over the last three months, he had suffered the added humiliation that his long-running list of purely-imaginary diseases had made him the laughing stock among their staff of cynical hotshot clinicians. The main thing—perhaps the only thing—that saved his sanity was he had managed to deal with his soul-wrenching, knee-weakening neuroses by treating them with humor. In his mind's eye, Collier saw himself as the personification of cartoonist Al Capp's character, Joe Blfsplk, from the comic strip "Lil' Abner." Like poor Blfsplk, Collier saw himself walking around with a black cloud discharging rain and lightning constantly hovering over his head.

True to their word, the oral surgeon, Hoot Gibson, and his ping-pong buddy, Sammy Lee, had pretty much cured him of his throat cancer symptoms, but those nagging, mind-numbing—however largely-imaginary—distractions had been quickly replaced by the current GI symptoms, which had recently escalated into gnawing pain in the sub-sternum region, abdominal cramps and sub-clinical diarrhea.

One thing for sure, it was not his imagination that his stools were loose and his bowels often moved several times a day. For the past several weeks, he feared he had fallen victim to either amoebiasis or some of its more exotic, sometimes deadly, related Korean organisms, or failing that, a gastric ulcer—or worse, maybe even stomach cancer.

Now, as he slowly gathered his senses, Collier remembered Major Mutch admitting him late the previous evening to run a series of diagnostic tests to determine what was at the bottom of his long-running case of the trots. Burning with embarrassment for having let Hughes talk him into his own hospital, further exposing his neurosis to the world, he lay without moving, not at all ready to betray his wakefulness until he had the opportunity to gather his wits about him and figure out how to extricate himself from this current humiliation.

"You know who wrote those lines, Tenente?" his volunteer, sonorous orator growled.

Collier stiffened at the realization his wakefulness had been found out. His fellow patient was clearly addressing him

Remaining stock-still, he resolved to continue to play dead. He was not in the mood for conversation with some damn-fool poetry lover.

"Quit laying there like a freaking bunny-rabbit, Lieutenant. Get up and report for duty like an officer and a gentleman in the fucking United States Army," after perhaps a minute the theatrical voice boomed again, this time followed by a raucous, almost insane laugh.

"Knock it off. This is a hospital. There are patients still trying to get some sleep." Coming to the conclusion he would get no peace by playing possum, Collier roused up on his elbow and severely admonished the shadowy orator.

"Whom do you think you're talking to, Lieutenant? I am Colonel Wilson K. Massey, General Staff G-3, I Corps, United States Army. Twice-wounded in the ETO and already awarded another Purple Heart here. I've given this Army over twenty of the best years of my fucking life since I graduated the Point."

"I don't care if you're General Matthew Taylor, Colonel Wilson K. Massey. This is a hospital. And—for your information—I am the Adjutant here. Your rank will get you some respect if you earn it, but, among this command, I am third ranking officer in charge." Angry now, Collier rose up on his right elbow and stared hard at the shadowy form outlined against the plastic-coated, chicken wire covering the window across the large VIP room. Collier had learned in OCS that in special situations, rank was location dependant. All things were relative in the combat zone.

"Ho, ho, ho...toy soldier, just who the fuck do you think you're fooling?" Against the window, the shadowy figure performed a series of three deep-knee bends. "You're quaking in your fucking boots."

"Where's your wound, Colonel? You look like you're doing okay to me."

"Listen, Smartass, I'm in here for a possible coronary. I'll have your balls for breakfast if you don't show me more respect."

"You don't act like you've had a heart attack. Shouldn't you stay in bed?"

"Beds are for pussies. I feel fine. As soon as I can get to a fucking field phone, I'm getting out of here."

"Well, that's all well and good. But, in the meantime, Colonel, have some consideration for the really sick people in this hospital...please." Collier requested reasonably.

"Do you know where those lines are from, Tenente?" Responsive to Collier's request, the man claiming to be Colonel Wilson K. Massey lowered his voice now, taking on a more conversational tone.

"They seem to have a familiar ring, Colonel, but I really can't put my finger on where I've heard them," Collier admitted, wanting to go back to sleep.

"A Book of Verses underneath the Bough, A Jug of Wine, a Loaf of Bread—and Thou, Beside me singing in the Wilderness—Oh, Wilderness were Paradise enow!" The Colonel recited theatrically, but in a softer tone.

"Okay, okay, now I remember. That's from The Rubaiyat of Omar Khyyham. I studied it in high school." Collier vaguely remembered his high school English teacher, Mr. Wendall Snapp, quoting the lines in front of the class. Much the same as this frustrated thespian of an Army colonel, Snapp loved to stand in front of the class quoting verse. He was famous at Andrew Lewis for his sessions on Shakespeare.

"Give the young Tenente a ceegar!" the colonel enthused and continued quoting, "The Moving Finger writes: and, having writ, Moves on: nor all thy Piety nor Wit Shall lure it back to cancel half a Line, Nor all thy Tears wash out a Word of it."

"I'm impressed, Sir. But it's early, Sir. I'd really like to get back to sleep." Collier turned over and pulled the cover almost over his face.

"What kind of officer are you, anyway, Tenente? The sun is up and you want to go back to sleep." The colonel was clearly in a mood for company and not ready to abandon his captive audience. "Do you think Omar Khyyham would have approved of sleeping one's life away?"

"If I recall my high school English teacher correctly, old Omar has been sleeping for hundreds of years now, Colonel. From his poetry, I'd guess he flat drank and fucked himself to death." Collier had to suppress a laugh. For an old fart who had supposedly suffered a coronary, he admired the officer's *joie de vivre*.

"I have a feeling you're probably right. Since they brought me in here last evening, I've been lying awake most of the night wishing I'd done a lot more of that myself. There was this general's wife back at Benning who tried her best to get me to go out behind a howitzer barn with her. Man, she had the most gorgeous pair of headlights..." The colonel's eyes took on a dreamy look.

"I guess we all have a few regrets, Colonel." Collier's thoughts flashed back to Madison lying naked on the bed at the Hotel Fujiya.

"Yeah—like how the pussies back in Washington sold us down the river and gave in to the Gooks up at Panmumjom. MacArthur wouldn't have stopped until we pushed the bastards back across the Yalu." The colonel had turned and was gazing out of the window now.

"I'm with you in that regard, Colonel. I enlisted for OCS, but I've applied for RA commission and am seriously thinking of staying for a career. However, I do feel our government betrayed us over here. How do we answer all the young men who died in this godforsaken place?" Collier was suddenly reminded of how much he believed in what he was doing when he went to the recruiting office and enlisted for OCS.

"I don't know the answer to that one, Tenente. How would you answer them?"

"I don't know either, Colonel. *Homo sapiens*—Man: humankind—is supposed to be at the top of the animal evolutionary chain and yet all lower animal forms seem to be able to peacefully coexist. Our lower brothers in the evolutionary chain never fight one another except for survival..." Collier let the thought trail off; the enormity of it all was overwhelming.

"Aren't you quite the young philosopher this morning, Tenente? Are you a religious man? The Bible is full of blood and guts." The colonel turned to face him, seeming to warm to the idea of a philosophical discussion.

"I'm not religious...but I wouldn't bet on Army this year against Notre Dame."

"Don't tell me you're a fucking Notre Dame fan?"

"Colonel, I wouldn't root for Notre Dame if they were playing the Chinese Communists ...but it looks to me like they are going undefeated this year."

"Yeah...you might be right...fucking Catholic Church is into mind control..."

"Do you believe in God, Colonel Massey?" Intrigued by the idea the colonel had suddenly been confronted with his own mortality, he might be doing a little soul-searching.

"Well, I'd be lying if I said that having been in two wars hadn't left me inflicted with a certain brand of 'foxhole religion.'" Massey laughed.

"I understand. But how do you reconcile the idea of an all-powerful creative force—supposedly a *benevolent*, all-powerful creative entity...God, if you will—who would create mankind in its own image, then stand by and let the whole damn thing dissolve into utter chaos? Can you imagine a God entity who is frivolous or capricious? Or just got frigging bored with the whole idea of creation? How am I supposed to deal with a concept like that?" Collier persisted. And, speaking of "foxhole religion," he wondered what this colonel would say if he confessed that he still occasionally said his prayers at night?

"What are you doing out of bed, Colonel Massey? Major Hughes ordered you to strict bed rest," the chief nurse, Major Olsen, fairly exploded as she entered the room carrying a breakfast tray.

"I remember no such thing, Major. Get your goddamn Major Hughes in here right away. This is all a comedy of errors. I feel fine. I need to call my orderly. I need to get back to I Corp HQ at Uijongbu."

"Major Hughes will be along after awhile. Until then, for the moment at least, you need to get yourself back in that bed or I will have a couple of my orderlies put you there and strap you in. Do you understand?"

"Just who do you think you're talking to, Major?" The colonel stood there glaring for a long moment.

"Get in bed, Colonel. I don't have time to waste with your childish shenanigans. If you continue to insist on making an ass out of yourself, I'll call Colonel Spaulding, the hospital CO. He's a full-bird, in case you're wondering," the unflappable Olsen threatened, setting the breakfast tray on the movable table beside the colonel's bed.

Considering the possibility of a confrontation with the hospital commandant— and a full bird colonel at that—after a long moment, Colonel Massey shrugged and climbed slowly back into bed.

"Now eat your breakfast—it might improve your disposition." Olsen glared at him.

Before she left the room Olsen paused at the foot of Collier's bed which was nearest the door to the hall leading to the adjoining medical ward. "I'm sorry, Collier, but you don't get to eat this morning. Major Hughes has scheduled you for some more tests."

"Come back here, Major. I haven't dismissed you. Do you really expect me to eat this shit? I want two eggs over easy with a rasher of bacon," the colonel barked as Major Olsen headed for the door.

"I could care less whether you eat it or not, Colonel, but you might as well get used to it. What you're calling 'shit' is a special diet for heart patients. If you don't self-destruct first, you'll be eating that shit for quite awhile," the no-nonsense veteran nurse fired a parting shot as she disappeared through the door into the hall.

"I'll have that cunt's rank...you can count on it, Tenente," the crusty, outraged Infantry officer blustered.

Not wanting to be involved in any disagreement between this irascible Infantry colonel and his own Chief of Nursing, Collier turned his back and pulled the covers almost completely over his head.

"I'm speaking to you, Tenente. Or don't you like to be called, 'Tenente?"

"I'd like to get back to sleep, Colonel, if you don't mind," Collier muttered from beneath the covers, staring at the war- and weather-loosened plaster peeling off the masonry wall.

"You need to show more respect, Tenente..."

"If you don't mind my asking, Colonel, what's with all the 'tenente' business?" Collier was hard put to follow the ranting of this runaway Sherman tank of a man.

"Don't you read Papa Hemingway, Lieutenant?"

"Oh, yeah, I get it now. Tenente is Italian for lieutenant." Collier vaguely recalled reading Hemingway's *A Farewell to Arms* during his one abortive summer school at Roanoke College.

"Colonel Wilson K. Massey in here?" Before the colonel could reply, Corporal Perry—a strapping ex-combat medic who Collier knew owned a chest full of ribbons with at least one Purple Heart and galaxy of battle stars—wheeled a portable EKG machine through the door.

"Good morning, Lieutenant Ramsay..." Perry said, surprised to see the hospital's adjutant, as he made a beeline for the Colonel in the only other occupied bed by the window.

While Perry busied himself hooking the ill-humored colonel up to the EKG, Collier drifted back to sleep. He didn't awaken again until a medic brought in a cart with lunch trays. Rubbing sleep from his eyes, he noted another patient had joined them in the six-bed ward.

"Major Olsen said to tell you she's holding a tray for you until after Major Hughes and Captain Mutch make rounds," the orderly with the lunch trays explained to Collier before he left the room.

"Glad you finally decided to quit playing possum, Tenente. While you slept, we were joined by Captain Thomas Hartley, United States Army Dental Corp. Captain Hartley is an Oral Surgeon from Allentown, P.A. Captain Hartley, I'd like to present our rather rude—but nonetheless likeable—fellow patient, Lieutenant Collier Ramsay. Although presently a patient just like us, Tenente Ramsay is the fucking Adjutant of this hospital. He is also a connoisseur of literature—a particular fan of Papa Ernesto Hemingway." The Colonel waved his right hand dramatically in Collier's direction.

"Major Olsen tells me you're feeling better, Colonel Massey." Major Hughes entered as the orderly with the lunch cart left the room.

"Look, Major, except I had a little bout of indigestion yesterday up at Uijongbu, there's nothing wrong with me. I need to get out of here. I'm an I Corp general staff officer. If I can just get to a phone, I'll call my orderly and he'll come get me in a Jeep." The Colonel took a more reasonable tone with Major Hughes.

"Just relax, Colonel, and enjoy our hospitality. Lean forward and let me loose your cute little nightgown so I can listen to your chest." Hughes smiled reassurance as he put the earpieces to his stethoscope in his ears, approaching the colonel's bedside.

"Well, how about it, Major? Have you read my cardiogram? Can I get to a phone now?" Massey resumed harassing Hughes as soon as he had finished listening to his heart sounds and taking his vital signs.

"Not yet, Colonel, so you might as well relax. I'll get back to you later this afternoon." Hughes turned away and moved across the aisle to the dental captain's bed separating Collier's bed from the moveable privacy screen around the VIP portable toilet.

"How're you feeling, Captain?" Hughes asked Hartley as he waited for him to untie the hospital gown and bare his chest.

"Better now, Major—a lot better than when they brought me in. Did you ever have an elephant sitting on your chest?" the dental captain asked, as pale as a ghost.

"No, but I can imagine. I've ordered an EKG for this afternoon. I'll know more about what we're going to do with you after I see the tracings. After the technician does the EKG, I'm going to give you something to help your pain. In the meantime, just relax and get some sleep." Hughes gave Hartley a reassuring smile.

"Feeling better?" Hughes asked Collier as he turned away from the dental captain.

"Yeah, at least I haven't had to use Smitty's fancy, portable Johnny house since I came in last night," Collier quipped, humiliated he had wound up in his own hospital with a case of chronic shits.

"We've gotten some preliminary lab results from the stool specimens. It looks like you've picked up at least one exotic intestinal organism—maybe even two or three—God knows there are a few floating around this cesspool country. Unless we find something else later, when the lab reports will be more definitive, I'm going to give you some sulfonimides to kill those bugs in your gut and let you out of here tomorrow before lunchtime. In the meantime, get some rest. Captain Mutch will look in on you later when he makes his rounds." Hughes gave Collier a thumbs-up and left the room.

When Collier woke up again, his watch showed a few ticks past 1340 hours.

"Well, welcome back, Tenente. I wondered if you were ever going to wake up again." The irascible Colonel Massey called as soon as Collier rose up on his elbow, squinting hard against the bright sunlight pouring in through the window.

"I can't believe I slept so long." Collier shook his head nodding at his watch.

"Yeah, you and Hartley both. They gave Hartley a shot of the good old, golden-buzzard elixir right after they unhooked his EKG, and he's been out like a light ever since."

"Golden-buzzard elixir, Colonel?" With Massey, Collier never knew what was coming next.

"Demerol. Obviously you've never had any, Tenente, or you'd know what I mean." Massey shrugged knowingly.

"No, I've never had Demerol. And just what *do* you mean?" The Colonel had his interest now.

"Well, when they stick the needle in your arm, you get this warm feeling and then your whole being is transported up on this beautiful pink cloud and off in the distance you can see this graceful formation of golden buzzards approaching. As they get nearer, they form a circle around your head, and there are these gorgeous, naked girls swinging from these little trapezes hanging from the buzzard's feet, performing all sorts of obscene gymnastics." The impish Colonel spread his hands in a benevolent gesture, like a priest pronouncing a blessing.

"Sounds like potent stuff, Colonel. "But I think I'll stick to beer and booze if you don't mind." Collier chuckled.

"Speaking of booze, Tenente, you're adjutant of this fucking place; how about getting us a couple of fifths of some decent bourbon whiskey up here. We'll have a few social drinks before they serve us that shit they call chow," the Colonel suggested slyly.

"You know I can't do that, Colonel. Besides, even if I could, you and Captain Hartley have just suffered serious heart attacks." Collier dismissed the suggestion with a wave of his hand.

"Heart attacks be damned, Tenente—anyway alcohol dilates the blood vessels. Ask Captain Hartley here. He's an oral surgeon. He knows medicine." Massey persisted in harassing Collier.

"That's true. Alcohol does have some vasodilatory effects. I can't think of any reason that a little drink could hurt anything." Hartley replied groggily and pulled the cover over his head. It was clear to Collier the dental officer wanted no part of the argument.

"You're wasting your time trying to convince me, Colonel. Major Hughes is your physician. If he wants you to have some booze, he can order it." Collier shook his head.

"How long have you been in Korea, Tenente?" the colonel suddenly changed the subject.

"I got here on six July..." Collier replied, unsure what was coming next.

"How long have you been in the service?" Colonel Massey continued.

"Since two January, fifty-two...I enlisted to go to OCS..." Collier began, briefly recounting his military history. He finished outlining his Army resume, with his recent recommendation for promotion to First Lieutenant and his application for Regular Army status, adding his tentative plans to apply for reassignment in Japan when he completed his tour of a year in Korea.

"Regular Army is an admirable career, Tenente, but there are some things you should know about the 'good old boy' system in the Officer Corps." The colonel's voice took on a serious tone.

"What's that, Colonel?" Collier asked, wondering what the colonel was driving at.

"A Regular Army officer commissioned from the reserve ranks is low man on the totem pole when it comes to the promotion list in the peacetime Army." The old colonel had taken on a fatherly demeanor now.

"But I've been virtually assured I'll get my silver bars any day now," Collier protested anxiously.

"Oh, I'm not surprised about that. It's pretty much a rite of passage for being in the combat zone. But getting your railroad tracks may be another thing altogether. When you come up on the list for promotion to captain, remember you won't be the only one on that list with approximately the same time in grade." The colonel pointed out.

"Sure, I understand, Sir. But I have all sixes on my Efficiency Reports so far and certainly don't expect to lower my standard of performance. Being Regular Army will certainly give me preference over reserve officers on the list," Collier replied, proudly.

"That's certainly a commendable record, but that's just what I'm trying to tell you. Having Regular Army status is not a magic 'open sesame' to a successful career in the Army. The promotion lists also include officers who have graduated The Point—it's an unspoken and unwritten rule that West Pointers always have preference. Then there are the other, similar, military schools in the 'good old boy system'. VMI graduates come next in line and then there is a descending order of preference beginning with The Citadel. After that, you have to contend with all the countless subtle other things, mostly dependent on what your fraternity was or if you are you a Mason—and don't let me forget—there's always the question of whose asses you've kissed. You know how that goes?" The colonel raised his eyebrows questioningly to see if Collier got his drift.

"Sure. I understand, Colonel. It's pretty much the same in civilian life." Collier nodded.

"Yeah, but in civilian life, it's easier to get a grip on who is performing best. In the peacetime military it has more to do with 'who you know and who you blow' or vice versa. Be careful you don't wind up like me, Tenente, washed up as a light colonel at the age of thirty-nine—and I graduated The Point. I'm going to have to retire in several years because I will be passed over for the third time for making full bird. In the Army, they push you out to make room for the next graduation class at the Point. I'm not saying you won't find a way to beat the system, Tenente. If anyone could do it, you most likely could." The colonel shrugged.

"Thanks, for the warning, Colonel. I'll keep that in mind." Collier surmised the veteran officer was more than a little depressed and frustrated, having difficulty coming to terms with a likely career-ending heart attack.

"Speaking from the point of view of an aspiring Regular Army career officer, what do you think of the Pentagon's decision to negotiate a truce, Tenente?" The Colonel suddenly changed the subject.

"I think Washington sold out all of the men who fought on Korean soil...I certainly believe they sold me out, Colonel. When I enlisted, I believed we were fighting for a worthwhile cause. I'm just naïve enough to believe that freedom is a worthwhile cause." For emphasis, Collier pumped his fist in the air.

"I too believe freedom is a worthwhile cause, and I agree the White House and the Pentagon sold us out. Ike predicted we would become pawns of an Industrial-Military complex. Anyone with any sense should be able to see he was right." The Colonel nodded agreement.

Collier merely nodded, not wanting to pursue the point.

"So you read Hemingway, Tenente?" The colonel abruptly changed the subject again.

Apparently, now he had finished his lecture on the pitfalls of a career in the Army and given up the idea of getting a drink, for the moment at least.

"Well, I've read a little Hemingway. I like some of his short stories and the novels *A Farewell to Arms* and *For Whom the Bell Tolls*. I frankly don't think *The Sun Also Rises* was much of a book." Collier ventured. (He'd read a lot of books, but didn't fancy himself much of a literary critic. And, besides, Erskine Caldwell, Raymond Chandler, Dashiell Hammett, Brett Halliday and Mickey Spillane were more his speed.)

"Here, try this one. It's Papa's latest. All about an Army colonel in Venice, Italy, after World War Two who knows he has a bum ticker and falls in love with a beautiful Italian countess but has trouble raising a hard-on. It's a great book. John O'Hara reviewed it and said Hemingway was the most important writer since Shakespeare.   Here, read it, Tenente—you're a romantic; you'll enjoy it." Without warning, the colonel tossed the paperback novel across the full length of the room. Collier almost fell out of bed catching it.

"Well, I don't know, Colonel. I'm not exactly up to reading a book right now, and I'm sure they'll be getting you out of here as fast as possible. We don't do long-term coronary treatment here." Collier turned the book over in his hands and examined it. It was easy to see why the colonel would be fascinated by any novel about an Army colonel with a bad heart.

"You should read this novel, Tenente. Certainly you're interested in pussy— you know, that warm, fuzzy little thing between a woman's legs that makes the world go round. I know it's hard to believe right now, but there may come a time when you have trouble raising a hard-on."

"Well...believe it or not, I do believe you. As a matter of fact, I've just experienced a brief episode of that problem myself..." Collier blurted, then poured out his tale about not being able to perform for the Japanese prostitute, only to find his powers restored a few hours later when he went to the Fujiya with Madison.

Collier concluded philosophically, "I guess the idea of paying for sex has never appealed to me. For a real male, I think the attraction is in the chase—I really enjoy the rituals of the seduction..."

"Are you married, Tenente?"

"Yeah...we have a baby son—born May 5. But you know, as much as I hate to admit it, I still have trouble with the idea of my being a father. You know the old fairytale about the high-school quarterback marrying the head cheerleader. We started having sex when we were juniors in high school and more or less— mostly more—went steady all the way through college when we got married. You know I remember wanting to walk out of the church on my wedding day. She thinks I'm pretty much a loser. And, truth be told, I really haven't loved her for a long time. I hate to admit it, but I really don't feel much affection for the kid...our...my son. I'm beginning to wonder if I'm some sort of sociopath..."

"I wouldn't worry. Happens all the time. You ever hear of divorce?" the old colonel asked, his voice gone kindly now.

"Yeah. I'd divorce Emma in a heartbeat I think if it wasn't for the...ah...baby. There's this friend of Emma's, her former nursing classmate, who I really have strong feelings for. But, on second thought, if I ever got out of this marriage, I'm not sure I'd want to be hooked up to just one woman again."

"If I were a boy, I wouldn't want to grow up knowing my father and mother hated each other. Ever think about that?" Massey gave him a serious look. "Besides, who's talking about getting remarried, anyway? I'd hate to die knowing there are poor suffering women who need me. You know what Budda says?"

"No?...what?"

"*That it will never come again is what makes life so sweet.* It's foolish to waste a second regretting what we've done...regret only the things left undone, Tenente."

"Uhm-m? You mean women?..." Collier asked.

"You know, for an officer in the United States Army, you're a disgrace, Lieutenant. All this talk about pussy is bad for a man in my condition. I think I'll catch a little nap. While I'm asleep, give Hemingstein a try." The Colonel rolled over and pulled the sheet over his head.

Thumbing through to the first page of Chapter One, Collier read the opening sentence of *Across the River and Into the Trees.*

They started two hours before daylight, and at first, it was not necessary to break the ice across the canal as other boats had gone on ahead.

He had read several chapters when the Colonel roused awake again.

"Well? What do you think, Tenente?" Clearly the colonel was pleased to find Collier reading the novel.

"I admit I admire Hemingway's style. Nobody else writes like him." It was true; Collier had always admired Hemingway's almost poetic use of language.

"Good. Keep the book. You'll enjoy it. You can write me and tell me what you think."

"Oh no, Colonel. I won't have any way to keep track of you."

"That's not a problem. If you have something to write with, I'll give you my stateside contact. Jot it down inside the cover of the book."

To humor him, Collier picked up a ballpoint pen lying on the bedside table. "Alright, Colonel, shoot."

"Colonel Wilson K. Massey care of General Delivery, Robishaw, Mississippi." The Colonel slowly recited the address.

"Is that all?" Collier looked up, surprised at the simplicity of the address.

"That's all. Don't worry. You can always reach me at that address. Now if you don't mind, I'm going to take a little nap." The colonel smiled, turned his back and pulled the blanket over his head. Within a short time, he was snoring lightly.

"Well, Tenente, what do you think?" At 1530 hours, the colonel roused Collier from reading. He had already read slightly more than a third of the way through the novel.

"It's classic Hemingway alright." Collier was careful not to hurt the colonels' feelings. As far as he was concerned, the famous author's new novel was almost an impersonation of his earlier war novels. Now only in his early fifties, apparently Hemingway had already become a parody of himself.

"Don't patronize me, Tenente. That's insulting. I know what you're thinking. You think I like the book because it's about a washed-up Army colonel with a bum ticker." The senior officer laughed.

"Not at all, Sir." Collier felt himself blushing, red-faced at being caught trying to bullshit the savvy officer.

"Never try your hand at poker, Tenente. You're a lousy liar." Massey laughed.

At a loss just what to say, Collier marked his place in the book and put it on the bedside table.

"Long time no see, Collier." Collier looked up to see Herb Rudolph standing at the foot of his bed, grinning ear to ear.

"Well, I'll be damned! How'd you know I was up here?" Collier was delighted to see his friend.

"They told me downstairs in the orderly room." Herb nodded vaguely in the direction of the window. "So how're you doing, anyway?"

"I'm fine, except I've been shitting my brains out for the past couple of weeks. They say I have some sort of exotic intestinal thing..." Collier explained, greatly relieved he had some real physical excuse for being in the hospital.

"Aren't you going to introduce me to your friend, Tenente?" after a few minutes of ignoring his presence, the colonel rudely interrupted their reminiscing over old times back at Sill.

"I'm sorry, Colonel. Please allow me to introduce Sergeant Herb Rudolph. We were in Basic Training together back at Fort Sill," Collier made the introduction, having difficulty holding his tongue at the colonel's imperious effrontery.

"I'm pleased to make your acquaintance, Sergeant," the colonel said rather officiously. He obviously felt himself above dealing with an EM as a social equal.

"Likewise, Colonel." Not particularly impressed by the rank of the bad-mannered, hawkish-looking old man wearing the standard hospital gown, Herb nodded casually, then turned back to Collier and resumed their conversation.

"Lieutenant Ramsay, I just had a brilliant idea." Collier had hardly resumed his conversation with Herb when the Colonel interrupted again.

"What's that, Colonel?" Collier struggled to hold his tongue.

"Why don't we let the sergeant make our liquor run?" Massey replied.

"Look, Colonel, you might as well give up the idea of bringing liquor into this hospital. It is strictly against regulations." Collier responded emphatically.

"Regulations be goddamned, Tenente. First I was wounded at Heartbreak Ridge, and now I have to deal with a bunch of idiots trying to say I've had a heart attack in this fucking godforsaken country. I want a drink. What's the harm in sending the sergeant here on a mission of mercy? I'm sure he wouldn't mind; would you sergeant?" Massey persisted, ignoring Collier completely now.

"I really wouldn't mind, Sir, but my outfit is about an hour from here by Jeep. I have to get my vehicle back to the motor pool by 1900 hours. I'd never make it there and back in time." Herb hedged, not wanting to hurt the colonel's feelings.

"Doesn't this chickenshit outfit have a NCO Club where the sergeant could buy a bottle of decent booze, Tenente?" Massey sneered at Herb's altogether limited perspective concerning the problem and the solution.

"Well sure, but..." Collier started to protest.

"'Butt' is another word for 'ass' which is what you're being right now, Tenente. As a matter of fact, I'll bet your buddy would join us in a drink if we could find one. Wouldn't a drink taste pretty good right now, Sergeant?" The sly colonel shot Herb a wink.

"Well, sure. I'm always in the mood for a drink, Colonel." Herb was still the same old Herb.

"Look, I'm adjutant of this hospital. If you two think I'm going to just sit idly by and help you bring booze into this hospital ward, you're both crazier than I think you are..." Collier resumed his protest.

"Where's the NCO Club, Tenente? How much does a bottle of good bourbon cost?" Massey was already out of bed, digging through his billfold, looking for some cash.

"I.W. Harper's the best. The last time I bought a whole bottle it was a buck-fifty at our NCO club over in Seoul." Herb had already moved over to the foot of the Colonel's bed and stood waiting with his hand out.

"Here's three bucks. If you can, you might as well go ahead and get two. I may be in here awhile before my orderly shows up to take me back to my outfit." The colonel handed over three badly-rumpled, one-dollar bills in military script.

"Where's your NCO Club, by the way?" Herb stopped to ask Collier as he prepared to leave the room.

"Actually you go down the steps outside the door on the right. It's just up the hill about twenty yards, across the street from the stairs leading up to the side entrances between Building Three and Building Four. When you come back in here, make sure no one sees you bringing liquor in," resignedly Collier gave Herb directions. He knew when he had been outvoted.

"Trust me, Collier; no one will be the wiser." Herb grinned over his shoulder as he left the room.

"You know I'm officially obligated to report this to the charge nurse, Major Olsen." Collier told the senior officer as soon as Herb had left.

"Yeah, I know, Tenente, but I'm betting you won't. Whatever else you are, I'll bet you were never a spoil sport or a wet blanket." The Colonel said, seriously.

"Save the bullshit, Colonel." Collier rejected the Colonel's attempt to blow smoke up his ass.

"Okay, I got the goods. Who wants this stuff? I don't want to wind up in the stockade." Herb asked when he reappeared about thirty minutes later. Each of the oversized side pockets of his field jacket was bulging from the bulky cargo of a fifth of I.W. Harper bourbon, bottled-in-bond.

"Grab that empty glass and bring the booze over here to me, Sergeant. We're going to have a fucking party." The Colonel pointed to a glass on the table by the unoccupied bed across from the bed Collier occupied. "While you're at it, Sergeant, bring the Tenente's glass, too."

"No thanks, Gents. Count me out. I can't be a part of this." Collier raised up on his elbow and watched with morbid fascination as the Colonel carefully stowed one bottle of the precious cargo in the duffel beside his bed, then broke the seal, uncapped the remaining bottle and poured himself a drink, tossing it down in one thirsty gulp before he poured a generous slug in the empty glass Herb had retrieved.

"How about a little splash of I.W. Harper bourbon, Captain?" Colonel Massey offered the dentist a slug of his newfound booty.

"Sure, why not?" Captain Hartley extended his glass, eager to have a drink, anything to help him forget his circumstances.

"Why don't you relax and join us, Tenente? Don't be such a tight-ass all your life," the Colonel chided as he tossed back a second drink. "Here, Sergeant, take the bottle and pour the Tenente a little drink so we can all drink a toast to a long life and good health."

"Oh, no, I can't afford to..." Collier raised his hand to protest as Herb picked up his bedside glass, sloshing in a healthy slug of the amber liquid.

"Quit being such a scaredy-cat, Tenente. *A votre sante*–to your good health. To the good health of us all." The colonel raised his glass, draining the contents again. Collier drank the toast.

"Pour the chickenshit Tenente another shot, Sergeant, and bring that fucking bottle back." The Colonel's sonorous voice boomed boozily from across the room.

"No thanks, Colonel. And, if I were you, I'd keep my voice down unless you're hell-bent on professional suicide," Collier warned as he realized there was a potent synergism taking place between the bourbon and the Demerol. Fearing the worse, he turned his back and pulled the covers over his head. Lying there shuddering at the imagined consequences if Major Olsen or Major Mutch walked in on this impromptu Bacchanalia, Collier felt the liquor warming him; just before he drifted off to sleep, inexplicably his thoughts drifted back to the afternoon in July he had spent across the street in Otis Owens' house in the village. Momentarily, he experienced a deep yearning akin to the first years of his courtship of Emma. He must be intoxicated, he reasoned sleepily. This was hardly the time to be falling in crush with Ginger Lipscomb.

"You're drunk as a hoot owl, Colonel Massey. I'm telling you for the last time, Colonel, you cannot use the telephone. If you don't get back in bed and stay there, I'm going to have the orderlies strap you into bed with cargo straps." Collier was roused abruptly back to consciousness at the strident sound of Major Olsen's voice. The room was dark except for the soft, reflected light from the medical ward down the hall. As his eyes rapidly adjusted in the darkness, Collier saw Major Olsen overseeing two medics who were escorting the uncooperative Colonel Massey back to bed.

"Listen, you goddamn, dried-up old cunt, just who the hell do you think you are? If you won't let me use that phone, I promise I will have those golden oak leaves before you eat lunch tomorrow." The recalcitrant senior officer shook free of the two medics, reluctantly climbing back up on his bed.

"You listen to me, Colonel Massey. I'm in command on this floor and the next time you get out of bed for any reason other than to use the toilet, I will see to it you are strapped to that bed frame with cargo straps." Olsen motioned for the orderlies to leave the room. As she turned to leave, she stopped and pointed the beam of her flashlight into the large trashcan beside the door. Suddenly interested in something in the can, she removed a surgical glove from the pocket of her uniform and put it on her right hand before she stooped over and lifted a single empty bottle of I.W. Harper from the trash receptacle, holding it by two fingers up to the beam of flashlight.

"Where did you get this liquor, Colonel Massey? I know it was not in your kit when you were admitted. We searched everything you had with you." Olsen moved back to the foot of Massey's bed and held the bottle in front of him.

"Don't ask me, Major. I never saw that fucking bottle before just now. Why don't you ask the Dentist or your own young lieutenant lying over there playing possum?" Massey's face was a study in self-righteous innocence.

"Well, we'll just see what the CID has to say when they examine this for fingerprints, Colonel. I'm going call the MPs as soon as I get back to the ward. They shouldn't have any trouble making a quick determination of this bottle's ownership." Olsen turned and headed for the door.

"Listen, you silly, old dried-up cunt, I never saw that fucking bottle before. If you don't let me use that fucking telephone to call my outfit and have someone come pick me up, I am going to come in that ward and cut your fucking heart out. Do you understand plain English or has all that estrogen raging through your veins killed what few brain cells you were born with?" Massey shook his fist at her.

"Listen yourself, Colonel. If you don't stay in that bed and shut up, I'm going to call Colonel Spaulding out of his nice warm bed. Colonel Spaulding is a devout Seventh Day Adventist teetotaler. If he comes down here, you can count on him calling the MPs and having them cart you out of here for making such an unseemly disturbance in this hospital. You are about a micro-millimeter away from a general court martial for drunk and disorderly." Olsen's tone left little doubt she had reached the end of her patience and meant serious business.

Blinking hard at her dangling the bottle in front of his face, the colonel apparently finally got the message loud and clear as he slowly settled back against the pillows and glared, his lower lip protruding in a bourbon-fueled childish pout.

Satisfied she had made her point, Olsen turned off her flashlight and, still holding the bottle by her fingertips, she left the room.

Collier lay stone still and held his breath, certain that Olsen would put two-and-two together regarding the source of the I.W. Harper. Wondering now what had transpired while he was sleeping, it suddenly occurred to him to wonder what happened to the second bottle.

"Hey, you self-righteous 'goody-two-shoes' over there in the corner, I know you're awake, so you might as well quit the possum act. Sit up and tell me just how serious is that Major Olsen—will that tight-ass bitch really try to make trouble?" the colonel whispered in the darkness from across the room.

"I can assure you, Colonel, the Major is not someone you want to piss off. She will have Spaulding up here in a heartbeat if you mess with her." Collier whispered back.

"Then I'd have to tell them the liquor was your idea, Tenente. You understand I am a General Staff officer and a graduate of The Point. You are a reserve lieutenant, the lowest form of officer life in this man's Army—I'm sorry, Tenente, but you're expendable." The Colonel's tone left little doubt he was serious.

"Goodnight, Colonel." Collier turned his back and pulled the cover over his head.

"Wake up, Tenente. Hughes is shipping me out of here." Collier roused out of a sound sleep to find the room bathed in the orange glow of the rising sun. His watch showed 0725 hours.

"Where are they taking you, Colonel?" Collier asked, as the memory of last night's confrontation with Major Olsen came sharply back to him. He was sure this was going to be the worst day of his young life.

"They didn't say. An orderly just came in and packed my bags. He told me he'd be back to get me in a wheelchair as soon as Hughes showed up to release me." The colonel looked a little peaked now. His demeanor showed none of the previous evening's bravado and *joie de vivre*.

"Well, I wish you all the best, Colonel Massey. Please stay in touch...let me know how you're getting along," Collier said. Even though it was quite likely he was going to suffer the consequences of the old reprobate's drunken rampage of the previous evening, it was impossible to stay mad at the crusty, old curmudgeon.

"One thing before I leave, Tenente. I want you to know that I was only kidding last night when I said you were expendable. I would never let you take the blame for my indiscretions."

"Well, thank you for telling me that, Sir. I never questioned your integrity," Collier lied. Besides, it really didn't matter what the old bastard said about how the liquor got in, Collier knew damn well that as Adjutant, Scroggs and Spaulding would hold him guilty by default. No doubt about it, he was in for a career-ending disaster—headed straight for Fort Levenworth.

"Also, Tenente, I want you to promise me you'll start writing down your thoughts about things. You have a fine mind and a wonderful philosophical outlook. I see you as the benign and benevolent philosopher sitting astride the planet contemplating his navel...pondering the perfect order of the universe. Whether you know it or not, you were born to become a writer," the Colonel told him seriously.

"Well, I thank you for your advice, but I'm sure I'm not deserving of such high opinion..." Collier began and stopped, not wanting to add that he would have plenty of time to contemplate his navel and the cosmos doing hard time at Levenworth. "If you don't mind my asking, Sir, where is the other liquor bottle?"

"It's safe and sound, Tenente." The Colonel winked and nodded toward his combat pack on the foot of his bed.

"Good morning, Colonel Massey. I see you're packed. We're sending you on a little airplane ride." Major Hughes came into the room followed by an orderly pushing a wheelchair.

"I demand to know where you're taking me, Major? I need to get back up to I Corp HQ at Uijongbu..." Massey blustered angrily.

"Calm down, Colonel Massey. You're in good hands, Sir," Major Hughes attempted to calm the angry colonel as a medic pushed him toward the door in a wheelchair. Just before they left the room, Massey turned to Collier for a farewell word.

"Good luck, Lieutenant. Here's a couple of tidbits of soldierly advice before I leave. The two most overrated things in the world are home cooking and home fucking. And never mess with cold collards or woke pussy." The crusty officer gave Collier a salute as he went out the door.

Collier returned the salute and sucked in his breath and held it as Major Hughes stopped at the foot of his bed just before following the colonel's wheelchair out of the room.

"How are you feeling this morning, Collier?" Hughes asked. If there was any hint of disapproval in his voice, Collier couldn't detect it.

"I'm fine, Sir," Collier answered meekly, expecting all hell to break loose.

"That's great. Colonel Spaulding is bugging me about when he's going to get you back. I'm going to let you out of here. As soon as Major Olsen sends your clothes in here, get dressed and go down to the officers' mess for a decent breakfast. I'll see you there in a half-hour." Hughes waved and headed out of the door behind the Colonel's wheelchair.

"We sent Colonel Massey to Osaka for coronary rehab," Major Hughes said when he showed up for breakfast just as Collier was finishing his third cup of coffee.

"Will he recover? Will he be sent back to duty, Major?" Collier asked, deeply touched by Colonel Wilson Massey's farewell speech to him.

"He's what the latest medical literature is calling a Type A personality. If I were a gambling man, I'd say he had about a forty-sixty chance." Hughes shook his head regretfully. It was clear the astute clinician thought the odds were not in the Colonel's favor.

"But he has a chance...I mean..." Collier sipped his coffee, letting the thought die on his lips.

"A chance, sure. I'm not counting him out. I'll say one thing for him: he has an indomitable spirit. But he also had a very serious heart attack. Almost one-fourth of the anterior surface of his heart is necrotic. That's a lot of dead heart muscle for even the best of candidates to survive." Hughes raised his eyebrows, questioning that Collier understood.

"I'll be pulling for him." Collier murmured, expecting Hughes to get around to last night's episode with the liquor bottle.

"So will I. If we get any feedback from Osaka, I'll be sure and let you know. I've got to run back up to the ward. Major Olsen has a suspicious-looking case she wants me to see. I'll see you at Officer's call." Hughes pushed back his chair and left.

To Collier's great puzzlement, Major Hughes had not mentioned anything about Colonel Massey's confrontation the previous night with Major Olsen over the I.W. Harper liquor bottle.

"Glad you're back to duty, Collier. Colonel Spaulding was just about to send me out to check the light bulbs in your absence. Get a move on and hurry back in time for officer's call." Colonel Scroggs barely looked up as Collier came into the orderly room door a few minutes later.

All day long, Collier tiptoed around waiting for the axe to fall, but much to his complete confusion, the subject was never even hinted at.

"Glad to see you back on your feet, Collier," completely expressionless, Major Olsen greeted him after duty that evening in the Quonset Lounge. "Can I buy you a drink? I.W. Harper bottled-in-bond, I believe?"

"No ma'am. I never drink bourbon. I'll have Vodka Collins. Thank you for the drink." Collier never blinked.

Surprisingly—and inexplicably—no mention of the brouhaha with the drunken Colonel Wilson K. Massey or the source of the empty I.W. Harper bottle ever came up again.

CHAPTER FORTY-SEVEN

THE ROANOKE TIMES
Roanoke, Virginia, Wednesday, November 11, 1953
BIG THREE MEETING SET FOR BURMUDA

WASHINGTON, November 11 (UP) - President Eisenhower will meet British Prime Minister Winston Churchill and French Premier Joseph Laniel in Burmuda December 4-8 to map western strategy toward Russia's new "get tough" attitude...

STARS AND STRIPES
UNOFFICIAL PUBLICATION OF UNITED STATES FORCES, FAR EAST

Vol. 9, No. 207   Friday, November 13, 1953
NIXON CONFERS WITH RHEE,
TO ADDRESS ASSEMBLY

SEOUL, November 13 (Pac. S&S) - Vice President Nixon, fresh from a two-hour conference with ROK President Syngman Rhee yesterday, was scheduled to address South Korea's National Assembly at noon today after receiving the key to the city of Seoul earlier.

1.

"COME IN AND MAKE YOURSELF RIGHT AT HOME. Happy Armistice Day, Major Smith...you, too, Lieutenant Ramsay." Wednesday evening, 11 November, barefoot on the spotless, well-scrubbed wooden floors, and wearing jeans and an outrageously-civilian, green-flowered, Hawaiian-style shirt, the crusty—ordinarily toothless, but now wearing a fine set of GI dentures—Staff Sergeant Otis Cook, *chief honcho extraordinare* and all-around miracle worker of Smitty's amazing indigenous Korean labor force, greeted them at the door of his hut on the outskirts of the village just across the Suwon road from the gate to the 121ˢ compound, and ushered them inside. On the far side of the room was a young Korean woman. Looking around, Collier wondered if the Sergeant would remember loaning him the use of this house when Ginger had visited back in September.

Stopping to remove their low-cut, Class A shoes—they had both dressed in Class A khakis for the auspicious occasion—Collier followed Smitty inside and remained standing, expecting an introduction to the Sergeant's "Korean wife" who looked to be in her late teens.

"I don't believe we've had the pleasure of meeting this young lady, Otis," Smitty prompted the unintentionally-cavalier, socially-inept sergeant when it became obvious he had forgotten—or was purposefully ignoring—his rather heavy-featured, somewhat-homely, young Korean wife.

Collier knew from Smitty's briefing as they walked across from the compound into the village that the Sarge already had a wife and a house full of snot-nose children back in south Alabama. Although frowned upon by the high command, taking a "Korean wife" was a not-so-unusual practice among enlisted men, and sometimes even among the occasional officer.

-667-

"Excuse me, sir. Major Smith...Lieutenant Ramsay...this here is Moon. Say hello to Major Smith and Lieutenant Ramsay, Moon." The sergeant introduced the girl with a sweeping wave of the hand.

"A pleasure to meet you, Miss Moon," Collier echoed the Major's acknowledgement of the Sergeant's introduction.

"Would you gentlemen care for a beer? I have Asahi and Nippon...but I also have Miller's High Life, if you'd rather have American beer—what's your pleasure, gentlemen?"

"Make mine Asahi," Major Smith replied.

"I'll have an Asahi, too. Can I help you serve the beer?" Collier asked, looking over at the ice box and recalling with a wistful pang the brief time he'd spent here with the heartbreakingly-lovely Ginger. His conversation with Colonel Wilson Massey about life being too short to waste it with the wrong woman, came sharply back to haunt him. Lately, during his secret moments, he'd contemplated divorcing Emma. But he couldn't get past the idea of abandoning his son. A boy needed a father.

"Just have a seat and relax, Lieutenant. Moon will get your beer," the rawboned sergeant spoke up, making sure Collier didn't spoil the perfect order of his private little universe.

"Is Moon her given name or family name?" Collier asked the rawboned sergeant as soon as the young woman had disappeared out of earshot, somewhere back in the neatly-kept Korean house.

"Moon is her given name. Her family name is Choi," the sergeant replied, somewhat surprised Collier had an understanding of the reversed order of the Korean naming system.

"If you are ready, gentlemen, we'll eat." After Moon had served the beer, the sergeant nodded to her to begin serving their dinner. "Just to ease your mind, the steaks are courtesy of our own Captain Richmond"—Richmond was an attached Quartermaster officer, in charge of the 121 patient mess—"and the vegetables were grown by me, right out back in my own garden, fertilized with buffalo dung...not honey-bucket waste." Otis carefully made the distinction, to avoid any embarrassing reluctance in partaking of the meal.

When she finished placing the food in front of them, Moon stood respectfully aside, waiting to serve them more food or drink—clearly the sergeant was not going to invite her to join them at the table.

"Moon's cousin, Ahn Myung was a ROK lieutenant when the war started. He was taken prisoner down south in July of nineteen-fifty. Myung was repatriated during Big Switch. Myung has an interesting tale to tell, but, now, no one wants to listen," the sergeant remarked after Moon had cleared the table and had taken the dishes away.

"What do you mean? Was he tortured in prison camp? I expect there was a lot of that." Major Smith shrugged and lit the Dutch Masters cigar Sergeant Cook offered him. Collier lit a Lucky—he had long-since given up ever getting used to the tasteless filtered Kents, and for some strange reason, cigars always gave him the hiccups. It was just as well; he'd never learned to like cigars anyway.

"No Sir, Major, I'm not talking about prison abuse. Just before Myung was captured in July of nineteen-fifty near Taejon, he says he was witness to two wholesale massacres of civilians—one by the ROKs and the other by the NKPA."

"Yeah...we've all heard rumors of atrocities. It was the same in Europe in forty-five." The major nodded without much interest.

"Yes, Sir, I've heard them rumors, but Myung says he can confirm it—apparently he was able to hide several photographs of at least one of the atrocities before he was taken prisoner. Trouble is, nobody wants to listen to him." The sergeant puffed his cigar and gave them both an appraising look.

"What do you mean, no one will listen? Who has he tried to tell this story to?" Major Smith spoke up, holding the half-inch-long ash from his expensive cigar over the palm of his left hand to keep it from falling on the rice-straw mat upon which they were seated, looking anxiously for an ashtray.

"Moon, bring the picture Myung gave you, and, while you're at it, get us an ashtray." The sergeant directed the girl with a wave of his hand.

Disappearing behind the wooden screen partitioning the room from the back of the house, Moon reappeared carrying a brown manila envelope—she also carried the cut-off, bottom-portion of an 155mm artillery shell casing to use for an ashtray.

"Myung gave me this. His father took it just a short while before he—Myung's father—and his mother and two sisters were shot and pushed into the same large ditch in the picture." Moon removed a small, yellowing snapshot from the envelope and passed it across to the Major who looked at it and shook his head in disbelief before passing it over to Collier.

Although it was slightly discolored with age, the photo image was still sharp, the detail crystal clear. The scene was a long ditch, at least six- to eight-feet deep, filled with the corpses of at least a hundred—most-likely more—civilians of both sexes and of disparate ages. Incredibly, the head of what appeared to be a toddler, who could well have been still alive, was clearly discernible in the foreground. The toddler's body was mostly obscured behind the legs of what looked to be a male corpse being drug by several soldiers deeper into the ditch and was surrounded by several—four at least—of a group of fifty or more soldiers and civilian workers under the direction of at least one ROK officer, in the familiar American-supplied uniform, going about the grizzly business of burying the evidence of what obviously seemed to be a slaughter.

To Collier, the scene was immediately evocative of photos he had seen of German atrocities during WWII.

"Well, this is certainly a gruesome scene, right enough, but it is hardly evidence of a massacre. These civilians could have been killed by artillery...or a strafing from the air and these soldiers and civilian workers could be simply burying their dead." Smitty cleared his throat as he took the photo back to give it a closer inspection.

"Oh, it is of a massacre all right. Myung saw the entire thing—he was only nineteen, but already a lieutenant in the ROK. He possesses signed statements of five unimpeachable civilians from the Taejon area who witnessed at least one other such slaughter. In prison, he heard of similar wholesale slaughters of civilians throughout other nearby areas in the path of that first disastrous retreat. Some were said to be done by the NKPA—but some, like this one near Taejon, were done by our own ROKs." Moon, like many other Koreans her age, spoke surprisingly good English. Collier vaguely recalled Otis saying Moon had been raised and schooled by Christian missionaries at the orphanage at the Severance Medical College Hospital compound in Seoul. Many children had been taken in by the several-hundred-odd orphanages which had sprung up like mushrooms under the fostering impetus of sympathetic GIs who had enlisted help from their hometown church groups and other benevolent organizations—like the Masonic

Lodge. Even so, Collier was appalled by the number of apparent orphans who still wandered the streets of Seoul fending for themselves as pickpockets and beggars.

"But, I don't understand. Why would ROK soldiers execute innocent civilians?" Major Smith asked.

"This was at the very beginning of the surprise invasion from the NKPA, and they—the ROK, sometimes even in the presence of, and under orders from, U.S. Military Advisor officers—were executing suspected Communist sympathizers wholesale. Myung says there were an estimated eighteen-hundred, innocent civilians gunned down in the mass-murder in this picture." Moon replied.

"Eighteen-hundred! Oh, come on, now! You can't expect me to believe that?" Smitty exploded.

"Myung has proof...he has these photos and a photo copy of a report to Washington written by a Light Colonel Bob E. Edwards, the U.S. military attaché. Myung says these killings were the result of mass hysteria—a bloody nightmare," Moon explained. "He says your General Dean was aware of them and sent a report to his higher command which was repressed."

"I can't believe the American high command would suppress a report by an authority like General Dean. And eighteen-hundred people murdered...my God, that's preposterous. Just burying them would have taken a month." Smitty was adamant in his disbelief.

"The executions took place the first week in July. Myung says it took the ROK soldiers three whole days to herd that many people into the trenches like cattle—then kill them execution style. But this was not the only incident..." Moon left the thought unfinished.

Collier simply sat there speechless, trying to imagine the horror as the simple people stood by, waiting their turn to be mowed down with machine guns and rifles.

Clearly Smitty was overwhelmed as he contemplated the photo again.

"Do you mean there were other massacres like this?" Smitty roused from his horror.

"Yes. Several. In prison camp, Myung heard eyewitness accounts of others—particularly one near a southern village called No Gun Ri. According to Myung, in late July or early August, the situation had become so desperate that the commander of your Twentieth-fifth Infantry Division told his officers that all civilians seen in the area were to be considered as enemy and action taken accordingly. American soldiers from the First Cavalry Division had driven the people out from two villages near No Gun Ri, warning them the North Korean invaders were coming. As the refugees neared No Gun Ri, U.S. soldiers ordered them off the road and onto a railroad track where U.S. planes strafed the area. Many were slaughtered. After dark, American soldiers then herded the surviving refugees into the railroad bridge underpass and opened fire on them. The few Korean survivors said there were no North Korean troops within miles and the killings were not related to combat. Survivors of No Gun Ri say over two-hundred innocent civilians were murdered. According to American prisoners captured with Myung, this was also reported to the American high authority defending the Pusan perimeter who—just like Colonel Edwards' report of the Taejon slaughter—ordered all evidence of these killings be kept secret."

"It unbelievable that mass murder of such proportion witnessed by U.S. troops could be kept secret. We're talking about hundreds of innocent women and children," Smitty protested.

"Myung says he heard of other, similar, mass slaughters of refugees at Suwon and at a warehouse in Cheongwon, both just south of here. He says from what he heard, the total number killed may have exceeded one-hundred thousand. Also, Myung mentioned another mass killing at a village called Ulsan, further south, near Pusan. Most of these mass murders occurred during the initial retreat from the North Korean Communists in July and August of 1950—Myung said many of them were sanctioned by your American generals."

"Hmm-m? And just to whom has your cousin tried to report this?" Major Smith asked doubtfully, not sure what kind of Pandora's Box he might be getting into.

"Myung went to the American Embassy last week as soon as he was repatriated." Moon held out her hand for the photo.

"Did he show them these photos?" Smitty asked.

"Copies of this as well as several others of the same scene he had made with a Minox miniature German-spy camera he bought on the black market in Seoul with back pay he had accumulated while he was prisoner. They took his statement and told him they would take it to your ambassador, Mister Ellis O. Briggs. The ambassador's staff told him to come back this week. When he went back yesterday, they said they wanted the originals of the photos—not copies he made with the Minox. They said for him to bring the original pictures back to them. He refused, but gave them copies of several more images he had made with the German spy camera. They insisted he move into a barracks room at the Embassy. He says they are giving him what you Americans call, 'the run-around.' He also thinks he is being held under a sort of house arrest." Moon looked anxiously across the low table to see their reaction.

"Do you mean they won't let him leave the compound?" the Major asked, showing increased interest now.

"Well, not exactly. He is free to go out during daylight hours, but must be back by dark. And he is certain is he is being followed. He came to visit me this afternoon and gave me this. He says he has hidden the other photos and the originals of the signed statements. He wouldn't tell me where because he was afraid to get me involved. I'm pretty sure they are somewhere in the village."

"Do you have copies of the Minox camera pictures?" Collier spoke up, no longer able to contain himself, apologizing, "Sorry, Smitty, I didn't mean to interrupt."

"Yes. Moon, do you have the Minox images here?" Smitty nodded understanding to Collier for his interest and concern.

"No. Myung gave the Embassy one film strip. He said he has made duplicates and has hidden them in a safe place," Moon replied.

"You mean other originals? Or copies of the copies?"

"Other originals. Two more complete sets, each on a separate strip of film."

"I would like to see one of those, and I wonder if I could talk to your cousin, Myung Ahn, face-to-face," Major Smith asked Moon, trying to keep his hand steady as he was relighting his cigar. He juxtaposed Ahn Myung's surname in the accustomed American way.

"I will ask him if he comes back tomorrow. He is afraid he may be casting suspicion on me. He suspects your embassy is trying to shut him up." Moon hung her head, uncertain about making such an outrageous suggestion.

"Why, that's pure paranoia! I assure you that our military and our ambassador—our government—would want to do everything they could to get to the bottom of these allegations." Smitty waved the well-chewed unlit cigar emphatically in the air. "Tell your cousin I will meet him anywhere he says, if he is afraid. Assure him that I will tell no one."

"Ahso, Major Smith, I will tell him if I see him. I will send his answer by Otis tomorrow—that is if I am able to contact Myung." Smiling hopefully, Moon looked Smitty directly in the eye, before she took the photos, bowed low and backed out of the room.

"What do you think, Smitty? Do you believe Moon's story?" Collier asked as they were returning through the gate to the compound about an hour later after lingering for a polite interval of after-dinner conversation with Otis and Moon.

"I'm not sure. If you mean do I believe the stories about the massacres, then I'm concerned enough to want to know more. If you mean do I believe the Eighth Army hierarchy and our State Department are giving this guy Ahn Myung the runaround, the answer is maybe. If what he is claiming happened actually happened, then he is handing them a can of worms that would surely tighten a lot of important assholes in Washington. And, truth be known, I've heard rumors of some of this shit—they've been whispered around...they're in the air. Nobody wants to believe we could have actually participated in anything like that. I certainly don't want to believe it. Do you?" Smitty had his Zippo out, but couldn't get it to work in his never-ending struggle to keep the Dutch Masters cigar lit.

Collier flicked his Zippo and held the flame while they stopped in the middle of the road and the older officer puffed his precious cigar back to life, before he replied. "No...I don't want to believe it, either, but I know things happen in war. We were up against a nightmare situation after the North Koreans made that first push south. I can certainly understand how the ROKs might panic and execute a bunch of North Korean sympathizers. I don't believe American officers would stand by and let it happen, though. We—our Army, our military—have always abided by the Geneva Convention."

"What could *we* do, anyway? I mean if the higher ups are trying to keep a lid on this, do you want to get your tail in a crack?" Collier asked as they resumed walking up the hill toward Quonset Row.

"No...I really don't want to get involved. The truce is still too new—still uneasy. Old Syngman Rhee keeps threatening to send the ROK Army back north across the no-fire zone. With all that going on, I don't imagine the stuffed shirts and brass in the White House and the Pentagon are feeling all that easy, yet."

"Yeah...I can certainly understand that..." Collier nodded.

"Still?...I wonder what's really going on. I smell a rat. Is the brass really giving this Myung Ahn a fast shuffle? There's more to this than meets the eye." The older officer's cigar traced a glowing arc as he made a sweeping gesture with his hand to emphasize his concern.

"You know Vice President Nixon is coming to Seoul tomorrow to pay Ike's respects to Syngman Rhee?" Collier's question was rhetorical. Colonel Spaulding and Colonel Scroggs had driven the entire compound half crazy the past three days, getting the place in apple-pie order on the basis of a simple phone call from Eighth Army HQ that they should "be prepared" just in case the V.P and his wife decided to pay them a courtesy call to visit our 'sick and shut-in' soldiers which, nowadays, were mostly cases of ingrown toenails, hemorrhoidectomies, a few emergency appendectomies, an infrequent gall bladder and more than a few cases of the venereal disease Lymphogranuloma Venereum which was basically almost completely preventable, simply the result of inexcuseable, poor post-coital hygiene. Collier hated to be caught up in such a shameless exercise as sucking up to Tricky Dick Nixon and his prissy wife, but, then, this kind of political ass-kissing was about the same in corporate civilian life as it was in the military.

"So what? Surely you're not suggesting there might be some way to get Myung Ahn in touch with Nixon? Forget it. You've got to be out of your mind." Smitty stopped dead in his tracks under the street light, searching Collier's face for seriousness.

"Hold on, Smitty, calm down. Do I look like I'm crazy? I'm expecting my RA commission and promotion to First Lieutenant to come through any day now. I'm sure not looking to rattle any cages." Collier held up his hands in a calming gesture.

"Okay, okay. I'm just jumpy, I guess. The increase of incidents of village people lately coming over the back fence to steal food from the storeroom and blankets from the Chicken Coop has me chasing shadows. By the way, I guess you're aware you have AOD day after tomorrow?" Smitty reminded him he had switched days with Captain Richmond who was in Tokyo on R&R and wouldn't be back until next week.

"Yeah, I know—just my luck to pull OD on Friday the thirteenth—and with an impromptu visit from the Vice President hanging over our head. Look, I'm not ready to turn in. Let's walk down to the O Club, and I'll buy you a drink"

"No thanks. You go ahead. I've got to stop by the Coop and write a couple of long-overdue letters. Maybe I'll catch up with you later." The older officer waved him ahead as he turned left onto the narrow walk, heading back toward the senior officer billet.

"Lieutenant Ramsay?" A captain, decked out in sharply-pressed fatigues with Judge Advocate insignia embroidered on the lapels, stopped him in the foyer separating the O Club Quonset lounge from the dining room of the officers' mess as he walked through the door.

"Yes, sir, Captain. I'm Ramsay. Can I help you?" Collier braced to a casual semblance of attention but didn't salute since he was inside the building.

"My name's Chandler. I'm Secret Service with the advance party of Vice President Nixon's visit to Seoul to visit President Rhee tomorrow. Since you're adjutant here and will also be AOD Friday, I thought I would check in with you, and maybe you could show me around, so I can get a lay of the land for briefing the security team who will be traveling with the Vice President and his wife. Also, your people in the areas Mr. and Mrs. Nixon will be touring will need to be vetted and briefed. I've already spoken to Colonel Spaulding and Colonel Scroggs and they have alerted those involved to be present tomorrow morning at an 0700 meeting in Colonel Scrogg's office. If you have a few minutes, now, I would appreciate a quick walk-through—I'm on a tight schedule, and I've already been waiting over an hour." Unsmiling, the obviously anal, tight-jawed, Secret Service mannequin spoke through clenched teeth, every inch an Ivy League fraternity man.

"I don't mean to be impudent, Sir, but I didn't know Secret Service wore military uniform," speaking respectfully, Collier remained at semi-attention.

"Ordinarily, we don't, but my superiors thought it might attract less attention if the advance party wore military uniforms. If you see me tomorrow, I'll be back in civilian mufti."

"If you don't mind, Captain...ah...Mr. Chandler, Sir, I'd like to see some ID." It was growing rather late to be giving tours. Feeling more than a little put upon, Collier stood his ground.

"Not at all, Lieutenant." Still unsmiling, the Secret Service agent pulled a thin black-leather billfold from his hip pocket and flashed his badge and photo ID. Collier took it from him and looked it over carefully, comparing the photo of the man dressed in civvies to the man who stood in front of him in an Army captain's uniform. As far as he could tell, Chandler's credentials seemed to be in order.

"Thank you, Sir. Now tell me again what you want to see." Collier returned the wallet.

"Why don't we begin by going in through the main entrance, and then you can walk me through the hospital...take me the way you will take the Vice President and Mrs. Nixon if they show up here during their visit. I'd also like to see the OR and some actual wards with patients..." the unsmiling SS goon explained his mission as they walked outside and headed for the main building.

Once inside the main building, Collier led Chandler up the steps through the lobby, pointing out the administrative offices on the right and continuing across the hall through the door to the stairway up to the second building higher up the hill.

"What's up here?" the tight-assed G-Man asked when he paused for breath, halfway up the long covered stairway.

"The OR, Recovery Room and Intensive Care." Collier replied.

"Is there a better way to get up here?" Chandler asked, breathing hard from the exertion of climbing.

"What do you mean?" Collier asked, not certain if the Secret Service agent were concerned about the difficulty of securing the area or about the physical difficulty of the stairs.

"Mrs. Nixon will have trouble with these steps." Chandler replied at the top of the stairs, standing looking back down the steep slope onto the bombed-out ruins of the top of the main building.

"Well...you could have her driven up the hill to the side entrance, but there are still some steps to climb even from the street side." Collier nodded toward the wooden stairs leading from the street, plainly visible on their right.

"I see." The Federal Agent pulled a little notebook from his shirt pocket and jotted down a notation.

"The OR is on the right." Collier pointed through the door to the darkened surgical room, empty now, at night, except on the rare occasion of an emergency. "Across the hall, is the Recovery Room and beyond that is Intensive Care. Back here are the post-surgical wards where most of the more-serious cases recuperate." Collier indicated the large open wards on both sides of the corridor. "Now, do you want to go up to building three?"

"Are there more steps to climb?" Chandler asked.

"Yessir, but not quite as many," Collier replied.

"What's up there?"

"Mostly just wards where we treat various infectious diseases. VD to pneumonia or severe cases of gastrointestinal disorders—we have quite a few exotic bugs in Korea we don't often see in the States."

"Okay, let's take a quick look, just in case. Mrs. Nixon is rather unpredictable. We never know what to expect from her." Chandler nodded for Collier to lead the way.

"Wait here, while I go find surgical masks. There is some scary stuff in building four."

"No...that won't be necessary. We couldn't think of placing the Nixons in that kind of jeopardy. Just take me back down now."

Smiling to himself, Collier turned and led the nerdy spook back the way they'd come.

"Thanks for the tour," Chandler said after they had come back down and were standing outside on the steps under the portico. His Army OD sedan was waiting at the foot of the steps.

"Excuse me, Sir, but I can't help but wonder how the Secret Service agency coordinates with the State Department. I mean does the Vice President go through Mr. Briggs' office to meet with President Rhee?"

"Well...yes and no. The Vice President is legally and diplomatically autonomous in a manner of speaking, but diplomatic protocol always calls for the Executive Branch to operate through our embassies when we're on foreign soil. Korea is different in the sense that the country is still under military rule of UN forces. Why do you ask?"

"Well...it's just a matter that came to my attention recently concerning suppressed reports of U.S. involvement in major atrocities during the early part of the conflict..." Collier stopped short, already regretting he had opened the door on Myung's apocryphal tales of the Taejon, Nu Gun Ri, Suwon, and Ulsan massacres.

"What do you mean atrocities?" Obviously interested now, the stuffed-shirt Ivy League G-man actually separated his tightly-clenched teeth when he spoke.

"Massacres..." Collier quickly summarized what Moon had told them earlier, including Myung's frustrated efforts to get his evidence in front of both the military and the embassy.

"Oh? The Secret Service wouldn't be involved in this type of investigation. You'll have to bring this to the attention of your commanders...you know, follow the proper chain of command." Chandler dropped his reptilian eyes deceitfully. "Well, thanks again for the tour. We may meet again." The devious agent gestured goodbye with a dismissive wave.

"Goodnight, Sir." Collier returned the offhand gesture and started to turn back to the hospital entrance.

"Wait up, a minute, Lieutenant." When Collier looked again, Chandler had turned back toward him again.

"Yes, Sir?" Collier wondered what was coming next.

"Where does this man with the photos and Minox evidence live?" Chandler asked, still trying to act offhand.

"I don't know, Sir." Collier was glad he could answer honestly.

"Well, where does his cousin, Moon, live?" Chandler persisted.

"In the village across the street."

"Could you direct me to her house?"

"Not if my life depended upon it, Sir. I've only been there once and it was dark. Those huts all look the same to me." Collier was unflinching in the bald-faced lie. He really didn't care for Chandler's holier-than-thou Washington attitude, and he was certain Chandler's interest was not altruistically directed in Myung's favor.

"What's the rest of her name? Moon what?"

"I wouldn't have a clue, sir."

"Where is your sergeant? Her boyfriend?"

"As far as I know, he spends his evenings with her, Sir."

"Will he be on duty here tomorrow morning?"

"As far as I know, Sir. He works for Major Smith."

"Well, I'll see you again in the morning at o-seven-hundred for the briefing, Lieutenant. Goodnight and thanks again for the tour." Without further questions, Chandler stepped into the back seat of the OD sedan and the driver pulled away.

" *Well, goodnight, yourself, you sneaky SOB.*" Collier breathed half-aloud as he watched the vehicle leave. Although he wasn't exactly sure why, watching Chandler's staff car round the corner and exit through the guard gate, Collier was left with an uneasy feeling in his gut. Without further deliberation, he headed for the Chicken Coop on the dead run to tell Smitty of his blundering indiscretion.

"I think I goofed, Smitty..." Not wanting to chance being overheard by Scroggs or Spaulding in their rooms just down the hall, as soon as Major Smith cracked the door to his room Collier recounted his encounter with Chandler in guarded whispers. He concluded, "We need to tell Otis, so he can warn Moon. I don't trust that conniving Secret Service bastard. He'd sell his own mother to get brownie points in Washington."

"Don't worry about it. No need to warn Otis this late. This Chandler isn't likely to go wandering around the village alone this time of night. I'll tell him the first thing bright and early tomorrow morning. Moon can warn Myung to lie low, if she thinks he should," standing in his military underwear, Smitty advised Collier through the cracked door.

2.

"Cha...come here. I'm glad I caught you before you left." making his way in the dark by the officers' communal showers and latrine back to the street between Building Four and Quonset Row, Collier hailed the houseboy, Cha, coming up from the street from the new location of The Broken Drum.

"Ahso, Rootenant Collier-san. What you need from Cha?" The pixyish houseboy came trotting up, always eager to serve.

"You live in the village. Do you know where Sergeant Cook lives there with Choi Moon?" Collier asked, still apprehensive Nixon's Secret Service flunky might be up to no good as far as Moon and Myung were concerned.

"Ahso. I go there many times before to deliver things to Moon for Sergeant Cook." Cha nodded his head affirmatively.

"I'm going take you down to the guard shack and clear you to come back through. I want you to take a message to Sergeant Cook for me, right now." Collier already had his notepad out and was jotting a terse warning as they walked between the huts toward the street fronting Quonset Row.

Tell your housekeeper to get very lost immediately. I mean tonight.
Right now. Tell her to tell her cousin to get lost, too. It would be a good
idea for them both to stay lost for a few days, at least. I'll find you and
explain tomorrow when I can find a private moment. Burn this note.

At the gate, Collier made a careful inspection of the entrance to the village directly across the street, sweeping his gaze up and down in both directions looking for suspicious vehicles parked in the shadows along the Suwon road. When he was satisfied the coast was clear, he explained to the Corporal on duty at the gate that he needed Cha to take a message to Sergeant Cook. Although it was strictly against Colonel Spaulding's orders, it was fairly common among enlisted personnel to spend the night in the village from time to time. Some, like Otis Cook, regularly lived there. An unspoken state of *laissez faire* existed between those men and the permanent cadre who manned the guard gate.

Grudgingly, the Corporal agreed to cooperate. "Okay, Lieutenant, but make sure he comes straight back. It's almost curfew."

As soon as the duty Corporal gave him the go-ahead, Collier led Cha out of the guard's earshot and pressed the folded note into the Korean houseboy's hand. "Give this to Sergeant Cook...no one else. If someone else tries to take the note, you found it lying on the ground. You don't know anything about it. After you've delivered it, come back here to me. Understand?"

"Ahso...." Holding the folded note tightly in his fist, Cha scooted quickly across the road, disappearing beyond the arc of the compound's streetlights. Only two days past the dark of the moon, Cha immediately disappeared into the murky shadows of the unlit village, directly across the street. Waiting in the shadows near the guard shack for what seemed an eternity—but was actually less than five minutes by his watch—Collier was taken quite by surprise when Cha appeared again returning ghostlike from the darkened village.

Sergeant Cook was trailing close behind.

"Thanks for the warning, Lieutenant. The situation is already handled. Right after you and Smitty left, some civilians from the Embassy came nosing around the village. Fortunately, some of Moon's friends stalled them long enough for her to get clean away. I assure you she is well out of circulation by now. She will try to get a message to Myung. What happened after you left tonight to get you so stirred up, anyway? What's going on?" Toothless with his GI dentures in his hand, when he formed words, the trusted Sergeant's shapeless mouth reminded Collier of Popeye the Sailor of the comic strip.

"When I got back, I had a visitor—a stuffed-shirt from Nixon's Secret Service crew..." Collier quickly filled the veteran NCO in on the details of his busy night. "If I were you, I'd spend the night over here. Is there anything across the street to connect you to Moon or Myung?"

"Not a thing, Lieutenant. I travel light." The Sergeant winked a knowing wink.

"Okay. Lay low and let's see what happens. I may be making more of this than it deserves. I'll catch up with you Friday after the Nixons leave...if, indeed, they show up at all. Now go and get some rest." Collier gave the Sergeant's shoulder a friendly pat as the noncom turned and trudged down the street in front of the main building toward his cubbyhole in back of Supply.

"Good morning, Collier, I'm sorry to give such short notice, but, since the Vice President and Mrs. Nixon will be paying us a visit first thing tomorrow morning, we're meeting with the front man for their security, Chandler, at o-seven-hundred in my office. I hope you don't mind?" Scroggs reminded Collier when he showed up early for duty just prior to 0625 the following morning. Collier had risen just before 0530 and walked in the pre-dawn darkness to the Coop to fill Smitty in on his late night escapades.

"Thanks, I'm already on the case." The wise old Major winked. "I just got back from Sergeant Owen's quarters in the carpenter shop. He should already be across the Han River by now. I sent him on a scavenger hunt to all the MASH units north of Seoul to borrow some tubing from the OR."

A few minutes after Scroggs reminded Collier of Chandler's visit, Lieutenant James showed up. James already had the AOD armband around the bicep of his left arm and was strapping the Colt holster's leather tie-downs around his right thigh when Collier saw the well-polished Army OD sedan pull up under the portico.

Nixon's Secret Service flunky, Chandler, got out and ambled up the front steps.

"Good morning, Mister Chandler, we weren't expecting you quite this early," Collier went to the top of the steps outside the entrance foyer to greet him, greatly relieved he had taken the precaution to remove Otis Owen from Chandler's nosey questions about Myung's damning—not to mention: embarrassing—evidence of the unthinkable, horrendous Taejon atrocity.

"Sorry, but I'm pressed for time. Can we round up your key people who may be involved in the Vice President's visit tomorrow. We don't like to leave anything to chance. I'd just like a last-minute word with them to make sure everything goes off in perfect order." Chandler wrinkled his nose as he sniffed the heavily fecal-scented air trailing in the wake of the old village papasan's bi-weekly visit to fill the enormous, leaky metal honey buckets on his rustic ox-cart to overflowing with the human waste from the more than several latrines in the compound. As was his custom, he left a wide, clearly-visible trail of the semi-liquid human waste glistening in the morning sunlight. Telltale evidence the denizens of the 121 were still living in rudimentary combat conditions characterized by the use of primitive communal pit latrines serving the ambulatory sections of the hospital wards, themselves, and both the enlisted and officer living quarters, the pervasively-malodorous trail ran down the middle of the dirt street, disappearing around the corner in front of Supply where the street started up the hill.

"Yes, Sir, my superiors have been expecting your visit. If you'll just come in and have a seat, I'll tell Colonel Scroggs you're here and go round up the appropriate personnel. This may take a minute, Sir. You caught us right in the middle of a shift change which involves morning rounds." Mightily resisting his strong aversion to Chandler, Collier struggled to keep a civil tongue in his head.

"What's that there on the ground? What's that stink?" Chandler demanded through his permanently-clenched teeth before he turned to follow Collier.

"Drippings from the honey-bucket cart," Collier replied. "It's a daily fact of life in these parts."

"Honey-bucket cart?" Chandler queried, completely at a loss to comprehend.

"You know, Sir. It's human feces. The honey-bucket man is an old papasan who comes two or three times a week and dips out the reservoirs under our latrines and hauls the excrement out of here in two giant metal vats fastened to an ox-drawn cart. The Koreans fertilize with human feces—it's a tradition stretching back to long before written history I suppose." Collier explained.

"You mean they fertilize their gardens...their crops...with human...ah...waste?" The Ivy-leaguer was aghast.

"Yes, Sir. It's traditional throughout the Orient." Collier tried to keep a straight face at the agent's delicate sensibilities.

"The Orient? Does that include Japan?" Chandler voiced with a croak.

"I'm told MacArthur made great strides in converting the Japanese to more civilized methods of agriculture and sanitation, but, yes, Sir, I think a large portion of the hinterlands of Japan still fertilize their crops with human feces." Collier replied.

"Does that include the rice?" Chandler asked, now his face had turned a shade of pale green.

"Of course, Sir. In this part of the world, over ninety-percent of the diet depends upon rice."

"I see..." Chandler gasped through tightly-clenched incisors.

"Yes, Sir. Now, if you'll follow me, Sir?" Leading the badly-traumatized agent inside the hospital, Collier was dying to let the Ivy-League asshole know that he was aware of last night's raid on the village, but discretion was the better part of valor. It wouldn't take a genius to figure out why Sergeant Owens was conveniently off scavenging for supplies in the hinterlands.

"Wait up, Lieutenant, are you telling me that Mrs. Nixon would have to use...ah...some sort of primitive Johnny-house facilities if she should have to avail herself of the...ah... 'powder room' while she is on the premises?" Chandler was still having trouble wrapping his Ivy-ententacled gray matter around the idea that— except for the Eighth Air Force Club in Seoul—there were no flushing toilets in military installations in the combat zone.

"I'm afraid so, Sir, but we do have a rather nice, private, portable, patient-Johnny in the VIP ward...President Syngman Rhee and several of our General staff officers—including General Matthew Ridgeway—have used that facility on occasion of dire need.

"I see..." Chandler thought that over. From the look on his face, Collier could see the idea of Pat Nixon on an outhouse toilet seat did not sit well with the agency front-man's cultured scheme of things. He could just imagine Chandler going back to Seoul to brief his superiors on the imperative that Mrs. Nixon should take care to evacuate her bladder and bowels before venturing beyond the civilized comforts of Seoul.

Overlooking Chandler's insufferably-superior attitude, the briefing went off well enough. In something less than an hour, Collier escorted the Brooks Brothers-outfitted security guard back down the steps to his waiting staff car.

"By the way, I can't help but ask if you've heard from your young Korean friend, Moon Choi, or her cousin, Myung Ahn, regarding his contact with the Embassy concerning the alleged massacre of civilians." Using the American juxtaposition of the Korean names, Chandler struggled unsuccessfully to maintain a studied affect of offhand interest.

"No, Sir. I only met the girl once and seriously doubt I will ever have occasion to cross paths with her again." Collier shrugged as he opened the door to the staff car and held it for the insufferable preppie.

Searching Collier's face for honesty, Chandler nodded and got in the car. Collier closed the door behind him.

Rolling down the window, Chandler got in a parting shot. "By the way, Lieutenant, if I were you I wouldn't be so anxious to show off that nickel-plated Colt 45. It's strictly against regulation to deface government-issue equipment you know."

"I'm glad you mentioned it, Sir. I took it off of a dead Gook up on Pork Chop. They've recommended me for a medal, Sir." Collier smiled. The Colt was Collier's prize possession, a real find in Black Market Alley in downtown Seoul.

"Please call me 'Pat.'" Escorted by Agent Chandler with several other Brooks Brothers-outfitted Secret Service men and a photographer, Vice President Nixon's patronizing wife, Patricia, stepped out of the war-weary, however shiny, black, Cadillac diplomatic-corps sedan shortly after 0945 hours on Friday the 13th and extended Collier her limp, gloved hand which—even through her expensive white gloves—felt something like a dead fish. Arriving just after a sudden downpour, Pat Nixon's glove, like the morning weather, was damp and rather gray which was altogether in keeping with Collier's mood at having to wear the AOD armband and Colt sidearm for the next twenty-four hours.

The previous afternoon, Scroggs had briefed Collier on Nixon's prior military experience. During World War II, the Vice President had served in the Navy as a reserve officer. A so-called "ninety-day-wonder," Nixon had received his military training at Quonset Point, Rhode Island and Ottumwa, Iowa, before serving in the supply corps on several islands in the South Pacific where he eventually rose to the rank of lieutenant commander (the Naval equivalent of an Army major) commanding cargo-handling units in the South Pacific Combat Air Transport Command (SCAT). During his non-combat service in the Navy, the Vice President gained quite a reputation as a cutthroat, high-stakes poker-player. It was rumored among those who had served with "Tricky-Dick" in the Navy that the Pinocchio-nosed politician had bankrolled his first campaign for Congress with his military poker winnings.

"We don't have long. I'm meeting with Rhee before lunch. We'd like a quick tour of the hospital. I'd particularly like to have photos of Pat and me chatting with some of the patients," Nixon arrogantly informed Spaulding and Scroggs even before he finished shaking hands.

"Isn't there a better way to get up there?" Nixon frowned at Chandler when they exited the rear door of the Main Building and approached the long flight of covered wooden stairs leading to Building Two.

"We could have the limo drive you around to the back of Building Four, Sir." Chandler informed the Vice President.

"Don't be silly, Richard. I'm not afraid of climbing a few stairs." The pampered VP's lady said and started up the steps. By the time she reached the first landing halfway up, she had turned quite pale and was struggling to get her breath. Still, Collier had to hand it to her; she quickly got a second wind and proceeded all the way to the top without pausing again.

Inside Building Two, Collier efficiently guided the entourage past the OR which was now a virtual beehive of activity with all five tables occupied by surgical procedures—five rosy, merthiolate-painted assholes pointing ceilingward toward God, in a fitting salute to the nation's VP and his snooty lady. Her composure quickly regained, Pat Nixon followed Collier on past the Recovery Room where he took them into one of the wards and introduced them to Major Hughes and

Major Olsen who, in turn, introduced their high-ranking visitors to a group of post-surgical cases—carefully selected to exclude any hemorrhoidectomy or ingrown toenail patients.

With minimal meaningful social exchange between the VP and Pat and the actual patients, the Nixons posed for a well-orchestrated series of photos taken by the efficient official photographer, expertly calculated to exhibit an atmosphere of cozy, folksy, down-home camaraderie. This accomplished within the space of ten minutes, the Nixons thanked Major Hughes and Major Olsen. That done, Chandler told Collier to take them back to administration in Building One where they thanked Spaulding and Scroggs. Then the officious party took their leave, hardly bothering to grunt goodbye to Collier as they went down the front steps.

Without warning, that afternoon, the temperature dropped precipitously from the noontime high in the low-sixties to a reading in the mid-forties just before the sun went down. By 2300, hours the temperature had plummeted below freezing—a grim reminder of the coming hardship of the dreaded Korean winter which had taken such a toll on U.N. troops retreating from the Yalu that first winter of the war.

Suffering from the effects of the minor frostbite he had received in Basic at Sill, after duty, Collier went up to the storage room in the new The Broken Drum and dug, from the bottom of his duffel, his winter field jacket with a zip-in lining, a pair of fur-lined gloves his mom had sent him, and a set of GI long johns to protect him from the cold.

As AOD, he was periodically required to walk the perimeter of the Compound at two-hour intervals checking the guards. Although now suitably bundled against the unexpected artic chill, the rest of the evening had passed rather slowly for Collier by the time he returned to his desk in the Orderly Room after completing his appointed rounds just past 2200 hours.

"Lieutenant Ramsay, Sir, come quick. The soldier walking post in the area out behind the carpenter shop spotted an intruder coming over the fence." Collier had just pulled his gloves off. He had poured himself a cup of lukewarm coffee from a canister sent down from the hospital kitchen and was just completing a cursory entry in the AOD log book. He was fondly contemplating stretching out on the old-fashioned, folding canvas Army cot for a well-deserved short nap when a corporal wearing a polished, white-banded helmet liner and the white Guard cross-chest web belt, with the garnet and white SOG (Sergeant of the Guard) armband, came bursting into the room. The SOG was carrying a drawn Colt .45 in his hand.

"Lead on...I'm right behind you." Grabbing his own helmet liner and flashlight, Collier stuffed his gloves in the pocket of his field jacket as he headed for the door. He pulled his own nickel-plated Colt 45 as he ran.

"How many of them were there?" blowing his steaming breath on his half-frozen hands, Collier asked the GI walking post when they reached the compound's fence line out back of Supply. The stars were brilliant against the blackness of space. Four days past the dark of the moon, the first-quarter sliver of moon was yet to have risen in the starry bowl of night.

"I only saw one, Sir. Last time I saw him, he was heading back along the fence behind the NCO club. He disappeared in the direction of the Chicken Coop. There's been a lot of blanket-stealing lately and the rear windows of the Chicken Coop open just a few feet from the back fence. C'mon, Lieutenant, follow me," the eager-beaver corporal with the SOG armband growled in a hushed whisper as he took off running at a half-trot.

Cocking the Colt, Collier followed, adrenalin coursing through his veins.

"I'll take the guard path along the fence line behind the Chicken Coop, and you go along the walk between the rear of Quonset Row and the Coop. Keep an eye out for open windows and don't turn on that flashlight, Corporal," Collier whispered authoritatively, watching the steaming trail of the SOG's frozen breath, back lit by the nearest boundary light as it feathered and dissolved against the ink-black sky as the corporal headed along the back of Quonset Row.

His eyes having difficulty adjusting to the Stygian darkness of the deep shadows as a result of the distracting glow of the widely-spaced street lights down the line behind Quonset Row, relying upon his peripheral vision, Collier swept the area looking for movement.

Nothing...nothing he could see.

Advancing slowly, step-by-step in a half-crouch, taking great care to avoid the spider web of nurses' clotheslines running in back of the Coop, Collier warily made his way down the pitch-black fence line, his Colt .45 cocked and at the ready. Across the fence, the dirt road ran along the ghostly silhouettes of the low gray stucco buildings of the village school. The school road ended at an empty field fifty yards behind him. The nearest street light outside the hospital compound was at least a hundred yards in front of him down near where the school street joined the MSR to Suwon.

"HALT! HALT OR I'LL SHOOT," the sound of the sharp command came from up ahead, around the far end of the lengthy Chicken Coop. Judging from the squeaky youthful sound of the voice, the order came from the guard walking the next post stretching along the fence line all the way down the short hill to the main gate at the Suwon highway.

Immediately, Collier struck out at a half-trot toward the far corner of the shadowy building, about twenty-five feet up ahead. As he neared the corner of the tarpapered, wooden building, there arose a tinny clatter of rattling beer cans and discarded aluminum mess kits and assorted other metal noise-making appurtenances hanging from the chest-high, combination barbed- and reinforced double cattle-wire fence—a dead giveaway someone was most likely trying to scramble over.

"POP!" From up ahead, the ominous sound of an M-2 Carbine reverberated into the frigid night air.

Nearing the corner of the Coop, Collier caught view of the shadowy silhouette of what appeared to be a civilian male trying to claw his way up and over the rickety barbed-wire fence. **"HALT! CLIMB DOWN NOW OR I'LL SHOOT!"**

"Halt! **Mŏmch'uda! Stop! Mŏmch'ugehada!**" from somewhere between the Coop and Quonset Row, Collier heard the SOG shout both in English and ill-pronounced pidgin Korean.

Showing no sign of hesitation, the shadowy intruder continued unintimidated in his desperate attempt to scramble over the unsteady wire.

"HALT OR I'LL SHOOT!" Collier shouted again and reflexively fired his Colt skyward. The sound of his trusty Colt sounded like a cannon reverberating between the walls of the nearby stucco school buildings and the Coop in the silence of the Korean night.

"**Halt, I say. Halt or I'll shoot to kill!**" Blinking to help his eyes adjust from the sudden muzzle flash, Collier heard the SOG warn the shadowy figure from somewhere behind the Coop.

Showing no sign of stopping, the wraith-like outline now was poised near the top strand, just about to make his escape into road along the village schoolyard.

"**POP!**" The SOG squeezed off another shot.

"**HALT OR I'LL SHOOT!**" Collier warned again as he lowered the barrel of the Colt handgun and took deadly aim.

Reaching back to free his clothing from the clutch of the barbwire, the shadowy figure raised himself, poised to leap. The interloper left no doubt that he was not going to stop.

"**POP! POP!**" With no further warning, the SOG fired off two more rounds from his position behind the Coop—the corporal was obviously closer now.

"**POP! POP! POP!**" Now, three muzzle flashes from up ahead, behind the eight-holer latrine and shower buildings, signaled the arrival of the guard walking the post up from the direction of the main gate. Recalling the ineptitude on the rifle range of the Medic recruits he'd trained at Pickett, Collier reflexively squatted and pressed himself against the tarpaper wall of the Coop as he heard a round ricochet off metal and go whining out into the night.

"**POW!**" Squinting down the barrel over the stubby blade sight, Collier squeezed off a single round, then watched as the shadowy silhouette stiffened and suddenly went limp, dangling from the clutch of the wire by a single leg over the outside of the fence.

"We got that one, Lieutenant...come on, the post behind Supply says they saw another one sneak in after we started chasing his companion." The SOG waved his hand-held "prick-six"—GI slang for the AN/PRC-6, Walkie-talkie—beckoning Collier to follow him back along the area behind Quonset Row.

By the time they retraced their steps down along the fence on the eastern perimeter behind Supply, if indeed there had been a second interloper, he had disappeared.

"I guess when he heard all the shooting, he panicked and went back down behind Supply, Lieutenant," the SOG said after their careful search revealed no trace of a second trespasser.

When they returned to the spot where they had shot the first intruder, the body had already been removed.

"They already took the corpse up to the morgue. He was an old papasan. He left a trail of blankets he had stolen from the Supply storeroom as he ran up behind the Coop. You hit him twice with the carbine, Sergeant. Once in the right shoulder and again in the upper part of his back, just above the shoulder blade. The lieutenant had the kill shot. Congratulations, Sir. Your Colt .45 hit him in the back of the head and blew his face clean off. Major Greenberg is MOD. I'm sure he'll do the autopsy first thing tomorrow morning." The guard walking post had waited to give Collier and the SOG the report.

"Thank you, Williams. You can return to your post." The SOG dismissed the guard.

"Jeezus...we killed a man just for trying to keep his family warm..." Watching the guard leave, Collier shook his head as the utter senselessness of the act slowly overtook him.

"In the dark, we had no way of knowing. Don't sweat it, Lieutenant, for all we knew, that old papasan could have been a guerilla intent on murder and rape.

I'm going to walk back down the fence again just to make sure we haven't missed anything." The SOG saluted Collier, waiting to be dismissed.

"Okay, Corporal. I'm going back down to the orderly room and write my report while it's still fresh in my head. I suggest you do the same as soon as you've made sure the perimeter is secure. I guarantee there will be an inquiry." Collier returned the salute, then turned and entered the rear of Building Four to make his way back down through the hospital. Still shaken by the futility of the senseless shooting, he decided to take a look at the corpse on his way back by the Quonset morgue. When he reached the morgue, Collier found the padlock had been secured. Exhausted now as he came down from adrenalin overload, Collier decided to skip trying to locate the keyholder. Woodenly, he continued back down to the OD desk in the orderly room in Building One.

Although his hands were shaking and badly hurting from being without his gloves in the bitter cold, Collier slowly warmed them by holding them near the space heater. It took a good quarter-hour to rub color back into them before he sat down and forced himself to sketch out a narrative report of the incident as he remembered it. When he finished writing down the facts, suddenly overcome with nausea, he put down his pen and barely made it to the trashcan. Reminiscent of the night outside Nuevo Laredo after seeing the women and donkey act, he threw up time and time again. Finally exhausted from dry heaves, wanting to rid the orderly room from the stink of his vomit, he carried the trashcan outside and set it on the bare ground away from the covered stairs leading up to Building Two. When he returned inside, he stretched out on the old-timey canvas cot provided for the AOD and pulled a pair of blankets over himself in an attempt to stop his almost uncontrollable trembling.

When the SOG shook him awake to make rounds again just before 0200, Collier managed to complete his required tour of the perimeter without betraying just how deeply affected he had been by the killing of the old papasan. When he finished making rounds, Collier finally drifted back into an uneasy sleep. At 0600, when the SOG shook him awake to make their final tour of the perimeter, walking the fence line in the early-morning light seemed to relegate the memory of the event to the nebulous fabric of a bad dream.

"Why don't you go up and try to grab some sleep. You've had a trying night." Scroggs released him from further duty after he had given his usually-impassive Exec both a verbal and written report of the incident.

After a long, coma-like sleep and a late lunch alone in the officers' mess, hunched against the turned-up collar of his fully-lined field jacket against the newly-arrived bitter cold, Collier returned to his office to find both Scroggs and Spaulding had gone to Seoul for a meeting at Eighth Army HQ Compound.

Absently sorting through the mail on his desk, Collier's heart started wildly pumping when he came across two official letters from the Pentagon addressed to him. The first letter informed him that his application for RA commission had been approved and he had been promoted to First Lieutenant, effective 1 November 1953. Then, his hands trembling as he opened it, even more incredibly the second letter was to the effect his application for early release from active duty under the terms of the cryptic Department of the Army bulletin he had received—and forgotten about—back in September had also been approved. To his utter disbelief the order basically read that, "...effective 1 November, the following officers are relieved from active duty and are immediately free to proceed to the nearest military air base or seaport to utilize the first available transportation back to the United States where they are to report to Fort Meade, Maryland on or before 13 December 1953."

At the very end of the alphabetical list was:

2nd LT COLLIER B RAMSAY 01936991
P.O. Box 162
Salem, Virginia

Just above Collier's name was: 2nd LT JOHN HENRY PEWTER.

Still unsettled from the traumatic events of the previous evening, Collier reread the two communiqués, staring blankly out of the window at the almost featureless, brown barren hills stretching in the distance to the south along the Suwon road, overwhelmed by such an ironic turn of fate. After perhaps ten minutes, the incredible irony of his quandary—or incredible good fortune, depending upon his perspective—finally hit him and he burst out laughing, contemplating what he should do.

His thoughts turning back to the advice the savvy Colonel Wilson K. Massey had given him about the "good 'ol boy" network of West Point graduates and the power of the inbred military hierarchy in the peacetime Army, Collier considered the irony of his situation. Now that he was no longer faced with the commitment of staying in the military for the indefinite term of his commission, did he really want to turn right around and sign on to make the Army a lifelong career faced with the almost-certain knowledge he would always be sucking hind tit, taking a back seat to a long line of West Point, VMI and Citadel prima donnas?

Could it be possible that he could beat the odds? After all, he had all "sixes" on his efficiency reports and had just been made First Lieutenant, certainly at least a year before almost all but the few West Pointers with the same time-in-rank who had served in Korea prior to 27 July. Still, according to Colonel Massey, there was an almost certain chance the "old-boy" system would keep him frozen in grade until these same West Pointers could catch up and eventually pass him on the promotion lists. Certainly, he didn't want to sign on for a future where he would eventually be passed over until he was forced out of the Army as being unpromoteable after investing the best part of his young life.

On the other hand, did he want to go back home to continue doing silk screen banners for Kroger Pork'n'Beans and Valleydale Bacon? Kroger's regional advertising manager was almost certain to stick around until Collier had a long white beard. And, when Collier had left home, the future looked dim for his chances of ever making it as an illustrator in Roanoke. That was two years ago. He felt certain his opportunities had become even dimmer in the interim. And, to further complicate his aspirations, he had a family to support.

What about the advice of Major Hughes and Captain Mutch, who counseled him to investigate the possibility of a future in the pharmaceutical industry which, since WWII, was literally exploding with new discoveries in the areas of streptomycin, sulfas and penicillin along with other fantastic antibiotics and miracle drugs like the sex hormones and cortisone and similar steroid hormone compounds?

Major Hughes had also suggested that there was still a shortage of physicians and he could use his GI Bill to finance Medical School and actually become a doctor. But, remembering how Emma's brother had struggled to go to Med School after being a fighter pilot in WWII, now Collier wondered if he wanted to make the same sacrifices. He didn't need an adding machine to figure that he'd be in his mid-thirties by the time he graduated.

A future in the ordered life of an Army officer was seductive. Knowing who was supposed to salute him and who he was supposed to salute had a nice order to it and it beat hell out of being insulted by a wife who had little sympathy for his ambition to become an artist. Besides, the Medical Corps was somewhat insulated from the tentacles of the "good old boys." After all, not a lot of West Pointers became physicians.

If he elected to stay in the Army, he could transfer to Japan next June after he had served a year in Korea—but he would have to sign on for a two-year-tour of FECOM. Even junior officers' wives lived a storybook life in Japan, with nice housing and nannies and maids—even gardeners—to do their slightest bidding. PX prices for luxury items were half as much as back in the States—it would be like living on a Major's salary. Unfortunately, in his earlier overtures on the subject, Emma had made it clear she had absolutely no desire to engage in the nomadic life of an Army wife and had rejected out-of-hand any suggestions she consider bringing little Kyle and joining him for a two-year tour in Japan.

If Emma only knew how exotic—how utterly idyllic, really—a two-year tour as an officer's wife in Japan would be, she would thank him after he surrounded her with the respect befitting a Regular Army Officer's wife and a pampered lifestyle.

And, the truth was that as a civilian he had been struggling to find himself as an artist. At best, he was only second-rate at lettering and mundane pen-and-ink drawing which was the bread-and-butter of the profession in the small-time markets around Roanoke. How long did he want to go on doing silkscreen grocery posters and lettering headlines for weekly grocery ads?

Still? If he accepted the RA commission, he would be signing a commitment to remain here in this hellhole for another eight months, at least. Since the intense early days before the truce, when the halls were clogged with critically wounded—and the stressful KHF and bulbar polio outbreaks following the signing of the truce had passed—peacetime duty had become a drudge.

Moreover, if truth be known, he had also become something of a pariah among his peers; except for Scroggs and Spaulding and Major Smith and Colonel Reed, he had come to be seen by his fellow officers as something of a prude when it came to drinking and horsing around with the nurses and Red Cross debutantes. He was certain that most of the officer staff regarded him as an all-around boor. Yet, he felt he was gradually redeeming his image with his recent popularity as the unofficial host at the newly-reincarnated version of The Broken Drum, the new center of after-hours social activity.

Yet—despite all his failures with his peers—in front of him lay proof positive he had won approval of his superior officers. He was actually being offered a hard-won career in the Regular Army.

The more he considered the two letters before him, the more he realized there were no easy answers—no free ride in life. Carefully folding both communiqués, Collier placed them in the pocket of his field jacket and headed down to the Quonset Lounge to get a drink.

"If you decide to take the early release, and if you fly, you could be home before one December—in time to do your Christmas shopping," Smitty enthused when Collier showed him the two communiqués, hinting that he was leaning heavily on taking an early release for active duty.

"I don't want to fly. After surviving a war, Korean Hemorrhagic Fever and bulbar poliomyelitis, it would just be my bad luck to be killed in a plane crash on the way back home." Chilled by the thought of ever volunteering to climb aboard an airplane again, Collier refused to consider flying Military Air Transport Service out of Kimpo. "First thing tomorrow, I'm going to check on troopships leaving out of Pusan. I might have a chance to see my brother. He's flying B-26s out of K-9."

"That sounds like a good idea. Seems I saw or heard somewhere there are stepped-up shipments out of Pusan to get troops back home for Christmas. I think the military is calling it Operation Santa Claus." Smitty raised his glass in a toast.

"A Lieutenant Pewter at the Forty-sixth MASH is on the line. The switchboard operator says he can put it through down here." The enlisted bartender pushed the phone down the bar.

When Collier picked up the phone, Pewter came on the line bubbling over with the news. "You were right. I just got the orders shipping us home for early release. I'll be flying MATS"—MATS was the Military Air Transport Service, the Army's airline— "out of Kimpo in a day or two—just as soon as I can turn my duties over to someone else . Have you seen your orders yet?"

"Yeah, they came through today. I don't know when I'll be leaving. I'm going to try to find a troopship out of Pusan." Wishing him luck, but not about to admit his fear of flying, Collier promised Pewter he'd get in touch as soon as he got back home and hung up the phone without telling his buddy he'd finally won his silver bars.

Back in The Broken Drum, Collier sorted through the stack of mail Cha had placed on the bedside table and found two letters from Emma and a letter from his folks. Both were filled with sentiments about how much they missed him and anecdotes about little Kyle's latest accomplishments. Emma's most recent letter included a fuzzy snapshot of the tiny lad in red-corduroy bib overalls and a yellow tee shirt. Try as he might to feel strong attachment to the baby, Collier still saw no family resemblance. His gut churned with apprehension, trying to imagine what it would be like to celebrate his son's first Christmas with Emma back at his parents' home.

The next morning, Sunday, 15 November, Collier was up early trying to find out about troopships leaving Inchon or Pusan. Despite the day being Sunday, he eventually learned that for at least the next two-weeks, there were no troopships scheduled in or out of Inchon. But, Smitty had been right. The port of Pusan was doing a land-office business in shipping troops home for Operation Santa Claus. During the upcoming two weeks, there were at least two troopships scheduled to depart Pusan for Seattle—the last one, the U.S.S Marine Phoenix, was due to depart Sunday, 29 November, three days after Thanksgiving. If he left soon enough, he might be able to connect with his brother, Jim, at K-9 airfield, which was quite close to Pusan.

After an hour-long ordeal of being transferred from switchboard to switchboard, miraculously, Collier finally reached Jim on the phone.

"Sure, all you have to do is get here. We can put you up for however long you can stay. I'm envious you're going home, but it will be great to see you." His brother was overjoyed at the prospect of a reunion.

That evening in Quonset Lounge, Colonel Reed was a veritable goldmine of Korean travel information. "You can take the train to Pusan. Leaves every night around midnight—takes all night. Officers are provided compartments on old-fashioned Pullman cars. It's slow and primitive but dependable."

Monday morning when Collier showed up bright and early, he should have known that Scroggs would have already gotten the scuttlebutt about his early release. Scroggs came around from behind his desk to shake his hand. "I'm really sorry you aren't accepting the RA commission, Collier. Your promotion to First Lieutenant was well-deserved and long overdue—and we still haven't received word on our commendation for your action at Pork Chop in early July. With your efficiency ratings and a medal on your chest, you'd have a fine future in the Army. It's not too late to change your mind, you know?" Scroggs asked seriously.

"Thank you, Sir. But, I've made up my mind..." Collier began, struggling to hide a sudden wave of emotion, overcome with an unexpected sense of guilt. After all, the Army had actually made a man of him.

Taking most of the rest of Monday and all day Tuesday and Wednesday to put his affairs in order, Collier was taken by complete surprise when he walked into the officers' mess with Smitty Thursday evening, to take his final dinner meal at the 121ˢᵗ Evac. With Colonel Spaulding's pet fireplace completed enough to have a roaring fire and the adjoining, yet-unclosed spaces in the wall still covered rather loosely with canvas tarps against the frigid air, the dining hall was gaily festooned with red, white and blue streamers of crepe paper, and his fellow officers, doctors, nurses, and administrative alike all stood and sang "For he's a jolly good fellow..." which, surprisingly seemed warmly well-intended.

After supper, the party adjourned to the Quonset Lounge. The celebrants were just warming up when Collier finally broke away at 2230. Stowing a large piece of his "going-away" cake—which Captain Richmond had carefully wrapped in wax paper—in the cargo pocket of his field jacket, he directed the waiting Jeep driver to take him up the hill to The Broken Drum. Inside the Drum, he quickly stuffed the two going away gifts he had been presented at dinner—a fifth of I.W. Harper and a still-unopened, match-box-sized package wrapped in cheap Christmas paper—alongside his prized Colt .45—into the half-full duffel which he had packed with uniforms for his journey by train and boat. He scooped up the latest, still-unopened letter from Emma and a picture postcard of the Emperor's Palace in Tokyo from Ginger Lipscomb with the hastily scrawled message: *Dearest Collier: I'm finally rotating back home next week. Too bad I didn't have a chance to get my claws into you while we were away from prying eyes. Here's my new address. Love (I really mean it!), Ginger.* Beneath the message was scrawled an address at Fort Belvoir, Virginia, just outside Washington.

Placing both the letter and Ginger's postcard inside his leather writing folio alongside the photo of Ginger in the bikini he had saved from her previous letter, Collier stuffed the folio into his only other luggage, his trusty AWOL bag holding his shaving kit and other bare necessities for travel. The rest of his belongings were already en route in his bulging duffel bag to the Rep'l Depot at the Port of Pusan.

Taking one final look at the ill-heated room where no number of GI blankets could insulate him from the bone-numbing, pervasive Korean winter chill, Collier hopped back into the Jeep waiting to take him to the Seoul railroad station, suddenly filled with morbid anxiety for running quite late, now in grave danger of missing the train and having to return for yet another night in this godforsaken place. "Okay, let's get the fuck out of here. I don't want to miss that train."

"Stick your bag behind the seat and hop in." At 11:30 A.M., Friday morning, November 20—exactly thirteen hours ahead of the time Collier left the 121st outside Yongdongpo heading for the Seoul railroad station—Emma Lowell Ramsay pulled up in front of the seedy terminal building at Woodrum Field, pushed open the passenger door of her Studebaker and peered out at the smartly-turned out, figure of Major Simpkins Moseley, III waiting at the curb, shivering in his expensive, hand-tailored, grey-gabardine Army topcoat.

"What took you so long? I'm about to freeze my *cojones* off, standing out here in the cold. So-o...that's the kid." Moseley stopped complaining and took a closer look when he saw the baby sleeping in the infant car seat.

"The spitting image of you, Trey. God forbid what's going to happen if Collier ever figures that out."

"Oh...come on. I think you're just feeling guilty. I really can't see that much resemblance." Trey got in and closed the door, but took a second look at the sleeping baby.

"See your resemblance or not, he's A-negative, just like the one we lost. Collier is O-positive. If little Kyle's genotype ever comes to Collier's attention, the well-known substance is going to hit the well-known fan." Emma issued a mirthless laugh as she eased the car around the terminal's traffic circle and headed in the direction of Mill Mountain, looming in the distance over the downtown skyline.

"Speaking of your husband, what's the latest from Korea?" Trey asked as Emma merged the Studebaker into the heavy, late-morning traffic on Williamson Road.

"Can you believe Collier was actually considering applying for a Regular Army commission and making the military a career? Not that he wouldn't be better off in the military...he certainly isn't much of an artist. Anyway, I put a stop to that nonsense when he suggested I bring Kyle to Japan for a couple of years. Can you imagine me living in Japan?" Emma shook her head in disbelief.

"Well...I wouldn't be too quick to judge what two years as an officer's wife in Japan would be like. It's a lot more civilized than you can imagine. And even a junior officer's wife would be treated like a princess over there. You'd have a Japanese maid and houseboy and even a gardener. Luxury items are unbelievably cheap in the PX, and the American dollar in military script buys at least twice as much as it does back here." Trey had made it as far as Tokyo for several months , before his daddy pulled enough strings with highly-placed friends in Senator Byrd's far-reaching political circle and got him transferred stateside again.

"Don't be absurd. Even Collier says the country smells like feces. He said that you get used to it after a day or two. Can you imagine? The nerve of him suggesting I get used to living in a place that smells like a toilet?" Emma sniffed disdainfully.

"So?...did he give up his plans for a career in the military? I must admit I was impressed with his soldierly expertise when I ran in to him at Fort Sam."

"Well...I haven't heard anymore about it. As a matter of fact, I haven't had a letter in several weeks..." Emma's voice trailed off as she turned into the main drive leading into Hotel Roanoke.

"Hey...what about the kid? You certainly don't plan on bringing that baby in here when I'm checking in?"

"Don't be silly. While you get checked in, I'm taking Kyle to my sister-in-law's over off of Franklin Road. She's volunteered to keep him for the afternoon—while I go Christmas shopping." Emma winked. "You get checked in, and I'll call in about a half-hour, and you can give me your room number. I'll just go directly to the elevator and come up to your room when I get back. Go ahead and get a shower. We won't have all that much time..."

"You're a foxy bitch...I've really missed you. Just wait until mid-December when I meet you in DC. No one knows us there, we'll have a ball."

"The Pusan train is on the platform just below. The stairs are about a hundred yards ahead. Watch out for the bomb craters, they sneak up on you in the dark." A sergeant in fatigues bearing insignia of the Transportation Corps directed him as Collier ran along the dark platform above the mainline railroad tracks. Rushing blindly in the frigid night air along the concrete cantilevered upper platform, Collier had barely heard the warning when he found himself rushing headlong at a yawning, inky-black, bomb hole—big enough to drive a three-quarter-ton truck through—in the middle of the platform. In the dark, carrying the bulky, half-filled duffel and his AWOL bag and beset with an overriding fear of missing the only train, until the very last second, he had failed to see the pale, flickering light of the kerosene flare pots, placed to warn passengers of the danger. Righting himself just in time to avoid plunging to certain disaster on the platform below, Collier managed to slow his pell-mell dash enough to narrowly dance around the gaping chasm, finally negotiating the steps and locating the antiquated Pullman car on the train waiting on the track below.

"Yessir, this is the officer car. Just climb aboard and pick an empty compartment. We'll be leaving right on time." The young military trainman welcomed him aboard, his breath steaming in the icy air.

Inside, the Pullman car was toasty, obviously heated by circulating steam from the old-fashioned Korean locomotive. Collier took the first "compartment"—actually just a made-up Pullman berth with the side-curtains pulled open—on his right just inside the door, tossed his bags on the bed and shucked out of his jacket, fur-lined cap and gloves. For the first time since June, he felt transported back to civilization. Stretching out on the Pullman bed and pulling a blanket over his head, he promptly went to sleep.

Except that he vaguely recalled a soldier wakening him in the night to see his travel orders, Collier slept right through the night. When he awoke the next morning and looked out the window, the train was pulling into a station platform. A sign in English told him he had arrived in Pusan.

Gathering his baggage, Collier made his way directly to the latrine and splashed his face with water, shaved and brushed his teeth. Outside the terminal, he found himself looking at a familiar quasi-urban—not exactly a cityscape, but not exactly a village either—Korean setting very similar to Yongdongpo except there was virtually no evidence the war had ever touched this southernmost Port which had served as the main Port of Entry for the entire war. Not about to eat until he could find the nearest offering of American or, at the very least, British or Australian fare, he bypassed several open Korean stalls offering bowls of rice with whatever-topping comprised breakfast for the indigenous population and was rewarded by coming upon a Red Cross booth offering free coffee and doughnuts to American service men.

In front of the terminal, Collier found a battered Renault taxi which took him directly to the docks and the office of the port authority featuring a prominent sign: PUSAN REPLACEMENT DEPOT, with an adjacent sign in red script:

The Home of Operation Santa Claus, where he reported in, presenting his orders. As he anticipated, he was informed that two ships, the U.S.S. General Black and the U.S.S. Marine Phoenix, were due in and out of port within the next two weeks. The General Black was due in the following day, Saturday, 21 November and scheduled to depart no later than high noon on Thanksgiving Day, Thursday the 26th. The last ship, the Marine Phoenix, was scheduled to depart Sunday morning 29 November at 1200 hours, high noon. All personnel hoping to leave on either ship were required to report no later than twelve hours before departure time.

"If I were you, I'd catch the early ship. These two are the last of Operation Santa Claus—your last chance to make it Stateside for Christmas. If you miss the General Black and if the Phoenix is full, you might have to wait right here in Pusan until after Christmas...maybe even after New Year's." The grizzled sergeant blinked owl-like as he passed on this sage advice. Then he directed Collier to a cavernous Quonset barracks.

"Just pick any vacant bunk and make yourself right at home, Lieutenant."

Collier thanked the sergeant, waited until he had left and then asked a passing soldier for directions to the bus out to K-9 air base.

On the blue-painted Air Force bus traversing the bumpy, poorly-paved road—between the small, rugged, treeless mountains, the newly-plowed fields and rice paddies, and the Sea of Japan toward K-9—an airstrip the Engineers had scraped out of the hard shale landscape along the Korean eastern coast several miles outside Pusan—Collier finally gave up trying to jot a note to Emma telling her he would be home for Christmas. The longer he thought about it, the more convinced he became that he should just wait and call when he was safely back in the States. It would make the best Christmas surprise he could ever give Emma or his folks. Warming to the idea as the bus approached the main gate of K-9, he smiled as he put away his ballpoint pen and writing pad, imagining the look of surprise on Emma's face when he stepped out of the taxi at Mother Lowell's unannounced.

K-9 airstrip—it was hardly more than a single strip—ran along the base of a range of the omnipresent small, barren, rugged Korean mountains scarred by large excavations of yellowish earth in what appeared to be a big quarrying operation along the slopes rising from their base. At the entrance, a large, yellow-orange sign proclaimed PUSAN EAST AIR BASE - K-9.

The Air Force bus deposited Collier directly in front of a low barracks-like building with a black, 1950 Chevy sedan and a Jeep parked in front and the sign, 17th Bomb Wing (L), over the front door—Collier presumed the (L) was Air Force lingo for Light. All around, he was surrounded by plain, single-story structures which presented more the look of a collection of small warehouses than the campus of an Air Force Base.

"You can't miss it." Inside the HQ, a sergeant gave him directions to his brother's sleeping quarters, which were within easy walking distance. Having no difficulty locating the officer billet, Collier glanced at his watch and—standing in the pale, watered-down, sunlight—was surprised to find it was almost high-noon. Inspecting his Canon to make sure he had some exposures left, he opened the door to Jim's BOQ and stepped inside.

Just inside the door, the weak, morning sunlight shone in the window above the first bunk where the long, lank form of a flamboyantly-mustachioed man lay dead asleep. It took Collier a second and then a third look before he realized he was looking down at his brother Jim. Initially, Collier was certain Jim had somehow seen him coming and had pasted on a false Wyatt Earp mustache as a joke. Then, bending low to take a closer look, Collier realized the brush was real. He stood and contemplated the theatrical 'Hairbreadth Harry' comic strip mustache for what was probably a full minute before he decided it would take a lot of getting used to. Before he reached to shake his brother awake, he stepped back and snapped a photo of Jim in all of his mustachioed glory.

"You're looking good. I'd about given up on you." His brother gave him a bear hug as he hastily retrieved his trousers, carelessly draped across a chair, and located a freshly-pressed uniform blouse on a hanger-bar beside his bunk.

"It's great to see you, too..." Collier enthused, still trying to get used to the cookie-duster.

"Let's go find a cup of joe...have you had breakfast yet?" Jim asked, locating his cunt cap and adjusting it on his head as he headed for the door.

"Coffee sounds great, but breakfast sounds even better," Collier said following close behind as they approached a gray, wooden, clapboard building with a large sign on the wall near the entrance: OFFICERS OPEN MESS, 17TH BOMB WING (L). Lettered in black Helvetica capitals, the words were arranged around the heraldic squadron motif of a winged dragon above a shield which was rendered in bright yellow paint, substituting for customary gold.

Inside the Open Mess, the foyer opened into an opulent, high-ceilinged dining room with open beams and a massive stone fireplace dominating the far wall. Set for lunch, the tables were neatly covered in white table cloths, complete with linen napkins. The setting hardly rivaled the grand elegance of the Air Force Officers' club in Seoul, but compared to the rough-hewn structure of the Officers Mess at the 121, it was lavish. The impressive, skillfully-crafted fireplace put the one Otis Owen's rather uninspired crew was working on back at the 121 to shame.

"You flyboys sure got it rough..." Collier remarked as his kid brother led him gawking back through the deserted main dining room into a smaller dining room where a Korean waiter took their order for coffee and a late breakfast. Over coffee and food, they took turns catching each other up on their adventures to date, with Collier carefully omitting any mention of his weekend at the Fujiya with Madison or his steamy, but abortive, tête-à-tête with Ginger.

"At least stay for Thanksgiving here with me and take the ship that sails on Sunday; you'll still make it home in plenty of time for Christmas," Jim argued when Collier told him of his travel options, believing Collier had opted to take the boat instead of flying directly out of Kimpo because he wanted to spend some time with him before leaving Korea.

He'd have rather undergone a orchidectomy without anesthesia than let his hot-shot, flyboy kid brother know he was deathly afraid to fly.

"Well, let's wait and see how things go. If you have to fly, there's no sense in my hanging around here." Collier made a valid point.

As the afternoon drifted into evening, one-by-one, Jim introduced Collier to members of his squadron and eventually, as the time approached for closing, they partnered and took on the current champs in an ongoing, long-running, ping-pong tournament. At closing time, they were still the undefeated champs and taking on all comers.

The following morning, Saturday, 21 November, Jim went to squadron ops and successfully pled his case to be relieved of flying duty until at least after Thanksgiving. "Okay, that's settled. You can stay here for Thanksgiving."

"Good, but I'm going back to the Rep'l Depot first thing Friday morning; I don't want to take any chances on getting stuck in Korea until only God knows when." Collier made it clearly understood.

Saturday afternoon, the reunited brothers returned to the O Club to continue the defense of their ping-pong supremacy. They started out drinking draft beer, then Jim switched to Scotch on the rocks and Collier switched to Vodka Collins.

"Ready for a refill?" Collier asked while they waited for their next opponents to step to the ping-pong table.

"I'm tired of Vodka Collins," Collier balked. After drinking the sweetish Collins all afternoon and evening, he was past-ready for something different.

"Ever hear of a Spin, Crash and Burn?" Jim asked impishly.

"Yeah. But I want a drink, not a death potion." Collier shook his head. Back at the 121, the Spin, Crash and Burn was the favorite of the sophomoric, horny flyboys from Kimpo who came over to the Quonset Lounge at the 121st to score some "genuine white pussy" and were desperate enough to latch onto one of the nurses they wouldn't have given a second look back home. These jet jockeys had the adept Korean seamstresses sew slender, pencil-like pockets onto the sleeves of their flying suits to accommodate their George Sticks—which they usually wore off base to make sure everyone knew they were flyboys. A George Stick was a brightly-lacquered, pencil-sized stick of wood ornately-carved with Oriental characters and motifs such as dragons and snarling devil dogs. Most likely inspired by the long-handled backscratchers in stateside novelty shops, these George Sticks had a thin leather-thong threaded through an eye at the top which was supposed to be used to loop over the pilot's wrist. They were ostensibly to enable the pilot to operate the autopilot control—which was familiarly known as "George"—without having to move from a comfortable, laid-back position in the aircraft's seat. To a man, these cocky fighter-jocks carried a folded, hand-lettered recipe for a Spin, Crash and Burn which they glibly called an "S, C and B" and which consisted of: One jigger each of Vodka, Gin, Bourbon, Scotch, Rum and Dry Vermouth, well-shaken with cracked ice in a cocktail mixer and served in a brandy snifter.

Predictably, after about a half of an old-fashioned glass full of this lethal concoction, these apple-cheeked airmen would be taken suddenly, seriously drunk and usually have to be escorted back out to their Jeeps. Shortly after the truce was signed, and after more than a few of such incidents, Smitty had banned the making of S,C and B in the Quonset Lounge. Hardly any of the hospital staff took notice of the exotic drink's demise. It was certainly no loss to Collier, as far as he was concerned an S, C and B tasted like warmed-over possum shit.

"Ever try a French Seventy-five?" Jim asked, quickly bored with drinking Scotch.

"Nope. That's a new one on me," Collier confessed, then asked. "What's it made of?" After the S, C and B, he thought he'd heard of them all.

"It's simple. You pour two-ounces of Cognac in a hollow-stemmed Champagne glass and fill the rest with Champagne.

"Where are you going to find hollow-stemmed Champagne glasses?" Collier laughed.

"We're very civilized in the Air Force. Come on, man, let's give 'em a try," his brother urged.

"Okay, why not?" Collier didn't exactly love Champagne, but he was ready for a change. Cognac and Champagne sounded pretty innocent to him.

"Well, what do you think?" his brother asked after Collier took a tentative sip.

"Not bad, not bad at all." Collier smacked his lips and took a bigger swallow.

The rest of the evening, French 75s became the drink of champions, as the brothers Ramsay took on all comers in the marathon ping-pong tournament, retiring again at closing undefeated.

"If I can get my Ops officer to let me have an airplane, will you let me take you for a little spin over Pusan before you leave?" Jim started pestering Collier the next morning when he took him out to show him the flight line and let him get a first-hand look at the Douglas B-26 Invader aircraft. Holdovers from WWII, formerly dubbed the A-26, the battle-weary, light attack bomber B-26's looked pretty beat up and worn out to Collier.

"No sense in going to all that trouble. A plane ride is just a plane ride to me. I've flown halfway around the world." Collier resisted, trying to act blasé.

"Yeah, but you haven't flown in an actual bomber. And you haven't flown with *me*." Jim persisted adamantly. Collier could just envision his daredevil baby brother buzzing low over rice paddies and in between those treacherous mountain ranges. In his mind's eye, Collier could see the ensuing fireball and erupting mushroom of black smoke as they crashed into some remote Korean mountainside.

"Look, we don't have much time together as it is; why waste a day flying in an airplane?" Collier protested, careful not to betray his fear.

"It would only take a couple hours. Come on, Brother, are you chicken? I think you're actually afraid to fly with me," Jim goaded.

"I'm not afraid. I just don't see the need. Why waste a day?"

"Not a day...not even an entire morning. If I can get an airplane and permission to take you up, I'll have you back in a couple hours tops. Wait here and finish your coffee. I'll see if they'll let us have a plane," Jim persisted as he left Collier waiting in the O Club bar.

Watching his brother go out the door, Collier felt a cold trickle of sweat run down the crack of his ass as he breathed a silent prayer for divine intervention on his behalf.

"Good news. Barring any sort of unexpected missions, and if the weather cooperates, we can have a plane tomorrow morning," Jim announced when he reappeared about an hour later.

"No sense in going sightseeing if the area is under an overcast." Collier cast a hopeful eye in the direction of the low-lying cloud cover.

"I told them over at Ops we'd wait until around ten. That gives us plenty of time to get breakfast before we go get you fitted in some flying duds," Jim reminded him when they finally crawled into bed, exhausted from a non-stop defense of their ping-pong superiority and half-drunk from untold amounts of French 75s.

"If it's cloudy, let's just sleep in. No sense in going to all that trouble for nothing," Collier said and breathed a prayer to the Korean Weather God.

Tuesday morning, 24 November, appeared bright and clear as Jim shook him awake. "Get up, Brud. It's a great day for flying."

So much for prayers to a god who didn't know him. Could this be divine payback for playing Peeping Tom at the ladies of the choir adjusting their garter belts through the rear windows of the new Sunday School building at the old Fort Lewis Baptist Church?

"Can't we just skip the flying and sleep in?"

"Come on, you're not scared of flying with me are you?"

"Of course not," Collier grumbled as they found an airman to drive them to Operations.

"Have a seat while I see if I can find you some flying gear." When they arrived at Ops, Jim left him in the locker room and came back in about fifteen minutes with helmet, flying coveralls and a parachute piled high in his overburdened arms.

"Put these on over your uniform. It can be cold as a witch's tit up there. You'll welcome the extra warmth." Jim handed Collier the coveralls and put the helmet and parachute on a nearby folding chair.

"Come on, Brother, we're wasting valuable flying time." As soon as Collier finished donning the flight suit, Jim helped him into the parachute harness and prodded him out of the door.

"I brought my camera. Can we get someone to take our picture when we get to the plane?" Collier asked, feeling like an Eskimo in the bulky flying suit.

"Sure, Hector here will be glad to snap our picture. It will be great to take home to Mom and Dad." His brother nodded toward a flight line mechanic standing near a Jeep waiting to take them to the tarmac where the aircraft were parked.

When they got out of the Jeep near a B-26 with a half-naked, big-titted female and bearing the legend, Rice Paddy Wagon, painted on its nose, the mechanic took the camera and, snapped a couple shots of Jim and Collier standing beside the plane.

"That'll be a great shot to show Mom and Dad," Jim laughed as he thanked Hector and watched him get back in the Jeep to leave.

"Here, you can help. See the list of items under Outside Visual Check?" Jim unfolded a much-handled piece of paper and handed it to Collier. The Outside Visual Checklist was on the first page and contained a long list of the aircraft's items needing to be verified in one way or another before the plane could be deemed suitable for flight.

"Do you want me to read this list as we go along?" Collier asked, more than a bit confused.

"Sure...that's the general idea." Jim walked closer to the aircraft and Collier followed.

"1. All Switches...OFF," Collier began reading the list.

"Just skip the number...and I give the answer." Jim corrected. "You say: All switches. I'll answer – OFF!"

"Okay. I get it now. Pilot Cover..." he read the second item on the checklist.

"OFF...check drain holes..." Jim responded, peering closer at the aircraft's fuselage.

"Nose hatch and Gun Cowling..." Collier continued.

"Looked..." Jim answered as he examined the front of the aircraft.

"Locked?..." Collier asked, not sure he had heard his brother right.

"No...just looked. Like I took a good look...I examined it, okay?"

"Oh...yeah. I get it now..." Collier shook his head. To him, "looked" seemed like a rather stupid answer.

"Nose Wheel..." Collier continued. There were at least a dozen subheadings on the checklist under Nose Wheel. "A: Snubbing Yoke..." he plowed ahead, calling the first sub-heading under Nose Wheel.

"All bolts in and safetied..." his brother responded.

"B: Strut..." Collier read the next item.

"Properly Extended. Just call the item on the list...skip the alpha designation. We'll be here all night." His brother grumbled impatiently.

"Tire..." Collier read on.

"Inflated, No Slippage, Valve Stem..." Jim responded in a droning voice.

Moving to the Left Engine, the Left Wing, the Left Wheel Well, the Rear Fuselage—checking the gun turret, the left-side elevator, vertical stabilizer, rudder—and around to the other side checking the same items plus a list including Camera Door, Radar Door, Bomb Bay (with Gun Platform, Bomb Shackles, etc.) and finally checking the Right Wing and Engine plus the Wing Guns, Ailerons, Antenna and the like, they completed the list.

"Okay, let's climb aboard and get this joy ride underway." When they reached the last item on the Outside Checklist, Jim pointed to toe- and hand-holds on the side of the fuselage and proceeded to pull himself up to a position where he was standing between the port side engine and the open two-man cockpit. Stepping inside the front part of the cockpit and remaining standing, he supervised and encouraged Collier's effort to climb aboard by the same route. Despite the bulky flying gear and despite his heart thumping wildly in his chest—more than certain no good was going to come of this—Collier made it up to the wing and stepped into the seat directly to the right, beside Jim's pilot position. When he was securely in his harness, Jim showed him where to plug in the cord to his helmet radio.

"Alright Big Brother, we can start the Inside Checklist anytime you're ready." Jim voice came inside Collier's helmet loud and clear.

"Form One..." Collier called into the mike, confused by the Air Force gobbledygook.

"Aircraft in flyable condition and pre-flighted," Jim's voice came back.

"Ladder..." Collier read, getting into the swing of it now. If he hadn't been so goddamned scared, he would have been having fun. It was just like in the movies.

"Pulled up..." Jim droned on automatically, busying himself in the front cockpit.

"Parachute and Safety Harness..." Collier read.

"On and adjusted. Check yours, too," Jim came back on the mike, reminding Collier he was wearing a chute. Back at Operations, Jim had shown him how to pull the cord in case, God forbid, they had to abandon ship.

"Seat and Rudder Pedals..." Collier read on.

"Adjusted..." Jim replied, still busy fiddling with switches and levers up front.

When Collier finished running Jim through the Visual Inside Checklist, Jim called the tower. "K-nine tower this is Kayo two-six, taxi for takeoff for a local flight."

"Roger, Kayo two-six. Taxi to runway nine. Wind is one-fifty at ten and the current altimeter is three zero one zero."

"Okay, Big Brother, let's taxi to the runway block and run up the engines. Looks like a fine day for flying." Collier felt the aircraft moving slowly forward along the taxiway, then turn and line up with the stripe marking the center of the surprisingly short runway with the white caps on the ocean clearly visible at the far end.

Fine day for a funeral, Collier thought, sweaty-palmed in the frigid air, but not because of his heavy gloves. Looking down the runaway as Jim ran the power up on the engines, he imagined the front-page headlines of tomorrow's newspaper back home.

THE ROANOKE TIMES
Roanoke, Virginia, Wednesday, November 25, 1953
COUNTY COUPLE LOSES BOTH
SONS IN KOREAN AIR CRASH

PUSAN, KOREA, November 26 (AP) – Mr. and Mrs. H. M. Ramsay of Route I, Salem, received the tragic news late yesterday of the death of both their sons in a tragic crash of a B-26 just off the runway at K-9 Air Base, Pusan, Korea...

"Wake up, Brother, and pay attention here! Read the BEFORE TAKE-OFFS checklist for me, please...while we're parked and running up the engines." Jim came back on. His voice was more insistent now.

"Gas..." Collier quickly located the place on the page and began reading again.

"On Main Tanks...Bomb Bay Off." Jim's voice droned on as he continued running up the engines.

"Trim Tabs..." Collier went on.

"As desired..." Jim called back the response as they went down the short pre-flight list.

"Kayo twenty-six is ready for takeoff." As soon as they finished the list, Jim alerted the tower and shouted over the engines, "Here we go, Brother..."

Collier tensed and clenched his fists, trying to savor his final moments on earth. He held his breath—too late now to resort to prayer.

"Roger, two-six, *hold* your position..." The tower ordered insistently, as the radio suddenly went silent with the dead air stretching out over seconds, then into more than several minutes.

"What's going on? Has the radio gone dead?" Collier asked, completely at a loss. The words were hardly out of his mouth when the tower came back on.

"Kayo two-six, this is K-nine tower; cancel your take off. The base has just been been put on alert, and you are to return to your hardstand immediately. Repeat. Return to your hardstand. You are cleared to taxi back to your revetment. Be alert for increased tug and other vehicular activity along taxiways..." Collier could scarcely believe his ears.

"Roger, K-nine, Kayo two-six taxiing back to thirty-fourth area." Jim acknowledged and slowly pivoted the aircraft around and headed back to the group of buildings at the far end of the taxiway.

"Well, shit, Brother, I'm sure this is just another freaking false alarm. But that's that for our flying today," Jim complained over the intercom, exasperation dripping from every word.

Back at the Officers' mess, a secretly much-relieved Collier, and a visibly much-chagrined, much disappointed Jim, took up the undefeated defense of their ping-pong supremacy, including their herculean quest to deplete the entire air base storehouse of both French and American Champagne and Courvoisier and Hennessey Cognac—the main ingredients of their championship-sustaining *aqua vitae*, French 75s—retiring again at closing time undefeated.

"*...and thank you, God, for saving my brother and me from certain death in that airplane, and if it isn't too much trouble, please fix it so we can't fly again tomorrow...*" Collier ended his prayer just before he drifted off to sleep.

The next morning, to Collier's amazement and relief, the base was socked-in under a solid low-lying overcast with below-freezing temperatures and blustery 30-knot gusts of wind off of the Sea of Japan—an all-around perfect day to stay close to the fireplace and continue the boozy long-running ping-pong contest.

Collier breathed a sigh of relief knowing that the following day was Thanksgiving, and even if the "Base Alert" were lifted, there would certainly be no frivolous sightseeing flights on an important holiday when the flight-line personnel were off duty. The first thing Friday morning, he would be going back to the Rep'l Depot in Pusan to make damn sure he had a berth on the USS Marine Phoenix when she sailed Sunday morning, November 29th.

"They will court-martial your ass if they catch you trying to sneak that forty-five on board a ship. I heard they arrested an infantry officer a few weeks back for trying the same thing with a carbine which he had broken down into minor-sized parts." That evening during a break in the ping-pong marathon, Collier listened as one of Jim's fellow pilots predicted a dire outcome if Collier tried to get the weapon home with him. Collier was quite aware the pistol was contraband, but others had told him he would have no problem with carrying the weapon in his duffel if he broke it down and concealed the parts scattered throughout his uniforms.

"Well...I don't know. It's too late to try to ship it by mail," Collier hedged, now concerned as to what to do.

"Shit, they're even tougher on mail. They X-ray the mail for contraband," his unwanted advisor volunteered.

"Yeah...I heard that, too," Collier agreed.

"If you want to get rid of it, I'll give you three fifths of bottled-in-bond booze for it." One of the Jim's group offered, hopefully.

"Three jugs of hooch? That's not quite five bucks. I paid twenty-five on the black market in Seoul." Collier sniffed at the insultingly low offer for his coveted weapon.

"Yeah, but what's a few bucks compared to several years in Leavenworth?" the envious pilot countered.

"I'm going back to Pusan tomorrow morning. I'm sure I can sell it on the black market there—maybe even get more than I paid in Seoul," Collier mused, half to himself.

"What the hell, I'll give you six fifths of I.W. Harper. Take it or leave it. You're an officer; you certainly don't want to get caught wandering the streets of Pusan trying to unload a contraband weapon. Hells bells, that pistol's been chromed. That's a court-martial offense for defacing government property," the pilot persisted.

"Okay. You're right. I'll take the deal...six fifths of I.W. Harper." Collier quickly decided.

Although Collier enjoyed Thanksgiving Day and the sumptuous turkey dinner with all the trimmings with his brother at the O Club, as the evening wore on, a palpable atmosphere of depression settled over him, probably enhanced, in part, by being overstuffed with food coupled with his abrupt withdrawal from his several-day-long steady diet of French 75s. He excused himself from further defense of their ping-pong crown and went off to get a good night's rest.

"Take good care, Brother...sorry we missed our plane ride." After breakfast Friday morning which included a double Bloody Mary to get his heart started, Collier carefully wrapped the six bottles of booze in items of his uniforms. Including the fifth he'd been given as a going-away present at the 121, Collier staggered a bit under the weight of his AWOL bag as he gave his brother a farewell hug and boarded the bus for Pusan.

On the bus-ride into Pusan, Collier extracted his writing folio from his AWOL bag and reread Ginger's postcard. Hastily jotting a note telling her he was taking an early release from active duty and would be sailing tomorrow on the Marine Phoenix, he stuffed the folded note into an envelope and carefully addressed it to Ginger's new address at the Fort Belvoir hospital. When he stepped off the bus at the Rep'l Depot, he dropped the envelope into the mail box outside the HQ Quonset.

CHAPTER FORTY-EIGHT

THE ROANOKE TIMES
Roanoke, Virginia, Sunday, November 29, 1953
REDS REJECT UN CONCESSION ON PEACE TALKS

PANMUNJOM, Sunday, Nov. 29 (AP) - The Reds yesterday scornfully rejected as of "no merit" a conciliatory UN 12-point package plan to set up a Korean peace conference and said they would counter with their own offer Monday.

STARS AND STRIPES
UNOFFICIAL PUBLICATION OF UNITED STATES FORCES, FAR EAST
Vol. 9, No. 346   KOREA EDITION Sunday, November 29, 1953
U. S. GIVES ATROCITY EVIDENCE

UNITED NATIONS, N.Y., November 28 (UP) - The U.S. provided the U.N. today with new evidence of Communist atrocities in Korea.

Henry Cabot Lodge Jr., presented the General Assembly with eyewitness accounts of how Allied prisoners were shot down in cold blood and others were burned alive by North Korean and Chinese Communist troops.

BACK IN PUSAN, Collier checked into the Quonset barracks at the Rep'l-depot, found the nearest empty bed and promptly went to sleep, out like a light straight through to evening chow. After chow, he found the PX and sat around and sipped a beer and read the latest TIME magazine until closing. Saturday, 28 November, he slept in and—despite the bitter cold and wind from the sea—after noontime chow, he walked the streets of Pusan shooting pictures of the people and the shops and houses which, compared to Seoul, were unmarked by the bitter war that had raged to the north for a full three years. When he tired of playing tourist, Collier aimlessly strolled the dockside, watching the crews loading the Marine Phoenix and two smaller, equally rust-stained, vessels, just killing time and wishing he had stayed on another day at K-9.

Sunday morning dawned bright and clear and cold. Dressing quickly in the breezy Quonset barracks, he went to the mess hall shortly after 0900 and had a bowl of oatmeal and a cup of coffee, glancing idly at the latest issue of the Stars and Stripes with news of war atrocities which sounded suspiciously like the rumors he'd heard about the slaughter of the 1800 civilians at Taejon and the bridge massacre at No Gun Ri. He wondered idly if Moon's cousin, Ahn Myang, had been successful in getting his evidence before the stuffed shirts in Washington.

When he exited the mess just before 1000 hours, the long lines of enlisted soldiers were already filing up the gangplank boarding the Marine Phoenix. Standing on the dock waiting for the last of the enlisted men to board, Collier caught sight of the familiar figure of Herb Rudolph just disappearing inside the large doors into the bowels of the ship. Too late to try to hail his old friend, Collier made a mental note to try to locate Herb as soon as the ship was underway.

The numbers of officers taking this last ship home before the holidays were quite few in comparison to hundreds of enlisted and were boarded last, shuffling up the narrow gangway to the main deck single file. Not wanting to have to settle for an inside berth in the cramped, twelve-berth cabins, Collier had stepped to the front of the line as soon as the officers were called to board. His wisdom paid off and he was able to claim the first bunk inside the doorway to the tiny, sardine-can sleeping compartment. Just across the narrow companionway was an incredible sandwich smorgasbord complete with fresh lettuce and potato salad and deviled eggs—there were even pitchers of fresh milk—food the likes of which Collier hadn't seen in months. As soon as his compartment was full and his claim to his berth firmly established, Collier slipped across the companionway and made himself a quadruple-deck Dagwood sandwich. Biting into it, he was certain he had died and gone to heaven.

Shortly before 1400 hours, Collier was roused from his overstuffed, narcoleptic doze by the boat's whistle—it sounded like a horn—and he joined the mob of his fellow travelers, outside at the crowded deck rail to watch as the ship cast off from the dock, heading for the open sea and home.

Busy snapping pictures of the dock and harbor, soon after the ship had cleared the seawall with its small, pagoda-like pylon marking the outer boundary of the virtually landlocked Pusan harbor, Collier began to notice a nagging queasiness. Suspecting that he might be suffering the accumulated effects of too many days running on a diet of French 75s with little else in the way of nourishment, with his watch showing slightly past 1550 hours, he decided to go back inside. One thing he'd learned at the hard-partying 121ˢᵗ was that a little hair of the dog was almost an infallible cure for a nasty hangover. After taking a surreptitious therapeutic shooter from his considerable stash of I.W. Harper, he took to his bunk to try to take a nap.

When he was awakened by one of his compartment-mates around 1745 alerting him to the fact they were serving evening mess across the companionway, Collier was much relieved to discover he felt somewhat better. He waited until the compartment was empty, snuck another shooter as a hedge against his rebellious digestive system, and followed the rest of the junior officers to chow.

After a delightful meal in a nearby officers dining room with some of the ships officers—which included a *fresh* fruit salad on a generous bed of genuine, *fresh* crisp lettuce leaves—something he hadn't had since he left Tokyo the end of June—Collier made his way back out on deck to smoke an après-dinner cigarette. He had barely lit the Lucky and had only taken a puff or two when the slight queasiness struck again. Watching the lighted end of the barely-smoked cigarette flipping sparks end-over-end against the deepening purple-hued evening twilight, Collier returned inside and took to his bed again. Sleeping by fits and starts, he awoke again before 2300 hours and returned on unsteady sea legs to the outside deck and lit another cigarette. Once again, much to his consternation and increasing chagrin, he only smoked a few puffs before the vague queasiness welled up to plague him again.

When he went inside and lay back down, almost instantaneously, the slight nausea left him and he went immediately to sleep.

On the following morning, it was the same. He only managed to eat a cup of fresh fruit and drink a half-cup of coffee before the nausea found him again—this time he didn't even venture out on deck for a stroll.

All day long Monday—then Tuesday and Wednesday, the following day and the day after—the slight sense of being unwell plagued him every time he left his bunk. Strangely, as long as he was prone, the seasickness—by now he had put a name to the problem—left him. Unfortunately, no manner of pleading would grant him immunity from having to vacate the sleeping compartment each morning around 1030 hours while the ship's crew busied themselves with morning cleaning.

Gradually, by trial and error, however, because of this enforced vacating of his bunk, he discovered he could sustain periods of nervous, very uncomfortable, ambulation, even partake of an entire cigarette, by having a large swallow or two—two was definitely better—of his newly-discovered substitute for golden-buzzard elixer, I.W. Harper. And although he strongly suspected from the sly, sometimes envious and malevolent, looks he got in the close confines of the cramped compartment, the companionway, and the brief forays to the officers' mess, that he must literally reek of booze, no one made any mention of it.

Miraculously, despite the irritating queasiness which plagued him while he was erect on his own two feet, the seasickness never quite reached the point where he actually had to throw up—it only made him wish he could vomit and dispense with this godawful debilitating nausea.

After six days and five nights storm-tossed on the arctic waters of the northern Pacific, on Friday evening, 4 December, quite against his better instincts, Collier gave into the urging of one of his bunkmates who had already seen it and found his way to a fairly good-sized compartment—the intercom announcer called it a "salon"—where they were nightly showing a recent Hollywood swashbuckler entitled "Raiders of the Seven Seas" which starred Roanoke's own John Payne, whom Collier's father had sometimes given a ride before the local youth had gone to Hollywood and made it big. Beginning with a series of musical films in the mid- to late-thirties and graduating to more serious roles during WWII— eventually starring in such notable films as *The Razor's Edge* in 1946 and the perennial Christmas classic, *Miracle on 34th Street*, circa 1947—since then, probably related to his turning forty a year or so ago, Payne's career seemed to be gradually taking something of a downward turn.

With a lot of trepidation for his delicate condition, Collier made it cautiously along the companionway to the designated Salon. Arriving early and being the only officer present, he was afforded the luxury of assuming a semi-prone position on the deck, which somewhat assuaged the fickle, highly-unpredictable exacerbations of his motion-sickness. When the lights went down and the movie came up on the small screen, at first, Collier was so offended by the lowbrow quality of the production, he was tempted to get up and leave.

The frivolous, superficial quality of this pseudo-Douglas Fairbanks, Jr. seagoing soap opera was immediately evident as the film opened with the pirate, Barbarossa (Red Beard, aka Payne), being discovered romancing a bevy of skimpily-clad harem ladies, whereupon he is furiously chased by the Sultan's or Emir's or Caliph's—or whomever's—soldiers. Managing to reach the seacoast, Payne (aka Barbarossa) swims out to the nearest ship. To put it all in proper perspective, this was actually the best (barely endurable) part of the film as Barbarossa surreptitiously climbs aboard and, rather than becoming a galley slave, he persuades the crew to mutiny and then to embark upon piracy with him as their leader. From that point on, over the next ninety minutes, the whole ridiculous business sank quickly into Davy Jones' Locker, with Lon Chaney, Jr. playing Barbarossa's sidekick, Peg-Leg, a-har!

Totally wasted in the hackneyed trashy plot, the experienced actors, Henry Brandon and Gerald Mohr were heartbreakingly effective as wealthy-but-dishonest Spanish schemers, but their modern Fifth Avenue haircuts were cartoonishly out-of-place with their elaborate 17th-century court costumes.

Donna Reed looked okay—and gave Collier a tingle in the crotch on occasion—but was completely unconvincing as the haughty, spoiled daughter of the Spanish governor. The film quickly deteriorated into an unintended slapstick with Chaney and Payne repeatedly getting separated and reuniting with such repetitious, ridiculously-corny, lines as, "Have you sailed the seven seas?" with the equally idiotic reply, "Ah, yes. I've sailed the seven seas, seven times around the world and seven times back again, a-har!"—or some-such garbage as that!

Sadly, against a plot which even Oliver and Hardy would have turned down, John Payne showed almost no flashes of the superb acting ability which won him starring roles in serious films like *The Razor's Edge*; however, truth be known, when "The End" faded from the screen and the lights came on, although Collier left the compartment totally disenchanted, he was nonetheless mildly amused.

Bored to the brink of insanity from lying in his bunk all day long for seven days, the following morning, Collier decided he had recovered enough from his *mal de mer* to risk a trip into the bowels of the ship to try to locate Herb Rudolph. After venturing only one deck below in his quest, however, he became so nauseous, he quickly retreated, weighing the pleasure of finding Herb against the expense of his physical and mental well-being.

Still afflicted with his delicate condition, Collier woke from his regular snooze that afternoon with the intercom blaring the tiresome announcement that the movie would be shown again in the same Salon that evening—apparently the USS Marine Phoenix only had this one film to show. Bored and not at all sleepy a full fifteen minutes before 1900 hours, Collier unenthusiastically made his way down the companionway to the Salon and stretched his lanky form on the deck, waiting for the lights to go down and the screen to light up. Idly watching the attendees for the current night's showing of the corny film file into the compartment, Collier felt a curious sense of camaraderie when he recognized at least a half-dozen faces from the screening on the previous evening. This was silent testimony that even a second-rate movie was preferable to trying to read or write letters aboard this creaking, storm-tossed bucket of rust.

After the lights went down and the film began, anticipating the first reconciliation between actor John Payne as Barbarossa and Lon Chaney, Jr. as Peg-Leg, Collier deepened his voice and announced in a deep, falsely-theatrical timbre, "Have you sailed the Caribees?" Collier mimicked John Payne's melodious voice, followed by Lon Chaney, Jr.'s moronic reply, "Arh, yes, matey. I've sailed the seven seas seven times around the world and seven times back again, a-har!"

Collier's sardonic mimicry engendered a titter of laughter from the equally-jaded attendees around the compartment. Encouraged by this newfound camaraderie of cynicism, Collier continued the good-natured parody throughout the remainder of the evening's showing. At the end, the audience of battle-weary soldiers was bordering upon hysterical at such highly irreverent behavior from a young commissioned officer.

Still confined mostly to his bunk during the day, Collier began to look forward to the ensuing evening's showing of the movie and was gratified to see a number of familiar faces when he walked into the room for the third night in a row. Again he began to mock the main character's inane dialogue with an occasional ad lib of a funny aside, commenting on some of the supporting actors' out-of-place modern haircuts and Miss Reed's attractive anatomy as well as the highly-suspect status of her precious virginity in the script.

As in the previous evening, when The End appeared on the screen, practically all of those in the compartment were holding their sides from near hysterics.

For Collier, savoring the warm afterglow of these spontaneous antics was not the most pleasurable thing about these shipboard evenings at the movies. The vicarious thrill he experienced from seeing all the half-naked females made his loins tingle. Obsessing on the remarkable resemblance of one of the movie harem girls to Ginger Lipscomb, he left the movie on lustful overload. When he returned to the compartment, he fished inside his AWOL bag for his writing folio and extracted the photo of Ginger in the bikini. Reflecting upon the hot, searching kisses and the feel of her warm skin upon his fingertips that sensuous afternoon in Sergeant Owens' house in the village sent a rush of blood to his crotch. Embarrassed—hesitant of being detected—he resisted the strong urge to masturbate underneath his blankets in the claustrophobic compartment, crowded to overflowing with a total complement of twelve young officers, finally drifting off to sleep with a throbbing hard-on. As a result of his six-month-long, self-imposed celibacy, in the early hours of the morning on Sunday, 6 December, Collier was visited by a powerfully-realistic, erotic dream in which he was being ravished by Ginger Lipscomb and Madison Argabright—annoyingly metamorphosing intermittently back and forth, in and out of the image of Donna Reed—who were taking turns fucking and sucking him and each other. As he quickly built to orgasm in the dream, he started to come in his sleep. When he awoke, a veritable Old Faithful of semen was gushing into his Jockey shorts. When the orgasmic geyser finally subsided, in great horror of leaving a tell-tale pool of cum in his bed, Collier stealthily arose and quietly slipped out of his fatigue pants and removed the semen-soaked Jockey briefs. Stuffing the sodden underwear into a pocket of his field jacket, he left the jacket on the bunk while he wrapped a towel around his waist, located a fresh pair of Jockeys, then headed for the small shower adjoining the ship's head (naval lingo for latrine), diagonally across the companionway.

When he showered clean of a week's accumulation of sweat and grime, Collier toweled dry and donned the fresh Jockeys. Returning furtively back across the companionway, he slipped into his fatigues and field jacket and headed out onto the deck into the early-morning darkness. Making certain no late-night smokers or other insomniacs were present to witness, he lost no time in walking to the rail and tossing the semen-soaked Jockey shorts high into the air, watching as the blustery gale caught them, spinning them like a drunken tern in an ever-widening gyre, down toward the storm-tossed northern Pacific. Then, still a-tingle with post-orgasmic afterglow, Collier lit a Lucky and smoked it in the lee of a lifeboat, reflecting curiously on why for a long time now, Emma never seemed to find her way into his erotic dreams. Taking a final drag from the cigarette and flipping the glowing butt into the sea, Collier retraced his steps to his tiny bed and drifted quickly back to sleep.

Up at first light Sunday morning, taking advantage of a rare window of solitude, Collier went out on deck to grab a smoke by the rail. Idly glancing down at the sea, his eyes suddenly fixed upon his surreptitiously discarded Jockeys flying ignominiously in the half-gale of the northern hemisphere, caught on some chance bolt or davit or other nautical anomaly halfway down the rusting hull of the ship. Red-faced that his semen-soaked underwear was waving there in broad daylight like a personal ensign for all to see, Collier flipped his half-smoked cigarette into the ocean and slunk guiltily back inside.

Thankfully, when Collier returned to the deck rail at mid-morning, his vagrant pennant had miraculously dislodged its tenuous perch, safely consigned to Davy Jones' Locker.

Still bedeviled by his niggling low-grade seasickness, the daylight hours Monday, Tuesday and Wednesday, December 7, 8, and 9 passed with agonizing slowness with Collier alternatingly browsing a copy of the November 2 issue of *TIME* magazine, which someone had left in the wardroom (and was distinguished by a surreal Boris Artzybasheff cover-painting entitled AMATEUR PHOTOGRAPHER, depicting a Daliesque creature with a 35mm Lieca (or Canon) camera for its head, a box of Kodak color film for a neck and a leather camera bag for a body) and occasionally reading from a copy of James Michener's new Korean War novel, *The Bridges at Toko Ri*, he had purchased in the PX back at K-9. The two-week-old issue of *TIME* featured an article entitled the "$75 Billion Question" which began: "In the twilight years between uneasy peace and total war, few questions weigh more heavily on the minds of U.S. planners than this one: How much money can the U.S. spend in peacetime for its defense without stifling its economy? This week the National Planning Association, a non-political group of business, labor, agricultural and professional leaders, came up with its own answer: nearly $75 billion a year."

Judaspriest, who gave a shit, anyway? Collier mused cynically. He still hadn't figured out if he wanted to go back to his old job doing Kroger's grocery ads...or maybe check out the possibilities of working for a pharmaceutical manufacturer selling penicillin and cortisone...or even go back to school—there was always that.

There would be time enough for all that crap when he got back home.

Quickly flipping through the pages, it didn't take Collier long to reaffirm that *TIME* was not the best source for pictures of scantily-clad females, so he discarded the magazine in favor of reading Michener's heroic—however tragic and depressing—tale about Korea.

In between reading Michener and thumbing magazines, sporadically, Collier snacked on the lavish smorgasbord adjoining the wardroom across the companionway, frequently going out on deck to smoke and back to napping—only to repeat the tiresome process all over again. Following the blur of days engaged in this mind-numbing tedium, during the intervening evenings, he continued to return and take the lead in an irreverently-sarcastic, rollicking free-for-all of ad-libbing and raucous asides directed at the sophomoric wooden dialogue at the nightly showing of the John Payne swashbuckler flick.

"Land ho!..." one of Collier's compartment mates came bursting in from a deck side smoking break.

"I'm in no mood for kidding around..." Collier responded grumpily from his bunk.

"I'm not kidding this time, guys. We're within sight of land." Around mid-morning on Thursday, 10 December, the excited young lieutenant assured them.

Taking his time to follow the rush to confirm this highly-suspicious announcement, Collier was rewarded with the unmistakable sight of shoreline off both sides of the bow when he emerged into the cloud-filtered, weak, hazy sunlight. All around, his shipmates were dancing joyously, while feeding a giant flock of seagulls which were screaming and dipping, catching pieces of sandwich bread purloined from the wardroom smorgasbord.

"Where are we? Are we in some sort of canal?" Collier asked the seaman nearest him as he elbowed his way to the rail, puzzled by the sight of land on both sides of the vessel.

"The Straits of Wandapooka," the seaman grinned pointing to the wide, island-clogged waterway ahead.

"W-A-N-D-A-P-O-O-K-A? Is that in the USA?" Collier asked, completely in the dark.

"It's Juan de Fuca. J-U-A-N...you know, like Don Juan?" Someone behind him said.

"And D-E...F-U..." another of his nearby compartment mates finished spelling out the exotic name. "And, no, it's not exactly a canal, but it's a seaway between Vancouver Island, British Columbia, and the northwesternmost tip of the state of Washington leading into the port of Seattle," the know-it-all young lieutenant went on to explain.

"But I don't understand...we've only been at sea a total of eleven days...twelve, maybe if you count the afternoon we left Pusan as a full day." Mentally, Collier recounted the days in his head. "I thought the crossing was supposed to take thirteen days?"

"Well, don't ask me. Maybe we had following seas or some-such thing," someone Collier didn't know suggested thoughtfully.

"Who gives a shit? What I want to know is how long will it be before we get off this bucket of rust and I can get a plane back to St. Louis?" A nearby Army captain from the less-crowded stateroom a few doors down their companionway laughed, rubbing his hands together in anticipation.

For the rest of the morning, Collier spent his time going back and forth from his bunk to assuage his intermittent nausea and slipping out on deck to grab a smoke and reassure himself they were indeed still in sight of land.

Finally, around 1600 hours, they steamed into the mouth of Seattle harbor with tugs and fireboats sounding a cacophony of horns and whistles and the fireboats sending up long streams of water from their fire hoses in salute.

"I believe you left this in the ship's laundry, Sir." As Collier entered the companionway to get his bags after the tugs had finally maneuvered the Marine Phoenix deftly alongside the docks and the terminal crew was making fast the lines, a young seaman discretely handed Collier a small package wrapped in plain, brown paper.

"Sorry, sailor, you've got the wrong guy. I didn't send any laundry out during the voyage." Collier politely rejected the extended package.

"There's no mistake, sir. They have your name and serial number. You probably just forgot." The seaman thrust the package into Collier's hands and turned and left before Collier could protest further. Back inside the compartment, Collier idly loosed one end of the brown-paper wrapping, then blushed bright red. There, freshly laundered were his previously semen-soaked Jockeys which he had last spied snagged on the side of the rusty hull, flapping in the ocean gale an unwelcome advertisement for his nocturnal accident.

After what seemed an eternity, but was only a little over an hour, at 1740 hours in the misty overcast of the surprisingly temperate day, Collier walked down the gangplank and stepped onto solid land. From there, he was herded onto a bus which took them to a large, nearby building for processing for available transportation home. While his fellow officers mobbed the booths of the various airlines trying to book flights to their various destinations east or—in the case of the west coasters—south, Collier spent the next hour waiting in line to book himself a Pullman compartment for a leisurely, four or five day railroad trip back to Roanoke, Virginia.

"What time's your flight?" Pullman ticket finally in hand, Collier overheard an anonymous voice behind him ask a fellow air-traveler.

"Twenty-ten hours. I change in Denver. I've got to call my old lady. I'll be in D.C. tomorrow in time for breakfast," the anonymous companion replied happily.

Upon hearing this happy exchange, almost immediately Collier began to regret giving in to his fear of flying as he stood waiting for the buses which would take the majority of his fellow travelers to the Seattle-Tacoma airport, with the pitiful few of the rest of them going to bus or train stations. Suddenly confronted by the reality that most of these young officers heading to the airport would be back home tomorrow morning, Collier's fear of flying gradually gave way to the quiet reality that he would be stuck on a boring train ride for the next four days, spending untold amounts on expensive meals and without the benefit of a long-overdue, much-needed, leisurely and luxurious, steamy-hot, fresh-water shower.

In a panic, Collier turned and bolted back up the short flight of steps to where he had purchased his railroad ticket.

"Is it too late to trade this in for a plane ticket?" Collier asked the grinning clerk as she reached for his ticket and started flipping through the airline schedules.

Because of his waiting so long to change his mind, the ticket agent had to book him on Northwest Orient into Minneapolis-St. Paul with a two-hour layover, changing planes in Detroit at three in the morning before continuing on into Washington, DC. Ticket finally in hand, Collier ran down the long steps in the light rain and boarded the waiting bus for Seattle-Tacoma airport. By midnight he was having a French 75—which he instructed the stewardess-bartender how to make—in the luxurious, padded-leather lounge at the bottom of the fancy spiral staircase of a Northwest Orient Boeing Stratocruiser as he watched the lights of what he assumed was Spokane disappear over the western horizon behind them far below.

After a miserable two hours pacing the chilly main concourse of the Detroit airport, which was filled with revolving platform displays of luxury-model automobiles of virtually every manufacture—although the idea of a reunion with her scared him half to death—Collier finally decided to call Emma and ask her to meet him in Washington. He could get a hotel room and get cleaned up before she arrived. They could have a second honeymoon of a sort—maybe rethink his troubling desire to dissolve his marriage.

After all, it would be bad form to suggest a divorce this close to Christmas...and, after all, what was the need to hurry?

"Hello?..." after depositing a handful of change, the call rang through; much to Collier's chagrin, he recognized Mother Lowell's voice on the line.

"Mother Lowell...it's Collier. I'm sorry to wake you. I was hoping Emma would answer...would it be too much trouble to get her on the line?" Collier stuttered, embarrassed he had woken his kindly mother-in-law out of a sound sleep in the middle of the night.

"I'm sorry, Collier, but she's not here. Are you all right?" Assuming he was calling from Korea, Mother Lowell didn't know quite what to make of the call.

"Emma's not there? Where on earth is she, anyway?" Collier had never once considered Emma would not be in bed at home.

"She's in Richmond Christmas shopping with some girlfriends. She's staying at the John Marshall. I'm sure you can reach her there. Are you all right?" his mother-in-law asked again.

"I'm fine. Are you keeping little Kyle?" Collier asked, trying to wrap his mind around the idea of Emma leaving their seven-and-a-half-month-old with her frail, aging Mother.

"Ann is here with me. She's taking care of Kyle," the elderly woman replied defensively.

"Oh, sure...well, again, I'm sorry I woke you up. I'll wait and try Emma later. I forgot about the difference in time," Collier apologized lamely and hastily hung up.

Overwhelmed with self-recrimination for not having let Emma know he was coming home, he absently dug through his bags and found the letter from his parents he'd received the night he left Yongdongpo. His mother had written that Bo was still hospitalized at Fort Belvoir, Virginia, just outside Washington and Jenny had taken a job up there to be with him during his recovery. His mother had included Jenny's address and phone number at her apartment in Belvoir.

Boarding a TWA DC-6 bound for Washington, DC at slightly after 0200 hours, disappointed and curiously angry from not reaching Emma by phone, Collier chided himself again for not letting her know he was coming home. Sensibly, he decided not to rouse her out of a sound sleep in her room at the John Marshall in Richmond which she was most likely sharing with one of her girlfriends. When he reached Washington around daylight, he would rent a car and drive the two-hour drive to Richmond. He would show up at the door of her hotel room, unannounced, in time to order a Champagne breakfast from room service. The problem of a babysitter for little Kyle had already been solved. His plan for a second-, or third- honeymoon had been handed him on a silver platter. Contemplating the surprised look on Emma's face, he closed his eyes and was fast asleep before the airplane had even taxied out for takeoff.

"Please fasten your seatbelts...we are beginning our approach to Washington National Airport..." the stewardess' voice intruded into a fretful dream about stacking dead bodies in a Quonset morgue. Rousing groggily awake, Collier rubbed the sleep out of his eyes and pulled his seatbelt snug as he watched excitedly as the big aircraft made its descent down the Potomac river by the Washington Monument, preparing to make the approach to National Airport.

It was only after the wheels kissed the ground with a screech and they had taxied to the terminal that he realized he had flown 3000 miles across the country and hadn't once thought about dying in an airplane crash.

He'd come a long way since the morning of January 3, 1952, when he had stepped off the Pullman car at the Washington terminal with Bo Bohon and Daryl Pogue—his first morning as a soldier in the Army.

CHAPTER FORTY-NINE

Vol. 9, No. 346   KOREA EDITION Sunday, Dec. 13, 1953

DEAN CHARGES REDS STILL HOLD PRISONERS

PANMUNJON, December 12 (AP) - U.S. Special Envoy Arthur H. Dean today accused the Communists of violating the armistice agreement and the Geneva Convention by still holding American and South Korean prisoners of war, despite their claim that all prisoners who requested repatriation were sent home.

THE ROANOKE TIMES
Roanoke, Virginia, Sunday, December 13, 1953
U.S. STALKS OUT OF PEACE TALKS

PANMUNJON, December 13 (AP) - Official Washington was obviously surprised today by the sudden breakdown of Panmunjon talks for a Korean peace conference...

THE ROANOKE TIMES
Roanoke, Virginia, Sunday, December 27, 1953
EISENHOWER CUTS U.S. TROOPS IN KOREA
TWO DIVISIONS TO RETURN HOME SOON
By Marvin L. Arrowsmith

AUGUSTA, Ga., Sunday, December 27 (AP) - President Eisenhower today ordered a progressive reduction of American ground force strength in Korea...

THE ROANOKE TIMES
Roanoke, Virginia, Monday, January 4, 1954
ANTI-COMMUNIST POWS
TO BECOME CIVILIANS

MUNSAN, Monday, January 4 (AP) - The United Nations Command today flatly declared that all non-communist prisoners will become civilians at midnight January 22 and be free to go where they choose...

"WELCOME HOME, LIEUTENANT. Let me help you with that smaller bag." Collier was rendered momentarily speechless at the sight of Ginger Lipscomb waiting at the top of the stairs inside the main lobby of the cavernous terminal. Wearing a dove-gray, light-weight-jersey sheath dress underneath a camel-tan designer topcoat with a cowl collar, she looked more like a fashion model than an Army nurse. After wrestling and lugging the more bulky-and-clumsy than actually-heavy canvas duffel and his little AWOL bag down the narrow steps of the rolling off-boarding stairs from the airplane across the tarmac, and up the steps into the terminal building, he was not only completely flabbergasted but somewhat out of breath.

"Ginger! How the hell did you know?...I mean...how?..." Collier stammered, as soon as he found his voice.

"I got the note you sent from Pusan just before you sailed. I called Salem this morning, early, looking for Emma to tell her I was back in the States and would be coming to Roanoke in a few days, and Emma's mom told me you'd called. Mother Lowell thinks you called from Korea. But I put two and two together and realized you were probably already back stateside and probably on an airplane from Seattle and, most likely, were intending to surprise them. I checked the Northwest schedule and decided to come over here and take a chance on finding you. Lucky me! Aren't I smart? Do I get a kiss?" Without waiting for an answer, she stepped forward and planted her lips solidly on his in a chaste but enthusiastic kiss.

After a long moment, she pulled back and gave his face a searching look. Apparently confirming her unspoken question by the hungry look in his eyes, she leaned forward and kissed him again, this time her hummingbird tongue insinuated itself inside his mouth.

Initially somewhat stiff from total shock at finding Ginger waiting, Collier slowly relaxed and dropped both bags. Then, with shy reservation, he let his own tongue timidly respond to her unexpected passion. Instantly, he became totally absorbed in the kiss. Merging the full length of her body against his when she felt his response, Ginger unblushingly pressed against the growing bulge inside his uniform pants.

"Wow! Of all the gin joints, in all the towns, in all the world, she walks into mine! This is a nice surprise." Collier pulled back when he finally came to his senses and realized they were standing in full view of at least a hundred people.

"You've been seeing too many Bogart movies." She laughed and hugged him closer.

"After twelve days on that rusty old tub with only one shower, I must smell like a wild goat."

"So come on; let's get out of here. I have a room at the Mayflower. We can grab a cab. I'll order us room service breakfast while you take a shower." Ginger reached down and picked up the smaller bag from where he had dropped them both to free his arms for her welcoming embrace.

"Well...I don't know. First I need to find a phone and try to call Emma again. Mother Lowell told me she's in Richmond, Christmas shopping with some girlfriends." Collier stooped, re-shouldering his bulky duffel bag.

"Don't waste your time. My guess is that Emma's not shopping in Richmond with the girls." Ginger gave him a knowing look.

"What do you mean?" Collier asked, not sure he understood.

"She's in Richmond, but not for Christmas shopping. Just take my word and let it go at that," Ginger hedged, clearly sorry she had been so quick to speak out of turn.

"How do you know? What are you saying?" Collier prodded. It was much too late to back off now.

"Collier, please just let it lie. I spoke too soon. Go ahead and call. I could be wrong. Come on; the phones are right over there by the main entrance doors." Ginger turned and started across the terminal with Collier lugging the duffel close behind.

"Watch the bags while I go find some change for the phone," Collier requested when they reached the long row of telephone booths just inside the main entrance doors.

"Wait! No need, I have almost a purse full of silver." Ginger opened her purse and fished out a handful of coins.

"I want to place a person-to-person call to Mrs. Emma Ramsay at the John Marshall Hotel in Richmond, Virginia." Leaving the door to the booth open, Collier stacked up the coins on the small shelf beside the phone while he waited for the operator to put him through.

"I'm sorry, Sir. Mrs. Ramsey doesn't answer her phone. Can I take a message?" after ringing Emma's room for the better part of a minute, the John Marshall operator asked Collier's long-distance operator.

"No message...thank you, Operator," Collier said and slowly replaced the phone.

"Well?..." Ginger asked, her voice trying not to imply 'I told you so.'

"You're wrong. They have her registered at the John Marshall. She just doesn't answer the phone." Ruefully, Collier shook his head as he exited the booth, not sure what to do next. "Emma is a late sleeper. It's just now only zero-seven-zero. It's over a full hour before Miller and Rhodes and Thalheimers department stores open their doors."

"You're right. of course. I wouldn't worry. If she's with friends Christmas shopping like her mother said, the stores don't close this time of year until ten at night. They probably stayed up half the night, catching up on the latest gossip." Ginger shrugged, backtracking not altogether convincingly. "Come on, let's grab a cab. You'll feel better after a shower and some chow."

"Well, I had planned on renting a car and driving to Richmond to surprise her. I could be there before eleven if I left right now." Collier looked down at his bags, undecided as to what to do next. It served him right for not having dropped Emma a note before he left Seoul, telling her the good news.

"Come on, take my advice. At least come with me to the Mayflower and clean up before you hit the road. You can try calling her again from my room," Ginger offered again.

"Okay, let's grab a cab. I don't want to wait all day before I get started." Collier picked up his bags; under the circumstances, what Ginger said made sense.

"The Mayflower," Ginger told the driver as he ushered them inside the clean, but rather hard-used Yellow cab. Once underway, Ginger snuggled close, but remained relatively silent as the driver efficiently drove them in the rush-hour traffic across the 14th Street Bridge to the Mayflower. When they alit to the sidewalk in front of the marquee awning, Ginger paid and tipped the driver and instructed the Mayflower bell captain to bring Collier's bags to her room. Against Collier's protests, when the bellman delivered his bags a few minutes later, Ginger tipped him again before Collier could wrestle his wallet out of his trousers' pocket.

After six months in Korea, Ginger's room at the elegant Mayflower seemed right out of a Selznick extravaganza to Collier as he took his kit into the bathroom and immediately got down to the business of shaving and taking a shower. Toweling dry and—blushing at the memory of tossing his semen-soaked undershorts into the storm-tossed night—he located the clean Jockeys the seaman had rescued, wrapped himself in a towel and went back into the room looking for a clean uniform in his duffel. To his amazement and great pleasure, while he had been in the bathroom, Ginger had had room service set up a mouth-watering breakfast on a table cart.

"Here, put this on while we eat." Ginger handed him a heavy, white terry-cloth robe with the Mayflower logo embroidered on the breast pocket. "Let's not let our food get cold."

"Looks delicious...I'm famished," Collier said, holding her chair before he went around and pulled up a large hassock for a seat.

"We should make a toast." Ginger picked up the large, salt-encrusted glass of tomato juice, removing the celery-stick-stirrer.

"*A votre sante.*" Collier raised his glass, clinking it lightly against Ginger's glass.

"*A votre sante...*" Ginger said and took a tiny sip.

"Wow, lady! That's my kind of tomato juice!" Taking a large swallow of the red liquid, Collier realized it was a Bloody Mary.

"Having a half-naked man in my room makes me feel rather depraved." Ginger giggled, taking another swallow of the potent drink. "What's *a votre sante* mean, anyway?"

"To your health...I think. My French is not that great." Collier sheepishly confessed.

"Hm-m...I was rather hoping it meant something more seductive. Besides, it seems superficial. I'm indecently healthy. And I must say, now that you're cleaned up, you look healthy enough to me. You hardly look the worse for having spent two weeks on that rusty tub. It's great to be back in the States, and you're a sight for sore eyes." Ginger regarded him appreciatively over the rim of her glass, licking the rock salt crust with her tongue. After contemplating him for a thoughtful moment, she stood and began lifting the warming lids from the plates.

Taken on an empty stomach, Collier was already feeling the heady, warming effect of the drink. Appraising the outline of Ginger's just slightly overripe figure against the clinging fabric of her sheath dress as she bent forward busying herself pouring them both cups of steaming coffee, Collier furtively adjusted his swelling penis as he took another swallow of the tasty drink.

"Eat your food before it gets cold," Ginger urged, seated again and tasting a bite of her scrambled eggs, washing them down with another swallow of the salty drink.

"Uhm-m, this is marvelous..." Collier groaned, wolfing down a fork-full of the lightest pancakes he'd ever sunk a tooth into.

Smiling, Ginger picked up her own fork again and began to eat in earnest.

"That was absolutely fan-damn-tastic. I'm so full I can hardly move. You're an angel in disguise." Collier said as he came back from locating his cigarettes. Offering Ginger one, he lit both with the sterling-silver Zippo he'd bought in Korea.

"Trust me. I'm no angel." Ginger gave him a hooded look.

"Angel or not, thank you for the rescue." Collier exhaled a perfect smoke ring before continuing. "I was disappointed we didn't get together in Japan. I still have the photo you sent me." He stopped himself from adding, "wearing the bikini."

"Well...I guess I got a bit carried away with that..." She blushed. "You must think I'm a hussy." From the way she handled the cigarette, it was easy to see she wasn't much of a smoker.

"Not at all. As a matter of fact, I have it right there in my AWOL bag." He got up and located the writing folio photo and handed her the seductive snapshot. He wondered what she'd say if he told her he had masturbated when he got it in the mail.

"I'm flattered—and a just a little embarrassed. If I were you, I don't think it would be such a good idea to let Emma find this." Ginger snubbed out her cigarette and drained the final sip from the Bloody Mary before she handed back the photo which he gave another appreciative look.

"It's already after nine. I guess I should try to call Emma again. Is it okay if I charge the call to your room? I'll leave the money to reimburse you," Collier asked as he nervously looked around for the phone.

"Sure. Do you want me to step outside and give you some privacy?" Ginger asked politely.

"Don't be silly. I'm sitting here in your hotel room looking at a picture of you practically naked—and I'm practically naked underneath this robe. There is very little left for us to hide from each other." Collier moved between the two oversized "queen" beds, sat down and picked up the telephone and flashed the hotel operator.

"Long distance, please; I want to make a person-to-person call charged to this room..." he began and gave the operator Emma's name and the name of the John Marshall hotel in Richmond. While he waited, he absently studied Ginger's photo. With breasts like hers, she should be a center-foldout in *Esquire*, he mused, his thoughts drifting back to his youth when *Esquire* ran the sexy—better than nude—Vargas and Petty paintings of luscious, overripe females, scantily-clad in transparent lingerie.

"Emma?..." Collier asked, abruptly coming back to reality as a female voice answered the ring on the other end of the line.

"Is that you, Trey? I thought Emma was with you?..." the unfamiliar, obviously-puzzled female voice replied.

"Ah-h...uh...I'm sorry...I uhm-m...I must have the wrong number..." Quite unprepared to hear the unfamiliar females' response, Collier stammered and hung up the phone. He sat there for a long moment too stunned to talk, before he finally placed the handset back on the cradle.

"What's the matter? What happened?" Ginger finally asked.

"I...ah...I'm not sure I know...I'm not sure I really want to know..." Collier muttered reflexively, still in shock.

"What do you mean?" Ginger got up and walked over and took a seat across from him on the other bed. "What on earth happened?"

"Well...I...the woman who answered thought I was someone named 'Trey' looking for Emma..." Collier began and recounted the brief exchange to Ginger.

"You're right. It must have been the wrong room..." Ginger sympathized lamely.

"But she said she thought '*Emma*' was with me—this guy, *Trey*, I mean."

Fishing another Lucky from the pocket of the robe, Collier fumbled for his Zippo as an uneasy suspicion began to grow inside his travel-weary consciousness. Ginger got up and retrieved the lighter he'd left on the room-service cart.

"Did you ever hear Emma mention anyone named Trey?" Collier looked up at her as she lit his dangling cigarette.

Ginger blushed, and shot him an uncertain look.

"You *do* know this Trey, don't you? Ginger's guilty look of confirmation opened up a yawning abyss of suspicion followed by a barrage of questions. "Who is this guy, anyway? Why would Emma be in Richmond Christmas shopping with him?"

"Well...there was an intern named Simpkins Moseley the Third when we were in training at Lewis-Gale. His father, Simpkins Moseley, Senior was a doctor at the Salem VA. Since the son was Simpkins Moseley the Third, he was sometimes addressed as Trey. But the last I heard, Trey Moseley had been drafted into the Army Medical Corp and was a Major stationed in San Antone." Ginger shrugged.

"Hm-m. Was he a little guy? Sort of like a banty-rooster?" Collier asked, recalling the comic-opera Major he had met when he and Pewter had been assigned as spur-of-the-moment drill instructors for the ragtag group of drafted doctors at the MFSS. Somehow the name Moseley rang a bell.

"That describes him to a tee." Ginger laughed. "Did Emma introduce you?"

"Well...now that I think about it, she might have introduced him once back at the VA in Salem, before I went into the Army. But, I'm pretty sure I ran into him at the MFSS." Collier muttered half-aloud, trying to get a grip on the idea that Emma might have been cheating on him and trying to recall if he had had any other contact with the Napoleonic physician.

Nothing suspicious came to mind.

"You're right. I remember now. I was there working the Bloodmobile the night she introduced you two at the Salem VA. Do you remember?" Ginger prompted.

"Okay...let's have it all. Emma and this doctor Simpkins were having a thing...right? It started way back in nursing training?" Collier wracked his brain struggling to remember any incidents that might have indicated she was having an affair.

"Well, I didn't say that. Back in training, when Trey was interning—actually the first summer he came there, he was only an extern, a senior med student—the little pantywaist was something of a rape artist. At night when he was on duty with student nurses, he would force his attentions on them. He knew they wouldn't tell and risk getting kicked out of training. He even tried to force himself on me one night, but I threatened to go to Dr. Bondurant. I wasn't the only one; I feel certain. There was some gossip among the nurses, but you know how that is. I've told you pretty much all I know for sure." Ginger nervously fumbled with the fancy sterling silver Zippo, flicking the top open and closed again.

"Come on, Ginger. You're not telling me everything. You might as well come clean. I can tell you right now, I hate to walk out and leave her with my son, but I'm not going back to her." Collier stood, uncertain what he should do next.

"I wouldn't worry about walking out on the kid. You can be damn well certain he's not yours," Ginger blurted with exasperation.

"Oh, I'm sure you're mistaken about that! That boy was conceived in Oklahoma City on my first weekend pass from OCS. It was Labor Day weekend and we met my brother, Jimmy, there. He drove down from Enid, Oklahoma, where he was in multi-engine training," Collier contradicted vehemently.

"All that may be well and good, but I hate to disappoint you. If you'll check back, you'll find Major Simpkins Moseley the Third was at the Fort Sill Army Hospital on TDY from Brooke Army Hospital in San Antonio that weekend." Ginger shot him an imperious look.

"Are you sure? How do you know that?" Collier searched her face for truthfulness.

"I was stationed at Brooke Army Hospital, remember? Trey was always pestering me, trying to add a pelt to his hunting belt. He bragged about seeing Emma in unmistakable and rather descriptive terms when he got back from his TDY at Sill."

Momentarily speechless, Collier was trying to take it all in.

"Are you saying Emma and this doctor have been having an affair since before we were married?" Collier found it difficult to believe Emma capable of such malicious, purposeful and ongoing betrayal.

"That's exactly what I'm saying. Listen, now that it's out in the open, you might as well know the ugly truth. In Emma's defense, Trey probably did rape her the first time—when she was on night duty with him back in training at Lewis-Gale. God knows the little worm doesn't have the finesse to seduce anyone. But, for whatever reason, she didn't report him—probably because his daddy was an important physician, or maybe just because she was afraid it would get her kicked out of training, whatever. Anyway, for whatever reason, she apparently let it continue. I know there were rumors and the nursing staff breathed a great sigh of relief when he finished his externship."

"But wait up a second; do I understand you're telling me that Kyle isn't mine? How could you possibly know that?" Overwhelmed with the flood of dark secrets, he was still unwilling to believe Emma had knowingly passed off Trey Moseley's baby as being his.

"You wouldn't remember, but I was in Roanoke on travel leave visiting some Lewis-Gale classmates before I shipped for Japan when Kyle was born. Knowing about Trey's TDY to Fort Sill to see Emma and remembering Emma's abortion of her first pregnancy, I had one of our ex-classmates check the chart. I always despised 'Miss Goody-two-shoes' Emma for the rotten way she treated you. I sent her flowers after the first abortion with a card with an inscription, 'O plus O equals A with a question mark.'"

"I remember that card. It made no sense to me at the time..." Collier interjected thoughtfully as the memory came flooding back.

"When I found out Baby Kyle has blood type A-positive just like that first fetus Emma lost before you went in service, I sent her flowers again with another card that read 'This time, I hope you got the genotype right.'"

"But I'm not sure what you're saying..." His mind still reeling from humiliation at being so cruelly cuckolded, Collier was perplexed.

"You do understand Mendel's Law, don't you?" Ginger stared in disbelief.

"You mean all that business about the color of pea blossoms? What are you driving at?"

"That same business about the pea flowers applies to animals—in this case, specifically to humans. Both you and Emma are blood type O. There is no way you could father a child with blood type A."

"Huh?..." Collier just stood there as the enormity of what Ginger was saying descended over him like a winter rain.

After a long moment, he walked over to the window and looked out at the gray, overcast sky. Finally he turned, looking around for his duffel with his fresh uniforms. "I'm going to rent a car and drive to Richmond. I still might catch her red-handed—that would give me grounds for a divorce right there."

"Don't waste your time. I told you, they're not in Richmond—besides you don't need to catch them red-handed. A good lawyer would take the medical evidence and skewer Emma in court. Just calm down. You're in no shape to go anywhere right now," Ginger cautioned and moved across and took him by the hand, leading him back to the bed.

"How do you know they aren't in Richmond? And how come you know so much about the babies' geno-ah...the blood types and all that stuff? And why do you give a shit about any of this, anyway?" Collier asked, frustration edging every syllable.

"Well...let's just say I always liked you...ah...admired you from the first time Emma introduced us way back when we started nursing training at Lewis Gale. You were playing basketball at Bluefield College, and I had a terrible crush on you. I liked to draw and paint, and you encouraged me after you started Art School at RPI in Richmond. We had a dance at the YWCA when we graduated and I got to dance with you several times. You wouldn't remember, but I thought I had died and gone to heaven. Emma really got upset and accused me of flirting with you...she always hated my guts. I always thought you deserved better; Emma was such a holier-than-thou bitch. I thought she treated you like shit long before Trey Moseley came into the picture. Now quit with the questions and take a nap. I'll be right here when you wake up. I'm not going anywhere." Ginger pushed him back down on the bed again.

"I still can't believe Emma was running around on me all that time." When Collier woke up an hour later, he sat on the side of the bed rubbing the sleep out of his eyes and shaking his head in utter disbelief. "It's really funny...well, not exactly humorous, but I've been feeling guilty for some time now. I really didn't love her...or at least I wasn't '*in love*' with her by the time we were married. I actually spent most of my wedding day entertaining fantasies about running away. But I just couldn't disappoint her and all those people. And even though I had steady work as an artist with Kroger Company, she really treated me like a worthless dreamer when I was struggling to make it as an artist. She made quite a bit more money than I did at the VA, and she acted like she was supporting us both. I've never really forgiven Emma for the way she treated me before I enlisted in the Army. Then, after I came home from Basic at Sill, she seemed to change. She insisted on coming back to Sill with me and was such a help when I was in OCS—I actually would never have made it through without her...I'm sure of that. To think she screwed Moseley the day before we went to Oklahoma City...but then, if truth be known, I had a transient fling with an older woman at Sill before Emma came back out to Lawton with me. It didn't amount to much..." Collier let the thought trail off.

"Well...look at this way. You can get over your guilt now. Besides, I lived at Army Hall in Tokyo and have heard a little from Madison Argabright about your weekend with her. I hate to confess, but it was me who let the cat out of the bag to Madison about Emma and her baby."

"It serves me right. I should have told Madison I was married...but you'd have to understand the circumstances of that weekend. It really was one of those 'no-questions-asked' situations. All's fair in love and war."

"Uhm-m, I know all about Madison and I understand. By the way, I guess you know her long-lost Naval aviator showed up alive during Operation Big Switch. That's why she abruptly transferred back to the States. She's taken a leave of absence from her hush-hush government job and is moving to Pensacola to marry him right after New Year's."

"No shit! Well, good for her." Collier brightened. He idly wondered if Ginger knew Madison had had an abortion, but, in his book, confession was definitely not good for the soul.

"Look, I'm sorry I had to break the news about Emma and the kid. It's a hell of a homecoming, but you just admitted you were feeling guilty about not loving her..."

"Well, not only that, but I've been carrying a lot of guilt about my lack of paternal instincts for the boy. It's hard to explain, but I just never did feel a connection to the baby."

"No wonder. But then you had no way of knowing about Emma then. So cut yourself some slack. I think your plan to turn the whole messy business over to an attorney and avoid a confrontation with her makes a lot of sense. Best of all worlds, you left home before the child was two months old. He's still only...what? Eight months? You'll never be an important factor in his life."

"That's true. Actually the guilt of abandoning little Kyle was the only thing that kept me from asking Emma for a divorce. I had asked her to join me in Japan, before I found out I was getting out on early release." Collier shrugged.

"Oh, well, go easy on yourself. I guess I haven't exactly been a saint myself." Ginger emitted a dry laugh.

"You're lucky I didn't run into you earlier in Tokyo. Emma or no Emma, I'm not as bad as you think I am, but I probably would have tried to make a move on you." Collier hung his head.

"I'm shameless. That night when I kissed you heading for the elevator at the Yuraku's Roof Garden, I dumped my date and headed back up there looking for you. Worst luck, you had already left with Madison."

"Damn...just my luck. But, anyway, you weren't looking to get laid..." Collier laughed.

"I wouldn't be so sure if I were you. Why do you think I volunteered to help deliver that iron lung to you in Korea?..." she began and stopped herself.

"Oh, sure. Now you're just trying to make me feel better about all this garbage with Emma..."

"Don't make that mistake. I mean...I don't want you to feel badly, but I'm talking way too much...I...ah...I really don't know what I mean."

"Oh, then so am I. I do remember quite well that dance at the YWCA when you were in training. I had such a case of the hots for you I could hardly talk when you were around. After we danced that night, I had to excuse myself and go outside and smoke a cigarette to calm down. It was ah...uh...quite embarrassing." He looked sheepishly up at her.

"Back then, I wasn't very popular with my classmates in training. Emma and a lot of the rest of them always hated me, because on weekends off, I was singing with that band. There were nasty rumors about my morals, but I got good grades and never broke the rules. In the end, I made some friends and graduated near the top of the class. I showed those snobs I was every bit as good as they were." Ginger clenched her fists as the memories of her unhappy times came back to her.

"I can't believe you felt inferior. Every girl in that nursing school—practically every nurse in that hospital—was jealous of your looks and that you were singing with that band. You *are* probably too damn good-looking for your own good." Collier shrugged and laughed.

"You are a dear...you're certainly too blind to be an artist," she reddened, obviously pleased. Leaning forward impulsively, she put her hands behind his head and hugged his face into her lower abdomen, just above the belly-button.

"Even a half-blind man would succumb to your beauty. If we hadn't been interrupted in Korea, I would have...ah..." Collier began but let the thought go unfinished. Needily, he wrapped his arms around her waist and pulled her closer, inhaling deeply of her woman scent.

"Uhm-m..." she sighed, pressing closer. The soft hollow of her navel and the texture of her pubic triangle were quite apparent to him beneath the flimsy fabric of her skirt.

"*Come fill the cup and in the fires of spring, your winter garments of repentance fling ...*" Collier murmured, letting his hands slowly move down, across the rounded form of her derriere, delicately tracing the curve with his fingertips.

"Uhm-m...I love it when you do that..."

"*For the Bird of Time has but a little way to flutter and the bird is on the wing...*" He completed the couplet as his busy hands caressed her just beneath the curve of her buttocks.

Leaning slightly forward without breaking his hold on her behind, impulsively she kissed him on the top of his head. Then, tilting his face upward, she kissed him full on the mouth.

"You know what the poet, Omar Khyham, was saying, don't you?" She pulled back and gave him a searching look.

"He was saying that man is a fool to waste a single, solitary moment of pleasure...the opportunity might not present itself again...' Collier turned his face upward, begging for another kiss.

"Wait! Here, unzip me. I want to get out of these clothes..." She kissed him one last time, then pulled back, turning to let him help her disrobe.

After he had unzipped the top of her dress, she shrugged the loose garment up and over her head, tossing it carelessly on the nearby chair. Then, with a matching economy of movement, she followed suit with her expensive rose-beige slip. When she turned to face him again, she was standing in only her matching rose-beige bra and panties.

"Oh, Collier, just look at you..." she exclaimed and dropped to her knees as she glimpsed the tip of his penis peeking out from between the folds of the terry robe. Pushing the robe from his shoulders, she helped him disrobe and started to take his organ into her mouth.

"Wait...I want you naked, too." Collier pushed her away, expertly unfastening her bra, freeing her perfect breasts—the large aureoles resembled two deep-pink camellia blossoms, nipples swollen in obvious arousal. Lowering her panties with a single maneuver of one hand and twist of the legs, she stepped free and stood there shyly in front of him naked as Eve in the Garden, her flaming-red pubic curls only inches from his face.

"What's this scar," he asked, tracing a light pink area along the outer aspect of her thigh.

"It was only a scratch, but you should treat me with more respect. I am a bona fide recipient of a Purple Heart, you know..." she teased, explaining she had been hit by a tiny fragment of shrapnel when she had flown into the combat zone on a chopper in April during the next-to-last battle for Pork Chop Hill.

"Come here, my brave Amazon warrior; I want you on the bed..." he murmured, reaching out his hand.

"No, wait! Pull back the covers and lie down. I need to go freshen up." She gently pushed his face away and headed for the bathroom.

"Wake up...I'm back. You're not going to get out of this, you know." She sniggered like a spoiled schoolgirl at her own birthday party when she returned a few minutes later to find Collier lightly snoring, spread-eagle naked on the bed.

"Here, sit astride me so I can get my tongue in you." Collier guided her right leg across his chest just below his chin and buried his face between her legs.

"Just where do you think you're going in such a hurry? I'm not nearly finished with you." When Collier finally roused awake shortly after noon, Ginger pulled him back in bed and kissed him lightly on the nose.

"That suits me fine, but you'd better let me pee or you'll be sorry." Collier pushed her gently away and headed for the bathroom.

"Come back to bed. I want you to ravish me again," Ginger crooned seductively when he returned.

"I really should be thinking about renting a car and heading for Roanoke. If I left soon, I could make it to my folks' house near Salem by suppertime," Collier mused aloud.

"Have you decided what you are going to do about Emma?" Ginger asked, more than casually interested.

"Not specifically in any detailed way. But, one thing for sure, I intend to let her know I'm aware of Kyle's paternity and I'm not coming back to her. Divorces in Virginia are not that easy. I'm going to get a good lawyer as soon as I get back and let him advise me exactly what course I should follow." Collier shrugged.

"It's Friday afternoon; you won't be able to see an attorney until Monday at the earliest. You said no one except me knows you're back in the States. Why don't you stay here with me for the weekend at least? Or are you tired of me already?" Ginger pouted prettily, reaching up to him.

"No...I'm not tired of you—not by a long shot. And you're right. For the first time in a long time I don't have to answer to anyone for a few days, at least. You are a silver-tongued fox. You talked me right into it. I'll stay the weekend, anyway." Collier plopped down on the bed beside her, kissing her hungrily.

"Oh, my! I think you must be Superman..." She exhaled a gasp of pleasure as he slipped between her legs again.

"Now that you won't be going back to Emma, are you planning to go back to work with your uncle...with the grocery chain?" Ginger asked sometime later, interrupting Collier's speculative, post-orgiastic reveries about a future without Emma. It seemed she could almost read his mind.

"I'm not sure. I hate to give up trying to become an illustrator, but reality tells me I probably haven't got what it takes to compete with the big boys in New York." Collier idly traced a circle around her nipples with his fingertips, reluctantly confiding his self-doubts. "Worse comes to worse, my RA commission came through just before I left Seoul. I could always ask the Army to take me back."

"I don't think they would take kindly to your wanting to go back to active duty after you just opted to shorten your tour in Korea." Ginger raised up on her right elbow.

"You're probably right about that...and besides, I know it's different with you Nurses, but I really don't think I want to make the peacetime Army a career." He recounted what Colonel Wilson Massey had told him about West Pointers and the "good-old-boy" system. He went on to tell her of his brief misadventure with the crusty old colonel and his love of Hemingway and his description of Demerol as 'golden buzzard elixir;' adding at the end, "...the crusty old romantic said he thought I should try my hand at writing."

"You'd make a damn good writer. I'm sure of it."

"Don't be absurd. I love to read, but trying to write scares me half to death."

"Oh, pooh! You're smart. What about Medical School...or even Pharmacy School?" Ginger's fingers idly twined tiny circlets in the thick hair on his chest.

"Med School, maybe, but not Pharmacy. Can you see me standing behind a drug store counter selling rubbers to pimple-faced teenage boys?" He laughed out loud.

"I see your point," she laughingly replied.

"Some of the doctors back in Korea suggested I should go into Hospital Administration, but when I looked into it, even that requires a special college degree nowadays," Collier reflected ironically. "That's another reason I decided to get out of the military. If I had stayed in, there would be too many other junior officers with college degrees in related disciplines. I'm afraid a two-year diploma in Accelerated Pre-med from a Junior College and two years study in Advertising Art doesn't add up to being very well-qualified as a Medical Service officer."

"Well, why not look into converting all that to a degree in Hospital Administration?" Ginger offered helpfully. "My guess is you could find a school where they would accept your experience for credit and you'd graduate in a year...two tops."

"You may well be right..." he reflected for a moment, "...but the simple truth is that I really don't want to be a civilian Hospital Administrator sitting behind a desk worried about quarrels between the medical and nursing staff and problems with the cafeteria. I'm just not cut out for that kind of life. Some of the doctors and our pharmacists back in Korea suggested I look into pharmaceutical sales. With the discovery of penicillin and cortisone, they seemed to think we're poised on the age of miracle drugs. I'm not sure I like the idea of being a salesman, but they said pharmaceutical salesmen were more like consultants or public relations people than salesmen. And, they said they got to play a lot of client golf." He gave her a playful tickle.

"I'm sure that would be right up your alley." She tickled him back, rolling her shapely right leg across him, edging closer for a kiss.

"Wait...we have all weekend. I need to call an old friend while I'm here." He kissed her and got up and went to his duffel to retrieve the letter with Jenny Bohon's phone number, he had gotten from his mother the night he left Yongdongpo.

"Jenny...it's Collier..." he began when Jenny picked up on the first ring and briefly told her about his good fortune and that no one knew he was coming home in time for Christmas.

"Oh...I'm sure Emma and your mother and dad will be out of their minds when they see you." Jenny laughed, imagining their surprise. "You'll hardly recognize little Kyle; he's growing like a weed."

"Ah...yes...I'm sure..." he said lamely. "How's Bo? From what I hear, he's lucky to still have his arm. Lucky to be alive."

"You're right. He was in Osaka for a month before they dared move him..." Jenny started in and recounted how they had flown Bo in a hospital plane to Wake Island, on to Midway Island, then to Tipler Hospital in Honolulu for awhile before they finally flew him to the states. "He's already had several operations here at Belvoir. The doctors think he's out of the woods as far as saving the arm, but he still has a rough road ahead." She concluded her account of Bo's five-month-long ordeal.

"I know it's been rough on you, too. My mom says you have an apartment and a job up here while Bo's at Belvoir." Collier offered lamely, anxious now to get off the phone.

"I do. I had to get a job. I can't live up here on the Army's one-thirty-seven a month. I work for Shenandoah Life near the White House...commute back and forth each day. Will you be able to come see Bo while you're here?" she asked, her voice alive with hopeful expectation. "I'll give you one of my apple cakes to take back home." Filled with nuts and only God knew what else, Jenny's apple cakes were dark and rich, but moister than most fruit cakes...even including his Grandma Ramsay's.

"Not this trip. You know the military. As much as my mouth is watering for a taste of your cake, I have to catch a plane. Please tell Bo I'll write him, and maybe I can visit when I come back up here to Meade to be processed out of Active Duty status," he lied—not able to stand the thought of looking at Bo lying in a hospital bed, knowing he would never be able to snap a clothesline throw to second base or hit another golf ball.

"He'll be so disappointed. Please make a special effort to see him when you come back to Meade..." Jenny pleaded just before Collier said goodbye and hung up the phone.

"I take it this Bo person is a hometown buddy—wounded in Korea?" Ginger asked.

"Yeah..." Collier recounted the highlights of his friendship with Bo.

"If he's at Belvoir, I could look in on him," Ginger offered tentatively.

"That would nice of you. It's probably best you don't let Bo or Jenny know about the upcoming divorce...they're both friends of Emma's. I'm sure you understand." Collier gave her a meaningful look.

"Of course. By the way, I just got back from FECOM and am officially on travel leave until after Christmas. What if I drove you to Roanoke Monday? I know the shit is going to hit the fan with Emma, and I'm sure finding out they don't really have a grandson will be a real emotional rollercoaster for your folks right at Christmas. I mean in the middle of all this mess, would you be able to see me while I'm there? Or...would you want me to come with you? Would we be able to *see* each other...you know what I mean?" Ginger broke off lamely, afraid she might be overstepping the bounds of their newly-begun relationship.

"Of course I want you to come with me. But, given the ah...circumstances, it wouldn't be the best time to introduce you to my parents, of course I will be able to see you, no matter what goes down with divorcing Emma. I'm turning that over to a lawyer. I've decided it would be best to avoid any sort of face-to-face confrontation over this. The boy's blood type speaks for itself. The less said the better, if you get my drift?"

"Yes. I think that's the best. Now, do you want to go out somewhere to eat or shall we order room service?" Ginger pulled him back down beside her, snuggling close to him.

"*Forget food, Sweethoit; you're all I need for now.*" Collier nuzzled her, growling his worst/best Bogart imitation."

"*Louie, I think this could be the beginning of a beautiful friendship,*" Ginger responded in her own best worst Bogartese.

EPILOGUE

The Washington Post

Friday, October 22, 2010

US ADMIRAL WARNS AGAINST
ANOTHER NKOREA NUKE TEST

By HYUNG-JIN KIM
The Associated Press
Friday, October 22, 2010, 5:49 AM

SEOUL, South Korea -- If North Korea carries out a third nuclear test, it would seriously undermine international and regional security, the U.S. Pacific commander warned Friday.

Adm. Robert Willard's comments were prompted by a South Korean newspaper report that said a U.S. spy satellite detected activity at the North's main nuclear test site and that a detonation could occur in three months. South Korean officials played down the report, saying the activity didn't seem unusual.

Responding to questions about the report, Willard told reporters that North Korea's nuclear capabilities pose a grave threat to the region and that another atomic bomb test - which would be the country's third - would be a "very serious matter."

———————

Tensions between the Koreas -- which are still technically at war because the 1950-53 Korean War ended with a truce, not a peace treaty - - have been high in recent months following the sinking of a South Korean warship that killed 46 sailors. Seoul blamed the sinking on North Korea, which denied involvement.

———————

NEATLY FOLDING THE *POST*, Collier Boyd Ramsay secured the paper tightly underneath his arm as he walked the short distance from the haunting metallic figures of the Korean War Memorial over to the nearby parking area and clicked open the electronic locks of the silver Audi cabriolet he had special-ordered from the rental agency via the internet before he left Key West. Except that it was this year's model, it was a virtual duplicate of the sporty car he drove back home.

Pausing to lower the black-canvas convertible top to take the pleasure of the warming Indian summer sun, he expertly tooled the sleek car into the busy traffic circle leading behind the Lincoln Memorial, looping back around to cross the Potomac over the Memorial Bridge, around Lady Bird Johnson Circle across the George Washington Memorial Parkway and the Jefferson Davis Highway, directly into the entrance to Arlington National Cemetery. Just ahead, the wide avenue dead-ended at the semicircular stone Memorial Gate. Taking advantage of the absence of early-morning traffic, he pulled over and consulted the map he had printed from the Arlington National Cemetery website before he slowly started the Audi rolling again.

Turning sharply left, then quickly bearing right at Roosevelt Drive, Collier passed Weeks Drive on his left where he could plainly see the connection with

Sheridan Drive at the entrance to the Eternal Flame marking JFK's grave. Continuing on Roosevelt, he crossed both Grant and McClelland Drive, climbing steadily up the slope between the sea of neatly-serried, white-marble markers. The vista called to his mind the lines, "*In Flanders Fields the poppies blow, between the crosses row on row,*" from John McCrae's moving World War I poem which he had memorized in Ms. Edna Morris's second grade at Fort Lewis School, lo' those seventy-odd long years ago.

Where Roosevelt dead-ended at Wilson Drive, he bore right and took the next left onto Memorial Drive passing the iconic amphitheater on his left. Taking the right hand fork where Memorial dead-ended at Porter Drive, ignoring the No Parking signs, he pulled off the pavement where the map indicated Section 21 with a numerical coding 9 embedded in a black circle corresponding to the Key indicating the Nurse's Memorial on his computer-generated map. Turning off the ignition, he retrieved the single long stem white rosebud lying on the passenger seat and exited the Audi. Wading through the lush carpet of freshly-mowed grass covering his shoe tops, he walked over to the imposing marble statue of a nurse and stood and read the inscription: THIS MONUMENT WAS ERECTED IN 1938 AND REDEDICATED IN 1971 TO COMMEMORATE DEVOTED SERVICE TO COUNTRY AND HUMANITY BY ARMY, NAVY AND AIR FORCE NURSES.

When he had finished reading, he turned to his right and threaded his way between the rows of markers. It had been several years since he had visited here, and at first he had trouble orienting himself, but after some minor trial and error, he finally located the marker he was seeking.

VIRGINIA
LIPSCOMB
RAMSAY
BRONZE STAR
PURPLE HEART OLC
MAJ
US ARMY NURSE CORPS
KOREA
VIETNAM
APR 13, 1929
FEB 14, 1968

After perhaps five minutes, the raucous, insistent shrill of a blue jay perched on a limb just across the way roused him from his silent reverie. Slowly, he knelt and kissed the white rosebud before he placed it on the ground in front of the marker. Bending forward, he gently touched his lips to the top of the austere cold marble stele and murmured "*Here's looking at you, kid.*"

Regaining his feet and brushing fresh grass clippings from his well-worn jeans, Collier turned and walked back to the Audi. Turning the car around, he retraced the route down Memorial Drive and stopped and briefly contemplated the stone Korean War Bench located just north of the Memorial Amphitheater, beside the Korean pine and ash trees planted by Korean Roh Tae Woo in 1989. Momentarily, he considered going to the Information Center to ask if CWO Reilly Yates or Sergeant Sandford Williams were buried here in Arlington, but, after a moment, he decided against it. Thomas Wolfe was probably right when he penned, "*You can't go home again....*"

Removing the dog-eared envelope from his topcoat pocket, he looked out across the cityscape at the White House and Capitol dome as he consulted the invitation again.

THE PRESIDENT OF THE UNITED STATES REQUESTS THE PRESENCE OF YOUR COMPANY FOR DINNER AT THE WHITE HOUSE
7PM, FRIDAY, OCTOBER 22, 2010.
SOCIAL HOUR AT 6PM
RSVP 202/456-1414

Too late to back out now, he mused. Putting the convertible in gear, he headed back toward the fondly-remembered Mayflower Hotel, located somewhere in the maze of buildings across the river. He still had plenty of time to take a nap.

In his restive dream, he was AOD back at the 121ˢᵗ running through the frigid, moonless Korean winter night and squeezing off one deadly shot from his Colt .45 as the shadowy figure of the old papasan climbing over the wire fence behind the Chicken Coop, stiffened and tumbled to the ground. When he reached the old papasan's body, he stood horror-stricken to find the old man's head had exploded like a watermelon and the children in the schoolyard across the street were picking up the pieces and grinning like jackals. One boy about six years of age picked up a piece and offered it to him, and Collier woke with a start to find himself soaked with sweat.

As promised by the White House, a liveried chauffeur pulled up in front of the Mayflower at precisely 1745. After a short ride, the limo deposited Collier Boyd Ramsay beneath the White House North Portico almost at 1800 hours on the button. To Collier's total disbelief, the President himself—dressed in a plain, dark-blue suit with a tasteful white and blue-striped red silk tie and the obligatory white shirt—was waiting at the top of the marble steps to greet him.

"It's good to finally meet you, at long last," the slightly overeager President said rather theatrically, giving the whole scenario an aura of insincerity.

"Dear, I would like to present Collier Boyd Ramsay, a true American hero," before Collier had hardly shook his hand, the self-important, Ivy-educated President introduced him to his wife, who had wasted a lot of money on her flamboyant designer gown.

"I'm honored to meet you, Madam...and Mister President, Sir," Collier murmured, at the moment not exactly the soul of grace and sincerity himself.

Inside, the main Entrance Hall was impressive, constructed almost completely of pink-and-white marble, traversed by a wide, rich-red carpet matching the gold-fringed, red swag window dressings. Sparsely furnished with a white painted and gilded wooden suite of furniture—which looked as if the pieces might have been stolen from one of the upper lobby salons at the famous Greenbrier resort, but was more likely the gift of some past foreign ruler—the Entrance Hall was further decorated with portraits of JKF and GHW Bush, and was about as inviting as a mausoleum. Ushering him across the wide runner of rich-red carpet through the narrow Cross Hall, then bearing slightly left into the large, rectangular—almost square—Red Room, the President made introductions to the Vice President, the Secretary of Defense, several high-ranking officers from all branches of the military, several senators from both parties rumored to have ambitions of replacing him in next election, the Speaker of the House and several other civilians he didn't recognize—a total of at least two-dozen expensively-dressed and well-coiffed warm bodies—if he had correctly counted the number of chairs at the long dinner table in the adjoining Blue Room. Declining a glass of sparkling wine which he assumed must be domestic Champagne, Collier managed to find a glass of plain quinine water with a wedge of lime to sip on while these self-important stuffed shirts ignored him, sipped judiciously of the free wine, and expertly "worked" the room.

Now, not at all looking forward to suffering the company of these egocentric politicians for an entire evening, Collier was having second thoughts and serious self-recriminations about why—at his advanced age—he had accepted this ill-motivated invitation in the first place.

Not that he was in anyway the least intimidated. Spending the better part of an hour during the afternoon in his room at the Mayflower on his laptop connected to the internet, pouring over the pages of *Department of the Army Pamphlet 600-60. Personnel—General: A Guide to Protocol and Etiquette for Official Entertainment*, Collier felt more-or-less relaxed in such sophisticated company when dinner was announced and the President guided him into the Blue Room. Walking in at the President's elbow, he was shown to his seat at the imposingly long table, which he had surmised from doing his homework was set using the protocol for large dinners that seated the host and hostess opposite each other at the center of the table. As guest of honor, he was seated at the right hand of the President. Casually glancing down each side of the table in both directions, he was able to assess the diminishing political importance of each guest in the impressive blue-and-gold-draped, beautiful, spacious oval-shaped room.

As soon as all the guests were seated, the President moved to a small lectern at the end of the room overlooking the Rose Garden before he began speaking, "We are gathered here tonight to honor Collier Boyd Ramsay, a true American hero, whose bravery has gone unacknowledged for over a half a century. Mr. Ramsay, please join me up here at the podium..."

Collier stood and made his way self-consciously to the lectern.

The President picked up a document from the lectern and began to read, "Official Citation. The President of the United States of America, authorized by Act of Congress, March 3, 1863, has awarded, in the name of Congress, the Distinguished Service Cross to First Lieutenant Collier Boyd Ramsay, United States Army, for conspicuous gallantry and intrepidity at the risk of his life above and beyond the call of duty. Lieutenant Collier Boyd Ramsay distinguished himself by acts of gallantry and intrepidity above and beyond the call of duty while serving as a Second Lieutenant, Assistant Batallion Surgeon, Eighth Army, Seoul, Korea in connection with combat operations against the North Korean Peoples Army and the Chinese Communist Army at the Fourth Battle for Pork Chop Hill in the I Corps sector of Korea north of the Thirty-eighth Parallel during the hours after midnight on July ninth, 1953..." the President paused and looked up, his eyes sweeping the room as if to make certain the attendees were properly respectful of the honor. After a brief moment he lowered his eyes and continued reading.

Humbly, Collier bowed his head as he listened to the President read the account of the events that rainy night over a half-century ago. *If they only knew the truth. I didn't volunteer...*he mused silently. *I'm certainly nobody's hero...*

"Lieutenant Ramsay's gallant action directly saved four men from further injury, certain captivity, or death. Second Lieutenant Ramsay's extraordinary heroism and selflessness at the peril of his own life, above and beyond the call of duty, are in keeping with the highest traditions of the military service and reflect great credit upon himself, his unit and the United States Army." The President concluded reading and turned to Collier.

"Before I present this high honor of our military—second only to the Medal of Honor—to Mr. Ramsay, I want to ask his son, Collier Boyd Ramsay, Jr. and his grandson, First Lieutenant Collier Boyd Ramsay the Third, to step forward and join us at the podium. First Lieutenant Ramsay the Third has already earned a Bronze Star and Purple Heart during his two tours in Iraq and one tour in Afghanistan."

Looking out beyond the assemblage of dignitaries, cabinet members, Pentagon bigwigs, reporters and cameramen to the back of the East Room, Collier was overcome with pride as his son and his husky, grandson—a former Academic All-American footballer, now attired in Army dress blues—stood from where they were sitting in the back of the room and came forward.

After Collier had lowered his head to allow the President to place the brilliant blue ribbon—bordered on both sides with red and white stripes—of the Distinguished Service Cross around his neck, he stepped to the microphone and said simply. "I am proud I served my country, but I would be remiss if I didn't confess that I am truly undeserving of this honor. I had the great pleasure of recommending the true heroes in this action, the brave chopper pilot, Chief Warrant Officer Reilly Yates and our courageous companion, Sergeant Sandford Williams—who volunteered for the mission to Pork Chop Hill that night—for our highest award, the Medal of Honor. Sadly...typical of military and political hierarchy...my commendation was ultimately downgraded by higher command to the Silver Star. Before I left Korea, however, it was my pleasure to present both of these true heroes with the Silver Star...which was far less than those brave soldiers deserved..." overcome with emotion as the memories of that fearful night swirled inside his head like this morning's fallen leaves twisting in the chill wind around the marble markers on that lonely hillside across the Potomac, Collier's voice broke, choking off any further words.

"It was indeed a distinct pleasure and an honor to have you and your son and grandson with us this evening here at the White House. Our country owes a great deal to its brave sons and daughters such as you..." the President pontificated sonorously, standing with his Chief of Staff just outside the Blue Room, looking anxiously over at the foot of the Grand Staircase leading up to the First Family's living quarters on the second floor. The media and the rest of the crowd had already dispersed.

Collier's son and grandson had already made their exits, saying they would meet him back at the Mayflower.

"It's too bad our lofty 'powers-that-be' have squandered this, their most precious, resource so recklessly," Collier snapped back, sorry he had opened his mouth barely before the words escaped his lips.

"And, just what do you mean by that?" the President asked defensively. His media opportunity passed, he was now no longer interested in currying favor.

"In my estimation, our plan to maintain a standing military has all but self-destructed. Within a generation, the day that we will be regarded as a world power will be hardly more than a memory." Collier shrugged.

"Are you advocating we reestablish the draft? Look what we've accomplished in Afghanistan and Iraq with our volunteer Army." The President gave him an imperious look.

"Well, yes, I would like to see our country establish a method of Universal Military Training. Patriotism has virtually lost its meaning in the vocabulary of our young—it has become almost an epithet, a concept for derision. If every one of our young men and women were required to enter active duty in the military—upon graduation from high school...or at age eighteen—then we could very quickly reestablish a strong sense of patriotism in our country. And we would also have a leg up if, or when, we should be called upon to mobilize a sizeable military force for our defense. And, while we're on that subject, Sir, just exactly what have we accomplished in Iraq and Afghanistan?"

"Well...I couldn't disagree more. It is far more important to the welfare of this country that the creative and leadership resource of our best families be developed appropriately by sending them to the best institutions of higher learning..." the President blustered, ignoring completely Collier's pointed question about the current debacle in the Middle East.

"Excluding of course West Point and the academies of our other arms of the military?" Collier asked and went on, his tone dripping sarcasm. "Since it has become a popular trend lately for our top schools to do away with ROTC as being...what?...beneath their dignity? Well, certainly unimportant—say, relative to winning an invitation to a top football bowl or being in the Final Four." Not at all intimidated, Collier held his ground.

"Well I'm certainly in favor of athletic programs, but I'm talking about the importance of curriculum in international commerce, world politics and important subjects like that. Are you insinuating that graduate programs in such worthwhile pursuits are a waste of time? I frankly believe that war among civilized nations will eventually become a thing of the past...obsolete. Besides, as we move deeper into an age of computerization, we have less and less employment for the formerly productive manpower of our nation's heartland, making a career in the military a more attractive...a...uh...a more viable option." The President's smirk betrayed the arrogance of his political power.

"Doesn't it worry you at all that we are already mired up to our eyeballs into that class-discrimination process? Just look at the state of our current military..."

"What do you mean class-discrimination?" The President bowed his back with self-righteous indignation.

"We could start with the fact that fewer than one-third of the five-hundred-thirty-five members of the current Congress have served in the military. This is compared to almost eighty percent in 1977. The end of the draft in 1973 marked the beginning of a declining number of veterans in Congress. It probably helps explain why so few children of lawmakers serve in uniform nowadays."

"Don't start that argument with me! Are you saying our nation's duly-elected lawmakers are unpatriotic? Are corrupt?" The President was purple-faced at the suggestion.

"If the shoe fits, wear it, as my Granny used to say." Collier couldn't help but smile at the politician's discomfort. "What I'm mainly saying, Mr. President, is that generations of inbreeding among our 'political class'—that large group of families like the Tafts, the Byrds, Kennedys, the Rockefellers and the Bushes—has undermined the overall character and intelligence level of our country's elected elite. Integrity in politics has become a joke, in my opinion. I think this can easily be demonstrated by an examination of the political platforms and outlandish promises made by almost any candidate running for election, compared with the about face and waffling after they are elected to office."

"I...ah-h..." the President sputtered; then merely stood speechless, glaring at him.

"What I'm saying, Mr. President, is that politicians have little, if any, business determining the future of our military. We certainly cannot continue the way we are going. The inbred deterioration of character in the upper—the political—classes is rapidly rotting our underbelly. If the present exercise of political favoritism continues, we are fast approaching the day when no one in Congress and no President or Cabinet Member will have served or have any children serving. Even with competent leadership generated at West Point, Annapolis and the Air Force Academy, in the eventual absence of civilian, political decision makers with real, knowledgeable, hands-on military experience, the military will be ill-used and poorly directed and government support will be non-existent for any project or cause which becomes a political liability, and, conversely, the military will become largely a chip in the game of international politics...which I hesitate to say more about..." Collier paused then asked. "Have you ever stopped to question the succession...the actual necessity and meaning of...Vietnam, Desert Storm, Bosnia, Iraq, Pakistan and now Afghanistan?"

"Are you questioning the intelligence...the integrity...the...ah...uh?...the motivations of our recent actions in...ah...the Middle East?" The President looked to be on the verge of apoplexy.

"I repeat, sir. If the shoe fits wear it. I'm saying, Sir, that I think President Dwight David Eisenhower hit the nail dead on the head when he warned back in the early fifties, *'In the councils of government, we must guard against the acquisition of unwarranted influence, whether sought or unsought, by the military-industrial complex. The potential for the disastrous rise of misplaced power exists and will persist.'* I remember my father telling me that he hated to admit it, but it seemed like this country couldn't survive economically without a 'good shooting war.' I'm sorry to say that I—and my son and grandson—have lived to see the bitter truth in my father's observation. I have great fear that my great-great grandchildren will continue to be victims of future generations of corrupt, self-important, economically-motivated leaders."

"I take umbrage, sir...but I refuse to dignify your rather obvious insult that our country's leadership is corrupt. I bid you goodnight and, again thank you for your heroism on behalf of a grateful nation." The badly-flustered Commander-in-Chief attempted to maintain an air of self-righteous indignation.

"Goodnight, Mr. President, but, I almost forgot...before I leave, I brought you this." From his pocket Collier removed a plain envelope containing images from the strip of microfilm from the Minox spy camera that had been the matchbox-sized package he had been handed as a going-away gift the night he had left Seoul. Enlarged to full size, the film reconstituted Ahn Myung's documents and photos documenting the damning evidence of the Taejon massacre.

"What is this?" the suspicious Chief Executive asked, removing the photocopies from the envelope.

"These are affidavits with confirming photographs detailing a massacre of up to several hundred—perhaps as many as several thousand, maybe even more— innocent Korean civilians near Taejon in July 1950. Word is that this was reported by one of our commanders, but his report was suppressed by his superiors. Just another idealistic example of American integrity. Anyway, I thought I'd warn you. I'm writing a book."

"Writing a book?" The worried President looked at his Chief of Staff, who looked like he had found half a cockroach in his crème brulee.

"I'm sure when you look into this you'll uncover evidence this information has been suppressed by our government for over fifty years. By comparison, this makes the Pulitzer-winning *The Bridge at No Gun Ri* and the more recent, infamous myth of 'weapons of mass destruction' look like innocent games of hide-and-seek."

"What with these latest reports of North Korea's nuclear brinksmanship, and the rising casualties in Iraq, we're having enough trouble as it is." Plainly ignoring Collier's reference to "weapons of mass destruction," the President's harried Chief of Staff replied, then asked, "Why do you want to drag all this slime out from under a rock now?"

"I think it was President Truman who said, '*If you can't stand the heat get out of the kitchen.*' It's something you politicians don't seem to understand. We common folk—this country's real heroes who get up and go to work, or to school, or to church, or to the VFW or to cemeteries on Memorial Day—we just call it truth in advertising."

Standing there in the empty entrance lobby, the President and his flunky simply glared, helpless to respond.

"Well, *here's looking at you, kid.*" Collier Boyd Ramsay gave a mock salute and left.

The Washington Post

Thursday, April 24, 2008

N. KOREANS TAPED AT SYRIAN REACTOR

Video Played a Role in Israeli Raid

By Robin Wright

Washington Post Staff Writer

A video taken inside a secret Syrian facility last summer convinced the Israeli government and the Bush administration that North Korea was helping to construct a reactor similar to one that produces plutonium for North Korea's nuclear arsenal, according to senior U.S. officials who said it would be shared with lawmakers today.

Vol. 9, No. 207   Monday, May 19, 2008

S. KOREA'S KILLING FIELDS

'Most tragic and brutal chapter of the Korean War'

By Charles J. Hanley and Jae-soon Chang

Associated Press Writers

DAEJEON, South Korea, May 19, 2008, (AP) – Grave by mass grave, South Korea is unearthing the skeletons and buried truths of a cold-blooded slaughter from early in the Korean War.

The nation's U.S.-backed regime killed untold thousands of leftists and peasants in a summer of terror in 1950.

With U.S. military officers sometimes present, and as North Korean invaders pushed down the peninsula, the southern army and police emptied South Korean prisons, lined up detainees and shot them in the head, dumping the bodies into hastily dug trenches.

Others were thrown into abandoned mines or into the sea. Women and children were among those killed. Many victims never faced charges or trial.

The extermination campaign, carried out over mere weeks and hidden from history for a half-century, is the "the most tragic and brutal chapter of the Korean War," said historian Kim Dong-choon, a member of a two-year-old government commission investigating the mass executions.

* * * * * *

The Washington Post

Monday, December 13, 2010; 5:45 AM

NKOREA THREATENS SKOREA WITH NUCLEAR WAR

By HYUNG-JIN KIM

The Associated Press

Monday, December 13, 2010; 2:53 AM

SEOUL, South Korea -- North Korea warned Monday that U.S.-South Korean cooperation could bring a nuclear war to the region, as the South began artillery drills amid lingering tension nearly three weeks after the North's deadly shelling of a South Korean island.

The South's naval live-fire drills are scheduled to run Monday through Friday at 27 sites. The regularly scheduled exercises are getting special attention following a North Korean artillery attack on front-line Yeonpyeong Island that killed two South Korean marines and two civilians.

The Nov. 23 artillery barrage, the North's first assault to target a civilian area since the end of the 1950-53 Korean War, began after the North said South Korea first fired artillery toward its territorial waters. South Korea says it fired shells southward, not toward North Korea, as part of routine exercises.

* * * * * *

North Korea, however, lashed out at Seoul, accusing South Korea of collaborating with the United States and Japan to ratchet up pressure on Pyongyang.

That cooperation "is nothing but treachery escalating the tension between the North and the South and bringing the dark clouds of a nuclear war to hang over the Korean peninsula," Pyongyang's main Rodong Sinmun newspaper said in a commentary carried by the North's official Korean Central News Agency.

North Korea has often issued similar threats during standoffs.

The End

Dedication

For my wife Charlotte, my true love, my inspiration and counsel and Chumbley, our adorable, cavalierly alpha English Bulldog.

For my spiritual brother and lifelong friends Al and Nancy Stump

For Rick Robotham, my erudite longtime good friend.

For Paul Golden Price my intrepid comrade in arms who posed with Marilyn Monroe and me in the doorway of a DC-3 at the SeaTac Airport in 1953.

And for my brother, James Harris Robertson; my friends Bruce Bohon (deceased); Donald Young (deceased); all my classmates of Class 30/1952 at Fort Sill, Oklahoma FAOCS and all our gallant military and UN civilians who served in Korea from June 24, 1950 through the early Fall of 1953—with a heartfelt salute to the many Allied military personnel who have steadfastly continued to maintain a U.S. vigilance in Korea to assure the ongoing, but uneasy, peace.

For the Class of 1946 of Andrew Lewis High School, Salem, Virginia and all persons who attended ALHS from 1941 through 1946.

Acknowledgements

Credit to Charles L. Wyrick, Jr. for his editorial erudition.

Thanks to my brother, Capt. (Ret.) James Harris Robertson—a skilled pilot who flew B-26s in Korea—for consultation on all matters aviation.

Special appreciation to Col. Nathan K. Slate, Lawton, OK, U.S. Army (Retired); Col. (Ret.) George Bannon and Ft. Sill FAOCS Secretary Randy Dunham for advice and inspiration.

Special recognition and appreciation to Alicia R. Sell and the Archivists in the Virginia Room of the Roanoke Public Libraries, Roanoke, Virginia, for the wealth of historic news headlines and articles from *The Roanoke Times, The Salem Times Register* and *Time* magazine.

Appreciation to Antoinette High with YGS Group. All material from AP articles "Used with permission of The Associated Press Copyright© 2008. All rights reserved."

Appreciation to Robin Davison, Joe Hight and the management of *The Oklahoman* for permission to use the headlines from *The Daily Oklahoman*.

Appreciation to Michael Knoop of the *San Antonio News-Express* for permission to use the headlines from the *San Antonio News-Express* and to Matt De Waelsche, Librarian/Archivist and Assistant Manager of the San Antonio Public Library for his diligent and most helpful research in finding these files in the Library's microfilm archives.

Appreciation to Andrea Nunes Pereira with UPI. All material from UPI articles "Used with permission from *UPI.* © 1953, 2008 *UPI.*"

Appreciation to Catharine Giordano and Jenifer Stepp of *Stars and Stripes.* All material from *Stars and Stripes* "Used with permission from *Stars and Stripes.* © 1953, 2007 *Stars and Stripes.*"

Appreciation to Sara Wakefield and Michelle Butler of the *ArmyTimes.*

Gratitude to Debbie and John Gonzales, author and Snoop Dawg for reinforcing the author's memories of Dallas, Texas during 1952.

Thanks to our friends Craig and Lynn Wanous for countless, invaluable favors both in Key West and also while we were summering in Maine.

In Memoriam

Harry Milton Robertson and Lida Brewster Robertson
March 8, 1899 – February 1, 1972 * July 6, 1904 – April 22, 2000
My parents who always loved me.

Blanche Brewster Pedneau
August 1902 – May 30, 2002
Librarian extraordinare, my aunt, my heroine.

Patricia Jolene Saunders
March 6, 1932 – January 6, 2008
My cousin, my original reader, my cheerleader, and lifelong friend.

George Palmer Garrett, Jr.
June 11, 1929 – May 30, 2008
Soldier, scholar, teacher, writer, friend and inspiration.

William Hoffman
May 16, 1925 – September 13, 2009
Soldier, scholar, teacher, writer, friend and inspiration.

Bruce E. Bohon Sr.
July 21, 1929 -- November 25, 2009
Lifelong friend, comrade-in-arms and personal hero.

www.ingramcontent.com/pod-product-compliance
Lightning Source LLC
Chambersburg PA
CBHW030737030726
47497CB00001B/11